THE ART
OF THE TALE

THE ART OF THE TALE

· ·

An International Anthology
of Short Stories
1945-1985

edited by Daniel Halpern

Elisabeth Sifton Books

VIKING

ELISABETH SIFTON BOOKS • VIKING
Viking Penguin Inc., 40 West 23rd Street,
New York, New York 10010, U.S.A.
Penguin Books Ltd, Harmondsworth,
Middlesex, England
Penguin Books Australia Ltd, Ringwood,
Victoria, Australia
Penguin Books Canada Limited, 2801 John Street,
Markham, Ontario, Canada L3R 1B4
Penguin Books (N.Z.) Ltd, 182–190 Wairau Road,
Auckland 10, New Zealand

First published in 1986 by Viking Penguin Inc.
Published simultaneously in Canada

LIBRARY OF CONGRESS CATALOGING IN PUBLICATION DATA
The Art of the tale.
"Elisabeth Sifton Books."
1. Short stories.   2. Fiction—20th century.
I. Halpern, Daniel, 1945–
PN6120.2.A75   1986   808.83′1   85-41061
ISBN 0-670-80592-0

Printed in the United States of America by
R. R. Donnelley & Sons Company, Harrisonburg, Virginia
Set in Electra

Grateful acknowledgment is made for permission to reprint the short stories in this anthology as follows:

"The Sacrificial Egg" from the book *Girls at War and Other Short Stories* by Chinua Achebe. Copyright © 1972, 1973 by Chinua Achebe. Reprinted by permission of Doubleday & Company, Inc.

"The Bound Man" from *The Bound Man* by Ilse Aichinger. Copyright © 1956, renewed 1984 by Ilse Aichinger. Copyright 1954 by S. Fischer Verlag, Frankfurt am Main. Reprinted by permission of Farrar, Straus and Giroux, Inc. and S. Fischer Verlag.

"Little Whale, Varnisher of Reality" from *The Steel Bird and Other Stories* by Vasily Aksenov, translated by Susan Brownsberger (Ardis, 1979). Copyright © 1979 by Ardis. Reprinted by permission.

"Hair Jewellery" from *Dancing Girls* by Margaret Atwood. Copyright © 1977, 1982 by O. W. Toad, Ltd. Reprinted by permission of Simon & Schuster, Inc. and Jonathan Cape Ltd.

"Everything" by Ingeborg Bachmann. From *Das Dreissigtste Jahr*, © R. Piper & Co. Verlag, Munich 1961. By permission of Joan Daves.

"Going to Meet the Man" from the book *Going to Meet the Man* by James Baldwin. Copyright © 1948, 1951, 1957, 1958, 1960, 1965 by James Baldwin. Reprinted by permission of Doubleday & Company, Inc.

(Pages 817–820 constitute an extension of this copyright page.)

Unlike the novel, a short story may be,
for all purposes, essential.

—JORGE LUIS BORGES

Acknowledgments

. . . .

For their considerable and conscientious work on this anthology, I would like to thank Lea Baechler, Kathleen Reddy, and Melora Wolff. I would also like to thank Jeanne Wilmot and Dana Cowin for their thoughtful reading of the stories, and Arthur Monke of the Bowdoin College Library for making hospitable those rooms where much of the reading for this volume was accomplished. And, again, for her unfailing good taste and supportive presence, my editor Elisabeth Sifton.

Contents

· ·

Introduction

· ·

Some aficionados of the short story would date the moment from the publication of Jorge Luis Borges's *Ficciones* or Vladimir Nabokov's first translated stories; others from the impressive volumes of collected stories that began to appear by such writers as Isaac Bashevis Singer, Graham Greene, Eudora Welty, V. S. Pritchett, John Cheever, Jean Stafford, Nadine Gordimer, and Gabriel Garcia Marquez; or in our recognition of the magnitude of Flannery O'Connor's achievement. Still others would locate that moment in the works of Julio Cortázar, Tommaso Landolfi, Juan Rulfo, R. K. Narayan and Italo Calvino, who picked up and extended the agreed-upon qualities of the folktale—fantasy and legend. But regardless of whose pen fired the important moment, there seems to be general agreement that a serious revival of the short story is under way, as if at this particular juncture in the parlous history of our race we especially need its singular purity and magic, its devotion to the crucial—though often eccentric and enigmatic—moments in human life. And yet how fickle we serious readers of fiction must seem to the practitioners: one year we are conned by critics into believing that our story writers have turned to the novel because the market for stories has evaporated; and then, as we peruse our favorite paper of a late Sunday morning over good coffee, we discover the novel has died.

It seems to me, after considering a great deal of short fiction written since World War II, that in any given period since the war both the short story and the novel have not only maintained themselves, but have flourished. The story, when it is written well, is like strong emotion: it is alive, convincing, and difficult to expel from the body's metabolism. The goal of this anthology is to present stories capable of surviving the vagrancies of time and fashion, the fecklessness of our short memory and our impatience. I have selected eighty-two writers, each of whom has already produced a body of work that argues for representation here. The stories in *The Art of the Tale* were all published in English, in book form, after 1945, although some of the stories were actually written before the war. Nabokov's "Spring in Fialta" is one example; it first appeared in the emigre review *Sovremennie Zapiski* (Paris) in 1938, under the pen name of

V. Sirin, but it did not appear in English, in book form, until *Nine Stories* was published in 1947.

The writers included in these pages inherited the pen that indelibly established the short story in modern terms. A list of precursors to the present volume would certainly include stories by the acknowledged masters of the form: Pushkin (b. 1799); Balzac (b. 1799); Hawthorne (b. 1804); Poe (b. 1809); Gogol (b. 1809)—Turgenev is quoted as saying, "We all came out from under Gogol's 'Overcoat' "; Turgenev (b. 1818)—"*A Sportsman's Notebook*," Frank O'Connor wrote, "may well be the greatest book of short stories ever written"; Flaubert (b. 1821); Dostoevsky (b. 1821); Maupassant (b. 1850); James (b. 1843); Conrad (b. 1857); Chekhov (b. 1860)—the writer most often cited as an influence by the writers in this collection; Gorky (b. 1868); Crane (b. 1871); Mann (b. 1875); Anderson (b. 1876); Joyce (b. 1882); Kafka (b. 1883); Lawrence (b. 1885); Porter (b. 1890); Babel (b. 1894); Faulkner (b. 1897); and Hemingway (b. 1899). With the exception of Isak Dinesen, born in 1885, 1899 is the year the oldest writers in this anthology were born: Jorge Luis Borges, Vladimir Nabokov, and Yasunari Kawabata.

No short story anthology could ever be quite large enough to encompass the editorial vision at work in the selection of stories from any given half-century. Naturally, the omissions are a source of sadness and, in some cases, even embarrassment. But space and cost—that is, the finite qualities of our world—must always have a say in the final choice. Randall Jarrell, in addressing the problem of a representative anthology of stories, likened it to starting a zoo in a closet, where the giraffe, the first to arrive, takes up more space than one has for the collection.

I have attempted to avoid stories that have been over-anthologized, but I have made exceptions when a story seemed the inevitable and inescapable choice. While I have also tried to represent stories from as many countries as possible, my ending up with many more pages devoted to the English-speaking world was unavoidable. This should not be surprising, given the enormous number of stories available in English from both emerging and established writers. Of course, many non-English writers worthy of inclusion have yet to be translated and thus remained beyond the net of my selection process. And there were other obstacles that made representation difficult to achieve; for example, very few French writers published collections of stories after the war; the same is true for writers in German—Günter Grass, Peter Handke, and Max Frisch, to name but three, have no story collections. On the other hand, there was a profusion of Italian and Latin American writers from whom to choose.

In the past forty years, which is the scope of *The Art of the Tale*, the story has been many things. For Chinua Achebe of Nigeria and R. K. Narayan of India, the story carries on the ancient art of the folktale, the retelling of village banter, superstition, local mythology, and gossip. For Yukio Mishima of Japan, it is the painful enactment of inherited tradition; however, his countryman Yasunari Kawabata's story "One Arm" is very much a brother to Tommaso Landolfi's fanciful "Gogol's Wife." For V. S. Pritchett, the story "resembles a ballad or a sonnet and depends on a spontaneity that conceals its architecture. A story twenty pages long, for example, will have run to at least a hundred of rewriting." And Peter Taylor writes, "The short story is a dramatic form, closer to plays than to novels." And William Gass: "For me, the short story is not a character sketch, a mouse trap, an epiphany, a slice of suburban life. It is the flowering of a symbol center. It is a poem grafted onto sturdier stock." Today, the various styles of the short story already in existence continue as viable forms; they are inherited by young writers in the same way they were inherited by writers coming of age forty years ago. The entire history of the short story is passed down, generation after generation, like a relay runner's baton, and the art of the story continues.

The conventional story is championed in this anthology by such writers as V. S. Pritchett, William Trevor, John Cheever, William Maxwell, Peter Taylor, Richard Ford, and Paul Bowles who has taken this conventional style of storytelling and added his own exotic English to it. In a more experimental vein, there is the work of Jorge Luis Borges, Guy Davenport, Italo Calvino, William Gass, and Julio Cortázar. The fable has a place here, by way of Abdeslam Boulaich of Morocco in his piece "Cowardice," executed in the oral tradition by tape recorder and translated from the Mogrebi, the Moroccan dialect. And exploring what approaches an allegorical fiction, there is Ilse Aichinger's tale, "The Bound Man." I have also included stories that employ the elusive vehicle of surrealism, as in Gabriel Garcia Marquez's "Eyes of a Blue Dog," Wolfgang Hildescheimer's "How I Transformed Myself into a Nightingale," and Luisa Valenzuela's evocative "I'm Your Horse in the Night." The political story, too, is represented: by Tadeusz Borowski, who bore witness to the camps of the Holocaust, and by James Baldwin, whose powerful "Going to Meet the Man" confronts the racial atmosphere of fifties America.

A number of stories are cast against an exotic setting, such as those by Italo Calvino, Albert Camus, Paul Bowles, and Donald Barthelme. Other stories rely on various modes of humor, such as William Maxwell's "A Pilgrimage," Stanley Elkin's "I Look Out for Ed Wolfe," and Tommaso Landolfi's "Gogol's Wife." Still others focus on love's endlessly inventive entanglements and stratagems: stories by Richard Yates, Patrick White, Eudora Welty, Jean Stafford, Joyce Carol Oates, and Samuel Beckett.

In reading the work of more than a hundred story writers, what soon became evident to me is that these stories have brought forth incredibly bountiful worlds; the fictional landscape that is their legacy illustrates with unmistakable clarity the prodigiously imaginative life of story writers around the world. Yet in the midst of this abundance of riches, I have tried to keep in mind Proust's cagey and inarguable dictum, that each reader reads only what is within himself.

DANIEL HALPERN

February 1986

THE ART
OF THE TALE

Chinua Achebe

· ·

THE SACRIFICIAL EGG

Julius Obi sat gazing at his typewriter. The fat Chief Clerk, his boss, was snoring at his table. Outside, the gatekeeper in his green uniform was sleeping at his post. You couldn't blame him; no customer had passed through the gate for nearly a week. There was an empty basket on the giant weighing machine. A few palm-kernels lay desolately in the dust around the machine. Only the flies remained in strength.

Julius went to the window that overlooked the great market on the bank of the River Niger. This market, though still called Nkwo, had long spilled over into Eke, Oye, and Afo with the coming of civilization and the growth of the town into a big palm-oil port. In spite of this encroachment, however, it was still busiest on its original Nkwo day, because the deity who had presided over it from antiquity still cast her spell only on her own day—let men in their greed spill over themselves. It was said that she appeared in the form of an old woman in the centre of the market just before cock-crow and waved her magic fan in the four directions of the earth—in front of her, behind her, to the right and to the left—to draw to the market men and women from distant places. And they came bringing the produce of their lands—palm-oil and kernels, kola nuts, cassava, mats, baskets and earthenware pots; and took home many-coloured cloths, smoked fish, iron pots and plates. These were the forest peoples. The other half of the world who lived by the great rivers came down also—by canoe, bringing yams and fish. Sometimes it was a big canoe with a dozen or more people in it; sometimes it was a lone fisherman and his wife in a small vessel from the swift-flowing Anambara. They moored their canoe on the bank and sold their fish, after much haggling. The woman then walked up the steep banks of the river to the heart of the market to buy salt and oil and, if the sales had been very good, even a length of cloth. And for her children at home she bought bean cakes and mai-mai which the Igara women cooked. As evening approached, they took up their paddles again and paddled away, the water shimmering in the sunset and their canoe becoming smaller and smaller in the distance until it was just a dark crescent on the water's face and two dark bodies swaying forwards and backwards in it. Umuru then was the meeting place of the forest people who were

5

called Igbo and the alien riverain folk whom the Igbo called Olu and beyond whom the world stretched in indefiniteness.

Julius Obi was not a native of Umuru. He had come like countless others from some bush village inland. Having passed his Standard Six in a mission school he had come to Umuru to work as a clerk in the offices of the all-powerful European trading company which bought palm-kernels at its own price and sold cloth and metalware, also at its own price. The offices were situated beside the famous market so that in his first two or three weeks Julius had to learn to work within its huge enveloping hum. Sometimes when the Chief Clerk was away he walked to the window and looked down on the vast anthill activity. Most of these people were not there yesterday, he thought, and yet the market had been just as full. There must be many, many people in the world to be able to fill the market day after day like this. Of course they say not all who came to the great market were real people. Janet's mother, Ma, had said so.

"Some of the beautiful young women you see squeezing through the crowds are not people like you or me but mammy-wota who have their town in the depths of the river," she said. "You can always tell them, because they are beautiful with a beauty that is too perfect and too cold. You catch a glimpse of her with the tail of your eye, then you blink and look properly, but she has already vanished in the crowd."

Julius thought about these things as he now stood at the window looking down on the silent, empty market. Who would have believed that the great boisterous market could ever be quenched like this? But such was the strength of Kitikpa, the incarnate power of smallpox. Only he could drive away all those people and leave the market to the flies.

When Umuru was a little village, there was an age-grade who swept its market-square every Nkwo day. But progress had turned it into a busy, sprawling, crowded and dirty river port, a no-man's-land where strangers outnumbered by far the sons of the soil, who could do nothing about it except shake their heads at this gross perversion of their prayer. For indeed they had prayed—who will blame them—for their town to grow and prosper. And it had grown. But there is good growth and there is bad growth. The belly does not bulge out only with food and drink; it might be the abominable disease which would end by sending its sufferer out of the house even before he was fully dead.

The strangers who came to Umuru came for trade and money, not in search of duties to perform, for they had those in plenty back home in their village which was real home.

And as if this did not suffice, the young sons and daughters of Umuru soil, encouraged by schools and churches were behaving no better than the strangers. They neglected all their old tasks and kept only the revelries.

Such was the state of the town when Kitikpa came to see it and to demand the sacrifice the inhabitants owed the gods of the soil. He came in confident knowledge of the terror he held over the people. He was an evil deity, and boasted it. Lest he be offended those he killed were not killed but decorated, and no one dared weep for them. He put an end to the coming and going between neighbours and between villages. They said, "Kitikpa is in that village," and immediately it was cut off by its neighbours.

Julius was sad and worried because it was almost a week since he had seen Janet, the girl he was going to marry. Ma had explained to him very gently that he should no longer go to see them "until this thing is over, by the power of Jehovah." (Ma was a very devout Christian convert and one reason why she approved of Julius for her only daughter was that he sang in the choir of the CMS church.)

"You must keep to your rooms," she had said in hushed tones, for Kitikpa strictly forbade any noise or boisterousness. "You never know whom you might meet on the streets. That family has got it." She lowered her voice even more and pointed surreptitiously at the house across the road whose doorway was barred with a yellow palm-frond. "He has decorated one of them already and the rest were moved away today in a big government lorry."

Janet walked a short way with Julius and stopped; so he stopped too. They seemed to have nothing to say to each other yet they lingered on. Then she said goodnight and he said goodnight. And they shook hands, which was very odd, as though parting for the night were something new and grave.

He did not go straight home, because he wanted desperately to cling, even alone, to this strange parting. Being educated he was not afraid of whom he might meet, so he went to the bank of the river and just walked up and down it. He must have been there a long time because he was still there when the wooden gong of the night-mask sounded. He immediately set out for home, half-walking and half-running, for night-masks were not a matter of superstition; they were real. They chose the night for their revelry because like the bat's their ugliness was great.

In his hurry he stepped on something that broke with a slight liquid explosion. He stopped and peeped down at the footpath. The moon was not up yet but there was a faint light in the sky which showed that it would not be long delayed. In this half-light he saw that he had stepped on an egg offered in sacrifice. Someone oppressed by misfortune had brought the offering to the crossroads in the dusk. And he had stepped on it. There were the usual young palm-fronds around it. But Julius saw it differently as a house where the terrible artist was at work. He wiped the sole of his foot on the sandy path and hurried away, carrying another vague worry in his mind. But hurrying was no use now; the fleet-footed mask was already abroad. Perhaps it was impelled to hurry by the threatening imminence of the moon. Its voice rose high and clear in the still night air like a flaming sword. It was yet a long way away, but Julius knew that distances vanished before it. So he made straight for the cocoyam farm beside the road and threw himself on his belly, in the shelter of the broad leaves. He had hardly done this when he heard the rattling staff of the spirit and a thundering stream of esoteric speech. He shook all over. The sounds came bearing down on him, almost pressing his face into the moist earth. And now he could hear the footsteps. It was as if twenty evil men were running together. Panic sweat broke all over him and he was nearly impelled to get up and run. Fortunately he kept a firm hold on himself . . . In no time at all the commotion in the air and on the earth—the thunder and torrential rain, the earthquake and flood—passed and disappeared in the distance on the other side of the road.

The next morning, at the office the Chief Clerk, a son of the soil spoke bitterly about last night's provocation of Kitikpa by the headstrong youngsters who had launched the noisy fleet-footed mask in defiance of their elders, who knew that Kitikpa would be enraged, and then . . .

The trouble was that the disobedient youths had never yet experienced the power of Kitikpa themselves; they had only heard of it. But soon they would learn.

As Julius stood at the window looking out on the emptied market he lived through the terror of that night again. It was barely a week ago but already it seemed like another life, separated from the present by a vast emptiness. This emptiness deepened with every passing day. On this side of it stood Julius, and on the other Ma and Janet whom the dread artist decorated.

Ilse Aichinger

• • • • • • • • • • • • • • • • • • •

THE BOUND MAN

Sunlight on his face woke him, but made him shut his eyes again; it streamed unhindered down the slope, collected itself into rivulets, attracted swarms of flies, which flew low over his forehead, circled, sought to land, and were overtaken by fresh swarms. When he tried to whisk them away he discovered that he was bound. A thin rope cut into his arms. He dropped them, opened his eyes again, and looked down at himself. His legs were tied all the way up to his thighs; a single length of rope was tied round his ankles, criss-crossed all the way up his legs, and encircled his hips, his chest and his arms. He could not see where it was knotted. He showed no sign of fear or hurry, though he thought he was unable to move, until he discovered that the rope allowed his legs some free play, and that round his body it was almost loose. His arms were tied to each other but not to his body, and had some free play too. This made him smile, and it occurred to him that perhaps children had been playing a practical joke on him.

He tried to feel for his knife, but again the rope cut softly into his flesh. He tried again, more cautiously this time, but his pocket was empty. Not only his knife, but the little money that he had on him, as well as his coat, were missing. His shoes had been pulled from his feet and taken too. When he moistened his lips he tasted blood, which had flowed from his temples down his cheeks, his chin, his neck, and under his shirt. His eyes were painful; if he kept them open for long he saw reddish stripes in the sky.

He decided to stand up. He drew his knees up as far as he could, rested his hands on the fresh grass and jerked himself to his feet. An elder-branch stroked his cheek, the sun dazzled him, and the rope cut into his flesh. He collapsed to the ground again, half out of his mind with pain, and then tried again. He went on trying until the blood started flowing from his hidden weals. Then he lay still again for a long while, and let the sun and the flies do what they liked.

When he awoke for the second time the elder-bush had cast its shadow over him, and the coolness stored in it was pouring from between its branches. He must have been hit on the head. Then they must have laid him down carefully, just as a mother lays her baby behind a bush when she goes to work in the fields.

9

His chances all lay in the amount of free play allowed him by the rope. He dug his elbows into the ground and tested it. As soon as the rope tautened he stopped, and tried again more cautiously. If he had been able to reach the branch over his head he could have used it to drag himself to his feet, but he could not reach it. He laid his head back on the grass, rolled over, and struggled to his knees. He tested the ground with his toes, and then managed to stand up almost without effort.

A few paces away lay the path across the plateau, and among the grass were wild pinks and thistles in bloom. He tried to lift his foot to avoid trampling on them, but the rope round his ankles prevented him. He looked down at himself.

The rope was knotted at his ankles, and ran round his legs in a kind of playful pattern. He carefully bent and tried to loosen it, but, loose though it seemed to be, he could not make it any looser. To avoid treading on the thistles with his bare feet he hopped over them like a bird.

The cracking of a twig made him stop. People in this district were very prone to laughter. He was alarmed by the thought that he was in no position to defend himself. He hopped on until he reached the path. Bright fields stretched far below. He could see no sign of the nearest village, and, if he could move no faster than this, night would fall before he reached it.

He tried walking, and discovered that he could put one foot before another if he lifted each foot a definite distance from the ground and then put it down again before the rope tautened. In the same way he could actually swing his arms a little.

After the first step he fell. He fell right across the path, and made the dust fly. He expected this to be a sign for the long-suppressed laughter to break out, but all remained quiet. He was alone. As soon as the dust had settled he got up and went on. He looked down and watched the rope slacken, grow taut, and then slacken again.

When the first glow-worms appeared he managed to look up. He felt in control of himself again, and his impatience to reach the nearest village faded.

Hunger made him light-headed, and he seemed to be going so fast that not even a motor-cycle could have overtaken him; alternatively he felt as if he were standing still and that the earth was rushing past him, like a river flowing past a man swimming against the stream. The stream carried branches which had been bent southwards by the north wind, stunted young trees, and patches of grass with bright, long-stalked flowers. It ended by submerging the bushes and the young trees, leaving only the sky and the man above water-level. The moon had risen, and illuminated the bare, curved summit of the plateau, the path, which was overgrown with young grass, the bound man making his way along it with quick, measured steps, and two hares, which ran across the hill just in front of him and vanished down the slope. Though the nights were still cool at this time of the year, before midnight the bound man lay down at the edge of the escarpment and went to sleep.

In the light of morning the animal-tamer who was camping with his circus in the field outside the village saw the bound man coming down the path, gazing thoughtfully at the ground. The bound man stopped and bent down. He held out one arm to help keep his balance and with the other picked up an empty wine-bottle. Then he straightened himself and stood erect again. He moved slowly, to avoid being cut by the rope, but to the circus proprietor what he did suggested the voluntary limitation of an enormous swiftness of movement. He was enchanted by its extraordinary gracefulness, and while the bound man looked about for a stone on which to break the bottle, so that he could use the splintered neck to cut the rope, the animal-tamer walked across the field and approached him. The first leaps of a young panther had never filled him with such delight.

"Ladies and gentlemen, the bound man!" His very first movements let loose a storm of applause, which out of sheer excitement caused the blood to rush to the cheeks of the animal-tamer standing at the edge of the arena. The bound man rose to his feet. His surprise whenever he did this was like that of a four-footed animal which has managed to stand on its hind-legs. He knelt, stood up, jumped, and turned cart-wheels. The spectators found it as astonishing as if they had seen a bird which voluntarily remained earthbound, and confined itself to hopping. The bound man became an enormous draw. His absurd steps and little jumps, his elementary exercises in movement, made the rope-dancer superfluous. His fame grew from village to village, but the motions he went through were few and always the same; they were really quite ordinary motions, which he had continually to practise in the day-time in the half-dark tent in order to retain his shackled freedom. In that he remained entirely within the limits set by his rope he was free of it, it did not confine him, but gave him wings and endowed his leaps and jumps with purpose; just as the flights of birds of passage have purpose when they take wing in the warmth of summer and hesitantly make small circles in the sky.

All the children of the neighbourhood started playing the game of "bound man." They formed rival gangs, and one day the circus people found a little girl lying bound in a ditch, with a cord tied round her neck so that she could hardly breathe. They released her, and at the end of the performance that night the bound man made a speech. He announced briefly that there was no sense in being tied up in such a way that you could not jump. After that he was regarded as a comedian.

Grass and sunlight, tent-pegs driven into the ground and then pulled up again, and on to the next village. "Ladies and gentlemen, the bound man!" The summer mounted towards its climax. It bent its face deeper over the fish-ponds in the hollows, taking delight in its dark reflection, skimmed the surface of the rivers, and made the plain into what it was. Everyone who could walk went to see the bound man.

Many wanted a close-up view of how he was bound. So the circus proprietor announced after each performance that anyone who wanted to satisfy himself that the knots were real and the rope not made of rubber was at liberty to do so. The bound man generally waited for the crowd in the area outside the tent. He laughed or remained serious, and held out his arms for inspection. Many took the opportunity to look him in the face, others gravely tested the rope, tried the knots on his ankles, and wanted to know exactly how the lengths compared with the length of his limbs. They asked him how he had come to be tied up like that, and he answered patiently, always saying the same thing. Yes, he had been tied up, he said, and when he awoke he found that he had been robbed as well. Those who had done it must have been pressed for time, because they had tied him up somewhat too loosely for someone who was not supposed to be able to move and somewhat too tightly for someone who was expected to be able to move. But he did move, people pointed out. Yes, he replied, what else could he do?

Before he went to bed he always sat for a time in front of the fire. When the circus proprietor asked him why he didn't make up a better story, he always answered that he hadn't made up that one, and blushed. He preferred staying in the shade.

The difference between him and the other performers was that when the show was over he did not take off his rope. The result was that every movement that he made was worth seeing, and the villagers used to hang about the camp for hours, just for the sake of seeing him get up from in front of the fire and roll himself in his blanket. Sometimes the sky was beginning to lighten when he saw their shadows disappear.

The circus proprietor often remarked that there was no reason why he should not be untied after the evening performance and tied up again next day. He pointed out that the rope-dancers, for instance, did not stay on their rope over night. But no-one took the idea of untying him seriously.

For the bound man's fame rested on the fact that he was always bound, that whenever he washed himself he had to wash his clothes too and *vice versa*, and that his only way of doing so was to jump in the river just as he was every morning when the sun came out, and that he had to be careful not to go too far out for fear of being carried away by the stream.

The proprietor was well aware that what in the last resort protected the bound man from the jealousy of the other performers was his helplessness; he deliberately left them the pleasure of watching him groping painfully from stone to stone on the river bank every morning with his wet clothes clinging to him. When his wife pointed out that even the best clothes would not stand up indefinitely to such treatment (and the bound man's clothes were by no means of the best) he replied curtly that it was not going to last for ever. That was his answer to all objections—it was for the summer season only. But when he said this he was not being serious; he was talking like a gambler who has no intention of giving up his vice. In reality he would have been prepared cheerfully to sacrifice his lions and his rope-dancers for the bound man.

He proved this on the night when the rope-dancers jumped over the fire. Afterwards he was convinced that they did it, not because it was midsummer's day, but because of the bound man, who as usual was lying and watching them, with that peculiar smile that might have been real or might have been only the effect of the glow on his face. In any case no-one knew anything about him, because he never talked about anything that had happened to him before he emerged from the wood that day.

But that evening two of the performers suddenly picked him up by the arms and legs, carried him to the edge of the fire and started playfully swinging him to and fro, while two others held out their arms to catch him on the other side. In the end they threw him, but too short. The two men on the other side drew back—they explained afterwards that they did so the better to take the shock. The result was that the bound man landed at the very edge of the flames and would have been burned if the circus proprietor had not seized his arms and quickly dragged him away to save the rope which was starting to get singed. He was certain that the object had been to burn the rope. He sacked the four men on the spot.

A few nights later the proprietor's wife was awakened by the sound of footsteps on the grass, and went outside just in time to prevent the clown from playing his last practical joke. He was carrying a pair of scissors. When he was asked for an explanation he insisted that he had had no intention of taking the bound man's life, but only wanted to cut his rope, because he felt sorry for him. But he was sacked too.

These antics amused the bound man, because he could have freed himself if he had wanted to whenever he liked, but perhaps he wanted to learn a few new jumps first. The children's rhyme: "We travel with the circus, we travel with the circus" sometimes occurred to him while he lay awake at night. He could hear the voices of spectators on the opposite bank who had been driven too far downstream on the way home. He could see the river gleaming in the moonlight, and the young shoots growing out of the thick tops of the willow trees, and did not think about autumn yet.

The circus proprietor dreaded the danger involved for the bound man by sleep. Attempts were continually made to release him while he slept. The chief culprits were sacked rope-dancers, or children who were bribed for the purpose. But measures could be taken to safeguard against these. A much bigger danger was that which he represented to himself. In his dreams he forgot his rope, and was surprised by it when he woke in the darkness of morning. He would angrily try to get up, but lose his balance and fall back again. The previous evening's applause was forgotten, sleep was still too near, his head and neck too free. He was just the opposite of a hanged man—his neck was the only part of him that was free. You had to make sure that at such moments no knife was within his reach. In the early hours of the morning the circus proprietor sometimes sent his wife to see whether the bound man was all right. If he was asleep she would bend over him and feel the rope. It had grown hard from dirt and damp. She would test the amount of free play it allowed him, and touch his tender wrists and ankles.

The most varied rumours circulated about the bound man. Some said he had tied himself up and invented the story of having been robbed, and towards the end of the summer that was the general opinion. Others maintained that he had been tied up at his own request, perhaps in league with the circus proprietor. The hesitant way in which he told his story, his habit of breaking off when the talk got round to the attack on him, contributed greatly to these rumours. Those who still believed in the robbery-with-violence story were laughed at. Nobody knew what difficulties the circus proprietor had in keeping the bound man, and how often he said he had had enough and wanted to clear off, for too much of the summer had passed.

Later, however, he stopped talking about clearing off. When the proprietor's wife brought him his food by the river and asked him how long he proposed to remain with them, he did not answer. She thought he had got used, not to being tied up, but to not forgetting for a moment that he was tied up—the only thing that anyone in his position could get used to. She asked him whether he did not think it ridiculous to be tied up all the time, but he answered that he did not. Such a variety of people—clowns, freaks, and comics, to say nothing of elephants and tigers—travelled with circuses that he did not see why a bound man should not travel with a circus too. He told her about the movements he was practising, the new ones he had discovered, and about a new trick that had occurred to him while he was whisking flies from the animals' eyes. He described to her how he always anticipated the effect of the rope and always restrained his movements in such a way as to prevent it from ever tautening; and she knew that there were days when he was hardly aware of the rope when he jumped down from the wagon and slapped the flanks of the horses in the morning, as if he were moving in a dream. She watched him vault over the bars almost without touching them, and saw the sun on his face, and he told her that sometimes he felt as if he were not tied up at all. She answered that if he were prepared to be untied there would never be any need for him to feel tied up. He agreed that he could be untied whenever he felt like it.

The woman ended by not knowing whether she were more concerned with the man or with the rope that tied him. She told him that he could go on travelling with the circus without his rope, but she did not believe it. For what would be the point of his antics without his rope, and what would he amount to without it? Without his rope he would leave them, and the happy days would be over. She would no longer be able to sit beside him on the stones by the river without rousing suspicion, and she knew that his continued presence, and her conversations with him, of which the rope was the only subject, depended on it. Whenever she agreed that the rope had its advantages he would start talking about how troublesome it was, and whenever he started talking about its advantages she would urge him to get rid of it. All this seemed as endless as the summer itself.

At other times she was worried at the thought that she was herself hastening the end by her talk. Sometimes she would get up in the middle of the night and run across the grass to where he slept. She wanted to shake him, wake him up and ask him to keep the rope. But then she would see him lying there; he had thrown off his blanket, and there he lay like a corpse, with his legs outstretched and his arms close together, with the rope tied round them. His clothes had suffered from the heat and the water, but the rope had grown no thinner. She felt that he would go on travelling with the circus until the flesh fell from him and exposed the joints. Next morning she would plead with him more ardently than ever to get rid of his rope.

The increasing coolness of the weather gave her hope. Autumn was coming, and he would not be able to go on jumping into the river with his clothes on much longer. But the thought of losing his rope, about which he had felt indifferent earlier in the season, now depressed him.

The songs of the harvesters filled him with foreboding. "Summer has gone, summer has gone." But he realized that soon he would have to change his clothes, and he was certain that when he had been untied it would be impossible to tie him up again in exactly the same way. About this time the proprietor started talking about travelling south that year.

The heat changed without transition into quiet, dry cold, and the fire was kept in all day long. When the bound man jumped down from the wagon he felt the coldness of the grass under his feet. The stalks were bent with ripeness. The horses dreamed on their feet and the wild animals, crouching to leap even in their sleep, seemed to be collecting gloom under their skins which would break out later.

On one of these days a young wolf escaped. The circus proprietor kept quiet about it, to avoid spreading alarm, but the wolf soon started raiding cattle in the neighbourhood. People at first believed that the wolf had been driven to these parts by the prospect of a severe winter, but the circus soon became suspect. The proprietor could not conceal the loss of the animal from his own employees, so the truth was bound to come out before long. The circus people offered their aid in tracking down the beast to the burgomasters of the neighbouring villagers, but all their efforts were vain. Eventually the circus was openly blamed for the damage and the danger, and spectators stayed away.

The bound man went on performing before half-empty seats without losing anything of his amazing freedom of movement. During the day he wandered among the surrounding hills under the thin-beaten silver of the autumn sky, and, whenever he could, lay down where the sun shone longest. Soon he found a place which the twilight reached last of all, and when at last it reached him he got up most unwillingly from the withered grass. In coming down the hill he had to pass through a little wood on its southern slope, and one evening he saw the gleam of two little green lights. He knew that they came from no church window, and was not for a moment under any illusion about what they were.

He stopped. The animal came towards him through the thinning foliage. He could make out its shape, the slant of its neck, its tail which swept the ground, and its receding head. If he had not been bound, perhaps he would have tried to run away, but as it was he did not even feel fear. He stood calmly with dangling arms and looked down at the wolf's bristling coat, under which the muscles played like his own underneath the rope. He thought the evening wind was still between him and the wolf when the beast sprang. The man took care to obey his rope.

Moving with the deliberate care that he had so often put to the test, he seized the wolf by the throat. Tenderness for a fellow-creature arose in him, tenderness for the upright being concealed in the four-footed. In a movement that resembled the drive of a great bird—he felt a sudden awareness that flying would be possible only if one were tied up in a special way—he flung himself at the animal and brought it to the ground. He felt a slight elation at having lost the fatal advantage of free limbs which causes men to be worsted.

The freedom he enjoyed in this struggle was having to adapt every movement of his limbs to the rope that tied him—the freedom of panthers, wolves, and the wild flowers that sway in the evening breeze. He ended up lying obliquely down the slope, clasping the animal's hind-legs between his own bare feet and its head between his hands. He felt the gentleness of the faded foliage stroking the back of his hands, and he felt his own grip almost effortlessly reaching its maximum, and he felt too how he was in no way hampered by the rope.

As he left the wood light rain began to fall and obscured the setting sun. He stopped for a while under the trees at the edge of the wood. Beyond the camp and the river he saw the fields where the cattle grazed, and the places where they crossed. Perhaps he would travel south with the circus after all. He laughed softly. It was against all reason. Even if he went on putting up with his joints' being covered with sores, which opened and bled when he made certain movements, his clothes would not stand up much longer to the friction of the rope.

The circus proprietor's wife tried to persuade her husband to announce the death of the wolf without mentioning that it had been killed by the bound man. She said that even at the time of his greatest popularity people would have refused to believe him capable of it, and in their present angry mood, with the nights getting cooler, they would be more incredulous than ever. The wolf had attacked a group of children at play that day, and nobody would believe that it had really been killed; for the circus proprietor had many wolves, and it was easy enough for him to hang a skin on the rail and allow free entry. But he was not to be dissuaded. He thought that the announcement of the bound man's act would revive the triumphs of the summer.

That evening the bound man's movements were uncertain. He stumbled in one of his jumps, and fell. Before he managed to get up he heard some low whistles and catcalls, rather like birds calling at dawn. He tried to get up too quickly, as he had done once or twice during the summer, with the result that he tautened the rope and fell back again. He lay still to regain his calm, and listened to the boos and catcalls growing into an uproar. "Well, bound man, and how did you kill the wolf?" they shouted, and: "Are you the man who killed the wolf?" If he had been one of them he would not have believed it himself. He thought they had a perfect right to be angry: a circus at this time of year, a bound man, an escaped wolf, and all ending up with this. Some groups of spectators started arguing with others, but the greater part of the audience thought the whole thing a bad joke. By the time he had got to his feet there was such a hubbub that he was barely able to make out individual words.

He saw people surging up all round him, like faded leaves raised by a whirlwind in a circular valley at the centre of which all was yet still. He thought of the golden sunsets of the last few days; and the cemetery light which lay over the blight of all that he had built up during so many nights, the gold frame which the pious hang round dark, old pictures, this sudden collapse of everything, filled him with anger.

They wanted him to repeat his battle with the wolf. He said that such a thing had no place in a circus performance, and the proprietor declared that he did not keep animals to have them slaughtered in front of an audience. But the mob stormed the ring and forced them towards the cages. The proprietor's wife made her way between the seats to the exit and managed to get round to the cages from the other side. She pushed aside the attendant whom the crowd had forced to open a cage door, but the spectators dragged her back and prevented the door from being shut.

"Aren't you the woman who used to lie with him by the river in the summer?" they called out. "How does he hold you in his arms?" She shouted back at them that they needn't believe in the bound man if they didn't want to, they had never deserved him—painted clowns were good enough for them.

The bound man felt as if the bursts of laughter were what he had been expecting ever since early May. What had smelt so sweet all through the summer now stank. But, if they insisted, he was ready to take on all the animals in the circus. He had never felt so much at one with his rope.

Gently he pushed the woman aside. Perhaps he would travel south with them after all. He stood in the open doorway of the cage, and he saw the wolf, a strong young animal, rise to its feet, and he heard the proprietor grumbling again about the loss of his exhibits. He clapped his hands to attract the animal's attention, and when it was near enough he turned to slam the cage door. He looked the woman in the face. Suddenly he remembered the proprietor's warning to suspect of murderous intentions anyone near him who had a sharp instrument in his hand. At the same moment he felt the blade on his wrists, as cool as the water of the river in autumn, which during the last few weeks he had been barely able to stand. The rope curled up in a tangle beside him while he struggled free. He pushed the woman back, but there was no point in anything he did now. Had he been insufficiently on his guard against those who wanted to release him, against the sympathy in which they wanted to lull him? Had he lain too long on the river bank? If she had cut the cord at any other moment it would have been better than this.

He stood in the middle of the cage, and rid himself of the rope like a snake discarding its skin. It amused him to see the spectators shrinking back. Did they realise that he had no choice now? Or that fighting the wolf now would prove nothing whatever? At the same time he felt all his blood rush to his feet. He felt suddenly weak.

The rope, which fell at its feet like a snare, angered the wolf more than the entry of a stranger into its cage. It crouched to spring. The man reeled, and grabbed the pistol that hung ready at the side of the cage. Then, before anyone could stop him, he shot the wolf between the eyes. The animal reared, and touched him in falling.

On the way to the river he heard the footsteps of his pursuers—spectators, the rope-dancers, the circus proprietor, and the proprietor's wife, who persisted in the chase longer than anyone else. He hid in a clump of bushes and listened to them hurrying past, and later on streaming in the opposite direction back to the camp. The moon shone on the meadow; in that light its colour was that of both growth and death.

When he came to the river his anger died away. At dawn it seemed to him as if lumps of ice were floating in the water, and as if snow had fallen, obliterating memory.

Translated from the German by Eric Musbacher

Vasily Aksenov

· ·

LITTLE WHALE, VARNISHER OF REALITY

"What's that thing you brought home?" Whale asked me.

"It's a cap."

"Let me see."

He seized my new leather cap and wonderingly began to look it over. Within seconds his curiosity had reached such a fierce pitch that he was trembling. He let out a shout: "Daddy, what is it?"

"Just a funny kind of a cap," I grunted.

"A cap to fly in?" he shouted, more fiercely still, and began leaping about with the cap in his hands.

I was willing to play along. "Yes, to fly in. We'll fly to the North Pole in this cap, you and I."

"Hooray! To see the polar bears?"

"Yes."

"The walruses?"

"Yes, and the walruses."

"And who else?"

My head was splitting: I'd had words with several people at the office that day, taken a dressing down from the manager, and made several mistakes. I was in a god-awful mood, but still, I racked my brains to recall the scant fauna of the Arctic Ocean. "The sharks," I said in desperation.

"That's a lie," he retorted indignantly. "They don't have sharks there. Sharks are evil, and all the animals at the North Pole are good."

"You're right," I agreed hastily. "Well then, we'll go and see the polar bears, the walruses . . ."

"The whales," he prompted.

"Uh-huh, the whales and the . . . er . . ."

"The limpedooza!" he shouted rapturously.

"Now what's a limpedooza?"

He stopped in confusion, laid the cap on the divan, went off to the far corner, and whispered from across the room. "A limpedooza is a kind of an animal."

18

"Right you are," I said. "How could I have forgotten? The limpedooza! A kind of slithery, clever little animal, right?"

"No! He's big and fluffy!" said Whale with conviction.

My wife came into the room and said to Whale, "Let's go tend to our business." They went out together, but my wife came back and asked, "Did you call him?"

"Who?"

"Don't pretend. You had all day and couldn't make a phone call?"

"All right, I'll do it now."

She went out, and for the first time that day I was left alone. Listening to the unusual stillness, I might have been taking a bath or a shower, a shower of solitude after a work day filled in all its dimensions with clamorous people, some of them friends, some strangers.

I sat down at the empty desk and laid my hands on it, felt with pleasure its cool empty surface, devoid of any business or papers, serving now only as a prop for my heavy hands.

Outside the window the sun, having noiselessly surmounted the thickety yellow garden next door, was rolling toward the corner of a multistory apartment house, a gigantic up-ended parallelepiped, dark now and seemingly lifeless.

In the courtyard below, some demonic ten-year-olds were tearing around on the toolshed roof. From their wide-open mouths, I could imagine what a ruckus they were raising there outside our window panes.

A proper little old lady came timidly around from the front yard and, watchfully as a doe, turned toward the toolshed. As soon as they spotted her the boys leaped down from the roof.

This little old lady, who came out to the courtyard every evening for a breath of oxygen, with an inflatable rubber pillow to put under her meager seat, was a constant target of evil small-boy tricks. She was long since used to them and patiently endured the antics of these courtyard terrorists, so puzzling to her, so crafty and fleet—patiently endured them, but was nonetheless afraid of them, always afraid.

Now the boys had turned the janitor's hose directly across her path; they were having a wonderful time, leaping wildly about with their mouths open in laughter, while the old lady stood there patiently waiting for them to tire of their game. The janitor's wife appeared, a friend of the old lady's, and rushed to the attack, opening her mouth wide and waving her arms as she ran.

This whole scene, had it been wired for sound, would surely have roused me to anger or pain, but now it passed before my indifferent gaze like the frames of an old silent film.

And so, the old lady successfully traversed the courtyard, while the terrorists raged on the toolshed roof, mindless that the old lady's death, even now impending, might bring about the first desolation—a slight one, to be sure—of their own souls.

Striving to maintain my indifference and providential languor, I pulled the phone over and began to dial that damned number, as if paying no attention, as if it were nothing for me to call him, but by the third digit my insides were already knotted up, my heart, my liver, my spleen had contracted into one madly pounding lump, and only the short quick beeps delivered me. Busy! ·

I pictured him sitting in an easy chair, or maybe lying on the divan, but in any case fiddling with his spectacles, twirling them on one finger while he talked to someone. To whom? Sadovnikov? Voynovsky? Ovsyannikov?

I swore, and at that moment I heard Whale's shout from the kitchen. He was acting up, for no good reason. Something comes over him sometimes.

"Go away!" he roared at the top of his lungs. "Go away!" he shouted to my wife. "We don't need you!"

I could hear my wife's indignant voice and then the click of the light switch. Sanctions had been applied to Whale—he was left in the kitchen, in solitude and darkness. He immediately quieted down.

My wife went off to the bedroom to sulk. She takes it very hard when she has a tiff with her Whale-child, with this baby boy, our sweet little male-child, this Tom Thumb of a man just over three years old.

I got up and started for the kitchen, stomping the parquet elephant-style, trumpeting gaily and sternly, "Too-roo-roo! Here comes the Elephant Dad! Out of the depths of the jungle, Bimbo the Elephant himself! Too-roo-roo! Daddy himself! The one and only! In person!"

A feeling of tranquillity and love sprang up in my heart like a whirlwind.

In the kitchen I saw his round head silhouetted against the dusky window. He was sitting on the potty whispering something, his finger raised toward the window, where the lights were already beginning to come on in the building across the way.

I'm almost used to Whale now. More and more seldom am I visited by that strange sense of illusoriness when he runs into the room or wheels in on his tricycle. The reverence before mystery, and the fear, that I felt the first few months of his life are almost gone. Now it's "Oh, there's Whale"—and that's it. Small boy, sweet son, magic marvel whale-fish beside the Humpback Horsey sits . . . He's the stuff the old rhymes are made of.

He was six months old when I named him Whale. The two of us, my wife and I, were bathing him in a little tub; he wiggled in the soapy water, his toothless mouth gaping. I held up his head and kept stuffing the bits of cotton back in his ears as they fell out. From time to time he lifted his blue gaze to me and smiled a sly little smile, as if in foreknowledge of the intricate relations we have now. First off it struck me he looked like a sausage in bouillon, and I told my wife so: "A sausage in bouillon, that's what he is."

After a moment's reflection my wife observed that this was scarcely an elegant comparison. Then I thought of the three whales that used to hold up the world in olden times:

"He's a baby Whale."

My wife was silent.

That evening, after the bath, I went out to Vnukovo airport and boarded a huge plane for the East. Then in Sakhalin, traveling around the little ports they have there, I would take out his picture in hotels and tourist homes and find myself thinking, "How's that little Whale of mine?"

Not that I didn't give him plenty of other nicknames later on. He was Bullyboy for a while, and Cupkins, and once he acquired this elaborate surname: Plumpkins-Bumpkins-Rumtumtumpkins-Sleepygrumpkins-Lunchkins-Munchkins. Yet little by little these nicknames all faded away and were forgotten, until there remained but one, the big one—Whale.

"Well, what happened, Whale?" I asked, as I settled myself on the kitchen stepstool and lit up a cigarette.

"Look," he said, pointing out the window, "pretty little lights!" He set about counting them: "One, two, three, eighteen, eleven, nine ... Look!" he exclaimed suddenly, "the moon!"

I turned toward the window. A pale moon with its side eaten away hung over the houses.

"Yes, the moon." It upset me, somehow, and I flicked my ash on the floor.

"Tolya, Tolya, we do have an ashtray," said Whale in his mother's tone of voice.

"You're right," I said. "Sorry."

We fell silent and sat for a while—I on the stepstool, he on the potty—in absolute stillness, broken only by my wife's sighs from the bedroom and the rustle of the pages of her book. Whale's eyes shone mysteriously. The lull was evidently to his liking.

"Y'know"—he suddenly roused himself—"Gagarin the pilot flies to the moon."

"Yes," I said.

"Y'know," he said, "Gagarin doesn't, and Titov doesn't, and Tereshkova doesn't, and John Glenn doesn't ..." A thoughtful pause.

"What?" I asked.

"And Cooper doesn't—they don't breathe anything into their mouth or nose," he completed his thought.

My wife came into the kitchen and lifted him off the potty. "You didn't do anything. Sit down again and try. You aren't trying at all."

"Tolya, do you try when you sit on the potty?" asked Whale.

"Yes," I said. "Bimbo the Elephant tries."

"And Tumba the Mama Elephant?"

"She does too."

"And Kuchka the Baby Elephant?"

"Sure he tries."

"And who else tries?"

"The dolphin," I said.

"Is the dolphin good?" he asked.

"Did you call him?" my wife asked.

"It was busy," I said.

"Then call him again."

"Listen here!" My temper flared. "This is my business, right? It's my business, and I'm the one who knows when to call."

"You're just chicken," she said scornfully.

I jumped up from the stool.

"Go take a walk, the both of you!" she said sharply. "Get dressed, fast! Out!"

Whale and I went out of the house and walked down our street toward the boulevard. It was already dark. Whale took big, business-like steps, his soft baby hand firmly clasping mine.

"So what about it?" he asked.

"What?" I was lost.

"Is the dolphin good?"

"Yes, of course he's good. Sharks are evil, but the dolphin is good."

How does he picture the sea, when he's never laid eyes on it, I thought. How does he picture the depth and boundlessness of the sea? How does he picture this city? What does Moscow mean to him? He doesn't know anything yet, at all. He doesn't know that the world is split into two camps. He doesn't know what it is, the world. We have already labelled . . . it's been catch as catch can, but we've managed to put a label to practically all the phenomena in our environment; we've built ourselves up this real world of ours. But right now he's living in a world strange and wonderful, not in the slightest like ours.

"And who bit off the side of the moon?" he asked.

"The Great Bear," I blurted, and at once felt alarmed, realizing how long it would take me to explain all that to him. I could tell from his tiny hand that once again he was quivering all over with curiosity.

"What do you mean, Tolya?" he asked carefully. "What kind of a bear?"

I picked him up in my arms and pointed to the sky. "See those little stars? Those right there—one, two, three, four, five, six, seven . . . In the shape of a dipper. That's called the Great Bear."

What are they, the stars? What is the Great Bear? Why has she hung over us like this since time immemorial?

"Yes, the great bear!" he cried happily, shaking his finger at her. "She's the one that bit off the side of the moon! Tch, tch!"

The ease with which he had grasped these fictions emboldened me. "And up a bit higher there," I said, "there's a Lesser Bear too. See the little small dipper? That's the Lesser Bear."

"Where's the Daddy Bear?" It was a reasonable question; he was trying to set up a bear family.

"The Daddy Bear . . ." I muttered, "the Daddy Bear . . ."

Whale came to my aid. "He's gone hunting in the woods, hasn't he?"

"That's it." I let him down from my shoulder.

We came out on to the boulevard. The benches here were all taken by old men and nannies, but promenading along the mall were packs of fourteen-year-old girls, followed by packs of fifteen-year-old boys. It was bright and bluish here: fluorescent lamps cast their light on a Humpback Horsey the size of a dinosaur; a Firebird that looked like a giant turkey; an enormous Puss-in-Boots, tall as two men, with a depraved expression on his round visage; another cat—this one with a totally corrupt look—on a golden chain by the curving sea; King Guidon, the Swan Princess, a rocket, the Queen of the Fields, Gulliver . . .

It was Fantasy World, a children's book fair set up on our boulevard. At this hour the stalls were closed; only here and there did a yellow light gleam through the cracks in the fabulous plywood giants—the vendors were inside counting their take.

Whale was overwhelmed. He did not know where to run first—the Cat, the

Prince, the Swan. For a moment or so he stood as if struck dumb: he just rolled his big eyes and whispered soundlessly. Then he tugged at my hand and let out a squeal, and practically skipping we took off for the stalls. I fought off a barrage of questions and was a long time telling him what was what, who was good and who was evil.

As it turned out, nearly all the figures stood for goodness and light, wisdom and the native wit of the people; there was only the wretched kite, hovering over the Swan, to represent the forces of evil, and Guidon's arrow was already aimed at him.

At length my Whale got tired and leaned heavily against the Humpback Horsey.

"Let's go, Whale," I said. "We should be getting home."

"Tolya, listen, let's take them all with us."

"But they're so big, how can we?"

"Who cares, we'll take them anyhow." He swatted the Horse with his small palm: "This one's taken!" He ran over and swatted the Cat: "And this one!"

Thus he captured them all to have with him at bedtime and after that departed for home—quite tranquil now—without a backward glance.

At the turnoff from the boulevard he was lagging behind. I stopped; what now?

"Look, Tolya," he said. "Look what a pretty lady."

And what should I see but a pretty lady, who was coming our way. Her gait called to mind a restrained, or rather a scarcely restrainable, dance. With each nudge of her marvelous knees she flung open the skirts of her marvelous coat, and the umbrella, incredibly sharp and slim, which she held under her arm was plainly nothing less than a spare inner pivot for her gyrations, and her eyes, secret and subtle, flashed brilliantly at the sight of us. It was three days since I had last seen her, this lady, and now a dismal, anxious mood came over me, as always when I saw her or thought of her. The more so now, with Whale there.

"Oh," said she, "so this is what he's like, your little Whale. How delightful!"

She bent down to him, but he touched the umbrella and asked, "What's this? An arrow? A gun?"

"It's an umbrella," she exclaimed, and in a trice she had it open. With a faint flip it unfolded over her head, lending her whole figure a supplemental buoyancy, an airiness almost of the circus.

"Let me hold it!" shouted Whale.

She handed him the umbrella.

"It is a pleasure, Signor, to see you engaged in such peaceful pursuits," said she to me.

"And you, Mam'selle, are a joy to behold," said I.

We really could have done without the fatuous badinage customary in our circle and plunged right into serious talk about whatever had lately been on our minds; but it was the thing to do—one had to start by displaying his sense of humor in this or some more felicitous manner—and neither she nor I could break with the custom.

Whale was circling about on the great umbrella, and we were able to talk in peace.

"Tolya, why so sour?"

"Am I offending you?"

"You're sick of me, aren't you?"

"How come?"

"You think I'm crowding you—"

"Do you have to play games?"

She said she was not playing games, we shouldn't have to quarrel, after all we hadn't seen each other in three days, she understood that I had a fox gnawing at my vitals, she understood all, I was always in her thoughts, and maybe that was helping me.

She was lying and not lying. How neatly the female heart combines sincerity and subtlety, I thought. Everlasting peace and the senseless, disgusting inner turmoil of vanity. They have it easier later on, pretty women do, I thought; they have no fear of death, never give it a thought, their only fear is old age. Silly things, they're afraid of old age.

I had the further thought, as she went on being sympathetic, that I'd better not enter into her world again; I wasn't up to it, I had nothing in my head but turmoil, I was in no mood for adventure just now and no mood for romance; how I yearned for tranquillity, yet only once that whole day had I been tranquil, amid the plywood monstrosities of Fantasy World.

"Darling," said the pretty lady to me, "I know how humiliating it is, but pluck up your courage and make that phone call. You *must* clear things up once and for all, and even if it turns out for the worse, it will still be for the better, I assure you."

She lifted her hand and put the palm of this hand to my cheek . . . stroked . . .

Just then Whale came squirming in between us. He tugged the pretty lady by the sleeve: "Hey, take your old umbrella and don't touch Daddy. He's my Daddy, not yours."

We parted from the pretty lady and started home. Ever so slightly false, affectedly amiable, possibly bitter, her laughter lingered a few seconds in our ears.

Along the way we stopped at the gate of the bus depot. Enormous buses kept driving in through the gate, and middle-sized ones, and micro-buses.

"Daddy Bus, Mama Bus, Baby Bus," said Whale, and laughed.

And so we returned home. While Whale had supper and told his Mama about the walk, I hung around in the livingroom, glancing at the phone from time to time, and got myself too upset to do anything at all.

I hate that instrument. It amazes me the way my wife can talk to her girl friends for hours on end, the way she can achieve a cordial intimacy with people by means of a telephone. Could it be that her affection for her friends is transferred to the telephone receiver, and all those hours it's really the receiver she's so fond of?

I do waste a lot of time out of dislike for the phone. Rather than pick up the receiver and make some gaffe, I drive clear across town, a waste of time and money. Maybe it's because I aspire to a life of realism, while any voice you hear in the receiver seems like make-believe, always make-believe, never the real thing.

Perhaps that's what I should do this time? Perhaps not call him today, but go over tomorrow and have this talk face to face. Once we are face to face I can use the art of mime, delicate, barely perceptible mimicry, to show him I'm not all that simple, it's not all that simple to humiliate me; give him to understand that I'm no milktoast but a man of courage, that this visit of mine, too, is an act of courage, and I care not a fig for him. A conversation over the phone gives him an enormous advantage, over the phone I might just as well be conversing with a supernatural power.

The phone rang. Jangled, the ugly thing! I picked up the receiver and heard the voice of my old pal Stasik.

"I'm mad at you, you're mad at me, I'm a skunk, you're a skunk," babbled Stasik.

With the overture out of the way, I asked what he was calling for.

"I'll tell you what for: don't be a fool, call that party immediately. You know yourself how much depends on him. I saw Voynovsky today, and he'd run into Ovsyannikov, who'd spoken to Sadovnikov yesterday; all of them feel you *must* do it. I'm about to call Ovsyannikov, and he'll try and get in touch with Sadovnikov, and Sadovnikov will be calling you. You wouldn't know Voynovsky's number?"

I hung up. The plungers clicked nastily. For fifteen minutes, sitting by the now silent instrument, I had an almost physical awareness of the telephonic hurry-scurry my friends had set in motion—pictured their words, sleek as mice, darting cleverly into the cables and slithering along in convergent streams.

Then Sadovnikov called, promising to hurry and get in touch with Ovsyannikov, who would give him Stasik's number, and Stasik would help him contact Voynovsky.

"Did you get through to him?" my wife asked as she came into the room.

"There's no one home," I lied.

"Of course not. You're just a man with no answers."

She left. I was in a state of complete confusion and disarray when in came Whale, smiling, his arms piled with books.

"Read me a story, Tolya?"

There were works by Marshak, Jacob Akim, Eugene Rein, and Henry Samgir, as well as an assortment of folk tales. We took up the folk tales. Whale leaned against me and listened attentively, pulling on my ear at tense moments.

The Indian story of the little elephant he rejected, however. When we came to the part where the crocodile seizes the little elephant by the trunk, Whale gave a shout, snatched the book, and hurled it to the floor.

"It's a lie!" He even flushed red. "That didn't happen! It's a bad story!"

"Now look, Whale," I said, "the story is a good one. It has a happy ending."

"No it's not. It's evil! Read this one here."

What he pulled from the pile was "The Wolf and the Seven Little Goats." My God, I thought, here too we have dramatic happenings—a dreadful act, the devouring of the baby goats—and even though it all ends happily, how am I going to read it to Whale, my baby fact-varnisher?

Whale, meanwhile, was leafing through the book, scrutinizing the crude illustrations.

"Here's the Mama Goat," he said, "bringing milk. Here are the little goat-children, playing."

The delightful idyll unfolded before us, and it gladdened Whale. Naive as he was, and ignorant of the laws of dramaturgy, he turned calmly to the next page, where a garishly ferocious wolf was taking the poor little white kid into his fearsome maw. I froze.

"And here's the nice Daddy Goat," said Whale, pointing to the wolf. "He's playing with the baby." He had set up the goat family in a most peaceful fashion.

"Whale, you're mistaken," I said cautiously. "That's not the Daddy Goat, it's the nasty gray wolf. He's about to swallow the little goat, but everything turns out all right, the wolf will be punished. This is Dramaturgy, my little Whale."

"No!" he shouted, on the verge of tears. "That's not a wolf! It's the Daddy Goat. He's playing. You don't understand anything, Tolya!"

"My mistake," I said hastily. "You're right. It's the Daddy Goat."

"Ivan dearest, time for bed," called his mother, and off he went, taking with him into his gentle dreams the family of heavenly bears, the "bus family," and the nice family of goats, the pretty lady's umbrella, the good monstrosities of Fantasy World, and my cap, which would of course grow overnight to the size of an airplane and which he would fly to the North Pole, to the kingdom of good animals.

When she had tucked him in my wife returned and sat down in the armchair opposite me. We lighted cigarettes. Normally these were happy moments, when we smoked together at the end of the day, but tonight it was no good.

"Who's the lady Ivan was telling me about?" asked my wife.

"Someone from the main office. A consultant on legal problems."

"Is that so," she said. "What do you intend to do now?"

"I don't know."

"Is that so," she said.

"My God, I wish it were winter!" I burst out.

"Why winter?"

"Winter's when I have vacation. I'll go skiing."

"But of course," she said caustically. "You're a great skier."

"Don't."

"No, it's true. You *are* a first-class skier. Everyone knows that."

She bit her lip, ever so slightly, to keep from breaking into tears. Whereupon I pulled the phone over and dialed that damned number at one fell swoop.

While the long slow tones rang in the receiver, I pictured him swinging his feet down from the divan and leisurely walking to the telephone, reading from one of his books on the way. Maybe he was rubbing his back or his seat, maybe thinking, "Who can this be? Most likely that sad sack with his fatuous requests." Here he was, picking up the receiver.

He spoke to me gently, confidingly. "Listen, my friend, they tell me you've had trouble bringing yourself to call me. I've been waiting for your call a long time. Come now, why the rigamarole and apprehension? Apparently it's all been due to a misconception. When last we met I wondered whether you hadn't misunderstood me. I do believe everything will be favorably resolved. Sleep in peace. With all my soul I am for you, and by its every fiber and by my every nerve, my heart, my liver, and my spleen, by my virtue and my honor, my fidelity, my sincerity and my love, by all that is sacred to humankind, by the ideals of all generations, by the earth's axis, by the solar system, by the wisdom of my best-beloved writers and philosophers, by history, geography, and botany, by the red sun, the blue sea, and the high and far off kingdom I vow to be unto you a faithful servant, your armor-bearer and your page."

Drenched in sweat, I hung up the receiver.

"There," said my wife to me, "that wasn't so dreadful, was it? You just have to make a wish, and . . ." She smiled at me.

I got up, went into the bathroom, washed, and then stopped by the bedroom for a look at Whale. He slept like an infant hero, arms and legs flung wide. The creases of his baby fat had not quite faded away; they still marked his wrists, his dimpled paws. In his sleep he smiled a sly little smile, evidently busy completing various droll and delightful turnabouts in his kingdom.

When I look at him I am filled with gladness, goodness, and light. I feel like drinking to the long, happy life of the Seven Little Goats.

Translated from the Russian by Susan Brownsberger

Margaret Atwood

· ·

HAIR JEWELLERY

There must be some approach to this, a method, a technique, that's the word I want, it kills germs. Some technique then, a way of thinking about it that would be bloodless and therefore painless; devotion recollected in tranquillity. I try to conjure up an image of myself at that time, also one of you, but it's like conjuring the dead. How do I know I'm not inventing both of us, and if I'm not inventing then it really is like conjuring the dead, a dangerous game. Why should I disturb those sleepers, sleepwalkers, as they make their automaton rounds through the streets where we once lived, fading from year to year, their voices thinning to the sound of a thumb drawn across a wet window: an insect squeak, transparent as glass, no words. You can never tell with the dead whether it is they who wish to return or the living who want them to. The usual explanation is that they have something to tell us. I'm not sure I believe it; in this case it's more likely that I have something to tell them.

Be careful, I want to write, *there is a future,* God's hand on the temple wall, clear and unavoidable in the new snow, just in front of them where they are walking—I see it as December—along the brick sidewalk in Boston, city of rotting dignities, she in her wavering high heels, getting her feet wet from sheer vanity. Boots were ugly then, heavy shapeless rubber like rhinoceros paws, flight boots they called them, or furred at the tops like old ladies' or bedroom slippers, with stringy bows; or there were those plastic wedge-shaped rain boots, they would yellow quickly and become encrusted with dirt on the inside, they looked like buried teeth.

That's my technique, I resurrect myself through clothes. In fact it's impossible for me to remember what I did, what happened to me, unless I can remember what I was wearing, and every time I discard a sweater or a dress I am discarding a part of my life. I shed identities like a snake, leaving them pale and shrivelled behind me, a trail of them, and if I want any memories at all I have to collect, one by one, those cotton and wool fragments, piece them together, achieving at last a patchwork self, no defence anyway against the cold. I concentrate, and this particular lost soul rises miasmic from the Crippled Civilians

Clothing Donation Box in the Loblaws parking lot in downtown Toronto, where I finally ditched that coat.

The coat was long and black. It was good quality—good quality mattered then, and the women's magazines had articles about basic wardrobes and correct pressing and how to get spots out of camel's hair—but it was far too big for me, the sleeves came to my knuckles, the hem to the tops of my plastic rain boots, which did not fit either. When I bought it I meant to alter it, but I never did. Most of my clothes were the same, they were all too big, perhaps I believed that if my clothes were large and shapeless, if they formed a sort of tent around me, I would be less visible. But the reverse was true; I must have been more noticeable than most as I billowed along the streets in my black wool shroud, my head swathed in, was it a plaid angora scarf, also good quality; at any rate, my head swathed.

I bought these clothes, when I bought clothes at all—for you must remember that, like you, I was poor, which accounts for at least some of our desperation—in Filene's Basement, where good quality clothes that failed to sell at the more genteel levels were disposed of at slashed prices. You often had to try them on in the aisles, as there were few dressing rooms, and the cellar, for it was a cellar, low-ceilinged, dimly lit, dank with the smell of anxious armpits and harassed feet, was filled on bargain days with struggling women in slips and bras, stuffing themselves into torn and soiled designer originals to the sound of heavy breathing and a hundred sticking zippers. It is customary to laugh at bargain-hunting women, at their voraciousness, their hysteria, but Filene's Basement was, in its own way, tragic. No one went there who did not aspire to a shape-change, a transformation, a new life, but the things never did quite fit.

Under the black coat I wear a heavy tweed skirt, grey in colour, and a brown sweater with only one not very noticeable hole, valued by me because it was your cigarette that burned it. Under the sweater I have a slip (too long), a brassiere (too small), some panties with little pink roses on them, also from Filene's Basement, only twenty-five cents, five for a dollar, and a pair of nylon stockings held up by a garter belt which, being too large, is travelling around my waist, causing the seams at the backs of my legs to spiral like barbers' poles. I am lugging a suitcase which is far too heavy—no one carried packsacks then except at summer camp—as it contains another set of my weighty, oversized clothes as well as six nineteenth-century Gothic novels and a sheaf of clean paper. On the other side, counterbalancing the suitcase, are my portable typewriter and my Filene's Basement handbag, gargantuan, bottomless as the tomb. It is February, the wind whips the black coat out behind me, my plastic rain boots skid on the ice of the sidewalk, in a passing store window I see a woman thick and red and bundled. I am hopelessly in love and I am going to the train station to escape.

If I had been richer it would have been the airport. I would have gone to California, Algiers, somewhere oily and alien and above all warm. As it was, I had just enough money for a return ticket and three days in Salem, the only other place both accessible and notable being Walden Pond, which was not much good in winter. I had already justified the trip to myself: it would be more educational to go to Salem than to Algiers, for I was supposed to be "doing work"

on Nathaniel Hawthorne. "Doing work," they called it; they still call it that. I
would be able to soak up atmosphere; perhaps from this experience, to which I
did not look forward, the academic paper required for my survival as a scholar
would emerge, like a stunted dandelion from a crack in the sidewalk. Those dismal streets, that Puritanical melancholy combined with the sodden February sea
winds would be like a plunge into cold water, shocking into action my critical
faculties, my talent for word-chopping and the construction of plausible foot-
notes which had assured so far the trickle of scholarship money on which I subsisted. For the past two months these abilities had been paralyzed by unrequited
love. I thought that several days away from you would give me time to think
things over. In my subsequent experience, this does no good at all.

Unrequited love was, at that period of my life, the only kind I seemed to be
capable of feeling. This caused me much pain, but in retrospect I see it had advantages. It provided all the emotional jolts of the other kind without any of the
risks, it did not interfere with my life, which, although meagre, was mine and
predictable, and it involved no decisions. In the world of stark physical reality it
might call for the removal of my ill-fitting garments (in the dark or the bathroom, if possible: no woman wants a man to see her safety pins), but it left undisturbed their metaphysical counterparts. At that time I believed in
metaphysics. My Platonic version of myself resembled an Egyptian mummy, a
mysteriously wrapped object that might or might not fall into dust if uncovered.
But unrequited love demanded no stripteases.

If, as had happened several times, my love was requited, if it became a question of the future, of making a decision that would lead inevitably to the sound
of one's beloved shaving with an electric razor while one scraped congealed egg
from his breakfast plate, I was filled with panic. My academic researches had
made me familiar with the moment at which one's closest friend and most
trusted companion grows fangs or turns into a bat; this moment was expected,
and held few terrors for me. Far more disconcerting was that other moment,
when the scales would fall from my eyes and my current lover would be revealed
not as a demigod or a monster, impersonal and irresistible, but as a human
being. What Psyche saw with the candle was not a god with wings but a pigeon-
chested youth with pimples, and that's why it took her so long to win her way
back to true love. It is easier to love a daemon than a man, though less heroic.

You were, of course, the perfect object. No banal shadow of lawn mowers and
bungalows lurked in your melancholy eyes, opaque as black marble, recondite as
urns, you coughed like Roderick Usher, you were, in your own eyes and therefore in mine, doomed and restless as Dracula. Why is it that dolefulness and a
sense of futility are so irresistible to young women? I watch this syndrome
among my students: those febrile young men who sprawl on the carpets which
this institution of higher learning has so thoughtfully provided for them, grubby
and slack as hookworm victims, each with some girl in tow who buys cigarettes
and coffee for him and who receives in turn his outpourings of spleen, his con-
demnations of the world and his mockery of her in particular, of the way she
dresses, of the recreation room and two television sets owned by her parents,
who may be in fact identical to his, of her friends, of what she reads, of how she
thinks. Why do they put up with it? Perhaps it makes them feel, by contrast,

healthful and life-giving; or perhaps these men are their mirrors, reflecting the misery and chaps they contain but are afraid to acknowledge.

Our case was different only in externals; the desperation, I'm sure, was identical. I had ended up in academia because I did not want to be a secretary, or, to put it another way, because I did not want always to have to buy my good-quality clothes in Filene's Basement; you, because you did not want to be drafted, and at that time the university dodge still worked. We were both from small, unimportant cities, whose Rotary Club denizens, unaware of our actual condition, believed that their minute bursaries were helping us to pursue arcane but glamourous careers which would in some vague way reflect credit on the community. But neither of us wanted to be a professional scholar, and the real ones, some of whom had brushcuts and efficient briefcases and looked like junior executives of shoe companies, filled us with dismay. Instead of "doing work" we would spend our time drinking draft beer in the cheapest of the local German restaurants, ridiculing the pomposity of our seminars and the intellectual mannerisms of our fellow students. Or we would wander through the stacks of the library, searching for recondite titles no one could possibly have heard of so we could drop them into the next literary debate in that reverential tone soon mastered by every future departmental chairman, and watch the ripples of dismay spread through the eyes of our fellow inmates. Sometimes we would sneak into the Music Department, co-opt a vacant piano and sing maudlin Victorian favourites or bouncy choruses from Gilbert and Sullivan, or a plaintive ballad by Edward Lear from which we had been compelled, earlier in the year, to extract the Freudian symbols. I associate it with a certain brown corduroy skirt which I had made myself, the hem of which was stapled in several places because I had not had the moral energy to sew it.

> On the coast of Coromandel,
> Where the early pumpkins blow
> In the middle of the woods
> Lived the Yonghy-Bonghy-Bo . . .
>
> Two old chairs, and half a candle
> One old jug without a handle,
> These were all his worldly goods
> In the middle of the woods . . .

The mutilated candle and the broken jug had caused much snide merriment at the seminar, but for us they held a compelling pathos. The state of affairs in Coromandel, its squalor and hopelessness, seemed too apt a comment on our own.

Our problem, I thought, was that neither the world around us nor the future stretching before us contained any image of what we might conceivably become. We were stranded in the present as in a stalled, otherwise empty subway train, and in this isolation we clutched morosely at each other's shadows. That at any rate was my analysis as I lugged my suitcase through the icy twilight towards the only hotel in Salem that was open, or so the conductor had told me. I have trouble seeing this, but I think the railroad station was condensed and dark, lit by a muddy orange light like the subway stations in Boston, and it too had the smell of weak disinfectant unsuccessfully applied to a layer of dried urine so old as to be almost respectable. It did not remind me of Puritans or witches or even of overstuffed shipbuilders, but of undernourished millworkers with lung trouble, a later generation.

The hotel, too, smelt of decay and better days. It was being repainted, and the painters' canvas cloths and stepladders almost blocked the corridors. The hotel was open only because of the renovations; otherwise, said the desk clerk, who seemed also to be the bellboy, the manager and possibly the owner, he would have shut it down and gone to Florida. "People only come here in the summer," he said, "to see the House of the Seven Gables and that." He resented my being there at all, and more especially for refusing to give a satisfactory explanation. I told him I had come to look at the tombstones but he did not believe this. As he hauled my suitcase and my typewriter towards the windswept cupboard in which he was about to deposit me, he kept looking back over my shoulder as though there ought to have been a man behind me. Illicit sex, he knew, was the only conceivable reason for Salem in February. He was right, of course.

The bed was narrow and hard as a mortuary slab, and I soon discovered that although there was a brisk sea breeze blowing through the closed window, the management was aware of it and had compensated; each fresh onslaught of central heating was announced by the sound of hammers and leaden gongs from the radiator.

Between my fits of sleep I thought about you, rehearsing our future, which I knew would be brief. Of course we would sleep together, though this topic had not yet been discussed. In those days, as you recall, it had to be discussed first, and so far we had not progressed beyond a few furtive outdoor gropings and one moment when, under a full moon on one of those deserted brick streets, you had put your hand on my throat and announced that you were the Boston Strangler; a joke which, for one with my literary predilections, amounted to a seduction. But though sex was a necessary and even a desirable ritual, I dwelt less on it than on our parting, which I visualized as sad, tender, inevitable and final. I rehearsed it in every conceivable location: doorways, ferry-boat docks, train, plane and subway stations, park benches. We would not say much, we would look at each other, we would *know* (though precisely what we would know I wasn't sure); then you would turn a corner and be lost forever. I would be wearing a trench coat, not yet purchased, though I had seen the kind of thing I wanted in Filene's Basement the previous autumn. The park bench scene—I set it in spring, to provide a contrast to the mood—was so affecting that I cried, though since I had a horror of being overheard, even in an empty hotel, I timed it to coincide with the radiator. Futility is so attractive to the young, and I had not yet exhausted its possibilities.

By the next morning I was tired of brooding and snivelling. I decided to seek out the main derelict graveyard, which might provide me with a quaint seventeenth-century tombstone epitaph suitable for my Hawthorne paper. In the hall the workmen were hammering and painting; as I walked down the corridor they stared after me like frogs in a pond. The desk clerk grudgingly relinquished a

Chamber of Commerce tourist brochure, which had a map and a short list of the points of interest.

There was no one in the streets outside, and very few cars. The houses, filmed with soot, their paint peeled by the salty air, seemed deserted, though in several of the front windows behind the greying lace curtains I could see the shadowy outline of a face. The sky was grey and furrowed, like the inside of a mattress, and there was a high wind blowing. I skidded over the sidewalks in my slippery boots, the wind pushing my black coat like a sail, making good progress until I turned a corner and the wind was no longer behind me. Soon after that I gave up the graveyard idea.

Instead I turned into a small restaurant; I had not yet had breakfast—the hotel had been surly about it—and I wanted to eat and to consider what to do next. I ordered an egg sandwich and a glass of milk and studied the brochure. The waitress and the proprietor, who were the only other people in the room, retreated to the far end and stood with folded arms, watching me suspiciously while I ate as though expecting me to leap up and perform some act of necromancy with the butter knife. Meanwhile, the House of the Seven Gables was closed for the winter. It had nothing to do with Hawthorne anyway; it was just an old house that had avoided being torn down, and which people now paid money to see because it had been given the name of a novel. No genuine author's sweat on the banisters. I think this was the moment at which I started to become cynical about literature.

The only other point of interest, according to the Chamber of Commerce, was the library. Unlike everything else it was open in February, and was apparently world-famous for its collection of genealogies. The last thing I wanted was a visit to the library, but returning to the hotel with its noise and chemical smells was pointless, and I couldn't stay in the restaurant all day.

The library was empty, except for a middle-aged man in a felt hat who was looking doggedly at the rows of genealogies, palpably killing time. An official woman with a bun and a scowl was sitting behind a blunt desk doing crossword puzzles. The library served also as a museum of sorts. There were several ships' figureheads, maidens with rigid eyes, wooden men, ornate fish and lions, their gilt worn thin; and, displayed in glass cases, a collection of Victorian hair jewellery; brooches and rings, each with a crystal front protecting a design of woven hair; flowers, initials, wreaths or weeping willows. The more elaborate ones had hair of different colours. Though originally they must have shone, the strands by now had aged to the texture of something you find under a chair cushion. It struck me that Donne had been wrong about the circlet of bright hair about the bone. A hand-lettered card explained that many of these pieces were memorial jewellery, intended for distribution to the mourners at funerals.

"The funeral ones," I said to the woman at the desk. "I mean, how did they . . . did they cut the hair off before or after?"

She looked up from her puzzle. She did not understand at all what I was talking about.

"Before or after the person died," I said. If it was before, it seemed to me a callous thing to do. If after, how did they have time to weave all those willow trees before the funeral? And why would they want to? I could not imagine wearing at my throat one of those heavy brooches, like a metal pillow, stuffed with the gradually dimming tresses of one I loved. It would be like a dried hand. It would be like a noose.

"I'm sure I don't know," she said with distaste. "This is a travelling exhibition."

The man in the felt hat was lying in wait for me outside the door. He asked me to join him for a drink. He must have been staying at the hotel.

"No, thank you," I said, adding, "I'm with someone." I said this to mollify him—women always feel compelled to mollify men by whom they are declining to be picked up—but as I said it I realized I had come here not to get away from you, as I had thought, but to be with you, more completely than your actual presence would allow. In the flesh your irony was impenetrable, but alone I could wallow uninterrupted in romantic doom. I've never understood why people consider youth a time of freedom and joy. It's probably because they have forgotten their own. Surrounded now by the doleful young, I can only feel grateful for having escaped, hopefully forever (for I no longer believe in reincarnation), from the intolerable bondage of being twenty-one.

I had told you I was going away for three days, but undiluted fantasy was too much for me. Salem was a vacuum and you were expanding to fill it. I knew whose hair that was in the massive black and gold *memento mori* in the second row of brooches, I knew who I had heard in the vacant hotel room to the left of mine, breathing almost inaudibly between the spasms of the radiator. Luckily there was an afternoon train; I took it, and fled back to the present.

I called you from the Boston train station. You accepted my early return with your usual fatalism, expressing neither glee nor surprise. You were supposed to be doing work on ambiguity in Tennyson's "Locksley Hall," which, you informed me, was clearly out of the question. Ambiguity was big in those days. We went for a walk instead. It was milder and the snow was turning to mush; we ended up at the Charles River, where we rolled snowballs and pitched them into the water. After that we constructed a damp statue of Queen Victoria, complete with jutting bosom, monumental bustle and hooked nose, then demolished it with snowballs and chunks of ice, sniggering at intervals with what I then thought was liberated abandon but now recognize as hysteria.

And then, and then. What did I have on? My coat, of course, and a different skirt, a sickly greenish plaid; the same sweater with the burnt hole in it. We slithered together through the partially frozen slush beside the river, holding each other's chilly hands. It was evening and getting colder. From time to time we stopped, to jump up and down and kiss each other, in order to keep warm. On the oily surface of the Charles were reflected, like bright mirages, the towers and belfries from which the spring examination hopeless ones would later hurl themselves, as they did every year; in its sludgy depths floated the literary suicides, Faulkner's among them, encrusted with crystalline words and glittering like eyes; but we were reckless, we sang in mockery of them, a ragged duet:

Two old chairs, and half a candle,
One old jug without a handle, . . .

For once you were laughing. I renounced my carefully constructed script, the ending I had planned for us. The future opened like a wide-screen vista, promising and dangerous, any direction was possible. I felt as if I was walking along the edge of a high bridge. It seemed to us—at least it seemed to me—that we were actually happy.

When the cold was finally too much for us and you had begun to sneeze, we went to one of the cheap restaurants where, it was rumoured, you could live for nothing by eating the free packets of ketchup, relish and sugar and drinking the cream out of the cream-jugs when no one was looking. There we debated the advisability of sleeping together, the pros and cons and, quite soon after that, the ways and means. It was not done lightly, especially by female graduate students, who were supposed to be like nuns, dedicated and unfleshly. Not that in those monastic surroundings they had much chance to be anything else, as the male ones mostly went to the opera together in little groups and had sherry parties to which they invited only each other. We both lived in residence; we both had cellmates who were always in the room, biting their nails and composing bibliographies. Neither of us had a car, and we were sure the local hotels would reject us. It would have to be somewhere else. We settled on New York at Easter Break.

The day before the trip I went to Filene's Basement and bought, after some deliberation, a red nylon baby-doll nightgown, only one size too big and with a shoulder strap that could easily be sewed back on. I lingered over a mauve one with Carmen-like flounces, but I could wear only one at a time and the money would be needed for other things. On Good Friday I took the bus down to New York. You had left several days earlier, but I had stayed to finish an overdue essay on Mrs. Radcliffe's *The Italian*. You yourself had three overdue papers by that time, but you no longer seemed to care. You had been spending a lot of time taking showers, which had annoyed your roommate; you had also been suffering from extended nightmares, which featured, as I recall, elephants, alligators and other large animals rolling down hills in wheelchairs, and people being nailed to crosses and incinerated. I viewed these as evidence of your sensitivity.

The plan was that you would stay at the apartment of an old friend from your hometown, while I was to get a single hotel room. This would defeat suspicion, we hoped; also it would be less expensive.

At that time I had never been to New York and I was not prepared for it. At first it made me dizzy. I stood in the Port Authority in my long black coat, with my heavy suitcase and my bottomless purse, looking for a phone booth. The crowd was like a political demonstration, though at that time I had never seen a real one. Women jostled each other and spat insults as if they were slogans, hauling grumpy children in their wake; there was a lineup of seedy old men on the benches, and the floor was dotted with gum, candy wrappers and cigarette stubs. I'm not sure but I think there were pinball machines; can that be possible? I wished now that I had asked you to meet the bus, but such dependencies were not part of our understanding.

As I headed for what I guessed was the exit, a black man grabbed hold of my suitcase and began to pull. He had a fresh cut on his forehead from which the blood was running, and his eyes were filled with such desperation that I almost let go. He was not trying to steal my suitcase, I realized after a minute; he just wanted to carry it to a taxi for me.

"No thank you," I said. "No money."

He glanced with scorn at my coat—it was, after all, good quality—and did not let go. I pulled harder and he gave up. He shouted something after me that I didn't understand; those words had not yet become common currency.

I knew the address of the hotel, but I didn't know how to get there. I began to walk. The sun was out and I was sweating, from fright as well as heat. I found a telephone booth: the phone had been eviscerated and was a tangle of wires. The next one was intact, but when I called you there was no answer. This was strange, as I'd told you what time I was arriving.

I leaned against the side of the phone booth, making an effort not to panic. New York had been designed like a barred window, so by looking at the street signs and counting, I should be able to deduce the location of the hotel. I did not want to ask anyone: the expressions of blank despair or active malice made me nervous, and I had passed several people who were talking out loud to themselves. New York, like Salem, appeared to be falling to pieces. A rich person might have seen it as potential urban renewal, but the buildings with chunks missing, the holes in the sidewalks, did not reassure me.

I set out to drag my suitcase to the hotel, stopping at every phone booth to dial your number. In one of these I left your copy of *The Education of Henry Adams*, by mistake. It was just as well, as it was the only thing of yours I had; it would have been unlucky to have kept it.

The hotel clerk was nearly as suspicious of me as the one in Salem had been. I had ascribed the distrust of me there to small-town xenophobia, but it occurred to me now for the first time that it might be the way I was dressed. With my cuffs down to my knuckles, I did not look like someone with a credit card.

I sat in my room, which was really very much like the one in Salem, wondering what had happened to you, where you were. I phoned every half hour. There was not much I could do while waiting. I unpacked the red nightgown with the broken strap, only to find I'd forgotten the needle and thread with which I'd intended to repair it; I didn't even have a safety pin. I wanted to take a bath, but the handle of my door kept turning, and although I had fastened the chain I did not want to take the chance. I even kept my coat on. I began to think that you had given me the wrong number, or, worse, that you were something I had invented.

Finally at about seven o'clock someone answered the phone at your end. It was a woman. When I asked for you she laughed, not pleasantly.

"Hey, Voice of Doom," I heard her say. "Some chick wants you." When you came on your voice was even more remote than usual.

"Where are you?" I said, trying not to sound like a nagging wife. "I've been trying to get hold of you since two-thirty."

"It's my friend," you said. "She swallowed a bottle of sleeping pills this morning. I had to walk her around a lot."

"Oh," I said. I'd had the impression that the friend was male. "Couldn't you have taken her to a hospital or something?"

"You don't take people to hospitals here unless you really have to."

"Why did she do it?" I asked.

"Who knows?" you said, in the voice of someone annoyed at being involved, however peripherally. "To pass the time, I guess." In the background the woman said something that sounded like "You shit."

The soles of my feet turned cold, my legs went numb. I had realized suddenly that she was not just an old friend, as you had told me. She had been a lover, she was still a lover, she was serious, she had taken the pills because she found out I was arriving that day and she was trying to stop you; yet all this time you were calmly writing down the room number, the phone number, that I was just as calmly giving you. We arranged to meet the next day. I spent the night lying on the bed with my coat on.

Of course you failed to arrive, and by that time I had thought twice about phoning. You did not even return to Boston. In May I got a cryptic note from you on a postcard with a picture of the Atlantic City boardwalk on the front:

> I ran off to join the Navy but they wouldn't have me, they didn't think Ancient Greek was a good enough qualification. I got a job in a hash joint by lying about my literacy. It's better than jumping off the bell tower. Give my regards to Coromandel. Ever yours, Bo.

As usual, I couldn't decide whether or not you were sneering.

Of course I mourned; not so much for your departure, as that had been, I now saw, a foregone conclusion, but for its suddenness. I had been deprived of that last necessary scene, the park bench, the light spring wind, the trench coat (which I was destined never to buy), your vanishing figure. Even after I realized that our future would have contained neither the dreaded bungalow and electric razor nor those vague, happy possibilities I had once imagined, but, inevitable as a rhymed couplet, an emptied bottle of sleeping pills whose effects you might not have helped me walk off, I continued to mourn.

Because you had not left in the proper way it seemed as though you had never left at all. You hung around, like a miasma or the smell of mice, waiting to deflate my attempts at optimism—for out of sheer fright I soon began to make them—with your own jaundiced view of my behaviour. As if you were my darker twin or an adept in sinister telepathy I could sense on every occasion what your opinion would be. When I became engaged (seven months later, to an architect who designed, and continues to design, apartment buildings), you let me know you had expected other things of me. The actual wedding, and yes, I had all the trimmings including a white gown, filled you with scorn. I could see you in your dingy room, surrounded by empty sardine tins and lint-covered socks, living on nothing but your derision and your refusal to sell out, as I was so palpably doing. (To what? To whom? Unlike later generations, we were never able to pinpoint the enemy.)

My two children did not impress you, nor did the academic position which I subsequently achieved. I have become, in a minor way, an authority on women domestic novelists of the nineteenth century. I discovered after my marriage that I really had more in common with them than I did with Gothic romances; I suppose this insight into my true character signifies maturity, a word you despise. The most prominent of my subjects is Mrs. Gaskell, but you may have heard of Mrs. J. H. Riddell as well; she wrote also under the pen name of F. G. Trafford. I gave quite a creditable paper on her *George Geith of Fen Court*, which was later published in a reputable journal. Needless to say I have tenure, as my department, averse to women for many years, has recently been under some pressure to justify its hiring policies. I am a token, as you never tire of pointing out. I dress well, too, as befits a token. The drab, defiantly woollen wardrobe you may remember vanished little by little into the bins of the Salvation Army as I grew richer, and was replaced by a moderately chic collection of pantsuits and brisk dresses. My male colleagues think of me as efficient and rather cold. I no longer have casual affairs, as I hate mementoes that cannot be thrown away. My coats no longer flap, and when I attend academic conferences nobody stares.

It was at one of these, the big one, the central flesh market and hiring fair, that I saw you last. Curiously enough, it was held in New York that year. I was giving a paper on Amelia Edwards and other female journalists of the period. When I saw your name on the agenda I thought it must be someone else. But it was you, all right, and you spent the entire session discussing whether or not John Keats had had syphilis. You had done a considerable amount of research on the medical uses of mercury in the early part of the century, and your last paragraph was a masterpiece of inconclusion. You had gained weight, in fact you looked healthy, you looked as if you played golf. Though I watched in vain for a sardonic smile: your delivery was deadpan.

Afterwards I went up to congratulate you. You were surprised to see me; you had never thought of me, you said, ending up quite like this, and your possibly dismayed gaze took in my salon haircut, my trim-fitting red jump suit, my jaunty boots. You yourself were married, with three children, and you hastily showed me wallet snapshots, holding them out like protective talismans. I matched them with my own. Neither of us suggested having a drink. We wished each other well; we were both disappointed. You had wanted me, I saw now, to die young of consumption or some equally operatic disease. Underneath it all you too were a romantic.

That should have been that, and I can't understand why it isn't. It is absolutely true that I love my husband and children. In addition to attending faculty meetings, where I crochet afghan squares during discussions of increments and curricula, I cook them nourishing meals, arrange birthday parties and make my own bread and pickles, most of the time. My husband admires my achievements and is supportive, as they say, during my depressions, which become rarer. I have a rich and rewarding sex life, and I can already hear you ridiculing the adjectives, but it is rich and rewarding in spite of you. And you have done no better than I have.

But when I returned from the conference to the house where I live, which is not a bungalow but a two-storey colonial and in which, ever since I moved in, you have occupied the cellar, you were not gone. I expected you to have been dispelled, exorcised: you had become real, you had a wife and three snapshots, and banality is after all the magic antidote for unrequited love. But it was not enough. There you were, in your accustomed place, over by the shelf to the right of the cellar stairs where I keep the preserves, standing dusty and stuffed like

Jeremy Bentham in his glass case, looking at me not with your former scorn, it's true, but with reproach, as if I had let it happen, as if it was my fault. Surely you don't want it back, that misery, those decaying buildings, that seductive despair and emptiness, that fear? Surely you don't want to be stuck on that slushy Boston street forever. You should have been more careful. I try to tell you it would have ended badly, that it was not the way you remember, you are deceiving yourself, but you refuse to be consoled. *Goodbye,* I tell you, waiting for your glance, pensive, regretful. You are supposed to turn and walk away, past the steamer trunks, around the corner into the laundry room, and vanish behind the twinset washer-dryer; but you do not move.

Ingeborg Bachmann

. . . .

EVERYTHING

When we sit down to a meal like two people who have been turned to stone, or meet in the evening at the door of the apartment because we have both thought of bolting it at the same time, I feel our mourning like a bow stretching from one end of the world to the other—that is to say, from Hanna to me—and to the bent bow is fitted an arrow that must strike the impassive sky in the heart. When we go back through the hall she walks two steps in front of me, she goes into the bedroom without saying good night, and I flee into my room, to my typewriter and then stare into space, her bowed head before my eyes and her silence in my ears. Is she lying down and trying to sleep or is she awake and waiting? What for?—since she isn't waiting for me.

When I married Hanna it was less for her own sake than because she was expecting a baby. I had no choice, needed to make no decision. I was moved because something was in preparation that was new and came from us, and because the world seemed to me to be waxing. Like the moon before which one is supposed to bow three times when it is new and stands tender and breath-coloured at the start of its course. I experienced moments of absence I had not known before. Even in the office—although I had enough to do—or during a conference, I would suddenly slip into this state in which I turned only to the child, to this unknown, spectral being, and went towards it with all my thoughts right into the warm, lightless womb in which it lay prisoner.

The child we expected changed us. We scarcely went out any more and neglected our friends; we looked for a larger apartment and arranged our living conditions better and more permanently. But on account of the child I was waiting for, everything began to change for me; I came upon unexpected thoughts, as one comes upon mines, of such explosive power that I ought to have drawn back in terror, but I went on, with no feeling for the danger.

Hanna misunderstood me. Because I couldn't decide whether the baby carriage should have big or small wheels I seemed indifferent. ('I really don't know. Whichever you like. Yes, I am listening.') When I stood around with her in shops where she was searching for bonnets, jackets and diapers, hesitating be-

40

tween pink and blue, synthetic wool and real wool, she reproached me with not having my mind on the subject. But it was only too much on it.

How am I to express what was going on inside me? I was like a savage who is suddenly made aware that the world in which he moves between hearth and encampment, between sunrise and sunset, between hunting and eating, is also the world that is millions of years old and will pass away, that occupies an insignificant place among many solar systems, that rotates at a great speed on its axis and at the same time round the sun. All at once I saw myself in other contexts, myself and the child whose turn to be born would come round at a particular point of time, the beginning or middle of November, just as it had once come for me, just as it had once come for all those before me.

One just has to visualize it clearly. This whole line of descent! Like the black and white sheep before you fall asleep (one black, one white, one black, one white, and so on), a mental image which can sometimes make one dull and drowsy and sometimes desperately wide awake. I have never been able to get to sleep by means of this prescription, although Hanna, who learnt it from her mother, swears that it is much more tranquillizing than a sleeping tablet. Perhaps it is tranquillizing to many people to think of this chain: And Shem begat Arphaxad. And Arphaxad lived five and thirty years and begat Salah. And Salah begat Eber. And Eber begat Peleg. And Peleg lived thirty years and begat Reu, and Reu begat Serug and Serug begat Nahor and each of them afterwards begat many sons and daughters, and the sons kept begetting sons, to wit Nahor begat Terah and Terah begat Abram, Nahor and Haran. I tried two or three times to think this process through, not only forwards, but also backwards to Adam and Eve from whom we are unlikely to be descended; but in every case there is a darkness, so that it makes no difference whether we attach ourselves to Adam and Eve or to two other exemplars. Only if we don't want to attach ourselves and prefer to ask why each one had his turn, we find ourselves completely baffled by the chain and don't know what to make of all the begettings, of the first and last lives. For each person has only one turn at the game which he finds waiting for him and is compelled to take up: procreation and education, economics and politics, and he is allowed to occupy himself with money and emotion, with work and invention and the justification of the rules of the game which is called thinking.

But since we so trustingly multiply we have to make the best of it. The game needs the players. (Or do the players need the game?) I too had been put so trustingly into the world, and now I had put a child into the world.

Now I trembled at the very thought.

I began to look at *everything* in relation to the child. My hands, for example, which would one day touch and hold him, our apartment on the third floor, the Kandlgasse, the 7th District, the roads running this way and that through the city down to the river meadows of the Prater and finally the whole wide world which I would explain to him. From me he should hear the names: table and bed, nose and foot. Also words like spirit and God and soul, in my view useless words, but they couldn't be hidden from him, and later complicated words like resonance, diapositive, chiliasm and astronautics. I should have to see to it that my child learnt what everything meant and how everything was to be used, a door-handle and a bicycle, a mouth-wash and a form. It was all spinning round in my head.

When the child came, of course, I could make no use of my great lesson. He lay there, jaundiced, wrinkled, pitiful, and there was one thing I was not prepared for—that I had to give him a name. I hurriedly came to an agreement with Hanna and we had three names entered in the register. My father's, her father's and my grandfather's. None of the three names was ever used. By the end of the first week the child was called Fipps. I don't know how this came about. Perhaps it was partly my fault because I tried, like Hanna who was quite inexhaustible in the invention and combination of meaningless syllables, to call him by pet names because his real names just didn't seem to fit the tiny naked creature. Various attempts at ingratiation produced this name that has annoyed me more and more with the passing of the years. Sometimes I even blamed it on the child, as though he could have defended himself, as though it was no coincidence. Fipps! I shall have to go on calling him that, making him ridiculous beyond death and us with him.

When Fipps lay in his blue and white cot, awake, asleep, and all I was good for was to wipe a few drops of saliva or sour milk from his mouth, to pick him up in the hope of giving him relief when he screamed, I thought to myself for the first time that he too had plans for me but that he was allowing me time to get to the bottom of them, was altogether determined to allow me time, like a ghost that appears to one and returns into the darkness and comes back, emitting the same unfathomable look. I often used to sit by his bed looking down at that almost immobile face, into those eyes that gazed without direction, and studying his features like an ancient script for whose decipherment there is no clue. I was glad to see that Hanna kept unerringly to the obvious things, feeding him, putting him to sleep, waking him, changing his bed and his diapers as laid down in the book. She cleaned his nose with little wads of cotton wool and dusted a cloud of powder between his chubby thighs as though this were of everlasting benefit to him and to her.

After a few weeks I tried to entice a first smile out of him. But when he did surprise us with one the grimace remained enigmatic and unrelated to us. Even when he directed his eyes more and more frequently and more and more exactly at us or stretched out his little arms, I had a suspicion that it meant nothing and that we were merely trying to find for him the reasons which he would later assume. It was impossible for Hanna, and perhaps for anybody, to understand me, but at this period my disquiet began. I'm afraid that I already started then to move away from Hanna, more and more to shut her out and keep her at a distance from my true thoughts. I discovered a weakness in myself—the child had made me discover it—and the feeling of moving towards a defeat. I was thirty like Hanna, who looked young and slender as never before. But the child had not given me any fresh youth. To the degree that his circle expanded, I contracted mine. I went to the wall, at every smile, every exultation, every cry. I hadn't the strength to nip this smiling, this chirping, these cries in the bud. Because that would have been the thing to do.

The time that remained to me passed quickly. Fipps sat upright in the pram, cut his first teeth, moaned a great deal; soon he stretched, stood up swaying, grew visibly steadier, crawled on his hands and knees across the room, and one day the first words came. There was no stopping it now and I still didn't know what was to be done.

What indeed? In the past I had thought I had to teach him the world. Since the mute dialogues with him I had become confused and been taught otherwise. Did I not have it in my power, for example, to refrain from telling him the names of things, from teaching him the use of objects? He was the first man. With him everything started, and it was impossible to say whether everything might not become quite different through him. Should I not leave the world to him, blank and without meaning? I didn't have to initiate him into purposes and aims, into good and evil, into what really is and what only seems to be. Why should I draw him over to me, why should I make him know and believe, rejoice and suffer? Here, where we are standing, the world is the worst of all worlds, and no one has understood it up to now, but where he was standing nothing had been decided. Not yet. How much longer?

And I suddenly knew, it is all a question of language and not merely of this one language of ours that was created with others in Babel to confuse the world. For underneath it there smoulders another language that extends to gestures and looks, the unwinding of thoughts and the passage of feelings, and in it is all our misfortune. It was all a question of whether I could preserve the child from our language until he had established a new one and could introduce a new era.

I often went out of the house alone with Fipps, and when I saw what Hanna had done to him in the way of sweet talk, coquetry, playfulness, I was horrified. He was taking after us. But not only after Hanna and me, no, after mankind in general. But there were moments in which he governed himself, and then I observed him earnestly. All paths were the same to him. All beings the same. Hanna and I undoubtedly stood closer to him only because we were continually busying ourselves close to him. It was all the same to him. How much longer?

He was afraid. Not yet of an avalanche or a mean act, however, but of a leaf that started moving on a tree. Of a butterfly. Flies utterly terrified him. And I thought: how will he be able to live when a whole tree bends in the wind and I leave him so unclear about everything!

He met a neighbour's child on the stairs; he clutched clumsily at his face, drew back, and perhaps didn't know that he was looking at a child. In the past he had screamed when he felt uncomfortable, but when he screamed now more was involved. It often happened before he fell asleep or when I picked him up to carry him to the table, or when a toy was taken away from him. There was a great rage in him. He could lie down on the floor, dig his nails into the carpet and scream till he was blue in the face and frothing at the mouth. He used to scream out in his sleep as though a vampire had settled on his chest. These screams confirmed my opinion that he still trusted himself to scream and that his screams worked.

Oh, one day!

Hanna went about with gentle reproaches and called him naughty. She pressed him to her, kissed him or looked at him gravely and told him not to distress his mother. She was a wonderful temptress. She stood unflinchingly bent over the nameless river and tried to draw him across, she walked up and down on our bank enticing him with chocolates and oranges, tops and teddy bears.

And when the trees cast shadows I thought I heard a voice: 'Teach him the language of shadows! The world is an experiment and it is enough that this experiment has always been repeated in the same way with the same result. Make another experiment! Let him go to shadows! The result till now has been a life in guilt, love and despair.' (I had begun to think of everything in universal terms; then words like this occurred to me.) But I could spare him guilt, love and any kind of fate and free him for another life.

Yes, on Sundays I wandered with him through the Vienna woods, and when we came to a stream a voice inside me said: 'Teach him the language of water!' It passed over stones. Over roots. 'Teach him the language of stones! Plant his roots afresh!' The leaves were falling because it was autumn again. 'Teach him the language of leaves!'

But since I knew and found no word of such languages, had only my own language and could not pass beyond its frontiers, I carried him up and down the paths in silence, and back home where he learnt to form sentences and walked into the trap. He was already expressing wishes, uttering requests and orders and talking for the sake of talking. On later Sunday walks he tore out blades of grass, picked up worms, caught beetles. Now they were no longer all the same to him, he examined them, killed them if I didn't take them out of his hand in time. At home he took to pieces books and boxes and his string puppet. He grabbed everything, bit it, felt everything, threw it away or accepted it. Oh, one day. One day he would know all about everything.

During this period, when she was more communicative, Hanna often used to draw my attention to what Fipps said; she was enchanted with his innocent looks, innocent talk and his doings. But I could see no innocence in the child at all since he was no longer defenceless and dumb as during the first weeks. And then no doubt he wasn't innocent but only incapable of expressing himself, a bundle of fine flesh and flax with thin breath, with an enormous, dull head that took the edge off the world's messages like a lightning conductor.

When he was older, Fipps was often allowed to play with other children in a blind alley near the house. Once, when I was coming home around midday, I saw him with three little boys catch water in a tin as it flowed along the gutter. Then they stood in a circle talking. It looked like a consultation. (This is how engineers consult together as to where they shall begin drilling, where they shall make the first hole.) They squatted down on the pavement and Fipps, who held the tin, was on the point of emptying it out when they stood up again and moved three paving-stones farther on. But this spot seemed not to be right either for what they had in mind. They stood up again. There was a tension in the air. What a male tension! Something had to happen! Then they found the spot, three feet farther on. They squatted down again, fell silent, and Fipps tipped the tin. The dirty water flowed over the paving-stones. They stared at it, silent and solemn. It was done, accomplished. Perhaps successful. It must have been successful. The world could rely on these little men who were carrying it on. They would carry it on, of that I was now quite sure. I entered the house, mounted the stairs and threw myself on the bed in our bedroom. The world had been carried forward, the spot had been found from which to carry it forward, always in the same direction. I had hoped that my child would not find the direction. And once, a long time ago, I had feared that he would not find his way. Fool that I was, I had feared that he wouldn't find the direction!

I got up and splashed a few handfuls of cold tap-water over my face. I didn't want this child any more. I hated him because he understood too well, because I already saw him treading in everyone's footsteps.

I walked around extending my hatred to everything that came of man, to the trams, the house numbers, titles, the division of time, this whole jumbled, ingenious chaos that is called order, to refuse disposal, lecture-lists, registration offices, all these wretched institutions against which it is no longer possible to kick, against which nobody ever does kick, these altars on which I had sacrificed but wasn't willing to let my child be sacrificed. Why should he be? He hadn't arranged the world, hadn't caused its injury. Why should he settle down in it? I yelled at the registration office and the schools and the barracks: 'Give him a chance! Give my child, before he is ruined, one single chance!' I raged against myself because I had forced my son into this world and was doing nothing to set him free. I owed it to him, I had to act, go away with him, withdraw with him to an island. But where is this island from which a new human being can found a new world? I was caught with the child and condemned from the outset to join in the old. Therefore I dropped the child. I dropped him from my love. This child was capable of anything, only not of stepping out, not of breaking through the devil's circle.

Fipps played away the years till he went to school. He played them away in the truest sense of the word. I was glad to see him play, but not those games that showed him the way to later games. Hide and seek, counting games, cops and robbers. I wanted quite different, pure games for him, other fairy stories than the familiar ones. But I couldn't think of anything and he was only interested in imitation. One doesn't believe it possible, but there is no way out for us. Again and again everything is divided into above and below, good and evil, light and dark, into quantity and quality, friend and enemy, and where other beings or animals appear in the fables they immediately take on the features of human beings.

Because I no longer knew how and to what purpose to educate him I gave it up. Hanna noticed that I no longer bothered about him. Once we tried to talk about it and she stared at me as if I were a monster. I couldn't get everything out because she stood up, cut me short and went into the nursery. It was evening, and from that evening on she, who formerly would no more have thought of it than I, began to pray with the child: Now I lay me down to sleep. Little Jesus meek and mild. And so on. I didn't bother about that either, but they will have gone a long way with their repertoire. I think she wanted thereby to put him under protection. Anything would have done for her, a cross or a mascot, a magic formula or anything else. Fundamentally she was right, since Fipps would soon fall among the wolves and soon howl with the wolves. 'God be with you' was perhaps the last chance. We were both delivering him up, each in his own way.

When Fipps came home from school with bad marks I didn't say a word, but
nor did I comfort him. Hanna was secretly anguished. She regularly sat down
after lunch and helped him with his homework, heard him on his lessons. She
did her job as well as it could be done. But I didn't believe in the cause. It was all
the same to me whether Fipps went to the grammar school later or not, whether
he developed into something worthwhile or not. A worker wants to see his son a
doctor, a doctor wants to see his son at least a doctor. I don't understand that. I
didn't want Fipps to become either cleverer or better than us. Nor did I want to
be loved by him; there was no need for him to obey me, no need for him to bend
to my will. No, I wanted . . . I only wanted him to begin from the beginning, to
show me with a single gesture that he didn't have to reflect *our* gestures. I didn't
see anything new in him. I was newborn, but he wasn't! It was I, yes, I was the
first man and had gambled everything away, and done nothing!

I wanted nothing for Fipps, absolutely nothing at all. I merely went on observing him. I don't know whether a man has a right to observe his own child
like this. As a research worker observes a 'case'. I watched this hopeless case of
human being. This child whom I couldn't love as I loved Hanna, Hanna whom I
never dropped completely because she couldn't disappoint me. She had already
been one of the same kind of people as myself when I met her, with a good figure, experienced, slightly special and yet not special, a woman and then my wife.
I put this child and myself on trial—him because he was destroying a lofty expectation, myself because I could not prepare the ground for him. I had expected that this child, because he was a child—yes, I had expected him to
redeem the world. It sounds monstrous. And I did indeed behave monstrously
towards the child, but there is nothing monstrous about what I hoped for. It was
simply that I wasn't prepared for the child, like everyone before me. I had no
thought in my mind when I embraced Hanna, when I was soothed in the darkness of her body—I couldn't think. It was good to marry Hanna, not only on
account of the child; but later I was never again happy with her but only concerned that she shouldn't have another. She wanted one, I have reason to believe
that, although she no longer talks about it now and does nothing to make it
happen. One might imagine that now of all times Hanna would think about a
child, but she is turned to stone. She doesn't go away from me and doesn't come
to me. She bickers with me in a way one ought never to bicker with anyone,
since a man is not master over such intangible things as death and life. At that
time she would have liked to bring up a whole litter and I prevented it. All the
conditions were right for her and none of them were right for me. She once explained to me, when we were quarrelling, all the things she wanted to do and
have for Fipps. *Everything:* a lighter room, more vitamins, a sailor suit, more
love, all the love there was, she wanted to set up a storehouse of love that would
last a lifetime, because of outside, because of people . . . a good education, foreign languages, to watch out for his talents. She cried and was offended because
I laughed at this. I don't believe it occurred to her for a moment that Fipps
would be one of the people 'outside', that like them he might wound, insult,
cheat, that he might be capable of so much as one mean action, and yet I had
every reason to assume that he would. For evil, as we call it, was present in the
child like an abscess in the body. I don't even need to think of the story of the

knife here. It began much earlier, when he was three or four. I came in when he was stamping round angry and snivelling; a tower he had built with bricks had fallen over. Suddenly he stopped his lamenting and said in a low, emphatic voice: 'I'll set the house on fire. I'll smash everything to bits. I'll smash you all to bits.' I lifted him up onto my knee, caressed him, promised to rebuild the tower for him. He repeated his threats. Hanna, who joined us, was for the first time unsure. She reproved him and asked him who said such things to him. He replied firmly: 'Nobody.'

Then he pushed a little girl who lived in the building down the stairs, was very frightened afterwards, wept, promised never to do it again and yet did it again. For a time he hit out at Hanna at every opportunity. This, too, passed.

Of course I forget to bear in mind how many charming things he said, how affectionate he could be, how pink and glowing he was when he woke in the morning. I often noticed all that, was often tempted to snatch him up, to kiss him, as Hanna did, but I didn't want to let myself be reassured and deceived by this. I was on the alert. Because there was nothing monstrous about what I hoped for. I had no grandiose plans for my child, but I did want this little thing, this slight deviation. Of course, when a child is called Fipps . . . Must he do such honour to his name? To come and go with a lapdog's name. To waste eleven years in one circus act after another. (Eat with the right hand. Hold yourself straight when you walk. Wave. Don't talk with your mouth full.)

After he went to school I was more often to be found out of the house than in it. I played chess in a café or, on the pretext of work, I shut myself up in my room and read. I met Betty, a salesgirl from the Maria Hilferstrasse, to whom I brought stockings, movie tickets or something to eat, and so got her used to me. She was offhand, undemanding, subservient and if she enjoyed anything during her joyless free evenings it was eating. I went to her pretty often throughout one year, lay down beside her on the bed in her furnished room where, as I drank a glass of wine, she read illustrated papers and then agreed to my suggestions without embarrassment. It was a time of the greatest confusion because of the child. I never made love to Betty, on the contrary, I was on the search for self-gratification, for the prohibited, light-shunning liberation from woman and the human race. In order not to be caught, in order to be independent. I didn't want to sleep with Hanna any more because I had given in to her.

Although I had not tried to conceal my evenings away from home over such a long period, it seemed to me that Hanna lived without suspicion. One day I discovered that it was not so; she had already seen me once with Betty in the Café Elsahof, where we often used to meet after work, and again two days later when I was standing with Betty in a line for tickets outside the Cosmos Cinema. Hanna behaved in a very unusual way, looking past me as though I were a stranger, so that I didn't know what to do. I nodded to her, feeling paralysed, and shifted forward to the box-office, feeling Betty's hand in mine, and, incredible as it seems to me now, actually went into the movie theatre. After the performance, while I prepared for reproaches and tested out my defence, I took a taxi for the short way home, as if I could thereby make reparation or prevent something. Since Hanna didn't say a word I plunged into my prepared text. She maintained a stubborn silence, as though I were speaking of things that didn't concern her. Finally she did open her mouth and said shyly that I should think of the child. 'For Fipps's sake . . .' was the expression she used. I was stricken, because of her embarrassment, begged her forgiveness, went down on my knees, promised never again, and I really did never see Betty again. I don't know why I nevertheless wrote her two letters, to which she undoubtedly attached no importance. No answer came and in fact I hadn't expected an answer. . . . As though I had wanted these letters to come to myself or Hanna, I had laid myself bare in them as never before to anyone. Sometimes I feared to be blackmailed by Betty. Why blackmailed? I sent her money. Why, since Hanna knew about her?

This bewilderment. This desolation.

I felt extinct as a man, impotent. I wanted to remain so. If a bill were presented it would go in my favour. To withdraw from the human race, to come to an end, an end, let it come to that!

But everything that happened was not a matter of me or Hanna or Fipps, but of father and son, a guilt and a death.

I once read in a book the sentence: 'It is not heaven's way to raise its head.' It would be a good thing if everyone knew of this sentence that speaks of the hardness of heaven. Oh no, it really isn't heaven's way to look down, to give signs to the bewildered people below it. At least not where such a sombre drama takes place in which it too, this fabricated 'above', plays a part. Father and son. A son—that such a thing exists, that is what is inconceivable. Words like this occur to me now because there is no lucid word for this gloomy business; merely to think about it deprives one of one's reason. A gloomy business: for there was my seed, indefinable and uncanny to me myself, and then Hanna's blood in which the child was nourished and which accompanied the birth, altogether a gloomy business. And it had ended with blood, with his resoundingly brilliant child's blood that flowed from the wound in his head.

He couldn't speak as he lay there on the jutting crag in the ravine. All he managed to get out was the name of the first schoolboy who reached him. He tried to raise his hand, to make some sign to him or to cling to him. But the hand wouldn't rise. In the end, however, a few moments later when the teacher bent over him, he did manage to say:

'I want to go home.'

I shall take care not to believe, on the strength of this sentence, that he felt an explicit longing for Hanna and me. One wants to go home when one feels that one is dying, and he did feel that. He was a child and had no great messages to leave. Fipps was only a quite ordinary child, there was nothing to block his path as he thought his last thoughts. The other children and the teacher collected sticks, made a stretcher of them and carried him to the upper village. He died on the way, almost at the first few steps. Passed away? Departed this life? In the obituary notice we wrote: '. . . our only child . . . was taken from us by an accident.' The man at the printer's who took the order asked if we didn't want to say 'our only, dearly beloved child', but Hanna, who was on the telephone, said no, that went without saying, beloved and dearly beloved, and that was no longer the point. I was so foolish as to try to embrace her for this statement; so morbid were my feelings for her. She pushed me away. Does she see me at all? What in heaven's name does she reproach me with?

Hanna, who for a long time had cared for him entirely on her own, goes around looking unrecognizable, as though no longer lit by the searchlight that had shone upon her when she stood with Fipps and through Fipps in the centre of the stage. There is no longer anything to be said about her, as though she had neither qualities nor characteristics. In the past she was gay and lively, anxious, gentle and strict, always ready to guide the child, to let him run and pull him back close to her. After the incident with the knife, for instance, she had her finest hour, she glowed with magnanimity and insight, she was able to take the part of the child and his faults, she stood up for him in front of every authority. It was in his third year at school. Fipps had gone for a schoolfellow with a pocket-knife. He tried to stab him in the chest; the knife slipped and went into the child's arm. We were called to the school and I had painful discussions with the headmaster and the teachers and the parents of the injured child—painful because I had no doubt that Fipps was quite capable of doing this and quite different things, but I couldn't say what I thought—painful because the views that were forced upon me didn't interest me in the least.

It wasn't clear to anybody what we ought to do with Fipps. He sobbed, now obstinate, now in despair, and if it is possible to draw a conclusion, then he regretted what had happened. Nevertheless we did not succeed in persuading him to go voluntarily to the child and beg his pardon. We forced him, and all three of us went to the hospital. But I believe that Fipps, who had had nothing against the child when he attacked him, began to hate him from the moment when he had to say his piece. It was no childish anger that was in him, but a very fine, very adult hate held down with great self-control. He had succeeded in developing a difficult emotion into which he let no one see, it was as if he had been struck into humanity.

Every time I think of the school outing in the course of which everything came to an end, I also remember the business with the knife as if there were some remote connexion between them, because of the shock that once more reminded me of the existence of my child. For apart from these two incidents the few school years appear empty in my recollection, because I paid no attention to his growing up, to the increasing lucidity of his intelligence and his sensibilities. He must have been like all children of that age: wild and gentle, noisy and taciturn—exceptional in Hanna's eyes, unique in Hanna's eyes.

The headmaster of the school phoned me at my office. This had never happened before; even when the affair with the knife took place they had phoned the flat and it was Hanna who got in touch with me. I met the man half an hour later in the firm's entrance hall. We crossed the street to a café on the other side. First, he tried to say what he had to say in the hall, then in the street, but even in the café he felt that it wasn't the proper place. Perhaps there is no proper place for the announcement that a child is dead.

It wasn't the teacher's fault, he said.

I nodded. I had no wish to disagree.

The condition of the path was good, but Fipps had broken away from the class, out of exuberance or curiosity, perhaps because he wanted to look for a stick.

The headmaster began to stammer.

Fipps had slipped on a rock and crashed down onto the one beneath.

The wound in his head had not been serious in itself, but the doctor had discovered the reason for his rapid death, a cyst, I probably knew ...

I nodded. Cyst? I didn't know what it was.

The school was profoundly affected, said the headmaster, a commission of inquiry had been set up, the police informed. ...

I wasn't thinking of Fipps but of the teacher, for whom I felt sorry, and I gave the headmaster to understand that there was nothing to fear from my side.

No one was to blame. No one.

I rose before we had time to order anything, put a shilling on the table, and we parted. I went back into the office and away again at once, to the café, to drink a coffee after all, although I would have preferred a brandy or a whisky. I didn't trust myself to drink a brandy. Midday had come and I had to go home and tell Hanna. I don't know how I managed it or what I said. While we walked away from the door of the apartment and through the hall she must already have realized. Things moved so fast. I had to put her to bed and call the doctor. She was out of her mind and until she lost consciousness she screamed. She screamed as terribly as at his birth, and I trembled for her again as I had then. Once again all I wished was that nothing should happen to Hanna. All the time I thought: Hanna! Never of the child.

During the days that followed I trod all the paths alone. At the cemetery—I had kept the time of the funeral secret from Hanna—the headmaster made a speech. It was a fine day, a light wind was blowing, the bows on the wreaths rose as though for a festival. The headmaster talked on and on. For the first time I saw the whole class, the children with whom Fipps had spent half of almost every day, a collection of little lads staring dully in front of them, and among them I knew that there was one whom Fipps had tried to stab. There is an inner coldness that makes what is nearest and what is farthest move simultaneously into the distance. The grave moved into the distance with those standing round it and the wreaths. I saw the whole Central Cemetery drift away to the east, and while people were still squeezing my hand I felt only squeeze after squeeze and saw the faces out there, precise and as though seen from close to, but very far away, tremendously far away.

Learn the language of shadows! Learn it yourself.

But now that it is all over and Hanna no longer sits for hours in his room, but has allowed me to lock the door through which he so often ran, I sometimes speak to him in the language that I cannot consider good.

My wild one. My heart.

I am ready to carry him on my back and I promise him a blue balloon, a boat trip on the old Danube and postage stamps. I blow on his knee when he has bumped himself and help him with his sums.

Even if I cannot thereby bring him back to life it is not too late to think: I have accepted him, this son. I couldn't be friendly to him because I went too far with him.

Don't go too far. First learn to walk forward. Learn it yourself.

But first one has to be able to tear to pieces the bow of sorrow that leads from a man to a woman. This distance, measurable with silence, how can it ever decrease? For time without end, where for me there is a minefield, there will be a garden for Hanna.

I no longer think but would like to stand up, cross the dark passage and, without saying a word, reach Hanna. I look at nothing that would serve this purpose, neither my hands that are to hold her, nor my mouth in which I can enclose hers. It is unimportant with what sound before each word I come to her, with what warmth before each act of sympathy. I would not go in order to have her back, but in order to keep her in the world and so that she should keep me in the world. Through union, mild and sombre. If there are children after this embrace, good, let them come, be there, grow up, become like all the others. I shall devour them like Chronos, beat them like a big, terrible father, spoil them, these sacred animals, and let myself be deceived like a Lear. I shall bring them up as the times demand, half aiming at the wolfish practice and half at the idea of morality—and I shall give them nothing to take on their way. Like a man of my times: no possessions, no good advice.

But I don't know whether Hanna is still awake.

I am no longer thinking. The flesh is strong and dark that buries a true feeling under the great laughter of night.

I don't know whether Hanna is still awake.

Translated from the German by Michael Bullock

James Baldwin

· ·

GOING TO MEET THE MAN

"What's the matter?" she asked.

"I don't know," he said, trying to laugh, "I guess I'm tired."

"You've been working too hard," she said. "I keep telling you."

"Well, goddammit, woman," he said, "it's not my fault!" He tried again; he wretchedly failed again. Then he just lay there, silent, angry, and helpless. Excitement filled him just like a toothache, but it refused to enter his flesh. He stroked her breast. This was his wife. He could not ask her to do just a little thing for him, just to help him out, just for a little while, the way he could ask a nigger girl to do it. He lay there, and he sighed. The image of a black girl caused a distant excitement in him, like a far-away light; but, again, the excitement was more like pain; instead of forcing him to act, it made action impossible.

"Go to sleep," she said, gently, "you got a hard day tomorrow."

"Yeah," he said, and rolled over on his side, facing her, one hand still on one breast. "Goddamn the niggers. The black stinking coons. You'd think they'd learn. Wouldn't you think they'd learn? I mean, *wouldn't* you?"

"They going to be out there tomorrow," she said, and took his hand away, "get some sleep."

He lay there, one hand between his legs, staring at the frail sanctuary of his wife. A faint light came from the shutters; the moon was full. Two dogs, far away, were barking at each other, back and forth, insistently, as though they were agreeing to make an appointment. He heard a car coming north on the road and he half sat up, his hand reaching for his holster, which was on a chair near the bed, on top of his pants. The lights hit the shutters and seemed to travel across the room and then went out. The sound of the car slipped away, he heard it hit gravel, then heard it no more. Some liverlipped students, probably, heading back to that college—but coming from where? His watch said it was two in the morning. They could be coming from anywhere, from out of state most likely, and they would be at the court-house tomorrow. The niggers were getting ready. Well, they would be ready, too.

He moaned. He wanted to let whatever was in him out; but it wouldn't come out. Goddamn! he said aloud, and turned again, on his side, away from Grace, staring at the shutters. He was a big, healthy man and he had never had any trouble sleeping. And he wasn't old enough yet to have any trouble getting it up—he was only forty-two. And he was a good man, a God-fearing man, he had tried to do his duty all his life, and he had been a deputy sheriff for several years. Nothing had ever bothered him before, certainly not getting it up. Sometimes, sure, like any other man, he knew that he wanted a little more spice than Grace could give him and he would drive over yonder and pick up a black piece or arrest her, it came to the same thing but he couldn't do that now, no more. There was no telling what might happen once your ass was in the air. And they were low enough to kill a man then, too, everyone of them, or the girl herself might do it, right while she was making believe you made her feel so good. The niggers. What had the good Lord Almighty had in mind when he made the niggers? Well. They were pretty good at that, all right. Damn. Damn. Goddamn.

This wasn't helping him to sleep. He turned again, toward Grace again, and moved close to her warm body. He felt something he had never felt before. He felt that he would like to hold her, hold her, hold her, and be buried in her like a child and never have to get up in the morning again and go downtown to face those faces, good Christ, they were ugly! and never have to enter that jail house again and smell that smell and hear that singing; never again feel that filthy, kinky, greasy hair under his hand, never again watch those black breasts leap against the leaping cattle prod, never hear those moans again or watch that blood run down or the fat lips split or the sealed eyes struggle open. They were animals, they were no better than animals, what could be done with people like that? Here they had been in a civilized country for years and they still lived like animals. Their houses were dark, with oil cloth or cardboard in the windows, the smell was enough to make you puke your guts out, and there they sat, a whole tribe, pumping out kids, it looked like, every damn five minutes, and laughing and talking and playing music like they didn't have a care in the world, and he reckoned they didn't, neither, and coming to the door, into the sunlight, just standing there, just looking foolish, not thinking of anything but just getting back to what they were doing, saying, Yes suh, Mr. Jesse. I surely will, Mr. Jesse. Fine weather, Mr. Jesse. Why, I thank you, Mr. Jesse. He had worked for a mail-order house for a while and it had been his job to collect the payments for the stuff they bought. They were too dumb to know that they were being cheated blind, but that was no skin off his ass—he was just supposed to do his job. They would be late—they didn't have the sense to put money aside; but it was easy to scare them, and he never really had any trouble. Hell, they all liked him, the kids used to smile when he came to the door. He gave them candy, sometimes, or chewing gum, and rubbed their rough bullet heads—maybe the candy should have been poisoned. Those kids were grown now. He had had trouble with one of them today.

"There was this nigger today," he said; and stopped; his voice sounded peculiar. He touched Grace. "You awake?" he asked. She mumbled something, impatiently, she was probably telling him to go to sleep. It was all right. He knew that he was not alone.

"What a funny time," he said, "to be thinking about a thing like that—you listening?" She mumbled something again. He rolled over on his back. "This nigger's one of the ringleaders. We had trouble with him before. We must have had him out there at the work farm three or four times. Well, Big Jim C. and some of the boys really had to whip that nigger's ass today." He looked over at Grace; he could not tell whether she was listening or not; and he was afraid to ask again. "They had this line you know, to register"—he laughed, but she did not—"and they wouldn't stay where Big Jim C. wanted them, no, they had to start blocking traffic all around the court house so couldn't nothing or nobody get through, and Big Jim C. told them to disperse and they wouldn't move, they just kept up that singing, and Big Jim C. figured that the others would move if this nigger would move, him being the ringleader, but he wouldn't move and he wouldn't let the others move, so they had to beat him and a couple of the others and they threw them in the wagon—but *I* didn't see this nigger till I got to the jail. They were still singing and I was supposed to make them stop. Well, I couldn't make them stop for me but I knew he could make them stop. He was lying on the ground jerking and moaning, they had threw him in a cell by himself, and blood was coming out his ears from where Big Jim C. and his boys had whipped him. Wouldn't you think they'd learn? I put the prod to him and he jerked some more and he kind of screamed—but he didn't have much voice left. 'You make them stop that singing,' I said to him, 'you hear me? You make them stop that singing.' He acted like he didn't hear me and I put it to him again, under his arms, and he just rolled around on the floor and blood started coming from his mouth. He'd pissed his pants already." He paused. His mouth felt dry and his throat was as rough as sandpaper; as he talked, he began to hurt all over with that peculiar excitement which refused to be released. "You all are going to stop your singing, I said to him, and you are going to stop coming down to the court house and disrupting traffic and molesting the people and keeping us from our duties and keeping doctors from getting to sick white women and getting all them Northerners in this town to give our town a bad name—!" As he said this, he kept prodding the boy, sweat pouring from beneath the helmet he had not yet taken off. The boy rolled around in his own dirt and water and blood and tried to scream again as the prod hit his testicles, but the scream did not come out, only a kind of rattle and a moan. He stopped. He was not supposed to kill the nigger. The cell was filled with a terrible odor. The boy was still. "You hear me?" he called. "You had enough?" The singing went on. "You had enough?" His foot leapt out, he had not known it was going to, and caught the boy flush on the jaw. *Jesus,* he thought, *this ain't no nigger, this is a goddamn bull,* and he screamed again, "You had enough? You going to make them stop that singing now?"

But the boy was out. And now he was shaking worse than the boy had been shaking. He was glad no one could see him. At the same time, he felt very close to a very peculiar, particular joy; something deep in him and deep in his memory was stirred, but whatever was in his memory eluded him. He took off his helmet. He walked to the cell door.

"White man," said the boy, from the floor, behind him.

He stopped. For some reason, he grabbed his privates.

"You remember Old Julia?"

The boy said, from the floor, with his mouth full of blood, and one eye, barely open, glaring like the eye of a cat in the dark, "My grandmother's name was Mrs. Julia Blossom. *Mrs.* Julia Blossom. You going to call our women by their right names yet.—And those kids ain't going to stop singing. We going to keep on singing until every one of you miserable white mothers go stark raving out of your minds. Then he closed the one eye; he spat blood; his head fell back against the floor.

He looked down at the boy, whom he had been seeing, off and on, for more than a year, and suddenly remembered him: Old Julia had been one of his mail-order customers, a nice old woman. He had not seen her for years, he supposed that she must be dead.

He had walked into the yard, the boy had been sitting in a swing. He had smiled at the boy, and asked, "Old Julia home?"

The boy looked at him for a long time before he answered. "Don't no Old Julia live here."

"This is her house. I know her. She's lived here for years."

The boy shook his head. "You might know a Old Julia someplace else, white man. But don't nobody by that name live here."

He watched the boy; the boy watched him. The boy certainly wasn't more than ten. *White man.* He didn't have time to be fooling around with some crazy kid. He yelled, "Hey! Old Julia!"

But only silence answered him. The expression on the boy's face did not change. The sun beat down on them both, still and silent; he had the feeling that he had been caught up in a nightmare, a nightmare dreamed by a child; perhaps one of the nightmares he himself had dreamed as a child. It had that feeling—everything familiar, without undergoing any other change, had been subtly and hideously displaced: the trees, the sun, the patches of grass in the yard, the leaning porch and the weary porch steps and the cardboard in the windows and the black hole of the door which looked like the entrance to a cave, and the eyes of the pickaninny, all, all, were charged with malevolence. *White man.* He looked at the boy. "She's gone out?"

The boy said nothing.

"Well," he said, "tell her I passed by and I'll pass by next week." He started to go; he stopped. "You want some chewing gum?"

The boy got down from the swing and started for the house. He said, "I don't want nothing you got, white man." He walked into the house and closed the door behind him.

Now the boy looked as though he were dead. Jesse wanted to go over to him and pick him up and pistol whip him until the boy's head burst open like a melon. He began to tremble with what he believed was rage, sweat, both cold and hot, raced down his body, the singing filled him as though it were a weird, uncontrollable, monstrous howling rumbling up from the depths of his own belly, he felt an icy fear rise in him and raise him up, and he shouted, he howled, "You lucky we *pump* some white blood into you every once in a while—your women! Here's what I got for all the black bitches in the world—!" Then he was, abruptly, almost too weak to stand; to his bewilderment, his horror, beneath his own fingers, he felt himself violently stiffen—with no warning at all; he dropped his hands and he stared at the boy and he left the cell.

"All that singing they do," he said. "All that singing." He could not remember the first time he had heard it; he had been hearing it all his life. It was the sound with which he was most familiar—though it was also the sound of which he had been least conscious—and it had always contained an obscure comfort. They were singing to God. They were singing for mercy and they hoped to go to heaven, and he had even sometimes felt, when looking into the eyes of some of the old women, a few of the very old men, that they were singing for mercy for his soul, too. Of course he had never thought of their heaven or of what God was, or could be, for them; God was the same for everyone, he supposed, and heaven was where good people went—he supposed. He had never thought much about what it meant to be a good person. He tried to be a good person and treat everybody right: it wasn't his fault if the niggers had taken it into their heads to fight against God and go against the rules laid down in the Bible for everyone to read! Any preacher would tell you that. He was only doing his duty: protecting white people from the niggers and the niggers from themselves. And there were still lots of good niggers around—he had to remember that; they weren't all like that boy this afternoon; and the good niggers must be mighty sad to see what was happening to their people. They would thank him when this was over. In that way they had, the best of them, not quite looking him in the eye, in a low voice, with a little smile: We surely thanks you, Mr. Jesse. From the bottom of our hearts, we thanks you. He smiled. They hadn't all gone crazy. This trouble would pass.—He knew that the young people had changed some of the words to the songs. He had scarcely listened to the words before and he did not listen to them now; but he knew that the words were different; he could hear that much. He did not know if the faces were different, he had never, before this trouble began, watched them as they sang, but he certainly did not like what he saw now. They hated him, and this hatred was blacker than their hearts, blacker than their skins, redder than their blood, and harder, by far, than his club. Each day, each night, he felt worn out, aching, with their smell in his nostrils and filling his lungs, as though he were drowning—drowning in niggers; and it was all to be done again when he awoke. It would never end. It would never end. Perhaps this was what the singing had meant all along. They had not been singing black folks into heaven, they had been singing white folks into hell.

Everyone felt this black suspicion in many ways, but no one knew how to express it. Men much older than he, who had been responsible for law and order much longer than he, were now much quieter than they had been, and the tone of their jokes, in a way that he could not quite put his finger on, had changed. These men were his models, they had been friends to his father, and they had taught him what it meant to be a man. He looked to them for courage now. It wasn't that he didn't know that what he was doing was right—he knew that, nobody had to tell him that; it was only that he missed the ease of former years. But they didn't have much time to hang out with each other these days. They tended to stay close to their families every free minute because nobody knew what might happen next. Explosions rocked the night of their tranquil town. Each time each man wondered silently if perhaps this time the dynamite had not fallen into the wrong hands. They thought that they knew where all the guns were; but they could not possibly know every move that was made in that secret place where the darkies lived. From time to time it was suggested that they form a posse and search the home of every nigger, but they hadn't done it yet. For one thing, this might have brought the bastards from the North down on their backs; for another, although the niggers were scattered throughout the town—down in the hollow near the railroad tracks, way west near the mills, up on the hill, the well-off ones, and some out near the college—nothing seemed to happen in one part of town without the niggers immediately knowing it in the other. This meant that they could not take them by surprise. They rarely mentioned it, but they *knew* that some of the niggers had guns. It stood to reason, as they said, since, after all, some of them had been in the Army. There were niggers in the Army right now and God knows they wouldn't have had any trouble stealing this half-assed government blind—the whole world was doing it, look at the European countries and all those countries in Africa. They made jokes about it—bitter jokes; and they cursed the government in Washington, which had betrayed them; but they had not yet formed a posse. Now, if their town had been laid out like some towns in the North, where all the niggers lived together in one locality, they could have gone down and set fire to the houses and brought about peace that way. If the niggers had all lived in one place, they could have kept the fire in one place. But the way this town was laid out, the fire could hardly be controlled. It would spread all over town—and the niggers would probably be helping it to spread. Still, from time to time, they spoke of doing it, anyway; so that now there was a real fear among them that somebody might go crazy and light the match.

They rarely mentioned anything not directly related to the war that they were fighting, but this had failed to establish between them the unspoken communication of soldiers during a war. Each man, in the thrilling silence which sped outward from their exchanges, their laughter, and their anecdotes, seemed wrestling, in various degrees of darkness, with a secret which he could not articulate to himself, and which, however directly it related to the war, related yet more surely to his privacy and his past. They could no longer be sure, after all, that they had all done the same things. They had never dreamed that their privacy could contain any element of terror, could threaten, that is, to reveal itself, to the scrutiny of a judgment day, while remaining unreadable and inaccessible to themselves; nor had they dreamed that the past, while certainly refusing to be forgotten, could yet so stubbornly refuse to be remembered. They felt themselves mysteriously set at naught, as no longer entering into the real concerns of other people—while here they were, outnumbered, fighting to save the civilized world. They had thought that people would care—people didn't care; not enough, anyway, to help them. It would have been a help, really, or at least a relief, even to have been forced to surrender. Thus they had lost, probably forever, their old and easy connection with each other. They were forced to depend on each other more and, at the same time, to trust each other less. Who could tell when one of them might not betray them all, for money, or for the ease of confession? But no one dared imagine what there might be to confess. They were soldiers fighting a war, but their relationship to each other was that of accomplices in a crime. They all had to keep their mouths shut.

I stepped in the river at Jordan.

Out of the darkness of the room, out of nowhere, the line came flying up at him, with the melody and the beat. He turned wordlessly toward his sleeping wife. *I stepped in the river at Jordan.* Where had he heard that song?

"Grace," he whispered. "You awake?"

She did not answer. If she was awake, she wanted him to sleep. Her breathing was slow and easy, her body slowly rose and fell.

I stepped in the river at Jordan.
The water came to my knees.

He began to sweat. He felt an overwhelming fear, which yet contained a curious and dreadful pleasure.

I stepped in the river at Jordan.
The water came to my waist.

It had been night, as it was now, he was in the car between his mother and his father, sleepy, his head in his mother's lap, sleepy, and yet full of excitement. The singing came from far away, across the dark fields. There were no lights anywhere. They had said good-bye to all the others and turned off on this dark dirt road. They were almost home.

I stepped in the river at Jordan,
The water came over my head,
I looked way over to the other side,
He was making up my dying bed!

"I guess they singing for him," his father said, seeming very weary and subdued now. "Even when they're sad, they sound like they just about to go and tear off a piece." He yawned and leaned across the boy and slapped his wife lightly on the shoulder, allowing his hand to rest there for a moment. "Don't they?"

"Don't talk that way," she said.

"Well, that's what we going to do," he said, "you can make up your mind to that." He started whistling. "You see? When I begin to feel it, I gets kind of musical, too."

Oh, Lord! Come on and ease my troubling mind!

He had a black friend, his age, eight, who lived nearby. His name was Otis. They wrestled together in the dirt. Now the thought of Otis made him sick. He began to shiver. His mother put her arm around him.

"He's tired," she said.

"We'll be home soon," said his father. He began to whistle again.

"We didn't see Otis this morning," Jesse said. He did not know why he said this. His voice, in the darkness of the car, sounded small and accusing.

"You haven't seen Otis for a couple of mornings," his mother said.

That was true. But he was only concerned about *this* morning.

"No," said his father, "I reckon Otis's folks was afraid to let him show himself this morning."

"But Otis didn't do nothing!" Now his voice sounded questioning.

"Otis *can't* do nothing," said his father, "he's too little." The car lights picked up their wooden house, which now solemnly approached them, the lights falling around it like yellow dust. Their dog, chained to a tree, began to bark.

"We just want to make sure Otis *don't* do nothing," said his father, and stopped the car. He looked down at Jesse. "And you tell him what your Daddy said, you hear?"

"Yes sir," he said.

His father switched off the lights. The dog moaned and pranced, but they ignored him and went inside. He could not sleep. He lay awake, hearing the night sounds, the dog yawning and moaning outside, the sawing of the crickets, the cry of the owl, dogs barking far away, then no sounds at all, just the heavy, endless buzzing of the night. The darkness pressed on his eyelids like a scratchy blanket. He turned, he turned again. He wanted to call his mother, but he knew his father would not like this. He was terribly afraid. Then he heard his father's voice in the other room, low, with a joke in it; but this did not help him, it frightened him more, he knew what was going to happen. He put his head under the blanket, then pushed his head out again, for fear, staring at the dark window. He heard his mother's moan, his father's sigh; he gritted his teeth. Then their bed began to rock. His father's breathing seemed to fill the world.

That morning, before the sun had gathered all its strength, men and women, some flushed and some pale with excitement, came with news. Jesse's father seemed to know what the news was before the first jalopy stopped in the yard, and he ran out, crying, "They got him, then? They got him?"

The first jalopy held eight people, three men and two women and three children. The children were sitting on the laps of the grown-ups. Jesse knew two of them, the two boys; they shyly and uncomfortably greeted each other. He did not know the girl.

"Yes, they got him," said one of the women, the older one, who wore a wide hat and a fancy, faded blue dress. "They found him early this morning."

"How far had he got?" Jesse's father asked.

"He hadn't got no further than Harkness," one of the men said. "Look like he got lost up there in all them trees—or maybe he just got so scared he couldn't move." They all laughed.

"Yes, and you know it's near a graveyard, too," said the younger woman, and they laughed again.

"Is that where they got him now?" asked Jesse's father.

By this time there were three cars piled behind the first one, with everyone looking excited and shining, and Jesse noticed that they were carrying food. It was like a Fourth of July picnic.

"Yeah, that's where he is," said one of the men, "declare, Jesse, you going to keep us here all day long, answering your damn fool questions. Come on, we ain't got no time to waste."

"Don't bother putting up no food," cried a woman from one of the other cars, "we got enough. Just come on."

"Why, thank you," said Jesse's father, "we be right along, then."

"I better get a sweater for the boy," said his mother, "in case it turns cold."

Jesse watched his mother's thin legs cross the yard. He knew that she also wanted to comb her hair a little and maybe put on a better dress, the dress she wore to church. His father guessed this, too, for he yelled behind her, "Now don't you go trying to turn yourself into no movie star. You just come on." But he laughed as he said this, and winked at the men; his wife was younger and prettier than most of the other women. He clapped Jesse on the head and started pulling him toward the car. "You all go on," he said, "I'll be right behind you. Jesse, you go tie up that there dog while I get this car started."

The cars sputtered and coughed and shook; the caravan began to move; bright dust filled the air. As soon as he was tied up, the dog began to bark. Jesse's mother came out of the house, carrying a jacket for his father and a sweater for Jesse. She had put a ribbon in her hair and had an old shawl around her shoulders.

"Put these in the car, son," she said, and handed everything to him. She bent down and stroked the dog, looked to see if there was water in his bowl, then went back up the three porch steps and closed the door.

"Come on," said his father, "ain't nothing in there for nobody to steal." He was sitting in the car, which trembled and belched. The last car of the caravan had disappeared but the sound of singing floated behind them.

Jesse got into the car, sitting close to his father, loving the smell of the car, and the trembling, and the bright day, and the sense of going on a great and unexpected journey. His mother got in and closed the door and the car began to move. Not until then did he ask, "Where are we going? Are we going on a picnic?"

He had a feeling that he knew where they were going, but he was not sure.

"That's right," his father said, "we're going on a picnic. You won't ever forget *this* picnic—!"

"Are we," he asked, after a moment, "going to see the bad nigger—the one that knocked down old Miss Standish?"

"Well, I reckon," said his mother, "that we *might* see him."

He started to ask, *Will a lot of niggers be there? Will Otis be there?*—but he did not ask his question, to which, in a strange and uncomfortable way, he already knew the answer. Their friends, in the other cars, stretched up the road as far as he could see; other cars had joined them; there were cars behind them. They were singing. The sun seemed, suddenly very hot, and he was, at once very happy and a little afraid. He did not quite understand what was happening, and he did not know what to ask—he had no one to ask. He had grown accustomed, for the solution of such mysteries, to go to Otis. He felt that Otis knew everything. But he could not ask Otis about this. Anyway, he had not seen Otis for two days; he had not seen a black face anywhere for more than two days; and he now realized, as they began chugging up the long hill which eventually led to Harkness, that there were no black faces on the road this morning, no black people anywhere. From the houses in which they lived, all along the road, no smoke curled, no life stirred—maybe one or two chickens were to be seen, that was all. There was no one at the windows, no one in the yard, no one sitting on the porches, and the doors were closed. He had come this road many a time and seen women washing in the yard (there were no clothes on the clotheslines) men working in the fields, children playing in the dust; black men passed them on the road other mornings, other days, on foot, or in wagons, sometimes in cars, tipping their hats, smiling, joking, their teeth a solid white against their skin, their eyes as warm as the sun, the blackness of their skin like dull fire against the white of the blue or the grey of their torn clothes. They passed the nigger church—dead-white, desolate, locked up; and the graveyard, where no one knelt or walked, and he saw no flowers. He wanted to ask, *Where are they? Where are they all?* But he did not dare. As the hill grew steeper, the sun grew colder. He looked at his mother and his father. They looked straight ahead, seeming to be listening to the singing which echoed and echoed in this graveyard silence. They were strangers to him now. They were looking at something he could not see. His father's lips had a strange, cruel curve, he wet his lips from time to time, and swallowed. He was terribly aware of his father's tongue, it was as though he had never seen it before. And his father's body suddenly seemed immense, bigger than a mountain. His eyes, which were grey-green, looked yellow in the sunlight; or at least there was a light in them which he had never seen before. His mother patted her hair and adjusted the ribbon, leaning forward to look into the car mirror. "You look all right," said his father, and laughed. "When that nigger looks at you, he's going to swear he threw his life away for nothing. Wouldn't be surprised if he don't come back to haunt you." And he laughed again.

The singing now slowly began to cease; and he realized that they were nearing their destination. They had reached a straight, narrow, pebbly road, with trees on either side. The sunlight filtered down on them from a great height, as though they were under-water; and the branches of the trees scraped against the cars with a tearing sound. To the right of them, and beneath them, invisible now, lay the town; and to the left, miles of trees which led to the high mountain range which his ancestors had crossed in order to settle in this valley. Now, all was silent, except for the bumping of the tires against the rocky road, the sputtering of motors, and the sound of a crying child. And they seemed to move more slowly. They were beginning to climb again. He watched the cars ahead as they toiled patiently upward, disappearing into the sunlight of the clearing. Presently, he felt their vehicle also rise, heard his father's changed breathing, the sunlight hit his face, the trees moved away from them, and they were there. As their car crossed the clearing, he looked around. There seemed to be millions, there were certainly hundreds of people in the clearing, staring toward something he could not see. There was a fire. He could not see the flames, but he smelled the smoke. Then they were on the other side of the clearing, among the trees again. His father drove off the road and parked the car behind a great many other cars. He looked down at Jesse.

"You all right?" he asked.

"Yes sir," he said.

"Well, come on, then," his father said. He reached over and opened the door on his mother's side. His mother stepped out first. They followed her into the clearing. At first he was aware only of confusion, of his mother and father greeting and being greeted, himself being handled, hugged, and patted, and told how much he had grown. The wind blew the smoke from the fire across the clearing into his eyes and nose. He could not see over the backs of the people in front of

him. The sounds of laughing and cursing and wrath—and something else—
rolled in waves from the front of the mob to the back. Those in front expressed
their delight at what they saw, and this delight rolled backward, wave upon
wave, across the clearing, more acrid than the smoke. His father reached down
suddenly and sat Jesse on his shoulders.

Now he saw the fire—of twigs and boxes, piled high; flames made pale orange
and yellow and thin as a veil under the steadier light of the sun; grey-blue smoke
rolled upward and poured over their heads. Beyond the shifting curtain of fire
and smoke, he made out first only a length of gleaming chain, attached to a great
limb of the tree; then he saw that this chain bound two black hands together at
the wrist, dirty yellow palm facing dirty yellow palm. The smoke poured up; the
hands dropped out of sight; a cry went up from the crowd. Then the hands
slowly came into view again, pulled upward by the chain. This time he saw the
kinky, sweating, bloody head—he had never before seen a head with so much
hair on it, hair so black and so tangled that it seemed like another jungle. The
head was hanging. He saw the forehead, flat and high, with a kind of arrow of
hair in the center, like he had, like his father had; they called it a widow's peak;
and the mangled eye brows, the wide nose, the closed eyes, and the glinting eye
lashes and the hanging lips, all streaming with blood and sweat. His hands were
straight above his head. All his weight pulled downward from his hands; and he
was a big man, a bigger man than his father, and black as an African jungle cat,
and naked. Jesse pulled upward; his father's hands held him firmly by the ankles.
He wanted to say something, he did not know what, but nothing he said could
have been heard, for now the crowd roared again as a man stepped forward and
put more wood on the fire. The flames leapt up. He thought he heard the hanging man scream, but he was not sure. Sweat was pouring from the hair in his
armpits, poured down his sides, over his chest, into his navel and his groin. He
was lowered again; he was raised again. Now Jesse knew that he heard him
scream. The head went back, the mouth wide open, blood bubbling from the
mouth; the veins of the neck jumped out; Jesse clung to his father's neck in terror as the cry rolled over the crowd. The cry of all the people rose to answer the
dying man's cry. He wanted death to come quickly. They wanted to make death
wait: and it was they who held death, now, on a leash which they lengthened
little by little. *What did he do?* Jesse wondered. *What did the man do? What
did he do?*—but he could not ask his father. He was seated on his father's shoulders, but his father was far away. There were two older men, friends of his father's, raising and lowering the chain; everyone, indiscriminately, seemed to be
responsible for the fire. There was no hair left on the nigger's privates, and the
eyes, now, were wide open, as white as the eyes of a clown or a doll. The smoke
now carried a terrible odor across the clearing, the odor of something burning
which was both sweet and rotten.

He turned his head a little and saw the field of faces. He watched his mother's
face. Her eyes were very bright, her mouth was open: she was more beautiful
than he had ever seen her, and more strange. He began to feel a joy he had never
felt before. He watched the hanging, gleaming body, the most beautiful and terrible object he had ever seen till then. One of his father's friends reached up and
in his hands he held a knife: and Jesse wished that he had been that man. It was

a long, bright knife and the sun seemed to catch it, to play with it, to caress it—it was brighter than the fire. And a wave of laughter swept the crowd. Jesse felt his father's hands on his ankles slip and tighten. The man with the knife walked toward the crowd, smiling slightly; as though this were a signal, silence fell; he heard his mother cough. Then the man with the knife walked up to the hanging body. He turned and smiled again. Now there was a silence all over the field. The hanging head looked up. It seemed fully conscious now, as though the fire had burned out terror and pain. The man with the knife took the nigger's privates in his hand, one hand, still smiling, as though he were weighing them. In the cradle of the one white hand, the nigger's privates seemed as remote as meat being weighed in the scales; but seemed heavier, too, much heavier, and Jesse felt his scrotum tighten; and huge, huge, much bigger than his father's, flaccid, hairless, the largest thing he had ever seen till then, and the blackest. The white hand stretched them, cradled them, caressed them. Then the dying man's eyes looked straight into Jesse's eyes—it could not have been as long as a second, but it seemed longer than a year. Then Jesse screamed, and the crowd screamed as the knife flashed, first up, then down, cutting the dreadful thing away, and the blood came roaring down. Then the crowd rushed forward, tearing at the body with their hands, with knives, with rocks, with stones, howling and cursing. Jesse's head, of its own weight, fell downward toward his father's head. Someone stepped forward and drenched the body with kerosene. Where the man had been, a great sheet of flame appeared. Jesse's father lowered him to the ground.

"Well, I told you," said his father, "you wasn't never going to forget *this* picnic." His father's face was full of sweat, his eyes were very peaceful. At that moment Jesse loved his father more than he had ever loved him. He felt that his father had carried him through a mighty test, had revealed to him a great secret which would be the key to his life forever.

"I reckon," he said. "I reckon."

Jesse's father took him by the hand and, with his mother a little behind them, talking and laughing with the other women, they walked through the crowd, across the clearing. The black body was on the ground, the chain which had held it was being rolled up by one of his father's friends. Whatever the fire had left undone, the hands and the knives and the stones of the people had accomplished. The head was caved in, one eye was torn out, one ear was hanging. But one had to look carefully to realize this, for it was, now, merely, a black charred object on the black, charred ground. He lay spread-eagled with what had been a wound between what had been his legs.

"They going to leave him here, then?" Jesse whispered.

"Yeah," said his father, "they'll come and get him by and by. I reckon we better get over there and get some of that food before it's all gone."

"I reckon," he muttered now to himself, "I reckon." Grace stirred and touched him on the thigh: the moonlight covered her like glory. Something bubbled up in him, his nature again returned to him. He thought of the boy in the cell; he thought of the man in the fire; he thought of the knife and grabbed himself and stroked himself and a terrible sound, something between a high laugh and a howl, came out of him and dragged his sleeping wife up on one elbow. She stared at him in a moonlight which had grown cold as ice. He thought of the morning and grabbed her, laughing and crying, crying and laughing, and he whispered, as he stroked her, as he took her, "Come on, sugar, I'm going to do you like a nigger, just like a nigger, come on, sugar, and love me just like you'd love a nigger." He thought of the morning as he labored and she moaned, thought of morning as he labored harder than he ever had before, and before his labors had ended, he heard the first cock crow and the dogs begin to bark, and the sound of tires on the gravel road.

Russell Banks

. . . .

THE CHILD SCREAMS
AND LOOKS BACK
AT YOU

Marcelle called her boys from the kitchen to hurry and get dressed for school. One of these mornings she was not going to keep after them like this and they would all be late for school and she would not write a note to the teacher to explain anything, she didn't give a damn if the teacher kept them after school, because it would teach them a lesson once and for all, and that lesson was when she woke them in the morning they had to hurry and get dressed and make their beds and get the hell out here to the kitchen and eat their breakfasts and brush their teeth and get the hell out the door to school so she could get dressed and eat her breakfast and go to work. There were four of them, the four sons of Marcelle and Richard Chagnon. Joel was the oldest at twelve, and then, separated by little more than nine months, came Raymond, Maurice, and Charles. The father had moved out, had been thrown out of the apartment by Marcelle's younger brother Steve and one of Steve's friends nearly nine years ago, when the youngest, Charles, was still an infant, and though for several years Richard had tried to convince Marcelle she should let him move back in with them and let him be her husband and the father of his four sons again, she had never allowed it, for his way of being a husband and father was to get drunk and beat her and the older boys and then to wake ashamed and beg their forgiveness. For years she had forgiven him, because to her when you forgive someone you make it possible for that person to change, and the boys also forgave him—they were, after all, her sons too, and she had taught them, in their dealings with each other, to forgive. If you don't forgive someone who has hurt you, he can't change into a new person. He is stuck in his life with you at the point where he hurt you. But her husband and their father Richard, after five years of it, had come to seem incapable of using their forgiveness in any way that allowed him to stop hurting them, so finally one night she had sent her oldest boy, Joel, who was then only four and a half years old, out the door and down the dark stairs to the street, down the street to the tenement where her brother Steve lived with his girlfriend, and Joel had found Steve sitting at the kitchen table drinking beer with a friend and had said to him, "Come and keep my daddy from hitting my mommy!" That night for Marcelle marked the end of the period of forgiveness, for she had permitted outsiders, her brother and his friend, to see how badly her husband Richard behaved. By that act she had ceased to protect her husband, and you cannot forgive someone you will not protect. Richard never perceived or understood that shift, just as all those years he had never perceived or understood what it meant to be protected and forgiven. If you don't know what you've got when you've got it, you won't know what you've lost when you've lost it. Marcelle was Catholic and even though she was not a diligent Catholic she was a loyal one, and she never remarried, which is not to say that over the years she did not now and again fall in love, once even with a married man, only briefly, however, until she became strong enough to reveal her affair to Father Brautigan, after which she had broken off with the man, to the relief of her sons, for they had not liked the way he had come sneaking around at odd hours to see their mother and talk with her in hushed tones in the kitchen until very late, when the lights would go off and an hour or two later he would leave. When in the morning the children got up and came out to the kitchen for breakfast, they would talk in low voices, as if the married man were still in the apartment and asleep in their mother's bed, and she would have deep circles under her eyes and would stir her coffee slowly and look out the window and now and then quietly remind them to hurry or they'd be late for school. They were more comfortable when she was hollering at them, standing at the door to their bedroom, her hands on her hips, her dressing gown flapping open as she whirled and stomped back to the kitchen, embarrassing her slightly, for beneath her dressing gown she wore men's long underwear, so that, by the time they got out to the kitchen themselves, her dressing gown would have been pulled back tightly around her and tied at the waist, and all they could see of the long underwear beneath it would be the top button at her throat, which she would try to cover casually with one hand while she set their breakfasts before them with the other. On this morning, however, only three of her sons appeared at the table, dressed for school, slumping grumpily into their chairs, for it was a gray, wintry day in early December, barely light outside. The oldest, Joel, had not come out with them, and she lost her temper, slammed three plates of scrambled eggs and toast down in front of the others and fairly jogged back to the bedroom, stalked to the narrow bed by the wall where the boy slept and yanked the covers away, to expose the boy, curled up on his side, eyes wide open, his face flushed and sweating, his hands clasped together as if in prayer. Horrified, she looked down at the gangly boy, and she saw him dead and quickly lay the covers back over him, gently straightening the blanket and top sheet. Then, slowly, she sat down on the edge of the bed and stroked his hot forehead, brushing his limp blond hair back, feeling beneath his jawbone as if for a pulse, touching his cheeks with the smooth backside of her cool hand. "Tell me how you feel, honey," she said to the boy. He didn't answer her. His tongue came out and touched his dry lips and went quickly back inside his mouth. "Don't worry, honey," she said, and she got up from the bed. "It's probably the flu, that's all. I'll take your temperature and maybe call Doctor Wickshaw, and he'll tell me what to do. If you're too sick, I'll stay home from the tannery today. All right?" she asked and took a tentative step away from the bed. "Okay," the boy said weakly. The room was dark and cluttered with clothing and toys, model airplanes and boats, weapons, costumes, tools, hockey equipment, portable radios, photographs of athletes and singers, like the prop room of a small theater group. As she left the room, Marcelle stopped in the doorway and looked back. The boy huddled in his bed looked like one of the props, a ventriloquist's dummy, perhaps, or a heap of clothes that, in this shadowy half-light, only resembled a human child for a second or two, and then, looked at from a second angle, came clearly to be no more than an impatiently discarded costume.

Most people, when they call in a physician, deal with him as they would a priest. They say that what they want is a medical opinion, a professional medical man's professional opinion, when what they really want is his blessing. Information is useful only insofar as it provides peace of mind, release from the horrifying visions of dead children, an end to this dream. Most physicians, like most priests, recognize the need and attempt to satisfy it. This story takes place almost twenty years ago, in the early 1960s, in a small mill town in central New Hampshire, and it was especially true then and there that the physician responded before all other needs to the patient's need for peace of mind, and only when that need had been met would he respond to the patient's need for bodily health. In addition, because he usually knew all the members of the family and frequently treated them for injuries and diseases, he tended to regard an injured or ill person as one part of an injured or ill family. Thus it gradually became the physician's practice to minimize the danger or seriousness of a particular injury or illness, so that a broken bone was often called a probable sprain, until x rays proved otherwise, and a concussion was called, with a laugh, a bump on the head, until the symptoms—dizziness, nausea, sleepiness—persisted, when the bump on the head became a possible mild concussion, which eventually may have to be upgraded all the way to fractured skull. It was the same with diseases. A virus, the flu that's going around, a low-grade intestinal infection, and so on, often came to be identified a week or two later as strep throat, bronchial pneumonia, dysentery, without necessarily stopping there. There was an obvious, if limited, use for this practice, because it soothed and calmed both the patient and the family members, which made it easier for the physician to make an accurate diagnosis and to secure the aid of the family members in providing treatment. It was worse than useless, however, when an overoptimistic diagnosis of a disease or injury led to the patient's sudden, crazed descent into sickness, pain, paralysis, and death.

Doctor Wickshaw, a man in his middle-forties, portly but in good physical condition, with horn-rimmed glasses and a Vandyke beard, told Marcelle that her son Joel probably had the flu, it was going around, half the school was out with it. "Keep him in bed a few days and give him lots of liquids," he instructed her after examining the boy. He made housecalls, if the call for help came during morning hours or if it was truly an emergency. Afternoons he was at his office, and evenings he made rounds at the Concord Hospital, twenty-five miles away. Marcelle asked what she should do about the fever, one hundred four degrees, and he told her to give the boy three aspirins now and two more every three or four hours. She saw the man to the door, and as he passed her in the narrow hallway he placed one hand on her rump, and he said to the tall, broad-shouldered woman, "How are things with you, Marcelle? I saw you walking home from the tannery the other day, and I said to myself, 'Now that's a woman who shouldn't be alone in the world.' " He smiled into her bladelike face, the face of a large, powerful bird, and showed her his excellent teeth. His hand was still pressed against her rump and they stood face to face, for she was as tall as he. She was not alone in the world, she reminded him, mentioning her four sons. The doctor's hand slipped to her thigh. She did not move. "But you get lonely," he told her. She had gray eyes and her face was filled with fatigue, tiny lines that broke her smooth pale skin like the cracks in a ceramic jar that long ago had broken and had been glued back together again, as good as new, they say, and even stronger than before, but nevertheless fragile-looking now, and brittle per-haps, more likely to break a second time, it seemed, than when it had not been broken at all. "Yes," she said, "I get lonely," and with both hands, she reached up to her temples and pushed her dark hair back, and holding on to the sides of her own head she leaned it forward and kissed the man for several seconds, pushing at him with her mouth, until he pulled away, red-faced, his hand at his side now, and moved self-consciously sideways toward the door. "I'll come by tomorrow," he said in a low voice. "To see how Joel's doing." She smiled slightly and nodded. "If he's better," she said, "I'll be at work. But the door is always open." From the doorway, he asked if she came home for lunch. "Yes," she said, "when one of the boys is home sick, I do. Otherwise, no." He said that he might be here then, and she said, "Fine," and reached forward and closed the door on him.

Sometimes you dream that you are walking across a meadow under sunshine and a cloudless blue sky, hand in hand with your favorite child, and soon you notice that the meadow is sloping uphill slightly, and so walking becomes some-what more difficult, although it remains a pleasure, for you are with your favorite child and he is beautiful and happy and confident that you will let nothing terri-ble happen to him. You cross the crest, a rounded, meandering ridge, and start downhill, walking faster and more easily. The sun is shining and there are wild-flowers all around you, and the grass is golden and drifting in long waves in the breeze. Soon you find that the hill is steeper than before, the slope is falling away beneath your feet, as if the earth were curving in on itself, so you dig in your heels and try to slow your descent. Your child looks up at you and there is fear in his eyes, as he realizes he is falling away from you. "My hand!" you cry. "Hold tightly to my hand!" And you grasp the child's hand, who has started to fly away from you, as if over the edge of a crevice, while you dig your heels deeper into the ground and grab with your free hand at the long grasses behind you. The child screams and looks back at you with a pitiful gaze, and suddenly he grows so heavy that his weight is pulling you free of the ground also. You feel your feet leave the ground, and your body falls forward and down, behind your child's body, even though with one hand you still cling to the grasses. You weep, and you let go of your child's hand. The child flies away and you wake up, shuddering.

.   .   .   .   .

That night the boy's fever went higher, to one hundred five degrees, and Marcelle moved the younger boys into her own room, so that she could sleep in the bed next to the sick boy's. She bathed him in cool water with washcloths, coaxed him into swallowing aspirin with orange juice, and sat there on the edge of the bed next to his and watched him sleep, although she knew he was not truly sleeping, he was merely lying there on his side, his legs out straight now, silent and breathing rapidly, like an injured dog, stunned and silently healing itself. But the boy was not healing himself, he was hourly growing worse. She could tell that. She tried to move him so that she could straighten the sheets, but when she touched him, he cried out in pain, as if his back or neck were broken, and frightened, she drew back from him. She wanted to call Doctor Wickshaw, and several times she got up and walked out to the kitchen where the telephone hung on the wall like a large black insect, and each time she stood for a few seconds before the instrument, remembered the doctor in the hallway and what she had let him promise her with his eyes, remembered then what he had told her about her son's illness, and turned and walked back to the boy and tried again to cool him with damp cloths. Her three other sons slept peacefully through the night and knew nothing of what happened until morning came.

When your child lives, he carries with him all his earlier selves, so that you cannot separate your individual memories of him from your view of him now, at this moment. When you recall a particular event in your and your child's shared past—a day at the beach, a Christmas morning, a sad, weary night of flight from the child's shouting father, a sweet, pathetic supper prepared by the child for your birthday—when you recall these events singly, you cannot see the child as a camera would have photographed him then. You see him simultaneously all the way from infancy to adolescence to adulthood and on, as if he has been moving through your life too rapidly for any camera to catch and still, so that the image is blurred, grayed out, a swatch of your own past pasted across the foreground of a studio photographer's carefully arranged backdrop.

When her son went into convulsions, Marcelle did not at first know it, for his voice was clear and what he said made sense. Suddenly, he spoke loudly and in complete sentences. "Ma, I'm not alone. I know that, and it helps me not be scared. For a while I thought I was alone," he went on, and she sat upright and listened alertly to him in the darkness of the bedroom. "And then I started to see things and think maybe there was someone else in the room here with me, and then I was scared, Ma. Because I didn't know for sure whether I was alone or not. But now I know I'm not alone, and knowing it helps me not be scared." She said that she was glad, because she thought he was talking about her presence in the room, and she took his recognition of her presence as a sign that the fever had broken. But when she reached out in the darkness and touched his neck, it was burning, like an empty, black pot left over a fire, and she almost cried out in pain, and might have, had the child not commenced to shout at her, bellowing at her as if she were a large, ugly animal that he wished to send cowering into the far corner of his room.

.   .   .   .   .

Most people, when they do what the physician has told them will cure them, expect to be cured. When they are not cured, they at first believe it is because they have not done properly what they have been told to do. Sickness is the mystery, the miracle, and the physician understands such things, you say, whereas you, who are not a physician, all you understand is health. This is not so, of course, for health is the mystery and the miracle, not sickness. Sickness can be penetrated, understood, predicted. Health cannot. No, the analogy between the physician and the priest will not hold, for sickness and injury are not at all like divine protection and forgiveness. Sadly, most people and most physicians and most priests do not know this, or if they do, they do not act as if they know it. It's only in dealing with their children that people treat life as if it were indeed the miracle, as if life itself were the mystery of divine protection and forgiveness, and in that way, it is only in dealing with their children that most people are like priests serving God, making it possible for poor sinners to obtain grace.

Doctor Wickshaw hurried into the boy's bedroom and this time knew that the boy had contracted meningitis, probably spinal meningitis, and he also knew that it was too late to save the boy, that if he did not die in the next few days, he would suffer irreparable damage to his central nervous system.

Marcelle knew that by her son's death she was now a lost soul, and she did not weep. She went grimly about her appointed rounds, she raised her three remaining sons, and each of them, in his turn, forgave her and protected her. The one that died, Joel, the oldest, never forgave her, never shielded her from judgment, never let grace fall on her. Late at night, when she lay in bed alone, she knew this to the very bottom of her mind, and the knowledge was the lamp that illuminated the mystery and the miracle of her remaining days.

Donald Barthelme

. . . .

CORTÉS AND MONTEZUMA

Because Cortés lands on a day specified in the ancient writings, because he is dressed in black, because his armor is silver in color, a certain *ugliness* of the strangers taken as a group—for these reasons, Montezuma considers Cortés to be Quetzalcoatl, the great god who left Mexico many years before, on a raft of snakes, vowing to return.

Montezuma gives Cortés a carved jade drinking cup.

Cortés places around Montezuma's neck a necklace of glass beads strung on a cord scented with musk.

Montezuma offers Cortés an earthenware platter containing small pieces of meat lightly breaded and browned which Cortés declines because he knows the small pieces of meat are human fingers.

Cortés sends Montezuma a huge basket of that Spanish bread of which Montezuma's messengers had said, on first encountering the Spaniards, "As to their food, it is like human food, it is white and not heavy, and slightly sweet . . ."

Cortés and Montezuma are walking, down by the docks. Little green flies fill the air. Cortés and Montezuma are holding hands; from time to time one of them disengages a hand to brush away a fly.

Montezuma receives new messages, in picture writing, from the hills. These he burns, so that Cortés will not learn their contents. Cortés is trimming his black beard.

Doña Marina, the Indian translator, is sleeping with Cortés in the palace given him by Montezuma. Cortés awakens; they share a cup of chocolate. *She looks tired*, Cortés thinks.

Down by the docks, Cortés and Montezuma walk, holding hands. "Are you acquainted with a Father Sanchez?" Montezuma asks. "Sanchez, yes, what's he been up to?" says Cortés. "Overturning idols," says Montezuma. "Yes," Cortés says vaguely, "yes, he does that, everywhere we go."

At a concert later that evening, Cortés is bitten on the ankle by a green insect. The bug crawls into his velvet slipper. Cortés removes the slipper, feels around inside, finds the bug and removes it. "Is this poisonous?" he asks Doña Marina. "Perfectly," she says.

Montezuma himself performs the operation upon Cortés's swollen ankle. He lances the bitten place with a sharp knife, then sucks the poison from the wound, spits. Soon they are walking again, down by the docks.

Montezuma writes, in a letter to his mother: "The new forwardness of the nobility has come as a welcome relief. Whereas formerly members of the nobility took pains to hide among the general population, to pretend that they were ordinary people, they are now flaunting themselves and their position in the most disgusting ways. Once again they wear scarlet sashes from shoulder to hip, even on the boulevards; once again they prance about in their great powdered wigs; once again they employ lackeys to stand in pairs on little shelves at the rear of their limousines. The din raised by their incessant visiting of one another is with us from noon until early in the morning . . .

"This flagrant behavior is, as I say, welcome. For we are all tired of having to deal with their manifold deceptions, of uncovering their places of concealment, of keeping track of their movements—in short, of having to think about them, of having to *remember* them. Their new assertiveness, however much it reminds us of the excesses of former times, is easier. The interesting question is, what has emboldened the nobility to emerge from obscurity at this time? Why now?

"Many people here are of the opinion that it is a direct consequence of the plague of devils we have had recently. It is easily seen that, against a horizon of devils, the reappearance of the nobility can only be considered a more or less tolerable circumstance—they themselves must have realized this. Not since the late years of the last Bundle have we had so many spitting, farting, hair-shedding devils abroad. Along with the devils there have been roaches, roaches big as ironing boards. Then, too, we have the Spaniards . . ."

A group of great lords hostile to Montezuma holds a secret meeting in Vera Cruz, under the special protection of the god Smoking Mirror. Debate is fierce; a heavy rain is falling; new arrivals crowd the room.

Doña Marina, although she is the mistress of Cortés, has an Indian lover of high rank as well. Making her confession to Father Sanchez, she touches upon this. "His name is Cuitlahuac? This may be useful politically. I cannot give you absolution, but I will remember you in my prayers."

In the gardens of Tenochtitlán, whisperers exchange strange new words: *guillotine, white pepper, sincerity, temperament.*

Cortés's men break through many more walls but behind these walls they find, invariably, only the mummified carcasses of dogs, cats, and sacred birds.

Down by the docks, Cortés and Montezuma walk, holding hands. Cortés has employed a detective to follow Montezuma; Montezuma has employed a detective to follow Father Sanchez. "There are only five detectives of talent in Tenochtitlán," says Montezuma. "There are others, but I don't use them. Visions are best—better than the best detective."

Atop the great Cue, or pyramid, Cortés strikes an effigy of the god Blue Hummingbird and knocks off its golden mask; an image of the Virgin is installed in its place.

"The heads of the Spaniards," says Doña Marina, "Juan de Escalante and the five others, were arranged in a row on a pike. The heads of their horses were arranged in another row on another pike, set beneath the first."
Cortés screams.
The guards run in, first Cristóbal de Olid, and following him Pedro de Alvarado and then de Ordás and de Tapia.
Cortés is raving. He runs from the palace into the plaza where he meets and is greeted by Montezuma. Two great lords stand on either side of Montezuma supporting his arms, which are spread wide in greeting. They fold Montezuma's arms around Cortés. Cortés speaks urgently into Montezuma's ear.
Montezuma removes from his bosom a long cactus thorn and pricks his ear with it repeatedly, until the blood flows.

Doña Marina is walking, down by the docks, with her lover Cuitlahuac, Lord of the Place of the Dunged Water. "When I was young," says Cuitlahuac, "I was at school with Montezuma. He was, in contrast to the rest of us, remarkably chaste. A very religious man, a great student—I'll wager that's what they talk about, Montezuma and Cortés. Theology." Doña Marina tucks a hand inside his belt, at the back.

Bernal Diaz del Castillo, who will one day write *The True History of the Conquest of New Spain*, stands in a square whittling upon a piece of mesquite. The Proclamation of Vera Cruz is read, in which the friendship of Cortés and Montezuma is denounced as contrary to the best interests of the people of Mexico, born and yet unborn.

Cortés and Montezuma are walking, down by the docks. "I especially like the Holy Ghost. Qua idea," says Montezuma. "The other God, the Father, is also—" "One God, three Persons," Cortés corrects gently. "That the Son should be sacrificed," Montezuma continues, "seems to me wrong. It seems to me He should be sacrificed *to*. Furthermore," Montezuma stops and taps Cortés meaningfully on the chest with a brown forefinger, "where is the Mother?"

Bernal asks Montezuma, as a great favor, for a young pretty woman; Montezuma sends him a young woman of good family, together with a featherwork mantle, some crickets in cages, and a quantity of freshly made soap. Montezuma observes, of Bernal, that "he seems to be a gentleman."

"The ruler prepares dramas for the people," Montezuma says.

Cortés, sitting in an armchair, nods.

"Because the cultivation of maize requires on the average only fifty days' labor per person per year, the people's energies may be invested in these dramas—for example the eternal struggle to win, to retain, the good will of Smoking Mirror, Blue Hummingbird, Quetzalcoatl . . ."

Cortés smiles and bows.

"Easing the psychological strain on the ruler who would otherwise be forced to face alone the prospect of world collapse, the prospect of the world folding in on itself . . ."

Cortés blinks.

"If the drama is not of my authorship, if events are not controllable by me—"

Cortés has no reply.

"Therefore it is incumbent upon you, dear brother, to disclose to me the ending or at least what you know of the drama's probable course so that I may attempt to manipulate it in a favorable direction with the application of what magic is left to me."

Cortés has no reply.

Breaking through a new wall, Cortés's men discover, on the floor of a chamber behind the wall, a tiny puddle of gold. The Proclamation is circulated throughout the city; is sent to other cities.

Bernal builds a stout hen coop for Doña Marina. The sky over Tenochtitlán darkens; flashes of lightning; then rain sweeping off the lake.

Down by the docks, Cortés and Montezuma take shelter in a doorway. "Doña Marina translated it; I have a copy," says Cortés.

"When you smashed Blue Hummingbird with the crowbar—"

"I was rash. I admit it."

"You may take the gold with you. All of it. My gift."

"Your Highness is most kind."

"Your ships are ready. My messengers say their sails are as many as the clouds over the water."

"I cannot leave until all of the gold in Mexico, past, present and future, is stacked in the holds."

"Impossible on the face of it."

"I agree. Let us talk of something else."

Montezuma notices that a certain amount of white lint has accumulated on his friend's black velvet doublet. He thinks: *She should take better care of him.*

In bed with Cortés, Doña Marina displays for his eyes her beautiful golden buttocks, which he strokes reverently. A tiny green fly is buzzing about the room; Cortés brushes it away with a fly whisk made of golden wire. She tells him about a vision. In the vision Montezuma is struck in the forehead by a large stone, and falls. His enraged subjects hurl more stones.

"Don't worry," says Cortés. "Trust me."

Father Sanchez confronts Cortés with the report of the detective he has hired to follow Doña Marina, together with other reports, documents, photographs. Cortés orders that all of the detectives in the city be arrested, that the profession of detective be abolished forever in Tenochtitlán, and that Father Sanchez be sent back to Cuba in chains.

In the marketplaces and theaters of the city, new words are passed about: *tranquillity, vinegar, entitlement, schnell.*

On another day Montezuma and Cortés and Doña Marina and the guard of Cortés and certain great lords of Tenochtitlán leave their palaces and are carried in palanquins to the part of the city called Cotaxtla.

There, they halt before a great house and dismount.

"What is this place?" Cortés asks, for he has never seen it before.

Montezuma replies that it is the meeting place of the Aztec council or legislature which formulates the laws of his people.

Cortés expresses surprise and states that it had been his understanding that Montezuma is an absolute ruler answerable to no one—a statement Doña Marina tactfully neglects to translate lest Montezuma be given offense by it.

Cortés, with his guard at his back and Montezuma at his right hand, enters the building.

At the end of a long hallway he sees a group of functionaries each of whom wears in his ears long white goose quills filled with powdered gold. Here Cortés and his men are fumigated with incense from large pottery braziers, but Montezuma is not, the major-domos fix their eyes on the ground and do not look at him but greet him with great reverence saying, "Lord, my Lord, my Great Lord."

The party is ushered through a pair of tall doors of fragrant cedar into a vast chamber hung with red and yellow banners. There, on low wooden benches divided by a broad aisle, sit the members of the council, facing a dais. There are perhaps three hundred of them, each wearing affixed to his buttocks a pair of mirrors as is appropriate to his rank. On the dais are three figures of considerable majesty, the one in the center raised somewhat above his fellows; behind them, on the wall, hangs a great wheel of gold with much intricate featherwork depicting a whirlpool with the features of the goddess Chalchihuitlicue in the center. The council members sit in attitudes of rigid attention, arms held at their sides, chins lifted, eyes fixed on the dais. Cortés lays a hand on the shoulder of one of them, then recoils. He raps with his knuckles on that shoulder which gives forth a hollow sound. "They are pottery," he says to Montezuma. Montezuma winks. Cortés begins to laugh. Montezuma begins to laugh. Cortés is choking, hysterical. Cortés and Montezuma run around the great hall, dodging in and out of the rows of benches, jumping into the laps of one or another of the clay figures, overturning some, turning others backwards in their seats. "I am the State!" shouts Montezuma, and Cortés shouts, "Mother of God, forgive this poor fool who doesn't know what he is saying!"

In the kindest possible way, Cortés places Montezuma under house arrest. "Best you come to stay with me a while."
"Thank you but I'd rather not."
"We'll have games and in the evenings, home movies."
"The people wouldn't understand."
"We've got Pitalpitoque shackled to the great chain."
"I thought it was Quintalbor."
"Pitalpitoque, Quintalbor, Tendile."
"I'll send them chocolate."
"Come away, come away, come away with me."
"The people will be frightened."
"What do the omens say?"
"I don't know I can't read them anymore."
"Cutting people's hearts out, forty, fifty, sixty at a crack."
"It's the custom around here."
"The people of the South say you take too much tribute."
"Can't run an empire without tribute."
"Our Lord Jesus Christ loves you."
"I'll send Him chocolate."
"Come away, come away, come away with me."

Down by the docks, Cortés and Montezuma are walking with Charles V, Emperor of Spain. Doña Marina follows at a respectful distance carrying two picnic baskets containing many delicacies: caviar, white wine, stuffed thrushes, gumbo.

Charles V bends to hear what Montezuma is saying; Cortés brushes from the person of the Emperor little green flies, using a fly whisk made of golden wire. "Was there no alternative?" Charles asks. "I did what I thought best," says Cortés, "proceeding with gaiety and conscience." "I am murdered," says Montezuma.

The sky over Tenochtitlán darkens; flashes of lightning; then rain sweeping off the lake.

The pair walking down by the docks, hand in hand, the ghost of Montezuma rebukes the ghost of Cortés. "Why did you not throw up your hand, and catch the stone?"

Ann Beattie

JACKLIGHTING

It is Nicholas's birthday. Last year he was alive, and we took him presents; a spiral notebook he pulled the pages out of, unable to write but liking the sound of paper tearing; magazines he flipped through, paying no attention to pictures, liking the blur of color. He had a radio, so we could not take a radio. More than the radio, he seemed to like the sound the metal drawer in his bedside table made, sliding open, clicking shut. He would open the drawer and look at the radio. He rarely took it out.

Nicholas's brother Spence has made jam. For days the cat has batted grapes around under the huge home-made kitchen table; dozens of bloody rags of cheesecloth have been thrown into the trash. There is grape jelly, raspberry jelly, strawberry, quince and lemon. Last month, a neighbor's pig escaped and ate Spence's newly planted fraise des bois plants, but overlooked the strawberry plants close to the house, heavy with berries. After that, Spence captured the pig and called his friend Andy, who came for it with his truck and took the pig to his farm in Warrenton. When Andy got home and looked in the back of the truck, he found three piglets curled against the pig.

In this part of Virginia, it is a hundred degrees in August. In June and July you can smell the ground, but in August it has been baked dry; instead of smelling the earth you smell flowers, hot breeze. There is a haze over the Blue Ridge Mountains that stays in the air like cigarette smoke. It is the same color as the eye shadow Spence's girlfriend, Pammy, wears. The rest of us are sunburned, with pink mosquito bites on our bodies, small scratches from gathering raspberries. Pammy has just arrived from Washington. She is winter-pale. Since she is ten years younger than the rest of us, a few scratches wouldn't make her look as if she belonged, anyway. She is in medical school at Georgetown, and her summer-school classes have just ended. She arrived with leather sandals that squeak. She is exhausted and sleeps half the day, upstairs, with the fan blowing on her. All weekend the big fan has blown on Spence, in the kitchen, boiling and bottling his jams and jellies. The small fan blows on Pammy.

Wynn and I have come from New York. Every year we borrow his mother's car and drive from Hoboken to Virginia. We used to take the trip to spend the week of Nicholas's birthday with him. Now we come to see Spence, who lives alone in the house. He is making jam early, so we can take jars back with us. He stays in the kitchen because he is depressed and does not really want to talk to us. He scolds the cat, curses when something goes wrong.

Wynn is in love. The girl he loves is twenty, or twenty-one. Twenty-two. When he told me (top down on the car, talking into the wind), I couldn't understand half of what he was saying. There were enough facts to daze me; she had a name, she was one of his students, she had canceled her trip to Rome this summer. The day he told me about her, he brought it up twice; first in the car, later in Spence's kitchen. "That was *not* my mother calling the other night to say she got the car tuned," Wynn said, smashing his glass on the kitchen counter. I lifted his hand off the large shard of glass, touching his fingers as gently as I'd touch a cactus. When I steadied myself on the counter, a chip of glass nicked my thumb. The pain shot through my body and pulsed in my ribs. Wynn examined my hands; I examined his. A dust of fine glass coated our hands, gently touching, late at night, looking out the window at the moon shining on Spence's lemon tree with its one lemon, too heavy to be growing on the slender branch. A jar of Lipton iced tea was next to the tub the lemon tree grew out of—a joke, put there by Wynn, to encourage it to bear more fruit.

Wynn is standing in the field across from the house, pacing, head down, the bored little boy grown up.

"When wasn't he foolish?" Spence says, walking through the living room. "What kind of sense does it make to turn against him now for being a fool?"

"He calls it mid-life crisis, Spence, and he's going to be thirty-two in September."

"I know when his birthday is. You hint like this every year. Last year at the end of August you dropped it into conversation that the two of you were doing something or other to celebrate *his birthday*."

"We went to one of those places where a machine shoots baseballs at you. His birthday present was ten dollars' worth of balls pitched at him, I gave him a Red Sox baseball cap. He lost it the same day."

"How did he lose it?"

"We came out of a restaurant and a Doberman was tied by its leash to a stop sign, barking like mad—a very menacing dog. He tossed the cap, and it landed on the dog's head. It was funny until he wanted to get it back, and he couldn't go near it."

"He's one in a million. He deserves to have his birthday remembered. Call me later in the month and remind me." Spence goes to the foot of the stairs. "Pammy," he calls.

"Come up and kill something for me," she says. The bed creaks. "Come kill a wasp on the bedpost. I hate to kill them. I hate the way they crunch."

He walks back to the living room and gets a newspaper and rolls it into a tight tube, slaps it against the palm of his hand.

Wynn, in the field, is swinging a broken branch, batting hickory nuts and squinting into the sun.

                                                              .   .   .   .   .

Nicholas lived for almost a year, brain-damaged, before he died. Even before the accident, he liked the way things felt. He always watched shadows. He was the man looking to the side in Cartier-Bresson's photograph, instead of putting his eye to the wall. He'd find pennies on the sidewalk when the rest of us walked down city streets obliviously, spot the chipped finger on a mannequin flawlessly dressed, sidestep the one piece of glass among shells scattered on the shoreline. It would really have taken something powerful to do him in. So that's what happened: a drunk in a van, speeding, head-on, Nicholas out for a midnight ride without his helmet. Earlier in the day he'd assembled a crazy nest of treasures in the helmet, when he was babysitting the neighbors' four-year-old daughter. Spence showed it to us—holding it forward as carefully as you'd hold a bomb, looking away the way you'd avoid looking at dead fish floating in a once nice aquarium, the way you'd look at an ugly scar, once the bandages had been removed, and want to lay the gauze back over it. While he was in the hospital, his fish tank overheated and all the black mollies died. The doctor unwound some of the bandages and the long brown curls had been shaved away, and there was a red scar down the side of his head that seemed as out of place as a line dividing a highway out west, a highway that nobody traveled anyway. It could have happened to any of us. We'd all ridden on the Harley, bodies pressed into his back, hair whipped across our faces. How were we going to feel ourselves again, without Nicholas? In the hospital, it was clear that the thin intravenous tube was not dripping life back into him—that was as farfetched as the idea that the too-thin branch of the lemon tree could grow one more piece of fruit. In the helmet had been dried chrysanthemums, half of a robin's blue shell, a cat's-eye marble, yellow twine, a sprig of grapes, a piece of a broken ruler. I remember Wynn actually jumping back when he saw what was inside. I stared at the strangeness such ordinary things had taken on. Wynn had been against his teaching me to ride his bike, but he had. He taught me to trust myself and not to settle for seeing things the same way. The lobster claw on a necklace he made me was funny and beautiful. I never felt the same way about lobsters or jewelry after that. "Psychologists have figured out that infants start to laugh when they've learned to be skeptical of danger," Nicholas had said. Laughing on the back of his motorcycle. When he lowered the necklace over my head, rearranging it, fingers on my throat.

It is Nicholas's birthday, and so far no one has mentioned it. Spence has made all the jam he can make from the fruit and berries and has gone to the store and returned with bags of flour to make bread. He brought the *Daily Progress* to Pammy, and she is reading it, on the side porch where there is no screening, drying her hair and stiffening when bees fly away from the Rose of Sharon bushes. Her new sandals are at the side of the chair. She has red toenails. She rubs the small pimples on her chin the way men finger their beards. I sit on the porch with her, catcher's mitt on my lap, waiting for Wynn to get back from his walk so we can take turns pitching to each other.

"Did he tell you I was a drug addict? Is that why you hardly speak to me?" Pammy says. She is squinting at her toes. "I'm older than I look," she says. "He says I'm twenty-one, because I look so young. He doesn't know when to let go of a joke, though. I don't like to be introduced to people as some child prodigy."

"What were you addicted to?" I say.

"Speed," she says. "I had another life." She has brought the bottle of polish with her, and begins brushing on a new layer of red, the fingers of her other hand stuck between her toes from underneath, separating them. "I don't get the feeling you people had another life," she says. "After all these years, I still feel funny when I'm around people who've never lived the way I have. It's just snobbishness, I'm sure."

I cup the catcher's mitt over my knee. A bee has landed on the mitt. This is the most Pammy has talked. Now she interests me; I always like people who have gone through radical changes. It's snobbishness—it shows me that other people are confused, too.

"That was the summer of sixty-seven," she says. "I slept with a stockbroker for money. Sat through a lot of horror movies. That whole period's a blur. What I remember about it is being underground all the time, going places on the subway. I only had one real friend in the city. I can't remember where I was going." Pammy looks at the newspaper beside her chair. "Charlottesville, Virginia," she says. "My, my. Who would have thought twitchy little Pammy would end up here?"

Spence tosses the ball. I jump, mitt high above my head, and catch it. Spence throws again. Catch. Again. A hard pitch that lets me know the palm of my hand will be numb when I take off the catcher's mitt. Spence winds up. Pitches. As I'm leaning to get the ball, another ball sails by on my right. Spence has hidden a ball in his pocket all this time. Like his brother, he's always trying to make me smile.

"It's too hot to play ball," he says. "I can't spend the whole day trying to distract you because Wynn stalked off into the woods today."

"Come on," I say. "It was working."

"Why don't we all go to Virginia Beach next year instead of standing around down here smouldering? This isn't any tribute to my brother. How did this get started?"

"We came to be with you because we thought it would be hard. You didn't tell us about Pammy."

"Isn't that something? What that tells you is that you matter, and Wynn matters, and Nicholas mattered, but I don't even think to mention the person who's supposedly my lover."

"She said she had been an addict."

"She probably tried to tell you she wasn't twenty-one, too, didn't she?"

I sidestep a strawberry plant, notice one croquet post stuck in the field.

"It was a lie?" I say.

"No," he says. "I never know when to let my jokes die."

When Nicholas was alive, we'd celebrate his birthday with mint juleps and croquet games, stuffing ourselves with cake, going for midnight skinny-dips. Even if he were alive, I wonder if today would be anything like those birthdays of the past, or whether we'd have bogged down so hopelessly that even his childish enthusiasm would have had little effect. Wynn is sure that he's having a crisis and that it's not the real thing with his student because he also has a crush on Pammy. We are open about everything: he tells me about taking long walks and thinking about nothing but sex; Spence bakes the french bread too long, finds that he's lightly tapping a rock, sits on the kitchen counter, puts his hands over his face, and cries. Pammy says that she does not feel close to any of us—that Virginia was just a place to come to cool out. She isn't sure she wants to go on with medical school. I get depressed and think that if the birds could talk, they'd say that they didn't enjoy flying. The mountains have disappeared in the summer haze.

Late at night, alone on the porch, toasting Nicholas with a glass of wine, I remember that when I was younger, I assumed he'd be our guide: he saw us through acid trips, planned our vacations, he was always there to excite us and to give us advice. He started a game that went on for years. He had us close our eyes after we'd stared at something and made us envision it again. We had to describe it with our eyes closed. Wynn and Spence could talk about the things and make them more vivid than they were in life. They remembered well. When I closed my eyes, I squinted until the thing was lost to me. It kept going backwards into darkness.

Tonight, Nicholas's birthday, it is dark and late and I have been trying to pay him some sort of tribute by seeing something and closing my eyes and imagining it. Besides realizing that two glasses of wine can make me drunk, I have had this revelation: that you can look at something, close your eyes and see it again and still know nothing—like staring at the sky to figure out the distances between stars.

The drunk in the van that hit Nicholas thought that he had hit a deer.

Tonight, stars shine over the field with the intensity of flashlights. Every year, Spence calls the state police to report that on his property, people are jacklighting.

Samuel Beckett

$\cdot$ $\cdot$ $\cdot$ $\cdot$ $\cdot$ $\cdot$ $\cdot$ $\cdot$ $\cdot$ $\cdot$ $\cdot$ $\cdot$ $\cdot$ $\cdot$ $\cdot$ $\cdot$ $\cdot$ $\cdot$ $\cdot$ $\cdot$ $\cdot$ $\cdot$ $\cdot$

FIRST LOVE

I associate, rightly or wrongly, my marriage with the death of my father, in time. That other links exist, on other planes, between these two affairs, is not impossible. I have enough trouble as it is in trying to say what I think I know.

I visited, not so long ago, my father's grave, that I do know, and noted the date of his death, of his death alone, for that of his birth had no interest for me, on that particular day. I set out in the morning and was back by night, having lunched lightly in the graveyard. But some days later, wishing to know his age at death, I had to return to the grave, to note the date of his birth. These two limiting dates I then jotted down on a piece of paper, which I now carry about with me. I am thus in a position to affirm that I must have been about twenty-five at the time of my marriage. For the date of my own birth, I repeat, my own birth, I have never forgotten, I never had to note it down, it remains graven in my memory, the year at least, in figures that life will not easily erase. The day itself comes back to me, when I put my mind to it, and I often celebrate it, after my fashion, I don't say each time it comes back, for it comes back too often, but often.

Personally I have nothing against graveyards, I take the air there willingly, perhaps more willingly than elsewhere, when take the air I must. The smell of corpses, distinctly perceptible under those of grass and humus mingled, I do not find unpleasant, a trifle on the sweet side perhaps, a trifle heady, but how infinitely preferable to what the living emit, their feet, teeth, armpits, arses, sticky foreskins and frustrated ovules. And when my father's remains join in, however modestly, I can almost shed a tear. The living wash in vain, in vain perfume themselves, they stink. Yes, as a place for an outing, when out I must, leave me my graveyards and keep—you—to your public parks and beauty-spots. My sandwich, my banana, taste sweeter when I'm sitting on a tomb, and when the time comes to piss again, as it so often does, I have my pick. Or I wander, hands clasped behind my back, among the slabs, the flat, the leaning and the upright, culling the inscriptions. Of these I never weary, there are always three or four of such drollery that I have to hold on to the cross, or the stele, or the angel, so as not to fall. Mine I composed long since and am still pleased with it, tolerably pleased. My other writings are no sooner dry than they revolt me, but my epi-

taph still meets with my approval. There is little chance unfortunately of its ever
being reared above the skull that conceived it, unless the State takes up the matter. But to be unearthed I must first be found, and I greatly fear those gentlemen
will have as much trouble finding me dead as alive. So I hasten to record it here
and now, while there is yet time:

> Hereunder lies the above who up below
> So hourly died that he survived till now.

The second and last or rather latter line limps a little perhaps, but that is no
great matter, I'll be forgiven more than that when I'm forgotten. Then with a
little luck you hit on a genuine interment, with real live mourners and the odd
relict rearing to throw herself into the pit. And nearly always that charming business with the dust, though in my experience there is nothing less dusty than
holes of this type, verging on muck for the most part, nor anything particularly
powdery about the deceased, unless he happen to have died, or she, by fire. No
matter, their little gimmick with the dust is charming. But my father's yard was
not among my favourite. To begin with it was too remote, way out in the wilds
of the country on the side of a hill, and too small, far too small, to go on with.
Indeed it was almost full, a few more windows and they'd be turning them away.
I infinitely preferred Ohlsdorf, particularly the Linne section, on Prussian soil,
with its nine hundred acres of corpses packed tight, though I knew no one there,
except by reputation the wild animal collector Hagenbeck. A lion, if I remember
right, is carved on his monument, death must have had for Hagenbeck the countenance of a lion. Coaches ply to and fro, crammed with widows, widowers,
orphans and the like. Groves, rottoes, artificial lakes with swans, purvey consolation to the inconsolable. It was December, I had never felt so cold, the eel soup
lay heavy on my stomach, I was afraid I'd die, I turned aside to vomit, I envied
them.

But to pass on to less melancholy matters, on my father's death I had to leave
the house. It was he who wanted me in the house. He was a strange man. One
day he said, Leave him alone, he's not disturbing anyone. He didn't know I was
listening. This was a view he must have often voiced, but the other times I
wasn't by. They would never let me see his will, they simply said he had left me
such a sum. I believed then, and still believe, that he had stipulated in his will
for me to be left the room I had occupied in his lifetime and for food to be
brought me there, as hitherto. He may even have given this the force of condition precedent. Presumably he liked to feel me under his roof, otherwise he
would not have opposed my eviction. Perhaps he merely pitied me. But somehow I think not. He should have left me the entire house, then I'd have been all
right, the others too for that matter, I'd have summoned them and said, Stay,
stay by all means, your home is here. Yes, he was properly had, my poor father, if
his purpose was really to go on protecting me from beyond the tomb. With regard to the money it is only fair to say they gave it to me without delay, on the
very day following the inhumation Perhaps they were legally bound to. I said to
them, Keep this money and let me live on here, in my room, as in Papa's lifetime. I added, God rest his soul, in the hope of melting them. But they refused.
I offered to place myself at their disposal, a few hours every day, for the little odd

maintenance jobs every dwelling requires, if it is not to crumble away. Pottering is still just possible, I don't know why. I proposed in particular to look after the hothouse. There I would have gladly whiled away the hours, in the heat, tending the tomatoes, hyacinths, pinks and seedlings. My father and I alone, in that household, understood tomatoes. But they refused. One day, on my return from stool, I found my room locked and my belongings in a heap before the door. This will give you some idea how constipated I was, at this juncture. It was, I am now convinced, anxiety constipation. But was I genuinely constipated? Somehow I think not. Softly, softly. And yet I must have been, for how otherwise account for those long, those cruel sessions in the necessary house? At such times I never read, any more than at other times, never gave way to revery or meditation, just gazed dully at the almanac hanging from a nail before my eyes, with its chromo of a bearded stripling in the midst of sheep, Jesus no doubt, parted the cheeks with both hands and strained, heave! ho! heave! ho!, with the motions of one tugging at the oar, and only one thought in my mind, to be back in my room and flat on my back again. What can that have been but constipation? Or am I confusing it with the diarrhoea? It's all a muddle in my head, graves and nuptials and the different varieties of motion. Of my scanty belongings they had made a little heap, on the floor, against the door. I can still see that little heap, in the kind of recess full of shadow between the landing and my room. It was in this narrow space, guarded on three sides only, that I had to change, I mean exchange my dressing-gown and nightgown for my travelling costume, I mean shoes, socks, trousers, shirt, coat, greatcoat and hat, I can think of nothing else. I tried other doors, turning the knobs and pushing, or pulling, before I left the house, but none yielded. I think if I'd found one open I'd have barricaded myself in the room, they would have had to gas me out. I felt the house crammed as usual, the usual pack, but saw no one. I imagined them in their various rooms, all bolts drawn, every sense on the alert. Then the rush to the window, each holding back a little, hidden by the curtain, at the sound of the street door closing behind me, I should have left it open. Then the doors fly open and out they pour, men, women and children, and the voices, the sighs, the smiles, the hands, the keys in the hands, the blessed relief, the precautions rehearsed, if this then that, but if that then this, all clear and joy in every heart, come let's eat, the fumigation can wait. All imagination to be sure, I was already on my way, things may have passed quite differently, but who cares how things pass, provided they pass. All those lips that had kissed me, those hearts that had loved me (it is with the heart one loves, is it not, or am I confusing it with something else?), those hands that had played with mine and those minds that had almost made their own of me! Humans are truly strange. Poor Papa, a nice mug he must have felt that day if he could see me, see us, a nice mug on my account I mean. Unless in his great disembodied wisdom he saw further than his son whose corpse was not yet quite up to scratch.

But to pass on to less melancholy matters, the name of the woman with whom I was soon to be united was Lulu. So at least she assured me and I can't see what interest she could have had in lying to me, on this score. Of course one can never tell. She also disclosed her family name, but I've forgotten it. I should have made a note of it, on a piece of paper, I hate forgetting a proper name. I

met her on a bench, on the bank of the canal, one of the canals, for our town
boasts two, though I never knew which was which. It was a well situated bench,
backed by a mound of solid earth and garbage, so that my rear was covered. My
flanks too, partially, thanks to a pair of venerable trees, more than venerable,
dead, at either end of the bench. It was no doubt these trees one fine day, aripple
with all their foliage, that had sown the idea of a bench, in someone's fancy. To
the fore, a few yards away, flowed the canal, if canals flow, don't ask me, so that
from that quarter too the risk of surprise was small. And yet she surprised me. I
lay stretched out, the night being warm, gazing up through the bare boughs in-
terlocking high above me, where the trees clung together for support, and
through the drifting cloud, at a patch of starry sky as it came and went. Shove
up, she said. My first movement was to go, but my fatigue, and my having nowhere to go, dissuaded me from acting on it. So I drew back my feet a little way
and she sat. Nothing more passed between us that evening and she soon took
herself off, without another word. All she had done was sing, *sotto voce*, as to
herself, and without the words fortunately, some old folk songs, and so disjointedly, skipping from one to another and finishing none, that even I found it
strange. The voice, though out of tune, was not unpleasant. It breathed of a soul
too soon wearied ever to conclude, that perhaps least arse-aching soul of all. The
bench itself was soon more than she could bear and as for me, one look had been
enough for her. Whereas in reality she was a most tenacious woman. She came
back next day and the day after and all went off more or less as before. Perhaps a
few words were exchanged. The next day it was raining and I felt in security.
Wrong again. I asked her if she was resolved to disturb me every evening. I disturb you? she said. I felt her eyes on me. They can't have seen much, two eyelids
at the most, with a hint of nose and brow, darkly, because of the dark. I thought
we were easy, she said. You disturb me, I said, I can't stretch out with you there.
The collar of my greatcoat was over my mouth and yet she heard me. Must you
stretch out? she said. The mistake one makes is to speak to people. You have
only to put your feet on my knees, she said. I didn't wait to be asked twice,
under my miserable calves I felt her fat thighs. She began stroking my ankles. I
considered kicking her in the cunt. You speak to people about stretching out and
they immediately see a body at full length. What mattered to me in my dispeo-
pled kingdom, that in regard to which the disposition of my carcass was the
merest and most futile of accidents, was supineness in the mind, the dulling of
the self and of that residue of execrable frippery known as the non-self and even
the world, for short. But man is still today, at the age of twenty-five, at the mercy
of an erection, physically too, from time to time, it's the common lot, even I was
not immune, if that may be called an erection. It did not escape her naturally,
women smell a rigid phallus ten miles away and wonder, How on earth did he
spot me from there? One is no longer oneself, on such occasions, and it is painful to be no longer oneself, even more painful if possible than when one is. For
when one is one knows what to do to be less so, whereas when one is not one is
any old one irredeemably. What goes by the name of love is banishment, with
now and then a postcard from the homeland, such is my considered opinion,
this evening. When she had finished and my self been resumed, mine own, the
mitigable, with the help of a brief torpor, it was alone. I sometimes wonder if

that is not all invention, if in reality things did not take quite a different course, one I had no choice but to forget. And yet her image remains bound, for me, to that of the bench, not the bench by day, nor yet the bench by night, but the bench at evening, in such sort that to speak of the bench, as it appeared to me at evening, is to speak of her, for me. That proves nothing, but there is nothing I wish to prove. On the subject of the bench by day no words need be wasted, it never knew me, gone before morning and never back till dusk. Yes, in the day-time I foraged for food and marked down likely cover. Were you to inquire, as undoubtedly you itch, what I had done with the money my father had left me, the answer would be I had done nothing with it but leave it lie in my pocket. For I knew I would not be always young, and that summer does not last for ever either, nor even autumn, my mean soul told me so. In the end I told her I'd had enough. She disturbed me exceedingly, even absent. Indeed she still disturbs me, but no worse now than the rest. And it matters nothing to me now, to be disturbed, or so little, what does it mean, disturbed, and what would I do with myself if I wasn't? Yes, I've changed my system, it's the winning one at last, for the ninth or tenth time, not to mention not long now, not long till curtain down, on disturbers and disturbed, no more tattle about that, all that, her and the others, the shitball and heaven's high halls. So you don't want me to come any more, she said. It's incredible the way they repeat what you've just said to them, as if they risked faggot and fire in believing their ears. I told her to come just the odd time. I didn't understand women at that period. I still don't for that matter. Nor men either. Nor animals either. What I understand best, which is not say-ing much, are my pains. I think them through daily, it doesn't take long, thought moves so fast, but they are not only in my thought, not all. Yes, there are moments, particularly in the afternoon, when I go all syncretist, à la Rein-hold. What equilibrium! But even them, my pains, I understand ill. That must come from my not being all pain and nothing else. There's the rub. Then they recede, or I, till they fill me with amaze and wonder, seen from a better planet. Not often, but I ask no more. Catch-cony life! To be nothing but pain, how that would simplify matters! Omnidolent! Impious dream. I'll tell them to you some day none the less, if I think of it, if I can, my strange pains, in detail, distin-guishing between the different kinds, for the sake of clarity, those of the mind, those of the heart or emotional conative, those of the soul (none prettier than these) and finally those of the frame proper, first the inner or latent, then those affecting the surface, beginning with the hair and scalp and moving methodi-cally down, without haste, all the way down to the feet beloved of the corn, the cramp, the kibe, the bunion, the hammer toe, the nail ingrown, the fallen arch, the common blain, the club foot, duck foot, goose foot, pigeon foot, flat foot, trench foot and other curiosities. And I'll tell by the same token, for those kind enough to listen, in accordance with a system whose inventor I forget, of those instants when, neither drugged, nor drunk, nor in ecstasy, one feels nothing. Next of course she desired to know what I meant by the odd time, that's what you get for opening your mouth. Once a week? Once in ten days? Once a fort-night? I replied less often, far less often, less often to the point of no more if she could, and if she could not the least often possible. And the next day (what is more) I abandoned the bench, less I must confess on her account than on its, for the site no longer answered my requirements, modest though they were, now that the air was beginning to strike chill, and for other reasons better not wasted on cunts like you, and took refuge in a deserted cowshed marked on one of my forays. It stood in the corner of a field richer on the surface in nettles than in grass and in mud than in nettles, but whose subsoil was perhaps possessed of exceptional qualities. It was in this byre, littered with dry and hollow cowclaps subsiding with a sigh at the poke of my finger, that for the first time in my life, and I would not hesitate to say the last if I had not to husband my cyanide, I had to contend with a feeling which gradually assumed, to my dismay, the dread name of love. What constitutes the charm of our country, apart of course from its scant population, and this without help of the meanest contraceptive, is that all is derelict, with the sole exception of history's ancient faeces. These are ardently sought after, stuffed and carried in procession. Wherever nauseated time has dropped a nice fat turd you will find our patriots, sniffing it up on all fours, their faces on fire. Elysium of the roofless. Hence my happiness at last. Lie down, all seems to say, lie down and stay down. I see no connexion between these remarks. But that one exists, and even more than one, I have little doubt, for my part. But what? Which? Yes, I loved her, it's the name I gave, still give alas, to what I was doing then. I had nothing to go by, having never loved before, but of course had heard of the thing, at home, in school, in brothel and at church, and read romances, in prose and verse, under the guidance of my tutor, in six or seven languages, both dead and living, in which it was handled at length. I was therefore in a position, in spite of all, to put a label on what I was about when I found myself inscribing the letters of Lulu in an old heifer pat or flat on my face in the mud under the moon trying to tear up the nettles by the roots. They were giant nettles, some full three foot high, to tear them up assuaged my pain, and yet it's not like me to do that to weeds, on the contrary, I'd smother them in manure if I had any. Flowers are a different matter. Love brings out the worst in man and no error. But what kind of love was this, exactly? Love-passion? Somehow I think not. That's the priapic one, is it not? Or is this a different variety? There are so many, are there not? All equally if not more delicious, are they not? Platonic love, for example, there's another just occurs to me. It's disinterested. Perhaps I loved her with a platonic love? But somehow I think not. Would I have been tracing her name in old cowshit if my love had been pure and disinterested? And with my devil's finger into the bargain, which I then sucked. Come now! My thoughts were all of Lulu, if that doesn't give you some idea nothing will. Anyhow I'm sick and tired of this name Lulu, I'll give her another, more like her, Anna for example, it's not more like her but no matter. I thought of Anna then, I who had learnt to think of nothing, nothing except my pains, a quick think through, and of what steps to take not to perish off-hand of hunger, or cold, or shame, but never on any account of living beings as such (I wonder what that means) whatever I may have said, or may still say, to the contrary or otherwise, on this subject. But I have always spoken, no doubt always shall, of things that never existed, or that existed if you insist, no doubt always will, but not with the existence I ascribe to them. Kepis, for example, exist beyond a doubt, indeed there is little hope of their ever disappearing, but personally I never wore a kepi. I wrote somewhere, They gave me . . . a hat. Now the truth is they never gave me a hat, I have always had my own hat, the one my father gave me, and I have never had any other hat than that hat. I may add it has followed me to the grave. I thought of Anna then, long long sessions, twenty minutes, twenty-five minutes and even as long as half an hour daily. I obtain these figures by the addition of other, lesser figures. That must have been my way of loving. Are we to infer from this I loved her with that intellectual love which drew from me such drivel, in another place? Somehow I think not. For had my love been of this kind would I have stooped to inscribe the letters of Anna in time's forgotten cowplats? To divellicate urtica *plenis manibus?* And felt, under my tossing head, her thighs to bounce like so many demon bolsters? Come now! In order to put an end, to try and put an end, to this plight, I returned one evening to the bench, at the hour she had used to join me there. There was no sign of her and I waited in vain. It was December already, if not January, and the cold was seasonable, that is to say reasonable, like all that is seasonable. But one is the hour of the dial, and another that of changing air and sky, and another yet again the heart's. To this thought, once back in the straw, I owed an excellent night. The next day I was earlier to the bench, much earlier, night having barely fallen, winter night, and yet too late, for she was there already, on the bench, under the boughs tinkling with rime, her back to the frosted mound, facing the icy water. I told you she was a highly tenacious woman. I felt nothing. What interest could she have in pursuing me thus? I asked her, without sitting down, stumping to and fro. The cold had embossed the path. She replied she didn't know. What could she see in me, would she kindly tell me that at least, if she could. She replied she couldn't. She seemed warmly clad, her hands buried in a muff. As I looked at this muff, I remember, tears came to my eyes. And yet I forget what colour it was. The state I was in then! I have always wept freely, without the least benefit to myself, till recently. If I had to weep this minute I could squeeze till I was blue, I'm convinced not a drop would fall. The state I am in now! It was things made me weep. And yet I felt no sorrow. When I found myself in tears for no apparent reason it meant I had caught sight of something unbeknownst. So I wonder if it was really the muff that evening, if it was not rather the path, so iron hard and bossy as perhaps to feel like cobbles to my tread, or some other thing, some chance thing glimpsed below the threshold, that so unmanned me. As for her, I might as well never have laid eyes on her before. She sat all huddled and muffled up, her head sunk, the muff with her hands in her lap, her legs pressed tight together, her heels clear of the ground. Shapeless, ageless, almost lifeless, it might have been anything or anyone, an old woman or a little girl. And the way she kept on saying, I don't know, I can't. I alone did not know and could not. Is it on my account you came? I said. She managed yes to that. Well here I am, I said. And I? Had I not come on hers? Here we are, I said. I sat down beside her but sprang up again immediately as though scalded. I longed to be gone, to know if it was over. But before going, to be on the safe side, I asked her to sing me a song. I thought at first she was going to refuse, I mean simply not sing, but no, after a moment she began to sing and sang for some time, all the time the same song it seemed to me, without change of attitude. I did not know the song, I had never heard it before and shall never hear it again. It had something to do with lemon trees, or orange trees, I forget, that is all I remember, and for me that is no mean feat, to remember it had something to do with lemon trees, or orange trees, I forget, for of all the other songs I have ever heard in my life, and I have heard plenty, it being apparently impossible, physically impossible short of being deaf, to get through this world, even my way, without hearing singing, I have retained nothing, not a word, not a note, or so few words, so few notes, that, that what, that nothing, this sentence has gone on long enough. Then I started to go and as I went I heard her singing another song, or perhaps more verses of the same, fainter and fainter the further I went, then no more, either because she had come to an end or because I was gone too far to hear her. To have to harbour such a doubt was something I preferred to avoid, at that period. I lived of course in doubt, on doubt, but such trivial doubts as this, purely somatic as some say, were best cleared up without delay, they could nag at me like gnats for weeks on end. So I retraced my steps a little way and stopped. At first I heard nothing, then the voice again, but only just, so faintly did it carry. First I didn't hear it, then I did, I must therefore have begun hearing it, at a certain point, but no, there was no beginning, the sound emerged so softly from the silence and so resembled it. When the voice ceased at last I approached a little nearer, to make sure it had really ceased and not merely been lowered. Then in despair, saying, No knowing, no knowing, short of being beside her, bent over her, I turned on my heel and went, for good, full of doubt. But some weeks later, even more dead than alive than usual, I returned to the bench, for the fourth or fifth time since I had abandoned it, at roughly the same hour, I mean roughly the same sky, no, I don't mean that either, for it's always the same sky and never the same sky, what words are there for that, none I know, period. She wasn't there, then suddenly she was, I don't know how, I didn't see her come, nor hear her, all ears and eyes though I was. Let us say it was raining, nothing like a change, if only of weather. She had her umbrella up, naturally, what an outfit. I asked if she came every evening. No, she said, just the odd time. The bench was soaking wet, we paced up and down, not daring to sit. I took her arm, out of curiosity, to see if it would give me pleasure, it gave me none, I let it go. But why these particulars? To put off the evil hour. I saw her face a little clearer, it seemed normal to me, a face like millions of others. The eyes were crooked, but I didn't know that till later. It looked neither young nor old, the face, as though stranded between the vernal and the sere. Such ambiguity I found difficult to bear, at that period. As to whether it was beautiful, the face, or had once been beautiful, or could conceivably become beautiful, I confess I could form no opinion. I had seen faces in photographs I might have found beautiful had I known even vaguely in what beauty was supposed to consist. And my father's face, on his death-bolster, had seemed to hint at some form of aesthetics relevant to man. But the faces of the living, all grimace and flush, can they be described as objects? I admired in spite of the dark, in spite of my fluster, the way still or scarcely flowing water reaches up, as though athirst, to that falling from the sky. She asked if I would like her to sing something. I replied no, I would like her to say something. I thought she would say she had nothing to say, it would have been like her, and so was agreeably surprised when she said she had a room, most agreeably surprised, though I suspected as much. Who has not a room? Ah I hear the clamour. I have two rooms, she said. Just how many rooms do you have? I said. She said she had two rooms and a kitchen. The premises were expanding steadily, given time she would remember a bathroom. Is it two rooms I heard you say? I said. Yes, she said. Adjacent? I said. At last conversation worthy of the name. Separated by the kitchen, she said. I asked her why she had not told me before. I must have been beside myself, at this period. I did not feel easy when I was with her, but at least free to think of something else than her, of the old trusty things, and so little by little, as down steps towards a deep, of nothing. And I knew that away from her I would forfeit this freedom.

There were in fact two rooms, separated by a kitchen, she had not lied to me. She said I should have fetched my things. I explained I had no things. It was at the top of an old house, with a view of the mountains for those who cared. She lit an oil-lamp. You have no current? I said. No, she said, but I have running water and gas. Ha, I said, you have gas. She began to undress. When at their wit's end they undress, no doubt the wisest course. She took off everything, with a slowness fit to enflame an elephant, except her stockings, calculated presumably to bring my concupiscence to the boil. It was then I noticed the squint. Fortunately she was not the first naked woman to have crossed my path, so I could stay. I knew she would not explode. I asked to see the other room which I had not yet seen. If I had seen it already I would have asked to see it again. Will you not undress? she said. Oh you know, I said, I seldom undress. It was the truth, I was never one to undress indiscriminately. I often took off my boots when I went to bed, I mean when I composed myself (composed!) to sleep, not to mention this or that outer garment according to the outer temperature. She was therefore obliged, out of common savoir faire, to throw on a wrap and light me the way. We went via the kitchen. We could just as well have gone via the corridor, as I realized later, but we went via the kitchen, I don't know why, perhaps it was the shortest way. I surveyed the room with horror. Such density of furniture defeats imagination. Not a doubt, I must have seen that room somewhere. What's this? I cried. The parlour, she said. The parlour! I began putting out the furniture through the door to the corridor. She watched, in sorrow I suppose, but not necessarily. She asked me what I was doing. She can't have expected an answer. I put it out piece by piece, and even two at a time, and stacked it all up in the corridor, against the outer wall. They were hundreds of pieces, large and small, in the end they blocked the door, making egress impossible, and a fortiori ingress, to and from the corridor. The door could be opened and closed, since it opened inwards, but had become impassable. To put it wildly. At least take off your hat, she said. I'll treat of my hat some other time perhaps. Finally the room was empty but for a sofa and some shelves fixed to the wall. The former I dragged to the back of the room, near the door, and next day took down the latter and put them out, in the corridor, with the rest. As I was taking them down, strange memory, I heard the word fibrome, or brone, I don't know which, never knew, never knew what it meant and never had the curiosity to find out. The things one recalls! And records! When all was in order at last I dropped on the sofa. She had not raised her little finger to help me. I'll get sheets and blankets, she said. But I wouldn't hear of sheets. You couldn't draw the curtain? I said. The window was frosted over. The effect was not white, because of the night, but faintly luminous none the less. This faint cold sheen, though I lay with my feet towards the door, was more than I could bear. I suddenly rose and changed the position of the sofa, that is to say turned it round so that the back, hitherto against the wall, was now on the outside and consequently the front, or way in, on the inside. Then I climbed back, like a dog into its basket. I'll leave you the lamp, she said, but I begged her to take it with her. And suppose you need something in the night, she said. She was going to start quibbling again, I could feel it. Do you know where the convenience is? she said. She was right, I was forgetting. To relieve oneself in bed is enjoyable at the time, but soon a source of discomfort. Give me a chamber-pot, I said. But she did not possess one. I have a close-stool of sorts, she said. I saw the grandmother on it, sitting up very stiff and grand, having just purchased it, pardon, picked it up, at a charity sale, or perhaps won it in a raffle, a period piece, and now trying it out, doing her best rather, almost wishing someone could see her. That's the idea, procrastinate. Any old recipient, I said, I don't have the flux. She came back with a kind of saucepan, not a true saucepan for it had no handle, it was oval in shape with two lugs and a lid. My stewpan, she said. I don't need the lid, I said. You don't need the lid? she said. If I had said I needed the lid she would have said, You need the lid? I drew this utensil down under the blanket, I like something in my hand when sleeping, it reassures me, and my hat was still wringing. I turned to the wall. She caught up the lamp off the mantelpiece where she had set it down, that's the idea, every particular, it flung her waving shadow over me, I thought she was off, but no, she came stooping down towards me over the sofa back. All family possessions, she said. I in her shoes would have tiptoed away, but not she, not a stir. Already my love was waning, that was all that mattered. Yes, already I felt better, soon I'd be up to the slow descents again, the long submersions, so long denied me through her fault. And I had only just moved in! Try and put me out now, I said. I seemed not to grasp the meaning of these words, nor even hear the brief sound they made, till some seconds after having uttered them. I was so unused to speech that my mouth would sometimes open, of its own accord, and void some phrase or phrases, grammatically unexceptionable but entirely devoid if not of meaning, for on close inspection they would reveal one, and even several, at least of foundation. But I heard each word no sooner spoken. Never had my voice taken so long to reach me as on this occasion. I turned over on my back to see what was going on. She was smiling. A little later she went away, taking the lamp with her. I heard her steps in the kitchen and then the door of her room close behind her. Why behind her? I was alone at last, in the dark at last. Enough about that. I thought I was all set for a good night, in spite of the strange surroundings, but no, my night was most agitated. I woke next morning quite spent, my clothes in disorder, the blanket likewise, and Anna beside me, naked naturally. One shudders to think of her exertions. I still had the stewpan in my grasp. It had not served. I looked at my member. If only it could have spoken! Enough about that. It was my night of love.

Gradually I settled down, in this house. She brought my meals at the appointed hours, looked in now and then to see if all was well and make sure I needed nothing, emptied the stewpan once a day and did out the room once a month. She could not always resist the temptation to speak to me, but on the whole gave me no cause to complain. Sometimes I heard her singing in her room, the song traversed her door, then the kitchen, then my door, and in this way won to me, faint but indisputable. Unless it travelled by the corridor. This did not greatly incommode me, this occasional sound of singing. One day I asked her to bring me a hyacinth, live, in a pot. She brought it and put it on the mantelpiece, now the only place in my room to put things, unless you put them on the floor. Not a day passed without my looking at it. At first all went well, it even put forth a bloom or two, then it gave up and was soon no more than a limp stem hung with limp leaves. The bulb, half clear of the clay as though in search of oxygen, smelt foul. She wanted to remove it, but I told her to leave it. She wanted to get me another, but I told her I didn't want another. I was more seriously disturbed by other sounds, stifled giggles and groans, which filled the dwelling at certain hours of the night, and even of the day. I had given up thinking of her, quite given up, but still I needed silence, to live my life. In vain I tried to listen to such reasonings as that air is made to carry the clamours of the world, including inevitably much groan and giggle, I obtained no relief. I couldn't make out if it was always the same gent or more than one. Lovers' groans are so alike, and lovers' giggles. I had such horror then of these paltry perplexities that I always fell into the same error, that of seeking to clear them up. It took me a long time, my lifetime so to speak, to realize that the colour of an eye half seen, or the source of some distant sound, are closer to Giudecca in the hell of unknowing than the existence of God, or the origins of protoplasm, or the existence of self, and even less worthy than these to occupy the wise. It's a bit much, a lifetime, to achieve this consoling conclusion, it doesn't leave you much time to profit by it. So a fat lot of help it was when, having put the question to her, I was told they were clients she received in rotation. I could obviously have got up and gone to look through the keyhole. But what can you see, I ask you, through holes the likes of those? So you live by prostitution, I said. We live by prostitution, she said. You couldn't ask them to make less noise? I said, as if I believed her. I added, Or a different kind of noise. They can't help but yap and yelp, she said. I'll have to leave, I said. She found some old hangings in the family junk and hung them before our doors, hers and mine. I asked her if it would not be possible, now and then, to have a parsnip. A parsnip! she cried, as if I had asked for a dish of sucking Jew. I reminded her that the parsnip season was fast drawing to a close and that if, before it finally got there, she could feed me nothing but parsnips I'd be grateful. I like parsnips because they taste like violets and violets because they smell like parsnips. Were there no parsnips on earth violets would leave me cold and if violets did not exist I would care as little for parsnips as I do for turnips, or radishes. And even in the present state of their flora, I mean on this planet where parsnips and violets contrive to coexist, I could do without both with the utmost ease, the uttermost ease. One day she had the impudence to announce she was with child, and four or five months gone into the bargain, by me of all people! She offered me a side view of her belly. She even undressed, no doubt to prove she wasn't hiding a cushion under her skirt, and then of course for the pure pleasure of undressing. Perhaps it's mere wind, I said, by way of consolation. She gazed at me with her big eyes whose colour I forget, with one big eye rather, for the other seemed riveted on the remains of the hyacinth. The more naked she was the more cross-eyed. Look, she said, stooping over her breasts, the haloes are darkening already. I summoned up my remaining strength and said, Abort, abort, and they'll blush like new. She had drawn back the curtain for a clear view of all her rotundities. I saw the mountain, impassible, cavernous, secret, where from morning to night I'd hear nothing but the wind, the curlews, the clink like distant silver of the stonecutters' hammers. I'd come out in the daytime to the heather and gorse, all warmth and scent, and watch at night the distant city lights, if I chose, and the other lights, the lighthouses and lightships my father had named for me, when I was small, and whose names I could find again, in my memory, if I chose, that I knew. From that day forth things went from bad to worse, to worse and worse. Not that she neglected me, she could never have neglected me enough, but the way she kept plaguing me with *our* child, exhibiting her belly and breasts and saying it was due any moment, she could feel it lepping already. If it's lepping, I said, it's not mine. I might have been worse off than I was, in that house, that was certain, it fell short of my ideal naturally, but I wasn't blind to its advantages. I hesitated to leave, the leaves were falling already, I dreaded the winter. One should not dread the winter, it too has its bounties, the snow gives warmth and deadens the tumult and its pale days are soon over. But I did not yet know, at that time, how tender the earth can be for those who have only her and how many graves in her giving, for the living. What finished me was the birth. It woke me up. What that infant must have been going through! I fancy she had a woman with her, I seemed to hear steps in the kitchen, on and off. It went to my heart to leave a house without being put out. I crept out over the back of the sofa, put on my coat, greatcoat and hat, I can think of nothing else, laced up my boots and opened the door to the corridor. A mass of junk barred my way, but I scrabbled and barged my way through it in the end, regardless of the clatter. I used the word marriage, it was a kind of union in spite of all. Precautions would have been superfluous, there was no competing with those cries. It must have been her first. They pursued me down the stairs and out into the street. I stopped before the house door and listened. I could still hear them. If I had not known there was crying in the house I might not have heard them. But knowing it I did. I was not sure where I was. I looked among the stars and constellations for the Wains, but could not find them. And yet they must have been there. My father was the first to show them to me. He had shown me others, but alone, without him beside me, I could never find any but the Wains. I began playing with the cries, a little in the same way as I had played with the song, on, back, on, back, if that may be called playing. As long as I kept walking I didn't hear them, because of the footsteps. But as soon as I halted I heard them again, a little fainter each time, admittedly, but what does it matter, faint or loud, cry is cry, all that matters is that it should cease. For years I thought they would cease. Now I don't think so any more. I could have done with other loves perhaps. But there it is, either you love or you don't.

Heinrich Böll

• •

ACTION WILL BE TAKEN

An Action-Packed Story

Probably one of the strangest interludes in my life was the time I spent as an employee in Alfred Wunsiedel's factory. By nature I am inclined more to pensiveness and inactivity than to work, but now and again prolonged financial difficulties compel me—for pensiveness is no more profitable than inactivity—to take on a so-called job. Finding myself once again at a low ebb of this kind, I put myself in the hands of the employment office and was sent with seven other fellow-sufferers to Wunsiedel's factory, where we were to undergo an aptitude test.

The exterior of the factory was enough to arouse my suspicions: the factory was built entirely of glass brick, and my aversion to well-lit buildings and well-lit rooms is as strong as my aversion to work. I became even more suspicious when we were immediately served breakfast in the well-lit, cheerful coffee shop: pretty waitresses brought us eggs, coffee and toast, orange juice was served in tastefully designed jugs, goldfish pressed their bored faces against the sides of pale-green aquariums. The waitresses were so cheerful that they appeared to be bursting with good cheer. Only a strong effort of will—so it seemed to me—restrained them from singing away all day long. They were as crammed with unsung songs as chickens with unlaid eggs.

Right away I realized something that my fellow-sufferers evidently failed to realize: that this breakfast was already part of the test; so I chewed away reverently, with the full appreciation of a person who knows he is supplying his body with valuable elements. I did something which normally no power on earth can make me do: I drank orange juice on an empty stomach, left the coffee and egg untouched, as well as most of the toast, got up, and paced up and down in the coffee shop, pregnant with action.

As a result I was the first to be ushered into the room where the questionnaires were spread out on attractive tables. The walls were done in a shade of green that would have summoned the word "delightful" to the lips of interior decoration enthusiasts. The room appeared to be empty, and yet I was so sure of being observed that I behaved as someone pregnant with action behaves when he believes himself unobserved: I ripped my pen impatiently from my pocket, unscrewed the top, sat down at the nearest table and pulled the questionnaire toward me, the way irritable customers snatch at the bill in a restaurant.

Question No. 1: Do you consider it right for a human being to possess only two arms, two legs, eyes, and ears?

Here for the first time I reaped the harvest of my pensive nature and wrote without hesitation: "Even four arms, legs and ears would not be adequate for my driving energy. Human beings are very poorly equipped."

Question No. 2: How many telephones can you handle at one time?

Here again the answer was as easy as simple arithmetic: "When there are only seven telephones," I wrote, "I get impatient; there have to be nine before I feel I am working to capacity."

Question No. 3: How do you spend your free time?

My answer: "I no longer acknowledge the term free time—on my fifteenth birthday I eliminated it from my vocabulary, for in the beginning was the act."

I got the job. Even with nine telephones I really didn't feel I was working to capacity. I shouted into the mouthpieces: "Take immediate action!" or: "Do something!—We must have some action—Action will be taken—Action has been taken—Action should be taken." But as a rule—for I felt this was in keeping with the tone of the place—I used the imperative.

Of considerable interest were the noon-hour breaks, when we consumed nutritious foods in an atmosphere of silent good cheer. Wunsiedel's factory was swarming with people who were obsessed with telling you the story of their lives, as indeed vigorous personalities are fond of doing. The story of their lives is more important to them than their lives, you have only to press a button, and immediately it is covered with spewed-out exploits.

Wunsiedel had a right-hand man called Broschek, who had in turn made a name for himself by supporting seven children and a paralyzed wife by working night-shifts in his student days, and successfully carrying on four business agencies, besides which he had passed two examinations with honors in two years. When asked by reporters: "When do you sleep, Mr. Broschek?" he had replied: "It's a crime to sleep!"

Wunsiedel's secretary had supported a paralyzed husband and four children by knitting, at the same time graduating in psychology and German history as well as breeding shepherd dogs, and she had become famous as a night-club singer where she was known as *Vamp Number Seven*.

Wunsiedel himself was one of those people who every morning, as they open their eyes, make up their minds to act. "I must act," they think as they briskly tie their bathrobe belts around them. "I must act," they think as they shave, triumphantly watching their beard hairs being washed away with the lather: these hirsute vestiges are the first daily sacrifices to their driving energy. The more intimate functions also give these people a sense of satisfaction: water swishes, paper is used. Action has been taken. Bread gets eaten, eggs are decapitated.

With Wunsiedel, the most trivial activity looked like action: the way he put on his hat, the way—quivering with energy—he buttoned up his overcoat, the kiss he gave his wife, everything was action.

When he arrived at his office he greeted his secretary with a cry of "Let's have some action!" And in ringing tones she would call back: "Action will be taken!" Wunsiedel then went from department to department, calling out his cheerful: "Let's have some action!" Everyone would answer: "Action will be taken!" And I would call back to him too, with a radiant smile, when he looked into my office: "Action will be taken!"

Within a week I had increased the number of telephones on my desk to eleven, within two weeks to thirteen, and every morning on the streetcar I enjoyed thinking up new imperatives, or chasing the words *take action* through various tenses and modulations: for two whole days I kept saying the same sentence over and over again because I thought it sounded so marvelous: "Action ought to have been taken;" for another two days it was: "Such action ought not to have been taken."

So I was really beginning to feel I was working to capacity when there actually was some action. One Tuesday morning—I had hardly settled down at my desk—Wunsiedel rushed into my office crying his "Let's have some action!" But an inexplicable something in his face made me hesitate to reply, in a cheerful gay voice as the rules dictated: "Action will be taken!" I must have paused too long, for Wunsiedel, who seldom raised his voice, shouted at me: "Answer! Answer, you know the rules!" And I answered, under my breath, reluctantly, like a child who is forced to say: I am a naughty child. It was only by a great effort that I managed to bring out the sentence: "Action will be taken," and hardly had I uttered it when there really was some action: Wunsiedel dropped to the floor. As he fell he rolled over onto his side and lay right across the open doorway. I knew at once, and I confirmed it when I went slowly around my desk and approached the body on the floor: he was dead.

Shaking my head I stepped over Wunsiedel, walked slowly along the corridor to Broschek's office, and entered without knocking. Broschek was sitting at his desk, a telephone receiver in each hand, between his teeth a ballpoint pen with which he was making notes on a writing pad, while with his bare feet he was operating a knitting machine under the desk. In this way he helps to clothe his family. "We've had some action," I said in a low voice.

Broschek spat out the ballpoint pen, put down the two receivers, reluctantly detached his toes from the knitting machine.

"What action?" he asked.

"Wunsiedel is dead," I said.

"No," said Broschek.

"Yes," I said, "come and have a look!"

"No," said Broschek, "that's impossible," but he put on his slippers and followed me along the corridor.

"No," he said, when we stood beside Wunsiedel's corpse, "no, no!" I did not contradict him. I carefully turned Wunsiedel over onto his back, closed his eyes, and looked at him pensively.

I felt something like tenderness for him, and realized for the first time that I had never hated him. On his face was that expression which one sees on children who obstinately refuse to give up their faith in Santa Claus, even though the arguments of their playmates sound so convincing.

"No," said Broschek, "no."

"We must take action," I said quietly to Broschek.

"Yes," said Broschek, "we must take action."

Action was taken: Wunsiedel was buried, and I was delegated to carry a wreath of artificial roses behind his coffin, for I am equipped with not only a penchant for pensiveness and inactivity but also a face and figure that go extremely well with dark suits. Apparently as I walked along behind Wunsiedel's coffin carrying the wreath of artificial roses I looked superb. I received an offer from a fashionable firm of funeral directors to join their staff as a professional mourner. "You are a born mourner," said the manager, "your outfit would be provided by the firm. Your face—simply superb!"

I handed in my notice to Broschek, explaining that I had never really felt I was working to capacity there; that, in spite of the thirteen telephones, some of my talents were going to waste. As soon as my first professional appearance as a mourner was over I knew: This is where I belong, this is what I am cut out for.

Pensively I stand behind the coffin in the funeral chapel, holding a simple bouquet, while the organ plays Handel's *Largo*, a piece that does not receive nearly the respect it deserves. The cemetery café is my regular haunt; there I spend the intervals between my professional engagements, although sometimes I walk behind coffins which I have not been engaged to follow, I pay for flowers out of my own pocket and join the welfare worker who walks behind the coffin of some homeless person. From time to time I also visit Wunsiedel's grave, for after all I owe it to him that I discovered my true vocation, a vocation in which pensiveness is essential and inactivity my duty.

It was not till much later that I realized I had never bothered to find out what was being produced in Wunsiedel's factory. I expect it was soap.

Translated from the German by Leila Vennewitz

Wolfgang Borchert

. . . .

DO STAY, GIRAFFE

He stood on the wind-howling night-empty platform in the great greysooted moon-lonely hall. Empty stations at night are the end of the world, extinct, grown meaningless. And void. Void, void, void. But if you go further, you are lost.

Then you are lost. For the darkness has a terrible voice. You cannot escape it and in a flash it has overwhelmed you. It assails you with memory—of the murder you committed yesterday. And it attacks you with foreknowledge—of the murder you'll commit tomorrow. And it presses up a cry in you: unheard fish-cry of the solitary animal, overwhelmed by its own sea. And the cry tears up your face and makes hollows in it full of fear and past danger, that terrify others. So silent is the dreadful darkness—cry of the solitary animal in its own sea.

And it mounts like a flood and rushes on, dark-winged, threatening, like breakers. And hisses wickedly, like foam.

He stood at the end of the world. The cold white arc-lamps were merciless and made everything naked and doleful. But behind them grew a terrible darkness. No black was as black as the darkness round the white lamps of the night-empty platforms.

I see you've got cigarettes, said the girl with the too red mouth in the pale face.

Yes, he said, I have some.

Why don't you come with me then? she whispered, close.

No, he said, what for?

You don't know what I'm like, she sniffed round about him.

I do, he answered, like them all.

You're a giraffe, big boy, a stubborn giraffe! D'you even know what I look like, eh?

Hungry, he said, naked and painted. Like them all.

You're long and dumb, you giraffe, she giggled close, but you look sweet. And you've cigarettes. Come on, boy, it's dark.

Then he looked at her. All right, he laughed, you get the cigarettes and I kiss you. But if I take hold of your dress, what then?

98

Then I'll blush, she said, and he thought her grin vulgar.

A freight train yowled through the station. And suddenly tore off. Its miserly, shimmering tail-light oozed away in embarrassment into the darkness. Banging, squeaking, crashing, rumbling—gone. Then he went with her.

Then there were hands, faces and lips. But all the faces are bleeding, he thought, bleeding from the mouth, and the hands hold hand-grenades. But then he tasted the make-up and her hand grasped his bony arm. Then there was a groan and a steel helmet fell and an eye broke.

You're dying, he screamed.

Dying, she gloated. That'd be something!

Then she pushed the helmet back on to the forehead. Her dark hair shone softly.

Ah, your hair, he whispered.

Will you stay? she asked softly.

Yes.

For long?

Yes.

For always?

Your hair smells like wet twigs, he said.

For always? she asked again.

And then from the distance: near, fat, great cry. Fish-cry, bat's cry, dungbeetle's cry. The never-heard animal cry of the locomotive. Did the train sway on its tracks, full of fear from that cry? New, never-known yellow-green cry beneath faded constellations. Did that cry make the stars shiver?

Then he tore open the window, so that the night clutched with cold hands at his naked breast, and said: I must go.

Do stay, giraffe! Her mouth shimmered sick-red in her pale face.

But the giraffe stalked away across the pavement with hollow, echoing steps. And behind him the moon-grey street, falling silent again, returned to its petrified loneliness. The reptile-eyed windows looked dead, as though glazed with a milky film. The curtains, sleep-heavy secretly breathing eyelids, billowed gently. Dangled. Dangled, white, soft, and waved sorrowfully after him.

The shutter miaowed. And her breast was cold. When he looked round, behind the pane was a too red mouth. Giraffe, it wept.

Translated from the German by David Porter

Jorge Luis Borges

· ·

THE ALEPH

O God! I could be bounded in a nutshell, and count myself a King of infinite space. . . .
HAMLET, II, 2

But they will teach us that Eternity is the Standing still of the Present Time, A Nunc-stans (as the Schools call it); which neither they, nor any else understand, no more than they would a Hic-stans for an Infinite greatness of Place.
LEVIATHAN, IV, 46

On the burning February morning Beatriz Viterbo died, after braving an agony that never for a single moment gave way to self-pity or fear, I noticed that the sidewalk billboards around Constitution Plaza were advertising some new brand or other of American cigarettes. The fact pained me, for I realized that the wide and ceaseless universe was already slipping away from her and that this slight change was the first of an endless series. The universe may change but not me, I thought with a certain sad vanity. I knew that at times my fruitless devotion had annoyed her; now that she was dead, I could devote myself to her memory, without hope but also without humiliation. I recalled that the thirtieth of April was her birthday; on that day to visit her house on Garay Street and pay my respects to her father and to Carlos Argentino Daneri, her first cousin, would be an irreproachable and perhaps unavoidable act of politeness. Once again I would wait in the twilight of the small, cluttered drawing room, once again I would study the details of her many photographs: Beatriz Viterbo in profile and in full color; Beatriz wearing a mask, during the Carnival of 1921; Beatriz at her First Communion; Beatriz on the day of her wedding to Roberto Alessandri; Beatriz soon after her divorce, at a luncheon at the Turf Club; Beatriz at a seaside resort in Quilmes with Delia San Marco Porcel and Carlos Argentino; Beatriz with the Pekinese lapdog given her by Villegas Haedo; Beatriz, front and three-quarter views, smiling, hand on her chin. . . . I would not be forced, as in the past, to justify my presence with modest offerings of books—books whose pages I finally learned to cut beforehand, so as not to find out, months later, that they lay around unopened.

Beatriz Viterbo died in 1929. From that time on, I never let a thirtieth of April go by without a visit to her house. I used to make my appearance at seven-fifteen sharp and stay on for some twenty-five minutes. Each year, I arrived a little later and stayed a little longer. In 1933, a torrential downpour coming to my aid, they were obliged to ask me to dinner. Naturally, I took advantage of that lucky precedent. In 1934, I arrived, just after eight, with one of those large Santa Fe sugared cakes, and quite matter-of-factly I stayed to dinner. It was in this way, on these melancholy and vainly erotic anniversaries, that I came into the gradual confidences of Carlos Argentino Daneri.

Beatriz had been tall, frail, slightly stooped; in her walk there was (if the oxymoron may be allowed) a kind of uncertain grace, a hint of expectancy. Carlos Argentino was pink-faced, overweight, gray-haired, fine-featured. He held a minor position in an unreadable library out on the edge of the Southside of Buenos Aires. He was authoritarian but also unimpressive. Until only recently, he took advantage of his nights and holidays to stay at home. At a remove of two generations, the Italian "S" and demonstrative Italian gestures still survived in him. His mental activity was continuous, deeply felt, far-ranging, and—all in all—meaningless. He dealt in pointless analogies and in trivial scruples. He had (as did Beatriz) large, beautiful, finely shaped hands. For several months he seemed to be obsessed with Paul Fort—less with his ballads than with the idea of a towering reputation. "He is the Prince of poets," Daneri would repeat fatuously. "You will belittle him in vain—but no, not even the most venomous of your shafts will graze him."

On the thirtieth of April, 1941, along with the sugared cake I allowed myself to add a bottle of Argentine cognac. Carlos Argentino tasted it, pronounced it "interesting," and, after a few drinks, launched into a glorification of modern man.

"I view him," he said with a certain unaccountable excitement, "in his inner sanctum, as though in his castle tower, supplied with telephones, telegraphs, phonographs, wireless sets, motion-picture screens, slide projectors, glossaries, timetables, handbooks, bulletins. . . ."

He remarked that for a man so equipped, actual travel was superfluous. Our twentieth century had inverted the story of Mohammed and the mountain; nowadays, the mountain came to the modern Mohammed.

So foolish did his ideas seem to me, so pompous and so drawn out his exposition, that I linked them at once to literature and asked him why he didn't write them down. As might be foreseen, he answered that he had already done so—that these ideas, and others no less striking, had found their place in the Proem, or Augural Canto, or, more simply, the Prologue Canto of the poem on which he had been working for many years now, alone, without publicity, without fanfare, supported only by those twin staffs universally known as work and solitude. First, he said, he opened the floodgates of his fancy; then, taking up hand tools, he resorted to the file. The poem was entitled *The Earth*; it consisted of a description of the planet, and, of course, lacked no amount of picturesque digressions and bold apostrophes.

I asked him to read me a passage, if only a short one. He opened a drawer of his writing table, drew out a thick stack of papers—sheets of a large pad im-

printed with the letterhead of the Juan Crisóstomo Lafinur Library—and, with
ringing satisfaction, declaimed:

> Mine eyes, as did the Greek's, have known men's towns and fame,
> The works, the days in light that fades to amber;
> I do not change a fact or falsify a name—
> The *voyage* I set down is . . . *autour de ma chambre.*

"From any angle, a greatly interesting stanza," he said, giving his verdict.
"The opening line wins the applause of the professor, the academician, and the
Hellenist—to say nothing of the would-be scholar, a considerable sector of the
public. The second flows from Homer to Hesiod (generous homage, at the very
outset, to the father of didactic poetry), not without rejuvenating a process
whose roots go back to Scripture—enumeration, congeries, conglomeration.
The third—baroque? decadent? example of the cult of pure form?—consists of
two equal hemistichs. The fourth, frankly bilingual, assures me the unstinted
backing of all minds sensitive to the pleasures of sheer fun. I should, in all fair-
ness, speak of the novel rhyme in lines two and four, and of the erudition that
allows me—without a hint of pedantry!—to cram into four lines three learned
allusions covering thirty centuries packed with literature—first to the *Odyssey*,
second to *Works and Days*, and third to the immortal bagatelle bequeathed us
by the frolicking pen of the Savoyard, Xavier de Maistre. Once more I've come
to realize that modern art demands the balm of laughter, the scherzo. Decidedly, Goldoni holds the stage!"

He read me many other stanzas, each of which also won his own approval and
elicited his lengthy explications. There was nothing remarkable about them. I
did not even find them any worse than the first one. Application, resignation,
and chance had gone into the writing; I saw, however, that Daneri's real work
lay not in the poetry but in his invention of reasons why the poetry should be
admired. Of course, this second phase of his effort modified the writing in his
eyes, though not in the eyes of others. Daneri's style of delivery was extravagant,
but the deadly drone of his metric regularity tended to tone down and to dull
that extravagance.*

Only once in my life have I had occasion to look into the fifteen thousand
alexandrines of the *Polyolbion*, that topographical epic in which Michael Dray-
ton recorded the flora, fauna, hydrography, orography, military and monastic
history of England. I am sure, however, that this limited but bulky production is
less boring than Carlos Argentino's similar vast undertaking. Daneri had in
mind to set to verse the entire face of the planet, and, by 1941, had already dispatched a number of acres of the State of Queensland, nearly a mile of the

---

* Among my memories are also some lines of a satire in which he lashed out unsparingly at bad
poets. After accusing them of dressing their poems in the warlike armor of erudition, and of flapping in vain their unavailing wings, he concluded with this verse:

> But they forget, alas, one foremost fact—BEAUTY!

Only the fear of creating an army of implacable and powerful enemies dissuaded him (he told
me) from fearlessly publishing this poem.

course run by the River Ob, a gasworks to the north of Veracruz, the leading shops in the Buenos Aires parish of Concepción, the villa of Mariana Cambaceres de Alvear in the Belgrano section of the Argentine capital, and a Turkish baths establishment not far from the well-known Brighton Aquarium. He read me certain long-winded passages from his Australian section, and at one point praised a word of his own coining, the color "celestewhite," which he felt "actually *suggests* the sky, an element of utmost importance in the landscape of the continent Down Under." But these sprawling, lifeless hexameters lacked even the relative excitement of the so-called Augural Canto. Along about midnight, I left.

Two Sundays later, Daneri rang me up—perhaps for the first time in his life. He suggested we get together at four o'clock "for cocktails in the salon-bar next door, which the forward-looking Zunino and Zungri—my landlords, as you doubtless recall—are throwing open to the public. It's a place you'll really want to get to know."

More in resignation than in pleasure, I accepted. Once there, it was hard to find a table. The "salon-bar," ruthlessly modern, was only barely less ugly than what I had expected; at the nearby tables, the excited customers spoke breathlessly of the sums Zunino and Zungri had invested in furnishings without a second thought to cost. Carlos Argentino pretended to be astonished by some feature or other of the lighting arrangement (with which, I felt, he was already familiar), and he said to me with a certain severity, "Grudgingly, you'll have to admit to the fact that these premises hold their own with many others far more in the public eye."

He then reread me four or five different fragments of the poem. He had revised them following his pet principle of verbal ostentation: where at first "blue" had been good enough, he now wallowed in "azures," "ceruleans," and "ultramarines." The word "milky" was too easy for him; in the course of an impassioned description of a shed where wool was washed, he chose such words as "lacteal," "lactescent," and even made one up—"lactinacious." After that, straight out, he condemned our modern mania for having books prefaced, "a practice already held up to scorn by the Prince of Wits in his own graceful preface to the *Quixote*." He admitted, however, that for the opening of his new work an attention-getting foreword might prove valuable—"an accolade signed by a literary hand of renown." He next went on to say that he considered publishing the initial cantos of his poem. I then began to understand the unexpected telephone call; Daneri was going to ask me to contribute a foreword to his pedantic hodgepodge. My fear turned out unfounded; Carlos Argentino remarked, with admiration and envy, that surely he could not be far wrong in qualifying with the epithet "solid" the prestige enjoyed in every circle by Álvaro Melián Lafinur, a man of letters, who would, if I insisted on it, be only too glad to dash off some charming opening words to the poem. In order to avoid ignominy and failure, he suggested I make myself spokesman for two of the book's undeniable virtues—formal perfection and scientific rigor—"inasmuch as this wide garden of metaphors, of figures of speech, of elegances, is inhospitable to the least detail not strictly upholding of truth." He added that Beatriz had always been taken with Álvaro.

I agreed—agreed profusely—and explained for the sake of credibility that I would not speak to Álvaro the next day, Monday, but would wait until Thursday, when we got together for the informal dinner that follows every meeting of the Writers' Club. (No such dinners are ever held, but it is an established fact that the meetings do take place on Thursdays, a point which Carlos Argentino Daneri could verify in the daily papers, and which lent a certain reality to my promise.) Half in prophecy, half in cunning, I said that before taking up the question of a preface I would outline the unusual plan of the work. We then said goodbye.

Turning the corner of Bernardo de Irigoyen, I reviewed as impartially as possible the alternatives before me. They were: *a*) to speak to Álvaro, telling him this first cousin of Beatriz' (the explanatory euphemism would allow me to mention her name) had concocted a poem that seemed to draw out into infinity the possibilities of cacophony and chaos; *b*) not to say a word to Álvaro. I clearly foresaw that my indolence would opt for *b*.

But first thing Friday morning, I began worrying about the telephone. It offended me that that device, which had once produced the irrecoverable voice of Beatriz, could now sink so low as to become a mere receptacle for the futile and perhaps angry remonstrances of that deluded Carlos Argentino Daneri. Luckily, nothing happened—except the inevitable spite touched off in me by this man, who had asked me to fulfill a delicate mission for him and then had let me drop.

Gradually, the phone came to lose its terrors, but one day toward the end of October it rang, and Carlos Argentino was on the line. He was deeply disturbed, so much so that at the outset I did not recognize his voice. Sadly but angrily he stammered that the now unrestrainable Zunino and Zungri, under the pretext of enlarging their already outsized "salon-bar," were about to take over and tear down his house.

"My home, my ancestral home, my old and inveterate Garay Street home!" he kept repeating, seeming to forget his woe in the music of his words.

It was not hard for me to share his distress. After the age of fifty, all change becomes a hateful symbol of the passing of time. Besides, the scheme concerned a house that for me would always stand for Beatriz. I tried explaining this delicate scruple of regret, but Daneri seemed not to hear me. He said that if Zunino and Zungri persisted in this outrage, Doctor Zunni, his lawyer, would sue *ipso facto* and make them pay some fifty thousand dollars in damages.

Zunni's name impressed me; his firm, although at the unlikely address of Caseros and Tacuarí, was nonetheless known as an old and reliable one. I asked him whether Zunni had already been hired for the case. Daneri said he would phone him that very afternoon. He hesitated, then with that level, impersonal voice we reserve for confiding something intimate, he said that to finish the poem he could not get along without the house because down in the cellar there was an Aleph. He explained that an Aleph is one of the points in space that contains all other points.

"It's in the cellar under the dining room," he went on, so overcome by his worries now that he forgot to be pompous. "It's mine—mine. I discovered it when I was a child, all by myself. The cellar stairway is so steep that my aunt and uncle forbade my using it, but I'd heard someone say there was a world down there. I found out later they meant an old-fashioned globe of the world, but at the time I thought they were referring to the world itself. One day when no one was home I started down in secret, but I stumbled and fell. When I opened my eyes, I saw the Aleph."

"The Aleph?" I repeated.

"Yes, the only place on earth where all places are—seen from every angle, each standing clear, without any confusion or blending. I kept the discovery to myself and went back every chance I got. As a child, I did not foresee that this privilege was granted me so that later I could write the poem. Zunino and Zungri will not strip me of what's mine—no, and a thousand times no! Legal code in hand, Doctor Zunni will prove that my Aleph is inalienable."

I tried to reason with him. "But isn't the cellar very dark?" I said.

"Truth cannot penetrate a closed mind. If all places in the universe are in the Aleph, then all stars, all lamps, all sources of light are in it, too."

"You wait there. I'll be right over to see it."

I hung up before he could say no. The full knowledge of a fact sometimes enables you to see all at once many supporting but previously unsuspected things. It amazed me not to have suspected until that moment that Carlos Argentino was a madman. As were all the Viterbos, when you came down to it. Beatriz (I myself often say it) was a woman, a child, with almost uncanny powers of clairvoyance, but forgetfulness, distractions, contempt, and a streak of cruelty were also in her, and perhaps these called for a pathological explanation. Carlos Argentino's madness filled me with spiteful elation. Deep down, we had always detested each other.

On Garay Street, the maid asked me kindly to wait. The master was, as usual, in the cellar developing pictures. On the unplayed piano, beside a large vase that held no flowers, smiled (more timeless than belonging to the past) the large photograph of Beatriz, in gaudy colors. Nobody could see us; in a seizure of tenderness, I drew close to the portrait and said to it, "Beatriz, Beatriz Elena, Beatriz Elena Viterbo, darling Beatriz, Beatriz now gone forever, it's me, it's Borges."

Moments later, Carlos came in. He spoke drily. I could see he was thinking of nothing else but the loss of the Aleph.

"First a glass of pseudo-cognac," he ordered, "and then down you dive into the cellar. Let me warn you, you'll have to lie flat on your back. Total darkness, total immobility, and a certain ocular adjustment will also be necessary. From the floor, you must focus your eyes on the nineteenth step. Once I leave you, I'll lower the trapdoor and you'll be quite alone. You needn't fear the rodents very much—though I know you will. In a minute or two, you'll see the Aleph—the microcosm of the alchemists and Kabbalists, our true proverbial friend, the *multum in parvo!*"

Once we were in the dining room, he added, "Of course, if you don't see it, your incapacity will not invalidate what I have experienced. Now, down you go. In a short while you can babble with *all* of Beatriz' images."

Tired of his inane words, I quickly made my way. The cellar, barely wider than the stairway itself, was something of a pit. My eyes searched the dark, looking in vain for the globe Carlos Argentino had spoken of. Some cases of empty bottles and some canvas sacks cluttered one corner. Carlos picked up a sack, folded it in two, and at a fixed spot spread it out.

"As a pillow," he said, "this is quite threadbare, but if it's padded even a half-inch higher, you won't see a thing, and there you'll lie, feeling ashamed and ridiculous. All right now, sprawl that hulk of yours there on the floor and count off nineteen steps."

I went through with his absurd requirements, and at last he went away. The trapdoor was carefully shut. The blackness, in spite of a chink that I later made out, seemed to me absolute. For the first time, I realized the danger I was in: I'd let myself be locked in a cellar by a lunatic, after gulping down a glassful of poison! I knew that back of Carlos' transparent boasting lay a deep fear that I might not see the promised wonder. To keep his madness undetected, to keep from admitting that he was mad, *Carlos had to kill me*. I felt a shock of panic, which I tried to pin to my uncomfortable position and not to the effect of a drug. I shut my eyes—I opened them. Then I saw the Aleph.

I arrive now at the ineffable core of my story. And here begins my despair as a writer. All language is a set of symbols whose use among its speakers assumes a shared past. How, then, can I translate into words the limitless Aleph, which my floundering mind can scarcely encompass? Mystics, faced with the same problem, fall back on symbols: to signify the godhead, one Persian speaks of a bird that somehow is all birds; Alanus de Insulis, of a sphere whose center is everywhere and circumference is nowhere; Ezekiel, of a four-faced angel who at one and the same time moves east and west, north and south. (Not in vain do I recall these inconceivable analogies; they bear some relation to the Aleph.) Perhaps the gods might grant me a similar metaphor, but then this account would become contaminated by literature, by fiction. Really, what I want to do is impossible, for any listing of an endless series is doomed to be infinitesimal. In that single gigantic instant I saw millions of acts both delightful and awful; not one of them amazed me more than the fact that all of them occupied the same point in space, without overlapping or transparency. What my eyes beheld was simultaneous, but what I shall now write down will be successive, because language is successive. Nonetheless, I'll try to recollect what I can.

On the back part of the step, toward the right, I saw a small iridescent sphere of almost unbearable brilliance. At first I thought it was revolving; then I realized that this movement was an illusion created by the dizzying world it bounded. The Aleph's diameter was probably little more than an inch, but all space was there, actual and undiminished. Each thing (a mirror's face, let us say) was infinite things, since I distinctly saw it from every angle of the universe. I saw the teeming sea; I saw daybreak and nightfall; I saw the multitudes of America; I saw a silvery cobweb in the center of a black pyramid; I saw a splintered labyrinth (it was London); I saw, close up, unending eyes watching themselves in me as in a mirror; I saw all the mirrors on earth and none of them reflected me; I saw in a backyard of Soler Street the same tiles that thirty years before I'd seen in the entrance of a house in Fray Bentos; I saw bunches of grapes, snow, tobacco, lodes of metal, steam; I saw convex equatorial deserts and each one of their grains of sand; I saw a woman in Inverness whom I shall never forget; I saw her tangled hair, her tall figure, I saw the cancer in her breast; I saw a ring of baked mud in a sidewalk, where before there had been a tree; I saw a summer house in Adrogué and a copy of the first English translation of Pliny— Philemon Holland's—and all at the same time saw each letter on each page (as a boy, I used to marvel that the letters in a closed book did not get scrambled and lost overnight); I saw a sunset in Querétaro that seemed to reflect the color of a rose in Bengal; I saw my empty bedroom; I saw in a closet in Alkmaar a terrestrial globe between two mirrors that multiplied it endlessly; I saw horses with flowing manes on a shore of the Caspian Sea at dawn; I saw the delicate bone structure of a hand; I saw the survivors of a battle sending out picture postcards; I saw in a showcase in Mirzapur a pack of Spanish playing cards; I saw the slanting shadows of ferns on a greenhouse floor; I saw tigers, pistons, bison, tides, and armies; I saw all the ants on the planet; I saw a Persian astrolabe; I saw in the drawer of a writing table (and the handwriting made me tremble) unbelievable, obscene, detailed letters, which Beatriz had written to Carlos Argentino; I saw a monument I worshiped in the Chacarita cemetery; I saw the rotted dust and bones that had once deliciously been Beatriz Viterbo; I saw the circulation of my own dark blood; I saw the coupling of love and the modification of death; I saw the Aleph from every point and angle, and in the Aleph I saw the earth and in the earth the Aleph and in the Aleph the earth; I saw my own face and my own bowels; I saw your face; and I felt dizzy and wept, for my eyes had seen that secret and conjectured object whose name is common to all men but which no man has looked upon—the unimaginable universe.

I felt infinite wonder, infinite pity.

"Feeling pretty cockeyed, are you, after so much spying into places where you have no business?" said a hated and jovial voice. "Even if you were to rack your brains, you couldn't pay me back in a hundred years for this revelation. One hell of an observatory, eh, Borges?"

Carlos Argentino's feet were planted on the topmost step. In the sudden dim light, I managed to pick myself up and utter, "One hell of a—yes, one hell of a."

The matter-of-factness of my voice surprised me. Anxiously, Carlos Argentino went on.

"Did you see everything—really clear, in colors?"

At that very moment I found my revenge. Kindly, openly pitying him, distraught, evasive, I thanked Carlos Argentino Daneri for the hospitality of his cellar and urged him to make the most of the demolition to get away from the pernicious metropolis, which spares no one—believe me, I told him, no one! Quietly and forcefully, I refused to discuss the Aleph. On saying goodbye, I embraced him and repeated that the country, that fresh air and quiet were the great physicians.

Out on the street, going down the stairways inside Constitution Station, riding the subway, every one of the faces seemed familiar to me. I was afraid that not a single thing on earth would ever again surprise me; I was afraid I would never again be free of all I had seen. Happily, after a few sleepless nights, I was visited once more by oblivion.

Postscript of March first, 1943—Some six months after the pulling down of a certain building on Garay Street, Procrustes & Co., the publishers, not put off by the considerable length of Daneri's poem, brought out a selection of its "Argentine sections." It is redundant now to repeat what happened. Carlos Argentino Daneri won the Second National Prize for Literature.* First Prize went to Dr. Aita; Third Prize, to Dr. Mario Bonfanti. Unbelievably, my own book *The Sharper's Cards* did not get a single vote. Once again dullness and envy had their triumph! It's been some time now that I've been trying to see Daneri; the gossip is that a second selection of the poem is about to be published. His felicitous pen (no longer cluttered by the Aleph) has now set itself the task of writing an epic on our national hero, General San Martín.

I want to add two final observations: one, on the nature of the Aleph; the other, on its name. As is well known, the Aleph is the first letter of the Hebrew alphabet. Its use for the strange sphere in my story may not be accidental. For the Kabbala, that letter stands for the *En Soph,* the pure and boundless godhead; it is also said that it takes the shape of a man pointing to both heaven and earth, in order to show that the lower world is the map and mirror of the higher; for Cantor's *Mengenlehre,* it is the symbol of transfinite numbers, of which any part is as great as the whole. I would like to know whether Carlos Argentino chose that name or whether he read it—applied to another point where all points converge—in one of the numberless texts that the Aleph in his cellar revealed to him. Incredible as it may seem, I believe that the Aleph of Garay Street was a false Aleph.

Here are my reasons. Around 1867, Captain Burton held the post of British Consul in Brazil. In July, 1942, Pedro Henríquez Ureña came across a manuscript of Burton's, in a library at Santos, dealing with the mirror which the Oriental world attributes to Iskander Zu al-Karnayn, or Alexander Bicornis of Macedonia. In its crystal the whole world was reflected. Burton mentions other similar devices—the sevenfold cup of Kai Kosru; the mirror that Tariq ibn-Ziyad found in a tower (*Thousand and One Nights,* 272); the mirror that Lucian of Samosata examined on the moon (*True History,* I, 26); the mirrorlike spear that the first book of Capella's *Satyricon* attributes to Jupiter; Merlin's universal mirror, which was "round and hollow . . . and seem'd a world of glas" (*The Faerie Queene,* III, 2, 19)—and adds this curious statement: "But the aforesaid objects (besides the disadvantage of not existing) are mere optical instruments. The Faithful who gather at the mosque of Amr, in Cairo, are acquainted with the fact that the entire universe lies inside one of the stone pillars that ring its central court. . . . No one, of course, can actually see it, but those who lay an ear against the surface tell that after some short while they perceive its busy hum. . . . The mosque dates from the seventh century; the pillars come from other temples of pre-Islamic religions, since, as ibn-Khaldun has written: 'In na-

---

* "I received your pained congratulations," he wrote me. "You rage, my poor friend, with envy, but you must confess—even if it chokes you!—that this time I have crowned my cap with the reddest of feathers; my turban with the most *caliph* of rubies."

tions founded by nomads, the aid of foreigners is essential in all concerning masonry.' "

Does this Aleph exist in the heart of a stone? Did I see it there in the cellar when I saw all things, and have I now forgotten it? Our minds are porous and forgetfulness seeps in; I myself am distorting and losing, under the wearing away of the years, the face of Beatriz.

Translated from the Spanish by Norman Thomas di Giovanni

Tadeusz Borowski

• • • • • • • • • • • • • • • • • • • •

THIS WAY
FOR THE GAS, LADIES
AND GENTLEMEN

All of us walk around naked. The delousing is finally over, and our striped suits are back from the tanks of Cyclone B solution, an efficient killer of lice in clothing and of men in gas chambers. Only the inmates in the blocks cut off from ours by the 'Spanish goats'* still have nothing to wear. But all the same, all of us walk around naked: the heat is unbearable. The camp has been sealed off tight. Not a single prisoner, not one solitary louse, can sneak through the gate. The labour Kommandos have stopped working. All day, thousands of naked men shuffle up and down the roads, cluster around the squares, or lie against the walls and on top of the roofs. We have been sleeping on plain boards, since our mattresses and blankets are still being disinfected. From the rear blockhouses we have a view of the F.K.L.—*Frauen Konzentration Lager*; there too the delousing is in full swing. Twenty-eight thousand women have been stripped naked and driven out of the barracks. Now they swarm around the large yard between the blockhouses.

The heat rises, the hours are endless. We are without even our usual diversion: the wide roads leading to the crematoria are empty. For several days now, no new transports have come in. Part of 'Canada'** has been liquidated and detailed to a labour Kommando—one of the very toughest—at Harmenz. For there exists in the camp a special brand of justice based on envy: when the rich and mighty fall, their friends see to it that they fall to the very bottom. And Canada, our Canada, which smells not of maple forests but of French perfume, has amassed great fortunes in diamonds and currency from all over Europe.

Several of us sit on the top bunk, our legs dangling over the edge. We slice the neat loaves of crisp, crunchy bread. It is a bit coarse to the taste, the kind that stays fresh for days. Sent all the way from Warsaw—only a week ago my mother held this white loaf in her hands . . . dear Lord, dear Lord . . .

We unwrap the bacon, the onion, we open a can of evaporated milk. Henri,

---

* Crossed wooden beams wrapped in barbed wire.

** 'Canada' designated wealth and well-being in the camp. More specifically, it referred to the members of the labour gang, or Kommando, who helped to unload the incoming transports of people destined for the gas chambers.

the fat Frenchman, dreams aloud of the French wine brought by the transports from Strasbourg, Paris, Marseille . . . Sweat streams down his body.

'Listen, *mon ami*, next time we go up on the loading ramp, I'll bring you real champagne. You haven't tried it before, eh?'

'No. But you'll never be able to smuggle it through the gate, so stop teasing. Why not try and "organize" some shoes for me instead—you know, the perforated kind, with a double sole, and what about that shirt you promised me long ago?'

'*Patience, patience.* When the new transports come, I'll bring all you want. We'll be going on the ramp again!'

'And what if there aren't any more "cremo" transports?' I say spitefully. 'Can't you see how much easier life is becoming around here: no limit on packages, no more beatings? You even write letters home . . . One hears all kind of talk, and, dammit, they'll run out of people!'

'Stop talking nonsense.' Henri's serious fat face moves rhythmically, his mouth is full of sardines. We have been friends for a long time, but I do not even know his last name. 'Stop talking nonsense,' he repeats, swallowing with effort. 'They can't run out of people, or we'll starve to death in this blasted camp. All of us live on what they bring.'

'All? We have our packages . . .'

'Sure, you and your friend, and ten other friends of yours. Some of you Poles get packages. But what about us, and the Jews, and the Russkis? And what if we had no food, no "organization" from the transports, do you think you'd be eating those packages of yours in peace? We wouldn't let you!'

'You would, you'd starve to death like the Greeks. Around here, whoever has grub, has power.'

'Anyway, you have enough, we have enough, so why argue?'

Right, why argue? They have enough, I have enough, we eat together and we sleep on the same bunks. Henri slices the bread, he makes a tomato salad. It tastes good with the commissary mustard.

Below us, naked, sweat-drenched men crowd the narrow barracks aisles or lie packed in eights and tens in the lower bunks. Their nude, withered bodies stink of sweat and excrement; their cheeks are hollow. Directly beneath me, in the bottom bunk, lies a rabbi. He has covered his head with a piece of rag torn off a blanket and reads from a Hebrew prayer book (there is no shortage of this type of literature at the camp), wailing loudly, monotonously.

'Can't somebody shut him up? He's been raving as if he'd caught God himself by the feet.'

'I don't feel like moving. Let him rave. They'll take him to the oven that much sooner.'

'Religion is the opium of the people,' Henri, who is a Communist and a *rentier*, says sententiously. 'If they didn't believe in God and eternal life, they'd have smashed the crematoria long ago.'

'Why haven't you done it then?'

The question is rhetorical; the Frenchman ignores it.

'Idiot,' he says simply, and stuffs a tomato in his mouth.

Just as we finish our snack, there is a sudden commotion at the door. The

Muslims* scurry in fright to the safety of their bunks, a messenger runs into the
Block Elder's shack. The Elder, his face solemn, steps out at once.

'Canada! *Antreten!* But fast! There's a transport coming!'

'Great God!' yells Henri, jumping off the bunk. He swallows the rest of his
tomato, snatches his coat, screams '*Raus*' at the men below, and in a flash is at
the door. We can hear a scramble in the other bunks. Canada is leaving for the
ramp.

'Henri, the shoes!' I call after him.

'*Keine Angst!*' he shouts back, already outside.

I proceed to put away the food. I tie a piece of rope around the suitcase where
the onions and the tomatoes from my father's garden in Warsaw mingle with
Portuguese sardines, bacon from Lublin (that's from my brother), and authentic
sweetmeats from Salonica. I tie it all up, pull on my trousers, and slide off the
bunk.

'*Platz!*' I yell, pushing my way through the Greeks. They step aside. At the
door I bump into Henri.

'*Was ist los?*'

'Want to come with us on the ramp?'

'Sure, why not?'

'Come along then, grab your coat! We're short of a few men. I've already told
the Kapo,' and he shoves me out of the barracks door.

We line up. Someone has marked down our numbers, someone up ahead
yells, 'March, march,' and now we are running towards the gate, accompanied
by the shouts of a multilingual throng that is already being pushed back to the
barracks. Not everybody is lucky enough to be going on the ramp . . . We have
almost reached the gate. *Links, zwei, drei, vier! Mützen ab!* Erect, arms
stretched stiffly along our hips, we march past the gate briskly, smartly, almost
gracefully. A sleepy S.S. man with a large pad in his hand checks us off, waving
us ahead in groups of five.

'*Hundert!*' he calls after we have all passed.

'*Stimmt!*' comes a hoarse answer from out front.

We march fast, almost at a run. There are guards all around, young men with
automatics. We pass camp II B, then some deserted barracks and a clump of unfamiliar green—apple and pear trees. We cross the circle of watchtowers and,
running, burst on to the highway. We have arrived. Just a few more yards.
There, surrounded by trees, is the ramp.

A cheerful little station, very much like any other provincial railway stop: a
small square framed by tall chestnuts and paved with yellow gravel. Not far off,
beside the road, squats a tiny wooden shed, uglier and more flimsy than the ug-
liest and flimsiest railway shack; farther along lie stacks of old rails, heaps of
wooden beams, barracks parts, bricks, paving stones. This is where they load
freight for Birkenau: supplies for the construction of the camp, and people for
the gas chambers. Trucks drive around, load up lumber, cement, people—a regular daily routine.

---

* 'Muslim' was the camp name for a prisoner who had been destroyed physically and spiritually,
and who had neither the strength nor the will to go on living—a man ripe for the gas chamber.

And now the guards are being posted along the rails, across the beams, in the green shade of the Silesian chestnuts, to form a tight circle around the ramp. They wipe the sweat from their faces and sip out of their canteens. It is unbearably hot; the sun stands motionless at its zenith.

'Fall out!'

We sit down in the narrow streaks of shade along the stacked rails. The hungry Greeks (several of them managed to come along, God only knows how) rummage underneath the rails. One of them finds some pieces of mildewed bread, another a few half-rotten sardines. They eat.

'*Schweinedreck*,' spits a young, tall guard with corn-coloured hair and dreamy blue eyes. 'For God's sake, any minute you'll have so much food to stuff down your guts, you'll bust!' He adjusts his gun, wipes his face with a handkerchief.

'Hey you, fatso!' His boot lightly touches Henri's shoulder. '*Pass mal auf*, want a drink?'

'Sure, but I haven't got any marks,' replies the Frenchman with a professional air.

'*Schade*, too bad.'

'Come, come, Herr Posten, isn't my word good enough any more? Haven't we done business before? How much?'

'One hundred. *Gemacht?*'

'*Gemacht.*'

We drink the water, lukewarm and tasteless. It will be paid for by the people who have not yet arrived.

'Now you be careful,' says Henri, turning to me. He tosses away the empty bottle. It strikes the rails and bursts into tiny fragments. 'Don't take any money, they might be checking. Anyway, who the hell needs money? You've got enough to eat. Don't take suits, either, or they'll think you're planning to escape. Just get a shirt, silk only, with a collar. And a vest. And if you find something to drink, don't bother calling me. I know how to shift for myself, but you watch your step or they'll let you have it.'

'Do they beat you up here?'

'Naturally. You've got to have eyes in your ass. *Arschaugen.*'

Around us sit the Greeks, their jaws working greedily, like huge human insects. They munch on stale lumps of bread. They are restless, wondering what will happen next. The sight of the large beams and the stacks of rails has them worried. They dislike carrying heavy loads.

'*Was wir arbeiten?*' they ask.

'*Niks. Transport kommen, alles Krematorium, compris?*'

'*Alles verstehen*,' they answer in crematorium Esperanto. All is well—they will not have to move the heavy rails or carry the beams.

In the meantime, the ramp has become increasingly alive with activity, increasingly noisy. The crews are being divided into those who will open and unload the arriving cattle cars and those who will be posted by the wooden steps. They receive instructions on how to proceed most efficiently. Motor cycles drive up, delivering S.S. officers, bemedalled, glittering with brass, beefy men with highly polished boots and shiny, brutal faces. Some have brought their briefcases, others hold thin, flexible whips. This gives them an air of military readi-

ness and agility. They walk in and out of the commissary—for the miserable little shack by the road serves as their commissary, where in the summertime they
drink mineral water, *Studentenquelle*, and where in winter they can warm up
with a glass of hot wine. They greet each other in the state-approved way, raising
an arm Roman fashion, then shake hands cordially, exchange warm smiles, discuss mail from home, their children, their families. Some stroll majestically on
the ramp. The silver squares on their collars glitter, the gravel crunches under
their boots, their bamboo whips snap impatiently.

We lie against the rails in the narrow streaks of shade, breathe unevenly, occasionally exchange a few words in our various tongues, and gaze listlessly at the
majestic men in green uniforms, at the green trees, and at the church steeple of a
distant village.

'The transport is coming,' somebody says. We spring to our feet, all eyes turn
in one direction. Around the bend, one after another, the cattle cars begin rolling in. The train backs into the station, a conductor leans out, waves his hand,
blows a whistle. The locomotive whistles back with a shrieking noise, puffs, the
train rolls slowly alongside the ramp. In the tiny barred windows appear pale,
wilted, exhausted human faces, terror-stricken women with tangled hair, unshaven men. They gaze at the station in silence. And then, suddenly, there is a stir
inside the cars and a pounding against the wooden boards.

'Water! Air!'—weary, desperate cries.

Heads push through the windows, mouths gasp frantically for air. They draw
a few breaths, then disappear; others come in their place, then also disappear.
The cries and moans grow louder.

A man in a green uniform covered with more glitter than any of the others
jerks his head impatiently, his lips twist in annoyance. He inhales deeply, then
with a rapid gesture throws his cigarette away and signals to the guard. The
guard removes the automatic from his shoulder, aims, sends a series of shots
along the train. All is quiet now. Meanwhile, the trucks have arrived, steps are
being drawn up, and the Canada men stand ready at their posts by the train
doors. The S.S. officer with the briefcase raises his hand.

'Whoever takes gold, or anything at all besides food, will be shot for stealing
Reich property. Understand? *Verstanden?*'

'*Jawohl!*' we answer eagerly.

'*Also los!* Begin!'

The bolts crack, the doors fall open. A wave of fresh air rushes inside the
train. People . . . inhumanly crammed, buried under incredible heaps of luggage,
suitcases, trunks, packages, crates, bundles of every description (everything that
had been their past and was to start their future). Monstrously squeezed together, they have fainted from heat, suffocated, crushed one another. Now they
push towards the opened doors, breathing like fish cast out on the sand.

'Attention! Out, and take your luggage with you! Take out everything. Pile all
your stuff near the exits. Yes, your coats too. It is summer. March to the left.
Understand?'

'Sir, what's going to happen to us?' They jump from the train on to the gravel,
anxious, worn-out.

'Where are you people from?'

'Sosnowiec-Będzin. Sir, what's going to happen to us?' They repeat the question stubbornly, gazing into our tired eyes.

'I don't know, I don't understand Polish.'

It is the camp law: people going to their death must be deceived to the very end. This is the only permissible form of charity. The heat is tremendous. The sun hangs directly over our heads, the white, hot sky quivers, the air vibrates, an occasional breeze feels like a sizzling blast from a furnace. Our lips are parched, the mouth fills with the salty taste of blood, the body is weak and heavy from lying in the sun. Water!

A huge, multicoloured wave of people loaded down with luggage pours from the train like a blind, mad river trying to find a new bed. But before they have a chance to recover, before they can draw a breath of fresh air and look at the sky, bundles are snatched from their hands, coats ripped off their backs, their purses and umbrellas taken away.

'But please, sir, it's for the sun, I cannot . . .'

'*Verboten!*' one of us barks through clenched teeth. There is an S.S. man standing behind your back, calm, efficient, watchful.

'*Meine Herrschaften*, this way, ladies and gentlemen, try not to throw your things around, please. Show some goodwill,' he says courteously, his restless hands playing with the slender whip.

'Of course, of course,' they answer as they pass, and now they walk alongside the train somewhat more cheerfully. A woman reaches down quickly to pick up her handbag. The whip flies, the woman screams, stumbles, and falls under the feet of the surging crowd. Behind her, a child cries in a thin little voice 'Mamele!'—a very small girl with tangled black curls.

The heaps grow. Suitcases, bundles, blankets, coats, handbags that open as they fall, spilling coins, gold, watches; mountains of bread pile up at the exits, heaps of marmalade, jams, masses of meat, sausages; sugar spills on the gravel. Trucks, loaded with people, start up with a deafening roar and drive off amidst the wailing and screaming of the women separated from their children, and the stupefied silence of the men left behind. They are the ones who had been ordered to step to the right—the healthy and the young who will go to the camp. In the end, they too will not escape death, but first they must work.

Trucks leave and return, without interruption, as on a monstrous conveyor belt. A Red Cross van drives back and forth, back and forth, incessantly: it transports the gas that will kill these people. The enormous cross on the hood, red as blood, seems to dissolve in the sun.

The Canada men at the trucks cannot stop for a single moment, even to catch their breath. They shove the people up the steps, pack them in tightly, sixty per truck, more or less. Near by stands a young, cleanshaven 'gentleman', an S.S. officer with a notebook in his hand. For each departing truck he enters a mark; sixteen gone means one thousand people, more or less. The gentleman is calm, precise. No truck can leave without a signal from him, or a mark in his notebook: *Ordnung muss sein*. The marks swell into thousands, the thousands into whole transports, which afterwards we shall simply call 'from Salonica', 'from

Strasbourg', 'from Rotterdam'. This one will be called 'Sosnowiec-Będzin'. The
new prisoners from Sosnowiec-Będzin will receive serial numbers 131–2–thousand, of course, though afterwards we shall simply say 131–2, for short.

The transports swell into weeks, months, years. When the war is over, they
will count up the marks in their notebooks—all four and a half million of them.
The bloodiest battle of the war, the greatest victory of the strong, united Germany. *Ein Reich, ein Volk, ein Führer*—and four crematoria.

The train has been emptied. A thin, pock-marked S.S. man peers inside,
shakes his head in disgust and motions to our group, pointing his finger at the
door.

'*Rein*. Clean it up!'

We climb inside. In the corners amid human excrement and abandoned
wrist-watches lie squashed, trampled infants, naked little monsters with enormous heads and bloated bellies. We carry them out like chickens, holding several in each hand.

'Don't take them to the trucks, pass them on to the women,' says the S.S.
man, lighting a cigarette. His cigarette lighter is not working properly; he examines it carefully.

'Take them, for God's sake!' I explode as the women run from me in horror,
covering their eyes.

The name of God sounds strangely pointless, since the women and the infants
will go on the trucks, every one of them, without exception. We all know what
this means, and we look at each other with hate and horror.

'What, you don't want to take them?' asks the pock-marked S.S. man with a
note of surprise and reproach in his voice, and reaches for his revolver.

'You mustn't shoot, I'll carry them.' A tall, grey-haired woman takes the little
corpses out of my hands and for an instant gazes straight into my eyes.

'My poor boy,' she whispers and smiles at me. Then she walks away, staggering along the path. I lean against the side of the train. I am terribly tired. Someone pulls at my sleeve.

'*En avant*, to the rails, come on!'

I look up, but the face swims before my eyes, dissolves, huge and transparent,
melts into the motionless trees and the sea of people . . . I blink rapidly: Henri.

'Listen, Henri, are we good people?'

'That's stupid. Why do you ask?'

'You see, my friend, you see, I don't know why, but I am furious, simply furious with these people—furious because I must be here because of them. I feel
no pity. I am not sorry they're going to the gas chamber. Damn them all! I could
throw myself at them, beat them with my fists. It must be pathological, I just
can't understand . . .'

'Ah, on the contrary, it is natural, predictable, calculated. The ramp exhausts
you, you rebel—and the easiest way to relieve your hate is to turn against someone weaker. Why, I'd even call it healthy. It's simple logic, *compris*?' He props
himself up comfortably against the heap of rails. 'Look at the Greeks, they know
how to make the best of it! They stuff their bellies with anything they find. One
of them has just devoured a full jar of marmalade.'

'Pigs! Tomorrow half of them will die of the shits.'

'Pigs? You've been hungry.'

'Pigs!' I repeat furiously. I close my eyes. The air is filled with ghastly cries, the earth trembles beneath me, I can feel sticky moisture on my eyelids. My throat is completely dry.

The morbid procession streams on and on—trucks growl like mad dogs. I shut my eyes tight, but I can still see corpses dragged from the train, trampled infants, cripples piled on top of the dead, wave after wave . . . freight cars roll in, the heaps of clothing, suitcases and bundles grow, people climb out, look at the sun, take a few breaths, beg for water, get into the trucks, drive away. And again freight cars roll in, again people . . . The scenes become confused in my mind—I am not sure if all of this is actually happening, or if I am dreaming. There is a humming inside my head; I feel that I must vomit.

Henri tugs at my arm.

'Don't sleep, we're off to load up the loot.'

All the people are gone. In the distance, the last few trucks roll along the road in clouds of dust, the train has left, several S.S. officers promenade up and down the ramp. The silver glitters on their collars. Their boots shine, their red, beefy faces shine. Among them there is a woman—only now I realize she has been here all along—withered, flat-chested, bony, her thin, colourless hair pulled back and tied in a 'Nordic' knot; her hands are in the pockets of her wide skirt. With a rat-like, resolute smile glued on her thin lips she sniffs around the corners of the ramp. She detests feminine beauty with the hatred of a woman who is herself repulsive, and knows it. Yes, I have seen her many times before and I know her well: she is the commandant of the F.K.L. She has come to look over the new crop of women, for some of them, instead of going on the trucks, will go on foot—to the concentration camp. There our boys, the barbers from Zauna, will shave their heads and will have a good laugh at their 'outside world' modesty.

We proceed to load the loot. We lift huge trunks, heave them on to the trucks. There they are arranged in stacks, packed tightly. Occasionally somebody slashes one open with a knife, for pleasure or in search of vodka and perfume. One of the crates falls open; suits, shirts, books drop out on the ground . . . I pick up a small, heavy package. I unwrap it—gold, about two handfuls, bracelets, rings, brooches, diamonds . . .

'*Gib hier*,' an S.S. man says calmly, holding up his briefcase already full of gold and colourful foreign currency. He locks the case, hands it to an officer, takes another, an empty one, and stands by the next truck, waiting. The gold will go to the Reich.

It is hot, terribly hot. Our throats are dry, each word hurts. Anything for a sip of water! Faster, faster, so that it is over, so that we may rest. At last we are done, all the trucks have gone. Now we swiftly clean up the remaining dirt: there must be 'no trace left of the *Schweinerei*'. But just as the last truck disappears behind the trees and we walk, finally, to rest in the shade, a shrill whistle sounds around the bend. Slowly, terribly slowly, a train rolls in, the engine whistles back with a deafening shriek. Again weary, pale faces at the windows, flat as though cut out of paper, with huge, feverishly burning eyes. Already trucks are pulling up, already the composed gentleman with the notebook is at his post, and the S.S. men emerge from the commissary carrying briefcases for the gold and money. We unseal the train doors.

It is impossible to control oneself any longer. Brutally we tear suitcases from their hands, impatiently pull off their coats. Go on, go on, vanish! They go, they vanish. Men, women, children. Some of them know.

Here is a woman—she walks quickly, but tries to appear calm. A small child with a pink cherub's face runs after her and, unable to keep up, stretches out his little arms and cries: 'Mama! Mama!'

'Pick up your child, woman!'

'It's not mine, sir, not mine!' she shouts hysterically and runs on, covering her face with her hands. She wants to hide, she wants to reach those who will not ride the trucks, those who will go on foot, those who will stay alive. She is young, healthy, good-looking, she wants to live.

But the child runs after her, wailing loudly: 'Mama, mama, don't leave me!'

'It's not mine, not mine, no!'

Andrei, a sailor from Sevastopol, grabs hold of her. His eyes are glassy from vodka and the heat. With one powerful blow he knocks her off her feet, then, as she falls, takes her by the hair and pulls her up again. His face twitches with rage.

'Ah, you bloody Jewess! So you're running from your own child! I'll show you, you whore!' His huge hand chokes her, he lifts her in the air and heaves her on to the truck like a heavy sack of grain.

'Here! And take this with you, bitch!' and he throws the child at her feet.

'*Gut gemacht*, good work. That's the way to deal with degenerate mothers,' says the S.S. man standing at the foot of the truck. '*Gut, gut, Russki.*'

'Shut your mouth,' growls Andrei through clenched teeth, and walks away. From under a pile of rags he pulls out a canteen, unscrews the cork, takes a few deep swallows, passes it to me. The strong vodka burns the throat. My head swims, my legs are shaky, again I feel like throwing up.

And suddenly, above the teeming crowd pushing forward like a river driven by an unseen power, a girl appears. She descends lightly from the train, hops on to the gravel, looks around inquiringly, as if somewhat surprised. Her soft, blonde hair has fallen on her shoulders in a torrent, she throws it back impatiently. With a natural gesture she runs her hands down her blouse, casually straightens her skirt. She stands like this for an instant, gazing at the crowd, then turns and with a gliding look examines our faces, as though searching for someone. Unknowingly, I continue to stare at her, until our eyes meet.

'Listen, tell me, where are they taking us?'

I look at her without saying a word. Here, standing before me, is a girl, a girl with enchanting blonde hair, with beautiful breasts, wearing a little cotton blouse, a girl with a wise, mature look in her eyes. Here she stands, gazing straight into my face, waiting. And over there is the gas chamber: communal death, disgusting and ugly. And over in the other direction is the concentration camp: the shaved head, the heavy Soviet trousers in sweltering heat, the sickening, stale odour of dirty, damp female bodies, the animal hunger, the inhuman labour, and later the same gas chamber, only an even more hideous, more terrible death . . .

Why did she bring it? I think to myself, noticing a lovely gold watch on her delicate wrist. They'll take it away from her anyway.

'Listen, tell me,' she repeats.

I remain silent. Her lips tighten.

'I know,' she says with a shade of proud contempt in her voice, tossing her head. She walks off resolutely in the direction of the trucks. Someone tries to stop her; she boldly pushes him aside and runs up the steps. In the distance I can only catch a glimpse of her blonde hair flying in the breeze.

I go back inside the train; I carry out dead infants; I unload luggage. I touch corpses, but I cannot overcome the mounting, uncontrollable terror. I try to escape from the corpses, but they are everywhere: lined up on the gravel, on the cement edge of the ramp, inside the cattle cars. Babies, hideous naked women, men twisted by convulsions. I run off as far as I can go, but immediately a whip slashes across my back. Out of the corner of my eye I see an S.S. man, swearing profusely. I stagger forward and run, lose myself in the Canada group. Now, at last, I can once more rest against the stack of rails. The sun has leaned low over the horizon and illuminates the ramp with a reddish glow; the shadows of the trees have become elongated, ghostlike. In the silence that settles over nature at this time of day, the human cries seem to rise all the way to the sky.

Only from this distance does one have a full view of the inferno on the teeming ramp. I see a pair of human beings who have fallen to the ground locked in a last desperate embrace. The man has dug his fingers into the woman's flesh and has caught her clothing with his teeth. She screams hysterically, swears, cries, until at last a large boot comes down over her throat and she is silent. They are pulled apart and dragged like cattle to the truck. I see four Canada men lugging a corpse: a huge, swollen female corpse. Cursing, dripping wet from the strain, they kick out of their way some stray children who have been running all over the ramp, howling like dogs. The men pick them up by the collars, heads, arms, and toss them inside the trucks, on top of the heaps. The four men have trouble lifting the fat corpse on to the car, they call others for help, and all together they hoist up the mound of meat. Big, swollen, puffed-up corpses are being collected from all over the ramp; on top of them are piled the invalids, the smothered, the sick, the unconscious. The heap seethes, howls, groans. The driver starts the motor, the truck begins rolling.

'Halt! Halt!' an S.S. man yells after them. 'Stop, damn you!'

They are dragging to the truck an old man wearing tails and a band around his arm. His head knocks against the gravel and pavement; he moans and wails in an uninterrupted monotone: '*Ich will mit dem Herrn Kommandanten sprechen*—I wish to speak with the commandant . . .' With senile stubbornness he keeps repeating these words all the way. Thrown on the truck, trampled by others, choked, he still wails: '*Ich will mit dem . . .*'

'Look here, old man!' a young S.S. man calls, laughing jovially. 'In half an hour you'll be talking with the top commandant! Only don't forget to greet him with a *Heil Hitler!*'

Several other men are carrying a small girl with only one leg. They hold her by the arms and the one leg. Tears are running down her face and she whispers faintly: 'Sir, it hurts, it hurts . . .' They throw her on the truck on top of the corpses. She will burn alive along with them.

The evening has come, cool and clear. The stars are out. We lie against the rails. It is incredibly quiet. Anaemic bulbs hang from the top of the high lamp-posts; beyond the circle of light stretches an impenetrable darkness. Just one step, and a man could vanish for ever. But the guards are watching, their automatics ready.

'Did you get the shoes?' asks Henri.

'No.'

'Why?'

'My God, man, I am finished, absolutely finished!'

'So soon? After only two transports? Just look at me, I . . . since Christmas, at least a million people have passed through my hands. The worst of all are the transports from around Paris—one is always bumping into friends.'

'And what do you say to them?'

'That first they will have a bath, and later we'll meet at the camp. What would you say?'

I do not answer. We drink coffee with vodka; somebody opens a tin of cocoa and mixes it with sugar. We scoop it up by the handful, the cocoa sticks to the lips. Again coffee, again vodka.

'Henri, what are we waiting for?'

'There'll be another transport.'

'I'm not going to unload it! I can't take any more.'

'So, it's got you down? Canada is nice, eh?' Henri grins indulgently and disappears into the darkness. In a moment he is back again.

'All right. Just sit here quietly and don't let an S.S. man see you. I'll try to find you your shoes.'

'Just leave me alone. Never mind the shoes.' I want to sleep. It is very late.

Another whistle, another transport. Freight cars emerge out of the darkness, pass under the lamp-posts, and again vanish in the night. The ramp is small, but the circle of lights is smaller. The unloading will have to be done gradually. Somewhere the trucks are growling. They back up against the steps, black, ghostlike, their searchlights flash across the trees. *Wasser! Luft!* The same all over again, like a late showing of the same film: a volley of shots, the train falls silent. Only this time a little girl pushes herself halfway through the small window and, losing her balance, falls out on to the gravel. Stunned, she lies still for a moment, then stands up and begins walking around in a circle, faster and faster, waving her rigid arms in the air, breathing loudly and spasmodically, whining in a faint voice. Her mind has given way in the inferno inside the train. The whining is hard on the nerves: an S.S. man approaches calmly, his heavy boot strikes between her shoulders. She falls. Holding her down with his foot, he draws his revolver, fires once, then again. She remains face down, kicking the gravel with her feet, until she stiffens. They proceed to unseal the train.

I am back on the ramp, standing by the doors. A warm, sickening smell gushes from inside. The mountain of people filling the car almost halfway up to the ceiling is motionless, horribly tangled, but still steaming.

'*Ausladen!*' comes the command. An S.S. man steps out from the darkness. Across his chest hangs a portable searchlight. He throws a stream of light inside.

'Why are you standing about like sheep? Start unloading!' His whip flies and falls across our backs. I seize a corpse by the hand; the fingers close tightly around mine. I pull back with a shriek and stagger away. My heart pounds, jumps up to my throat. I can no longer control the nausea. Hunched under the train I begin to vomit. Then, like a drunk, I weave over to the stack of rails.

I lie against the cool, kind metal and dream about returning to the camp, about my bunk, on which there is no mattress, about sleep among comrades who are not going to the gas tonight. Suddenly I see the camp as a haven of peace. It is true, others may be dying, but one is somehow still alive, one has enough food, enough strength to work . . .

The lights on the ramp flicker with a spectral glow, the wave of people—feverish, agitated, stupefied people—flows on and on, endlessly. They think that now they will have to face a new life in the camp, and they prepare themselves emotionally for the hard struggle ahead. They do not know that in just a few moments they will die, that the gold, money, and diamonds which they have so prudently hidden in their clothing and on their bodies are now useless to them. Experienced professionals will probe into every recess of their flesh, will pull the gold from under the tongue and the diamonds from the uterus and the colon. They will rip out gold teeth. In tightly sealed crates they will ship them to Berlin.

The S.S. men's black figures move about, dignified, businesslike. The gentleman with the notebook puts down his final marks, rounds out the figures: fifteen thousand.

Many, very many, trucks have been driven to the crematoria today.

It is almost over. The dead are being cleared off the ramp and piled into the last truck. The Canada men, weighed down under a load of bread, marmalade and sugar, and smelling of perfume and fresh linen, line up to go. For several days the entire camp will live off this transport. For several days the entire camp will talk about 'Sosnowiec-Będzin'. 'Sosnowiec-Będzin' was a good, rich transport.

The stars are already beginning to pale as we walk back to the camp. The sky grows translucent and opens high above our heads—it is getting light.

Great columns of smoke rise from the crematoria and merge up above into a huge black river which very slowly floats across the sky over Birkenau and disappears beyond the forests in the direction of Trzebinia. The 'Sosnowiec-Będzin' transport is already burning.

We pass a heavily armed S.S. detachment on its way to change guard. The men march briskly, in step, shoulder to shoulder, one mass, one will.

'*Und morgen die ganze Welt . . .*' they sing at the top of their lungs.

'*Rechts ran!* To the right march!' snaps a command from up front. We move out of their way.

Translated from the Polish by Barbara Vedder

Abdeslam Boulaich

. . . .

COWARDICE

A Moslem, a Jew, and a Christian were sitting in a café talking about Heaven. They agreed that it was a difficult place to get into, but each one thought he would have a better chance than the others.

You have to have the right clothes, the Christian told them. I always wear a jacket and a tie.

Let's go and see, said the other two.

They started out, and when they got close to Heaven, the Moslem and the Jew stopped walking, and the Christian kept going until he reached the door of Heaven.

Our Lord Solomon, who guards the door, said to him: Where are you going?

Inside, the Nazarene answered.

Who are you?

My name is John.

Stand back, said Our Lord Solomon.

Then the Jew and the Moslem spoke together. The Moslem said: He didn't get in. But we will.

I'll go first, said the Jew.

That's right. You go, the Moslem told him.

So the Jew walked up to the door of Heaven. And Our Lord Solomon said to him: Where are you going?

Inside.

Who are you?

Yaqoub, said the Jew.

Stand back!

The Moslem saw this and said to himself: That's that. Neither one of them got in. Now I'll try.

He walked until he got to the door of Heaven. Then he pulled the hood of his djellaba down over his face. And Our Lord Solomon said to him: Where are you going?

Inside.

Who are you? Our Lord Solomon asked him.

I am the Prophet Mohammed, he said. And he went in. The Jew was watching. He said to himself: If he can get in there, so can I.

And he took a sack and filled it with sticks of wood and slung it over his shoulder. Then he walked up to the door.

Where are you going? asked Our Lord Solomon.

The Jew stuck his foot in the door.

Who are you?

The Prophet Mohammed's manservant, he said. And the Jew went in.

The Christian had been watching. He was afraid to try to get in by lying, and so he went back to his country and told everyone that Heaven did not exist.

Translated from the Mogrebi by Paul Bowles

Paul Bowles

. . . .

A DISTANT EPISODE

The September sunsets were at their reddest the week the Professor decided to visit Aïn Tadouirt, which is in the warm country. He came down out of the high, flat region in the evening by bus, with two small overnight bags full of maps, sun lotions and medicines. Ten years ago he had been in the village for three days; long enough, however, to establish a fairly firm friendship with a café-keeper, who had written him several times during the first year after his visit, if never since. "Hassan Ramani," the Professor said over and over, as the bus bumped downward through ever warmer layers of air. Now facing the flaming sky in the west, and now facing the sharp mountains, the car followed the dusty trail down the canyons into air which began to smell of other things besides the endless ozone of the heights: orange blossoms, pepper, sun-baked excrement, burning olive oil, rotten fruit. He closed his eyes happily and lived for an instant in a purely olfactory world. The distant past returned—what part of it, he could not decide.

The chauffeur, whose seat the Professor shared, spoke to him without taking his eyes from the road. "*Vous étes géologue?*"

"A geologist? Ah, no! I'm a linguist."

"There are no languages here. Only dialects."

"Exactly. I'm making a survey of variations on Moghrebi."

The chauffeur was scornful. "Keep on going south," he said. "You'll find some languages you never heard of before."

As they drove through the town gate, the usual swarm of urchins rose up out of the dust and ran screaming beside the bus. The Professor folded his dark glasses, put them in his pocket; and as soon as the vehicle had come to a standstill he jumped out, pushing his way through the indignant boys who clutched at his luggage in vain, and walked quickly into the Grand Hotel Saharien. Out of its eight rooms there were two available—one facing the market and the other, a smaller and cheaper one, giving onto a tiny yard full of refuse and barrels, where two gazelles wandered about. He took the smaller room, and pouring the entire pitcher of water into the tin basin, began to wash the grit from his face and ears. The afterglow was nearly gone from the sky, and the pinkness in objects was disappearing, almost as he watched. He lit the carbide lamp and winced at its odor.

After dinner the Professor walked slowly through the streets to Hassan Ramani's café, whose back room hung hazardously out above the river. The entrance was very low, and he had to bend down slightly to get in. A man was tending the fire. There was one guest sipping tea. The *qaouaji* tried to make him take a seat at the other table in the front room, but the Professor walked airily ahead into the back room and sat down. The moon was shining through the reed latticework and there was not a sound outside but the occasional distant bark of a dog. He changed tables so he could see the river. It was dry, but there was a pool here and there that reflected the bright night sky. The *qaouaji* came in and wiped off the table.

"Does this café still belong to Hassan Ramani?" he asked him in the Moghrebi he had taken four years to learn.

The man replied in bad French: "He is deceased."

"Deceased?" repeated the Professor, without noticing the absurdity of the word. "Really? When?"

"I don't know," said the *qaouaji*. "One tea?"

"Yes. But I don't understand . . ."

The man was already out of the room, fanning the fire. The Professor sat still, feeling lonely, and arguing with himself that to do so was ridiculous. Soon the *qaouaji* returned with the tea. He paid him and gave him an enormous tip, for which he received a grave bow.

"Tell me," he said, as the other started away. "Can one still get those little boxes made from camel udders?"

The man looked angry. "Sometimes the Reguibat bring in those things. We do not buy them here." Then insolently, in Arabic: "And why a camel-udder box?"

"Because I like them," retorted the Professor. And then because he was feeling a little exalted, he added, "I like them so much I want to make a collection of them, and I will pay you ten francs for every one you can get me."

"*Khamstache*," said the *qaouaji*, opening his left hand rapidly three times in succession.

"Never. Ten."

"Not possible. But wait until later and come with me. You can give me what you like. And you will get camel-udder boxes if there are any."

He went out into the front room, leaving the Professor to drink his tea and listen to the growing chorus of dogs that barked and howled as the moon rose higher into the sky. A group of customers came into the front room and sat talking for an hour or so. When they had left, the *qaouaji* put out the fire and stood in the doorway putting on his burnous. "Come," he said.

Outside in the street there was very little movement. The booths were all closed and the only light came from the moon. An occasional pedestrian passed, and grunted a brief greeting to the *qaouaji*.

"Everyone knows you," said the Professor, to cut the silence between them. "Yes."

"I wish everyone knew me," said the Professor, before he realized how infantile such a remark must sound.

"No one knows you," said his companion gruffly.

They had come to the other side of the town, on the promontory above the desert, and through a great rift in the wall the Professor saw the white endlessness, broken in the foreground by dark spots of oasis. They walked through the opening and followed a winding road between rocks, downward toward the nearest small forest of palms. The Professor thought: "He may cut my throat. But his café—he would surely be found out."

"Is it far?" he asked, casually.

"Are you tired?" countered the *qaouaji*.

"They are expecting me back at the Hotel Saharien," he lied.

"You can't be there and here," said the *qaouaji*.

The Professor laughed. He wondered if it sounded uneasy to the other.

"Have you owned Ramani's café long?"

"I work there for a friend." The reply made the Professor more unhappy than he had imagined it would.

"Oh. Will you work tomorrow?"

"That is impossible to say."

The Professor stumbled on a stone, and fell, scraping his hand. The *qaouaji* said: "Be careful."

The sweet black odor of rotten meat hung in the air suddenly.

"Agh!" said the Professor, choking. "What is it?"

The *qaouaji* had covered his face with his burnous and did not answer. Soon the stench had been left behind. They were on flat ground. Ahead the path was bordered on each side by a high mud wall. There was no breeze and the palms were quite still, but behind the walls was the sound of running water. Also, the odor of human excrement was almost constant as they walked between the walls.

The Professor waited until he thought it seemed logical for him to ask with a certain degree of annoyance: "But where are we going?"

"Soon," said the guide, pausing to gather some stones in the ditch.

"Pick up some stones," he advised. "Here are bad dogs."

"Where?" asked the Professor, but he stooped and got three large ones with pointed edges.

They continued very quietly. The walls came to an end and the bright desert lay ahead. Nearby was a ruined marabout, with its tiny dome only half standing, and the front wall entirely destroyed. Behind it were clumps of stunted, useless palms. A dog came running crazily toward them on three legs. Not until it got quite close did the Professor hear its steady low growl. The *qaouaji* let fly a large stone at it, striking it square in the muzzle. There was a strange snapping of jaws and the dog ran sideways in another direction, falling blindly against rocks and scrambling haphazardly about like an injured insect.

Turning off the road, they walked across the earth strewn with sharp stones, past the little ruin, through the trees, until they came to a place where the ground dropped abruptly away in front of them.

"It looks like a quarry," said the Professor, resorting to French for the word "quarry," whose Arabic equivalent he could not call to mind at the moment. The *qaouaji* did not answer. Instead he stood still and turned his head, as if listening. And indeed, from somewhere down below, but very far below, came the faint sound of a low flute. The *qaouaji* nodded his head slowly several times. Then he said: "The path begins here. You can see it well all the way. The rock is white and the moon is strong. So you can see well. I am going back now and sleep. It is late. You can give me what you like."

Standing there at the edge of the abyss which at each moment looked deeper, with the dark face of the *qaouaji* framed in its moonlit burnous close to his own face, the Professor asked himself exactly what he felt. Indignation, curiosity, fear, perhaps, but most of all relief and the hope that this was not a trick, the hope that the *qaouaji* would really leave him alone and turn back without him.

He stepped back a little from the edge, and fumbled in his pocket for a loose note, because he did not want to show his wallet. Fortunately there was a fifty-franc bill there, which he took out and handed to the man. He knew the *qaouaji* was pleased, and so he paid no attention when he heard him saying: "It is not enough. I have to walk a long way home and there are dogs. . . ."

"Thank you and good night," said the Professor, sitting down with his legs drawn up under him, and lighting a cigarette. He felt almost happy.

"Give me only one cigarette," pleaded the man.

"Of course," he said, a bit curtly, and he held up the pack.

The *qaouaji* squatted close beside him. His face was not pleasant to see. "What is it?" thought the Professor, terrified again, as he held out his lighted cigarette toward him.

The man's eyes were almost closed. It was the most obvious registering of concentrated scheming the Professor had ever seen. When the second cigarette was burning, he ventured to say to the still-squatting Arab: "What are you thinking about?"

The other drew on his cigarette deliberately, and seemed about to speak. Then his expression changed to one of satisfaction, but he did not speak. A cool wind had risen in the air, and the Professor shivered. The sound of the flute came up from the depths below at intervals, sometimes mingled with the scraping of nearby palm fronds one against the other. "These people are not primitives," the Professor found himself saying in his mind.

"Good," said the *qaouaji*, rising slowly. "Keep your money. Fifty francs is enough. It is an honor." Then he went back into French: "*Ti n'as qu'd discendre, to' droit.*" He spat, chuckled (or was the Professor hysterical?), and strode away quickly.

The Professor was in a state of nerves. He lit another cigarette, and found his lips moving automatically. They were saying: "Is this a situation or a predicament? This is ridiculous." He sat very still for several minutes, waiting for a sense of reality to come to him. He stretched out on the hard, cold ground and looked up at the moon. It was almost like looking straight at the sun. If he shifted his gaze a little at a time, he could make a string of weaker moons across the sky. "Incredible," he whispered. Then he sat up quickly and looked about. There was no guarantee that the *qaouaji* really had gone back to town. He got to his feet and looked over the edge of the precipice. In the moonlight the bottom seemed miles away. And there was nothing to give it scale; not a tree, not a house, not a person. . . . He listened for the flute, and heard only the wind going by his ears. A sudden violent desire to run back to the road seized him, and he turned and looked in the direction the *qaouaji* had taken. At the same time he felt softly of his wallet in his breast pocket. Then he spat over the edge of the cliff. Then he made water over it, and listened intently, like a child. This gave him the impetus to start down the path into the abyss. Curiously enough, he was not dizzy. But prudently he kept from peering to his right, over the edge. It was a steady and steep downward climb. The monotony of it put him into a frame of mind not unlike that which had been induced by the bus ride. He was murmuring "Hassan Ramani" again, repeatedly and in rhythm. He stopped, furious with himself for the sinister overtones the name now suggested to him. He decided he was exhausted from the trip. "And the walk," he added.

He was now well down the gigantic cliff, but the moon, being directly overhead, gave as much light as ever. Only the wind was left behind, above, to wander among the trees, to blow through the dusty streets of Aïn in Tadouirt, into the hall of the Grand Hotel Saharien, and under the door of his little room.

It occurred to him that he ought to ask himself why he was doing this irrational thing, but he was intelligent enough to know that since he was doing it, it was not so important to probe for explanations at that moment.

Suddenly the earth was flat beneath his feet. He had reached the bottom sooner than he had expected. He stepped ahead distrustfully still, as if he expected another treacherous drop. It was so hard to know in this uniform, dim brightness. Before he knew what had happened the dog was upon him, a heavy mass of fur trying to push him backwards, a sharp nail rubbing down his chest, a straining of muscles against him to get the teeth into his neck. The Professor thought: "I refuse to die this way." The dog fell back; it looked like an Eskimo dog. As it sprang again, he called out, very loud: "Ay!" It fell against him, there was a confusion of sensations and a pain somewhere. There was also the sound of voices very near to him, and he could not understand what they were saying. Something cold and metallic was pushed brutally against his spine as the dog still hung for a second by his teeth from a mass of clothing and perhaps flesh. The Professor knew it was a gun, and he raised his hands, shouting in Moghrebi: "Take away the dog!" But the gun merely pushed him forward, and since the dog, once it was back on the ground, did not leap again, he took a step ahead. The gun kept pushing; he kept taking steps. Again he heard voices, but the person directly behind him said nothing. People seemed to be running about; it sounded that way, at least. For his eyes, he discovered, were still shut tight against the dog's attack. He opened them. A group of men was advancing toward him. They were dressed in the black clothes of the Reguibat. "The Reguiba is a cloud across the face of the sun." "When the Reguiba appears the righteous man turns away." In how many shops and market-places he had heard these maxims uttered banteringly among friends. Never to a Reguiba, to be sure, for these men do not frequent towns. They send a representative in disguise, to arrange with shady elements there for the disposal of captured goods. "An opportunity," he thought quickly, "of testing the accuracy of such statements." He did not doubt for a moment that the adventure would prove to be a kind of warning against such foolishness on his part—a warning which in retrospect would be half sinister, half farcical.

Two snarling dogs came running from behind the oncoming men and threw themselves at his legs. He was scandalized to note that no one paid any attention to this breach of etiquette. The gun pushed him harder as he tried to sidestep the animals' noisy assault. Again he cried: "The dogs! Take them away!" The gun shoved him forward with great force and he fell, almost at the feet of the crowd of men facing him. The dogs were wrenching at his hands and arms. A boot kicked them aside, yelping, and then with increased vigor it kicked the Professor in the hip. Then came a chorus of kicks from different sides, and he was rolled violently about on the earth for a while. During this time he was conscious of hands reaching into his pockets and removing everything from them. He tried to say: "You have all my money; stop kicking me!" But his bruised facial muscles would not work; he felt himself pouting, and that was all. Someone dealt him a terrific blow on the head, and he thought: "Now at least I shall lose consciousness, thank Heaven." Still he went on being aware of the guttural voices he could not understand, and of being bound tightly about the ankles and chest. Then there was black silence that opened like a wound from time to time, to let in the soft, deep notes of the flute playing the same succession of notes again and again. Suddenly he felt excruciating pain everywhere—pain and cold. "So I have been unconscious, after all," he thought. In spite of that, the present seemed only like a direct continuation of what had gone before.

It was growing faintly light. There were camels near where he was lying; he could hear their gurgling and their heavy breathing. He could not bring himself to attempt opening his eyes, just in case it should turn out to be impossible. However, when he heard someone approaching, he found that he had no difficulty in seeing.

The man looked at him dispassionately in the gray morning light. With one hand he pinched together the Professor's nostrils. When the Professor opened his mouth to breathe, the man swiftly seized his tongue and pulled on it with all his might. The Professor was gagging and catching his breath; he did not see what was happening. He could not distinguish the pain of the brutal yanking from that of the sharp knife. Then there was an endless choking and spitting that went on automatically, as though he were scarcely a part of it. The word "operation" kept going through his mind; it calmed his terror somewhat as he sank back into darkness.

The caravan left sometime toward midmorning. The Professor, not unconscious, but in a state of utter stupor, still gagging and drooling blood, was dumped doubled-up into a sack and tied at one side of a camel. The lower end of the enormous amphitheater contained a natural gate in the rocks. The camels, swift *mehara*, were lightly laden on this trip. They passed through single file, and slowly mounted the gentle slope that led up into the beginning of the desert. That night, at a stop behind some low hills, the men took him out, still in a state which permitted no thought, and over the dusty rags that remained of his clothing they fastened a series of curious belts made of the bottoms of tin cans strung together. One after another of these bright girdles was wired about his torso, his arms and legs, even across his face, until he was entirely within a suit of armor that covered him with its circular metal scales. There was a good deal of merriment during this decking-out of the Professor. One man brought out a flute and a younger one did a not ungraceful caricature of an Ouled Naïl executing a cane dance. The Professor was no longer conscious; to be exact, he existed in the middle of the movements made by these other men. When they had finished dressing him the way they wished him to look, they stuffed some food under the tin bangles hanging over his face. Even though he chewed mechanically, most of it eventually fell out onto the ground. They put him back into the sack and left him there.

Two days later they arrived at one of their own encampments. There were women and children here in the tents, and the men had to drive away the snarling dogs they had left there to guard them. When they emptied the Professor out of his sack, there were screams of fright, and it took several hours to convince the last woman that he was harmless, although there had been no doubt from the start that he was a valuable possession. After a few days they began to move on again, taking everything with them, and traveling only at night as the terrain grew warmer.

Even when all his wounds had healed and he felt no more pain, the Professor did not begin to think again; he ate and defecated, and he danced when he was bidden, a senseless hopping up and down that delighted the children, principally because of the wonderful jangling racket it made. And he generally slept through the heat of the day, in among the camels.

Wending its way southeast, the caravan avoided all stationary civilization. In a few weeks they reached a new plateau, wholly wild and with a sparse vegetation. Here they pitched camp and remained, while the *mehara* were turned loose to graze. Everyone was happy here; the weather was cooler and there was a well only a few hours away on a seldom-frequented trail. It was here they conceived the idea of taking the Professor to Fogara and selling him to the Touareg.

It was a full year before they carried out this project. By this time the Professor was much better trained. He could do a handspring, make a series of fearful growling noises which had, nevertheless, a certain element of humor; and when the Reguibat removed the tin from his face they discovered he could grimace admirably while he danced. They also taught him a few basic obscene gestures which never failed to elicit delighted shrieks from the women. He was now brought forth only after especially abundant meals, when there was music and festivity. He easily fell in with their sense of ritual, and evolved an elementary sort of "program" to present when he was called for: dancing, rolling on the ground, imitating certain animals, and finally rushing toward the group in feigned anger, to see the resultant confusion and hilarity.

When three of the men set out for Fogara with him, they took four *mehara* with them, and he rode astride his quite naturally. No precautions were taken to guard him, save that he was kept among them, one man always staying at the rear of the party. They came within sight of the walls at dawn, and they waited among the rocks all day. At dusk the youngest started out, and in three hours he returned with a friend who carried a stout cane. They tried to put the Professor through his routine then and there, but the man from Fogara was in a hurry to get back to town, so they all set out on the *mehara*.

In the town they went directly to the villager's home, where they had coffee in the courtyard sitting among the camels. Here the Professor went into his act again, and this time there was prolonged merriment and much rubbing together of hands. An agreement was reached, a sum of money paid, and the Reguibat withdrew, leaving the Professor in the house of the man with the cane, who did not delay in locking him into a tiny enclosure off the courtyard.

The next day was an important one in the Professor's life, for it was then that pain began to stir again in his being. A group of men came to the house, among whom was a venerable gentleman, better clothed than those others who spent their time flattering him, setting fervent kisses upon his hands and the edges of his garments. This person made a point of going into classical Arabic from time to time, to impress the others, who had not learned a word of the Koran. Thus his conversation would run more or less as follows: "Perhaps at In Salah. The French there are stupid. Celestial vengeance is approaching. Let us not hasten it. Praise the highest and cast thine anathema against idols. With paint on his face. In case the police wish to look close." The others listened and agreed, nodding their heads slowly and solemnly. And the Professor in his stall beside them listened, too. That is, he was *conscious* of the sound of the old man's Arabic. The words penetrated for the first time in many months. Noises, then: "Celestial vengeance is approaching." Then: "It is an honor. Fifty francs is enough. Keep your money. Good." And the *qaouaji* squatting near him at the edge of the precipice. Then "anathema against idols" and more gibberish. He turned over panting on the sand and forgot about it. But the pain had begun. It operated in a kind of delirium, because he had begun to enter into consciousness again. When the man opened the door and prodded him with his cane, he cried out in a rage, and everyone laughed.

They got him onto his feet, but he would not dance. He stood before them, staring at the ground, stubbornly refusing to move. The owner was furious, and so annoyed by the laughter of the others that he felt obliged to send them away, saying that he would await a more propitious time for exhibiting his property, because he dared not show his anger before the elder. However, when they had left he dealt the Professor a violent blow on the shoulder with his cane, called him various obscene things, and went out into the street, slamming the gate behind him. He walked straight to the street of the Ouled Naïl, because he was sure of finding the Reguibat there among the girls, spending the money. And there in a tent he found one of them still abed, while an Ouled Naïl washed the tea glasses. He walked in and almost decapitated the man before the latter had even attempted to sit up. Then he threw his razor on the bed and ran out.

The Ouled Naïl saw the blood, screamed, ran out of her tent into the next, and soon emerged from that with four girls who rushed together into the coffee house and told the *qaouaji* who had killed the Reguiba. It was only a matter of an hour before the French military police had caught him at a friend's house, and dragged him off to the barracks. That night the Professor had nothing to eat, and the next afternoon, in the slow sharpening of his consciousness caused by increasing hunger, he walked aimlessly about the courtyard and the rooms that gave onto it. There was no one. In one room a calendar hung on the wall. The Professor watched nervously, like a dog watching a fly in front of its nose. On the white paper were black objects that made sounds in his head. He heard them: "*Grande Epicerie du Sahel. Juin. Lundi, Mardi, Mercredi. . . .*"

The tiny inkmarks of which a symphony consists may have been made long ago, but when they are fulfilled in sound they become imminent and mighty. So a kind of music of feeling began to play in the Professor's head, increasing in volume as he looked at the mud wall, and he had the feeling that he was performing what had been written for him long ago. He felt like weeping; he felt like roaring through the little house, upsetting and smashing the few breakable objects. His emotion got no further than this one overwhelming desire. So, bellowing as loud as he could, he attacked the house and its belongings. Then he attacked the door into the street, which resisted for a while and finally broke. He climbed through the opening made by the boards he had ripped apart, and still bellowing and shaking his arms in the air to make as loud a jangling as possible, he began to gallop along the quiet street toward the gateway of the town. A few people looked at him with great curiosity. As he passed the garage, the last building before the high mud archway that framed the desert beyond, a French soldier saw him. *"Tiens,"* he said to himself, "a holy maniac."

Again it was sunset time. The Professor ran beneath the arched gate, turned his face toward the red sky, and began to trot along the Piste d'In Salah, straight into the setting sun. Behind him, from the garage, the soldier took a pot shot at him for good luck. The bullet whistled dangerously near the Professor's head, and his yelling rose into an indignant lament as he waved his arms more wildly, and hopped high into the air at every few steps, in an access of terror.

The soldier watched a while, smiling, as the cavorting figure grew smaller in the oncoming evening darkness, and the rattling of the tin became a part of the great silence out there beyond the gate. The wall of the garage as he leaned against it still gave forth heat, left there by the sun, but even then the lunar chill was growing in the air.

T. Coraghessan Boyle

· ·

GREASY LAKE

It's about a mile down on the dark side of Route 88.   —BRUCE SPRINGSTEEN

There was a time when courtesy and winning ways went out of style, when it was good to be bad, when you cultivated decadence like a taste. We were all dangerous characters then. We wore torn-up leather jackets, slouched around with toothpicks in our mouths, sniffed glue and ether and what somebody claimed was cocaine. When we wheeled our parents' whining station wagons out into the street we left a patch of rubber half a block long. We drank gin and grape juice, Tango, Thunderbird, and Bali Hai. We were nineteen. We were bad. We read André Gide and struck elaborate poses to show that we didn't give a shit about anything. At night, we went up to Greasy Lake.

Through the center of town, up the strip, past the housing developments and shopping malls, street lights giving way to the thin streaming illumination of the headlights, trees crowding the asphalt in a black unbroken wall: that was the way out to Greasy Lake. The Indians had called it Wakan, a reference to the clarity of its waters. Now it was fetid and murky, the mud banks glittering with broken glass and strewn with beer cans and the charred remains of bonfires. There was a single ravaged island a hundred yards from shore, so stripped of vegetation it looked as if the air force had strafed it. We went up to the lake because everyone went there, because we wanted to snuff the rich scent of possibility on the breeze, watch a girl take off her clothes and plunge into the festering murk, drink beer, smoke pot, howl at the stars, savor the incongruous full-throated roar of rock and roll against the primeval susurrus of frogs and crickets. This was nature.

I was there one night, late, in the company of two dangerous characters. Digby wore a gold star in his right ear and allowed his father to pay his tuition at Cornell; Jeff was thinking of quitting school to become a painter/musician/head-shop proprietor. They were both expert in the social graces, quick with a sneer, able to manage a Ford with lousy shocks over a rutted and gutted blacktop road at eighty-five while rolling a joint as compact as a Tootsie Roll Pop stick. They could lounge against a bank of booming speakers and trade "man"'s with the best of them or roll out across the dance floor as if their joints worked on bearings. They were slick and quick and they wore their mirror shades at breakfast and dinner, in the shower, in closets and caves. In short, they were bad.

I drove. Digby pounded the dashboard and shouted along with Toots & the Maytals while Jeff hung his head out the window and streaked the side of my mother's Bel Air with vomit. It was early June, the air soft as a hand on your cheek, the third night of summer vacation. The first two nights we'd been out till dawn, looking for something we never found. On this, the third night, we'd cruised the strip sixty-seven times, been in and out of every bar and club we could think of in a twenty-mile radius, stopped twice for bucket chicken and forty-cent hamburgers, debated going to a party at the house of a girl Jeff's sister knew, and chucked two dozen raw eggs at mailboxes and hitchhikers. It was 2:00 A.M.; the bars were closing. There was nothing to do but take a bottle of lemon-flavored gin up to Greasy Lake.

The taillights of a single car winked at us as we swung into the dirt lot with its tufts of weed and washboard corrugations; '57 Chevy, mint, metallic blue. On the far side of the lot, like the exoskeleton of some gaunt chrome insect, a chopper leaned against its kickstand. And that was it for excitement: some junkie half-wit biker and a car freak pumping his girlfriend. Whatever it was we were looking for, we weren't about to find it at Greasy Lake. Not that night.

But then all of a sudden Digby was fighting for the wheel. "Hey, that's Tony Lovett's car! Hey!" he shouted, while I stabbed at the brake pedal and the Bel Air nosed up to the gleaming bumper of the parked Chevy. Digby leaned on the horn, laughing, and instructed me to put my brights on. I flicked on the brights. This was hilarious. A joke. Tony would experience premature withdrawal and expect to be confronted by grim-looking state troopers with flashlights. We hit the horn, strobed the lights, and then jumped out of the car to press our witty faces to Tony's windows; for all we knew we might even catch a glimpse of some little fox's tit, and then we could slap backs with red-faced Tony, roughhouse a little, and go on to new heights of adventure and daring.

The first mistake, the one that opened the whole floodgate, was losing my grip on the keys. In the excitement, leaping from the car with the gin in one hand and a roach clip in the other, I spilled them in the grass—in the dark, rank, mysterious nighttime grass of Greasy Lake. This was a tactical error, as damaging and irreversible in its way as Westmoreland's decision to dig in at Khe Sanh. I felt it like a jab of intuition, and I stopped there by the open door, peering vaguely into the night that puddled up round my feet.

The second mistake—and this was inextricably bound up with the first—was identifying the car as Tony Lovett's. Even before the very bad character in greasy jeans and engineer boots ripped out of the driver's door, I began to realize that this chrome blue was much lighter than the robin's-egg of Tony's car, and that Tony's car didn't have rear-mounted speakers. Judging from their expressions, Digby and Jeff were privately groping toward the same inevitable and unsettling conclusion as I was.

In any case, there was no reasoning with this bad greasy character—clearly he was a man of action. The first lusty Rockette kick of his steel-toed boot caught me under the chin, chipped my favorite tooth, and left me sprawled in the dirt. Like a fool, I'd gone down on one knee to comb the stiff hacked grass for the keys, my mind making connections in the most dragged-out, testudineous way, knowing that things had gone wrong, that I was in a lot of trouble, and that the lost ignition key was my grail and my salvation. The three or four succeeding blows were mainly absorbed by my right buttock and the tough piece of bone at the base of my spine.

Meanwhile, Digby vaulted the kissing bumpers and delivered a savage kung-fu blow to the greasy character's collarbone. Digby had just finished a course in martial arts for phys-ed credit and had spent the better part of the past two nights telling us apocryphal tales of Bruce Lee types and of the raw power invested in lightning blows shot from coiled wrists, ankles, and elbows. The greasy character was unimpressed. He merely backed off a step, his face like a Toltec mask, and laid Digby out with a single whistling roundhouse blow . . . but by now Jeff had got into the act, and I was beginning to extricate myself from the dirt, a tinny compound of shock, rage, and impotence wadded in my throat.

Jeff was on the guy's back, biting at his ear. Digby was on the ground, cursing. I went for the tire iron I kept under the driver's seat. I kept it there because bad characters always keep tire irons under the driver's seat, for just such an occasion as this. Never mind that I hadn't been involved in a fight since sixth grade, when a kid with a sleepy eye and two streams of mucus depending from his nostrils hit me in the knee with a Louisville slugger; never mind that I'd touched the tire iron exactly twice before, to change tires: it was there. And I went for it.

I was terrified. Blood was beating in my ears, my hands were shaking, my heart turning over like a dirtbike in the wrong gear. My antagonist was shirtless, and a single cord of muscle flashed across his chest as he bent forward to peel Jeff from his back like a wet overcoat. "Motherfucker," he spat, over and over, and I was aware in that instant that all four of us—Digby, Jeff, and myself included—were chanting "motherfucker, motherfucker," as if it were a battle cry. (What happened next? the detective asks the murderer from beneath the turned-down brim of his porkpie hat. I don't know, the murderer says, something came over me. Exactly.)

Digby poked the flat of his hand in the bad character's face and I came at him like a kamikaze, mindless, raging, stung with humiliation—the whole thing, from the initial boot in the chin to this murderous primal instant involving no more than sixty hyperventilating, gland-flooding seconds—I came at him and brought the tire iron down across his ear. The effect was instantaneous, astonishing. He was a stunt man and this was Hollywood, he was a big grimacing toothy balloon and I was a man with a straight pin. He collapsed. Wet his pants. Went loose in his boots.

A single second, big as a zeppelin, floated by. We were standing over him in a circle, gritting our teeth, jerking our necks, our limbs and hands and feet twitching with glandular discharges. No one said anything. We just stared down at the guy, the car freak, the lover, the bad greasy character laid low. Digby looked at me; so did Jeff. I was still holding the tire iron, a tuft of hair clinging to the crook like dandelion fluff, like down. Rattled, I dropped it in the dirt, already envisioning the headlines, the pitted faces of the police inquisitors, the gleam of handcuffs, clank of bars, the big black shadows rising from the back of the cell . . . when suddenly a raw torn shriek cut through me like all the juice in all the electric chairs in the country.

It was the fox. She was short, barefoot, dressed in panties and a man's shirt. "Animals!" she screamed, running at us with her fists clenched and wisps of blow-dried hair in her face. There was a silver chain round her ankle, and her toenails flashed in the glare of the headlights. I think it was the toenails that did it. Sure, the gin and the cannabis and even the Kentucky Fried may have had a hand in it, but it was the sight of those flaming toes that set us off—the toad emerging from the loaf in *Virgin Spring*, lipstick smeared on a child: she was already tainted. We were on her like Bergman's deranged brothers—see no evil, hear none, speak none—panting, wheezing, tearing at her clothes, grabbing for flesh. We were bad characters, and we were scared and hot and three steps over the line—anything could have happened.

It didn't.

Before we could pin her to the hood of the car, our eyes masked with lust and greed and the purest primal badness, a pair of headlights swung into the lot. There we were, dirty, bloody, guilty, dissociated from humanity and civilization, the first of the Ur-crimes behind us, the second in progress, shreds of nylon panty and spandex brassiere dangling from our fingers, our flies open, lips licked—there we were, caught in the spotlight. Nailed.

We bolted. First for the car, and then, realizing we had no way of starting it, for the woods. I thought nothing. I thought escape. The headlights came at me like accusing fingers. I was gone.

Ram-bam-bam, across the parking lot, past the chopper and into the feculent undergrowth at the lake's edge, insects flying up in my face, weeds whipping, frogs and snakes and red-eyed turtles splashing off into the night: I was already ankle-deep in muck and tepid water and still going strong. Behind me, the girl's screams rose in intensity, disconsolate, incriminating, the screams of the Sabine women, the Christian martyrs, Anne Frank dragged from the garret. I kept going, pursued by those cries, imagining cops and bloodhounds. The water was up to my knees when I realized what I was doing: I was going to swim for it. Swim the breadth of Greasy Lake and hide myself in the thick clot of woods on the far side. They'd never find me there.

I was breathing in sobs, in gasps. The water lapped at my waist as I looked out over the moon-burnished ripples, the mats of algae that clung to the surface like scabs. Digby and Jeff had vanished. I paused. Listened. The girl was quieter now, screams tapering to sobs, but there were male voices, angry, excited, and the high-pitched ticking of the second car's engine. I waded deeper, stealthy, hunted, the ooze sucking at my sneakers. As I was about to take the plunge—at the very instant I dropped my shoulder for the first slashing stroke—I blundered into something. Something unspeakable, obscene, something soft, wet, mossgrown. A patch of weed? A log? When I reached out to touch it, it gave like a rubber duck, it gave like flesh.

In one of those nasty little epiphanies for which we are prepared by films and TV and childhood visits to the funeral home to ponder the shrunken painted forms of dead grandparents, I understood what it was that bobbed there so inadmissibly in the dark. Understood, and stumbled back in horror and revulsion, my mind yanked in six different directions (I was nineteen, a mere child, an infant, and here in the space of five minutes I'd struck down one greasy character and blundered into the waterlogged carcass of a second), thinking, The keys, the keys, why did I have to go and lose the keys? I stumbled back, but the muck took hold of my feet—a sneaker snagged, balance lost—and suddenly I was pitching face forward into the buoyant black mass, throwing out my hands in desperation while simultaneously conjuring the image of reeking frogs and muskrats revolving in slicks of their own deliquescing juices. AAAAArrrgh! I shot from the water like a torpedo, the dead man rotating to expose a mossy beard and eyes cold as the moon. I must have shouted out, thrashing around in the weeds, because the voices behind me suddenly became animated.

"What was that?"

"It's them, it's them: they tried to, tried to . . . *rape* me!" Sobs.

A man's voice, flat Midwestern accent. "You sons a bitches, we'll kill you!"

Frogs, crickets.

Then another voice, harsh, *r*-less, Lower East Side: "Motherfucker!" I recognized the verbal virtuosity of the bad greasy character in the engineer boots. Tooth chipped, sneakers gone, coated in mud and slime and worse, crouching breathless in the weeds waiting to have my ass thoroughly and definitively kicked and fresh from the hideous stinking embrace of a three-days-dead-corpse, I suddenly felt a rush of joy and vindication: the son of a bitch was alive! Just as quickly, my bowels turned to ice. "Come on out of there, you pansy motherfuckers!" the bad greasy character was screaming. He shouted curses till he was out of breath.

The crickets started up again, then the frogs. I held my breath. All at once there was a sound in the reeds, a swishing, a splash: thunk-a-thunk. They were throwing rocks. The frogs fell silent. I cradled my head. Swish, swish, thunk-a-thunk. A wedge of feldspar the size of a cue ball glanced off my knee. I bit my finger.

It was then that they turned to the car. I heard a door slam, a curse, and then the sound of the headlights shattering—almost a good-natured sound, celebratory, like corks popping from the necks of bottles. This was succeeded by the dull booming of the fenders, metal on metal, and then the icy crash of the windshield. I inched forward, elbows and knees, my belly pressed to the muck, thinking of guerrillas and commandos and *The Naked and the Dead*. I parted the weeds and squinted the length of the parking lot.

The second car—it was a Trans-Am—was still running, its high beams washing the scene in a lurid stagy light. Tire iron flailing, the greasy bad character was laying into the side of my mother's Bel Air like an avenging demon, his shadow riding up the trunks of the trees. Whomp. Whomp. Whomp-whomp. The other two guys—blond types, in fraternity jackets—were helping out with tree branches and skull-sized boulders. One of them was gathering up bottles, rocks, muck, candy wrappers, used condoms, poptops, and other refuse and pitching it through the window on the driver's side. I could see the fox, a white bulb behind the windshield of the '57 Chevy. "Bobbie," she whined over the thumping, "come *on*." The greasy character paused a moment, took one good swipe at the left taillight, and then heaved the tire iron halfway across the lake. Then he fired up the '57 and was gone.

Blond head nodded at blond head. One said something to the other, too low for me to catch. They were no doubt thinking that in helping to annihilate my mother's car they'd committed a fairly rash act, and thinking too that there were three bad characters connected with that very car watching them from the woods. Perhaps other possibilities occurred to them as well—police, jail cells, justices of the peace, reparations, lawyers, irate parents, fraternal censure. Whatever they were thinking, they suddenly dropped branches, bottles, and rocks and sprang for their car in unison, as if they'd choreographed it. Five seconds. That's all it took. The engine shrieked, the tires squealed, a cloud of dust rose from the rutted lot and then settled back on darkness.

I don't know how long I lay there, the bad breath of decay all around me, my jacket heavy as a bear, the primordial ooze subtly reconstituting itself to accommodate my upper thighs and testicles. My jaws ached, my knee throbbed, my coccyx was on fire. I contemplated suicide, wondered if I'd need bridgework, scraped the recesses of my brain for some sort of excuse to give my parents—a tree had fallen on the car, I was blindsided by a bread truck, hit and run, vandals had got to it while we were playing chess at Digby's. Then I thought of the dead man. He was probably the only person on the planet worse off than I was. I thought about him, fog on the lake, insects chirring eerily, and felt the tug of fear, felt the darkness opening up inside me like a set of jaws. Who was he, I wondered, this victim of time and circumstance bobbing sorrowfully in the lake at my back. The owner of the chopper, no doubt, a bad older character come to this. Shot during a murky drug deal, drowned while drunkenly frolicking in the lake. Another headline. My car was wrecked; he was dead.

When the eastern half of the sky went from black to cobalt and the trees began to separate themselves from the shadows, I pushed myself up from the mud and stepped out into the open. By now the birds had begun to take over for the crickets, and dew lay slick on the leaves. There was a smell in the air, raw and sweet at the same time, the smell of the sun firing buds and opening blossoms. I contemplated the car. It lay there like a wreck along the highway, like a steel sculpture left over from a vanished civilization. Everything was still. This was nature.

I was circling the car, as dazed and bedraggled as the sole survivor of an air blitz, when Digby and Jeff emerged from the trees behind me. Digby's face was crosshatched with smears of dirt; Jeff's jacket was gone and his shirt was torn across the shoulder. They slouched across the lot, looking sheepish, and silently came up beside me to gape at the ravaged automobile. No one said a word. After a while Jeff swung open the driver's door and began to scoop the broken glass and garbage off the seat. I looked at Digby. He shrugged. "At least they didn't slash the tires," he said.

It was true: the tires were intact. There was no windshield, the headlights were staved in, and the body looked as if it had been sledge-hammered for a quarter a shot at the countyfair, but the tires were inflated to regulation pressure. The car was drivable. In silence, all three of us bent to scrape the mud and shattered glass from the interior. I said nothing about the biker. When we were finished, I reached in my pocket for the keys, experienced a nasty stab of recollection, cursed myself, and turned to search the grass. I spotted them almost immediately, no more than five feet from the open door, glinting like jewels in the first tapering shaft of sunlight. There was no reason to get philosophical about it: I eased into the seat and turned the engine over.

It was at that precise moment that the silver Mustang with the flame decals rumbled into the lot. All three of us froze; then Digby and Jeff slid into the car and slammed the door. We watched as the Mustang rocked and bobbed across the ruts and finally jerked to a halt beside the forlorn chopper at the far end of the lot. "Let's go," Digby said. I hesitated, the Bel Air wheezing beneath me.

Two girls emerged from the Mustang. Tight jeans, stiletto heels, hair like frozen fur. They bent over the motorcycle, paced back and forth aimlessly, glanced once or twice at us, and then ambled over to where the reeds sprang up in a green fence round the perimeter of the lake. One of them cupped her hands to her mouth. "Al," she called. "Hey, Al!"

"Come on," Digby hissed. "Let's get out of here."

But it was too late. The second girl was picking her way across the lot, unsteady on her heels, looking up at us and then away. She was older—twenty-five or -six—and as she came closer we could see there was something wrong with her: she was stoned or drunk, lurching now and waving her arms for balance. I gripped the steering wheel as if it were the ejection lever of a flaming jet, and Digby spat out my name, twice, terse and impatient.

"Hi," the girl said.

We looked at her like zombies, like war veterans, like deaf-and-dumb pencil peddlers.

She smiled, her lips cracked and dry. "Listen," she said, bending from the waist to look in the window, "you guys seen Al?" Her pupils were pinpoints, her eyes glass. She jerked her neck. "That's his bike over there—Al's. You seen him?"

Al. I didn't know what to say. I wanted to get out of the car and retch. I wanted to go home to my parents' house and crawl into bed. Digby poked me in the ribs. "We haven't seen anybody," I said.

The girl seemed to consider this, reaching out a slim veiny arm to brace herself against the car. "No matter," she said, slurring the *t*'s, "he'll turn up." And then, as if she'd just taken stock of the whole scene—the ravaged car and our battered faces, the desolation of the place—she said: "Hey, you guys look like some pretty bad characters—been fightin', huh?" We stared straight ahead, rigid as catatonics. She was fumbling in her pocket and muttering something. Finally she held out a handful of tablets in glassine wrappers: "Hey, you want to party, you want to do some of these with me and Sarah?"

I just looked at her. I thought I was going to cry. Digby broke the silence. "No thanks," he said, leaning over me. "Some other time."

I put the car in gear and it inched forward with a groan, shaking off pellets of glass like an old dog shedding water after a bath, heaving over the ruts on its worn springs, creeping toward the highway. There was a sheen of sun on the lake. I looked back. The girl was still standing there, watching us, her shoulders slumped, hand outstretched.

Harold Brodkey

· ·
CEIL

I have to imagine Ceil—I did not know her; I did not know my mother. I cannot imagine Ceil. She is the initial word. Everything in me having to do with knowing refers to her. The heart of the structures of my speech is my mother. It is not with my mother but with Ceil in her own life that my speech begins. My mother as an infant, and then a child, and then a girl, a hoyden maybe, seven years old, ten and coldly angular, and then a girl of twelve, then a girl of nineteen, tall, thin-bodied, long-legged in a fashion inconceivable to me. What I am is her twisted and bereaved and altered and ignorant heir. She died when I was two. I died as well, but I came to life again in another family, and no one was like her, everything was different. I was told I was not like her. I see that she is not human in the ways I am: she is more wise, more pathetic—whichever—in some way larger than my life, which, after all, she contained for a while. I was her dream, her punishment. She dreams me but she bears me, too. Her dream is real. It is a clouded and difficult legend.

I tend to feel an almost theatrical fright when I am near a subject that hints of her. I've felt this way since I was six and learned that my real mother had died and that I did not know her.

In the last year before the war that shaped her life, in 1913, she was nineteen; and she has a too stylishly formed, too stylized a body, too sexual, too strongly marked for me to be comfortable with the thought of her. Her body when she was that age I recognize; I invent it. I know her feet, her hands, her hair—as a girl: they are unlike mine. She has longish brown hair, very fine-drawn, so that, although it is curly, its own weight straightens it except at the ends. Fine hair, which sets an uneasy and trembling too thin silkiness, a perilously sexual lack of weight around her face, which bobs nakedly forward from what might have framed or hidden her vitality; beneath the too fine hair is one of those girlishly powerful faces atop a tall body, a face large-lipped, eyes set very wide; a face bold with an animal and temperamental and intellectual electricity. She is both regal and peasantlike, gypsyish—or like a red Indian—a noticeable presence, physically exhilarated and willful. She is muscular. She is direct in glance. She has a long neck and a high rear end and longish feet and short-fingered hands with oddly unimpressive nails—her hands are not competent; they are cut off a little from life because her mind is active and her hands consequently stumble, but her energy and a somewhat hot and comic and even farcical grace of attention she has make up for that, and she is considered by others and by herself to be very good at manual things anyway.

And she is literate—she is bookish and given to quoting and argument—and she is active physically, and she is given to bad temper rather than to depression. In comparative poverty, in an era of grave terrors, she has lived in enough danger that she has become courteous and ironic, and has been ever since she was a small child, but the courtesy and the irony lie atop a powerful other self. As a personality, she was a striking image for others from the beginning—she was what would be called by some people A Great Favorite: much pawed is what that comes down to. This is among Jews and Russians. Things were asked of her often by her mother and her father and by others: errands and talk and company, physical company. She was noticeable and had that quality of mind which made people take her as *special*, as being destined and far-seeing, more *reasonable* than others. She was (in a sense) the trademark or logo of the community, of the family—sought after, liked, used, I would imagine, but she was patient with that because she was praised, and so admiringly looked at as well. People close their minds off and charge and butt at their favorites—or tease and torment them: A Peasant Beauty.

Here are some sentences from Chekhov: *The village was never free of fever, and there was boggy mud there even in the summer, especially under the fences over which hung old willow-trees that gave deep shade. Here there was always a smell from the factory refuse and the acetic acid which was used in the finishing of cotton print. . . . The tanyard often made the little river stink . . .* [Bribes to the chief of police and the district doctor kept the factory open.] *In the whole village there were only two decent houses made of brick with tin roofs.*

And: *The sonorous, joyful clang of the church bells hung over the town unceasingly, setting the spring air aquiver.*

And: *The charming street in spring, on each side of it was a row of poplars. . . . And acacias, tall bushes of lilacs, wild cherries and appletrees hung over the fence and the palings.*

Barefoot, in Russia near a small ravine, she moves, much too showily present, not discreet, not slipping and sliding along in the Oriental fashion, not devious or subterranean or flirtatious or in any masquerade, but obvious and present, forthright in a local manner, a common enough manner in that part of the world where women ran farms and inns and stores and had that slightly masculinized swagger or march, that alive-in-the-world-of-men, alert, and roughened air, that here-and-now way of presenting themselves.

Ceil, almost nervously, always overrated rebellion—and discipline—loyalty to the absent *king*, complete law-abidingness as rebellion, the claim of following the true law, the truer one.

In Illinois, where money was comparatively plentiful, she would despise money, which she liked; but despising it was a further mode of bandit independence and religious, soaring freedom. She would be confused by the utter secrecy of the actual politics of the county and the state, the bribes and the use of force and the criminal nature of much that goes on; she will not understand the sheer power of the lie in creating a password-based social class of rule, of stability: this Christian doubleness, perhaps largely English in style in Illinois, will strike her as contemptible.

(*She was always talking about being realistic; she wanted everyone to be realistic about everything all the time; she lorded it over everyone because she was so realistic.* The woman who became my mother, Lila Silenowicz, told me this.)

She never lived in a city. Well, actually she did try to live in St. Louis for a while, but the urban sophistications, the interplay of things, of money and information and shibboleth—respectabilities and concealed coercions—upset her, and I believe she lost out in whatever she tried to do, in whatever she attempted in the way of dignity there.

And Max's proposal, my father's proposal, offered her a life in a small town, a really small town—thirty-five hundred people. Long after Ceil died, my mother by adoption said, "Ceil wanted a foothold. She wasn't really under anyone's protection. She could do what she wanted; no one could stop her. No one wanted her to listen to Max; he was no good, no good for a woman; but it didn't matter what anyone thought; she could do as she liked." Max's proposal involved her going to live in that small town, under an enormous canopy of sky like that pale canopy that overhangs plains anywhere, and it's true that her pride and victories took root again once she was in so small a place.

My mother's mind, and to some extent her language, tribal and local but influenced by St. Petersburg, and her conceit are somewhat like those of the poet Mandelstam, who was born not far from where she was born. He lived at the same time; similar dates cover his life, too, but it was a different life, of course, except that it, too, was stubborn and mad, and his death was as empty of reason as Ceil's.

Mandelstam went to St. Petersburg, and he went south a number of times, to the Crimea. He went to school in St. Petersburg, and he was considerably more *civilized* than Ceil was, early or late, and stiff-necked and romantic and unromantic, and as passionately self-willed and oddly placed in the world as she was: he was deathful and lifeful in similar ways. He has a line in a poem which I will say goes into English as (it is about the dome of Hagia Sophia, in Istanbul) "*It is swimming in the world.*" It is swimming in the world at the end of a long gold chain let down from Heaven.

On a dusty road, here is Ceil, here is my mother, and she is like that in her mind.

Ceil thought of herself as a Jew first, then as a woman, and, when I knew her, she thought of herself as an American—she had no interest in being European.

Her father, it was known, could talk to God; he could influence God; God cared about him. On certain special (cathedral, or sanctified) occasions, Ceil's father could tug the gold chain let down from Heaven.

"Ceil didn't like him so much—she loved him; she was a good daughter, don't get me wrong—but everyone thought only about him, and it suffocated her. She had a bad streak; she thought she was as smart as anyone." (Lila. My mother by adoption.)

Ceil was an immensely passionate woman, who loved steadily and somewhat harshly in the nature of things; that is, that was the form her energy and attention outwardly took.

"She loved to work; she loved to keep things clean. She loved to have you on her arm. She loved to have her hair done. She didn't giggle none." (This is Old Ruthie talking. My grandmother by adoption.) "She had no foolishness; she liked to work."

"She was a cold woman, pardon me for saying it—very cold. But you couldn't tell with her. She liked that little town; she liked Max for a while. You never knew with her—she sometimes seemed very hot, even sentimental, to me; I was colder in the long run. But she said she was alone; she said she had always been alone until you were born, and now she had someone and she was happy. It's too bad it didn't last." (Lila.)

"Ceil was big; she carried herself like a queen; she couldn't come into a room quietly, you know." (Lila.)

My grandfather was a ferocious Jewish charlatan. Unless he actually was a magician. Ceil believed in him. The family myth is that he was a wonder-working rebbe, who had a private army and a small group of industries that he ran and, because he was a religious genius, fifteen thousand loyal followers at his command—a man six feet six or seven or four or five, a man unashamed of his power in the world, his influence over men and over women, a man who could *scare a Cossack.*

But I don't believe it. It is not true. It is mostly untrue, I think. He was poor, and his congregation was poor.

Lila: "Ceil said she hardly knew her mother. There were fifteen, twenty, twenty-five children by the same woman. Ceil said she was a shadow. Ceil said she paid no attention to anyone but the father. Ceil was the youngest, the last one. It used to embarrass Ceil to tell this. Ceil said the father was too smart and too religious to like women. If you ask me, he didn't care about anything but himself; your grandmother got the benefit and the work. . . ."

And: *She was his shadow; she liked it like that; Ceil didn't like that, she didn't want to be like that, she told me she didn't want a man she had to feel obligated to at all.*

Ceil's mother spun and flamed and guttered out her life, my grandma, in hero worship (maybe).

Lila: "Your mother was raised by her older sister."

Lila: "Ceil never knew what kind of man Max was. What could she know? She was ignorant; she only knew what she knew, you know what I mean? She knew what she could know. I wish you understood me, Wiley."

The stories of women go unheard, I understood her to say, Lila.

"No one knows what happens to women. No one knows how bad it is, or how good it is, either. Women can't talk—we know too much."

Ceil's father, my grandfather, claimed literally to be the unnamable God's vicar on earth, his voice on earth—poor or not.

I mean, within four walls he was magnificent, not boastful but merely dutiful toward his powers: he was as powerful as Bach.

She, Ceil, was his pet. She is physically very striking, even exotic, not Jewish-exotic but Tatar-exotic—Byzantine, Saracen. And she has a mind of notable quality, a rankling form of forwardness that shows itself early, and she is educated more than a Jewish woman usually is in such communities, since her father considers her remarkable in her way, and thinks that she might be a prophet and his true heir more than his thickwitted and numberless sons.

For a woman, surely, words are the prime element of force, of being able to enforce things on others, to coerce them. The prime *realistic* thing, in a certain sense, for women in this world, is words, words insofar as they contain law and announcements of principles, the semi-minor apocalypses of utopia, or at least of peace on earth. For Lila, too, it was criticism, judgment, social and psychological coercion. But for Ceil most words were God's, and were cabalistic: the right terms could summon happiness.

Lila: "She hated the Communists by the time they were through; she said they wouldn't give anyone any peace; she said they were mean and stupid, amen."

And: "She had wonderful skin, and she was a good sleeper: I think she had a good conscience; she was very strict. She wasn't shy with people. She wasn't scared; she could talk to anyone; she was like a queen. Your mother had a nice laugh, but she wouldn't laugh in front of men—she said it was like showing her drawers. I never saw anyone as sure of herself as she was—it could drive you crazy sometimes. I never saw her tired."

Life is unlivable, but we live it. No virgin would have married Max Stein. No good-hearted daughter of a strikingly holy man would have left such a presence.

He wants to marry her to a scholar, a rachitic and skinny scholar, devoted to *pilpulim* and to certain Chassidic songs, certain spells of rapture, certain kinds of cunning wit, and, above all, to him, the rebbe, the physical and sexual and worldly power who has been the holy body for the thinner bodies who are his flock. The skinny and lesser mystic he has chosen, and Ceil will preserve the line. In the past Ceil was intoxicated by such notions, but now it is too late. Events have aged her. The war. A brother's disappearance. Perhaps something personal—a man, a woman. A book. A movie. A grief. Or greed: *she wanted a chance to live.* Ceil will choose sin and will be an outcast.

Tall, long-legged, the odd-eyed young woman resists, refuses the marriage. ("There was real trouble between her and her father. He forgave her and he put a curse on her both. He was ugly about her. But she was selfish. She wasn't afraid of him anymore.")

Ceil wasn't ashamed of anything. That's one reason she married Max, so she wouldn't be ashamed of the people back in the old country—the court. *She did things, oddly, for her father and against him. She straightened out her life for his sake, in a way.*

Lila: "She went to the beauty parlor twice a week and she liked Garbo. She didn't speak English and she worked as a maid, I think. She wanted to have her own money, her own life, right away. She had offers, but she turned them all down. She always acted as if she knew what she was doing."

I start with Garbo; I think of scenes of Garbo *travelling*—that almost impossibly powerful presence on the screen, at once challenging and Nordically disciplined, costumed, unafraid.

And: "Your mother was always quick to dress herself up. You'd say about another woman she was putting on airs, but you wouldn't say it about her—it was just one of the things she liked and she made it seem religious almost, a duty. She was like a queen that way."

My father, Max, came from Odessa. My mother did not meet him there, but she sailed from Odessa on a grain ship, and she landed in New Orleans.

Lila: "No one met her, not one of her relatives—she only had one sister in this country—but I swear to God she wasn't frightened. The first thing she did was have her hair done. I won't say she was vain; it wasn't like vanity in her, it was something else. But she went out on the street afterward, and she saw what she had done to it was wrong. What money she had she was never afraid to spend on herself. Oh, you don't have any grip on what she was like. She could live on cabbage or on air; she could walk and not take a streetcar. She had a terrible amount of energy, you know. Anyway, she went to a better beauty parlor right away, the same day, the same hour, and had her hair done all over again, so no one would laugh at her. She was an immigrant, but she knew what was what from the beginning."

And: "After a while, she married Max and went to that little town. She did laugh a lot, always, but it was often cruel, very cruel—her jokes were mean. But sometimes she was just like a girl. She would never go shopping with me. I used to give her things—silk scarves, jewelry—but then she stopped taking things. I never knew what to make of her."

Giggling, she journeys by bus or train up the Mississippi Valley, Memphis, St. Louis, inland in Illinois.

Lila: "She used to let us all lie on her bed, and she would tell stories until we were faint with laughter. If you ask me, she wasn't prepared for her sister's not being high society. Her sister must have lied a lot when she wrote home—you know how it is—and Ceil made jokes about it."

And: "Ceil made money from the first, writing letters for people to the old country, and she worked in a restaurant, but that was dirty and hard, and then she took to working in people's houses because she was safer there from men, and after the first year she started speaking English better."

One story about Ceil's father, who was killed nearly ten years after Ceil died, was that the Russians (in another war) ordered him and his congregation to evacuate, to retreat to the east. He, for one reason or another—disloyalty to Stalin among his reasons—refused to accede to that order to migrate to Siberia. He was in his eighties. Eighteen shots—so the family myth goes—were fired at him by the Russians, but the Germans were near and the Russians fled, and he was healed or miraculously had not been hit or was so wounded it didn't matter to him if he lived or died, and he lived in an in-between state until the Germans came, and he confronted them, too, a living dead man in his anger, and the Germans shot him, in midcurse, in front of the Ark. Some part of this is true, is verifiable.

Lila: "Ceil betook herself from her sister's, and she went to St. Louis, where some educated Jews lived and there was a good rabbi. Some people took her in, but she worked as a maid, and they used her—she didn't know how not to work; she was accustomed to doing everything for her father—and she thought the St. Louis rabbi was silly and knew nothing—she said he had no God—and she had offers, but they didn't interest her. But everybody liked her, we all liked her, and wondered what would happen to her, and she married Max. We warned her, but she was stubborn—she would never listen to anyone."

Here is Ceil in America, in Illinois—in a little town of thirty-five hundred— among American faces, cornfields, American consciences and violence; and her earlier memories never leave her, never lose their power among the sophistications of this traveller in her costumes, her days, her mornings and evenings. I think it was like that. Of course, I know none of this part as a fact.

She lived at the edge of the farm town, in a wooden house—it had five finished rooms in it. Across the road, the farm fields begin on the other side of a shallow ditch. Those fields stretch without a hill to the horizon. Never is the landscape as impressive as the skyscape here. From the rear of the house to the center of town is perhaps two and a half blocks. The houses are close together. Nowadays, there are trailers set up permanently on these streets where there were lawns once. It's not a rich town. To the east, between the town and the superhighway, which is seven miles away, two slag heaps rise in the middle of cornfields. In the course of a day, the shadows of the slag heaps make a clocklike round on the leaves of the corn around them.

In the summer, the laboring factory sky and the rows of corn in their long vegetable avenues form an obscene unity of heat. In winter, the sky is a cloud-jammed attic, noisy and hollow.

She was ashamed, you know—her accent, her size. She knew she was something and that people admired her, and still she hid herself away. She could see her way to a dime, her eyes would light up over seventy-five cents—I could never do that. She was good at arithmetic, she could do numbers in her head better than a man, and she could make people laugh, and no one thought she was a liar: you don't know what that means in a little town—everyone keeps track of who makes money, and if anyone makes money people think he's gouging everyone else. She had a good eye for just how good she could do on a deal and still go on in that town; she was honest, but she was a good liar, and she socked some money away so people wouldn't hold it against her; she was getting richer by the day, by leaps and bounds, and she wanted a child to make her life complete.

You were her success in the world, you were her success in America in a nutshell.

I was born in her bedroom, at home.
I *feel* her; I feel her moods.

Alongside the house and running at a diagonal to it is a single-track railroad. It
is set on a causeway six feet high. I think I can remember the house begin to
shake with an amazing faint steadiness until, as if in an arithmetical theatre, the
house begins to slide and shimmy in a quickening rhythm that is not human. It
is as if pebbles in a shaking drum became four, then eight, then rocks, perhaps
like numbers made of brass in a tin cylinder, antic and chattering like birds, but
more logically. In lunacy, the sound increases mathematically, with a vigor that
is nothing at all like the beating of a pulse or the rhythms of rain. It is loud and
real and unpicturable. The clapboards and nails, glass panes and furniture and
wooden and tin objects in drawers tap and whine and scratch with an unremit-
ting increase in noise so steadily there is nothing you can do to resist or shut off
these signals of approach. The noise becomes a yawing thing, as if the wall had
been torn off the house and we were flip-flopping in chaos. The noise and echoes
come from all directions now. The almost unbearable bass of the large interior
timbers of the house has no discernible pattern but throbs in an aching shape-
lessness, isolated.

At night, the light on the locomotive comes sweeping past the trembling window shades, and a blind glare pours on us an unstable and intangible milk in the
middle of the noise. The rolling and rollicking thing that rides partway in the sky
among its battering waves of air does this to you. Noise is all over you and then it
dwindles; the shaking and noise and light flow off, trickle down and away, and
the smell of the grass and of the night that was there before is mixed with the
smell of ozone, traces of burnt metal, a stink of vanished sparks, bits of smoke
from the engine if the night is without wind.

The train withdraws and moves over the fields, over the corn. The house ticks
and thumps, tings and subsides. The train moves southwest, toward St. Louis.

The wooden-odored shade of a porch, the slightly acid smell of the house:
soap and wood—a country smell.

My mother's torso in a flowered print dress.

A summer, an autumn, a winter—those that I had with Ceil.

The house had very large windows that went down quite close to the floor.
These windows had drawn shades that were an inhumanly dun-yellow color, a
color like that of old lions in the zoo, or the color of corn tassels, of cottonwood
leaves after they have lain on the ground for a while—that bleached and earthen
clayey white-yellow.

My mother's happiness was not the concern of the world.

I half believe that my mother had a lover. I half remember going with her to
see him; she took me with her on a train that ran by electricity among the flat
farm fields. I stood on the seat and looked out the train window. My hand marks
and nose marks and breath marks—I remember those and her hand wiping the

marks away. I see wheeling rows of corn, occasional trees, windmills, farm-houses.

Maybe I am mistaken.

Lila: *She had more character than any woman I ever knew, but a lot of good it did her.*

Your mother knew she'd made a mistake marrying Max; she gave him money and she knew he would spend it and go off; she was no one's fool, but how she had the nerve to live in that little town alone I just don't know; everyone's watching; you can fall flat on your face.

Ceil's business did well in hard times and in good times. My brother said she was a genius at business—she had such a good head men were interested in doing business with her—men enjoyed talking to her, she was their size, and you could see she was religious, she was serious; it tickled people that someone so smart lived in such a little town and worked so hard and didn't speak English well and was getting ahead in the world anyway.

You won't understand this, but she wasn't ashamed of being a woman.

I often think I would have disliked Ceil—at least at times. My mother. I imagine the lunatic and pitiable arrogance, the linguistic drunkenness of my mother on her bed of language and anathema.

I was her child—her infant, really—and the most important thing in her life, she said, but never to the exclusion of her rising in the world or the operations of her will.

In my dreams at night, often the people of a small town crowd around the white-painted wooden farmhouse, carrying torches, to celebrate my election, my revealed glory of destiny; if they applaud or cheer too loudly, I awake and leave them behind in the dream that is a lost planet, a wandering asteroid from which they cannot escape. My mother's dreams and her life were of her election. As in most lives, there is quiet in it, but not often.

Ceil's pride kept her from making friends; friends would have preserved her life but altered the workings and turns of her mind. "She was comfortable only with people who worked for her; she had to be the best; she had great pride in her mind; she thought she knew everything."

Ceil dresses herself in her efforts and her decisions.

Your mother was cursed by your grandfather if she should ever stop being Jewish: look, not just Jewish, strict, you know what I mean—you know what I mean by strict? I don't know if I have the wherewithal to tell you the story if you don't make an effort to understand it on your own; he said she was supposed to die in a bad way if she wasn't a Jew just the way he was, the way he said Jews should be; you know what people are like who have those kinds of minds, don't you? Well, Ceil got taken ill, and she said it was because she wasn't a Jew any-more that her father would let in his house.

Now I want to switch to another woman's voice, away from Lila—not a woman I know well. *You want to hear? Mostly, men don't want to know. My mother went to see Ceil in the hospital when she was dying, she went every day, even when Ceil couldn't speak; she said it was good for her* [edifying for her mother: the nobility, the piety, the strength in suffering]—*but maybe not. There's truth in those old things, but how can you tell? Everybody dies anyway. Maybe she didn't keep it up, Ceil, but she had a lot of dignity. She liked God, you know, better than people—maybe except for you. She said she owed it to God. She said she had no right to complain. I don't know if I understood it. She had one sister here, and the sister didn't like her children; they were too American, they weren't good to her—you know how some young people are—and she was afraid they were no good. Ceil told me in confidence that her sister was nothing special: she was a stupid woman and greedy and not very nice. Ceil was different; she talked different; she looked at things different. Her sister hacked herself up with a meat cleaver. You know, it's funny how many suicides I know about. People hide it from children, you know. She made sure no one was in the house; she sent all the children to the movies. Ceil's sister was twenty years older than her. I think there was a curse on her, too. She took the cleaver and she chopped up everything—all her furniture and all her clothes, everything, hand-kerchiefs and stockings. And then she hit herself over and over, over and over— are you sure you want to hear this—until she was dead. Then Ceil had been having trouble with Max, and she did something she was ashamed of; it was the abortion, but she did it to herself with the help of a Frenchwoman who knew her. And Ceil got a little sick; it was nothing bad, but she went to her sister's funeral and sat shiva and she took you with her, and she said to me that the voice of her father was in that room and she tried not to listen. Ceil had a lot of money in the bank, a lot of money, and she loved you, it was nice to see. She didn't want to die, I promise you that. When she was sick, she said you would feel she ran out on you. A woman is always wrong. I was lucky. It never got so serious for me I couldn't laugh. Oh, maybe once or twice I thought I would die from it. I wanted to go be in an asylum, but it wasn't my children who saved me. They take, they don't give. She said who would ever give you now what she did, what a mother gives, for no good reason, who would take care of a child like a mother. A woman has her own children or she is ignorant. How can you let a mother go when you're that little and then you have to take what you can get— it's a terrible story, as I said—but she got ill, it was in her soul, she was disgusted with all of us—it happens to a lot of women. She didn't give in right away; the doctors said she would die in a week, but she lived on six months because of you—in pain that was terrible. It couldn't even be God's anger, it was so terri- ble; it came from the Devil, she said, and the drugs weren't strong enough to touch it. It's terrible when nothing can help. She stank from an infection so bad it made people throw up—it made her sick, her own stench. It was like some- thing out of Hell. They put her on a floor where everyone was dying. You know how doctors run away when they can't help you. And it got worse and worse and worse. She lay there and she plotted to find someone to save you. And to tell you the truth, she didn't want Lila to have you—she didn't like Lila at all; Lila is trash, she said—but when Lila brought you to see her and you were better than* you'd been and Lila had on her diamonds and a lot of perfume and you liked her, Ceil said it was better maybe you were saved, no matter what, no matter who it was—even someone, practically a Gentile whore, like Lila: Ceil talked like a rabbi, very strict. She said Lila wasn't as bad as some people thought. Lila was brave. No one could tell Lila what to do. Lila brought you to your mother and she put you in your mother's arms, and you cried when she held you; you can't blame yourself: it was horrible; you knew your mother only when she was well, a strong woman like that and here is this bag of bones, this woman who prays in a crazy way, and she is crazy with worry about you; and she prayed you'd live and be all right and do something for the Jews. You cried and you turned and you held your arms out to Lila. I'll tell you the truth, it killed Ceil, but she wasn't surprised—she said to me it's easy to die, it was hard to live, I want to die now, and she died that night. Don't blame yourself. The only thing she asked me to tell you is to tell you to remember her.

I remember her. I hate Jews.

No. I don't really remember her and I don't hate Jews.

In the tormented and torn silence of certain dreams—in the night court of my sleep—sometimes words, like fingers, move and knead and shape the tableaux: shadowy lives in night streets. There is a pearly strangeness to the light. Love and children appear as if in daylight, but it is always a sleeping city, on steep hills, with banked fires and ghosts lying in the streets in the dully reflectant gray light of a useless significance.

I do not believe there was any justice in Ceil's life.

Dino Buzzati

· · · · · · · · · · · · · · · · · · · ·

SEVEN FLOORS

One morning in March, after a night's train journey, Giovanni Corte arrived in the town where the famous nursing home was. He was a little feverish, but he was still determined to walk from the station to the hospital, carrying his small bag.

Although his was an extremely slight case, in the very earliest stages, Giovanni Corte had been advised to go to the well-known sanatorium, which existed solely for the care of the particular illness from which he was suffering. This meant that the doctors were particularly competent and the equipment particularly pertinent and efficient.

Catching sight of it from a distance—he recognised it from having seen photos in some brochure—Giovanni Corte was most favourably impressed. The building was white, seven storeys high; its mass was broken up by a series of recesses which gave it a vague resemblance to a hotel. It was surrounded by tall trees.

After a brief visit from the doctor, prior to a more thorough one later on, Giovanni Corte was taken to a cheerful room on the seventh and top floor. The furniture was light and elegant, as was the wallpaper, there were wooden arm-chairs and brightly coloured cushions. The view was over one of the loveliest parts of the town. Everything was peaceful, welcoming and reassuring.

Giovanni Corte went to bed immediately, turned on the reading-lamp at his bedside and began to read a book he had brought with him. After a few moments a nurse came in to see whether he needed anything.

He didn't, but was delighted to chat with the young woman and ask her questions about the nursing home. That was how he came to know its one extremely odd characteristic: the patients were housed on each floor according to the gravity of their state. The seventh, or top, floor, was for extremely mild cases. The sixth was still for mild cases, but ones needing a certain amount of attention. On the fifth floor there were quite serious cases and so on, floor by floor. The second floor was for the very seriously ill. On the first floor were the hopeless cases.

This extraordinary system, apart from facilitating the general services consid-

152

erably, meant that a patient only mildly affected would not be troubled by a dying co-sufferer next door and ensured a uniformity of atmosphere on each floor. Treatment, of course, would thus vary from floor to floor.

This meant that the patients were divided into seven successive castes. Each floor was a world apart, with its own particular rules and traditions. And as each floor was in the charge of a different doctor, slight but definite differences in the methods of treatment had grown up, although initially the director had given the institution a single basic bent.

As soon as the nurse had left the room Giovanni Corte, no longer feeling feverish, went to the window and looked out, not because he wanted to see the view of the town (although he was not familiar with it) but in the hopes of catching a glimpse, through the windows, of the patients on the lower floors. The structure of the building, with its large recesses, made this possible. Giovanni Corte concentrated particularly on the first floor windows, which looked a very long way away, and which he could see only obliquely. But he could see nothing interesting. Most of the windows were completely hidden by grey venetian blinds.

But Corte did see someone, a man, standing at a window right next to his own. The two looked at each other with a growing feeling of sympathy but did not know how to break the silence. At last Giovanni Corte plucked up courage and said: 'Have you just arrived too?'

'Oh no,' said his neighbour, 'I've been here two months.' He was silent for a few moments and then, apparently not sure how to continue the conversation, added: 'I was watching my brother down there.'

'Your brother?'

'Yes. We both came here at the same time, oddly enough, but he got worse—he's on the fourth now.'

'Fourth what?'

'Fourth floor,' explained the man, pronouncing the two words with such pixy and horror that Giovanni Corte was vaguely alarmed.

'But in that case'—Corte proceeded with his questioning with the light-heartedness one might adopt when speaking of tragic matters which don't concern one—'if things are already so serious on the fourth floor, whom do they put on the first?'

'Oh, the dying. There's nothing for the doctors to do down there. Only the priests. And of course . . .'

'But there aren't many people down there,' interrupted Giovanni Corte as if seeking confirmation, 'almost all the blinds are down.'

'There aren't many now, but there were this morning,' replied the other with a slight smile. 'The rooms with the blinds down are those where someone has died recently. As you can see, on the other floors the shutters are all open. Will you excuse me,' he continued, moving slowly back in, 'it seems to be getting rather cold. I'm going back to bed. May I wish you all the best . . .'

The man vanished from the window sill and shut the window firmly; a light was lit inside the room. Giovanni Corte remained standing at the window, his eyes fixed on the lowered blinds of the first floor. He stared at them with morbid intensity, trying to visualise the ghastly secrets of that terrible first floor where patients were taken to die; he felt relieved that he was so far away. Meanwhile, the shadows of evening crept over the city. One by one the thousand windows of the sanatorium lit up, from the distance it looked like a great house lit up for a ball. Only on the first floor, at the foot of the precipice, did dozens of windows remain blank and empty.

Giovanni Corte was considerably reassured by the doctor's visit. A natural pessimist, he was already secretly prepared for an unfavourable verdict and wouldn't have been surprised if the doctor had sent him down to the next floor.

His temperature however showed no signs of going down, even though his condition was otherwise satisfactory. But the doctor was pleasant and encouraging. Certainly he was affected—the doctor said—but only very slightly; in two or three weeks he would probably be cured. 'So I'm to stay on the seventh floor?' enquired Giovanni Corte anxiously at this point.

'Well of course!' replied the doctor, clapping a friendly hand on his shoulder. 'Where did you think you were going? Down to the fourth perhaps?' He spoke jokingly, as though it were the most absurd thought in the world.

'I'm glad about that,' said Giovanni Corte. 'You know how it is, when one's ill one always imagines the worst.' In fact he stayed in the room which he had originally been given. On the rare afternoons when he was allowed up he made the acquaintance of some of his fellow-patients. He followed the treatment scrupulously, concentrated his whole attention on making a rapid recovery, yet his condition seemed to remain unchanged.

About ten days later, the head nurse of the seventh floor came to see Giovanni Corte. He wanted to ask an entirely personal favour: the following day a woman with two children was coming to the hospital: there were two free rooms right next to his, but a third was needed; would Signor Corte mind very much moving into another, equally comfortable room?

Naturally, Giovanni Corte made no objection; he didn't mind what room he was in; indeed, he might have a new and prettier nurse.

'Thank you so much,' said the head nurse with a slight bow; 'though, mark you, such a courteous act doesn't surprise me coming from a person such as yourself. We'll start moving your things in about an hour, if you don't mind. By the way, it's one floor down' he added in a quieter tone, as though it were a negligible detail. 'Unfortunately there are no free rooms on this floor. Of course it's a purely temporary arrangement,' he hastened to add, seeing that Corte had sat up suddenly and was about to protest, 'a purely temporary arrangement. You'll be coming up again as soon as there's a free room, which should be in two or three days.'

'I must confess,' said Giovanni Corte smiling, to show that he had no childish fears, 'I must confess that this particular sort of change of room doesn't appeal to me in the least.'

'But it has no medical basis; I quite understand what you mean, but in this case it's simply to do a favour for this woman who doesn't want to be separated from her children. . . . Now please' he added, laughing openly, 'please don't get it into your head that there are other reasons!'

'Very well,' said Giovanni Corte, 'but it seems to me to bode ill.'

So Giovanni Corte went down to the sixth floor, and though he was convinced that this move did not correspond to any worsening in his own condition, he felt unhappy at the thought that there was now a definite barrier between himself and the everyday world of healthy people. The seventh floor was an embarkation point, with a certain degree of contact with society; it could be regarded as a sort of annexe to the ordinary world. But the sixth was already part of the real hospital; the attitudes of the doctors, nurses, of the patients themselves were just slightly different. It was admitted openly that the patients on that floor were really sick, even if not seriously so. From his initial conversation with his neighbours, staff and doctors, Giovanni Corte gathered that here the seventh floor was regarded as a joke, reserved for amateurs, all affectation and caprice; it was only on the sixth floor that things began in earnest.

One thing Giovanni Corte did realise, however, was that he would certainly have some difficulty in getting back up to the floor where, medically speaking, he really belonged; to get back to the seventh floor he would have to set the whole complex organism of the place in motion, even for such a small move; it was quite plain that, were he not to insist, no one would ever have thought of putting him back on the top floor, with the 'almost-well'.

So Giovanni Corte decided not to forfeit anything that was his by right and not to yield to the temptations of habit. He was much concerned to impress upon his companions that he was with them only for a few days, that it was he who had agreed to go down a floor simply to oblige a lady, that he'd be going up again as soon as there was a free room. The others listened without interest and nodded, unconvinced.

Giovanni Corte's convictions, however, were confirmed by the judgement of the new doctor. He agreed that Giovanni Corte could most certainly be on the seventh floor; the form the disease had taken was ab-so-lute-ly negligible—he stressed each syllable so as to emphasise the importance of his diagnosis—but after all it might well be that Giovanni Corte would be better taken care of on the sixth floor.

'I don't want all that nonsense all over again,' Giovanni Corte interrupted firmly at this point, 'you say I should be on the seventh floor, and that's where I want to be.'

'No one denies that,' retorted the doctor. 'I was advising you not as a doc-tor, but as a re-al friend. As I say, you're very slightly affected, it wouldn't even be an exaggeration to say that you're not ill at all, but in my opinion what makes your case different from other similarly mild ones is its greater extension: the intensity of the disease is minimal, but it is fairly widespread; the destructive process of the cells'—it was the first time Giovanni Corte had heard the sinister expression—'the destructive process of the cells is absolutely in the initial stage, it may not even have begun yet, but it is tending, I say tending, to affect large expanses of the organism. This is the only reason, in my opinion, why you might be better off down here on the sixth floor, where the methods of treatment are more highly specialised and more intensive.'

One day he was informed that the Director of the nursing home, after lengthy consultation with his colleagues, had decided to make a change in the subdivision of the patients. Each person's grade—so to speak—was to be lowered by half a point. From now on the patients on each floor were to be divided into two categories according to the seriousness of their condition (indeed the respective doctors had already made this subdivision, though exclusively for their own personal use) and the lower of these two halves was to be officially moved one floor down. For example, half the patients on the sixth floor, those who were slightly more seriously affected, were to go down to the fifth; the less slightly affected of the seventh floor would go down to the sixth. Giovanni Corte was pleased to hear this, because his return to the seventh floor would certainly be much easier amid this highly complicated series of removals.

However, when he mentioned this hope to the nurse he was bitterly disappointed. He learned that he was indeed to be moved, not up to the seventh but down to the floor below. For reasons that the nurse was unable to explain, he had been classed among the more 'serious' patients on the sixth floor and so had to go down to the fifth.

Once he had recovered from his initial surprise, Giovanni Corte completely lost his temper; he shouted that they were cheating him, that he refused to hear of moving downwards, that he would go back home, that rights were rights and that the hospital administration could not afford to ignore the doctors' diagnosis so brazenly.

He was still shouting when the doctor arrived to explain matters more fully. He advised Corte to calm down unless he wanted his temperature to rise and explained that there had been a misunderstanding, at least in a sense. He agreed once again that Giovanni Corte would have been equally suitably placed on the seventh floor, but added that he had a slightly different, though entirely personal, view of the case. Basically, in a certain sense, his condition could be considered as needing treatment on the sixth floor, because the symptoms were so widespread. But he himself failed to understand why Corte had been listed among the more serious cases of the sixth floor. In all probability the secretary, who had phoned him that very morning to ask about Giovanni Corte's exact medical position, had made a mistake in copying out his report. Or more likely still the administrative staff had purposely depreciated his own judgement, since he was considered an expert doctor but over optimistic. Finally, the doctor advised Corte not to worry, to accept the move without protest; what counted was the disease, not the floor on which the patient was placed.

As far as the treatment was concerned—added the doctor—Giovanni Corte would certainly not have cause for complaint: the doctor on the floor below was undoubtedly far more experienced; it was almost part of the system that the doctors became more experienced, at least in the eyes of the administration, the further down you went. The rooms were equally comfortable and elegant. The view was equally good; it was only from the third floor that it was cut off by the surrounding trees.

It was evening, and Giovanni Corte's temperature had risen accordingly; he listened to this meticulous ratiocination with an increasing feeling of exhaustion. Finally he realised that he had neither the strength nor the desire to resist this unfair removal any further. Unprotesting, he allowed himself to be taken one floor down.

Giovanni Corte's one meagre consolation on the fifth floor was the knowledge that, in the opinion of doctors, nurses and patients alike, he was the least seriously ill of anyone on the whole floor. In short, he could consider himself much the most fortunate person in that section. On the other hand he was haunted by the thought that there were now two serious barriers between himself and the world of ordinary people.

As spring progressed the weather became milder, but Giovanni Corte no longer liked to stand at the window as he used to do; although it was stupid to feel afraid, he felt a strange movement of terror at the sight of the first floor windows, always mostly closed and now so much nearer.

His own state seemed unchanged; though after three days on the fifth floor a patch of eczema appeared on his right leg and showed no signs of clearing up during the following days. The doctor assured him that this was something absolutely independent of the main disease; it could have happened to the most healthy person in the world. Intensive treatment with digamma rays would clear it up in a few days.

'And can't one have that here?' asked Giovanni Corte.

'Certainly,' replied the doctor delighted; 'we have everything here. There's only one slight inconvenience . . .'

'What?' asked Giovanni Corte with vague foreboding.

'Inconvenience in a manner of speaking,' the doctor corrected himself. 'The fourth floor is the only one with the relevant apparatus and I wouldn't advise you to go up and down three times a day.'

'So it's out of the question?'

'It would really be better if you would be good enough to go down to the fourth floor until the eczema has cleared up.'

'That's enough,' shrieked Giovanni Corte exasperated. 'I've had enough of going down! I'd rather die than go down to the fourth floor!'

'As you wish,' said the doctor soothingly, so as not to annoy him, 'but as the doctor responsible, I must point out that I forbid you to go up and down three times a day.'

The unfortunate thing was that the eczema, rather than clearing up, began to spread gradually. Giovanni Corte couldn't rest, he tossed and turned in bed. His anger held out for three days but finally he gave in. Of his own accord, he asked the doctor to arrange for the ray treatment to be carried out, and to move to the floor below.

Here Corte noticed, with private delight, that he really was an exception. The other patients on the floor were certainly much more seriously affected and unable to move from their beds at all. He, on the other hand, could afford the luxury of walking from his bedroom to the room where the rays were, amid the compliments and amazement of the nurses themselves.

He made a point of stressing the extremely special nature of his position to the new doctor. A patient who, basically, should have been on the seventh floor was in fact on the fourth. As soon as his eczema was better, he would be going up again. This time there could be absolutely no excuse. He, who could still legitimately have been on the seventh floor!

'On the seventh?' exclaimed the doctor who had just finished examining him, with a smile. 'You sick people do exaggerate so! I'd be the first to agree that you should be pleased with your condition; from what I see from your medical chart, it hasn't changed much for the worse. But—forgive my rather brutal honesty—there's quite a difference between that and the seventh floor. You're one of the least worrying cases, I quite agree, but you're definitely ill.'

'Well then,' said Giovanni Corte, scarlet in the face, 'what floor would you personally put me on?'

'Well really, it's not easy to say, I've only examined you briefly, for any final judgement I'd have to observe you for at least a week.'

'All right,' insisted Corte, 'but you must have some idea.'

To calm him, the doctor pretended to concentrate on the matter for a moment and then, nodding to himself, said slowly: 'Oh dear! Look, to please you, I think after all one might say the sixth. Yes,' he added as if to persuade himself of the rightness of what he was saying, 'the sixth would probably be all right.'

The doctor thought that this would please his patient. But an expression of terror spread over Giovanni Corte's face: he realised that the doctors of the upper floors had deceived him; here was this new doctor, plainly more expert and honest, who in his heart of hearts—it was quite obvious—would place him not on the seventh but on the sixth floor, possibly even the lower fifth! The unexpected disappointment prostrated Corte. That evening his temperature rose appreciably.

His stay on the fourth floor was the most peaceful period he had had since coming to the hospital. The doctor was a delightful person, attentive and pleasant; he often stayed for whole hours to talk about all kinds of things. Giovanni Corte too was delighted to have an opportunity to talk, and drew the conversation around to his normal past life as a lawyer and man of the world. He tried to convince himself that he still belonged to the society of healthy men, that he was still connected with the world of business, that he was really still interested in matters of public import. He tried, but unsuccessfully. The conversation invariably came round, in the end, to the subject of his illness.

The desire for any sign of improvement had become an obsession. Unfortunately the digamma rays had succeeded in preventing the spread of the eczema but they had not cured it altogether. Giovanni Corte talked about this at length with the doctor every day and tried to appear philosophical, even ironic about it, without ever succeeding.

'Tell me, doctor,' he said one day, 'how is the destructive process of the cells coming along?'

'What a frightful expression,' said the doctor reprovingly. 'Wherever did you come across that? That's not at all right, particularly for a patient. I never want to hear anything like that again.'

'All right,' objected Corte, 'but you still haven't answered.'

'I'll answer right away,' replied the doctor pleasantly. 'The destructive process of your cells, to use your own horrible expression is, in your very minor case, absolutely negligible. But obstinate, I must say.'

'Obstinate, you mean chronic?'

'Now don't credit me with things I haven't said. I only said obstinate. Anyhow that's how it is in minor cases. Even the mildest infections often need long and intensive treatment.'

'But tell me, doctor, when can I expect to see some improvement?'

'When? It's difficult to say in these cases. . . . But listen,' he added after pausing for thought, 'I can see that you're positively obsessed with the idea of recovery . . . if I weren't afraid of angering you, do you know what I'd suggest?'

'Please do say . . .'

'Well, I'll put the situation very clearly. If I had this disease even slightly and were to come to this sanatorium, which is probably the best there is, I would arrange of my own accord, and from the first day—I repeat from the first day—to go down to one of the lower floors. In fact I'd even go to the . . .'

'To the first?' suggested Corte with a forced smile.

'Oh dear no!' replied the doctor with a deprecating smile, 'Oh dear no! But to the third or even the second. On the lower floors the treatment is far better, you know, the equipment is more complete, more powerful, the staff are more expert. And then you know who is the real soul of this hospital?'

'Isn't it Professor Dati?'

'Exactly. It was he who invented the treatment carried out here, he really planned the whole place. Well, Dati, the master-mind, operates, so to speak, between the first and second floors. His driving force radiates from there. But I assure you that it never goes beyond the third floor: further up than that the details of his orders are glossed over, interpreted more slackly; the heart of the hospital is on the lowest floors, and that's where you must be to have the best treatment.'

'So in short,' said Giovanni Corte, his voice shaking, 'so you would advise me. . . .'

'And there's something else,' continued the doctor unperturbed, 'and that is that in your case there's also the eczema to be considered. I agree that it's quite unimportant, but it is rather irritating, and in the long run it might lower your morale; and you know how important peace of mind is for your recovery. The rays have been only half successful. Now why? It might have been pure chance, but it might also have been that they weren't sufficiently intense. Well, on the third floor the apparatus is far more powerful. The chances of curing your eczema would be much greater. And the point is that once the cure is under way, the hardest part is over. Once you really feel better, there's absolutely no reason why you shouldn't come up here again, or indeed higher still, according to your "deserts", to the fifth, the sixth, possibly even the seventh . . .'

'But do you think this will hasten my recovery?'

'I've not the slightest doubt it will. I've already said what I'd do if I were in your place.'

The doctor talked like this to Giovanni Corte every day. And at last, tired of the inconveniences of the eczema, despite his instinctive reluctance to go down a floor, he decided to take the doctor's advice and move to the floor below.

He noticed immediately that the third floor was possessed of a special gaiety affecting both doctors and nurses, even though the cases treated on that floor were very serious. He noticed too that this gaiety increased daily; consumed with curiosity, as soon as he got to know the nurse, he asked why on earth they were all so cheerful.

'Oh, didn't you know?' she replied, 'in three days time we're all going on holiday.'

'On holiday?'

'That's right. The whole floor closes for a fortnight and the staff go off and enjoy themselves. Each floor takes it in turn to have a holiday.'

'And what about the patients?'

'There are relatively few of them, so two floors are converted into one.'

'You mean you put the patients of the third and fourth floors together?'

'No no,' the nurse corrected him, 'of the third and second. The patients on this floor will have to go down.'

'Down to the second?' asked Giovanni Corte, suddenly pale as death. 'You mean I'll have to go down to the second?'

'Well, yes. What's so odd about that? When we come back, in a fortnight, you'll come back here, in this same room. I can't see anything so terrifying about it.'

But Giovanni Corte—as if forewarned by some strange instinct—was horribly afraid. However, since he could hardly prevent the staff from going on their holidays, and convinced that the new treatment with the stronger rays would do him good—the eczema had almost cleared up—he didn't dare offer any formal opposition to this new move. But he did insist, despite nurses' banter, that the label on the door of his new room should read 'Giovanni Corte, third floor, temporary'. Such a thing had never been done before in the whole history of the sanatorium, but the doctors didn't object, fearing that the prohibition of even such a minor matter might cause a serious shock to a patient as highly strung as Giovanni Corte.

After all, it was simply a question of waiting for fourteen days, neither more nor less. Giovanni Corte began to count them with stubborn eagerness, lying motionless on his bed for hours on end, staring at the furniture, which wasn't as pleasant and modern here as on the higher floors, but more cumbersome, gloomy and severe. Every now and again he would listen intently, thinking he heard sounds from the floor below, the floor of the dying, the 'condemned'— vague sounds of death in action.

Naturally he found all this very dispiriting. His agitation seemed to nourish the disease, his temperature began to rise, the state of continued weakness began to affect him vitally. From the window—which was almost always open, since it was now mid-summer—he could no longer see the roofs nor even the houses, but only the green wall of the surrounding trees.

A week later, one afternoon about two o'clock, his room was suddenly invaded by the head nurse and three nurses, with a trolley. 'All ready for the move, then?' asked the head nurse jovially.

'What move?' asked Giovanni Corte weakly, 'what's all this? The third floor staff haven't come back after a week have they?'

'Third floor?' repeated the head nurse uncomprehendingly, 'my orders are to take you down to the first floor,' and he produced a printed form for removal to the first floor signed by none other than Professor Dati himself.

Giovanni Corte gave vent to his terror, his diabolical rage in long angry shrieks, which resounded throughout the whole floor. 'Less noise, please,' begged the nurses, 'there are some patients here who are not at all well.' But it would have taken more than that to calm him.

At last the second floor doctor appeared—a most attentive person. After being given the relevant information he looked at the form and listened to Giovanni Corte's side of the story. He then turned angrily to the head nurse and told him there had been a mistake, he himself had had no such orders, for some time now the place had been an impossible muddle, he himself knew nothing about what was going on . . . at last, when he had had his say with his inferior, he turned politely to his patient, highly apologetic.

'Unfortunately, however,' he added, 'unfortunately Professor Dati left the hospital about an hour ago—he'll be away for a couple of days. I'm most awfully sorry, but his orders can't be overlooked. He would be the first to regret it, I assure you . . . an absurd mistake! I fail to understand how it could have happened!'

Giovanni Corte had begun to tremble piteously. He was now completely unable to control himself, overcome with fear like a small child. His slow desperate sobbing echoed throughout the room.

It was as a result of this execrable mistake, then, that he was removed to his last resting place: he who basically, according to the most stringent medical opinion, was fit for the sixth, if not the seventh floor as far as his illness was concerned! The situation was so grotesque that from time to time Giovanni Corte felt inclined simply to roar with laughter.

Stretched out on his bed, while the afternoon warmth flowed calmly over the city, he would stare at the green of the trees through the window and feel that he had come to a completely unreal world, walled in with sterilised tiles, full of deathly arctic passages and soulless white figures. It even occurred to him that the trees he thought he saw through the window were not real; finally, when he noticed that the leaves never moved, he was certain of it.

Corte was so upset by this idea that he called the nurse and asked for his spectacles, which he didn't use in bed, being short-sighted; only then was he a little reassured: the lenses proved that they were real leaves and that they were shaken, though very slightly, by the wind.

When the nurse had gone out, he spent half an hour in complete silence. Six floors, six solid barriers, even if only because of a bureaucratic mistake, weighed implacably above Giovanni Corte. How many years (for obviously it was now a question of years) would it be before he could climb back to the top of that precipice?

But why was the room suddenly going so dark? It was still mid-afternoon. With a supreme effort, for he felt himself paralysed by a strange lethargy,

Giovanni Corte turned to look at his watch on the locker by his bed. Three-thirty. He turned his head the other way and saw that the venetian blinds, in obedience to some mysterious command, were dropping slowly, shutting out the light.

Translated from the Italian by Judith Landry

Italo Calvino

. . . .

THE ADVENTURE
OF A TRAVELER

Federico V., who lived in a northern Italian city, was in love with Cinzia U., a resident of Rome. Whenever his work permitted, he would take the train to the capital. Accustomed to budgeting his time strictly, at the job and in his pleasures, he always traveled at night: there was one train, the last, that was not crowded—except in the holiday season—and Federico could stretch out and sleep.

Federico's days in his own city went by nervously, like the hours of someone between trains who, as he goes about his business, cannot stop thinking of the schedule. But when the evening of his departure finally came and his tasks were done and he was walking with his suitcase toward the station, then, even in his haste to avoid missing his train, he began to feel a sense of inner calm pervade him. It was as if all the bustle around the station—now at its last gasp, given the late hour—were part of a natural movement, and he also belonged to it. Everything seemed to be there to encourage him, to give a spring to his steps like the rubberized pavement of the station, and even the obstacles—the wait, his minutes numbered, at the last ticket window still open, the difficulty of breaking a large bill, the lack of small change at the newsstand—seemed to exist for his pleasure in confronting and overcoming them.

Not that he betrayed any sign of this mood: a staid man, he liked being undistinguishable from the many travelers arriving and leaving, all in overcoats like him, a case in hand; and yet he felt as if he were borne on the crest of a wave, because he was rushing toward Cinzia.

The hand in his overcoat pocket toyed with a telephone token. Tomorrow morning, as soon as he landed at the Stazione Termini in Rome, he would run, token in hand, to the nearest public telephone, dial the number, and say, "Hello, darling, I'm here. . . ." And he clutched the token as if it were a most precious object, the only one in the world, the sole tangible proof of what awaited him on his arrival.

The trip was expensive and Federico wasn't rich. If he saw a second-class coach with padded seats and empty compartments, Federico would buy a second-class ticket. Or, rather, he always bought a second-class ticket, with the idea that, if he found too many people there, he would move into first, paying the difference to the conductor. In this operation, he enjoyed the pleasure of economy (besides, when the cost of first-class was paid in two installments, and through necessity, it upset him less), the satisfaction of profiting by his own experience, and a sense of freedom and expansiveness in his actions and in his thoughts.

As sometimes happens with men whose lives are more conditioned by others, exterior, poured out, Federico tended constantly to defend his own inner concentration, and actually it took very little, a hotel room, a train compartment all to himself, for him to adjust the world into harmony with his life; the world seemed created specially for him, as if the railroads that swathed the peninsula had been built deliberately to bear him triumphantly to Cinzia. That evening, again, second-class was almost empty. Every sign was favorable.

Federico V. chose an empty compartment, not over the wheels but not too far into the coach, either, because he knew that as a rule people who board a train in haste tend to reject the first few compartments. The defense of the space necessary to stretch out and travel lying down is made up of tiny psychological devices; Federico knew them and employed them all. For example, he drew the curtains over the door, an act that, performed at this point, might even seem excessive; but it aimed, in fact, at a psychological effect. Seeing those drawn curtains, the traveler who arrives later is almost always overcome by an instinctive scruple and prefers, if he can find it, a compartment with perhaps two or three people in it already but with the curtains open. Federico strewed his bag, overcoat, newspapers on the seats opposite and beside him. Another elementary move, abused and apparently futile but actually of use. Not that he wanted to make people believe those places were occupied: such a subterfuge would have been contrary to his civic conscience and to his sincere nature. He wanted only to create a rapid impression of a cluttered, not very inviting compartment, a simple, rapid impression.

He sat down and heaved a sigh of relief. He had learned that being in a setting where everything can only be in its place, the same as always, anonymous, without possible surprises, filled him with calm, with self-awareness, freedom of thought. His whole life rushed along in disorder, but now he found the perfect balance between interior stimulus and the impassive neutrality of material things.

It lasted an instant (if he was in second; a minute if he was in first); then he was immediately seized by a pang: the squalor of the compartment, the plush threadbare in places, the suspicion of dust all about, the faded texture of the curtains in the old-style coaches, gave him a sensation of sadness, the uneasy prospect of sleeping in his clothes, on a bunk not his, with no possible intimacy between him and what he touched. But he immediately recalled the reason he was traveling, and he felt caught up again in that natural rhythm, as of the sea or the wind, that festive, light impulse; he had only to seek it within himself, closing his eyes or clasping the telephone token in his hand, and that sense of squalor was defeated; only he existed, alone, facing the adventure of his journey.

But something was still missing: what? Ah: he heard the bass voice approaching under the marquee: "Pillows!" He had already stood up, was lowering the window, extending his hand with the two hundred-lire pieces, shouting, "I'll take one!" It was the pillow man who, every time, gave the journey its starting signal. He passed by the window a minute before departure, pushing in front of him the wheeled rack with pillows hanging from it. He was a tall old man, thin, with white mustache and large hands, long, thick fingers: hands that inspire trust. He was dressed all in black: military cap, uniform, overcoat, a scarf wound tight around his neck. A character from the times of King Umberto; perhaps an old colonel, or only a faithful quartermaster sergeant. Or a postman, an old rural messenger: with those big hands, when he extended the thin pillow to Federico, holding it with his fingertips, he seemed to be delivering a letter, or perhaps to be posting it through the window. The pillow now was in Federico's arms, square, flat, just like an envelope, and, what's more, covered with postmarks: it was the daily letter to Cinzia, also departing this evening, and instead of the page of eager scrawl there was Federico in person to take the invisible path of the night mail, through the hand of the old winter messenger, the last incarnation of the rational, disciplined North before the incursion among the unruly passions of the Center-South.

But still, and above all, it was a pillow; namely, a soft object (though pressed and compact) and white (though covered with postmarks) from the steam laundry. It contained in itself, as a concept is enclosed within an ideographic sign, the idea of the bed, the twisting and turning, the privacy; and Federico was already anticipating with pleasure the island of freshness it would be for him, that night, amid that rough and treacherous plush. And further: that slender rectangle of comfort prefigured later comforts, later intimacy, later sweetnesses, whose enjoyment was the reason he was setting out on this journey; indeed, the very fact of departing, the hiring of the cushion, was a form of enjoying them, a way of entering the dimension where Cinzia reigned, the circle enclosed by her soft arms.

And it was with an amorous, caressing motion that the train began to glide among the columns of the marquees, snaking through the iron-clad fields of the switches, hurling itself into the darkness, and becoming one with the impulse that till then Federico had felt within himself. And as if the release of his tension in the speeding of the train had made him lighter, he began to accompany its race, humming the tune of a song that this speed brought to his mind: *"J'ai deux amours. . . . Mon pays et Paris . . . Paris toujours . . ."*

A man entered; Federico fell silent. "Is this place free?" He sat down. Federico had already made a quick mental calculation: strictly speaking, if you want to make your journey lying down, it's best to have someone else in the compartment. One person stretched out on one side and the other on the other, for then nobody dares disturb you; but if, on the other hand, half the compartment remains free, when you least expect it a family of six boards the train, complete with children, all bound for Siracusa, and you're forced to sit up. Federico was quite aware, then, that the wisest thing to do, on entering an uncrowded train, was to take a seat not in an empty compartment but in a compartment where there was already one traveler. But he never did this: he preferred to aim at total solitude, and when, through no choice of his, he acquired a traveling companion, he could always console himself with the advantages of the new situation.

And so he did now. "Are you going to Rome?" he asked the newcomer, so that he could then add: Fine, let's draw the curtains, turn off the light, and nobody else will come in. But instead the man answered, "No, Genoa." It would be fine for him to get off at Genoa and leave Federico alone again, but for a few hours' journey he wouldn't want to stretch out, would probably remain awake, wouldn't allow the light to be turned off; and other people could come in at the stations along the way. Thus Federico had the disadvantages of traveling in company, with none of the corresponding advantages.

But he didn't dwell on this. His forte had always been his ability to dismiss from the area of his thoughts any aspect of reality that upset him or was of no use to him. He erased the man seated in the corner opposite his, reduced him to a shadow, a gray patch. The newspapers that both held open before their faces assisted the reciprocal impermeability. Federico could go on soaring in his amorous flight. "*Paris toujours . . .*" No one could imagine that in that sordid setting of people coming and going, driven by necessity and by forbearance, he was flying to the arms of a woman the like of Cinzia U. And to feel this sense of pride, Federico felt impelled to consider his traveling companion (at whom he had not even glanced so far) to compare—with the cruelty of the *nouveau riche*—his own fortunate state with the grayness of other existences.

The stranger, however, didn't look the least downcast. He was still a young man, sturdy, hefty; his manner was satisfied, active; he was reading a sports magazine and had a large suitcase at his side. He looked, in other words, like the agent for some firm, a commercial traveler. For a moment, Federico V. was gripped by the feeling of envy always inspired in him by people who seemed more practical and vital than he; but it was the impression of a moment, which he immediately dismissed, thinking: He's a man who travels in corrugated iron, or paints, whereas I . . . And he was seized again by that desire to sing, in a release of euphoria, clearing his mind. "*Je voyage en amour!*" he warbled in his mind, to the earlier rhythm that he felt harmonized with the race of the train, adapting words specially invented to enrage the salesman, if he could have heard him. "*Je voyage en volupté!*," underlining as much as he could the lilt and the languor of the tune, "*Je voyage toujours . . . l'hiver et l'été. . . .*" He was thus becoming more and more worked up—"*l'hiver et . . . l'été!*"—to such a degree that a smile of complete mental beatitude must have appeared on his lips. At that moment he realized the salesman was staring at him.

He promptly resumed his staid mien and concentrated on reading his paper, denying even to himself that he had been caught a moment before in such a childish mood. Childish? Why? Nothing childish about it: his journey put him in a propitious condition of spirit, a condition characteristic, in fact, of the mature man, of the man who knows the good and the evil of life and is now preparing himself to enjoy, deservedly, the good. Serene, his conscience perfectly at peace, he leafed through the illustrated weeklies, shattered images of a fast, frantic life, in which he sought some of the same things that moved him. Soon he discovered that the magazines didn't interest him in the least, mere scribbles of immediacy, of the life that flows on the surface. His impatience was voyaging through loftier heavens. *"L'hiver et . . . l'été!"* Now it was time to settle down to sleep.

He received an unexpected satisfaction: the salesman had fallen asleep sitting up, without changing position, the newspaper in his lap. Federico considered people who were capable of sleeping in a seated position with a sense of estrangement that didn't even manage to be envy: for him, sleeping on the train involved an elaborate procedure, a detailed ritual, but this, too, was precisely the arduous pleasure of his journeys.

First, he had to take off his good trousers and put on an old pair, so he wouldn't arrive all rumpled. The operation would take place in the W.C.; but before—to have greater freedom of movement—it was best to change his shoes for slippers. From his bag Federico took out his old trousers and the slipper bag, took off his shoes, put on the slippers, hid the shoes under the seat, went to the W.C. to change his trousers. *"Je voyage toujours!"* He came back, arranged his good trousers on the rack so they would keep their crease. *"Trallala-la-la!"* He placed the pillow at the end of the seat toward the corridor, because it was better to hear the sudden opening of the door above your head than to be struck by it visually as you suddenly opened your eyes. *"Du voyage, je sais tout!"* At the other end of the seat he put a newspaper, because he didn't lie down barefoot, but kept his slippers on. He hung his jacket from a hook over the pillow, and in one pocket he put his change purse and his money clip, which would have pressed against his leg if left in his trouser pocket. But he kept his ticket in the little pocket below his belt. *"Je sais bien voyager. . . ."* He replaced his good sweater, so as not to wrinkle it, with an old one; he would change his shirt in the morning.

The salesman, waking when Federico came back into the compartment, had followed his maneuvering as if not completely understanding what was going on. *"Jusqu'à mon amour . . ."* He took off his tie and hung it up, took the celluloid stiffeners from his shirt collar and put them in a pocket of his jacket, along with his money. *". . . j'arrive avec le train!"* He took off his suspenders (like all men devoted to an elegance not merely external, he wore suspenders) and his garters; he undid the top button of his trousers so they wouldn't be too tight over the belly. *"Trallala-la-la!"* He didn't put the jacket on again over his old pullover, but his overcoat instead, after having taken his house keys from the pocket; he left the precious token, though, with the heart-rending fetishism of a child who puts his favorite toy under the pillow. He buttoned up the overcoat completely, turned up the collar; if he was careful, he could sleep in it without leaving a wrinkle. *"Maintenant voilà!"* Sleeping on the train meant waking with your hair all disheveled and maybe finding yourself in the station without even the time to comb it; so he pulled a beret all the way down on his head. *"Je suis prêt, alors!"* He swayed across the compartment in the overcoat, which, worn without a jacket, hung on him like a priestly vestment; he drew the curtains across the door, pulling them until the metallic buttons reached the leather buttonholes. With a gesture toward his companion, he asked permission to turn off the light; the salesman was sleeping. He turned the light off; in the bluish penumbra of the little safety light, he moved just enough to close the curtains at the window, or, rather, to draw them almost closed: here he always left a crack open: in the morning he liked to have a ray of sunshine in his bedroom. One more operation: wind his watch. There, now he could go to bed. With one bound, he had flung himself horizontally on the seat, on his side, the overcoat smooth, his legs bent, hands in his pockets, token in his hand, his feet—still in his slippers—on the newspaper, nose against the pillow, beret over his eyes. Now, with a deliberate relaxation of all his feverish inner activity, a vague anticipation of tomorrow, he would fall asleep.

The conductor's curt intrusion (he opened the door with a yank, with confident hand unbuttoned both curtains in a single movement as he raised his other hand to turn on the light) was foreseen. Federico, however, preferred not to wait for it: if the man arrived before he had fallen asleep, fine; if his first sleep had already begun, a habitual and anonymous appearance like the conductor's interrupted it only for a few seconds, just as a sleeper in the country wakes at the cry of a nocturnal bird but then rolls over as if he hadn't waked at all. Federico had the ticket ready in his pocket and held it out, not getting up, almost not opening his eyes, his hand remaining open until he felt the ticket again between his fingers; he pocketed it and would immediately have fallen back to sleep if he hadn't been obliged to perform an operation that nullified all his earlier effort at immobility: namely, to get up and fasten the curtains again. On this trip he was still awake, and the ticket check lasted a bit longer than usual, because the salesman, caught in his sleep, took a while to get his bearings and find his ticket. He doesn't have prompt reflexes like mine, Federico thought, and took the opportunity to overwhelm him with new variations of his imaginary song. "*Je voyage l'amour . . .*" he crooned. The idea of using the verb *voyager* transitively gave him the sense of fullness that poetic inspiration, even the slightest, gives, and the satisfaction of having finally found an expression adequate to his spiritual state. "*Je voyage amour! Je voyage liberté! Jour et nuit je cours . . . pars les chemins-de-fer. . . .*"

The compartment was again in darkness. The train devoured its invisible road. Could Federico ask more of life? From such bliss to sleep, the transition is brief. Federico dozed off as if sinking into a pit of feathers. Five or six minutes only: then he woke. He was hot, all in a sweat. The coaches were already heated, since it was well into autumn, but he, recalling the cold he had felt on his previous trip, had thought to lie down in his overcoat. He rose, took it off, flung it over himself like a blanket, leaving his shoulders and chest free but still trying to spread it out so as not to make ugly wrinkles. He turned onto his other side. The sweat had spread over his body a network of itching. He unbuttoned his shirt, scratched his chest, scratched one leg. The constricted condition of his body that he now felt evoked thoughts of physical freedom, the sea, nakedness, swimming, running, and all this culminated in the embracing of Cinzia, the sum of the good of existence. And there, half asleep, he could no longer distinguish present discomforts from the yearned-for good; he had everything at once; he writhed in an uneasiness that presupposed and almost contained every possible well-being. He fell asleep again.

The loudspeakers of the stations that woke him every so often are not as disagreeable as many people suppose. Waking and knowing at once where you are offers two different possibilities of satisfaction: you can think, if the station is farther along than you imagined: How much I've slept! How far I've gone without realizing it! Or, if the station is way behind: Good, now I have plenty of time to fall asleep again and continue sleeping without any concern.

Now he was in the second of these situations. The salesman was there, now also stretched out asleep, softly snoring. Federico was still warm. He rose, half-sleeping, groped for the regulator of the electric heating system, found it on the wall opposite his, just above the head of his traveling companion, extended his hands, balancing on one foot because one of his slippers had come off, and angrily turned the dial to "Low." The salesman had to open his eyes at that moment and see the clawing hand over his head: he gulped, swallowed saliva, then sank back into his haze. Federico flung himself down. The electric regulator let out a hum, a red light came on, as if it were trying to explain, to start a dialogue. Federico impatiently waited for the heat to be dispelled; he rose to lower the window a crack, but since the train was now moving very fast, he felt cold and closed it again. He shifted the regulator toward "Automatic." His face on the amorous pillow, he lay for a while listening to the buzzes of the regulator like mysterious messages from ultraterrestrial worlds. The train was traveling over the earth, surmounted by endless spaces, and in all the universe he and he alone was the man who was speeding toward Cinzia U.

The next awakening was at the cry of a coffee vendor in the Stazione Principe, Genoa. The salesman had vanished. Carefully, Federico stopped up the gaps in the wall of curtains, and listened with apprehension to every footstep approaching along the passage, to every opening of a door. No, nobody came in. But at Genoa-Brignole, a hand opened a breach, groped, tried to part the curtains, failed; a human form appeared, crouching, and cried in dialect toward the corridor, "Come on! It's empty here!" A heavy shuffling of boots replied, with scattered voices, and four Alpine soldiers entered the darkness of the compartment and almost sat down on top of Federico. As they bent over him, as if over an unknown animal—"Oh! Who's this here?"—he pulled himself up abruptly on his arms and confronted them: "Aren't there any other compartments?" "No. All full," they answered, "but never mind. We'll all sit over on this side. Stay comfortable." They seemed intimidated, but actually they were simply accustomed to curt manners and paid no attention to anything; brawling, they flung themselves on the other seat. "Are you going far?" Federico asked, meeker now, from his pillow. No, they were getting off at one of the first stations. "And where are you going?" "To Rome." "Madonna! All the way to Rome!" Their tone of amazed compassion was transformed, in Federico's heart, into a heroic, melting pride.

And so the journey continued. "Could you turn off the light?" They turned it off, and remained faceless in the dark, noisy, cumbersome, shoulder to shoulder. One raised a curtain at the window and peered out: it was a moonlit night. Lying down, Federico saw only the sky and now and then the row of lights of a little station that dazzled his eyes and cast a rake of shadows on the ceiling. The *alpini* were rough country boys, going home on leave; they never stopped talking loud and hailing one another, and at times in the darkness they punched and slapped one another, except one of them who was sleeping and another who coughed. They spoke a murky dialect. Federico could grasp words now and then—talk about the barracks, the brothel. For some reason, he felt he didn't hate them. Now he was with them, almost one of them, and he identified with them for the pleasure of then imagining himself tomorrow at the side of Cinzia U., feeling the dizzying, sudden shift of fate. But this was not to belittle them, as with the stranger earlier; now he remained obscurely on their side; their unaware blessing accompanied him toward Cinzia; in everything that was most remote from her lay the value of having her, the sense of his being the one who had her.

Now Federico's arm was numb. He lifted it, shook it; the numbness wouldn't go away, turned into pain; the pain turned into slow well-being as he flapped his bent arm in the air. The *alpini*, all four of them, sat there staring at him, mouths agape. "What's come over him? . . . He's dreaming. . . . Hey, what are you doing? . . ." Then, with youthful fickleness, they went back to teasing one another. Federico now tried to revive the circulation in one leg, putting his foot on the floor and stamping hard.

Between dozing and clowning, an hour went by. And he didn't feel he was their enemy; perhaps he was no one's enemy; perhaps he had become a good man. He didn't hate them even when, a little before their station, they went out, leaving the door and the curtains wide open. He got up, barricaded himself again, savored once more the pleasure of solitude, but with no bitterness toward anyone.

Now his legs were cold. He pushed the cuffs of his trousers inside his socks, but he was still cold. He wrapped the folds of his overcoat around his legs. Now his stomach and shoulders were cold. He turned the regulator up almost to "High," tucked himself in again, pretended not to notice that the overcoat was getting ugly creases though he felt them under him. Now he was ready to renounce everything for his immediate comfort; the awareness of being good to his neighbor drove him to be good to himself and, in this general indulgence, to find once more the road to sleep.

From now on the awakenings were intermittent and mechanical. The entrances of the conductor, with his practiced movement in opening the curtains, were easily distinguishable from the uncertain attempts of the night travelers who had got on at an intermediate station and were bewildered at finding a series of compartments with the curtains drawn. Equally professional but more brusque and grim was the appearance of the policeman, who abruptly turned on the light in the sleeper's face, examined him, turned it off, and went out in silence, leaving behind him a prison chill.

Then a man came in, at some station buried in the night. Federico became aware of him when he was already huddled in one corner, and from the damp odor of his coat realized that outside it was raining. When he woke again the man had vanished, at God knows what other invisible station, and for Federico he had been only a shadow smelling of rain, with heavy respiration.

He was cold; he turned the regulator all the way to "High," then stuck his hand under the seat to feel the warmth rise. He felt nothing; he groped there; everything must have been cut off. He put his overcoat on again, then removed it; he hunted for his good sweater, took off the old one, put on the good one, put the old one on over it, put the overcoat on again, huddled down, and tried to achieve once more the sensation of fullness that earlier had led him to sleep; but he couldn't manage to recall anything, and when he remembered the song he was already sleeping, and that rhythm continued cradling him triumphantly in his sleep.

The first morning light came through the cracks like the cries of "Hot coffee!" and "Newspapers!" at a station perhaps still in Tuscany, or at the very beginning of Latium. It wasn't raining; beyond the damp windows the sky already displayed a southern indifference to autumn. The desire for something hot, and also the automatic reaction of the city man who begins all his mornings by glancing at the newspapers, acted on Federico's reflexes; and he felt that he should rush to the window and buy coffee or the paper or both. But he succeeded so well in convincing himself that he was still asleep and hadn't heard anything that this persuasion still held when the compartment was invaded by the usual people from Civitavecchia who take the early-morning trains into Rome. And the best part of his sleep, that of the first hours of daylight, had almost no breaks.

When he really did wake up, he was dazzled by the light that came in through the panes, now without curtains. On the seat opposite him a row of people were lined up, including even a little boy on a fat woman's lap, and a man was seated on Federico's own seat, in the space left free by his bent legs. The men had various faces but all had something vaguely bureaucratic about them, with the one possible variant of an air-force officer in a uniform laden with ribbons; it was also obvious that the women were going to call on relatives who worked in some government office. In any case, these were people going to Rome to deal with red tape for themselves or for others. And all of them, some looking up from the conservative newspaper *Il Tempo*, observed Federico stretched out there at the level of their knees, shapeless, bundled into that overcoat, without feet, like a seal; as he was detaching himself from the saliva-stained pillow, disheveled, the beret on the back of his head, one cheek marked by the wrinkles in the pillowcase; as he got up, stretched with awkward, seal-like movements, gradually rediscovering the use of his legs, slipping the slippers on the wrong feet, and now unbuttoning and scratching himself between the double sweaters and the rumpled shirt, while running his still sticky eyes over them and smiling.

At the window, the broad Roman *campagna* spread out. Federico sat there for a moment, his hands on his knees, still smiling; then, with a gesture, he asked permission to take the newspaper from the knees of the man facing him. He glanced at the headlines, felt as always the sense of finding himself in a remote country, looked olympically at the arches of the aqueducts that sped past outside the window, returned the newspaper, and got up to look for his toilet kit in his suitcase.

At the Stazione Termini the first to jump down from the car, fresh as a daisy, was Federico. He was clasping the token in his hand. In the niches between the columns and the newsstands, the gray telephones were waiting only for him. He put the token in the slot, dialed the number, listened with beating heart to the distant ring, heard Cinzia's "Hello . . ." still suffused with sleep and soft warmth, and he was already in the tension of their days together, in the desperate battle against the hours; and he realized he would never manage to tell her anything of the significance of that night, which he now sensed was fading, like every perfect night of love, at the cruel explosion of day.

Translated from the Italian by William Weaver

Albert Camus

· · · · · · · · · · · · · · · · · · · ·

THE ADULTEROUS
WOMAN

A house fly had been circling for the last few minutes in the bus, though the windows were closed. An odd sight here, it had been silently flying back and forth on tired wings. Janine lost track of it, then saw it light on her husband's motionless hand. The weather was cold. The fly shuddered with each gust of sandy wind that scratched against the windows. In the meagre light of the winter morning, with a great fracas of sheet metal and axles, the vehicle was rolling, pitching, and making hardly any progress. Janine looked at her husband. With wisps of greying hair growing low on a narrow forehead, a broad nose, a flabby mouth, Marcel looked like a pouting faun. At each hollow in the roadway she felt him jostle against her. Then his heavy torso would slump back on his wide-spread legs and he would become inert again and absent, with vacant stare. Nothing about him seemed active but his thick hairless hands, made even shorter by the flannel underwear extending below his cuffs and covering his wrists. His hands were holding so tight to a little canvas suitcase set between his knees that they appeared not to feel the fly's halting progress.

Suddenly the wind was distinctly heard to howl and the gritty fog surrounding the bus became even thicker. The sand now struck the windows in packets as if hurled by invisible hands. The fly shook a chilled wing, flexed its legs, and took flight. The bus slowed and seemed on the point of stopping. But the wind apparently died down, the fog lifted slightly, and the vehicle resumed speed. Gaps of light opened up in the dust-drowned landscape. Two or three frail, whitened palm trees which seemed cut out of metal flashed into sight in the window only to disappear the next moment.

'What a country!' Marcel said.

The bus was full of Arabs pretending to sleep, shrouded in their burnouses. Some had folded their legs on the seat and swayed more than the others in the car's motion. Their silence and impassivity began to weigh upon Janine; it seemed to her as if she had been travelling for days with that mute escort. Yet the bus had left only at dawn from the end of the railroad line and for two hours in the cold morning it had been advancing on a stony, desolate plateau which, in the beginning at least, extended its straight lines all the way to reddish horizons.

But the wind had risen and gradually swallowed up the vast expanse. From that moment on, the passengers had seen nothing more; one after another, they had ceased talking and were silently progressing in a sort of sleepless night, occasionally wiping their lips and eyes irritated by the sand that filtered into the car.

'Janine!' She gave a start at her husband's call. Once again she thought how ridiculous that name was for someone tall and sturdy like her. Marcel wanted to know where his sample-case was. With her foot she explored the empty space under the seat and encountered an object which she decided must be it. She could not stoop over without gasping somewhat. Yet in school she had won the first prize in gymnastics and hadn't known what it was to be winded. Was that so long ago? Twenty-five years. Twenty-five years were nothing, for it seemed to her only yesterday when she was hesitating between an independent life and marriage, just yesterday when she was thinking anxiously of the time she might be growing old alone. She was not alone and that law student who always wanted to be with her was now at her side. She had eventually accepted him although he was a little shorter than she and she didn't much like his eager, sharp laugh or his black protruding eyes. But she liked his courage in facing up to life, which he shared with all the French of this country. She also liked his crestfallen look when events or men failed to live up to his expectations. Above all, she liked being loved, and he had showered her with attentions. By so often making her aware that she existed for him he made her exist in reality. No, she was not alone. . . .

The bus, with many loud honks, was ploughing its way through invisible obstacles. Inside the car, however, no one stirred. Janine suddenly felt someone staring at her and turned towards the seat across the aisle. He was not an Arab, and she was surprised not to have noticed him from the beginning. He was wearing the uniform of the French regiments of the Sahara and an unbleached linen cap above his tanned face, long and pointed like a jackal's. His grey eyes were examining her with a sort of glum disapproval, in a fixed stare. She suddenly blushed and turned back to her husband, who was still looking straight ahead in the fog and wind. She snuggled down in her coat. But she could still see the French soldier, long and thin, so thin in his fitted tunic that he seemed constructed of a dry, friable material, a mixture of sand and bone. Then it was that she saw the thin hands and burned faces of the Arabs in front of her and noticed that they seemed to have plenty of room, despite their ample garments, on the seat where she and her husband felt wedged in. She pulled her coat around her knees. Yet she wasn't so fat—tall and well-rounded rather, plump and still desirable, as she was well aware when men looked at her, with her rather childish face, her bright, naïve eyes contrasting with this big body she knew to be warm and inviting.

No, nothing had happened as she had expected. When Marcel had wanted to take her along on his trip she had protested. For some time he had been thinking of this trip—since the end of the war, to be precise, when business had returned to normal. Before the war the small dry-goods business he had taken over from his parents on giving up his study of law had provided a fairly good living. On the coast the years of youth can be happy ones. But he didn't much like physical effort and very soon had given up taking her to the beaches. The little car took them out of town solely for the Sunday-afternoon ride. The rest of the time he preferred his shop full of multi-coloured piece-goods shaded by the arcades of this half-native, half-European quarter. Above the shop they lived in three rooms furnished with Arab hangings and furniture from the Galerie Barbès. They had not had children. The years had passed in the semi-darkness behind the half-closed shutters. Summer, the beaches, excursions, the mere sight of the sky were things of the past. Nothing seemed to interest Marcel but business. She felt she had discovered his true passion to be money, and, without really knowing why, she didn't like that. After all, it was to her advantage. Far from being miserly, he was generous, especially where she was concerned. 'If something happened to me,' he used to say, 'you'd be provided for.' And, in fact, it is essential to provide for one's needs. But for all the rest, for what is not the most elementary need, how to provide? This is what she felt vaguely, at infrequent intervals. Meanwhile she helped Marcel keep his books and occasionally substituted for him in the shop. Summer was always the hardest, when the heat stifled even the sweet sensation of boredom.

Suddenly, in summer as it happened, the war, Marcel called up then rejected on grounds of health, the scarcity of piece-goods, business at a standstill, the streets empty and hot. If something happened now, she would no longer be provided for. This is why, as soon as piece-goods came back on the market, Marcel had thought of covering the villages of the upper plateaux and of the south himself in order to do without a middleman and sell directly to the Arab merchants. He had wanted to take her along. She knew that travel was difficult, she had trouble breathing, and she would have preferred staying at home. But he was obstinate and she had accepted because it would have taken too much energy to refuse. Here they were and, truly, nothing was like what she had imagined. She had feared the heat, the swarms of flies, the filthy hotels reeking of aniseed. She had not thought of the cold, of the biting wind, of these semi-polar plateaux cluttered with moraines. She had dreamed too of palm trees and soft sand. Now she saw that the desert was not that at all, but merely stone, stone everywhere, in the sky full of nothing but stone-dust, rasping and cold, as on the ground, where nothing grew among the stones except dry grasses.

The bus stopped abruptly. The driver shouted a few words in that language she had heard all her life without ever understanding it. 'What's the matter?' Marcel asked. The driver, in French this time, said that the sand must have clogged the carburettor, and again Marcel cursed this country. The driver laughed hilariously and asserted that it was nothing, that he would clean the carburettor and they'd be off again. He opened the door and the cold wind blew into the bus, lashing their faces with a myriad grains of sand. All the Arabs silently plunged their noses into their burnouses and huddled up. 'Shut the door,' Marcel shouted. The driver laughed as he came back to the door. Without hurrying, he took some tools from under the dashboard, then, tiny in the fog, again disappeared ahead without closing the door. Marcel sighed. 'You may be sure he's never seen a motor in his life.' 'Oh, be quiet!' said Janine. Suddenly she gave a start. On the shoulder of the road close to the bus, draped forms were standing still. Under the burnous's hood and behind a rampart of veils, only their eyes were visible. Mute, come from nowhere, they were staring at the travellers. 'Shepherds,' Marcel said.

Inside the car there was total silence. All the passengers, heads lowered, seemed to be listening to the voice of the wind loosed across these endless plateaux. Janine was all of a sudden struck by the almost complete absence of luggage. At the end of the railroad line the driver had hoisted their trunk and a few bundles on to the roof. In the racks inside the bus could be seen nothing but gnarled sticks and shopping-baskets. All these people of the South apparently were travelling empty-handed.

But the driver was coming back, still brisk. His eyes alone were laughing above the veils with which he too had masked his face. He announced that they would soon be under way. He closed the door, the wind became silent, and the rain of sand on the windows could be heard better. The motor coughed and died. After having been urged at great length by the starter, it finally sparked and the driver raced it by pressing on the accelerator. With a big hiccough the bus started off. From the ragged clump of shepherds, still motionless, a hand rose and then faded into the fog behind them. Almost at once the vehicle began to bounce on the road, which had become worse. Shaken up, the Arabs constantly swayed. None the less, Janine was feeling overcome with sleep when there suddenly appeared in front of her a little yellow box filled with lozenges. The jackal-soldier was smiling at her. She hesitated, took one, and thanked him. The jackal pocketed the box and simultaneously swallowed his smile. Now he was staring at the road, straight in front of him. Janine turned towards Marcel and saw only the solid back of his neck. Through the window he was watching the denser fog rising from the crumbly embankment.

They had been travelling for hours and fatigue had extinguished all life in the bus when shouts burst forth outside. Children wearing burnouses, whirling like tops, leaping, clapping their hands, were running around the bus. It was now going down a long street lined with low houses; they were entering the oasis. The wind was still blowing, but the walls intercepted the grains of sand which had previously cut off the light. Yet the sky was still cloudy. Amidst shouts, in a great screeching of brakes, the bus stopped in front of the adobe arcades of a hotel with dirty windows. Janine got out and, once on the pavement, staggered. Above the houses she could see a slim yellow minaret. On her left rose the first palm trees of the oasis, and she would have liked to go towards them. But although it was close to noon, the cold was bitter; the wind made her shiver. She turned towards Marcel and saw the soldier coming towards her. She expected him to smile or salute. He passed without looking at her and disappeared. Marcel was busy getting down the trunk of piece-goods, a black foot-locker perched on the bus's roof. It would not be easy. The driver was the only one to take care of the luggage and he had already stopped, standing on the roof, to hold forth to the circle of burnouses gathered around the bus. Janine, surrounded with faces that seemed cut out of bone and leather, besieged by guttural shouts, suddenly became aware of her fatigue. 'I'm going in,' she said to Marcel, who was shouting impatiently at the driver.

She entered the hotel. The manager, a thin, laconic Frenchman, came to meet her. He led her to a second-floor balcony overlooking the street and into a room which seemed to have but an iron bed, a white-enamelled chair, an uncurtained wardrobe, and, behind a rush screen, a washbasin covered with fine sand-dust. When the manager had closed the door, Janine felt the cold coming from the bare, whitewashed walls. She didn't know where to put her bag, where to put herself. She had either to lie down or to remain standing, and to shiver in either case. She remained standing, holding her bag and staring at a sort of window-slit that opened on to the sky near the ceiling. She was waiting, but she didn't know for what. She was aware only of her solitude, and of the penetrating cold, and of a greater weight in the region of her heart. She was in fact dreaming, almost deaf to the sounds rising from the street along with Marcel's vocal outbursts, more aware on the other hand of that sound of a river coming from the window-slit and caused by the wind in the palm trees, so close now, it seemed to her. Then the wind seemed to increase and the gentle ripple of waters became a hissing of waves. She imagined, beyond the walls, a sea of erect, flexible palm trees unfurling in the storm. Nothing was like what she had expected, but those invisible waves refreshed her tired eyes. She was standing, heavy, with dangling arms, slightly stooped, as the cold climbed her thick legs. She was dreaming of the erect and flexible palm trees and of the girl she had once been.

After having washed, they went down to the dining-room. On the bare walls had been painted camels and palm trees drowned in a sticky background of pink and lavender. The arcaded windows let in a meagre light. Marcel questioned the hotel manager about the merchants. Then an elderly Arab wearing a military decoration on his tunic served them. Marcel, preoccupied, tore his bread into little pieces. He kept his wife from drinking water. 'It hasn't been boiled. Take wine.' She didn't like that, for wine made her sleepy. Besides, there was pork on the menu. 'They don't eat it because of the Koran. But the Koran didn't know that well-done pork doesn't cause illness. We French know how to cook. What are you thinking about?' Janine was not thinking of anything, or perhaps of that victory of the cooks over the prophets. But she had to hurry. They were to leave the next morning for still farther south; that afternoon they had to see all the important merchants. Marcel urged the elderly Arab to hurry the coffee. He nodded without smiling and pattered out. 'Slowly in the morning, not too fast in the afternoon,' Marcel said, laughing. Yet eventually the coffee came. They barely took time to swallow it and went out into the dusty, cold street. Marcel called a young Arab to help him carry the trunk, but as a matter of principle quibbled about the payment. His opinion, which he once more expressed to Janine, was in fact based on the vague principle that they always asked for twice as much in the hope of settling for a quarter of the amount. Janine, ill at ease, followed the two trunk-bearers. She had put on a wool dress under her heavy coat and would have liked to take up less space. The pork, although well done, and the small quantity of wine she had drunk also bothered her somewhat.

They walked along a diminutive public garden planted with dusty trees. They encountered Arabs who stepped out of their way without seeming to see them, wrapping themselves in their burnouses. Even when they were wearing rags, she felt they had a look of dignity unknown to the Arabs of her town. Janine followed the trunk, which made a way for her through the crowd. They went through the gate in an earthen rampart and emerged on a little square planted with the same mineral trees and bordered on the far side, where it was widest, with arcades and shops. But they stopped in the square itself in front of a small construction shaped like an artillery shell and painted chalky blue. Inside, in the single room lighted solely by the entrance, an old Arab with a white moustache stood behind a shiny plank. He was serving tea, raising and lowering the teapot over three tiny multi-coloured glasses. Before they could make out anything else in the darkness, the cool scent of mint tea greeted Marcel and Janine at the door. Marcel had barely crossed the threshold and dodged the garlands of pewter tea-pots, cups and trays, and the postcard displays when he was up against the counter. Janine stayed at the door. She stepped a little aside so as not to cut off the light. At that moment she perceived in the darkness behind the old merchant two Arabs smiling at them, seated on the bulging sacks that filled the back of the shop. Red-and-black rugs and embroidered scarves hung on the walls; the floor was cluttered with sacks and little boxes filled with aromatic seeds. On the counter, beside a sparkling pair of brass scales and an old yardstick with figures effaced, stood a row of loaves of sugar. One of them had been unwrapped from its coarse blue paper and cut into on top. The smell of wool and spices in the room became apparent behind the scent of tea when the old merchant set down the teapot and said good day.

Marcel talked rapidly in the low voice he assumed when talking business. Then he opened the trunk, exhibited the wools and silks, pushed back the scale and yardstick to spread out his merchandise in front of the old merchant. He got excited, raised his voice, laughed nervously, like a woman who wants to make an impression and is not sure of herself. Now, with hands spread wide, he was going through the gestures of selling and buying. The old man shook his head, passed the tea tray to the two Arabs behind him, and said just a few words that seemed to discourage Marcel. He picked up his goods, piled them back into the trunk, then wiped an imaginary sweat from his forehead. He called the little porter and they started off towards the arcades. In the first shop, although the merchant began by exhibiting the same Olympian manner, they were a little luckier. 'They think they're God almighty,' Marcel said, 'but they're in business too! Life is hard for everyone.'

Janine followed without answering. The wind had almost ceased. The sky was clearing in spots. A cold, harsh light came from the deep holes that opened up in the thickness of the clouds. They had now left the square. They were walking in narrow streets along earthen walls over which hung rotted December roses or, from time to time, a pomegranate, dried and wormy. An odour of dust and cof-fee, the smoke of a wood fire, the smell of stone and of sheep permeated this quarter. The shops, hollowed out of the walls, were far from one another; Janine felt her feet getting heavier. But her husband was gradually becoming more cheerful. He was beginning to sell and was feeling more kindly; he called Janine 'Baby'; the trip would not be wasted. 'Of course,' Janine said mechanically, 'it's better to deal directly with them.'

They came back by another street, towards the centre. It was late in the after-noon; the sky was now almost completely clear. They stopped in the square. Marcel rubbed his hands and looked affectionately at the trunk in front of them.

'Look,' said Janine. From the other end of the square was coming a tall Arab, thin, vigorous, wearing a sky-blue burnous, soft brown boots and gloves and bearing his bronzed aquiline face loftily. Nothing but the *chèche* that he was wearing swathed as a turban distinguished him from those French officers in charge of native affairs whom Janine had occasionally admired. He was advancing steadily towards them, but seemed to be looking beyond their group as he slowly removed the glove from one hand. 'Well,' said Marcel as he shrugged his shoulders, 'there's one who thinks he's a general.' Yes, all of them here had that look of pride; but this one, really, was going too far. Although they were surrounded by the empty space of the square, he was walking straight towards the trunk, without seeing it, without seeing them. Then the distance separating them decreased rapidly and the Arab was upon them when Marcel suddenly seized the handle of the foot-locker and pulled it out of the way. The Arab passed without seeming to notice anything and headed with the same regular step towards the ramparts. Janine looked at her husband; he had his crestfallen look. 'They think they can get away with anything now,' he said. Janine did not reply. She loathed that Arab's stupid arrogance and suddenly felt unhappy. She wanted to leave and thought of her little flat. The idea of going back to the hotel, to that icy room, discouraged her. It suddenly occurred to her that the manager had advised her to climb up to the terrace around the fort to see the desert. She said this to Marcel and that he could leave the trunk at the hotel. But he was tired and wanted to sleep a little before dinner. 'Please,' said Janine. He looked at her, suddenly attentive. 'Of course, my dear,' he said.

She waited for him in the street in front of the hotel. The white-robed crowd was becoming larger and larger. Not a single woman could be seen, and it seemed to Janine that she had never seen so many men. Yet none of them looked at her. Some of them, without appearing to see her, slowly turned towards her that thin, tanned face that made them all look alike to her, the face of the French soldier in the bus and that of the gloved Arab, a face both shrewd and proud. They turned that face towards the foreign woman, they didn't see her, and then, light and silent, they walked around her as she stood there with swelling ankles. And her discomfort, her need of getting away increased. 'Why did I come?' But already Marcel was coming back.

When they climbed the stairs to the fort, it was five o'clock. The wind had died down altogether. The sky, completely clear, was now periwinkle blue. The cold, now drier, made their cheeks smart. Half-way up the stairs an old Arab, stretched out against the wall, asked them if they wanted a guide, but didn't budge, as if he had been sure of their refusal in advance. The stairs were long and steep despite several landings of packed earth. As they climbed, the space widened and they rose into an ever broader light, cold and dry, in which every sound from the oasis reached them pure and distinct. The bright air seemed to vibrate around them with a vibration increasing in length as they advanced, as if their progress struck from the crystal of light a sound-wave that kept spreading out. And as soon as they reached the terrace and their gaze was lost in the vast horizon beyond the palm grove, it seemed to Janine that the whole sky rang with a single short and piercing note, whose echoes gradually filled the space above her, then suddenly died and left her silently facing the limitless expanse.

From east to west, in fact, her gaze swept slowly, without encountering a single obstacle, along a perfect curve. Beneath her, the blue-and-white terraces of the Arab town overlapped one another, splattered with the dark-red spots of peppers drying in the sun. Not a soul could be seen, but from the inner courts, together with the aroma of roasting coffee, there rose laughing voices or incomprehensible stamping of feet. Farther off, the palm grove, divided into uneven squares by clay walls, rustled its upper foliage in a wind that could not be felt up on the terrace. Still farther off and all the way to the horizon extended the ochre-and-grey realm of stones, in which no life was visible. At some distance from the oasis, however, near the wadi that bordered the palm grove on the west could be seen broad black tents. All around them a flock of motionless dromedaries, tiny at that distance, formed against the grey ground the black signs of a strange handwriting, the meaning of which had to be deciphered. Above the desert, the silence was as vast as the space.

Janine, leaning her whole body against the parapet, was speechless, unable to tear herself away from the void opening before her. Beside her, Marcel was getting restless. He was cold; he wanted to go back down. What was there to see here, after all? But she could not take her gaze from the horizon. Over yonder, still farther south, at that point where sky and earth met in a pure line—over yonder it suddenly seemed there was awaiting her something of which, though it had always been lacking, she had never been aware until now. In the advancing afternoon the light relaxed and softened; it was passing from the crystalline to the liquid. Simultaneously, in the heart of a woman brought there by pure chance a knot tightened by the years, habit, and boredom was slowly loosening. She was looking at the nomads' encampment. She had not even seen the men living in it; nothing was stirring among the black tents, and yet she could think only of them whose existence she had barely known until this day. Homeless, cut off from the world, they were a handful wandering over the vast territory she could see, which however was but a paltry part of an even greater expanse whose dizzying course stopped only thousands of miles farther south, where the first river finally waters the forest. Since the beginning of time, on the dry earth of this limitless land scraped to the bone, a few men had been ceaselessly trudging, possessing nothing but serving no one, poverty-stricken but free lords of a strange kingdom. Janine did not know why this thought filled her with such a sweet, vast melancholy that it closed her eyes. She knew that this kingdom had been eternally promised her and yet that it would never be hers, never again, except in this fleeting moment perhaps when she opened her eyes again on the suddenly motionless sky and on its waves of steady light, while the voices rising from the Arab town suddenly fell silent. It seemed to her that the world's course had just stopped and that, from that moment on, no one would ever age any more or die. Everywhere, henceforth, life was suspended—except in her heart, where, at the same moment, someone was weeping with affliction and wonder.

But the light began to move; the sun, clear and devoid of warmth, went down towards the west, which became slightly pink, while a grey wave took shape in the east ready to roll slowly over the vast expanse. A first dog barked and its distant bark rose in the now even colder air. Janine noticed that her teeth were chattering. 'We are catching our death of cold,' Marcel said. 'You're a fool.

Let's go back.' But he took her hand awkwardly. Docile now, she turned away from the parapet and followed him. Without moving, the old Arab on the stairs watched them go down towards the town. She walked along without seeing anyone, bent under a tremendous and sudden fatigue, dragging her body, the weight of which now seemed to her unbearable. Her exaltation had left her. Now she felt too tall, too thick, too white too for this world she had just entered. A child, the girl, the dry man, the furtive jackal were the only creatures who could silently walk that earth. What would she do there henceforth except to drag herself towards sleep, towards death?

She dragged herself, in fact, towards the restaurant with a husband suddenly taciturn unless he was telling how tired he was, while she was struggling weakly against a cold, aware of a fever rising within her. Then she dragged herself towards her bed, where Marcel came to join her and put the light out at once without asking anything of her. The room was frigid. Janine felt the cold creeping up while the fever was increasing. She breathed with difficulty, her blood pumped without warming her; a sort of fear grew within her. She turned over and the old iron bedstead groaned under her weight. No, she didn't want to fall ill. Her husband was already asleep; she too had to sleep; it was essential. The muffled sounds of the town reached her through the window-slit. With a nasal twang old phonographs in the Moorish cafés ground out tunes she recognized vaguely; they reached her borne on the sound of a slow-moving crowd. She must sleep. But she was counting black tents; behind her eyelids motionless camels were grazing; immense solitudes were whirling within her. Yes, why had she come? She fell asleep on that question.

She awoke a little later. The silence around her was absolute. But, on the edges of town, hoarse dogs were howling in the soundless night. Janine shivered. She turned over, felt her husband's hard shoulder against hers, and suddenly, half asleep, huddled against him. She was drifting on the surface of sleep without sinking in and she clung to that shoulder with unconscious eagerness as her safest haven. She was talking, but no sound issued from her mouth. She was talking, but she herself hardly heard what she was saying. She could feel only Marcel's warmth. For more than twenty years every night thus, in his warmth, just the two of them, even when ill, even when travelling, as at present. . . . Besides, what would she have done alone at home? No child! Wasn't that what she lacked? She didn't know. She simply followed Marcel, pleased to know that someone needed her. The only joy he gave her was the knowledge that she was necessary. Probably he didn't love her. Love, even when filled with hate, doesn't have that sullen face. But what is his face like? They made love in the dark by feel, without seeing each other. Is there another love than that of darkness, a love that would cry aloud in daylight? She didn't know, but she did know that Marcel needed her and that she needed that need, that she lived on it night and day, at night especially—every night, when he didn't want to be alone, or to age or die, with that set expression he assumed which she occasionally recognized on other men's faces, the only common expression of those madmen hiding under an appearance of wisdom until the madness seizes them and hurls them desperately towards a woman's body to bury in it, without desire, everything terrifying that solitude and night reveals to them.

Marcel stirred as if to move away from her. No, he didn't love her; he was merely afraid of what was not she, and she and he should long ago have separated and slept alone until the end. But who can always sleep alone? Some men do, cut off from others by a vocation or misfortune, who go to bed every night in the same bed as death. Marcel never could do so—he above all, a weak and disarmed child always frightened by suffering, her own child indeed who needed her and who, just at that moment, let out a sort of whimper. She cuddled a little closer and put her hand on his chest. And to herself she called him with the little love-name she had once given him, which they still used from time to time without even thinking of what they were saying.

She called him with all her heart. After all, she too needed him, his strength, his little eccentricities, and she too was afraid of death. 'If I could overcome that fear, I'd be happy. . . .' Immediately, a nameless anguish seized her. She drew back from Marcel. No, she was overcoming nothing, she was not happy, she was going to die, in truth, without having been liberated. Her heart pained her; she was stifling under a huge weight that she suddenly discovered she had been dragging about for twenty years. Now she was struggling under it with all her strength. She wanted to be liberated even if Marcel, even if the others, never were! Fully awake, she sat up in bed and listened to a call that seemed very close. But from the edges of night the exhausted and yet indefatigable voices of the dogs of the oasis were all that reached her ears. A slight wind had risen and she heard its light waters flow in the palm grove. It came from the south, where desert and night mingled now under the again unchanging sky, where life stopped, where no one would ever age or die any more. Then the waters of the wind dried up and she was not even sure of having heard anything except a mute call that she could, after all, silence or notice. But never again would she know its meaning unless she responded to it at once. At once—yes, that much was certain at least!

She got up gently and stood motionless beside the bed, listening to her husband's breathing. Marcel was asleep. The next moment, the bed's warmth left her and the cold gripped her. She dressed slowly, feeling for her clothes in the faint light coming through the blinds from the street-lamps. Her shoes in her hand, she reached the door. She waited a moment more in the darkness, then gently opened the door. The knob squeaked and she stood still. Her heart was beating madly. She listened with her body tense and, reassured by the silence, turned her hand a little more. The knob's turning seemed to her interminable. At last she opened the door, slipped outside, and closed the door with the same stealth. Then, with her cheek against the wood, she waited. After a moment she made out, in the distance, Marcel's breathing. She faced about, felt the icy night air against her cheek, and ran the length of the balcony. The outer door was closed. While she was slipping the bolt, the night watchman appeared at the top of the stairs, his face blurred with sleep, and spoke to her in Arabic. 'I'll be back,' said Janine as she stepped out into the night.

Garlands of stars hung down from the black sky over the palm trees and houses. She ran along the short avenue, now empty, that led to the fort. The cold, no longer having to struggle against the sun, had invaded the night; the icy air burned her lungs. But she ran, half blind, in the darkness. At the top of the avenue, however, lights appeared, then descended towards her zigzagging. She stopped, caught the whirr of turning sprockets and, behind the enlarging lights, soon saw vast burnouses surmounting fragile bicycle wheels. The burnouses flapped against her; then three red lights sprang out of the black behind her and disappeared at once. She continued running towards the fort. Half-way up the stairs, the air burned her lungs with such cutting effect that she wanted to stop. A final burst of energy hurled her despite herself on to the terrace, against the parapet, which was now pressing her belly. She was panting and everything was hazy before her eyes. Her running had not warmed her and she was still trembling all over. But the cold air she was gulping down soon flowed evenly inside her and a spark of warmth began to glow amidst her shivers. Her eyes opened at last on the expanse of night.

Not a breath, not a sound—except at intervals the muffled crackling of stones that the cold was reducing to sand—disturbed the solitude and silence surrounding Janine. After a moment, however, it seemed to her that the sky above her was moving in a sort of slow gyration. In the vast reaches of the dry, cold night, thousands of stars were constantly appearing, and their sparkling icicles, loosened at once, began to slip gradually towards the horizon. Janine could not tear herself away from contemplating those drifting flares. She was turning with them, and the apparently stationary progress little by little identified her with the core of her being, where cold and desire were now vying with each other. Before her the stars were falling one by one and being snuffed out among the stones of the desert, and each time Janine opened a little more to the night. Breathing deeply, she forgot the cold, the dead weight of others, the craziness or stuffiness of life, the long anguish of living and dying. After so many years of mad, aimless fleeing from fear, she had come to a stop at last. At the same time, she seemed to recover her roots and the sap again rose in her body, which had ceased trembling. Her whole belly pressed against the parapet as she strained towards the moving sky; she was merely waiting for her fluttering heart to calm down and establish silence within her. The last stars of the constellations dropped their clusters a little lower on the desert horizon and became still. Then, with unbearable gentleness, the water of night began to fill Janine, drowned the cold, rose gradually from the hidden core of her being and overflowed in wave after wave, rising up even to her mouth full of moans. The next moment, the whole sky stretched out over her, fallen on her back on the cold earth.

When Janine returned to the room, with the same precautions, Marcel was not awake. But he whimpered as she got back in bed and a few seconds later sat up suddenly. He spoke and she didn't understand what he was saying. He got up, turned on the light, which blinded her. He staggered towards the washbasin and drank a long draught from the bottle of mineral water. He was about to slip between the sheets when, one knee on the bed, he looked at her without understanding. She was weeping copiously, unable to restrain herself. 'It's nothing, dear,' she said, 'it's nothing.'

Translated from the French by Justin O'Brien

Truman Capote

. . . .

CHILDREN ON THEIR
BIRTHDAYS

Yesterday afternoon the six-o'clock bus ran over Miss Bobbit. I'm not sure what there is to be said about it; after all, she was only ten years old, still I know no one of us in this town will forget her. For one thing, nothing she ever did was ordinary, not from the first time that we saw her, and that was a year ago. Miss Bobbit and her mother, they arrived on that same six-o'clock bus, the one that comes through from Mobile. It happened to be my cousin Billy Bob's birthday, and so most of the children in town were here at our house. We were sprawled on the front porch having tutti-frutti and devil cake when the bus stormed around Deadman's Curve. It was the summer that never rained; rusted dryness coated everything; sometimes when a car passed on the road, raised dust would hang in the still air an hour or more. Aunt El said if they didn't pave the highway soon she was going to move down to the seacoast; but she'd said that for such a long time. Anyway, we were sitting on the porch, tutti-frutti melting on our plates, when suddenly, just as we were wishing that something would happen, something did; for out of the red road dust appeared Miss Bobbit. A wiry little girl in a starched, lemon-colored party dress, she sassed along with a grownup mince, one hand on her hip, the other supporting a spinsterish umbrella. Her mother, lugging two cardboard valises and a wind-up victrola, trailed in the background. She was a gaunt shaggy woman with silent eyes and a hungry smile.

All the children on the porch had grown so still that when a cone of wasps started humming the girls did not set up their usual holler. Their attention was too fixed upon the approach of Miss Bobbit and her mother, who had by now reached the gate. "Begging your pardon," called Miss Bobbit in a voice that was at once silky and childlike, like a pretty piece of ribbon, and immaculately exact, like a movie-star or a schoolmarm, "but might we speak with the grownup persons of the house?" This, of course, meant Aunt El; and, at least to some degree, myself. But Billy Bob and all the other boys, no one of whom was over thirteen, followed down to the gate after us. From their faces you would have thought

184

they'd never seen a girl before. Certainly not like Miss Bobbit. As Aunt El said, whoever heard tell of a child wearing make-up? Tangee gave her lips an orange glow, her hair, rather like a costume wig, was a mass of rosy curls, and her eyes had a knowing, penciled tilt; even so, she had a skinny dignity, she was a lady, and, what is more, she looked you in the eye with manlike directness. "I'm Miss Lily Jane Bobbit, Miss Bobbit from Memphis, Tennessee," she said solemnly. The boys looked down at their toes, and, on the porch, Cora McCall, who Billy Bob was courting at the time, led the girls into a fanfare of giggles. "Country children," said Miss Bobbit with an understanding smile, and gave her parasol a saucy whirl. "My mother," and this homely woman allowed an abrupt nod to acknowledge herself, "my mother and I have taken rooms here. Would you be so kind as to point out the house? It belongs to a Mrs. Sawyer." Why, sure, said Aunt El, that's Mrs. Sawyer's, right there across the street. The only boarding house around here, it is an old tall dark place with about two dozen lightning rods scattered on the roof: Mrs. Sawyer is scared to death in a thunderstorm.

Coloring like an apple, Billy Bob said, please ma'am, it being such a hot day and all, wouldn't they rest a spell and have some tutti-frutti? and Aunt El said yes, by all means, but Miss Bobbit shook her head. "Very fattening, tutti-frutti; but *merci* you kindly," and they started across the road, the mother half-dragging her parcels in the dust. Then, and with an earnest expression, Miss Bobbit turned back; the sunflower yellow of her eyes darkened, and she rolled them slightly sideways, as if trying to remember a poem. "My mother has a disorder of the tongue, so it is necessary that I speak for her," she announced rapidly and heaved a sigh. "My mother is a very fine seamstress; she has made dresses for the society of many cities and towns, including Memphis and Tallahassee. No doubt you have noticed and admired the dress I am wearing. Every stitch of it was hand-sewn by my mother. My mother can copy any pattern, and just recently she won a twenty-five-dollar prize from the *Ladies' Home Journal.* My mother can also crochet, knit and embroider. If you want any kind of sewing done, please come to my mother. Please advise your friends and family. Thank you." And then, with a rustle and a swish, she was gone.

Cora McCall and the girls pulled their hair-ribbons nervously, suspiciously, and looked very put out and prune-faced. I'm *Miss* Bobbit, said Cora, twisting her face into an evil imitation, and I'm Princess Elizabeth, that's who I am, ha, ha, ha. Furthermore, said Cora, that dress was just as tacky as could be; personally, Cora said, all my clothes come from Atlanta; plus a pair of shoes from New York, which is not even to mention my silver turquoise ring all the way from Mexico City, Mexico. Aunt El said they ought not to behave that way about a fellow child, a stranger in the town, but the girls went on like a huddle of witches, and certain boys, the sillier ones that liked to be with the girls, joined in and said things that made Aunt El go red and declare she was going to send them all home and tell their daddies, to boot. But before she could carry forward this threat Miss Bobbit herself intervened by traipsing across the Sawyer porch, costumed in a new and startling manner.

The older boys, like Billy Bob and Preacher Star, who had sat quiet while the girls razzed Miss Bobbit, and who had watched the house into which she'd disappeared with misty, ambitious faces, they now straightened up and ambled down to the gate. Cora McCall sniffed and poked out her lower lip, but the rest of us went and sat on the steps. Miss Bobbit paid us no mind whatever. The Sawyer yard is dark with mulberry trees and it is planted with grass and sweet shrub. Sometimes after a rain you can smell the sweet shrub all the way into our house; and in the center of this yard there is a sundial which Mrs. Sawyer installed in 1912 as a memorial to her Boston bull, Sunny, who died after having lapped up a bucket of paint. Miss Bobbit pranced into the yard toting the victrola, which she put on the sundial; she wound it up, and started a record playing, and it played the Count of Luxemborg. By now it was almost nightfall, a firefly hour, blue as milkglass; and birds like arrows swooped together and swept into the folds of trees. Before storms, leaves and flowers appear to burn with a private light, color, and Miss Bobbit, got up in a little white skirt like a powder-puff and with strips of gold-glittering tinsel ribboning her hair, seemed, set against the darkening all around, to contain this illuminated quality. She held her arms arched over her head, her hands lily-limp, and stood straight up on the tips of her toes. She stood that way for a good long while, and Aunt El said it was right smart of her. Then she began to waltz around and around, and around and around she went until Aunt El said, why, she was plain dizzy from the sight. She stopped only when it was time to re-wind the victrola; and when the moon came rolling down the ridge, and the last supper bell had sounded, and all the children had gone home, and the night iris was beginning to bloom, Miss Bobbit was still there in the dark turning like a top.

We did not see her again for some time. Preacher Star came every morning to our house and stayed straight through to supper. Preacher is a rail-thin boy with a butchy shock of red hair; he has eleven brothers and sisters, and even they are afraid of him, for he has a terrible temper, and is famous in these parts for his green-eyed meanness: last fourth of July he whipped Ollie Overton so bad that Ollie's family had to send him to the hospital in Pensacola; and there was another time he bit off half a mule's ear, chewed it and spit it on the ground. Before Billy Bob got his growth, Preacher played the devil with him, too. He used to drop cockleburrs down his collar, and rub pepper in his eyes, and tear up his homework. But now they are the biggest friends in town: talk alike, walk alike; and occasionally they disappear together for whole days, Lord knows where to. But during these days when Miss Bobbit did not appear they stayed close to the house. They would stand around in the yard trying to slingshot sparrows off telephone poles; or sometimes Billy Bob would play his ukulele, and they would sing so loud Uncle Billy Bob, who is Judge for this county, claimed he could hear them all the way to the courthouse: *send me a letter, send it by mail, sent it in care of the Birming-ham jail.* Miss Bobbit did not hear them; at least she never poked her head out the door. Then one day Mrs. Sawyer, coming over to borrow a cup of sugar, rattled on a good deal about her new boarders. You know, she said, squinting her chicken-bright eyes, the husband was a crook, uh huh, the child told me herself. Hasn't an ounce of shame, not a mite. Said her daddy was the dearest daddy and the sweetest singing man in the whole of Tennessee. . . . And I said, honey, where is he? and just as offhand as you please she says, Oh, he's in the penitentiary and we don't hear from him no more. Say, now, does that make your blood run cold? Uh huh, and I been thinking, her mama, I been thinking she's some kinda foreigner: never says a word, and some-times it looks like she don't understand what nobody says to her. And you know, they eat everything *raw*. *Raw* eggs, *raw* turnips, carrots—no meat whatsoever. For reasons of health, the child says, but ho! she's been straight out on the bed running a fever since last Tuesday.

That same afternoon Aunt El went out to water her roses, only to discover them gone. These were special roses, ones she'd planned to send to the flower show in Mobile, and so naturally she got a little hysterical. She rang up the Sher-iff, and said, listen here, Sheriff, you come over here right fast. I mean some-body's got off with all my Lady Anne's that I've devoted myself to heart and soul since early spring. When the Sheriff's car pulled up outside our house, all the neighbors along the street came out on their porches, and Mrs. Sawyer, layers of cold cream whitening her face, trotted across the road. Oh shoot, she said, very disappointed to find no one had been murdered, oh shoot, she said, nobody's stole them roses. Your Billy Bob brought them roses over and left them for little Bobbit. Aunt El did not say one word. She just marched over to the peach tree, and cut herself a switch. Ohhh, Billy Bob, she stalked along the street calling his name, and then she found him down at Speedy's garage where he and Preacher were watching Speedy take a motor apart. She simply lifted him by the hair and, switching blueblazes, towed him home. But she couldn't make him say he was sorry and she couldn't make him cry. And when she was finished with him he ran into the backyard and climbed high into the tower of a pecan tree and swore he wasn't ever going to come down. Then his daddy came home, and it was time to have supper. His daddy stood at the window and called to him: Son, we aren't mad with you, so come down and eat your supper. But Billy Bob wouldn't budge. Aunt El went and leaned against the tree. She spoke in a voice soft as the gathering light. I'm sorry, son, she said, I didn't mean whipping you so hard like that. I've fixed a nice supper, son, potato salad and boiled ham and deviled eggs. Go away, said Billy Bob, I don't want no supper, and I hate you like all-fire. His daddy said he ought not to talk like that to his mother, and she began to cry. She stood there under the tree and cried, raising the hem of her skirt to dab at her eyes. I don't hate you, son. . . . If I didn't love you I wouldn't whip you. The pecan leaves began to rattle; Billy Bob slid slowly to the ground, and Aunt El, rushing her fingers through his hair, pulled him against her. Aw, Ma, he said, Aw, Ma.

After supper Billy Bob came and flung himself on the foot of my bed. He smelled all sour and sweet, the way boys do, and I felt very sorry for him, espe-cially because he looked so worried. His eyes were almost shut with worry. You're s'posed to send sick folks flowers, he said righteously. About this time we heard the victrola, a lilting faraway sound, and a night moth flew through the window, drifting in the air delicate as the music. But it was dark now, and we couldn't tell if Miss Bobbit was dancing. Billy Bob, as though he were in pain, doubled up on the bed like a jackknife; but his face was suddenly clear, his grubby boy-eyes twitching like candles. She's so cute, he whispered, she's the cutest dickens I ever saw, gee, to hell with it, I don't care, I'd pick all the roses in China.

Preacher would have picked all the roses in China, too. He was as crazy about

her as Billy Bob. But Miss Bobbit did not notice them. The sole communication
we had with her was a note to Aunt El thanking her for the flowers. Day after
day she sat on her porch, always dressed to beat the band, and doing a piece of
embroidery, or combing curls in her hair, or reading a Webster's dictionary—
formal, but friendly enough; if you said good-day to her she said good-day to
you. Even so, the boys never could seem to get up the nerve to go over and talk
with her, and most of the time she simply looked through them, even when they
tomcatted up and down the street trying to get her eye. They wrestled, played
Tarzan, did foolheaded bicycle tricks. It was a sorry business. A great many girls
in town strolled by the Sawyer house two and three times within an hour just on
the chance of getting a look. Some of the girls who did this were: Cora McCall,
Mary Murphy Jones, Janice Ackerman. Miss Bobbit did not show any interest in
them either. Cora would not speak to Billy Bob any more. The same was true
with Janice and Preacher. As a matter of fact, Janice wrote Preacher a letter in
red ink on lace-trimmed paper in which she told him he was vile beyond all
human beings and words, that she considered their engagement broken, that he
could have back the stuffed squirrel he'd given her. Preacher, saying he wanted
to act nice, stopped her the next time she passed our house, and said, well, hell,
she could keep that old squirrel if she wanted to. Afterwards, he couldn't understand why Janice ran away bawling the way she did.

Then one day the boys were being crazier than usual; Billy Bob was sagging
around in his daddy's World War khakis, and Preacher, stripped to the waist,
had a naked woman drawn on his chest with one of Aunt El's old lipsticks. They
looked like perfect fools, but Miss Bobbit, reclining in a swing, merely yawned.
It was noon, and there was no one passing in the street, except a colored girl,
baby-fat and sugar-plum shaped, who hummed along carrying a pail of blackberries. But the boys, teasing at her like gnats, joined hands and wouldn't let her
go by, not until she paid a tariff. I ain't studyin' no tariff, she said, what kinda
tariff you talkin' about, mister? A party in the barn, said Preacher, between
clenched teeth, mighty nice party in the barn. And she, with a sulky shrug, said,
huh, she intended studyin' no barn parties. Whereupon Billy Bob capsized her
berry pail, and when she, with despairing, piglike shrieks, bent down in futile
gestures of rescue, Preacher, who can be mean as the devil, gave her behind a
kick which sent her sprawling jellylike among the blackberries and the dust.
Miss Bobbit came tearing across the road, her finger wagging like a metronome;
like a schoolteacher she clapped her hands, stamped her foot, said: "It is a well-
known fact that gentlemen are put on the face of this earth for the protection of
ladies. Do you suppose boys behave this way in towns like Memphis, New York,
London, Hollywood or Paris?" The boys hung back, and shoved their hands in
their pockets. Miss Bobbit helped the colored girl to her feet; she dusted her off,
dried her eyes, held out a handkerchief and told her to blow. "A pretty pass,"
she said, "a fine situation when a lady can't walk safely in the public daylight."

Then the two of them went back and sat on Mrs. Sawyer's porch; and for the
next year they were never far apart, Miss Bobbit and this baby elephant, whose
name was Rosalba Cat. At first, Mrs. Sawyer raised a fuss about Rosalba being
so much at her house. She told Aunt El that it went against the grain to have a
nigger lolling smack there in plain sight on her front porch. But Miss Bobbit had

a certain magic, whatever she did she did it with completeness, and so directly, so solemnly, that there was nothing to do but accept it. For instance, the trades-people in town used to snicker when they called her *Miss* Bobbit; but by and by she was Miss Bobbit, and they gave her stiff little bows as she whirled by spin-ning her parasol. Miss Bobbit told everyone that Rosalba was her sister, which caused a good many jokes; but like most of her ideas, it gradually seemed natu-ral, and when we would overhear them calling each other Sister Rosalba and Sister Bobbit none of us cracked a smile. But Sister Rosalba and Sister Bobbit did some queer things. There was the business about the dogs. Now there are a great many dogs in this town, rat-terriers, bird-dogs, bloodhounds; they trail along the forlorn noon-hot streets in sleepy herds of six to a dozen, all waiting only for dark and the moon, when straight through the lonesome hours you can hear them howling: someone is dying, someone is dead. Miss Bobbit com-plained to the Sheriff; she said that certain of the dogs always planted them-selves under her window, and that she was a light sleeper to begin with; what is more, and as Sister Rosalba said, she did not believe they were dogs at all, but some kind of devil. Naturally the Sheriff did nothing; and so she took the matter into her own hands. One morning, after an especially loud night, she was seen stalking through the town with Rosalba at her side, Rosalba carrying a flower basket filled with rocks; whenever they saw a dog they paused while Miss Bobbit scrutinized him. Sometimes she would shake her head, but more often she said, "Yes, that's one of them, Sister Rosalba," and Sister Rosalba, with ferocious aim, would take a rock from her basket and crack the dog between the eyes.

Another thing that happened concerns Mr. Henderson. Mr. Henderson has a back room in the Sawyer house; a tough runt of a man who formerly was a wild-cat oil prospector in Oklahoma, he is about seventy years old and, like a lot of old men, obsessed by functions of the body. Also, he is a terrible drunk. One time he had been drunk for two weeks; whenever he heard Miss Bobbit and Sis-ter Rosalba moving around the house, he would charge to the top of the stairs and bellow down to Mrs. Sawyer that there were midgets in the walls trying to get at his supply of toilet paper. They've already stolen fifteen cents' worth, he said. One evening, when the two girls were sitting under a tree in the yard, Mr. Henderson, sporting nothing more than a nightshirt, stamped out after them. Steal all my toilet paper, will you? he hollered, I'll show you midgets. . . . Some-body come help me, else these midget bitches are liable to make off with every sheet in town. It was Billy Bob and Preacher who caught Mr. Henderson and held him until some grown men arrived and began to tie him up. Miss Bobbit, who had behaved with admirable calm, told the men they did not know how to tie a proper knot, and undertook to do so herself. She did such a good job that all the circulation stopped in Mr. Henderson's hands and feet and it was a month before he could walk again.

It was shortly afterwards that Miss Bobbit paid us a call. She came on Sunday and I was there alone, the family having gone to church. "The odors of a church are so offensive," she said, leaning forward and with her hands folded primly be-fore her. "I don't want you to think I'm a heathen, Mr. C.; I've had enough ex-perience to know that there is a God and that there is a Devil. But the way to tame the Devil is not to go down there to church and listen to what a sinful mean fool he is. No, love the Devil like you love Jesus: because he is a powerful man, and will do you a good turn if he knows you trust him. He has frequently done me good turns, like at dancing school in Memphis. . . . I always called in the Devil to help me get the biggest part in our annual show. That is common sense; you see, I knew Jesus wouldn't have any truck with dancing. Now, as a matter of fact, I have called in the Devil just recently. He is the only one who can help me get out of this town. Not that I live here, not exactly. I think always about somewhere else, somewhere else where everything is dancing, like people dancing in the streets, and everything is pretty, like children on their birthdays. My precious papa said I live in the sky, but if he'd lived more in the sky he'd be rich like he wanted to be. The trouble with my papa was he did not love the Devil, he let the Devil love him. But I am very smart in that respect; I know the next best thing is very often the best. It was the next best thing for us to move to this town; and since I can't pursue my career here, the next best thing for me is to start a little business on the side. Which is what I have done. I am sole subscription agent in this county for an impressive list of magazines, including *Reader's Digest, Popular Mechanics, Dime Detective* and *Child's Life*. To be sure, Mr. C., I'm not here to sell you anything. But I have a thought in mind. I was thinking those two boys that are always hanging around here, it occurred to me that they are men, after all. Do you suppose they would make a pair of likely assistants?"

Billy Bob and Preacher worked hard for Miss Bobbit, and for Sister Rosalba, too. Sister Rosalba carried a line of cosmetics called Dewdrop, and it was part of the boys' job to deliver purchases to her customers. Billy Bob used to be so tired in the evening he could hardly chew his supper. Aunt El said it was a shame and a pity, and finally one day when Billy Bob came down with a touch of sunstroke she said, all right, that settled it, Billy Bob would just have to quit Miss Bobbit. But Billy Bob cussed her out until his daddy had to lock him in his room; whereupon he said he was going to kill himself. Some cook we'd had told him once that if you ate a mess of collards all slopped over with molasses it would kill you sure as shooting; and so that is what he did. I'm dying, he said, rolling back and forth on his bed, I'm dying and nobody cares.

Miss Bobbit came over and told him to hush up. "There's nothing wrong with you, boy," she said. "All you've got is a stomach ache." Then she did something that shocked Aunt El very much: she stripped the covers off Billy Bob and rubbed him down with alcohol from head to toe. When Aunt El told her she did not think that was a nice thing for a little girl to do, Miss Bobbit replied: "I don't know whether it's nice or not, but it's certainly very refreshing." After which Aunt El did all she could to keep Billy Bob from going back to work for her, but his daddy said to leave him alone, they would have to let the boy lead his own life.

Miss Bobbit was very honest about money. She paid Billy Bob and Preacher their exact commission, and she would never let them treat her, as they often tried to do, at the drugstore or to the picture-show. "You'd better save your money," she told them. "That is, if you want to go to college. Because neither one of you has got the brains to win a scholarship, not even a football scholarship." But it was over money that Billy Bob and Preacher had a big falling out;

that was not the real reason, of course: the real reason was that they had grown cross-eyed jealous over Miss Bobbit. So one day, and he had the gall to do this right in front of Billy Bob, Preacher said to Miss Bobbit that she'd better check her accounts carefully because he had more than a suspicion that Billy Bob wasn't turning over to her *all* the money he collected. That's a damned lie, said Billy Bob, and with a clean left hook he knocked Preacher off the Sawyer porch and jumped after him into a bed of nasturtiums. But once Preacher got a hold on him, Billy Bob didn't stand a chance. Preacher even rubbed dirt in his eyes. During all this, Mrs. Sawyer, leaning out an upper-story window, screamed like an eagle, and Sister Rosalba, fatly cheerful, ambiguously shouted, Kill him! Kill him! Kill him! Only Miss Bobbit seemed to know what she was doing. She plugged in the lawn hose, and gave the boys a closeup, blinding bath. Gasping, Preacher staggered to his feet. Oh, honey, he said, shaking himself like a wet dog, honey, you've got to decide. "Decide *what*?" said Miss Bobbit, right away in a huff. Oh, honey, wheezed Preacher, you don't want us boys killing each other. You got to decide who is your real true sweetheart. "Sweetheart, my eye," said Miss Bobbit. "I should've known better than to get myself involved with a lot of country children. What sort of businessman are you going to make? Now, you listen here, Preacher Star: I don't want a sweetheart, and if I did, it wouldn't be you. As a matter of fact, you don't even get up when a lady enters the room."

Preacher spit on the ground and swaggered over to Billy Bob. Come on, he said, just as though nothing had happened, she's a hard one, she is, she don't want nothing but to make trouble between two good friends. For a moment it looked as if Billy Bob was going to join him in a peaceful togetherness; but suddenly, coming to his senses, he drew back and made a gesture. The boys regarded each other a full minute, all the closeness between them turning an ugly color: you can't hate so much unless you love, too. And Preacher's face showed all of this. But there was nothing for him to do except go away. Oh, yes, Preacher, you looked so lost that day that for the first time I really liked you, so skinny and mean and lost going down the road all by yourself.

They did not make it up, Preacher and Billy Bob; and it was not because they didn't want to, it was only that there did not seem to be any straight way for their friendship to happen again. But they couldn't get rid of this friendship: each was always aware of what the other was up to; and when Preacher found himself a new buddy, Billy Bob moped around for days, picking things up, dropping them again, or doing sudden wild things, like purposely poking his finger in the electric fan. Sometimes in the evenings Preacher would pause by the gate and talk with Aunt El. It was only to torment Billy Bob, I suppose, but he stayed friendly with all of us, and at Christmas time he gave us a huge box of shelled peanuts. He left a present for Billy Bob, too. It turned out to be a book of Sherlock Holmes; and on the flyleaf there was scribbled, "Friends Like Ivy On The Wall Must Fall." That's the corniest thing I ever saw, Billy Bob said. Jesus, what a dope he is! But then, and though it was a cold winter day, he went in the backyard and climbed up into the pecan tree, crouching there all afternoon in the blue December branches.

But most of the time he was happy, because Miss Bobbit was there, and she was always sweet to him now. She and Sister Rosalba treated him like a man;

that is to say, they allowed him to do everything for them. On the other hand, they let him win at three-handed bridge, they never questioned his lies, nor discouraged his ambitions. It was a happy while. However, trouble started again when school began. Miss Bobbit refused to go. "It's ridiculous," she said, when one day the principal, Mr. Copland, came around to investigate, "really ridiculous; I can read and write and there are *some* people in this town who have every reason to know that I can count money. No, Mr. Copland, consider for a moment and you will see neither of us has the time nor energy. After all, it would only be a matter of whose spirit broke first, yours or mine. And besides, what is there for you to teach me? Now, if you knew anything about dancing, that would be another matter; but under the circumstances, yes, Mr. Copland, under the circumstances, I suggest we forget the whole thing." Mr. Copland was perfectly willing to. But the rest of the town thought she ought to be whipped. Horace Deasley wrote a piece in the paper which was titled "A Tragic Situation." It was, in his opinion, a tragic situation when a small girl could defy what he, for some reason, termed the Constitution of the United States. The article ended with a question: *Can she get away with it?* She did; and so did Sister Rosalba. Only she was colored, so no one cared. Billy Bob was not as lucky. It was school for him, all right; but he might as well have stayed home for the good it did him. On his first report card he got three F's, a record of some sort. But he is a smart boy. I guess he just couldn't live through those hours without Miss Bobbit; away from her he always seemed half-asleep. He was always in a fight, too; either his eye was black, or his lip was split, or his walk had a limp. He never talked about these fights, but Miss Bobbit was shrewd enough to guess the reason why. "You are a dear, I know, I know. And I appreciate you, Billy Bob. Only don't fight with people because of me. Of course they say mean things about me. But do you know why that is, Billy Bob? It's a compliment, kind of. Because deep down they think I'm absolutely wonderful."

And she was right: if you are not admired no one will take the trouble to disapprove. But actually we had no idea of how wonderful she was until there appeared the man known as Manny Fox. This happened late in February. The first news we had of Manny Fox was a series of jovial placards posted up in the stores around town: Manny Fox Presents the Fan Dancer Without the Fan; then, in smaller print: Also, Sensational Amateur Program Featuring Your Own Neighbors—First Prize, A Genuine Hollywood Screen Test. All this was to take place the following Thursday. The tickets were priced at one dollar each, which around here is a lot of money; but it is not often that we get any kind of flesh entertainment, so everybody shelled out their money and made a great todo over the whole thing. The drugstore cowboys talked dirty all week, mostly about the fan dancer without the fan, who turned out to be Mrs. Manny Fox. They stayed down the highway at the Chucklewood Tourist Camp; but they were in town all day, driving around in an old Packard which had Manny Fox's full name stenciled on all four doors. His wife was a deadpan pimento-tongued redhead with wet lips and moist eyelids; she was quite large actually, but compared to Manny Fox she seemed rather frail, for he was a fat cigar of a man.

They made the pool hall their headquarters, and every afternoon you could find them there, drinking beer and joking with the town loafs. As it developed,

Manny Fox's business affairs were not restricted to theatrics. He also ran a kind of employment bureau: slowly he let it be known that for a fee of $150 he could get for any adventurous boys in the county high-class jobs working on fruit ships sailing from New Orleans to South America. The chance of a lifetime, he called it. There are not two boys around here who readily lay their hands on so much as five dollars; nevertheless, a good dozen managed to raise the money. Ada Willingham took all she'd saved to buy an angel tombstone for her husband and gave it to her son, and Acey Trump's papa sold an option on his cotton crop.

But the night of the show! That was a night when all was forgotten: mortgages, and the dishes in the kitchen sink. Aunt El said you'd think we were going to the opera, everybody so dressed up, so pink and sweet-smelling. The Odeon had not been so full since the night they gave away the matched set of sterling silver. Practically everybody had a relative in the show, so there was a lot of nervousness to contend with. Miss Bobbit was the only contestant we knew real well. Billy Bob couldn't sit still; he kept telling us over and over that we mustn't applaud for anybody but Miss Bobbit; Aunt El said that would be very rude, which sent Billy Bob off into a state again; and when his father bought us all bags of popcorn he wouldn't touch his because it would make his hands greasy, and please, another thing, we mustn't be noisy and eat ours while Miss Bobbit was performing. That she was to be a contestant had come as a last-minute surprise. It was logical enough, and there were signs that should've told us; the fact, for instance, that she had not set foot outside the Sawyer house in how many days? And the victrola going half the night, her shadow whirling on the windowshade, and the secret, stuffed look on Sister Rosalba's face whenever asked after Sister Bobbit's health. So there was her name on the program, listed second, in fact, though she did not appear for a long while. First came Manny Fox, greased and leering, who told a lot of peculiar jokes, clapping his hands, ha, ha. Aunt El said if he told another joke like that she was going to walk straight out: he did, and she didn't. Before Miss Bobbit came on there were eleven contestants, including Eustacia Bernstein, who imitated movie stars so that they all sounded like Eustacia, and there was an extraordinary Mr. Buster Riley, a jug eared old wool-hat from way in the back country who played "Waltzing Matilda" on a saw. Up to that point, he was the hit of the show; not that there was any marked difference in the various receptions, for everybody applauded generously, everybody, that is, except Preacher Star. He was sitting two rows ahead of us, greeting each act with a donkey-loud boo. Aunt El said she was never going to speak to him again. The only person he ever applauded was Miss Bobbit. No doubt the Devil was on her side, but she deserved it. Out she came, tossing her hips, her curls, rolling her eyes. You could tell right away it wasn't going to be one of her classical numbers. She tapped across the stage, daintily holding up the sides of a cloud-blue skirt. That's the cutest thing I ever saw, said Billy Bob, smacking his thigh, and Aunt El had to agree that Miss Bobbit looked real sweet. When she started to twirl the whole audience broke into spontaneous applause; so she did it all over again, hissing, "Faster, faster," at poor Miss Adelaide, who was at the piano doing her Sunday-school best. "I was born in China, and raised in Jay-pan . . ." We had never heard her sing before, and she had a rowdy sandpaper voice. ". . . if you don't like my peaches, stay away from my can, o-ho o-ho!" Aunt El gasped; she gasped again when Miss Bobbit, with a bump, up-ended her skirt to display blue-lace underwear, thereby collecting most of the whistles the boys had been saving for the fan dancer without the fan, which was just as well, as it later turned out, for that lady, to the tune of "An Apple for the Teacher" and cries of gyp gyp, did her routine attired in a bathing suit. But showing off her bottom was not Miss Bobbit's final triumph. Miss Adelaide commenced an ominous thundering in the darker keys, at which point Sister Rosalba, carrying a lighted Roman candle, rushed onstage and handed it to Miss Bobbit, who was in the midst of a full split; she made it, too, and just as she did the Roman candle burst into fiery balls of red, white and blue, and we all had to stand up because she was singing "The Star Spangled Banner" at the top of her lungs. Aunt El said afterwards that it was one of the most gorgeous things she'd ever seen on the American stage.

Well, she surely did deserve a Hollywood screen test and, inasmuch as she won the contest, it looked as though she were going to get it. Manny Fox said she was: honey, he said, you're real star stuff. Only he skipped town the next day, leaving nothing but hearty promises. Watch the mails, my friends, you'll all be hearing from me. That is what he said to the boys whose money he'd taken, and that is what he said to Miss Bobbit. There are three deliveries daily, and this sizable group gathered at the post office for all of them, a jolly crowd growing gradually joyless. How their hands trembled when a letter slid into their mailbox. A terrible hush came over them as the days passed. They all knew what the other was thinking, but no one could bring himself to say it, not even Miss Bobbit. Postmistress Patterson said it plainly, however: the man's a crook, she said, I knew he was a crook to begin with, and if I have to look at your faces one more day I'll shoot myself.

Finally, at the end of two weeks, it was Miss Bobbit who broke the spell. Her eyes had grown more vacant than anyone had ever supposed they might, but one day, after the last mail was up, all her old sizzle came back. "O.k., boys, it's lynch law now," she said, and proceeded to herd the whole troupe home with her. This was the first meeting of the Manny Fox Hangman's Club, an organization which, in a more social form, endures to this day, though Manny Fox has long since been caught and, so to say, hung. Credit for this went quite properly to Miss Bobbit. Within a week she'd written over three hundred descriptions of Manny Fox and dispatched them to Sheriffs throughout the South; she also wrote letters to papers in the larger cities, and these attracted wide attention. As a result, four of the robbed boys were offered good-paying jobs by the United Fruit Company, and late this spring, when Manny Fox was arrested in Uphigh, Arkansas, where he was pulling the same old dodge, Miss Bobbit was presented with a Good Deed Merit award from the Sunbeam Girls of America. For some reason, she made a point of letting the world know that this did not exactly thrill her. "I do not approve of the organization," she said. "All that rowdy bugle blowing. It's neither good-hearted nor truly feminine. And anyway, what is a good deed? Don't let anybody fool you, a good deed is something you do because you want something in return." It would be reassuring to report she was wrong, and that her just reward, when at last it came, was given out of kindness and love. However, this is not the case. About a week ago the boys involved in the swindle all received from Manny Fox checks covering their losses, and Miss Bobbit, with clodhopping determination, stalked into a meeting of the Hangman's Club, which is now an excuse for drinking beer and playing poker every Thursday night. "Look, boys," she said, laying it on the line, "none of you ever thought to see that money again, but now that you have, you ought to invest it in something practical—like me." The proposition was that they should pool their money and finance her trip to Hollywood; in return, they would get ten percent of her life's earnings which, after she was a star, and that would not be very long, would make them all rich men. "At least," as she said, "in this part of the country." Not one of the boys wanted to do it: but when Miss Bobbit looked at you, what was there to say?

Since Monday, it has been raining buoyant summer rain shot through with sun, but dark at night and full of sound, full of dripping leaves, watery chimings, sleepless scuttlings. Billy Bob is wide-awake, dry-eyed, though everything he does is a little frozen and his tongue is as stiff as a bell tongue. It has not been easy for him, Miss Bobbit's going. Because she'd meant more than that. Than what? Than being thirteen years old and crazy in love. She was the queer things in him, like the pecan tree and liking books and caring enough about people to let them hurt him. She was the things he was afraid to show anyone else. And in the dark the music trickled through the rain: won't there be nights when we will hear it just as though it were really there? And afternoons when the shadows will be all at once confused, and she will pass before us, unfurling across the lawn like a pretty piece of ribbon? She laughed to Billy Bob; she held his hand, she even kissed him. "I'm not going to die," she said. "You'll come out there, and we'll climb a mountain, and we'll all live there together, you and me and Sister Rosalba." But Billy Bob knew it would never happen that way, and so when the music came through the dark he would stuff the pillow over his head.

Only there was a strange smile about yesterday, and that was the day she was leaving. Around noon the sun came out, bringing with it into the air all the sweetness of wisteria. Aunt El's yellow Lady Anne's were blooming again, and she did something wonderful, she told Billy Bob he could pick them and give them to Miss Bobbit for good-bye. All afternoon Miss Bobbit sat on the porch surrounded by people who stopped by to wish her well. She looked as though she were going to Communion, dressed in white and with a white parasol. Sister Rosalba had given her a handkerchief, but she had to borrow it back because she couldn't stop blubbering. Another little girl brought a baked chicken, presumably to be eaten on the bus; the only trouble was she'd forgotten to take out the insides before cooking it. Miss Bobbit's mother said that was all right by her, chicken was chicken; which is memorable because it is the single opinion she ever voiced. There was only one sour note. For hours Preacher Star had been hanging around down at the corner, sometimes standing at the curb tossing a coin, and sometimes hiding behind a tree, as if he didn't want anyone to see him. It made everybody nervous. About twenty minutes before bus time he sauntered up and leaned against our gate. Billy Bob was still in the garden picking roses; by now he had enough for a bonfire, and their smell was as heavy as wind. Preacher stared at him until he lifted his head. As they looked at each other the rain began again, falling fine as sea spray and colored by a rainbow.

Without a word, Preacher went over and started helping Billy Bob separate the roses into two giant bouquets: together they carried them to the curb. Across the street there were bumblebees of talk, but when Miss Bobbit saw them, two boys whose flower-masked faces were like yellow moons, she rushed down the steps, her arms outstretched. You could see what was going to happen; and we called out, our voices like lightning in the rain, but Miss Bobbit, running toward those moons of roses, did not seem to hear. That is when the six-o'clock bus ran over her.

Raymond Carver

. . . .

FAT

I am sitting over coffee and cigarets at my friend Rita's and I am telling her about it.

Here is what I tell her.

It is late of a slow Wednesday when Herb seats the fat man at my station.

This fat man is the fattest person I have ever seen, though he is neat-appearing and well dressed enough. Everything about him is big. But it is the fingers I remember best. When I stop at the table near his to see to the old couple, I first notice the fingers. They look three times the size of a normal person's fingers—long, thick, creamy fingers.

I see to my other tables, a party of four businessmen, very demanding, another party of four, three men and a woman, and this old couple. Leander has poured the fat man's water, and I give the fat man plenty of time to make up his mind before going over.

Good evening, I say. May I serve you? I say.

Rita, he was big, I mean big.

Good evening, he says. Hello. Yes, he says. I think we're ready to order now, he says.

He has this way of speaking—strange, don't you know. And he makes a little puffing sound every so often.

I think we will begin with a Caesar salad, he says. And then a bowl of soup with some extra bread and butter, if you please. The lamb chops, I believe, he says. And baked potato with sour cream. We'll see about dessert later. Thank you very much, he says, and hands me the menu.

God, Rita, but those were fingers.

I hurry away to the kitchen and turn in the order to Rudy, who takes it with a face. You know Rudy. Rudy is that way when he works.

As I come out of the kitchen, Margo—I've told you about Margo? The one who chases Rudy? Margo says to me, Who's your fat friend? He's really a fatty.

Now that's part of it. I think that is really part of it.

I make the Caesar salad there at his table, him watching my every move, meanwhile buttering pieces of bread and laying them off to one side, all the time making this puffing noise. Anyway, I am so keyed up or something, I knock over his glass of water.

I'm so sorry, I say. It always happens when you get into a hurry. I'm very sorry, I say. Are you all right? I say. I'll get the boy to clean up right away, I say.

It's nothing, he says. It's all right, he says, and he puffs. Don't worry about it, we don't mind, he says. He smiles and waves as I go off to get Leander, and when I come back to serve the salad, I see the fat man has eaten all his bread and butter.

A little later, when I bring him more bread, he has finished his salad. You know the size of those Caesar salads?

You're very kind, he says. This bread is marvelous, he says.

Thank you, I say.

Well, it is very good, he says, and we mean that. We don't often enjoy bread like this, he says.

Where are you from? I ask him. I don't believe I've seen you before, I say.

He's not the kind of person you'd forget, Rita puts in with a snicker.

Denver, he says.

I don't say anything more on the subject, though I am curious.

Your soup will be along in a few minutes, sir, I say, and I go off to put the finishing touches to my party of four businessmen, very demanding.

When I serve his soup, I see the bread has disappeared again. He is just putting the last piece of bread into his mouth.

Believe me, he says, we don't eat like this all the time, he says. And puffs. You'll have to excuse us, he says.

Don't think a thing about it, please, I say. I like to see a man eat and enjoy himself, I say.

I don't know, he says. I guess that's what you'd call it. And puffs. He arranges the napkin. Then he picks up his spoon.

God, he's fat! says Leander.

He can't help it, I say, so shut up.

I put down another basket of bread and more butter. How was the soup? I say.

Thank you. Good, he says. Very good, he says. He wipes his lips and dabs his chin. Do you think it's warm in here, or is it just me? he says.

No, it is warm in here, I say.

Maybe we'll take off our coat, he says.

Go right ahead, I say. A person has to be comfortable, I say.

That's true, he says, that is very, very true, he says.

But I see a little later that he is still wearing his coat.

My large parties are gone now and also the old couple. The place is emptying out. By the time I serve the fat man his chops and baked potato, along with more bread and butter, he is the only one left.

I drop lots of sour cream onto his potato. I sprinkle bacon and chives over his sour cream. I bring him more bread and butter.

Is everything all right? I say.

Fine, he says, and he puffs. Excellent, thank you, he says, and puffs again.

Enjoy your dinner, I say. I raise the lid of his sugar bowl and look in. He nods and keeps looking at me until I move away.

I know now I was after something. But I don't know what.

How is old tub-of-guts doing? He's going to run your legs off, says Harriet. You know Harriet.

For dessert, I say to the fat man, there is the Green Lantern Special, which is a pudding cake with sauce, or there is cheesecake or vanilla ice cream or pineapple sherbet.

We're not making you late, are we? he says, puffing and looking concerned.

Not at all, I say. Of course not, I say. Take your time, I say. I'll bring you more coffee while you make up your mind.

We'll be honest with you, he says. And he moves in the seat. We would like the Special, but we may have a dish of vanilla ice cream as well. With just a drop of chocolate syrup, if you please. We told you we were hungry, he says.

I go off to the kitchen to see after his dessert myself, and Rudy says, Harriet says you got a fat man from the circus out there. That true?

Rudy has his apron and hat off now, if you see what I mean.

Rudy, he is fat, I say, but that is not the whole story.

Rudy just laughs.

Sounds to me like she's sweet on fat-stuff, he says.

Better watch out, Rudy, says Joanne, who just that minute comes into the kitchen.

I'm getting jealous, Rudy says to Joanne.

I put the Special in front of the fat man and a big bowl of vanilla ice cream with chocolate syrup to the side.

Thank you, he says.

You are very welcome, I say—and a feeling comes over me.

Believe it or not, he says, we have not always eaten like this.

Me, I eat and I eat and I can't gain, I say. I'd like to gain, I say.

No, he says. If we had our choice, no. But there is no choice.

Then he picks up his spoon and eats.

What else? Rita says, lighting one of my cigarets and pulling her chair closer to the table. This story's getting interesting now, Rita says.

That's it. Nothing else. He eats his desserts, and then he leaves and then we go home, Rudy and me.

Some fatty, Rudy says, stretching like he does when he's tired. Then he just laughs and goes back to watching the TV.

I put the water on to boil for tea and take a shower. I put my hand on my middle and wonder what would happen if I had children and one of them turned out to look like that, so fat.

I pour the water in the pot, arrange the cups, the sugar bowl, carton of half and half, and take the tray in to Rudy. As if he's been thinking about it, Rudy says, I knew a fat guy once, a couple of fat guys, really fat guys, when I was a kid. They were tubbies, my God. I don't remember their names. Fat, that's the only name this one kid had. We called him Fat, the kid who lived next door to me.

He was a neighbor. The other kid came along later. His name was Wobbly. Everybody called him Wobbly except the teachers. Wobbly and Fat. Wish I had their pictures, Rudy says.

I can't think of anything to say, so we drink our tea and pretty soon I get up to go to bed. Rudy gets up too, turns off the TV, locks the front door, and begins his unbuttoning.

I get into bed and move clear over to the edge and lie there on my stomach. But right away, as soon as he turns off the light and gets into bed, Rudy begins. I turn on my back and relax some, though it is against my will. But here is the thing. When he gets on me, I suddenly feel I am fat. I feel I am terrifically fat, so fat that Rudy is a tiny thing and hardly there at all.

That's a funny story, Rita says, but I can see she doesn't know what to make of it.

I feel depressed. But I won't go into it with her. I've already told her too much.

She sits there waiting, her dainty fingers poking her hair.

Waiting for what? I'd like to know.

It is August.

My life is going to change. I feel it.

John Cheever

. . . .

THE COUNTRY
HUSBAND

To begin at the beginning, the airplane from Minneapolis in which Francis Weed was traveling East ran into heavy weather. The sky had been a hazy blue, with the clouds below the plane lying so close together that nothing could be seen of the earth. Then mist began to form outside the windows, and they flew into a white cloud of such density that it reflected the exhaust fires. The color of the cloud darkened to gray, and the plane began to rock. Francis had been in heavy weather before, but he had never been shaken up so much. The man in the seat beside him pulled a flask out of his pocket and took a drink. Francis smiled at his neighbor, but the man looked away; he wasn't sharing his pain killer with anyone. The plane began to drop and flounder wildly. A child was crying. The air in the cabin was overheated and stale, and Francis' left foot went to sleep. He read a little from a paper book that he had bought at the airport, but the violence of the storm divided his attention. It was black outside the ports. The exhaust fires blazed and shed sparks in the dark, and, inside, the shaded lights, the stutfness, and the window curtains gave the cabin an atmosphere of intense and misplaced domesticity. Then the lights flickered and went out. "You know what I've always wanted to do?" the man beside Francis said suddenly. "I've always wanted to buy a farm in New Hampshire and raise beef cattle." The stewardess announced that they were going to make an emergency landing. All but the children saw in their minds the spreading wings of the Angel of Death. The pilot could be heard singing faintly, "I've got sixpence, jolly, jolly sixpence. I've got sixpence to last me all my life . . ." There was no other sound.

The loud groaning of the hydraulic valves swallowed up the pilot's song, and there was a shrieking high in the air, like automobile brakes, and the plane hit flat on its belly in a cornfield and shook them so violently that an old man up forward howled, "Me kidneys! Me kidneys!" The stewardess flung open the door, and someone opened an emergency door at the back, letting in the sweet noise of their continuing mortality—the idle splash and smell of a heavy rain. Anxious for their lives, they filed out of the doors and scattered over the cornfield in all directions, praying that the thread would hold. It did. Nothing happened. When it was clear that the plane would not burn or explode, the crew and the stewardess gathered the passengers together and led them to the shelter of a barn. They were not far from Philadelphia, and in a little while a string of taxis took them into the city. "It's just like the Marne," someone said, but there was surprisingly little relaxation of that suspiciousness with which many Americans regard their fellow travelers.

In Philadelphia, Francis Weed got a train to New York. At the end of that journey, he crossed the city and caught just as it was about to pull out the commuting train that he took five nights a week to his home in Shady Hill.

He sat with Trace Bearden. "You know, I was in that plane that just crashed outside Philadelphia," he said. "We came down in a field . . ." He had traveled faster than the newspapers or the rain, and the weather in New York was sunny and mild. It was a day in late September, as fragrant and shapely as an apple. Trace listened to the story, but how could he get excited? Francis had no powers that would let him re-create a brush with death—particularly in the atmosphere of a commuting train, journeying through a sunny countryside where already, in the slum gardens, there were signs of harvest. Trace picked up his newspaper, and Francis was left alone with his thoughts. He said good night to Trace on the platform at Shady Hill and drove in his secondhand Volkswagen up to the Blenhollow neighborhood, where he lived.

The Weeds' Dutch Colonial house was larger than it appeared to be from the driveway. The living room was spacious and divided like Gaul into three parts. Around an ell to the left as one entered from the vestibule was the long table, laid for six, with candles and a bowl of fruit in the center. The sounds and smells that came from the open kitchen door were appetizing, for Julia Weed was a good cook. The largest part of the living room centered on a fireplace. On the right were some bookshelves and a piano. The room was polished and tranquil, and from the windows that opened to the west there was some late-summer sunlight, brilliant and as clear as water. Nothing here was neglected; nothing had not been burnished. It was not the kind of household where, after prying open a stuck cigarette box, you would find an old shirt button and a tarnished nickel. The hearth was swept, the roses on the piano were reflected in the polish of the broad top, and there was an album of Schubert waltzes on the rack. Louisa Weed, a pretty girl of nine, was looking out the western windows. Her younger brother Henry was standing beside her. Her still younger brother, Toby, was studying the figures of some tonsured monks drinking beer on the polished brass of the woodbox. Francis, taking off his hat and putting down his paper, was not consciously pleased with the scene; he was not that reflective. It was his element, his creation, and he returned to it with that sense of lightness and strength with which any creature returns to his home. "Hi, everybody," he said. "The plane from Minneapolis . . ."

Nine times out of ten, Francis would be greeted with affection, but tonight the children are absorbed in their own antagonisms. Francis had not finished his sentence about the plane crash before Henry plants a kick in Louisa's behind. Louisa swings around, saying, "*Damn* you!" Francis makes the mistake of scolding Louisa for bad language before he punishes Henry. Now Louisa turns on her father and accuses him of favoritism. Henry is always right; she is persecuted and lonely; her lot is hopeless. Francis turns to his son, but the boy has justification for the kick—she hit him first; she hit him on the ear, which is dangerous. Louisa agrees with this passionately. She hit him on the ear, and she *meant* to hit him on the ear, because he messed up her china collection. Henry says that this is a lie. Little Toby turns away from the woodbox to throw in some evidence for Louisa. Henry claps his hand over little Toby's mouth. Francis separates the two boys but accidentally pushes Toby into the woodbox. Toby begins to cry. Louisa is already crying. Just then, Julia Weed comes into that part of the room where the table is laid. She is a pretty, intelligent woman, and the white in her hair is premature. She does not seem to notice the fracas. "Hello, darling," she says serenely to Francis. "Wash your hands, everyone. Dinner is ready." She strikes a match and lights the six candles in this vale of tears.

This simple announcement, like the war cries of the Scottish chieftains, only refreshes the ferocity of the combatants. Louisa gives Henry a blow on the shoulder. Henry, although he seldom cries, has pitched nine innings and is tired. He bursts into tears. Little Toby discovers a splinter in his hand and begins to howl. Francis says loudly that he has been in a plane crash and that he is tired. Julia appears again from the kitchen and, still ignoring the chaos, asks Francis to go upstairs and tell Helen that everything is ready. Francis is happy to go; it is like getting back to headquarters company. He is planning to tell his oldest daughter about the airplane crash, but Helen is lying on her bed reading a *True Romance* magazine, and the first thing Francis does is to take the magazine from her hand and remind Helen that he has forbidden her to buy it. She did not buy it, Helen replies. It was given to her by her best friend, Bessie Black. Everybody reads *True Romance*. Bessie Black's father reads *True Romance*. There isn't a girl in Helen's class who doesn't read *True Romance*. Francis expresses his detestation of the magazine and then tells her that dinner is ready—although from the sounds downstairs it doesn't seem so. Helen follows him down the stairs. Julia has seated herself in the candlelight and spread a napkin over her lap. Neither Louisa nor Henry has come to the table. Little Toby is still howling, lying face down on the floor. Francis speaks to him gently: "Daddy was in a plane crash this afternoon, Toby. Don't you want to hear about it?" Toby goes on crying. "If you don't come to the table now, Toby," Francis says, "I'll have to send you to bed without any supper." The little boy rises, gives him a cutting look, flies up the stairs to his bedroom, and slams the door. "Oh dear," Julia says, and starts to go after him. Francis says that she will spoil him. Julia says that Toby is ten pounds underweight and has to be encouraged to eat. Winter is coming, and he will spend the cold months in bed unless he has his dinner. Julia goes upstairs. Francis sits down at the table with Helen. Helen is suffering from the dismal feeling of having read too intently on a fine day, and she gives her father and the room a jaded look. She doesn't understand about the plane crash, because there wasn't a drop of rain in Shady Hill.

Julia returns with Toby, and they all sit down and are served. "Do I have to look at that big, fat slob?" Henry says, of Louisa. Everybody but Toby enters into this skirmish, and it rages up and down the table for five minutes. Toward the end, Henry puts his napkin over his head and, trying to eat that way, spills spinach all over his shirt. Francis asks Julia if the children couldn't have their dinner earlier. Julia's guns are loaded for this. She can't cook two dinners and lay two tables. She paints with lightning strokes that panorama of drudgery in which her youth, her beauty, and her wit have been lost. Francis says that he must be understood; he was nearly killed in an airplane crash, and he doesn't like to come home every night to a battlefield. Now Julia is deeply concerned. Her voice trembles. He doesn't come home every night to a battlefield. The accusation is stupid and mean. Everything was tranquil until he arrived. She stops speaking, puts down her knife and fork, and looks into her plate as if it is a gulf. She begins to cry. "Poor Mummy!" Toby says, and when Julia gets up from the table, drying her tears with a napkin, Toby goes to her side. "Poor Mummy," he says. "Poor Mummy!" And they climb the stairs together. The other children drift away from the battlefield, and Francis goes into the back garden for a cigarette and some air.

It was a pleasant garden, with walks and flower beds and places to sit. The sunset had nearly burned out, but there was still plenty of light. Put into a thoughtful mood by the crash and the battle, Francis listened to the evening sounds of Shady Hill. "Varmints! Rascals!" old Mr. Nixon shouted to the squirrels in his bird-feeding station. "Avaunt and quit my sight!" A door slammed. Someone was cutting grass. Then Donald Goslin, who lived at the corner, began to play the "Moonlight Sonata." He did this nearly every night. He threw the tempo out the window and played it *rubato* from beginning to end, like an outpouring of tearful petulance, lonesomeness, and self-pity—of everything it was Beethoven's greatness not to know. The music rang up and down the street beneath the trees like an appeal for love, for tenderness, aimed at some lovely housemaid—some fresh-faced, homesick girl from Galway, looking at old snapshots in her third-floor room. "Here, Jupiter, here, Jupiter," Francis called to the Mercers' retriever. Jupiter crashed through the tomato vines with the remains of a felt hat in his mouth.

Jupiter was an anomaly. His retrieving instincts and his high spirits were out of place in Shady Hill. He was as black as coal, with a long, alert, intelligent, rakehell face. His eyes gleamed with mischief, and he held his head high. It was the fierce, heavily collared dog's head that appears in heraldry, in tapestry, and that used to appear on umbrella handles and walking sticks. Jupiter went where he pleased, ransacking wastebaskets, clotheslines, garbage pails, and shoe bags. He broke up garden parties and tennis matches, and got mixed up in the processional at Christ Church on Sunday, barking at the men in red dresses. He crashed through old Mr. Nixon's rose garden two or three times a day, cutting a wide swath through the Condesa de Sastagos, and as soon as Donald Goslin lighted his barbecue fire on Thursday nights, Jupiter would get the scent. Nothing the Goslins did could drive him away. Sticks and stones and rude commands only moved him to the edge of the terrace, where he remained, with his gallant and heraldic muzzle, waiting for Donald Goslin to turn his back and reach for the salt. Then he would spring onto the terrace, lift the steak lightly off the fire, and run away with the Goslins' dinner. Jupiter's days were numbered. The Wrightsons' German gardener or the Farquarsons' cook would soon poison him.

Even old Mr. Nixon might put some arsenic in the garbage that Jupiter loved. "Here, Jupiter, Jupiter!" Francis called, but the dog pranced off, shaking the hat in his white teeth. Looking at the windows of his house, Francis saw that Julia had come down and was blowing out the candles.

Julia and Francis Weed went out a great deal. Julia was well liked and gregarious, and her love of parties sprang from a most natural dread of chaos and loneliness. She went through her morning mail with real anxiety, looking for invitations, and she usually found some, but she was insatiable, and if she had gone out seven nights a week, it would not have cured her of a reflective look— the look of someone who hears distant music—for she would always suppose that there was a more brilliant party somewhere else. Francis limited her to two week-night parties, putting a flexible interpretation on Friday, and rode through the weekend like a dory in a gale. The day after the airplane crash, the Weeds were to have dinner with the Farquarsons.

Francis got home late from town, and Julia got the sitter while he dressed, and then hurried him out of the house. The party was small and pleasant, and Francis settled down to enjoy himself. A new maid passed the drinks. Her hair was dark, and her face was round and pale and seemed familiar to Francis. He had not developed his memory as a sentimental faculty. Wood smoke, lilac, and other such perfumes did not stir him, and his memory was something like his appendix—a vestigial repository. It was not his limitation at all to be unable to escape the past; it was perhaps his limitation that he had escaped it so successfully. He might have seen the maid at other parties, he might have seen her taking a walk on Sunday afternoons, but in either case he would not be searching his memory now. Her face was, in a wonderful way, a moon face—Norman or Irish—but it was not beautiful enough to account for his feeling that he had seen her before, in circumstances that he ought to be able to remember. He asked Nellie Farquarson who she was. Nellie said that the maid had come through an agency, and that her home was Trenon, in Normandy—a small place with a church and a restaurant that Nellie had once visited. While Nellie talked on about her travels abroad, Francis realized where he had seen the woman before. It had been at the end of the war. He had left a replacement depot with some other men and taken a three-day pass in Trenon. On their second day, they had walked out to a crossroads to see the public chastisement of a young woman who had lived with the German commandant during the Occupation.

It was a cool morning in the fall. The sky was overcast, and poured down onto the dirt crossroads a very discouraging light. They were on high land and could see how like one another the shapes of the clouds and the hills were as they stretched off toward the sea. The prisoner arrived sitting on a three-legged stool in a farm cart. She stood by the cart while the Mayor read the accusation and the sentence. Her head was bent and her face was set in that empty half smile behind which the whipped soul is suspended. When the Mayor was finished, she undid her hair and let it fall across her back. A little man with a gray mustache cut off her hair with shears and dropped it on the ground. Then, with a bowl of soapy water and a straight razor, he shaved her skull clean. A woman approached and began to undo the fastenings of her clothes, but the prisoner pushed her aside and undressed herself. When she pulled her chemise over her head and threw it on the ground, she was naked. The women jeered; the men were still. There was no change in the falseness or the plaintiveness of the prisoner's smile. The cold wind made her white skin rough and hardened the nipples of her breasts. The jeering ended gradually, put down by the recognition of their common humanity. One woman spat on her, but some inviolable grandeur in her nakedness lasted through the ordeal. When the crowd was quiet, she turned—she had begun to cry—and, with nothing on but a pair of worn black shoes and stockings, walked down the dirt road alone away from the village. The round white face had aged a little, but there was no question but that the maid who passed his cocktails and later served Francis his dinner was the woman who had been punished at the crossroads.

The war seemed now so distant and that world where the cost of partisanship had been death or torture so long ago. Francis had lost track of the men who had been with him in Vesey. He could not count on Julia's discretion. He could not tell anyone. And if he had told the story now, at the dinner table, it would have been a social as well as a human error. The people in the Farquarsons' living room seemed united in their tacit claim that there had been no past, no war— that there was no danger or trouble in the world. In the recorded history of human arrangements, this extraordinary meeting would have fallen into place, but the atmosphere of Shady Hill made the memory unseemly and impolite. The prisoner withdrew after passing the coffee, but the encounter left Francis feeling languid; it had opened his memory and his senses, and left them dilated. Julia went into the house. Francis stayed in the car to take the sitter home.

Expecting to see Mrs. Henlein, the old lady who usually stayed with the children, he was surprised when a young girl opened the door and came out onto the lighted stoop. She stayed in the light to count her textbooks. She was frowning and beautiful. Now, the world is full of beautiful young girls, but Francis saw here the difference between beauty and perfection. All those endearing flaws, moles, birthmarks, and healed wounds were missing, and he experienced in his consciousness that moment when music breaks glass, and felt a pang of recognition as strange, deep, and wonderful as anything in his life. It hung from her frown, from an impalpable darkness in her face—a look that impressed him as a direct appeal for love. When she had counted her books, she came down the steps and opened the car door. In the light, he saw that her cheeks were wet. She got in and shut the door.

"You're new," Francis said.

"Yes. Mrs. Henlein is sick. I'm Anne Murchison."

"Did the children give you any trouble?"

"Oh, no, no." She turned and smiled at him unhappily in the dim dashboard light. Her light hair caught on the collar of her jacket, and she shook her head to set it loose.

"You've been crying."

"Yes."

"I hope it was nothing that happened in our house."

"No, no, it was nothing that happened in your house." Her voice was bleak. "It's no secret. Everybody in the village knows. Daddy's an alcoholic, and he just called me from some saloon and gave me a piece of his mind. He thinks I'm immoral. He called just before Mrs. Weed came back."

"I'm sorry."

"Oh, *Lord!*" She gasped and began to cry. She turned toward Francis, and he took her in his arms and let her cry on his shoulder. She shook in his embrace, and this movement accentuated his sense of the fineness of her flesh and bone. The layers of their clothing felt thin, and when her shuddering began to diminish, it was so much like a paroxysm of love that Francis lost his head and pulled her roughly against him. She drew away. "I live on Belleview Avenue," she said. "You go down Lansing Street to the railroad bridge."

"All right." He started the car.

"You turn left at that traffic light. . . . Now you turn right here and go straight on toward the tracks."

The road Francis took brought him out of his own neighborhood, across the tracks, and toward the river, to a street where the near-poor lived, in houses whose peaked gables and trimmings of wooden lace conveyed the purest feelings of pride and romance, although the houses themselves could not have offered much privacy or comfort, they were all so small. The street was dark, and, stirred by the grace and beauty of the troubled girl, he seemed, in turning into it, to have come into the deepest part of some submerged memory. In the distance, he saw a porch light burning. It was the only one, and she said that the house with the light was where she lived. When he stopped the car, he could see beyond the porch light into a dimly lighted hallway with an old-fashioned clothes tree. "Well, here we are," he said, conscious that a young man would have said something different.

She did not move her hands from the books, where they were folded, and she turned and faced him. There were tears of lust in his eyes. Determinedly—not sadly—he opened the door on his side and walked around to open hers. He took her free hand, letting his fingers in between hers, climbed at her side the two concrete steps, and went up a narrow walk through a front garden where dahlias, marigolds, and roses—things that had withstood the light frosts—still bloomed, and made a bittersweet smell in the night air. At the steps, she freed her hand and then turned and kissed him swiftly. Then she crossed the porch and shut the door. The porch light went out, then the light in the hall. A second later, a light went on upstairs at the side of the house, shining into a tree that was still covered with leaves. It took her only a few minutes to undress and get into bed, and then the house was dark.

Julia was asleep when Francis got home. He opened a second window and got into bed to shut his eyes on that night, but as soon as they were shut—as soon as he had dropped off to sleep—the girl entered his mind, moving with perfect freedom through its shut doors and filling chamber after chamber with her light, her perfume, and the music of her voice. He was crossing the Atlantic with her on the old *Mauretania* and, later, living with her in Paris. When he woke from his dream, he got up and smoked a cigarette at the open window. Getting back into bed, he cast around in his mind for something he desired to do that would injure no one, and he thought of skiing. Up through the dimness in his mind rose the image of a mountain deep in snow. It was late in the day. Wherever his eyes looked, he saw broad and heartening things. Over his shoulder, there was a snow-filled valley, rising into wooded hills where the trees dimmed the whiteness like a sparse coat of hair. The cold deadened all sound but the loud, iron clanking of the lift machinery. The light on the trails was blue, and it was harder than it had been a minute or two earlier to pick the turns, harder to judge—now that the snow was all deep blue—the crust, the ice, the bare spots, and the deep piles of dry powder. Down the mountain he swung, matching his speed against the contours of a slope that had been formed in the first ice age, seeking with ardor some simplicity of feeling and circumstance. Night fell then, and he drank a Martini with some old friend in a dirty country bar.

In the morning, Francis' snow-covered mountain was gone, and he was left with his vivid memories of Paris and the *Mauretania*. He had been bitten gravely. He washed his body, shaved his jaws, drank his coffee, and missed the seven-thirty-one. The train pulled out just as he brought his car to the station, and the longing he felt for the coaches as they drew stubbornly away from him reminded him of the humors of love. He waited for the eight-two, on what was now an empty platform. It was a clear morning; the morning seemed thrown like a gleaming bridge of light over his mixed affairs. His spirits were feverish and high. The image of the girl seemed to put him into a relationship to the world that was mysterious and enthralling. Cars were beginning to fill up the parking lot, and he noticed that those that had driven down from the high land above Shady Hill were white with hoarfrost. This first clear sign of autumn thrilled him. An express train—a night train from Buffalo or Albany—came down the tracks between the platforms, and he saw that the roofs of the foremost cars were covered with a skin of ice. Struck by the miraculous physicalness of everything, he smiled at the passengers in the dining car, who could be seen eating eggs and wiping their mouths with napkins as they traveled. The sleeping-car compartments, with their soiled bed linen, trailed through the fresh morning like a string of rooming-house windows. Then he saw an extraordinary thing; at one of the bedroom windows sat an unclothed woman of exceptional beauty, combing her golden hair. She passed like an apparition through Shady Hill, combing and combing her hair, and Francis followed her with his eyes until she was out of sight. Then old Mrs. Wrightson joined him on the platform and began to talk.

"Well, I guess you must be surprised to see me here the third morning in a row," she said, "but because of my window curtains I'm becoming a regular commuter. The curtains I bought on Monday I returned on Tuesday, and the curtains I bought Tuesday I'm returning today. On Monday, I got exactly what I wanted—it's a wool tapestry with roses and birds—but when I got them home, I found they were the wrong length. Well, I exchanged them yesterday, and when I got them home, I found they were still the wrong length. Now I'm praying to high heaven that the decorator will have them in the right length, because you know my house, you *know* my living-room windows, and you can imagine what a problem they present. I don't know what to do with them."

"I know what to do with them," Francis said.

"What?"

"Paint them black on the inside, and shut up."

There was a gasp from Mrs. Wrightson, and Francis looked down at her to be sure that she knew he meant to be rude. She turned and walked away from him, so damaged in spirit that she limped. A wonderful feeling enveloped him, as if light were being shaken about him, and he thought again of Venus combing and combing her hair as she drifted through the Bronx. The realization of how many years had passed since he had enjoyed being deliberately impolite sobered him. Among his friends and neighbors, there were brilliant and gifted people—he saw that—but many of them, also, were bores and fools, and he had made the mistake of listening to them all with equal attention. He had confused a lack of discrimination with Christian love, and the confusion seemed general and destructive. He was grateful to the girl for this bracing sensation of independence. Birds were singing—cardinals and the last of the robins. The sky shone like enamel. Even the smell of ink from his morning paper honed his appetite for life, and the world that was spread out around him was plainly a paradise.

If Francis had believed in some hierarchy of love—in spirits armed with hunting bows, in the capriciousness of Venus and Eros—or even in magical potions, philters, and stews, in scapulae and quarters of the moon, it might have explained his susceptibility and his feverish high spirits. The autumnal loves of middle age are well publicized, and he guessed that he was face to face with one of these, but there was not a trace of autumn in what he felt. He wanted to sport in the green woods, scratch where he itched, and drink from the same cup.

His secretary, Miss Rainey, was late that morning—she went to a psychiatrist three mornings a week—and when she came in, Francis wondered what advice a psychiatrist would have for him. But the girl promised to bring back into his life something like the sound of music. The realization that this music might lead him straight to a trial for statutory rape at the county courthouse collapsed his happiness. The photograph of his four children laughing into the camera on the beach at Gay Head reproached him. On the letterhead of his firm there was a drawing of the Laocoon, and the figure of the priest and his sons in the coils of the snake appeared to him to have the deepest meaning.

He had lunch with Pinky Trabert. At a conversational level, the mores of his friends were robust and elastic, but he knew that the moral card house would come down on them all—on Julia and the children as well—if he got caught taking advantage of a baby-sitter. Looking back over the recent history of Shady Hill for some precedent, he found there was none. There was no turpitude; there had not been a divorce since he lived there; there had not even been a breath of scandal. Things seemed arranged with more propriety even than in the Kingdom of Heaven. After leaving Pinky, Francis went to a jeweler's and bought the girl a bracelet. How happy this clandestine purchase made him, how stuffy and comical the jeweler's clerks seemed, how sweet the women who passed at his back smelled! On Fifth Avenue, passing Atlas with his shoulders bent under the weight of the world, Francis thought of the strenuousness of containing his physicalness within the patterns he had chosen.

He did not know when he would see the girl next. He had the bracelet in his inside pocket when he got home. Opening the door of his house, he found her in the hall. Her back was to him, and she turned when she heard the door close. Her smile was open and loving. Her perfection stunned him like a fine day—a day after a thunderstorm. He seized her and covered her lips with his, and she struggled but she did not have to struggle for long, because just then little Gertrude Flannery appeared from somewhere and said, "Oh, Mr. Weed . . ."

Gertrude was a stray. She had been born with a taste for exploration, and she did not have it in her to center her life with her affectionate parents. People who did not know the Flannerys concluded from Gertrude's behavior that she was the child of a bitterly divided family, where drunken quarrels were the rule. This was not true. The fact that little Gertrude's clothing was ragged and thin was her own triumph over her mother's struggle to dress her warmly and neatly. Garrulous, skinny, and unwashed, she drifted from house to house around the Blenhollow neighborhood, forming and breaking alliances based on an attachment to babies, animals, children her own age, adolescents, and sometimes adults. Opening your front door in the morning, you would find Gertrude sitting on your stoop. Going into the bathroom to shave, you would find Gertrude using the toilet. Looking into your son's crib, you would find it empty, and, looking further, you would find that Gertrude had pushed him in his baby carriage into the next village. She was helpful, pervasive, honest, hungry, and loyal. She never went home of her own choice. When the time to go arrived, she was indifferent to all its signs. "Go home, Gertrude," people could be heard saying in one house or another, night after night. "Go home, Gertrude. It's time for you to go home now, Gertrude." "You had better go home and get your supper, Gertrude." "I told you to go home twenty minutes ago, Gertrude." "Your mother will be worrying about you, Gertrude." "Go home, Gertrude, go home."

There are times when the lines around the human eye seem like shelves of eroded stone and when the staring eye itself strikes us with such a wilderness of animal feeling that we are at a loss. The look Francis gave the little girl was ugly and queer, and it frightened her. He reached into his pockets—his hands were shaking—and took out a quarter. "Go home, Gertrude, go home, and don't tell anyone, Gertrude. Don't—" He choked and ran into the living room as Julia called down to him from upstairs to hurry and dress.

The thought that he would drive Anne Murchison home later that night ran like a golden thread through the events of the party that Francis and Julia went to, and he laughed uproariously at dull jokes, dried a tear when Mabel Mercer told him about the death of her kitten, and stretched, yawned, sighed, and grunted like any other man with a rendezvous at the back of his mind. The bracelet was in his pocket. As he sat talking, the smell of grass was in his nose, and he was wondering where he would park the car. Nobody lived in the old Parker mansion, and the driveway was used as a lovers' lane. Townsend Street was a dead end, and he could park there, beyond the last house. The old lane that used to connect Elm Street to the riverbanks was overgrown, but he had walked there with his children, and he could drive his car deep enough into the brushwoods to be concealed.

The Weeds were the last to leave the party, and their host and hostess spoke of their own married happiness while they all four stood in the hallway saying good night. "She's my girl," their host said, squeezing his wife. "She's my blue sky. After sixteen years, I still bite her shoulders. She makes me feel like Hannibal crossing the Alps."

The Weeds drove home in silence. Francis brought the car up the driveway and sat still, with the motor running. "You can put the car in the garage," Julia said as she got out. "I told the Murchison girl she could leave at eleven. Someone drove her home." She shut the door, and Francis sat in the dark. He would be spared nothing then, it seemed, that a fool was not spared: ravening lewdness, jealousy, this hurt to his feelings that put tears in his eyes, even scorn—for he could see clearly the image he now presented, his arms spread over the steering wheel and his head buried in them for love.

Francis had been a dedicated Boy Scout when he was young, and, remembering the precepts of his youth, he left his office early the next afternoon and played some round-robin squash, but, with his body toned up by exercise and a shower, he realized that he might better have stayed at his desk. It was a frosty night when he got home. The air smelled sharply of change. When he stepped into the house, he sensed an unusual stir. The children were in their best clothes, and when Julia came down, she was wearing a lavender dress and her diamond sunburst. She explained the stir: Mr. Hubber was coming at seven to take their photograph for the Christmas card. She had put out Francis' blue suit and a tie with some color in it, because the picture was going to be in color this year. Julia was lighthearted at the thought of being photographed for Christmas. It was the kind of ceremony she enjoyed.

Francis went upstairs to change his clothes. He was tired from the day's work and tired with longing, and sitting on the edge of the bed had the effect of deepening his weariness. He thought of Anne Murchison, and the physical need to express himself, instead of being restrained by the pink lamps of Julia's dressing table, engulfed him. He went to Julia's desk, took a piece of writing paper, and began to write on it. "Dear Anne, I love you, I love you, I love you . . ." No one would see the letter, and he used no restraint. He used phrases like "heavenly bliss," and "love nest." He salivated, sighed, and trembled. When Julia called him to come down, the abyss between his fantasy and the practical world opened so wide that he felt it affected the muscles of his heart.

Julia and the children were on the stoop, and the photographer and his assistant had set up a double battery of floodlights to show the family and the architectural beauty of the entrance to their house. People who had come home on a late train slowed their cars to see the Weeds being photographed for their Christmas card. A few waved and called to the family. It took half an hour of smiling and wetting their lips before Mr. Hubber was satisfied. The heat of the lights made an unfresh smell in the frosty air, and when they were turned off, they lingered on the retina of Francis' eyes.

Later that night, while Francis and Julia were drinking their coffee in the living room, the doorbell rang. Julia answered the door and let in Clayton Thomas. He had come to pay for some theatre tickets that she had given his mother some time ago, and that Helen Thomas had crupulously insisted on paying for, though Julia had asked her not to. Julia invited him in to have a cup of coffee. "I won't have any coffee," Clayton said, "but I will come in for a minute." He followed her into the living room, said good evening to Francis, and sat awkwardly in a chair.

Clayton's father had been killed in the war, and the young man's fatherlessness surrounded him like an element. This may have been conspicuous in Shady Hill because the Thomases were the only family that lacked a piece; all the other marriages were intact and productive. Clayton was in his second or third year of college, and he and his mother lived alone in a large house, which she hoped to sell. Clayton had once made some trouble. Years ago, he had stolen some money and run away; he had got to California before they caught up with him. He was tall and homely, wore horn-rimmed glasses, and spoke in a deep voice.

"When do you go back to college, Clayton?" Francis asked.

"I'm not going back," Clayton said. "Mother doesn't have the money, and there's no sense in all this pretense. I'm going to get a job, and if we sell the house, we'll take an apartment in New York."

"Won't you miss Shady Hill?" Julia asked.

"No," Clayton said. "I don't like it."

"Why not?" Francis asked.

"Well, there's a lot here I don't approve of," Clayton said gravely. "Things like the club dances. Last Saturday night, I looked in toward the end and saw Mr. Granner trying to put Mrs. Minot into the trophy case. They were both drunk. I disapprove of so much drinking."

"It was Saturday night," Francis said.

"And all the dovecotes are phony," Clayton said. "And the way people clutter up their lives. I've thought about it a lot, and what seems to me to be really wrong with Shady Hill is that it doesn't have any future. So much energy is spent in perpetuating the place—in keeping out undesirables, and so forth—that the only idea of the future anyone has is just more and more commuting trains and more parties. I don't think that's healthy. I think people ought to be able to dream big dreams about the future. I think people ought to be able to dream great dreams."

"It's too bad you couldn't continue with college," Julia said.

"I wanted to go to divinity school," Clayton said.

"What's your church?" Francis asked.

"Unitarian, Theosophist, Transcendentalist, Humanist," Clayton said.

"Wasn't Emerson a transcendentalist?" Julia asked.

"I mean the English transcendentalists," Clayton said. "All the American transcendentalists were goops."

"What kind of job do you expect to get?" Francis asked.

"Well, I'd like to work for a publisher," Clayton said, "but everyone tells me there's nothing doing. But it's the kind of thing I'm interested in. I'm writing a long verse play about good and evil. Uncle Charlie might get me into a bank, and that would be good for me. I need the discipline. I have a long way to go in forming my character. I have some terrible habits. I talk too much. I think I ought to take vows of silence. I ought to try not to speak for a week, and discipline myself. I've thought of making a retreat at one of the Episcopalian monasteries, but I don't like Trinitarianism."

"Do you have any girl friends?" Francis asked.

"I'm engaged to be married," Clayton said. "Of course, I'm not old enough or rich enough to have my engagement observed or respected or anything, but I bought a simulated emerald for Anne Murchison with the money I made cutting lawns this summer. We're going to be married as soon as she finishes school."

Francis recoiled at the mention of the girl's name. Then a dingy light seemed to emanate from his spirit, showing everything—Julia, the boy, the chairs—in their true colorlessness. It was like a bitter turn of the weather.

"We're going to have a large family," Clayton said. "Her father's a terrible rummy, and I've had my hard times, and we want to have lots of children. Oh, she's wonderful, Mr. and Mrs. Weed, and we have so much in common. We like all the same things. We sent out the same Christmas card last year without planning it, and we both have an allergy to tomatoes, and our eyebrows grow together in the middle. Well, goodnight."

Julia went to the door with him. When she returned, Francis said that Clayton was lazy, irresponsible, affected, and smelly. Julia said that Francis seemed to be getting intolerant; the Thomas boy was young and should be given a chance. Julia had noticed other cases where Francis had been short-tempered. "Mrs. Wrightson has asked everyone in Shady Hill to her anniversary party but us," she said.

"I'm sorry, Julia."

"Do you know why they didn't ask us?"

"Why?"

"Because you insulted Mrs. Wrightson."

"Then you know about it?"

"June Masterson told me. She was standing behind you."

Julia walked in front of the sofa with a small step that expressed, Francis knew, a feeling of anger.

"I did insult Mrs. Wrightson, Julia, and I meant to. I've never liked her parties, and I'm glad she's dropped us."

"What about Helen?"

"How does Helen come into this?"

"Mrs. Wrightson's the one who decides who goes to the assemblies."

"You mean she can keep Helen from going to the dances?"

"Yes."

"I hadn't thought of that."

"Oh. I knew you hadn't thought of it," Julia cried, thrusting hilt-deep into this chink of his armor. "And it makes me furious to see this kind of stupid thoughtlessness wreck everyone's happiness."

"I don't think I've wrecked anyone's happiness."

"Mrs. Wrightson runs Shady Hill and has run it for the last forty years. I don't know what makes you think that in a community like this you can indulge every impulse you have to be insulting, vulgar, and offensive."

"I have very good manners," Francis said, trying to give the evening a turn toward the light.

"Damn you, Francis Weed!" Julia cried, and the spit of her words struck him in the face. "I've worked hard for the social position we enjoy in this place, and I won't stand by and see you wreck it. You must have understood when you settled here that you couldn't expect to live like a bear in a cave."

"I've got to express my likes and dislikes."

"You can conceal your dislikes. You don't have to meet everything head on, like a child. Unless you're anxious to be a social leper. It's no accident that we get asked out a great deal! It's no accident that Helen has so many friends. How would you like to spend your Saturday nights at the movies? How would you like to spend your Sundays raking up dead leaves? How would you like it if your daughter spent the assembly nights sitting at her window, listening to the music from the club? How would you like it—" He did something then that was, after all, not so unaccountable, since her words seemed to raise up between them a wall so deadening that he gagged. He struck her full in the face. She staggered and then, a moment later, seemed composed. She went up the stairs to their room. She didn't slam the door. When Francis followed, a few minutes later, he found her packing a suitcase.

"Julia, I'm very sorry."

"It doesn't matter," she said. She was crying.

"Where do you think you're going?"

"I don't know. I just looked at a timetable. There's an eleven-sixteen into New York. I'll take that."

"You can't go, Julia."

"I can't stay. I know that."

"I'm sorry about Mrs. Wrightson, Julia, and I'm—"

"It doesn't matter about Mrs. Wrightson. That isn't the trouble."

"What is the trouble?"

"You don't love me."

"I do love you, Julia."

"No, you don't."

"Julia, I do love you, and I would like to be as we were—sweet and bawdy and dark—but now there are so many people."

"You hate me."

"I don't hate you, Julia."

"You have no idea of how much you hate me. I think it's subconscious. You don't realize the cruel things you've done."

"What cruel things, Julia?"

"The cruel acts your subconscious drives you to in order to express your hatred of me."

"What, Julia?"

"I've never complained."

"Tell me."

"You don't know what you're doing."

"Tell me."

"Your clothes."

"What do you mean?"

"I mean the way you leave your dirty clothes around in order to express your subconscious hatred of me."

"I don't understand."

"I mean your dirty socks and your dirty pajamas and your dirty underwear and your dirty shirts!" She rose from kneeling by the suitcase and faced him, her eyes blazing and her voice ringing with emotion. "I'm talking about the fact that you've never learned to hang up anything. You just leave your clothes all over the floor where they drop, in order to humiliate me. You do it on purpose!" She fell on the bed, sobbing.

"Julia, darling!" he said, but when she felt his hand on her shoulder she got up.

"Leave me alone," she said. "I have to go." She brushed past him to the closet and came back with a dress. "I'm not taking any of the things you've given me," she said. "I'm leaving my pearls and the fur jacket."

"Oh, Julia!" Her figure, so helpless in its self-deceptions, bent over the suitcase made him nearly sick with pity. She did not understand how desolate her life would be without him. She didn't understand the hours that working women have to keep. She didn't understand that most of her friendships existed within the framework of their marriage, and that without this she would find herself alone. She didn't understand about travel, about hotels, about money. "Julia, I can't let you go! What you don't understand, Julia, is that you've come to be dependent on me."

She tossed her head back and covered her face with her hands. "Did you say that *I* was dependent on *you*?" she asked. "Is that what you said? And who is it that tells you what time to get up in the morning and when to go to bed at night? Who is it that prepares your meals and picks up your dirty clothes and invites your friends to dinner? If it weren't for me, your neckties would be greasy and your clothing would be full of moth holes. You were alone when I met you, Francis Weed, and you'll be alone when I leave. When Mother asked you for a list to send out invitations to our wedding, how many names did you have to give her? Fourteen!"

"Cleveland wasn't my home, Julia."

"And how many of your friends came to the church? Two!"

"Cleveland wasn't my home, Julia."

"Since I'm not taking the fur jacket," she said quietly, "you'd better put it back into storage. There's an insurance policy on the pearls that comes due in January. The name of the laundry and the maid's telephone number—all those things are in my desk. I hope you won't drink too much, Francis. I hope that nothing bad will happen to you. If you do get into serious trouble, you can call me."

"Oh, my darling, I can't let you go!" Francis said. "I can't let you go, Julia!" He took her in his arms.

"I guess I'd better stay and take care of you for a little while longer," she said.

Riding to work in the morning, Francis saw the girl walk down the aisle of the coach. He was surprised; he hadn't realized that the school she went to was in the city, but she was carrying books, she seemed to be going to school. His surpise delayed his reaction, but then he got up clumsily and stepped into the aisle. Several people had come between them, but he could see her ahead of him, waiting for someone to open the car door, and then, as the train swerved, putting out her hand to support herself as she crossed the platform into the next car. He followed her through that car and halfway through another before calling her name—"Anne! Anne!"—but she didn't turn. He followed her into still another

car, and she sat down in an aisle seat. Coming up to her, all his feelings warm
and bent in her direction, he put his hand on the back of her seat—even this
touch warmed him—and leaning down to speak to her, he saw that it was not
Anne. It was an older woman wearing glasses. He went on deliberately into another car, his face red with embarrassment and the much deeper feeling of having his good sense challenged; for if he couldn't tell one person from another,
what evidence was there that his life with Julia and the children had as much
reality as his dreams of iniquity in Paris or the litter, the grass smell, and the
cave-shaped trees in Lovers' Lane.

Late that afternoon, Julia called to remind Francis that they were going out
for dinner. A few minutes later, Trace Bearden called. "Look, fellar," Trace said.
"I'm calling for Mrs. Thomas. You know? Clayton, that boy of hers, doesn't
seem able to get a job, and I wondered if you could help. If you'd call Charlie
Bell—I know he's indebted to you—and say a good word for the kid, I think
Charlie would—"

"Trace, I hate to say this," Francis said, "but I don't feel that I can do anything for that boy. The kid's worthless. I know it's a harsh thing to say, but it's a
fact. Any kindness done for him would backfire in everybody's face. He's just a
worthless kid, Trace, and there's nothing to be done about it. Even if we got him
a job, he wouldn't be able to keep it for a week. I know that to be a fact. It's an
awful thing, Trace, and I know it is, but instead of recommending that kid, I'd
feel obligated to warn people against him—people who knew his father and
would naturally want to step in and do something. I'd feel obliged to warn them.
He's a thief . . ."

The moment this conversation was finished, Miss Rainey came in and stood
by his desk. "I'm not going to be able to work for you any more, Mr. Weed," she
said. "I can stay until the seventeenth if you need me, but I've been offered a
whirlwind of a job, and I'd like to leave as soon as possible."

She went out, leaving him to face alone the wickedness of what he had done
to the Thomas boy. His children in their photograph laughed and laughed,
glazed with all the bright colors of summer, and he remembered that they had
met a bagpiper on the beach that day and he had paid the piper a dollar to play
them a battle song of the Black Watch. The girl would be at the house when he
got home. He would spend another evening among his kind neighbors, picking
and choosing dead-end streets, cart tracks, and the driveways of abandoned
houses. There was nothing to mitigate his feeling—nothing that laughter or a
game of softball with the children would change—and, thinking back over the
plane crash, the Farquarsons' new maid, and Anne Murchison's difficulties with
her drunken father, he wondered how he could have avoided arriving at just
where he was. He was in trouble. He had been lost once in his life, coming back
from a trout stream in the north woods, and he had now the same bleak realization that no amount of cheerfulness or hopefulness or valor or perseverance
could help him find, in the gathering dark, the path that he'd lost. He smelled
the forest. The feeling of bleakness was intolerable, and he saw clearly that he
had reached the point where he would have to make a choice.

He could go to a psychiatrist, like Miss Rainey; he could go to church and
confess his lusts; he could go to a Danish massage parlor in the West Seventies

that had been recommended by a salesman; he could rape the girl or trust that he would somehow be prevented from doing this; or he could get drunk. It was his life, his boat, and, like every other man, he was made to be the father of thousands, and what harm could there be in a tryst that would make them both feel more kindly toward the world? This was the wrong train of thought, and he came back to the first, the psychiatrist. He had the telephone number of Miss Rainey's doctor, and he called and asked for an immediate appointment. He was insistent with the doctor's secretary—it was his manner in business—and when she said that the doctor's schedule was full for the next few weeks, Francis demanded an appointment that day and was told to come at five.

The psychiatrist's office was in a building that was used mostly by doctors and dentists, and the hallways were filled with the candy smell of mouthwash and memories of pain. Francis' character had been formed upon a series of private resolves—resolves about cleanliness, about going off the high diving board or repeating any other feat that challenged his courage, about punctuality, honesty, and virtue. To abdicate the perfect loneliness in which he had made his most vital decisions shattered his concept of character and left him now in a condition that felt like shock. He was stupefied. The scene for his *miserere mei Deus* was, like the waiting room of so many doctor's offices, a crude token gesture toward the sweets of domestic bliss: a place arranged with antiques, coffee tables, potted plants, and etchings of snow-covered bridges and geese in flight, although there were no children, no marriage bed, no stove, even, in this travesty of a house, where no one had ever spent the night and where the curtained windows looked straight onto a dark air shaft. Francis gave his name and address to a secretary and then saw, at the side of the room, a policeman moving toward him. "Hold it, hold it," the policeman said. "Don't move. Keep your hands where they are."

"I think it's all right, Officer," the secretary began. "I think it will be—"

"Let's make sure," the policeman said, and he began to slap Francis' clothes, looking for what—pistols, knives, an icepick? Finding nothing, he went off and the secretary began a nervous apology: "When you called on the telephone, Mr. Weed, you seemed very excited, and one of the doctor's patients has been threatening his life, and we have to be careful. If you want to go in now?" Francis pushed open a door connected to an electrical chime, and in the doctor's lair sat down heavily, blew his nose into a handkerchief, searched in his pockets for cigarettes, for matches, for something, and said hoarsely, with tears in his eyes, "I'm in love, Dr. Herzog."

It is a week or ten days later in Shady Hill. The seven-fourteen has come and gone, and here and there dinner is finished and the dishes are in the dish-washing machine. The village hangs, morally and economically, from a thread; but it hangs by its thread in the evening light. Donald Goslin has begun to worry the "Moonlight Sonata" again. *Marcato ma sempre pianissimo!* He seems to be wringing out a wet bath towel, but the housemaid does not heed him. She is writing a letter to Arthur Godfrey. In the cellar of his house, Francis Weed is building a coffee table. Dr. Herzog recommends woodwork as a therapy, and Francis finds some true consolation in the simple arithmetic involved and in the holy smell of new wood. Francis is happy. Upstairs, little Toby is crying, because he is tired. He puts off his cowboy hat, gloves, and fringed jacket, unbuckles the belt studded with gold and rubies, the silver bullets and holsters, slips off his suspenders, his checked shirt, and Levi's, and sits on the edge of his bed to pull off his high boots. Leaving this equipment in a heap, he goes to the closet and takes his space suit off a nail. It is a struggle for him to get into the long tights, but he succeeds. He loops the magic cape over his shoulders and, climbing onto the footboard of his bed, he spreads his arms and flies the short distance to the floor, landing with a thump that is audible to everyone in the house but himself.

"Go home, Gertrude, go home," Mrs. Masterson says. "I told you to go home an hour ago, Gertrude. It's way past your suppertime, and your mother will be worried. Go home!" A door on the Babcocks' terrace flies open, and out comes Mrs. Babcock without any clothes on, pursued by a naked husband. (Their children are away at boarding school, and their terrace is screened by a hedge.) Over the terrace they go and in at the kitchen door, as passionate and handsome a nymph and satyr as you will find on any wall in Venice. Cutting the last of the roses in her garden, Julia hears old Mr. Nixon shouting at the squirrels in his bird-feeding station. "Rapscallions! Varmints! Avaunt and quit my sight!" A miserable cat wanders into the garden, sunk in spiritual and physical discomfort. Tied to its head is a small straw hat—a doll's hat—and it is securely buttoned into a doll's dress, from the skirts of which protrudes its long, hairy tail. As it walks, it shakes its feet, as if it had fallen into water.

"Here, pussy, pussy, pussy!" Julia calls.

"Here, pussy, here, poor pussy!" But the cat gives her a skeptical look and stumbles away in its skirts. The last to come is Jupiter. He prances through the tomato vines, holding in his generous mouth the remains of an evening slipper. Then it is dark; it is a night where kings in golden suits ride elephants over the mountains.

Robert Coover

· ·

QUENBY AND OLA, SWEDE AND CARL

Night on the lake. A low cloud cover. The boat bobs silently, its motor for some reason dead. There's enough light in the far sky to see the obscure humps of islands a mile or two distant, but up close: nothing. There are islands in the intermediate distance, but their uncertain contours are more felt than seen. The same might be said, in fact, for the boat itself. From either end, the opposite end seems to melt into the blackness of the lake. It feels like it might rain.

Imagine Quenby and Ola at the barbecue pit. Their faces pale in the gathering dusk. The silence after the sudden report broken only by the whine of mosquitos in the damp grass, a distant whistle. Quenby has apparently tried to turn Ola away, back toward the house, but Ola is staring back over her shoulder. What is she looking at, Swede or the cat? Can she even see either?

In the bow sat Carl. Carl was from the city. He came north to the lake every summer for a week or two of fishing. Sometimes he came along with other guys, this year he came alone.

He always told himself he liked it up on the lake, liked to get away, that's what he told the fellows he worked with, too: get out of the old harness, he'd say. But he wasn't sure. Maybe he didn't like it. Just now, on a pitchblack lake with a stalled motor, miles from nowhere, cold and hungry and no fish to show for the long day, he was pretty sure he didn't like it.

You know the islands are out there, not more than a couple hundred yards probably, because you've seen them in the daylight. All you can make out now is here and there the pale stroke of what is probably a birch trunk, but you know there are spruce and jack pines as well, and balsam firs and white cedars and Norway pines and even maples and tamaracks. Forests have collapsed upon forests on these islands.

The old springs crush and grate like crashing limbs, exhausted trees, rocks tumbling into the bay, like the lake wind rattling through dry branches and pine needles. She is hot, wet, rich, softly spread. Needful. "Oh yes!" she whispers.

Walking on the islands, you've noticed saxifrage and bellwort, clintonia, shinleaf, and stemless lady's slippers. Sioux country once upon a time, you've heard tell, and Algonquin, mostly Cree and Ojibwa. Such things you know. Or the names of the birds up here: like spruce grouse and whiskey jack and American three-toed woodpecker. Blue-headed vireo. Scarlet tanager. Useless information. Just now, anyway. You don't even know what makes that strange whistle that pierces the stillness now.

"Say, what's that whistling sound, Swede? Sounds like a goddamn traffic whistle!" That was pretty funny, but Swede didn't laugh. Didn't say anything. "Some bird, I guess. Eh, Swede? Some goddamn bird."

"Squirrels," Swede said finally.

"Squirrels!" Carl was glad Swede had said something. At least he knew he was still back there. My Jesus, it was dark! He waited hopefully for another response from Swede, but it didn't come. "Learn something new every day."

Ola, telling the story, laughed brightly. The others laughed with her. What had she seen that night? It didn't matter, it was long ago. There were more lemon pies and there were more cats. She enjoyed being at the center of attention and she told the story well, imitating her father's laconic ways delightfully. She strode longleggedly across the livingroom floor at the main house, gripping an imaginary cat, her face puckered in a comic scowl. Only her flowering breasts under the orange shirt, her young hips packed snugly in last year's bright white shorts, her soft girlish thighs, slender calves: these were not Swede's.

She is an obscure teasing shape, now shattering the sheen of moonlight on the bay, now blending with it. Is she moving toward the shore, toward the house? No, she is in by the boats near the end of the docks, dipping in among shadows. You follow.

By day, there is a heavy greenness, mostly the deep dense greens of pines and shadowed undergrowth, and glazed blues and the whiteness of rocks and driftwood. At night, there is only darkness. Branches scrape gently on the roof of the guests' lodge; sometimes squirrels scamper across it. There are bird calls, the burping of frogs, the rustle of porcupines and muskrats, and now and then what sounds like the crushing footfalls of deer. At times, there is the sound of wind or rain, waves snapping in the bay. But essentially a deep stillness prevails, a stillness and darkness unknown to the city. And often, from far out on the lake, miles out perhaps, yet clearly ringing as though just outside the door: the conversation of men in fishing boats.

"Well, I guess you know your way around this lake pretty well. Eh, Swede?"

"Oh yah."

"Like the back of your hand, I guess." Carl felt somehow encouraged that

Swede had answered him. That "oh yah" was Swede's trademark. He almost never talked, and when he did, it was usually just "oh yah." Up on the "oh," down on the "yah." Swede was bent down over the motor, but what was he looking at? Was he looking at the motor or was he looking back this way? It was hard to tell. "It all looks the same to me, just a lot of trees and water and sky, and now you can't even see that much. Those goddamn squirrels sure make a lot of noise, don't they?" Actually, they were probably miles away.

Carl sighed and cracked his knuckles. "Can you hunt ducks up here?" Maybe it was better up here in the fall or winter. Maybe he could get a group interested. Probably cold, though. It was cold enough right now. "Well, I suppose you can. Sure, hell, why not?"

Quenby at the barbecue pit, grilling steaks. Thick T-bones, because he's back after two long weeks away. He has poured a glass of whiskey for himself, splashed a little water in it, mixed a more diluted one for Quenby. He hands her her drink and spreads himself into a lawnchair. Flames lick and snap at the steaks, and smoke from the burning fat billows up from the pit. Quenby wears pants, those relaxed faded bluejeans probably, and a soft leather jacket. The late evening sun gives a gentle rich glow to the leather. There is something solid and good about Quenby. Most women complain about hunting trips. Quenby bakes lemon pies to celebrate returns. Her full buttocks flex in the soft blue denim as, with tongs, she flips the steaks over. Imagine.

Her hips jammed against the gunwales, your wet bodies sliding together, shivering, astonished, your lips meeting—you wonder at your madness, what an island can do to a man, what an island girl can do. Later, having crossed the bay again, returning to the rocks, you find your underwear is gone. Yes, here's the path, here's the very tree—but gone. A childish prank? But she was with you all the time. Down by the kennels, the dogs begin to yelp.

Swede was a native of sorts. He and his wife Quenby lived year-round on an island up here on the lake. They operated a kind of small rustic lodge for men from the city who came up to fish and hunt. Swede took them out to the best places, Quenby cooked and kept the cabin up. They could take care of as many as eight at a time. They moved here years ago, shortly after marrying. Real natives, folks born and bred on the lake, are pretty rare; their 14-year-old daughter Ola is one of the few.

How far was it to Swede's island? This is a better question maybe than "Who is Swede?" but you are even less sure of the answer. You've been fishing all day and you haven't been paying much attention. No lights to be seen anywhere, and Swede always keeps a dock light burning, but you may be on the back side of his island, cut off from the light by the thick pines, only yards away from home, so to speak. Or maybe miles away. Most likely miles.

Yes, goddamn it, it was going to rain. Carl sucked on a beer in the bow. Swede tinkered quietly with the motor in the stern.

What made a guy move up into these parts? Carl wondered. It was okay for maybe a week or two, but he couldn't see living up here all the time. Well, of course, if a man really loved to fish. Fish and hunt. If he didn't like the ratrace in the city, and so on. Must be a bitch for Swede's wife and kid, though. Carl knew his own wife would never stand still for the idea. And Swede was probably pretty hard on old Quenby. With Swede there were never two ways about it. That's the idea Carl got.

Carl tipped the can of beer back, drained it. Stale and warm. It disgusted him. He heaved the empty tin out into the darkness, heard it plunk somewhere on the black water. He couldn't see if it sank or not. It probably didn't sink. He'd have to piss again soon. Probably he should do it before they got moving again. He didn't mind pissing from the boat, in a way he even enjoyed it, he felt like part of things up here when he was pissing from a boat, but right now it seemed too quiet or something.

Then he got to worrying that maybe he shouldn't have thrown it out there on the water, that beercan, probably there was some law about it, and anyway you could get things like that caught in boat motors, couldn't you? Hell, maybe that was what was wrong with the goddamn motor now. He'd just shown his ignorance again probably. That was what he hated most about coming up here, showing his ignorance. In groups it wasn't so bad, they were all green and could joke about it, but Carl was all alone this trip. Never again.

The Coleman lantern is lit. Her flesh glows in its eery light and the starched white linens are ominously alive with their thrashing shadows. She has brought clean towels; or perhaps some coffee, a book. Wouldn't look right to put out the lantern while she's down here, but its fierce gleam is disquieting. Pine boughs scratch the roof. The springs clatter and something scurries under the cabin. "Hurry!" she whispers.

"Listen, Swede, you need some help?" Swede didn't reply, so Carl stood up in a kind of crouch and made a motion as though he were going to step back and give a hand. He could barely make Swede out back there. He stayed carefully in the middle of the boat. He wasn't completely stupid.

Swede grunted. Carl took it to mean he didn't want any help, so he sat down again. There was one more can of beer under his seat, but he didn't much care to drink it. His pants, he had noticed on rising and sitting, were damp, and he felt stiff and sore. It was late. The truth was, he didn't know the first goddamn thing about outboard motors anyway.

There's this story about Swede. Ola liked to tell it and she told it well. About three years ago, when Ola was eleven, Swede had come back from a two-week hunting trip up north. For ducks. Ola, telling the story, would make a big thing about the beard he came back with and the jokes her mother made about it.

Quenby had welcomed Swede home with a big steak supper: thick T-bones, potatos wrapped in foil and baked in the coals, a heaped green salad. And lemon pie. Nothing in the world like Quenby's homemade lemon pie, and she'd baked it just for Swede. It was a great supper. Ola skipped most of the details, but one could imagine them. After supper, Swede said he'd bring in the pie and coffee.

In the kitchen, he discovered that Ola's cat had tracked through the pie. Right through the middle of it. It was riddled with cat tracks, and there was lemon pie all over the bench and floor. Daddy had been looking forward to that lemon pie for two weeks, Ola would say, and now it was full of cat tracks.

He picked up his gun from beside the back door, pulled some shells out of his jacket pocket, and loaded it. He found the cat in the laundryroom with lemon pie still stuck to its paws and whiskers. He picked it up by the nape and carried it outside. It was getting dark, but you could still see plainly enough. At least against the sky.

He walked out past the barbecue pit. It was dark enough that the coals seemed to glow now. Just past the pit, he stopped. He swung his arm in a lazy arc and pitched the cat high in the air. Its four paws scrambled in space. He lifted the gun to his shoulder and blew the cat's head off. Her daddy was a good shot.

Her mock pout, as she strides across the room, clutching the imaginary cat, makes you laugh. She needs a new pair of shorts. Last year they were loose on her, wrinkled where bunched at the waist, gaping around her small thighs. But she's grown, filled out a lot, as young girls her age do. When her shirt rides up over her waist, you notice that the zipper gapes in an open V above her hip bone. The white cloth is taut and glossy over her firm bottom; the only wrinkle is the almost painful crease between her legs.

Carl scrubbed his beard. It was pretty bristly, but that was because it was still new. He could imagine what his wife would say. He'd kid his face into a serious frown and tell her, hell, he was figuring on keeping the beard permanently now. Well, he wouldn't, of course, he'd feel like an ass at the office with it on, he'd just say that to rile his wife a little. Though, damn it, he did enjoy the beard. He wished more guys where he worked wore beards. He liked to scratch the back of his hand and wrist with it.

"You want this last beer, Swede?" he asked. He didn't get an answer. Swede was awful quiet. He was a quiet type of guy. Reticent, that's how he is, thought Carl. "Maybe Quenby's baked a pie," he said, hoping he wasn't being too obvious. Sure was taking one helluva long time.

He lifts the hem of his tee shirt off his hairy belly, up his chest, but she can't seem to wait for that—her thighs jerk up, her ankles lock behind his buttocks, and they crash to the bed, the old springs shrieking and thumping like a speeding subway, traffic at noon, arriving trains. His legs and buttocks, though pale and flabby, seem dark against the pure white spectacle of the starched sheets, the flushed glow of her full heaving body, there in the harsh blaze of the Coleman lantern. Strange, they should keep it burning. His short stiff beard scrubs the hollow of her throat, his broad hands knead her trembling flesh. She sighs, whimpers, pleads, as her body slaps rhythmically against his. "Yes!" she cries hoarsely.

You turn silently from the window. At the house, when you arrive, you find Ola washing dishes.

What did Quenby talk about? Her garden probably, pie baking, the neighbors. About the wind that had come up one night while he'd been gone, and how she'd had to move some of the boats around. His two-week beard: looked like a darned broom, she said. He'd have to sleep down with the dogs if he didn't cut it off. Ola would giggle, imagining her daddy sleeping with the dogs. And, yes, Quenby would probably talk about Ola, about the things she'd done or said while he was away, what she was doing in sixth grade, about her pets and her friends and the ways she'd helped around the place.

Quenby at the barbecue pit, her full backside to him, turning the steaks, sipping the whiskey, talking about life on the island. Or maybe not talking at all. Just watching the steaks maybe. Ola inside setting the table. Or swimming down by the docks. A good thing here. The sun now an orangish ball over behind the pines. Water lapping at the dock and the boats, curling up on the shore, some minutes after a boat passes distantly. The flames and the smoke. Down at the kennels, the dogs were maybe making a ruckus. Maybe Ola's cat had wandered down there. The cat had a habit of teasing them outside their pen. The dogs had worked hard, they deserved a rest. Mentally, he gave the cat a boot in the ribs. He had already fed the dogs, but later he would take the steak bones down.

Quenby's thighs brush together when she walks. In denim, they whistle; bare, they whisper. Not so, Ola's. Even with her knees together (they rarely are), there is space between her thighs. A pressure there, not of opening, but of awkwardness.

Perhaps, too, island born, her walk is different. Her mother's weight is settled solidly beneath her buttocks; she moves out from there, easily, calmly, weightlessly. Ola's center is still between her narrow shoulders, somewhere in the midst of her fine new breasts, and her quick astonished stride is guided by the tips of her hipbones, her knees, her toes. Quenby's thick black cushion is a rich locus of movement; her daughter still arches uneasily out and away from the strange outcropping of pale fur that peeks out now at the inner edges of the white shorts.

It is difficult for a man to be alone on a green island.

Carl wished he had a cigarette. He'd started out with cigarettes, but he'd got all excited once when he hooked a goddamn fish, and they had all spilled out on the wet bottom of the boat. What was worse, the damn fish—a great northern, Swede had said—had broke his line and got away. My Jesus, the only strike he'd got all day, and he'd messed it up! Swede had caught two. Both bass. A poor day, all in all. Swede didn't smoke.

To tell the truth, even more than a cigarette, he wished he had a good stiff drink. A hot supper. A bed. Even that breezy empty lodge at Swede's with its stale piney smell and cold damp sheets and peculiar noises filled him with a terrific longing. Not to mention home, real home, the TV, friends over for bridge or poker, his own electric blanket.

"Sure is awful dark, ain't it?" Carl said "ain't" out of deference to Swede.

Swede always said "ain't" and Carl liked to talk that way when he was up here. He liked to drink beer and say "ain't" and "he don't" and stomp heavily around with big boots on. He even found himself saying "oh yah!" sometimes, just like Swede did. Up on the "oh," down on the "yah." Carl wondered how it would go over back at the office. They might even get to know him by it. When he was dead, they'd say: "Well, just like good old Carl used to say: oh yah!"

In his mind, he watched the ducks fall. He drank the whiskey and watched the steaks and listened to Quenby and watched the ducks fall. They didn't just plummet, they fluttered and flopped. Sometimes they did seem to plummet, but in his mind he saw the ones that kept trying to fly, kept trying to understand what the hell was happening. It was the rough flutter sound and the soft loose splash of the fall that made him like to hunt ducks.

Swede, Quenby, Ola, Carl . . . Having a drink after supper, in the livingroom around the fireplace, though there's no fire in it. Ola's not drinking, of course. She's telling a story about her daddy and a cat. It is easy to laugh. She's a cute girl. Carl stretches. "Well, off to the sack, folks. Thanks for the terrific supper. See you in the morning, Swede." Quenby: "Swede or I'll bring you fresh towels, Carl. I forgot to put any this morning."

You know what's going on out here, don't you? You're not that stupid. You know why the motor's gone dead, way out here, miles from nowhere. You know the reason for the silence. For the wait. Dragging it out. Making you feel it. After all, there was the missing underwear. Couldn't find it in the morning sunlight either.

But what could a man do? You remember the teasing buttocks as she dog-paddled away, the taste of her wet belly on the gunwales of the launch, the terrible splash when you fell. Awhile ago, you gave a tug on the stringer. You were hungry and you were half-tempted to paddle the boat to the nearest shore and cook up the two bass. The stringer felt oddly weighted. You had a sudden vision of a long cold body at the end of it, hooked through a cheek, eyes glazed over, childish limbs adrift. What do you do with a vision like that? You forget it. You try to.

They go in to supper. He mixes a couple more drinks on the way. The whiskey plup-plup-plups out of the bottle. Outside, the sun is setting. Ola's cat rubs up against his leg. Probably contemplating the big feed when the ducks get cleaned. Brownnoser. He lifts one foot and scrubs the cat's ears with the toe of his boot. Deep-throated purr. He grins, carries the drinks in and sits down at the dining-room table.

Quenby talks about town gossip, Ola talks about school and Scouts, and he talks about shooting ducks. A pretty happy situation. He eats with enthusiasm. He tells how he got the first bird, and Ola explains about the Golden Gate Bridge, cross-pollination, and Tom Sawyer, things she's been reading in school.

He cleans his plate and piles on seconds and thirds of everything. Quenby smiles to see him eat. She warns him to save room for the pie, and he replies that he could put away a herd of elephants and still have space for ten pies. Ola laughs gaily at that. She sure has a nice laugh. Ungainly as she is just now, she's going to be a pretty girl, he decides. He drinks his whiskey off, announces he'll bring in the pie and coffee.

How good it had felt! In spite of the musty odors, the rawness of the stiff sheets, the gaudy brilliance of the Coleman lantern, the anxious haste, the cool air teasing the hairs on your buttocks, the scamper of squirrels across the roof, the hurried by-passing of preliminaries (one astonishing kiss, then shirt and jacket and pants had dropped away in one nervous gesture, and down you'd gone, you in teeshirt and socks still): once it began, it was wonderful! Lunging recklessly into that steaming softness, your lonely hands hungering over her flesh, her heavy thighs kicking up and up, then slamming down behind your knees, hips rearing up off the sheets, her voice rasping: "Hurry!"—everything else forgotten, how good, how good!

And then she was gone. And you lay in your teeshirt and socks, staring half-dazed at the Coleman lantern, smoking a cigarette, thinking about tomorrow's fishing trip, idly sponging away your groin's dampness with your shorts. You stubbed out the cigarette, pulled on your khaki pants, scratchy on your bare and agitated skin, slipped out the door to urinate. The light leaking out your shuttered window caught your eye. You went to stand there, and through the broken shutter, you stared at the bed, the roughed-up sheets, watched yourself there. Well. Well. You pissed on the wall, staring up toward the main house, through the pines. Dimly, you could see Ola's head in the kitchen window.

You know. You know.

"Listen, uh, Swede . . ."

"Yah?"

"Oh, nothing. I mean, well, what I started to say was, maybe I better start putting my shoulder to, you know, one of the paddles or whatever the hell you call them. I—well, unless you're sure you can get it—"

"Oh yah. I'm sure."

"Well . . ."

Swede, Carl, Ola, Quenby . . . One or more may soon be dead. Swede or Carl, for example, in revenge or lust or self-defense. And if one or both of them do return to the island, what will they find there? Or perhaps Swede is long since dead, and Carl only imagines his presence. A man can imagine a lot of things, alone on a strange lake in a dark night.

Carl, Quenby, Swede, Ola . . . Drinks in the livingroom. An after-dinner sleepiness on all of them. Except Ola. Wonderful supper. Nothing like fresh lake bass. And Quenby's lemon pie. "Did you ever hear about Daddy and the cat?" Ola asks. "No!" All smile. Ola perches forward on the hassock. "Well, Daddy had been away for two weeks . . ."

.   .   .   .   .

Listen: alone, far from your wife, nobody even to play poker with, a man does foolish things sometimes. You're stretched out in your underwear on an uncomfortable bed in the middle of the night; for example, awakened perhaps by the footfalls of deer outside the cabin, or the whistle of squirrels, the cry of loons, unable now to sleep. You step out, barefoot, to urinate by the front wall of the lodge. There seems to be someone swimming down in the bay, over near the docks, across from the point here. No lights up at the main house, just the single dull bulb glittering as usual out on the far end of the dock, casting no light. A bright moon.

You pad quietly down toward the bay, away from the kennels, hoping the dogs don't wake. She is swimming this way. She reaches the rocks near the point here, pulls herself up on them, then stands shivering, her slender back to you, gazing out on the way she's come, out toward the boats and docks, heavy structures crouched in the moonglazed water. Pinpricks of bright moonlight sparkle on the crown of her head, her narrow shoulders and shoulderblades, the crest of her buttocks, her calves and heels.

Hardly thinking, you slip off your underwear, glance once at the house, then creep out on the rock beside her. "How's the water?" you whisper.

She huddles over her breasts, a little surprised, but smiles up at you. "It's better in than out," she says, her teeth chattering a little with the chill.

You stoop to conceal, in part, your burgeoning excitement, which you'd hoped against, and dip your fingers in the water. Is it cold? You hardly notice, for you are glancing back up now, past the hard cleft nub where fine droplets of water, catching the moonlight, bejewel the soft down, past the flat gleaming tummy and clutched elbows, at the young girl's dark shivering lips. She, too, seems self-conscious, for like you, she squats now, presenting you only her bony knees and shoulders, trembling, and her smile. "It's okay," you say, "I have a daughter just your age." Which is pretty stupid.

They were drifting between two black islands. Carl squinted and concentrated, but he couldn't see the shores, couldn't guess how far away the islands were. Didn't matter anyway. Nobody on them. "Hey, listen, Swede, you need a light? I think I still got some matches here if they're not wet—"

"No, sit down. Just be a moment . . ."

Well, hell, stop and think, goddamn it, you can't stick a lighted match around a gasoline motor. "Well, I just thought . . ." Carl wondered why Swede didn't carry a flashlight. My Jesus, a man live up here on a lake all these years and doesn't know enough to take along a goddamn flashlight. Maybe he wasn't so bright, after all.

He wondered if Swede's wife wasn't worrying about them by now. Well, she was probably used to it. A nice woman, friendly, a good cook, probably pretty well built in her day, though not Carl's type really. A little too slack in the britches. Skinny little daughter, looked more like Swede. Filling out, though. Probably be a cute girl in a couple years. Carl got the idea vaguely that Quenby, Swede's wife, didn't really like it up here. Too lonely or something. Couldn't blame her.

He knew it was a screwy notion, but he kept wishing there was a goddamn neon light or something around. He fumbled under the seat for the other beer.

"I asked Daddy why he shot my cat," she said. She stood at the opposite end of the livingroom, facing them, in her orange shirt and bright white shorts, thin legs apart. It was a sad question, but her lips were smiling, her small white teeth glittering gaily. She'd just imitated her daddy lobbing the cat up in the air and blowing its head off. " 'Well, honey, I gave it a sporting chance,' he said. 'I threw it up in the air, and if it'd flown away, I wouldn't have shot it!' " She joined in the general laughter, skipping awkwardly, girlishly, back to the group. It was a good story.

She slips into the water without a word, and dogpaddles away, her narrow bottom bobbing in and out of sight. What the hell, the house is dark, the dogs silent: you drop into the water—wow! sudden breathtaking impact of the icy envelope! whoopee!—and follow her, a dark teasing shape rippling the moonlit surface.

You expect her to bend her course in toward the shore, toward the house, and, feeling suddenly exposed and naked and foolish in the middle of the bright bay, in spite of your hunger to see her again, out of the water, you pause, prepare to return to the point. But, no, she is in by the boats, near the end of the docks, disappearing into the wrap of shadows. You sink out of sight, swim underwater to the docks—a long stretch for a man your age—and find her there, holding onto the rope ladder of the launch her father uses for guiding large groups. The house is out of sight, caution out of mind.

She pulls herself up the ladder and you follow close behind, her legs brushing your face and shoulders. At the gunwales, she emerges into full moonlight, and as she bends forward to crawl into the launch, drugged by the fantasy of the moment, you lean up to kiss her glistening buttocks. In your throbbing mind is the foolish idea that, if she protests, you will make some joke about your beard.

He punched the can and the beer exploded out. He ducked just in time, but got part of it in his ear. "Hey! Did I get you, Swede?" he laughed. Swede didn't say anything. Hell, it was silly even to ask. The beer had shot off over his shoulder, past the bow, the opposite direction from Swede. He had asked only out of habit. Because he didn't like the silence. He punched a second hole and put the can to his lips. All he got at first was foam. But by tipping the can almost straight up, he managed a couple swallows of beer. At first, he thought it tasted good, but a moment later, the flat warm yeasty taste sliming his mouth, he wondered why the hell he had opened it up. He considered dumping the rest of it in the lake. But, damn it, Swede would hear him and wonder why he was doing it. This time, though, he would remember and not throw the empty can away.

Swede, Quenby, Carl, Ola . . . The story and the laughter and off to bed. The girl has omitted one detail from her story. After her daddy's shot, the cat had plummeted to the earth. But afterwards, there was a fluttering sound on the ground where it hit. Still, late at night, it caused her wonder. Branches scrape softly on the roof. Squirrels whistle and scamper. There is a rustling of beavers, foxes, skunks, and porcupines. A profound stillness, soon to be broken surely by rain. And, from far out on the lake, men in fishing boats, arguing, chattering, opening beercans. Telling stories.

Julio Cortázar

• •

BESTIARY

Between the last spoonful of rice pudding with milk (very little cinnamon, a shame) and the goodnight kisses before going up to bed, there was a tinkling in the telephone room and Isabel hung around until Inés came from answering it and said something into their mother's ear. They looked at one another, then both of them looked at Isabel who was thinking about the broken birdcage and the long division problems and briefly of old lady Lucera being angry because she'd pushed her doorbell on the way back from school. She wasn't all that worried, Inés and her mother were looking as if they were gazing past her somewhere, almost taking her as an excuse; but they were looking at her.

"I don't like the idea of her going, believe you me," Inés said. "Not so much because of the tiger, after all they're very careful in that respect. But it's such a depressing house and only that boy to play with her . . ."

"I don't like the idea either," her mother said, and Isabel knew, as if she were on a toboggan, that they were going to send her to the Funes' for the summer. She flung herself into the news, into the great green wave, the Funes', the Funes', sure they were going to send her. They didn't like it, but it was convenient. Delicate lungs, Mar del Plata so very expensive, difficult to manage such a spoiled child, stupid, the way she always acted up with that wonderful Miss Tania, a restless sleeper, toys underfoot everyplace, questions, buttons to be sewn back on, filthy knees. She felt afraid, delighted, smell of the willow trees and the *u* in Funes was getting mixed in with the rice pudding, so late to be still up, and get up to bed, right now.

Lying there, the light out, covered with kisses and rueful glances from Inés and their mother, not fully decided but already decided in spite of everything to send her. She was enjoying beforehand the drive up in the phaeton, the first breakfast, the happiness of Nino, hunter of cockroaches, Nino the toad, Nino the fish (a memory of three years before, Nino showing her some small cutouts he'd glued in an album and telling her gravely, "This-is-a-toad, and THIS is-a-fish"). Now Nino in the park waiting for her with the butterfly net, and also Rema's soft hands—she saw them coming out of the darkness, she had her eyes open and instead of Nino's face—zap!—Rema's hands, the Funes' younger daughter. "Aunt Rema loves me a lot," and Nino's eyes got large and wet, she saw Nino again disjointedly floating in the dim light of the bedroom, looking at her contentedly. Nino the fish. Falling asleep wanting the week to be over that same night, and the goodbyes, the train, the last half-mile in the phaeton, the gate, the eucalyptus trees along the road leading up to the house. Just before falling asleep, she had a moment of terror when she imagined that she was maybe dreaming. Stretching out all at once, her feet hit the brass bars at the foot of the bed, they hurt through the covers, and she heard her mother and Inés talking in the big dining room, baggage, see the doctor about those pimples, cod-liver oil and concentrate of witch hazel. It wasn't a dream, it wasn't a dream.

It wasn't a dream. They took her down to Constitution Station one windy morning, small flags blowing from the pushcarts in the plaza, a piece of pie in the railroad station restaurant, and the enormous entrance to platform 14. Between Inés and her mother they kissed her so much that her face felt like it'd been walked on, soft and smelly, rouge and Coty powder, wet around the mouth, a squeamish feeling of filth that the wind eradicated with one large smack. She wasn't afraid to travel alone because she was a big girl, with nothing less than twenty pesos in her pocketbook, Sansinena Co., Frozen Meats a sweetish stink seeping in the window, the railroad trestle over the yellow brook and Isabel already back to normal from having had to have that crying spell at the station, happy, dead with fear, active, using fully the seat by the window, almost the only traveler in that portion of the coach from which one could examine all the different places and see oneself in the small mirrors. She thought once or twice of her mother, of Inés—they'd already be on the 97 car, leaving Constitution—she read no smoking, spitting is forbidden by law, seating capacity 42 passengers, they were passing through Banfield at top speed, vavooom! country more country more country intermingled with the taste of Milky Way and the menthol drops. Inés had reminded her that she would be working on the green wool in such a way that Isabel packed the knitting into the most inaccessible part of the suitcase, poor Inés, and what a stupid idea.

At the station she was a little bit worried because if the phaeton . . . But there it was, with don Nicanor very red and respectful, yes miss, this miss, that miss, was the trip fine, was her mother as well as ever, of course it had rained— Oh the swinging motion of the phaeton to get her back into the whole aquarium of her previous visit to Los Horneros. Everything smaller, more crystalline and pink, without the tiger then, don Nicanor with fewer white hairs, barely three years ago, Nino a toad, Nino a fish, and Rema's hands which made you want to cry and feel them on your head forever, a caress like death almost and pastries with vanilla cream, the two best things on earth.

They gave her a room upstairs all to herself, the loveliest room. A grownup's room (Nino's idea, all black curls and eyes, handsome in his blue overalls; in the afternoon, of course, Luis made him dress up, his slate-grey suit and a red tie) and inside, another tiny room with an enormous wild cardinal. The bathroom was two doors away (but inside doors through the rooms so that you could go without checking beforehand where the tiger was), full of spigots and metal things, though they did not fool Isabel easily, you could tell it was a country bathroom, things were not as perfect as in a city bath. And it smelled old, the second morning she found a waterbug taking a walk in the washbasin. She barely touched it, it rolled itself into a timid ball and disappeared down the gurgling drain.

Dear mama, I'm writing to— They were eating in the dining room with the chandelier because it was cooler. The Kid was complaining every minute about the heat, Luis said nothing, but every once in a while you could see the sweat break out on his forehead or his chin. Only Rema was restful, she passed the plates slowly and always as if the meal were a birthday party, a little solemnly and impressively. (Isabel was secretly studying her way of carving and of ordering the servants.) For the most part, Luis was always reading, fist to brow, and the book leaning against a siphon. Rema touched his arm before passing him a plate, and the Kid would interrupt him once in a while to call him philosopher. It hurt Isabel that Luis might be a philosopher, not because of that, but because of the Kid, that he had an excuse then to joke and call him that.

They ate like this: Luis at the head of the table, Rema and Nino on one side, the Kid and Isabel on the other, so that there was an adult at the end and a child and a grownup at either side. When Nino wanted to tell her something serious, he'd give her a kick on the shin with his shoe. Once Isabel yelled and the Kid got angry and said she was badly brought up. Rema looked at her continuously until Isabel was comforted by the gaze and the potato soup.

Mama, before you go in to eat it's like all the rest of the time, you have to look and see if— Almost always it was Rema who went to see if they could go into the dining room with the crystal chandelier. The second day she came to the big living room and said they would have to wait. It was a long time before a farmhand came to tell them that the tiger was in the clover garden, then Rema took the children's hands and everyone went in to eat. The fried potatoes were pretty dry that morning, though only Nino and the Kid complained.

You told me I was not supposed to go around making— Because Rema seemed to hold off all questions with her terse sweetness. The setup worked so well that it was unnecessary to worry about the business of the rooms. It was an absolutely enormous house, and at worst, there was only one room they couldn't go into; never more than one, so it didn't matter. Isabel was as used to it as Nino, after a couple of days. From morning until evening they played in the grove of willows, and if they couldn't play in the willow grove, there was always the clover garden, the park with its hammocks, and the edge of the brook. It was the same in the house, they had their bedrooms, the hall down the center, the library downstairs (except one Thursday when they couldn't go into the library) and the dining room with the chandelier. They couldn't go into Luis' study because Luis was reading all the time, once in a while he would call to his son and give him picture books; but Nino always took them out, they went to the living room or to the front garden to look at them. They never went into the Kid's study because they were afraid he would throw a tantrum. Rema told them that it was better that way, she said it as though she were warning them; they'd already learned how to read her silences.

After all's said, it was a sad life. Isabel wondered one night why the Funes' had invited her for the summer. She wasn't old enough to understand that it was for Nino not for her, a summer plaything to keep Nino happy. She only managed to see the sadness of the house, that Rema seemed always tired, that it hardly ever rained and that, nonetheless, things had that air of being damp and abandoned. After a few days she got used to the rules of the house and the not-difficult discipline of that summer at Los Horneros. Nino was beginning to learn to use the microscope Luis had given him; they spent a magnificent week growing insects in a trough with stagnant water and lily pads, putting drops on the glass slide to look at the microbes. "They're mosquito larvae, you're not going to see microbes with that microscope," Luis told them, his smile somewhat pained and distant. They could never believe that that wriggling horror was not a microbe. Rema brought them a kaleidoscope which she kept in her wardrobe, but they still preferred detecting microbes and counting their legs. Isabel carried a notebook and kept notations of their experiments, she combined biology with chemistry and putting together a medicine chest. They made the medicine chest in Nino's room after ransacking the whole house to get things for it. Isabel told Luis, "We want some of everything: things." Luis gave them Andreu lozenges, pink cotton, a test tube. The Kid came across with a rubber bag and a bottle of green pills with the label worn off. Rema came to see the medicine chest, read the inventory in the notebook, and told them that they were learning a lot of useful things. It occurred to her or to Nino (who always got excited and wanted to show off in front of Rema) to assemble an herbarium. As it was possible that morning to go down to the clover garden, they went about collecting samples and by nightfall they had both their bedroom floors filled with leaves and flowers on bits of paper, there was hardly room to step. Before going to bed, Isabel noted: "Leaf #74: green, heart-shaped, with brown spots." It annoyed her a little that almost all the leaves were green, nearly all smooth, and nearly all lanceolate.

The day they went out ant-hunting she saw the farmhands. She knew the foreman and the head groom because they brought reports to the house. But these other younger hands stood there against the side of the sheds with an air of siesta, yawning once in a while and watching the kids play. One of them asked Nino, "Why'ya collectin' all them bugs?" and tapped him on top of his head with all the curls, using two fingers. Isabel would have liked Nino to lose his temper, to show that he was the boss's son. They already had the bottle crawling with ants and on the bank of the brook they ran across a bug with an enormous hard shell and stuck him in the bottle too, to see what would happen. The idea of an ant-farm they'd gotten out of *The Treasure of Youth*, and Luis loaned them a big, deep glass tank. As they left, both of them carrying it off, Isabel heard him say to Rema, "Better this way, they'll be quiet in the house." Also it seemed to her that Rema sighed. Before dropping off to sleep, when faces appear in the darkness, she remembered again the Kid going out onto the porch for a smoke, thin, humming to himself, saw Rema who was bringing him out coffee and he made a mistake taking the cup so clumsily that he caught Rema's fingers while trying to get the cup, Isabel had seen from the dining room Rema pulling her hand back and the Kid was barely able to keep the cup from falling and laughed at the tangle. Black ants better than the red ones: bigger, more ferocious. Afterward let loose a pile of red ones, watch the war from outside the glass, all very safe. Except they didn't fight. Made two anthills, one in each corner of the glass tank. They consoled one another by studying the distinctive habits, a special notebook for each kind of ant. But almost sure they would fight, look through the glass at war without quarter, and just one notebook.

Rema didn't like to spy on them, she passed by the bedrooms sometimes and would see them with the ant-farm beside the window, impassioned and important. Nino was particularly good at pointing out immediately any new galleries, and Isabel enlarged the diagram traced in ink on double pages. On Luis' advice they collected black ants only, and the ant-farm was already enormous, the ants appeared to be furious and worked until nightfall, excavating and moving earth with a thousand methods and maneuvers, the careful rubbing of feelers and feet, abrupt fits of fury or vehemence, concentrations and dispersals for no apparent reason. Isabel no longer knew what to take notes on, little by little she put the notebook aside and hours would pass in studying and forgetting what had been discovered. Nino began to want to go back to the garden, he mentioned the hammocks and the colts. Isabel was somewhat contemptuous of him for that. The ant-farm was worth the whole of Los Horneros, and it gave her immense pleasure to think that the ants came and went without fear of any tiger, sometimes she tried to imagine a tiny little tiger like an eraser, roaming the galleries of the ant-farm; maybe that was why the dispersals and concentrations. And now she liked to rehearse the real world in the one of glass, now that she felt a little like a prisoner, now that she was forbidden to go down to the dining room until Rema said so.

She pushed her nose against one of the glass sides, promptly all attention because she liked for them to look at her; she heard Rema stop in the doorway, just silent, looking at her. She heard those things with such a sharp brightness when it was Rema.

"You're alone here? Why?"

"Nino went off to the hammocks. This big one must be a queen, she's huge."

Rema's apron was reflected in the glass. Isabel saw one of her hands slightly raised, with the reflection it looked as if it were inside the ant-farm; suddenly she thought about the same hand offering a cup of coffee to the Kid, but now there were ants running along her fingers, ants instead of the cup and the Kid's hand pressing the fingertips.

"Take your hand out, Rema," she asked.

"My hand?"

"Now it's all right. The reflection was scaring the ants."

"Ah. It's all right in the dining room now, you can go down."

"Later. Is the Kid mad at you, Rema?"

The hand moved across the glass like a bird through a window. It looked to Isabel as though the ants were really scared this time, that they ran from the reflection. You couldn't see anything now, Rema had left, she went down the hall as if she were escaping something. Isabel felt afraid of the question herself, a dull fear, made no sense, maybe it wasn't the question but seeing Rema run off that way, or the once-more-clear empty glass where the galleries emptied out and twisted like twitching fingers inside the soil.

It was siesta one afternoon, watermelon, handball against the wall which overlooked the brook, and Nino was terrific, catching shots that looked impossible and climbing up to the roof on a vine to get the ball loose where it was caught between two tiles. A son of one of the farmhands came out from beside the willows and played with them, but he was slow and clumsy and shots got away from him. Isabel could smell the terebinth leaves and at one moment, returning with a backhand an insidious low shot of Nino's, she felt the summer's happiness very deep inside her. For the first time she understood her being at Los Horneros, the vacation, Nino. She thought of the ant-farm up there and it was an oozy dead thing, a horror of legs trying to get out, false air, poisonous. She hit the ball angrily, happily, she bit off a piece of a terebinth leaf with her teeth, bitter, she spit it out in disgust, happy for the first time really, and at last, under the sun in the country.

The window glass fell like hail. It was in the Kid's study. They saw him rise in his shirtsleeves and the broad black eyeglasses.

"Filthy pains-in-the-ass!"

The little peon fled. Nino set himself alongside Isabel, she felt him shaking with the same wind as the willows.

"We didn't mean to do it, uncle."

"Honest, Kid, we didn't mean to do it."

He wasn't there any longer.

She had asked Rema to take away the ant-farm and Rema promised her. After, chatting while she helped her hang up her clothes and get into her pajamas, they forgot. When Rema put out the light, Isabel felt the presence of the ants, Rema went down the hall to say goodnight to Nino who was still crying and repentant, but she didn't have the nerve to call her back again. Rema would have thought that she was just a baby. She decided to go to sleep immediately, and was wider awake than ever. When the moment came when there were faces in the darkness, she saw her mother and Inés looking at one another and smiling like accomplices and pulling on gloves of phosphorescent yellow. She saw Nino weeping, her mother and Inés with the gloves on that now were violet hairdos that twirled and twirled round their heads, Nino with enormous vacant eyes—maybe from having cried too much—and thought that now she would see Rema and Luis, she wanted to see them, she didn't want to see the Kid, but she saw the Kid without his glasses with the same tight face that he'd had when he began hitting Nino and Nino fell backwards until he was against the wall and looked at him as though expecting that would finish it, and the Kid continued to whack back and forth across his face with a loose soft slap that sounded moist, until Rema intruded herself in front of Nino and the Kid laughed, his face almost touching Rema's, and then they heard Luis returning and saying from a distance that now they could go into the dining room. Everything had happened so fast because Nino had been there and Rema had come to tell them not to leave the living room until Luis found out what room the tiger was in and she stayed there with them watching the game of checkers. Nino won and Rema praised him, then Nino was so happy that he put his arms around her waist and wanted to kiss her. Rema had bent down, laughing, and Nino kissed her on the nose and eyes, the two of them laughing and Isabel also, they were so happy playing. They didn't see the Kid coming, when he got up to them he grabbed Nino, jerked at him, said something about the ball breaking the window in his room and started to hit him, he looked at Rema while he hit him, he seemed furious with Rema and she defied him with her eyes for a moment. Terrified, Isabel saw her face up to him, then she stepped in between to protect Nino. The whole evening meal was a deceit, a lie, Luis thought that Nino was crying from having taken a tumble, the Kid looked at Rema as if to order her to shut up, Isabel saw him now with his hard, handsome mouth, very red lips; in the dimness they were even more scarlet, she could see his teeth, barely revealed, glittering. A puffed cloud emerged from his teeth, a green triangle, Isabel blinked her eyes to wipe out the images and Inés and her mother appeared again with their yellow gloves; she gazed at them for a moment, then thought of the ant-farm: that was there and you couldn't see it; the yellow gloves were not there and she saw them instead as if in bright sunlight. It seemed almost curious to her, she couldn't make the ant-farm come out, instead she felt it as a kind of weight there, a chunk of thick, live space. She felt it so strongly that she reached about for the matches, the night-lamp. The ant-farm leaped from the nothingness, wrapped in shifting shadow. Isabel lifted the lamp and came closer. Poor ants, they were going to think that the sun was up. When she could see one of the sides, she was frightened; the ants had been working in all that blackness. She watched them swarm up and down, in silence, so visible, palpable. They were working away inside there as though they had not yet lost their hope of getting out.

It was almost always the foreman who kept them advised of the tiger's movements; Luis had the greatest confidence in him, and since he passed almost the whole day working in his study, he neither emerged nor let those who came down from the next floor move about until don Roberto sent in his report. But they had to rely on one another also. Busy with the household chores inside, Rema knew exactly what was happening upstairs and down. At other times, it was the children who brought the news to the Kid or to Luis. Not that they'd seen anything, just that don Roberto had run into them outside, indicated the tiger's whereabouts to them, and they came back in to pass it on. They believed Nino without question, Isabel less, she was new and might make a mistake. Later, though, since she always went about with Nino stuck to her skirt, they finally believed both of them equally. That was in the morning and afternoon; at night it was the Kid who went out to check and see that the dogs were tied up or that no live coals had been left close to the houses. Isabel noticed that he carried the revolver and sometimes a stick with a silver handle.

She hadn't wanted to ask Rema about it because Rema clearly found it something so obvious and necessary; to pester her would have meant looking stupid, and she treasured her pride before another woman. Nino was easy, he talked

straight. Everything clear and obvious when he explained it. Only at night, if she
wanted to reconstruct that clarity and obviousness, Isabel noticed that the important reasons were still missing. She learned quickly what was really important: if you wanted to leave the house, or go down to the dining room, to Luis'
study, or to the library, find out first. "You have to trust don Roberto," Rema
had said. Her and Nino as well. She hardly ever asked Luis because he hardly
ever knew. The Kid, who always knew, she never asked. And so it was always
easy, the life organized itself for Isabel with a few more obligations as far as her
movements went, and a few less when it came to clothes, meals, the time to go
to bed. A real summer, the way it should be all year round.

   *. . . see you soon. They're all fine. I have an ant-farm with Nino and we play
and are making a very large herbarium. Rema sends her kisses, she is fine. I think
she's sad, the same as Luis who is very nice. I think that Luis has some trouble
although he studies all the time. Rema gave me some lovely colored handkerchiefs, Inés is going to like them. Mama, it's nice here and I'm enjoying myself
with Nino and don Roberto, he's the foreman and tells us when we can go out
and where, one afternoon he was almost wrong and sent us to the edge of the
brook, when a farmhand came to tell us no, you should have seen how awful don
Roberto felt and then Rema, she picked Nino up and was kissing him, and she
squeezed me so hard. Luis was going about saying that the house was not for
children, and Nino asked him who the children were, and everybody laughed,
even the Kid laughed. Don Roberto is the foreman.*

   *If you come to get me you could stay a few days and be with Rema and cheer
her up. I think that she . . .*

But to tell her mother that Rema cried at night, that she'd heard her crying
going down the hall, staggering a little, stop at Nino's door, continue, go downstairs (she must have been drying her eyes) and Luis' voice in the distance:
"What's the matter, Rema? Aren't you well?", a silence, the whole house like an
enormous ear, then a murmur and Luis' voice again: "He's a bastard, a miserable bastard . . ." almost as though he were coldly confirming a fact, making a
connection, a fate.

   *. . . is a little ill, it would do her good if you came and kept her company. I
have to show you the herbarium and some stones from the brook the farmhands
brought me. Tell Inés . . .*

It was the kind of night she liked, insects, damp, reheated bread, and custard
with Greek raisins. The dogs barked constantly from the edge of the brook, and
an enormous praying mantis flew in and landed on the mantelpiece and Nino
went to fetch the magnifying glass; they trapped it with a wide-mouthed glass
and poked at it to make it show the color of its wings.

"Throw that bug away," Rema pleaded. "They make me so squeamish."

"It's a good specimen," Luis admitted. "Look how he follows my hand with
his eyes. The only insect that can turn its head."

"What a goddamned night," the Kid said from behind his newspaper.

Isabel would have liked to cut the mantis' head off, a good snip with the scissors, and see what would happen.

                                                   .   .   .   .   .

"Leave it in the glass," she asked Nino. "Tomorrow we can put it in the ant-farm and study it."

It got hotter, by ten-thirty you couldn't breathe. The children stayed with Rema in the inside dining room, the men were in their studies. Nino was the first to say that he was getting sleepy.

"Go on up by yourself, I'll come see you later. Everything is all right up-stairs." And Rema took him about the waist with that expression he liked so well.

"Tell us a story, Aunt Rema?"

"Another night."

They were down there alone, with the mantis which looked at them. Luis came to say his goodnights to them, muttering something about the hour that children ought to go to bed, Rema smiled at him when she kissed him.

"Growly bear," she said, and Isabel, bent over the mantis' glass, thought that she'd never seen Rema kissing the Kid or a praying mantis that was so so green. She moved the glass a little and the mantis grew frantic. Rema came over to tell her to go to bed.

"Throw that bug away, it's horrible."

"Rema, tomorrow."

She asked her to come up and say goodnight to her. The Kid had the door of his study left partly open and was pacing up and down in his shirtsleeves, the collar open. He whistled to her as she passed.

"I'm going to bed, Kid."

"Listen to me: tell Rema to make me a nice cold lemonade and bring it to me here. Then you go right up to your room."

Of course she was going to go up to her room, she didn't see why he had to tell her to. She went back to the dining room to tell Rema, she saw her hesitate.

"Don't go upstairs yet. I'm going to make the lemonade and you take it down yourself."

"He said for you . . ."

"Please."

Isabel sat down at the side of the table. Please. There were clouds of insects whirling under the carbide lamp, she would have stayed there for hours looking at nothing, repeating: Please, please. Rema, Rema. How she loved her, and that unhappy voice, bottomless, without any possible reason, the voice of sadness it-self. Please. Rema, Rema . . . A feverish heat reached her face, a wish to throw herself at Rema's feet, to let Rema pick her up in her arms, a wish to die looking at her and Rema be sorry for her, pass her cool, delicate fingers through her hair, over the eyelids . . .

Now she was holding out a green tumbler full of ice and sliced lemons.

"Take it to him."

"Rema . . ."

Rema seemed to tremble, she turned her back on the table so that she shouldn't see her eyes.

"I'll throw the mantis out right now, Rema."

.   .   .   .   .

One sleeps poorly in the viscous heat and all that buzzing of mosquitoes. Twice she was on the point of getting up, to go out into the hall or to go to the bathroom to put cold water on her face and wrists. But she could hear someone walking, downstairs, someone was going from one side of the dining room to the other, came to the bottom of the stairway, turned around . . . They weren't the confused, long steps of Luis' walk, nor was it Rema's. How warm the Kid had felt that night, how he'd drunk the lemonade in great gulps. Isabel saw him drinking the tumblerful, his hands holding the green tumbler, the yellow discs wheeling in the water under the lamp; but at the same time she was sure the Kid had never drunk the lemonade, that he was still staring at the glass she had brought him, over to the table, like someone looking at some kind of infinite naughtiness. She didn't want to think about the Kid's smile, his going to the door as though he were about to go into the dining room for a look, his slow turning back.

"She was supposed to bring it to me. You, I told you to go up to your room."

And the only thing that came to her mind was a very idiot answer:

"It's good and cold, Kid."

And the tumbler, green as the praying mantis.

Nino was the first one up, it was his idea that they go down to the brook to look for snails. Isabel had hardly slept at all, she remembered rooms full of flowers, tinkling bells, hospital corridors, sisters of charity, thermometers in jars of bichlorate, scenes from her first communion, Inés, the broken bicycle, the restaurant in the railroad station, the gypsy costume when she had been eight. Among all this, like a delicate breeze between the pages of an album, she found herself wide awake, thinking of things that were not flowers, bells, hospital corridors. She got out of bed grudgingly, washed her face hard, especially the ears. Nino said that it was ten o'clock and that the tiger was in the music room, so that they could go down to the brook right away. They went downstairs together, hardly saying good morning to Luis and the Kid who were both reading with their doors open. You could find the snails mostly on the bank nearest the wheatfields. Nino moved along blaming Isabel for her distraction, said she was no kind of friend at all and wasn't helping form the collection. She saw him suddenly as so childish, such a little boy with his snails and his leaves.

She came back first, when they raised the flag at the house for lunch. Don Roberto came from his inspection and Isabel asked him the same question as always. Then Nino was coming up slowly, carrying the box of snails and the rakes; Isabel helped him put the rakes away on the porch and they went in together. Rema was standing there, white and silent. Nino put a blue snail into her hand.

"The nicest one, for you."

The Kid was eating already, the newspaper beside him, there was hardly enough room for Isabel to rest her arm. Luis was the last to come from his room, contented as he always was at noon. They ate, Nino was talking about the snails, the snail eggs in the reeds, the collection itself, the sizes and the colors. He was going to kill them by himself, it hurt Isabel to do it, they'd put them to dry on a zinc sheet. After the coffee came and Luis looked at them with the usual question, Isabel got up first to look for don Roberto, even though don Roberto had

already told her before. She made the round of the porch and when she came in
again, Rema and Nino had their heads together over the snail box, it was like a
family photograph, only Luis looked up at her and she said, "It's in the Kid's
study," and stayed watching how the Kid shrugged his shoulders, annoyed, and
Rema who touched a snail with a fingertip, so delicately that her finger even
seemed part snail. Afterwards, Rema got up to go look for more sugar, and Isabel
tailed along behind her babbling until they came back in laughing from a joke
they'd shared in the pantry. When Luis said he had no tobacco and ordered
Nino to look in his study, Isabel challenged him that she'd find the cigarettes
first and they went out together. Nino won, they came back in running and
pushing, they almost bumped into the Kid going to the library to read his newspaper, complaining because he couldn't use his study. Isabel came over to look
at the snails, and Luis waiting for her to light his cigarette as always saw that she
was lost, studying the snails which were beginning to ooze out slowly and move
about, looking at Rema suddenly, but dropping her like a flash, captivated by
the snails, so much so that she didn't move at the Kid's first scream, they were
all running and she was still standing over the snails as if she did not hear the
Kid's new choked cry, Luis beating against the library door, don Roberto coming
in with the dogs, the Kid's moans amid the furious barking of the dogs, and Luis
saying over and over again, "But if it was in his study! She said it was in his own
study!", bent over the snails willowy as fingers, like Rema's fingers maybe, or it
was Rema's hand on her shoulder, made her raise her head to look at her, to
stand looking at her for an eternity, broken by her ferocious sob into Rema's
skirt, her unsettled happiness, and Rema running her hand over her hair, quiet-
ing her with a soft squeeze of her fingers and a murmuring against her ear, a
stuttering as of gratitude, as of an unnameable acquiescence.

Translated from the Spanish by Paul Blackburn

Guy Davenport

THE HAILE SELASSIE FUNERAL TRAIN

The Haile Selassie Funeral Train pulled out of Deauville at 1500 hours sharp, so slowly that we glided in silence past the platform on which gentlemen in Prince Alberts stood mute under their umbrellas, ladies in picture hats held handkerchiefs to their mouths, and porters in blue smocks stood at attention. A brass band played Stanford in A.

We picked up speed at the gasworks and the conductor and the guards began to work their way down the car, punching tickets and looking at passports. Most of us sat with our hands folded in our laps. I thought of the cool fig trees of Addis Ababa and of the policemen with white spats painted on their bare feet, of the belled camel that had brought the sunburnt and turbaned Rimbaud across the Danakil.

We passed neat farms and pig sties, olive groves and vineyards. Once the conductor and guards were in the next car, we began to make ourselves comfortable and to talk.

—Has slept with his eyes open for forty years! a woman behind me said to her companion, who replied that it runs in the family.

—The Jews, a fat man said to the car at large.

Years later, when I was telling James Johnson Sweeney of this solemn ride on the Haile Selassie Funeral Train, he was astonished that I had been aboard.

—My God, what a train! he exclaimed. What a time! It is incredible now to remember the people who were on that train. James Joyce was there, I was there, ambassadors, professors from the Sorbonne and Oxford, at least one Chinese field marshal, and the entire staff of *La Prensa*.

James Joyce, and I had not seen him! The world in 1936 was quite different from what it is now. I knew that Apollinaire was on board. I had seen him in his crumpled lieutenant's uniform, his head wrapped in a gauze bandage, his small Croix de Guerre caught under his Sam Brown belt. He sat bolt upright, his wide hands on his knees, his chin lifted and proud.

A bearded little man in pince-nez must have seen with what awe I was watching Apollinaire, for he got out of his seat and came and put his hand on my arm.

—Don't go near that man, he said softly in my ear, he says that he is the Kaiser.

The compassion I felt for the wounded poet seemed to be reflected in the somber little farms we passed. We saw cows goaded home from the pasture, gypsies squatting around their evening fire, soldiers marching behind a flag and a drummer with his mouth open.

Once we heard a melody played on a harmonica but could see only the great wheel of a colliery.

Apollinaire could look so German from time to time that you could see the pickelhaube on his bandaged head, the swallow-wing moustache, the glint of disciplinary idiocy in his sweet eyes. He was Guillaume, Wilhelm. Forms deteriorate, transformation is not always growth, there is a hostage light in shadows, vagrom shadow in desert noon, burgundy in the green of a vine, green in the reddest wine.

We passed a city that like Richmond had chinaberry trees in the yards of wooden houses hung with wistaria at the eaves, women with shears and baskets standing in the yards. I saw a girl with a lamp standing at a window, an old Negro shuffling to the music of a banjo, a mule wearing a straw hat.

Joyce sat at a kitchen table in the first compartment to the right, a dingy room, as you entered the fourth wagon-lit counting from the locomotive and tender. His eyes enlarged by his glasses seemed to be goldfish swimming back and forth in a globe. There was a sink behind him, a bit of soap by the faucet, a window with lace half-curtains yellowed with the years. Tacked to the green tongue-and-groove wall was a Sacred Heart in mauve, rose, and gilt, a postcard photograph of a bathing beauty of the eighties, one hand on the bun of her hair, the other with fingers spread level with her dimpled knee, and a neatly clipped newspaper headline: A United Ireland and Trieste Belongs to Italy Says Mayor Curley at Fete.

He was talking about Orpheus preaching to the animals.

—The wild harp had chimed, I heard him say, and the elk had come with regal tread, superb under the tree of his antlers, a druid look in his eye.

He described Orpheus on a red cow of the Ashanti, Eurydice beneath him underground making her way through the roots of trees.

Apollinaire stuffed shag into a small clay pipe and lit it with an Italian match from a scarlet box bearing in an oval wreathed with scrolled olive and wheat a portrait of King Umberto. He tapped his knee as he smoked. He batted his eyes. King Umberto looked like Velasquez's Rey Filipe.

—My wife, Joyce says, keeps looking for Galway in Paris. We move every six weeks.

There came to Orpheus a red mouse with her brood, chewing a leaf of thoroughwax, a yawning leopard, a pair of coyotes walking on their toes.

Joyce's fingers were crowded with rings, the blob of magnified eye sloshed in its lens, he spoke of the sidhe turning alder leaves the whole of a night on the ground until they all faced downward toward China. Of creation he said we had no idea because of the fineness of the stitch. The ear of a flea, scales on the wing of a moth, peripheral nerves of the sea hare, great God! beside the anatomy of a grasshopper Chartres is a kind of mudpie and all the grand pictures in their frames in the Louvre the tracks of a hen.

Our train was going down the boulevard Montparnasse, which was in Barcelona.

—How a woman beats a batter for a cake, Joyce was saying, is how the king's horses, white and from Galway, champing in their foam and thundering against rock like the January Atlantic, maul the sward, the dust, the sty, the garden. Energy is in the race, handed down from cave to public house. Isben kept a mirror in his hat to comb his mane by, your Norse earl eyed his blue tooth in a glass he'd given the pelts of forty squirrels for in Byzantium, glory to Freya.

Apollinaire was showing his passport to a guard who had come by with the conductor. They whispered, head to head, the conductor and the guard. Apollinaire took his hat from the rack and put it on. It sat high on the bandage.

—*Je ne suis pas Balzac,* he said.

We passed the yellow roofs and red warehouses of Brindisium.

—*Ni Michel Larionoff.*

—Whale fish, Joyce was saying, listen from the sea, porpoises, frilly jellyfish, walrusses, whelks and barnacles. Owl listens from the olive, ringdove from the apple. And to all he says: *Il n'y a que l'homme qui est immonde.*

Somewhere on the train lay the Lion of Judah, Ras Taffari, the son of Ras Makonnen. His spearmen had charged the armored cars of the Italian Corpo d'Armata Africano leaping and baring their teeth.

His leopards had a car to themselves.

When we rounded a long curve I could see that our locomotive bore the Imperial Standard of Ethiopia: a crowned lion bearing a bannered cross within a pentad of Magen Davids on three stripes green, yellow, and red. There was writing on it in Coptic.

We passed the ravaged and eroded hills of the Dalmatian coast, combed with gullies like stains on an ancient wall. There was none of us who looked at the desolation of these hills without thinking of the wastes of the Danakil, the red rock valleys of Edom, the black sand marches of Beny Taámir.

From time to time we could hear from the car that bore Haile Selassie the long notes of some primitive horn and the hard clang of a bell.

Moths quivered on the dusty panes, Mamestras, Eucalypteras, Antiblemmas. And O! the gardens we could see beyond walls and fences. Outside Barcelona, as in a dream, we saw La Belle Jardinière herself, with her doves and wasps, her sure signs in full view among the flowers: her bennu tall on its blue legs, her crown of butterflies, her buckle of red jasper, her lovely hair. She was busy beside a sycamore, pulling water out in threads.

—Rue Vavin! Apollinaire said quite clearly, as if to the car at large. It was there that La Laurencin set out for Spain with a bird on her hat, an ear of wheat in her teeth. As her train pulled out of the Gare St. Lazare, taking her and Otto van Waetjen to the shorescapes of Boudin at Deauville, where we all boarded this train, where we were all of us near the umbrellas of Proust, the Great War began. They burnt the library at Louvain. What in the name of God could humanity be if man is an example of it?

Deftly she drew the crystal water from the sycamore, deftly. Her helper, perhaps her lord, wore a mantle of leaves and a mask that made his head that of Thoth, beaked, with fixed and painted eyes.

We were in Genoa, on tracks that belonged to trolleys. Walls as long and fortresslike as those of Peking were stuck all over up to a height with posters depicting corsets, Cinzano, Mussolini, shoe wax, the Fascist ax, boys and girls marching to *Giovanezza! Giovanezza!* Trees showed their topmost branches above these long gray walls, and many of us must have tried to imagine the secluded gardens with statues and belvederes which they enclosed.

He lay with his hands folded over his sword, the Conquering Lion, somewhere on the train. Four spearmen in scarlet capes stood barefoot around him, two at his head, two at his feet. A priest in a golden hat read constantly from a book. If only one could hear the words, they described Saaba on an ivory chair, on cushions deep as a bath, a woman with a bright mind and red blood. They described Shulaman in his cedar house beyond the stone desert it takes forty years to cross. The priest's words were as bees in an orchard, as bells in a holy city. He read aloud in a melodious drone of saints, dragons, underworlds, forests with eyes in every leaf, Mariamne, Italian airplanes.

—An unweeded garden, Joyce was saying, is all an inspired poet rode rickrack the river to usher to us. Her wick is all ears, the lady in the garden. There is an adder in the girl of her eye, dew on the lashes, and an apple in the mirror of the dew. Does anybody on this buggering train know the name of the engineer?

—King's Counsel Jones, cried James Johnson Sweeney.

He had pushed his way between *federales* of the Guardia Civil, Ethiopian infantrymen in tunics and pith helmets, quilted sergeants of the Kwomintang.

I thought of the engineer Elrod Singbell, who used to take the mile-long descending curve of Stump House Mountain in the Blue Ridge playing *Amazing Grace* on the whistle. I remembered the sharp sweet perfume of chinaberry blossoms in earliest spring.

Joyce spoke of an Orpheus in yellow dancing through bamboo, followed by cheetahs, macaws, canaries, tigers. And an Orpheus in the canyons at the bottom of the sea leading a gelatin of hydras, fylfot starfish, six-eyed medusas, feather-boa sealilies, comb-jelly cydippidas, scarlet crabs, and gleaming mackerel as old as the moon.

—Noé, Apollinaire said in a brown study.

—Mice whisker to whisker, Joyce said, white-shanked quaggas trotting *presto presto e delicatamente*, cackling pullets, grave hogs, whistling tapirs.

La Belle Jardinière. We saw her selling flowers in Madrid, corn marigolds, holy thistles, great silver knapweed, and white wild campions. In Odessa she pranced in a turn of sparrows. She was in the azaleas when we went through Atlanta, shaking fire from her wrists.

—Would that be the castellum, Joyce said, where the graaf put his twin sons together with a commentary on the Babylonian Talmud in a kerker dark as the ka of Osiris until a certain lady in jackboots and eyepatch found her way to them by lightning a squally night she had put the *Peahen* into the cove above Engelanker and kidnapped them tweeling as they were sweetening Yehonathan and

Dawidh a sugarplum's midge from Luther into the wind and stars but not before twisting her heel by the doorpost and wetting the premises?

—Shepherds! Apollinaire cried to the car, startling us all. We had no shepherds at Ypres. We have no shepherds now.

We were crossing the gardens of Normandy, coming back to Deauville.

Somewhere on the train, behind us, before us, Haile Selassie lay on his bier, his open eyes looking up through the roof of his imperial car to the double star Gamma in Triangulum, twin suns, the one orange, the other green.

Isak Dinesen

. . . .

THE CLOAK

When the great old master, the sculptor Leonidas Allori, whom they called the Lion of the Mountains, was arrested for rebellion and high treason and condemned to death, his pupils wept and stormed. For to them he had been spiritual father, archangel and immortal. They assembled in Pierino's hostelry outside the town, in a studio or in an attic, where they could sob, two or three, in each other's arms, or—like a big tree in a gale with its bare branches reaching upward—crowded in a cluster could shake ten pairs of clenched fists to the sky, in a cry for rescue of their beloved, and for revenge on tyranny.

Only one out of all of them in those days continued to live as if he had neither heard nor understood the terrible news. And that one was the disciple whom the master had loved above all others, whom he had called son, as the young man had called him father. Angelo Santasilia's schoolfellows took his silence to be the expression of infinite sorrow; they respected his pain and left him alone. But the real reason for Angelo's absence of mind was that his heart was filled with passion for the master's young wife, Lucrezia. The love and understanding between her and him just at this time had gone so far that she had promised him her total surrender.

In vindication of the faithless wife it must be pleaded that for a long time, and in deep agitation and alarm, she had resisted the divine and merciless power which held her in its hands. With the most sacred names she had sealed—and had made her lover seal—an oath: that never again should word or glance at which the master himself could not have rejoiced pass between the two. As she felt that neither of them could keep the oath, she entreated Angelo to go to Paris to study. Everything was prepared for his journey. It was only when she realized that this resolve could not be carried out, either, that she gave herself up to her destiny.

The faithless disciple, too, might have pleaded extenuating circumstances, even if these might not have been accepted by every judge or juryman. Angelo in his young life had had many love affairs, and in every single case had surrendered himself utterly to his passion, but none of these adventures had ever for any

246

length of time left a deep impression on his being. It was inevitable that, some-day, one of them must become the most important of all. And it was reasonable, it was perhaps inevitable, that the chosen mistress should be the wife of his teacher. He had loved no human being as he had loved Leonidas Allori; no other human being had he at any time whole-heartedly admired. He felt that he had been created by the hands of his master, as Adam by the hands of the Lord; from these same hands he was to accept his mate. The Duke of Alba, in Spain, who was a handsome and brilliant man, married a plain and simple-minded lady of the court and remained faithful to her, and when his friends, amazed at the fact, jestingly questioned him upon it, he answered them that the Duchess of Alba must needs, in her own right, and irrespective of personal qualities, be the most desirable woman in the world. So it was with the disloyal pupil. Once his strong amorous urge was joined with that great art which to him was the highest ideal of all—and was, moreover, coupled with a deep personal devotion—a fire was kindled, which later on he himself could not restrict.

Neither was Leonidas himself without blame in regard to the two young people. Day by day, in conversations with his favorite pupil, he had dwelt on Lucrezia's beauty. While making the young woman pose for his lovely and immortal Psyche with the Lamp he called upon Angelo to try, at his side in the studio, his hand at the same task, and did indeed interrupt his own work in order to point out the beauties in the living, breathing and blushing body before them, enraptured and inspired as in front of a classic work of art. Of this strange understanding between the old and the young artist neither of them was really conscious, and if a third person had spoken to them of it, they would have rebuffed him with indifference, perhaps with impatience. The one who suspected it was the woman, Lucrezia. And through it she suspected—at the same time with a kind of dismay and giddiness—the hardness and coldness which may be found in the hearts of men and artists, even with regard to the ones whom these hearts do embrace with deepest tenderness. Her own heart lamented, in complete loneliness, much as a lamb laments when led by its shepherd to the shamble.

As now, through various unusual occurrences in his daily life, Leonidas realized that he was being watched and followed, and as from this fact he concluded that he was in great danger, he was seized so deeply by the idea of his own death, and of the approaching end to his artistic career, that his whole being closed round it. He spoke no word of his danger to the people surrounding him, because these people, in the course of a few weeks, to him had become infinitely distant and thus, in accordance with the law of perspective, infinitely small. He might have wished to complete the work on which he was engaged, but soon his work, too, to him seemed an unreasonable and inconvenient distraction from the matter which really engrossed him. In the last days before his arrest, he stepped out of his isolation, unwontedly gentle and considerate toward all those around him. He now also sent Lucrezia away to the house of a friend, the owner of a vineyard, in the mountains a few miles from town. As, in order to give a reason for this arrangement—for he did not wish her to have any suspicion of the actual position—he explained to her that she looked pale and feverish, he himself believed that he was using a casual pretense to persuade her to leave him, and he smiled at the deep concern with which she received his command.

She at once sent word to Angelo and told him of her husband's decision. The lovers, who in anguish had been seeking an opportunity to meet and fulfill their love, looked each other in the eyes in triumphant certainty that now, and from now on, all powers of life were uniting to serve them, and that their passion was the loadstone which according to its will attracted and ranged everything around them. Lucrezia before now had visited the farm; she instructed Angelo as to how, by a certain path in the mountains, he could approach the house unseen, and come to her window. The window faced west, the moon would be in her first quarter, she would be able to discern the figure of her lover between the vines. When he picked up a pebble from the ground and threw it against the windowpane, she would open the window. As, in the course of their deliberation, they came to this moment, the voices of both faltered. To regain his equilibrium Angelo told her that for the nocturnal journey he had bought himself a large and fine cloak of violet goat's wool with brown embroidery, which a friend from the country, who was hard up for the moment, had offered him. All this they discussed in Lucrezia's room next to the studio where the master was working, and with the door to it open. The meeting, they decided, was to take place on the second Saturday evening.

They parted; and just as, all through the following week, the thought of death and eternity accompanied the master, the thought of Lucrezia's body against his own accompanied the young disciple. This thought, without having at any time really left him, constantly seemed to return to him anew like a forgotten, surprising, joyful message—"Open to me, my sister, my love, my dove, my undefiled: for my head is filled with dew, and my locks with the drops of the night. Thou art all fair, my love; there is no spot in thee. I am my beloved's, and my beloved is mine."

On Sunday morning Leonidas Allori was arrested and taken to prison. In the course of the week several interrogations of him followed, and possibly the old patriot might have justified himself in some of the accusations brought against him. But in the first place the government was resolved this time to make an end of such a dangerous enemy, and in the second place the accused himself was resolved not to upset, by any ups and downs, the sublime balance of mind he had attained. There was from the very beginning no real doubt as to the outcome of the case. Judgment was passed, and orders were given that next Sunday morning that most famous son of the people should be stood up against the prison wall, to fall against the cobbles with six bullets in his breast.

Toward the end of the week the old artist asked to be paroled for twelve hours in order to go to the place where his wife was staying, and to take leave of her.

His plea was refused. But such great strength had this man still in him, and with such an aura of radiance did his fame and his integrity of heart surround his person, that his words could not die quickly in the ears of those to whom they were addressed. The last request of the condemned man was brought up again and weighed by his judges, even after he himself had given up hope.

It so happened that the topic was raised in a house where Cardinal Salviati was present.

"No doubt," said His Eminence, "clemency here might set a dangerous precedent. But the country—and the royal house itself which possesses some of his works—is in debt to Allori. This man has often by his art restored men's faith in themselves—maybe men should now have faith in him."

He thought the matter over and continued: "It is said that the master—do they not call him the Lion of the Mountains?—is deeply loved by his pupils. We might find out if he has really been able to awaken a devotion which will defy death. We might, in his case, make use of the old rule which will allow a prisoner to leave his prison for a specified period, on the condition that he produce a hostage to die in his stead, if he does not return in time.

"Allori," said the Cardinal, "last summer did me the honor of executing the reliefs on my villa at Ascoli. He had with him there his beautiful young wife and a very handsome young disciple, Angelo by name, whom he called his son. We might let Leonidas know that he can obtain his freedom for a period of twelve hours, during which, as he wishes, he can take leave of his wife. But the condition will be that this young Angelo shall enter the prison cell as he himself leaves it, and that it will be made clear to both the old and the young artist that at the expiration of the twelve hours, at all events an execution will be carried out in the prison yard."

A feeling that in the circumstances it would be correct to decide on something unconventional made the powerful gentlemen with whom the matter rested accept the Cardinal's suggestion. The condemned man was informed that his request had been granted, and on which conditions. Leonidas sent word to Angelo.

The young artist was not in his room when his schoolfellows came to bring him the message and to fetch him to prison. Even though he had not paid any attention to the sorrow of his friends, it had nevertheless upset and distressed him, since at this moment he himself conceived the universe as perfect in beauty and harmony, and life in itself as boundless grace. He had kept apart from his fellows in a sort of antagonism, just as in respect and commiseration they had kept apart from him. He had traveled afoot the long way to the Duke of Miranda's villa to see a recently unearthed Greek statue of the god Dionysus. Still without really knowing it, he had wished and resolved to have a powerful work of art confirm his conviction of the divinity of the world.

His friends thus had to wait for him a long time in a small room high above the narrow street. When the chosen one finally entered, they pounced on him from all sides and informed him of the sad honor that awaited him.

So little had the master's favorite understood the nature and extent of the misfortune that had befallen himself and all of them, that the messengers had to repeat their tidings to him. When at last he comprehended, he stood petrified for a while, in the deepest grief. In the manner of a sleepwalker he inquired about the sentence and the execution, and his comrades, with tears in their eyes, gave him their answers. But when they came to the offer made to Leonidas, and the prisoner's request for Angelo, light returned to the young man's eyes and

color to his cheeks. He asked his friends, indignantly, why they had not informed him at once—then without words he tore himself from their grasp to
hasten to the prison.

But on the doorstep he stopped, seized by the solemnity of the moment. He
had walked a long way and had slept on the grass, his clothes were covered with
dust, and he had torn a rent in one sleeve. He did not wish to appear before his
master like this today. He lifted his big new cloak from the hook on which it
hung, and put it on.

The warders in the prison knew in advance of his coming. He was led to the
condemned man's cell, and let in. He threw himself into his master's arms.

Leonidas Allori calmed him. To make the young man forget the present, he
turned the conversation round to the stellar heavens, of which he had often
talked with his son, and in the knowledge of which he had instructed him. Soon
his great gaze and deep, clear voice lifted his pupil up there with him, as if the
two of them, hand in hand, had slipped back many years, and were now speaking together all by themselves in a lofty, carefree world. Only when the teacher
had seen the tears dry on the pale young face did he return to the ground, and he
asked his pupil if he was indeed prepared to spend, in his place, the night in the
prison. Angelo replied that he knew he was.

"I thank you, my son," said Leonidas, "for giving me twelve hours which will
be of boundless importance to me.

"Aye, I believe in the immortality of the soul," he continued, "and perhaps
the eternal life of the spirit is the one true reality. I do not know yet, but I shall
know tomorrow. But this physical world around us, these four elements—earth,
water, air and fire—are these not realities as well? And is not also my own
body—my marrow-filled bones, my flowing, never-pausing blood, and my five
glorious senses—divinely true? Others think that I am old. But I am a peasant
and of peasant stock, and our soil to us has been a stern, bountiful nurse. My
muscles and sinews are but firmer and harder than when I was a youth, my hair
is as luxurious as it was then, my sight is not in the least impaired. All these my
faculties I shall now leave here behind me, for as my spirit goes forth on new
paths, the earth—my own well-loved Campania—will take my honest body in
her honest arms and will make it one with herself. But I wish to meet Nature
face to face once more, and to hand it over to her in full consciousness, as in a
gentle and solemn conversation between friends. Tomorrow I shall look to the
future, I shall collect myself and prepare myself for the unknown. But tonight I
shall go out, free in a free world, among things familiar to me. I shall observe the
rich play of light of the sunset, and after that the moon's divine clarity, and the
ancient constellations of the stars round her. I shall hear the song of running
water and taste its freshness, breathe the sweetness and bitterness of trees and
grass in the darkness and feel the soil and the stones under the soles of my feet.
What a night awaits me! All gifts given to me I shall gather together into my
embrace, to give them back again in profound understanding, and with thanks."

"Father," said Angelo, "the earth, the water, the air and the fire must needs
love you, the one in whom none of their gifts have been wasted."

"I believe that myself, son," said Leonidas. "Always, from the time when I
was a child in my home in the country, have I believed that God loved me.

"I cannot explain to you—for the time is now but short—how, or by what path, I have come to understand in full God's infinite faithfulness toward me. Or how I have come to realize the fact that faithfulness is the supreme divine factor by which the universe is governed. I know that in my heart I have always been faithful to this earth and to this life. I have pleaded for liberty tonight in order to let them know that our parting itself is a pact.

"Then tomorrow I shall be able to fulfill my pact with great Death and with things to come." He spoke slowly, and now stopped and smiled. "Forgive my talking so much," he said. "For a week I have not talked to a person whom I loved."

But when he spoke again his voice and mien were deeply serious.

"And you, my son," he said, "you, whom I thank for your faithfulness throughout our long happy years—and tonight—be you also always faithful to me. I have thought of you in these days, between these walls. I have fervently wished to see you once again, not for my own sake, but in order to tell you something. Yes, I had got much to say to you, but I must be brief. Only this, then, I enjoin and implore you: keep always in your heart the divine law of proportion, the golden section."

"Gladly, gladly do I remain here tonight," said Angelo. "But even more gladly would I tonight go with you, such as, many nights, we have wandered together."

Leonidas smiled again. "My road tonight," he said, "under the stars, by the grass-grown, dewy mountain paths, takes me to one thing, and to one alone. I will be, for one last night, with my wife, with Lucrezia. I tell you, Angelo, that in order that man—His chief work, into the nostrils of whom He had breathed the breath of life—might embrace and become one with the earth, the sea, the air and the fire, God gave him woman. In Lucrezia's arms I shall be sealing, in the night of leave-taking, my pact with all these." He was silent for a few moments, and motionless.

"Lucrezia," he then said, "is a few miles from here, in the care of good friends. I have, through them, made sure that she has learned nothing of my imprisonment or my sentence. I do not wish to expose my friends to danger, and they shall not know, tonight, that I come to their house. Neither do I wish to come to her as a man condemned to death, with the breath of the grave on me, but our meeting shall be like our first night together, and its secrecy to her shall mean a young man's fancy and a young lover's folly."

"What day is it today?" Angelo suddenly asked.

"What day?" Leonidas repeated. "Do you ask that of me—me who have been living in eternity, not in time? To me this day is called: the last day. But stay, let me think. Why, my child, to you, and to the people around you, today is named Saturday. Tomorrow is Sunday.

"I know the road well," he said a short while later, thoughtfully, as if he were already on his journey. "By a mountain path I approach her window from behind the farm. I shall pick up a pebble and throw it against the windowpane. Then she will awake and wonder, she will go to her window, discern me amongst the vines, and open it."

His mighty chest moved as he drew his breath.

"Oh, my child and my friend," he exclaimed, "you know this woman's beauty. You have dwelt in our house and have eaten at our table, you know, too, the gentleness and gaiety of her mind, its childlike tranquillity and its inconceivable innocence. But what you do not know, what nobody knows in the whole world but I, is the infinite capacity of her body and soul for surrender. How that snow can burn! She has been to me all glorious works of art of the world, all of them in one single woman's body. Within her embrace at night my strength to create in the daytime was restored. As I speak to you of her, my blood lifts like a wave." After some seconds he closed his eyes. "When I come back here tomorrow," he said, "I shall come with my eyes closed. They will lead me in here from the gate, and later, at the wall, they will bind a cloth before my eyes. I shall have no need of these eyes of mine. And it shall not be the black stones, nor the gun barrels, that I shall leave behind in these my dear, clear eyes when I quit them." Again he was silent for a while, then said in a soft voice: "At times, this week, I have not been able to recall the line of her jaw from ear to chin. At daybreak tomorrow morning I shall look upon it, so that I shall never again forget it."

When again he opened his eyes, his radiant gaze met the gaze of the young man. "Do not look at me in such pain and dread," he said, "and do not pity me. I do not deserve that of you. Nor—you will know it—am I to be pitied tonight. My son, I was wrong: tomorrow, as I come back, I shall open my eyes once more in order to see your face, which has been so dear to me. Let me see it happy and at peace, as when we were working together."

The prison warder now turned the heavy key in the lock and came in. He informed the prisoners that the clock in the prison tower showed a quarter to six. Within a quarter of an hour one of the two must leave the building. Allori answered that he was ready, but he hesitated a moment.

"They arrested me," he said to Angelo, "in my studio and in my working smock. But the air may grow colder as I get into the mountains. Will you lend me your cloak?"

Angelo removed the violet cloak from his shoulders and handed it to his teacher. As he fumbled at his throat with the hook, with which he was unfamiliar, the master took the young hand that helped him, and held it.

"How grand you are, Angelo," he said. "This cloak of yours is new and costly. In my native parish a bridegroom wears a cloak like this on his wedding day.

"Do you remember," he added as he stood ready to go, in the cloak, "one night, when together we lost our way in the mountains? Suddenly you collapsed, exhausted and cold as ice, and whispered that it was impossible for you to go any farther. I took off my cloak then—just as you did now—and wrapped it around us both. We lay the whole night together in each other's arms, and in my cloak you fell asleep almost immediately, like a child. You are to sleep tonight too."

Angelo collected his thoughts, and remembered the night of which the master was speaking. Leonidas had always been a far more experienced mountaineer than he himself, as altogether his strength had always exceeded his own. He recalled the warmth of that big body, like that of a big friendly animal in the dark, against his own numb limbs. He remembered, further, that as he woke up the sun had risen, and all mountain slopes had become luminous in its rays. He had sat up, then, and had cried out, "Father, this night you have saved my life." From his breast came a groan, wordless.

"We will not take leave tonight," said Leonidas, "but tomorrow morning I shall kiss you."

The jailer opened the door and held it open, while the towering, straight figure stepped over the threshold. Then the door was once more shut, the key turned in the lock, and Angelo was alone.

Within the first seconds he felt the fact that the door was locked, and that nobody could come in to him, as an incomparable favor. But immediately after, he fell to the floor, like a man struck by, and crushed beneath, a falling rock.

In his ears echoed the voice of the master. And before his eyes stood the figure of the master, illuminated by the radiance of a higher world, of Art's infinite universe. From this world of light, which his father had once opened to him, he was now cast down into darkness. After the one whom he had betrayed had gone from him, he was completely alone. He dared not think of the stellar heavens, nor of the earth, nor of the sea, nor of the rivers, nor of the marble statues that he had loved. If at this moment Leonidas Allori himself had wanted to save him, it would not have been possible. For to be unfaithful is to be annihilated.

The word "unfaithful" was now flung on him from all angles, like a shower of flints on the man who is being stoned, and he met it on his knees, with hanging arms, like a man stoned. But when at last the shower slackened, and after a silence the words "the golden section" rose and echoed, subdued and significant, he raised his hands and pressed them against his ears.

And unfaithful, he thought after a time, *for the sake of a woman. What is a woman? She does not exist until we create her, and she has no life except through us. She is nothing but body, but she is not body, even, if we do not look at her. She claims to be brought to life, and requires our soul as a mirror, in which she can see that she is beautiful. Men must burn, tremble and perish, in order that she may know that she exists and is beautiful. When we weep, she weeps, too, but with happiness—for now she has proof that she is beautiful. Our anguish must be kept alive every hour, or she is no longer alive.*

All my creative power, his thoughts went on, *if things had gone as she wished, would have been used up in the task of creating her, and of keeping her alive. Never, nver again would I have produced a great work of art. And when I grieved over my misfortune, she would not understand, but would declare, "Why, but you have me!" While with him—with him, I was a great artist!*

Yet he was not really thinking of Lucrezia, for to him there was in the world no other human being than the father whom he had betrayed.

Did I ever believe, Angelo thought, *that I was, or that I might become, a great artist, a creator of glorious statues? I am no artist, and I shall never create a glorious statue. For I know now that my eyes are gone—I am blind!*

After a further lapse of time his thoughts slowly turned away from eternity and back to the present.

His master, he thought, would walk up the path and stop near the house, among the vines. He would pick up a pebble from the ground and throw it against the windowpane, and then she would open the window. She would call to the man in the violet cloak, such as she was wont to do at their meetings,

"Angelo!" And the great master, the unfailing friend, the immortal man, the man sentenced to death, would understand that his disciple had betrayed him.

During the previous day and night Angelo had walked far and slept but little, and the whole of the last day he had not eaten. He now felt that he was tired unto death. His master's command: "You are to sleep tonight," came back to him. Leonidas' commands, when he had obeyed them, had always led him right. He slowly rose to his feet and fumbled his way to the pallet where his master had lain. He fell asleep almost immediately.

But as he slept, he dreamed.

He saw once more, and more clearly than before, the big figure in the cloak walk up the mountain path, stop and bend down for the pebble and throw it against the pane. But in the dream he followed him farther, and he saw the woman in the man's arms—Lucrezia! And he awoke.

He sat up on the bed. Nothing sublime or sacred was any longer to be found in the world, but the deadly pain of physical jealousy stopped his breath and ran through him like fire. Gone was the disciple's reverence for his master, the great artist; in the darkness the son ground his teeth at his father. The past had vanished, there was no future to come, all the young man's thoughts ran to one single point—the embrace there, a few miles away.

He came to a sort of consciousness, and resolved not to fall asleep again.

But he did fall asleep again, and dreamed the same, but now more vividly and with a multitude of details, which he himself disowned, which his imagination could only have engendered when in his sleep he no longer had control of it.

As after this dream he was once more wide awake, a cold sweat broke out over his limbs. From the pallet he noticed some glowing embers on the fireplace; he now got up, set his naked foot upon them and kept it there. But the embers were almost dead, and went out under his foot.

In the next dream he himself, silent and lurking, followed the wanderer on the mountain path and through the window. He had his knife in his hand, he leaped forward, and plunged it first in the man's heart, then in hers, as they lay clasped in one another's arms. But the sight of their blood, mingled, soaking into the sheet, like a red-hot iron, burned out his eyes. Half awake, once more sitting up, he thought, *But I do not need to use the knife. I can strangle them with my hands.*

Thus passed the night.

When the turnkey of the prison awakened him, it was light. "So you can sleep?" said the turnkey. "So you really trust the old fox? If you ask me, I should say he has played you a fine trick. The clock shows a quarter to six. When it strikes, the warden and the colonel will come in, and take whichever bird they find in the cage. The priest is coming later. But your old lion is never coming. Honestly—would you or I come, if we were in his shoes?"

When Angelo succeeded in understanding the words of the turnkey, his heart filled with indescribable joy. There was nothing more to fear. God had granted him this way out: death. This happy, easy way out. Vaguely, through his aching head one thought ran: *And it is for him that I die.* But the thought sank away again, for he was not really thinking of Leonidas Allori, or of any person in the world round him. He felt only one thing: that he himself, within the last moment, had been pardoned.

He got up, washed his face in a basin of water brought by his guard, and combed his hair back. He now felt the pain of the burn in his foot and again was filled with gratitude. Now he also remembered the master's words about God's faithfulness.

The turnkey looked at him and said, "I took you for a young man yesterday."

After some time footsteps could be heard up the stone-paved passage, and a faint rattling. Angelo thought, *Those are the soldiers with their carbines.* The heavy door swung open, and between two gendarmes, who held his arms, entered Allori. In accordance with his words the evening before, he let himself be led forward with closed eyes by the warders. But he felt or perceived where Angelo was standing and took a step toward him. He stood silent before him, unhooked his cloak, lifted it from his own shoulders and laid it around the young man's. In this movement the two were brought close, body to body, and Angelo said to himself, *Perhaps, after all, he will not open his eyes and look at me.* But whenever had Allori not kept a given word? The hand which—as it put the cloak round him—rested against Angelo's neck forced his head a little forward, the large eyelids trembled and lifted, and the master looked into the eyes of the disciple. But the disciple could never afterward remember or recall the look. A moment later he felt Allori's lips on his cheek.

"Well, now!" cried the turnkey with surprise in his voice. "Welcome back! We were not expecting you. Now you must take potluck! And you," he added, turning to Angelo, "you can go your way. There are still a few minutes to six o'clock. My lords are not coming till after it has struck. The priest is coming later. Things are done with precision here. And fair—as you know—is fair."

E. L. Doctorow

. . . .

THE HUNTER

The town is terraced in the hill, along the river, a factory town of clapboard houses and public buildings faced in red stone. There is a one-room library called the Lyceum. There are several taverns made from porched homes, Miller and Bud signs hanging in neon in the front windows. Down at water's edge sits the old brassworks, a long two-story brick building with a tower at one end and it is behind locked fences and many of its windows are broken. The river is frozen. The town is dusted in new snow. Along the sides of the streets the winter's ac-cumulated snow is banked high as a man's shoulder. Smoke drifts from the chimneys of the houses and is quickly sucked into the sky. The wind comes up off the river and sweeps up the hill through the houses.

A school bus makes its way through the narrow hill streets. The mothers and fathers stand on the porches above to watch the bus accept their children. It's the only thing moving in the town. The fathers fill their arms with firewood stacked by the front doors and go back inside. Trees are black in the woods be-hind the homes; they are black against the snow. Sparrow and finch dart from branch to branch and puff their feathers to keep warm. They flutter to the ground and hop on the snow-crust under the trees.

The children enter the school through the big oak doors with the push bars. It is not a large school but its proportions, square and high, create hollow rooms and echoing stairwells. The children sit in their rows with their hands folded and watch their teacher. She is cheery and kind. She has been here just long enough for her immodest wish to transform these children to have turned to awe at what they are. Their small faces have been rubbed raw by the cold; the weakness of their fair skin is brought out in blotches on their cheeks and in the blue pallor of their eyelids. Their eyelids are translucent membranes, so thin and so delicate that she wonders how they sleep, how they keep from seeing through their closed eyes.

She tells them she is happy to see them here in such cold weather, with a hard wind blowing up the valley and another storm coming. She begins the day's work with their exercise, making them squat and bend and jump and swing their arms and somersault so that they can see what the world looks like upside down.

How does it look? she cries, trying it herself, somersaulting on the gym mat until she's dizzy.

They are not animated but the exercise alerts them to the mood she's in. They watch her with interest to see what is next. She leads them out of the small, dimly lit gymnasium through the empty halls, up and down the stairs, telling them they are a lost patrol in the caves of a planet somewhere far out in space. They are looking for signs of life. They wander through the unused schoolrooms, where crayon drawings hang from one thumbtack and corkboards have curled away from their frames. Look, she calls, holding up a child's red rubber boot, fished from the depths of a classroom closet. You never can tell!

When they descend to the basement, the janitor dozing in his cubicle is startled awake by a group of children staring at him. He is a large bearish man and wears fatigue pants and a red plaid woolen shirt. The teacher has never seen him wear anything different. His face has a gray stubble. We're a lost patrol, she says to him, have you seen any living creatures hereabouts? The janitor frowns. What? he says. What?

It is warm in the basement. The furnace emits its basso roar. She has him open the furnace door so the children can see the source of heat, the fire in its pit. They are each invited to cast a handful of coal through the door. They do this as a sacrament.

Then she insists that the janitor open the storage rooms and the old lunchroom kitchen, and here she notes unused cases of dried soup mix and canned goods, and then large pots and thick aluminum cauldrons and a stack of metal trays with food compartments. Here, you can't take those, the janitor says. And why not, she answers, this is their school, isn't it? She gives each child a tray or pot, and they march upstairs, banging them with their fists to scare away the creatures of wet flesh and rotating eyes and pulpy horns who may be lying in wait round the corners.

In the afternoon it is already dark, and the school bus receives the children in the parking lot behind the building. The new street lamps installed by the county radiate an amber light. The yellow school bus in the amber light is the color of a dark egg yolk. As it leaves, the children, their faces indistinct behind the windows, turn to stare out at the young teacher. She waves, her fingers opening and closing like a fluttering wing. The bus windows slide past, breaking her image and re-forming it, and giving her the illusion of the stone building behind her sliding along its foundations in the opposite direction.

The bus has turned into the road. It goes slowly past the school. The children's heads lurch in unison as the driver shifts gears. The bus plunges out of sight in the dip of the hill. At this moment the teacher realizes that she did not recognize the driver. He was not the small, burly man with eyeglasses without rims. He was a young man with long light hair and white eyebrows, and he looked at her in the instant he hunched over the steering wheel, with his arms about to make the effort of putting the bus into a turn.

That evening at home the young woman heats water for a bath and pours it in the tub. She bathes and urinates in the bathwater. She brings her hands out of the water and lets it pour through her fingers. She hums a made-up tune. The bathroom is large, with wainscoting of wood strips painted gray. The tub rests on four cast-iron claws. A small window high on the wall is open just a crack and through it the night air sifts into the room. She lies back and the cold air comes along the water line and draws its finger across her neck.

In the morning she dresses and combs her hair back and ties it behind her head and wears small opal teardrop earrings given to her for her graduation from college. She walks to work, opens up the school, turns up the radiator, cleans the blackboard, and goes to the front door to await the children on the yellow bus.

They do not come.

She goes to her teaching room, rearranges the day's lesson on the desk, distributes a sheet of stiff paper to each child's desk. She goes back to the front door and awaits the children.

They are nowhere in sight.

She looks for the school janitor in the basement. The furnace makes a kind of moaning sound, there is rhythmic intensification of its running pitch, and he's staring at it with a perplexed look on his face. He tells her the time, and it is the time on her watch. She goes back upstairs and stands at the front door with her coat on.

The yellow bus comes into the school driveway and pulls up before the front door. She puts her hand on the shoulder of each child descending the steps from the bus. The young man with the blond hair and eyebrows smiles at her.

There have been sacred rites and legendary events in this town. In a semi-pro football game a player was killed. A presidential candidate once came and spoke. A mass funeral was held here for the victims of a shoe-factory fire. She understands the new bus driver has no knowledge of any of this.

On Saturday morning the teacher goes to the old people's home and reads aloud. They sit there and listen to the story. They are the children's faces in another time. She thinks she can even recognize some of the grandmothers and grandfathers by family. When the reading is over those who can walk come up to her and pluck at her sleeves and her collar, interrupting each other to tell her who they are and what they used to be. They shout at each other. They mock each other's words. They waggle their hands in her face to get her to look at them.

She cannot get out of there fast enough. In the street she breaks into a run. She runs until the old people's home is out of sight.

It is very cold, but the sun shines. She decides to walk up to the mansion at the top of the highest hill in town. The hill streets turn abruptly back on themselves like a series of chutes. She wears lace-up boots and jeans. She climbs through snowdrifts in which she sinks up to the thighs.

The old mansion sits in the sun above the tree line. It is said that one of the factory owners built it for his bride, and that shortly after taking possession he killed her with a shotgun. The Greek columns have great chunks missing and she sees chicken wire exposed under the plaster. The portico is hung with icicles, and snow is backed against the house. There is no front door. She goes in. The light of the sun and a fall of snow fill the entrance hall and its grand stairway.

She can see the sky through the collapsed ceiling and a crater in the roof. She moves carefully and goes to the door of what must have been the dining room. She opens it. It smells of rot. There is a rustle and a hissing sound and she sees several pairs of eyes constellated in the dark. She opens the door wider. Many cats are backed into a corner of the room. They growl at her and twitch their tails.

She goes out and walks around to the back, an open field white in the sun. There is a pitted aluminum straight ladder leaning against a windowsill in the second floor. She climbs the ladder. The window is punched out and she climbs through the frame and stands in a light and airy bedroom. A hemisphere of ice hangs from the ceiling. It looks like the bottom of the moon. She stands at the window and sees at the edge of the field a man in an orange jacket and red hat. She wonders if he can see her from this distance. He raises a rifle to his shoulder and a moment later she hears an odd smack as if someone has hit the siding of the house with an open palm. She does not move. The hunter lowers his rifle and steps back into the woods at the edge of the field.

That evening the young teacher calls the town physician to ask for something to take. What seems to be the trouble? the doctor says. She conceives of a self-deprecating answer, sounding confident and assertive, even managing a small laugh. He says he will call the druggist and prescribe Valiums, two-milligram so that she won't be made drowsy by them. She walks down to Main Street, where the druggist opens his door and without turning on the store light leads her to the prescription counter in the rear. The druggist puts his hand into a large jar and comes up with a handful of tablets, and feeds the Valium one by one, from his thumb and forefinger, into a vial.

She goes to the movie theater on Main Street and pays her admission. The theater bears the same name as the town. She sits in the dark and swallows a handful of tabs. She cannot discern the picture. The screen is white. Then what she sees forming on the white screen is the town in its blanket of snow, the clapboard houses on the hill, the frozen river, the wind blowing snow along the streets. She sees the children coming out of their doors with their schoolbooks and walking down their steps to the street. She sees her life exactly as it is outside the movie theater.

Later she walks through the downtown. The only thing open is the State News. Several men stand thumbing the magazines. She turns down Mechanic Street and walks past the tool-and-die company and crosses the railroad tracks to the bridge. She begins to run. In the middle of the bridge the wind is a force and she feels it wants to press her through the railing into the river. She runs bent over, feeling as if she is pushing through something, as if it is only giving way to her by tearing.

Across the bridge the road turns sharply left and at the curve, at the foot of a hill of pine trees, is a brown house with a neon sign in the window: The Rapids. She climbs up the porch steps into the Rapids, and looking neither left nor right, walks to the back, where she finds the ladies' room. When she comes out she sits in one of the varnished plywood booths and stares at the table. After a while a man in an apron comes over and she orders a beer. Only then does she look up. The light is dim. A couple of elderly men are at the bar. But alone down at the end, established with his glass and a pack of cigarettes, is the new bus driver with the long blond hair, and he is smiling at her.

He has joined her. For a while nothing is said. He raises his arm and turns in his seat to look toward the bar. He turns his head to look back at her. You want another, he says. She shakes her head no but doesn't say thank you. She digs in her coat pocket and puts a wrinkled dollar beside her bottle. He holds up one finger.

You from around here? he says.

From the eastern part of the state, she says.

I'm from Valdese, he says. Down on Sixteen.

Oh yes.

I know you're their teacher, he says. I'm their driver.

He wears a wool shirt and a denim jacket and jeans. It is what he wears in his bus. He would not own a coat. There is something on a chain around his neck but it is hidden under the shirt. Blond beard stubble lies sparsely on his chin and along the line of his jaw. His cheeks are smooth. He is smiling. One of his front teeth is chipped.

What do you do to get to be a teacher?

You go to college. She sighs: What do you do to be a driver?

It's a county job, he says. You need a chauffeur's license and a clean record.

What is a dirty record?

Why, if you been arrested, you know? If you have any kind of record. Or if you got a bad service discharge.

She waits.

I had a teacher once in the third grade, he says. I believe she was the most beautiful woman I have ever seen. I believe now she was no more'n a girl. Like you. But she was very proud and she had a way of tossing her head and walking that made me wish to be a better student.

She laughs.

He picks up her beer bottle and feigns reproach and holds up his arm to the bartender and signals for two.

It is very easy, she says, to make them fall in love with you. Boys or girls, it's very easy.

And to herself she admits that she tries to do it, to make them love her, she takes on a grace she doesn't really have at any other time. She moves like a dancer, she touches them and brushes against them. She is outgoing and shows no terror, and the mystery of her is created in their regard.

Do you have sisters? she says.

Two. How'd you know that?

They're older than you?

One older, one younger.

What do they do?

Work in the office of the lumber mill down there.

She says: I would trust a man who had sisters.

He tilts his head back and takes a long pull at his beer bottle, and she watches his Adam's apple rise and fall, and the sparse blond stubble on his throat move like reeds lying on the water.

Later they come out of the Rapids and he leads her to his pickup. He is rather short. She climbs in and notices his workboots when he comes up into the cab from the other side. They're clean good boots, new yellow leather. He has trouble starting the engine.

What are you doing here at night if you live in Valdese? she says.

Waiting for you. He laughs and the engine turns over.

They drive slowly across the bridge, and across the tracks. Following her instructions, he goes to the end of the main street and turns up into the hills and brings her to her house. He pulls up in the yard by the side door.

It is a small house and it looks dark and cold. He switches off the engine and the headlights and leans across her lap and presses the button of the glove compartment. He says: Happens I got me some party wine right here. He removes a flat bottle in a brown bag and slams the door, and as he moves back, his arm brushes her thigh.

She stares through the windshield. She says: Stupid goddamn mill hand. Making his play with the teacher. Look at that, with his party wine in a sack. I can't believe it.

She jumps down from the cab, runs around the truck, and up the back steps into her kitchen. She slams the door. There is silence. She waits in the kitchen, not moving, in the dark, standing behind the table, facing the door.

She hears nothing but her own breathing.

All at once the back door is flooded with light, the white curtain on the door glass becomes a white screen, and then the light fades, and she hears the pickup backing out to the street. She is panting and now her rage breaks, and she is crying.

She stands alone in her dark kitchen crying, a bitter scent coming off her body, a smell of burning, which offends her. She heats water on the stove and takes it up to her bath.

On Monday morning the teacher waits for her children at the front door of the school. When the bus turns into the drive, she steps back and stands inside the door. She can see the open door of the bus but she cannot see if he is trying to see her.

She is very animated this morning. This is a special day, children, she announces, and she astonishes them by singing them a song while she accompanies herself on the Autoharp. She lets them strum the Autoharp while she presses the chords. Look, she says to each one, you are making music.

At eleven the photographer arrives. He is a man with a potbelly and a black string tie. I don't get these school calls till spring, he says.

This is a special occasion, the teacher says. We want a picture of ourselves now. Don't we, children?

They watch intently as he sets up his tripod and camera. He has a black valise with brass latches that snap as he opens them. Inside are cables and floodlamps.

Used to be classes of kids, he says. Now look at what's left of you. Heat this whole building for one room.

By the time he is ready, the young teacher has pushed the benches to the blackboard and grouped the children in two rows, the taller ones sitting on the benches, the shorter ones sitting in front of them on the floor, cross-legged. She herself stands at one side. There are fifteen children staring at the camera and their smiling teacher holding her hands in front of her, like an opera singer.

The photographer looks at the scene and frowns. Why, these children ain't fixed up for their picture.

What do you mean?

Why, they ain't got on their ties and their new shoes. You got girls here wearing trousers.

Just take it, she says.

They don't look right. Their hair ain't combed, these boys here.

Take us as we are, the teacher says. She steps suddenly out of line and with a furious motion removes the barrette fastening her hair and shakes her head until her hair falls to her shoulders. The children are startled. She kneels down on the floor in front of them, facing the camera, and pulls two of them into her arms. She brings all of them around her with an urgent opening and closing of her hands, and they gather about her. One girl begins to cry.

She pulls them in around her, feeling their bodies, the thin bones of their arms, their small shoulders, their legs, their behinds.

Take it, she says in a fierce whisper. Take it as we are. We are looking at you. Take it.

Stanley Elkin

. . . .

I LOOK OUT
FOR ED WOLFE

He was an orphan, and, to himself, he seemed like one, looked like one. His orphan's features were as true of himself as are their pale, pinched faces to the blind. At twenty-seven he was a neat, thin young man in white shirts and light suits with lintless pockets. Something about him suggested the ruthless isolation, the hard self-sufficiency of the orphaned, the peculiar dignity of men seen eating alone in restaurants on national holidays. Yet it was this perhaps which shamed him chiefly, for there was a suggestion, too, that his impregnability was a myth, a smell not of the furnished room which he did not inhabit, but of the three-room apartment on a good street which he did. The very excellence of his taste, conditioned by need and lack, lent to him the odd, maidenly primness of the lonely.

He saved the photographs of strangers and imprisoned them behind clear plastic windows in his wallet. In the sound of his own voice he detected the accent of the night school and the correspondence course, and nothing of the fat, sunny ring of the word's casually afternooned. He strove against himself, a supererogatory enemy, and sought by a kind of helpless abrasion, as one rubs wood, the gleaming self beneath. An orphan's thinness, he thought, was no accident.

Returning from lunch, he entered the office building where he worked. It was an old building, squat and gargoyled, brightly patched where sandblasters had once worked and then, for some reason, quit before they had finished. He entered the lobby, which smelled always of disinfectant, and walked past the wide, dirty glass of the cigarette-and-candy counter to the single elevator, as thickly barred as a cell.

The building was an outlaw. Low rents and a downtown address and the landlord's indifference had brought together from the peripheries of business and professionalism a strange band of entrepreneurs and visionaries, men desperately but imaginatively failing: an eye doctor who corrected vision by massage; a radio evangelist; a black-belt judo champion; a self-help organization for crippled veterans; dealers in pornographic books, in paper flowers, in fireworks, in

263

264

STANLEY ELKIN

plastic jewelry, in the artificial, in the artfully made, in the imitated, in the copied, in the stolen, the unreal, the perversion, the plastic, the *schlak*.

On the third floor the elevator opened and the young man, Ed Wolfe, stepped out.

He passed the Association for the Indians, passed Plasti-Pens, passed *Coffin & Tombstone*, passed Soldier Toys, passed Prayer-a-Day. He walked by the open door of C. Morris Brut, Chiropractor, and saw him, alone, standing at a mad attention, framed in the arching golden nimbus of his inverted name on the window, squeezing handballs.

He looked quickly away, but Dr. Brut saw him and came toward him, putting the handballs in his shirt pocket, where they bulged awkwardly. He held him by the elbow. Ed Wolfe looked down at the yellowing tile, infinitely diamonded, chipped, the floor of a public toilet, and saw Dr. Brut's dusty shoes. He stared sadly at the jagged, broken glass of the mail chute.

"Ed Wolfe, take care of yourself," Dr. Brut said.

"Right."

"Regard your position in life. A tall man like yourself looks terrible when he slumps. Don't be a *schlump*. It's no good for the organs."

"I'll watch it."

"When the organs get out of line the man begins to die."

"I know."

"You say so. How many guys make promises. Brains in the brainpan. Balls in the strap. The bastards downtown." Dr. Brut meant doctors in hospitals, in clinics, on boards, non-orphans with M.D. degrees and special license plates and respectable patients who had Blue Cross, charts, died in clean hospital rooms. They were the bastards downtown, his personal New Deal, his neighborhood Wall Street banker. A disease cartel. "They won't tell you. The white bread kills you. The cigarettes. The whiskey. The sneakers. The high heels. They won't tell you. Me, *I'll* tell you."

"I appreciate it."

"Wise guy. Punk. I'm a friend. I give a father's advice."

"I'm an orphan."

"I'll adopt you."

"I'm late to work."

"We'll open a clinic. 'C. Morris Brut and Adopted Son.'"

"It's something to think about."

"Poetry," Dr. Brut said and walked back to his office, his posture stiff, awkward, a man in a million who knew how to hold himself.

Ed Wolfe went on to his own office. The sad-faced telephone girl was saying, "Cornucopia Finance Corporation." She pulled the wire out of the board and slipped her headset around her neck, where it hung like a delicate horse collar. "Mr. La Meck wants to see you. But don't go in yet. He's talking to somebody."

He went toward his desk at one end of the big main office. Standing, fists on the desk, he turned to the girl. "What happened to my call cards?"

"Mr. La Meck took them," she said.

"Give me the carbons," Ed Wolfe said. "I've got to make some calls."

The girl looked embarrassed. Her face went through a weird change, the sadness taking on an impossible burden of shame, so that she seemed massively tragic, like a hit-and-run driver. "I'll get them," she said, moving out of the chair heavily. Ed Wolfe thought of Dr. Brut.

He took the carbons and fanned them out on the desk, then picked one in an intense, random gesture like someone drawing a number on a public stage. He dialed rapidly.

As the phone buzzed brokenly in his ear he felt the old excitement. Someone at the other end greeted him sleepily.

"Mr. Flay? This is Ed Wolfe at Cornucopia Finance." (Can you cope, can you cope? he hummed to himself.)

"Who?"

"Ed Wolfe. I've got an unpleasant duty," he began pleasantly. "You've skipped two payments."

"I didn't skip nothing. I called the girl. She said it was okay."

"That was three months ago. She meant it was all right to miss a few days. Listen, Mr. Flay, we've got that call recorded, too. Nothing gets by."

"I'm a little short."

"Grow."

"I couldn't help it," the man said. Ed Wolfe didn't like the cringing tone. Petulance and anger he could meet with his own petulance, his own anger. But guilt would have to be met with his own guilt, and that, here, was irrelevant.

"Don't con me, Flay. You're a troublemaker. What are you, Flay, a Polish person? Flay isn't a Polish name, but your address . . ."

"What's that?"

"What are you? Are you Polish?"

"What's that to you? What difference does it make?" That's more like it, Ed Wolfe thought warmly.

"That's what you are, Flay. You're a Pole. It's guys like you who give your race a bad name. Half our bugouts are Polish persons."

"Listen. You can't . . ."

He began to shout. "*You* listen. You wanted the car. The refrigerator. The chintzy furniture. The sectional you saw in the funny papers. And we paid for it, right?"

"Listen. The money I owe is one thing, the way . . ."

"We paid for it, right?"

"That doesn't . . ."

"Right? *Right?*"

"Yes, you . . ."

"*Okay.* You're in trouble, Warsaw. You're in terrible trouble. It means a lien. A judgment. We've got lawyers. You've got nothing. We'll pull the furniture the hell out of there. The car. Everything."

"Wait," he said. "Listen, my brother-in-law . . ."

Ed Wolfe broke in sharply. "He's got money?"

"I don't know. A little. I don't know."

"Get it. If you're short, grow. This is America."

"I don't know if he'll let me have it."

"Steal it. This is America. Good-by."

"Wait a minute. Please."

"That's it. There are other Polish persons on my list. This time it was just a friendly warning. Cornucopia wants its money. Cornucopia. Can you cope? Can you cope? Just a friendly warning, Polish-American. Next time we come with the lawyers and the machine guns. Am I making myself clear?"

"I'll try to get it to you."

Ed Wolfe hung up. He pulled a handkerchief from his drawer and wiped his face. His chest was heaving. He took another call card. The girl came by and stood beside his desk. "Mr. La Meck can see you now," she mourned.

"Later. I'm calling." The number was already ringing.

"Please, Mr. Wolfe."

"Later, I said. In a minute." The girl went away. "Hello. Let me speak with your husband, madam. I am Ed Wolfe of Cornucopia Finance. He can't cope. Your husband can't cope."

The woman made an excuse. "Put him on, goddamn it. We know he's out of work. Nothing gets by. Nothing."

There was a hand on the receiver beside his own, the wide male fingers pink and vaguely perfumed, the nails manicured. For a moment he struggled with it fitfully, as though the hand itself were all he had to contend with. Then he recognized La Meck and let go. La Meck pulled the phone quickly toward his mouth and spoke softly into it, words of apology, some ingenious excuse Ed Wolfe couldn't hear. He put the receiver down beside the phone itself and Ed Wolfe picked it up and returned it to its cradle.

"Ed," La Meck said, "come into the office with me."

Ed Wolfe followed La Meck, his eyes on La Meck's behind.

La Meck stopped at his office door. Looking around, he shook his head sadly, and Ed Wolfe nodded in agreement. La Meck let him enter first. While La Meck stood, Ed Wolfe could discern a kind of sadness in his slouch, but once the man was seated behind his desk he seemed restored, once again certain of the world's soundness. "All right," La Meck began, "I won't lie to you."

Lie to me. Lie to me, Ed Wolfe prayed silently.

"You're in here for me to fire you. You're not being laid off. I'm not going to tell you that I think you'd be happier some place else, that the collection business isn't your game, that profits don't justify our keeping you around. Profits are terrific, and if collection isn't your game it's because you haven't got a game. As far as your being happier some place else, that's bullshit. You're not supposed to be happy. It isn't in the cards for you. You're a fall guy type, God bless you, and though I like you personally I've got no use for you in my office."

I'd like to get you on the other end of a telephone some day, Ed Wolfe thought miserably.

"Don't ask me for a reference," La Meck said. "I couldn't give you one."

"No, no," Ed Wolfe said. "I wouldn't ask you for a reference." A helpless civility was all he was capable of. If you're going to suffer, *suffer*, he told himself.

"Look," La Meck said, his tone changing, shifting from brutality to compassion as though there were no difference between the two, "you've got a kind of quality, a real feeling for collection. I'm frank to tell you, when you first came to work for us I figured you wouldn't last. I put you on the phones because I wanted you to see the toughest part first. A lot of people can't do it. You take a guy who's already down and bury him deeper. It's heart-wringing work. But you, you were amazing. An artist. You had a real thing for the deadbeat soul, I thought. But we started to get complaints, and I had to warn you. Didn't I warn you? I should have suspected something when the delinquent accounts started to turn over again. It was like rancid butter turning sweet. So I don't say this to knock your technique. Your technique's terrific. With you around we could have laid off the lawyers. But Ed, you're a gangster. A gangster."

That's it. Ed Wolfe thought. I'm a gangster. Babyface Wolfe at nobody's door.

"Well," La Meck said, "I guess we owe you some money."

"Two weeks' pay," Ed Wolfe said.

"And two weeks in lieu of notice," La Meck said grandly.

"And a week's pay for my vacation."

"You haven't been here a year," La Meck said.

"It would have been a year in another month. I've earned the vacation."

"What the hell," La Meck said. "A week's pay for vacation."

La Meck figured on a pad, and tearing off a sheet, handed it to Ed Wolfe. "Does that check with your figures?" he asked.

Ed Wolfe, who had no figures, was amazed to see that his check was so large. After the deductions he made $92.73 a week. Five $92.73's was evidently $463.65. It was a lot of money. "That seems to be right," he told La Meck.

La Meck gave him a check and Ed Wolfe got up. Already it was as though he had never worked there. When La Meck handed him the check he almost couldn't think what it was for. There should have been a photographer there to record the ceremony: ORPHAN AWARDED CHECK BY BUSINESSMAN.

"Good-by, Mr. La Meck," he said. "It has been an interesting association," he added foolishly.

"Good-by, Ed," La Meck answered, putting his arm around Ed Wolfe's shoulders and leading him to the door. "I'm sorry it had to end this way." He shook Ed Wolfe's hand seriously and looked into his eyes. He had a hard grip.

Quantity and quality, Ed Wolfe thought.

"One thing, Ed. Watch yourself. Your mistake here was that you took the job too seriously. You hated the chiselers."

No, no, I loved them, he thought.

"You've got to watch it. Don't love. Don't hate. That's the secret. Detachment and caution. Look out for Ed Wolfe."

"I'll watch out for him," he said giddily, and in a moment he was out of La Meck's office, and the main office, and the elevator, and the building itself, loose in the world, as cautious and as detached as La Meck could want him.

He took the car from the parking lot, handing the attendant the two dollars. The man gave him back fifty cents. "That's right," Ed Wolfe said, "it's only two o'clock." He put the half-dollar in his pocket, and, on an impulse, took out his wallet. He had twelve dollars. He counted his change. Eighty-two cents. With his finger, on the dusty dashboard, he added $12.82 to $463.65. He had $476.47. Does that check with your figures? he asked himself and drove in the crowded traffic.

Proceeding slowly, past his old building, past garages, past bar-and-grills, past second-rate hotels, he followed the traffic further downtown. He drove into the deepest part of the city, down and downtown to the bottom, the foundation, the city's navel. He watched the shoppers and tourists and messengers and men with appointments. He was tranquil, serene. It was something he could be content to do forever. He could use his check to buy gas, to take his meals at drive-in restaurants, to pay tolls. It would be a pleasant life, a great life, and he contemplated it thoughtfully. To drive at fifteen or twenty miles an hour through eternity, stopping at stoplights and signs, pulling over to the curb at the sound of sirens and the sight of funerals, obeying all traffic laws, making obedience to them his very code. Ed Wolfe, the Flying Dutchman, the Wandering Jew, the Off and Running Orphan, "Look Out for Ed Wolfe," a ghostly wailing down the city's corridors. What would be bad? he thought.

In the morning, out of habit, he dressed himself in a white shirt and light suit. Before he went downstairs he saw that his check and his twelve dollars were still in his wallet. Carefully he counted the eighty-two cents that he had placed on the dresser the night before, put the coins in his pocket, and went downstairs to his car.

Something green had been shoved under the wiper blade on the driver's side. YOUR CAR WILL NEVER BE WORTH MORE THAN IT IS WORTH RIGHT NOW! WHY WAIT FOR DEPRECIATION TO MAKE YOU AUTOMATICALLY BANKRUPT? I WILL BUY THIS CAR AND PAY YOU CASH! I WILL NOT CHEAT YOU!

Ed Wolfe considered his car thoughtfully a moment and then got in. That day he drove through the city, playing the car radio softly. He heard the news on the hour and half-hour. He listened to Art Linkletter, far away and in another world. He heard Bing Crosby's ancient voice, and thought sadly, Depreciation. When his tank was almost empty he thought wearily of having it filled and could see himself, bored and discontented behind the bug-stained glass, forced into a patience he did not feel, having to decide whether to take the Green Stamps the attendant tried to extend. Put money in your purse, Ed Wolfe, he thought. Cash! he thought with passion.

He went to the address on the circular.

He drove up onto the gravel lot but remained in his car. In a moment a man came out of a small wooden shack and walked toward Ed Wolfe's car. If he was appraising it he gave no sign. He stood at the side of the automobile and waited while Ed Wolfe got out.

"Look around," the man said. "No pennants, no strings of electric lights." He saw the advertisement in Ed Wolfe's hand. "I ran the ad off on my brother-in-law's mimeograph. My kid stole the paper from his school."

Ed Wolfe looked at him.

"The place looks like a goddamn parking lot. When the snow starts falling I get rid of the cars and move the Christmas trees in. No overhead. That's the beauty of a volume business."

Ed Wolfe looked pointedly at the nearly empty lot.

"That's right," the man said. "It's slow. I'm giving the policy one more chance. Then I cheat the public just like everybody else. You're just in time. Come on, I'll show you a beautiful car."

"I want to sell my car," Ed Wolfe said.

"Sure, sure," the man said. "You want to trade with me. I give top allowances. I play fair."

"I want you to buy my car."

The man looked at him closely. "What do you want? You want me to go into the office and put on the ten-gallon hat? It's my only overhead, so I guess you're entitled to see it. You're paying for it. I put on this big frigging hat, see, and I become Texas Willie Waxelman, the Mad Cowboy. If that's what you want, I can get it in a minute."

It's incredible, Ed Wolfe thought. There are bastards everywhere who hate other bastards downtown everywhere. "I don't want to trade my car in," he said. "I want to sell it. I, too, want to reduce my inventory."

The man smiled sadly. "You want me to buy *your* car. You run in and put on the hat. I'm an automobile *salesman*, kid."

"No, you're not," Ed Wolfe said. "I was with Cornucopia Finance. We handled your paper. You're an automobile *buyer*. Your business is in buying up four- and five-year-old cars like mine from people who need dough fast and then auctioning them off to the trade."

The man turned away and Ed Wolfe followed him. Inside the shack the man said, "I'll give you two hundred."

"I need six hundred," Ed Wolfe said.

"I'll lend you the hat. Hold up a goddamn stagecoach."

"Give me five."

"I'll give you two-fifty and we'll part friends."

"Four hundred and fifty."

"Three hundred. Here," the man said, reaching his hand into an opened safe and taking out three sheaves of thick, banded bills. He held the money out to Ed Wolfe. "Go ahead, count it."

Absently Ed Wolfe took the money. The bills were stiff, like money in a teller's drawer, their value as decorous and untapped as a sheet of postage stamps. He held the money, pleased by its weight. "Tens and fives," he said, grinning.

"You bet," the man said, taking the money back. "You want to sell your car?"

"Yes," Ed Wolfe said. "Give me the money," he said hoarsely.

He had been to the bank, had stood in the patient, slow, money-conscious line, had presented his formidable check to the impassive teller, hoping the four hundred and sixty-three dollars and sixty-five cents she counted out would seem his week's salary to the man who waited behind him. Fool, he thought, it will seem two weeks' pay and two weeks in lieu of notice and a week for vacation for the hell of it, the three-week margin of an orphan.

"Thank you," the teller said, already looking beyond Ed Wolfe to the man behind him.

"Wait," Ed Wolfe said. "Here." He handed her a white withdrawal slip.

She took it impatiently and walked to a file. "You're closing your savings account?" she asked loudly.

"Yes," Ed Wolfe answered, embarrassed.

"I'll have a cashier's check made out for this."

"No, no," Ed Wolfe said desperately. "Give me cash."

"Sir, we make out a cashier's check and cash it for you," the teller explained.

"Oh," Ed Wolfe said. "I see."

When the teller had given him the two hundred fourteen dollars and twenty-three cents, he went to the next window, where he made out a check for $38.91. It was what he had in his checking account.

On Ed Wolfe's kitchen table was a thousand dollars. That day he had spent one dollar and ninety cents. He had twenty-seven dollars and seventy-one cents in his pocket. For expenses. "For attrition," he said aloud. "The cost of living. For streetcars and newspapers and half-gallons of milk and loaves of white bread. For the movies. For a cup of coffee." He went to his pantry. He counted the cans and packages, the boxes and bottles. "The three weeks again," he said. "The orphan's nutritional margin." He looked in his icebox. In the freezer he poked around among white packages of frozen meat. He looked brightly into the vegetable tray. A whole lettuce. Five tomatoes. Several slices of cucumber. Browning celery. On another shelf four bananas. Three and a half apples. A cut pineapple. Some grapes, loose and collapsing darkly in a white bowl. A quarter-pound of butter. A few eggs. Another egg, broken last week, congealing in a blue dish. Things in plastic bowls, in jars, forgotten, faintly mysterious left overs, faintly rotten, vaguely futured, equivocal garbage. He closed the door, feeling a draft. "Really," he said, "it's quite cozy." He looked at the thousand dollars on the kitchen table. "It's not enough," he said. "It's not enough," he shouted. "It's not enough to be cautious on. La Meck, you bastard, detachment comes higher, what do you think? You think it's cheap?" He raged against himself. It was the way he used to speak to people on the telephone. "Wake up. Orphan! Jerk! Wake up. It costs to be detached."

He moved solidly through the small apartment and lay down on his bed with his shoes still on, putting his hands behind his head luxuriously. It's marvelous, he thought. Tomorrow I'll buy a trench coat. I'll take my meals in piano bars. He lit a cigarette. "*I'll never smile again*," he sang, smiling. "All right, Eddie, play it again," he said. "Mistuh Wuf, you don' wan' to heah dat ol' song no maw. You know whut it do to you. She ain' wuth it, Mistuh Wuf." He nodded. "Again, Eddie." Eddie played his black ass off. "The way I see it, Eddie," he said, taking a long, sad drink of warm Scotch, "there are orphans and there are orphans." The overhead fan chuffed slowly, stirring the potted palmetto leaves.

He sat up in the bed, grinding his heels across the sheets. "There are orphans and there are orphans," he said. "I'll move. I'll liquidate. I'll sell out."

He went to the phone, called his landlady and made an appointment to see her.

It was a time of ruthless parting from his things, but there was no bitterness in it. He was a born salesman, he told himself. A disposer, a natural dumper. He administered severance. As detached as a funeral director, what he had learned was to say good-by. It was a talent of a sort. And he had never felt quite so interested. He supposed he was doing what he had been meant for—what, perhaps, everyone was meant for. He sold and he sold, each day spinning off little pieces of himself, like controlled explosions of the sun. Now his life was a series of speeches, of nearly earnest pitches. What he remembered of the day was what he had said. What others said to him, or even whether they spoke at all, he was unsure of.

Tuesday he told his landlady, "Buy my furniture. It's new. It's good stuff. It's expensive. You can forget about that. Put it out of your mind. I want to sell it. I'll show you bills for over seven hundred dollars. Forget the bills. Consider my character. Consider the man. Only the man. That's how to get your bargains. Examine. Examine. I could tell you about inner springs; I could talk to you of leather. But I won't. I don't. I smoke, but I'm careful. I can show you the ashtrays. You won't find cigarette holes in *my* tables. Examine. I drink. I'm a drinker. I drink. But I hold it. You won't find alcohol stains. May I be frank? I make love. Again, I could show you the bills. But I'm cautious. My sheets are virginal, white.

"Two hundred fifty dollars, landlady. Sit on that sofa. That chair. Buy my furniture. Rent the apartment furnished. Deduct what you pay from your taxes. Collect additional rents. Realize enormous profits. Wallow in gravy. Get it, landlady? Get it, landlady! Two hundred fifty dollars. Don't disclose the figure or my name. I want to remain anonymous."

He took her into his bedroom. "The piece of resistance, landlady. What you're really buying is the bedroom stuff. This is where I do all my dreaming. What do you think? Elegance. *Elegance!* I throw in the living-room rug. That I throw in. You have to take that or it's no deal. Give me cash and I move tomorrow."

Wednesday he said, "I heard you buy books. That must be interesting. And sad. It must be very sad. A man who loves books doesn't like to sell them. It would be the last thing. Excuse me. I've got no right to talk to you this way. You buy books and I've got books to sell. There. It's business now. As it should be. My library—" He smiled helplessly. "Excuse me. Such a grand name. Library." He began again slowly. "My books, my books are in there. Look them over. I'm afraid my taste has been rather eclectic. You see, my education has not been formal. There are over eleven hundred. Of course, many are paperbacks. Well, you can see that. I feel as if I'm selling my mind."

The book buyer gave Ed Wolfe one hundred twenty dollars for his mind.

On Thursday he wrote a letter:

American Annuity & Life Insurance Company,
Suite 410,
Lipton-Hill Building,
2007 Beverly Street, S.W.,
Boston 19, Massachusetts

Dear Sirs,
    I am writing in regard to Policy Number 593-000-34-78, a $5,000, twenty-year annuity held by Edward Wolfe of the address below.

Although only four payments have been made, and sixteen years remain before the policy matures, I find I must make application for the immediate return of my payments and cancel the policy.

I have read the "In event of cancellation" clause in my policy, and realize that I am entitled to only a flat three percent interest on the "total paid-in amount of the partial amortizement." Your records will show that I have made four payments of $198.45 each. If your figures check with mine this would come to $793.80. Adding three percent interest to this amount $23.81.), your company owes me $817.61.

Your prompt attention to my request would be gratefully appreciated, although I feel, frankly, as though I were selling my future.

On Monday someone came to buy his record collection. "What do you want to hear? I'll put something comfortable on while we talk. What do you like? Here, try this. Go ahead, put it on the machine. By the edges, man. By the edges! I feel as if I'm selling my throat. Never mind about that. Dig the sounds. Orphans up from Orleans singing the news of chain gangs to café society. You can smell the freight trains, man. Recorded during actual performance. You can hear the ice cubes clinkin' in the glasses, the waiters picking up their tips. I have jazz. Folk. Classical. Broadway. Spoken word. Spoken word, man! I feel as though I'm selling my ears. The stuff lives in my heart or I wouldn't sell. I have a one-price throat, one-price ears. Sixty dollars for the noise the world makes, man. But remember, I'll be watching. By the edges. *Only by the edges!*"

On Friday he went to a pawnshop in a Checker cab.

"*You?* You buy gold? You buy clothes? You buy Hawaiian guitars? You buy pistols for resale to suicides? I wouldn't have recognized you. Where's the skull-cap, the garters around the sleeves? The cigar I wouldn't ask you about. You look like anybody. You look like everybody. I don't know what to say. I'm stuck. I don't know how to deal with you. I was going to tell you something sordid, you know? You know what I mean? Okay, I'll give you facts.

"The fact is, I'm the average man. That's what the fact is. Eleven shirts, 15 neck, 34 sleeve. Six slacks, 32 waist. Five suits at 38 long. Shoes 10-C. A 7½) hat. You know something? Those marginal restaurants where you can never remember whether they'll let you in without a jacket? Well, the jackets they lend you in those places always fit me. That's the kind of guy you're dealing with. You can have confidence. Look at the clothes. Feel the material. And there's one thing about me. I'm fastidious. Fastidious. Immaculate. You think I'd be clumsy. A fall guy falls down, right? There's not a mark on the clothes. Inside? Inside it's another story. I don't speak of inside. Inside it's all Band-Aids, plaster, iodine, sticky stuff for burns. But outside—fastidiousness, immaculation, reality! My clothes will fly off your racks. I promise, I feel as if I'm selling my skin. Does that check with your figures?

"So now you know. It's me, Ed Wolfe. Ed Wolfe, the orphan? I lived in the orphanage for sixteen years. They gave me a name. It was a Jewish orphanage, so they gave me a Jewish name. Almost. That is, they couldn't know for sure themselves, so they kept it deliberately vague. I'm a foundling. A lostling. Who needs it, right? Who the hell needs it? I'm at loose ends, pawnbroker. I'm at loose ends out of looser beginnings. I need the money to stay alive. All you can give me.

"Here's a good watch. Here's a bad one. For good times and bad. That's life, right? You can sell them as a package deal. Here are radios. You like Art Link-letter? A phonograph. Automatic. Three speeds. Two speakers. One thing and another thing, see? And a pressure cooker. It's valueless to me, frankly. No pressure. I can live only on cold meals. Spartan. Spartan.

"I feel as if I'm selling—this is the last of it, I have no more things—I feel as if I'm selling my things."

On Saturday he called the phone company: "Operator? Let me speak to your supervisor, please.

"Supervisor? Supervisor, I am Ed Wolfe, your subscriber at TErrace 7-3572. There is nothing wrong with the service. The service has been excellent. No one calls, but you have nothing to do with that. However, I must cancel. I find that I no longer have any need of a telephone. Please connect me with the business office.

"Business office? Business office, this is Ed Wolfe. My telephone number is TErrace 7-3572. I am closing my account with you. When the service was first installed I had to surrender a twenty-five dollar deposit to your company. It was understood that the deposit was to be refunded when our connection with each other had been terminated. Disconnect me. Deduct what I owe on my current account from my deposit and refund the rest immediately. Business office, I feel as if I'm selling my mouth."

When he had nothing left to sell, when that was finally that, he stayed until he had finished all the food and then moved from his old apartment into a small, thinly furnished room. He took with him a single carton of clothing—the suit, the few shirts, the socks, the pajamas, the underwear and overcoat he did not sell. It was in preparing this carton that he discovered the hangers. There were hundreds of them. His own, previous tenants'. Hundreds. In each closet, on rods, in dark, dark corners, was this anonymous residue of all their lives. He unpacked his carton and put the hangers inside. They made a weight. He took them to the pawnshop and demanded a dollar for them. They were worth more, he argued. In an A&P he got another carton for nothing and went back to repack his clothes.

At the new place the landlord gave him his key.

"You got anything else?" the landlord asked. "I could give you a hand."

"No," he said. "Nothing."

Following the landlord up the deep stairs he was conscious of the $2,479.03 he had packed into the pockets of the suit and shirts and pajamas and overcoat inside the carton. It was like carrying a community of economically viable dolls.

When the landlord left him he opened the carton and gathered all his money together. In fading light he reviewed the figures he had entered in the pages of an old spiral notebook:

Pay	Pawned:	$463.65
Cash		12.82
Car		300.00
Savings		214.23
Checking		38.91
Furniture (& bedding)		250.00
Books		120.00
Insurance		817.61
Records		60.00
Clothes		110.00
2 watches		18.00
2 radios		12.00
Phonograph		35.00
Pressure cooker		6.00
Phone deposit (less bill)		19.81
Hangers		1.00
	Total	$2,479.03

So, he thought, that was what he was worth. That was the going rate for orphans in a wicked world. Something under $2,500. He took his pencil and crossed out all the nouns on his list. He tore the list carefully from top to bottom and crumpled the half which inventoried his expossessions. Then he crumpled the other half.

He went to the window and pushed aside the loose, broken shade. He opened the window and set both lists on the ledge. He made a ring of his forefinger and thumb and flicked the paper balls into the street. "Look out for Ed Wolfe," he said softly.

In six weeks the season changed. The afternoons failed. The steam failed. He was as unafraid of the dark as he had been of the sunlight. He longed for a special grief, to be touched by anguish or terror, but when he saw the others in the street, in the cafeteria, in the theater, in the hallway, on the stairs, at the newsstand, in the basement rushing their fouled linen from basket to machine, he stood as indifferent to their errand, their appetite, their joy, their greeting, their effort, their curiosity, their grime, as he was to his own. No envy wrenched him, no despair unhoped him, but, gradually, he became restless.

He began to spend, not recklessly so much as indifferently. At first he was able to recall for weeks what he spent on a given day. It was his way of telling time. Now he had difficulty remembering, and could tell how much his life was costing only by subtracting what he had left from his original two thousand four hundred seventy-nine dollars and three cents. In eleven weeks he had spent six hundred and seventy-seven dollars and thirty-four cents. It was almost three times more than he had planned. He became panicky. He had come to think of his money as his life. Spending it was the abrasion again, the old habit of self-buffing to come to the thing beneath. He could not draw infinitely on his credit. It was limited. Limited. He checked his figures. He had eighteen hundred and one dollars, sixty-nine cents. He warned himself, "Rothschild, child. Rockefeller, feller. Look out, Ed Wolfe. Look out."

He argued with his landlord and won a five-dollar reduction in his rent. He was constantly hungry, wore clothes stingily, realized an odd reassurance in his thin pain, his vague fetidness. He surrendered his dimes, his quarters, his half-dollars in a kind of sober anger. In seven more weeks he spent only one hundred and thirty dollars and fifty-one cents. He checked his figures. He had sixteen hundred seventy-one dollars, eighteen cents. He had spent almost twice what he had anticipated. "It's all right," he said. "I've reversed the trend. I can catch up." He held the money in his hand. He could smell his soiled underwear. "Nah, nah," he said. "It's not enough."

It was not enough, it was not enough, it was not enough. He had painted himself into a corner. Death by *cul-de-sac*. He had nothing left to sell, the born salesman. The born champion, long-distance, Ed Wolfe of a salesman lay in his room, winded, wounded, wondering where his next pitch was coming from, at one with the ages.

He put on his suit, took his sixteen hundred seventy-one dollars and eighteen cents and went down into the street. It was a warm night. He would walk downtown. The ice which just days before had covered the sidewalk was dissolved to slush. In darkness he walked through a thawing, melting world. There was something on the edge of the air, the warm, moist odor of the change of the season. He was touched despite himself. "I'll take a bus," he threatened. "I'll take a bus and close the windows and ride over the wheel."

He had dinner and some drinks in a hotel. When he finished he was feeling pretty good. He didn't want to go back. He looked at the bills thick in his wallet and went over to the desk clerk. "Where's the action?" he whispered. The clerk looked at him, startled. He went over to the bell captain. "Where's the action?" he asked and gave the man a dollar. He winked. The man stared at him helplessly.

"Sir?" the bell captain said, looking at the dollar.

Ed Wolfe nudged him in his gold buttons. He winked again. "Nice town you got here," he said expansively. "I'm a salesman, you understand, and this is new territory for me. Now if I were in Beantown or Philly or L.A. or Vegas or Big D or Frisco or Cincy—why, I'd know what was what. I'd be okay, know what I mean?" He winked once more. "Keep the buck, kid," he said. "Keep it, keep it," he said, walking off.

In the lobby a man sat in a deep chair, *The Wall Street Journal* opened wide across his face. "Where's the action?" Ed Wolfe said, peering over the top of the paper into the crown of the man's hat.

"What's that?" the man asked.

Ed Wolfe, surprised, saw that the man was a Negro.

"What's that?" the man repeated, vaguely nervous. Embarrassed, Ed Wolfe watched him guiltily, as though he had been caught in an act of bigotry.

"I thought you were someone else," he said lamely. The man smiled and lifted the paper to his face. Ed Wolfe stood before the opened paper, conscious of mildly teetering. He felt lousy, awkward, complicatedly irritated and ashamed, the mere act of hurting someone's feelings suddenly the most that could be held against him. It came to him how completely he had failed to make himself felt. "Look out for Ed Wolfe, indeed," he said aloud. The man lowered his paper. "Some of my best friends are Comanches," Ed Wolfe said. "Can I buy you a drink?"

"No," the man said.

"Resistance, eh?" Ed Wolfe said. "That's good. Resistance is good. A deal closed without resistance is no deal. Let me introduce myself. I'm Ed Wolfe. What's your name?"

"Please, I'm not bothering anybody. Leave me alone."

"Why?" Ed Wolfe asked.

The man stared at him and Ed Wolfe sat suddenly down beside him. "I won't press it," he said generously. "Where's the action? Where *is* it? Fold the paper, man. You're playing somebody else's gig." He leaned across the space between them and took the man by the arm. He pulled at him gently, awed by his own boldness. It was the first time since he had shaken hands with La Meck that he had touched anyone physically. What he was risking surprised and puzzled him. In all those months to have touched only two people, to have touched *even* two people! To feel their life, even, as now, through the unyielding wool of clothing, was disturbing. He was unused to it, frightened and oddly moved. Bewildered, the man looked at Ed Wolfe timidly and allowed himself to be taken toward the cocktail lounge.

They took a table near the bar. There, in the alcoholic dark, within earshot of the easy banter of the regulars, Ed Wolfe seated the Negro and then himself. He looked around the room and listened for a moment, then turned back to the Negro. Smoothly boozy, he pledged the man's health when the girl brought their drinks. He drank stolidly, abstractedly. Coming to life briefly, he indicated the men and women around them, their suntans apparent even in the dark. "Pilots," he said. "All of them. Airline pilots. The girls are all stewardesses and the pilots lay them." He ordered more drinks. He did not like liquor, and liberally poured ginger ale into his bourbon. He ordered more drinks and forgot the ginger ale. "*Goyim*," he said. "White *goyim*. American *goyim*." He stared at the Negro. He leaned across the table. "Little Orphan Annie, what the hell kind of an orphan is that with all her millions and her white American *goyim* friends to bail her out?"

He watched them narrowly, drunkenly. He had seen them before—in good motels, in airports, in bars—and he wondered about them, seeing them, he supposed, as Negroes or children of the poor must have seen him when he had sometimes driven his car through slums. They were removed, aloof—he meant it—a different breed. He turned and saw the Negro, and could not think for a moment what the man was doing there. The Negro slouched in his chair, his great white eyes hooded. "You want to hang around here?" Ed Wolfe asked him.

"It's your party," the man said.

"Then let's go some place else," Ed Wolfe said. "I get nervous here."

"I know a place," the Negro said.

"*You* know a place. You're a stranger here."

"No, man," the Negro said. "This is my home town. I come down here sometimes just to sit in the lobby and read the newspapers. It looks good, you know
what I mean? It looks good for the race."

"*The Wall Street Journal?* You're kidding Ed Wolfe. Watch that."

"No," the Negro said. "Honest."

"I'll be damned," Ed Wolfe said. "I come for the same reasons."

"Yeah," the Negro said. "No shit?"

"Sure, the same reasons." He laughed. "Let's get out of here." He tried to
stand, but fell back again in his chair. "Hey, help me up," he said loudly. The
Negro got up and came around to Ed Wolfe's side of the table. Leaning over, he
raised him to his feet. Some of the others in the room looked at them curiously.
"It's all right," Ed Wolfe said. "He's my man. I take him with me everywhere.
It looks good for the race." With their arms around each other's shoulders they
stumbled out of the bar and through the lobby.

In the street Ed Wolfe leaned against the building, and the Negro hailed a
cab, the dark left hand shooting up boldly, the long black body stretching
forward, raised on tiptoes, the head turned sharply along the left shoulder. Ed
Wolfe knew that he had never done it before. The Negro came up beside him
and guided Ed Wolfe toward the curb. Holding the door open, he shoved him
into the cab with his left hand. Ed Wolfe lurched against the cushioned seat
awkwardly. The Negro gave the driver an address and the cab moved off. Ed
Wolfe reached for the window handle and rolled it down rapidly. He shoved his
head out the window of the taxi and smiled and waved at the people along the
curb.

"Hey, man, close the window," the Negro said after a moment. "Close the
window. The cops, the cops."

Ed Wolfe laid his head on the edge of the taxi window and looked up at the
Negro, who was leaning over him, smiling; he seemed to be trying to tell him
something.

"Where we going, man?" Ed Wolfe asked.

"We're there," the Negro said, sliding along the seat toward the door.

"One ninety-five," the driver said.

"It's your party," Ed Wolfe told the Negro, waving away responsibility.

The Negro looked disappointed, but reached into his pocket.

Did he see what I had on me? Ed Wolfe wondered anxiously. Jerk, drunk,
you'll be rolled. They'll cut your throat and leave your skin in an alley. Be
careful.

"Come on, Ed," the Negro said. He took Ed Wolfe by the arm and got him
out of the taxi.

Fake. Fake, Ed Wolfe thought. Murderer. Nigger. Razor man.

The Negro pulled him toward a doorway. "You'll meet my friends," he said.

"Yeah, yeah," Ed Wolfe said. "I've heard so much about them."

"Hold it a second," the Negro said. He went up to the window and pressed
his ear against the opaque glass.

Ed Wolfe watched him without making a move.

"Here's the place," the Negro said proudly.

"Sure," Ed Wolfe said. "Sure it is."

"Come on, man," the Negro urged him.

"I'm coming, I'm coming," Ed Wolfe said. "But my head is bending low," he mumbled.

The Negro took out a ring of keys, selected one and put it in the door. Ed Wolfe followed him through.

"Hey, Oliver," somebody called. "Hey, baby, it's Oliver. Oliver looks good. He looks *good*."

"Hello, Mopiani," the Negro said to a short black man.

"How is stuff, Oliver?" Mopiani said to him.

"How's the market?" a man next to Mopiani asked, with a laugh.

"Ain't no mahket, baby. It's a *sto'*," somebody else said.

A woman stopped, looked at Ed Wolfe for a moment, and asked, "Who's the ofay, Oliver?"

"That's Oliver's broker, baby."

"Oliver's broker looks good," Mopiani said. "He looks *good*."

"This is my friend, Mr. Ed Wolfe," Oliver told them.

"Hey there," Mopiani said.

"Charmed," Ed Wolfe said.

"How's it going, man," a Negro said indifferently.

"Delighted," Ed Wolfe said.

He let Oliver lead him to a table.

"I'll get the drinks, Ed," Oliver said, leaving him.

Ed Wolfe looked at the room glumly. People were drinking steadily, gaily. They kept their bottles under their chairs in paper bags. He watched a man take a bag from beneath his chair, raise it and twist the open end of the bag carefully around the neck of the bottle so that it resembled a bottle of champagne swaddled in its toweling. The man poured liquor into his glass grandly. At the dark far end of the room some musicians were playing and three or four couples danced dreamily in front of them. He watched the musicians closely and was vaguely reminded of the airline pilots.

In a few minutes Oliver returned with a paper bag and some glasses. A girl was with him. "Mary Roberta, Ed Wolfe," he said, very pleased. Ed Wolfe stood up clumsily and the girl nodded.

"No more ice," Oliver explained.

"What the hell," Ed Wolfe said.

Mary Roberta sat down and Oliver pushed her chair up to the table. She sat with her hands in her lap and Oliver pushed her as though she were a cripple.

"Real nice little place here, Ollie," Ed Wolfe said.

"Oh, it's just the club," Oliver said.

"Real nice," Ed Wolfe said.

Oliver opened the bottle, then poured liquor into their glasses and put the paper bag under his chair. Oliver raised his glass. Ed Wolfe touched it lamely with his own and leaned back, drinking. When he put it down empty, Oliver filled it again from the paper bag. Ed Wolfe drank sluggishly, like one falling asleep, and listened, numbed, to Oliver and the girl. His glass never seemed to be empty any more. He drank steadily, but the liquor seemed to remain at the same level in the glass. He was conscious that someone else had joined them at the table. "Oliver's broker looks good," he heard somebody say. Mopiani. Warm and drowsy and gently detached, he listened, feeling as he had in barbershops, having his hair cut, conscious of the barber, unseen behind him, touching his hair and scalp with his warm fingers. "You see, Bert? He looks good," Mopiani was saying.

With great effort Ed Wolfe shifted in his chair, turning to the girl.

"Thought you were giving out on us, Ed," Oliver said. "That's it. That's it."

The girl sat with her hands folded in her lap.

"Mary Roberta," Ed Wolfe said.

"Uh huh," the girl said.

"Mary Roberta."

"Yes," the girl said. "That's right."

"You want to dance?" Ed Wolfe asked.

"All right," she said. "I guess so."

"That's it, that's it," Oliver said. "Stir yourself."

Ed Wolfe rose clumsily, cautiously, like one standing in a stalled Ferris wheel, and went around behind her chair, pulling it far back from the table with the girl in it. He took her warm, bare arm and moved toward the dancers. Mopiani passed them with a bottle. "Looks good, looks good," Mopiani said approvingly. He pulled her against him to let Mopiani pass, tightening the grip of his pale hand on her brown arm. A muscle leaped beneath the girl's smooth skin, filling his palm. At the edge of the dance floor he leaned forward into the girl's arms and they moved slowly, thickly across the floor. He held the girl close, conscious of her weight, the life beneath her body, just under her skin. Sick, he remembered a jumping bean he had held once in his palm, awed and frightened by the invisible life, jerking and hysterical, inside the stony shell. The girl moved with him in the music, Ed Wolfe astonished by the burden of her life. He stumbled away from her deliberately. Grinning, he moved ungently back against her. "Look out for Ed Wolfe," he crooned.

The girl stiffened and held him away from her, dancing self-consciously. Brooding, Ed Wolfe tried to concentrate on the lost rhythm. They danced in silence for a while.

"What do you do?" she asked him finally.

"I'm a salesman," he told her gloomily.

"Door to door?"

"Floor to ceiling. Wall to wall."

"Too much," she said.

"I'm a pusher," he said, suddenly angry. She looked frightened. "But I'm not hooked myself. It's a weakness in my character. I can't get hooked. Ach, what would you *goyim* know about it?"

"Take it easy," she said. "What's the matter with you? Do you want to sit down?"

"I can't push sitting down," he said.

"Hey," she said, "don't talk so loud."

"Boy," he said, "you black Protestants. What's the song you people sing?"

"Come on," she said.

"*Sometimes I feel like a motherless child,*" he sang roughly. The other dancers watched him nervously. "That's our national anthem, man," he said to a couple that had stopped dancing to look at him. "That's our song, sweethearts," he said, looking around him. "All right, *mine* then. I'm an orphan."

"Oh, come on," the girl said, exasperated, "an orphan. A grown man."

He pulled away from her. The band stopped playing. "Hell," he said loudly, "from the beginning. Orphan. Bachelor. Widower. Only child. All my names scorn me. I'm a survivor. I'm a goddamned survivor, that's what." The other couples crowded around him now. People got up from their tables. He could see them, on tiptoes, stretching their necks over the heads of the dancers. No, he thought. No, no. Detachment and caution. The La Meck Plan. They'll kill you. They'll kill you and kill you. He edged away from them, moving carefully backward against the bandstand. People pushed forward onto the dance floor to watch him. He could hear their questions, could see heads darting from behind backs and suddenly appearing over shoulders as they strained to get a look at him.

He grabbed Mary Roberta's hand, pulling her to him fiercely. He pulled and pushed her up onto the bandstand and then climbed up beside her. The trumpet player, bewildered, made room for him. "Tell you what I'm going to do," he shouted over their heads. "Tell you what I'm going to do."

Everyone was listening to him now.

"Tell you what I'm going to do," he began again.

Quietly they waited for him to go on.

"I don't *know* what I'm going to do," he shouted. "I don't *know* what I'm going to do. Isn't that a hell of a note?

"*Isn't it?*" he demanded.

"Brothers and sisters," he shouted, "and as an only child bachelor orphan I use the term playfully, you understand. Brothers and sisters, I tell you what I'm *not* going to do. I'm no consumer. Nobody's death can make me that. I won't consume. I mean, it's a question of identity, right? Closer, come up closer, buddies. You don't want to miss any of this."

"Oliver's broker looks good up there. Mary Roberta looks good. She looks good," Mopiani said below him.

"Right, Mopiani. She looks good, she looks *good*," Ed Wolfe called loudly. "So I tell you what I'm going to do. What am I bid? What am I bid for this fine strong wench? Daughter of a chief, masters. Dear dark daughter of a dead dinge chief. Look at those arms. Those arms, those arms. What am I bid?"

They looked at him, astonished.

"What am I bid?" he demanded. "Reluctant, masters? Reluctant masters, masters? Say, what's the matter with you darkies? Come on, what am I bid?" He turned to the girl. "No one wants you, honey," he said. "Folks, folks, I'd buy her myself, but I've already told you. I'm not a consumer. Please forgive me, miss."

He heard them shifting uncomfortably.

"Look," he said patiently, "the management has asked me to remind you that this is a living human being. This is the real thing, the genuine article, the goods. Oh, I told them I wasn't the right man for this job. As an orphan I have no conviction about the product. Now, you should have seen me in my old job. I could be rough. *Rough!* I hurt people. Can you imagine? I actually caused them pain. I mean, what the hell, I was an orphan. I *could* hurt people. An orphan doesn't have to bother with love. An orphan's like a nigger in that respect. Emancipated. But you people are another problem entirely. That's why I came here tonight. There are parents among you. I can feel it. There's even a sense of parents behind those parents. My God, don't any of you folks ever die? So what's holding us up? We're not making any money. Come on, what am I bid?"

"Shut up, mister." The voice was raised hollowly some place in the back of the crowd.

Ed Wolfe could not see the owner of the voice.

"He's not in," Ed Wolfe said.

"Shut up. What right you got to come down here and speak to us like that?"

"He's not in, I tell you. I'm his brother."

"You're a guest. A guest got no call to talk like that."

"He's out. I'm his father. He didn't tell me and I don't know when he'll be back."

"You can't make fun of us," the voice said.

"He isn't here. I'm his son."

"Bring that girl down off that stage!"

"Speaking," Ed Wolfe said brightly.

"Let go of that girl!" someone called angrily.

The girl moved closer to him.

"She's mine," Ed Wolfe said. "I danced with her."

"Get her down from there!"

"Okay," he said giddily. "Okay. All right." He let go of the girl's hand and pulled out his wallet. The girl did not move. He took out the bills and dropped the wallet to the floor.

"Damned drunk!" someone shouted.

"That whitey's crazy," someone else said.

"Here," Ed Wolfe said. "There's over sixteen hundred dollars here," he yelled, waving the money. It was, for him, like holding so much paper. "I'll start the bidding. I hear over sixteen hundred dollars once. I hear over sixteen hundred dollars twice. I hear it three times. Sold! A deal's a deal," he cried, flinging the money high over their heads. He saw them reach helplessly, noiselessly toward the bills, heard distinctly the sound of paper tearing.

He faced the girl. "Good-by," he said.

She reached forward, taking his hand.

"Good-by," he said again, "I'm leaving."

She held his hand, squeezing it. He looked down at the luxuriant brown hand, seeing beneath it the fine articulation of bones, the rich sudden rush of muscle. Inside her own he saw, indifferently, his own pale hand, lifeless and serene, still and infinitely free.

Richard Ford

. . . .

COMMUNIST

My mother once had a boyfriend named Glen Baxter. This was in 1961. We—my mother and I—were living in the little house my father had left her up the Sun River, near Victory, Montana, west of Great Falls. My mother was thirty-one at the time. I was sixteen. Glen Baxter was somewhere in the middle, between us, though I cannot be exact about it.

We were living then off the proceeds of my father's life insurance policies, with my mother doing some part-time waitressing work up in Great Falls and going to the bars in the evenings, which I know is where she met Glen Baxter. Sometimes he would come back with her and stay in her room at night, or she would call up from town and explain that she was staying with him in his little place on Lewis Street by the GN yards. She gave me his number every time, but I never called it. I think she probably thought that what she was doing was terrible, but simply couldn't help herself. I thought it was all right, though. Regular life it seemed and still does. She was young, and I knew that even then.

Glen Baxter was a Communist and liked hunting, which he talked about a lot. Pheasants. Ducks. Deer. He killed all of them, he said. He had been to Vietnam as far back as then, and when he was in our house he often talked about shooting the animals over there—monkeys and beautiful parrots—using military guns just for sport. We did not know what Vietnam was then, and Glen, when he talked about that, referred to it only as "the far east." I think now he must've been in the CIA and been disillusioned by something he saw or found out about and had been thrown out, but that kind of thing did not matter to us. He was a tall, dark-eyed man with thick black hair, and was usually in a good humor. He had gone halfway through college in Peoria, Illinois, he said, where he grew up. But when he was around our life he worked wheat farms as a ditcher, and stayed out of work winters and in the bars drinking with women like my mother, who had work and some money. It is not an uncommon life to lead in Montana.

What I want to explain happened in November. We had not been seeing Glen Baxter for some time. Two months had gone by. My mother knew other men, but she came home most days from work and stayed inside watching television in her bedroom and drinking beers. I asked about Glen once, and she said only that she didn't know where he was, and I assumed they had had a fight and that he was gone off on a flyer back to Illinois or Massachusetts, where he said he had relatives. I'll admit that I liked him. He had something on his mind always. He was a labor man as well as a Communist, and liked to say that the country was poisoned by the rich, and strong men would need to bring it to life again, and I liked that because my father had been a labor man, which was why we had a house to live in and money coming through. It was also true that I'd had a few boxing bouts by then—just with town boys and one with an Indian from Choteau—and there were some girlfriends I knew from that. I did not like my mother being around the house so much at night, and I wished Glen Baxter would come back, or that another man would come along and entertain her somewhere else.

At two o'clock on a Saturday, Glen drove up into our yard in a car. He had had a big brown Harley-Davidson that he rode most of the year, in his black-and-red irrigators and a baseball cap turned backwards. But this time he had a car, a blue Nash Ambassador. My mother and I went out on the porch when he stopped inside the olive trees my father had planted as a shelter belt, and my mother had a look on her face of not much pleasure. It was starting to be cold in earnest by then. Snow was down already onto the Fairfield Bench, though on this day a chinook was blowing, and it could as easily have been spring, though the sky above the Divide was turning over in silver and blue clouds of winter.

"We haven't seen you in a long time, I guess," my mother said coldly.

"My little retarded sister died," Glen said, standing at the door of his old car. He was wearing his orange VFW jacket and canvas shoes we called wino shoes, something I had never seen him wear before. He seemed to be in a good humor. "We buried her in Florida near the home."

"That's a good place," my mother said in a voice that meant she was a wronged party in something.

"I want to take this boy hunting today, Aileen," Glen said. "There're snow geese down now. But we have to go right away or they'll be gone to Idaho by tomorrow."

"He doesn't care to go," my mother said.

"Yes I do," I said and looked at her.

My mother frowned at me. "Why do you?"

"Why does he need a reason?" Glen Baxter said and grinned.

"I want him to have one, that's why." She looked at me oddly. "I think Glen's drunk, Les."

"No, I'm not drinking," Glen said, which was hardly ever true. He looked at both of us, and my mother bit down on the side of her lower lip and stared at me in a way to make you think she thought something was being put over on her and she didn't like you for it. She was very pretty, though when she was mad her features were sharpened and less pretty by a long way. "All right then, I don't care," she said to no one in particular. "Hunt, kill, maim. Your father did that too." She turned to go back inside.

"Why don't you come with us, Aileen?" Glen was smiling still, pleased.

"To do what?" my mother said. She stopped and pulled a package of cigarettes out of her dress pocket and put one in her mouth.

"It's worth seeing."

"See dead animals?" my mother said.

"These geese are from Siberia, Aileen," Glen said. "They're not like a lot of geese. Maybe I'll buy us dinner later. What do you say?"

"Buy what with?" my mother said. To tell the truth, I didn't know why she was so mad at him. I would've thought she'd be glad to see him. But she just suddenly seemed to hate everything about him.

"I've got some money," Glen said. "Let me spend it on a pretty girl tonight."

"Find one of those and you're lucky," my mother said, turning away toward the front door.

"I already found one," Glen Baxter said. But the door slammed behind her, and he looked at me then with a look I think now was helplessness, though I could not see a way to change anything.

My mother sat in the back seat of Glen's Nash and looked out the window while we drove. My double gun was in the seat between us beside Glen's Belgian pump, which he kept loaded with five shells in case, he said, he saw something beside the road he wanted to shoot. I had hunted rabbits before, and had ground-sluiced pheasants and other birds, but I had never been on an actual hunt before, one where you drove out to some special place and did it formally. And I was excited. I had a feeling that something important was about to happen to me and that this would be a day I would always remember.

My mother did not say anything for a long time, and neither did I. We drove up through Great Falls and out the other side toward Fort Benton, which was on the benchland where wheat was grown.

"Geese mate for life," my mother said, just out of the blue, as we were driving. "I hope you know that. They're special birds."

"I know that," Glen said in the front seat. "I have every respect for them."

"So where were you for three months?" she said. "I'm only curious."

"I was in the Big Hole for a while," Glen said, "and after that I went over to Douglas, Wyoming."

"What were you planning to do there?" my mother asked.

"I wanted to find a job, but it didn't work out."

"I'm going to college," she said suddenly, and this was something I had never heard about before. I turned to look at her, but she was staring out her window and wouldn't see me.

"I knew French once," Glen said. "Rose's pink. Rouge's red." He glanced at me and smiled. "I think that's a wise idea, Aileen. When are you going to start?"

"I don't want Les to think he was raised by crazy people all his life," my mother said.

"Les ought to go himself," Glen said.

"After I go, he will."

"What do you say about that, Les?" Glen said, grinning.

"He says it's just fine," my mother said.

"It's just fine," I said.

.   .   .   .   .

Where Glen Baxter took us was out onto the high flat prairie that was disked for wheat and had high, high mountains out to the east, with lower heartbreak hills in between. It was, I remember, a day for blues in the sky, and down in the distance we could see the small town of Floweree and the state highway running past it toward Fort Benton and the high line. We drove out on top of the prairie on a muddy dirt road fenced on both sides, until we had gone about three miles, which is where Glen stopped.

"All right," he said, looking up in the rearview mirror at my mother. "You wouldn't think there was anything here, would you?"

"*We're* here," my mother said. "You brought us here."

"You'll be glad though," Glen said, and seemed confident to me. I had looked around myself but could not see anything. No water or trees, nothing that seemed like a good place to hunt anything. Just wasted land. "There's a big lake out there, Les," Glen said. "You can't see it now from here because it's low. But the geese are there. You'll see."

"It's like the moon out here, I recognize that," my mother said, "only it's worse." She was staring out at the flat, disked wheatland as if she could actually see something in particular and wanted to know more about it. "How'd you find this place?"

"I came once on the wheat push," Glen said.

"And I'm sure the owner told you just to come back and hunt any time you like and bring anybody you wanted. Come one, come all. Is that it?"

"People shouldn't own land anyway," Glen said. "Anybody should be able to use it."

"Les, Glen's going to poach here," my mother said. "I just want you to know that, because that's a crime and the law will get you for it. If you're a man now, you're going to have to face the consequences."

"That's not true," Glen Baxter said, and looked gloomily out over the steering wheel down the muddy road toward the mountains. Though for myself I believed it was true, and didn't care. I didn't care about anything at that moment except seeing geese fly over me and shooting them down.

"Well, I'm certainly not going out there," my mother said. "I like towns better, and I already have enough trouble."

"That's okay," Glen said. "When the geese lift up you'll get to see them. That's all I wanted. Les and me'll go shoot them, won't we, Les?"

"Yes," I said, and I put my hand on my shotgun, which had been my father's and was heavy as rocks.

"Then we should go on," Glen said, "or we'll waste our light."

We got out of the car with our guns. Glen took off his canvas shoes and put on his pair of black irrigators out of the trunk. Then we crossed the barbed-wire fence and walked out into the high, tilled field toward nothing. I looked back at my mother when we were still not so far away, but I could only see the small, dark top of her head, low in the back seat of the Nash, staring out and thinking what I could not then begin to say.

On the walk toward the lake, Glen began talking to me. I had never been alone with him and knew little about him except what my mother said—that he drank too much, or other times that he was the nicest man she had ever known in the world and that some day a woman would marry him, though she didn't think it would be her. Glen told me as we walked that he wished he had finished college, but that it was too late now, that his mind was too old. He said he had liked "the far east" very much, and that people there knew how to treat each other, and that he would go back some day but couldn't go now. He said also that he would like to live in Russia for a while and mentioned the names of people who had gone there, names I didn't know. He said it would be hard at first, because it was so different, but that pretty soon anyone would learn to like it and wouldn't want to live anywhere else, and that Russians treated Americans who came to live there like kings. There were Communists everywhere now, he said. You didn't know them, but they were there. Montana had a large number, and he was in touch with all of them. He said that Communists were always in danger and that he had to protect himself all the time. And when he said that he pulled back his VFW jacket and showed me the butt of a pistol he had stuck under his shirt against his bare skin. "There are people who want to kill me right now," he said, "and I would kill a man myself if I thought I had to." And we kept walking. Though in a while he said, "I don't think I know much about you, Les. But I'd like to. What do you like to do?"

"I like to box," I said. "My father did it. It's a good thing to know."

"I suppose you have to protect yourself too," Glen said.

"I know how to," I said.

"Do you like to watch TV?" Glen said, and smiled.

"Not much."

"I love to," Glen said. "I could watch it instead of eating if I had one."

I looked out straight ahead over the green tops of sage that grew at the edge of the disked field, hoping to see the lake Glen said was there. There was an airishness and a sweet smell that I thought might be the place we were going, but I couldn't see it. "How will we hunt these geese?" I said.

"It won't be hard," Glen said. "Most hunting isn't even hunting. It's only shooting. And that's what this will be. In Illinois you would dig holes in the ground to hide in and set out your decoys. Then the geese come to you, over and over again. But we don't have time for that here." He glanced at me. "You have to be sure the first time here."

"How do you know they're here now?" I asked. And I looked toward the Highwood Mountains twenty miles away, half in snow and half dark blue at the bottom. I could see the little town of Floweree then, looking shabby and dimly lighted in the distance. A red bar sign shone. A car moved slowly away from the scattered buildings.

"They always come November first," Glen said.

"Are we going to poach them?"

"Does it make any difference to you?" Glen asked.

"No, it doesn't."

"Well then we aren't," he said.

We walked then for a while without talking. I looked back once to see the Nash far and small in the flat distance. I couldn't see my mother, and I thought that she must've turned on the radio and gone to sleep, which she always did, letting it play all night in her bedroom. Behind the car the sun was nearing the rounded mountains southwest of us, and I knew that when the sun was gone it would be cold. I wished my mother had decided to come along with us, and I thought for a moment of how little I really knew her at all.

Glen walked with me another quarter mile, crossed another barbed-wire fence where sage was growing, then went a hundred yards through wheatgrass and spurge until the ground went up and formed a kind of long hillock bunker built by a farmer against the wind. And I realized the lake was just beyond us. I could hear the sound of a car horn blowing and a dog barking all the way down in the town, then the wind seemed to move and all I could hear then and after then were geese. So many geese, from the sound of them, though I still could not see even one. I stood and listened to the high-pitched shouting sound, a sound I had never heard so close, a sound with size to it—though it was not loud. A sound that meant great numbers and that made your chest rise and your shoulders tighten with expectancy. It was a sound to make you feel separate from it and everything else, as if you were of no importance in the grand scheme of things.

"Do you hear them singing?" Glen asked. He held his hand up to make me stand still. And we both listened. "How many do you think, Les, just hearing?"

"A hundred," I said. "More than a hundred."

"Five thousand," Glen said. "More than you can believe when you see them. Go see."

I put down my gun and on my hands and knees crawled up the earthwork through the wheatgrass and thistle until I could see down to the lake and see the geese. And they were there, like a white bandage laid on the water, wide and long and continuous, a white expanse of snow geese, seventy yards from me, on the bank, but stretching onto the lake, which was large itself—a half mile across, with thick tules on the far side and wild plums farther and the blue mountain behind them.

"Do you see the big raft?" Glen said from below me, in a whisper.

"I see it," I said, still looking. It was such a thing to see, a view I had never seen and have not since.

"Are any on the land?" he said.

"Some are in the wheatgrass," I said, "but most are swimming."

"Good," Glen said. "They'll have to fly. But we can't wait for that now."

And I crawled backwards down the heel of land to where Glen was, and my gun. We were losing our light, and the air was purplish and cooling. I looked toward the car but couldn't see it, and I was no longer sure where it was below the lighted sky.

"Where do they fly to?" I said in a whisper, since I did not want anything to be ruined because of what I did or said. It was important to Glen to shoot the geese, and it was important to me.

"To the wheat," he said. "Or else they leave for good. I wish your mother had come, Les. Now she'll be sorry."

I could hear the geese quarreling and shouting on the lake surface. And I wondered if they knew we were here now. "She might be," I said with my heart pounding, but I didn't think she would be much.

It was a simple plan he had. I would stay behind the bunker, and he would crawl on his belly with his gun through the wheatgrass as near to the geese as he could. Then he would simply stand up and shoot all the ones he could close up, both in the air and on the ground. And when all the others flew up, with luck some would turn toward me as they came into the wind, and then I could shoot them and turn them back to him, and he would shoot them again. He could kill ten, he said, if he was lucky, and I might kill four. It didn't seem hard.

"Don't show them your face," Glen said. "Wait till you think you can touch them, then stand up and shoot. To hesitate is lost in this."

"All right," I said. "I'll try it."

"Shoot one in the head, and then shoot another one," Glen said. "It won't be hard." He patted me on the arm and smiled. Then he took off his VFW jacket and put it on the ground, climbed up the side of the bunker, cradling his shotgun in his arms, and slid on his belly into the dry stalks of yellow grass out of my sight.

Then for the first time in that entire day I was alone. And I didn't mind it. I sat squat down in the grass, loaded my double gun, and took my other two shells out of my pocket to hold. I pushed the safety off and on to see that it was right. The wind rose a little then, scuffed the grass and made me shiver. It was not the warm chinook now, but a wind out of the north, the one geese flew away from if they could.

Then I thought about my mother in the car alone, and how much longer I would stay with her, and what it might mean to her for me to leave. And I wondered when Glen Baxter would die and if someone would kill him, or whether my mother would marry him and how I would feel about it. And though I didn't know why, it occurred to me then that Glen Baxter and I would not be friends when all was said and done, since I didn't care if he ever married my mother or didn't.

Then I thought about boxing and what my father had taught me about it. To tighten your fists hard. To strike out straight from the shoulder and never punch backing up. How to cut a punch by snapping your fist inwards, how to carry your chin low, and to step toward a man when he is falling so you can hit him again. And most important, to keep your eyes open when you are hitting in the face and causing damage, because you need to see what you're doing to encourage yourself, and because it is when you close your eyes that you stop hitting and get hurt badly. "Fly all over your man, Les," my father said. "When you see your chance, fly on him and hit him till he falls." That, I thought, would always be my attitude in things.

And then I heard the geese again, their voices in unison, louder and shouting, as if the wind had changed and put all new sounds in the cold air. And then a *boom.* And I knew Glen was in among them and had stood up to shoot. The noise of geese rose and grew worse, and my fingers burned where I held my gun too tight to the metal, and I put it down and opened my fist to make the burning stop so I could feel the trigger when the moment came. *Boom,* Glen shot again, and I heard him shuck a shell, and all the sounds out beyond the bunker seemed to be rising—the geese, the shots, the air itself going up. *Boom,* Glen shot another time, and I knew he was taking his careful time to make his shots good.

And I held my gun and started to crawl up the bunker so as not to be surprised when the geese came over me and I could shoot.

From the top I saw Glen Baxter alone in the wheatgrass field, shooting at a white goose with black tips of wings that was on the ground not far from him, but trying to run and pull into the air. He shot it once more, and it fell over dead with its wings flapping.

Glen looked back at me and his face was distorted and strange. The air around him was full of white rising geese and he seemed to want them all. "Behind you, Les," he yelled at me and pointed. "They're all behind you now." I looked behind me, and there were geese in the air as far as I could see, more than I knew how many, moving so slowly, their wings wide out and working calmly and filling the air with noise, though their voices were not as loud or as shrill as I had thought they would be. And they were so close! Forty feet, some of them. The air around me vibrated and I could feel the wind from their wings and it seemed to me I could kill as many as the times I could shoot—a hundred or a thousand—and I raised my gun, put the muzzle on the head of a white goose and fired. It shuddered in the air, its wide feet sank below its belly, its wings cradled out to hold back air, and it fell straight down and landed with an awful sound, a noise a human would make, a thick, soft, *hump* noise. I looked up again and shot another goose, could hear the pellets hit its chest, but it didn't fall or even break its pattern for flying. *Boom*, Glen shot again. And then again. "Hey," I heard him shout. "Hey, hey." And there were geese flying over me, flying in line after line. I broke my gun and reloaded, and thought to myself as I did: I need confidence here, I need to be sure with this. I pointed at another goose and shot it in the head, and it fell the way the first one had, wings out, its belly down, and with the same thick noise of hitting. Then I sat down in the grass on the bunker and let geese fly over me.

By now the whole raft was in the air, all of it moving in a slow swirl above me and the lake and everywhere, finding the wind and heading out south in long wavering lines that caught the last sun and turned to silver as they gained a distance. It was a thing to see, I will tell you now. Five thousand white geese all in the air around you, making a noise like you have never heard before. And I thought to myself then: This is something I will never see again. I will never forget this. And I was right.

Glen Baxter shot twice more. One shot missed, but with the other he hit a goose flying away from him and knocked it half-falling and flying into the empty lake not far from shore, where it began to swim as though it was fine and make its noise.

Glen stood in the stubbly grass, looking out at the goose, his gun lowered. "I didn't need to shoot that, did I, Les?"

"I don't know," I said, sitting on the little knoll of land, looking at the goose swimming in the water.

"I don't know why I shoot 'em. They're so beautiful." He looked at me.

"I don't know either," I said.

"Maybe there's nothing else to do with them." Glen stared at the goose again and shook his head. "Maybe this is exactly what they're put on earth for."

I did not know what to say because I did not know what he could mean by that, though what I felt was embarrassment at the great number of geese there were, and a dulled feeling like a hunger because the shooting had stopped and it was over for me now.

Glen began to pick up his geese, and I walked down to my two that had fallen close together and were dead. One had hit with such an impact that its stomach had split and some of its inward parts were knocked out. Though the other looked unhurt, its soft white belly turned up like a pillow, its head and jagged bill-teeth and its tiny black eyes looking as if it were alive.

"What's happened to the hunters out here?" I heard a voice speak. It was my mother, standing in her pink dress on the knoll above us, hugging her arms. She was smiling though she was cold. And I realized that I had lost all thought of her in the shooting. "Who did all this shooting? Is this your work, Les?"

"No," I said.

"Les is a hunter, though, Aileen," Glen said. "He takes his time." He was holding two white geese by their necks, one in each hand, and he was smiling. He and my mother seemed pleased.

"I see you didn't miss too many," my mother said and smiled. I could tell she admired Glen for his geese, and that she had done some thinking in the car alone. "It *was* wonderful, Glen," she said. "I've never seen anything like that. They were like snow."

"It's worth seeing once, isn't it?" Glen said. "I should've killed more, but I got excited."

My mother looked at me then. "Where's yours, Les?"

"Here," I said and pointed to my two geese on the ground beside me.

My mother nodded in a nice way, and I think she liked everything then and wanted the day to turn out right and for all of us to be happy. "Six, then. You've got six in all."

"One's still out there," I said and motioned where the one goose was swimming in circles on the water.

"Okay," my mother said and put her hand over her eyes to look. "Where is it?"

Glen Baxter looked at me then with a strange smile, a smile that said he wished I had never mentioned anything about the other goose. And I wished I hadn't either. I looked up in the sky and could see the lines of geese by the thousands shining silver in the light, and I wished we could just leave and go home.

"That one's my mistake there," Glen Baxter said and grinned. "I shouldn't have shot that one, Aileen. I got too excited."

My mother looked out on the lake for a minute, then looked at Glen and back again. "Poor goose." She shook her head. "How will you get it, Glen?"

"I can't get that one now," Glen said.

My mother looked at him. "What do you mean?" she said.

"I'm going to leave that one," Glen said.

"Well, no. You can't leave one," my mother said. "You shot it. You have to get it. Isn't that a rule?"

"No," Glen said.

And my mother looked from Glen to me. "Wade out and get it, Glen," she said, in a sweet way, and my mother looked young then for some reason, like a young girl, in her flimsy short-sleeved waitress dress, and her skinny, bare legs in the wheatgrass.

"No." Glen Baxter looked down at his gun and shook his head. And I didn't know why he wouldn't go, because it would've been easy. The lake was shallow. And you could tell that anyone could've walked out a long way before it got deep, and Glen had on his boots.

My mother looked at the white goose, which was not more than thirty yards from the shore, its head up, moving in slow circles, its wings settled and relaxed so you could see the black tips. "Wade out and get it, Glenny, won't you please?" she said. "They're special things."

"You don't understand the world, Aileen," Glen said. "This can happen. It doesn't matter."

"But that's so cruel, Glen," she said, and a sweet smile came on her lips.

"Raise up your own arms, Leeny," Glen said. "I can't see any angel's wings, can you Les?" He looked at me, but I looked away.

"Then you go on and get it, Les," my mother said. "You weren't raised by crazy people." I started to go, but Glen Baxter suddenly grabbed me by my shoulder and pulled me back hard, so hard his fingers made bruises in my skin that I saw later.

"Nobody's going," he said. "This is over with now."

And my mother gave Glen a cold look then. "You don't have a heart, Glen," she said. "There's nothing to love in you. You're just a son of a bitch, that's all."

And Glen Baxter nodded at my mother as if he understood something that he had not understood before, but something that he was willing to know. "Fine," he said, "that's fine." And he took his big pistol out from against his belly, the big blue revolver I had only seen part of before and that he said protected him, and he pointed it out at the goose on the water, his arm straight away from him, and shot and missed. And then he shot and missed again. The goose made its noise once. And then he hit it dead, because there was no splash. And then he shot it three times more until the gun was empty and the goose's head was down and it was floating toward the middle of the lake where it was empty and dark blue. "Now who has a heart?" Glen said. But my mother was not there when he turned around. She had already started back to the car and was almost lost from sight in the darkness. And Glen smiled at me then and his face had a wild look on it. "Okay, Les?" he said.

"Okay," I said.

"There're limits to everything, right?"

"I guess so," I said.

"Your mother's a beautiful woman, but she's not the only beautiful woman in Montana." I did not say anything. And Glen Baxter suddenly said, "Here," and he held the pistol out at me. "Don't you want this? Don't you want to shoot me? Nobody thinks they'll die. But I'm ready for it right now." And I did not know what to do then. Though it is true that what I wanted to do was to hit him, hit him as hard in the face as I could, and see him on the ground bleeding and crying and pleading for me to stop. Only at that moment he looked scared to me, and I had never seen a grown man scared before—though I have seen one since—and I felt sorry for him, as though he was already a dead man. And I did not end up hitting him at all.

A light can go out in the heart. All of this went on years ago, but I still can feel now how sad and remote the world was to me. Glen Baxter, I think now, was not a bad man, only a man scared of something he'd never seen before— something soft in himself—his life going a way he didn't like. A woman with a son. Who could blame him there? I don't know what makes people do what they do or call themselves what they call themselves, only that you have to live someone's life to be the expert.

My mother had tried to see the good side of things, tried to be hopeful in the situation she was handed, tried to look out for us both, and it hadn't worked. It was a strange time in her life then and after that, a time when she had to adjust to being an adult just when she was on the thin edge of things. Too much awareness too early in life was her problem, I think.

And what I felt was only that I had somehow been pushed out into the world, into the real life then, the one I hadn't lived yet. In a year I was gone to hardrock mining and no-paycheck jobs and not to college. And I have thought more than once about my mother saying that I had not been raised by crazy people, and I don't know what that could mean or what difference it could make, unless it means that love is a reliable commodity, and even that is not always true, as I have found out.

Late on the night that all this took place I was in bed when I heard my mother say, "Come outside, Les. Come and hear this." And I went out onto the front porch barefoot and in my underwear, where it was warm like spring, and there was a spring mist in the air. I could see the lights of the Fairfield Coach in the distance on its way up to Great Falls.

And I could hear geese, white birds in the sky, flying. They made their high-pitched sound like angry yells, and though I couldn't see them high up, it seemed to me they were everywhere. And my mother looked up and said, "Hear them?" I could smell her hair wet from the shower. "They leave with the moon," she said. "It's still half wild out here."

And I said, "I hear them," and I felt a chill come over my bare chest, and the hair stood up on my arms the way it does before a storm. And for a while we listened.

"When I first married your father, you know, we lived on a street called Blue-bird Canyon, in California. And I thought that was the prettiest street and the prettiest name. I suppose no one brings you up like your first love. You don't mind if I say that, do you?" She looked at me hopefully.

"No," I said.

"We have to keep civilization alive somehow." And she pulled her little housecoat together because there was a cold vein in the air, a part of the cold that would be on us the next day. "I don't feel part of things tonight, I guess."

"It's all right," I said.

"Do you know where I'd like to go?" she said.

"No," I said. And I suppose I knew she was angry then, angry with life but did not want to show me that.

"To the Straits of Juan de Fuca. Wouldn't that be something? Would you like that?"

"I'd like it," I said. And my mother looked off for a minute, as if she could see the Straits of Juan de Fuca out against the line of mountains, see the lights of things alive and a whole new world.

"I know you liked him," she said after a moment. "You and I both suffer fools too well."

"I didn't like him too much," I said. "I didn't really care."

"He'll fall on his face. I'm sure of that," she said. And I didn't say anything because I didn't care about Glen Baxter anymore, and was happy not to talk about him. "Would you tell me something if I asked you? Would you tell me the truth?"

"Yes," I said.

And my mother did not look at me. "Just tell the truth," she said.

"All right," I said.

"Do you think I'm still very feminine? I'm thirty-two years old now. You don't know what that means. But do you think I am?"

And I stood at the edge of the porch, with the olive trees before me, looking straight up into the mist where I could not see geese but could still hear them flying, could almost feel the air move below their white wings. And I felt the way you feel when you are on a trestle all alone and the train is coming, and you know you have to decide. And I said, "Yes, I do." Because that was the truth. And I tried to think of something else then and did not hear what my mother said after that.

And how old was I then? Sixteen. Sixteen is young, but it can also be a grown man. I am forty-one years old now, and I think about that time without regret, though my mother and I never talked in that way again, and I have not heard her voice now in a long, long time.

. . . .

THE DOLL QUEEN

I

I went because that card—such a strange card—reminded me of her existence. I found it in a forgotten book whose pages had revived the ghost associated
with the childish calligraphy. For the first time in a long time I was rearranging
my books. I met surprise after surprise since some, placed on the highest shelves,
had not been read for a long time. So long a time that the edges of the leaves
were grainy, and a mixture of gold dust and greyish scale fell onto my open
palm, reminiscent of the lacquer covering certain bodies glimpsed first in dreams
and later in the deceptive reality of the first ballet performance to which we're
taken. It was a book from my childhood—perhaps from that of many children—that related a series of more or less truculent exemplary tales which had
the virtue of precipitating us upon our elders' knees to ask them, over and over
again: Why? Children who are ungrateful to their parents; maidens kidnapped
by flashy horsemen and returned home in shame—as well as those who willingly
abandon hearth and home; old men who in exchange for an overdue mortgage
demand the hand of the sweetest and most long-suffering daughter of the threatened family. . . . Why? I do not recall their answers, I only know that from
among the stained pages fell, fluttering, a white card in Amilamia's atrocious
hand: *Amilamia wil not forget her good frend—com see me here lik I draw it.*

And on the other side was that map of a path starting from an X that indicated, doubtlessly, the park bench where I, an adolescent rebelling against prescribed and tedious education, forgot my classroom schedule in order to spend
several hours reading books which if not actually written by me, seemed to be:
who could doubt that only from *my* imagination could spring all those corsairs,
those couriers of the tsar, all those boys slightly younger than I who rowed all
day up and down the great American rivers on a raft. Clutching the arm of the
park bench as if it were the frame of a magical saddle, at first I didn't hear the
sound of the light steps and of the little girl who would stop behind me after
running down the graveled garden path. It was Amilamia, and I don't know how
long the child would have kept me silent company if her mischievous spirit, one
afternoon, had not chosen to tickle my ear with down from a dandelion she blew
towards me, her lips puffed out and her brow furrowed in a frown.

She asked my name and after considering it very seriously, she told me hers with a smile which if not candid, was not too rehearsed. Quickly I realized that Amilamia had discovered, if discovered is the word, a form of expression midway between the ingenuousness of her years and the forms of adult mimicry that well-brought-up children have to know, particularly those for the solemn moments of introduction and of leave-taking. Amilamia's seriousness, apparently, was a gift of nature, whereas her moments of spontaneity, by contrast, seemed artificial. I like to remember her, afternoon after afternoon, in a succession of snapshots that in their totality sum up the complete Amilamia. And it never ceases to surprise me that I cannot think of her as she really was, or remember how she actually moved, light, questioning, constantly looking around her. I must remember her fixed forever in time, as in a photograph album. Amilamia in the distance, a point on the spot where the hill began to descend from a lake of clover towards the flat meadow where I, sitting on the bench, used to read: a point of fluctuating shadow and sunshine and a hand that waved to me from high on the hill. Amilamia frozen in her flight down the hill, her white skirt billowing, the flowered panties gathered around her thighs with elastic, her mouth open and eyes half-closed against the streaming air, the child crying with pleasure. Amilamia sitting beneath the eucalyptus trees, pretending to cry so that I would go over to her. Amilamia lying on her stomach with a flower in her hand: the petals of a flower which I discovered later didn't grow in this garden, but somewhere else, perhaps in the garden of Amilamia's house, since the single pocket of her blue-checked apron was often filled with those white blossoms. Amilamia watching me read, holding with both hands to the bars of the green bench, asking questions with her grey eyes: I recall that she never asked me what I was reading, as if she could divine in my eyes the images born of the pages. Amilamia laughing with pleasure when I lifted her by the waist and whirled her around my head; she seemed to discover a new perspective on the world in that slow flight. Amilamia turning her back to me and waving goodbye, her arm held high, the fingers waving excitedly. And Amilamia in the thousand postures she affected around my bench, hanging upside down, her bloomers billowing; sitting on the gravel with her legs crossed and her chin resting on her fist; lying on the grass, baring her belly-button to the sun; weaving tree branches, drawing animals in the mud with a twig, licking the bars of the bench, hiding beneath the seat, silently breaking off the loose bark from the ancient treetrunks, staring at the horizon beyond the hill, humming with her eyes closed, imitating the voices of birds, dogs, cats, hens, and horses. All for me, and nevertheless, nothing. It was her way of being with me, all these things I remember, but at the same time her manner of being alone in the park. Yes, perhaps my memory of her is fragmentary because reading alternated with the contemplation of the chubby-cheeked child with smooth hair changing in the reflection of the light: now wheat-colored, now burnt chestnut. And it is only today that I think how Amilamia in that moment established the other point of support for my life, the one that created the tension between my own irresolute childhood and the open world, the promised land that was beginning to be mine through my reading.

Not then. Then I dreamed about the women in my books, about the quintessential female—the word disturbed me—who assumed the disguise of the

Queen in order to buy the necklace secretly, about the imagined beings of mythology—half recognizable, half white-breasted, damp-bellied salamanders—
who awaited monarchs in their beds. And thus, imperceptibly, I moved from indifference towards my childish companion to an acceptance of the child's
gracefulness and seriousness and from there to an unexpected rejection of a presence that became useless to me. She irritated me, finally. I who was fourteen was
irritated by that child of seven who was not yet memory or nostalgia, but rather
the past and its reality. I had let myself be dragged along by weakness. We had
run together, holding hands, across the meadow. Together we had shaken the
pines and picked up the cones that Amilamia guarded jealously in her apron
pocket. Together we had constructed paper boats and followed them, happy and
gay, to the edge of the drain. And that afternoon amidst shouts of glee, when we
tumbled together down the hill and rolled to a stop at its foot, Amilamia was on
my chest, her hair between my lips; but when I felt her panting breath in my ear
and her little arms sticky from sweets around my neck, I angrily pushed away her
arms and let her fall. Amilamia cried, rubbing her wounded elbow and knee, and
I returned to my bench. Then Amilamia went away and the following day she
returned, handed me the paper without a word, and disappeared, humming, into
the woods. I hesitated whether to tear up the card or keep it in the pages of the
book: *Afternoons on the Farm.* Even my reading had become childish because
of Amilamia. She did not return to the park. After a few days I left for my vacation and when I returned it was to the duties of my first year of prep school. I
never saw her again.

II

And now, almost rejecting the image that is unaccustomed without being
fantastic, but is all the more painful for being so real, I return to that forgotten park and stopping before the grove of pines and eucalyptus I recognize
the smallness of the bosky enclosure that my memory has insisted on drawing
with an amplitude that allowed sufficient space for the vast swell of my imagination. After all, Strogoff and Huckleberry, Milady de Winter and Geneviève
de Brabante were born, lived and died here: in a little garden surrounded by
mossy iron railings, sparsely planted with old, neglected trees, barely adorned by
a concrete bench painted to look like wood that forces me to believe that my
beautiful wrought-iron green-painted bench never existed, or else was a part of
my orderly, retrospective delirium. And the hill . . . How could I believe the
promontory that Amilamia climbed and descended during her daily coming and
going, that steep slope we rolled down together, was *this*. A barely elevated
patch of dark stubble with no more heights and depths than those my memory
had created.

Com see me here lik I draw it. So I would have to cross the garden, leave the
woods behind, descend the hill in three loping steps, cut through that narrow
grove of chestnuts—it was here, surely, where the child gathered the white
petals—open the squeaking park gate and suddenly recall . . . , know . . . , find
oneself in the street, realize that every afternoon of one's adolescence, as if by a

miracle, he had succeeded in suspending the beat of the surrounding city, annulling that flood-tide of whistles, bells, voices, sobs, engines, radios, imprecations. Which was the true magnet, the silent garden or the feverish city?

I wait for the light to change and cross to the other sidewalk, my eyes never leaving the red iris detaining the traffic. I consult Amilamia's paper. After all, that rudimentary map is the true magnet of the moment I am living, and just thinking about it startles me. I was obliged, after the lost afternoons of my fourteenth year, to follow the channels of discipline; now I find myself, at twenty-nine, duly certified with a diploma, owner of an office, assured of a moderate income, a bachelor still, with no family to maintain, slightly bored with sleeping with secretaries, scarcely excited by an occasional outing to the country or to the beach, feeling the lack of a central attraction such as those once afforded me by my books, my park, and Amilamia. I walk down the street of this grey, low-buildinged suburb. The one-story houses with their doorways scaling paint succeed each other monotonously. Faint neighborhood sounds barely interrupt the general uniformity: the squeal of a knife-sharpener here, the hammering of a shoe-repairman there. The children of the neighborhood are playing in the dead-end streets. The music of an organ-grinder reaches my ears, mingled with the voices of children's rounds. I stop a moment to watch them with the sensation, also fleeting, that Amilamia must be among these groups of children, immodestly exhibiting her flowered panties, hanging by her knees from some balcony, still fond of acrobatic excesses, her apron pocket filled with white petals. I smile, and for the first time I am able to imagine the young lady of twenty-two who, even if she still lives at this address, will laugh at my memories, or who perhaps will have forgotten the afternoons spent in the garden.

The house is identical to all the rest. The heavy entry door, two grilled windows with closed shutters. A one-story house, topped by a false neoclassic balustrade that probably conceals the practicalities of the flat-roofed *azotea*: clothes hanging on lines, tubs of water, servants' quarters, a chicken coop. Before I ring the bell, I want to free myself of any illusion. Amilamia no longer lives here. Why would she stay fifteen years in the same house? Besides, in spite of her precocious independence and aloneness, she seemed like a well-brought-up, well-behaved child, and this neighborhood is no longer elegant; Amilamia's parents, without doubt, have moved. But perhaps the new renters will know where.

I press the bell and wait. I ring again. Here is another contingency: no one is home. And will I feel the need again to look for my childhood friend? No. Because it will not be possible a second time to open a book from my adolescence and accidentally find Amilamia's card. I would return to my routine, I would forget the moment whose importance lay in its fleeting surprise.

I ring once more. I press my ear to the door and am surprised: I can hear a harsh and irregular breathing on the other side; the sound of labored breathing, accompanied by the disagreeable odor of stale tobacco, filters through the cracks in the hall.

"Good afternoon. Could you tell me . . . ?"

As soon as he hears my voice, the person moves away with heavy and unsure steps. I press the bell again, shouting this time:

"Hey! Open up! What's the matter? Don't you hear me?"

No response. I continue ringing the bell, without result. I move back from the door, still staring at the small cracks, as if distance might give me perspective, or even penetration. With all my attention fixed on that damned door, I cross the street, walking backwards; a piercing scream, followed by a prolonged and ferocious blast of a whistle, saves me in time; dazed, I seek the person whose voice has just saved me. I see only the automobile moving down the street and I hang on to a lamp post, a hold that more than security offers me a point of support during the sudden rush of icy blood to my burning, sweaty skin. I look towards the house that has been, that was, that must be, Amilamia's. There, behind the balustrade, as I had known there would be, fluttering clothes are drying. I don't know what else is hanging there—skirts, pajamas, blouses—I don't know. All I can see is that starched little blue-checked apron, clamped by clothespins to the long cord that swings between an iron bar and a nail in the white wall of the *azotea.*

III

In the Bureau of Records they have told me that the property is in the name of a Señor R. Valdivia, who rents the house. To whom? That they don't know. Who is Valdivia? He has declared himself a businessman. Where does he live? Who are *you?* the young lady asked me with haughty curiosity. I haven't been able to present a calm and sure appearance. Sleep has not relieved my nervous fatigue. Valdivia. As I leave the Bureau the sun offends me. I associate the repugnance provoked by the hazy sun sifting through the clouds—therefore all the more intense—with the desire to return to the damp, shadowy park. No. It is only the desire to know whether Amilamia lives in that house and why they refuse to let me enter. But the first thing I must do is reject the absurd idea that kept me awake all night. Having seen the apron drying on the flat roof, the one where she kept the flowers, and so believing that in that house lived a seven-year-old girl that I had known fourteen or fifteen years before. . . . She must have a little girl! Yes. Amilamia, at twenty-two, is the mother of a girl who dressed the same, looked the same, repeated the same games, and—who knows—perhaps even went to the same park. And deep in thought I again arrived at the door of the house. I ring the bell and await the whistling breathing on the other side of the door. I am mistaken. The door is opened by a woman who can't be more than fifty. But wrapped in a shawl, dressed in black and in black low-heeled shoes, with no make-up and her salt and pepper hair pulled into a knot, she seems to have abandoned all illusion or pretext of youth; she is observing me with eyes so indifferent they seem almost cruel.

"You want something?"

"Señor Valdivia sent me." I cough and run my hand over my hair. I should have picked up my briefcase at the office. I realize that without it I cannot play my role very well.

"Valdivia?" the woman asks without alarm, without interest.

"Yes. The owner of this house."

One thing is clear. The woman will reveal nothing in her face. She looks at me, calmly.

"Oh, yes. The owner of the house."

"May I come in?"

I think that in bad comedies the traveling salesman sticks a foot in the door so they can't close the door in his face. I do the same, but the woman steps back and with a gesture of her hand invites me to come into what must have been a garage. On one side there is a glass-paned door, its paint faded. I walk towards the door over the yellow tiles of the entryway and ask again, turning towards the woman who follows me with tiny steps:

"This way?"

I notice for the first time that in her white hands she is carrying a chapelet which she toys with ceaselessly. I haven't seen one of those old-fashioned rosaries since my childhood and I want to comment on it, but the brusque and decisive manner with which the woman opens the door precludes any gratuitous conversation. We enter a long narrow room. The woman hastens to open the shutters. But because of four large perennial plants growing in porcelain and crusted glass pots the room remains in shadow. The only other objects in the room are an old high-backed cane-trimmed sofa and a rocking chair. But it is neither the plants nor the sparseness of the furniture that draws my attention.

The woman invites me to sit on the sofa before she sits in the rocking chair. Beside me, on the cane arm of the sofa, there is an open magazine.

"Señor Valdivia sends his apologies for not having come in person."

The woman rocks, unblinkingly. I peer at the comic book out of the corner of my eye.

"He sends his greetings and. . . ."

I stop, awaiting a reaction from the woman. She continues to rock. The magazine is covered with red-penciled scribbling.

". . . and asks me to inform you that he must disturb you for a few days. . . ."

My eyes search rapidly.

". . . A new evaluation of the house must be made for the tax lists. It seems it hasn't been done for. . . . You have been living here since . . . ?"

Yes. That is a stubby lipstick lying under the chair. If the woman smiles, it is only with the slow-moving hands caressing the chapelet; I sense, for an instant, a swift flash of ridicule that does not quite disturb her features. She still does not answer.

". . . for at least fifteen years, isn't that true?"

She does not agree. She does not disagree. And on the pale thin lips there is not the least sign of lipstick. . . .

". . . you, your husband, and . . . ?"

She stares at me, never changing expression, almost daring me to continue. We sit a moment in silence, she playing with the rosary, I leaning forwards, my hands on my knees. I rise.

"Well, then, I'll be back this afternoon with the papers. . . ."

The woman nods while, in silence, she picks up the lipstick and the comic book and hides them in the folds of her shawl.

IV

The scene has not changed. This afternoon, while I am writing down false figures in my notebook and feigning interest in establishing the quality of the dulled floor-boards and the length of the living room, the woman rocks, as the three decades of the chapelet whisper through her fingers. I sigh as I finish the supposed inventory of the living room and I ask her for permission to go to the other rooms in the house. The woman rises, bracing her long black-clad arms on the seat of the rocking chair and adjusting the shawl on her narrow bony shoulders.

She opens the opaque glass door and we enter a dining room with very little more furniture. But the table with the aluminum legs and the four nickel and plastic chairs lack even the slight hint of distinction of the living room furniture. Another window with wrought-iron grille and closed shutters must at times illuminate this bare-walled dining room, bare of either shelves or bureau. The only object on the table is a plastic fruit dish with a cluster of black grapes, two peaches, and a buzzing corona of flies. The woman, her arms crossed, her face expressionless, stops behind me. I take the risk of breaking the order of things: it is evident that these rooms will not tell me anything that I really want to know.

"Couldn't we go up to the roof?" I ask. "I believe that is the best way of measuring the total area."

The woman's eyes light up as she looks at me, or perhaps it is only the contrast with the penumbra of the dining room.

"What for?" she says finally. "Señor . . . Valdivia . . . knows the dimensions very well."

And those pauses, one before and one after the owner's name, are the first indications that something is at last perturbing the woman and forcing her, in defense, to resort to a certain irony.

"I don't know." I make an effort to smile. "Perhaps I prefer to go from top to bottom and not . . ." my false smile drains away, ". . . from bottom to top."

"You will go the way I show you," the woman says, her arms crossed across her chest, the silver cross hanging against her dark belly.

Before smiling weakly, I force myself to think how, in this shadow, my gestures are useless, not even symbolic. I open the notebook with a crunch of the cardboard cover and continue making my notes with the greatest possible speed, never glancing up, the numbers and estimates of this task whose fiction—the light flush in my cheeks and the perceptible dryness of my tongue tell me—is deceiving no one. And after filling the graph paper with absurd signs, with square roots and algebraic formulas, I ask myself what is preventing me from getting to the point, from asking about Amilamia and getting out of here with a satisfactory answer. Nothing. And nevertheless, I am sure that even if I obtained a response, the truth does not lie along this road. My slim and silent companion is a person I wouldn't look twice at in the street, but in this almost uninhabited house with the coarse furniture, she ceases to be an anonymous face in the crowd and is converted into a stock character of mystery. Such is the paradox, and if memories of Amilamia have once again awakened my appetite for the imaginary, I shall follow the rules of the game, I shall exhaust all the appearances, and I shall not rest until I find the answer—perhaps simple and clear, immediate and evident—that lies beyond the unexpected veils the señora of the rosary places in my path. Do I bestow a more-than-justified strangeness upon my reluctant Amphitryon? If that is so, I shall only take more pleasure in the labyrinths of my own invention. And the flies are still buzzing around the fruit dish, occasionally pausing on the damaged end of the peach, a nibbled bite—I lean closer using the pretext of my notes—where little teeth have left their mark in the velvety skin and ochre flesh of the fruit. I do not look towards the señora. I pretend I am taking notes. The fruit seems to be bitten but not touched. I crouch down to see it better, rest my hands upon the table, moving my lips closer as if I wished to repeat the act of biting without touching. I look down and I see another sign close to my feet: the track of two tires that seem to be bicycle tires, the print of two rubber tires that come as far as the edge of the table and then lead away, growing fainter, the length of the room, towards the señora. . . .

I close my notebook.

"Let us continue, señora."

As I turn towards her, I find her standing with her hands resting on the back of a chair. Seated before her, coughing the smoke of his black cigarette, is a man with heavy shoulders and hidden eyes: these eyes, hardly visible behind swollen wrinkled lids as thick and droopy as the neck of an ancient turtle, seem nevertheless to follow my every movement. The half-shaven cheeks, criss-crossed by a thousand grey furrows, hang from protruding cheekbones, and his greenish hands are folded beneath his arms. He is wearing a coarse blue shirt, and his rumpled hair is so curly it looks like the bottom of a barnacle-covered ship. He does not move, and the true sign of his existence is that difficult whistling breathing (as if every breath must breach a flood-gate of phlegm, irritation, and abuse) that I had already heard through the chinks of the entry hall.

Ridiculously, he murmurs: "Good afternoon . . . ," and I am disposed to forget everything: the mystery, Amilamia, the assessment, the bicycle tracks. The apparition of this asthmatic old bear justifies a prompt retreat. I repeat "Good afternoon," this time with an inflection of farewell. The turtle's mask dissolves into an atrocious smile: every pore of that flesh seems fabricated of brittle rubber, of painted, peeling oilcloth. The arm reaches out and detains me.

"Valdivia died four years ago," says the man in a distant, choking voice that issues from his belly instead of his larynx: a weak, high-pitched voice.

Held by that strong, almost painful, claw, I tell myself it is useless to pretend. But the wax and rubber faces observing me say nothing and for that reason I am able, in spite of everything, to pretend one last time, to pretend that I am speaking to myself when I say:

"Amilamia. . . ."

Yes; no one will have to pretend any longer. The fist that clutches my arm affirms its strength for only an instant, immediately its grip loosens, then it falls, weak and trembling, before rising to take the waxen hand touching the shoulder: the señora, perplexed for the first time, looks at me with the eyes of a violated bird and sobs with a dry moan that does not disturb the rigid astonishment of her features. Suddenly the ogres of my imagination are two solitary, abandoned, wounded old people, scarcely able to console themselves in the shuddering clasp of hands that fills me with shame. My fantasy has brought me to this stark dining room to violate the intimacy and the secret of two human beings exiled from life by something I no longer have the right to share. I have never despised myself more. Never have words failed me in such a clumsy way. Any gesture of mine would be in vain: shall I approach them, shall I touch them, shall I caress the woman's head, shall I ask them to excuse my intrusion? I return the notebook to my jacket pocket. I toss into oblivion all the clues in my detective story: the comic book, the lipstick, the nibbled fruit, the bicycle tracks, the blue-checked apron. . . . I decide to leave this house in silence. The old man, from behind those thick eyelids, must have noticed me. The high breathy voice says:

"Did you know her?"

That past, so natural they must use it every day, finally destroys my illusions. There is the answer. Did you know her? How many years? How many years must the world have lived without Amilamia, assassinated first by my forgetfulness, and revived, scarcely yesterday, by a sad impotent memory? When did those serious grey eyes cease to be astonished by the delight of an always solitary garden? When did those lips cease to pout or press together thinly in that ceremonious seriousness with which, I now realize, Amilamia must have discovered and consecrated the objects and events of life that, she knew perhaps intuitively, was fleeting?

"Yes, we played together in the park. A long time ago."

"How old was she?" says the old man, his voice even more muffled.

"She must have been about seven. No, older than seven."

The woman's voice rises, along with the arms that seem to implore:

"What was she like, señor? Tell us what she was like, please."

I close my eyes. "Amilamia is my memory, too. I can only compare her to the things that she touched, that she brought, that she discovered in the park. Yes. Now I see her, coming down the hill. No. It isn't true that it was a barely elevated patch of stubble. It was a hill, with grass, and Amilamia's coming and going had traced a path, and she waved to me from the top before she started down, accompanied by the music, yes, the music I saw, the painting I smelled, the tastes I heard, the odors I touched . . . my hallucination. . . ." Do they hear me? "She came, waving, dressed in white, in a blue-checked apron . . . the one you have hanging on the *azotea*. . . ."

They take my arms and still I do not open my eyes.

"What was she like, señor?"

"Her eyes were gray and the color of her hair changed in the reflection of the sun and the shadow of the trees. . . ."

They lead me gently, the two of them; I hear the man's labored breathing, the cross on the rosary hitting against the woman's body.

"Tell us, please. . . ."

"The air brought tears to her eyes when she ran; when she reached my bench her cheeks were silvered with happy tears. . . ."

I do not open my eyes. Now we are going upstairs. Two, five, eight, nine, twelve steps. Four hands guide my body.

"What was she like, what was she like?"

"She sat beneath the eucalyptus and wove garlands from the branches and pretended to cry so I would quit my reading and go over to her. . . ."

Hinges creak. The odor overpowers everything else: it routs the other senses, it takes its seat like a yellow Mogul upon the throne of my hallucination; heavy as a coffin, insinuating as the slither of draped silk, ornamented as a Turkish sceptre, opaque as a deep, lost vein of ore, brilliant as a dead star. The hands no longer hold me. More than the sobbing, it is the trembling of the old people that envelops me. Slowly, I open my eyes: first through the dizzying liquid of my cornea then through the web of my eyelashes, the room suffocated in that enormous battle of perfumes is disclosed, effluvia and frosty, almost flesh-like petals; the presence of the flowers is so strong here they seem to take on the quality of living flesh—the sweetness of the jasmine, the nausea of the lilies, the tomb of the tuberose, the temple of the gardenia. Illuminated through the incandescent wax lips of heavy sputtering candles, the small windowless bedroom with its aura of wax and humid flowers assaults the very center of my plexus, and from there, only there at the solar center of life, am I able to revive and to perceive beyond the candles, among the scattered flowers, the accumulation of used toys: the colored hoops and wrinkled balloons, cherries dried to transparency, wooden horses with scraggly manes, the scooter, blind and hairless dolls, bears spilling their sawdust, punctured oilcloth ducks, moth-eaten dogs, wornout jumping ropes, glass jars of dried candy, wornout shoes, the tricycle (three wheels? no, two, and not like a bicycle—two *parallel* wheels below), little woolen and leather shoes; and, facing me, within reach of my hand, the small coffin raised on paper flower-decorated blue boxes, flowers of life this time, carnations and sunflowers, poppies and tulips, but like the others, the ones of death, all part of a potion brewed by the atmosphere of this funeral hot-house in which reposes, inside the silvered coffin, between the black silk sheets, upon the pillow of white satin, that motionless and serene face framed in lace, highlighted with rose-colored tints, eyebrows traced by the lightest trace of pencil, closed lids, real eyelashes, thick, that cast a tenuous shadow on cheeks as healthy as those of the days in the park. Serious red lips, set almost in the angry pout that Amilamia feigned so I would come to play. Hands joined over the breast. A chapelet, identical to the mother's, strangling that cardboard neck. Small white shroud on the clean, prepubescent, docile body.

The old people, sobbing, have knelt.

I reach out my hand and run my fingers over the porcelain face of my friend. I feel the coldness of those painted features, of the doll-queen who presides over the pomp of this royal chamber of death. Porcelain, cardboard, and cotton. *Amilamia wil not forget her good frend—com see me here lik I draw it.*

I withdraw my fingers from the false cadaver. Traces of my fingerprints remain where I touched the skin of the doll.

And nausea crawls in my stomach where the candle smoke and the sweet stench of the lilies in the enclosed room have settled. I turn my back on Amilamia's sepulchre. The woman's hand touches my arm. Her wildly staring eyes do not correspond with the quiet, steady voice.

"Don't come back, señor. If you truly loved her, don't come back again."

I touch the hand of Amilamia's mother. I see through nauseous eyes the old man's head buried between his knees, and I go out of the room to the stairway, to the living room, to the patio, to the street.

V

If not a year, nine or ten months have passed. The memory of that idolatry no longer frightens me. I have forgotten the odor of the flowers and the image of the petrified doll. The real Amilamia has returned to my memory and I have felt, if not content, sane again: the park, the living child, my hours of adolescent reading, have triumphed over the spectres of a sick cult. The image of life is the more powerful. I tell myself that I shall live forever with my real Amilamia, the conqueror of the caricature of death. And one day I dare look again at that note-book with graph paper where I wrote the information of the false assessment. And from its pages, once again, falls Amilamia's card with its terrible childish scrawl and its map for getting from the park to her house. I smile as I pick it up. I bite one of the edges, thinking that in spite of everything, the poor old people would accept this gift.

Whistling, I put on my jacket and knot my tie. Why not visit them and offer them this paper with the child's own writing?

I am running as I approach the one-story house. Rain is beginning to fall in large isolated drops that bring from the earth with magical immediacy an odor of damp benediction that seems to stir the humus and precipitate the fermentation of everything living with its roots in the dust.

I ring the bell. The shower increases and I become insistent. A shrill voice shouts: "I'm going!" and I wait for the figure of the mother with her eternal rosary to open the door for me. I turn up the collar of my jacket. My clothes, my body, too, smell different in the rain. The door opens:

"What do you want? How wonderful you've come!"

The misshapen girl sitting in the wheelchair lays one hand on the doorknob and smiles at me with an indecipherably wry grin. The hump on her chest converts the dress into a curtain over her body, a piece of white cloth that nonetheless lends an air of coquetry to the blue-checked apron. The little woman extracts a pack of cigarettes from her apron pocket and rapidly lights a cigarette, staining the end with orange-painted lips. The smoke causes the beautiful grey eyes to squint. She arranges the coppery, wheat-colored, permanently waved hair: She stares at me all the time with a desolate, inquisitive, and hopeful—but at the same time fearful—expression.

"No Carlos. Go away. Don't come back."

And from the house, at the same moment, I hear the high breathy breathing of the old man, coming closer and closer.

"Where are you? Don't you know you're not supposed to answer the door? Go back! Devil's spawn! Do I have to beat you again?"

And the water from the rain trickles down my forehead, over my cheeks, and into my mouth, and the little frightened hands drop the comic book onto the damp stones.

Translated from the Spanish by Margaret S. Peden

Mavis Gallant

· · · · · · · · · · · · · · · · · · · ·

THE CHOSEN HUSBAND

In 1949, a year that contained no other news of value, Mme. Carette came into a legacy of eighteen thousand dollars from a brother-in-law who had done well in Fall River. She had suspected him of being a Freemason, as well as of other offenses, none of them trifling, and so she did not make a show of bringing out his photograph; instead, she asked her daughters, Berthe and Marie, to mention him in their prayers. They may have, for a while. The girls were twenty-two and twenty, and Berthe, the elder, hardly prayed at all.

The first thing that Mme. Carette did was to acquire a better address. Until now she had kept the Montreal habit of changing her rented quarters every few seasons, a conversation with a landlord serving as warranty, rent paid in cash. This time she was summoned by appointment to a rental agency to sign a two-year lease. She had taken the first floor of a stone house around the corner from the church of St. Louis de France. This was her old parish (she held to the network of streets near Parc Lafontaine) but a glorious strand of it, Rue St. Hubert.

Before her inheritance Mme. Carette had crept to church, eyes lowered; had sat where she was unlikely to disturb anyone whose life seemed more fortunate, therefore more deserving, than her own. She had not so much prayed as petitioned. Now she ran a glove along the pew to see if it was dusted, straightened the unread pamphlets that called for more vocations for missionary service in Africa, told a confessor that, like all the prosperous, she was probably without fault. When the holy-water font looked mossy, she called the parish priest and had words with his housekeeper, even though scrubbing the church was not her job. She still prayed every day for the repose of her late husband, and the unlikelier rest of his Freemason brother, but a tone of briskness caused her own words to rattle in her head. Church was a hushed annex to home. She prayed to insist upon the refinement of some request, and instead of giving thanks simply acknowledged that matters used to be worse.

Her daughter Berthe had been quick to point out that Rue St. Hubert was in decline. Otherwise, how could the Carettes afford to live here? (Berthe worked in an office and was able to pay half the rent.) A family of foreigners were installed across the road. A seamstress had placed a sign in a ground-floor win-

305

dow—a sure symptom of decay. True, but Mme. Carette had as near neighbors a retired opera singer and the first cousins of a city councillor—calm, courteous people who had never been on relief. A few blocks north stood the mayor's private dwelling, with a lamppost on each side of his front door. (During the recent war the mayor had been interned, like an enemy alien. No one quite remembered why. Mme. Carette believed that he had refused an invitation to Buckingham Palace, and that the English had it in for him. Berthe had been told that he had tried to annex Montreal to the State of New York and that someone had minded. Marie, who spoke to strangers on the bus, once came home with a story about Fascist views; but as she could not spell "Fascist," and did not know if it was a kind of landscape or something to eat, no one took her seriously. The mayor had eventually been released, was promptly reelected, and continued to add lustre to Rue St. Hubert.)

Mme. Carette looked out upon long façades of whitish stone, windowpanes with bevelled edges that threw rainbows. In her childhood this was how notaries and pharmacists had lived, before they began to copy the English taste for freestanding houses, blank lawns, ornamental willows, leashed dogs. She recalled a moneyed aunt and uncle, a family of well-dressed, soft-spoken children, heard the echo of a French more accurately expressed than her own. She had tried to imitate the peculiarity of every syllable, sounded like a plucked string, had tried to make her little girls speak that way. But they had rebelled, refused, said it made them laughed at.

When she had nothing to request, or was tired of repeating the same reminders, she shut her eyes and imagined her funeral. She was barely forty-five, but a long widowhood strictly observed had kept her childish, not youthful. She saw the rosary twined round her hands, the vigil, the candles perfectly still, the hillock of wreaths. Until the stunning message from Fall River, death had been her small talk. She had never left the subject, once entered, without asking, "And what will happen then to my poor little Marie?" Nobody had ever taken the question seriously except her Uncle Gildas. This was during their first Christmas dinner on Rue St. Hubert. He said that Marie should pray for guidance, the sooner the better. God had no patience with last-minute appeals. (Uncle Gildas was an elderly priest with limited social opportunities, though his niece believed him to have wide and worldly connections.)

"Prayer can fail," said Berthe, testing him.

Instead of berating her he said calmly, "In that case, Berthe can look after her little sister."

She considered him, old and eating slowly. His cassock exhaled some strong cleaning fluid—tetrachloride; he lived in a rest home, and nuns took care of him.

Marie was dressed in one of Berthe's castoffs—marine-blue velvet with a lace collar. Mme. Carette wore a gray-white dress Berthe thought she had seen all her life. In her first year of employment Berthe had saved enough for a dyed rabbit coat. She also had an electric seal, and was on her way to sheared raccoon. "Marie had better get married," she said.

Mme. Carette still felt cruelly the want of a husband, someone—not a daughter—to help her up the step of a streetcar, read *La Presse* and tell her what was in it, lay down the law to Berthe. When Berthe was in adolescence, laughing and whispering and not telling her mother the joke, Mme. Carette had asked Uncle Gildas to speak as a father. He sat in the parlor, in a plush chair, all boots and cassock, knees apart and a hand on each knee, and questioned Berthe about her dreams. She said she had never in her life dreamed anything. Uncle Gildas replied that anyone with a good conscience could dream events pleasing to God; he himself had been doing it for years. God kept the dreams of every living person on record, like great rolls of film. He could have them projected whenever he wanted. Montreal girls, notoriously virtuous, had his favor, but only up to a point. He forgave, but never forgot. He was the embodiment of endless time—though one should not take "embodiment" literally. Eternal remorse in a pit of flames was the same to him as a rap on the fingers with the sharp edge of a ruler. Marie, hearing this, had fainted dead away. That was the power of Uncle Gildas.

Nowadays, shrunken and always hungry, he lived in retirement, had waxed linoleum on his floor, no carpet, ate tapioca soup two or three times a week. He would have stayed in bed all day, but the nuns who ran the place looked upon illness as fatigue, fatigue as shirking. He was not tired or lazy; he had nothing to get up for. The view from his window was a screen of trees. When Mme. Carette came to visit—a long streetcar ride, then a bus—she had just the trees to look at: she could not stare at her uncle the whole time. The trees put out of sight a busy commercial garage. It might have distracted him to watch trucks backing out, perhaps to witness a bloodless accident. In the morning he went downstairs to the chapel, ate breakfast, sat on his bed after it was made. Or crossed the gleaming floor to a small table, folded back the oilcloth cover, read the first sentence of a memoir he was writing for his great-nieces: "I was born in Montreal, on the 22nd of May, 1869, of pious Christian parents, connected to Montreal families for whom streets and bridges have been named." Or shuffled out to the varnished corridor, where there was a pay phone. He liked dialling, but out of long discipline never did without a reason.

Soon after Christmas Mme. Carette came to see him, wearing Berthe's velvet boots with tassels, Berthe's dyed rabbit coat, and a feather turban of her own. Instead of praying for guidance Marie had fallen in love with one of the Greeks who were starting to move into their part of Montreal. There had never been a foreigner in the family, let alone a pagan. Her uncle interrupted to remark that Greeks were usually Christians, though of the wrong kind for Marie. Mme. Carette implored him to find someone, not a Greek, of the right kind: sober, established, Catholic, French-speaking, natively Canadian. "Not Canadian from New England," she said, showing a brief ingratitude to Fall River. She left a store of nickels, so that he could ring her whenever he liked.

Louis Driscoll, French in all but name, called on Marie for the first time on the twelfth of April, 1950. Patches of dirty snow still lay against the curb. The trees on Rue St. Hubert looked dark and brittle, as though winter had killed them at last. From behind the parlor curtain, unseen from the street, the Carette women watched him coming along from the bus stop. To meet Marie he had put on a beige tweed overcoat, loosely belted, a beige scarf, a bottle-green snap-brim fedora, crêpe-soled shoes, pigskin gloves. His trousers were sharply pressed, a shade darker than the hat. Under his left arm he held close a parcel in white paper, the size and shape of a two-pound box of Laura Secord chocolates. He stopped frequently to consult the house numbers (blue-and-white, set rather high, Montreal style), which he compared with a slip of paper brought close to his eyes.

It was too bad that he had to wear glasses; the Carettes were not prepared for that, or for the fringe of ginger hair below his hat. Uncle Gildas had said he was of distinguished appearance. He came from Moncton, New Brunswick, and was employed at the head office of a pulp-and-paper concern. His age was twenty-six. Berthe thought that he must be a failed seminarist; they were the only Catholic bachelors Uncle Gildas knew.

Peering at their front door, he walked into a puddle of slush. Mme. Carette wondered if Marie's children were going to be nearsighted. "How can we be sure he's the right man?" she said.

"Who else could he be?" Berthe replied. What did he want with Marie? Uncle Gildas could not have promised much in her name, apart from a pliant nature. There could never be a meeting in a notary's office to discuss a dowry, unless you counted some plates and furniture. The old man may have frightened Louis, reminded him that prolonged celibacy—except among the clergy—is displeasing to God. Marie is poor, he must have said, though honorably connected. She will feel grateful to you all her life.

Their front steps were painted pearl gray, to match the building stone. Louis's face, upturned, was the color of wood ash. Climbing the stair, ringing the front doorbell could change his life in a way he did not wholly desire. Probably he wanted a woman without sin or risk or coaxing or remorse; but did he want her enough to warrant setting up a household? A man with a memory as transient as his, who could read an address thirty times and still let it drift, might forget to come to the wedding. He crumpled the slip of paper, pushed it inside a tweed pocket, withdrew a large handkerchief, blew his nose.

Mme. Carette swayed back from the curtain as though a stone had been flung. She concluded some private thought by addressing Marie: ". . . although I will feel better on my deathbed if I know you are in your own home." Louis meanwhile kicked the bottom step, getting rid of snow stuck to his shoes. (Rustics kicked and stamped. Marie's Greek had wiped his feet.) Still he hesitated, sliding a last pale look in the direction of buses and streetcars. Then, as he might have turned a gun on himself, he climbed five steps and pressed his finger to the bell.

"Somebody has to let him in," said Mme. Carette.

"Marie," said Berthe.

"It wouldn't seem right. She's never met him."

He stood quite near, where the top step broadened to a small platform level with the window. They could have leaned out, introduced him to Marie. Marie at this moment seemed to think he would do; at least, she showed no sign of distaste, such as pushing out her lower lip or crumpling her chin. Perhaps she had been getting ready to drop her Greek: Mme. Carette had warned her that she would have to be a servant to his mother, and eat peculiar food. "He's never asked me to," said Marie, and that was part of the trouble. He hadn't asked anything. For her twenty-first birthday he had given her a locket on a chain and a box from Maitland's, the West End confectioner, containing twenty-one chocolate mice. "He loves me," said Marie. She kept counting the mice and would not let anyone eat them.

In the end it was Berthe who admitted Louis, accepted the gift of chocolates on behalf of Marie, showed him where to leave his hat and coat. She approved of the clean white shirt, the jacket of a tweed similar to the coat but lighter in weight, the tie with a pattern of storm-tossed sailboats. Before shaking hands he removed his glasses, which had misted over, and wiped them dry. His eyes meeting the bright evening at the window (Marie was still there, but with her back to the street) flashed ultra-marine. Mme. Carette hoped Marie's children would inherit that color.

He took Marie's yielding hand and let it drop. Freed of the introduction, she pried open the lid of the candy box and said, distinctly, "No mice." He seemed not to hear, or may have thought she was pleased to see he had not played a practical joke. Berthe showed him to the plush armchair, directly underneath a chandelier studded with light bulbs. From this chair Uncle Gildas had explained the whims of God; against its linen antimacassar the Greek had recently rested his head.

Around Louis's crêpe soles pools of snow water formed. Berthe glanced at her mother, meaning that she was not to mind; but Mme. Carette was trying to remember where Berthe had said that she and Marie were to sit. (On the sofa, facing Louis.) Berthe chose a gilt upright chair, from which she could rise easily to pass refreshments. These were laid out on a marble-topped console: vanilla wafers, iced sultana cake, maple fudge, marshmallow biscuits, soft drinks. Behind the sofa a large pier glass reflected Louis in the armchair and the top of Mme. Carette's head. Berthe could tell from her mother's posture, head tilted, hands clasped, that she was silently asking Louis to trust her. She leaned forward and asked him if he was an only child. Berthe closed her eyes. When she opened them, nothing had changed except that Marie was eating chocolates. Louis seemed to be reflecting on his status.

He was the oldest of seven, he finally said. The others were Joseph, Raymond, Vincent, Francis, Rose, and Claire. French was their first language, in a way. But, then, so was English. A certain Louis Joseph Raymond Driscoll, Irish, veteran of Waterloo on the decent side, proscribed in England and Ireland as a result, had come out to Canada and grafted on pure French stock a number of noble traits: bright, wavy hair, a talent for public speaking, another for social aplomb. In every generation of Driscolls, there had to be a Louis, a Joseph, a Raymond. (Berthe and her mother exchanged a look. He wanted three sons.)

His French was slow and muffled, as though strained through wool. He used English words, or French words in an English way. Mme. Carette lifted her shoulders and parted her clasped hands as if to say, Never mind, English is better than Greek. At least, they could be certain that the Driscolls were Catholic. In August his father and mother were making the Holy Year pilgrimage to Rome.

Rome was beyond their imagining, though all three Carettes had been to

Maine and Old Orchard Beach. Louis hoped to spend a vacation in Old Orchard (in response to an ardent question from Mme. Carette), but he had more feeling for Quebec City. His father's people had entered Canada by way of Quebec.

"The French part of the family?" said Mme. Carette.

"Yes, yes," said Berthe, touching her mother's arm.

Berthe had been to Quebec City, said Mme. Carette. She was brilliant, reliable, fully bilingual. Her office promoted her every January. They were always sending her away on company business. She knew Plattsburgh, Saranac Lake. In Quebec City, at lunch at the Château Frontenac, she had seen well-known politicians stuffing down oysters and fresh lobster, at taxpayers' expense.

Louis's glance tried to cross Berthe's, as he might have sought out and welcomed a second man in the room. Berthe reached past Mme. Carette to take the candy box away from Marie. She nudged her mother with her elbow.

"The first time I ever saw Old Orchard," Mme. Carette resumed, smoothing the bodice of her dress, "I was sorry I had not gone there on my honeymoon." She paused, watching Louis accept a chocolate. "My husband and I went to Fall River. He had a brother in the lumber business."

At the mention of lumber, Louis took on a set, bulldog look. Berthe wondered if the pulp-and-paper firm had gone bankrupt. Her thoughts rushed to Uncle Gildas—how she would have it out with him, not leave it to her mother, if he had failed to examine Louis's prospects. But then Louis began to cough and had to cover his mouth. He was in trouble with a caramel. The Carettes looked away, so that he could strangle unobserved. "How dark it is," said Berthe, to let him think he could not be seen. Marie got up, with a hiss and rustle of taffeta skirt, and switched on the twin floor lamps with their cerise silk shades.

There, she seemed to be saying to Berthe. Have I done the right thing? Is this what you wanted?

Louis still coughed, but weakly. He moved his fingers, like a child made to wave goodbye. Mme. Carette wondered how many contagious children's diseases he had survived; in a large family everything made the rounds. His eyes, perhaps seeking shade, moved across the brown wallpaper flecked with gold and stopped at the only familiar sight in the room—his reflection in the pier glass. He sat up straighter and quite definitely swallowed. He took a long drink of ginger ale. "When Irish eyes are smiling," he said, in English, as if to himself. "When Irish eyes are smiling. There's a lot to be said for that. A lot to be said."

Of course he was at a loss, astray in an armchair, with the Carettes watching like friendly judges. When he reached for another chocolate, they looked to see if his nails were clean. When he crossed his legs, they examined his socks. They were fixing their first impression of the stranger who might take Marie away, give her a modern kitchen, children to bring up, a muskrat coat, a charge account at Dupuis Frères department store, a holiday in Maine. Louis continued to examine his bright Driscoll hair, the small nose along which his glasses slid. Holding the glasses in place with a finger, he answered Mme. Carette: His father was a dental surgeon, with a degree from Pennsylvania. It was the only degree worth mentioning. Before settling into a dentist's chair the patient should always read the writing on the wall. His mother was born Lucarne, a big name in Moncton.

She could still get into her wedding dress. Everything was so conveniently arranged at home—cavernous washing machine, giant vacuum cleaner—that she seldom went out. When she did, she wore a two-strand cultured-pearl necklace and a coat and hat of Persian lamb.

The Carettes could not match this, though they were related to families for whom bridges were named. Mme. Carette sat on the edge of the sofa, ankles together. Gentility was the brace that kept her upright. She had once been a young widow, hard pressed, had needed to sew for money. Berthe recalled a stricter, an unsmiling mother, straining over pleats and tucks for clients who reneged on pennies. She wore the neutral shades of half-mourning, the whitish grays of Rue St. Hubert, as though everything had to be used up—even remnants of grief.

Mme. Carette tried to imagine Louis's mother. She might one day have to sell the pearls; even a dentist trained in Pennsylvania could leave behind disorder and debts. Whatever happened, she said to Louis, she would remain in this flat. Even after the girls were married. She would rather beg on the steps of the parish church than intrude upon a young marriage. When her last, dreadful illness made itself known, she would creep away to the Hôtel Dieu and die without a murmur. On the other hand, the street seemed to be filling up with foreigners. She might have to move.

Berthe and Marie were dressed alike, as if to confound Louis, force him to choose the true princess. Leaving the sight of his face in the mirror, puzzled by death and old age, he took notice of the two moiré skirts, organdie blouses, patent-leather belts. "I can't get over those twins of yours," he said to Mme. Carette. "I just can't get over them."

Once, Berthe had tried Marie in her own office—easy work, taking messages when the switchboard was closed. She knew just enough English for that. After two weeks the office manager, Mr. Macfarlane, had said to Berthe, "Your sister is an angel, but angels aren't in demand at Prestige Central Burners."

It was the combination of fair hair and dark eyes, the enchanting misalliance, that gave Marie the look of an angel. She played with the locket the Greek had given her, twisting and unwinding the chain. What did she owe her Greek? Fidelity? An explanation? He was punctual and polite, had never laid a hand on her, in temper or eagerness, had travelled a long way by streetcar to bring back the mice. True, said Berthe, reviewing his good points, while Louis ate the last of the fudge. It was true about the mice, but he should have become more than "Marie's Greek." In the life of a penniless unmarried young woman, there was no room for a man merely in love. He ought to have presented himself as *something*: Marie's future.

In May true spring came, moist and hot. Berthe brought home new dress patterns and yards of flowered rayon and piqué. Louis called three evenings a week, at seven o'clock, after the supper dishes were cleared away. They played hearts in the dining room, drank Salada tea, brewed black, with plenty of sugar and cream, ate éclairs and mille-feuilles from Celentano, the bakery on Avenue Mont Royal. (Celentano had been called something else for years now, but Mme. Carette did not take notice of change of that kind, and did not care to have it pointed out.) Louis, eating coffee éclairs one after the other, told stories set in Moncton that showed off his family. Marie wore a blue dress with a red collar, once Berthe's, and a red barrette in her hair. Berthe, a master player, held back to let Louis win. Mme. Carette listened to Louis, kept some of his stories, discarded others, garnering information useful to Marie. Marie picked up cards at random, disrupting the game. Louis's French was not as woolly as before, but he had somewhere acquired a common Montreal accent. Mme. Carette wondered who his friends were and how Marie's children would sound.

They began to invite him to meals. He arrived at half past five, straight from work, and was served at once. Mme. Carette told Berthe that she hoped he washed his hands at the office, because he never did here. They used the blue-willow-pattern china that would go to Marie. One evening, when the tablecloth had been folded and put away, and the teacups and cards distributed, he mentioned marriage—not his own, or to anyone in particular, but as a way of life. Mme. Carette broke in to say that she had been widowed at Louis's age. She recalled what it had been like to have a husband she could consult and admire. "Marriage means children," she said, looking fondly at her own. She would not be alone during her long, final illness. The girls would take her in. She would not be a burden; a couch would do for a bed.

Louis said he was tired of the game. He dropped his hand and spread the cards in an arc.

"So many hearts," said Mme. Carette, admiringly.

"Let me see." Marie had to stand: there was a large teapot in the way. "Ace, queen, ten, eight, five . . . a wedding." Before Berthe's foot reached her ankle, she managed to ask, sincerely, if anyone close to him was getting married this year.

Mme. Carette considered Marie as good as engaged. She bought a quantity of embroidery floss and began the ornamentation of guest towels and tea towels, placemats and pillow slips. Marie ran her finger over the pretty monogram with its intricate frill of vine leaves. Her mind, which had sunk into hibernation when she accepted Louis and forgot her Greek, awoke and plagued her with a nightmare. "I became a nun" was all she told her mother. Mme. Carette wished it were true. Actually, the dream had stopped short of vows. Barefoot, naked under a robe of coarse brown wool, she moved along an aisle in and out of squares of sunlight. At the altar they were waiting to shear her hair. A strange man—not Uncle Gildas, not Louis, not the Greek—got up out of a pew and stood barring her way. The rough gown turned out to be frail protection. All that kept the dream from sliding into blasphemy and abomination was Marie's entire unacquaintance, awake or asleep, with what could happen next.

Because Marie did not like to be alone in the dark, she and Berthe still shared a room. Their childhood bed had been taken away and supplanted by twin beds with quilted satin headboards. Berthe had to sleep on three pillows, because the aluminum hair curlers she wore ground into her scalp. First thing every morning, she clipped on her pearl earrings, sat up, and unwound the curlers, which she handed one by one to Marie. Marie put her own hair up and kept it that way until suppertime.

In the dark, her face turned to the heap of pillows dimly seen, Marie told Berthe about the incident in the chapel. If dreams are life's opposite, what did it mean? Berthe saw that there was more to it than Marie was able to say. Speaking softly, so that their mother would not hear, she tried to tell Marie about men— what they were like and what they wanted. Marie suggested that she and Berthe enter a cloistered convent together, now, while there was still time. Berthe supposed that she had in mind the famous Martin sisters of Lisieux, in France, most of them Carmelites and one a saint. She touched her own temple, meaning that Marie had gone soft in the brain. Marie did not see; if she had, she would have thought that Berthe was easing a curler. Berthe reminded Marie that she was marked out not for sainthood in France but for marriage in Montreal. Berthe had a salary and occasional travel. Mme. Carette had her Fall River bounty. Marie, if she put her mind to it, could have a lifetime of love.

"Is Louis love?" said Marie.

There were girls ready to line up in the rain for Louis, said Berthe.

"What girls?" said Marie, perplexed rather than disbelieving.

"Montreal girls," said Berthe. "The girls who cry with envy when you and Louis walk down the street."

"We have never walked down a street," said Marie.

The third of June was Louis's birthday. He arrived wearing a new seersucker suit. The Carettes offered three monogrammed hemstitched handkerchiefs—he was always polishing his glasses or mopping his face. Mme. Carette had prepared a meal he particularly favored—roast pork and coconut layer cake. The sun was still high. His birthday unwound in a steady, blazing afternoon. He suddenly put his knife and fork down and said that if he ever decided to get married he would need more than his annual bonus to pay for the honeymoon. He would have to buy carpets, lamps, a refrigerator. People talked lightly of marriage without considering the cost for the groom. Priests urged the married condition on bachelors—priests, who did not know the price of eight ounces of tea.

"Some brides bring lamps and lampshades," said Mme. Carette. "A glass-front bookcase. Even the books to put in it." Her husband had owned a furniture shop on Rue St. Denis. Household goods earmarked for Berthe and Marie had been stored with relatives for some twenty years, waxed and polished and free of dust. "An oak table that seats fourteen," she said, and stopped with that. Berthe had forbidden her to draw up an inventory. They were not bartering Marie.

"Some girls have money," said Marie. Her savings—eighteen dollars—were in a drawer of her mother's old treadle sewing machine.

A spasm crossed Louis's face; he often choked on his food. Berthe knew more about men than Marie—more than her mother, who knew only how children come about. Mr. Ryder, of Berthe's office, would stand in the corridor, letting elevators go by, waiting for a chance to squeeze in next to Berthe. Mr. Sexton had offered her money, a regular allowance, if she would go out with him every Friday, the night of his Legion meeting. Mr. Macfarlane had left a lewd poem on her desk, then a note of apology, then a poem even worse than the first. Mr. Wright-Ashburton had offered to leave his wife—for, of course, they had wives, Mr. Ryder, Mr. Sexton, Mr. Macfarlane, none of whom she had ever encouraged, and Mr. Wright-Ashburton, with whom she had been to Plattsburgh and Saranac Lake, and whose private behavior she had described, kneeling, in remote parishes, where the confessor could not have known her by voice.

When Berthe accepted Mr. Wright-Ashburton's raving proposal to leave his wife, saying that Irene probably knew about them anyway, would be thankful to have it in the clear, his face had wavered with fright, like a face seen underwater—rippling, uncontrolled. Berthe had to tell him she hadn't meant it. She could not marry a divorced man. On Louis's face she saw that same quivering dismay. He was afraid of Marie, of her docility, her monogrammed towels, her dependence, her glass-front bookcase. Having seen this, Berthe was not surprised when he gave no further sign of life until the twenty-fifth of June.

During his absence the guilt and darkness of rejection filled every corner of the flat. There was not a room that did not speak of humiliation—oh, not because Louis had dropped Marie but because the Carettes had honored and welcomed a clodhopper, a cheap-jack, a ginger-haired nobody. Mme. Carette and Marie made many telephone calls to his office, with a variety of names and voices, to be told every time he was not at his desk. One morning Berthe, on her way to work, saw someone very like him hurrying into Windsor Station. By the time she had struggled out of her crowded streetcar, he was gone. She followed him into the great concourse and looked at the times of the different trains and saw where they were going. A trapped sparrow fluttered under the glass roof. She recalled an expression of Louis's, uneasy and roguish, when he had told Berthe that Marie did not understand the facts of life. (This in English, over the table, as if Mme. Carette and Marie could not follow.) When Berthe asked what these facts might be, he had tried to cross her glance, as on that first evening, one man to another. She was not a man; she had looked away.

Mme. Carette went on embroidering baskets of flowers, ivy leaves, hunched over her work, head down. Marie decided to find a job as a receptionist in a beauty salon. It would be pleasant work in clean surroundings. A girl she had talked to on the bus earned fourteen dollars a week. Marie would give her mother eight and keep six. She did not need Louis, she said, and she was sure she could never love him.

"No one expected you to love him," said her mother, without looking up.

On the morning of the twenty-fifth of June he rang the front doorbell. Marie was eating breakfast in the kitchen, wearing Berthe's aluminum curlers under a mauve chiffon scarf, and Berthe's mauve-and-black kimono. He stood in the middle of the room, refusing offers of tea, and said that the whole world was engulfed in war. Marie looked out the kitchen window, at bare yards and storage sheds.

"Not there," said Louis. "In Korea."

Marie and her mother had never heard of the place. Mme. Carette took it for granted that the British had started something again. She said, "They can't take you, Louis, because of your eyesight." Louis replied that this time they would take everybody, bachelors first. A few married men might be allowed to make themselves useful at home. Mme. Carette put her arms around him. "You are my son now," she said. "I'll never let them ship you to England. You can hide in our coal shed." Marie had not understood that the mention of war was a marriage proposal, but her mother had grasped it at once. She wanted to call Berthe and tell her to come home immediately, but Louis was in a hurry to publish the banns. Marie retired to the bedroom and changed into Berthe's white sharkskin sundress and jacket and toeless white suède shoes. She smoothed Berthe's suntan makeup on her legs, hoping that her mother would not see she was not wearing stockings. She combed out her hair, put on lipstick and earrings, and butterfly sunglasses belonging to Berthe. Then, for the first time, she and Louis together walked down the front steps to the street.

At Marie's parish church they found other couples standing about, waiting for advice. They had heard the news and decided to get married at once. Marie and Louis held hands, as though they had been engaged for a long time. She hoped no one would notice that she had no engagement ring. Unfortunately, their banns could not be posted until July, or the marriage take place until August. His parents would not be present to bless them: at the very day and hour of the ceremony they would be on their way to Rome.

The next day, Louis went to a jeweller on Rue St. Denis, recommended by Mme. Carette, but he was out of engagement rings. He had sold every last one that day. Louis did not look anywhere else; Mme. Carette had said he was the only man she trusted. Louis's mother sent rings by registered mail. They had been taken from the hand of her dead sister, who had wanted them passed on to her son, but the son had vanished into Springfield and no longer sent Christmas cards. Mme. Carette shook her own wedding dress out of tissue paper and made a few adjustments so that it would fit Marie. Since the war it had become impossible to find silk of that quality.

Waiting for August, Louis called on Marie every day. They rode the streetcar up to Avenue Mont Royal to eat barbecued chicken. (One evening Marie let her engagement ring fall into a crack of the corrugated floor of the tram, and a number of strangers told her to be careful, or she would lose her man, too.) The chicken arrived on a bed of chips, in a wicker basket. Louis showed Marie how to eat barbecue without a knife and fork. Fortunately, Mme. Carette was not there to watch Marie gnawing on a bone. She was sewing the rest of the trousseau and had no time to act as chaperon.

Berthe's office sent her to Buffalo for a long weekend. She brought back match folders from Polish and German restaurants, an ashtray on which was written "Buffalo Hofbrau," and a number of articles that were much cheaper down there, such as nylon stockings. Marie asked if they still ate with knives and forks in Buffalo, or if they had caught up to Montreal. Alone together, Mme. Carette and Berthe sat in the kitchen and gossiped about Louis. The white summer curtains were up; the coal-and-wood range was covered with clean white oilcloth. Berthe had a new kimono—white, with red pagodas on the sleeves. She propped her new red mules on the oven door. She smoked now, and carried everywhere the Buffalo Hofbrau ashtray. Mme. Carette made Berthe promise not to smoke in front of Uncle Gildas, or in the street, or at Marie's wedding reception, or in the front parlor, where the smell might get into the curtains. Sometimes they had just tea and toast and Celentano pastry for supper. When Berthe ate a coffee éclair, she said, "Here's one Louis won't get."

The bright evenings of suppers and card games slid into the past, and by August seemed long ago. Louis said to Marie, "We knew how to have a good time. People don't enjoy themselves anymore." He believed that the other customers in the barbecue restaurant had secret, nagging troubles. Waiting for the wicker basket of chicken, he held Marie's hand and stared at men who might be Greeks. He tried to tell her what had been on his mind between the third and twenty-fifth of June, but Marie did not care, and he gave up. They came to their first important agreement: neither of them wanted the blue-willow-pattern plates. Louis said he would ask his parents to start them off with six place settings of English Rose. She seemed still to be listening, and so he told her that the name of her parish church, St. Louis de France, had always seemed to him to be a personal sign of some kind: an obscure force must have guided him to Rue St. Hubert and Marie. Her soft brown eyes never wavered. They forgot about Uncle Gildas, and whatever it was Uncle Gildas had said to frighten them.

Louis and Marie were married on the third Saturday of August, with flowers from an earlier wedding banked along the altar rail, and two other wedding parties waiting at the back of the church. Berthe supposed that Marie, by accepting the ring of a dead woman and wearing the gown of another woman widowed at twenty-six, was calling down the blackest kind of misfortune. She remembered her innocent nakedness under the robe of frieze. Marie had no debts. She owed Louis nothing. She had saved him from a long journey to a foreign place, perhaps even from dying. As he placed the unlucky ring on her finger, Berthe wept. She knew that some of the people looking on—Uncle Gildas, or Joseph and Raymond Driscoll, amazing in their ginger likeness—were mistaking her for a jealous older sister, longing to be in Marie's place.

Marie, now Mme. Driscoll, turned to Berthe and smiled, as she used to when they were children. Once again, the smile said, Have I done the right thing? Is this what you wanted? Yes, yes, said Berthe silently, but she went on crying. Marie had always turned to Berthe; she had started to walk because she wanted to be with Berthe. She had been standing, holding on to a kitchen chair, and she suddenly smiled and let go. Later, when Marie was three, and in the habit of taking her clothes off and showing what must never be seen, Mme. Carette locked her into the storage shed behind the kitchen. Berthe knelt on her side of the door, sobbing, calling, "Don't be afraid, Marie. Berthe is here." Mme. Carette relented and unlocked the door, and there was Marie, wearing just her undershirt, smiling for Berthe.

Leading her mother, Berthe approached the altar rail. Marie seemed contented; for Berthe, that was good enough. She kissed her sister, and kissed the chosen husband. He had not separated them but would be a long incident in their lives. Among the pictures that were taken on the church steps, there is one of Louis with an arm around each sister and the sisters trying to clasp hands behind his back.

The wedding party walked in a procession down the steps and around the corner: another impression in black-and-white. The August pavement burned under the women's thin soles. Their fine clothes were too hot. Children playing in the road broke into applause when they saw Marie. She waved her left hand, showing the ring. The children were still French-Canadian; so were the neighbors, out on their balconies to look at Marie. Three yellow leaves fell—white, in a photograph. One of the Driscoll boys raced ahead and brought the party to a stop. There is Marie, who does not yet understand that she is leaving home, and confident Louis, so soon to have knowledge of her bewildering ignorance.

Berthe saw the street as if she were bent over the box camera, trying to keep the frame straight. It was an important picture, like a precise instrument of measurement: so much duty, so much love, so much reckless safety—the distance between last April and now. She thought, It had to be done. They began to walk again. Mme. Carette realized for the first time what she and Uncle Gildas and Berthe had brought about: the unredeemable loss of Marie. She said to Berthe, "Wait until I am dead before you get married. You can marry a widower. They make good husbands." Berthe was nearly twenty-four, just at the limit. She had turned away so many attractive prospects, with no explanation, and had frightened so many others with her skill at cards and her quick blue eyes that word had spread, and she was not solicited as before.

Berthe and Marie slipped away from the reception—moved, that is, from the parlor to the bedroom—so that Berthe could help her sister pack. It turned out that Mme. Carette had done the packing. Marie had never had to fill a suitcase, and would not have known what to put in first. For a time, they sat on the edge of a bed, talking in whispers. Berthe smoked, holding the Buffalo Hofbrau ashtray. She showed Marie a black lacquer cigarette lighter she had not shown her mother. Marie had started to change her clothes; she was just in her slip. She looked at the lighter on all sides and handed it back. Louis was taking her to the Château Frontenac, in Quebec City, for three nights—the equivalent of ten days in Old Orchard, he had said. After that, they would go straight to the duplex property, quite far north on Boulevard Pie IX, that his father was helping him buy. "I'll call you tomorrow morning," said Marie, for whom tomorrow was still the same thing as today. If Uncle Gildas had been at Berthe's mercy, she would have held his head underwater. Then she thought, Why blame him? She and Marie were Montreal girls, not trained to accompany heroes, or to hold out for dreams, but just to be patient.

William Gass

• • • • • • • • • • • • • • • • • • • •

ORDER OF INSECTS

We certainly had no complaints about the house after all we had been through in the other place, but we hadn't lived there very long before I began to notice every morning the bodies of a large black bug spotted about the down-stairs carpet; haphazardly, as earth worms must die on the street after a rain; looking when I first saw them like rolls of dark wool or pieces of mud from the children's shoes, or sometimes, if the drapes were pulled, so like ink stains or deep burns they terrified me, for I had been intimidated by that thick rug very early and the first week had walked over it wishing my bare feet would swallow my shoes. The shells were usually broken. Legs and other parts I couldn't then identify would be scattered near like flakes of rust. Occasionally I would find them on their backs, their quilted undersides showing orange, while beside them were smudges of dark-brown powder that had to be vacuumed carefully. We believed our cat had killed them. She was frequently sick during the night then—a rare thing for her—and we could think of no other reason. Overturned like that they looked pathetic even dead.

I could not imagine where the bugs had come from. I am terribly meticulous myself. The house was clean, the cupboards tight and orderly, and we never saw one alive. The other place had been infested with those flat brown fuzzy roaches, all wires and speed, and we'd seen *them* all right, frightened by the kitchen light, sifting through the baseboards and the floor's cracks; and in the pantry I had nearly closed my fingers on one before it fled, tossing its shadow across the starch like an image of the startle in my hand.

Dead, overturned, their three pairs of legs would be delicately drawn up and folded shyly over their stomachs. When they walked I suppose their forelegs were thrust out and then bent to draw the body up. I still wonder if they jumped. More than once I've seen our cat hook one of her claws under a shell and toss it in the air, crouching while the insect fell, feigning leaps—but there was daylight; the bug was dead; she was not really interested any more; and she would walk immediately away. That image takes the place of jumping. Even if I actually saw those two back pairs of legs unhinge, as they would have to if one leaped, I think I'd find the result unreal and mechanical, a poor try measured by that sudden, high, head-over-heels flight from our cat's paw. I could look it up, I guess, but it's no study for a woman . . . bugs.

At first I reacted as I should, bending over, wondering what in the world; yet even before I recognized them I'd withdrawn my hand, shuddering. Fierce, ugly, armored things: they used their shadows to seem large. The machine sucked them up while I looked the other way. I remember the sudden thrill of horror I had hearing one rattle up the wand. I was relieved that they were dead, of course, for I could never have killed one, and if they had been popped, alive, into the dust bag of the cleaner, I believe I would have had nightmares again as I did the time my husband fought the red ants in our kitchen. All night I lay awake thinking of the ants alive in the belly of the machine, and when toward morning I finally slept I found myself in the dreadful elastic tunnel of the suction tube where ahead of me I heard them: a hundred bodies rustling in the dirt.

I never think of their species as alive but as comprised entirely by the dead ones on our carpet, all the new dead manufactured by the action of some mysterious spoor—perhaps that dust they sometimes lie in—carried in the air, solidified by night and shaped, from body into body, spontaneously, as maggots were before the age of science. I have a single book about insects, a little dated handbook in French which a good friend gave me as a joke—because of my garden, the quaintness of the plates, the fun of reading about worms in such an elegant tongue—and my bug has his picture there climbing the stem of an orchid. Beneath the picture is his name: *Periplaneta orientalis L. Ces répugnants insectes ne sont que trop communs dans les cuisines des vieilles habitations des villes, dans les magasins, entrepôts, boulangeries, brasseries, restaurants, dans la cale des navires, etc.*, the text begins. Nevertheless they are a new experience for me and I think that I am grateful for it now.

The picture didn't need to show me there were two, adult and nymph, for by that time I'd seen the bodies of both kinds. Nymph. My god the names we use. The one was dark, squat, ugly, sly. The other, slimmer, had hard sheath-like wings drawn over its back like another shell, and you could see delicate interwoven lines spun like fossil gauze across them. The nymph was a rich golden color deepening in its interstices to mahogany. Both had legs that looked under a glass like the canes of a rose, and the nymph's were sufficiently transparent in a good light you thought you saw its nerves merge and run like a jagged crack to each ultimate claw.

Tipped, their legs have fallen shut, and the more I look at them the less I believe my eyes. Corruption, in these bugs, is splendid. I've a collection now I keep in typewriter-ribbon tins, and though, in time, their bodies dry and the interior flesh decays, their features hold, as I suppose they held in life, an Egyptian determination, for their protective plates are strong and death must break bones to get in. Now that the heavy soul is gone, the case is light.

I suspect if we were as familiar with our bones as with our skin, we'd never bury dead but shrine them in their rooms, arranged as we might like to find them on a visit; and our enemies, if we could steal their bodies from the battle sites, would be museumed as they died, the steel still eloquent in their sides, their metal hats askew, the protective toes of their shoes unworn, and friend and enemy would be so wondrously historical that in a hundred years we'd find the jaws still hung for the same speech and all the parts we spent our life with tilted as they always were—rib cage, collar, skull—still repetitious, still defiant, angel light, still worthy of memorial and affection. After all, what does it mean to say that when our cat has bitten through the shell and put confusion in the pulp, the life goes out of them? Alas for us, I want to cry, our bones are secret, showing last, so we must love what perishes: the muscles and the waters and the fats.

Two prongs extend like daggers from the rear. I suppose I'll never know their function. That kind of knowledge doesn't take my interest. At first I had to screw my eyes down, and as I consider it now, the whole change, the recent alteration in my life, was the consequence of finally coming near to something. It was a self-mortifying act, I recall, a penalty I laid upon myself for the evil-tempered words I'd shouted at my children in the middle of the night. I felt instinctively the insects were infectious and their own disease, so when I knelt I held a handkerchief over the lower half of my face . . . saw only horror . . . turned, sick, masking my eyes . . . yet the worst of angers held me through the day: vague, searching, guilty, and ashamed.

After that I came near often; saw, for the first time, the gold nymph's difference; put between the mandibles a tinted nail I'd let grow long; observed the movement of the jaws, the stalks of the antennae, the skull-shaped skull, the lines banding the abdomen, and found an intensity in the posture of the shell, even when tipped, like that in the gaze of Gauguin's natives' eyes. The dark plates glisten. They are wonderfully shaped; even the buttons of the compound eyes show a geometrical precision which prevents my earlier horror. It isn't possible to feel disgust toward such an order. Nevertheless, I reminded myself, a roach . . . and you a woman.

I no longer own my own imagination. I suppose they came up the drains or out of the registers. It may have been the rug they wanted. Crickets, too, I understand, will feed on wool. I used to rest by my husband . . . stiffly . . . waiting for silence to settle in the house, his sleep to come, and then the drama of their passage would take hold of me, possess me so completely that when I finally slept I merely passed from one dream to another without the slightest loss of vividness or continuity. Never alive, they came with punctures; their bodies formed from little whorls of copperish dust which in the downstairs darkness I couldn't possibly have seen; and they were dead and upside down when they materialized, for it was in that moment that our cat, herself darkly invisible, leaped and brought her paws together on the true soul of the roach; a soul so static and intense, so immortally arranged, I felt, while I lay shell-like in our bed, turned inside out, driving my mind away, it was the same as the dark soul of the world itself—and it was this beautiful and terrifying feeling that took possession of me finally, stiffened me like a rod beside my husband, played caesar to my dreams.

The weather drove them up, I think . . . moisture in the tubes of the house. The first I came on looked put together in Japan; broken, one leg bent under like a metal cinch; unwound. It rang inside the hollow of the wand like metal too; brightly, like a stream of pins. The clatter made me shiver. Well I always see what I fear. Anything my eyes have is transformed into a threatening object: mud, or stains, or burns, or if not these, then toys in unmendable metal pieces. Not fears to be afraid of. The ordinary fears of daily life. Healthy fears. Womanly, wifely, motherly ones: the children may point at the wretch with the hunch and speak in a voice he will hear; the cat has fleas again, they will get in the sofa; one's face looks smeared, it's because of the heat; is the burner on under the beans? The washing machine's obscure disease may reoccur, it rumbles on rinse and rattles on wash; my god it's already eleven o'clock; which one of you has lost a galosh? So it was amid the worries of our ordinary life I bent, innocent and improperly armed, over the bug that had come undone. Let me think back on the shock. . . . My hand would have fled from a burn with the same speed; any-one's death or injury would have weakened me as well; and I could have gone cold for a number of reasons, because I felt in motion in me my own murderous disease, for instance; but none could have produced the revulsion that dim rec-ognition did, a reaction of my whole nature that flew ahead of understanding and made me withdraw like a spider.

I said I was innocent. Well I was not. Innocent. My god the names we use. What do we live with that's alive we haven't tamed—people like me?—even our houseplants breathe by our permission. All along I had the fear of what it was—something ugly and poisonous, deadly and terrible—the simple insect, worse and wilder than fire—and I should rather put my arms in the heart of a flame than in the darkness of a moist and webby hole. But the eye never ceases to change. When I examine my collection now it isn't any longer roaches I observe but gracious order, wholeness, and divinity. . . . My handkerchief, that time, was useless. . . . O my husband, they are a terrible disease.

The dark soul of the world . . . a phrase I should laugh at. The roach shell sickened me. And my jaw has broken open. I lie still, listening, but there is nothing to hear. Our cat is quiet. They pass through life to immortality between her paws.

Am I grateful now my terror has another object? From time to time I think so, but I feel as though I'd been entrusted with a kind of eastern mystery, sacred to a dreadful god, and I am full of the sense of my unworthiness and the clay of my vessel. So strange. It is the sewing machine that has the fearful claw. I live in a scatter of blocks and children's voices. The chores are my clock, and time is every other moment interrupted. I had always thought that love knew nothing of order and that life itself was turmoil and confusion. Let us leap, let us shout! I have leaped, and to my shame, I have wrestled. But this bug that I hold in my hand and know to be dead is beautiful, and there is a fierce joy in its composi-tion that beggars every other, for its joy is the joy of stone, and it lives in its tomb like a lion.

I don't know which is more surprising: to find such order in a roach, or such ideas in a woman.

I could not shake my point of view, infected as it was, and I took up their study with a manly passion. I sought out spiders and gave them sanctuary; played host to worms of every kind; was generous to katydids and lacewings, aphids, ants and various grubs; pampered several sorts of beetle; looked after crickets; sheltered bees; aimed my husband's chemicals away from the grasshop-pers, mosquitoes, moths, and flies. I have devoted hours to watching caterpillars feed. You can see the leaves they've eaten passing through them; their bodies thin and swell until the useless pulp is squeezed in perfect rounds from their rectal end; for caterpillars are a simple section of intestine, a decorated stalk of yearning muscle, and their whole being is enlisted in the effort of digestion. *Le tube digestif des Insectes est situé dans le grand axe de la cavité générale du corps . . . de la bouche vers l'anus . . . Le pharynx . . . L'œophage . . . Le jabot . . . Le ventricule chylifique . . . Le rectum et l'iléon . . .* Yet when they crawl their curves conform to graceful laws.

My children ought to be delighted with me as my husband is, I am so diligent, it seems, on their behalf, but they have taken fright and do not care to pry or to collect. My hobby's given me a pair of dreadful eyes, and sometimes I fancy they start from my head; yet I see, perhaps, no differently than Galileo saw when he found in the pendulum its fixed intent. Nonetheless my body resists such knowledge. It wearies of its edge. And I cannot forget, even while I watch our moonvine blossoms opening, the simple principle of the bug. It is a squat black cockroach after all, such a bug as frightens housewives, and it's only come to chew on rented wool and find its death absurdly in the teeth of the renter's cat.

Strange. Absurd. I am the wife of the house. This point of view I tremble in is the point of view of a god, and I feel certain, somehow, that could I give myself entirely to it, were I not continuing a woman, I could disarm my life, find peace and order everywhere; and I lie by my husband and I touch his arm and consider the temptation. But I am a woman. I am not worthy. Then I want to cry O husband, husband, I am ill, for I have seen what I have seen. What should he do at that, poor man, starting up in the night from his sleep to such nonsense, but comfort me blindly and murmur dream, small snail, only dream, bad dream, as I do to the children. I could go away like the wise cicada who abandons its shell to move to other mischief. I could leave and let my bones play cards and spank the children. . . . Peace. How can I think of such ludicrous things—beauty and peace, the dark soul of the world—for I am the wife of the house, concerned for the rug, tidy and punctual, surrounded by blocks.

Natalia Ginzburg

. . . .

THE MOTHER

Their mother was small and thin, and slightly round-shouldered; she always wore a blue skirt and a red woollen blouse. She had short, curly black hair which she kept oiled to control its bushiness; every day she plucked her eyebrows, making two black fish of them that swam towards her temples; and she used yellow powder on her face. She was very young; how old, they didn't know, but she seemed much younger than the mothers of the boys at school; they were always surprised to see their friends' mothers, how old and fat they were. She smoked a great deal and her fingers were stained with smoke; she even smoked in bed in the evening, before going to sleep. All three of them slept together, in the big double bed with the yellow quilt; their mother was on the side nearest the door, and on the bedside table she had a lamp with its shade wrapped in a red cloth, because at night she read and smoked; sometimes she came in very late, and the boys would wake up and ask her where she had been: she nearly always answered: 'At the cinema', or else 'With a girl friend of mine'; who this friend was they didn't know, because no woman friend had ever been to the house to see their mother. She told them they must turn the other way while she undressed, they heard the quick rustle of her clothes, and shadows danced on the walls; she slipped into bed beside them, her thin body in its cold silk nightdress, and they moved away from her because she always complained that they came too close and kicked while they slept; sometimes she put out the light so that they should go to sleep and smoked in silence in the darkness.

Their mother was not important. Granny, Grandpa, Aunt Clementina who lived in the country and turned up now and then with chestnuts and maize-flour were important; Diomira the maid was important, Giovanni the tubercular porter who made cane chairs was important; all these were very important to the two boys because they were strong people you could trust, strong people in allowing and forbidding, very good at everything they did and always full of wisdom and strength; people who could defend you from storms and robbers. But if they were at home with their mother the boys were frightened, just as if they had been alone; as for allowing or forbidding, she never allowed or forbade anything, at the most she complained in a weary voice: 'Don't make such a row because I've got a headache,' and if they asked permission to do something or other she answered at once: 'Ask Granny', or she said no first and then yes and then no and it was all a muddle. When they went out alone with their mother they felt uncertain and insecure because she always took wrong turnings and had to ask a policeman the way, and then she had such a funny, timid way of going into shops to ask for things to buy, and in the shops she always forgot something, gloves or handbag or scarf, and had to go back to look and the boys were ashamed.

Their mother's drawers were untidy and she left all her things scattered about and Diomira grumbled about her when she did out the room in the morning. She even called Granny in to see and together they picked up stockings and clothes and swept up the ash that was scattered all over the place. In the morning their mother went to do the shopping: she came back and flung the string bag on the marble table in the kitchen and took her bicycle and dashed off to the office where she worked. Diomira looked at all the things in the string bag, touched the oranges one by one and the meat, and grumbled and called Granny to see what poor meat it was. Their mother came home at two o'clock when they had all eaten and ate quickly with the newspaper propped up against her glass and then rushed off again to the office on her bicycle and they saw her for a minute at supper again, but after supper she nearly always dashed off.

The boys did their homework in the bedroom. There was their father's picture, large at the head of the bed, with his square black beard and bald head and tortoiseshell-rimmed spectacles, and then another small portrait on the table, with the younger of the boys in his arms. Their father had died when they were very small, they remembered nothing about him: or rather in the older boy's memory there was the shadow of a very distant afternoon, in the country at Aunt Clementina's: his father was pushing him across the meadow in a green wheelbarrow; afterwards he had found some pieces of this wheelbarrow, a handle and a wheel, in Aunt Clementina's attic; when it was new it was a splendid wheelbarrow and he was glad to have it; his father ran along pushing him and his long beard flapped. They knew nothing about their father but they thought he must be the sort of person who is strong and wise in allowing and forbidding; when Grandpa or Diomira got angry with their mother Granny said that they should be sorry for her because she had been very unfortunate, and she said that if Eugenio, the boys' father, had been there she would have been an entirely different woman, whereas she had had the misfortune to lose her husband when she was still young. For a time there had been their father's mother as well, they never saw her because she lived in France but she used to write and send Christmas presents: then in the end she died because she was very old.

At tea-time they ate chestnuts, or bread with oil and vinegar, and then if they had finished their homework they could go and play in the small piazza or among the ruins of the public baths, which had been blown up in an air raid. In the small piazza there were a great many pigeons and they took them bread or got Diomira to give them a paper bag of left-over rice. There they met all the local boys, boys from school and others they met in the youth clubs on Sundays when they had football matches with Don Vigliani, who hitched up his black cassock and kicked. Sometimes they played football in the small piazza too or else cops and robbers. Their grandmother appeared on the balcony occasionally and called to them not to get hurt: it was nice seeing the lighted windows of their home, up there on the third floor, from the dark piazza, and knowing that they could go back there, warm up at the stove and guard themselves from the night. Granny sat in the kitchen with Diomira and mended the linen; Grandpa was in the dining-room with his cap on, smoking his pipe. Granny was very fat, and wore black, and on her breast a medal with a picture of Uncle Oreste who had died in the war: she was very good at cooking pizzas and things. Sometimes she took them on her knee, even now when they were quite big boys; she was fat, she had a large soft bosom; from under the neck of her black dress you could see the thick white woollen vest with a scolloped edge which she had made herself. She would take them on her knee and say tender and slightly pitiful-sounding words in dialect; then she would take a long iron hair-pin out of her bun and clean their ears, and they would shriek and try to get away and Grandpa would come to the door with his pipe.

Grandpa had taught Greek and Latin at the high school. Now he was pensioned off and was writing a Greek grammar: many of his old pupils used to come and see him now and then. Then Diomira would make coffee; in the lavatory there were exercise book pages with Latin and Greek unseens on them, and his corrections in red and blue. Grandpa had a small white beard, a sort of goatee, and they were not to make a racket because his nerves were tired after all those years at school; he was always rather alarmed because prices kept going up and Granny always had a bit of a row with him in the morning because he was always surprised at the money they needed; he would say that perhaps Diomira pinched the sugar and made coffee in secret and Diomira would hear and rush at him and yell that the coffee was for the students who kept coming; but these were small incidents that quietened down at once and the boys were not alarmed, whereas they were alarmed when there was a quarrel between Grandpa and their mother; this happened sometimes if their mother came home very late at night, he would come out of his room with his overcoat over his pyjamas and bare feet, and he and their mother would shout: he said: 'I know where you've been, I know where you've been, I know what you are,' and their mother said: 'What do I care?' and then: 'Look, now you've woken the children,' and he said: 'A fat lot you care what happens to your children. Don't say anything because I know what you are. You're a bitch. You run around at night like the mad bitch you are.' And then Granny and Diomira would come out in their nightdresses and push him into his room and say: 'Shush, shush,' and their mother would get into bed and sob under the bedclothes, her deep sobs echoing in the dark room: the boys thought that Grandpa must be right, they thought their mother was wrong to go to the cinema and to her girl friends at night. They felt very unhappy, frightened and unhappy, and lay huddled close together in the deep, warm, soft bed, and the older boy who was in the middle pushed away so as not to touch his mother's body: there seemed to him something disgusting in his mother's tears, in the wet pillow: he thought: 'It gives a chap the creeps when his mother cries.' They never spoke between themselves of these rows their mother and Grandpa had, they carefully avoided mentioning them: but they loved each other very much and clung close together at night when their mother cried: in the morning they were faintly embarrassed, because they had hugged so tightly as if to protect themselves, and because there was that thing they didn't want to talk about; besides, they soon forgot that they had been unhappy, the day began and they went to school, and met their friends in the street, and played for a moment at the school door.

In the grey light of morning, their mother got up: with her petticoat wound round her waist she soaped her neck and arms standing bent over the basin: she always tried not to let them see her but in the looking glass they could make out her thin brown shoulders and small naked breasts: in the cold the nipples became dark and protruding, she raised her arms and powdered her armpits: in her armpits she had thick curly hair. When she was completely dressed she started plucking her eyebrows, staring at herself in the mirror from close to and biting her lips hard: then she smothered her face with cream and shook the pink swansdown puff hard and powdered herself: then her face became all yellow. Sometimes she was quite gay in the mornings and wanted to talk to the boys, she asked them about school and their friends and told them things about her time at school: she had a teacher called 'Signorina Dirce' and she was an old maid who tried to seem young. Then she put on her coat and picked up her string shopping bag, leant down to kiss the boys and ran out with her scarf wound round her head and her face all perfumed and powdered with yellow powder.

The boys thought it strange to have been born of her. It would have been much less strange to have been born of Granny or Diomira, with their large warm bodies that protected you from fear, that defended you from storms and robbers. It was very strange to think she was their mother, that she had held them for a while in her small womb. Since they learnt that children are in their mother's tummy before being born, they had felt very surprised and also a little ashamed that that womb had once held them. And that she had given them milk from her breasts as well: this was even more unlikely. But now she no longer had small children to feed and cradle, and every day they saw her dash off on her bicycle when the shopping was done, her body jerking away, free and happy. She certainly didn't belong to them: they couldn't count on her. You couldn't ask her anything: there were other mothers, the mothers of their school friends, whom clearly you could ask about all sorts of things; their friends ran to their mothers when school was over and asked them heaps of things, got their noses blown and their overcoats buttoned, showed their homework and their comics: these mothers were pretty old, with hats or veils or fur collars and they came to talk to the master practically every day: they were people like Granny or like Diomira, large soft imperious bodies of people who didn't make mistakes: people who didn't lose things, who didn't leave their drawers untidy, who didn't come home late at night. But their mother ran off free after the shopping; besides, she was bad at shopping, she got cheated by the butcher and was often given wrong change: she went off and it was impossible to join her where she went, deep down they marvelled at her enormously when they saw her go off: who knows what that office of hers was like, she didn't talk about it much; she had to type and write letters in French and English: who knows, maybe she was pretty good at that.

One day when they were out for a walk with Don Vigliani and with other boys from the youth club, on the way back they saw their mother in a suburban café. She was sitting inside the café; they saw her through the window, and a man was sitting with her. Their mother had laid her tartan scarf on the table and the old crocodile handbag they knew well: the man had a loose light overcoat and a brown moustache and was talking to her and smiling: their mother's face was happy, relaxed and happy, as it never was at home. She was looking at the man and they were holding hands and she didn't see the boys: the boys went on walking beside Don Vigliani who told them all to hurry because they must catch the tram: when they were on the tram the younger boy moved over to his brother and said: 'Did you see Mummy?' and his brother said: 'No, I didn't.' The younger one laughed softly and said: 'Oh yes you did, it was Mummy and there was a man with her.' The older boy turned his head away: he was big, nearly thirteen: his younger brother irritated him because he made him feel sorry for him, he couldn't understand why he felt sorry for him but he was sorry for himself as well and he didn't want to think of what he had seen, he wanted to behave as if he had seen nothing.

They said nothing to Granny. In the morning while their mother was dressing the younger boy said: 'Yesterday when we were out for a walk with Don Vigliani we saw you and there was a man with you.' Their mother jerked round, looking nasty: the black fish on her forehead quivered and met. She said: 'But it wasn't me. What an idea. I've got to stay in the office till late in the evening, as you know. Obviously you made a mistake.' The older boy then said, in a tired calm voice: 'No, it wasn't you. It was someone who looked like you.' And both boys realized that the memory must disappear: and they both breathed hard to blow it away.

But the man in the light overcoat once came to the house. He hadn't got his overcoat because it was summer, he wore blue spectacles and a light linen suit, he asked leave to take off his jacket while they had lunch. Granny and Grandpa had gone to Milan to meet some relations and Diomira had gone to her village, so they were alone with their mother. It was then the man came. Lunch was pretty good: their mother had bought nearly everything at the cooked meat shop: there was chicken with chips and this came from the shop: their mother had done the pasta, it was good, only the sauce was a bit burnt. There was wine, too. Their mother was nervous and gay, she wanted to say so much at once: she wanted to talk of the boys to the man and of the man to the boys. The man was called Max and he had been in Africa, he had lots of photographs of Africa and showed them: there was a photograph of a monkey of his, the boys asked him about this monkey a lot; it was so intelligent and so fond of him and had such a funny, pretty way with it when it wanted a sweet. But he had left it in Africa because it was ill and he was afraid it would die on the steamer. The boys became friendly with this Max. He promised to take them to the cinema one day. They showed him their books, they hadn't got many: he asked them if they had read *Saturnino Farandola* and they said no and he said he would give it to them, and *Robinson delle praterie* as well, as it was very fine. After lunch their mother told them to go and play in the recreation ground. They wished they could stay on with Max. They protested a bit but their mother, and Max too, said they must go; then in the evening when they came home Max was no longer there. Their mother hurriedly prepared the supper, coffee with milk and potato salad: they were happy, they wanted to talk about Africa and the monkey, they were extraordinarily happy and couldn't really understand why: and their mother seemed happy too and told them things, about a monkey she had once seen dancing to a little street organ. And then she told them to go to bed and said she was going out for a minute, they mustn't be scared, there was no reason to be; she bent down to kiss them and told them there was no point in telling Granny and Grandpa about Max because they never liked one inviting people home.

So they stayed on their own with their mother for a few days: they ate unusual things because their mother didn't want to cook, ham and jam and coffee with milk and fried things from the cooked meat shop. Then they washed up together. But when Granny and Grandpa came back the boys felt relieved: the tablecloth was on the dining-room table again, and the glasses and everything there should be: Granny was sitting in her rocking chair again, with her soft body and her smell: Grandma couldn't dash off, she was too old and too fat, it was nice having someone who stayed at home and couldn't ever dash away.

The boys said nothing to Granny about Max. They waited for the book *Saturnino Farandola* and waited for Max to take them to the cinema and show them more photographs of the monkey. Once or twice they asked their mother when they'd be going to the cinema with signor Max. But their mother answered harshly that signor Max had left now. The younger boy asked if he'd gone to Africa. Their mother didn't answer. But he thought he must have gone to Africa to fetch the monkey. He imagined that someday or other he would come and fetch them at school, with a black servant and a monkey in his arms. School began again and Aunt Clementina came to stay with them for a while; she had brought a bag of pears and apples which they put in the oven to cook with marsala and sugar. Their mother was in a very bad temper and quarrelled continually with Grandpa. She came home late and stayed awake smoking. She had got very much thinner and ate nothing. Her face became ever smaller and yellower, she now put black on her eyelashes too, she spat into a little box and picked up the black where she had spat with a brush; she put on masses of powder, Granny tried to wipe it off her face with a handkerchief and she turned her face away. She hardly ever spoke and when she did it seemed an effort, her voice was so weak. One day she came home in the afternoon at about six o'clock: it was strange, usually she came home much later; she locked herself in the bedroom. The younger boy came and knocked because he needed an exercise book: their mother answered angrily from inside that she wanted to sleep and that they were to leave her in peace: the boy explained timidly that he needed the exercise book; then she came to open up and her face was all swollen and wet: the boy realized she was crying, he went back to Granny and said: 'Mummy's crying,' and Granny and Aunt Clementina talked quietly together for a long time, they spoke of their mother but you couldn't make out what they were saying.

One night their mother didn't come home. Grandpa kept coming to see, barefoot, with his overcoat over his pyjamas; Granny came too and the boys slept badly, they could hear Granny and Grandpa walking about the house, opening and shutting the windows. The boys were very frightened. Then in the morning, they rang up from the police station: their mother had been found dead in an hotel, she had taken poison, she had left a letter: Grandpa and Aunt Clementina went along, Granny shrieked, the boys were sent to an old lady on the floor below who said continually: 'Heartless, leaving two babes like this.' Their mother was brought home. The boys went to see her when they had her laid out on the bed: Diomira had dressed her in her patent leather shoes and the red silk dress from the time she was married: she was small, a small dead doll.

It was strange to see flowers and candles in the same old room. Diomira and Aunt Clementina and Granny were kneeling and praying: they had said she took the poison by mistake, otherwise the priest wouldn't come and bless her, if he knew she had done it on purpose. Diomira told the boys they must kiss her: they were terribly ashamed and kissed her cold cheek one after the other. Then there was the funeral, it took ages, they crossed the entire town and felt very tired, Don Vigliani was there too and a great many children from school and from the youth club. It was cold, and very windy in the cemetery. When they went home again, Granny started crying and bawling at the sight of the bicycle in the passage: because it was really just like seeing her dashing away, with her free body and her scarf flapping in the wind: Don Vigliani said she was now in heaven, perhaps because he didn't know she had done it on purpose, or he knew and pretended not to: but the boys didn't really know if heaven existed, because Grandpa said no, and Granny said yes, and their mother had once said there was no heaven, with little angels and beautiful music, but that the dead went to a place where they were neither well nor ill, and that where you wish for nothing you rest and are wholly at peace.

The boys went to the country for a time, to Aunt Clementina's. Everyone was very kind to them, and kissed and caressed them, and they were very ashamed. They never spoke together of their mother nor of signor Max either; in the attic at Aunt Clementina's they found the book of *Saturnino Farandola* and they read it over and over and found it very fine. But the older boy often thought of his mother, as he had seen her that day in the café with Max, holding her hands and with such a relaxed, happy face; he thought then that maybe their mother had taken poison because Max had gone back to Africa for good. The boys played with Aunt Clementina's dog, a fine dog called Bubi, and they learnt to climb trees, as they couldn't do before. They went bathing in the river, too, and it was nice going back to Aunt Clementina's in the evening and doing crosswords all together. The boys were very happy at Aunt Clementina's. Then they went back to Granny's and were very happy. Granny sat in the rocking chair, and wanted to clean their ears with her hairpins. On Sunday they went to the cemetery, Diomira came too, they bought flowers and on the way back stopped at a bar to have hot punch. When they were in the cemetery, at the grave, Granny prayed and cried, but it was very hard to think that the grave and the crosses and the cemetery had anything to do with their mother, who had been cheated by the butcher and dashed off on her bicycle, and smoked, and took wrong turnings, and sobbed at night. The bed was very big for them now and they had a pillow each. They didn't often think of their mother because it hurt them a little and made them ashamed to think of her. Sometimes they tried to remember how she was, each on his own in silence: and they found it harder and harder to reassemble her short curly hair and the fish on her forehead and her lips: she put on a lot of yellow powder, this they remembered quite well; little by little there was a yellow dot, it was impossible to get the shape of her cheeks and face. Besides, they now realized that they had never loved her much, perhaps she too hadn't loved them much, if she had loved them she wouldn't have taken poison, they had heard Diomira and the porter and the lady on the floor below and so many other people say so. The years went by and the boys grew and so many things happened and that face which they had never loved very much disappeared for ever.

Translated from the Italian by Isabel Quigly

Nadine Gordimer

. . . .

THE LIFE OF THE IMAGINATION

As a child she did not inhabit their world, a place where whether the so-and-sos would fit in at dinner, and whose business it was to see that the plumber was called, and whether the car should be traded in or overhauled were the daily entries in a ledger of living. The sum of it was the comfortable, orderly house, beds with turned-down sheets from which nightmares and dreams never overstepped the threshold of morning, goodnight kisses as routine as the cleaning of teeth, a woman stating her truth, 'Charles would never eat a warmed-over meal,' a man defining his creed, 'One thing I was taught young, the value of money'.

From the beginning, for her, it was the mystery and not the carefully knotted net with which they covered it, as the highwire performer is protected from the fall. Instead of dust under the beds there was (for her) that hand that Malte Laurids Brigge saw reaching out towards him in the dark beneath his mother's table. Only she was not afraid, as she read, later, he was; she recognized, and grasped it.

And she never let go.

She did not make the mistake of thinking that because of this she must inevitably be able to write or paint; that was just another of the axioms that did for them (Barbara has such a vivid imagination, she is so artistic). She knew it was one thing to have entry to the other world, and another entirely to bring something of it back with you. She studied biology at the university for a while (the subject, incising soft fur and skin to get at the complexities beneath, lured her, and they heard there were good positions going for girls with a B.Sc. degree) but then left and took a job in a municipal art gallery. She began by sorting sepia postcards and went on to dust Chinese ceramic roof-tiles and to learn how to clean paintings. The smell of turpentine, size, and coffee in the room where she and the director worked was her first intimacy. They wondered how she could be so happy there, cut off from the company of young people, and once her father remarked half-meaningfully that he hoped the director wouldn't get any ideas.

The director had many ideas, including the only one her father thought of. He was an oldish man—to her, at the time, anyway—with the proboscis-face that often goes with an inquiring mind, and a sudden nakedness of tortoiseshell-

coloured eyes when he took off his huge glasses. His wife said, 'It's wonderful for
Dan to have you working for him. He's always been one of those men who are at
their best mentally only when they are more or less in love.' He told his assistant
the story of Wu Ch'eng-ên's characters, the monkey, the pilgrim Tripitaka,
Sandy, Pigsy and the two horses she had dusted, as well as giving her a masterly
analysis of the breakdown of feudalism in relation to the success of the Long
March. He had a collection of photographs he had taken of intricate machinery
and microphotography of the cells of plants, and together, using her skill in dis-
secting rats and frogs and grasshoppers, they added blow-ups of animal tissue.
He kissed her occasionally, but rather as if that were simply part of the order of
the cosmos; his lips were thin, now, and he knew it. It was through him that she
met and fell in love with the young architect whom she married, and with whom
she went to Japan, where he had won a scholarship to the University of Tokyo.
They wandered about the East and Europe together for a year or two (it was just
as her parents expected; she had no proper home) and then came back to South
Africa where he became a very successful architect indeed and made an excellent
living.

It was as simple and confounding as that. Government administration as well
as the great mining and industrial companies employed him to design one public building after another. He and Barbara had a serene, self-effacing house on a
kopje outside Pretoria—the garden demonstrated how well the spare, indige-
nous thorn trees of the Middle Veld followed the Japanese architectural idiom.
They had children. Barbara remained, in her late thirties, a thin, tall creature
with a bony face darkened by freckles, good-looking and much given to her own
company. Money changed her dress little, and her tastes not at all; she was able
to indulge them rather more. She had a *pondokkie* down in the Low Veld, on
the Crocodile River, where she went sometimes in the winter to stay for a week
or two on her own. Marriage was not possible, of course. Certainly not of true
minds, because if one is ever going to find release from the mesmerism of appearances one is condemned to make the effort by oneself. And daily intimacy
was an inevitable attempt to avoid this that left one sharing bed, bathroom, and
table, solitary as in any crowd. She and Arthur, her husband, knew it; they got
on almost wordlessly well, now and then turned instinctively to each other, and
were alone, he with his work and she with her books and her *pondokkie*. They
made their children happy. The school headmaster said they were the most
'creative' children that had ever passed through his hands (Barbara's children are
so artistic, Barbara's children are so imaginative).

They got measles and ran sudden fevers at awkward times, just like other
children, however, and one evening when Barbara and Arthur were about to go
out to dinner, Pete was discovered to have a high temperature. The dinner was
for a visiting Danish architect who had particularly requested to meet Arthur, so
he went on ahead while Barbara stayed to see what the doctor would say. She
had not been particularly pleased to hear that the family doctor was away on holiday in Europe and his locum tenens would be coming instead. He was perhaps
a little surprised to be met at the door by a woman in evening dress—the house
itself was something that made unexpected demands on the attention of people
who had not seen anything like it before. She felt the necessity to explain her

appearance, partly to disguise the slight hostility she felt towards him for being a substitute for a reassuring face—'We were just going out when I noticed my son looked like a beetroot.'

He smiled. 'It's a change from curlers and dressing-gowns.' And they stood there, she in her long dress, he with coat and brown bag, as if for a split second the situation of their confrontation was not clear; had they bumped into one another, stupidly both dodging in the same direction to avoid colliding in the street? Then the lapse closed and they proceeded to the bedroom where Pete and Bruce sat up in their beds expectantly. Pete said, 'That's not our doctor.'

'No, I know, this is Doctor Asher, he's looking after everybody while Doctor Dickson's away.'

'You won't give me an injection?' said Pete.

'I don't think you've got the sort of sickness that's going to need an injection,' the man said. 'Anyway, I give injections so fast you don't even know they've happened. Really.'

The little one, Bruce, giggled, flopped back in bed and pulled the sheet over his mouth.

The doctor said, 'You mustn't laugh at me. You can ask my children. One, two—before you can count three—it's done.'

Bruce said to him, 'It's not nice to swank.'

The doctor looked up over his open bag and appeared to flinch at this grown-up dictum. 'I'm sorry. I won't do it any more.'

When he had examined Pete he prescribed a mixture that Dr Dickson had often given the children; Barbara went to look in the medicine chest, and there was an almost full bottle there. Pete had swollen glands at the base of his skull and under the jawline. 'We'll watch it,' the doctor said, as Barbara preceded him down the passage. 'I've seen several cases of glandular fever since I've been here. Ring me in the morning if you're worried.' Again they stood in the entrance, she with her hands hanging at the sides of her long skirt, he getting into his coat. He was no taller than she, and probably about the same age, but tired, with the travel-worn look of general practitioners, perpetually lugging a bag around with them. His hair was a modified version of the sort of Julius Caesar cut affected by architects, journalists and advertising men; doctors usually stuck to short back and sides. She thanked him, using his name, and he remarked, pausing at the door, 'By the way, it's Usher—with a U.'

'Oh, I'm sorry—I misheard, over the phone. Usher.'

He was looking up and around the house. 'Japanese style, isn't it? They grow those miniature trees—amazing. There was an article about them the other day, I can't remember where I . . . What d'you call it?'

She had kept from childhood an awkward gesture of jerking her chin when embarrassed. One look at the house and people racked their brains for something apposite to say and up came those horrible little stunted trees. 'Oh yes. Bonsai. Thank you very much. Good night.'

When he had gone she went at once to give Pete his medicine and the nanny the telephone number of the hotel where the dinner was being held. Afterwards, she remembered with a detached clarity those few minutes before she left the house, when she was in and out of her sons' room: the light that seemed reddish, with the stuffy warmth of childhood colouring it, the stained rugs, the nursery-school daubs stuck on the walls, Dora's cheerfully scornful African voice and the hoist of her big rump as she bent about tidying up, the smell of fever on Pete's lips as she kissed him and the encounter, under the hand she leaned on, with the comforting midden of a child's bed—bits of raw potato he had been using as ammunition in a pea-shooter, the hard shape of a piece of jigsaw puzzle, the wooden spatula the doctor had used to flatten his tongue. And it seemed to her that even at the time, she had had a rare momentary vision of herself (she was not a woman given to awareness of creating effects). She had thought—moving between the small beds slowly because of the long dress, perfumed and painted—this is the image of the mother that men have often chosen to perpetu-ate, the autobiographers, the Prousts. This is what I may be for one of these lit-tle boys when I have become an old woman with bristles on her chin, dead.

Pete was better next day. The doctor came at about half past one, when the child was asleep and she was eating her lunch off a tray in the sun. The servant led the doctor out onto the terrace. He didn't want to disturb her; but she was simply having a snack, as he could see. He sat down while she told him about the child. She had a glass of white wine beside her plate of left-over fish salad—the wine was a left-over, too, but still, what interest could that be to him, whether or not she habitually bibbed wine alone at lunch? The man looked with real pleasure round the calm and sunny terrace and she felt sorry for him be-cause he thought bonsai trees were wonderful. 'Have a glass of wine—it's lovely and cold.' Her bony feet were bare in the winter sun. He refused; of course, a doctor can't do as he likes. But he took out a pipe, and smoked that. 'The sun's so pleasant, I must say Pretoria has its points.' They were both looking at her toes, on each foot the second one was crooked; it was because the child was asleep, of course, that he sat there. He told her that he came from Cape Town, where it rained all winter. They went upstairs to look at the child; he was breathing evenly and soundlessly. 'Leave him,' the doctor said. Downstairs he added, 'Another day or two in bed, I'd say. I'd like to check those glands again.'

He came just before two the following day. This time he accepted a cup of coffee. It was just as it had been yesterday; it might have been yesterday. It was almost the same time of day. The sun had exactly the same strength. They sat on the broad brick seat with its thick cushion. His pipe smoke hung a little haze before their eyes. She was telling him the child was so much better that it really was impossible to keep him in bed, when he looked at her amusedly, as if he had found them both out—himself and her—and his arm, with the hand curved to bring her to him, drew her in. They kissed and without thinking at all whether she wanted to kiss him or not, she found herself anxious to be skilful. She seemed to manage very well because the kissing went on for minutes, their heads turning this way and that as their mouths slowly detached and met.

And so it began. When they drew back from each other the words flew to her: why this man, for heaven's sake—why you? And because she was ashamed of the thought, she said aloud instead, 'Why me?'

He found this apparent unawareness of her own attractions so moving that he kissed her fiercely, answering, for her, both questions, the spoken and unspoken.

While they were kissing she became aware of the slightest, quickest sideways movement of the one slate-coloured eye she could see, a second before she herself heard the squeak of the servant's sandshoes approaching from within the house. They drew apart, she in jerky haste, he with composed swiftness so that the intimacy between them held good even while he put his pipe in his pocket, took out a prescription pad and was remarking, when the servant picked up the coffee tray, 'It mightn't be a bad idea to keep some sort of mild antipyretic in the house, not as strong as that mixture he's been having, I mean, but . . .'

So it began. The love-making, the absurdities of concealment; even the acceptance of the knowledge that this hard-working doctor with the sickle-line of a smile cut down either side of his mouth, and the brown, coarse-grained forehead, had gone through it all before, perhaps many times. So it began, exactly as it was to be.

They made love the first time in the flat he was living in temporarily. It was a ravishing experience for both of them and when it was over—for the moment—they knew that they must turn their attention urgently and at once to the intensely practical business of how, when and where they were to continue to be together. After a month his wife came up from Cape Town and things were more difficult. He had taken a house for his family; the sublet flat with other people's books and sheets and bric-à-brac, in which he and Barbara were the only objects familiar to each other, became a paradise lost. They drove then, separately, all the way to Johannesburg to spend an afternoon together in an hotel (Pretoria was too small a place for one to expect to go unrecognized). He was tied to his endless working hours; they had nowhere to go. Their problem was passion but they could hope for only the most down-to-earth, realistic solutions. One could not flinch from them. After the last patient left the consulting rooms in the evening the building was deserted—an office block. He made little popping noises on his pipe as he decided they would be quite safe there. Deaf and blind with anticipation of the meeting, she would come from the side street where her car was parked, through the dark foyer, past the mops and bucket of the African cleaner, up in the lift with its glowing eye showing as it rose through successive levels, then along the corridors of closed doors and commercial nameplates until she was there: Dr. J. McDow Dickson, M.B.B.Ch. Edin. Consulting Hours, Mornings 11–1, Afternoons 4–6. On the old daybed in Dr Dickson's anteroom they made love, among the medical insurance calendars and the desk accessories advertising antibiotics. Once the cleaner was heard turning his pass-key in the waiting-room door; once someone (a patient, no doubt) hammered at it for a while, and then went away. She had always been sure, without censure, that shabby love-affairs would be useless, for her. She learnt that shabbiness is the judgment of the outsider, the one left in the cold; there are no shabby love-affairs for those who are the lovers.

They met wherever and however and for whatever length of time they could, but still by far the greater part of their time was spent apart. Communications, movements, meeting-places—all this had to be settled as between two secret agents whom the world must not suspect to be in contact. In order to plan strategy, each had to brief the other about the normal pattern of his life: this was how they got to know, bit by bit, that yawning area of each other's lives that existed outside one another's arms. 'On Thursday nights I'm always alone because

Arthur takes a seminar at the university.' 'You can safely ring me any Sunday morning between eight and nine because Yvonne goes to Mass.'

So his wife was a Catholic. Well, yes, but he was not. Of course that meant that his children were being brought up as Catholics. One evening when he and Barbara were putting on their clothes again in the consulting rooms she had seen the picture of the three little girls, under the transparent plastic slot in his wallet. White-blond hair, short and straight as a nylon toothbrush, ribbon sashes, net petticoats, white socks held by elastic—the children of one of those nice, neat pretty women who look after them just as carefully as they used to take care of their dolls. Barbara never met her. He said that the local doctors' wives were being very kind—she was playing tennis regularly at the house of one, and another had little girls the same age who had become inseparable from his girls. If he and Barbara met at the consulting rooms on Friday evenings, he had to keep an eye on his watch—'Bridge night,' he said, doggedly, resignedly. Sometimes he said, 'Blast bridge night.'

Between embraces, confessions, questions came easily, up to a point. 'You lead a very different life,' he said.

He meant 'from mine'. Or from hers, perhaps—his wife's.

Lying there, Barbara pulled a dismissing face.

'Oh yes.' He did not want to be excepted, indulged, out of love; he had his own regard for the truth. 'What was wrong about the Japanese trees, that time—that first night I came to your house—what did I say? There was such a look on your face.'

'Oh that. The bonsai business.' The reproach was for herself; he didn't understand the shrinking in repugnance from 'good taste'—well, wasn't the shrinking as daintily fastidious, in its way, as the 'good taste' itself? You went whoring after one concept or the other of your own sensibility. 'Not different at all,'—she returned to his original remark; she had this quality, he noticed, of keeping a series of remarks you had passed laid out before her, and then unhesitatingly turning to pick up this one or that—'It's like putting a net into the sea. You bring up small fish or big fish, weeds, muck, little bright bits of things. But the water, the element that's living—that's drained away.'

'—So tonight it's bridge,' she added, putting out her hand to caress his chest.

He took the pipe out of his mouth. 'When you're down at the Crocodile,' he said—they called her *pondokkie* that because it was on the Crocodile River— 'What are you doing there, when you're alone?'

She lay under his gaze; she felt the quality she had for him, awkwardly, as if he had stuck a jewel on her forehead. She didn't answer.

'Reading, eh? Reading and thinking your own thoughts.' For years he had barely had time to get through the medical journals.

She was seeing the still, dry stretch to the horizon, each thorn bush like every other thorn bush, the narrow cattle paths leading back on themselves through the clean, dry grass, the silence into which one seemed to fall, at midday, as if into an airpocket; the silence there would be one day when one's heart stopped, while everything went on as it did in that veld silence, the hard trees waiting for sap to rise, the dead grass waiting to be sloughed off the new under rain, the boulders cracking into new forms under frost and sun.

But alive under her hand was the hair of his breast, still damp and soft from contact with her body, and she said, keeping her teeth together, 'I wish we could go there. I wish we were in bed there now.'

That winter she did not go once to the shack. It had become nothing but a shelter where they could have made love, whole nights and days. There were so many hours when they could not see each other. Could not even telephone; he was at home with his family, she with hers. Such slow stretches of mornings, thawing in the sun; such long afternoons when the interruption of her children was a monstrous breaking-in upon—what? She was doing nothing. She saw him as she had once watched him without his being aware of her, crossing the street and walking the length of a block to their meeting-place: a slight man with a pipe held between his teeth in a rather brutal way, a smiling curve of the mouth denied by the downward, inward lines of brow and eyelids as his head bobbed. In his hand the elegant pigskin bag she had given him because it was easy to explain away as the gift of some grateful patient. He sees nobody, only where he is going. Sitting at dinner-parties or reading at night, she saw him like this in broad daylight, crossing the street, bag in hand. It seemed she could follow him through all the hill-cupped small city, make out his back among all others, crossing the square past Dr Dolittle in his top hat (that was what her little boys thought the statue of President Kruger was), doing the rounds in the suburbs, the car full of pipe-smoke and empty phials with their necks snapped off, the smile a grim habit, greeting no one.

Sometimes he materialized at her own door—he'd had a call in the neighbourhood, or told the nurse so, anyway. It would be in the morning, when the boys were at school and Arthur was at the town studio. He always went straight to the telephone and rang up the consulting rooms, so that he'd be covered if his car happened to be seen: 'Oh Birdie, I'm around Muckleneuk—if there's anyone I ought to drop in on out this way? My next call will be the Wilson child, Waterkloof Road, so—' Then they would sit on the terrace again and have coffee. And he would give his expert glance round doors and windows before kissing her; he smelt of the hospital theatre he had been in, or the soap he had washed his hands with in other people's houses. He wore a pullover his mother had sent him, he had pigskin gloves Yvonne had bought him—he smiled, telling it—because she thought the smart new bag made his old ones look so shabby. For Barbara there was the bloom on him of the times when he was not with her.

She had never been in his house, of course, and she did not know the disposition of the rooms, or the sound of voices calling through it in the early morning rush to get to school and hospital rounds (she knew he got up very early, before she would even be awake), or the kind of conversation that came to life over drinks when friends were there, or the atmosphere, so strongly personal in every house, of the hour late at night when outsiders have gone and doors are being locked and lights switched off, one by one.

She had never been with him in the company of other people (unless one counted Pete and Bruce) and she did not know how he would appear in their eyes, or what his manner would be. She listened with careful detachment when he telephoned the nurse; he had a tired, humorous way with her—but that was just professional camaraderie, with a touch of the flirtatiousness that pleases old ladies. Once or twice he had had to phone his wife in Barbara's presence: it was the anonymous telecommunication of long marriage—'Yvonne? I'm on my way. Oh, twenty minutes or so. Well, if he does, say I'll be in any time after nine. Yes. No, I won't. See you.'

When they were together after love-making they talked about their past lives and discussed his future. He intended, within the next year, to go to America to do what he had always wanted—biological research. They discussed in great detail the planning of his finances: he had sold his practice in Cape Town in order to be able to keep his family while studying on a grant he'd been promised. The six months' locum-tenancy was a stop-gap between selling the practice and taking up the grant in Boston. He had moments of deep uncertainty: he should have gone ten years ago, young and single-minded—but, helplessly, even then there was a girl, marriage, babies. From the depths of his uncertainty, he and Barbara looked at each other like two prisoners who wake up and find themselves on the floor of the same cell. He said, as if for what it was worth, 'I love you.' They became absorbed again in the questions of how he should best use his opportunities in America, and under whom he should try to get the chance to work. And then it was time to get dressed, time up, time to go, time to be home to change for his bridge evening, time to be home to receive Arthur's friends. Standing in the lift together they were silent, weary, at one. They left the consulting-room building separately; as she walked away he became again that figure crossing streets, going in and out of houses and car, pigskin doctor's bag in hand, seeing nobody, only where he was going.

Her mind constructed snatches of dialogue, like remembered fragments of a play. She was following him home to the bridge table (she had never played card games) or the dinner-table—there was a roast, that would be the sort of thing, a brown leg of pork with apple sauce, and he was carving, knowing what cut each member of the little family liked best. The white-haired, white-socked little girls had washed their hands. The bridge players talked with the ease of colleagues, the wives were saying, 'John wouldn't touch it,' 'I must say the only thing he always does remember is when to pay the insurance,' 'I can't get anyone to do shirt collars properly.' She had the feeling his wife bought his clothes for him; but the haircut—that he chose for himself. As he chose her, Barbara, and other women. On Sundays she lay with an unread book on the terrace or laughed and talked without listening among Arthur's friends (they all seemed to be Arthur's friends, now) and he was running about some clean, hard tennis court, red in the face, agile, happy perhaps, in the mindless happiness of physical exercise. She was not jealous, only slightly excited by the thought of him with her completely out of mind. Or perhaps this Sunday they had taken the children on some outing. Once when she had visualized him all afternoon on that tennis court, he had happened to mention that Sunday afternoon had been swallowed up in a family outing—the children had heard about a game park in Krugersdorp. The plain, white-haired little girl clambered over him to see better; was he irritated? Or was he smoothing the hair behind the child's ears with that lover's gesture of his, also, perhaps, a father's gesture? She read over again a paragraph in the book lying between her elbows on the grass: '. . . the word *lolo* means both "soul" and "butterfly" . . . the dual meaning is due to the fact that the chrysalis resembles a shrouded corpse and that the butterfly emerges from it like the soul from the body of a sleeping man.' But the idea had no meaning for her. The words floated on her mind; no, a moth, quite an ordinary-looking, protectively-coloured moth, not noticed going about the streets, quickly crossing the square in the early evening, coming softly along the corridor, touching softly. Fierily, making quick the sleeping body.

One night when she had the good luck to be alone for a few days (Arthur was in the Cape), he was able to slip away and come to her at home. This rare opportunity required careful planning, like every other arrangement between them. He said he was going to a meeting of the medical association; she had an early dinner, to be sure the servants would be out of the way. She saw to it that all the windows of the house except those of her bedroom should be in darkness, so that any unexpected caller would presume she had gone to bed and not disturb her. In fact, she did lie on her bed, fully dressed, waiting for him. She had given him the key of the side door, off the terrace, that afternoon. He came with a quiet, determined hesitancy, through another man's house. He had never been into the bedroom before but he knew where the children's rooms were. When she heard him reach the passage where a turn divided the parents' quarters from the children's, she got up and went softly to meet him. But the little boys were asleep, long ago. She took his two clean hands, dryly cold from the winter night, in hers, and then they crept along together. In the bedroom, when she had shut the door behind them, she was cold and trembling, as if she too had just found shelter.

He had to leave not long after the time the meeting would end; now, because this was her own bed, in her own home, she lay there naked, flung back under the disarray of bedclothes, and watched him dress alone. He took her brush and put it through his hair before the mirror, with a quick, knowing look at himself. He sat on the bed, like a doctor, to embrace her a last time. She watched him softly release the handle of the door, almost without a click, as he closed it on her, heard him going evenly, quietly down the corridor, listened to the faint creak and stir of him making his way through the big living room, and then, after a pause, heard the clip of his footsteps dying away across the terrace. The engine of the car started up: shadows from its lights flew across the bedroom windows.

She put up her hand to switch off the bed lamp but did not move her head or body. She lay in the dark for a long time just as he had left her; perhaps she slept. There seemed to be a dark wind blowing through her hollow mind; she was awake, and there was a night wind come up, the cold gale of the winter veld, pressing against the walls and windows like pressure in one's ears. A thorn branch scrabbled on the terrace wall. She heard dry leaves swirl and trail across the flagstones. And irregularly, at long intervals, a door banged without engaging its latch. She tried to sleep or to return to sleep, but some part of her mind waited for the impact of the door in the wind. And it came, again and again. Slowly, reasoned thought cohered round the sound: she identified the direction from which it came, her mind travelled through the house the way he had gone, and arrived at the terrace door. The door banged, with a swinging shudder, again.

He's left the door open. She saw it; saw the gaping door, and the wind belly-ing the long curtains and sending papers skimming about the room, the leaves sailing in and slithering across the floors. The whole house was filling up with the wind. There had been burglaries in the suburb lately. This was one of the few houses without an alarm system—she and Arthur had refused to imprison themselves in the white man's fear of attack on himself and his possessions. Yet now the door was open like the door of a deserted house and she found herself believing, like any other suburban matron, that someone must enter. They would come in unheard, with that wind, and approach through the house, black men with their knives in their hands. She, who had never submitted to this sort of fear ever in her life, could hear them coming, hear them breathe under their dirty rag masks and their *tsotsi* caps. They had killed an old man on a farm out-side Pretoria last week; someone described in the papers as a mother of two had held them off, at her bedside, with a golf club. Multiple wounds, the old man had received, multiple wounds.

She was empty, unable to summon anything but this stale fantasy, shared with the whole town, the whole white population. She lay there possessed by it, and she thought, she violently longed—they will come straight into the room and stick a knife in me. No time to cry out. Quick. Deep. Over.

The light came instead. Her sons began to play the noisy whispering games of children, about the house in the very early morning.

Graham Greene

· ·

TWO GENTLE PEOPLE

They sat on a bench in the Parc Monceau for a long time without speaking to one another. It was a hopeful day of early summer with a spray of white clouds lapping across the sky in front of a small breeze: at any moment the wind might drop and the sky become empty and entirely blue, but it was too late now—the sun would have set first.

In younger people it might have been a day for a chance encounter—secret behind the long barrier of perambulators with only babies and nurses in sight. But they were both of them middle-aged, and neither was inclined to cherish an illusion of possessing a lost youth, though he was better looking than he believed, with his silky old-world moustache like a badge of good behaviour, and she was prettier than the looking-glass ever told her. Modesty and disillusion gave them something in common; though they were separated by five feet of green metal they could have been a married couple who had grown to resemble each other. Pigeons like old grey tennis balls rolled unnoticed around their feet. They each occasionally looked at a watch, though never at one another. For both of them this period of solitude and peace was limited.

The man was tall and thin. He had what are called sensitive features, and the cliché fitted him; his face was comfortably, though handsomely, banal—there would be no ugly surprises when he spoke, for a man may be sensitive without imagination. He had carried with him an umbrella which suggested caution. In her case one noticed first the long and lovely legs as unsensual as those in a society portrait. From her expression she found the summer day sad, yet she was reluctant to obey the command of her watch and go—somewhere—inside.

They would never have spoken to each other if two teen-aged louts had not passed by, one with a blaring radio slung over his shoulder, the other kicking out at the preoccupied pigeons. One of his kicks found a random mark, and on they went in a din of pop, leaving the pigeon lurching on the path.

The man rose, grasping his umbrella like a riding-whip. 'Infernal young scoundrels,' he exclaimed, and the phrase sounded more Edwardian because of the faint American intonation—Henry James might surely have employed it.

'The poor bird,' the woman said. The bird struggled upon the gravel, scatter-

ing little stones. One wing hung slack and a leg must have been broken too, for
the pigeon swivelled round in circles unable to rise. The other pigeons moved
away, with disinterest, searching the gravel for crumbs.

'If you would look away for just a minute,' the man said. He laid his umbrella
down again and walked rapidly to the bird where it thrashed around; then he
picked it up, and quickly and expertly he wrung its neck—it was a kind of skill
anyone of breeding ought to possess. He looked round for a refuse bin in which
he tidily deposited the body.

'There was nothing else to do,' he remarked apologetically when he returned.

'I could not myself have done it,' the woman said, carefully grammatical in a
foreign tongue.

'Taking life is *our* privilege,' he replied with irony rather than pride.

When he sat down the distance between them had narrowed; they were able
to speak freely about the weather and the first real day of summer. The last week
had been unseasonably cold, and even today. . . . He admired the way in which
she spoke English and apologized for his own lack of French, but she reassured
him: it was no ingrained talent. She had been 'finished' at an English school at
Margate.

'That's a seaside resort, isn't it?'

'The sea always seemed very grey,' she told him, and for a while they lapsed
into separate silences. Then perhaps thinking of the dead pigeon she asked him
if he had been in the army. 'No, I was over forty when the war came,' he said. 'I
served on a government mission, in India. I became very fond of India.' He
began to describe to her Agra, Lucknow, the old city of Delhi, his eyes alight
with memories. The new Delhi he did not like, built by a Britisher—Lut-Lut-
Lut? No matter. It reminded him of Washington.

'Then you do not like Washington?'

'To tell you the truth,' he said, 'I am not very happy in my own country. You
see, i like old things. I found myself more at home—can you believe it?—in
India, even with the British. And now in France I find it's the same. My grandfather was British Consul in Nice.'

'The Promenade des Anglais was very new then,' she said.

'Yes, but it aged. What we Americans build never ages beautifully. The
Chrysler Building, Hilton hotels . . .'

'Are you married?' she asked. He hesitated a moment before replying, 'Yes,'
as though he wished to be quite, quite accurate. He put out his hand and felt for
his umbrella—it gave him confidence in this surprising situation of talking so
openly to a stranger.

'I ought not to have asked you,' she said, still careful with her grammar.

'Why not?' He excused her awkwardly.

'I was interested in what you said.' She gave him a little smile. 'The question
came. It was *imprévu.*'

'Are *you* married?' he asked, but only to put her at her ease, for he could see
her ring.

'Yes.'

By this time they seemed to know a great deal about each other, and he felt it was churlish not to surrender his identity. He said, 'My name is Greaves. Henry C. Greaves.'

'Mine is Marie-Claire. Marie-Claire Duval.'

'What a lovely afternoon it has been,' the man called Greaves said.

'But it gets a little cold when the sun sinks.' They escaped from each other again with regret.

'A beautiful umbrella you have,' she said, and it was quite true—the gold band was distinguished, and even from a few feet away one could see there was a monogram engraved there—an H certainly, entwined perhaps with a C or a G.

'A present,' he said without pleasure.

'I admired so much the way you acted with the pigeon. As for me I am *lâche*.'

'That I am quite sure is not true,' he said kindly.

'Oh, it is. It is.'

'Only in the sense that we are all cowards about something.'

'You are not,' she said, remembering the pigeon with gratitude.

'Oh yes, I am,' he replied, 'in one whole area of life.' He seemed on the brink of a personal revelation, and she clung to his coat-tail to pull him back; she literally clung to it, for lifting the edge of his jacket she exclaimed, 'You have been touching some wet paint.' The ruse succeeded; he became solicitous about her dress, but examining the bench they both agreed the source was not there. 'They have been painting on my staircase,' he said.

'You have a house here?'

'No, an apartment on the fourth floor.'

'With an *ascenseur?*'

'Unfortunately not,' he said sadly. 'It's a very old house in the *dix-septième*.'

The door of his unknown life had opened a crack, and she wanted to give something of her own life in return, but not too much. A 'brink' would give her vertigo. She said, 'My apartment is only too depressingly new. In the *huitième*. The door opens electrically without being touched. Like in an airport.'

A strong current of revelation carried them along. He learned how she always bought her cheeses in the Place de la Madeleine—it was quite an expedition from her side of the *huitième*, near the Avenue George V, and once she had been rewarded by finding Tante Yvonne, the General's wife, at her elbow choosing a Brie. He on the other hand bought his cheeses in the Rue de Tocqueville, only round the corner from his apartment.

'You yourself?'

'Yes, I do the marketing,' he said in a voice suddenly abrupt.

She said, 'It is a little cold now. I think we should go.'

'Do you come to the Parc often?'

'It is the first time.'

'What a strange coincidence,' he said. 'It's the first time for me too. Even though I live close by.'

'And I live quite far away.'

They looked at one another with a certain awe, aware of the mysteries of providence. He said, 'I don't suppose you would be free to have a little dinner with me.'

Excitement made her lapse into French. *'Je suis libre, mais vous . . . votre femme . . . ?'*

'She is dining elsewhere,' he said. 'And your husband?'

'He will not be back before eleven.'

He suggested the Brasserie Lorraine, which was only a few minutes' walk away, and she was glad that he had not chosen something more chic or more flamboyant. The heavy bourgeois atmosphere of the *brasserie* gave her confidence, and, though she had small appetite herself, she was glad to watch the comfortable military progress down the ranks of the sauerkraut trolley. The menu too was long enough to give them time to readjust to the startling intimacy of dining together. When the order had been given, they both began to speak at once. 'I never expected . . .'

'It's funny the way things happen,' he added, laying unintentionally a heavy inscribed monument over that conversation.

'Tell me about your grandfather, the consul.'

'I never knew him,' he said. It was much more difficult to talk on a restaurant sofa than on a park bench.

'Why did your father go to America?'

'The spirit of adventure perhaps,' he said. 'And I suppose it was the spirit of adventure which brought me back to live in Europe. America didn't mean Coca-Cola and *Time-Life* when my father was young.'

'And have you found adventure? How stupid of me to ask. Of course you married here?'

'I brought my wife with me,' he said. 'Poor Patience.'

'Poor?'

'She is fond of Coca-Cola.'

'You can get it here,' she said, this time with intentional stupidity.

'Yes.'

The wine-waiter came and he ordered a Sancerre. 'If that will suit you?'

'I know so little about wine,' she said.

'I thought all French people . . .'

'We leave it to our husbands,' she said, and in his turn he felt an obscure hurt. The sofa was shared by a husband now as well as a wife, and for a while the *sole meunière* gave them an excuse not to talk. And yet silence was not a genuine escape. In the silence the two ghosts would have become more firmly planted, if the woman had not found the courage to speak.

'Have you any children?' she asked.

'No. Have you?'

'No.'

'Are you sorry?'

She said, 'I suppose one is always sorry to have missed something.'

'I'm glad at least I did not miss the Parc Monceau today.'

'Yes, I am glad too.'

The silence after that was a comfortable silence: the two ghosts went away and left them alone. Once their fingers touched over the sugar-castor (they had chosen strawberries). Neither of them had any desire for further questions; they seemed to know each other more completely than they knew anyone else. It was like a happy marriage; the stage of discovery was over—they had passed the test of jealousy, and now they were tranquil in their middle age. Time and death remained the only enemies, and coffee was like the warning of old age. After that it was necessary to hold sadness at bay with a brandy, though not successfully. It was as though they had experienced a lifetime, which was measured as with butterflies in hours.

He remarked of the passing head waiter, 'He looks like an undertaker.'

'Yes,' she said. So he paid the bill and they went outside. It was a death-agony they were too gentle to resist for long. He asked, 'Can I see you home?'

'I would rather not. Really not. You live so close.'

'We could have another drink on the *terrasse?*' he suggested with half a sad heart.

'It would do nothing more for us,' she said. 'The evening was perfect. *Tu es vraiment gentil.*' She noticed too late that she had used '*tu*' and she hoped his French was bad enough for him not to have noticed. They did not exchange addresses or telephone numbers, for neither of them dared to suggest it: the hour had come too late in both their lives. He found her a taxi and she drove away towards the great illuminated Arc, and he walked home by the Rue Jouffroy, slowly. What is cowardice in the young is wisdom in the old, but all the same one can be ashamed of wisdom.

Marie-Claire walked through the self-opening doors and thought, as she always did, of airports and escapes. On the sixth floor she let herself into the flat. An abstract painting in cruel tones of scarlet and yellow faced the door and treated her like a stranger.

She went straight to her room, as softly as possible, locked the door and sat down on her single bed. Through the wall she could hear her husband's voice and laugh. She wondered who was with him tonight—Toni or François. François had painted the abstract picture, and Toni, who danced in ballet, always claimed, especially before strangers, to have modelled for the little stone phallus with painted eyes that had a place of honour in the living-room. She began to undress. While the voice next door spun its web, images of the bench in the Parc Monceau returned and of the sauerkraut trolley in the Brasserie Lorraine. If he had heard her come in, her husband would soon proceed to action: it excited him to know that she was a witness. The voice said, 'Pierre, Pierre,' reproachfully. Pierre was a new name to her. She spread her fingers on the dressing-table to take off her rings and she thought of the sugar-castor for the strawberries, but at the sound of the little yelps and giggles from next door the sugar-castor turned into the phallus with painted eyes. She lay down and screwed beads of wax into her ears, and she shut her eyes and thought how different things might have been if fifteen years ago she had sat on a bench in the Parc Monceau, watching a man with pity killing a pigeon.

'I can smell a woman on you,' Patience Greaves said with pleasure, sitting up against two pillows. The top pillow was punctured with brown cigarette burns.

'Oh no, you can't. It's your imagination, dear.'

'You said you would be home by ten.'

'It's only twenty past now.'

'You've been up in the Rue de Douai, haven't you, in one of those bars, look-ing for a *fille*.'

'I sat in the Parc Monceau and then I had dinner at the Brasserie Lorraine. Can I give you your drops?'

'You want me to sleep so that I won't expect anything. That's it, isn't it, you're too old now to do it twice.'

He mixed the drops from the carafe of water on the table between the twin beds. Anything he might say would be wrong when Patience was in a mood like this. Poor Patience, he thought, holding out the drops towards the face crowned with red curls, how she misses America—she will never believe that the Coca-Cola tastes the same here. Luckily this would not be one of their worst nights, for she drank from the glass without further argument, while he sat beside her and remembered the street outside the *brasserie* and how—by accident he was sure—he had been called '*tu*'.

'What are you thinking?' Patience asked. 'Are you still in the Rue de Douai?'

'I was only thinking that things might have been different,' he said.

It was the biggest protest he had ever allowed himself to make against the condition of life.

Wolfgang Hildesheimer

. . . .

WHY I TRANSFORMED MYSELF INTO A NIGHTINGALE

Acting on the strength of my convictions, I transformed myself into a nightingale. Since neither the reason nor the resolve necessary for this sort of action lies within the realm of the ordinary, I think the story of this metamorphosis is worth telling.

My father was a zoologist. Because he thought the literature on batrachia was incompetent and rather inaccurate, he spent his life writing a multivolume study on the subject which became famous in scholarly circles. This work never really appealed to me, although we had lots of frogs and salamanders at home whose lives and patterns of development would have merited my study.

My mother had been an actress before she married, and she achieved her greatest triumph as Ophelia at the Zwickau State Theater; she never surpassed this high watermark. To this I owe my name Laertes, certainly a euphonious but somewhat peculiar name. Nevertheless, I am grateful that she didn't name me Polonius or Guildenstern—but of course it doesn't matter now.

When I was five years old, my parents gave me a magic set. I learned how to make a certain amount of childish magic before I could read or write. With the powder and instruments contained in the kit, I could turn colorless water red and back to colorless water again, halve a wooden egg simply by turning it upside down (while the other half disappeared without a trace), and make a handkerchief change colors by pulling it through a ring. In short, there wasn't anything in the kit—as is the case with most toys—which represented reality in miniature. The manufacturer of this toy seemed intent on ignoring its educational value and suppressing the child's awakening sense of utility. This experience had a decided influence on my later development in that the joy of changing one useless object into another taught me to search for happiness in knowledge which serves no practical purpose. Certainly, I hadn't found this happiness before my metamorphosis.

Above all, my ambition was aroused. Soon the magic kit no longer satisfied me because in the meantime I had learned to read, and on the cover I read the demeaning phrase "The Little Magician."

I still remember the afternoon when I went into my father's study and asked him if I could have magic lessons. He was deep in the world of batrachia and looked at me absentmindedly. I kept on asking; soon he gave in. I can't escape the impression that he thought it had something to do with piano lessons, which I also took, because he asked me a few times afterward whether I could play Czerny etudes yet. I said yes because I was sure I would never have to prove it.

I took lessons from a magician who appeared at several vaudeville shows in town and who, I had heard, had been a great success in London and Paris. After a few years—I went to high school in the meantime—I had progressed far enough so that I could pull a rabbit out of a top hat. I remember the first performance I gave for my parents and close relatives. My parents were proud of my talents, which I had acquired on the side, so to speak. They thought I could practice them in the future, instead of playing chamber music with friends, while I worked at my career (something about which they had no really definite ideas). But I had other plans.

I outgrew my teacher and began experimenting on my own. I didn't neglect my academic education, though. I read a lot and went around with school friends whose patterns of development I observed. One friend who had been given an electric train in his childhood was preparing for a career with the railroad; another who had played with tin soldiers decided on a career as a military officer. In this way, the work force was regulated by early influences, and each person latched on to his occupation, or rather, the occupation latched on to him. But I decided to arrange my life according to other considerations.

I might mention here that I did not arrive at the decision I made during the next year because I wanted to appear eccentric or unique in the eyes of others. It was more my growing awareness that I couldn't select a conventional, bourgeois profession without in some way interfering with other people's lives. The career of a bureaucrat seemed particularly immoral to me, but I rejected other, more accepted humanitarian careers as well. To me, the work of a doctor who could save human life through his interference was highly suspect, because it might be that the person he saved was an out-and-out scoundrel whose life hundreds of oppressed people fervently wished would end.

When I came to this realization, I came to yet another, namely that only the momentary state of things can be perceived, that it is merely idle speculation to try to draw conclusions or gather knowledge from experience. I decided to spend my life in leisure and contemplate nothing. I got two turtles, sat down on a lounge chair, and watched the birds above me and the turtles beneath me. I had given up magic because my art had reached a state of perfection. I felt that I was able to change people into animals. I didn't make use of this ability, though, because I believed that this sort of interference into another person's life was completely unjustifiable.

It was at this time that my desire to become a bird first appeared. At first I didn't want to admit this wish to myself because it meant defeat to a certain extent: I hadn't yet succeeded in enjoying the pure existence of a bird without wishing for more beyond that; my feelings were tainted by desire. However, I was weak enough to toy with the idea of doing it, and indeed, I was proud of being able to fulfill my wish when and as soon as it pleased me. I needed only a test of my art.

The opportunity soon presented itself. One afternoon while I was sitting in the garden observing my turtles, my friend Mr. Werhahn visited me. He was a newspaper editor. (Someone had given him a typewriter when he was young.) He sat down on the lounge chair next to me and began to complain, first about malicious readers, then about incompetent journalists. I didn't say anything; people who are complaining usually don't appreciate interruptions. At last he finished and said, "I've had it," and as one of my turtles crawled under the lounge chair, he said, "Boy, I wish I were a turtle." These were his last words, because I waved my magic wand and transformed him. Mr. Werhahn's journalistic career was over, but his life was probably lengthened by this metamorphosis because turtles live to be quite old. It was a great triumph for me. What's more, I now had three turtles. (Just for the record, I'd like to assure you that I purchased the other two animals as such.)

I used my art one other time before my own metamorphosis. I remember this incident not without a twinge of uneasiness, because I am not completely certain that I handled things properly.

One afternoon in June—I had spent the day in the country—I was sitting in the garden of an inn under a linden tree, drinking a glass of apple cider. I was enjoying the solitude. But soon a group of five young girls came and sat down at a table near mine. The girls were gay and pretty, but I was irritated by the disturbance and became even more irritated when they began to sing, accompanied by one of them on the mandolin. First they sang "Must I then, Must I then be gone from the town," and next:

> "Oh, if I were a sparrow,
> And I had two wings,
> Into your arms I'd fly."

This song always seemed rather silly to me because a bird naturally has two wings, doesn't it? But here was an express wish to be a bird, which prompted me, when the song was over, to transform the singers into a flock of sparrows. I went over to their table and waved my magic wand, so that for a moment it seemed as if I wanted to conduct the quintet—but not for long, because the five shrieking sparrows flew up and away. Only five half-empty glasses of cider, a couple of nibbled sandwiches, and the fallen mandolin testified that a few seconds before, full, young lives were being lived.

Surveying this desolate scene, I felt a slight sense of remorse come over me, because I thought that perhaps the singing of the song did not express absolutely and unequivocally the desire to be a bird; and besides, the phrase "If I were bird" doesn't necessarily express the desire to be bird, even though that is the natural implication of the song (if you can speak of an implication in such a song). I had the feeling that I had acted emotionally, under the influence of my (certainly justified) irritation. I thought that this wasn't worthy of me, so I decided not to delay my own metamorphosis any longer. I would like to make clear that it wasn't fear of the consequences of my deed, of any criminal prosecution, which finally persuaded me to take on another form. (After all, I could easily have changed the police officers at the time of my arrest into toy fox terriers!) It was more the certainty that, for technical reasons, I would never find the unspoiled peace I needed for the pure enjoyment of things, undisturbed by the will. Somewhere a dog would always bark, a child scream, or a young girl sing.

My choice of the form of the nightingale was by no means arbitrary. I wanted to be a bird because the thought of being able to fly from one tree to another was very appealing. Furthermore, I wanted to sing because I love music. The thought that I would interfere in the life of someone else whose sleep I might disturb did occur to me. But now that I am no longer human, I have put away my human thoughts and interests. My ethic is now the ethic of a nightingale.

In September of last year, I went to my bedroom, opened the window wide, cast my spell, and flew away. I've had no regrets ever since.

Now it is May. It is dusk, and soon it will be dark. Then I begin to sing, or, as humans say, strike up my song.

Translated from the German by Susan Perry Alexander

Yasunari Kawabata

. . . .

ONE ARM

"I can let you have one of my arms for the night," said the girl. She took off her right arm at the shoulder and, with her left hand, laid it on my knee.

"Thank you." I looked at my knee. The warmth of the arm came through.

"I'll put the ring on. To remind you that it's mine." She smiled and raised her left arm to my chest. "Please." With but one arm, it was difficult for her to take the ring off.

"An engagement ring?"

"No. A keepsake. From my mother."

It was silver, set with small diamonds.

"Perhaps it does look like an engagement ring, but I don't mind. I wear it, and then when I take it off it's as if I were leaving my mother."

Raising the arm on my knee, I removed the ring and slipped it on the ring finger.

"Is this the one?"

"Yes." She nodded. "It will seem artificial unless the elbow and fingers bend. You won't like that. Let me make them bend for you."

She took her right arm from my knee and pressed her lips gently to it. Then she pressed them to the finger joints.

"Now they'll move."

"Thank you." I took the arm back. "Do you suppose it will speak? Will it speak to me?"

"It only does what an arm does. If it talks I'll be afraid to have it back. But try anyway. It should at least listen to what you say, if you're good to it."

"I'll be good to it."

"I'll see you again," she said, touching the right arm with her left hand, as if to infuse it with a spirit of its own. "You're his, but just for the night."

As she looked at me she seemed to be fighting back tears.

"I don't suppose you'll try to change it for your own arm," she said. "But it will be all right. Go ahead, do."

"Thank you."

I put her arm in my raincoat and went out into the foggy streets. I feared I

351

might be thought odd if I took a taxi or a streetcar. There would be a scene if the arm, now separated from the girl's body, were to cry out, or to weep.

I held it against my chest, toward the side, my right hand on the roundness at the shoulder joint. It was concealed by the raincoat, and I had to touch the coat from time to time with my left hand to be sure that the arm was still there. Probably I was making sure not of the arm's presence but of my own happiness.

She had taken off the arm at the point I liked. It was plump and round—was it at the top of the arm or the beginning of the shoulder? The roundness was that of a beautiful Occidental girl, rare in a Japanese. It was in the girl herself, a clean, elegant roundness, like a sphere glowing with a faint, fresh light. When the girl was no longer clean that gentle roundness would fade, grow flabby. Something that lasted for a brief moment in the life of a beautiful girl, the roundness of the arm made me feel the roundness of her body. Her breasts would not be large. Shy, only large enough to cup in the hands, they would have a clinging softness and strength. And in the roundness of the arm I could feel her legs as she walked along. She would carry them lightly, like a small bird, or a butterfly moving from flower to flower. There would be the same subtle melody in the tip of her tongue when she kissed.

It was the season for changing to sleeveless dresses. The girl's shoulder, newly bared, had the color of skin not used to the raw touch of the air. It had the glow of a bud moistened in the shelter of spring and not yet ravaged by summer. I had that morning bought a magnolia bud and put it in a glass vase; and the roundness of the girl's arm was like the great, white bud. Her dress was cut back more radically than most sleeveless dresses. The joint at the shoulder was exposed, and the shoulder itself. The dress, of dark green silk, almost black, had a soft sheen. The girl was in the rounded slope of the shoulders, which drew a gentle wave with the swelling of the back. Seen obliquely from behind, the flesh from the round shoulders to the long, slender neck came to an abrupt halt at the base of the upswept hair, and the black hair seemed to cast a glowing shadow over the roundness of the shoulders.

She had sensed that I thought her beautiful, and so she lent me her right arm for the roundness there at the shoulder.

Carefully hidden under my raincoat, the girl's arm was colder than my hand. I was giddy from the racing of my heart, and I knew that my hand would be hot. I wanted the warmth to stay as it was, the warmth of the girl herself. And the slight coolness in my hand passed on to me the pleasure of the arm. It was like her breasts, not yet touched by a man.

The fog yet thicker, the night threatened rain, and wet my uncovered hair. I could hear a radio speaking from the back room of a closed pharmacy. It announced that three planes unable to land in the fog had been circling the airport for a half hour. It went on to draw the attention of listeners to the fact that on damp nights clocks were likely to go wrong, and that on such nights the springs had a tendency to break if wound too tight. I looked for the lights of the circling planes, but could not see them. There was no sky. The pressing dampness invaded my ears, to give a wet sound like the wriggling of myriads of distant earthworms. I stood before the pharmacy awaiting further admonitions. I learned that on such nights the fierce beasts in the zoo, the lions and tigers and leopards and the rest, roared their resentment at the dampness, and that we were now to hear it. There was a roaring like the roaring of the earth. I then learned that pregnant women and despondent persons should go to bed early on such nights, and that women who applied perfume directly to their skins would find it difficult to remove afterwards.

At the roaring of the beasts, I moved off, and the warning about perfume followed me. That angry roaring had unsettled me, and I moved on lest my uneasiness be transmitted to the girl's arm. The girl was neither pregnant nor despondent, but it seemed to me that tonight, with only one arm, she should take the advice of the radio and go quietly to bed. I hoped that she would sleep peacefully.

As I started across the street I pressed my left hand against my raincoat. A horn sounded. Something brushed my side, and I twisted away. Perhaps the arm had been frightened by the horn. The fingers were clenched.

"Don't worry," I said. "It was a long way off. It couldn't see. That's why it honked."

Because I was holding something important to me, I had looked in both directions. The sound of the horn had been so far away that I had thought it must be meant for someone else. I looked in the direction from which it came, but could see no one. I could see only the headlights. They widened into a blur of faint purple. A strange color for headlights. I stood on the curb when I had crossed and watched it pass. A young woman in vermilion was driving. It seemed to me that she turned toward me and bowed. I wanted to run off, fearing that the girl had come for her arm. Then I remembered that she would hardly be able to drive with only one. But had not the woman in the car seen what I was carrying? Had she not sensed it with a woman's intuition? I would have to take care not to encounter another of the sex before I reached my apartment. The rear lights were also a faint purple. I still did not see the car. In the ashen fog a lavender blur floated up and moved away.

"She is driving for no reason, for no reason at all except to be driving. And while she drives she will simply disappear," I muttered to myself. "And what was that sitting in the back seat?"

Nothing, apparently. Was it because I went around carrying girls' arms that I felt so unnerved by emptiness? The car she drove carried the clammy night fog. And something about her had turned it faintly purple in the headlights. If not from her own body, whence had come that purplish light? Could the arm I concealed have so clothed in emptiness a woman driving alone on such a night? Had she nodded at the girl's arm from her car? Perhaps on such a night there were angels and ghosts abroad protecting women. Perhaps she had ridden not in a car but in a purple light. Her drive had not been empty. She had spied out my secret.

I made my way back to my apartment without further encounters. I stood listening outside the door. The light of a firefly skimmed over my head and disappeared. It was too large and too strong for a firefly. I recoiled backwards. Several more lights like fireflies skimmed past. They disappeared even before the heavy fog could suck them in. Had a will-o'-the-wisp, a deathfire of some sort, run on ahead of me, to await my return? But then I saw that it was a swarm of small moths. Catching the light at the door, the wings of the moths glowed like fireflies. Too large to be fireflies, and yet, for moths, so small as to invite the mistake.

Avoiding the automatic elevator, I made my way stealthily up the narrow stairs to the third floor. Not being left-handed, I had difficulty unlocking the door. The harder I tried the more my hand trembled—as if in terror after a crime. Something would be waiting for me inside the room, a room where I lived in solitude; and was not the solitude a presence? With the girl's arm I was no longer alone. And so perhaps my own solitude waited there to intimidate me.

"Go on ahead," I said, taking out the girl's arm when at length I had opened the door. "Welcome to my room. I'll turn on the light."

"Are you afraid of something?" the arm seemed to say. "Is something here?"

"You think there might be?"

"I smell something."

"Smell? It must be me that you smell. Don't you see traces of my shadow, up there in the darkness? Look carefully. Maybe my shadow was waiting for me to come back."

"It's a sweet smell."

"Ah—the magnolia," I answered brightly. I was glad it was not the moldy smell of my loneliness. A magnolia bud befitted my winsome guest. I was getting used to the dark. Even in pitch blackness I knew where everything was.

"Let me turn on the light." Coming from the arm, a strange remark. "I haven't been in your room before."

"Thank you. I'll be very pleased. No one but me has ever turned on the lights here before."

I held the arm to the switch by the door. All five lights went on at once: at the ceiling, on the table, by the bed, in the kitchen, in the bathroom. I had not thought they could be so bright.

The magnolia was in enormous bloom. That morning it had been in bud. It could have only just bloomed, and yet there were stamens on the table. Curious, I looked more closely at the stamens than at the white flower. As I picked up one or two and gazed at them, the girl's arm, laid on the table, began to move, the fingers like spanworms, and gathered the stamens in its hand. I went to throw them in the wastebasket.

"What a strong smell. It sinks right into my skin. Help me."

"You must be tired. It wasn't an easy trip. Suppose you rest awhile."

I laid the arm on the bed and sat down beside it. I stroked it gently.

"How pretty. I like it." The arm would be speaking of the bed cover. Flowers were printed in three colors on an azure ground, somewhat lively for a man who lived alone. "So this is where we spend the night. I'll be very quiet."

"Oh?"

"I'll be beside you and not beside you."

The hand took mine gently. The nails, carefully polished, were a faint pink. The tips extended well beyond the fingers.

Against my own short, thick nails, hers possessed a strange beauty, as if they belonged to no human creature. With such fingertips, a woman perhaps transcended mere humanity. Or did she pursue womanhood itself? A shell luminous from the pattern inside it, a petal bathed in dew—I thought of the obvious likenesses. Yet I could think of no shell or petal whose color and shape resembled them. They were the nails on the girl's fingers, comparable to nothing else. More translucent than a delicate shell, than a thin petal, they seemed to hold a dew of tragedy. Every day and every night her energies were poured into the polishing of this tragic beauty. It penetrated my solitude. Perhaps my yearning, my solitude, transformed them into dew.

I rested her little finger on the index finger of my free hand, gazing at the long, narrow nail as I rubbed it with my thumb. My finger touched the tip of hers, sheltered by the nail. The finger bent, and the elbow too.

"Does it tickle?" I asked. "It must."

I had spoken carelessly. I knew that the tips of a woman's fingers were sensitive when the nails were long. And so I had told the girl's arm that I had known other women.

From one who was not a great deal older than the girl who had lent me the arm but far more mature in her experience of men, I had heard that fingertips thus hidden by nails were often acutely sensitive. One became used to touching things not with the fingertips but with the nails, and the fingertips therefore tickled when something came against them.

I had shown astonishment at this discovery, and she had gone on: "You're, say, cooking—or eating—and something touches your fingers, and you find yourself hunching your shoulders, it seems so dirty."

Was it the food that seemed unclean, or the tip of the nail? Whatever touched her fingers made her writhe with its uncleanness. Her own cleanness would leave behind a drop of tragic dew, there under the long shadow of the nail. One could not assume that for each of the ten fingers there would be a separate drop of dew.

It was natural that I should want all the more to touch those fingertips, but I held myself back. My solitude held me back. She was a woman on whose body few tender spots could be expected to remain.

And on the body of the girl who had lent me the arm they would be beyond counting. Perhaps, toying with the fingertips of such a girl, I would feel not guilt but affection. But she had not lent me the arm for such mischief. I must not make a comedy of her gesture.

"The window." I noticed not that the window itself was open but that the curtain was undrawn.

"Will anything look in?" asked the girl's arm.

"Some man or woman. Nothing else."

"Nothing human would see me. If anything it would be a self. Yours."

"Self? What is that? Where is it?"

"Far away," said the arm, as if singing in consolation. "People walk around looking for selves, far away."

"And do they come upon them?"

"Far away," said the arm once more.

It seemed to me that the arm and the girl herself were an infinity apart.

Would the arm be able to return to the girl, so far away? Would I be able to take it back, so far away? The arm lay peacefully trusting me; and would the girl be sleeping in the same peaceful confidence? Would there not be harshness, a nightmare? Had she not seemed to be fighting back tears when she parted with it? The arm was now in my room, which the girl herself had not visited.

The dampness clouded the window, like a toad's belly stretched over it. The fog seemed to withhold rain in mid-air, and the night outside the window lost distance, even while it was wrapped in limitless distance. There were no roofs to be seen, no horns to be heard.

"I'll close the window," I said, reaching for the curtain. It too was damp. My face loomed up in the window, younger than my thirty-three years. I did not hesitate to pull the curtain, however. My face disappeared.

Suddenly a remembered window. On the ninth floor of a hotel, two little girls in wide red skirts were playing in the window. Very similar children in similar clothes, perhaps twins, Occidentals. They pounded at the glass, pushing it with their shoulders and shoving at each other. Their mother knitted, her back to the window. If the large pane were to have broken or come loose, they would have fallen from the ninth floor. It was only I who thought them in danger. Their mother was quite unconcerned. The glass was in fact so solid that there was no danger.

"It's beautiful," said the arm on the bed as I turned from the window. Perhaps she was speaking of the curtain, in the same flowered pattern as the bed cover.

"Oh? But it's faded from the sun and almost ready to go." I sat down on the bed and took the arm on my knee. "This is what is beautiful. More beautiful than anything."

Taking the palm of the hand in my own right palm, and the shoulder in my left hand, I flexed the elbow, and then again.

"Behave yourself," said the arm, as if smiling softly. "Having fun?"

"Not in the least."

A smile did come over the arm, crossing it like light. It was exactly the fresh smile on the girl's cheek.

I knew the smile. Elbows on the table, she would fold her hands loosely and rest her chin or cheek on them. The pose should have been inelegant in a young girl; but there was about it a lightly engaging quality that made expressions like "elbows on the table" seem inappropriate. The roundness of the shoulders, the fingers, the chin, the cheeks, the ears, the long, slender neck, the hair, all came together in a single harmonious movement. Using knife and fork deftly, first and little fingers bent, she would raise them ever so slightly from time to time. Food would pass the small lips and she would swallow—I had before me less a person at dinner than an inviting music of hands and face and throat. The light of her smile flowed across the skin of her arm.

The arm seemed to smile because, as I flexed it, very gentle waves passed over the firm, delicate muscles, to send waves of light and shadow over the smooth skin. Earlier, when I had touched the fingertips under the long nails, the light passing over the arm as the elbow bent had caught my eye. It was that, and not any impulse toward mischief, that had made me bend and unbend her arm. I stopped, and gazed at it as it lay stretched out on my knee. Fresh lights and shadows were still passing over it.

"You ask if I'm having fun. You realize that I have permission to change you for my own arm?"

"I do."

"Somehow I'm afraid to."

"Oh?"

"May I?"

"Please."

I heard the permission granted, and wondered whether I could accept it. "Say it again. Say 'please.'"

"Please, please."

I remembered. It was like the voice of a woman who had decided to give herself to me, one not as beautiful as the girl who had lent me the arm. Perhaps there was something a little strange about her.

"Please," she had said, gazing at me. I had put my fingers on her eyelids and closed them. Her voice was trembling. "'Jesus wept. Then said the Jews, Behold how he loved her!'"

"Her" was a mistake for "him." It was the story of the dead Lazarus. Perhaps, herself a woman, she had remembered it wrong, perhaps she had made the substitution intentionally.

The words, so inappropriate to the scene, had shaken me. I gazed at her, wondering if tears would start from the closed eyes.

She opened them and raised her shoulders. I pushed her down with my arm. "You're hurting me!" She put her hand to the back of her head.

There was a small spot of blood on the white pillow. Parting her hair, I put my lips to the drop of blood swelling on her head.

"It doesn't matter." She took out all her hairpins. "I bleed easily. At the slightest touch."

A hairpin had pierced her skin. A shudder seemed about to pass through her shoulders, but she controlled herself.

Although I think I understand how a woman feels when she gives herself to a man, there is still something unexplained about the act. What is it to her? Why should she wish to do it, why should she take the initiative? I could never really accept the surrender, even knowing that the body of every woman was made for it. Even now, old as I am, it seems strange. And the ways in which various women go about it: unalike if you wish, or similar perhaps, or even identical. Is that not strange? Perhaps the strangeness I find in it all is the curiosity of a younger man, perhaps the despair of one advanced in years. Or perhaps some spiritual debility I suffer from.

Her anguish was not common to all women in the act of surrender. And it was with her only the one time. The silver thread was cut, the golden bowl destroyed.

"Please," the arm had said, and so reminded me of the other girl; but were the two voices in fact similar? Had they not sounded alike because the words were the same? Had the arm acquired independence in this measure of the body from which it was separated? And were the words not the act of giving itself up, of being ready for anything, without restraint or responsibility or remorse? It seemed to me that if I were to accept the invitation and change the arm for my own I would be bringing untold pain to the girl.

I gazed at the arm on my knee. There was a shadow at the inside of the elbow. It seemed that I might be able to suck it in. I pressed it to my lips, to gather in the shadow.

"It tickles. Do behave yourself." The arm was around my neck, avoiding my lips.

"Just when I was having a good drink."

"And what were you drinking?"

I did not answer.

"What were you drinking?"

"The smell of light? Of skin."

The fog seemed thicker; even the magnolia leaves seemed wet. What other warnings would issue from the radio? I started toward my table radio and stopped. To listen to it with the arm around my neck seemed altogether too much. But I suspected I would hear something like this: because of the wet branches and their own wet feet and wings, small birds have fallen to the ground and cannot fly. Automobiles passing through parks should take care not to run over them. And if a warm wind comes up, the fog will perhaps change color. Strange-colored fogs are noxious. Listeners should therefore lock their doors if the fog should turn pink or purple.

"Change color?" I muttered. "Turn pink or purple?"

I pulled at the curtain and looked out. The fog seemed to press down with an empty weight. Was it because of the wind that a thin darkness seemed to be moving about, different from the usual black of night? The thickness of the fog seemed infinite, and yet beyond it something fearsome writhed and coiled.

I remembered that earlier, as I was coming home with the borrowed arm, the head and tail beams of the car driven by the woman in vermilion had come up indistinctly in the fog. A great, blurred sphere of faint purple now seemed to come toward me. I hastily pulled away from the curtain.

"Let's go to bed. Us too."

It seemed as if no one else in the world would be up. To be up was terror.

Taking the arm from my neck and putting it on the table, I changed into a fresh night-kimono, a cotton print. The arm watched me change. I was shy at being watched. Never before had a woman watched me undress in my room.

The arm in my own, I got into bed. I lay facing it, and brought it lightly to my chest. It lay quiet.

Intermittently I could hear a faint sound as of rain, a very light sound, as if the fog had not turned to rain but were itself forming drops. The fingers clasped in my hand beneath the blanket grew warmer; and it gave me the quietest of sensations, the fact that they had not warmed to my own temperature.

"Are you asleep?"

"No," replied the arm.

"You were so quiet, I thought you might be asleep."

"What do you want me to do?"

Opening my kimono, I brought the arm to my chest. The difference in warmth sank in. In the somehow sultry, somehow chilly night, the smoothness of the skin was pleasant.

The lights were still on. I had forgotten to turn them out as I went to bed. "The lights." I got up, and the arm fell from my chest.

I hastened to pick it up. "Will you turn out the lights?" I started toward the door. "Do you sleep in the dark? Or with lights on?"

The arm did not answer. It would surely know. Why had it not answered? I did not know the girl's nocturnal practices. I compared the two pictures, of her asleep in the dark and with the lights on. I decided that tonight, without her arm, she would have them on. Somehow I too wanted them on. I wanted to gaze at the arm. I wanted to stay awake and watch the arm after it had gone to sleep. But the fingers stretched to turn off the switch by the door.

I went back and lay down in the darkness, the arm by my chest. I lay there silently, waiting for it to go to sleep. Whether dissatisfied or afraid of the dark, the hand lay open at my side, and presently the five fingers were climbing my chest. The elbow bent of its own accord, and the arm embraced me.

There was a delicate pulse at the girl's wrist. It lay over my heart, so that the two pulses sounded against each other. Hers was at first somewhat slower than mine, then they were together. And then I could feel only mine. I did not know which was faster, which slower.

Perhaps this identity of pulse and heartbeat was for a brief period when I might try to exchange the arm for my own. Or had it gone to sleep? I had once heard a woman say that women were less happy in the throes of ecstasy than sleeping peacefully beside their men; but never before had a woman slept beside me as peacefully as this arm.

I was conscious of my beating heart because of the pulsation above it. Between one beat and the next, something sped far away and sped back again. As I listened to the beating, the distance seemed to increase. And however far the something went, however infinitely far, it met nothing at its destination. The next beat summoned it back. I should have been afraid, and was not. Yet I groped for the switch beside my pillow.

Before turning it on, I quietly rolled back the blanket. The arm slept on, unaware of what was happening. A gentle band of faintest white encircled my naked chest, seeming to rise from the flesh itself, like the glow before the dawning of a tiny, warm sun.

I turned on the light. I put my hands to the fingers and shoulder and pulled the arm straight. I turned it quietly in my hands, gazing at the play of light and shadow, from the roundness at the shoulder over the narrowing and swelling of the forearm, the narrowing again at the gentle roundness of the elbow, the faint depression inside the elbow, the narrowing roundness to the wrist, the palm and back of the band, and on to the fingers.

"I'll have it." I was not conscious of muttering the words. In a trance, I removed my right arm and substituted the girl's.

There was a slight gasp—whether from the arm or from me I could not tell—and a spasm at my shoulder. So I knew of the change.

The girl's arm—mine now—was trembling and reaching for the air. Bending it, I brought it close to my mouth.

"Does it hurt? Do you hurt?"

"No. Not at all. Not at all." The words were fitful.

A shudder went through me like lightning. I had the fingers in my mouth.

Somehow I spoke my happiness, but the girl's fingers were at my tongue, and whatever it was I spoke did not form into words.

"Please. It's all right," the arm replied. The trembling stopped. "I was told you could. And yet—"

I noticed something. I could feel the girl's fingers in my mouth, but the fingers of her right hand, now those of my own right hand, could not feel my lips or teeth. In panic I shook my right arm and could not feel the shaking. There was a break, a stop, between arm and shoulder.

"The blood doesn't go," I blurted out. "Does it or doesn't it?"

For the first time I was swept by fear. I rose up in bed. My own arm had fallen beside me. Separated from me, it was an unsightly object. But more important—would not the pulse have stopped? The girl's arm was warm and pulsing; my own looked as if it were growing stiff and cold. With the girl's, I grasped my own right arm. I grasped it, but there was no sensation.

"Is there a pulse?" I asked the arm. "Is it cold?"

"A little. Just a little colder than I am. I've gotten very warm." There was something especially womanly in the cadence. Now that the arm was fastened to my shoulder and made my own, it seemed womanly as it had not before.

"The pulse hasn't stopped?"

"You should be more trusting."

"Of what?"

"You changed your arm for mine, didn't you?"

"Is the blood flowing?"

" 'Woman, whom seekest thou?' You know the passage?"

" 'Woman, why weepest thou? Whom seekest thou?' "

"Very often when I'm dreaming and wake up in the night I whisper it to myself."

This time of course the "I" would be the owner of the winsome arm at my shoulder. The words from the Bible were as if spoken by an eternal voice, in an eternal place.

"Will she have trouble sleeping?" I too spoke of the girl herself. "Will she be having a nightmare? It's a fog for herds of nightmares to wander in. But the dampness will make even demons cough."

"To keep you from hearing them." The girl's arm, my own still in its hand, covered my right ear.

It was now my own right arm, but the motion seemed to have come not of my volition but of its own, from its heart. Yet the separation was by no means so complete.

"The pulse. The sound of the pulse."

I heard the pulse of my own right arm. The girl's arm had come to my ear with my own arm in its hand, and my own wrist was at my ear. My arm was warm—as the girl's arm had said, just perceptibly cooler than her fingers and my ear.

"I'll keep away the devils." Mischievously, gently, the long, delicate nail of her little finger stirred in my ear. I shook my head. My left hand—mine from the start—took my right wrist—actually the girl's. As I threw my head back, I caught sight of the girl's little finger.

Four fingers of her hand were grasping the arm I had taken from my right shoulder. The little finger alone—shall we say that it alone was allowed to play free?—was bent toward the back of the hand. The tip of the nail touched my right arm lightly. The finger was bent in a position possible only to a girl's supple hand, out of the question for a stiff-jointed man like me. From its base it rose at right angles. At the first joint it bent in another right angle, and at the next in yet another. It thus traced a square, the fourth side formed by the ring finger.

It formed a rectangular window at the level of my eye. Or rather a peep-hole, or an eyeglass, much too small for a window; but somehow I thought of a window. The sort of window a violet might look out through. The window of the little finger, the finger-rimmed eyeglass, so white that it gave off a faint glow—I brought it nearer my eye. I closed the other eye.

"A peep show?" asked the arm. "And what do you see?"

"My dusky old room. Its five lights." Before I had finished the sentence I was almost shouting. "No, no! I see it!"

"And what do you see?"

"It's gone."

"And what did you see?"

"A color. A blur of purple. And inside it little circles, little beads of red and gold, whirling around and around."

"You're tired." The girl's arm put down my right arm, and her fingers gently stroked my eyelids.

"Were the beads of gold and red spinning around in a huge cogwheel? Did I see something in the cogwheel, something that came and went?"

I did not know whether I had actually seen something there or only seemed to—a fleeting illusion, not to stay in the memory. I could not remember what it might have been.

"Was it an illusion you wanted to show me?"

"No. I came to erase it."

"Of days gone by. Of longing and sadness."

On my eyelids the movement of her fingers stopped.

I asked an unexpected question. "When you let down your hair does it cover your shoulders?"

"It does. I wash it in hot water, but afterward—a special quirk of mine, maybe—I pour cold water over it. I like the feel of cold hair against my shoulders and arms, and against my breasts too."

It would of course be the girl again. Her breasts had never been touched by a man, and no doubt she would have had difficulty describing the feel of the cold, wet hair against them. Had the arm, separated from the body, been separated too from the shyness and the reserve?

Quietly I took in my left hand the gentle roundness at the shoulder, now my own. It seemed to me that I had in my hand the roundness, not yet large, of her breasts. The roundness of the shoulder became the soft roundness of breasts.

Her hand lay gently on my eyelids. The fingers and the hand clung softly and sank through, and the underside of the eyelids seemed to warm at the touch. The warmth sank into my eyes.

"The blood is going now," I said quietly. "It is going."

It was not a cry of surprise as when I had noticed that my arm was changed for hers. There was no shuddering and no spasm, in the girl's arm or my shoulder. When had my blood begun to flow through the arm, her blood through me? When had the break at the shoulder disappeared? The clean blood of the girl was now, this very moment, flowing through me; but would there not be unpleasantness when the arm was returned to the girl, this dirty male blood flowing through it? What if it would not attach itself to her shoulder?

"No such betrayal," I muttered.

"It will be all right," whispered the arm.

There was no dramatic awareness that between the arm and my shoulder the blood came and went. My left hand, enfolding my right shoulder, and the shoulder itself, now mine, had a natural understanding of the fact. They had come to know it. The knowledge pulled them down into slumber.

I slept.

I floated on a great wave. It was the encompassing fog turned a faint purple, and there were pale green ripples at the spot where I floated on the great wave, and there alone. The dank solitude of my room was gone. My left hand seemed to rest lightly on the girl's right arm. It seemed that her fingers held magnolia stamens. I could not see them, but I could smell them. We had thrown them away—and when and how had she gathered them up again? The white petals, but a day old, had not yet fallen; why then the stamens? The automobile of the woman in vermilion slid by, drawing a great circle with me at the center. It seemed to watch over our sleep, the arm's and mine.

Our sleep was probably light, but I had never before known sleep so warm, so sweet. A restless sleeper, I had never before been blessed with the sleep of a child.

The long, narrow, delicate nail scratched gently at the palm of my hand, and the slight touch made my sleep deeper. I disappeared.

I awoke screaming. I almost fell out of bed, and staggered three or four steps.

I had awakened to the touch of something repulsive. It was my right arm.

Steadying myself, I looked down at the arm on the bed. I caught my breath, my heart raced, my whole body trembled. I saw the arm in one instant, and the next I had torn the girl's from my shoulder and put back my own. The act was like murder upon a sudden, diabolic impulse.

I knelt by the bed, my chest against it, and rubbed at my insane heart with my restored hand. As the beating slowed down a sadness welled up from deeper than the deepest inside me.

"Where is her arm?" I raised my head.

It lay at the foot of the bed, flung palm up into the heap of the blanket. The outstretched fingers did not move. The arm was faintly white in the dim light.

Crying out in alarm I swept it up and held it tight to my chest. I embraced it as one would a small child from whom life was going. I brought the fingers to my lips. If the dew of woman would but come from between the long nails and the fingertips!

Translated from the Japanese by Edward Seidensticker

Milan Kundera

· ·

LET THE OLD DEAD
MAKE ROOM FOR THE
YOUNG DEAD

1

He was returning home along the street of a small Czech town, where he had been living for several years. He was reconciled to his not too exciting life, his backbiting neighbors, and the monotonous rowdiness which surrounded him at work, and he was walking so totally without seeing (as one walks along a path traversed a hundred times) that he almost passed her by. But she had already recognized him from a distance, and coming toward him she gave him that gentle smile of hers. Only at the last moment, when they had almost passed each other, that smile rang a bell in his memory and snapped him out of his drowsy state.

"I wouldn't have recognized you!" he apologized, but it was a stupid apology, because it brought them precipitately to a painful subject, about which it would have been advisable to keep silent; they had not seen each other for fifteen years and during this time they had both aged. "Have I changed so much?" she asked and he replied that she hadn't, and even if this was a lie it wasn't an out-and-out lie, because that gentle smile (expressing demurely and restrainedly a capacity for some sort of eternal enthusiasm) emerged from the distance of many years quite unchanged, and it confused him. It evoked for him so distinctly the former appearance of this woman that he had to make a definite effort to disregard it and to see her as she was now: she was almost an old woman.

He asked her where she was going and what was on her agenda, and she replied that she had nothing else to do but wait for the train which would take her back to Prague that evening. He evinced pleasure at their unexpected meeting, and because they agreed (with good reason) that the two local cafes were overcrowded and dirty, he invited her to his bachelor apartment, which wasn't very far away. He had both coffee and tea there, and, more important, it was clean and peaceful.

2

Right from the start it had been a bad day. Twenty-five years ago she had lived here with her husband for a short time as a new bride, then they had

364

moved to Prague, where he'd died ten years back. He was buried, thanks to an eccentric wish in his last will and testament, in the local cemetery. At that time she had paid in advance for a ten-year lease on the grave, but a few days before, she had become afraid that the time limit had expired and that she had forgotten to renew the lease. Her first impulse had been to write to the cemetery administration, but then she had realized how futile it was to correspond with the authorities and she had come out here.

She knew the path to her husband's grave from memory, and yet today she felt all at once as if she were in this cemetery for the first time. She couldn't find the grave and it seemed to her that she had gone astray. It took her a while to understand. There, where the gray sandstone monument with the name of her husband in gold lettering used to be, precisely on that spot (she confidently recognized the two neighboring graves) now stood a black marble headstone with a quite different name in gilt.

Upset, she went to the cemetery administration. There they told her that upon expiration of the leases, the graves were canceled. She reproached them for not having advised her that she should renew the lease, and they replied that there was little room in the cemetery and that the *old dead ought to make room for the young dead*. This exasperated her and she told them, holding back her tears, that they knew absolutely nothing of humaneness or respect for man, but she soon understood that the conversation was useless. Just as she could not have prevented her husband's death, so also she was defenseless against his second death, this death "of an old dead man," which no longer permitted him to exist even as a dead man.

She went off into town and anxiety quickly began to get mixed in with her sorrow. She tried to imagine how she would explain to her son the disappearance of his father's grave and how she would justify her neglect. At last fatigue overtook her. She didn't know how to pass the long hours until time for the departure of her train. She no longer knew anyone here, and nothing encouraged her to take even a sentimental stroll, because over the years the town had changed too much and the once familiar places looked quite strange to her now. That is why she gratefully accepted the invitation of the (half-forgotten) old acquaintance, whom she'd met by chance. She could wash her hands in his bathroom and then sit in his soft armchair (her legs ached), look around his room, and listen to the boiling water bubbling away behind the screen which separated the kitchen nook from the room.

3

Not long ago he had turned thirty-five, and exactly at that time he had noticed that the hair on the top of his head was thinning very visibly. The bald spot still wasn't there yet, but its appearance was quite conceivable (the scalp was showing beneath the hair) and, more important, it was certain to one cup of coffee on it in front of the couch (where he later sat down), the other in front of the armchair, in which his visitor was sitting. He said to himself that there was a curious malice in the fact that he had met this woman, with whom he'd once been head over heels in love and whom in those days he'd let escape (through his own fault, his own blunders), precisely when he found himself in this state of mind and at a time when it was no longer possible to rectify anything.

4

She would hardly have guessed that she appeared to him as that woman who had escaped him; still, she was aware all the time of the night they'd spent together. She remembered how he had looked then. (He was twenty, didn't know how to dress; he used to blush and his boyishness amused her.) And she remembered herself. (She had been thirty-five, and a certain desire for beauty drove her into the arms of other men, but at the same time drove her away from them. She always imagined that her life should have resembled a *beautiful ball* and she feared that her unfaithfulness to her husband might turn into an ugly habit.)

Yes, she had decreed beauty for herself, as people decree moral injunctions for themselves. If she had noticed any ugliness in her own life, she would perhaps have fallen into despair. And because she was now aware that after fifteen years she must seem old to her host (with all the ugliness that this brings with it), she wanted quickly to unfold an imaginary fan in front of her own face, and to this end she deluged him with hasty questions: she asked him how he had come to this town; she asked him about his job. She complimented him on the coziness of his bachelor apartment, and praised the view from the window over the rooftops of the town (she said that it was in no way a special view, but that there was a certain airiness and freedom about it). She named the painters of several framed reproductions of Impressionist pictures (this was not difficult, in the apartments of poor Czech intellectuals you will unfailingly find these cheap prints). Then she got up from the table with her unfinished cup of coffee in her hand and bent over a small writing desk, upon which were a few photographs in a stand (it didn't escape her that among them there was no photo of a young woman), and she asked whether the face of the old woman in one of them belonged to his mother. (He confirmed this.)

Then he asked her what she'd meant when she'd told him earlier that she had come here to settle "some affairs." She really dreaded speaking about the cemetery (here on the fifth floor she not only felt high above the roofs, but also pleasantly high above her own life). When he insisted, though, she finally confessed (but very briefly, because the immodesty of hasty frankness had always been foreign to her) that she had lived here many years before, that her husband was buried here (she was silent about the cancellation of the grave), and that she and her son had been coming here for the last ten years without fail on All Souls' Day.

5

"Every year?" This statement saddened him and once again he thought that a spiteful trick was being played on him. If only he'd met her six years ago when he'd moved here, perhaps it would have been possible to save everything. She wouldn't have been so marked by her age, her appearance wouldn't have been so different from the image he had of the woman he had loved fifteen years before. It would have been within his power to surmount the difference and perceive both images (the past and the present) as one. But now they stood hopelessly far apart.

She drank her coffee and talked. He tried hard to determine precisely the extent of the transformation by means of which she was eluding him *for the second time*. Her face was wrinkled (in vain did the layer of powder try to deny this). Her neck was withered (in vain did the high collar try to hide this). Her cheeks sagged. Her hair (but it was almost beautiful!) had grown gray. However, her hands drew his attention most of all (unfortunately, it was not possible to touch them up with powder or paint): blue bunches of veins stood out on them, so that all at once they were the hands of a man.

In him, pity was mixed with anger and he felt like drowning their too-long-put-off meeting in alcohol; he asked her if she fancied some cognac (he had an opened bottle in the cabinet behind the screen). She replied that she didn't and he remembered that even years before she had drunk almost not at all, perhaps so that alcohol wouldn't make her behave contrary to the demands of good taste and decorum. And when he saw the delicate movement of her hand with which she refused the offer of cognac, he realized that this charm, this magic, this grace, which had enraptured him, was still the same in her, though hidden beneath the mask of old age, and was in itself still attractive, though doubly cut off from him.

When it crossed his mind that she was *cut off by old age*, he felt immense pity for her, and this pity brought her nearer to him (this woman who had once been so dazzling, before whom he used to be tonguetied), and he wanted to have a long conversation with her and to talk the way a man would talk with his girl friend when he really felt down. He started to talk (and it did indeed turn into a long talk) and eventually he got to the pessimistic thoughts, which had visited him of late. Naturally he was silent about the bald spot that was beginning to appear (it was just like her silence about the canceled grave). On the other hand, the vision of the bald spot was transubstantiated into quasi-philosophical maxims to the effect that time passes more quickly than man is able to live, and that life is terrible, because everything in it is necessarily doomed to extinction. He voiced these and similar maxims, to which he awaited a sympathetic response; but he didn't get it.

"I don't like that kind of talk," she said almost vehemently. "All that you've been saying is awfully superficial."

6

She didn't like conversations about growing old or dying, because they contained images of physical ugliness, which went against the grain with her. Several times, almost in a fluster, she repeated to her host that his opinion was *superficial*. After all, she said, man is more than just a body which wastes away, a man's work is substantial and that is what he leaves behind for others. Her advocacy of this opinion wasn't new; it had first come to her aid when, twenty-five years earlier, she had fallen in love with her former husband, who was nineteen years older than she. She had never ceased to respect him wholeheartedly (in spite of all her infidelities, about which he either didn't know or didn't want to know) and she took pains to convince herself that her husband's intellect and importance would fully outweigh the heavy load of his years.

"What kind of work, I ask you! What kind of work do we leave behind!" protested her host with a bitter smile.

She didn't want to refer to her dead husband, though she firmly believed in the lasting value of everything that he had accomplished. She therefore only said that every man accomplishes something, which in itself may be most modest, but that in this and only in this is his value. Then she went on to talk about herself, how she worked in a house of culture in a suburb of Prague, how she organized lectures and poetry readings. She spoke (with an excitement that seemed out of proportion to him) about "the grateful faces" of the public, and straight after that she expatiated upon how beautiful it was to have a son and to see her own features (her son looked like her) changing into the face of a man, how it was beautiful to give him everything that a mother can give a son and then to fade quietly into the background of his life.

It was not by chance that she had begun to talk about her son, because all day her son had been in her thoughts, a reproachful reminder of the morning's failure at the cemetery. It was strange; she had never let any man impose his will on her, but her own son subjugated her, and she didn't know how. The failure at the cemetery had upset her so much today, above all because she felt guilty before him and feared his reproaches. Of course she had long suspected that her son so jealously watched over the way she honored his father's memory (after all it was he who insisted every All Souls' Day that they should not fail to visit the cemetery), not so much out of love for his dead father, as from a desire to usurp his mother, to assign her to a widow's proper confines. For it was like this, even if he never voiced it and she tried hard (without success) not to know it, the idea that his mother could still have a sex life disgusted him. Everything in her that remained sexual (at least in the realm of possibility and chance) disgusted him, and because the idea of sex is connected with the idea of youthfulness, he was disgusted by everything that was still youthful in her. He was no longer a child and his mother's youthfulness (combined with the aggressiveness of her motherly care) disagreeably thwarted his relationship with girls, who had begun to interest him. He wanted to have an old mother. Only from such a mother would he tolerate love and only of such a mother could he be fond. And although at times she realized that in this way he was pushing her toward the grave, she had finally submitted to him, succumbed to his pressure, and even idealized her capitulation, persuading herself that the beauty of her life consisted precisely in quietly fading out in the shadow of another life. In the name of this idealization (without which the wrinkles on her face would after all have made her far more uneasy), she now conducted with such unexpected warmth this dispute with her host.

But he suddenly leaned across the little table which stood between them, stroked her hand, and said, "Forgive me for my chatter. You know, I always was an idiot."

Their dispute didn't irritate him; on the contrary, his visitor yet again confirmed her identity for him. In her protest against his pessimistic talk (wasn't this above all a protest against ugliness and bad taste?), he recognized her as the person he had once known, so her former appearance and their old story filled his thoughts all the more. Now he wished only that nothing destroy the intimate mood, so favorable to their conversation (for that reason he stroked her hand and called himself an idiot), and he wanted to tell her about the thing that seemed most important to him at this moment: their adventure together. For he was convinced that he had experienced something very special with her, which she didn't suspect and which he alone could, if he made the effort, put into words.

He no longer even remembered how they had met. Apparently, she sometimes came in contact with his student friends, but he remembered perfectly the out-of-the-way Prague cafe where they had been alone together for the first time. He had been sitting opposite her in a plush booth, depressed and silent, but at the same time thoroughly elated by her delicate hints that she was favorably disposed toward him. He had tried hard to visualize (without daring to hope for the fulfillment of these fancies) how she would look if he kissed her, undressed her, and made love to her—but he just couldn't bring it off. Yes, there was something odd about it: he had tried a thousand times to imagine her in bed, but in vain. Her face kept on looking at him with its calm, gentle smile and he couldn't (even with the most dogged efforts of his imagination) distort it with the grimace of physical ecstasy. *She absolutely defied his imagination.*

And that was the situation, which had never since been repeated in his life. At that time he had stood face to face with the unimaginable. Obviously he was experiencing that very short period (a *heavenly* period) when fancy is not yet satiated by experience, has not become routine, knows little, and knows how to do little, so that the unimaginable still exists; and should the unimaginable become reality (without the mediation of the imaginable, without that narrow bridge of fancies), a man will be seized by panic and vertigo. Such vertigo did actually overtake him, when after several further meetings, in the course of which he hadn't resolved anything, she began to ask him in detail and with meaningful curiosity about his student room in the dormitory, so that she soon forced him to invite her there.

He shared the little room in the dorm with another student, who for a glass of rum had promised not to return till after midnight. It bore little resemblance to his bachelor apartment of today: two metal cots, two chairs, a cupboard, a glaring, unshaded lightbulb, and frightful disorder. He tidied up the room and at seven o'clock (it went with her refinement that she was habitually on time) she knocked on the door. It was September and only gradually did it begin to get dark. They sat down on the edge of a cot and kissed. Then it got even darker and he didn't want to switch on the light, because he was glad that he couldn't be seen, and hoped that the darkness would relieve the state of embarrassment in which he would find himself having to undress in front of her. (If he knew tolerably well how to unbutton women's blouses, he himself would undress in front of them with bashful haste.) This time, however, he didn't for a long time dare to undo her first button (it seemed to him that in the matter of beginning to undress there must exist some tasteful and elegant procedure, which only men who were *experts* knew, and he was afraid of betraying his ignorance), so that in the end she herself stood up and, asking with a smile, "Shouldn't I take off this armor? . . ." began to undress. It was dark, however, and he saw only the shadows of her movements. He hastily undressed too and gained some confidence only when they began (thanks to her patience) to make love. He looked into her face, but in the dusk her expression entirely eluded him, and he couldn't even make out her features. He regretted that it was dark, but it seemed impossible for him to get up and move away from her at that moment to turn on the switch by the door, so vainly he went on straining his eyes! But he didn't recognize her. It seemed to him that he was making love with someone else—with someone spurious or else someone quite unreal and unindividuated.

Then she got on top of him (at that time he saw only her raised shadow), and moving her hips, she said something in a muffled tone, in a whisper, and it wasn't clear whether she was talking to him or to herself. He couldn't make out the words and asked her what she had said. She went on whispering, and even when he clasped her to him again, he couldn't understand what she was saying.

8

She listened to her host and became increasingly absorbed in the details, which she had long ago forgotten: for instance, in those days she used to wear a pale blue summer suit, in which, they said, she looked like an inviolable angel (yes, she recalled that suit). She used to wear a large ivory comb stuck in her hair, which they said gave her a majestically old-fashioned look; at the cafe she always used to order tea with rum (her only alcoholic vice), and all this pleasantly carried her away from the cemetery, away from her sore feet, and away from the reproachful eyes of her son. Look, it flashed across her mind, regardless of what I am like today, if a bit of my youth lives on in this man, I haven't lived in vain. This immediately struck her as a new corroboration of her conviction that the worth of a man lies in his ability to extend beyond himself, to go outside himself, to exist in and for other people.

She listened, and didn't resist him when from time to time he stroked her hand. The stroking merged with the soothing tone of the conversation and had a disarming indefiniteness about it (for whom was it intended? For the woman *about whom* he was speaking or for the woman *to whom* he was speaking?); after all, she liked the man who was caressing her; she even said to herself that she liked him better than the youth of fifteen years ago, whose boyishness, if she remembered correctly, had been rather a nuisance.

When he got to the place in his account where her moving shadow had risen above him and he had vainly endeavored to understand her whispering, for a moment he fell silent and she (foolishly, as if he would know these words and would want to remind her of them after so many years like some forgotten mystery) asked softy: "And what did I say then?"

"I don't know," he replied. He didn't know. At that time she had eluded not only his fancies, but also his perceptions; she had eluded his sight and hearing. When he had switched on the light in the dormitory room, she was already dressed. Everything about her was once again sleek, dazzling, perfect, and he vainly sought a connection between her face in the light and the face which a moment before he had been guessing at in the darkness. They hadn't parted yet, but he was already trying to remember her. He tried to imagine how her (unseen) face and (unseen) body had looked when they'd made love a little while before—but without success. She still defied his imagination.

He made up his mind that next time he must make love to her with the light on. Only there wasn't a next time. From that day on she adroitly and tactfully avoided him. He had failed hopelessly, yet it wasn't clear why. They'd certainly made love beautifully, but he also knew how impossible he had been *beforehand*, and he was ashamed of this. He now felt condemned by her avoidance and no longer dared to pursue her.

"Tell me, why did you avoid me then?"

"I beg you," she said in the gentlest of voices, "it's so long ago, that I don't know . . ." And when he pressed her further she protested, "You shouldn't always return to the past. It's enough that we have to devote so much time to it against our will." She said this only to ward off his insistence (and perhaps the last sentence, spoken with a light sigh, referred to her morning visit to the cemetery). But he perceived her statement differently: as an intense and purposeful clarification for him of the fact (this obvious thing) that there were not two women (a past and a present), but only one and the same woman, and that she, who had eluded him fifteen years earlier, was here now, was within reach of his hand.

"You're right, the present is more important," he said in a meaningful tone and looked intently at her face. She was smiling with her mouth half-open and he glimpsed a row of white teeth. At that instant a recollection flashed through his head: that time in his dorm room she had put his fingers into her mouth, bitten them hard until it had hurt. Meanwhile he had been feeling the whole inside of her mouth and still knew that on one side at the top the back upper teeth were all missing (this had not discouraged him at the time; on the contrary, such a trivial imperfection went with her age, which attracted and excited him). But now, looking into the crack between her teeth and the corner of her mouth, he saw that her teeth were strikingly white and none were missing, and this made him shudder. Both images got loose again, but he didn't want to admit it. He wanted to reunite them by force and violence, and so said, "Don't you really feel like having some cognac?" When with a charming smile and a mildly raised eyebrow she shook her head, he went behind the screen, took out the bottle, put it to his lips, and took a swig. Then it occurred to him that she would be able to detect his secret action from his breath, and so he picked up two small glasses and the bottle and carried them into the room. Once more she shook her head. "At least symbolically," he said and filled both glasses. He clinked her glass. "To speaking about you only in the present tense!" He

downed his drink, she moistened her lips. He took a seat on the arm of her chair
and seized her hand.

10

She hadn't suspected when she went to his bachelor apartment, that it could
come to *this* sort of intimacy, and at first she felt dismay, as if it had come before
she had been able to prepare herself (that *perpetual preparedness*, familiar to the
mature woman, she had lost long ago). (We should perhaps find in this dismay
something akin to the dismay of a very young girl who has been kissed for the
first time, for if the young girl is *not yet* and she was *no longer* prepared, then
this "no longer" and "not yet" are mysteriously related, as the peculiarities of
old age and childhood are related.) Then he moved her from the armchair to the
couch, clasped her to him, and stroked her whole body, and in his arms she felt
amorphously soft (yes, soft, because her body had long ago lost the sensuality
that had once ruled it, that sensuality which had readily endowed her muscles
with the rhythm of contractions and with the relaxation and activity of a hundred delicate movements).

The moment of dismay, however, soon melted away in his embrace and she,
though far removed from the beautiful mature woman she had once been, now
almost immediately rediscovered her former character. She regained a feeling of
herself, she regained her knowledge, and once again found the confidence of an
erotically adept woman; and because this was a confidence long untasted she felt
it now more intensely than ever before. Her body, which a short while before
had been trapped, alarmed, passive, and soft, revived and responded now with
its own caresses and she felt the nicety and expertise of these caresses and it
gratified her. These caresses, the way she put her face to his body, the delicate
movements with which her body answered his embrace, she found all this not
like something she was merely affecting, something that she knew how to do and
which she was now performing with cold complaisance, but like something *essential*, of which she was elatedly and enthusiastically a part, as if this were her
homeland (ah, land of beauty!), from which she had been exiled, and to which
she now returned in triumph.

Her son was now infinitely far away. When her host had grabbed her, in a corner of her mind she caught sight of the boy warning her of the danger, but then
he quickly disappeared. Now there remained only she and the man, who was
stroking and embracing her. But when he placed his lips on her lips and wanted
to open her mouth with his tongue, everything was suddenly reversed: she woke
up. She firmly clenched her teeth (she imagined the bitter unfamiliarity of the
substance, which would press against the roof of her mouth, and how her mouth
would be full), and she didn't give herself to him; then she gently pushed him
away and said: "No. Really, please, I'd rather not."

When he kept on insisting, she held him by the wrists of both hands and repeated her refusal. Then she said (it was hard for her to speak, but she knew that
she must speak if she wanted him to obey her) that it was too late for them to
make love. She reminded him of her age, if they did make love he would be dis-

gusted with her and she would feel wretched about this, because what he had told her about the two of them was for her immensely beautiful and important. Her body was mortal and wasted, but she now knew that of it there still remained something incorporeal, something like the glow which shines even after a star has burned out. What did it matter that she was growing old if her youth remained preserved—intact—within someone. "You've erected a memorial to me within yourself. We cannot allow it to be destroyed. Please understand me," she warded him off. "Don't let it happen. No, don't let it happen!"

11

He assured her that she was still beautiful, that in fact nothing had changed, that a human being always remains the same, but he knew that he was deceiving her and that she was right. After all, he was well aware of his physical supersensitivity, his increasing fastidiousness about the external defects of a woman's body, which in recent years had driven him to ever younger and therefore, as he bitterly realized, also ever emptier and stupider women. Yes, there was no doubt about it; if he got her to make love it would end in disgust, and this disgust would then splatter with mud not only the present, but also the image of the beloved woman of long ago, an image cherished like a jewel in his memory.

He knew all this, but only intellectually, and the intellect meant nothing in the face of this desire, which knew only one thing: the woman whom he had thought of as unattainable and elusive for a whole fifteen years—was here. At last he could see her in broad daylight, at last he might discern from her body of today what her body had been like then, from her face of today what her face had been like then. At last he might discern her (unimaginable) love-making, first the movements and then the orgasm.

He put his arms around her shoulders and looked into her eyes: "Don't fight me. It's absurd to fight me."

12

But she shook her head, because she knew that it wasn't absurd for her to refuse him. She knew men and their approach to the female body. She was aware that in love even the most passionate idealism will not rid the body's surface of its terrible, basic importance. It is true that she still had a nice figure, which had preserved its original proportions, and especially in her clothes she looked quite youthful. But she knew that when she undressed she would expose the wrinkles in her neck, the long scar from a stomach operation ten years before, and her gray hair. She wasn't ashamed of the gray hair on her head, but that which she had in the center of her body she wore like a secret badge of dishonor.

And just as the consciousness of her present physical appearance, which she had forgotten a short while before, returned to her, so there arose from the street below (until now, this room had seemed to her safely high above her life) the anxieties of the morning. They were filling the room, they were alighting on the prints behind glass, on the armchair, on the table, on the empty coffee cup--and her son's face dominated their procession. When she caught sight of it, she blushed and fled somewhere deep inside herself. Foolishly, she had been on the point of wishing to escape from the path he had assigned to her and which she had trodden up to now with a smile and words of enthusiasm. She had been on the point of wishing (at least for a moment) to escape, and now she must obediently return and admit that it was the only path suitable for her. Her son's face was so derisive that, in shame, she felt herself growing smaller and smaller before him until, humiliated, she turned into the mere scar on her stomach.

Her host held her by the shoulders and once again repeated: "It's absurd for you to fight me," and she shook her head, but quite mechanically, because what she was seeing was not her host but her own youthful features in the face of her son-enemy, whom she hated the more the smaller and the more humiliated she felt. She heard him reproaching her about the canceled grave, and now, from the chaos of her memory, illogically there leaped out the sentence, which she enragedly threw into his face: *The old dead must make room for the young dead, my boy!*

13

He didn't have the slightest doubt that this would actually end in disgust. After all, he couldn't even give her a look (a searching and penetrating look) without feeling a certain disgust. But the curious thing was that it didn't make any difference to him. The very opposite, it excited him and goaded him on as if he were wishing for this disgust. The desire to read, finally, from her body what he had for so long not been permitted to know, was mixed with the desire to debase this reading immediately.

Where did this come from? Whether he realized it or not, a unique opportunity was presenting itself. To him, his visitor stood for everything that he had not had, that had eluded him, that he had overlooked, that by its absence amounted to what was so intolerable to him—his present age, his thinning hair, his dismally meager balance sheet. And he, whether he realized it or only vaguely suspected it, could now strip all these pleasures that had been denied him of their significance and color (for it was precisely their colorfulness that made his life so sadly dull). He could reveal that they were worthless, that they were only appearances doomed to destruction, that they were only dust transforming itself. He could take revenge upon them, demean them.

"Don't fight me," he repeated, and made an effort to draw her close.

14

Before her eyes she still saw her son's derisive face, and when now her host drew her to him by force she said, "Please, leave me alone for a minute," and released herself from his embrace. She didn't want to interrupt what was racing through her head: the old dead must make room for the young dead and memorials were no good and her memorial, which this man beside her had honored for fifteen years in his thoughts, was no good, and her husband's memorial was no good, and yes, my boy, all memorials were no good, she said inwardly to her son. And with vengeful delight she watched his contorted face and heard him yell,

"You never spoke like this, Mother!" Of course she knew that she'd never spoken like this, but this moment was full of a light, under which everything became quite different.

There was no reason why she should give preference to memorials over life. Her own memorial had a single meaning for her: that at this moment she could abuse it for the sake of her disparaged body. The man who was sitting beside her appealed to her. He was young and very likely (almost certainly) he was the last man who would appeal to her and whom, at the same time, she could have—and that alone was important. If he then became disgusted with her and destroyed her memorial in his thoughts, it made no difference because her memorial was outside her, just as his thoughts and memory were outside her, and everything that was outside her made no difference. "You never spoke like that, Mother!" She heard her son's cry, but she paid no attention to him. She was smiling.

"You're right, why should I fight you," she said quietly, and got up. Then she slowly began to unbutton her dress. Evening was still a long way off. This time the room was full of light.

Translated from the Czech by Suzanne Rappaport

Tommaso Landolfi

. . . .

GOGOL'S WIFE

At this point, confronted with the whole complicated affair of Nikolai Vassilevitch's wife, I am overcome by hesitation. Have I any right to disclose something which is unknown to the whole world, which my unforgettable friend himself kept hidden from the world (and he had his reasons), and which I am sure will give rise to all sorts of malicious and stupid misunderstandings? Something, moreover, which will very probably offend the sensibilities of all sorts of base, hypocritical people, and possibly of some honest people too, if there are any left? And finally, have I any right to disclose something before which my own spirit recoils, and even tends toward a more or less open disapproval?

But the fact remains that, as a biographer, I have certain firm obligations. Believing as I do that every bit of information about so lofty a genius will turn out to be of value to us and to future generations, I cannot conceal something which in any case has no hope of being judged fairly and wisely until the end of time. Moreover, what right have we to condemn? Is it given to us to know, not only what intimate needs, but even what higher and wider ends may have been served by those very deeds of a lofty genius which perchance may appear to us vile? No indeed, for we understand so little of these privileged natures. "It is true," a great man once said, "that I also have to pee, but for quite different reasons."

But without more ado I will come to what I know beyond doubt, and can prove beyond question, about this controversial matter, which will now—I dare to hope—no longer be so. I will not trouble to recapitulate what is already known of it, since I do not think this should be necessary at the present stage of development of Gogol studies.

Let me say it at once: Nikolai Vassilevitch's wife was not a woman. Nor was she any sort of human being, nor any sort of living creature at all, whether animal or vegetable (although something of the sort has sometimes been hinted). She was quite simply a balloon. Yes, a balloon; and this will explain the perplexity, or even indignation, of certain biographers who were also the personal friends of the Master, and who complained that, although they often went to his house, they never saw her and "never even heard her voice." From this they deduced all sorts of dark and disgraceful complications—yes, and criminal ones too. No, gentlemen, everything is always simpler than it appears. You did not hear her voice simply because she could not speak, or to be more exact, she could only speak in certain conditions, as we shall see. And it was always, except once, in tête-à-tête with Nikolai Vassilevitch. So let us not waste time with any cheap or empty refutations but come at once to as exact and complete a description as possible of the being or object in question.

Gogol's so-called wife was an ordinary dummy made of thick rubber, naked at all seasons, buff in tint, or as is more commonly said, flesh-colored. But since women's skins are not all of the same color, I should specify that hers was a light-colored, polished skin, like that of certain brunettes. It, or she, was, it is hardly necessary to add, of feminine sex. Perhaps I should say at once that she was capable of very wide alterations of her attributes without, of course, being able to alter her sex itself. She could sometimes appear to be thin, with hardly any breasts and with narrow hips more like a young lad than a woman, and at other times to be excessively well-endowed or—let us not mince matters—fat. And she often changed the color of her hair, both on her head and elsewhere on her body, though not necessarily at the same time. She could also seem to change in all sorts of other tiny particulars, such as the position of moles, the vitality of the mucous membranes and so forth. She could even to a certain extent change the very color of her skin. One is faced with the necessity of asking oneself who she really was, or whether it would be proper to speak of a single "person"—and in fact we shall see that it would be imprudent to press this point.

The cause of these changes, as my readers will already have understood, was nothing else but the will of Nikolai Vassilevitch himself. He would inflate her to a greater or lesser degree, would change her wig and her other tufts of hair, would grease her with ointments and touch her up in various ways so as to obtain more or less the type of woman which suited him at that moment. Following the natural inclinations of his fancy, he even amused himself sometimes by producing grotesque or monstrous forms; as will be readily understood, she became deformed when inflated beyond a certain point or if she remained below a certain pressure.

But Gogol soon tired of these experiments, which he held to be "after all, not very respectful" to his wife, whom he loved in his own way—however inscrutable it may remain to us. He loved her, but which of these incarnations, we may ask ourselves, did he love? Alas, I have already indicated that the end of the present account will furnish some sort of an answer. And how can I have stated above that it was Nikolai Vassilevitch's will which ruled that woman? In a certain sense, yes, it is true; but it is equally certain that she soon became no longer his slave but his tyrant. And here yawns the abyss, or if you prefer it, the Jaws of Tartarus. But let us not anticipate.

I have said that Gogol obtained with his manipulations *more or less* the type of woman which he needed from time to time. I should add that when, in rare cases, the form he obtained perfectly incarnated his desire, Nikolai Vassilevitch fell in love with it "exclusively," as he said in his own words, and that this was enough to render "her" stable for a certain time—until he fell out of love with "her." I counted no more than three or four of these violent passions—or, as I suppose they would be called today, infatuations—in the life (dare I say in the conjugal life?) of the great writer. It will be convenient to add here that a few years after what one may call his marriage, Gogol had even given a name to his wife. It was Caracas, which is, unless I am mistaken, the capital of Venezuela. I have never been able to discover the reason for this choice: great minds are so capricious!

Speaking only of her normal appearance, Caracas was what is called a fine woman—well built and proportioned in every part. She had every smallest attribute of her sex properly disposed in the proper location. Particularly worthy of attention were her genital organs (if the adjective is permissible in such a context). They were formed by means of ingenious folds in the rubber. Nothing was forgotten, and their operation was rendered easy by various devices, as well as by the internal pressure of the air.

Caracas also had a skeleton, even though a rudimentary one. Perhaps it was made of whalebone. Special care had been devoted to the construction of the thoracic cage, of the pelvic basin and of the cranium. The first two systems were more or less visible in accordance with the thickness of the fatty layer, if I may so describe it, which covered them. It is a great pity that Gogol never let me know the name of the creator of such a fine piece of work. There was an obstinacy in his refusal which was never quite clear to me.

Nikolai Vassilevitch blew his wife up through the anal sphincter with a pump of his own invention, rather like those which you hold down with your two feet and which are used today in all sorts of mechanical workshops. Situated in the anus was a little one-way valve, or whatever the correct technical description would be, like the mitral valve of the heart, which, once the body was inflated, allowed more air to come in but none to go out. To deflate, one unscrewed a stopper in the mouth, at the back of the throat.

And that, I think, exhausts the description of the most noteworthy peculiarities of this being. Unless perhaps I should mention the splendid rows of white teeth which adorned her mouth and the dark eyes which, in spite of their immobility, perfectly simulated life. Did I say simulate? Good heavens, simulate is not the word! Nothing seems to be the word, when one is speaking of Caracas! Even these eyes could undergo a change of color, by means of a special process to which, since it was long and tiresome, Gogol seldom had recourse. Finally, I should speak of her voice, which it was only once given to me to hear. But I cannot do that without going more fully into the relationship between husband and wife, and in this I shall no longer be able to answer to the truth of everything with absolute certitude. On my conscience I could not—so confused, both in itself and in my memory, is that which I now have to tell.

Here, then, as they occur to me, are some of my memories.

The first and, as I said, the last time I ever heard Caracas speak to Nikolai Vassilevitch was one evening when we were absolutely alone. We were in the room where the woman, if I may be allowed the expression, lived. Entrance to this room was strictly forbidden to everybody. It was furnished more or less in the Oriental manner, had no windows and was situated in the most inaccessible part of the house. I did know that she could talk, but Gogol had never explained to me the circumstances under which this happened. There were only the two of us, or three, in there. Nikolai Vassilevitch and I were drinking vodka and discussing Butkov's novel. I remember that we left this topic, and he was maintaining the necessity for radical reforms in the laws of inheritance. We had almost forgotten her. It was then that, with a husky and submissive voice, like Venus on the nuptial couch, she said point-blank: "I want to go poo poo."

I jumped, thinking I had misheard, and looked across at her. She was sitting on a pile of cushions against the wall; that evening she was a soft, blonde beauty, rather well-covered. Her expression seemed commingled of shrewdness and slyness, childishness and irresponsibility. As for Gogol, he blushed violently and, leaping on her, stuck two fingers down her throat. She immediately began to shrink and to turn pale; she took on once again that lost and astonished air which was especially hers, and was in the end reduced to no more than a flabby skin on a perfunctory bony armature. Since, for practical reasons which will readily be divined, she had an extraordinarily flexible backbone, she folded up almost in two, and for the rest of the evening she looked up at us from where she had slithered to the floor, in utter abjection.

All Gogol said was: "She only does it for a joke, or to annoy me, because as a matter of fact she does not have such needs." In the presence of other people, that is to say of me, he generally made a point of treating her with a certain disdain.

We went on drinking and talking, but Nikolai Vassilevitch seemed very much disturbed and absent in spirit. Once he suddenly interrupted what he was saying, seized my hand in his and burst into tears. "What can I do now?" he exclaimed. "You understand, Foma Paskalovitch, that I loved her?"

It is necessary to point out that it was impossible, except by a miracle, ever to repeat any of Caracas' forms. She was a fresh creation every time, and it would have been wasted effort to seek to find again the exact proportions, the exact pressure, and so forth, of a former Caracas. Therefore the plumpish blonde of that evening was lost to Gogol from that time forth forever; this was in fact the tragic end of one of those few loves of Nikolai Vassilevitch, which I described above. He gave me no explanation; he sadly rejected my proffered comfort, and that evening we parted early. But his heart had been laid bare to me in that outburst. He was no longer so reticent with me, and soon had hardly any secrets left. And this, I may say in parenthesis, caused me very great pride.

It seems that things had gone well for the "couple" at the beginning of their life together. Nikolai Vassilevitch had been content with Caracas and slept regularly with her in the same bed. He continued to observe this custom till the end, saying with a timid smile that no companion could be quieter or less importunate than she. But I soon began to doubt this, especially judging by the state he was sometimes in when he woke up. Then, after several years, their relationship began strangely to deteriorate.

All this, let it be said once and for all, is no more than a schematic attempt at an explanation. About that time the woman actually began to show signs of independence or, as one might say, of autonomy. Nikolai Vassilevitch had the extraordinary impression that she was acquiring a personality of her own, indecipherable perhaps, but still distinct from his, and one which slipped through his fingers. It is certain that some sort of continuity was established between each of her appearances—between all those brunettes, those blondes, those redheads and auburn-headed girls, between those plump, those slim, those dusky or snowy or golden beauties, there was a certain something in common. At the beginning of this chapter I cast some doubt on the propriety of considering Caracas as a unitary personality; nevertheless I myself could not quite, whenever I saw her, free myself of the impression that, however unheard of it may seem, this was fundamentally the same woman. And it may be that this was why Gogol felt he had to give her a name.

An attempt to establish in what precisely subsisted the common attributes of the different forms would be quite another thing. Perhaps it was no more and no less than the creative afflatus of Nikolai Vassilevitch himself. But no, it would have been too singular and strange if he had been so much divided off from himself, so much averse to himself. Because whoever she was, Caracas was a disturbing presence and even—it is better to be quite clear—a hostile one. Yet neither Gogol nor I ever succeeded in formulating a remotely tenable hypothesis as to her true nature; when I say formulate, I mean in terms which would be at once rational and accessible to all. But I cannot pass over an extraordinary event which took place at this time.

Caracas fell ill of a shameful disease—or rather Gogol did—though he was not then having, nor had he ever had, any contact with other women. I will not even try to describe how this happened, or where the filthy complaint came from; all I know is that it happened. And that my great, unhappy friend would say to me: "So, Foma Paskalovitch, you see what lay at the heart of Caracas; it was the spirit of syphilis."

Sometimes he would even blame himself in a quite absurd manner; he was always prone to self-accusation. This incident was a real catastrophe as far as the already obscure relationship between husband and wife, and the hostile feelings of Nikolai Vassilevitch himself, were concerned. He was compelled to undergo long-drawn-out and painful treatment—the treatment of those days—and the situation was aggravated by the fact that the disease in the woman did not seem to be easily curable. Gogol deluded himself for some time that, by blowing his wife up and down and furnishing her with the most widely divergent aspects, he could obtain a woman immune from the contagion, but he was forced to desist when no results were forthcoming.

I shall be brief, seeking not to tire my readers, and also because what I remember seems to become more and more confused. I shall therefore hasten to the tragic conclusion. As to this last, however, let there be no mistake. I must once again make it clear that I am very sure of my ground. I was an eyewitness. Would that I had not been!

The years went by. Nikolai Vassilevitch's distaste for his wife became stronger, though his love for her did not show any signs of diminishing. Toward the end, aversion and attachment struggled so fiercely with each other in his heart that he became quite stricken, almost broken up. His restless eyes, which habitually assumed so many different expressions and sometimes spoke so sweetly to the heart of his interlocutor, now almost always shone with a fevered light, as if he were under the effect of a drug. The strangest impulses arose in him, accompanied by the most senseless fears. He spoke to me of Caracas more and more often, accusing her of unthinkable and amazing things. In these regions I could not follow him, since I had but a sketchy acquaintance with his wife, and hardly any intimacy—and above all since my sensibility was so limited compared with his. I shall accordingly restrict myself to reporting some of his accusations, without reference to my personal impressions.

"Believe it or not, Foma Paskalovitch," he would, for example, often say to me: "Believe it or not, *she's aging!*" Then, unspeakably moved, he would, as was his way, take my hands in his. He also accused Caracas of giving herself up to solitary pleasures, which he had expressly forbidden. He even went so far as to charge her with betraying him, but the things he said became so extremely obscure that I must excuse myself from any further account of them.

One thing that appears certain is that toward the end Caracas, whether aged or not, had turned into a bitter creature, querulous, hypocritical and subject to religious excess. I do not exclude the possibility that she may have had an influence on Gogol's moral position during the last period of his life, a position which is sufficiently well known. The tragic climax came one night quite unexpectedly when Nikolai Vassilevitch and I were celebrating his silver wedding— one of the last evenings we were to spend together. I neither can nor should attempt to set down what it was that led to his decision, at a time when to all appearances he was resigned to tolerating his consort. I know not what new events had taken place that day. I shall confine myself to the facts; my readers must make what they can of them.

That evening Nikolai Vassilevitch was unusually agitated. His distaste for Caracas seemed to have reached an unprecedented intensity. The famous "pyre of vanities"—the burning of his manuscripts—had already taken place; I should not like to say whether or not at the instigation of his wife. His state of mind had been further inflamed by other causes. As to his physical condition, this was ever more pitiful, and strengthened my impression that he took drugs. All the same, he began to talk in a more or less normal way about Belinsky, who was giving him some trouble with his attacks on the *Selected Correspondence.* Then suddenly, tears rising to his eyes, he interrupted himself and cried out: "No. No. It's too much, too much. I can't go on any longer," as well as other obscure and disconnected phrases which he would not clarify. He seemed to be talking to himself. He wrung his hands, shook his head, got up and sat down again after having taken four or five anxious steps round the room. When Caracas appeared, or rather when we went in to her later in the evening in her Oriental chamber, he controlled himself no longer and began to behave like an old man, if I may so express myself, in his second childhood, quite giving way to his absurd impulses. For instance, he kept nudging me and winking and senselessly repeating: "There she is, Foma Paskalovitch; there she is!" Meanwhile she seemed to look up at us with a disdainful attention. But behind these "mannerisms" one could feel in him a real repugnance, a repugnance which had, I suppose, now reached the limits of the endurable. Indeed . . .

After a certain time Nikolai Vassilevitch seemed to pluck up courage. He burst into tears, but somehow they were more manly tears. He wrung his hands again, seized mine in his, and walked up and down, muttering: "That's enough! We can't have any more of this. This is an unheard of thing. How can such a thing be happening to me? How can a man be expected to put up with *this*?"

He then leapt furiously upon the pump, the existence of which he seemed just to have remembered, and, with it in his hand, dashed like a whirlwind to Caracas. He inserted the tube in her anus and began to inflate her. . . . Weeping the while, he shouted like one possessed: "Oh, how I love her, how I love her, my poor, poor darling! . . . But she's going to burst! Unhappy Caracas, most pitiable of God's creatures! But die she must!"

Caracas was swelling up. Nikolai Vassilevitch sweated, wept and pumped. I wished to stop him but, I know not why, I had not the courage. She began to become deformed and shortly assumed the most monstrous aspect; and yet she had not given any signs of alarm—she was used to these jokes. But when she began to feel unbearably full, or perhaps when Nikolai Vassilevitch's intentions became plain to her, she took on an expression of bestial amazement, even a little beseeching, but still without losing that disdainful look. She was afraid, she was even committing herself to his mercy, but still she could not believe in the immediate approach of her fate; she could not believe in the frightful audacity of her husband. He could not see her face because he was behind her. But I looked at her with fascination, and did not move a finger.

At last the internal pressure came through the fragile bones at the base of her skull, and printed on her face an indescribable rictus. Her belly, her thighs, her lips, her breasts and what I could see of her buttocks had swollen to incredible proportions. All of a sudden she belched, and gave a long hissing groan; both these phenomena one could explain by the increase in pressure, which had suddenly forced a way out through the valve in her throat. Then her eyes bulged frantically, threatening to jump out of their sockets. Her ribs flared wide apart and were no longer attached to the sternum, and she resembled a python digesting a donkey. A donkey, did I say? An ox! An elephant! At this point I believed her already dead, but Nikolai Vassilevitch, sweating, weeping and repeating: "My dearest! My beloved! My best!" continued to pump.

She went off unexpectedly and, as it were, all of a piece. It was not one part of her skin which gave way and the rest which followed, but her whole surface at the same instant. She scattered in the air. The pieces fell more or less slowly, according to their size, which was in no case above a very restricted one. I distinctly remember a piece of her cheek, with some lip attached, hanging on the corner of the mantelpiece. Nikolai Vassilevitch stared at me like a madman. Then he pulled himself together and, once more with furious determination, he began carefully to collect those poor rags which once had been the shining skin of Caracas, and all of her.

"Good-by, Caracas," I thought I heard him murmur, "Good-by! You were too pitiable!" And then suddenly and quite audibly: "The fire! The fire! She too must end up in the fire." He crossed himself—with his left hand, of course. Then, when he had picked up all those shriveled rags, even climbing on the furniture so as not to miss any, he threw them straight on the fire in the hearth, where they began to burn slowly and with an excessively unpleasant smell.

Nikolai Vassilevitch, like all Russians, had a passion for throwing important things in the fire.

Red in the face, with an inexpressible look of despair, and yet of sinister triumph too, he gazed on the pyre of those miserable remains. He had seized my arm and was squeezing it convulsively. But those traces of what had once been a being were hardly well alight when he seemed yet again to pull himself together, as if he were suddenly remembering something or making a painful decision. In one bound he was out of the room.

A few seconds later I heard him speaking to me through the door in a broken, plaintive voice: "Foma Paskalovitch, I want you to promise not to look. *Golubchik*, promise not to look at me when I come in."

I don't know what I answered, or whether I tried to reassure him in any way. But he insisted, and I had to promise him, as if he were a child, to hide my face against the wall and only turn round when he said I might. The door then opened violently and Nikolai Vassilevitch burst into the room and ran to the fireplace.

And here I must confess my weakness, though I consider it justified by the extraordinary circumstances. I looked round before Nikolai Vassilevitch told me I could; it was stronger than me. I was just in time to see him carrying something in his arms, something which he threw on the fire with all the rest, so that it suddenly flared up. At that, since the desire to *see* had entirely mastered every other thought in me, I dashed to the fireplace. But Nikolai Vassilevitch placed himself between me and it and pushed me back with a strength of which I had not believed him capable. Meanwhile the object was burning and giving off clouds of smoke. And before he showed any sign of calming down there was nothing left but a heap of silent ashes.

The true reason why I wished to see was because I had already glimpsed. But it was only a glimpse, and perhaps I should not allow myself to introduce even the slightest element of uncertainty into this true story. And yet, an eyewitness account is not complete without a mention of that which the witness knows with less than complete certainty. To cut a long story short, that something was a baby. Not a flesh and blood baby, of course, but more something in the line of a rubber doll or a model. Something, which, to judge by its appearance, could have been called *Caracas' son.*

Was I mad too? That I do not know, but I do know that this was what I saw, not clearly, but with my own eyes. And I wonder why it was that when I was writing this just now I didn't mention that when Nikolai Vassilevitch came back into the room he was muttering between his clenched teeth: "Him too! Him too!"

And that is the sum of my knowledge of Nikolai Vassilevitch's wife. In the next chapter I shall tell what happened to him afterwards, and that will be the last chapter of his life. But to give an interpretation of his feelings for his wife, or indeed for anything, is quite another and more difficult matter, though I have attempted it elsewhere in this volume, and refer the reader to that modest effort. I hope I have thrown sufficient light on a most controversial question and that I have unveiled the mystery, if not of Gogol, then at least of his wife. In the course of this I have implicitly given the lie to the insensate accusation that he ill-treated or even beat his wife, as well as other like absurdities. And what else can be the goal of a humble biographer such as the present writer but to serve the memory of that lofty genius who is the object of his study?

Translated from the Italian by Wayland Young

Doris Lessing

. . . .

THE HABIT OF LOVING

In 1947 George wrote again to Myra, saying that now the war was well over she should come home and marry him. She wrote back from Australia, where she had gone with her two children in 1943 because there were relations there, saying she felt they had drifted apart; she was no longer sure she wanted to marry George. He did not allow himself to collapse. He cabled her the air fare and asked her to come over and see him. She came, for two weeks, being unable to leave the children for longer. She said she liked Australia; she liked the climate; she did not like the English climate any longer; she thought England was, very probably, played out; and she had become used to missing London. Also, presumably, to missing George Talbot.

For George this was a very painful fortnight. He believed it was painful for Myra, too. They had met in 1938, had lived together for five years, and had exchanged for four years the letters of lovers separated by fate. Myra was certainly the love of his life. He had believed he was of hers until now. Myra, an attractive woman made beautiful by the suns and beaches of Australia, waved goodbye at the airport, and her eyes were filled with tears.

George's eyes, as he drove away from the airport, were dry. If one person has loved another truly and wholly, then it is more than love that collapses when one side of the indissoluble partnership turns away with a tearful goodbye. George dismissed the taxi early and walked through St. James's Park. Then it seemed too small for him, and he went to the Green Park. Then he walked into Hyde Park and through to Kensington Gardens. When the dark came and they closed the great gates of the park he took a taxi home. He lived in a block of flats near the Marble Arch. For five years Myra had lived with him there, and it was here he had expected to live with her again. Now he moved into a new flat near Covent Garden. Soon after that he wrote Myra a very painful letter. It occurred to him that he had often received such letters, but had never written one before. It occurred to him that he had entirely underestimated the amount of suffering he must have caused in his life. But Myra wrote him a sensible letter back, and George Talbot told himself that now he must finally stop thinking about Myra.

Therefore he became rather less of a dilettante in his work than he had been recently, and he agreed to produce a new play written by a friend of his. George Talbot was a man of the theatre. He had not acted in it for many years now; but he wrote articles, he sometimes produced a play, he made speeches on important occasions and was known by everyone. When he went into a restaurant people tried to catch his eye, and he often did not know who they were. During the four years since Myra had left, he had had a number of affairs with young women round and about the theatre, for he had been lonely. He had written quite frankly to Myra about these affairs, but she had never mentioned them in her letters. Now he was very busy for some months and was seldom at home; he earned quite a lot of money, and he had a few more affairs with women who were pleased to be seen in public with him. He thought about Myra a great deal, but he did not write to her again, nor she to him, although they had agreed they would always be great friends.

One evening in the foyer of a theatre he saw an old friend of his he had always admired, and he told the young woman he was with that that man had been the most irresistible man of his generation—no woman had been able to resist him. The young woman stared briefly across the foyer and said, "Not really?"

When George Talbot got home that night he was alone, and he looked at himself with honesty in the mirror. He was sixty, but he did not look it. Whatever had attracted women to him in the past had never been his looks, and he was not much changed: a stoutish man, holding himself erect, grey-haired, carefully brushed, well-dressed. He had not paid much attention to his face since those many years ago when he had been an actor; but now he had an uncharacteristic fit of vanity and remembered that Myra had admired his mouth, while his wife had loved his eyes. He took to taking glances at himself in foyers and restaurants where there were mirrors, and he saw himself as unchanged. He was becoming conscious, though, of a discrepancy between that suave exterior and what he felt. Beneath his ribs his heart had become swollen and soft and painful, a monstrous area of sympathy playing enemy to what he had been. When people made jokes he was often unable to laugh; and his manner of talking, which was light and allusive and dry, must have changed, because more than once old friends asked him if he was depressed, and they no longer smiled appreciatively as he told his stories. He gathered he was not being good company. He understood he might be ill, and he went to the doctor. The doctor said there was nothing wrong with his heart, he had thirty years of life in him yet—luckily, he added respectfully, for the British theatre.

George came to understand that the word "heartache" meant that a person could carry a heart that ached around with him day and night for, in his case, months. Nearly a year now. He would wake in the night, because of the pressure of pain in his chest; in the morning he woke under a weight of grief. There seemed to be no end to it; and this thought jolted him into two actions. First, he wrote to Myra a tender, carefully phrased letter, recalling the years of their love. To this he got, in due course, a tender and careful reply. Then he went to see his wife. With her he was, and had been for many years, good friends. They saw each other often, but not so often now the children were grownup; perhaps once or twice a year, and they never quarrelled.

His wife had married again after they divorced, and now she was a widow. Her second husband had been a member of Parliament, and she worked for the Labour Party, and she was on a Hospital Advisory Committee and on the Board of Directors of a progressive school. She was fifty, but did not look it. On this afternoon she was wearing a slim grey suit and grey shoes, and her grey hair had a wave of white across the front which made her look distinguished. She was animated, and very happy to see George; and she talked about some deadhead on her hospital committee who did not see eye to eye with the progressive minority about some reform or other. They had always had their politics in common, a position somewhere left of center in the Labour Party. She had sympathised with his being a pacifist in the First World War—he had been for a time in prison because of it; he had sympathised with her militant feminism. Both had helped the strikers in 1926. In the Thirties, after they were divorced, she had helped with money when he went on tour with a company acting Shakespeare to people on the dole, or hunger-marching.

Myra had not been at all interested in politics, only in her children. And in George, of course.

George asked his first wife to marry him again, and she was so startled that she let the sugar tongs drop and crack a saucer. She asked what had happened to Myra, and George said: "Well, dear, I think Myra forgot about me during those years in Australia. At any rate, she doesn't want me now." When he heard his voice saying this it sounded pathetic, and he was frightened, for he could not remember ever having to appeal to a woman. Except to Myra.

His wife examined him and said briskly: "You're lonely, George. Well, we're none of us getting any younger."

"You don't think you'd be less lonely if you had me around?"

She got up from her chair in order that she could attend to something with her back to him, and she said that she intended to marry again quite soon. She was marrying a man considerably younger than herself, a doctor who was in the progressive minority at her hospital. From her voice George understood that she was both proud and ashamed of this marriage, and that was why she was hiding her face from him. He congratulated her and asked her if there wasn't perhaps a chance for him yet? "After all, dear, we were happy together, weren't we? I've never really understood why that marriage ever broke up. It was you who wanted to break it up."

"I don't see any point in raking over that old business," she said, with finality, and returned to her seat opposite him. He envied her very much, looking young with her pink and scarcely lined face under that brave lock of deliberately whitened hair.

"But dear, I wish you'd tell me. It doesn't do any harm now, does it? And I always wondered. . . . I've often thought about it and wondered." He could hear the pathetic note in his voice again, but he did not know how to alter it.

"You wondered," she said, "when you weren't occupied with Myra."

"But I didn't know Myra when we got divorced."

"You knew Phillipa and Georgina and Janet and Lord knows who else."

"But I didn't care about them."

She sat with her competent hands in her lap, and on her face was a look he remembered seeing when she told him she would divorce him. It was bitter and full of hurt. "You didn't care about me either," she said.

"But we were happy. Well, I was happy ..." he trailed off, being pathetic against all his knowledge of women. For, as he sat there, his old rake's heart was telling him that if only he could find them, there must be the right words, the right tone. But whatever he said came out in this hopeless, old dog's voice, and he knew that this voice could never defeat the gallant and crusading young doctor. "And I did care about you. Sometimes I think you were the only woman in my life."

At this she laughed. "Oh, George, don't get maudlin now, please."

"Well, dear, there was Myra. But when you threw me over there was bound to be Myra, wasn't there? There were two women, you and then Myra. And I've never never understood why you broke it all up when we seemed to be so happy."

"You didn't care for me," she said again. "If you had, you would never have come home from Phillipa, Georgina, Janet, et al., and said calmly, just as if it didn't matter to me in the least, that you had been with them in Brighton or wherever it was."

"But if I had cared about them I would never have told you."

She was regarding him incredulously, and her face was flushed. With what? Anger? George did not know.

"I remember being so proud," he said pathetically, "that we had solved this business of marriage and all that sort of thing. We had such a good marriage that it didn't matter, the little flirtations. And I always thought one should be able to tell the truth. I always told you the truth, didn't I?"

"Very romantic of you, dear George," she said dryly; and soon he got up, kissed her fondly on the cheek, and went away.

He walked for a long time through the parks, hands behind his erect back, and he could feel his heart swollen and painful in his side. When the gates shut, he walked through the lighted streets he had lived in for fifty years of his life, and he was remembering Myra and Molly, as if they were one woman, merging into each other, a shape of warm easy intimacy, a shape of happiness walking beside him. He went into a little restaurant he knew well, and there was a girl sitting there who knew him because she had heard him lecture once on the state of the British theatre. He tried hard to see Myra and Molly in her face, but he failed; and he paid for her coffee and his own and went home by himself. But his flat was unbearably empty, and he left it and walked down by the Embankment for a couple of hours to tire himself, and there must have been a colder wind blowing than he knew, for next day he woke with a pain in his chest which he could not mistake for heartache.

He had 'flu and a bad cough, and he stayed in bed by himself and did not ring up the doctor until the fourth day, when he was getting lightheaded. The doctor said it must be the hospital at once. But he would not go to the hospital. So the doctor said he must have day and night nurses. This he submitted to until the cheerful friendliness of the nurses saddened him beyond bearing, and he asked the doctor to ring up his wife, who would find someone to look after him who would be sympathetic. He was hoping that Molly would come herself to nurse him, but when she arrived he did not like to mention it, for she was busy with preparations for her new marriage. She promised to find him someone who would not wear a uniform and make jokes. They naturally had many friends in common; and she rang up an old flame of his in the theatre who said she knew of a girl who was looking for a secretary's job to tide her over a patch of not working, but who didn't really mind what she did for a few weeks.

So Bobby Tippett sent away the nurses and made up a bed for herself in his study. On the first day she sat by George's bed sewing. She wore a full dark skirt and a demure printed blouse with short frills at the wrist, and George watched her sewing and already felt much better. She was a small, thin, dark girl, probably Jewish, with sad black eyes. She had a way of letting her sewing lie loose in her lap, her hands limp over it; and her eyes fixed themselves, and a bloom of dark introspection came over them. She sat very still at these moments, like a small china figure of a girl sewing. When she was nursing George, or letting in his many visitors, she put on a manner of cool and even languid charm; it was the extreme good manners of heartlessness, and at first George was chilled: but then he saw through the pose; for whatever world Bobby Tippett had been born into he did not think it was the English class to which these manners belonged. She replied with a "yes," or a "no," to questions about herself; he gathered that her parents were dead, but there was a married sister she saw sometimes; and for the rest she had lived around and about London, mostly by herself, for ten or more years. When he asked her if she had not been lonely, so much by herself, she drawled, "Why, not at all, I don't mind being alone." But he saw her as a small, brave child, a waif against London, and was moved.

He did not want to be the big man of the theatre; he was afraid of evoking the impersonal admiration he was only too accustomed to; but soon he was asking her questions about her career, hoping that this might be the point of her enthusiasm. But she spoke lightly of small parts, odd jobs, scene-painting and understudying, in a jolly good-little-trouper's voice; and he could not see that he had come any closer to her at all. So at last he did what he had tried to avoid and, sitting up against his pillows like a judge or an impresario, he said: "Do something for me, dear. Let me see you." She went next door like an obedient child, and came back in tight black trousers, but still in her demure little blouse, and stood on the carpet before him, and went into a little song-and-dance act. It wasn't bad. He had seen a hundred worse. But he was very moved; he saw her now above all as the little urchin, the gamin, boy-girl and helpless. And utterly touching. "Actually," she said, "this is half of an act. I always have someone else."

There was a big mirror that nearly filled the end wall of the large, dark room. George saw himself in it, an elderly man sitting propped up on pillows watching the small doll-like figure standing before him on the carpet. He saw her turn her head towards her reflection in the darkened mirror, study it, and then she began to dance with her own reflection, dance against it, as it were. There were two small, light figures dancing in George's room; there was something uncanny in it. She began singing, a little broken song in stage cockney, and George felt that she was expecting the other figure in the mirror to sing with her; she was singing at the mirror as if she expected an answer.

"That's very good, dear," he broke in quickly, for he was upset, though he did not know why. "Very good indeed." He was relieved when she broke off and came away from the mirror, so that the uncanny shadow of her went away.

"Would you like me to speak to someone for you, dear? It might help. You know how things are in the theatre," he suggested apologetically.

"I don't maind if I dew," she said in the stage cockney of her act; and for a moment her face flashed into a mocking, reckless, gaminlike charm. "Perhaps I'd better change back into my skirt?" she suggested. "More natural-like for a nurse, ain't it?"

But he said he liked her in her tight black trousers, and now she always wore them, and her neat little shirts; and she moved about the flat as a charming feminine boy, chattering to him about the plays she had had small parts in and about the big actors and actresses and producers she had spoken to, who were, of course, George's friends or, at least, equals. George sat up against his pillows and listened and watched, and his heart ached. He remained in bed longer than there was need, because he did not want her to go. When he transferred himself to a big chair, he said: "You mustn't think you're bound to stay here, dear, if there's somewhere else you'd rather go." To which she replied, with a wide flash of her black eyes, "But I'm resting, darling, resting. I've nothing better to do with myself." And then: "Oh aren't I aw*ful*, the things wot I sy?"

"But you do like being here? You don't mind being here with me, dear?" he insisted.

There was the briefest pause. She said: "Yes, oddly enough I do like it." The "oddly enough" was accompanied by a quick, half-laughing, almost flirtatious glance; and for the first time in many months the pressure of loneliness eased around George's heart.

Now it was a happiness to him because when the distinguished ladies and gentlemen of the theatre or of letters came to see him, Bobby became a cool, silky little hostess; and the instant they had gone she relapsed into urchin charm. It was a proof of their intimacy. Sometimes he took her out to dinner or to the theatre. When she dressed up she wore bold, fashionable clothes and moved with the insolence of a mannequin; and George moved beside her, smiling fondly, waiting for the moment when the black, reckless, freebooting eyes would flash up out of the languid stare of the woman presenting herself for admiration, exchanging with him amusement at her posing, amusement at the world; promising him that soon, when they got back to the apartment, by themselves, she would again become the dear little girl or the gallant, charming waif.

Sometimes, sitting in the dim room at night, he would let his hand close over the thin point of her shoulder; sometimes, when they said goodnight, he bent to kiss her, and she lowered her head, so that his lips encountered her demure, willing forehead.

George told himself that she was unawakened. It was a phrase that had been the prelude to a dozen warm discoveries in the past. He told himself that she knew nothing of what she might be. She had been married, it seemed—she dropped this information once, in the course of an anecdote about the theatre; but George had known women in plenty who after years of marriage had been unawakened. George asked her to marry him; and she lifted her small sleek head with an animal's startled turn and said: "Why do you want to marry me?"

"Because I like being with you, dear. I love being with you."

"Well, I like being with you." It had a questioning sound. She was questioning herself? "Strainge," she said in cockney, laughing. "Strainge but trew."

The wedding was to be a small one, but there was a lot about it in the papers. Recently several men of George's generation had married young women. One of them had fathered a son at the age of seventy. George was flattered by the newspapers, and told Bobby a good deal about his life that had not come up before. He remarked, for instance, that he thought his generation had been altogether more successful about this business of love and sex than the modern generation. He said, "Take my son, for instance. At his age I had had a lot of affairs and knew about women; but there he is, nearly thirty, and when he stayed here once with a girl he was thinking of marrying I know for a fact they shared the same bed for a week and nothing ever happened. She told me so. Very odd it all seems to me. But it didn't seem odd to her. And now he lives with another young man and listens to that long-playing record thing of his, and he's engaged to a girl he takes out twice a week, like a schoolboy. And there's my daughter, she came to me a year after she was married, and she was in an awful mess, really awful. . . . It seems to me your generation are very frightened of it all. I don't know why."

"Why my generation?" she asked, turning her head with that quick listening movement. "It's not my generation."

"But you're nothing but a child," he said fondly.

He could not decipher what lay behind the black, full stare of her sad eyes as she looked at him now; she was sitting cross-legged in her black glossy trousers before the fire, like a small doll. But a spring of alarm had been touched in him and he didn't dare say any more.

"At thirty-five, I'm the youngest child alive," she sang, with a swift sardonic glance at him over her shoulder. But it sounded gay.

He did not talk to her again about the achievements of his generation.

After the wedding he took her to a village in Normandy where he had been once, many years ago, with a girl called Eve. He did not tell her he had been there before.

It was spring, and the cherry trees were in flower. The first evening he walked with her in the last sunlight under the white-flowering branches, his arm around her thin waist, and it seemed to him that he was about to walk back through the gates of a lost happiness.

They had a large comfortable room with windows which overlooked the cherry trees and there was a double bed. Madame Cruchot, the farmer's wife, showed them the room with shrewd, non-commenting eyes, said she was always happy to shelter honeymoon couples, and wished them a good night.

George made love to Bobby, and she shut her eyes, and he found she was not at all awkward. When they had finished, he gathered her in his arms, and it was then that he returned simply, with an incredulous awed easing of the heart, to a

happiness which—and now it seemed to him fantastically ungrateful that he
could have done—he had taken for granted for so many years of his life. It was
not possible, he thought, holding her compliant body in his arms, that he could
have been by himself, alone, for so long. It had been intolerable. He held her
silent breathing body, and he stroked her back and thighs, and his hands remembered the emotions of nearly fifty years of loving. He could feel the mem-
oried emotions of his life flooding through his body, and his heart swelled with a
joy it seemed to him he had never known, for it was a compound of a dozen
loves.

He was about to take final possession of his memories when she turned
sharply away, sat up, and said: "I want a fag. How about yew?"

"Why, yes, dear, if you want."

They smoked. The cigarettes finished, she lay down on her back, arms folded
across her chest, and said, "I'm sleepy." She closed her eyes. When he was sure
she was asleep, he lifted himself on his elbow and watched her. The light still
burned, and the curve of her cheek was full and soft, like a child's. He touched it
with the side of his palm, and she shrank away in her sleep, but clenched up, like
a fist; and her hand, which was white and unformed, like a child's hand, was
clenched in a fist on the pillow before her face.

George tried to gather her in his arms, and she turned away from him to the
extreme edge of the bed. She was deeply asleep, and her sleep was unsharable.
George could not endure it. He got out of bed and stood by the window in the
cold spring night air, and saw the white cherry trees standing under the white
moon, and thought of the cold girl asleep in her bed. He was there in the chill
moonlight until the dawn came; in the morning he had a very bad cough and
could not get up. Bobby was charming, devoted, and gay. "Just like old times,
me nursing you," she commented, with a deliberate roll of her black eyes. She
asked Madame Cruchot for another bed, which she placed in the corner of the
room, and George thought it was quite reasonable she should not want to catch
his cold; for he did not allow himself to remember the times in his past when
quite serious illness had been no obstacle to the sharing of the dark; he decided
to forget the sensualities of tiredness, or of fever, or of the extremes of sleepless-
ness. He was even beginning to feel ashamed.

For a fortnight the Frenchwoman brought up magnificent meals, twice a day,
and George and Bobby drank a great deal of red wine and of calvados and made
jokes with Madame Cruchot about getting ill on honeymoons. They returned
from Normandy rather earlier than had been arranged. It would be better for
George, Bobby said, at home, where his friends could drop in to see him. Besides, it was sad to be shut indoors in springtime, and they were both eating too
much.

On the first night back in the flat, George waited to see if she would go into
the study to sleep, but she came to the big bed in her pyjamas, and for the second time he held her in his arms for the space of the act, and then she smoked,
sitting up in bed and looking rather tired and small and, George thought, terribly young and pathetic. He did not sleep that night. He did not dare move out
of bed for fear of disturbing her, and he was afraid to drop off to sleep for fear his
limbs remembered the habits of a lifetime and searched for hers. In the morning

she woke smiling, and he put his arms around her, but she kissed him with small gentle kisses and jumped out of bed.

That day she said she must go and see her sister. She saw her sister often during the next few weeks and kept suggesting that George should have his friends around more than he did. George asked why didn't the sister come to see her here, in the flat? So one afternoon she came to tea. George had seen her briefly at the wedding and disliked her, but now for the first time he had a spell of revulsion against the marriage itself. The sister was awful—a commonplace, middleaged female from some suburb. She had a sharp, dark face that poked itself inquisitively into the corners of the flat, pricing the furniture, and a thin acquisitive nose bent to one side. She sat, on her best behaviour, for two hours over the teacups, in a mannish navy blue suit, a severe black hat, her brogued feet set firmly side by side before her; and her thin nose seemed to be carrying on a silent, satirical conversation with her sister about George. Bobby was being cool and well-mannered, as it were, deliberately tired of life, as she always was when guests were there, but George was sure this was simply on his account. When the sister had gone, George was rather querulous about her; but Bobby said, laughing, that of course she had known George wouldn't like Rosa; she *was* rather ghastly; but then who had suggested inviting her? So Rosa came no more, and Bobby went out to meet her for a visit to the pictures, or for shopping. Meanwhile, George sat alone and thought uneasily about Bobby, or visited his old friends. A few months after they returned from Normandy, someone suggested to George that perhaps he was ill. This made George think about it, and he realised he was not far from being ill. It was because he could not sleep. Night after night he lay beside Bobby, after her cheerfully affectionate submission to him; and he saw the soft curve of her cheek on the pillow, the long dark lashes lying close and flat. Never had anything in his life moved him so deeply as that childish cheek, the shadow of those lashes. A small crease in one cheek seemed to him the signature of emotion; and the lock of black glossy hair falling across her forehead filled his throat with tears. His nights were long vigils of locked tenderness.

Then one night she woke and saw him watching her.

"What's the matter?" she asked, startled. "Can't you sleep?"

"I'm only watching you, dear," he said hopelessly.

She lay curled up beside him, her fist beside her on the pillow, between him and her. "Why aren't you happy?" she asked suddenly; and as George laughed with a sudden bitter irony, she sat up, arms around her knees, prepared to consider this problem practically.

"This isn't marriage; this isn't love," he announced. He sat up beside her. He did not know that he had never used that tone to her before. A portly man, his elderly face flushed with sorrow, he had forgotten her for the moment, and he was speaking across her from his past, resurrected in her, to his past. He was dignified with responsible experience and the warmth of a lifetime's responses. His eyes were heavy, satirical, and condemning. She rolled herself up against him and said with a small smile, "Then show me, George."

"Show you?" he said, almost stammering. "Show you?" But he held her, the obedient child, his cheek against hers, until she slept; then a too close pressure of his shoulder on hers caused her to shrink and recoil from him away to the edge of the bed.

In the morning she looked at him oddly, with an odd sad little respect, and said, "You know what, George? You've just got into the habit of loving."

"What do you mean, dear?"

She rolled out of bed and stood beside it, a waif in her white pyjamas, her black hair ruffled. She slid her eyes at him and smiled. "You just want something in your arms, that's all. What do you do when you're alone? Wrap yourself around a pillow?"

He said nothing; he was cut to the heart.

"My husband was the same," she remarked gaily. "Funny thing is, he didn't care anything about me." She stood considering him, smiling mockingly. "Strainge, ain't it?" she commented and went off to the bathroom. That was the second time she had mentioned her husband.

That phrase, "the habit of loving," made a revolution in George. It was true, he thought. He was shocked out of himself, out of the instinctive response to the movement of skin against his, the pressure of a breast. It seemed to him that he was seeing Bobby quite newly. He had not really known her before. The delightful little girl had vanished, and he saw a young woman toughened and wary because of defeats and failures he had never stopped to think of. He saw that the sadness that lay behind the black eyes was not at all impersonal; he saw the first sheen of grey lying on her smooth hair; he saw that the full curve of her cheek was the beginning of the softening into middleage. He was appalled at his egotism. Now, he thought, he would really know her, and she would begin to love him in response to it.

Suddenly, George discovered in himself a boy whose existence he had totally forgotten. He had been returned to his adolescence. The accidental touch of her hand delighted him; the swing of her skirt could make him shut his eyes with happiness. He looked at her through the jealous eyes of a boy and began questioning her about her past, feeling that he was slowly taking possession of her. He waited for a hint of emotion in the drop of her voice, or a confession in the wrinkling of the skin by the full, dark, comradely eyes. At night, a boy again, reverence shut him into ineptitude. The body of George's sensuality had been killed stone dead. A month ago he had been a man vigorous with the skilled harbouring of memory; the long use of his body. Now he lay awake beside this woman, longing—not for the past, for that past had dropped away from him, but dreaming of the future. And when he questioned her, like a jealous boy, and she evaded him, he could see it only as the locked virginity of the girl who would wake in answer to the worshipping boy he had become.

But still she slept in a citadel, one fist before her face.

Then one night she woke again, roused by some movement of his. "What's the matter *now*, George?" she asked, exasperated.

In the silence that followed, the resurrected boy in George died painfully. "Nothing," he said. "Nothing at all." He turned away from her, defeated.

It was he who moved out of the big bed into the narrow bed in the study. She said with a sharp, sad smile, "Fed up with me, George? Well I can't help it, you know. I didn't ever like sleeping beside someone very much."

George, who had dropped out of his work lately, undertook to produce another play, and was very busy again; and he became drama critic for one of the big papers and was in the swim and at all the first nights. Sometimes Bobby was with him, in her startling, smart clothes, being amused with him at the whole business of being fashionable. Sometimes she stayed at home. She had the capacity of being by herself for hours, apparently doing nothing. George would come home from some crowd of people, some party, and find her sitting crosslegged before the fire in her tight trousers, chin in hand, gone off by herself into some place where he was now afraid to try and follow. He could not bear it again, putting himself in a position where he might hear the cold, sharp words that showed she had never had an inkling of what he felt, because it was not in her nature to feel it. He would come in late, and she would make them both some tea; and they would sit hand in hand before the fire, his flesh and memories quiet. Dead, he thought. But his heart ached. He had become so used to the heavy load of loneliness in his chest that when, briefly, talking to an old friend, he became the George Talbot who had never known Bobby, and his heart lightened and his oppression went, he would look about him, startled, as if he had lost something. He felt almost lightheaded without the pain of loneliness.

He asked Bobby if she weren't bored, with so little to do, month after month after month, while he was so busy. She said no, she was quite happy doing nothing. She wouldn't like to take up her old work again.

"I wasn't ever much good, was I?" she said.

"If you'd enjoy it, dear, I could speak to someone for you."

She frowned at the fire but said nothing. Later he suggested it again, and she sparked up with a grin and: "Well, I don't maind if I dew. . . ."

So he spoke to an old friend, and Bobby returned to the theatre, to a small act in a little intimate revue. She had found somebody, she said, to be the other half of her act. George was very busy with a production of *Romeo and Juliet,* and did not have time to see her at rehearsal, but he was there on the night *The Offbeat Revue* opened. He was rather late and stood at the back of the gimcrack little theatre, packed tight with fragile little chairs. Everything was so small that the well-dressed audience looked too big, like oversize people crammed in a box. The tiny stage was left bare, with a few black-and-white posters stuck here and there, and there was one piano. The pianist was good, a young man with black hair falling limp over his face, playing as if he were bored with the whole thing. But he played very well. George, the man of the theatre, listened to the first number, so as to catch the mood, and thought, Oh Lord, not again. It was one of the songs from the First World War, and he could not stand the flood of easy emotion it aroused. He refused to feel. Then he realised that the emotion was, in any case, blocked; the piano was mocking the song; There's a Long, Long Trail was being played like a five-finger exercise; and Keep the Home Fires Burning and Tipperary followed, in the same style, as if the piano were bored. People were beginning to chuckle, they had caught the mood. A young blond man with a moustache and wearing the uniform of 1914 came in and sang fragments of the songs, like a corpse singing; and then George understood he was supposed to be one of the dead of that war singing. George felt all his responses blocked, first because he could not allow himself to feel any emotion from that time at all—it

was too painful; and then because of the five-finger exercise style, which contradicted everything, all pain or protest, leaving nothing, an emptiness. The show
went on; through the Twenties, with bits of popular songs from that time, a
number about the General Strike, which reduced the whole thing to the scale of
marionettes without passion, and then on to the Thirties. George saw it was a
sort of potted history, as it were—Nöel Coward's falsely heroic view of his time
parodied. But it wasn't even that. There was no emotion, nothing. George did
not know what he was supposed to feel. He looked curiously at the faces of the
people around him and saw that the older people looked puzzled, affronted, as if
the show were an insult to them. But the younger people were in the mood of
the thing. But what mood? It was the parody of a parody. When the Second
World War was evoked by Run Rabbit Run, played like *Lohengrin*, while the
soldiers in the uniforms of the time mocked their own understated heroism from
the other side of death, then George could not stand it. He did not look at the
stage at all. He was waiting for Bobby to come on, so he could say that he had
seen her. Meanwhile he smoked and watched the face of a very young man near
him; it was a pale, heavy, flaccid face, but it was responding, it seemed from a
habit of rancour, to everything that went on on the stage. Suddenly, the young
face lit into sarcastic delight, and George looked at the stage. On it were two urchins, identical, it seemed, in tight black glossy trousers, tight crisp white shirts.
Both had short black hair, neat little feet placed side by side. They were standing
together, hands crossed loosely before them at the waist, waiting for the music to
start. The man at the piano, who had a cigarette in the corner of his mouth,
began playing something very sentimental. He broke off and looked with sardonic enquiry at the urchins. They had not moved. They shrugged and rolled
their eyes at him. He played a marching song, very loud and pompous. The urchins twisted a little and stayed still. Then the piano broke fast and sudden into
a rage of jazz. The two puppets on the stage began a furious movement, their
limbs clashing with each other and with the music, until they fell into poses of
helpless despair while the music grew louder and more desperate. They tried
again, whirling themselves into a frenzied attempt to keep up with the music.
Then, two waifs, they turned their two small white sad faces at each other, and,
with a formal nod, each took a phrase of music from the fast flood of sound that
had already swept by them, held it, and began to sing. Bobby sang her bad
stage-cockney phrases, meaningless, jumbled up, flat, hopeless; the other urchin
sang drawling languid phrases from the upperclass jargon of the moment. They
looked at each other, offering the phrases, as it were, to see if they would be accepted. Meanwhile, the hard, cruel, hurtful music went on. Again the two went
limp and helpless, unwanted, unaccepted. George, outraged and hurt, asked
himself again: What am I feeling? What am I supposed to be feeling? For that
insane nihilistic music demanded some opposition, some statement of affirma-
tion, but the two urchins, half-boy, half-girl, as alike as twins (George had to
watch Bobby carefully so as not to confuse her with "the other half of her act"),
were not even trying to resist the music. Then, after a long, sad immobility, they
changed roles. Bobby took the languid jaw-writhing part of a limp young man,
and the other waif sang false-cockney phrases in a cruel copy of a woman's voice.
It was the parody of a parody. George stood tense, waiting for a resolution. His

nature demanded that now, and quickly, for the limp sadness of the turn was unbearable, the two false urchins should flash out in some sort of rebellion. But there was nothing. The jazz went on like hammers; the whole room shook— stage, walls, ceiling—and it seemed the people in the room jigged lightly and helplessly. The two children on the stage twisted their limbs into the wilful mockery of a stage convention, and finally stood side by side, hands hanging limp, heads lowered meekly, twitching a little while the music rose into a final crashing discord and the lights went out. George could not applaud. He saw that the damp-faced young man next to him was clapping wildly, while his lank hair fell all over his face. George saw that the older people were all, like himself, bewildered and insulted.

When the show was over, George went backstage to fetch Bobby. She was with "the other half of the act," a rather good-looking boy of about twenty, who was being deferential to the impressive husband of Bobby. George said to her: "You were very good, dear, very good indeed." She looked smilingly at him, half-mocking, but he did not know what it was she was mocking now. And she had been good. But he never wanted to see it again.

The revue was a success and ran for some months before it was moved to a bigger theatre. George finished his production of *Romeo and Juliet*, which, so the critics said, was the best London had seen for many years, and refused other offers of work. He did not need the money for the time being, and besides, he had not seen very much of Bobby lately.

But of course now she was working. She was at rehearsals several times a week, and away from the flat every evening. But George never went to her theatre. He did not want to see the sad, unresisting children twitching to the cruel music.

It seemed Bobby was happy. The various little parts she had played with him—the urchin, the cool hostess, the dear child—had all been absorbed into the hard-working female who cooked him his meals, looked after him, and went out to her theatre giving him a friendly kiss on the cheek. Their relationship was most pleasant and amiable. George lived beside this good friend, his wife Bobby, who was doing him so much credit in every way, and ached permanently with loneliness.

One day he was walking down the Charing Cross Road, looking into the windows of bookshops, when he saw Bobby strolling up the other side with Jackie, the other half of her act. She looked as he had never seen her: her dark face was alive with animation, and Jackie was looking into her face and laughing. George thought the boy very handsome. He had a warm gloss of youth on his hair and in his eyes; he had the lithe, quick look of a young animal.

George was not jealous at all. When Bobby came in at night, gay and vivacious, he knew he owed this to Jackie and did not mind. He was even grateful to him. The warmth Bobby had for "the other half of the act" overflowed towards him; and for some months Myra and his wife were present in his mind, he saw and felt them, two loving presences, young women who loved George, brought into being by the feeling between Jackie and Bobby. Whatever that feeling was.

The Offbeat Revue ran for nearly a year, and then it was coming off, and Bobby and Jackie were working out another act. George did not know what it was. He thought Bobby needed a rest, but he did not like to say so. She had been tired recently, and when she came in at night there was strain beneath her gaiety. Once, at night, he woke to see her beside his bed. "Hold me for a little, George," she asked. He opened his arms and she came into them. He lay holding her, quite still. He had opened his arms to the sad waif, but it was an unhappy woman lying in his arms. He could feel the movement of her lashes on his shoulder, and the wetness of tears.

He had not lain beside her for a long time—years, it seemed. She did not come to him again.

"You don't think you're working too hard, dear?" he asked once, looking at her strained face; but she said briskly, "No, I've got to have something to do, can't stand doing nothing."

One night it was raining hard, and Bobby had been feeling sick that day, and she did not come home at her usual time. George became worried and took a taxi to the theatre and asked the doorman if she was still there. It seemed she had left some time before. "She didn't look too well to me, sir," volunteered the doorman, and George sat for a time in the taxi, trying not to worry. Then he gave the driver Jackie's address; he meant to ask him if he knew where Bobby was. He sat limp in the back of the taxi, feeling the heaviness of his limbs, thinking of Bobby ill.

The place was in a mews, and he left the taxi and walked over rough cobbles to a door which had been the door of stables. He rang, and a young man he didn't know let him in, saying yes, Jackie Dickson was in. George climbed narrow, steep, wooden stairs slowly, feeling the weight of his body, while his heart pounded. He stood at the top of the stairs to get his breath, in a dark which smelled of canvas and oil and turpentine. There was a streak of light under a door; he went towards it, knocked, heard no answer, and opened it. The scene was a high, bare, studio sort of place, badly lighted, full of pictures, frames, junk of various kinds. Jackie, the dark, glistening youth, was seated cross-legged before the fire, grinning as he lifted his face to say something to Bobby, who sat in a chair, looking down at him. She was wearing a formal dark dress and jewellery, and her arms and neck were bare and white. She looked beautiful, George thought, glancing once, briefly, at her face, and then away; for he could see on it an emotion he did not want to recognise. The scene held for a moment before they realised he was there and turned their heads, with the same lithe movement of disturbed animals, to see him standing there in the doorway. Both faces froze. Bobby looked quickly at the young man, and it was in some kind of fear. Jackie looked sulky and angry.

"I've come to look for you, dear," said George to his wife. "It was raining and the doorman said you seemed ill."

"It's very sweet of you," she said and rose from the chair, giving her hand formally to Jackie, who nodded with bad grace at George.

The taxi stood in the dark, gleaming rain, and George and Bobby got into it and sat side by side, while it splashed off into the street.

"Was that the wrong thing to do, dear?" asked George, when she said nothing.

"No," she said.

"I really did think you might be ill."

She laughed. "Perhaps I am."

"What's the matter, my darling? What is it? He was angry, wasn't he? Because I came?"

"He thinks you're jealous," she said shortly.

"Well, perhaps I am rather," said George.

She did not speak.

"I'm sorry, dear, I really am. I didn't mean to spoil anything for you."

"Well, that's certainly *that*," she remarked, and she sounded impersonally angry.

"Why? But why should it be?"

"He doesn't like—having things asked of him," she said, and he remained silent while they drove home.

Up in the warmed, comfortable old flat, she stood before the fire, while he brought her a drink. She smoked fast and angrily, looking into the fire.

"Please forgive me, dear," he said at last. "What is it? Do you love him? Do you want to leave me? If you do, of course you must. Young people should be together."

She turned and stared at him, a black strange stare he knew well.

"George," she said, "I'm nearly forty."

"But darling, you're a child still. At least, to me."

"And he," she went on, "will be twenty-two next month. I'm old enough to be his mother." She laughed, painfully. "Very painful, maternal love . . . or so it seems . . . but then how should I know?" She held out her bare arm and looked at it. Then, with the fingers of one hand she creased down the skin of that bare arm toward the wrist, so that the ageing skin lay in creases and folds. Then, setting down her glass, her cigarette held between tight, amused, angry lips, she wriggled her shoulders out of her dress, so that it slipped to her waist, and she looked down at her two small, limp, unused breasts. "Very painful, dear George," she said, and shrugged her dress up quickly, becoming again the formal woman dressed for the world. "He does not love me. He does not love me at all. Why should he?" She began singing:

> "He does not love me
> With a love that is trew. . . ."

Then she said, in stage cockney, "Repeat; I could 'ave bin 'is muvver, see?" And with the old rolling derisive black flash of her eyes she smiled at George.

George was thinking only that this girl, his darling, was suffering now what he had suffered, and he could not stand it. She had been going through this for how long now? But she had been working with that boy for nearly two years. She had been living beside him, George, and he had had no idea at all of her unhappiness. He went over to her, put his old arms around her, and she stood with her head on his shoulder and wept. For the first time, George thought, they were together. They sat by the fire a long time that night, drinking, smoking, and her head was on his knee and he stroked it, and thought that now, at last, she had been admitted into the world of emotion and they would learn to be really together. He could feel his strength stirring along his limbs for her. He was still a man, after all.

Next day she said she would not go on with the new show. She would tell
Jackie he must get another partner. And besides, the new act wasn't really any
good. "I've had one little act all my life," she said, laughing. "And sometimes
it's fitted in, and sometimes it hasn't."

"What was the new act? What's it about?" he asked her.

She did not look at him. "Oh, nothing very much. It was Jackie's idea,
really. . . ." Then she laughed. "It's quite good really, I suppose. . . ."

"But what is it?"

"Well, you see. . . ." Again he had the impression she did not want to look at
him. "It's a pair of lovers. We make fun . . . it's hard to explain, without doing
it."

"You make fun of love?" he asked.

"Well, you know, all the attitudes . . . the things people say. It's a man and a
woman—with music, of course. All the music you'd expect, played offbeat. We
wear the same costume as for the other act. And then we go through all the motions. . . . It's rather funny, really . . ." she trailed off, breathless, seeing George's
face. "Well," she said, suddenly very savage, "if it isn't all bloody funny, what is
it?" She turned away to take a cigarette.

"Perhaps you'd like to go on with it after all?" he asked ironically.

"No. I can't. I really can't stand it. I can't stand it any longer, George," she
said, and from her voice he understood she had nothing to learn from him of
pain.

He suggested they both needed a holiday, so they went to Italy. They travelled from place to place, never stopping anywhere longer than a day, for George
knew she was running away from any place around which emotion could gather.
At night he made love to her, but she closed her eyes and thought of the other
half of the act; and George knew it and did not care. But what he was feeling
was too powerful for his old body; he could feel a lifetime's emotions beating
through his limbs, making his brain throb.

Again they curtailed their holiday, to return to the comfortable old flat in
London.

On the first morning after their return, she said: "George, you know you're
getting too old for this sort of thing—it's not good for you; you look ghastly."

"But, darling, why? What else am I still alive for?"

"People'll say I'm killing you," she said, with a sharp, half-angry, half-amused,
black glance.

"But, my darling, believe me . . ."

He could see them both in the mirror; he, an old pursy man, head lowered in
sullen obstinacy; she . . . but he could not read her face.

"And perhaps *I'm* getting too old?" she remarked suddenly.

For a few days she was gay, mocking, then suddenly tender. She was provocative, teasing him with her eyes; then she would deliberately yawn and say, "I'm
going to sleep. Goodnight George."

"Well of course, my darling, if you're tired."

One morning she announced she was going to have a birthday party; it would
be her fortieth birthday soon. The way she said it made George feel uneasy.

On the morning of her birthday she came into his study where he had been sleeping, carrying his breakfast tray. He raised himself on his elbow and gazed at her, appalled. For a moment he had imagined it must be another woman. She had put on a severe navy blue suit, cut like a man's; heavy black-laced shoes; and she had taken the wisps of black hair back off her face and pinned them into a sort of clumsy knot. She was suddenly a middleaged woman.

"But, my darling," he said, "my darling, what have you done to yourself?"

"I'm forty," she said. "Time to grow up."

"But, my darling, I do so love you in your nice clothes. I do so love you being beautiful in your lovely clothes."

She laughed, and left the breakfast tray beside his bed, and went clumping out on her heavy shoes.

That morning she stood in the kitchen beside a very large cake, on which she was carefully placing forty small pink candles. But it seemed only the sister had been asked to the party, for that afternoon the three of them sat around the cake and looked at one another. George looked at Rosa, the sister, in her ugly, straight, thick suit, and at his darling Bobby, all her grace and charm submerged into heavy tweed, her hair dragged back, without makeup. They were two middleaged women, talking about food and buying.

George said nothing. His whole body throbbed with loss.

The dreadful Rosa was looking with her sharp eyes around the expensive flat, and then at George and then at her sister.

"You've let yourself go, haven't you, Bobby?" she commented at last. She sounded pleased about it.

Bobby glanced defiantly at George. "I haven't got time for all this nonsense any more," she said. "I simply haven't got time. We're all getting on now, aren't we?"

George saw the two women looking at him. He thought they had the same black, hard, inquisitive stare over sharp-bladed noses. He could not speak. His tongue was thick. The blood was beating through his body. His heart seemed to be swelling and filling his whole body, an enormous soft growth of pain. He could not hear for the tolling of the blood through his ears. The blood was beating up into his eyes, but he shut them so as not to see the two women.

Mario Vargas Llosa

· ·

THE CHALLENGE

We were drinking beer, like every Saturday, when Leonidas appeared in the doorway of the River Bar. We saw at once from his face that something had happened.

"What's up?" Leon asked.

Leonidas pulled up a chair and sat down next to us.

"I'm dying of thirst."

I filled a glass up to the brim for him and the head spilled over onto the table. Leonidas blew gently and sat pensively, watching how the bubbles burst. Then he drank it down to the last drop in one gulp.

"Justo's going to be fighting tonight," he said in a strange voice.

We kept silent for a moment. Leon drank; Briceño lit a cigarette.

"He asked me to let you know," Leonidas added. "He wants you to come."

Finally, Briceño asked: "How did it go?"

"They met this afternoon at Catacaos." Leonidas wiped his forehead and lashed the air with his hand; a few drops of sweat slipped from his fingers to the floor. "You can picture the rest."

"After all," Leon said, "if they had to fight, better that way, according to the rules. No reason to get scared either. Justo knows what he's doing."

"Yeah," Leonidas agreed, absent-mindedly. "Maybe it's better like that."

The bottles stood empty. A breeze was blowing and just a few minutes earlier, we had stopped listening to the neighborhood band from the garrison at Grau playing in the plaza. The bridge was covered with people coming back from the open-air concert and the couples who had sought out the shade of the embankment also began leaving their hiding places. A lot of people were going by the door of the River Bar. A few came in. Soon the sidewalk café was full of men and women talking loudly and laughing.

"It's almost nine," Leon said. "We better get going."

"Okay, boys," Leonidas said. "Thanks for the beer."

We left.

"It's going to be at 'the raft,' right?" Briceño asked.

"Yeah. At eleven. Justo'll look for you at ten-thirty, right here."

The old man waved good-bye and went off down Castilla Avenue. He lived on the outskirts of town, where the dunes started, in a lonely hut that looked as if it was standing guard over the city. We walked toward the plaza. It was nearly deserted. Next to the Tourist Hotel some young guys were arguing loudly. Passing by, we noticed a girl in the middle, listening, smiling. She was pretty and seemed to be enjoying herself.

"The Gimp's going to kill him," Briceño said suddenly.

"Shut up!" Leon snapped.

We went our separate ways at the corner by the church. I walked home quickly. Nobody was there. I put on overalls and two pullovers and hid my knife, wrapped in a handkerchief, in the back pocket of my pants. As I was leaving, I met my wife, just getting home.

"Going out again?" she asked.

"Yeah. I've got some business to take care of."

The boy was asleep in her arms and I had the impression he was dead.

"You've got to get up early," she insisted. "You work Sundays, remember?"

"Don't worry," I replied. "I'll be back in a few minutes."

I walked back down to the River Bar and sat at the bar. I asked for a beer and a sandwich, which I didn't finish. I'd lost my appetite. Somebody tapped me on the shoulder. It was Moses, the owner of the place.

"The fight's on?"

"Yeah. It's going to be at 'the raft.' Better keep quiet."

"I don't need advice from you," he said. "I heard about it a little while ago. I feel sorry for Justo, but really, he's been asking for it for some time. And the Gimp's not very patient—we all know that by now."

"The Gimp's an asshole."

"He used to be your friend . . ." Moses started to say, but checked himself. Somebody was calling him from an outside table and he went off, but in a few minutes he was back at my side.

"Want me to go?" he asked.

"No. There's enough with us, thanks."

"Okay. Let me know if I can help some way. Justo's my friend too." He took a sip of my beer without asking. "Last night the Gimp was here with his bunch. All he did was talk about Justo and swear he was going to cut him up into little pieces. I was praying you guys wouldn't decide to come by here."

"I'd like to have seen the Gimp," I said. "His face is really funny when he's mad."

Moses laughed. "Last night he looked like the devil. And he's so ugly you can't look at him without feeling sick."

I finished my beer and left to walk along the embankment, but from the doorway of the River Bar I saw Justo, all alone, sitting at an outside table. He had on rubber sneakers and a faded pullover that came up to his ears. Seen from the side and against the darkness outside, he looked like a kid, a woman: from that angle, his features were delicate, soft. Hearing my footsteps, he turned around, showing me the purple scar wounding the other side of his face, from the corner of his mouth up to his forehead. (Some people say it was from a punch he took in a fight when he was a kid, but Leonidas insisted he'd been

born the day of the flood and that scar was his mother's fright when she saw the
water come right up to the door of the house.)

"I just got here," he said. "What's with the others?"

"They're coming. They must be on their way."

Justo looked at me straight on. He seemed about to smile, but got very serious
and turned his head.

"What happened this afternoon?"

He shrugged and made a vague gesture.

"We met at the Sunken Cart. I just went in to have a drink and I bump into
the Gimp and his guys face to face. Get it? If the priest hadn't stepped in, they'd
have cut my throat right there. They jumped me like dogs. Like mad dogs. The
priest pulled us apart."

"*Are you a man?*" *the Gimp shouted.*

"*More than you,*" *Justo shouted.*

"*Quiet, you animals,*" *the priest said.*

"*At 'the raft' tonight, then?*" *the Gimp shouted.*

"*Okay,*" *said Justo.*

"That was all."

The crowd at the River Bar had dwindled. A few people were left at the bar
but we were alone at an outside table.

"I brought this," I said, handing him the handkerchief.

Justo opened the knife and hefted it. The blade was exactly the size of his
hand, from his wrist to his fingernails. Then he took another knife out of his
pocket and compared them.

"They're the same," he said. "I'll stick with mine."

He asked for a beer and we drank it without speaking, just smoking.

"I haven't got the time," said Justo, "but it must be past ten. Let's go catch
up with them."

At the top of the bridge we met Briceño and Leon. They greeted Justo, shaking his hand.

"Listen, brother," Leon said, "you're going to cut him to shreds."

"That goes without saying," said Briceño. "The Gimp couldn't touch
you."

They both had on the same clothes as before and seemed to have agreed on
showing confidence and even a certain amount of light-heartedness in front of
Justo.

"Let's go down this way," Leon said. "It's shorter."

"No," Justo said. "Let's go around. I don't feel like breaking my leg just
now."

That fear was funny because we always went down to the riverbed by lowering
ourselves from the steel framework holding up the bridge. We went a block farther on the street, then turned right and walked for a good while in silence.
Going down the narrow path to the riverbed, Briceño tripped and swore. The
sand was lukewarm and our feet sank in as if we were walking on a sea of cotton.
Leon looked attentively at the sky.

"Lots of clouds," he said. "The moon's not going to help much tonight."

"We'll light bonfires," Justo said.

"Are you crazy?" I said. "You want the police to come?"

"It can be arranged," Briceño said without conviction. "It could be put off till tomorrow. They're not going to fight in the dark."

Nobody answered and Briceño didn't persist.

"Here's 'the raft,' " Leon said.

At one time—nobody knew when—a carob tree had fallen into the riverbed and it was so huge that it stretched three quarters of the way across the dry riverbed. It was very heavy and once it went down, the water couldn't raise it, could only drag it along for a few yards, so that each year "the raft" moved a little farther from the city. Nobody knew, either, who had given it the name "the raft," but that's what everybody called it.

"They're here already," Leon said.

We stopped about five yards short of "the raft." In the dim glow of night we couldn't make out the faces of whoever was waiting for us, only their silhouettes. There were five of them. I counted, trying in vain to find the Gimp.

"You go," Justo said.

I moved toward the tree trunk slowly, trying to keep a calm expression on my face.

"Stop!" somebody shouted. "Who's there?"

"Julian," I called out. "Julian Huertas. You blind?"

A small shape came out to meet me. It was Chalupas.

"We were just leaving," he said. "We figured little Justo had gone to the police to ask them to take care of him."

"I want to come to terms with a man," I shouted without answering him. "Not with this dwarf."

"Are you real brave?" Chalupas asked, with an edge in his voice.

"Silence!" the Gimp shouted. They had all drawn near and the Gimp advanced toward me. He was tall, much taller than all the others. In the dark I couldn't see but could only imagine the face armored in pimples, the skin, deep olive and beardless, the tiny pinholes of his eyes, sunken like two dots in that lump of flesh divided by the oblong bumps of his cheekbones, and his lips, thick as fingers, hanging from his chin, triangular like an iguana's. The Gimp's left foot was lame. People said he had a scar shaped like a cross on that foot, a souvenir from a pig that bit him while he was sleeping, but nobody had ever seen that scar.

"Why'd you bring Leonidas?" the Gimp asked hoarsely.

"Leonidas? Who's brought Leonidas?"

With his finger the Gimp pointed off to one side. The old man had been a few yards behind on the sand and when he heard his name mentioned he came near.

"What about me!" he said. He looked at the Gimp fixedly. "I don't need them to bring me along. I came along, on my own two feet, just because I felt like it. If you're looking for an excuse not to fight, say so."

The Gimp hesitated before answering. I thought he was going to insult the old man and I quickly moved my hand to my back pocket.

"Don't get involved, Pop," said the Gimp amiably. "I'm not going to fight with you."

"Don't think I'm so old," Leonidas said. "I've walked over a lot better than you."

"It's okay, Pop," the Gimp said. "I believe you." He turned to me. "Are you ready?"

"Yeah. Tell your friends not to butt in. If they do, so much the worse for them."

The Gimp laughed. "Julian, you know I don't need any backup. Especially today. Don't worry."

One of the men behind the Gimp laughed too. The Gimp handed something toward me. I reached out my hand: his knife blade was out and I had taken it by the cutting edge. I felt a small scratch in my palm and a trembling. The metal felt like a piece of ice.

"Got matches, Pop?"

Leonidas lit a match and held it between his fingers until the flame licked his fingernails. In the feeble light of the flame I thoroughly examined the knife. I measured its width and length; I checked the edge of its blade and its weight. "It's okay," I said.

"Chunga," the Gimp ordered. "Go with him."

Chunga walked between Leonidas and me. When we reached the others, Briceño was smoking and every drag he took lit up, for an instant, the faces of Justo, impassive, tight-lipped; Leon, chewing on something, maybe a blade of grass; and Briceño himself, sweating.

"Who told you you could come?" Justo asked harshly.

"Nobody told me," Leonidas asserted loudly. "I came because I wanted to. You want explanations from me?"

Justo didn't answer. I signaled to him and pointed out Chunga, who had kept a little ways back. Justo took out his knife and threw it. The weapon fell somewhere near Chunga's body and he shrank back.

"Sorry," I said, groping on the sand in search of the knife. "It got away from me. Here it is."

"You're not going to be so cute in a while," Chunga said.

Then, just as I had done, he passed his fingers over the blade by match light; he returned it to us without saying anything and went back to "the raft" in long strides. For a few minutes we were silent, inhaling the perfume from the cotton plants nearby, borne by a warm breeze in the direction of the bridge. On the two sides of the riverbed in back of us the twinkling lights of the city were visible. The silence was almost total; from time to time barking or braying ruptured it abruptly.

"Ready!" shouted a voice from the other side.

"Ready!" I shouted.

There was shuffling and whispering among the group of men next to "the raft." Then a limping shadow slid toward the center of the space the two groups had marked off. I saw the Gimp test the ground out there with his feet, checking whether there were stones, holes. My eyes sought out Justo: Leon and Briceño had put their arms on his shoulders. Justo detached himself from them quickly. When he was beside me, he smiled. I put out my hand to him. He started to back away but Leonidas jumped and grabbed him by the shoulders. The old man took off a poncho he was wearing over his back. He stood at my side.

"Don't get close to him even for a second." The old man spoke slowly, his voice trembling slightly. "Always at a distance. Dance round him till he's worn out. Most of all, guard your stomach and face. Keep your arm up all the time. Crouch down, feet firm on the ground. If you slip, kick in the air until he pulls back. . . . All right, get going. Carry yourself like a man. . . ."

Justo listened to Leonidas with his head lowered. I thought he was going to hug him but he confined himself to a brusque gesture. He yanked the poncho out of the old man's hands and wrapped it around his arm. Then he withdrew, walking on the sand with firm steps, his head up. As he walked away from us, the short piece of metal in his right hand shot back glints. Justo halted two yards away from the Gimp.

For a few seconds they stood motionless, silent, surely saying with their eyes how much they hated each other, observing each other, their muscles tight under their clothing, right hands angrily crushing their knives. From a distance, half hidden by the night's warm darkness, they didn't look so much like two men getting ready to fight as shadowy statues cast in some black material or the shadows of two young, solid carob trees on the riverbank, reflected in the air, not on the sand. As if answering some urgently commanding voice, they started moving almost simultaneously. Maybe Justo was first, a second earlier. Fixed to the spot, he began to sway slowly from his knees on up to his shoulders and the Gimp imitated him, also rocking without spreading his feet. Their postures were identical: right arm in front, slightly bent, with the elbow turned out, hands pointing directly at the adversary's middle, and the left arm, disproportionate, gigantic, wrapped in a poncho and crossed over like a shield at face height. At first only their bodies moved; their heads, feet and hands remained fixed. Imperceptibly, they both had been bending forward, arching their backs, flexing their legs as if to dive into the water. The Gimp was the first to attack: he jumped forward suddenly, his arm tracing a rapid circle. Grazing Justo without wounding him, the weapon had followed an incomplete path through the air when Justo, who was fast, spun around. Without dropping his guard, he wove a circle around the other man, sliding gently over the sand, at an ever increasing rate. The Gimp spun in place. He had bent lower, and as he turned himself round and round, following the direction of his rival, he trailed him constantly with his eyes, like a man hypnotized. Unexpectedly, Justo stood upright: we saw him fall on the other with his whole body and spring back to his spot in a second, like a jack-in-the-box.

"There," whispered Briceño. "He nicked him."

"On the shoulder," said Leonidas. "But barely."

Without having given a yell, still steady in his position, the Gimp went on dancing, while Justo no longer held himself to circling around him: he moved in and away from the Gimp at the same time, shaking the poncho, dropping and keeping up his guard, offering his body and whisking it away, slippery, agile, tempting and rejecting his opponent like a woman in heat. He wanted to get him dizzy, but the Gimp had experience as well as tricks. He broke out of the circle by retreating, still bent over, forcing Justo to pause and to chase after him, pursuing in very short steps, neck out, face protected by the poncho draped over his arm. The Gimp drew back, dragging his feet, crouching so low his knees nearly touched the sand. Justo jabbed his arm out twice and both times hit only thin air. "Don't get so close," Leonidas said next to me in a voice so low only I could hear him, just when that shape—the broad, deformed shadow that had shrunk by folding into itself like a caterpillar—brutally regained its normal height and, in growing as well as charging, cut Justo out of our view. We were breathless for one, two, maybe three seconds, watching the immense figure of the clinched fighters, and we heard a brief sound, the first we'd heard during the duel, similar to a belch. An instant later, to one side of the gigantic shadow another sprang up, this one thinner and more graceful, throwing up an invisible wall between the two fighters in two leaps. This time the Gimp began to revolve: he moved his right foot and dragged his left. I strained my eyes vainly to penetrate the darkness and read on Justo's skin what had happened in those three seconds when the adversaries, as close as two lovers, formed a single body. "Get out of there!" Leonidas said very slowly. "Why the hell you fighting so close?" Mysteriously, as if the light breeze that was blowing had carried that secret message to him, Justo also began to bounce up and down, like the Gimp. Stalking, watchful, fierce, they went from defense to attack and then back to defense with the speed of lightning, but the feints fooled neither one: to the swift move of the enemy's arm poised as if to throw a stone, which was intended not to wound but to balk the adversary, to confuse him for an instant, to throw him off guard, the other man would respond automatically, raising his left arm without budging. I wasn't able to see their faces, but I closed my eyes and saw them better than if I'd been in their midst: the Gimp sweating, his mouth shut, his little pig eyes aflame and blazing behind his eyelids, his skin throbbing, the wings of his flattened nose and the slit of his mouth shaken by an inconceivable quivering; and Justo, with his usual sneering mask intensified by anger and his lips moist with rage and fatigue. I opened my eyes just in time to see Justo pounce madly, blindly on the other man, giving him every advantage, offering his face, foolishly exposing his body. Anger and impatience lifted him off the ground, held him oddly up in the air, outlined against the sky, smashed him violently into his prey. The savage outburst must have surprised the Gimp, who briefly remained indecisive, and when he bent down, lengthening his arm like an arrow, hiding from our view the shining blade we followed in our imagination, we knew that Justo's crazy action hadn't been totally wasted. At the impact, the night enveloping us became populated with deep, blood-curdling roars bursting like sparks from the fighters. We didn't know then, we will never know, how long they were clenched in that convulsive polyhedron; but even without distinguishing who was who, without knowing whose arm delivered which blows, whose throat offered up those roars that followed one another like echoes, we repeatedly saw the naked knife blades in the ar, quivering toward the heavens or in the midst of the darkness, down at their sides, swift, blazing, in and out of sight, hidden or brandished in the night as in some magician's spectacular show.

We must have been gasping and eager, holding our breath, our eyes popping, maybe whispering gibberish, until the human pyramid cracked, suddenly cleaved through its center by an invisible slash: the two were flung back, as if magnetized from behind, at the same moment, with the same violent force. They stayed a yard apart, panting. "We've got to stop them," said Leon's voice. "It's enough." But before we tried to move, the Gimp had left his position like a meteor. Justo didn't side-step the lunge and they both rolled on the ground. They twisted in the sand, rolling over on top of each other, splitting the air with slashes and silent gasps. This time the fight was over quickly. Soon they were still, stretched out in the riverbed, as if sleeping. I was ready to run toward them when, perhaps guessing my intention, someone suddenly stood up and remained standing next to the fallen man, swaying worse than a drunk. It was the Gimp.

In the struggle they had lost their ponchos, which lay a little way off, looking like a many-faceted rock. "Let's go," Leon said. But this time as well something happened that left us motionless. Justo got up with difficulty, leaning his entire weight on his right arm and covering his head with his free hand as if he wanted to drive some horrible sight away from his eyes. When he was up the Gimp stepped back a few feet. Justo swayed. He hadn't taken his arm from his face. Then we heard a voice we all knew but which we wouldn't have recognized if it had taken us by surprise in the dark.

"Julian!" the Gimp shouted. "Tell him to give up!"

I turned to look at Leonidas but I found his face blocked out by Leon's: he was watching the scene with a horrified expression. I turned back to look at them: they were joined once again. Roused by the Gimp's words, Justo, no doubt about it, had taken his arm from his face the second I looked away from the fight and he must have thrown himself on his enemy, draining the last strength out of his pain, out of the bitterness of his defeat. Jumping backward, the Gimp easily escaped this emotional and useless attack.

"Leonidas!" he shouted again in a furious, imploring tone. "Tell him to give up."

"Shut up and fight!" Leonidas bellowed without hesitating.

Justo had attempted another attack, but all of us, especially Leonidas, who was old and had seen many fights in his day, knew there was nothing to be done now, that his arm didn't have enough strength even to scratch the Gimp's olive-toned skin. With an anguish born in his depths and rising to his lips, making them dry, and even to his eyes, clouding them over, he struggled in slow motion as we watched for still another moment until the shadow crumpled once more: someone collapsed onto the ground with a dry sound.

When we reached the spot where Justo was lying, the Gimp had withdrawn to his men and they started leaving all together without speaking. I put my face next to his chest, hardly noticing that a hot substance dampened my neck and shoulder as my hand, through the rips in the cloth, explored his stomach and back, sometimes plunging into the limp, damp, cold body of a beached jellyfish. Briceño and Leon took off their jackets, wrapped him carefully and picked him up by his feet and arms. I looked for Leonidas' poncho, which lay a few feet away, and not looking, just groping, I covered his face. Then, in two rows, the four of us carried him on our shoulders like a coffin and we walked, matching our steps, in the direction of the path that climbed up the riverbank and back to the city.

"Don't cry, old-timer," Leon said. "I've never known anyone brave as your son. I really mean that."

Leonidas didn't answer. He walked behind me, so I couldn't see him.

At the first huts in Castilla, I asked: "Want us to carry him to your house, Leonidas?"

"Yes," the old man said hastily, as if he hadn't been listening.

Translated from the Spanish by Ronald Christ
and Gregory Kolovakas

Naguib Mahfouz

. . . .

THE CONJURER MADE OFF WITH THE DISH

'The time has come for you to be useful,' said my mother to me, and she slipped her hand into her pocket, saying:

'Take this piastre and go off and buy some beans. Don't play on the way and keep away from the cars.'

I took the dish, put on my clogs and went out, humming a tune. Finding a crowd in front of the bean-seller, I waited until I discovered a way through to the marble table.

'A piastre's worth of beans, mister,' I called out in my shrill voice.

He asked me impatiently:

'Beans alone? With oil? With cooking butter?'

I didn't answer and he said to me roughly:

'Make way for someone else.'

I withdrew, overcome by embarrassment and returned home defeated.

'Returning with an empty dish?' my mother shouted at me. 'What did you do—spill the beans or lose the piastre, you naughty boy?'

'Beans alone? With oil? With cooking butter?—you didn't tell me,' I protested.

'You stupid, what do you eat every morning?'

'I don't know.'

'You good-for-nothing, ask him for beans with oil.'

I went off to the man and said:

'A piastre's worth of beans with oil, mister.'

With a frown of impatience he asked:

'Linseed oil? Nut oil? Olive oil?'

I was taken aback and again made no answer:

'Make way for someone else,' he shouted at me.

I returned in a rage to my mother, who called out in astonishment:

'You've come back empty-handed—no beans and no oil.'

'Linseed oil? Nut oil? Olive oil?—you didn't tell me,' I said angrily.

'Beans with oil means beans with linseed oil.'

'How should I know?'

411

'You're a good-for-nothing and he's a tiresome man—tell him beans with lin-seed oil.'

'How should I know?'

I went off quickly and called out to the man while still some yards from his shop:

'Beans with linseed oil, mister.'

'Put the piastre on the counter,' he said, plunging the ladle into the pot.

I put my hand into my pocket but didn't find the piastre. I searched round for it anxiously. I turned my pocket inside out but found no trace of it. The man withdrew the ladle empty, saying with disgust:

'You've lost the piastre—you're not a boy to be depended on.'

'I haven't lost it,' I said, looking under my feet and round about me. 'It's been in my pocket all the time.'

'Make way for someone else and don't make trouble.'

I returned to my mother with an empty dish.

'Good grief, you idiot boy!'

'The piastre. . . .'

'What of it?'

'It wasn't in my pocket.'

'Did you buy sweets with it?'

'I swear I didn't.'

'How did you lose it?'

'I don't know.'

'Do you swear by the Koran you didn't buy anything with it?'

'I swear.'

'There's a hole in your pocket.'

'No there isn't.'

'Maybe you gave it to the man the first time or the second.'

'Maybe.'

'Are you sure of nothing?'

'I'm hungry.'

She clapped her hands together in a gesture of resignation.

'Never mind,' she said. 'I'll give you another piastre but I'll take it out of your money-box, and if you come back with an empty dish I'll break your head.'

I went off at a run, dreaming of a delicious breakfast. At the turning leading to the alleyway where the bean-seller was I saw a crowd of children and heard merry, festive sounds. My feet dragged as my heart was pulled towards them. At least let me have a fleeting glance. I slipped in amongst them and found the con-jurer looking straight at me. A stupefying joy overwhelmed me; I was completely taken out of myself. With the whole of my being I became involved in the tricks of the rabbits and the eggs, and the snakes and the ropes. When the man came up to collect money, I drew back mumbling, 'I haven't got any money.'

He rushed at me savagely and I escaped only with difficulty. I ran off, my back almost broken by his blow, and yet I was utterly happy as I made my way to the seller of beans.

'Beans with linseed oil for a piastre, mister,' I said.

He went on looking at me without moving, so I repeated my request.

'Give me the dish,' he demanded angrily.

The dish! Where was the dish? Had I dropped it while running? Had the conjurer made off with it?

'Boy, you're out of your mind.'

I turned back, searching along the way for the lost dish. The place where the conjurer had been I found empty, but the voices of children led me to him in a nearby lane. I moved round the circle; when the conjurer spotted me he shouted out threateningly:

'Pay up or you'd better scram.'

'The dish!' I called out despairingly.

'What dish, you little devil?'

'Give me back the dish.'

'Scram or I'll make you into food for snakes.'

He had stolen the dish, yet fearfully I moved away out of sight and wept. Whenever a passer-by asked me why I was crying I would reply:

'The conjurer made off with the dish.'

Through my misery I became aware of a voice saying:

'Come along and watch.'

I looked behind me and saw a peep-show had been set up. I saw dozens of children hurrying towards it and taking it in turns to stand in front of the peep-holes, while the man began making his commentary on the pictures:

'There you've got the gallant knight and the most beautiful of all ladies, Zainat al-Banat.'

Drying my tears, I gazed up in fascination at the box, completely forgetting the conjurer and the dish. Unable to overcome the temptation, I paid over the piastre and stood in front of the peep-hole next to a girl who was standing in front of the other one, and there flowed across our vision enchanting picture stories. When I came back to my own world I realized I had lost both the piastre and the dish, and there was no sign of the conjurer. However, I gave no thought to the loss, so taken up was I with the pictures of chivalry, love and deeds of daring. I forgot my hunger; I forgot the fear of what threatened me back home. I took a few paces back so as to lean against an ancient wall of what had once been a Treasury and the seat of office of the Cadi, and gave myself up wholly to my reveries. For a long while I dreamt of chivalry, of Zainat al-Banat and the ghoul. In my dream I spoke aloud, giving meaning to my words with gestures. Thrusting home the imaginary lance, I said:

'Take that, O ghoul, right in the heart!'

'And he raised Zainat al-Banat up behind him on his horse,' came back a gentle voice.

I looked to my right and saw the young girl who had been beside me at the performance. She was wearing a dirty dress and coloured clogs and was playing with her long plait of hair; in her other hand were the red and white sweets called 'Lady's fleas', which she was leisurely sucking. We exchanged glances and I lost my heart to her.

'Let's sit down and rest,' I said to her.

She appeared to be agreeable to my suggestion, so I took her by the arm and we went through the gateway of the ancient wall and sat down on the step of a

stairway that went nowhere, a stairway that rose up until it ended in a platform
behind which there could be seen a blue sky and minarets. We sat in silence,
side by side. I pressed her hand and we sat on in silence, not knowing what to
say. I experienced feelings that were new, strange and obscure. Putting my face
close to hers, I breathed in the natural smell of her hair, mingled with an odour
of earth, and the fragrance of breath mixed with the aroma of sweets. I kissed her
lips. I swallowed my saliva which had taken on a sweetness from the dissolved
'Lady's fleas'. I put my arm round her, without her uttering a word, kissing her
cheek and lips. Her lips grew still as they received the kiss, then went back to
sucking at the sweets. At last she decided we should get up. I seized her arm
anxiously.

'Sit down,' I said.

'I'm going,' she said simply.

'Where to?' I asked irritably.

'To the midwife Umm Ali,' and she pointed to a house at the bottom of
which was a small ironing shop.

'Why?'

'To tell her to come quickly.'

'Why?'

'My mother's crying in pain at home. She told me to go to the midwife Umm
Ali and to take her along quickly.'

'And you'll come back after that?'

She nodded her head in assent. Her mentioning her mother reminded me of
my own and my heart missed a beat. Getting up from the ancient stairway, I
made my way back home. I wept out loud, a tried method by which I would defend myself. I expected she would come to me but she did not. I wandered from
the kitchen to the bedroom but found no trace of her. Where had my mother
gone? When would she return? I was bored with being in the empty house. An
idea occurred to me: I took a dish from the kitchen and a piastre from my savings and went off immediately to the seller of beans. I found him asleep on a
bench outside the shop, his face covered over by his arm. The pots of beans had
vanished and the long-necked bottles of oil had been put back on the shelf and
the marble top washed down.

'Mister,' I whispered, approaching.

Hearing nothing but his snoring, I touched his shoulder. He raised his arm in
alarm and looked at me through reddened eyes.

'Mister.'

'What do you want?' he asked roughly, becoming aware of my presence and
recognizing me.

'A piastre's worth of beans with linseed oil.'

'Eh?'

'I've got the piastre and I've got the dish.'

'You're crazy, boy,' he shouted at me. 'Get out or I'll bash your brains in.'

When I didn't move he pushed me so violently I went sprawling on to my
back. I got up painfully, struggling to hold back the crying that was twisting my
lips. My hands were clenched, one on the dish and the other on the piastre. I
threw him an angry look. I thought about returning with my hopes dashed, but

dreams of heroism and valour altered my plan of action. Resolutely, I made a quick decision and with all my strength threw the dish at him. It flew through the air and struck him on the head, while I took to my heels, heedless of everything. I was convinced I'd killed him, just as the knight had killed the ghoul. I didn't stop running till I was near the ancient wall. Panting, I looked behind me but saw no signs of any pursuit. I stopped to get my breath back, then asked myself what I should do now that the second dish was lost? Something warned me not to return home directly, and soon I had given myself over to a wave of indifference that bore me off where it willed. It meant a beating, neither more nor less, on my return, so let me put it off for a time. Here was the piastre in my hand and I could have some sort of enjoyment with it before being punished. I decided to pretend I had forgotten my having done wrong—but where was the conjurer, where was the peep-show? I looked everywhere for them but to no avail.

Worn out by this fruitless searching, I went off to the ancient stairway to keep my appointment. I sat down to wait, imagining to myself the meeting. I yearned for another kiss redolent with the fragrance of sweets. I admitted to myself that the little girl had given me sensations I had never experienced before. As I waited and dreamed, a whispering sound came to me from faraway behind me. I climbed the stairs cautiously and at the final landing I lay down flat on my face in order to see what was behind it, without anyone being able to spot me. I saw some ruins surrounded by a high wall, the last of what remained of the Treasury and the Chief Cadi's house. Directly under the stairs sat a man and a woman, and it was from them that the whispering came. The man looked like a tramp; the woman like one of those gypsies that tend sheep. An inner voice told me that their meeting was similar to the one I had had. Their lips and eyes revealed this, but they showed astonishing expertise in the extraordinary things they did. My gaze became rooted upon them with curiosity, surprise, pleasure, and a certain amount of disquiet. At last they sat down side by side, neither of them taking any notice of the other. After quite a while the man said:

'The money!'

'You're never satisfied,' she said irritably.

Spitting on the ground, he said: 'You're crazy.'

'You're a thief.'

He slapped her hard with the back of his hand, and she gathered up a handful of earth and threw it in his face. Then he sprang at her, fastening his fingers on her windpipe. In vain she gathered all her strength to escape from his grip. Her voice failed her, her eyes bulged out of their sockets, while her feet struck out at the air. In dumb terror I stared at the scene till I saw a thread of blood trickling down from her nose. A scream escaped from my mouth. Before the man raised his head, I had crawled backwards; descending the stairs at a jump, I raced off like mad to wherever my legs might carry me. I didn't stop running till I was out of breath. Gasping for breath, I was quite unaware of my whereabouts, but when I came to myself I found I was under a raised vault at the middle of a crossroads. I had never set foot there before and had no idea of where I was in relation to our quarter. On both sides sat sightless beggars, and crossing it from all directions were people who paid attention to no one. In terror I realized I had lost my way and that countless difficulties lay in wait for me before I would find my way home. Should I resort to asking one of the passers-by to direct me? What, though, would happen if chance should lead me to a man like the vendor of beans or the tramp of the waste plot? Would a miracle come about whereby I'd see my mother approaching so that I could eagerly hurry towards her? Should I try to make my own way, wandering about till I came across some familiar land-mark that would indicate the direction I should take? I told myself that I should be resolute and take a quick decision: the day was passing and soon mysterious darkness would descend.

Translated from the Arabic by Denys Johnson-Davis

Bernard Malamud

. . . .

THE LAST MOHICAN

Fidelman, a self-confessed failure as a painter, came to Italy to prepare a critical study of Giotto, the opening chapter of which he had carried across the ocean in a new pigskin-leather briefcase, now gripped in his perspiring hand. Also new were his gum-soled oxblood shoes, a tweed suit he had on despite the late-September sun slanting hot in the Roman sky, although there was a lighter one in his bag; and a dacron shirt and set of cotton-dacron underwear, good for quick and easy washing for the traveler. His suitcase, a bulky, two-strapped affair which embarrassed him slightly, he had borrowed from his sister Bessie. He planned, if he had any money left at the end of the year, to buy a new one in Florence. Although he had been in not much of a mood when he had left the U.S.A., Fidelman revived in Naples, and at the moment, as he stood in front of the Rome railroad station, after twenty minutes still absorbed in his first sight of the Eternal City, he was conscious of a certain exaltation that devolved on him after he had discovered that directly across the many-vehicled piazza stood the remains of the Baths of Diocletian. Fidelman remembered having read that Michelangelo had had a hand in converting the baths into a church and convent, the latter ultimately changed into the museum that presently was there. "Imagine," he muttered. "Imagine all that history."

In the midst of his imagining, Fidelman experienced the sensation of suddenly seeing himself as he was, to the pinpoint, outside and in, not without bittersweet pleasure; and as the well-known image of his face rose before him he was taken by the depth of pure feeling in his eyes, slightly magnified by glasses, and the sensitivity of his elongated nostrils and often tremulous lips, nose divided from lips by a mustache of recent vintage that looked, Fidelman thought, as if it had been sculptured there, adding to his dignified appearance although he was a little on the short side. But almost at the same moment, this unexpectedly intense sense of his being—it was more than appearance—faded, exaltation having gone where exaltation goes, and Fidelman became aware that there was an exterior source to the strange, almost tri-dimensional reflection of himself he had felt as well as seen. Behind him, a short distance to the right, he had noticed a stranger—give a skeleton a couple of pounds—loitering near a bronze statue on a stone pedestal of the heavy-dugged Etruscan wolf suckling the infants Romulus and Remus, the man contemplating Fidelman already acquisitively so as to suggest to the traveler that he had been mirrored (lock, stock, barrel) in the other's gaze for some time, perhaps since he had stepped off the train. Casually studying him, though pretending no, Fidelman beheld a person of about his own height, oddly dressed in brown knickers and black, knee-length woolen socks drawn up over slightly bowed, broomstick legs, these grounded in small, porous, pointed shoes. His yellowed shirt was open at the gaunt throat, both sleeves rolled up over skinny, hairy arms. The stranger's high forehead was bronzed, his black hair thick behind small ears, the dark, close-shaven beard tight on the face; his experienced nose was weighted at the tip, and the soft brown eyes, above all, *wanted*. Though his expression suggested humility, he all but licked his lips as he approached the ex-painter.

"Shalom," he greeted Fidelman.

"Shalom," the other hesitantly replied, uttering the word—so far as he recalled—for the first time in his life. My God, he thought, a handout for sure. My first hello in Rome and it has to be a schnorrer.

The stranger extended a smiling hand. "Susskind," he said, "Shimon Susskind."

"Arthur Fidelman." Transferring his briefcase to under his left arm while standing astride the big suitcase, he shook hands with Susskind. A blue-smocked porter came by, glanced at Fidelman's bag, looked at him, then walked away.

Whether he knew it or not Susskind was rubbing his palms contemplatively together.

"Parla italiano?"

"Not with ease, although I read it fluently. You might say I need practice."

"Yiddish?"

"I express myself best in English."

"Let it be English then." Susskind spoke with a slight British intonation. "I knew you were Jewish," he said, "the minute my eyes saw you."

Fidelman chose to ignore the remark. "Where did you pick up your knowledge of English?"

"In Israel."

Israel interested Fidelman. "You live there?"

"Once, not now," Susskind answered vaguely. He seemed suddenly bored.

"How so?"

Susskind twitched a shoulder. "Too much heavy labor for a man of my modest health. Also I couldn't stand the suspense."

Fidelman nodded.

"Furthermore, the desert air makes me constipated. In Rome I am lighthearted."

"A Jewish refugee from Israel, no less," Fidelman said good-humoredly.

"I'm always running," Susskind answered mirthlessly. If he was lighthearted, he had yet to show it.

"Where else from, if I may ask?"

"Where else but Germany, Hungary, Poland? Where not?"

"Ah, that's so long ago." Fidelman then noticed the gray in the man's hair. "Well, I'd better be going," he said. He picked up his bag as two porters hovered uncertainly nearby.

But Susskind offered certain services. "You got a hotel?"

"All picked and reserved."

"How long are you staying?"

What business is it of his? However, Fidelman courteously replied, "Two weeks in Rome, the rest of the year in Florence, with a few side trips to Siena, Assisi, Padua, and maybe also Venice."

"You wish a guide in Rome?"

"Are you a guide?"

"Why not?"

"No," said Fidelman. "I'll look as I go along to museums, libraries, et cetera."

This caught Susskind's attention. "What are you, a professor?"

Fidelman couldn't help blushing. "Not exactly, really just a student."

"From which institution?"

He coughed a little. "By that I mean a professional student, you might say. Call me Trofimov, from Chekhov. If there's something to learn I want to learn it."

"You have some kind of a project?" the other persisted. "A grant?"

"No grant. My money is hard-earned. I worked and saved a long time to take a year in Italy. I made certain sacrifices. As for a project, I'm writing on the painter Giotto. He was one of the most important—"

"You don't have to tell me about Giotto," Susskind interrupted with a little smile.

"You've studied his work?"

"Who doesn't know Giotto?"

"That's interesting to me," said Fidelman, secretly irritated. "How do you happen to know him?"

"How do you mean?"

"I've given a good deal of time and study to his work."

"So I know him too."

I'd better get this over with before it begins to amount to something, Fidelman thought. He set down his bag and fished with a finger in his leather coin purse. The two porters watched with interest, one taking a sandwich out of his pocket, unwrapping the newspaper, and beginning to eat.

"This is for yourself," Fidelman said.

Susskind hardly glanced at the coin as he let it drop into his pants pocket. The porters then left.

The refugee had an odd way of standing motionless, like a cigar store Indian about to burst into flight. "In your luggage," he said vaguely, "would you maybe have a suit you can't use? I could use a suit."

At last he comes to the point. Fidelman, though annoyed, controlled himself. "All I have is a change from the one you now see me wearing. Don't get the wrong idea about me, Mr. Susskind. I'm not rich. In fact, I'm poor. Don't let a few new clothes deceive you. I owe my sister money for them."

Susskind glanced down at his shabby, baggy knickers. "I haven't had a suit for

years. The one I was wearing when I ran away from Germany fell apart. One day
I was walking around naked."

"Isn't there a welfare organization that could help you out—some group in
the Jewish community interested in refugees?"

"The Jewish organizations wish to give me what they wish, not what I wish,"
Susskind replied bitterly. "The only thing they offer me is a ticket back to Israel."

"Why don't you take it?"

"I told you already, here I feel free."

"Freedom is a relative term."

"Don't tell me about freedom."

He knows all about that, too, Fidelman thought. "So you feel free," he said,
"but how do you live?"

Susskind coughed, a brutal cough.

Fidelman was about to say something more on the subject of freedom but left
it unsaid. Jesus, I'll be saddled with him all day if I don't watch out.

"I'd better be getting off to the hotel." He bent again for his bag.

Susskind touched him on the shoulder and when Fidelman exasperatedly
straightened up, the half dollar he had given the man was staring him in the eye.

"On this we both lose money."

"How do you mean?"

"Today the lira sells six twenty-three on the dollar, but for specie they only
give you five hundred."

"In that case, give it here and I'll let you have a dollar." From his wallet Fidelman quickly extracted a crisp bill and handed it to the refugee.

"Not more?" Susskind sighed.

"Not more," the student answered emphatically.

"Maybe you would like to see Diocletian's bath? There are some enjoyable
Roman coffins inside. I will guide you for another dollar."

"No thanks." Fidelman said goodbye and, lifting the suitcase, lugged it to the
curb. A porter appeared and the student, after some hesitation, let him carry it
toward the line of small dark-green taxis in the piazza. The porter offered to
carry the briefcase too, but Fidelman wouldn't part with it. He gave the cab
driver the address of the hotel, and the taxi took off with a lurch. Fidelman at
last relaxed. Susskind, he noticed, had disappeared. Gone with his breeze, he
thought. But on the way to the hotel he had an uneasy feeling that the refugee,
crouched low, might be clinging to the little tire on the back of the cab; he
didn't look out to see.

Fidelman had reserved a room in an inexpensive hotel not far from the station, with its very convenient bus terminal. Then, as was his habit, he got himself quickly and tightly organized. He was always concerned with not wasting
time, as if it were his only wealth—not true, of course, though Fidelman admitted he was ambitious—and he soon arranged a schedule that made the most of
his working hours. Mornings he usually visited the Italian libraries, searching
their catalogues and archives, read in poor light, and made profuse notes. He
napped for an hour after lunch, then at four, when the churches and museums

were reopening, hurried off to them with lists of frescoes and paintings he must see. He was anxious to get to Florence, at the same time a little unhappy at all he would not have time to take in in Rome. Fidelman promised himself to return again if he could afford it, perhaps in the spring, and look at anything he pleased.

After dark he managed to unwind and relax. He ate as the Romans did, late, enjoyed a half liter of white wine and smoked a cigarette. Afterwards he liked to wander—especially in the old sections near the Tiber. He had read that here, under his feet, were the ruins of ancient Rome. It was an inspiring business, he, Arthur Fidelman, after all born a Bronx boy, walking around in all this history. History was mysterious, the remembrance of things unknown, in a way burdensome, in a way a sensuous experience. It uplifted and depressed, why he did not know, except that it excited his thoughts more than he thought good for him. This kind of excitement was all right up to a point, perfect maybe for a creative artist, but less so for a critic. A critic, he thought, should live on beans. He walked for miles along the winding river, gazing at the star-strewn skies. Once, after a couple of days in the Vatican Museum, he saw flights of angels—gold, blue, white—intermingled in the sky. "My God, I got to stop using my eyes so much," Fidelman said to himself. But back in his room he sometimes wrote till morning.

Late one night, about a week after his arrival in Rome, as Fidelman was writing notes on the Byzantine-style mosaics he had seen during the day, there was a knock on the door, and though the student, immersed in his work, was not conscious he had said "Avanti," he must have, for the door opened, and instead of an angel, in came Susskind in his shirt and baggy knickers.

Fidelman, who had all but forgotten the refugee, certainly never thought of him, half rose in astonishment. "Susskind," he exclaimed, "how did you get in here?"

Susskind for a moment stood motionless, then answered with a weary smile, "I'll tell you the truth, I know the desk clerk."

"But how did you know where I live?"

"I saw you walking in the street so I followed you."

"You mean you saw me accidentally?"

"How else? Did you leave me your address?"

Fidelman resumed his seat. "What can I do for you, Susskind?" He spoke grimly.

The refugee cleared his throat. "Professor, the days are warm but the nights are cold. You see how I go around naked." He held forth bluish arms, goose-fleshed. "I came to ask you to reconsider about giving away your old suit."

"And who says it's an old suit?" Despite himself, Fidelman's voice thickened.

"One suit is new, so the other is old."

"Not precisely. I am afraid I have no suit for you, Susskind. The one I presently have hanging in the closet is a little more than a year old and I can't afford to give it away. Besides, it's gabardine, more like a summer suit."

"On me it will be for all seasons."

After a moment's reflection, Fidelman drew out his billfold and counted four single dollars. These he handed to Susskind.

"Buy yourself a warm sweater."

Susskind also counted the money. "If four," he said, "why not five?"

Fidelman flushed. The man's warped nerve. "Because I happen to have four available," he answered. "That's twenty-five hundred lire. You should be able to buy a warm sweater and have something left over besides."

"I need a suit," Susskind said. "The days are warm but the nights are cold." He rubbed his arms. "What else I need I won't tell you."

"At least roll down your sleeves if you're so cold."

"That won't help me."

"Listen, Susskind," Fidelman said gently, "I would gladly give you the suit if I could afford to, but I can't. I have barely enough money to squeeze out a year for myself here. I've already told you I am indebted to my sister. Why don't you try to get yourself a job somewhere, no matter how menial? I'm sure that in a short while you'll work yourself up into a decent position."

"A job, he says," Susskind muttered gloomily. "Do you know what it means to get a job in Italy? Who will give me a job?"

"Who gives anybody a job? They have to go out and look for it."

"You don't understand, professor. I am an Israeli citizen and this means I can only work for an Israeli company. How many Israeli companies are there here?—maybe two, El Al and Zim, and even if they had a job, they wouldn't give it to me because I have lost my passport. I would be better off now if I were stateless. A stateless person shows his laissez-passer and sometimes he can find a small job."

"But if you lost your passport why didn't you put in for a duplicate?"

"I did, but did they give it to me?"

"Why not?"

"Why not? They say I sold it."

"Had they reason to think that?"

"I swear to you somebody stole it from me."

"Under such circumstances," Fidelman asked, "how do you live?"

"How do I live?" He chomped with his teeth. "I eat air."

"Seriously?"

"Seriously, on air. I also peddle," he confessed, "but to peddle you need a license, and that the Italians won't give me. When they caught me peddling I was interned for six months in a work camp."

"Didn't they attempt to deport you?"

"They did, but I sold my mother's old wedding ring that I kept in my pocket so many years. The Italians are a humane people. They took the money and let me go, but they told me not to peddle any more."

"So what do you do now?"

"I peddle. What should I do, beg?—I peddle. But last spring I got sick and gave my little money away to the doctors. I still have a bad cough." He coughed fruitily. "Now I have no capital to buy stock with. Listen, professor, maybe we can go in partnership together? Lend me twenty thousand lire and I will buy ladies' nylon stockings. After I sell them I will return you your money."

"I have no funds to invest, Susskind."

"You will get it back, with interest."

"I honestly am sorry for you," Fidelman said, "but why don't you at least do something practical? Why don't you go to the Joint Distribution Committee, for instance, and ask them to assist you? That's their business."

"I already told you why. They wish me to go back, but I wish to stay here."

"I still think going back would be the best thing for you."

"No," cried Susskind angrily.

"If that's your decision, freely made, then why pick on me? Am I responsible for you then, Susskind?"

"Who else?" Susskind loudly replied.

"Lower your voice, please, people are sleeping around here," said Fidelman, beginning to perspire. "Why should I be?"

"You know what responsibility means?"

"I think so."

"Then you are responsible. Because you are a man. Because you are a Jew, aren't you?"

"Yes, goddamn it, but I'm not the only one in the whole wide world. Without prejudice, I refuse the obligation. I am a single individual and can't take on everybody's personal burden. I have the weight of my own to contend with."

He reached for his billfold and plucked out another dollar.

"This makes five. It's more than I can afford, but take it and after this please leave me alone. I have made my contribution."

Susskind stood there, oddly motionless, an impassioned statue, and for a moment Fidelman wondered if he would stay all night, but at last the refugee thrust forth a stiff arm, took the fifth dollar, and departed.

Early the next morning Fidelman moved out of the hotel into another, less convenient for him, but far away from Shimon Susskind and his endless demands.

This was Tuesday. On Wednesday, after a busy morning in the library, Fidelman entered a nearby trattoria and ordered a plate of spaghetti with tomato sauce. He was reading his *Messaggero*, anticipating the coming of the food, for he was unusually hungry, when he sensed a presence at the table. He looked up, expecting the waiter, but beheld instead Susskind standing there, alas, unchanged.

Is there no escape from him? thought Fidelman, severely vexed. Is this why I came to Rome?

"Shalom, professor," Susskind said, keeping his eyes off the table. "I was passing and saw you sitting here alone, so I came in to say shalom."

"Susskind," Fidelman said in anger, "have you been following me again?"

"How could I follow you?" asked the astonished Susskind. "Do I know where you live now?"

Though Fidelman blushed a little, he told himself he owed nobody an explanation. So he had found out he had moved—good.

"My feet are tired. Can I sit five minutes?"

"Sit."

Susskind drew out a chair. The spaghetti arrived, steaming hot. Fidelman sprinkled it with cheese and wound his fork into several tender strands. One of the strings of spaghetti seemed to stretch for miles, so he stopped at a certain point and swallowed the forkful. Having foolishly neglected to cut the long spaghetti string he was left sucking it, seemingly endlessly. This embarrassed him.

Susskind watched with rapt attention.

Fidelman at last reached the end of the long spaghetti, patted his mouth with a napkin, and paused in his eating.

"Would you care for a plateful?"

Susskind, eyes hungry, hesitated. "Thanks," he said.

"Thanks yes or thanks no?"

"Thanks no." The eyes looked away.

Fidelman resumed eating, carefully winding his fork; he had had not too much practice with this sort of thing and was soon involved in the same dilemma with the spaghetti. Seeing Susskind still watching him, he became tense.

"We are not Italians, professor," the refugee said. "Cut it in small pieces with your knife. Then you will swallow it easier."

"I'll handle it as I please," Fidelman responded testily. "This is my business. You attend to yours."

"My business," Susskind sighed, "don't exist. This morning I had to let a wonderful chance get away from me. I had a chance to buy ladies' stockings at three hundred lire if I had money to buy half a gross. I could easily sell them for five hundred a pair. We would have made a nice profit."

"The news doesn't interest me."

"So if not ladies' stockings, I can also get sweaters, scarves, men's socks, also cheap leather goods, ceramics—whatever would interest you."

"What interests me is what you did with the money I gave you for a sweater."

"It's getting cold, professor," Susskind said worriedly. "Soon comes the November rains, and in winter the tramontana. I thought I ought to save your money to buy a couple of kilos of chestnuts and a bag of charcoal for my burner. If you sit all day on a busy street corner you can sometimes make a thousand lire. Italians like hot chestnuts. But if I do this I will need some warm clothes, maybe a suit."

"A suit," Fidelman remarked sarcastically, "why not an overcoat?"

"I have a coat, poor that it is, but now I need a suit. How can anybody come in company without a suit?"

Fidelman's hand trembled as he laid down his fork. "To my mind you are utterly irresponsible and I won't be saddled with you. I have the right to choose my own problems and the right to my privacy."

"Don't get excited, professor, it's bad for your digestion. Eat in peace." Susskind got up and left the trattoria.

Fidelman hadn't the appetite to finish his spaghetti. He paid the bill, waited ten minutes, then departed, glancing around from time to time to see if he was being followed. He headed down the sloping street to a small piazza where he saw a couple of cabs. Not that he could afford one, but he wanted to make sure Susskind didn't tail him back to his new hotel. He would warn the clerk at the desk never to allow anybody of the refugee's name or description even to make inquiries about him.

Susskind, however, stepped out from behind a plashing fountain at the center of the little piazza. Modestly addressing the speechless Fidelman, he said, "I don't wish to take only, professor. If I had something to give you, I would gladly give it to you."

"Thanks," snapped Fidelman, "just give me some peace of mind."

"That you have to find yourself," Susskind answered.

In the taxi Fidelman decided to leave for Florence the next day, rather than at the end of the week, and once and for all be done with the pest.

That night, after returning to his room from an unpleasurable walk in the Trastevere—he had a headache from too much wine at supper—Fidelman found his door ajar and at once recalled that he had forgotten to lock it, although he had as usual left the key with the desk clerk. He was at first frightened, but when he tried the armadio in which he kept his clothes and suitcase, it was shut tight. Hastily unlocking it, he was relieved to see his blue gabardine suit—a one-button-jacket affair, the trousers a little frayed at the cuffs, but all in good shape and usable for years to come—hanging amid some shirts the maid had pressed for him; and when he examined the contents of the suitcase he found nothing missing, including, thank God, his passport and traveler's checks. Gazing around the room, Fidelman saw all in place. Satisfied, he picked up a book and read ten pages before he thought of his briefcase. He jumped to his feet and began to search everywhere, remembering distinctly that it had been on the night table as he had lain on the bed that afternoon, rereading his chapter. He searched under the bed and behind the night table, then again throughout the room, even on top of and behind the armadio. Fidelman hopelessly opened every drawer, no matter how small, but found neither the briefcase nor, what was worse, the chapter in it.

With a groan he sank down on the bed, insulting himself for not having made a copy of the manuscript, because he had more than once warned himself that something like this might happen to it. But he hadn't because there were some revisions he had contemplated making, and he had planned to retype the entire chapter before beginning the next. He thought now of complaining to the owner of the hotel, who lived on the floor below, but it was already past midnight and he realized nothing could be done until morning. Who could have taken it? The maid or the hall porter? It seemed unlikely they would risk their jobs to steal a piece of leather goods that would bring them only a few thousand lire in a pawnshop. Possibly a sneak thief? He would ask tomorrow if other persons on the floor were missing something. He somehow doubted it. If a thief, he would then and there have ditched the chapter and stuffed the briefcase with Fidelman's oxblood shoes, left by the bed, and the fifteen-dollar R. H. Macy sweater that lay in full view of the desk. But if not the maid or porter or a sneak thief, then who? Though Fidelman had not the slightest shred of evidence to support his suspicions, he could think of only one person—Susskind. This thought stung him. But if Susskind, why? Out of pique, perhaps, that he had not been given the suit he had coveted, nor was able to pry it out of the armadio? Try as he would, Fidelman could think of no one else and no other reason. Somehow the peddler had followed him home (he suspected their meeting at the fountain) and had got into his room while he was out to supper.

Fidelman's sleep that night was wretched. He dreamed of pursuing the refugee in the Jewish catacombs under the ancient Appian Way, threatening him with a blow on the presumptuous head with a seven-flamed candelabrum he clutched in his hand; while Susskind, clever ghost, who knew the ins and outs of all the crypts and alleys, eluded him at every turn. Then Fidelman's candles all blew out, leaving him sightless and alone in the cemeterial dark; but when the student arose in the morning and wearily drew up the blinds, the yellow Italian sun winked him cheerfully in both bleary eyes.

Fidelman postponed going to Florence. He reported his loss to the Questura, and though the police were polite and eager to help, they could do nothing for him. On the form on which the inspector noted the complaint, he listed the briefcase as worth ten thousand lire, and for "valore del manuscritto" he drew a line. Fidelman, after giving the matter a good deal of thought, did not report Susskind, first, because he had absolutely no proof, for the desk clerk swore he had seen no stranger around in knickers; second, because he was afraid of the consequences for the refugee if he was written down "suspected thief" as well as "unlicensed peddler" and inveterate refugee. He tried instead to rewrite the chapter, which he felt sure he knew by heart, but when he sat down at the desk, there were important thoughts, whole paragraphs, even pages, that went blank in the mind. He considered sending to America for his notes for the chapter, but they were in a barrel in his sister's attic in Levittown, among many notes for other projects. The thought of Bessie, a mother of five, poking around in his things, and the work entailed in sorting the cards, then getting them packaged and mailed to him across the ocean, wearied Fidelman unspeakably; he was certain she would send the wrong ones. He laid down his pen and went into the street, seeking Susskind. He searched for him in neighborhoods where he had seen him before, and though Fidelman spent hours looking, literally days, Susskind never appeared; or if he perhaps did, the sight of Fidelman caused him to vanish. And when the student inquired about him at the Israeli consulate, the clerk, a new man on the job, said he had no record of such a person or his lost passport; on the other hand, he was known at the Joint Distribution Committee, but by name and address only, an impossibility, Fidelman thought. They gave him a number to go to but the place had long since been torn down to make way for an apartment house.

Time went without work, without accomplishment. To put an end to this appalling waste Fidelman tried to force himself back into his routine of research and picture viewing. He moved out of the hotel, which he now could not stand for the harm it had done him (leaving a telephone number and urging he be called if the slightest clue turned up), and he took a room in a small pensione near the stazione and here had breakfast and supper rather than go out. He was much concerned with expenditures and carefully recorded them in a notebook he had acquired for the purpose. Nights, instead of wandering in the city, feasting himself upon its beauty and mystery, he kept his eyes glued to paper, sitting steadfastly at his desk in an attempt to re-create his initial chapter, because he was lost without a beginning. He had tried writing the second chapter from notes in his possession, but it had come to nothing. Always Fidelman needed something solid behind him before he could advance, some worthwhile accomplishment upon which to build another. He worked late, but his mood, or in-spiration, or whatever it was, had deserted him, leaving him with growing anxi-ety, almost disorientation; of not knowing—it seemed to him for the first time in months—what he must do next, a feeling that was torture. Therefore he again took up his search for the refugee. He thought now that once he had settled it, knew that the man had or hadn't stolen his chapter—whether he recovered it or not seemed at the moment immaterial—just the knowing of it would ease his mind and again he would *feel* like working, the crucial element.

Daily he combed the crowded streets, searching for Susskind wherever people peddled. On successive Sunday mornings he took the long ride to the Porta Por-tese market and hunted for hours among the piles of secondhand goods and junk lining the back streets, hoping his briefcase would magically appear, though it never did. He visited the open market at Piazza Fontanella Borghese, and ob-served the ambulant vendors at Piazza Dante. He looked among fruit and vege-table stalls set up in the streets, whenever he chanced upon them, and dawdled on busy street corners after dark, among beggars and fly-by-night peddlers. After the first cold snap at the end of October, when the chestnut sellers appeared throughout the city, huddled over pails of glowing coals, he sought in their faces the missing Susskind. Where in all of modern and ancient Rome was he? The man lived in the open air—he had to appear somewhere. Sometimes when rid-ing in a bus or tram, Fidelman thought he had glimpsed somebody in a crowd, dressed in the refugee's clothes, and he invariably got off to run after whoever it was—once a man standing in front of the Banco di Santo Spirito, gone when Fidelman breathlessly arrived; and another time he overtook a person in knick-ers, but this one wore a monocle. Sir Ian Susskind?

In November it rained. Fidelman wore a blue beret with his trench coat and a pair of black Italian shoes, smaller, despite their pointed toes, than his burly ox-bloods which overheated his feet and whose color he detested. But instead of vis-iting museums he frequented movie houses, sitting in the cheapest seats and regretting the cost. He was, at odd hours in certain streets, several times accosted by prostitutes, some heartbreakingly pretty, one a slender, unhappy-looking girl with bags under her eyes whom he desired mightily, but Fidelman feared for his health. He had got to know the face of Rome and spoke Italian fairly fluently, but his heart was burdened, and in his blood raged a murderous hatred of the bandy-legged refugee—although there were times when he bethought himself he might be wrong—so Fidelman more than once cursed him to perdition.

One Friday night, as the first star glowed over the Tiber, Fidelman, walking aimlessly along the left riverbank, came upon a synagogue and wandered in among a crowd of Sephardim with Italianate faces. One by one they paused be-fore a sink in an antechamber to dip their hands under a flowing faucet, then in the house of worship touched with loose fingers their brows, mouths, and breasts as they bowed to the Ark, Fidelman doing likewise. Where in the world am I? Three rabbis rose from a bench and the service began, a long prayer, sometimes chanted, sometimes accompanied by invisible organ music, but no Susskind any-where. Fidelman sat at a desk-like pew in the last row, where he could inspect the congregants yet keep an eye on the door. The synagogue was unheated and the cold rose like an exudation from the marble floor. The student's freezing nose burned like a lit candle. He got up to go, but the beadle, a stout man in a high hat and short caftan, wearing a long thick silver chain around his neck, fixed the student with his powerful left eye.

"From New York?" he inquired, slowly approaching.

Half the congregation turned to see who.

"State, not city," answered Fidelman, nursing an active guilt for the attention he was attracting. Then, taking advantage of a pause, he whispered, "Do you happen to know a man named Susskind? He wears knickers."

"A relative?" The beadle gazed at him sadly.

"Not exactly."

"My own son—killed in the Ardeatine Caves." Tears stood forth in his eyes.

"Ah, for that I'm sorry."

But the beadle had exhausted the subject. He wiped his wet lids with pudgy fingers and the curious Sephardim turned back to their prayer books.

"Which Susskind?" the beadle wanted to know.

"Shimon."

He scratched his ear. "Look in the ghetto."

"I looked."

"Look again."

The beadle walked slowly away and Fidelman sneaked out.

The ghetto lay behind the synagogue for several crooked, well-packed blocks, encompassing aristocratic palazzi ruined by age and unbearable numbers, their discolored façades strung with lines of withered wet wash, the fountains in the piazzas, dirt-laden, dry. And dark stone tenements, built partly on centuries-old ghetto walls, inclined toward one another across narrow, cobblestoned streets. In and among the impoverished houses were the wholesale establishments of wealthy Jews, dark holes ending in jeweled interiors, silks and silver of all colors. In the mazed streets wandered the present-day poor, Fidelman among them, oppressed by history, although, he joked to himself, it added years to his life.

A white moon shone upon the ghetto, lighting it like dark day. Once he thought he saw a ghost he knew by sight, and hastily followed him through a thick stone passage to a blank wall where shone in white letters under a tiny electric bulb: VIETATO URINARE. Here was a smell but no Susskind.

For thirty lire the student bought a dwarfed, blackened banana from a street vendor (not S) on a bicycle, and stopped to eat. A crowd of ragazzi gathered to watch.

"Anybody here know Susskind, a refugee wearing knickers?" Fidelman announced, stooping to point the banana where the pants went beneath the knees. He also made his legs a trifle bowed but nobody noticed.

There was no response until he had finished his fruit, then a thin-faced boy with brown liquescent eyes out of Murillo piped: "He sometimes works in the Cimitero Verano, the Jewish section."

There too? thought Fidelman. "Works in the cemetery?" he inquired. "With a shovel?"

"He prays for the dead," the boy answered, "for a small fee."

Fidelman bought him a quick banana and the others dispersed.

In the cemetery, deserted on the Sabbath—he should have come Sunday— Fidelman went among the graves, reading legends carved on tombstones, many topped with small brass candelabra, whilst withered yellow chrysanthemums lay on the stone tablets of other graves, dropped stealthily, Fidelman imagined, on All Souls' Day—a festival in another part of the cemetery—by renegade sons and daughters unable to bear the sight of their dead bereft of flowers, while the crypts of the goyim were lit and in bloom. Many were burial places, he read on the stained stones, of those who, for one reason or another, had died in the late large war, including an empty place, it said under a six-pointed star engraved upon a marble slab that lay on the ground, for "My beloved father/Betrayed by the damned Fascists/Murdered at Auschwitz by the barbarous Nazis/O *Crime Orribile*." But no Susskind.

Three months had gone by since Fidelman's arrival in Rome. Should he, he many times asked himself, leave the city and this foolish search? Why not off to Florence, and there amid the art splendors of the world, be inspired to resume his work? But the loss of his first chapter was like a spell cast over him. There were times he scorned it as a man-made thing, like all such, replaceable; other times he feared it was not the chapter per se, but that his volatile curiosity had become somehow entangled with Susskind's strange personality— Had he repaid generosity by stealing a man's life work? Was he so distorted? To satisfy himself, to know man, Fidelman had to know, though at what a cost in precious time and effort. Sometimes he smiled wryly at all this; ridiculous, the chapter grieved him for itself only—the precious thing he had created, then lost—especially when he got to thinking of the long diligent labor, how painstakingly he had built each idea, how cleverly mastered problems of order, form, how impressive the finished product, Giotto reborn! It broke the heart. What else, if after months he was here, still seeking?

And Fidelman was unchangingly convinced that Susskind had taken it, or why would he still be hiding? He sighed much and gained weight. Mulling over his frustrated career, on the backs of envelopes containing unanswered letters from his sister Bessie he aimlessly sketched little angels flying. Once, studying his minuscule drawings, it occurred to him that he might someday return to painting, but the thought was more painful than Fidelman could bear.

One bright morning in mid-December, after a good night's sleep, his first in weeks, he vowed he would have another look at the Navicella and then be off to Florence. Shortly before noon he visited the porch of St. Peter's, trying, from his remembrance of Giotto's sketch, to see the mosaic as it had been before its many restorations. He hazarded a note or two in shaky handwriting, then left the church and was walking down the sweeping flight of stairs, when he beheld at the bottom—his heart misgave him, was he still seeing pictures, a sneaky apostle added to the overloaded boatful?—ecco Susskind! The refugee, in beret and long green G.I. raincoat, from under whose skirts showed his black-stockinged, rooster's ankles—indicating knickers going on above though hidden—was selling black and white rosaries to all who would buy. He had several strands of beads in one hand, while in the palm of the other a few gilded medallions glinted in the winter sun. Despite his outer clothing, Susskind looked, it must be

said, unchanged, not a pound more of meat or muscle, the face though aged,
ageless. Gazing at him, the student ground his teeth in remembrance. He was
tempted quickly to hide, and unobserved observe the thief; but his impatience,
after the long unhappy search, was too much for him. With controlled trepida-
tion he approached Susskind on his left as the refugee was busily engaged on the
right, urging a sale of beads upon a woman drenched in black.

"Beads, rosaries, say your prayers with holy beads."

"Greetings, Susskind," Fidelman said, coming shakily down the stairs, dis-
sembling the Unified Man, all peace and contentment. "One looks for you
everywhere and finds you here. Wie gehts?"

Susskind, though his eyes flickered, showed no surprise to speak of. For a moment his expression seemed to say he had no idea who this was, had forgotten
Fidelman's existence, but then at last remembered—somebody long ago from
another country, whom you smiled on, then forgot.

"Still here?" he perhaps ironically joked.

"Still." Fidelman was embarrassed at his voice slipping.

"Rome holds you?"

"Rome," faltered Fidelman, "—the air." He breathed deep and exhaled with
emotion.

Noticing the refugee was not truly attentive, his eyes roving upon potential
customers, Fidelman, girding himself, remarked, "By the way, Susskind, you
didn't happen to notice—did you?—the briefcase I was carrying with me around
the time we met in September?"

"Briefcase—what kind?" This he said absently, his eyes on the church doors.

"Pigskin. I had in it"—here Fidelman's voice could be heard cracking—"a
chapter of critical work on Giotto I was writing. You know, I'm sure, the Tre-
cento painter?"

"Who doesn't know Giotto?"

"Do you happen to recall whether you saw, if, that is—" He stopped, at a loss
for words other than accusatory.

"Excuse me—business." Susskind broke away and bounced up the steps two
at a time. A man he approached shied away. He had beads, didn't need others.

Fidelman had followed the refugee. "Reward," he muttered up close to his
ear. "Fifteen thousand for the chapter, and who has it can keep the brand-new
briefcase. That's his business, no questions asked. Fair enough?"

Susskind spied a lady tourist, including camera and guide book. "Beads—holy
beads." He held up both hands but she was just a Lutheran, passing through.

"Slow today," Susskind complained as they walked down the stairs, "but
maybe it's the items. Everybody has the same. If I had some big ceramics of the
Holy Mother, they go like hot cakes—a good investment for somebody with a
little cash."

"Use the reward for that," Fidelman cagily whispered, "buy Holy Mothers."

If he heard, Susskind gave no sign. At the sight of a family of nine emerging
from the main portal above, the refugee, calling addio over his shoulder, fairly
flew up the steps. But Fidelman uttered no response. I'll get the rat yet. He went
off to hide behind a high fountain in the square. But the flying spume raised by

the wind wet him, so he retreated behind a massive column and peeked out at short intervals to keep the peddler in sight.

At two o'clock, when St. Peter's closed to visitors, Susskind dumped his goods into his raincoat pockets and locked up shop. Fidelman followed him all the way home, indeed the ghetto, although along a street he had not consciously been on before, which led into an alley where the refugee pulled open a left-handed door and, without transition, was "home." Fidelman, sneaking up close, caught a dim glimpse of an overgrown closet containing bed and table. He found no address on wall or door, nor, to his surprise, any door lock. This for a moment depressed him. It meant Susskind had nothing worth stealing. Of his own, that is. The student promised himself to return tomorrow, when the occupant was elsewhere.

Return he did, in the morning, while the entrepreneur was out selling religious articles, glanced around once, and was quickly inside. He shivered—a pitch-black freezing cave. Fidelman scratched up a thick match and confirmed bed and table, also a rickety chair, but no heat or light except a drippy candle stub in a saucer on the table. He lit the yellow candle and searched all over the place. In the table drawer a few eating implements plus safety razor, though where he shaved was a mystery, probably a public toilet. On a shelf above the thin-blanketed bed stood half a flask of red wine, part of a package of spaghetti, and a hard panino. Also an unexpected little fish bowl with a bony goldfish swimming around in arctic seas. The fish, reflecting the candle flame, gulped repeatedly, threshing its frigid tail as Fidelman watched. He loves pets, thought the student. Under the bed he found a chamber pot, but nowhere a briefcase with a fine critical chapter in it. The place was not more than an icebox someone probably had lent the refugee to come in out of the rain. Alas, Fidelman sighed. Back in the pensione, it took a hot-water bottle two hours to thaw him out; but from the visit he never fully recovered.

In this latest dream of Fidelman's he was spending the day in a cemetery all crowded with tombstones, when up out of an empty grave rose this long-nosed brown shade, Virgilio Susskind, beckoning.

Fidelman hurried over.

"Have you read Tolstoy?"

"Sparingly."

"Why is art?" asked the shade, drifting off.

Fidelman, willy-nilly, followed, and the ghost, as it vanished, led him up steps going through the ghetto and into a marble synagogue.

The student, left alone, for no reason he could think of lay down upon the stone floor, his shoulders keeping strangely warm as he stared at the sunlit vault above. The fresco therein revealed this saint in fading blue, the sky flowing from his head, handing an old knight in a thin red robe his gold cloak. Nearby stood a humble horse and two stone hills.

Giotto. San Francesco dona le vesti al cavaliere povero.

Fidelman awoke running. He stuffed his blue gabardine into a paper bag, caught a bus, and knocked early on Susskind's heavy portal.

"Avanti." The refugee, already garbed in beret and raincoat (probably his pajamas), was standing at the table, lighting the candle with a flaming sheet of paper. To Fidelman the paper looked like the underside of a typewritten page. Despite himself, the student recalled in letters of fire his entire chapter.

"Here, Susskind," he said in a trembling voice, offering the bundle, "I bring you my suit. Wear it in good health."

The refugee glanced at it without expression. "What do you wish for it?"

"Nothing at all." Fidelman laid the bag on the table, called goodbye, and left.

He soon heard footsteps clattering after him across the cobblestones.

"Excuse me, I kept this under my mattress for you." Susskind thrust at him the pigskin briefcase.

Fidelman savagely opened it, searching frenziedly in each compartment, but the bag was empty. The refugee was already in flight. With a bellow the student started after him. "You bastard, you burned my chapter!"

"Have mercy," cried Susskind, "I did you a favor."

"I'll do you one and cut your throat."

"The words were there but the spirit was missing."

In a towering rage, Fidelman forced a burst of speed, but the refugee, light as the wind in his marvelous knickers, his green coattails flying, rapidly gained ground.

The ghetto Jews, framed in amazement in their medieval windows, stared at the wild pursuit. But in the middle of it, Fidelman, stout and short of breath, moved by all he had lately learned, had a triumphant insight.

"Susskind, come back," he shouted, half sobbing. "The suit is yours. All is forgiven."

He came to a dead halt but the refugee ran on. When last seen he was still running.

Gabriel Garcia Marquez

· ·

EYES OF A BLUE DOG

Then she looked at me. I thought that she was looking at me for the first time. But then, when she turned around behind the lamp and I kept feeling her slippery and oily look in back of me, over my shoulder, I understood that it was I who was looking at her for the first time. I lit a cigarette. I took a drag on the harsh, strong smoke, before spinning in the chair, balancing on one of the rear legs. After that I saw her there, as if she'd been standing beside the lamp looking at me every night. For a few brief minutes that's all we did: look at each other. I looked from the chair, balancing on one of the rear legs. She stood, with a long and quiet hand on the lamp, looking at me. I saw her eyelids lighted up as on every night. It was then that I remembered the usual thing, when I said to her: "Eyes of a blue dog." Without taking her hand off the lamp she said to me: "That. We'll never forget that." She left the orbit, sighing: "Eyes of a blue dog. I've written it everywhere."

I saw her walk over to the dressing table. I watched her appear in the circular glass of the mirror looking at me now at the end of a back and forth of mathematical light. I watched her keep on looking at me with her great hot-coal eyes: looking at me while she opened the little box covered with pink mother of pearl. I saw her powder her nose. When she finished, she closed the box, stood up again, and walked over to the lamp once more, saying: "I'm afraid that someone is dreaming about this room and revealing my secrets." And over the flame she held the same long and tremulous hand that she had been warming before sitting down at the mirror. And she said: "You don't feel the cold." And I said to her: "Sometimes." And she said to me: "You must feel it now." And then I understood why I couldn't have been alone in the seat. It was the cold that had been giving me the certainty of my solitude. "Now I feel it," I said. "And it's strange because the night is quiet. Maybe the sheet fell off." She didn't answer. Again she began to move toward the mirror and I turned again in the chair, keeping my back to her. Without seeing her, I knew what she was doing. I knew that she was sitting in front of the mirror again, seeing my back, which had had time to reach the depths of the mirror and be caught by her look, which had also had just enough time to reach the depths and return—before the hand had time to start the second turn—until her lips were anointed now with crimson, from the first turn of her hand in front of the mirror. I saw, opposite me, the smooth wall, which was like another blind mirror in which I couldn't see her—sitting behind me—but could imagine her where she probably was as if a mirror had been hung in place of the wall. "I see you," I told her. And on the wall I saw what was as if she had raised her eyes and had seen me with my back turned toward her from the chair, in the depths of the mirror, my face turned toward the wall. Then I saw her lower her eyes again and remain with her eyes always on her brassiere, not talking. And I said to her again: "I see you." And she raised her eyes from her brassiere again. "That's impossible," she said. I asked her why. And she, with her eyes quiet and on her brassiere again: "Because your face is turned toward the wall." Then I spun the chair around. I had the cigarette clenched in my mouth. When I stayed facing the mirror she was back by the lamp. Now she had her hands open over the flame, like the two wings of a hen, toasting herself, and with her face shaded by her own fingers. "I think I'm going to catch cold," she said. "This must be a city of ice." She turned her face to profile and her skin, from copper to red, suddenly became sad. "Do something about it," she said. And she began to get undressed, item by item, starting at the top with the brassiere. I told her: "I'm going to turn back to the wall." She said: "No. In any case, you'll see me the way you did when your back was turned." And no sooner had she said it than she was almost completely undressed, with the flame licking her long copper skin. "I've always wanted to see you like that, with the skin of your belly full of deep pits, as if you'd been beaten." And before I realized that my words had become clumsy at the sight of her nakedness, she became motionless, warming herself on the globe of the lamp, and she said: "Sometimes I think I'm made of metal." She was silent for an instant. The position of her hands over the flame varied slightly. I said: "Sometimes, in other dreams, I've thought you were only a little bronze statue in the corner of some museum. Maybe that's why you're cold." And she said: "Sometimes, when I sleep on my heart, I can feel my body growing hollow and my skin is like plate. Then, when the blood beats inside me, it's as if someone were calling by knocking on my stomach and I can feel my own copper sound in the bed. It's like— what do you call it—laminated metal." She drew closer to the lamp. "I would have liked to hear you," I said. And she said: "If we find each other sometime, put your ear to my ribs when I sleep on the left side and you'll hear me echoing. I've always wanted you to do it sometime." I heard her breathe heavily as she talked. And she said that for years she'd done nothing different. Her life had been dedicated to finding me in reality, through that identifying phrase: "Eyes of a blue dog." And she went along the street saying it aloud, as a way of telling the only person who could have understood her:

"I'm the one who comes into your dreams every night and tells you: 'Eyes of a blue dog.' " And she said that she went into restaurants and before ordering said to the waiters: "Eyes of a blue dog." But the waiters bowed reverently, without remembering ever having said that in their dreams. Then she would write on the napkins and scratch on the varnish of the tables with a knife: "Eyes of a blue dog." And on the steamed-up windows of hotels, stations, all public buildings, she would write with her forefinger: "Eyes of a blue dog." She said that once she went into a drugstore and noticed the same smell that she had smelled in her room one night after having dreamed about me. "He must be near," she thought, seeing the clean, new tiles of the drugstore. Then she went over to the clerk and said to him: "I always dream about a man who says to me: 'Eyes of a blue dog.'" And she said the clerk had looked at her eyes and told her: "As a matter of fact, miss, you do have eyes like that." And she said to him: "I have to find the man who told me those very words in my dreams." And the clerk started to laugh and moved to the other end of the counter. She kept on seeing the clean tile and smelling the odor. And she opened her purse and on the tiles, with her crimson lipstick, she wrote in red letters: "Eyes of a blue dog." The clerk came back from where he had been. He told her: "Madam, you have dirtied the tiles." He gave her a damp cloth, saying: "Clean it up." And she said, still by the lamp, that she had spent the whole afternoon on all fours, washing the tiles and saying: "Eyes of a blue dog," until people gathered at the door and said she was crazy.

Now, when she finished speaking, I remained in the corner, sitting, rocking in the chair. "Every day I try to remember the phrase with which I am to find you," I said. "Now I don't think I'll forget it tomorrow. Still, I've always said the same thing and when I wake up I've always forgotten what the words I can find you with are." And she said: "You invented them yourself on the first day." And I said to her: "I invented them because I saw your eyes of ash. But I never remember the next morning." And she, with clenched fists, beside the lamp, breathed deeply: "If you could at least remember now what city I've been writing it in."

Her tightened teeth gleamed over the flame. "I'd like to touch you now," I said. She raised the face that had been looking at the light; she raised her look, burning, roasting, too, just like her, like her hands, and I felt that she saw me, in the corner where I was sitting, rocking in the chair. "You'd never told me that," she said. "I tell you now and it's the truth," I said. From the other side of the lamp she asked for a cigarette. The butt had disappeared between my fingers. I'd forgotten that I was smoking. She said: "I don't know why I can't remember where I wrote it." And I said to her: "For the same reason that tomorrow I won't be able to remember the words." And she said sadly: "No. It's just that sometimes I think that I've dreamed that too." I stood up and walked toward the lamp. She was a little beyond, and I kept on walking with the cigarettes and matches in my hand, which would not go beyond the lamp. I held the cigarette out to her. She squeezed it between her lips and leaned over to reach the flame before I had time to light the match. "In some city in the world, on all the walls, those words have to appear in writing: 'Eyes of a blue dog,'" I said. "If I remembered them tomorrow I could find you." She raised her head again and now the lighted coal was between her lips. "Eyes of a blue dog," she sighed, remembered, with the cigarette drooping over her chin and one eye half closed. Then she sucked in the smoke with the cigarette between her fingers and exclaimed: "This is something else now. I'm warming up." And she said it with her voice a little lukewarm and fleeting, as if she hadn't really said it, but as if she had written it on a piece of paper and had brought the paper close to the flame while I read: "I'm warming," and she had continued with the paper between her thumb and forefinger, turning it around as it was being consumed and I had just read "... up," before the paper was completely consumed and dropped all wrinkled to the floor, diminished, converted into light ash dust. "That's better, "I said. "Sometimes it frightens me to see you that way. Trembling beside a lamp."

We had been seeing each other for several years. Sometimes, when we were already together, somebody would drop a spoon outside and we would wake up. Little by little we'd been coming to understand that our friendship was subordinated to things, to the simplest of happenings. Our meetings always ended that way, with the fall of a spoon early in the morning.

Now, next to the lamp, she was looking at me. I remembered that she had also looked at me in that way in the past, from that remote dream where I made the chair spin on its back legs and remained facing a strange woman with ashen eyes. It was in that dream that I asked her for the first time: "Who are you?" And she said to me: "I don't remember." I said to her: "But I think we've seen each other before." And she said, indifferently: "I think I dreamed about you once, about this same room." And I told her: "That's it. I'm beginning to remember now." And she said: "How strange. It's certain that we've met in other dreams."

She took two drags on the cigarette. I was still standing, facing the lamp, when suddenly I kept looking at her. I looked her up and down and she was still copper; no longer hard and cold metal, but yellow, soft, malleable copper. "I'd like to touch you," I said again. And she said: "You'll ruin everything." I said: "It doesn't matter now. All we have to do is turn the pillow over in order to meet again." And I held my hand out over the lamp. She didn't move. "You'll ruin everything," she said again before I could touch her. "Maybe, if you come around behind the lamp, we'd wake up frightened in who knows what part of the world." But I insisted: "It doesn't matter." And she said: "If we turned over the pillow, we'd meet again. But when you wake up you'll have forgotten." I began to move toward the corner. She stayed behind, warming her hands over the flame. And I still wasn't beside the chair when I heard her say behind me: "When I wake up at midnight, I keep turning in bed, with the fringe of the pillow burning my knee, and repeating until dawn: 'Eyes of a blue dog.' "

Then I remained with my face toward the wall. "It's already dawning," I said without looking at her. "When it struck two I was awake and that was a long time back." I went to the door. When I had the knob in my hand, I heard her voice again, the same, invariable. "Don't open that door," she said. "The hallway is full of difficult dreams." And I asked her: "How do you know?" And she told me: "Because I was there a moment ago and I had to come back when I discovered I was sleeping on my heart." I had the door half opened. I moved it a little and a cold, thin breeze brought me the fresh smell of vegetable earth, damp fields. She spoke again. I gave the turn, still moving the door, mounted on silent hinges, and I told her: "I don't think there's any hallway outside here. I'm getting the smell of country." And she, a little distant, told me: "I know that better than you. What's happening is that there's a woman outside dreaming about the country." She crossed her arms over the flame. She continued speaking: "It's that woman who always wanted to have a house in the country and was never able to leave the city." I remembered having seen the woman in some previous dream, but I knew, with the door ajar now, that within half an hour I would have to go down for breakfast. And I said: "In any case, I have to leave here in order to wake up."

Outside the wind fluttered for an instant, then remained quiet, and the breathing of someone sleeping who had just turned over in bed could be heard. The wind from the fields had ceased. There were no more smells. "Tomorrow I'll recognize you from that," I said. "I'll recognize you when on the street I see a woman writing 'Eyes of a blue dog' on the walls." And she, with a sad smile—which was already a smile of surrender to the impossible, the unreachable—said: "Yet you won't remember anything during the day." And she put her hands back over the lamp, her features darkened by a bitter cloud. "You're the only man who doesn't remember anything of what he's dreamed after he wakes up."

Translated from the Spanish by Gregory Rabassa

William Maxwell

· ·

THE PILGRIMAGE

In a rented Renault, with exactly as much luggage as the back seat would hold, Ray and Ellen Ormsby were making a little tour of France. It had so far included Vézelay, the mountain villages of Auvergne, the roses and Roman ruins of Provence, and the gorges of the Tarn. They were now on their way back to Paris by a route that was neither the most direct nor particularly scenic, and that had been chosen with one thing in mind—dinner at the Hôtel du Domino in Périgueux. The Richardsons, who were close friends of the Ormsbys in America, had insisted that they go there. "The best dinner I ever had in my entire life," Jerry Richardson had said. "Every course was something with truffles." "And the dessert," Anne Richardson had said, "was little balls of various kinds of ice cream in a beautiful basket of spun sugar with a spun-sugar bow." Putting the two statements together, Ray Ormsby had persisted in thinking that the ice cream also had truffles in it, and Ellen had given up trying to correct this impression.

At seven o'clock, they were still sixty-five kilometres from Périgueux, on a winding back-country road, and beginning to get hungry. The landscape was gilded with the evening light. Ray was driving. Ellen read aloud to him from the "Guide Gastronomique de la France" the paragraph on the Hôtel du Domino: "*Bel et confortable établissement à la renommée bien assise et que Mme. Lasgrezas dirige avec beaucoup de bonheur. Grâce à un maître queux qualifié, vous y ferez un repas de grande classe qui vous sera servi dans une élégante salle à manger ou dans un délicieux jardin d'été. . . .*"

As they drove through village after village, they saw, in addition to the usual painted Cinzano and Rasurel signs, announcements of the *spécialité* of the restaurant of this or that Hôtel des Sports or de la Poste or du Lion d'Or—always with truffles. In Montignac, there were so many of these signs that Ellen said anxiously, "Do you think we ought to eat *here*?"

"No," Ray said. "Périgueux is the place. It's the capital of Périgord, and so it's bound to have the best food."

Outside Thenon, they had a flat tire—the seventh in eight days of driving—

438

and the casing of the spare tire was in such bad condition that Ray was afraid to drive on until the inner tube had been repaired and the regular tire put back on. It was five minutes of nine when they drove up before the Hôtel du Domino, and they were famished. Ray went inside and found that the hotel had accommodations for them. The car was driven into the hotel garage and emptied of its formidable luggage, and the Ormsbys were shown up to their third-floor room, which might have been in any plain hotel anywhere in France. "What I'd really like is the roast chicken stuffed with truffles," Ellen said from the washstand. "But probably it takes a long time."

"What if it does," Ray said. "We'll be eating other things first."

He threw open the shutters and discovered that their room looked out on a painting by Dufy—the large, bare, open square surrounded by stone buildings, with the tricolor for accent, and the sky a rich, stained-glass blue. From another window, at the turning of the stairs on their way down to dinner, they saw the delicious garden, but it was dark, and no one was eating there now. At the foot of the stairs, they paused.

"You wanted the restaurant?" the concierge asked, and when they nodded, she came out from behind her mahogany railing and led them importantly down a corridor. The maître d'hôtel, in a grey business suit, stood waiting at the door of the dining room, and put them at a table for two. Then he handed them the menu with a flourish. They saw at a glance how expensive the dinner was going to be. A waitress brought plates, glasses, napkins, knives, and forks.

While Ellen was reading the menu, Ray looked slowly around the room. The "*élégante salle à manger*" looked like a hotel coffee shop. There weren't even any tablecloths. The walls were painted a dismal shade of off-mustard. His eyes came to rest finally on the stippled brown dado a foot from his face. "It's a perfect room to commit suicide in," he said, and reached for the menu. A moment later he exclaimed, "I don't see the basket of ice cream!"

"It must be there," Ellen said. "Don't get so excited."

"Well, where? Just show me!"

Together they looked through the two columns of desserts, without finding the marvel in question. "Jerry and Anne were here several days," Ellen said. "They may have had it in some other restaurant."

This explanation Ray would not accept. "It was the same dinner, I remember distinctly." The full horror of their driving all the way to Périgueux in order to eat a very expensive meal at the wrong restaurant broke over him. In a cold sweat he got up from the table.

"Where are you going?" Ellen asked.

"I'll be right back," he said, and left the dining room. Upstairs in their room, he dug the "Guide Michelin" out of a duffel-bag. He had lost all faith in the "Guide Gastronomique," because of its description of the dining room; the person who wrote that had never set eyes on the Hôtel du Domino or, probably, on Périgueux. In the "Michelin," the restaurant of the Hôtel du Domino rated one star and so did the restaurant Le Montaigne, but Le Montaigne also had three crossed forks and spoons, and suddenly it came to him, with the awful clarity of a long-submerged memory at last brought to the surface through layer after layer of consciousness, that it was at Le Montaigne and not at the Hôtel du Domino that the Richardsons had meant them to eat. He picked up Ellen's coat and, still carrying the "Michelin," went back downstairs to the dining room.

"I've brought you your coat," he said to Ellen as he sat down opposite her. "We're in the wrong restaurant."

"We aren't either," Ellen said. "And even if we were, I've *got* to have something to eat. I'm starving, and it's much too late now to go looking for—"

"It won't be far," Ray said. "Come on." He looked up into the face of the maître d'hôtel, waiting with his pencil and pad to take their order.

"You speak English?" Ray asked.

The maître d'hôtel nodded, and Ray described the basket of spun sugar filled with different kinds of ice cream.

"And a spun-sugar bow," Ellen said.

The maître d'hôtel looked blank, and so Ray tried again, speaking slowly and distinctly.

"*Omelette?*" the maître d'hôtel said.

"No—ice cream!"

"*Glace,*" Ellen said.

"*Et du sucre,*" Ray said. "*Une*—" He and Ellen looked at each other. Neither of them could think of the word for "basket."

The maître d'hôtel went over to a sideboard and returned with another menu. "*Le menu des glaces,*" he said coldly. "*Vanille,*" they read, "*chocolat, pistache, framboise, fraise, tutti-frutti, praliné . . .*"

Even if the spun-sugar basket had been on the *menu des glaces* (which it wasn't), they were in too excited a state to have found it—Ray because of his fear that they were making an irremediable mistake in having dinner at this restaurant and Ellen because of the dreadful way he was acting.

"We came here on a pilgrimage," he said to the maître d'hôtel, in a tense, excited voice that carried all over the dining room. "We have these friends in America who ate in Périgueux, and it is absolutely necessary that we eat in the place they told us about."

"This is a very good restaurant," the maître d'hôtel said. "We have many *spécialités. Foie gras truffé, poulet du Périgord noir, truffes sous la cendre*—"

"I know," Ray said, "but apparently it isn't the right one." He got up from his chair, and Ellen, shaking her head—because there was no use arguing with him when he was like this—got up, too. The other diners had all turned around to watch.

"Come," the maître d'hôtel said, taking hold of Ray's elbow. "In the lobby is a lady who speaks English very well. She will understand what it is you want."

In the lobby, Ray told his story again—how they had come to Périgueux because their friends in America had told them about a certain restaurant here, and how it was this restaurant and no other that they must find. They had thought it was the restaurant in the Hôtel du Domino, but since the restaurant of the Hôtel du Domino did not have the dessert that their friends in America had particularly recommended, little balls of ice cream in—

The concierge, her eyes large with sudden comprehension, interrupted him. "You wanted truffles?"

· · · · ·

Out on the sidewalk, trying to read the "Michelin" map of Périgueux by the feeble light of a tall street lamp, Ray said, "Le Montaigne has a star just like the Hôtel du Domino, but it also has three crossed forks and spoons, so it must be better than the hotel."

"All those crossed forks and spoons mean is that it is a very comfortable place to eat in," Ellen said. "It has nothing to do with the quality of the food. I don't care where we eat, so long as I don't have to go back there."

There were circles of fatigue under her eyes. She was both exasperated with him and proud of him for insisting on getting what they had come here for, when most people would have given in and taken what there was. They walked on a couple of blocks and came to a second open square. Ray stopped a man and woman.

"*Pardon, m'sieur,*" he said, removing his hat. "*Le restaurant La Montagne, c'est par là*"—he pointed—"*ou par là?*"

"*La Montagne? Le restaurant La Montagne?*" the man said dubiously. "*Je regrette, mais je ne le connais pas.*"

Ray opened the "Michelin" and, by the light of the nearest neon sign, the man and woman read down the page.

"*Ooh,* LE MONTAIGNE!" the woman exclaimed suddenly.

"LE MONTAIGNE!" the man echoed.

"*Oui, Le Montaigne,*" Ray said, nodding.

The man pointed across the square.

Standing in front of Le Montaigne, Ray again had doubts. It was much larger than the restaurant of the Hôtel du Domino, but it looked much more like a bar than a first-class restaurant. And again there were no tablecloths. A waiter approached them as they stood undecided on the sidewalk. Ray asked to see the menu, and the waiter disappeared into the building. A moment later, a second waiter appeared. "*Le menu,*" he said, pointing to a standard a few feet away. Le Montaigne offered many specialties, most of them *truffés,* but not the Richardsons' dessert.

"Couldn't we just go someplace and have an ordinary meal?" Ellen said. "I don't think I feel like eating anything elaborate any longer."

But Ray had made a discovery. "The restaurant is upstairs," he said. "What we've been looking at is the café, so naturally there aren't any tablecloths."

Taking Ellen by the hand, he started up what turned out to be a circular staircase. The second floor of the building was dark. Ellen, convinced that the restaurant had stopped serving dinner, objected to going any farther, but Ray went on, and, protesting, she followed him. The third floor was brightly lighted—was, in fact, a restaurant, with white tablecloths, gleaming crystal, and the traditional dark-red plush upholstery, and two or three clients who were lingering over the end of dinner. The maître d'hôtel, in a black dinner jacket, led them to a table and handed them the same menu they had read downstairs.

"I don't see any roast chicken stuffed with truffles," Ellen said.

"Oh, I forgot that's what you wanted!" Ray said, conscience-stricken. "Did they have it at the Domino?"

"No, but they had *poulet noir*—and here they don't even have that."

"I'm so sorry," he said. "Are you sure they don't have it here?" He ran his eyes down the list of dishes with truffles and said suddenly, "There it is!"

"Where?" Ellen demanded. He pointed to "*Tournedos aux truffes du Périgord.*" "That's not chicken," Ellen said.

"Well, it's no good, then," Ray said.

"No good?" the maître d'hôtel said indignantly. "It's *very* good! *Le tournedos aux truffes du Périgord* is a *spécialité* of the restaurant!"

They were only partly successful in conveying to him that that was not what Ray had meant.

No, there was no roast chicken stuffed with truffles.

No chicken of any kind.

"I'm very sorry," Ray said, and got up from his chair.

He was not at all sure that Ellen would go back to the restaurant in the Hôtel du Domino with him, but she did. Their table was just as they had left it. A waiter and a busboy, seeing them come in, exchanged startled whispers. The maître d'hôtel did not come near them for several minutes after they had sat down, and Ray carefully didn't look around for him.

"Do you think he is angry because we walked out?" Ellen asked.

Ray shook his head. "I think we hurt his feelings, though. I think he prides himself on speaking English, and now he will never again be sure that he does speak it, because of us."

Eventually, the maître d'hôtel appeared at their table. Sickly smiles were exchanged all around, and the menu was offered for the second time, without the flourish.

"What is *les truffes sous la cendre?*" Ellen asked.

"It takes forty-five minutes," the maître d'hôtel said.

"*Le foie gras truffé,*" Ray said. "For two."

"*Le foie gras,* O.K.," the maître d'hôtel said. "*Et ensuite?*"

"*Œufs en gelée,*" Ellen said.

"*Œufs en gelée,* O.K."

"*Le poulet noir,*" Ray said.

"*Le poulet noir,* O.K."

"*Et deux Cinzano,*" Ray said, on solid ground at last, "*avec un morceau de glace et un zeste de citron. S'il vous plaît.*"

The apéritif arrived, with ice and lemon peel, but the wine list was not presented, and Ray asked the waitress for it. She spoke to the maître d'hôtel, and that was the last the Ormsbys ever saw of her. The maître d'hôtel brought the wine list, they ordered the dry white *vin du pays* that he recommended, and their dinner was served to them by a waiter so young that Ray looked to see whether he was in knee pants.

The pâté was everything the Richardsons had said it would be, and Ray, to make up for all he had put his wife through in the course of the evening, gave her a small quantity of his, which, protesting, she accepted. The maître d'hôtel stopped at their table and said, "Is it good?"

"Very good," they said simultaneously.

The *œufs en gelée* arrived and were also very good, but were they any better than or even as good as the *œufs en gelée* the Ormsbys had had in the restaurant of a hotel on the outskirts of Aix-en-Provence was the question.

"Is it good?" the maître d'hôtel asked.

"Very good," they said. "So is the wine."

The boy waiter brought in the *poulet noir*—a chicken casserole with a dark-brown Madeira sauce full of chopped truffles.

"Is it good?" Ray asked when the waiter had finished serving them and Ellen had tasted the *pièce de résistance.*

"It's very good," she said. "But I'm not sure I can taste the truffles."

"I think I can," he said, a moment later.

"With the roast chicken, it probably would have been quite easy," Ellen said.

"Are you sure the Richardsons had roast chicken stuffed with truffles?" Ray asked.

"I think so," Ellen said. "Anyway, I know I've read about it."

"Is it good?" the maître d'hôtel, their waiter, and the waiter from a neighboring table asked, in succession.

"Very good," the Ormsbys said.

Since they couldn't have the little balls of various kinds of ice cream in a basket of spun sugar with a spun-sugar bow for dessert, they decided not to have any dessert at all. The meal came to an abrupt end with *café filtre.*

Intending to take a short walk before going to bed, they heard dance music in the square in front of Le Montaigne, and found a large crowd there, celebrating the annual fair of Périgueux. There was a seven-piece orchestra on a raised platform under a canvas, and a few couples were dancing in the street. Soon there were more.

"Do you feel like dancing?" Ray asked.

The pavement was not as bad for dancing as he would have supposed, and something happened to them that had never happened to them anywhere in France before—something remarkable. In spite of their clothes and their faces and the "Michelin" he held in one hand, eyes constantly swept over them or past them without pausing. Dancing in the street, they aroused no curiosity and, in fact, no interest whatever.

At midnight, standing on the balcony outside their room, they could still hear the music, a quarter of a mile away.

"Hasn't it been a lovely evening!" Ellen said. "I'll always remember dancing in the street in Périgueux."

Two people emerged from the cinema, a few doors from the Hôtel du Domino. And then a few more—a pair of lovers, a woman, a boy, a woman and a man carrying a sleeping child.

"The pâté was the best I ever ate," Ellen said.

"The Richardsons probably ate in the garden," Ray said. "I don't know that the dinner as a whole was all *that* good," he added thoughtfully. And then, "I don't know that we need tell them."

"The poor people who run the cinema," Ellen said.

"Why?"

"No one came to see the movie."

"I suppose Périgueux really isn't the kind of town that would support a movie theatre," Ray said.

"That's it," Ellen said. "Here, when people want to relax and enjoy themselves, they have an apéritif, they walk up and down in the evening air, they dance in the street, the way people used to do before there were any movies. It's another civilization entirely from anything we're accustomed to. Another world."

They went back into the bedroom and closed the shutters. A few minutes later, some more people emerged from the movie theatre, and some more, and some more, and then a great crowd came streaming out and, walking gravely, like people taking part in a religious procession, fanned out across the open square.

Ian McEwan

. . . .

FIRST LOVE, LAST RITES

From the beginning of summer until it seemed pointless, we lifted the thin mattress on to the heavy oak table and made love in front of the large open window. We always had a breeze blowing into the room and smells of the quayside four floors down. I was drawn into fantasies against my will, fantasies of the creature, and afterwards when we lay on our backs on the huge table, in those deep silences I heard it faintly running and clawing. It was new to me, all this, and I worried, I tried to talk to Sissel about it for reassurance. She had nothing to say, she did not make abstractions or discuss situations, she lived inside them. We watched the seagulls wheeling about in our square of sky and wondered if they had been watching us up there, that was the kind of thing we talked about, mildly entertaining hypotheses of the present moment. Sissel did things as they came to her, stirred her coffee, made love, listened to her records, looked out the window. She did not say things like I'm happy, or confused, or I want to make love, or I don't, or I'm tired of the fights in my family, she had no language to split herself in two, so I suffered alone what seemed like crimes in my head while we fucked, and afterwards listened alone to it scrabbling in the silence. Then one afternoon Sissel woke from a doze, raised her head from the mattress and said, 'What's that scratching noise behind the wall?'

My friends were far away in London, they sent me anguished and reflective letters, what would they do now? Who were they, and what was the point of it all? They were my age, seventeen and eighteen, but I pretended not to understand them. I sent back postcards, find a big table and an open window, I told them. I was happy and it seemed easy, I was making eel traps, it was so easy to have a purpose. The summer went on and I no longer heard from them. Only Adrian came to see us, he was Sissel's ten-year-old brother and he came to escape the misery of his disintegrating home, the quick reversals of his mother's moods, the endless competitive piano playing of his sisters, the occasional bitter visits of his father. Adrian and Sissel's parents after twenty-seven years of marriage and six children hated each other with sour resignation, they could no longer bear to live in the same house. The father moved out to a hostel a few streets away to be near his children. He was a businessman who was out of work and looked like

445

Gregory Peck, he was an optimist and had a hundred schemes to make money in an interesting way. I used to meet him in the pub. He did not want to talk about his redundancy or his marriage, he did not mind me living in a room over the quayside with his daughter. Instead he told me about his time in the Korean war, and when he was an international salesman, and of the legal fraudery of his friends who were now at the top and knighted, and then one day of the eels in the River Ouse, how the river bed swarmed with eels, how there was money to be made catching them and taking them live to London. I told him how I had eighty pounds in the bank, and the next morning we bought netting, twine, wire hoops and an old cistern tank to keep eels in. I spent the next two months making eel traps.

On fine days I took my net, hoops and twine outside and worked on the quay, sitting on a bollard. An eel trap is cylinder-shaped, sealed at one end, and at the other is a long tapering funnel entrance. It lies on the river bed, the eels swim in to eat the bait and in their blindness cannot find their way out. The fishermen were friendly and amused. There's eels down there, they said, and you'll catch a few but you won't make no living on it. The tide'll lose your nets fast as you make them. We're using iron weights, I told them, and they shrugged in a good-natured way and showed me a better way to lash the net to the hoops, they believed it was my right to try it for myself. When the fishermen were out in their boats and I did not feel like working I sat about and watched the tidal water slip across the mud, I felt no urgency about the eel traps but I was certain we would be rich.

I tried to interest Sissel in the eel adventure, I told her about the rowing-boat someone was lending to us for the summer, but she had nothing to say. So instead we lifted the mattress on to the table and lay down with our clothes on. Then she began to talk. We pressed our palms together, she made a careful examination of the size and shape of our hands and gave a running commentary. Exctly the same size, your fingers are thicker, you've got this extra bit here. She measured my eyelashes with the end of her thumb and wished hers were as long, she told me about the dog she had when she was small, it had long white eyelashes. She looked at the sunburn on my nose and talked about that, which of her brothers and sisters went red in the sun, who went brown, what her youngest sister said once. We slowly undressed. She kicked off her plimsolls and talked about her foot rot. I listened with my eyes closed, I could smell mud and seaweed and dust through the open window. Wittering on, she called it, this kind of talk. Then once I was inside her I was moved, I was inside my fantasy, there could be no separation now of my mushrooming sensations from my knowledge that we could make a creature grow in Sissel's belly. I had no wish to be a father, that was not in it at all. It was eggs, sperms, chromosomes, feathers, gills, claws, inches from my cock's end the unstoppable chemistry of a creature growing out of a dark red slime, my fantasy was of being helpless before the age and strength of this process and the thought alone could make me come before I wanted. When I told Sissel she laughed. Oh, Gawd, she said. To me Sissel was right inside the process, she *was* the process and the power of its fascination grew. She was meant to be on the pill and every month she forgot it at least two or three times. Without discussion we came to the arrangement that I was to come outside her, but it rarely worked. As we were swept down the long slopes to our orgasms, in those last desperate seconds I struggled to find my way out but I was caught like an eel in my fantasy of the creature in the dark, waiting, hungry, and I fed it great white gobs. In those careless fractions of a second I abandoned my life to feeding the creature, whatever it was, in or out of the womb, to fucking only Sissel, to feeding more creatures, my whole life given over to this in a moment's weakness. I watched out for Sissel's periods, everything about women was new to me and I could take nothing for granted. We made love in Sissel's copious, effortless periods, got good and sticky and brown with the blood and I thought we were the creatures now in the slime, we were inside fed by gobs of cloud coming through the window, by gases drawn from the mudflats by the sun. I worried about my fantasies, I knew I could not come without them. I asked Sissel what she thought about and she giggled. Not feathers and gills, anyway. What *do* you think about, then? Nothing much, nothing really. I pressed my question and she withdrew into silence.

I knew it was my own creature I heard scrabbling, and when Sissel heard it one afternoon and began to worry, I realized her fantasies were involved too, it was a sound which grew out of our lovemaking. We heard it when we were finished and lying quite still on our backs, when we were empty and clear, perfectly quiet. It was the impression of small claws scratching blindly against a wall, such a distant sound it needed two people to hear it. We thought it came from one part of the wall. When I knelt down and put my ear to the skirting-board it stopped, I sensed it on the other side of the wall, frozen in its action, waiting in the dark. As the weeks passed we heard it at other times in the day, and now and then at night. I wanted to ask Adrian what he thought it was. Listen, there it is, Adrian, shut up a moment, what do you think that noise is, Adrian? He strained impatiently to hear what we could hear but he would not be still long enough. There's nothing there, he shouted. Nothing, nothing, nothing. He became very excited, jumped on his sister's back, yelling and yodelling. He did not want whatever it was to be heard, he did not want to be left out. I pulled him off Sissel's back and we rolled about on the bed. Listen again, I said, pinning him down, there it was again. He struggled free and ran out of the room shouting his two-tone police-car siren. We listened to it fade down the stairs and when I could hear him no more I said, Perhaps Adrian is really afraid of mice. Rats, you mean, said his sister, and put her hands between my legs.

By mid-July we were not so happy in our room, there was a growing dishevelment and unease, and it did not seem possible to discuss it with Sissel. Adrian was coming to us every day now because it was the summer holidays and he could not bear to be at home. We would hear him four floors down, shouting and stamping on the stairs on his way up to us. He came in noisily, doing handstands and showing off to us. Frequently he jumped on Sissel's back to impress me, he was anxious, he was worried we might not find him good company and send him away, send him back home. He was worried too because he could no longer understand his sister. At one time she was always ready for a fight, and she was a good fighter, I heard him boast that to his friends, he was proud of her. Now changes had come over his sister, she pushed him off sulkily, she wanted to be left alone to do nothing, she wanted to listen to records. She was angry when he got his shoes on her skirt, and she had breasts now like his mother, she talked to him now like his mother. Get down off there, Adrian. Please, Adrian, please, not now, later. He could not quite believe it all the same, it was a mood of his sister's, a phase, and he went on taunting and attacking her hopefully, he badly wanted things to stay as they were before his father left home. When he locked his forearms round Sissel's neck and pulled her backwards on to the bed his eyes were on me for encouragement, he thought the real bond was between us, the two men against the girl. He did not see there was no encouragement, he wanted it so badly. Sissel never sent Adrian away, she understood why he was here, but it was hard for her. One long afternoon of torment she left the room almost crying with frustration. Adrian turned to me and raised his eyebrows in mock horror. I tried to talk to him then but he was already making his yodelling sound and squaring up for a fight with me. Nor did Sissel have anything to say to me about her brother, she never made general remarks about people because she never made general remarks. Sometimes when we heard Adrian on his way up the stairs she glanced across at me and seemed to betray herself by a slight pursing of her beautiful lips.

There was only one way to persuade Adrian to leave us in peace. He could not bear to see us touch, it pained him, it genuinely disgusted him. When he saw one of us move across the room to the other he pleaded with us silently, he ran between us, pretending playfulness, wanted to decoy us into another game. He imitated us frantically in a desperate last attempt to show us how fatuous we appeared. Then he could stand it no more, he ran out of the room machine-gunning German soldiers and young lovers on the stairs.

But Sissel and I were touching less and less now, in our quiet ways we could not bring ourselves to it. It was not that we were in decline, not that we did not delight in each other, but that our opportunities were faded. It was the room itself. It was no longer four floors up and detached, there was no breeze through the window, only a mushy heat rising off the quayside and dead jellyfish and clouds of flies, fiery grey flies who found our armpits and bit fiercely, houseflies who hung in clouds over our food. Our hair was too long and dank and hung in our eyes. The food we bought melted and tasted like the river. We no longer lifted the mattress on to the table, the coolest place now was the floor and the floor was covered with greasy sand which would not go away. Sissel grew tired of her records, and her foot rot spread from one foot to the other and added to the smell. Our room stank. We did not talk about leaving because we did not talk about anything. Every night now we were woken by the scrabbling behind the wall, louder now and more insistent. When we made love it listened to us behind the wall. We made love less and our rubbish gathered around us, milk bottles we could not bring ourselves to carry away, grey sweating cheese, butter wrappers, yogurt cartons, overripe salami. And among it all Adrian cart-wheeling, yodelling, machine-gunning and attacking Sissel. I tried to write poems about my fantasies, about the creature, but I could see no way in and I wrote nothing down, not even a first line. Instead I took long walks long the river dyke into the Norfolk hinterland of dull beet fields, telegraph poles, uniform grey skies. I had two more eel nets to make, I was forcing myself to sit down to them each day. But in my heart I was sick of them, I could not really believe that eels would ever go inside them and I wondered if I wanted them to, if it was not better that the eels should remain undisturbed in the cool mud at the bottom of the river. But I went on with it because Sissel's father was ready to begin, because I had to expiate all the money and hours I had spent so far, because the idea had its own tired, fragile momentum now and I could no more stop it than carry the milk bottles from our room.

Then Sissel found a job and it made me see we were different from no one, they all had rooms, houses, jobs, careers, that's what they all did, they had cleaner rooms, better jobs, we were anywhere's striving couple. It was one of the windowless factories across the river where they canned vegetables and fruit. For ten hours a day she was to sit in the roar of machines by a moving conveyor belt, talk to no one and pick out the rotten carrots before they were canned. At the end of her first day Sissel came home in a pink-and-white nylon raincoat and pink cap. I said, Why don't you take it off? Sissel shrugged. It was all the same to her, sitting around in the room, sitting around in a factory where they relayed Radio One through speakers strung along the steel girders, where four hundred women half listened, half dreamed, while their hands spun backwards and forwards like powered shuttles. On Sissel's second day I took the ferry across the river and waited for her at the factory gates. A few women stepped through a small tin door in a great windowless wall and a wailing siren sounded all across the factory complex. Other small doors opened and they streamed out, converging on the gates, scores of women in pink-and-white nylon coats and pink caps. I stood on a low wall and tried to see Sissel, it was suddenly very important. I thought that if I could not pick her out from this rustling stream of pink nylon then she was lost, we were both lost and our time was worthless. As it approached the factory gates the main body was moving fast. Some were half running in the splayed, hopeless way that women have been taught to run, the others walked as fast as they could. I found out later they were hurrying home to cook suppers for their families, to make an early start on the housework. Latecomers on the next shift tried to push their way through in the opposite direction. I could not see Sissel and I felt on the edge of panic, I shouted her name and my words were trampled underfoot. Two older women who stopped by the wall to light cigarettes grinned up at me. Sizzle yerself. I walked home by the long way, over the bridge, and decided not to tell Sissel I had been to wait for her because I would have to explain my panic and I did not know how. She was sitting on the bed when I came in, she was still wearing her nylon coat. The cap was on the floor. Why don't you take that thing off? I said. She said, Was that you outside the factory? I nodded. Why didn't you speak to me if you saw me standing there? Sissel turned and lay face downwards on the bed. Her coat was stained and smelled of machine oil and earth. I dunno, she said into the pillow, I didn't think. I didn't think of anything after my shift. Her words had a deadening finality, I glanced around our room and fell silent.

Two days later, on Saturday afternoon, I bought pounds of rubbery cows' lungs sodden with blood (lights, they were called) for bait. That same afternoon we filled the traps and rowed out into mid-channel at low tide to lay them on the river bed. Each of the seven traps was marked by a buoy. Four o'clock Sunday morning Sissel's father called for me and we set out in his van to where we kept the borrowed boat. We were rowing out now to find the marker buoys and pull the traps in, it was the testing time, would there be eels in the nets, would it be profitable to make more nets, catch more eels and drive them once a week to Billingsgate market, would we be rich? It was a dull windy morning, I felt no anticipation, only tiredness and a continuous erection. I half dozed in the warmth of the van's heater. I had spent many hours of the night awake listening to the scrabbling noises behind the wall. Once I got out of bed and banged the skirting-board with a spoon. There was a pause, then the digging continued. It seemed certain now that it was digging its way into the room. While Sissel's father rowed I watched over the side for markers. It was not as easy as I thought to find them, they did not show up white against the water but as dark low silhouettes. It was twenty minutes before we found the first. As we pulled it up I was amazed at how soon the clean white rope from the chandlers had become like all other rope near the river, brown and hung about with fine strands of green weed. The net too was old-looking and alien, I could not believe that one of us had made it. Inside were two crabs and a large eel. He untied the closed end of the trap, let the two crabs drop into the water and put the eel in the plastic bucket we had brought with us. We put fresh lights in the trap and dropped it over the side. It took another fifteen minutes to find the next trap and that one had nothing inside. We rowed up and down the channel for half an hour after that without finding another trap, and by this time the tide was coming up and covering the markers. It was then that I took the oars and made for the shore.

We went back to the hostel where Sissel's father was staying and he cooked breakfast. We did not want to discuss the lost traps, we pretended to ourselves and to each other that we would find them when we went out at the next low tide. But we knew they were lost, swept up or downstream by the powerful tides, and I knew I could never make another eel trap in my life. I knew also that my partner was taking Adrian with him on a short holiday, they were leaving that afternoon. They were going to visit military airfields, and hoped to end up at the Imperial War Museum. We ate eggs, bacon and mushrooms and drank coffee. Sissel's father told me of an idea he had, a simple but lucrative idea. Shrimps cost very little on the quayside here and they were very expensive in Brussels. We could drive two vanloads across there each week, he was optimistic in his relaxed, friendly way and for a moment I was sure his scheme would work. I drank the last of my coffee. Well, I said, I suppose that needs some thinking about. I picked up the bucket with the eel in, Sissel and I could eat that one. My partner told me as we shook hands that the surest way of killing an eel was to cover it with salt. I wished him a good holiday and we parted, still maintaining the silent pretence that one of us would be rowing out at the next low tide to search for the traps.

After a week at the factory I did not expect Sissel to be awake when I got home, but she was sitting up in bed, pale and clasping her knees. She was staring into one corner of the room. It's in here, she said. It's behind those books on the floor. I sat down on the bed and took off my wet shoes and socks. The mouse? You mean you heard the mouse? Sissel spoke quietly. It's a rat. I saw it run across the room, and it's a rat. I went over to the books and kicked them, and instantly it was out, I heard its claws on the floorboards and then I saw it run along the wall, the size of a small dog it seemed to me then, a rat, a squat, power-ful grey rat dragging its belly along the floor. It ran the whole length of the wall and crept behind a chest of drawers. We've got to get it out of here, Sissel wailed, in a voice which was strange to me. I nodded, but I could not move for the moment, or speak, it was so big, the rat, and it had been with us all summer, scrabbling at the wall in the deep, clear silences after our fucking, and in our sleep, it was our familiar. I was terrified, more afraid than Sissel, I was certain the rat knew us as well as we knew it, it was aware of us in the room now just as we were aware of it behind the chest of drawers. Sissel was about to speak again when we heard a noise outside on the stairs, a familiar stamping, machine-gun-ning noise. I was relieved to hear it. Adrian came in the way he usually did, he kicked the door and leaped in, crouching low, a machine gun ready at his hip. He sprayed us with raw noises from the back of his throat, we crossed our lips with our fingers and tried to hush him. You're dead, both of you, he said, and got ready for a cartwheel across the room. Sissel shushed him again, she tried to wave him towards the bed. Why sshh? What's wrong with you? We pointed to the chest of drawers. It's a rat, we told him. He was down on his knees at once, peering. A rat? he gasped. Fantastic, it's a big one, look at it. Fantastic. What are you going to do? Let's catch it. I crossed the room quickly and picked up a poker from the fireplace, I could lose my fear in Adrian's excitement, pretend it was just a fat rat in our room, an adventure to catch it. From the bed Sissel wailed again. What are you going to do with that? For a moment I felt my grip loosen on the poker, it was not just a rat, it was not an adventure, we both knew that. Meanwhile Adrian danced his dance, Yes, that, use that. Adrian helped me carry the books across the room, we built a wall right round the chest of drawers with only one gap in the middle where the rat could get through. Sissel went on asking, What are you doing? What are you going to do with that? but she did not dare leave the bed. We had finished the wall and I was giving Adrian a coat hanger to drive the rat out with when Sissel jumped across the room and tried to snatch the poker from my hand. Give me that, she cried, and hung on to my lifted arm. At that moment the rat ran out through the gap in the books, it ran straight at us and I thought I saw its teeth bared and ready. We scattered, Adrian jumped on the table, Sissel and I were back on the bed. Now we all had time to see the rat as it paused in the centre of the room and then ran forward again, we had time to see how powerful and fat and fast it was, how its whole body quiv-ered, how its tail slid behind it like an attendant parasite. It knows us, I thought, it wants us. I could not bring myself to look at Sissel. As I stood up on the bed, raised the poker and aimed it, she screamed. I threw it as hard as I could, it struck the floor point first several inches from the rat's narrow head. It turned instantly and ran back between the gap in the books. We heard the scratch of its claws on the floor as it settled itself behind the chest of drawers to wait.

I unwound the wire coat-hanger, straightened it and doubled it over and gave it to Adrian. He was quieter now, slightly more fearful. His sister sat on the bed with her knees drawn up again. I stood several feet from the gap in the books with the poker held tight in both hands. I glanced down and saw my pale bare feet and saw a ghost rat's teeth bared and tearing nail from flesh. I called out, Wait, I want to get my shoes. But it was too late, Adrian was jabbing the wire behind the chest of drawers and now I dared not move. I crouched a little lower over the poker, like a batsman. Adrian climbed on to the chest and thrust the wire right down into the corner. He was in the middle of shouting something to me, I did not hear what it was. The frenzied rat was running through the gap, it was running at my feet to take its revenge. Like the ghost rat its teeth were bared. With both hands I swung the poker down, caught it clean and whole smack under its belly, and it lifted clear off the ground, sailed across the room, borne up by Sissel's long scream through her hand in her mouth, it dashed against the wall and I thought in an instant, It must have broken its back. It dropped to the ground, legs in the air, split from end to end like a ripe fruit. Sissel did not take her hand from her mouth, Adrian did not move from the chest, I did not shift my weight from where I had struck, and no one breathed out. A faint smell crept across the room, musty and intimate, like the smell of Sissel's monthly blood. Then Adrian farted and giggled from his held-back fear, his human smell mingled with the wide-open rat smell. I stood over the rat and prodded it gently with the poker. It rolled on its side, and from the mighty gash which ran its belly's length there obtruded and slid partially free from the lower abdomen a translucent purple bag, and inside five pale crouching shapes, their knees drawn up around their chins. As the bag touched the floor I saw a movement, the leg of one unborn rat quivered as if in hope, but the mother was hopelessly dead and there was no more for it.

Sissel knelt by the rat, Adrian and I stood behind her like guards, it was as if she had some special right, kneeling there with her long red skirt spilling round her. She parted the gash in the mother rat with her forefinger and thumb, pushed the bag back inside and closed the blood-spiked fur over it. She remained kneeling a little while and we still stood behind her. Then she cleared some dishes from the sink to wash her hands. We all wanted to get outside now, so Sissel wrapped the rat in newspaper and we carried it downstairs. Sissel lifted the lid of the dustbin and I placed it carefully inside. Then I remembered something, I told the other two to wait for me and I ran back up the stairs. It was the eel I came back for, it lay quite still in its few inches of water and for a moment I thought that it too was dead till I saw it stir when I picked up the bucket. The wind had dropped now and the cloud was breaking up, we walked to the quay in alternate light and shade. The tide was coming in fast. We walked down the stone steps to the water's edge and there I tipped the eel back in the river and we watched him flick out of sight, a flash of white underside in the brown water. Adrian said goodbye to us, and I thought he was going to hug his sister. He hesitated and then ran off, calling out something over his shoulder. We shouted after him to have a good holiday. On the way back Sissel and I stopped to look at the factories on the other side of the river. She told me she was going to give up her job there.

We lifted the mattress on to the table and lay down in front of the open window, face to face, the way we did at the beginning of summer. We had a light breeze blowing in, a distant smoky smell of autumn, and I felt calm, very clear. Sissel said, This afternoon let's clean the room up and then go for a long walk, a walk along the river dyke. I pressed the flat of my palm against her warm belly and said, Yes.

Leonard Michaels

. . . .

THE DEAL

Twenty were jammed together on the stoop; tiers of heads made one central head, and the wings rested along the banisters: a raggedy monster of boys studying her approach. Her white face and legs. She passed without looking, poked her sunglasses against the bridge of her nose and tucked her bag between her arm and ribs. She carried it at her hip like a rifle stock. On her spine forty eyes hung like poison berries. Bone dissolved beneath her lank beige silk, and the damp circle of her belt cut her in half. Independent legs struck toward the points of her shoes. Her breasts lifted and rode the air like porpoises. She would cross to the grocery as usual, buy cigarettes, then cross back despite their eyes. As if the neighborhood hadn't changed one bit. She slipped the bag forward to crack it against her belly and pluck out keys and change. In the gesture she was home from work. Her keys jangled in the sun as if they opened everything and the air received her. The monster, watching, saw the glove fall away.

Pigeons looped down to whirl between buildings, and a ten-wheel truck came slowly up the street. As it passed she emerged from the grocery, then stood at the curb opposite the faces. She glanced along the street where she had crossed it. No glove. Tar reticulated between the cobbles. A braid of murky water ran against the curb, twisting bits of flotsam toward the drain. She took off her sunglasses, dropped them with her keys into the bag, then stepped off the curb toward the faces. Addressing them with a high, friendly voice, she said: "Did you guys see a glove? I dropped it a moment ago."

The small ones squinted up at her from the bottom step. On the middle steps sat boys fourteen or fifteen years old. The oldest ones made the wings. Dandies and introverts, they sprawled, as if with a common corruption in their bones. In the center, his eyes level with hers, a boy waited for her attention in the matter of gloves. To his right sat a very thin boy with a pocked face. A narrow-brimmed hat tipped toward his nose and shaded the continuous activity of his eyes. She spoke to the green eyes of the boy in the center and held up the glove she had: "Like this."

Teeth appeared below the hat, then everywhere as the boys laughed. Did she hold up a fish? Green eyes said: "Hello, Miss Calile."

453

She looked around at the faces, then laughed with them at her surprise. "You know my name?"

"I see it on the mailbox," said the hat. "He can't read. I see it."

"My name is Duke Francisco," said the illiterate.

"My name is Abbe Carlyle," she said to him.

The hat smirked. "His name Francisco Lopez."

Green eyes turned to the hat. "Shut you mouth, baby. I tell her my name, not you."

"His name Francisco Lopez," the hat repeated.

She saw pocks and teeth, the thin oily face and the hat, as he spoke again, nicely to her: "My name Francisco Pacheco, the Prince. I seen you name on the mailbox."

"Did either of you . . ."

"You name is shit," said green eyes to the hat.

"My name is Tito." A small one on the bottom step looked up for the effect of his name. She looked down at him. "I am Tito," he said.

"Did you see my glove, Tito?"

"This is Tomato," he answered, unable to bear her attention. He nudged the boy to his left. Tomato nudged back, stared at the ground.

"I am happy to know you, Tito," she said, "and you, Tomato. Both of you." She looked back up to green eyes and the hat. The hat acknowledged her courtesy. He tilted back to show her his eyes, narrow and black except for bits of white reflected in the corners. His face was thin, high-boned and fragile. She pitied the riddled skin.

"This guy," he said, pointing his thumb to the right, "is Monkey," and then to the left beyond green eyes, "and this guy is Beans." She nodded to the hat, then Monkey, then Beans, measuring the respect she offered, doling it out in split seconds. Only one of them had the glove.

"Well, did any of you guys see my glove?"

Every tier grew still, like birds in a tree waiting for a sign that would move them all at once.

Tito's small dark head snapped forward. She heard the slap an instant late. The body lurched after the head and pitched off the stoop at her feet. She saw green eyes sitting back slowly. Tito gaped up at her from the concrete. A sacrifice to the lady. She stepped back as if rejecting it and frowned at green eyes. He gazed indifferently at Tito, who was up, facing him with coffee-bean fists. Tito screamed, "I tell her you got it, dick-head."

The green eyes swelled in themselves like a light blooming in the ocean. Tito's fists opened, he turned, folded quickly and sat back into the mass. He began to rub his knees.

"May I have my glove, Francisco?" Her voice was still pleasant and high. She now held her purse in the crook of her arm and pressed it against her side.

Some fop had a thought and giggled in the wings. She glanced up at him immediately. He produced a toothpick. With great delicacy he stuck it into his ear. She looked away. Green eyes again waited for her. A cup of darkness formed in the hollow that crowned his chestbone. His soiled gray polo shirt hooked below it. "You think I have you glove?" She didn't answer. He stared between his knees, between heads and shoulders to the top of Tito's head. "Hey, Tito, you tell her I got the glove?"

"I didn't tell nothing," muttered Tito rubbing his knees harder as if they were still bitter from his fall.

"He's full of shit, Miss Calile. I break his head later. What kind of glove you want?"

"This kind," she said wearily, "a white glove like this."

"Too hot." He grinned.

"Yes, too hot, but I need it."

"What for? Too hot." He gave her full green concern.

"It's much too hot, but the glove is mine, mister."

She rested her weight on one leg and wiped her brow with the glove she had. They watched her do it, the smallest of them watched her, and she moved the glove slowly to her brow again and drew it down her cheek and neck. She could think of nothing to say, nothing to do without expressing impatience. Green eyes changed the subject. "You live there." He pointed toward her building.

"That's right."

A wooden front door with a window in it showed part of the shadowy lobby, mailboxes, and a second door. Beyond her building and down the next street were warehouses. Beyond them, the river. A meat truck started toward them from a packing house near the river. It came slowly, bug-eyed with power. The driver saw the lady standing in front of the boys. He yelled as the truck went past. Gears yowled, twisting the sound of his voice. She let her strength out abruptly: "Give me the glove, Francisco."

The boy shook his head at the truck, at her lack of civilization. "What you give me?"

That tickled the hat. "*Vaya*, baby. What she give you, eh?" He spoke fast, his tone decorous and filthy.

"All right, baby," she said fast as the hat, "what do you want?" The question had New York and much man in it. The hat swiveled to the new sound. A man of honor, let him understand the terms. He squinted at her beneath the hat brim.

"Come on, Francisco, make your deal." She presented brave, beautiful teeth, smiling hard as a skull.

"Tell her, Duke. Make the deal." The hat lingered on "deal," grateful to the lady for this word.

The sun shone in his face and the acknowledged duke sat dull, green eyes blank with possibilities. Her question, not "deal," held him. It had come too hard, too fast. He laughed in contempt of something and glanced around at the wings. They offered nothing. "I want a dollar," he said.

That seemed obvious to the hat: he sneered, "He wants a dollar." She had to be stupid not to see it.

"No deal. Twenty-five cents." Her gloves were worth twenty dollars. She had paid ten for them at a sale. At the moment they were worth green eyes' life.

"I want ten dollars," said green eyes flashing the words like extravagant meaningless things; gloves of his own. He lifted his arms, clasped his hands behind his head and leaned against the knees behind him. His belly filled with air, the polo shirt rolled out on its curve. He made a fat man doing business. "Ten dollars." Ten fingers popped up behind his head like grimy spikes. Keeper of the glove, cocky duke of the stoop. The number made him happy: it bothered her. He drummed the spikes against his head: "I wan' you ten dol-lar." Beans caught the beat in his hips and rocked it on the stoop.

"Francisco," she said, hesitated, then said, "dig me, please. You will get twenty-five cents. Now let's have the glove." Her bag snapped open, her fingers hooked, stiffened on the clasp. Monkey leered at her and bongoed his knees with fists. "The number is ten dol-lar." She waited, said nothing. The spikes continued drumming, Monkey rocked his hips, Beans pummeled his knees. The hat sang sadly: "Twany fyiv not d'nummer, not d'nummer, not d'nummer." He made claves of his fingers and palms, tocked, clicked his tongue against the beat. "Twan-ny fyiv—na t'nomma." She watched green eyes. He was quiet now in the center of the stoop, sitting motionless, waiting, as though seconds back in time his mind still touched the question: what did he want? He seemed to wonder, now that he had the formula, what *did* he want? The faces around him, dopey in the music, wondered nothing, grinned at her, nodded, clicked, whined the chorus: "Twany fyiv not t'nomma, twany fyiv not t'nomma."

Her silk blouse stained and stuck flat to her breasts and shoulders. Water chilled her sides.

"Ten dol-lar iss t'nomma."

She spread her feet slightly, taking better possession of the sidewalk and resting on them evenly, the bag held open for green eyes. She could see he didn't want that, but she insisted in her silence he did. Tito spread his little feet and lined the points of his shoes against hers. Tomato noticed the imitation and cackled at the concrete. The music went on, the beat feeding on itself, pulverizing words, smearing them into liquid submission: "Iss t'nomma twany fyiv? Dat iss not t'nomma."

"Twenty-five cents," she said again.

Tito whined, "Gimme twenty-five cents."

"Shut you mouth," said the hat, and turned a grim face to his friend. In the darkness of his eyes there were deals. The music ceased. "Hey, baby, you got no manners? Tell what you want." He spoke in a dreamy voice, as if to a girl.

"I want a kiss," said green eyes.

She glanced down with this at Tito and studied the small shining head. "Tell him to give me my glove, Tito," she said cutely, nervously. The wings shuffled and looked down bored. Nothing was happening. Twisting backwards Tito shouted up to green eyes, "Give her the glove." He twisted front again and crouched over his knees. He shoved Tomato for approval and smiled. Tomato shoved him back, snarled at the concrete and spit between his feet at a face which had taken shape in the grains.

"I want a kiss," said the boy again.

She sighed, giving another second to helplessness. The sun was low above the river and the street three quarters steeped in shade. Sunlight cut across the building tops where pigeons swept by loosely and fluttered in to pack the stone foliage of the eaves. Her bag snapped shut. Her voice was business: "Come on, Francisco. I'll give you the kiss."

He looked shot among the faces.

"Come on," she said, "it's a deal."

The hat laughed out loud with childish insanity. The others shrieked and jiggled, except for the wings. But they ceased to sprawl, and seemed to be getting bigger, to fill with imminent motion. "Gimme a kiss, gimme a kiss," said the little ones on the lowest step. Green eyes sat with a quiet, open mouth.

"Let's go," she said. "I haven't all day."

"Where I go?"

"That doorway." She pointed to her building and took a step toward it. "You know where I live, don't you?"

"I don't want no kiss."

"What's the matter now?"

"You scared?" asked the hat. "Hey, Duke, you scared?"

The wings leaned toward the center, where green eyes hugged himself and made a face.

"Look, Mr. Francisco, you made a deal."

"Yeah," said the wings.

"Now come along."

"I'm not scared," he shouted and stood up among them. He sat down. "I don't want no kiss."

"You're scared?" she said.

"You scared chicken," said the hat.

"Yeah," said the wings. "Hey, punk. Fairy. Hey, Duke Chicken."

"Duke scared," mumbled Tito. Green eyes stood up again. The shoulders below him separated. Tito leaped clear of the stoop and trotted into the street. Green eyes passed through the place he had vacated and stood at her side, his head not so high as her shoulder. She nodded at him, tucked her bag up and began walking toward her building. A few others stood up on the stoop and the hat started down. She turned. "Just him." Green eyes shuffled after her. The hat stopped on the sidewalk. Someone pushed him forward. He resisted, but called after them, "He's my cousin." She walked on, the boy came slowly after her. They were yelling from the stoop, the hat yelling his special point, "He's my brother." He stepped after them and the others swarmed behind him down the stoop and onto the sidewalk. Tito jumped out of the street and ran alongside the hat. He yelled, "He's got the glove." They all moved down the block, the wings trailing sluggishly, the young ones jostling, punching each other, laughing, shrieking things in Spanish after green eyes and the lady. She heard him, a step behind her. "I give you the glove and take off."

She put her hand out to the side a little. The smaller hand touched hers and took it. "You made a deal."

She tugged him through the doorway into the tight, square lobby. The hand snapped free and he swung by, twisting to face her as if to meet a blow. He put his back against the second door, crouched a little. His hands pressed the sides of his legs. The front door shut slowly and the shadows deepened in the lobby. He crouched lower, his eyes level with her breasts, as she took a step toward him. The hat appeared, a black rock in the door window. Green eyes saw it, straightened up, one hand moving quickly toward his pants pocket. The second and third head, thick dark bulbs, lifted beside the hat in the window. Bodies piled against the door behind her. Green eyes held up the glove. "Here, you lousy glove."

She smiled and put out her hand. The hat screamed, "Hey, you made a deal, baby. Hey, you got no manners."

"Don't be scared," she whispered, stepping closer.

The glove lifted toward her and hung in the air between them, gray, languid as smoke. She took it and bent toward his face. "I won't kiss you. Run." The window went black behind her, the lobby solid in darkness, silent but for his breathing, the door breathing against the pressure of the bodies, and the scraping of fingers spread about them like rats in the walls. She felt his shoulder, touched the side of his neck, bent the last inch and kissed him. White light cut the walls. They tumbled behind it, screams and bright teeth. Spinning to face them she was struck, pitched against green eyes and the second door. He twisted hard, shoved away from her as the faces piled forward popping eyes and lights, their fingers accumulating in the air, coming at her. She raised the bag, brought it down swishing into the faces, and wrenched and twisted to get free of the fingers, screaming against their shrieks, "Stop it, stop it, stop it." The bag sprayed papers and coins, and the sunglasses flew over their heads and cracked against the brass mailboxes. She dropped amid shrieks, "Gimme a kiss, gimme a kiss," squirming down the door onto her knees to get fingers out from under her and she thrust up with the bag into bellies and thighs until a fist banged her mouth. She cursed, flailed at nothing.

There was light in the lobby and leather scraping on concrete as they crashed out the door into the street. She shut her eyes instantly as the fist came again, big as her face. Then she heard running in the street. The lobby was silent. The door shut slowly, the shadows deepened. She could feel the darkness getting thicker. She opened her eyes. Standing in front of her was the hat.

He bowed slightly. "I get those guys for you. They got no manners." The hat shook amid the shadows, slowly, sadly.

She pressed the smooth leather of her bag against her cheek where the mouths had kissed it. Then she tested the clasp, snapping it open and shut. The hat shifted his posture and waited. "You hit me," she whispered and did not look up at him. The hat bent and picked up her keys and the papers. He handed the keys to her, then the papers, and bent again for the coins. She dropped the papers into her bag and stuffed them together in the bottom. "Help me up!" She took his hands and got to her feet without looking at him. As she put the key against the lock of the second door she began to shiver. The key rattled against the slot. "Help me!" The hat leaned over the lock, his long thin fingers squeezing the key. It caught, angled with a click. She pushed him aside. "You give me something? Hey, you give me something?" The door shut on his voice.

Yukio Mishima

. . . .

PATRIOTISM

1

On the twenty-eighth of February, 1936 (on the third day, that is, of the February 26 Incident), Lieutenant Shinji Takeyama of the Konoe Transport Battalion—profoundly disturbed by the knowledge that his closest colleagues had been with the mutineers from the beginning, and indignant at the imminent prospect of Imperial troops attacking Imperial troops—took his officer's sword and ceremonially disemboweled himself in the eight-mat room of his private residence in the sixth block of Aoba-chō, in Yotsuya Ward. His wife, Reiko, followed him, stabbing herself to death. The lieutenant's farewell note consisted of one sentence: "Long live the Imperial Forces." His wife's, after apologies for her unfilial conduct in thus preceding her parents to the grave, concluded: "The day which, for a soldier's wife, had to come, has come. . . ." The last moments of this heroic and dedicated couple were such as to make the gods themselves weep. The lieutenant's age, it should be noted, was thirty-one, his wife's twenty-three; and it was not half a year since the celebration of their marriage.

2

Those who saw the bride and bridegroom in the commemorative photograph—perhaps no less than those actually present at the lieutenant's wedding—had exclaimed in wonder at the bearing of this handsome couple. The lieutenant, majestic in military uniform, stood protectively beside his bride, his right hand resting upon his sword, his officer's cap held at his left side. His expression was severe, and his dark brows and wide-gazing eyes well conveyed the clear integrity of youth. For the beauty of the bride in her white over-robe no comparisons were adequate. In the eyes, round beneath soft brows, in the slender, finely shaped nose, and in the full lips, there was both sensuousness and refinement. One hand, emerging shyly from a sleeve of the over-robe, held a fan, and the tips of the fingers, clustering delicately, were like the bud of a moonflower.

After the suicide, people would take out this photograph and examine it, and sadly reflect that too often there was a curse on these seemingly flawless unions.

459

Perhaps it was no more than imagination, but looking at the picture after the tragedy it almost seemed as if the two young people before the gold-lacquered screen were gazing, each with equal clarity, at the deaths which lay before them.

Thanks to the good offices of their go-between, Lieutenant General Ozeki, they had been able to set themselves up in a new home at Aoba-chō in Yotsuya. "New home" is perhaps misleading. It was an old three-room rented house backing onto a small garden. As neither the six- nor the four-and-a-half-mat room downstairs was favored by the sun, they used the upstairs eight-mat room as both bedroom and guest room. There was no maid, so Reiko was left alone to guard the house in her husband's absence.

The honeymoon trip was dispensed with on the grounds that these were times of national emergency. The two of them had spent the first night of their marriage at this house. Before going to bed, Shinji, sitting erect on the floor with his sword laid before him, had bestowed upon his wife a soldierly lecture. A woman who had become the wife of a soldier should know and resolutely accept that her husband's death might come at any moment. It could be tomorrow. It could be the day after. But, no matter when it came—he asked—was she steadfast in her resolve to accept it? Reiko rose to her feet, pulled open a drawer of the cabinet, and took out what was the most prized of her new possessions, the dagger her mother had given her. Returning to her place, she laid the dagger without a word on the mat before her, just as her husband had laid his sword. A silent understanding was achieved at once, and the lieutenant never again sought to test his wife's resolve.

In the first few months of her marriage Reiko's beauty grew daily more radiant, shining serene like the moon after rain.

As both were possessed of young, vigorous bodies, their relationship was passionate. Nor was this merely a matter of the night. On more than one occasion, returning home straight from maneuvers, and begrudging even the time it took to remove his mud-splashed uniform, the lieutenant had pushed his wife to the floor almost as soon as he had entered the house. Reiko was equally ardent in her response. For a little more or a little less than a month, from the first night of their marriage Reiko knew happiness, and the lieutenant, seeing this, was happy too.

Reiko's body was white and pure, and her swelling breasts conveyed a firm and chaste refusal; but, upon consent, those breasts were lavish with their intimate, welcoming warmth. Even in bed these two were frighteningly and awesomely serious. In the very midst of wild, intoxicating passions, their hearts were sober and serious.

By day the lieutenant would think of his wife in the brief rest periods between training; and all day long, at home, Reiko would recall the image of her husband. Even when apart, however, they had only to look at the wedding photograph for their happiness to be once more confirmed. Reiko felt not the slightest surprise that a man who had been a complete stranger until a few months ago should now have become the sun about which her whole world revolved.

All these things had a moral basis, and were in accordance with the Education Rescript's injunction that "husband and wife should be harmonious." Not once did Reiko contradict her husband, nor did the lieutenant ever find reason to scold his wife. On the god shelf below the stairway, alongside the tablet from the Great Ise Shrine, were set photographs of their Imperial Majesties, and regularly every morning, before leaving for duty, the lieutenant would stand with his wife at this hallowed place and together they would bow their heads low. The offering water was renewed each morning, and the sacred sprig of *sasaki* was always green and fresh. Their lives were lived beneath the solemn protection of the gods and were filled with an intense happiness which set every fiber in their bodies trembling.

3

Although Lord Privy Seal Saitō's house was in their neighborhood, neither of them heard any noise of gunfire on the morning of February 26. It was a bugle, sounding muster in the dim, snowy dawn, when the ten-minute tragedy had already ended, which first disrupted the lieutenant's slumbers. Leaping at once from his bed, and without speaking a word, the lieutenant donned his uniform, buckled on the sword held ready for him by his wife, and hurried swiftly out into the snow-covered streets of the still darkened morning. He did not return until the evening of the twenty-eighth.

Later, from the radio news, Reiko learned the full extent of this sudden eruption of violence. Her life throughout the subsequent two days was lived alone, in complete tranquility, and behind locked doors.

In the lieutenant's face, as he hurried silently out into the snowy morning, Reiko had read the determination to die. If her husband did not return, her own decision was made: she too would die. Quietly she attended to the disposition of her personal possessions. She chose her sets of visiting kimonos as keepsakes for friends of her schooldays, and she wrote a name and address on the stiff paper wrapping in which each was folded. Constantly admonished by her husband never to think of the morrow, Reiko had not even kept a diary and was now denied the pleasure of assiduously rereading her record of the happiness of the past few months and consigning each page to the fire as she did so. Ranged across the top of the radio were a small china dog, a rabbit, a squirrel, a bear, and a fox. There were also a small vase and a water pitcher. These comprised Reiko's one and only collection. But it would hardly do, she imagined, to give such things as keepsakes. Nor again would it be quite proper to ask specifically for them to be included in the coffin. It seemed to Reiko, as these thoughts passed through her mind, that the expressions on the small animals' faces grew even more lost and forlorn.

Reiko took the squirrel in her hand and looked at it. And then, her thoughts turning to a realm far beyond these childlike affections, she gazed up into the distance at the great sunlike principle which her husband embodied. She was ready, and happy, to be hurtled along to her destruction in that gleaming sun chariot—but now, for these few moments of solitude, she allowed herself to luxuriate in this innocent attachment to trifles. The time when she had genuinely loved these things, however, was long past. Now she merely loved the memory of having once loved them, and their place in her heart had been filled by more intense passions, by a more frenzied happiness. . . . For Reiko had never, even to

herself, thought of those soaring joys of the flesh as a mere pleasure. The February cold, and the icy touch of the china squirrel, had numbed Reiko's slender
fingers; yet, even so, in her lower limbs, beneath the ordered repetition of the
pattern which crossed the skirt of her trim *meisen* kimono, she could feel now,
as she thought of the lieutenant's powerful arms reaching out toward her, a hot
moistness of the flesh which defied the snows.

She was not in the least afraid of the death hovering in her mind. Waiting
alone at home, Reiko firmly believed that everything her husband was feeling or
thinking now, his anguish and distress, was leading her—just as surely as the
power in his flesh—to a welcome death. She felt as if her body could melt away
with ease and be transformed to the merest fraction of her husband's thought.

Listening to the frequent announcements on the radio, she heard the names
of several to her husband's colleagues mentioned among those of the insurgents.
This was news of death. She followed the developments closely, wondering anxiously, as the situation became daily more irrevocable, why no Imperial ordinance was sent down, and watching what had at first been taken as a movement
to restore the nation's honor come gradually to be branded with the infamous
name of mutiny. There was no communication from the regiment. At any moment, it seemed, fighting might commence in the city streets, where the remains
of the snow still lay.

Toward sundown on the twenty-eighth Reiko was startled by a furious
pounding on the front door. She hurried downstairs. As she pulled with fumbling fingers at the bolt, the shape dimly outlined beyond the frosted-glass panel
made no sound, but she knew it was her husband. Reiko had never known the
bolt on the sliding door to be so stiff. Still it resisted. The door just would not
open.

In a moment, almost before she knew she had succeeded, the lieutenant was
standing before her on the cement floor inside the porch, muffled in a khaki
greatcoat, his top boots heavy with slush from the street. Closing the door behind him, he returned the bolt once more to its socket. With what significance,
Reiko did not understand.

"Welcome home."

Reiko bowed deeply, but her husband made no response. As he had already
unfastened his sword and was about to remove his greatcoat, Reiko moved
around behind to assist. The coat, which was cold and damp and had lost the
odor of horse dung it normally exuded when exposed to the sun, weighed heavily
upon her arm. Draping it across a hanger, and cradling the sword and leather
belt in her sleeves, she waited while her husband removed his top boots and then
followed behind him into the "living room." This was the six-mat room downstairs.

Seen in the clear light from the lamp, her husband's face, covered with a
heavy growth of bristle, was almost unrecognizably wasted and thin. The cheeks
were hollow, their luster and resilience gone. In his normal good spirits he would
have changed into old clothes as soon as he was home and have pressed her to
get supper at once, but now he sat before the table still in his uniform, his head
drooping dejectedly. Reiko refrained from asking whether she should prepare
the supper.

After an interval the lieutenant spoke.

"I knew nothing. They hadn't asked me to join. Perhaps out of consideration, because I was newly married. Kanō, and Homma too, and Yamaguchi."

Reiko recalled momentarily the faces of high-spirited young officers, friends of her husband, who had come to the house occasionally as guests.

"There may be an Imperial ordinance sent down tomorrow. They'll be posted as rebels, I imagine. I shall be in command of a unit with orders to attack them. . . . I can't do it. It's impossible to do a thing like that."

He spoke again.

"They've taken me off guard duty, and I have permission to return home for one night. Tomorrow morning, without question, I must leave to join the attack. I can't do it, Reiko."

Reiko sat erect with lowered eyes. She understood clearly that her husband had spoken of his death. The lieutenant was resolved. Each word, being rooted in death, emerged sharply and with powerful significance against this dark, unmovable background. Although the lieutenant was speaking of his dilemma, already there was no room in his mind for vacillation.

However, there was a clarity, like the clarity of a stream fed from melting snows, in the silence which rested between them. Sitting in his own home after the long two-day ordeal, and looking across at the face of his beautiful wife, the lieutenant was for the first time experiencing true peace of mind. For he had at once known, though she said nothing, that his wife divined the resolve which lay beneath his words.

"Well, then . . ." The lieutenant's eyes opened wide. Despite his exhaustion they were strong and clear, and now for the first time they looked straight into the eyes of his wife. "Tonight I shall cut my stomach."

Reiko did not flinch.

Her round eyes showed tension, as taut as the clang of a bell.

"I am ready," she said. "I ask permission to accompany you."

The lieutenant felt almost mesmerized by the strength in those eyes. His words flowed swiftly and easily, like the utterances of a man in delirium, and it was beyond his understanding how permission in a matter of such weight could be expressed so casually.

"Good. We'll go together. But I want you as a witness, first, for my own suicide. Agreed?"

When this was said a sudden release of abundant happiness welled up in both their hearts. Reiko was deeply affected by the greatness of her husband's trust in her. It was vital for the lieutenant, whatever else might happen, that there should be no irregularity in his death. For that reason there had to be a witness. The fact that he had chosen his wife for this was the first mark of his trust. The second, and even greater, mark was that though he had pledged that they should die together he did not intend to kill his wife first—he had deferred her death to a time when he would no longer be there to verify it. If the lieutenant had been a suspicious husband, he would doubtless, as in the usual suicide pact, have chosen to kill his wife first.

When Reiko said, "I ask permission to accompany you," the lieutenant felt these words to be the final fruit of the education which he had himself given his wife, starting on the first night of their marriage, and which had schooled her, when the moment came, to say what had to be said without a shadow of hesitation. This flattered the lieutenant's opinion of himself as a self-reliant man. He was not so romantic or conceited as to imagine that the words were spoken spontaneously, out of love for her husband.

With happiness welling almost too abundantly in their hearts, they could not help smiling at each other. Reiko felt as if she had returned to her wedding night.

Before her eyes was neither pain nor death. She seemed to see only a free and limitless expanse opening out into vast distances.

"The water is hot. Will you take your bath now?"

"Ah yes, of course."

"And supper . . . ?"

The words were delivered in such level, domestic tones that the lieutenant came near to thinking, for the fraction of a second, that everything had been a hallucination.

"I don't think we'll need supper. But perhaps you could warm some sake?"

"As you wish."

As Reiko rose and took a *tanzen* gown from the cabinet for after the bath, she purposely directed her husband's attention to the opened drawer. The lieutenant rose, crossed to the cabinet, and looked inside. From the ordered array of paper wrappings he read, one by one, the addresses of the keepsakes. There was no grief in the lieutenant's response to this demonstration of heroic resolve. His heart was filled with tenderness. Like a husband who is proudly shown the childish purchases of a young wife, the lieutenant, overwhelmed by affection, lovingly embraced his wife from behind and implanted a kiss upon her neck.

Reiko felt the roughness of the lieutenant's unshaven skin against her neck. This sensation, more than being just a thing of this world, was for Reiko almost the world itself, but now—with the feeling that it was soon to be lost forever—it had freshness beyond all her experience. Each moment had its own vital strength, and the senses in every corner of her body were reawakened. Accepting her husband's caresses from behind, Reiko raised herself on the tips of her toes, letting the vitality seep through her entire body.

"First the bath, and then, after some sake . . . lay out the bedding upstairs, will you?"

The lieutenant whispered the words into his wife's ear. Reiko silently nodded.

Flinging off his uniform, the lieutenant went to the bath. To faint background noises of slopping water Reiko tended the charcoal brazier in the living room and began the preparations for warming the sake.

Taking the *tanzen*, a sash, and some underclothes, she went to the bathroom to ask how the water was. In the midst of a coiling cloud of steam the lieutenant was sitting cross-legged on the floor, shaving, and she could dimly discern the rippling movements of the muscles on his damp, powerful back as they responded to the movement of his arms.

There was nothing to suggest a time of any special significance. Reiko, going busily about her tasks, was preparing side dishes from odds and ends in stock. Her hands did not tremble. If anything, she managed even more efficiently and smoothly than usual. From time to time, it is true, there was a strange throbbing deep within her breast. Like distant lightning, it had a moment of sharp intensity and then vanished without trace. Apart from that, nothing was in any way out of the ordinary.

The lieutenant, shaving in the bathroom, felt his warmed body miraculously healed at last of the desperate tiredness of the days of indecision and filled—in spite of the death which lay ahead—with pleasurable anticipation. The sound of his wife going about her work came to him faintly. A healthy physical craving, submerged for two days, reasserted itself.

The lieutenant was confident there had been no impurity in that joy they had experienced when resolving upon death. They had both sensed at that moment—though not, of course, in any clear and conscious way—that those permissible pleasures which they shared in private were once more beneath the protection of Righteousness and Divine Power, and of a complete and unassailable morality. On looking into each other's eyes and discovering there an honorable death, they had felt themselves safe once more behind steel walls which none could destroy, encased in an impenetrable armor of Beauty and Truth. Thus, so far from seeing any inconsistency or conflict between the urges of his flesh and the sincerity of his patriotism, the lieutenant was even able to regard the two as parts of the same thing.

Thrusting his face close to the dark, cracked, misted wall mirror, the lieutenant shaved himself with great care. This would be his death face. There must be no unsightly blemishes. The clean-shaven face gleamed once more with a youthful luster, seeming to brighten the darkness of the mirror. There was a certain elegance, he even felt, in the association of death with this radiantly healthy face.

Just as it looked now, this would become his death face! Already, in fact, it had half departed from the lieutenant's personal possession and had become the bust above a dead soldier's memorial. As an experiment he closed his eyes tight. Everything was wrapped in blackness, and he was no longer a living, seeing creature.

Returning from the bath, the traces of the shave glowing faintly blue beneath his smooth cheeks, he seated himself beside the now well-kindled charcoal brazier. Busy though Reiko was, he noticed, she had found time lightly to touch up her face. Her cheeks were gay and her lips moist. There was no shadow of sadness to be seen. Truly, the lieutenant felt, as he saw this mark of his young wife's passionate nature, he had chosen the wife he ought to have chosen.

As soon as the lieutenant had drained his sake cup he offered it to Reiko. Reiko had never before tasted sake, but she accepted without hesitation and sipped timidly.

"Come here," the lieutenant said.

Reiko moved to her husband's side and was embraced as she leaned backward across his lap. Her breast was in violent commotion, as if sadness, joy, and the potent sake were mingling and reacting within her. The lieutenant looked down into his wife's face. It was the last face he would see in this world, the last face he would see of his wife. The lieutenant scrutinized the face minutely, with the eyes of a traveler bidding farewell to splendid vistas which he will never revisit. It was a face he could not tire of looking at—the features regular yet not cold, the lips lightly closed with a soft strength. The lieutenant kissed those lips, unthinkingly. And suddenly, though there was not the slightest distortion of the face into the unsightliness of sobbing, he noticed that tears were welling slowly from beneath the long lashes of the closed eyes and brimming over into a glistening stream.

When, a little later, the lieutenant urged that they should move to the upstairs bedroom, his wife replied that she would follow after taking a bath. Climbing the stairs alone to the bedroom, where the air was already warmed by the gas heater, the lieutenant lay down on the bedding with arms outstretched and legs apart. Even the time at which he lay waiting for his wife to join him was no later and no earlier than usual.

He folded his hands beneath his head and gazed at the dark boards of the ceiling in the dimness beyond the range of the standard lamp. Was it death he was now waiting for? Or a wild ecstasy of the senses? The two seemed to overlap, almost as if the object of this bodily desire was death itself. But, however that might be, it was certain that never before had the lieutenant tasted such total freedom.

There was the sound of a car outside the window. He could hear the screech of its tires skidding in the snow piled at the side of the street. The sound of its horn re-echoed from near-by walls. . . . Listening to these noises he had the feeling that this house rose like a solitary island in the ocean of a society going as restlessly about its business as ever. All around, vastly and untidily, stretched the country for which he grieved. He was to give his life for it. But would that great country, with which he was prepared to remonstrate to the extent of destroying himself, take the slightest heed of his death? He did not know; and it did not matter. His was a battlefield without glory, a battlefield where none could display deeds of valor: it was the front line of the spirit.

Reiko's footsteps sounded on the stairway. The steep stairs in this old house creaked badly. There were fond memories in that creaking, and many a time, while waiting in bed, the lieutenant had listened to its welcome sound. At the thought that he would hear it no more he listened with intense concentration, striving for every corner of every moment of this precious time to be filled with the sound of those soft footfalls on the creaking stairway. The moments seemed transformed to jewels, sparkling with inner light.

Reiko wore a Nagoya sash about the waist of her *yukata*, but as the lieutenant reached toward it, its redness sobered by the dimness of the light, Reiko's hand moved to his assistance and the sash fell away, slithering swiftly to the floor. As she stood before him, still in her *yukata*, the lieutenant inserted his hands through the side slits beneath each sleeve, intending to embrace her as she was; but at the touch of his finger tips upon the warm naked flesh, and as the armpits closed gently about his hands, his whole body was suddenly aflame.

In a few moments the two lay naked before the glowing gas heater.

Neither spoke the thought, but their hearts, their bodies, and their pounding breasts blazed with the knowledge that this was the very last time. It was as if the words "The Last Time" were spelled out, in invisible brushstrokes, across every inch of their bodies.

The lieutenant drew his wife close and kissed her vehemently. As their tongues explored each other's mouths, reaching out into the smooth, moist interior, they felt as if the still-unknown agonies of death had tempered their senses to the keenness of red-hot steel. The agonies they could not yet feel, the distant pains of death, had refined their awareness of pleasure.

"This is the last time I shall see your body," said the lieutenant. "Let me look at it closely." And, tilting the shade on the lampstand to one side, he directed the rays along the full length of Reiko's outstretched form.

Reiko lay still with her eyes closed. The light from the low lamp clearly revealed the majestic sweep of her white flesh. The lieutenant, not without a touch of egocentricity, rejoiced that he would never see this beauty crumble in death.

At his leisure, the lieutenant allowed the unforgettable spectacle to engrave itself upon his mind. With one hand he fondled the hair, with the other he softly stroked the magnificent face, implanting kisses here and there where his eyes lingered. The quiet coldness of the high, tapering forehead, the closed eyes with their long lashes beneath faintly etched brows, the set of the finely shaped nose, the gleam of teeth glimpsed between full, regular lips, the soft cheeks and the small, wise chin . . . these things conjured up in the lieutenant's mind the vision of a truly radiant death face, and again and again he pressed his lips tight against the white throat—where Reiko's own hand was soon to strike—and the throat reddened faintly beneath his kisses. Returning to the mouth he laid his lips against it with the gentlest of pressures, and moved them rhythmically over Reiko's with the light rolling motion of a small boat. If he closed his eyes, the world became a rocking cradle.

Wherever the lieutenant's eyes moved his lips faithfully followed. The high, swelling breasts, surmounted by nipples like the buds of a wild cherry, hardened as the lieutenant's lips closed about them. The arms flowed smoothly downward from each side of the breast, tapering toward the wrists, yet losing nothing of their roundness or symmetry, and at their tips were those delicate fingers which had held the fan at the wedding ceremony. One by one, as the lieutenant kissed them, the fingers withdrew behind their neighbor as if in shame. . . . The natural hollow curving between the bosom and the stomach carried in its lines a suggestion not only of softness but of resilient strength, and while it gave forewarning of the rich curves spreading outward from here to the hips it had, in itself, an appearance only of restraint and proper discipline. The whiteness and richness of the stomach and hips was like milk brimming in a great bowl, and the sharply shadowed dip of the navel could have been the fresh impress of a raindrop, fallen there that very moment. Where the shadows gathered more thickly, hair clustered, gentle and sensitive, and as the agitation mounted in the now no longer passive body there hung over this region a scent like the smoldering of fragrant blossoms, growing steadily more pervasive.

At length, in a tremulous voice, Reiko spoke.

"Show me. . . . Let me look too, for the last time."

Never before had he heard from his wife's lips so strong and unequivocal a request. It was as if something which her modesty had wished to keep hidden to the end had suddenly burst its bonds of constraint. The lieutenant obediently lay back and surrendered himself to his wife. Lithely she raised her white, trembling body, and—burning with an innocent desire to return to her husband what he had done for her—placed two white fingers on the lieutenant's eyes, which gazed fixedly up at her, and gently stroked them shut.

Suddenly overwhelmed by tenderness, her cheeks flushed by a dizzying uprush of emotion, Reiko threw her arms about the lieutenant's close-cropped head. The bristly hairs rubbed painfully against her breast, the prominent nose was cold as it dug into her flesh, and his breath was hot. Relaxing her embrace, she gazed down at her husband's masculine face. The severe brows, the closed eyes, the splendid bridge of the nose, the shapely lips drawn firmly together . . . the blue, clean-shaven cheeks reflecting the light and gleaming smoothly. Reiko kissed each of these. She kissed the broad nape of the neck, the strong, erect shoulders, the powerful chest with its twin circles like shields and its russet nipples. In the armpits, deeply shadowed by the ample flesh of the shoulders and chest, a sweet and melancholy odor emanated from the growth of hair, and in the sweetness of this odor was contained, somehow, the essence of young death. The lieutenant's naked skin glowed like a field of barley, and everywhere the muscles showed in sharp relief, converging on the lower abdomen about the small, unassuming navel. Gazing at the youthful, firm stomach, modestly covered by a vigorous growth of hair, Reiko thought of it as it was soon to be, cruelly cut by the sword, and she laid her head upon it, sobbing in pity, and bathed it with kisses.

At the touch of his wife's tears upon his stomach the lieutenant felt ready to endure with courage the cruelest agonies of his suicide.

What ecstasies they experienced after these tender exchanges may well be imagined. The lieutenant raised himself and enfolded his wife in a powerful embrace, her body now limp with exhaustion after her grief and tears. Passionately they held their faces close, rubbing cheek against cheek. Reiko's body was trembling. Their breasts, moist with sweat, were tightly joined, and every inch of the young and beautiful bodies had become so much one with the other that it seemed impossible there should ever again be a separation. Reiko cried out. From the heights they plunged into the abyss, and from the abyss they took wing and soared once more to dizzying heights. The lieutenant panted like the regimental standard-bearer on a route march. . . . As one cycle ended, almost immediately a new wave of passion would be generated, and together—with no trace of fatigue—they would climb again in a single breathless movement to the very summit.

4

When the lieutenant at last turned away, it was not from weariness. For one thing, he was anxious not to undermine the considerable strength he would need in carrying out his suicide. For another, he would have been sorry to mar the sweetness of these last memories by overindulgence.

Since the lieutenant had clearly desisted, Reiko too, with her usual compliance, followed his example. The two lay naked on their backs, with fingers interlaced, staring fixedly at the dark ceiling. The room was warm from the heater, and even when the sweat had ceased to pour from their bodies they felt no cold. Outside, in the hushed night, the sounds of passing traffic had ceased. Even the noises of the trains and streetcars around Yotsuya station did not penetrate this far. After echoing through the region bounded by the moat, they were lost in the heavily wooded park fronting the broad driveway before Akasaka Palace. It was hard to believe in the tension gripping this whole quarter, where the two factions of the bitterly divided Imperial Army now confronted each other, poised for battle.

Savoring the warmth glowing within themselves, they lay still and recalled the ecstasies they had just known. Each moment of the experience was relived. They remembered the taste of kisses which had never wearied, the touch of naked flesh, episode after episode of dizzying bliss. But already, from the dark boards of the ceiling, the face of death was peering down. These joys had been final, and their bodies would never know them again. Not that joy of this intensity—and the same thought had occurred to them both—was ever likely to be re-experienced, even if they should live on to old age.

The feel of their fingers intertwined—this too would soon be lost. Even the wood-grain patterns they now gazed at on the dark ceiling boards would be taken from them. They could feel death edging in, nearer and nearer. There could be no hesitation now. They must have the courage to reach out to death themselves, and to seize it.

"Well, let's make our preparations," said the lieutenant. The note of determination in the words was unmistakable, but at the same time Reiko had never heard her husband's voice so warm and tender.

After they had risen, a variety of tasks awaited them.

The lieutenant, who had never once before helped with the bedding, now cheerfully slid back the door of the closet, lifted the mattress across the room by himself, and stowed it away inside.

Reiko turned off the gas heater and put away the lamp standard. During the lieutenant's absence she had arranged this room carefully, sweeping and dusting it to a fresh cleanness, and now—if one overlooked the rosewood table drawn into one corner—the eight-mat room gave all the appearance of a reception room ready to welcome an important guest.

"We've seen some drinking here, haven't we? With Kanō and Homma and Noguchi . . ."

"Yes, they were great drinkers, all of them."

"We'll be meeting them before long, in the other world. They'll tease us, I imagine, when they find I've brought you with me."

Descending the stairs, the lieutenant turned to look back into this calm, clean room, now brightly illuminated by the ceiling lamp. There floated across his mind the faces of the young officers who had drunk there, and laughed, and innocently bragged. He had never dreamed then that he would one day cut open his stomach in this room.

In the two rooms downstairs husband and wife busied themselves smoothly and serenely with their respective preparations. The lieutenant went to the toilet, and then to the bathroom to wash. Meanwhile Reiko folded away her husband's padded robe, placed his uniform tunic, his trousers, and a newly cut bleached loincloth in the bathroom, and set out sheets of paper on the living-room table for the farewell notes. Then she removed the lid from the writing box and began rubbing ink from the ink tablet. She had already decided upon the wording of her own note.

Reiko's fingers pressed hard upon the cold gilt letters of the ink tablet, and the water in the shallow well at once darkened, as if a black cloud had spread across it. She stopped thinking that this repeated action, this pressure from her fingers, this rise and fall of faint sound, was all and solely for death. It was a routine domestic task, a simple paring away of time until death should finally stand before her. But somehow, in the increasingly smooth motion of the tablet rubbing on the stone, and in the scent from the thickening ink, there was unspeakable darkness.

Neat in his uniform, which he now wore next to his skin, the lieutenant emerged from the bathroom. Without a word he seated himself at the table, bolt upright, took a brush in his hand, and stared undecidedly at the paper before him.

Reiko took a white silk kimono with her and entered the bathroom. When she reappeared in the living room, clad in the white kimono and with her face lightly made up, the farewell note lay completed on the table beneath the lamp. The thick black brushstrokes said simply:

"Long Live the Imperial Forces—Army Lieutenant Takeyama Shinji."

While Reiko sat opposite him writing her own note, the lieutenant gazed in silence, intensely serious, at the controlled movement of his wife's pale fingers as they manipulated the brush.

With their respective notes in their hands—the lieutenant's sword strapped to his side, Reiko's small dagger thrust into the sash of her white kimono—the two of them stood before the god shelf and silently prayed. Then they put out all the downstairs lights. As he mounted the stairs the lieutenant turned his head and gazed back at the striking, white-clad figure of his wife, climbing behind him, with lowered eyes, from the darkness beneath.

The farewell notes were laid side by side in the alcove of the upstairs room. They wondered whether they ought not to remove the hanging scroll, but since it had been written by their go-between, Lieutenant General Ozeki, and consisted, moreover, of two Chinese characters signifying "Sincerity," they left it where it was. Even if it were to become stained with splashes of blood, they felt that the lieutenant general would understand.

The lieutenant, sitting erect with his back to the alcove, laid his sword on the floor before him.

Reiko sat facing him, a mat's width away. With the rest of her so severely white the touch of rouge on her lips seemed remarkably seductive.

Across the dividing mat they gazed intently into each other's eyes. The lieutenant's sword lay before his knees. Seeing it, Reiko recalled their first night and was overwhelmed with sadness. The lieutenant spoke, in a hoarse voice:

"As I have no second to help me I shall cut deep. It may look unpleasant, but please do not panic. Death of any sort is a fearful thing to watch. You must not be discouraged by what you see. Is that all right?"

"Yes."

Reiko nodded deeply.

Looking at the slender white figure of his wife the lieutenant experienced a bizarre excitement. What he was about to perform was an act in his public capacity as a soldier, something he had never previously shown his wife. It called for a resolution equal to the courage to enter battle; it was a death of no less degree and quality than death in the front line. It was his conduct on the battlefield that he was now to display.

Momentarily the thought led the lieutenant to a strange fantasy. A lonely death on the battlefield, a death beneath the eyes of his beautiful wife . . . in the sensation that he was now to die in these two dimensions, realizing an impossible union of them both, there was sweetness beyond words. This must be the very pinnacle of good fortune, he thought. To have every moment of his death observed by those beautiful eyes—it was like being borne to death on a gentle, fragrant breeze. There was some special favor here. He did not understand precisely what it was, but it was a domain unknown to others; a dispensation granted to no one else had been permitted to himself. In the radiant, bridelike figure of his white-robed wife the lieutenant seemed to see a vision of all those things he had loved and for which he was to lay down his life—the Imperial Household, the Nation, the Army Flag. All these, no less than the wife who sat before him, were presences observing him closely with clear and never-faltering eyes.

Reiko too was gazing intently at her husband, so soon to die, and she thought that never in this world had she seen anything so beautiful. The lieutenant always looked well in uniform, but now, as he contemplated death with severe brows and firmly closed lips, he revealed what was perhaps masculine beauty at its most superb.

"It's time to go," the lieutenant said at last.

Reiko bent her body low to the mat in a deep bow. She could not raise her face. She did not wish to spoil her make-up with tears, but the tears could not be held back.

When at length she looked up she saw hazily through the tears that her husband had wound a white bandage around the blade of his now unsheathed sword, leaving five or six inches of naked steel showing at the point.

Resting the sword in its cloth wrapping on the mat before him, the lieutenant rose from his knees, resettled himself cross-legged, and unfastened the hooks of his uniform collar. His eyes no longer saw his wife. Slowly, one by one, he undid the flat brass buttons. The dusky brown chest was revealed, and then the stomach. He unclasped his belt and undid the buttons of his trousers. The pure whiteness of the thickly coiled loincloth showed itself. The lieutenant pushed the cloth down with both hands, further to ease his stomach, and then reached for the white-bandaged blade of his sword. With his left hand he massaged his abdomen, glancing downward as he did so.

To reassure himself on the sharpness of his sword's cutting edge the lieutenant folded back the left trouser flap, exposing a little of his thigh, and lightly drew the blade across the skin. Blood welled up in the wound at once, and several streaks of red trickled downward, glistening in the strong light.

It was the first time Reiko had ever seen her husband's blood, and she felt a violent throbbing in her chest. She looked at her husband's face. The lieutenant was looking at the blood with calm appraisal. For a moment—though thinking at the same time that it was hollow comfort—Reiko experienced a sense of relief.

The lieutenant's eyes fixed his wife with an intense, hawk-like stare. Moving the sword around to his front, he raised himself slightly on his hips and let the upper half of his body lean over the sword point. That he was mustering his whole strength was apparent from the angry tension of the uniform at his shoulders. The lieutenant aimed to strike deep into the left of his stomach. His sharp cry pierced the silence of the room.

Despite the effort he had himself put into the blow, the lieutenant had the impression that someone else had struck the side of his stomach agonizingly with a thick rod of iron. For a second or so his head reeled and he had no idea what had happened. The five or six inches of naked point had vanished completely into his flesh, and the white bandage, gripped in his clenched fist, pressed directly against his stomach.

He returned to consciousness. The blade had certainly pierced the wall of the stomach, he thought. His breathing was difficult, his chest thumped violently, and in some far deep region, which he could hardly believe was a part of himself, a fearful and excruciating pain came welling up as if the ground had split open to disgorge a boiling stream of molten rock. The pain came suddenly nearer, with terrifying speed. The lieutenant bit his lower lip and stifled an instinctive moan.

Was this *seppuku?*—he was thinking. It was a sensation of utter chaos, as if the sky had fallen on his head and the world was reeling drunkenly. His will power and courage, which had seemed so robust before he made the incision, had now dwindled to something like a single hairlike thread of steel, and he was assailed by the uneasy feeling that he must advance along this thread, clinging to it with desperation. His clenched fist had grown moist. Looking down, he saw that both his hand and the cloth about the blade were drenched in blood. His loincloth too was dyed a deep red. It struck him as incredible that, amidst this terrible agony, things which could be seen could still be seen, and existing things existed still.

The moment the lieutenant thrust the sword into his left side and she saw the deathly pallor fall across his face, like an abruptly lowered curtain, Reiko had to struggle to prevent herself from rushing to his side. Whatever happened, she must watch. She must be a witness. That was the duty her husband had laid upon her. Opposite her, a mat's space away, she could clearly see her husband biting his lip to stifle the pain. The pain was there, with absolute certainty, before her eyes. And Reiko had no means of rescuing him from it.

The sweat glistened on her husband's forehead. The lieutenant closed his eyes, and then opened them again, as if experimenting. The eyes had lost their luster, and seemed innocent and empty like the eyes of a small animal.

The agony before Reiko's eyes burned as strong as the summer sun, utterly remote from the grief which seemed to be tearing herself apart within. The pain grew steadily in stature, stretching upward. Reiko felt that her husband had already become a man in a separate world, a man whose whole being had been resolved into pain, a prisoner in a cage of pain where no hand could reach out to him. But Reiko felt no pain at all. Her grief was not pain. As she thought about this, Reiko began to feel as if someone had raised a cruel wall of glass high between herself and her husband.

Ever since her marriage her husband's existence had been her own existence, and every breath of his had been a breath drawn by herself. But now, while her husband's existence in pain was a vivid reality, Reiko could find in this grief of hers no certain proof at all of her own existence.

With only his right hand on the sword the lieutenant began to cut sideways across his stomach. But as the blade became entangled with the entrails it was pushed constantly outward by their soft resilience; and the lieutenant realized that it would be necessary, as he cut, to use both hands to keep the point pressed deep into his stomach. He pulled the blade across. It did not cut as easily as he had expected. He directed the strength of his whole body into his right hand and pulled again. There was a cut of three or four inches.

The pain spread slowly outward from the inner depths until the whole stomach reverberated. It was like the wild clanging of a bell. Or like a thousand bells which jangled simultaneously at every breath he breathed and every throb of his pulse, rocking his whole being. The lieutenant could no longer stop himself from moaning. But by now the blade had cut its way through to below the navel, and when he noticed this he felt a sense of satisfaction, and a renewal of courage.

The volume of blood had steadily increased, and now it spurted from the wound as if propelled by the beat of the pulse. The mat before the lieutenant was drenched red with splattered blood, and more blood overflowed onto it from pools which gathered in the folds of the lieutenant's khaki trousers. A spot, like a bird, came flying across to Reiko and settled on the lap of her white silk kimono.

By the time the lieutenant had at last drawn the sword across to the right side of his stomach, the blade was already cutting shallow and had revealed its naked tip, slippery with blood and grease. But, suddenly stricken by a fit of vomiting, the lieutenant cried out hoarsely. The vomiting made the fierce pain fiercer still, and the stomach, which had thus far remained firm and compact, now abruptly heaved, opening wide its wound, and the entrails burst through, as if the wound too were vomiting. Seemingly ignorant of their master's suffering, the entrails gave an impression of robust health and almost disagreeable vitality as they slipped smoothly out and spilled over into the crotch. The lieutenant's head drooped, his shoulders heaved, his eyes opened to narrow slits, and a thin trickle of saliva dribbled from his mouth. The gold markings on his epaulettes caught the light and glinted.

Blood was scattered everywhere. The lieutenant was soaked in it to his knees, and he sat now in a crumpled and listless posture, one hand on the floor. A raw smell filled the room. The lieutenant, his head drooping, retched repeatedly, and the movement showed vividly in his shoulders. The blade of the sword, now pushed back by the entrails and exposed to its tip, was still in the lieutenant's right hand.

It would be difficult to imagine a more heroic sight than that of the lieutenant at this moment, as he mustered his strength and flung back his head. The movement was performed with sudden violence, and the back of his head struck with a sharp crack against the alcove pillar. Reiko had been sitting until now with her face lowered, gazing in fascination at the tide of blood advancing toward her knees, but the sound took her by surprise and she looked up.

The lieutenant's face was not the face of a living man. The eyes were hollow, the skin parched, the once so lustrous cheeks and lips the color of dried mud. The right hand alone was moving. Laboriously gripping the sword, it hovered shakily in the air like the hand of a marionette and strove to direct the point at the base of the lieutenant's throat. Reiko watched her husband make this last, most heart-rending, futile exertion. Glistening with blood and grease, the point was thrust at the throat again and again. And each time it missed its aim. The strength to guide it was no longer there. The straying point struck the collar and the collar badges. Although its hooks had been unfastened, the stiff military collar had closed together again and was protecting the throat.

Reiko could bear the sight no longer. She tried to go to her husband's help, but she could not stand. She moved through the blood on her knees, and her white skirts grew deep red. Moving to the rear of her husband, she helped no more than by loosening the collar. The quivering blade at last contacted the naked flesh of the throat. At that moment Reiko's impression was that she herself had propelled her husband forward; but that was not the case. It was a movement planned by the lieutenant himself, his last exertion of strength. Abruptly he threw his body at the blade, and the blade pierced his neck, emerging at the nape. There was a tremendous spurt of blood and the lieutenant lay still, cold blue-tinged steel protruding from his neck at the back.

5

Slowly, her socks slippery with blood, Reiko descended the stairway. The upstairs room was now completely still.

Switching on the ground-floor lights, she checked the gas jet and the main gas plug and poured water over the smoldering, half-buried charcoal in the brazier. She stood before the upright mirror in the four-and-a-half-mat room and held up her skirts. The bloodstains made it seem as if a bold, vivid pattern was printed across the lower half of her white kimono. When she sat down before the mirror, she was conscious of the dampness and coldness of her husband's blood in the region of her thighs, and she shivered. Then, for a long while, she lingered over her toilet preparations. She applied the rouge generously to her cheeks, and her lips too she painted heavily. This was no longer make-up to please her husband. It was make-up for the world which she would leave behind, and there was a touch of the magnificent and the spectacular in her brushwork. When she rose, the mat before the mirror was wet with blood. Reiko was not concerned about this.

Returning from the toilet, Reiko stood finally on the cement floor of the porchway. When her husband had bolted the door here last night it had been in preparation for death. For a while she stood immersed in the consideration of a simple problem. Should she now leave the bolt drawn? If she were to lock the door, it could be that the neighbors might not notice their suicide for several days. Reiko did not relish the thought of their two corpses putrifying before discovery. After all, it seemed, it would be best to leave it open. . . . She released the bolt, and also drew open the frosted-glass door a fraction. . . . At once a chill wind blew in. There was no sign of anyone in the midnight streets, and stars glittered ice-cold through the trees in the large house opposite.

Leaving the door as it was, Reiko mounted the stairs. She had walked here and there for some time and her socks were no longer slippery. About halfway up, her nostrils were already assailed by a peculiar smell.

The lieutenant was lying on his face in a sea of blood. The point protruding from his neck seemed to have grown even more prominent than before. Reiko walked heedlessly across the blood. Sitting beside the lieutenant's corpse, she stared intently at the face, which lay on one cheek on the mat. The eyes were opened wide, as if the lieutenant's attention had been attracted by something. She raised the head, folding it in her sleeve, wiped the blood from the lips, and bestowed a last kiss.

Then she rose and took from the closet a new white blanket and a waist cord. To prevent any derangement of her skirts, she wrapped the blanket about her waist and bound it there firmly with the cord.

Reiko sat herself on a spot about one foot distant from the lieutenant's body. Drawing the dagger from her sash, she examined its dully gleaming blade intently, and held it to her tongue. The taste of the polished steel was slightly sweet.

Reiko did not linger. When she thought how the pain which had previously opened such a gulf between herself and her dying husband was now to become a part of her own experience, she saw before her only the joy of herself entering a realm her husband had already made his own. In her husband's agonized face there had been something inexplicable which she was seeing for the first time. Now she would solve that riddle. Reiko sensed that at last she too would be able to taste the true bitterness and sweetness of that great moral principle in which her husband believed. What had until now been tasted only faintly through her husband's example she was about to savor directly with her own tongue.

Reiko rested the point of the blade against the base of her throat. She thrust hard. The wound was only shallow. Her head blazed, and her hands shook uncontrollably. She gave the blade a strong pull sideways. A warm substance flooded into her mouth, and everything before her eyes reddened, in a vision of spouting blood. She gathered her strength and plunged the point of the blade deep into her throat.

Translated from the Japanese by Geoffrey W. Sargent

Alberto Moravia

. . . .

JEWELLERY

You can be quite sure that, when a woman finds her way into a group of men friends, that group, without the slightest doubt, is bound to disintegrate and each member of it to go off on his own account. That year we formed a group of young men who were all in the closest sympathy with each other, always united, always in agreement, always together. We were all of us earning a very good living, Tore with his garage, the two Modesti brothers with their meat-broker's business, Pippo Morganti with his pork-butcher's shop, Rinaldo with his bar, and I with a varied assortment of things: at that moment I was dealing in resin and products allied to it. Although we were all under thirty, none of us weighed less than twelve or thirteen stone: we all knew how to wield a knife and fork. During the day we were at work; but from seven o'clock onwards we were always together, first at Rinaldo's bar in the Corso Vittorio, and then in a restaurant with a garden in the neighbourhood of the Chiesa Nuova. We spent Sundays together, of course: either at the stadium watching football matches, or on expeditions to the Castelli Romani, or, in the warm weather, at Ostia or Ladispoli. There were six of us, yet it might be said that we were one single person. So, supposing that one of us was smitten by a caprice, the other five were soon smitten too. With regard to jewellery, it was Tore who started it: he came one evening to the restaurant wearing a wristwatch of massive gold, with a plaited gold strap nearly an inch wide. We asked him who had given it to him. "The Director of the Bank of Italy," he said, by which he meant that he had bought it with his own money. Then he slipped it off and showed it to us: it was a watch of a well-known make, double-cased and with a second hand, and, together with its stiff plaited strap, it weighed goodness knows how much. It made a great impression upon us. "An investment," said somebody. But Tore replied: "What d'you mean, an investment? I like wearing it on my wrist, that's all." When we met next day at the usual restaurant, Morganti already had a wristwatch of his own, with a gold strap too, but not such a heavy one. Then it was the turn of the Modesti brothers who each bought one—larger ones than Tore's and with plaited straps that were less solid but broader. As for Rinaldo and me, as we both liked

Tore's watch, we asked him where he had got it and then went together to a good shop in the Corso and each bought one.

It was now May, and often in the evenings we used to go to Monte Mario, to the inn there, to drink wine and eat fresh beans and sheep's milk cheese. One evening Tore put out his hand to help himself to beans and we all saw a ring on his finger, a massive ring containing a diamond of no very great size but a fine one nevertheless. "My goodness!" we exclaimed. "Now look here," he said roughly, "you're not to imitate me, you pack of monkeys. . . . I bought this so as to be different." However, he took it off and we passed it round: it was really a very fine diamond, limpid, perfect. But Tore is a big, rather soft-looking chap, with a flat, flabby face, two little pig-like eyes, a nose that looks as if it were made of butter and a mouth like a purse with broken hinges. With that ring on his small, fat finger and that watch on his stumpy wrist, he looked almost like a woman. The diamond ring, as he wished, was not copied. However, we each of us bought a nice ring for ourselves. The Modesti brothers had two similar rings made both of red gold but with different stones in them, one green and one blue; Rinaldo bought himself a ring of a more or less antique style, pierced and carved, with a brown cameo containing a little white figure of a nude woman; Morganti, always anxious to cut a dash, acquired one actually made of platinum, with a black stone; while I myself, being more conventional, contented myself with a ring which had a square setting and a flat yellow stone upon which I had my initials cut, so that I could use it for sealing parcels. After the rings came cigarette-cases. It was Tore, as usual, who began it, by producing a long, flat case—made of gold, of course—with crossed lines incised on it, and snapping it open under our noses; and then everyone imitated him, some in one way and some in another. After the cigarette-cases, we all indulged our own whims: somebody bought a bracelet with a medal, to wear on his other wrist; somebody else a pressure-controlled fountain pen; somebody else a little chain with a cross and a medallion of the Madonna to hang round his neck; and somebody else a cigarette-lighter. Tore, vainest of all, acquired three more rings; and now he looked more like a woman than ever, especially when he took off his jacket and appeared in a short-sleeved shirt, displaying his big, soft arms and hands covered with rings.

We were all laden with jewellery now; and I don't know why, but it was just at that moment that things began to go wrong. It didn't amount to much—a little teasing, a few rather caustic remarks, a few sharp retorts. And then one evening Rinaldo, who owned the bar, arrived at our usual restaurant with a girl, his new cashier. Her name was Lucrezia and she was perhaps not yet even twenty, but she was as fully developed as a woman of thirty. Her skin was white as milk, her eyes black, large, steady and expressionless, her mouth red, her hair black. She looked indeed like a statue, especially as she always remained still and composed and hardly spoke at all. Rinaldo confided to us that he had found her by means of a commercial advertisement, and he said he knew nothing about her, not even whether she had a family or whom she lived with. She was just the right person, he added, for the cash-desk: a girl like that attracted clients by her good looks and then, by her serious demeanour, kept them at a distance; a plain girl fails to attract, and a pretty but forthcoming one does no work and creates disorder. The presence of Lucrezia that evening caused considerable constraint among us: we sat very upright the whole time, with our jackets on, talking in a reserved manner without any jokes or coarse words and eating very politely; even Tore tried to eat his fruit with a knife and fork, without much success however. Next day we all rushed to the bar to see her at her duties. She was sitting on a tiny stool, her hips—which were already too broad for her age—bulging over its sides: and her haughty bosom was almost pressing against the keys of the cash-register. We all stood there open-mouthed as we watched her calmly, precisely, unhurriedly distributing price-dockets, continually pressing down the keys of the machine without even looking at them, her eyes fixed straight ahead of her in the direction of the bar counter. She notified the barman, each time, in a quiet, impersonal voice: "Two coffees.... One bitter.... One orangeade.... One beer." She never smiled, she never looked at the customer; and certainly there were some who went up very close to her in the hope of being looked at. She was dressed with propriety, but like the poor girl that she was: in a simple, sleeveless white dress. But clean, fresh, well ironed. *She* wore no jewellery, not even ear-rings, although the lobes of her ears had been pierced. We, of course, when we saw how pretty she was, started making jokes, encouraged by Rinaldo, who was proud of her. But she, after the first few jokes, said: "We shall meet at the restaurant this evening, shan't we? So leave me in peace now. . . . I don't like being disturbed while I'm working." Tore, to whom these words were addressed because he was the most prying and ill-mannered, said with feigned surprise: "I say, I'm sorry . . . we're only poor people, and we didn't know we had to do with a princess. . . . I'm sorry . . . we didn't mean any offence." She replied, drily: "I'm not a princess but a poor girl who works for her living . . . and I'm not offended. . . . One coffee and one bitter." And so we went away feeling rather humiliated.

In the evening we all met, as usual, at the restaurant. Rinaldo and Lucrezia were the last to arrive; and we immediately ordered our dinner. For a short time, while we were waiting for our food, there was again a feeling of constraint; then the proprietor brought in a big dish of chicken *alla romana*, already cut up, with tomato sauce and red peppers. We all looked at each other, and Tore, interpreting our common feeling, exclaimed: "You know what I say? When I eat I like to feel free . . . do as I do and you'll feel better." As he spoke he seized hold of a leg of chicken and, lifting it to his mouth with his two ring-covered hands, started to devour it. This was the signal; after a moment of hesitation we all began eating with our hands—all except Rinaldo and, of course, Lucrezia who nibbled delicately at a little piece of breast. After the first moment we recovered ourselves and went back, in every possible respect, to our old noisy ways. We talked as we ate and ate as we talked; we gulped down brimming glasses of wine with our mouths full; we slouched back in our chairs; we told our usual racy stories. In fact, perhaps out of defiance, we behaved worse than usual; and I don't remember ever having eaten so much, and with so much enjoyment, as I did that evening. When we had finished dinner, Tore loosened the buckle of his trouser-band and uttered a profound belch, which would have shaken the ceiling if it hadn't happened that we were out of doors, under a pergola. "Ugh, I feel better," he declared. He took a toothpick and, as he always did, started prodding at his teeth, all of them, one by one, and then all over again; and finally, with the toothpick stuck into the corner of his mouth, he told us a really indecent story. At this, Lucrezia rose to her feet and said: "Rinaldo, I feel tired. . . . If you don't mind, will you take me home now?" We all exchanged meaning glances: she had been Rinaldo's cashier for barely two days and already she was talking to him familiarly and calling him by his Christian name. A commercial advertisement in the paper, indeed! They went out and, the moment they had gone, Tore gave another belch and said: "About time too . . . I'd had enough. . . . Did you see the haughtiness of it? And him following behind as good as gold . . . as meek as a lamb! As for that commercial advertisement—matrimonial advertisement, I should say!"

For two or three days the same scenes were repeated: Lucrezia eating composedly and silently; the rest of us trying to pretend she wasn't there; Rinaldo divided between Lucrezia and us and not knowing what line to take. But there was something brewing, we all felt that. The girl—still waters run deep—gave no sign, but all the time she was wanting Rinaldo to choose between herself and us. At last, one evening, for no precise reason—perhaps because it was hot and, as one knows, heat gets on people's nerves—Rinaldo, half-way through dinner, made an attack upon us, in this way: "This is the last time I'm coming to eat with you." We were all astonished, and Tore asked: "Oh, is that really so? And may we ask why?" "Because I don't like you." "You don't like us? Well, I'm sure we're all very sorry for that—really terribly sorry." "You're a bunch of swine, that's what you are." "Now be careful what you say, but . . . are you crazy?" "Yes, you're a bunch of swine; I say it and I repeat it. . . . Eating with you makes me feel sick." By this time we were all red in the face with anger, and some of us had jumped up from the table. "It's you," said Tore, "who's the biggest swine of all. Who gave you the right to judge us? Haven't we always been all together? Haven't we always done the same things?" "You be quiet," Rinaldo said to him; "with all that jewellery on you, you look like one of those women— you know who I mean. . . . All you need is some scent. . . . I say, haven't you ever thought of putting on some scent?" This blow was aimed at all of us; and, realizing the source from which it came, we all looked at Lucrezia: but she, hypocritically, kept on pulling Rinaldo by the sleeve and urging him to stop and come away. Then Tore said: "You've got jewellery too . . . you've got a watch and a ring and a bracelet . . . just as much as anyone else." Rinaldo was beside himself now. "But you know what I'm going to do?" he cried. "I'm taking them all off and giving them to her. . . . Come on, take them, Lucrezia, I'm giving them to you." As he spoke, he slipped off his ring, his bracelet, his wristwatch, pulled his cigarette-case out of his pocket and threw the whole lot into the girl's lap. "None of the rest of you," he said insultingly, "would ever do that . . . you *couldn't* do it." "Go to hell," said Tore; but you could see, now, that he was ashamed of having all those rings on his fingers. "Rinaldo," said Lucrezia calmly, "take your things and let's go." She gathered all the things Rinaldo had given her into a heap and put them into his pocket. Rinaldo, however, owing to some kind of grudge that he had against us, continued to abuse us even while allowing Lucrezia to drag him away. "You're a bunch of swine, I tell you. . . . Why don't you learn how to eat; why don't you learn how to live. . . . Swine!" "Idiot!" shouted Tore, mad with rage. "Imbecile! . . . You've allowed yourself to be led away by that other idiot who's standing beside you!" If you could have seen Rinaldo! He jumped right over the table and seized hold of Tore by the collar of his shirt. We had to pull them apart.

That evening, after they had gone, we did not breathe a word and we all left after a few minutes. Next evening we met again, but now our old gaiety was gone. We noticed, on this occasion, that several of the rings had vanished and some of the watches too. After two evenings we none of us had any jewellery left, and we were duller than ever. A week went by and then, with one excuse and another, we ceased to meet at all. It was all finished, and, as one knows, when things are finished they don't begin again: no one likes warmed-up soup. Later on I heard that Rinaldo had married Lucrezia; I was told that, at the church, she was more thickly covered with jewellery than a statue of the Madonna. And Tore? I saw him at his garage a short time ago. He had a ring on his finger, but it was not of gold and it had no diamond in it: it was one of those silver rings that mechanics wear.

Translated from the Italian by Angus Davidson

Mohammed Mrabet

. . . .

DOCTOR SAFI

Safi lived by himself. It was a small village, and he lived the same as everyone else, except that he had a special pleasure, which was to take qoqa. He would collect all the red poppies he could find and carry them home. There he would pull off their petals and crush their two green seed pods in a cup with a stick. He would put a little of the qoqa pulp into the teapot, add tea, sugar and boiling water, and set the pot on the fire. When he took it off he would stuff fresh mint into the top of the pot. Finally he would pour himself a glass of the tea and take some snuff. But his snuff too had qoqa in it. He made a powder of the dried pods and sprinkled it in with the tobacco.

One day after he had drunk his tea and taken his snuff he was resting. From where he sat he could see his donkey in the courtyard outside, and as he looked at it he saw that it was not doing what it usually did. It rolled on the ground in a different way, and there was a little foam coming out of its mouth. Safi got up and went out to it. It was an old donkey and he knew its teeth were bad. He looked into its mouth, and then he pulled out four of its teeth.

You have a few good teeth left, he told the donkey. But it's all right. If I have to take them out too, I'll make you a set of false ones. You'll still be able to chew.

Later, at the end of the day, Safi was sitting with his friends in front of the village mosque. A taleb came by, holding his hand over his face. My tooth! he was crying. Safi, being full of qoqa and still remembering the teeth he had just pulled for the donkey, said to the taleb: Come home with me. I can pull your tooth.

He took the taleb with him to his house. There he told him to sit down on the mat, and he gave him a glass of his special tea. Then he had the taleb take a few pinches of his qoqa snuff.

Soon Safi said to the taleb: Open your mouth. Where's the tooth? Here?

He tied a cord to it. Say *Al-lah!* he told the taleb. Then he yanked out the tooth and gave him a glass of hot water with salt in it and told him to wash his mouth.

How much do I owe you? the taleb asked.

Safi was busy thinking. It's free this time, he told him. Because you're my first patient.

The taleb thanked him and went away. As Safi watched him go, he said to himself: And now I'm going to build myself a clinic.

On his extra land Safi began to build a shack. When it was finished he put benches along its walls. He bought three mirrors and a table to hold the pliers and knives. He filled several bottles with salted water. The room had two entrance doors side by side. On one he hung a sign which read: DOCTOR SAFI— PEOPLE, and on the other: DOCTOR SAFI—ANIMALS.

One afternoon not much later, a man came to the clinic with his wife. She wanted two teeth taken out. Safi was very full of qoqa, and he scarcely knew what he was doing. He tied the woman's hands behind her and bound her legs together before looking into her mouth.

Hold her head tight, he told the man. Then he took a pair of pliers in his hand. Open your mouth. Is this the tooth?

Yes! she cried.

Say Al-lah! And while she was saying it he pulled out the tooth. The woman began to groan. He gave her a glass of salt water. Then he reached in and pulled out the other tooth. This time she fainted and fell on the floor.

When Safi saw her lying there with blood coming from her mouth he was afraid. But he went to his room and got some soft soap to stuff into the holes he had left in her gums. When she came to she began to talk to her husband, and it was not many minutes before she had masses of foam coming out of her mouth. This frightened her husband, but Safi merely kept working. He brought in a brazier and some benzoin. With the woman sitting beside the pot of coals, he sprinkled the pieces of benzoin over the fire, and she breathed the smoke. Finally he gave her a glass of qoqa tea. Drink it while it's hot, he told her.

Soon the woman was telling her husband that all the pain had gone away. And Safi said to himself: I've found the right medicine for teeth.

How much? said the man. Safi took the two teeth in his hand and looked at them for a while. The big one will be five rials and the small one two.

Another day a man came and knocked on his door. Salaam aleikoum, said the farmer. I have a cow and I think her teeth are bad.

Come in, said Safi. And bring the cow through the other door. The man led his cow into the office. Safi opened her mouth and looked in. He could not tell whether anything was the matter or not. He got a piece of bread and spread it thick with qoqa paste. After she had eaten it, he opened her mouth again and began to tap her teeth one by one with a hammer.

There's nothing wrong with her teeth, he told the farmer. Here's some medicine for her. She'll feel better. He gave the farmer a mass of qoqa paste.

How much do I owe you?

A rial and a half.

The man paid and left. When he got home he gave the cow the qoqa and put her in with the other animals, but the qoqa soon got into her head. She began to kick and bellow, and she attacked the other livestock. When the farmer went out to see what was happening, she came running at him and tossed him into the air.

Then she turned and pushed one horn into his thigh and began to tear open the flesh. The neighbors came running and tied the cow up.

We must take him to see Dr. Safi, said the neighbors. They carried the farmer to the clinic and Safi looked at his leg. He got a needle and some heavy thread. Lie still, he told the farmer. I'm going to sew up your leg.

He put the needle into the man's flesh, and the man began to yell. He pulled it out, and went to get him a glass of tea. When he had drunk it, Safi brought him another glass. He tried the needle again, and the man yelled again. I've got to find the right medicine for things like this, Safi said to himself. He brought a handful of powdered qoqa and a third glass of the tea. Put the powder into your mouth and drink this, he told him. He waited for a quarter of an hour, and the farmer fell back asleep. Then Safi sewed up his leg. Now take him home and put him to bed.

The neighbors said: How much do we owe you?

This was a lot of work, Safi told them. I used a lot of expensive thread and broke four needles on him. So I'll have to charge you twenty rials.

Each neighbor gave a little. They paid Safi and carried the farmer home. When they had gone, Safi went and sat on his sheepskin to enjoy himself. He poured himself a glass of tea and ate a spoonful of qoqa paste as he drank it. He was thinking that now that he was a doctor he must go down to the city and buy medicines. I've got to make a list of what I need. He got up and brought a board to write on and a pen made from a piece of cane.

The first medicine I need is red pepper. And then I need cumin and black pepper. And henna. He went on writing out the names of many other things he wanted to buy. Soon he got onto his horse and started out for the city.

He tethered his horse in the fondouk. Then he went to see a man who had a stall inside the gate. Give me two pesetas worth of red pepper and two of black. And the same of cumin and cinnamon and anise. He paid the man and went on to another stall. Give me two pesetas worth of rasoul and a bottle of orange flower water, and two pesetas worth of chibb. He paid and went out into the street, where a woman sat on the curb. She was holding an open umbrella over her head, and she had many kinds of resins and powders spread out in front of her. He bought a rial's worth of benzoin. And he went to a bacal and bought a pound of honey, and string and needles.

Before leaving the city he collected three big wooden crates, because he wanted to build benches for his patients to lie on. He tied everything onto his horse and set out for the village.

When Safi was back home again he got to work. He built fires in both of his braziers and put a pail of water over each fire. From the other room he brought a collection of bottles of all sizes. While the water heated he pulled the three crates to pieces and took out the nails. When it was boiling, he put anise seed in one pail and cumin in the other, and left them both on the fire to boil. After they had boiled for a long time, he began to fill the bottles. Then he corked them and put them on the shelf. The rest of the things he arranged in tins, and piled them on another shelf. Finally he built the benches out of the crates, and covered them with burlap bags so they would be comfortable to lie on.

One evening when he had taken a great deal of qoqa, he heard a knocking on the door and the sound of a voice calling. He opened the door and saw a man. What is it?

My wife's having a baby and the midwife can't manage it.

I'll go and look at her, said Safi. He took a bottle of boiled anise and one of cumin, and followed the man.

They went into the man's house. Give me a glass, said Safi. He mixed the anise and the cumin water and told the man to make his wife drink it.

When she had swallowed the stuff the woman opened her eyes and began to move around in the bed. Safi seized her hips and pushed, and the baby slipped out. The woman took the child in her hands and cut it loose.

Everything will be fine now, said Safi.

How much money is it going to cost?

That's the best medicine I have, Safi told him, and it's made of the most expensive materials. I gave you forty rials' worth of it.

I have a young cow, said the man. I can give her to you if you like.

Fine, said Safi. We'll close the deal tomorrow in front of the cheikh.

The man agreed.

The following morning Safi went out to meet the man with the young cow, and together they went to the cheikh. He took the calf back to his house and tied it up with the other cows, very much pleased because it was worth much more than forty rials.

One day a group of men brought the pacha of a distant city to see Safi. He was a man who was always sick, and wherever he went in his travels he looked for a doctor. When his hosts told him that there was a doctor in the village, straightway he wanted to see him, and they carried him on a litter to the clinic.

The pacha was thinking: Maybe at last this one will give me the right medicine.

When they arrived at the clinic Safi was just finishing another large shack he had been building. *Salaamou aleikoum.*

Aleikoum salaam. This is the Pacha of Bzou who has come to our town.

I'm very sick, the Pacha said.

Take him inside, Safi told them. How many of you are there?

There are six of us.

I'll have this room finished in ten minutes. You'll be needing it to sleep in, because you'll all have to stay here until he's cured.

They agreed. Safi finished hammering, and put some mats on the floor. Then the pacha and his friends went inside. Safi followed them, and knelt down to prepare tea for his visitors, and he put qoqa into the tea as he worked. And he set out a plate of qoqa mixed with honey for them, so they could eat it along with their tea.

Then they sat back to drink. Safi said to the pacha: Where do you feel sick?

I don't know. There's no such disease as what I have.

But try and tell me what it's like, Safi said.

The pacha shut his eyes. When I fall asleep I don't know whether I'm really asleep or not, he said. And when I eat I don't know whether I've eaten or not. And if I go out for a walk I'm not sure whether I'm taking a walk or not. Even if

I sit still, I'm not certain whether I'm really sitting there or not. And right now, am I talking? Or do I just think I'm talking?

Safi jumped up. What luck! he cried. I've got exactly the medicine for that. I've seen many cases of the same thing, and I've cured them all.

You have? The pacha was delighted.

This man is not sick, thought Safi. He's just rich. And he's afraid of dying. That's all.

He took a pail of water and put it on the fire. When the water began to boil, he threw in a lot of red peppers. And he let them boil for many hours, as if they had been cow's flesh. When they were ready, he took a fine cloth and placed it over the top of another pail. The liquid went into the pail and the pieces of red pepper stayed in the cloth. He filled a bottle with the water and picked up a piece of rasoul, the clay that women wash their hair with. Then he walked over to the pacha.

Ya, Sidi Bacha, he said. Here's the medicine. It's not medicine. Take it or don't take it. It will either cure you or it won't.

The pacha looked at Safi. And what does all that nonsense mean?

You tell me you sleep and you don't sleep, and you eat and don't eat, and sit and don't sit. I'm giving you the medicine for all those things. Drink half a glass of this the first thing every morning and eat a piece of this rasoul while you drink it. And do the same thing when you go to bed.

Good.

When evening came, the pacha decided he would begin his treatment. First I'll put the solid stuff into my mouth and then I'll wash it down with the liquid, he thought.

So he put the clay into his mouth and drained the glass of pepper water. As it reached his stomach he felt fire inside him, burning his throat and his heart. And although he had not got up from bed by himself in many months, he sprang up now without any help from anyone and began to walk back and forth very quickly. His face turned the color of fire and he breathed with his mouth opened wide. Soon he went outside and looked at the sky, and suddenly it occurred to him that he was cured. He called to his friends: It's a fine night! Come out and smell the air!

They all went out and raised their heads and sniffed, and told him that it was indeed a beautiful night. When they went back inside, the pacha sat in a corner for three hours talking to himself. After that he fell asleep.

In the morning when he awoke, the pacha decided that he felt so well he would not bother taking any more medicine. He went to speak with Safi. I'm cured, hamdoul'lah! My health is perfect. I feel like a man of twenty. How much do I owe you?

Speak with your own image, said Safi. You know what your health is worth to you.

The pacha took out a small pouch full of gold coins and handed it to Safi. And he and his friends went out.

Safi was not satisfied with his clinic, because he still had not discovered a medicine strong enough for serious cases where he had to cut and sew flesh. He worked at this each day, and went on mixing things together and trying them himself afterward. One day he picked some datura leaves and dried them over the fire. Then he made a powder of them, and pounded kif seeds in a mortar. He mixed these two with powdered qoqa. He added argan oil to some of this, and honey to some more. The powder that was left he stored away in a box.

Let's see what this does, he said to himself. He took a spoonful and drank a glass of tea. Then he leaned back and shut his eyes.

Three different people pounded on his door that afternoon, and Safi went on sleeping. Night came, and a man arrived with his son to have Dr. Safi look at the boy's tooth, but still he did not awaken.

In the morning Safi heard the donkeys braying and the cocks crowing, and he got up and opened the door to look out. What's the matter with them all? he thought. As he stood in the doorway some men walked past. And Safi said to them: Good afternoon.

It's early yet, they said. It's still morning.

It's not Monday?

Not any more. That was yesterday, they said.

Safi went inside. Aha! he thought. I've found what I was looking for.

That evening a neighbor woman sent Safi a big pot of spinach and a cauldron of snails cooked with tarragon, because she knew he liked those dishes. He was very much pleased with what she had sent him, and he sat down to eat his dinner in a good state of mind. But he had scarcely taken a few mouthfuls when someone began to hammer on his door with great force.

Wait! he shouted. Don't break it down! And he jumped up and opened the door. There were two men holding up a woman between them. They dragged her into the clinic.

What's the matter with her? said Safi. Put her there on the bench, poor thing.

She's dizzy and she has a fever, they said. And her vomit is bright yellow.

Safi put his hand on her forehead, and saw that the woman was very ill. Her eyes and her face were as yellow as eggyolks. He was afraid, because he did not know what to do for her. But he said: This woman has bousfar. We must get rid of all this yellowness. Has she eaten anything?

Not for the last three days, they said.

Snail broth is what she needs, said Safi. He went across to his rooms and brought the water from the snails he had been eating. When he carried it into the clinic he added four spoonfuls of his new powder, and stirred it into the broth.

The woman drank it all, and then Safi gave her a glass of qoqa tea. Ten minutes afterward she was sitting up talking with her husband, and she seemed very lively.

That's wonderful medicine you've got there, the two men told him. We'd like to buy the whole bowl full, if you'll sell it.

Safi looked at the woman's eyes, and was afraid again. But he agreed to sell the men the bowl of powder for sixty rials. They paid him and led the woman away with them.

After they had gone, Safi sat at his table thinking. He thought of his pouch full of gold coins that the Pacha of Bzou had given him, and of all the rest of the money that he had saved. Suddenly he got up and went out to the house of a neighbor who lived nearby. He sold the man his cows and his donkey, and went back home. There he collected his clothes and medicines, and packed everything onto his horse. He looked up the road and said to himself: This is the right way. Then he got astride his horse and set out along the road, leaving his clinic behind.

About midnight two men came to the door of the clinic and began to pound on it. One carried a club and the other carried an axe, and they were shouting for Doctor Safi. When they broke in the door and searched the place, they did not find him. By then everyone in the village was outside the clinic. The cheikh came running.

The man holding the axe cried: Doctor Safi sold me medicine. When I gave it to my wife she went crazy. Screaming, running, and we couldn't hold her. When she fell down, blood came out of her mouth, and then she was dead. We're looking for him. Where is he?

The cheikh waited a moment before he spoke. Then he said: Your wife is dead. Take her to the cemetery and bury her. Then you can marry a younger one. And here's Doctor Safi's clinic for you to live in. You can have it. The house you're living in now you can sell or rent.

The man looked at the cheikh. Thank you, he said. That's what I'm going to do. You are a very good man.

Everyone went home to bed. Safi was still riding along the road in the dark, happy and with his head full of qoqa.

Translated from the Mogrebi by Paul Bowles

Vladimir Nabokov

· · · · · · · · · · · · · · · · · · · ·

SPRING IN FIALTA

Spring in Fialta is cloudy and dull. Everything is damp: the piebald trunks of the plane trees, the juniper shrubs, the railings, the gravel. Far away, in a watery vista between the jagged edges of pale bluish houses, which have tottered up from their knees to climb the slope (a cypress indicating the way), the blurred Mount St. George is more than ever remote from its likeness on the picture post cards which since 1910, say (those straw hats, those youthful cabmen), have been courting the tourist from the sorry-go-round of their prop, among amethyst-toothed lumps of rock and the mantelpiece dreams of sea shells. The air is windless and warm, with a faint tang of burning. The sea, its salt drowned in a solution of rain, is less glaucous than gray with waves too sluggish to break into foam.

It was on such a day in the early thirties that I found myself, all my senses wide open, on one of Fialta's steep little streets, taking in everything at once, that marine rococo on the stand, and the coral crucifixes in a shopwindow, and the dejected poster of a visiting circus, one corner of its drenched paper detached from the wall, and a yellow bit of unripe orange peel on the old, slate-blue sidewalk, which retained here and there a fading memory of ancient mosaic design. I am fond of Fialta; I am fond of it because I feel in the hollow of those violaceous syllables the sweet dark dampness of the most rumpled of small flowers, and because the altolike name of a lovely Crimean town is echoed by its viola; and also because there is something in the very somnolence of its humid Lent that especially anoints one's soul. So I was happy to be there again, to trudge uphill in inverse direction to the rivulet of the gutter, hatless, my head wet, my skin already suffused with warmth although I wore only a light mackintosh over my shirt.

I had come on the Capparabella express, which, with that reckless gusto peculiar to trains in mountainous country, had done its thundering best to collect throughout the night as many tunnels as possible. A day or two, just as long as a breathing spell in the midst of a business trip would allow me, was all I expected to stay. I had left my wife and children at home, and that was an island of happiness always present in the clear north of my being, always floating beside me, and even through me, I dare say, but yet keeping on the outside of me most of the time.

A pantless infant of the male sex, with a taut mud-gray little belly, jerkily stepped down from a doorstep and waddled off, bowlegged, trying to carry three oranges at once, but continuously dropping the variable third, until he fell himself, and then a girl of twelve or so, with a string of heavy beads around her dusky neck and wearing a skirt as long as that of a gypsy, promptly took away the whole lot with her more nimble and more numerous hands. Nearby, on the wet terrace of a café, a waiter was wiping the slabs of tables; a melancholy brigand hawking local lollipops, elaborate-looking things with a lunar gloss, had placed a hopelessly full basket on the cracked balustrade, over which the two were conversing. Either the drizzle had stopped or Fialta had got so used to it that she herself did not know whether she was breathing moist air or warm rain. Thumb-filling his pipe from a rubber pouch as he walked, a plus-foured Englishman of the solid exportable sort came from under an arch and entered a pharmacy, where large pale sponges in a blue vase were dying a thirsty death behind their glass. What luscious elation I felt rippling through my veins, how gratefully my whole being responded to the flutters and effluvia of that gray day saturated with a vernal essence which itself it seemed slow in perceiving! My nerves were unusually receptive after a sleepless night; I assimilated everything: the whistling of a thrush in the almond trees beyond the chapel, the peace of the crumbling houses, the pulse of the distant sea, panting in the mist, all this together with the jealous green of bottle glass bristling along the top of a wall and the fast colors of a circus advertisement featuring a feathered Indian on a rearing horse in the act of lassoing a boldly endemic zebra, while some thoroughly fooled elephants sat brooding upon their star-spangled thrones.

Presently the same Englishman overtook me. As I absorbed him along with the rest, I happened to notice the sudden side-roll of his big blue eye straining at its crimson canthus, and the way he rapidly moistened his lips—because of the dryness of those sponges, I thought; but then I followed the direction of his glance, and saw Nina.

Every time I had met her during the fifteen years of our—well, I fail to find the precise term for our kind of relationship—she had not seemed to recognize me at once; and this time too she remained quite still for a moment, on the opposite sidewalk, half turning toward me in sympathetic incertitude mixed with curiosity, only her yellow scarf already on the move like those dogs that recognize you before their owners do—and then she uttered a cry, her hands up, all her ten fingers dancing, and in the middle of the street, with merely the frank impulsiveness of an old friendship (just as she would rapidly make the sign of the cross over me every time we parted), she kissed me thrice with more mouth than meaning, and then walked beside me, hanging on to me, adjusting her stride to mine, hampered by her narrow brown skirt perfunctorily slit down the side.

"Oh yes, Ferdie is here too," she replied and immediately in her turn inquired nicely after Elena.

"Must be loafing somewhere around with Segur," she went on in reference to her husband. "And I have some shopping to do; we leave after lunch. Wait a moment, where are you leading me, Victor dear?"

Back into the past, back into the past, as I did every time I met her, repeating the whole accumulation of the plot from the very beginning up to the last increment—thus in Russian fairy tales the already told is bunched up again at every new turn of the story. This time we had met in warm and misty Fialta, and I could not have celebrated the occasion with greater art, could not have adorned with brighter vignettes the list of fate's former services, even if I had known that this was to be the last one; the last one, I maintain, for I cannot imagine any heavenly firm of brokers that might consent to arrange me a meeting with her beyond the grave.

My introductory scene with Nina had been laid in Russia quite a long time ago, around 1917 I should say, judging by certain left-wing theater rumblings backstage. It was at some birthday party at my aunt's on her country estate, near Luga, in the deepest folds of winter (how well I remember the first sign of nearing the place: a red barn in a white wilderness). I had just graduated from the Imperial Lyceum; Nina was already engaged: although she was of my age and of that of the century, she looked twenty at least, and this in spite or perhaps because of her neat slender build, whereas at thirty-two that very slightness of hers made her look younger. Her fiancé was a guardsman on leave from the front, a handsome heavy fellow, incredibly well-bred and stolid, who weighed every word on the scales of the most exact common sense and spoke in a velvety baritone, which grew even smoother when he addressed her; his decency and devotion probably got on her nerves; and he is now a successful if somewhat lonesome engineer in a most distant tropical country.

Windows light up and stretch their luminous lengths upon the dark billowy snow, making room for the reflection of the fan-shaped light above the front door between them. Each of the two side-pillars is fluffily fringed with white, which rather spoils the lines of what might have been a perfect ex libris for the book of our two lives. I cannot recall why we had all wandered out of the sonorous hall into the still darkness, peopled only with firs, snow-swollen to twice their size; did the watchmen invite us to look at a sullen red glow in the sky, portent of nearing arson? Possibly. Did we go to admire an equestrian statue of ice sculptured near the pond by the Swiss tutor of my cousins? Quite as likely. My memory revives only on the way back to the brightly symmetrical mansion towards which we tramped in single file along a narrow furrow between snowbanks, with that crunch-crunch-crunch which is the only comment that a taciturn winter night makes upon humans. I walked last; three singing steps ahead of me walked a small bent shape; the firs gravely showed their burdened paws. I slipped and dropped the dead flashlight someone had forced upon me; it was devilishly hard to retrieve; and instantly attracted by my curses, with an eager, low laugh in anticipation of fun, Nina dimly veered toward me. I call her Nina, but I could hardly have known her name yet, hardly could we have had time, she and I, for any preliminary; "Who's that?" she asked with interest—and I was already kissing her neck, smooth and quite fiery hot from the long fox fur of her coat collar, which kept getting into my way until she clasped my shoulder, and with the candor so peculiar to her gently fitted her generous, dutiful lips to mine.

But suddenly parting us by its explosion of gaiety, the theme of a snowball fight started in the dark, and someone, fleeing, falling, crunching, laughing and panting, climbed a drift, tried to run, and uttered a horrible groan: deep snow had performed the amputation of an arctic. And soon after, we all dispersed to our respective homes, without my having talked with Nina, nor made any plans about the future, about those fifteen itinerant years that had already set out toward the dim horizon, loaded with the parts of our unassembled meetings; and as I watched her in the maze of gestures and shadows of gestures of which the rest of that evening consisted (probably parlor games—with Nina persistently in the other camp), I was astonished, I remember, not so much by her inattention to me after that warmth in the snow as by the innocent naturalness of that inattention, for I did not yet know that had I said a word it would have changed at once into a wonderful sunburst of kindness, a cheerful, compassionate attitude with all possible co-operation, as if woman's love were spring water containing salubrious salts which at the least notice she ever so willingly gave anyone to drink.

"Let me see, where did we last meet," I began (addressing the Fialta version of Nina) in order to bring to her small face with prominent cheekbones and dark-red lips a certain expression I knew; and sure enough, the shake of her head and the puckered brow seemed less to imply forgetfulness than to deplore the flatness of an old joke; or to be more exact, it was as if all those cities where fate had fixed our various rendezvous without ever attending them personally, all those platforms and stairs and three-walled rooms and dark back alleys, were trite settings remaining after some other lives all brought to a close long before and were so little related to the acting out of our own aimless destiny tht it was almost bad taste to mention them.

I accompanied her into a shop under the arcades; there, in the twilight beyond a beaded curtain, she fingered some red leather purses stuffed with tissue paper, peering at the price tags, as if wishing to learn their museum names. She wanted, she said, exactly that shape but in fawn, and when after ten minutes of frantic rustling the old Dalmatian found such a freak by a miracle that has puzzled me ever since, Nina, who was about to pick some money out of my hand, changed her mind and went through the streaming beads without having bought anything.

Outside it was just as milky dull as before; the same smell of burning, stirring my Tartar memories, drifted from the bare windows of the pale houses; a small swarm of gnats was busy darning the air above a mimosa, which bloomed listlessly, her sleeves trailing to the very ground; two workmen in broad-brimmed hats were lunching on cheese and garlic, their backs against a circus billboard, which depicted a red hussar and an orange tiger of sorts; curious—in his effort to make the beast as ferocious as possible, the artist had gone so far that he had come back from the other side, for the tiger's face looked positively human.

"*Au fond,* I wanted a comb," said Nina with belated regret.

How familiar to me were her hesitations, second thoughts, third thoughts mirroring first ones, ephemeral worries between trains. She had always either just arrived or was about to leave, and of this I find it hard to think without feeling humiliated by the variety of intricate routes one feverishly follows in order to keep that final appointment which the most confirmed dawdler knows to be un-avoidable. Had I to submit before judges of our earthly existence a specimen of her average pose, I would have perhaps placed her leaning upon a counter at Cook's, left calf crossing right shin, left toe tapping floor, sharp elbows and coin-spilling bag on the counter, while the employee, pencil in hand, pondered with her over the plan of an eternal sleeping car.

After the exodus from Russia, I saw her—and that was the second time—in Berlin at the house of some friends. I was about to get married; she had just broken with her fiancé. As I entered that room I caught sight of her at once and, having glanced at the other guests, I instinctively determined which of the men knew more about her than I. She was sitting in the corner of a couch, her feet pulled up, her small comfortable body folded in the form of a Z; an ash tray stood aslant on the couch near one of her heels; and, having squinted at me and listened to my name, she removed her stalklike cigarette holder from her lips and proceeded to utter slowly and joyfully, "Well, of all people—" and at once it became clear to everyone, beginning with her, that we had long been on inti-mate terms: unquestionably, she had forgotten all about the actual kiss, but somehow because of that trivial occurrence she found herself recollecting a vague stretch of warm, pleasant friendship, which in reality had never existed between us. Thus the whole cast of our relationship was fraudulently based upon an imaginary amity—which had nothing to do with her random good will. Our meeting proved quite insignificant in regard to the words we said, but al-ready no barriers divided us; and when that night I happened to be seated beside her at supper, I shamelessly tested the extent of her secret patience.

Then she vanished again; and a year later my wife and I were seeing my brother off to Posen, and when the train had gone, and we were moving toward the exit along the other side of the platform, suddenly near a car of the Paris express I saw Nina, her face buried in the bouquet she held, in the midst of a group of people whom she had befriended without my knowledge and who stood in a circle gaping at her as idlers gape at a street row, a lost child, or the victim of an accident. Brightly she signaled to me with her flowers; I introduced her to Elena, and in that life-quickening atmosphere of a big railway station where everything is something trembling on the brink of something else, thus to be clutched and cherished, the exchange of a few words was enough to enable two totally dissimilar women to start calling each other by their pet names the very next time they met. That day, in the blue shade of the Paris car, Ferdinand was first mentioned: I learned with a ridiculous pang that she was about to marry him. Doors were beginning to slam; she quickly but piously kissed her friends, climbed into the vestibule, disappeared; and then I saw her through the glass settling herself in her compartment, having suddenly forgotten about us or passed into another world, and we all, our hands in our pockets, seemed to be spying upon an utterly unsuspecting life moving in that aquarium dimness, until she grew aware of us and drummed on the windowpane, then raised her eyes, fumbling at the frame as if hanging a picture, but nothing happened; some fel-low passenger helped her, and she leaned out, audible and real, beaming with pleasure; one of us, keeping up with the stealthily gliding car, handed her a magazine and a Tauchnitz (she read English only when traveling); all was slipping away with beautiful smoothness, and I held a platform ticket crumpled beyond recognition, while a song of the last century (connected, it has been rumored, with some Parisian drama of love) kept ringing and ringing in my head, having emerged, God knows why, from the music box of memory, a sobbing ballad which often used to be sung by an old maiden aunt of mine, with a face as yellow as Russian church wax, but whom nature had given such a powerful, ecstatically full voice that it seemed to swallow her up in the glory of a fiery cloud as soon as she would begin:

> On dit que tu te maries,
>   tu sais que j'en vais mourir,

and that melody, the pain, the offense, the link between hymen and death evoked by the rhythm, and the voice itself of the dead singer, which accompanied the recollection as the sole owner of the song, gave me no rest for several hours after Nina's departure and even later arose at increasing intervals like the last flat little waves sent to the beach by a passing ship, lapping ever more infrequently and dreamily, or like the bronze agony of a vibrating belfry after the bell ringer has already reseated himself in the cheerful circle of his family. And another year or two later, I was in Paris on business; and one morning on the landing of a hotel, where I had been looking up a film-actor fellow, there she was again, clad in a gray tailored suit, waiting for the elevator to take her down, a key dangling from her fingers. "Ferdinand has gone fencing," she said conversationally; her eyes rested on the lower part of my face if as she were lip reading, and after a moment of reflection (her amatory comprehension was matchless), she turned and rapidly swaying on slender ankles led me along the sea-blue carpeted passage. A chair at the door of her room supported a tray with the remains of breakfast—a honeystained knife, crumbs on the gray porcelain; but the room had already been done, and because of our sudden draft a wave of muslin embroidered with white dahlias got sucked in, with a shudder and knock, between the responsive halves of the French window, and only when the door had been locked did they let go that curtain with something like a blissful sigh; and a little later I stepped out on the diminutive cast-iron balcony beyond to inhale a combined smell of dry maple leaves and gasoline—the dregs of the hazy blue morning street; and as I did not yet realize the presence of that growing morbid pathos which was to embitter so my subsequent meetings with Nina, I was probably quite as collected and carefree as she was, when from the hotel I accompanied her to some office or other to trace a suitcase she had lost, and thence to the café where her husband was holding session with his court of the moment.

I will not mention the name (and what bits of it I happen to give here appear in decorous disguise) of that man, that Franco-Hungarian writer. . . . I would rather not dwell upon him at all, but I cannot help it—he is surging up from under my pen. Today one does not hear much about him; and this is good, for it proves that I was right in resisting his evil spell, right in experiencing a creepy chill down my spine whenever this or that new book of his touched my hand. The fame of his likes circulates briskly but soon grows heavy and stale; and as for history it will limit his life story to the dash between two dates. Lean and arrogant, with some poisonous pun ever ready to fork out and quiver at you, and with a strange look of expectancy in his dull brown veiled eyes, this false wag had, I daresay, an irresistible effect on small rodents. Having mastered the art of verbal invention to perfection, he particularly prided himself on being a weaver of words, a title he valued higher than that of a writer; personally, I never could understand what was the good of thinking up books, of penning things that had not really happened in some way or other; and I remember once saying to him as I braved the mockery of his encouraging nods that, were I a writer, I should allow only my heart to have imagination, and for the rest rely upon memory, that long-drawn sunset shadow of one's personal truth.

I had known his books before I knew him; a faint disgust was already replacing the aesthetic pleasure which I had suffered his first novel to give me. At the beginning of his career, it had been possible perhaps to distinguish some human landscape, some old garden, some dream-familiar disposition of trees through the stained glass of his prodigious prose . . . but with every new book the tints grew still more dense, the gules and purpure still more ominous; and today one can no longer see anything at all through that blazoned, ghastly rich glass, and it seems that were one to break it, nothing but a perfectly black void would face one's shivering soul. But how dangerous he was in his prime, what venom he squirted, with what whips he lashed when provoked! The tornado of his passing satire left a barren waste where felled oaks lay in a row, and the dust still twisted, and the unfortunate author of some adverse review, howling with pain, spun like a top in the dust.

At the time we met, his "Passage à niveau" was being acclaimed in Paris; he was, as they say, "surrounded," and Nina (whose adaptability was an amazing substitute for the culture she lacked) had already assumed if not the part of a muse at least that of a soul mate and subtle adviser, following Ferdinand's creative convolutions and loyally sharing his artistic tastes; for although it is wildly improbable that she had ever waded through a single volume of his, she had a magic knack of gleaning all the best passages from the shop talk of literary friends.

An orchestra of women was playing when we entered the café; first I noted the ostrich thigh of a harp reflected in one of the mirror-faced pillars, and then I saw the composite table (small ones drawn together to form a long one) at which, with his back to the plush wall, Ferdinand was presiding; and for a moment his whole attitude, the position of his parted hands, and the faces of his table companions all turned toward him reminded me in a grotesque, nightmarish way of something I did not quite grasp, but when I did so in retrospect, the suggested comparison struck me as hardly less sacrilegious than the nature of his art itself. He wore a white turtle-neck sweater under a tweed coat; his glossy hair was combed back from the temples, and above it cigarette smoke hung like a halo; his bony, Pharaohlike face was motionless: the eyes alone roved this way and that, full of dim satisfaction. Having forsaken the two or three obvious haunts where naïve amateurs of Montparnassian life would have expected to find him, he had started patronizing this perfectly bourgeois establishment because of his peculiar sense of humor, which made him derive ghoulish fun from the pitiful *specialité de la maison*—this orchestra composed of half a dozen weary-looking, self-conscious ladies interlacing mild harmonies on a crammed platform and not knowing, as he put it, what to do with their motherly bosoms, quite superfluous in the world of music. After each number he would be convulsed by a fit of epileptic applause, which the ladies had stopped acknowledging and which was already arousing, I thought, certain doubts in the minds of the proprietor of the café and its fundamental customers, but which seemed highly diverting to Ferdinand's friends. Among these I recall: an artist with an impeccably bald though slightly chipped head, which under various pretexts he constantly painted into his eye-and-guitar canvases; a poet, whose special gag was the ability to represent, if you asked him, Adam's Fall by means of five matches; a humble business man who financed surrealist ventures (and paid for the *apéritifs*) if permitted to print in a corner eulogistic allusions to the actress he kept; a pianist, presentable insofar as the face was concerned, but with a dreadful expression of the fingers; a jaunty but linguistically impotent Soviet writer fresh from Moscow, with an old pipe and a new wrist watch, who was completely and ridiculously unaware of the sort of company he was in; there were several other gentlemen present who have become confused in my memory, and doubtless two or three of the lot had been intimate with Nina. She was the only woman at the table; there she stooped, eagerly sucking at a straw, the level of her lemonade sinking with a kind of childish celerity, and only when the last drop had gurgled and squeaked, and she had pushed away the straw with her tongue, only then did I finally catch her eye, which I had been obstinately seeking, still not being able to cope with the fact that she had had time to forget what had occurred earlier in the morning—to forget it so thoroughly that upon meeting my glance, she replied with a blank questioning smile, and only after peering more closely did she remember suddenly what kind of answering smile I was expecting. Meanwhile, Ferdinand (the ladies having temporarily left the platform after pushing away their instruments like so many pieces of furniture) was juicily drawing his cronies' attention to the figure of an elderly luncher in a far corner of the café, who had, as some Frenchmen for some reason or other have, a little red ribbon or something on his coat lapel and whose gray beard combined with his mustaches to form a cosy yellowish nest for his sloppily munching mouth. Somehow the trappings of old age always amused Ferdie.

I did not stay long in Paris, but that week proved sufficient to engender between him and me that fake chumminess the imposing of which he had such a talent for. Subsequently I even turned out to be of some use to him: my firm acquired the film rights of one of his more intelligible stories, and then he had a good time pestering me with telegrams. As the years passed, we found ourselves every now and then beaming at each other in some place, but I never felt at ease in his presence, and that day in Fialta, too, I experienced a familiar depression upon learning that he was on the prowl nearby; one thing, however, considerably cheered me up: the flop of his recent play.

And here he was coming toward us, garbed in an absolutely waterproof coat with belt and pocket flaps, a camera across his shoulder, double rubber soles to his shoes, sucking with an imperturbability that was meant to be funny a long stick of moonstone candy, that specialty of Fialta's. Beside him, walked the dapper, doll-like, rosy Segur, a lover of art and a perfect fool; I never could discover for what purpose Ferdinand needed him; and I still hear Nina exclaiming with a moaning tenderness that did not commit her to anything: "Oh, he is such a darling, Segur!" They approached; Ferdinand and I greeted each other lustily, trying to crowd into hand shake and back slap as much fervor as possible, knowing by experience that actually that was all but pretending it was only a preface; and it always happened like that: after every separation we met to the accompaniment of strings being excitedly tuned, in a bustle of geniality, in the hubbub of sentiments taking their seats; but the ushers would close the doors, and after that no one was admitted.

Segur complained to me about the weather, and at first I did not understand what he was talking about; even if the moist, gray, greenhouse essence of Fialta might be called "weather," it was just as much outside of anything that could serve us as a topic of conversation as was, for instance, Nina's slender elbow, which I was holding between finger and thumb, or a bit of tin foil someone had dropped, shining in the middle of the cobbled street in the distance.

We four moved on, vague purchases still looming ahead. "God, what an Indian!" Ferdinand suddenly exclaimed with fierce relish, violently nudging me and pointing at a poster. Further on, near a fountain, he gave his stick of candy to a native child, a swarthy girl with beads round her pretty neck; we stopped to wait for him: he crouched saying something to her, addressing her sooty-black lowered eyelashes, and then he caught up with us, grinning and making one of those remarks with which he loved to spice his speech. Then his attention was drawn by an unfortunate object exhibited in a souvenir shop: a dreadful marble imitation of Mount St. George showing a black tunnel at its base, which turned out to be the mouth of an inkwell, and with a compartment for pens in the semblance of railroad tracks. Open-mouthed, quivering, all agog with sardonic triumph, he turned that dusty, cumbersome, and perfectly irresponsible thing in his hands, paid without bargaining, and with his mouth still open came out carrying the monster. Like some autocrat who surrounds himself with hunchbacks and dwarfs, he would become attached to this or that hideous object; this infatuation might last from five minutes to several days or even longer if the thing happened to be animate.

Nina wistfully alluded to lunch, and seizing the opportunity when Ferdinand and Segur stopped at a post office, I hastened to lead her away. I still wonder what exactly she meant to me, that small dark woman of the narrow shoulders and "lyrical limbs" (to quote the expression of a mincing émigré poet, one of the few men who had sighed platonically after her), and still less do I understand what was the purpose of fate in bringing us constantly together. I did not see her for quite a long while after my sojourn in Paris, and then one day when I came home from my office I found her having tea with my wife and examining on her silk-hosed hand, with her wedding ring gleaming through, the texture of some stockings bought cheap in Tauentzienstrasse. Once I was shown her photograph in a fashion magazine full of autumn leaves and gloves and wind-swept golf links. On a certain Christmas she sent me a picture post card with snow and stars. On a Riviera beach she almost escaped my notice behind her dark glasses and terra-cotta tan. Another day, having dropped in on an ill-timed errand at the house of some strangers where a party was in progress, I saw her scarf and fur coat among alien scarecrows on a coat rack. In a bookshop she nodded to me from a page of one of her husband's stories, a page referring to an episodic servant girl, but smuggling in Nina in spite of the author's intention: "Her face," he wrote, "was rather nature's snapshot than a meticulous portrait, so that when . . . tried to imagine it, all he could visualize were fleeting glimpses of disconnected features: the downy outline of her pommettes in the sun, the amber-tinted brown darkness of quick eyes, lips shaped into a friendly smile which was always ready to change into an ardent kiss."

Again and again she hurriedly appeared in the margins of my life, without influencing in the least its basic text. One summer morning (Friday—because housemaids were thumping out carpets in the sun-dusted yard), my family was away in the country and I was lolling and smoking in bed when I heard the bell ring with tremendous violence—and there she was in the hall having burst in to leave (incidentally) a hairpin and (mainly) a trunk illuminated with hotel labels, which a fortnight later was retrieved for her by a nice Austrian boy, who (according to intangible but sure symptoms) belonged to the same very cosmopolitan association of which I was a member. Occasionally, in the middle of a conversation her name would be mentioned, and she would run down the steps of a chance sentence, without turning her head. While traveling in the Pyrenees, I spent a week at the château belonging to people with whom she and Ferdinand happened to be staying, and I shall never forget my first night there: how I waited, how certain I was that without my having to tell her she would steal to my room, how she did not come, and the din thousands of crickets made in the delirious depth of the rocky garden dripping with moonlight, the mad bubbling brooks, and my struggle between blissful southern fatigue after a long day of hunting on the screes and the wild thirst for her stealthy coming, low laugh, pink ankles above the swan's-down trimming of high-heeled slippers; but the night raved on, and she did not come, and when next day, in the course of a general ramble in the montains, I told her of my waiting, she clasped her hands in dismay—and at once with a rapid glance estimated whether the backs of the gesticulating Ferd and his friend had sufficiently receded. I remember talking to her on the telephone across half of Europe (on her husband's business) and not recognizing at first her eager barking voice; and I remember once dreaming of her: I dreamt that my eldest girl had run in to tell me the doorman was sorely in trouble—and when I had gone down to him, I saw lying on a trunk, a roll of burlap under her head, pale-lipped and wrapped in a woolen kerchief, Nina fast asleep, as miserable refugees sleep in Godforsaken railway stations. And regardless of what happened to me or to her, in between, we never discussed anything, as we never thought of each other during the intervals in our destiny, so that when we met the pace of life altered at once, all its atoms were recombined, and we lived in another, lighter time-medium, which was measured not by the lengthy separations but by those few meetings of which a short, supposedly frivolous life was thus artificially formed. And with each new meeting I grew more and more apprehensive; no—I did not experience any inner emotional collapse, the shadow of tragedy did not haunt our revels, my married life remained unimpaired, while on the other hand her eclectic husband ignored her casual affairs

although deriving some profit from them in the way of pleasant and useful connections. I grew apprehensive because something lovely, delicate, and unrepeat-
able was being wasted: something which I abused by snapping off poor bright
bits in gross haste while neglecting the modest but true core which perhaps it
kept offering me in a pitiful whisper. I was apprehensive because, in the long
run, I was somehow accepting Nina's life, the lies, the futility, the gibberish of
that life. Even in the absence of any sentimental discord, I felt myself bound to
seek for a rational, if not moral, interpretation of my existence, and this meant
choosing between the world in which I sat for my portrait, with my wife, my
young daughters, the Doberman pinscher (idyllic garlands, a signet ring, a slender cane), between that happy, wise, and good world . . . and what? Was there
any practical chance of life together with Nina, life I could barely imagine, for it
would be penetrated, I knew, with a passionate, intolerable bitterness and every
moment of it would be aware of a past, teeming with protean partners. No, the
thing was absurd. And moreover was she not chained to her husband by something stronger than love—the stanch friendship between two convicts? Absurd!
But then what should I have done with you, Nina, how should I have disposed
of the store of sadness that had gradually accumulated as a result of our seemingly carefree, but really hopeless meetings?

Fialta consists of the old town and of the new one; here and there, past and
present are interlaced, struggling either to disentangle themselves or to thrust
each other out; each one has its own methods: the newcomer fights honestly—
importing palm trees, setting up smart tourist agencies, painting with creamy
lines the red smoothness of tennis courts; whereas the sneaky old-timer creeps
out from behind a corner in the shape of some little street on crutches or the
steps of stairs leading nowhere. On our way to the hotel, we passed a half-built
white villa, full of litter within, on a wall of which again the same elephants,
their monstrous baby knees wide apart, sat on huge, gaudy drums; in ethereal
bundles the equestrienne (already with a penciled mustache) was resting on a
broad-backed steed; and a tomato-nosed clown was walking a tightrope, balancing an umbrella ornamented with those recurrent stars—a vague symbolic recollection of the heavenly fatherland of circus performers. Here, in the Riviera part
of Fialta, the wet gravel crunched in a more luxurious manner, and the lazy
sighing of the sea was more audible. In the back yard of the hotel, a kitchen boy
armed with a knife was pursuing a hen which was clucking madly as it raced for
its life. A bootblack offered me his ancient throne with a toothless smile. Under
the plane trees stood a motorcycle of German make, a mud-bespattered limou-
sine, and a yellow long-bodied Icarus that looked like a giant scarab: ("That's
ours—Segur's, I mean," said Nina, adding, "Why don't you come with us, Victor?" although she knew very well that I could not come); in the lacquer of its
elytra a gouache of sky and branches was engulfed; in the metal of one of the
bomb-shaped lamps we ourselves were momentarily reflected, lean filmland pe-
destrians passing along the convex surface; and then, after a few steps, I glanced
back and foresaw, in an almost optical sense, as it were, what really happened an
hour or so later: the three of them wearing motoring helmets, getting in, smiling
and waving to me, transparent to me like ghosts, with the color of the world
shining through them, and then they were moving, receding, diminishing

(Nina's last ten-fingered farewell); but actually the automobile was still standing quite motionless, smooth and whole like an egg, and Nina under my outstretched arm was entering a laurel-flanked doorway, and as we sat down we could see through the window Ferdinand and Segur, who had come by another way, slowly approaching.

There was no one on the veranda where we lunched except the Englishman I had recently observed; in front of him, a long glass containing a bright crimson drink threw an oval reflection on the tablecloth. In his eyes, I noticed the same bloodshot desire, but now it was in no sense related to Nina; that avid look was not directed at her at all, but was fixed on the upper right-hand corner of the broad window near which he was sitting.

Having pulled the gloves off her small thin hands, Nina, for the last time in her life, was eating the shellfish of which she was so fond. Ferdinand also busied himself with food, and I took advantage of his hunger to begin a conversation which gave me the semblance of power over him: to be specific, I mentioned his recent failure. After a brief period of fashionable religious conversion, during which grace descended upon him and he undertook some rather ambiguous pilgrimages, which ended in a decidedly scandalous adventure, he had turned his dull eyes toward barbarous Moscow. Now, frankly speaking, I have always been irritated by the complacent conviction that a ripple of stream consciousness, a few healthy obscenities, and a dash of communism in any old slop pail will alchemically and automatically produce ultramodern literature; and I will contend until I am shot that art as soon as it is brought into contact with politics inevitably sinks to the level of any ideological trash. In Ferdinand's case, it is true, all this was rather irrelevant: the muscles of his muse were exceptionally strong, to say nothing of the fact that he didn't care a damn for the plight of the underdog; but because of certain obscurely mischievous undercurrents of that sort, his art had become still more repulsive. Except for a few snobs none had understood the play; I had not seen it myself, but could well imagine that elaborate Kremlinesque night along the impossible spirals of which he spun various wheels of dismembered symbols; and now, not without pleasure, I asked him whether he had read a recent bit of criticism about himself.

"Criticism!" he exclaimed. "Fine criticism! Every slick jackanapes sees fit to read me a lecture. Ignorance of my work is their bliss. My books are touched gingerly, as one touches something that may go bang. Criticism! They are examined from every point of view except the essential one. It is as if a naturalist, in describing the equine genus, started to jaw about saddles or Mme. de V. (he named a well-known literary hostess, who indeed strongly resembled a grinning horse). I would like some of that pigeon's blood, too," he continued in the same loud, ripping voice, addressing the waiter, who understood his desire only after he had looked in the direction of the long-nailed finger which unceremoniously pointed at the Englishman's glass. For some reason or other, Segur mentioned Ruby Rose, the lady who painted flowers on her breast, and the conversation took on a less insulting character. Meanwhile the big Englishman suddenly made up his mind, got up on a chair, stepped from there on to the window sill, and stretched up till he reached that coveted corner of the frame where rested a compact furry moth, which he deftly slipped into a pillbox.

". . . rather like Wouwerman's white horse," said Ferdinand, in regard to something he was discussing with Segur.

"*Tu es très hippique ce matin,*" remarked the latter.

Soon they both left to telephone. Ferdinand was particularly fond of long-distance calls, and particularly good at endowing them, no matter what the distance, with a friendly warmth when it was necessary, as for instance now, to make sure of free lodgings.

From afar came the sounds of music—a trumpet, a zither. Nina and I set out to wander again. The circus on its way to Fialta had apparently sent out runners: an advertising pageant was tramping by; but we did not catch its head, as it had turned uphill into a side alley: the gilded back of some carriage was receding, a man in a burnoose led a camel, a file of four mediocre Indians carried placards on poles, and behind them, by special permission, a tourist's small son in a sailor suit sat reverently on a tiny pony.

We wandered by a café where the tables were now almost dry but still empty; the waiter was examining (I hope he adopted it later) a horrible foundling, the absurd inkstand affair, stowed by Ferdinand on the banisters in passing. At the next corner we were attracted by an old stone stairway, and we climbed up, and I kept looking at the sharp angle of Nina's step as she ascended, raising her skirt, its narrowness requiring the same gesture as formerly length had done; she diffused a familiar warmth, and going up beside her, I recalled the last time we had come together. It had been in a Paris house, with many people around, and my dear friend Jules Darboux, wishing to do me a refined aesthetic favor, had touched my sleeve and said, "I want you to meet—" and led me to Nina, who sat in the corner of a couch, her body folded Z-wise, with an ash tray at her heel, and she took a long turquoise cigarette holder from her lips and joyfully, slowly exclaimed, "Well, of all people—" and then all evening my heart felt like breaking, as I passed from group to group with a sticky glass in my fist, now and then looking at her from a distance (she did not look . . .), and listened to scraps of conversation, and overheard one man saying to another, "Funny, how they all smell alike, burnt leaf through whatever perfume they use, those angular dark-haired girls," and as it often happens, a trivial remark related to some unknown topic coiled and clung to one's own intimate recollection, a parasite of its sadness.

At the top of the steps, we found ourselves on a rough kind of terrace. From here one could see the delicate outline of the dove-colored Mount St. George with a cluster of bone-white flecks (some hamlet) on one of its slopes; the smoke of an indiscernible train undulated along its rounded base—and suddenly disappeared; still lower, above the jumble of roofs, one could perceive a solitary cypress, resembling the moist-twirled black tip of a water-color brush; to the right, one caught a glimpse of the sea, which was gray, with silver wrinkles. At our feet lay a rusty old key, and on the wall of the half-ruined house adjoining the terrace, the ends of some wire still remained hanging . . . I reflected that formerly there had been life here, a family had enjoyed the coolness at nightfall, clumsy children had colored pictures by the light of a lamp . . . We lingered there as if listening to something; Nina, who stood on higher ground, put a hand on my shoulder and smiled, and carefully, so as not to crumple her smile, kissed me.

With an unbearable force, I relived (or so it now seems to me) all that had ever been between us beginning with a similar kiss; and I said (substituting for our cheap, formal "thou" that strangely full and expressive "you" to which the circumnavigator, enriched all around, returns), "Look here—what if I love you?" Nina glanced at me, I repeated those words, I wanted to add . . . but something like a bat passed swiftly across her face, a quick, queer, almost ugly expression, and she, who would utter coarse words with perfect simplicity, became embarrassed; I also felt awkward . . . "Never mind, I was only joking," I hastened to say, lightly encircling her waist. From somewhere a firm bouquet of small dark, unselfishly smelling violets appeared in her hands, and before she returned to her husband and car, we stood for a little while longer by the stone parapet, and our romance was even more hopeless than it had ever been. But the stone was as warm as flesh, and suddenly I understood something I had been seeing without understanding—why a piece of tin foil had sparkled so on the pavement, why the gleam of a glass had trembled on a tablecloth, why the sea was ashimmer: somehow, by imperceptible degrees, the white sky above Fialta had got saturated with sunshine, and now it was sun-pervaded throughout, and this brimming white radiance grew broader and broader, all dissolved in it, all vanished, all passed, and I stood on the station platform of Mlech with a freshly bought newspaper, which told me that the yellow car I had seen under the plane trees had suffered a crash beyond Fialta, having run at full speed into the truck of a traveling circus entering the town, a crash from which Ferdinand and his friend, those invulnerable rogues, those salamanders of fate, those basilisks of good fortune, had escaped with local and temporary injury to their scales, while Nina, in spite of her long-standing, faithful imitation of them, had turned out after all to be mortal.

Translated from the Russian by the author
in collaboration with Peter Pertzov

R. K. Narayan

. . . .

NAGA

The boy took off the lid of the circular wicker basket and stood looking at the cobra coiled inside, and then said, "Naga, I hope you are dead, so that I may sell your skin to the pursemakers; at least that way you may become useful." He poked it with a finger. Naga raised its head and looked about with a dull wonder. "You have become too lazy even to open your hood. You are no cobra. You are an earthworm. I am a snake charmer attempting to show you off and make a living. No wonder so often I have to stand at the bus stop pretending to be blind and beg. The trouble is, no one wants to see you, no one has any respect for you and no one is afraid of you, and do you know what that means? I starve, that is all."

Whenever the boy appeared at the street door, householders shooed him away. He had seen his father operate under similar conditions. His father would climb the steps of the house unmindful of the discouragement, settle down with his basket and go through his act heedless of what anyone said. He would pull out his gourd pipe from the bag and play the snake tune over and over, until its shrill, ear-piercing note induced a torpor and made people listen to his preamble: "In my dream, God Shiva appeared and said, 'Go forth and thrust your hand into that crevice in the floor of my sanctum.' As you all know, Shiva is the Lord of Cobras, which he ties his braid with, and its hood canopies his head; the great God Vishnu rests in the coils of Adi-Shesha, the mightiest serpent, who also bears on his thousand heads this Universe. Think of the armlets on goddess Parvathi! Again, elegant little snakes. How can we think that we are wiser than our gods? Snake is a part of a god's ornament, and not an ordinary creature. I obeyed Shiva's command—at midnight walked out and put my arm into the snake hole."

At this point his audience would shudder and someone would ask, "Were you bitten?"

"Of course I was bitten, but still you see me here, because the same god commanded, 'Find that weed growing on the old fort wall.' No, I am not going to mention its name, even if I am offered a handful of sovereigns."

"What did you do with the weed?"

"I chewed it; thereafter no venom could enter my system. And the terrible fellow inside this basket plunged his fangs into my arms like a baby biting his mother's nipple, but I laughed and pulled him out, and knocked off with a piece of stone the fangs that made him so arrogant; and then he understood that I was only a friend and well-wisher, and no trouble after that. After all, what is a serpent? A great soul in a state of penance waiting to go back to its heavenly world. That is all, sirs."

After this speech, his father would flick open the basket lid and play the pipe again, whereupon the snake would dart up like springwork, look about and sway a little; people would be terrified and repelled, but still enthralled. At the end of the performance, they gave him coins and rice, and sometimes an old shirt, too, and occasionally he wangled an egg if he observed a hen around; seizing Naga by the throat, he let the egg slide down its gullet, to the delight of the onlookers. He then packed up and repeated the performance at the next street or at the bazaar, and when he had collected sufficient food and cash he returned to his hut beside the park wall, in the shade of a big tamarind tree. He cooked the rice and fed his son, and they slept outside the hut, under the stars.

The boy had followed his father ever since he could walk, and when he attained the age of ten his father let him handle Naga and harangue his audience in his own style. His father often said, "We must not fail to give Naga two eggs a week. When he grows old, he will grow shorter each day; someday he will grow wings and fly off, and do you know that at that time he will spit out the poison in his fangs in the form of a brilliant jewel, and if you possessed it you could become a king?"

One day when the boy had stayed beside the hut out of laziness, he noticed a tiny monkey gambolling amidst the branches of the tamarind tree and watched it with open-mouthed wonder, not even noticing his father arrive home.

"Boy, what are you looking at? Here, eat this," said the father, handing him a packet of sweets. "They gave it to me at that big house, where some festival is going on. Naga danced to the pipe wonderfully today. He now understands all our speech. At the end of his dance, he stood six feet high on the tip of his tail, spread out his hood, hissed and sent a whole crowd scampering. Those people enjoyed it, though, and gave me money and sweets." His father looked happy as he opened the lid of the basket. The cobra raised its head. His father held it up by the neck, and forced a bit of a sweet between its jaws, and watched it work its way down. "He is now one of our family and should learn to eat what we eat," he said. After struggling through the sweet, Naga coiled itself down, and the man clapped the lid back.

The boy munched the sweet with his eyes still fixed on the monkey. "Father, I wish I were a monkey. I'd never come down from the tree. See how he is nibbling all that tamarind fruit. . . . Hey, monkey, get me a fruit!" he cried.

The man was amused, and said, "This is no way to befriend him. You should give him something to eat, not ask him to feed you."

At which the boy spat out his sweet, wiped it clean with his shirt, held it up and cried, "Come on, monkey! Here!"

His father said, "If you call him 'monkey,' he will never like you. You must give him a nice name."

"What shall we call him?"

"Rama, name of the master of Hanuman, the Divine Monkey. Monkeys adore that name."

The boy at once called, "Rama, here, take this." He flourished his arms, holding up the sweet, and the monkey did pause in its endless antics and notice him. The boy hugged the tree trunk, and heaved himself up, and carefully placed the sweet on the flat surface of a forking branch, and the monkey watched with round-eyed wonder. The boy slid back to the ground and eagerly waited for the monkey to come down and accept the gift. While he watched and the monkey was debating within himself, a crow appeared from somewhere and took away the sweet. The boy shrieked out a curse.

His father cried, "Hey, what? Where did you learn this foul word? No monkey will respect you if you utter bad words." Ultimately, when the little monkey was tempted down with another piece of sweet, his father caught him deftly by the wrist, holding him off firmly by the scruff to prevent his biting.

Fifteen days of starvation, bullying, cajoling and dangling of fruit before the monkey's eyes taught him what he was expected to do. First of all, he ceased trying to bite or scratch. And then he realized that his mission in life was to please his master by performing. At a command from his master, he could demonstrate how Hanuman, the Divine Monkey of the *Ramayana*, strode up and down with tail ablaze and set Ravana's capital on fire; how an oppressed village daughter-in-law would walk home carrying a pitcher of water on her head; how a newlywed would address his beloved (chatter, blink, raise the brow and grin); and, finally, what was natural to him—tumbling and acrobatics on top of a bamboo pole. When Rama was ready to appear in public, his master took him to a roadside-tailor friend of his and had him measured out for a frilled jacket, leaving the tail out, and a fool's cap held in position with a band under his small chin. Rama constantly tried to push his cap back and rip it off, but whenever he attempted it he was whacked with a switch, and he soon resigned himself to wearing his uniform until the end of the day. When his master stripped off Rama's clothes, the monkey performed spontaneous somersaults in sheer relief.

Rama became popular. Schoolchildren screamed with joy at the sight of him. Householders beckoned to him to step in and divert a crying child. He performed competently, earned money for his master and peanuts for himself. Discarded baby clothes were offered to him as gifts. The father-son team started out each day, the boy with the monkey riding on his shoulder and the cobra basket carried by his father at some distance away—for the monkey chattered and shrank, his face disfigured with fright, whenever the cobra hissed and reared itself up. While the young fellow managed to display the tricks of the monkey to a group, he could hear his father's pipe farther off. At the weekly market fairs in the villages around, they were a familiar pair, and they became prosperous enough to take a bus home at the end of the day. Sometimes as they started to get on, a timid passenger would ask, "What's to happen if the cobra gets out?"

"No danger. The lid is secured with a rope," the father replied.

There would always be someone among the passengers to remark, "A snake minds its business until you step on its tail."

"But this monkey?" another passenger said. "God knows what he will be up to!"

"He is gentle and wise," said the father, and offered a small tip to win the conductor's favor.

They travelled widely, performing at all market fairs, and earned enough money to indulge in an occasional tiffin at a restaurant. The boy's father would part company from him in the evening, saying, "Stay, I've a stomach ache; I'll get some medicine for it and come back," and return tottering late at night. The boy felt frightened of his father at such moments, and, lying on his mat, with the monkey tethered to a stake nearby, pretended to be asleep. Father kicked him and said, "Get up, lazy swine. Sleeping when your father slaving for you all day comes home for speech with you. You are not my son but a bastard." But the boy would not stir.

One night the boy really fell asleep, and woke up in the morning to find his father gone. The monkey was also missing. "They must have gone off together!" he cried. He paced up and down and called, "Father!" several times. He then peered into the hut and found the round basket intact in its corner. He noticed on the lid of the basket some coins, and felt rather pleased when he counted them and found eighty paise in small change. "It must all be for me," he said to himself. He felt promoted to adulthood, handling so much cash. He felt rich but also puzzled at his father's tactics. Ever since he could remember, he had never woken up without finding his father at his side. He had a foreboding that he was not going to see his father anymore. Father would never at any time go out without announcing his purpose—for a bath at the street tap, or to seek medicine for a "stomach ache," or to do a little shopping.

The boy lifted the lid of the basket to make sure that the snake at least was there. It popped up the moment the lid was taken off. He looked at it, and it looked at him for a moment. "I'm your master now. Take care." As if understanding the changed circumstances, the snake darted its forked tongue and half-opened its hood. He tapped it down with his finger, saying, "Get back. Not yet." Would it be any use waiting for his father to turn up? He felt hungry. Wondered if it'd be proper to buy his beakfast with the coins left on the basket lid. If his father should suddenly come back, he would slap him for taking the money. He put the lid back on the snake, put the coins back on the lid as he had found them and sat at the mouth of the hut, vacantly looking at the tamarind tree and sighing for his monkey, which would have displayed so many fresh and unexpected pranks early in the morning. He reached for a little cloth bag in which was stored a variety of nuts and fried pulses to feed the monkey. He opened the bag, examined the contents and put a handful into his mouth and chewed: "Tastes so good. Too good for a monkey, but Father will . . ." His father always clouted his head when he caught him eating nuts meant for the monkey. Today he felt free to munch the nuts, although worried at the back of his mind lest his father should suddenly remember and come back for the monkey food. He found the gourd pipe in its usual place, stuck in the thatch. He snatched it up and blew through its reeds, feeling satisfied that he could play as well as his father and that the public would not know the difference; only it made him cough a little and gasp for breath. The shrill notes attracted the attention of people passing by the hut, mostly day labourers carrying spades and pickaxes and women carrying baskets, who nodded their heads approvingly and remarked, "True son of the father." Everyone had a word with him. All knew him in that colony of huts, which had cropped up around the water fountain. All the efforts of the municipality to dislodge these citizens had proved futile; the huts sprang up as often as they were destroyed, and when the municipal councillors realized the concentration of voting power in this colony, they let the squatters alone, except when some V.I.P. from Delhi passed that way, and then they were asked to stay out of sight, behind the park wall, till the eminent man had flashed past in his car.

"Why are you not out yet?" asked a woman.

"My father is not here," the boy said pathetically. "I do not know where he is gone." He sobbed a little.

The woman put down her basket, sat by his side and asked, "Are you hungry?"

"I have money," he said.

She gently patted his head and said, "Ah, poor child! I knew your mother. She was a good girl. That she should have left you adrift like this and gone heavenward!" Although he had no memory of his mother, at the mention of her, tears rolled down his cheeks, and he licked them off with relish at the corner of his mouth. The woman suddenly said, "What are you going to do now?"

"I don't know," he said. "Wait till my father comes."

"Foolish and unfortunate child. Your father is gone."

"Where?" asked the boy.

"Don't ask me," the woman said. "I talked to a man who saw him go. He saw him get into the early-morning bus, which goes up the mountains, and that strumpet in the blue sari was with him."

"What about the monkey?" the boy asked. "Won't it come back?"

She had no answer to this question. Meanwhile, a man hawking rice cakes on a wooden tray was crying his wares at the end of the lane. The woman hailed him in a shrill voice and ordered, "Sell this poor child two *idlies*. Give him freshly made ones, not yesterday's."

"Yesterday's stuff not available even for a gold piece," said the man.

"Give him the money," she told the boy. The boy ran in and fetched some money. The woman pleaded with the hawker, "Give him something extra for the money."

"What extra?" he snarled.

"This is an unfortunate child."

"So are others. What can I do? Why don't you sell your earrings and help him? I shall go bankrupt if I listen to people like you and start giving more for less money." He took the cash and went on. Before he reached the third hut, the boy had polished off the *idlies*—so soft and pungent, with green chutney spread on top.

The boy felt more at peace with the world now, and able to face his problems. After satisfying herself that he had eaten well, the woman rose to go, muttering, "Awful strumpet, to seduce a man from his child." The boy sat and brooded over her words. Though he gave no outward sign of it, he knew who the strumpet in the blue sari was. She lived in one of those houses beyond the park wall and was always to be found standing at the door, and seemed to be a fixture there. At the sight of her, his father would slow down his pace and tell the boy, "You keep going. I'll join you." The first time it happened, after waiting at the street corner, the boy tied the monkey to a lamppost and went back to the house. He did not find either his father or the woman where he had left them. The door of the house was shut. He raised his hand to pound on it, but restrained himself and sat down on the step, wondering. Presently the door opened and his father emerged, with the basket slung over his shoulder as usual; he appeared displeased at the sight of the boy and raised his hand to strike him, muttering, "Didn't I say, 'Keep going'?" The boy ducked and ran down the street, and heard the blue-sari woman remark, "Bad, mischievous devil, full of evil curiosity!" Later, his father said, "When I say go, you must obey."

"What did you do there?" asked the boy, trying to look and sound innocent, and the man said severely, "You must not ask questions."

"Who is she? What is her name?"

"Oh, she is a relative," the man said. To further probing questions he said, "I went in to drink tea. You'll be thrashed if you ask more questions, little devil."

The boy said, as an afterthought, "I only came back thinking that you might want me to take the basket," whereupon his father said sternly, "No more talk. You must know, she is a good and lovely person." The boy did not accept this description of her. She had called him names. He wanted to shout from rooftops, "Bad, bad, and bad woman and not at all lovely!" but kept it to himself. Whenever they passed that way again, the boy quickened his pace, without looking left or right, and waited patiently for his father to join him at the street corner. Occasionally his father followed his example and passed on without glancing at the house if he noticed, in place of the woman, a hairy-chested man standing at the door, massaging his potbelly.

The boy found that he could play the pipe, handle the snake and feed it also—all in the same manner as his father used to. Also, he could knock off the fangs whenever they started to grow. He earned enough each day, and as the weeks and months passed he grew taller, and the snake became progressively tardy and flabby and hardly stirred its coils. The boy never ceased to sigh for the monkey. The worst blow his father had dealt him was the kidnapping of his monkey.

When a number of days passed without any earnings, he decided to rid himself of the snake, throw away the gourd pipe and do something else for a living. Perhaps catch another monkey and train it. He had watched his father and knew how to go about this. A monkey on his shoulder would gain him admission anywhere, even into a palace. Later on, he would just keep it as a pet and look for some other profession. Start as a porter at the railway station—so many trains to watch every hour—and maybe get into one someday and out into the wide world. But the first step would be to get rid of Naga. He couldn't afford to find eggs and milk for him.

. . . . .

He carried the snake basket along to a lonely spot down the river course, away from human habitation, where a snake could move about in peace without getting killed at sight. In that lonely part of Nallappa's grove, there were many mounds, crevasses and anthills. "You could make your home anywhere there, and your cousins will be happy to receive you back into their fold," he said to the snake. "You should learn to be happy in your own home. You must forget me. You have become useless, and we must part. I don't know where my father is gone. He'd have kept you until you grew wings and all that, but I don't care." He opened the lid of the basket, lifted the snake and set it free. It lay inert for a while, then raised its head, looked at the outside world without interest, and started to move along tardily, without any aim. After a few yards of slow motion, it turned about, looking for its basket home. At once the boy snatched up the basket and flung it far out of the snake's range. "You will not go anywhere else as long as I am nearby." He turned the snake round, to face an anthill, prodded it on and then began to run at full speed in the opposite direction. He stopped at a distance, hid himself behind a tree and watched. The snake was approaching the slope of the anthill. The boy had no doubt now that Naga would find the hole on its top, slip itself in and vanish from his life forever. The snake crawled half-way up the hill, hesitated and then turned round and came along in his direction again. The boy swore, "Oh, damned snake! Why don't you go back to your world and stay there? You won't find me again." He ran through Nallappa's grove and stopped to regain his breath. From where he stood, he saw his Naga glide along majestically across the ground, shining like a silver ribbon under the bright sun. The boy paused to say "Goodbye" before making his exit. But looking up he noticed a white-necked Brahmany kite sailing in the blue sky. "Garuda," he said in awe. As was the custom, he made obeisance to it by touching his eyes with his fingertips. Garuda was the vehicle of God Vishnu and was sacred. He shut his eyes in a brief prayer to the bird. "You are a god, but I know you eat snakes. Please leave Naga alone." He opened his eyes and saw the kite skimming along a little nearer, its shadow almost trailing the course of the lethargic snake. "Oh!" he screamed. "I know your purpose." Garuda would make a swoop and dive at the right moment and stab his claws into that foolish Naga, who had refused the shelter of the anthill, and carry him off for his dinner. The boy dashed back to the snake, retrieving his basket on the way. When he saw the basket, Naga slithered back into it, as if coming home after a strenuous public performance.

Naga was eventually reinstated in his corner at the hut beside the park wall. The boy said to the snake, "If you don't grow wings soon enough, I hope you will be hit on the head with a bamboo staff, as it normally happens to any cobra. Know this: I will not be guarding you forever. I'll be away at the railway station, and if you come out of the basket and adventure about, it will be your end. No one can blame me afterward."

Joyce Carol Oates

. . . .

THE TRYST

She was laughing. At first he thought she might be crying, but she was laughing.

Raggedy Ann, she said. You asked about nicknames—I've forgotten about it for years—but Raggedy Ann it was, for a while. They called me Raggedy Ann.

She lay sprawled on her stomach, her face pressed into the damp pillow, one arm loose and gangly, falling over the edge of the bed. Her hair was red-orange and since it had the texture of straw he had thought it was probably dyed. The bed jiggled, she was laughing silently. Her arms and shoulders were freckled and pale, her long legs were unevenly tanned, the flesh of her young body not so soft as it appeared but rather tough, ungiving. She was in an exuberant mood; her laughter was childlike, bright, brittle.

What were you called?—when you were a boy? she asked. Her voice was muffled by the pillow. She did not turn to look at him.

John, he said.

What! John! Never a nickname, never Johnny or Jack or Jackie?

I don't think so, he said.

She found that very funny. She laughed and kicked her legs and gave off an air, an odor, of intense fleshy heat. I won't survive this one, she giggled.

He was one of the adults of the world now. He was in charge of the world.

Sometimes he stood at the bedroom window and surveyed the handsome sloping lawn, the houses of his neighbors and their handsome lawns, his eye moving slowly along the memorized street. He knew it. The Tilsons . . . the Dwyers . . . the Pitkers . . . the Reddingers . . . the Schells. Like beads on a string were the houses, solid and baronial, each inhabited, each protected. Day or night he knew them and the knowledge made him pleasurably intoxicated.

He was Reddinger. Reddinger, John.

Last Saturday night, late, his wife asked: Why are you standing there, why aren't you undressing? It's after two.

He was not thinking of Annie. That long restless rangy body, that rather angular, bony face, her fingers stained with ink, her fingernails never very clean, the throaty mocking voice: he had pushed her out of his mind. He was breathing the night air and the sharp autumnal odor of pine needles stirred him, moved him deeply. He was in charge of the world but why should he not shiver with delight of the world? For he did love it. He loved it.

I loved it—this—all of you—

He spoke impulsively. She did not hear. Advancing upon him, her elbows raised as she labored to unfasten a hook at the back of her neck, she did not look at him; she spoke with a sleepy absentmindedness, as if they had had this conversation before. Were you drunk, when you were laughing so much? she asked. It wasn't like you. Then, at dinner, you were practically mute. Poor Frances Mason, trying to talk to you! That wasn't like you either, John.

There must have been a party at the Buhls', across the way. Voices lifted. Car doors were slammed. John Reddinger felt his spirit stirred by the acrid smell of the pines and the chilly bright-starred night and his wife's warm, perfumed, familiar closeness. His senses leaped, his eyes blinked rapidly as if he might burst into tears. In the autumn of the year he dwelt upon boyhood and death and pleasures of a harsh, sensual nature, the kind that are torn out of human beings, like cries; he dwelt upon the mystery of his own existence, that teasing riddle. The world itself was an intoxicant to him.

Wasn't it like me? he asked seriously. What am I like, then?

I don't ask you about your family, the girl pointed out. Why should you ask me about other men?

He admired her brusque, comic manner, the tomboyish wag of her foot.

Natural curiosity, he said.

Your wife! Your children!—I don't ask, do I?

They were silent and he had the idea she was waiting for him to speak, to volunteer information. But he was disingenuous. Her frankness made him uncharacteristically passive; for once he was letting a woman take the lead, never quite prepared for what happened. It was a novelty, a delight. It was sometimes unnerving.

You think I'm too proud to ask for money, I mean for a loan—for my rent, Annie said. I'm not, though. I'm not too proud.

Are you asking for it, then?

No. But not because I'm proud or because I'm afraid of altering our relationship. You understand? Because I want you to know I could have asked and I didn't—you understand?

I think so, John said, though in fact he did not.

At Christmas, somehow, they lost contact with each other. Days passed. Twelve days. Fifteen. His widowed mother came to visit them in the big red-brick colonial in Lathrup Park, and his wife's sister and her husband and two young children, and his oldest boy, a freshman at Swarthmore, brought his Japanese roommate home with him; life grew dense, robustly complicated. He telephoned her at the apartment but no one answered. He telephoned the gallery where she worked but the other girl answered and when he said softly and hopefully, Annie? Is that Annie?, the girl told him that it was *not* Annie; and the gallery owner, Mr. Helnutt, disapproved strongly of personal calls. She was certain Annie knew about this policy and surprised that Annie had not told him about it.

He hung up guiltily, like a boy.

A previous autumn, years ago, he had made a terrible mistake. What a blunder!

The worst blunder of my life, he said.

What was it? Annie asked at once.

But his mood changed. A fly was buzzing somewhere in her small, untidy apartment, which smelled of cats. His mood changed. His spirit changed.

He did not reply. After a while Annie yawned. I've never made any really bad mistakes, she said. Unless I've forgotten.

You're perfect, he said.

She laughed, irritated.

. . . Perfect. So beautiful, so confident. . . . So much at home in your body. . . .

He caressed her and forced himself to think of her, only of her. It was not true that she was beautiful but she was striking—red hair, brown eyes, a quick tense dancer's body—and he saw how other people looked at her, women as well as men. It was a fact. He loved her, he was silly and dizzy and sickened with love for her, and he did not wish to think of his reckless mistake of that other autumn. It had had its comic aspects, but it had been humiliating. And dangerous. While on a business trip to Atlanta he had strolled downtown and in a dimly lit bar had drifted into a conversation with a girl, a beautiful blonde in her twenties, soft-spoken and sweet and very shy. She agreed to come back with him to his hotel room for a nightcap, but partway back, on the street, John sensed something wrong, something terribly wrong, he heard his voice rattling on about the marvelous view from his room on the twentieth floor of the hotel and about how fine an impression Atlanta was making on him—then in midsentence he stopped, staring at the girl's heavily made-up face and at the blond hair which was certainly a wig—he stammered that he had made a mistake, he would have to say good night now; he couldn't bring her back to the room after all. She stared at him belligerently. She asked what was wrong, just what in hell was wrong?—her voice cracking slightly so that he knew she wasn't a girl, a woman, at all. It was a boy of about twenty-five. He backed away and the creature asked why he had changed his mind, wasn't she good enough for him, who did he think he was? Bastard! Shouting after John as he hurried away: *who did he think he was?*

I never think about the past, Annie said lazily. She was smoking in bed, her long bare legs crossed at the knee. I mean what the hell?—it's all over with.

He had not loved any of the others as he loved Annie. He was sure of that.

He thought of her, raking leaves. A lawn crew serviced the Reddingers' immense lawn but he sometimes raked leaves on the weekend, for the pleasure of it. He worked until his arm and shoulder muscles ached. Remarkable, he thought. Life, living. In this body. Now.

She crowded out older memories. Ah, she was ruthless! An Amazon, a Valkyrie maiden. Beautiful. Unpredictable. She obliterated other women, other sweetly painful memories of women. That was her power.

Remarkable, he murmured.

Daddy!

He looked around. His eleven-year-old daughter, Sally, was screaming at him.

Daddy, I've been calling and calling you from the porch, couldn't you hear me?—Momma wants you for something! A big grin. Amused, she was, at her father's absentmindedness; and she had a certain sly, knowing look as well, as if she could read his thoughts.

But of course that was only his imagination.

He's just a friend of mine, an old friend, Annie said vaguely. He doesn't count.

A friend from where?

From around town.

Meaning—?

From around town.

A girl in a raw, unfinished painting. Like the crude canvases on exhibit at the gallery, that day he had drifted by: something vulgar and exciting about the mere droop of a shoulder, the indifference of a strand of hair blown into her eyes. And the dirt-edged fingernails. And the shoes with the run-over heels. She was raw, unfinished, lazy, slangy, vulgar, crude, mouthing in her cheerful insouciant voice certain words and phrases John Reddinger would never have said aloud, in the presence of a member of the opposite sex; but at the same time it excited him to know that she was highly intelligent, and really well-educated, with a master's degree in art history and a studied, if rather flippant, familiarity with the monstrousness of contemporary art. He could not determine whether she was as impoverished as she appeared or whether it was a pose, an act. Certain items of clothing, he knew, were expensive. A suede leather coat, a pair of knee-high boots, a long skirt of black soft wool. And one of her rings might have been genuine. But much of the time she looked shabby—ratty. She nearly fainted once, at the airport; she had confessed she hadn't eaten for a while, had run out of money that week. In San Francisco, where she spent three days with him, she had eaten hungrily enough and it had pleased him to feed her, to nourish her on so elementary a level.

Who bought you this? he asked, fingering the sleeve of her coat.

What? This? I bought it myself.

Who paid for it?

It's a year old, I bought it myself.

It's very beautiful.

Yes?

He supposed, beforehand, that they would lose contact with each other when Christmas approached. The routine of life was upset, schedules were radically altered, obligations increased. He disliked holidays; yet in a way he liked them, craved them. Something wonderful must happen! Something wonderful must happen soon.

He was going to miss her, he knew.

She chattered about something he wasn't following. A sculptor she knew, his odd relationship with his wife. A friend. A former friend. She paused and he realized it was a conversation and he must reply, must take his turn. What was she talking about? Why did these girls talk so, when he wanted nothing so much as to stare at them, in silence, in pained awe? I don't really have friends any longer, he said slowly. It was a topic he and his wife had discussed recently. She had read an article on the subject in a woman's magazine: American men of middle age, especially in the higher income brackets, tended to have very few close friends, very few indeed. It was sad. It was unfortunate. I had friends in high school and college, he said, but I've lost touch . . . we've lost touch. It doesn't seem to happen afterward, after you grow up. Friendship, I mean.

God, that's sad. That's really sad. She shivered, staring at him. Her eyes were darkly brown and lustrous, at times almost too lustrous. They reminded him of a puppy's eyes.

Yes, I suppose it is, he said absently.

On New Year's Eve, driving from a party in Lathrup Park to another party in Wausau Heights, he happened to see a young woman who resembled Annie—in mink to midcalf, her red hair fastened in a bun, being helped out of a sports car by a young man. That girl! Annie! His senses leaped, though he knew it wasn't Annie.

For some reason the connection between them had broken. He didn't know why. He had had to fly to London; and then it was mid-December and the holiday season; then it was early January. He had tried to telephone two or three times, without success. His feeling for her ebbed. It was curious—other faces got in the way of hers, distracting him. Over the holidays there were innumerable parties: brunches and luncheons and cocktail parties and open houses and formal dinner parties and informal evening parties, a press of people, friends and acquaintances and strangers, all demanding his attention. He meant to telephone her, meant to send a small gift, but time passed quickly and he forgot.

After seeing the girl on New Year's Eve, however, he found himself thinking again of Annie. He lay in bed, sleepless, a little feverish, thinking of her. They had done certain things together and now he tried to picture them, from a distance. How he had adored her! Bold, silly, gawky, beautiful, not afraid to sit slumped in a kitchen chair, naked, pale, her uncombed hair in her eyes, drinking coffee with him as he prepared to leave. Not afraid of him—not afraid of anyone. That had been her power.

His imagination dwelt upon her. The close, stale, half-pleasant odor of her apartment, the messy bed, the lipstick- and mascara-smeared pillows, the ghostly presence of other men, strangers to him, and yet brothers of a kind: brothers. He wondered if any of them knew about *him*. (And what would she say?—what might her words be, describing him?) It excited him to imagine her haphazard, promiscuous life; he knew she was entirely without guilt or shame or self-consciousness, as if, born of a different generation, she were of a different species as well.

At the same time, however, he was slightly jealous. When he thought at length about the situation he was slightly jealous. Perhaps, if he returned to her, he would ask her not to see any of the others.

What have you been doing? What is your life, now?
Why do you want to know?
I miss you—missed you.
Did you really?
In early March he saw her again, but only for lunch. She insisted he return to the gallery to see their current show--ugly, frantic, oversized hunks of sheet metal and aluminum, seemingly thrown at will onto the floor. She was strident, talkative from the several glasses of wine she had had at lunch, a lovely girl, really, whose nearness seemed to constrict his chest, so that he breathed with difficulty. And so tall—five feet ten, at least. With her long red hair and her dark, intense eyes and her habit of raising her chin, as if in a gesture of hostility, she was wonderfully attractive; and she knew it. But she would not allow him to touch her.

I think this is just something you're doing, she said. I mean—something you're watching yourself do.
When can I see you?
I don't know. I don't want to.
What?
I'm afraid.
They talked for a while, pointlessly. He felt his face redden. She was backing away, with that pose of self-confidence, and he could not stop her. But I love you! I love you! Had he said these words aloud? She looked so frightened, he could not be certain.
Afraid! he laughed. Don't be ridiculous.

One day in early summer he came to her, in a new summer suit of pale blue, a lover, his spirit young and gay and light as dandelion seed. She was waiting for him in a downtown square. She rose from the park bench as he appeared, the sun gleaming in her hair, her legs long and elegant in a pair of cream-colored trousers. They smiled. They touched hands. Was it reckless, to meet the girl here, where people might see him?—at midday? He found that he did not care.
We can't go to my apartment.
We can go somewhere else.
He led her to his car. They were both smiling.
Where are we going? she asked.
For the past several weeks a girl cousin of hers had been staying with her in the apartment, so they had been going to motels; the motels around the airport were the most convenient. But today he drove to the expressway and out of the city, out along the lake, through the suburban villages north of the city: Elmwood Farms, Spring Arbor, Wausau Heights, Lathrup Park. He exited at Lathrup Park.
Where are we going? she asked.
He watched her face as he drove along Washburn Lane, which was graveled and tranquil and hilly. Is this—? Do you live—? she asked. He brought her to the big red-brick colonial he had bought nearly fifteen years ago; it seemed to

him that the house had never looked more handsome, and the surrounding trees and blossoming shrubs had never looked more beautiful.

Do you like it? he asked.

He watched her face. He was very excited.

But—Where is—Aren't you afraid—?

There's no one home, he said.

He led her through the foyer, into the living room with its thick wine-colored rug, its gleaming furniture, its many windows. He led her through the formal dining room and into the walnut-paneled recreation room where his wife had hung lithographs and had arranged innumerable plants, some of them hanging from the ceiling in clay pots, spidery-leafed, lovely. He saw the girl's eyes dart from place to place.

You live here, she said softly.

In an alcove he kissed her and made them each a drink. He kissed her again. She shook her hair from her eyes and pressed her forehead against his face and made a small convulsive movement—a shudder, or perhaps it was suppressed laughter. He could not tell.

You live here, she said.

What do you mean by that? he asked.

She shrugged her shoulders and moved away. Outside, birds were calling to one another excitedly. It was early summer. It was summer again. The world renewed itself and was beautiful. Annie wore the cream-colored trousers and a red jersey blouse that fitted her tightly and a number of bracelets that jingled as she walked. Her ears were pierced: she wore tiny loop earrings. On her feet, however, were shoes that pleased him less—scruffy sandals, once black, now faded to no color at all.

Give me a little more of this, she said, holding out the glass.

My beauty, he said. My beautiful girl.

She asked him why he had brought her here and he said he didn't know. Why had he taken the risk?—why was he taking it at this moment, still? He said he didn't know, really; he didn't usually analyze his own motives.

Maybe because it's here in this room, in this bed, that I think about you so much, he said.

She was silent for a while. Then she kicked about, and laughed, and chattered. He was sleepy, pleasantly sleepy. He did not mind her chatter, her high spirits. While she spoke of one thing or another—of childhood memories, of nicknames—Raggedy Ann they had called her, and it fitted her, he thought, bright red hair like straw and a certain ungainly but charming manner—what had been the boy's name, the companion to Raggedy Ann?—Andy?—he watched through half-closed eyes the play of shadows on the ceiling, imagining that he could smell the pines, the sunshine, the rich thick grass, remembering himself at the windows of this room not long ago, staring out into the night, moved almost to tears by an emotion he could not have named. You're beautiful, he told Annie, there's no one like you. No one. He heard his mother's voice: Arthritis, you don't know what it's like—you don't *know!* A woman approached him, both hands held out, palms up, appealing to him, the expanse of bare pale flesh troubling to him because he did not know what it meant. You don't know, don't *know*. He tried to protest but no words came to him. Don't know, don't know. Don't *know*. His snoring disturbed him. For an instant he woke, then sank again into a warm grayish ether. His wife was weeping. The sound of her weeping was angry. You brought that creature here—that filthy sick thing—you brought her to our bed to soil it, to soil me—to kill me— Again he wanted to protest. He raised his hands in a gesture of innocence and helplessness. But instead of speaking he began to laugh. His torso and belly shook with laughter. The bed shook. It was mixed suddenly with a gigantic fly that hovered over the bed, a few inches from his face; then his snoring woke him again and he sat up.

Annie?

Her things were still lying on the floor. The red blouse lay draped across a chintz-covered easy chair whose bright red and orange flowers, glazed, dramatic, seemed to be throbbing with energy. Annie? Are you in the bathroom?

The bathroom door was ajar, the light was not on. He got up. He saw that it was after two. A mild sensation of panic rose in his chest, for no reason. He was safe. They were safe here. No one would be home for hours—the first person to come home, at about three-thirty, would be Sally. His wife had driven with several other women to a bridge luncheon halfway across the state and would not be home, probably, until after six. The house was silent. It was empty.

He thought: What if she steals something?

But that was ridiculous and cruel. Annie would never do anything like that.

No one was in this bathroom, which was his wife's. He went to a closet and got a robe and put it on, and went out into the hallway, calling Annie?— Honey?—and knew, before he turned the knob to his own bathroom, that she was in there and that she would not respond. Annie? What's wrong?

The light switch to the bathroom operated a fan; the fan was on; he pressed his ear against the door and listened. Had she taken a shower? He didn't think so. Had not heard any noises. Annie, he said, rattling the knob, are you in there, is anything wrong? He waited. He heard the fan whirring. Annie? His voice was edged with impatience. Annie, will you unlock the door? Is anything wrong?

She said something—the words were sharp and unintelligible.

Annie? What? What did you say?

He rattled the knob again, angrily.

What did you say? I couldn't—

Again her high, sharp voice. It sounded like an animal's shriek. But the words were unintelligible.

Annie? Honey? Is something wrong?

He tried to fight his panic. He knew, he knew. Must get the bitch out of there. Out of the house. He knew. But if he smashed the paneling on the door?—how could he explain it? He began to plead with her, in the voice he used on Sally, asking her to please be good, be good, don't make trouble, don't make a fuss, why did she want to ruin everything? Why did she want to worry him?

He heard the lock being turned, suddenly.

He opened the door.

She must have taken the razor blade out of his razor, which she had found in the medicine cabinet. Must have leaned over the sink and made one quick, deft, hard slash with it—cutting the fingers of her right hand also. The razor blade slipped from her then and fell into the sink. There was blood on the powder-blue porcelain of the sink and the toilet, and on the fluffy black rug, and on the mirror, and on the blue-and-white tiled walls. When he opened the door and saw her, she screamed, made a move as if to strike him with her bleeding arm, and for an instant he could not think: could not think: what had happened, what was happening, what had this girl done to him? Her face was wet and distorted. Ugly. She was sobbing, whimpering. There was blood, bright blood, smeared on her breasts and belly and thighs: he had never seen anything so repulsive in his life.

My God—

He was paralyzed. Yet, in the next instant, a part of him came to life. He grabbed a towel and wrapped it around her arm, struggling with her. Stop! Stand still! For God's sake! He held her; she went limp; her head fell forward. He wrapped the towel tight around her arm. Tight, tight. They were both panting.

Why did you do it? Why? Why? You're crazy! You're sick! This is a—this is a terrible, terrible—a terrible thing, a crazy thing—

Her teeth were chattering. She had begun to shiver convulsively.

Did you think you could get away with it? With this? he cried.

I hate you—

Stop, be still! I hate you—I don't want to live—

She pushed past him, she staggered into the bedroom. The towel came loose. He ran after her and grabbed her and held the towel against the wound again, wrapping it tight, so tight she flinched. His brain reeled. He saw blood, splotches of blood, starlike splashes on the carpet, on the yellow satin bedspread that had been pulled onto the floor. Stop. Don't fight. Annie, stop. Goddamn you, stop!

I don't want to live—

You're crazy, you're sick! Shut up!

The towel was soaked. He stooped to get something else—his shirt—he wrapped that around the outside of the towel, trembling so badly himself that he could hardly hold it in place. The girl's teeth were chattering. His own teeth were chattering.

Why did you do it! Oh, you bitch, you bitch!

After some time the bleeding was under control. He got another towel, from his wife's bathroom, and wrapped it around her arm again. It stained, but not so quickly. The bleeding was under control; she was not going to die.

He had forced her to sit down. He crouched over her, breathing hard, holding her in place. What if she sprang up, what if she ran away?—through the house? He held her still. She was spiritless, weak. Her eyes were closed. In a softer voice he said, as if speaking to a child: Poor Annie, poor sweet girl, why did you do it, why, why did you want to hurt yourself, why did you do something so ugly . . . ? It was an ugly, ugly thing to do. . . .

Her head slumped against his arm.

He walked her to the cab, holding her steady. She was white-faced, haggard, subdued. Beneath the sleeve of her blouse, wound tightly and expertly, were strips of gauze and adhesive tape. The bleeding had stopped. The wound was probably not too deep—had probably not severed an important vein.

Seeing her, the taxi driver got out and offered to help. But there was no need. John waved him away.

Slide in, he told Annie. Can you make it? Watch out for your head.

He told the driver her address in the city. He gave the man a fifty-dollar bill, folded.

Thanks, the man said gravely.

It was 2:55.

From the living room, behind one of the windows, he watched the cab descend the drive—watched it turn right on Washburn Lane—watched its careful progress along the narrow street. He was still trembling. He watched the blue-and-yellow cab wind its way along Washburn Lane until it was out of sight. Then there was nothing more to see: grass, trees, foliage, blossoms, his neighbors' homes.

Tilsons . . . Dwyers . . . Pitkers . . . Reddingers . . . Schells.

He must have spoken aloud; he heard his own slow dazed voice. But what he had said, what words those were, he did not know.

Edna O'Brien

. . . .

SISTER IMELDA

Sister Imelda did not take classes on her first day back in the convent but we spotted her in the grounds after the evening Rosary. Excitement and curiosity impelled us to follow her and try to see what she looked like, but she thwarted us by walking with head bent and eyelids down. All we could be certain of was that she was tall and limber and that she prayed while she walked. No looking at nature for her, or no curiosity about seventy boarders in gaberdine coats and black shoes and stockings. We might just as well have been crows, so impervious was she to our stares and to abortive attempts at trying to say "Hello, Sister."

We had returned from our long summer holiday and we were all wretched. The convent, with its high stone wall and green iron gates enfolding us again, seemed more of a prison than ever—for after our spell in the outside world we all felt very much older and more sophisticated, and my friend Baba and I were dreaming of our final escape, which would be in a year. And so, on that damp autumn evening when I saw the chrysanthemums and saw the new nun intent on prayer I pitied her and thought how alone she must be, cut off from her friends and conversation, with only God as her intangible spouse.

The next day she came into our classroom to take geometry. Her pale, slightly long face I saw as formidable, but her eyes were different, being blue-black and full of verve. Her lips were very purple, as if she had put puce pencil on them. They were the lips of a woman who might sing in a cabaret, and unconsciously she had formed the habit of turning them inward, as if she, too, was aware of their provocativeness. She had spent the last four years—the same span that Baba and I had spent in the convent—at the university in Dublin, where she studied languages. We couldn't understand how she had resisted the temptations of the hectic world and willingly come back to this. Her spell in the outside world made her different from the other nuns; there was more bounce in her walk, more excitement in the way she tackled teaching, reminding us that it was the most important thing in the world as she uttered the phrase "Praise be the Incarnate World." She began each day's class by reading from Cardinal Newman, who was a favorite of hers. She read how God dwelt in light unapproachable, and how with Him there was neither change nor shadow of alteration. It was amazing how her looks changed. Some days, when her eyes were flashing, she looked almost profane and made me wonder what events inside the precincts of the convent caused her to be suddenly so excited. She might have been a girl going to a dance, except for her habit.

"Hasn't she wonderful eyes," I said to Baba. That particular day they were like blackberries, large and soft and shiny.

"Something wrong in her upstairs department," Baba said, and added that with makeup Imelda would be a cinch.

"Still, she has a vocation!" I said, and even aired the idiotic view that I might have one. At certain moments it did seem enticing to become a nun, to lead a life unspotted by sin, never to have to have babies, and to wear a ring that singled one out as the Bride of Christ. But there was the other side to it, the silence, the gravity of it, having to get up two or three times a night to pray and, above all, never having the opportunity of leaving the confines of the place except for the funeral of one's parents. For us boarders it was torture, but for the nuns it was nothing short of doom. Also, we could complain to each other, and we did, food being the source of the greatest grumbles. Lunch was either bacon and cabbage or a peculiar stringy meat followed by tapioca pudding; tea consisted of bread dolloped with lard and occasionally, as a treat, fairly green rhubarb jam, which did not have enough sugar. Through the long curtainless windows we saw the conifer trees and a sky that was scarcely ever without the promise of rain or a downpour.

She was a right lunatic, then, Baba said, having gone to university for four years and willingly come back to incarceration, to poverty, chastity, and obedience. We concocted scenes of agony in some Dublin hostel, while a boy, or even a young man, stood beneath her bedroom window throwing up chunks of clay or whistles or a supplication. In our version of it he was slightly older than her, and possibly a medical student, since medical students had a knack with women, because of studying diagrams and skeletons. His advances, like those of a sudden storm, would intermittently rise and overwhelm her, and the memory of these sudden flaying advances of his would haunt her until she died, and if ever she contracted fever, these secrets would out. It was also rumored that she possessed a fierce temper and that, while a postulant, she had hit a girl so badly with her leather strap that the girl had to be put to bed because of wounds. Yet another black mark against Sister Imelda was that her brother Ambrose had been sued by a nurse for breach of promise.

That first morning when she came into our classroom and modestly introduced herself, I had no idea how terribly she would infiltrate my life, how in time she would be not just one of those teachers or nuns but rather a special one, almost like a ghost who passed the boundaries of common exchange and who crept inside one, devouring so much of one's thoughts, so much of one's passion, invading the place that was called one's heart. She talked in a low voice, as if she did not want her words to go beyond the bounds of the wall, and constantly she stressed the value of work both to enlarge the mind and to discipline the thought. One of her eyelids was red and swollen, as if she was getting a sty. I reckoned that she overmortified herself by not eating at all. I saw in her some terrible premonition of sacrifice which I would have to emulate. Then, in direct contrast, she absently held the stick of chalk between her first and second fingers, the very same as if it were a cigarette, and Baba whispered to me that she might have been a smoker when in Dublin. Sister Imelda looked down sharply at me and said what was the secret and would I like to share it, since it seemed so comical. I said, "Nothing, Sister, nothing," and her dark eyes exuded such vehemence that I prayed she would never have occasion to punish me.

November came and the tiled walls of the recreation hall oozed moisture and gloom. Most girls had sore throats and were told to suffer this inconvenience to mortify themselves in order to lend a glorious hand in that communion of spirit that linked the living with the dead. It was the month of the Suffering Souls in Purgatory, and as we heard of their twofold agony, the yearning for Christ and the ferocity of the leaping flames that burned and charred their poor limbs, we were asked to make acts of mortification. Some girls gave up jam or sweets and some gave up talking, and so in recreation time they were like dummies making signs with thumb and finger to merely say "How are you?" Baba said that saner people were locked in the lunatic asylum, which was only a mile away. We saw them in the grounds, pacing back and forth, with their mouths agape and dribble coming out of them, like melting icicles. Among our many fears was that one of those lunatics would break out and head straight for the convent and assault some of the girls.

Yet in the thick of all these dreads I found myself becoming dreadfully happy. I had met Sister Imelda outside of class a few times and I felt that there was an attachment between us. Once it was in the grounds, when she did a reckless thing. She broke off a chrysanthemum and offered it to me to smell. It had no smell, or at least only something faint that suggested autumn, and feeling this to be the case herself, she said it was not a gardenia, was it? Another time we met in the chapel porch, and as she drew her shawl more tightly around her body, I felt how human she was, and prey to the cold.

In the classroom things were not so congenial between us. Geometry was my worst subject, indeed, a total mystery to me. She had not taught more than four classes when she realized this and threw a duster at me in a rage. A few girls gasped as she asked me to stand up and make a spectacle of myself. Her face had reddened, and presently she took out her handkerchief and patted the eye which was red and swollen. I not only felt a fool but felt in imminent danger of sneezing as I inhaled the smell of chalk that had fallen onto my gym frock. Suddenly she fled from the room, leaving us ten minutes free until the next class. Some girls said it was a disgrace, said I should write home and say I had been assaulted. Others welcomed the few minutes in which to gabble. All I wanted was to run after her and say that I was sorry to have caused her such distemper, because I knew dimly that it was as much to do with liking as it was with dislike. In me then there came a sort of speechless tenderness for her, and I might have known that I was stirred.

"We could get her defrocked," Baba said, and elbowed me in God's name to sit down.

That evening at Benediction I had the most overwhelming surprise. It was a particularly happy evening, with the choir nuns in full soaring form and the rows of candles like so many little ladders to the golden chalice that glittered all the more because of the beams of fitful flame. I was full of tears when I discovered a new holy picture had been put in my prayer book, and before I dared look on the back to see who had given it to me, I felt and guessed that this was no ordinary picture from an ordinary girl friend, that this was a talisman and a peace offering from Sister Imelda. It was a pale-blue picture, so pale that it was almost gray, like the down of a pigeon, and it showed a mother looking down on the infant child. On the back, in her beautiful ornate handwriting, she had written a verse:

> Trust Him when dark doubts assail thee,
> Trust Him when thy faith is small,
> Trust Him when to simply trust Him
> Seems the hardest thing of all.

This was her atonement. To think that she had located the compartment in the chapel where I kept my prayer book and to think that she had been so naked as to write in it and give me a chance to boast about it and to show it to other girls. When I thanked her next day, she bowed but did not speak. Mostly the nuns were on silence and only permitted to talk during class.

In no time I had received another present, a little miniature prayer book with a leather cover and gold edging. The prayers were in French and the lettering so minute it was as if a tiny insect had fashioned them. Soon I was publicly known as her pet. I opened the doors for her, raised the blackboard two pegs higher (she was taller than other nuns), and handed out the exercise books which she had corrected. Now in the margins of my geometry propositions I would find "Good" or "Excellent," when in the past she used to splash "Disgraceful." Baba said it was foul to be a nun's pet and that any girl who sucked up to a nun could not be trusted.

About a month later Sister Imelda asked me to carry her books up four flights of stairs to the cookery kitchen. She taught cookery to a junior class. As she walked ahead of me, I thought how supple she was and how thoroughbred, and when she paused on the landing to look out through the long curtainless window, I too paused. Down below, two women in suede boots were chatting and smoking as they moved along the street with shopping baskets. Nearby a lay nun was on her knees scrubbing the granite steps, and the cold air was full of the raw smell of Jeyes Fluid. There was a potted plant on the landing, and Sister Imelda put her fingers in the earth and went "Tch tch tch," saying it needed water. I said I would water it later on. I was happy in my prison then, happy to be near her, happy to walk behind her as she twirled her beads and bowed to the servile nun. I no longer cried for my mother, no longer counted the days on a pocket calendar until the Christmas holidays.

"Come back at five," she said as she stood on the threshold of the cookery kitchen door. The girls, all in white overalls, were arranged around the long wooden table waiting for her. It was as if every girl was in love with her. Because, as she entered, their faces broke into smiles, and in different tones of audacity they said her name. She must have liked cookery class, because she beamed and called to someone, anyone, to get up a blazing fire. Then she went across to the cast-iron stove and spat on it to test its temperature. It was hot, because her spit rose up and sizzled.

When I got back later, she was sitting on the edge of the table swaying her legs. There was something reckless about her pose, something defiant. It seemed as if any minute she would take out a cigarette case, snap it open, and then archly offer me one. The wonderful smell of baking made me realize how hungry I was, but far more so, it brought back to me my own home, my mother testing orange cakes with a knitting needle and letting me lick the line of half-baked dough down the length of the needle. I wondered if she had supplanted my mother, and I hoped not, because I had aimed to outstep my original world and take my place in a new and hallowed one.

"I bet you have a sweet tooth," she said, and then she got up, crossed the kitchen, and from under a wonderful shining silver cloche she produced two jam tarts with a crisscross design on them where the pastry was latticed over the dark jam. They were still warm.

"What will I do with them?" I asked.

"Eat them, you goose," she said, and she watched me eat as if she herself derived some peculiar pleasure from it, whereas I was embarrassed about the pastry crumbling and the bits of blackberry jam staining my lips. She was amused. It was one of the most awkward yet thrilling moments I had lived, and inherent in the pleasure was the terrible sense of danger. Had we been caught, she, no doubt, would have had to make massive sacrifice. I looked at her and thought how peerless and how brave, and I wondered if she felt hungry. She had a white overall over her black habit and this made her warmer and freer, and caused me to think of the happiness that would be ours, the laissez-faire if we were away from the convent in an ordinary kitchen doing something easy and customary. But we weren't. It was clear to me then that my version of pleasure was inextricable from pain, that they existed side by side and were interdependent, like the two forces of an electric current.

"Had you a friend when you were in Dublin at university?" I asked daringly.

"I shared a desk with a sister from Howth and stayed in the same hostel," she said.

But what about boys? I thought, and what of your life now and do you long to go out into the world? But could not say it.

We knew something about the nuns' routine. It was rumored that they wore itchy wool underwear, ate dry bread for breakfast, rarely had meat, cakes, or dainties, kept certain hours of strict silence with each other, as well as constant vigil on their thoughts; so that if their minds wandered to the subject of food or pleasure, they would quickly revert to thoughts of God and their eternal souls. They slept on hard beds with no sheets and hairy blankets. At four o'clock in the morning while we slept, each nun got out of bed, in her habit—which was also her death habit—and chanting, they all flocked down the wooden stairs like ravens, to fling themselves on the tiled floor of the chapel. Each nun—even the Mother Superior—flung herself in total submission, saying prayers in Latin and offering up the moment to God. Then silently back to their cells for one more hour of rest. It was not difficult to imagine Sister Imelda face downward, arms outstretched, prostrate on the tiled floor. I often heard their chanting when I wakened suddenly from a nightmare, because, although we slept in a different building, both adjoined, and if one wakened one often heard that monotonous Latin chanting, long before the birds began, long before our own bell summoned us to rise at six.

"Do you eat nice food?" I asked.

"Of course," she said, and smiled. She sometimes broke into an eager smile, which she did much to conceal.

"Have you ever thought of what you will be?" she asked.

I shook my head. My design changed from day to day.

She looked at her man's silver pocket watch, closed the damper of the range, and prepared to leave. She checked that all the wall cupboards were locked by running her hand over them.

"Sister," I called, gathering enough courage at last—we must have some secret, something to join us together—"what color hair have you?"

We never saw the nuns' hair, or their eyebrows, or ears, as all that part was covered by a stiff white wimple.

"You shouldn't ask such a thing," she said, getting pink in the face, and then she turned back and whispered, "I'll tell you on your last day here, provided your geometry has improved."

She had scarcely gone when Baba, who had been lurking behind some pillar, stuck her head in the door and said, "Christsake, save me a bit." She finished the second pastry, then went around looking in kitchen drawers. Because of everything being locked, she found only some castor sugar in a china shaker. She ate a little and threw the remainder into the dying fire, so that it flared up for a minute with a yellow spluttering flame. Baba showed her jealousy by putting it around the school that I was in the cookery kitchen every evening, gorging cakes with Sister Imelda and telling tales.

I did not speak to Sister Imelda again in private until the evening of our Christmas theatricals. She came to help us put on makeup and get into our stage clothes and fancy headgear. These clothes were kept in a trunk from one year to the next, and though sumptuous and strewn with braiding and gold, they smelled of camphor. Yet as we donned them we felt different, and as we sponged pancake makeup onto our faces, we became saucy and emphasized these new guises by adding dark pencil to the eyes and making the lips bright carmine. There was only one tube of lipstick and each girl clamored for it. The evening's entertainment was to comprise scenes from Shakespeare and laughing sketches. I had been chosen to recite Mark Antony's lament over Caesar's body, and for this I was to wear a purple toga, white knee-length socks, and patent buckle shoes. The shoes were too big and I moved in them as if in clogs. She said to take them off, to go barefoot. I realized that I was getting nervous and that in an effort to memorize my speech, the words were getting all askew and flying about in my head, like the separate pieces of a jigsaw puzzle. She sensed my panic and very slowly put her hand on my face and enjoined me to look at her. I looked into her eyes, which seemed fathomless, and saw that she was willing me to be calm and obliging me to be master of my fears, and I little knew that one day she would have to do the same as regards the swoop of my feelings for her. As we continued to stare I felt myself becoming calm and the words were restored to me in their right and fluent order. The lights were being lowered out in the recreation hall, and we knew now that all the nuns had arrived, had settled themselves down, and were eagerly awaiting this annual hotchpotch of amateur entertainment. There was that fearsome hush as the hall went dark and the few spotlights were turned on. She kissed her crucifix and I realized that she was saying a prayer for me. Then she raised her arm as if depicting the stance of a Greek goddess; walking onto the stage, I was fired by her ardor.

Baba could say that I bawled like a bloody bull, but Sister Imelda, who stood in the wings, said that temporarily she had felt the streets of Rome, had seen the corpse of Caesar, as I delivered those poignant, distempered lines. When I came off stage she put her arms around me and I was encased in a shower of silent kisses. After we had taken down the decorations and put the fancy clothes back in the trunk, I gave her two half-pound boxes of chocolates—bought for me illicitly by one of the day girls—and she gave me a casket made from the insides of match boxes and covered over with gilt paint and gold dust. It was like holding moths and finding their powder adhering to the fingers.

"What will you do on Christmas Day, Sister?" I said.

"I'll pray for you," she said.

It was useless to say, "Will you have turkey?" or "Will you have plum pudding?" or "Will you loll in bed?" because I believed that Christmas Day would be as bleak and deprived as any other day in her life. Yet she was radiant as if such austerity was joyful. Maybe she was basking in some secret realization involving her and me.

On the cold snowy afternoon three weeks later when we returned from our holidays, Sister Imelda came up to the dormitory to welcome me back. All the other girls had gone down to the recreation hall to do barn dances and I could hear someone banging on the piano. I did not want to go down and clump around with sixty other girls, having nothing to look forward to, only tea and the Rosary and early bed. The beds were damp after our stay at home, and when I put my hand between the sheets, it was like feeling dew but did not have the freshness of outdoors. What depressed me further was that I had seen a mouse in one of the cupboards, seen its tail curl with terror as it slipped away into a crevice. If there was one mouse, there were God knows how many, and the cakes we hid in secret would not be safe. I was still unpacking as she came down the narrow passage between the rows of iron beds and I saw in her walk such agitation.

"Tut, tut, tut, you've curled your hair," she said, offended.

Yes, the world outside was somehow declared in this perm, and for a second I remembered the scalding pain as the trickles of ammonia dribbled down my forehead and then the joy as the hairdresser said that she would make me look like Movita, a Mexican star. Now suddenly that world and those aspirations seemed trite and I wanted to take a brush and straighten my hair and revert to the dark gawky somber girl that I had been. I offered her iced queen cakes that my mother had made, but she refused them and said she could only stay a second. She lent me a notebook of hers, which she had had as a pupil, and into which she had copied favorite quotations, some religious, some not. I read at random:

> Twice or thrice had I loved thee,
> Before I knew thy face or name.
> So in a voice, so in a shapeless flame,
> Angels affect us oft . . .

"Are you well?" I asked.

She looked pale. It may have been the day, which was wretched and gray with sleet, or it may have been the white bedspreads, but she appeared to be ailing.

"I missed you," she said.

"Me too," I said.

At home, gorging, eating trifle at all hours, even for breakfast, having little ratafias to dip in cups of tea, fitting on new shoes and silk stockings, I wished that she could be with us, enjoying the fire and the freedom.

"You know it is not proper for us to be so friendly."

"It's not wrong," I said.

I dreaded that she might decide to turn away from me, that she might stamp on our love and might suddenly draw a curtain over it, a black crepe curtain that would denote its death. I dreaded it and knew it was going to happen.

"We must not become attached," she said, and I could not say we already were, no more than I could remind her of the day of the revels and the intimacy between us. Convents were dungeons and no doubt about it.

From then on she treated me as less of a favorite. She said my name sharply in class, and once she said if I must cough, could I wait until class had finished. Baba was delighted, as were the other girls, because they were glad to see me receding in her eyes. Yet I knew that the crispness was part of her love, because no matter how callously she looked at me, she would occasionally soften. Reading her notebook helped me, and I copied out her quotations into my own book, trying as accurately as possible to imitate her handwriting.

But some little time later when she came to supervise our study one evening, I got a smile from her as she sat on the rostrum looking down at us all. I continued to look up at her and by slight frowning indicated that I had a problem with my geometry. She beckoned to me lightly and I went up, bringing my copybook and the pen. Standing close to her, and also because her wimple was crooked, I saw one of her eyebrows for the first time. She saw that I noticed it and said did that satisfy my curiosity. I said not really. She said what else did I want to see, her swan's neck perhaps, and I went scarlet. I was amazed that she would say such a thing in the hearing of other girls, and then she said a worse thing, she said that G. K. Chesterton was very forgetful and had once put on his trousers backward. She expected me to laugh. I was so close to her that a rumble in her stomach seemed to be taking place in my own, and about this she also laughed. It occurred to me for one terrible moment that maybe she had decided to leave the convent, to jump over the wall. Having done the theorem for me, she marked it "100 out of 100" and then asked if I had any other problems. My eyes filled with tears, I wanted her to realize that her recent coolness had wrought havoc with my nerves and my peace of mind.

"What is it?" she said.

I could cry, or I could tremble to try to convey the emotion, but I could not tell her. As if on cue, the Mother Superior came in and saw this glaring intimacy and frowned as she approached the rostrum.

"Would you please go back to your desk," she said, "and in future kindly allow Sister Imelda to get on with her duties."

I tiptoed back and sat with head down, bursting with fear and shame. Then she looked at a tray on which the milk cups were laid, and finding one cup of milk untouched, she asked which girl had not drunk her milk.

"Me, Sister," I said, and I was called up to drink it and stand under the clock as a punishment. The milk was tepid and dusty, and I thought of cows on the fairs days at home and the farmers hitting them as they slid and slithered over the muddy streets.

For weeks I tried to see my nun in private; I even lurked outside doors where I knew she was due, only to be rebuffed again and again. I suspected the Mother Superior had warned her against making a favorite of me. But I still clung to a belief that a bond existed between us and that her coldness and even some glares which I had received were a charade, a mask. I would wonder how she felt alone in bed and what way she slept and if she thought of me, or refusing to think of me, if she dreamed of me as I did of her. She certainly got thinner, because her nun's silver ring slipped easily and sometimes unavoidably off her marriage finger. It occurred to me that she was having a nervous breakdown.

One day in March the sun came out, the radiators were turned off, and, though there was a lashing wind, we were told that officially spring had arrived and that we could play games. We all trooped up to the games field and, to our surprise, saw that Sister Imelda was officiating that day. The daffodils in the field tossed and turned; they were a very bright shocking yellow, but they were not as fetching as the little timid snowdrops that trembled in the wind. We played rounders, and when my turn came to hit the ball with the long wooden pound, I crumbled and missed, fearing that the ball would hit me.

"Champ . . ." said Baba, jeering.

After three such failures Sister Imelda said that if I liked I could sit and watch, and when I was sitting in the greenhouse swallowing my shame, she came in and said that I must not give way to tears, because humiliation was the greatest test of Christ's love, or indeed *any* love.

"When you are a nun you will know that," she said, and instantly I made up my mind that I would be a nun and that though we might never be free to express our feelings, we would be under the same roof, in the same cloister, in mental and spiritual conjunction all our lives.

"Is it very hard at first?" I said.

"It's awful," she said, and she slipped a little medal into my gym-frock pocket. It was warm from being in her pocket, and as I held it, I knew that once again we were near and that in fact we had never severed. Walking down from the playing field to our Sunday lunch of mutton and cabbage, everyone chattered to Sister Imelda. The girls milled around her, linking her, trying to hold her hand, counting the various keys on her bunch of keys, and asking impudent questions.

"Sister, did you ever ride a motorbicycle?"
"Sister, did you ever wear seamless stockings?"
"Sister, who's your favorite film star—male?"
"Sister, what's your favorite food?"
"Sister, if you had a wish, what would it be?"
"Sister, what do you do when you want to scratch your head?"

Yes, she had ridden a motorbicycle, and she had worn silk stockings, but they were seamed. She liked bananas best, and if she had a wish, it would be to go home for a few hours to see her parents and her brother.

That afternoon as we walked through the town, the sight of closed shops with porter barrels outside and mongrel dogs did not dispel my refound ecstasy. The medal was in my pocket, and every other second I would touch it for confirmation. Baba saw a Swiss roll in a confectioner's window laid on a doily and dusted with castor sugar, and it made her cry out with hunger and rail against being in a bloody reformatory, surrounded by drips and mopes. On impulse she took her nail file out of her pocket and dashed across to the window to see if she could cut the glass. The prefect rushed up from the back of the line and asked Baba if she wanted to be locked up.

"I am anyhow," Baba said, and sawed at one of her nails, to maintain her independence and vent her spleen. Baba was the only girl who could stand up to a prefect. When she felt like it, she dropped out of a walk, sat on a stone wall, and waited until we all came back. She said that if there was one thing more boring than studying it was walking. She used to roll down her stockings and examine her calves and say that she could see varicose veins coming from this bloody daily walk. Her legs, like all our legs, were black from the dye of the stockings; we were forbidden to bathe, because baths were immoral. We washed each night in an enamel basin beside our beds. When girls splashed cold water onto their chests, they let out cries, though this was forbidden.

After the walk we wrote home. We were allowed to write home once a week; our letters were always censored. I told my mother that I had made up my mind to be a nun, and asked if she could send me bananas when a batch arrived at our local grocery shop. That evening, perhaps as I wrote to my mother on the ruled white paper, a telegram arrived which said that Sister Imelda's brother had been killed in a van while on his way home from a hurling match. The Mother Superior announced it, and asked us to pray for his soul and write letters of sympathy to Sister Imelda's parents. We all wrote identical letters, because in our first year at school we had been given specimen letters for various occasions, and we all referred back to our specimen letter of sympathy.

Next day the town hire-car drove up to the convent, and Sister Imelda, accompanied by another nun, went home for the funeral. She looked as white as a sheet, with eyes swollen, and she wore a heavy knitted shawl over her shoulders. Although she came back that night (I stayed awake to hear the car), we did not see her for a whole week, except to catch a glimpse of her back, in the chapel. When she resumed class, she was peaky and distant, making no reference at all to her recent tragedy.

The day the bananas came I waited outside the door and gave her a bunch wrapped in tissue paper. Some were still a little green, and she said that Mother Superior would put them in the glasshouse to ripen. I felt that Sister Imelda would never taste them; they would be kept for a visiting priest or bishop.

"Oh, Sister, I'm sorry about your brother," I said in a burst.

"It will come to us all, sooner or later," Sister Imelda said dolefully.

I dared to touch her wrist to communicate my sadness. She went quickly, probably for fear of breaking down. At times she grew irritable and had a boil on her cheek. She missed some classes and was replaced in the cookery kitchen by a younger nun. She asked me to pray for her brother's soul and to avoid seeing her alone. Each time as she came down a corridor toward me, I was obliged to turn the other way. Now Baba or some other girl moved the blackboard two pegs higher and spread her shawl, when wet, over the radiator to dry.

I got flu and was put to bed. Sickness took the same bleak course, a cup of hot senna delivered in person by the head nun, who stood there while I drank it, tea at lunchtime with thin slices of brown bread (because it was just after the war, food was still rationed, so the butter was mixed with lard and had white streaks running through it and a faintly rancid smell), hours of just lying there surveying the empty dormitory, the empty iron beds with white counterpanes on each one, and metal crucifixes laid on each white, frilled pillow slip. I knew that she would miss me and hoped that Baba would tell her where I was. I counted the number of tiles from the ceiling to the head of my bed, thought of my mother at home on the farm mixing hen food, thought of my father, losing his temper perhaps and stamping on the kitchen floor with nailed boots, and I recalled the money owing for my school fees and hoped that Sister Imelda would never get to hear of it. During the Christmas holiday I had seen a bill sent by the head nun to my father which said, "Please remit this week without fail." I hated being in bed causing extra trouble and therefore reminding the head nun of the unpaid liability. We had no clock in the dormitory, so there was no way of guessing the time, but the hours dragged.

Marigold, one of the maids, came to take off the counterpanes at five and brought with her two gifts from Sister Imelda—an orange and a pencil sharpener. I kept the orange peel in my hand, smelling it, and planning how I would thank her. Thinking of her I fell into a feverish sleep and was wakened when the girls came to bed at ten and switched on the various ceiling lights.

At Easter Sister Imelda warned me not to give her chocolates, so I got her a flashlamp instead and spare batteries. Pleased with such a useful gift (perhaps she read her letters in bed), she put her arms around me and allowed one cheek to adhere but not to make the sound of a kiss. It made up for the seven weeks of withdrawal, and as I drove down the convent drive with Baba, she waved to me, as she had promised, from the window of her cell.

In the last term at school, studying was intensive because of the examinations which loomed at the end of June. Like all the other nuns, Sister Imelda thought

only of these examinations. She crammed us with knowledge, lost her temper
every other day, and gritted her teeth whenever the blackboard was too greasy to
take the imprint of the chalk. If ever I met her in the corridor, she asked if I
knew such and such a thing, and coming down from Sunday games, she went
over various questions with us. The fateful examination day arrived and we sat at
single desks supervised by some strange woman from Dublin. Opening a locked
trunk, she took out the pink examination papers and distributed them around.
Geometry was on the fourth day. When we came out from it, Sister Imelda was
in the hall with all the answers, so that we could compare our answers with hers.
Then she called me aside and we went up toward the cookery kitchen and sat on
the stairs while she went over the paper with me, question for question. I knew
that I had three right and two wrong, but did not tell her so.

"It is black," she said then, rather suddenly. I thought she meant the dark
light where we were sitting.

"It's cool, though," I said.

Summer had come; our white skins baked under the heavy uniform, and dark
violet pansies bloomed in the convent grounds. She looked well again, and her
pale skin was once more unblemished.

"My hair," she whispered, "is black." And she told me how she had spent her
last night before entering the convent. She had gone cycling with a boy and ridden for miles, and they'd lost their way up a mountain, and she became afraid
she would be so late home that she would sleep it out the next morning. It was
understood between us that I was going to enter the convent in September and
that I could have a last fling, too.

Two days later we prepared to go home. There were farewells and outlandish
promises, and autograph books signed, and girls trudging up the recreation hall,
their cases bursting open with clothes and books. Baba scattered biscuit crumbs
in the dormitory for the mice and stuffed all her prayer books under a mattress.
Her father promised to collect us at four. I had arranged with Sister Imelda secretly that I would meet her in one of the summerhouses around the walks,
where we would spend our last half hour together. I expected that she would tell
me something of what my life as a postulant would be like. But Baba's father
came an hour early. He had something urgent to do later and came at three instead. All I could do was ask Marigold to take a note to Sister Imelda.

> Remembrance is all I ask,
> But if remembrance should prove a task,
> Forget me.

I hated Baba, hated her busy father, hated the thought of my mother standing
in the doorway in her good dress, welcoming me home at last. I would have become a nun that minute if I could.

I wrote to my nun that night and again the next day and then every week for a
month. Her letters were censored, so I tried to convey my feelings indirectly. In
one of her letters to me (they were allowed one letter a month) she said that she
looked forward to seeing me in September. But by September Baba and I had

left for the university in Dublin. I stopped writing to Sister Imelda then, reluctant to tell her that I no longer wished to be a nun.

In Dublin we enrolled at the college where she had surpassed herself. I saw her maiden name on a list, for having graduated with special honors, and for days was again sad and remorseful. I rushed out and bought batteries for the flashlamp I'd given her, and posted them without any note enclosed. No mention of my missing vocation, no mention of why I had stopped writing.

One Sunday about two years later, Baba and I were going out to Howth on a bus. Baba had met some businessmen who played golf there and she had done a lot of scheming to get us invited out. The bus was packed, mostly mothers with babies and children on their way to Dollymount Strand. We drove along the coast road and saw the sea, bright green and glinting in the sun, and because of the way the water was carved up into millions of little wavelets, its surface seemed like an endless heap of dark-green broken bottles. Near the shore the sand looked warm and was biscuit-colored. We never swam or sunbathed, we never did anything that was good for us. Life was geared to work and to meeting men, and yet one knew that mating could only lead to one's being a mother and hawking obstreperous children out to the seaside on Sunday. "They know not what they do" could surely be said of us.

We were very made up; even the conductor seemed to disapprove and snapped at having to give change of ten shillings. For no reason at all I thought of our makeup rituals before the school play and how innocent it was in comparison, because now our skins were smothered beneath layers of it and we never took it off at night. Thinking of the convent, I suddenly thought of Sister Imelda, and then, as if prey to a dream, I heard the rustle of serge, smelled the Jeyes Fluid and the boiled cabbage, and saw her pale shocked face in the months after her brother died. Then I looked around and saw her in earnest, and at first thought I was imagining things. But no, she had got on accompanied by another nun and they were settling themselves in the back seat nearest the door. She looked older, but she had the same aloof quality and the same eyes, and my heart began to race with a mixture of excitement and dread. At first it raced with a prodigal strength, and then it began to falter and I thought it was going to give out. My fear of her and my love came back in one fell realization. I would have gone through the window except that it was not wide enough. The thing was how to escape her. Baba gurgled with delight, stood up, and in the most flagrant way looked around to make sure that it was Imelda. She recognized the other nun as one with the nickname of Johnny who taught piano lessons. Baba's first thought was revenge, as she enumerated the punishments they had meted out to us and said how nice it would be to go back and shock them and say, "Mud in your eye, Sisters," or "Get lost," or something worse. Baba could not understand why I was quaking, no more than she could understand why I began to wipe off the lipstick. Above all, I knew that I could not confront them.

"You're going to have to," Baba said.

"I can't," I said.

It was not just my attire; it was the fact of my never having written and of my broken promise. Baba kept looking back and said they weren't saying a word and that children were gawking at them. It wasn't often that nuns traveled in buses, and we speculated as to where they might be going.

"They might be off to meet two fellows," Baba said, and visualized them in the golf club getting blotto and hoisting up their skirts. For me it was no laughing matter. She came up with a strategy: it was that as we approached our stop and the bus was still moving, I was to jump up and go down the aisle and pass them without even looking. She said most likely they would not notice us, as their eyes were lowered and they seemed to be praying.

"I can't run down the bus," I said. There was a matter of shaking limbs and already a terrible vertigo.

"You're going to," Baba said, and though insisting that I couldn't, I had already begun to rehearse an apology. While doing this, I kept blessing myself over and over again, and Baba kept reminding me that there was only one more stop before ours. When the dreadful moment came, I jumped up and put on my face what can only be called an apology of a smile. I followed Baba to the rear of the bus. But already they had gone. I saw the back of their two sable, identical figures with their veils being blown wildly about in the wind. They looked so cold and lost as they hurried along the pavement and I wanted to run after them. In some way I felt worse than if I had confronted them. I cannot be certain what I would have said. I knew that there is something sad and faintly distasteful about love's ending, particularly love that has never been fully realized. I might have hinted at that, but I doubt it. In our deepest moments we say the most inadequate things.

Flannery O'Connor

. . . .

THE ARTIFICIAL NIGGER

Mr. Head awakened to discover that the room was full of moonlight. He sat up and stared at the floor boards—the color of silver—and then at the ticking on his pillow, which might have been brocade, and after a second, he saw half of the moon five feet away in his shaving mirror, paused as if it were waiting for his permission to enter. It rolled forward and cast a dignifying light on everything. The straight chair against the wall looked stiff and attentive as if it were awaiting an order and Mr. Head's trousers, hanging to the back of it, had an almost noble air, like the garment some great man had just flung to his servant; but the face on the moon was a grave one. It gazed across the room and out the window where it floated over the horse stall and appeared to contemplate itself with the look of a young man who sees his old age before him.

Mr. Head could have said to it that age was a choice blessing and that only with years does a man enter into that calm understanding of life that makes him a suitable guide for the young. This, at least, had been his own experience.

He sat up and grasped the iron posts at the foot of his bed and raised himself until he could see the face on the alarm clock which sat on an overturned bucket beside the chair. The hour was two in the morning. The alarm on the clock did not work but he was not dependent on any mechanical means to awaken him. Sixty years had not dulled his responses; his physical reactions, like his moral ones, were guided by his will and strong character, and these could be seen plainly in his features. He had a long tube-like face with a long rounded open jaw and a long depressed nose. His eyes were alert but quiet, and in the miraculous moonlight they had a look of composure and of ancient wisdom as if they belonged to one of the great guides of men. He might have been Vergil summoned in the middle of the night to go to Dante, or better, Raphael, awakened by a blast of God's light to fly to the side of Tobias. The only dark spot in the room was Nelson's pallet, underneath the shadow of the window.

Nelson was hunched over on his side, his knees under his chin and his heels under his bottom. His new suit and hat were in the boxes that they had been sent in and these were on the floor at the foot of the pallet where he could get his hands on them as soon as he woke up. The slop jar, out of the shadow and made snow-white in the moonlight, appeared to stand guard over him like a small personal angel. Mr. Head lay back down, feeling entirely confident that he could carry out the moral mission of the coming day. He meant to be up before Nelson and to have the breakfast cooking by the time he awakened. The boy was always irked when Mr. Head was the first up. They would have to leave the house at four to get to the railroad junction by five-thirty. The train was to stop for them at five forty-five and they had to be there on time for this train was stopping merely to accommodate them.

This would be the boy's first trip to the city though he claimed it would be his second because he had been born there. Mr. Head had tried to point out to him that when he was born he didn't have the intelligence to determine his whereabouts but this had made no impression on the child at all and he continued to insist that this was to be his second trip. It would be Mr. Head's third trip. Nelson had said, "I will've already been there twict and I ain't but ten."

Mr. Head had contradicted him.

"If you ain't been there in fifteen years, how you know you'll be able to find your way about?" Nelson had asked. "How you know it hasn't changed some?"

"Have you ever," Mr. Head had asked, "seen me lost?"

Nelson certainly had not but he was a child who was never satisfied until he had given an impudent answer and he replied, "It's nowhere around here to get lost at."

"The day is going to come," Mr. Head prophesied, "when you'll find you ain't as smart as you think you are." He had been thinking about this trip for several months but it was for the most part in moral terms that he conceived it. It was to be a lesson that the boy would never forget. He was to find out from it that he had no cause for pride merely because he had been born in a city. He was to find out that the city is not a great place. Mr. Head meant him to see everything there is to see in a city so that he would be content to stay at home for the rest of his life. He fell asleep thinking how the boy would at last find out that he was not as smart as he thought he was.

He was awakened at three-thirty by the smell of fatback frying and he leaped off his cot. The pallet was empty and the clothes boxes had been thrown open. He put on his trousers and ran into the other room. The boy had a corn pone on cooking and had fried the meat. He was sitting in the half-dark at the table, drinking cold coffee out of a can. He had on his new suit and his new gray hat pulled low over his eyes. It was too big for him but they had ordered it a size large because they expected his head to grow. He didn't say anything but his entire figure suggested satisfaction at having arisen before Mr. Head.

Mr. Head went to the stove and brought the meat to the table in the skillet. "It's no hurry," he said. "You'll get there soon enough and it's no guarantee you'll like it when you do neither," and he sat down across from the boy whose hat teetered back slowly to reveal a fiercely expressionless face, very much the same shape as the old man's. They were grandfather and grandson but they looked enough alike to be brothers and brothers not too far apart in age, for Mr. Head had a youthful expression by daylight, while the boy's look was ancient, as if he knew everything already and would be pleased to forget it.

Mr. Head had once had a wife and daughter and when the wife died, the daughter ran away and returned after an interval with Nelson. Then one morning, without getting out of bed, she died and left Mr. Head with sole care of the year-old child. He had made the mistake of telling Nelson that he had been born in Atlanta. If he hadn't told him that, Nelson couldn't have insisted that this was going to be his second trip.

"You may not like it a bit," Mr. Head continued. "It'll be full of niggers."

The boy made a face as if he could handle a nigger.

"All right," Mr. Head said. "You ain't ever seen a nigger."

"You wasn't up very early," Nelson said.

"You ain't ever seen a nigger," Mr. Head repeated. "There hasn't been a nigger in this county since we run that one out twelve years ago and that was before you were born." He looked at the boy as if he were daring him to say he had ever seen a Negro.

"How you know I never saw a nigger when I lived there before?" Nelson asked. "I probably saw a lot of niggers."

"If you seen one you didn't know what he was," Mr. Head said, completely exasperated. "A six-month-old child don't know a nigger from anybody else."

"I reckon I'll know a nigger if I see one," the boy said and got up and straightened his slick sharply creased gray hat and went outside to the privy.

They reached the junction some time before the train was due to arrive and stood about two feet from the first set of tracks. Mr. Head carried a paper sack with some biscuits and a can of sardines in it for their lunch. A coarse-looking orange-colored sun coming up behind the east range of mountains was making the sky a dull red behind them, but in front of them it was still gray and they faced a gray transparent moon, hardly stronger than a thumbprint and completely without light. A small tin switch box and a black fuel tank were all there was to mark the place as a junction; the tracks were double and did not converge again until they were hidden behind the bends at either end of the clearing. Trains passing appeared to emerge from a tunnel of trees and, hit for a second by the cold sky, vanish terrified into the woods again. Mr. Head had had to make special arrangements with the ticket agent to have this train stop and he was secretly afraid it would not, in which case, he knew Nelson would say, "I never thought no train was going to stop for you." Under the useless morning moon the tracks looked white and fragile. Both the old man and the child stared ahead as if they were awaiting an apparition.

Then suddenly, before Mr. Head could make up his mind to turn back, there was a deep warning bleat and the train appeared, gliding very slowly, almost silently around the bend of trees about two hundred yards down the track, with one yellow front light shining. Mr. Head was still not certain it would stop and he felt it would make an even bigger idiot of him if it went by slowly. Both he and Nelson, however, were prepared to ignore the train if it passed them.

The engine charged by, filling their noses with the smell of hot metal, and then the second coach came to a stop exactly where they were standing. A conductor with the face of an ancient bloated bulldog was on the step as if he expected them, though he did not look as if it mattered one way or the other to him if they got on or not. "To the right," he said.

Their entry took only a fraction of a second and the train was already speeding on as they entered the quiet car. Most of the travelers were still sleeping, some with their heads hanging off the chair arms, some stretched across two seats, and some sprawled out with their feet in the aisle. Mr. Head saw two unoccupied seats and pushed Nelson toward them. "Get in there by the winder," he said in his normal voice which was very loud at this hour of the morning. "Nobody cares if you sit there because it's nobody in it. Sit right there."

"I heard you," the boy muttered. "It's no use in you yelling," and he sat down and turned his head to the glass. There he saw a pale ghost-like face scowling at him beneath the brim of a pale ghost-like hat. His grandfather, looking quickly too, saw a different ghost, pale but grinning, under a black hat.

Mr. Head sat down and settled himself and took out his ticket and started reading aloud everything that was printed on it. People began to stir. Several woke up and stared at him. "Take off your hat," he said to Nelson and took off his own and put it on his knee. He had a small amount of white hair that had turned tobacco-colored over the years and this lay flat across the back of his head. The front of his head was bald and creased. Nelson took off his hat and put it on his knee and they waited for the conductor to come ask for their tickets.

The man across the aisle from them was spread out over two seats, his feet propped on the window and his head jutting into the aisle. He had on a light blue suit and a yellow shirt unbuttoned at the neck. His eyes had just opened and Mr. Head was ready to introduce himself when the conductor came up from behind and growled, "Tickets."

When the conductor had gone, Mr. Head gave Nelson the return half of his ticket and said, "Now put that in your pocket and don't lose it or you'll have to stay in the city."

"Maybe I will," Nelson said as if this were a reasonable suggestion.

Mr. Head ignored him. "First time this boy has ever been on a train," he explained to the man across the aisle, who was sitting up now on the edge of his seat with both feet on the floor.

Nelson jerked his hat on again and turned angrily to the window.

"He's never seen anything before," Mr. Head continued. "Ignorant as the day he was born, but I mean for him to get his fill once and for all."

The boy leaned forward, across his grandfather and toward the stranger. "I was born in the city," he said. "I was born there. This is my second trip." He said it in a high positive voice but the man across the aisle didn't look as if he understood. There were heavy purple circles under his eyes.

Mr. Head reached across the aisle and tapped him on the arm.

"The thing to do with a boy," he said sagely, "is to show him all it is to show. Don't hold nothing back."

"Yeah," the man said. He gazed down at his swollen feet and lifted the left one about ten inches from the floor. After a minute he put it down and lifted the other. All through the car people began to get up and move about and yawn and stretch. Separate voices could be heard here and there and then a general hum. Suddenly Mr. Head's serene expression changed. His mouth almost closed and a light, fierce and cautious both, came into his eyes. He was looking down the length of the car. Without turning, he caught Nelson by the arm and pulled him forward. "Look," he said.

A huge coffee-colored man was coming slowly forward. He had on a light suit and a yellow satin tie with a ruby pin in it. One of his hands rested on his stomach which rode majestically under his buttoned coat, and in the other he held the head of a black walking stick that he picked up and set down with a deliberate outward motion each time he took a step. He was proceeding very slowly, his large brown eyes gazing over the heads of the passengers. He had a small white mustache and white crinkly hair. Behind him there were two young women, both coffee-colored, one in a yellow dress and one in a green. Their progress was kept at the rate of his and they chatted in low throaty voices as they followed him.

Mr. Head's grip was tightening insistently on Nelson's arm. As the procession passed them, the light from a sapphire ring on the brown hand that picked up the cane reflected in Mr. Head's eye, but he did not look up nor did the tremendous man look at him. The group proceeded up the rest of the aisle and out of the car. Mr. Head's grip on Nelson's arm loosened. "What was that?" he asked.

"A man," the boy said and gave him an indignant look as if he were tired of having his intelligence insulted.

"What kind of a man?" Mr. Head persisted, his voice expressionless.

"A fat man," Nelson said. He was beginning to feel that he had better be cautious.

"You don't know what kind?" Mr. Head said in a final tone.

"An old man," the boy said and had a sudden foreboding that he was not going to enjoy the day.

"That was a nigger," Mr. Head said and sat back.

Nelson jumped up on the seat and stood looking backward to the end of the car but the Negro had gone.

"I'd of thought you'd know a nigger since you seen so many when you was in the city on your first visit," Mr. Head continued. "That's his first nigger," he said to the man across the aisle.

The boy slid down into the seat. "You said they were black," he said in an angry voice. "You never said they were tan. How do you expect me to know anything when you don't tell me right?"

"You're just ignorant is all," Mr. Head said and he got up and moved over in the vacant seat by the man across the aisle.

Nelson turned backward again and looked where the Negro had disappeared. He felt that the Negro had deliberately walked down the aisle in order to make a fool of him and he hated him with a fierce raw fresh hate; and also, he understood now why his grandfather disliked them. He looked toward the window and the face there seemed to suggest that he might be inadequate to the day's exactions. He wondered if he would even recognize the city when they came to it.

After he had told several stories, Mr. Head realized that the man he was talking to was asleep and he got up and suggested to Nelson that they walk over the train and see the parts of it. He particularly wanted the boy to see the toilet so they went first to the men's room and examined the plumbing. Mr. Head demonstrated the ice-water cooler as if he had invented it and showed Nelson the bowl with the single spigot where the travelers brushed their teeth. They went through several cars and came to the diner.

This was the most elegant car in the train. It was painted a rich egg-yellow and had a wine-colored carpet on the floor. There were wide windows over the tables and great spaces of the rolling view were caught in miniature in the sides of the coffee pots and in the glasses. Three very black Negroes in white suits and aprons were running up and down the aisle, swinging trays and bowing and bending over the travelers eating breakfast. One of them rushed up to Mr. Head and Nelson and said, holding up two fingers, "Space for two!" but Mr. Head replied in a loud voice, "We eaten before we left!"

The waiter wore large brown spectacles that increased the size of his eye whites. "Stan' aside then please," he said with an airy wave of the arm as if he were brushing aside flies.

Neither Nelson nor Mr. Head moved a fraction of an inch. "Look," Mr. Head said.

The near corner of the diner, containing two tables, was set off from the rest by a saffron-colored curtain. One table was set but empty but at the other, facing them, his back to the drape, sat the tremendous Negro. He was speaking in a soft voice to the two women while he buttered a muffin. He had a heavy sad face and his neck bulged over his white collar on either side. "They rope them off," Mr. Head explained. Then he said, "Let's go see the kitchen," and they walked the length of the diner but the black waiter was coming fast behind them.

"Passengers are not allowed in the kitchen!" he said in a haughty voice. "Passengers are NOT allowed in the kitchen!"

Mr. Head stopped where he was and turned. "And there's good reason for that," he shouted into the Negro's chest, "because the cockroaches would run the passengers out!"

All the travelers laughed and Mr. Head and Nelson walked out, grinning. Mr. Head was known at home for his quick wit and Nelson felt a sudden keen pride in him. He realized the old man would be his only support in the strange place they were approaching. He would be entirely alone in the world if he were ever lost from his grandfather. A terrible excitement shook him and he wanted to take hold of Mr. Head's coat and hold on like a child.

As they went back to their seats they could see through the passing windows that the countryside was becoming speckled with small houses and shacks and that a highway ran alongside the train. Cars sped by on it, very small and fast. Nelson felt that there was less breath in the air than there had been thirty minutes ago. The man across the aisle had left and there was no one near for Mr. Head to hold a conversation with so he looked out the window, through his own reflection, and read aloud the names of the buildings they were passing. "The Dixie Chemical Corp!" he announced. "Southern Maid Flour! Dixie Doors! Southern Belle Cotton Products! Patty's Peanut Butter! Southern Mammy Cane Syrup!"

"Hush up!" Nelson hissed.

All over the car people were beginning to get up and take their luggage off the overhead racks. Women were putting on their coats and hats. The conductor stuck his head in the car and snarled, "Firstopppppmry," and Nelson lunged out of his sitting position, trembling. Mr. Head pushed him down by the shoulder.

"Keep your seat," he said in dignified tones. "The first stop is on the edge of town. The second stop is at the main railroad station." He had come by this knowledge on his first trip when he had got off at the first stop and had had to pay a man fifteen cents to take him into the heart of town. Nelson sat back down, very pale. For the first time in his life, he understood that his grandfather was indispensable to him.

The train stopped and let off a few passengers and glided on as if it had never ceased moving. Outside, behind rows of brown rickety houses, a line of blue buildings stood up, and beyond them a pale rose-gray sky faded away to nothing. The train moved into the railroad yard. Looking down, Nelson saw lines and lines of silver tracks multiplying and criss-crossing. Then before he could start counting them, the face in the window started out at him, gray but distinct, and he looked the other way. The train was in the station. Both he and Mr. Head jumped up and ran to the door. Neither noticed that they had left the paper sack with the lunch in it on the seat.

They walked stiffly through the small station and came out of a heavy door into the squall of traffic. Crowds were hurrying to work. Nelson didn't know where to look. Mr. Head leaned against the side of the building and glared in front of him.

Finally Nelson said, "Well, how do you see what all it is to see?"

Mr. Head didn't answer. Then as if the sight of people passing had given him the clue, he said, "You walk," and started off down the street. Nelson followed, steadying his hat. So many sights and sounds were flooding in on him that for the first block he hardly knew what he was seeing. At the second corner, Mr. Head turned and looked behind him at the station they had left, a putty-colored terminal with a concrete dome on top. He thought that if he could keep the dome always in sight, he would be able to get back in the afternoon to catch the train again.

As they walked along, Nelson began to distinguish details and take note of the store windows, jammed with every kind of equipment—hardware, drygoods, chicken feed, liquor. They passed one that Mr. Head called his particular attention to where you walked in and sat on a chair with your feet upon two rests and let a Negro polish your shoes. They walked slowly and stopped and stood at the entrances so he could see what went on in each place but they did not go into any of them. Mr. Head was determined not to go into any city store because on his first trip here, he had got lost in a large one and had found his way out only after many people had insulted him.

They came in the middle of the next block to a store that had a weighing machine in front of it and they both in turn stepped up on it and put in a penny and received a ticket. Mr. Head's ticket said, "You weigh 120 pounds. You are upright and brave and all your friends admire you." He put the ticket in his pocket, surprised that the machine should have got his character correct but his weight wrong, for he had weighed on a grain scale not long before and knew he weighed 110. Nelson's ticket said, "You weigh 98 pounds. You have a great destiny ahead of you but beware of dark women." Nelson did not know any women and he weighed only 68 pounds but Mr. Head pointed out that the machine had probably printed the number upside down, meaning the 9 for a 6.

They walked on and at the end of five blocks the dome of the terminal sank out of sight and Mr. Head turned to the left. Nelson could have stood in front of every store window for an hour if there had not been another more interesting one next to it. Suddenly he said, "I was born here!" Mr. Head turned and looked at him with horror. There was a sweaty brightness about his face. "This is where I come from!" he said.

Mr. Head was appalled. He saw the moment had come for drastic action. "Lemme show you one thing you ain't seen yet," he said and took him to the corner where there was a sewer entrance. "Squat down," he said, "and stick your head in there," and he held the back of the boy's coat while he got down and put his head in the sewer. He drew it back quickly, hearing a gurgling in the depths under the sidewalk. Then Mr. Head explained the sewer system, how the entire city was underlined with it, how it contained all the drainage and was full of rats and how a man could slide into it and be sucked along down endless pitchblack tunnels. At any minute any man in the city might be sucked into the sewer and never heard from again. He described it so well that Nelson was for some seconds shaken. He connected the sewer passages with the entrance to hell and understood for the first time how the world was put together in its lower parts. He drew away from the curb.

Then he said, "Yes, but you can stay away from the holes," and his face took on that stubborn look that was so exasperating to his grandfather. "This is where I come from!" he said.

Mr. Head was dismayed but he only muttered, "You'll get your fill," and they walked on. At the end of two more blocks he turned to the left, feeling that he was circling the dome; and he was correct for in a half-hour they passed in front of the railroad station again. At first Nelson did not notice that he was seeing the same stores twice but when they passed the one where you put your feet on the rests while the Negro polished your shoes, he perceived that they were walking in a circle.

"We done been here!" he shouted. "I don't believe you know where you're at!"

"The direction just slipped my mind for a minute," Mr. Head said and they turned down a different street. He still did not intend to let the dome get too far away and after two blocks in their new direction, he turned to the left. This street contained two- and three-story wooden dwellings. Anyone passing on the sidewalk could see into the rooms and Mr. Head, glancing through one window, saw a woman lying on an iron bed, looking out, with a sheet pulled over her. Her knowing expression shook him. A fierce-looking boy on a bicycle came driving down out of nowhere and he had to jump to the side to keep from being hit. "It's nothing to them if they knock you down," he said. "You better keep closer to me."

They walked on for some time on streets like this before he remembered to turn again. The houses they were passing now were all unpainted and the wood in them looked rotten; the street between was narrower. Nelson saw a colored man. Then another. Then another. "Niggers live in these houses," he observed.

"Well come on and we'll go somewheres else," Mr. Head said. "We didn't come to look at niggers," and they turned down another street but they continued to see Negroes everywhere. Nelson's skin began to prickle and they stepped along at a faster pace in order to leave the neighborhood as soon as possible. There were colored men in their undershirts standing in the doors and colored women rocking on the sagging porches. Colored children played in the gutters and stopped what they were doing to look at them. Before long they began to pass rows of stores with colored customers in them but they didn't pause at the entrances of these. Black eyes in black faces were watching them from every direction. "Yes," Mr. Head said, "this is where you were born—right here with all these niggers."

Nelson scowled. "I think you done got us lost," he said.

Mr. Head swung around sharply and looked for the dome. It was nowhere in sight. "I ain't got us lost either," he said. "You're just tired of walking."

"I ain't tired, I'm hungry," Nelson said. "Give me a biscuit."

They discovered then that they had lost the lunch.

"You were the one holding the sack," Nelson said. "I would have kepaholt of it."

"If you want to direct this trip, I'll go on by myself and leave you right here," Mr. Head said and was pleased to see the boy turn white. However, he realized they were lost and drifting farther every minute from the station. He was hungry himself and beginning to be thirsty and since they had been in the colored neighborhood, they had both begun to sweat. Nelson had on his shoes and he was unaccustomed to them. The concrete sidewalks were very hard. They both wanted to find a place to sit down but this was impossible and they kept on walking, the boy muttering under his breath, "First you lost the sack and then you lost the way," and Mr. Head growling from time to time, "Anybody wants to be from this nigger heaven can be from it!"

By now the sun was well forward in the sky. The odor of dinners cooking drifted out to them. The Negroes were all at their doors to see them pass. "Whyn't you ast one of these niggers the way?" Nelson said. "You got us lost."

"This is where you were born," Mr. Head said. "You can ast one yourself if you want to."

Nelson was afraid of the colored men and he didn't want to be laughed at by the colored children. Up ahead he saw a large colored woman leaning in a doorway that opened onto the sidewalk. Her hair stood straight out from her head for about four inches all around and she was resting on bare brown feet that turned pink at the sides. She had on a pink dress that showed her exact shape. As they came abreast of her, she lazily lifted one hand to her head and her fingers disappeared into her hair.

Nelson stopped. He felt his breath drawn up by the woman's dark eyes. "How do you get back to town?" he said in a voice that did not sound like his own.

After a minute she said, "You in town now," in a rich low tone that made Nelson feel as if a cool spray had been turned on him.

"How do you get back to the train?" he said in the same reedlike voice.

"You can catch you a car," she said.

He understood she was making fun of him but he was too paralyzed even to scowl. He stood drinking in every detail of her. His eyes traveled up from her great knees to her forehead and then made a triangular path from the glistening sweat on her neck down and across her tremendous bosom and over her bare arm back to where her fingers lay hidden in her hair. He suddenly wanted her to reach down and pick him up and draw him against her and then he wanted to feel her breath on his face. He wanted to look down and down into her eyes while she held him tighter and tighter. He had never had such a feeling before. He felt as if he were reeling down through a pitchblack tunnel.

"You can go a block down yonder and catch you a car take you to the railroad station, Sugarpie," she said.

Nelson would have collapsed at her feet if Mr. Head had not pulled him roughly away. "You act like you don't have any sense!" the old man growled.

They hurried down the street and Nelson did not look back at the woman. He pushed his hat sharply forward over his face which was already burning with shame. The sneering ghost he had seen in the train window and all the foreboding feelings he had on the way returned to him and he remembered that his ticket from the scale had said to beware of dark women and that his grandfather's had said he was upright and brave. He took hold of the old man's hand, a sign of dependence that he seldom showed.

They headed down the street toward the car tracks where a long yellow rattling trolley was coming. Mr. Head had never boarded a streetcar and he let that one pass. Nelson was silent. From time to time his mouth trembled slightly but his grandfather, occupied with his own problems, paid him no attention. They stood on the corner and neither looked at the Negroes who were passing, going about their business just as if they had been white, except that most of them stopped and eyed Mr. Head and Nelson. It occurred to Mr. Head that since the streetcar ran on tracks, they could simply follow the tracks. He gave Nelson a slight push and explained that they would follow the tracks on into the railroad station, walking, and they set off.

Presently to their great relief they began to see white people again and Nelson sat down on the sidewalk against the wall of a building. "I got to rest myself some," he said. "You lost the sack and the direction. You can just wait on me to rest myself."

"There's the tracks in front of us," Mr. Head said. "All we got to do is keep them in sight and you could have remembered the sack as good as me. This is where you were born. This is your old home town. This is your second trip. You ought to know how to do," and he squatted down and continued in this vein but the boy, easing his burning feet out of his shoes, did not answer.

"And standing there grinning like a chim-pan-zee while a nigger woman gives you direction. Great Gawd!" Mr. Head said.

"I never said I was nothing but born here," the boy said in a shaky voice. "I never said I would or wouldn't like it. I never said I wanted to come. I only said I was born here and I never had nothing to do with that. I want to go home. I never wanted to come in the first place. It was all your big idea. How you know you ain't following the tracks in the wrong direction?"

This last had occurred to Mr. Head too. "All these people are white," he said.

"We ain't passed here before," Nelson said. This was a neighborhood of brick buildings that might have been lived in or might not. A few empty automobiles were parked along the curb and there was an occasional passerby. The heat of the pavement came up through Nelson's thin suit. His eyelids began to droop, and after a few minutes his head tilted forward. His shoulders twitched once or twice and then he fell over on his side and lay sprawled in an exhausted fit of sleep.

Mr. Head watched him silently. He was very tired himself but they could not both sleep at the same time and he could not have slept anyway because he did not know where he was. In a few minutes Nelson would wake up, refreshed by his sleep and very cocky, and would begin complaining that he had lost the sack and the way. You'd have a mighty sorry time if I wasn't here, Mr. Head thought; and then another idea occurred to him. He looked at the sprawled figure for several minutes; presently he stood up. He justified what he was going to do on the grounds that it is sometimes necessary to teach a child a lesson he won't forget, particularly when the child is always reasserting his position with some new impudence. He walked without a sound to the corner about twenty feet away and sat down on a covered garbage can in the alley where he could look out and watch Nelson wake up alone.

The boy was dozing fitfully, half conscious of vague noises and black forms moving up from some dark part of him into the light. His face worked in his sleep and he had pulled his knees up under his chin. The sun shed a dull dry light on the narrow street; everything looked like exactly what it was. After a while Mr. Head, hunched like an old monkey on the garbage can lid, decided that if Nelson didn't wake up soon, he would make a loud noise by bamming his foot against the can. He looked at his watch and discovered that it was two o'clock. Their train left at six and the possibility of missing it was too awful for him to think of. He kicked his foot backwards on the can and a hollow boom reverberated in the alley.

Nelson shot up onto his feet with a shout. He looked where his grandfather should have been and stared. He seemed to whirl several times and then, picking up his feet and throwing his head back, he dashed down the street like a wild maddened pony. Mr. Head jumped off the can and galloped after but the child was almost out of sight. He saw a streak of gray disappearing diagonally a block ahead. He ran as fast as he could, looking both ways down every intersection, but without sight of him again. Then as he passed the third intersection, completely winded, he saw about half a block down the street a scene that stopped him altogether. He crouched behind a trash box to watch and get his bearings.

Nelson was sitting with both legs spread out and by his side lay an elderly woman, screaming. Groceries were scattered about the sidewalk. A crowd of women had already gathered to see justice done and Mr. Head distinctly heard the old woman on the pavement shout, "You've broken my ankle and your daddy'll pay for it! Every nickel! Police! Police!" Several of the women were plucking at Nelson's shoulder but the boy seemed too dazed to get up.

Something forced Mr. Head from behind the trash box and forward, but only at a creeping pace. He had never in his life been accosted by a policeman. The women were milling around Nelson as if they might suddenly all dive on him at once and tear him to pieces, and the old woman continued to scream that her ankle was broken and to call for an officer. Mr. Head came on so slowly that he could have been taking a backward step after each forward one, but when he was about ten feet away, Nelson saw him and sprang. The child caught him around the hips and clung panting against him.

The women all turned on Mr. Head. The injured one sat up and shouted, "You sir! You'll pay every penny of my doctor's bill that your boy has caused. He's a juve-nile deliquent! Where is an officer? Somebody take this man's name and address!"

Mr. Head was trying to detach Nelson's fingers from the flesh in the back of his legs. The old man's head had lowered itself into his collar like a turtle's; his eyes were glazed with fear and caution.

"Your boy has broken my ankle!" the old woman shouted. "Police!"

Mr. Head sensed the approach of the policeman from behind. He stared straight ahead at the women who were massed in their fury like a solid wall to block his escape, "This is not my boy," he said. "I never seen him before."

He felt Nelson's fingers fall out of his flesh.

The women dropped back, staring at him with horror, as if they were so repulsed by a man who would deny his own image and likeness that they could not bear to lay hands on him. Mr. Head walked on, through a space they silently cleared, and left Nelson behind. Ahead of him he saw nothing but a hollow tunnel that had once been the street.

The boy remained standing where he was, his neck craned forward and his hands hanging by his sides. His hat was jammed on his head so that there were no longer any creases in it. The injured woman got up and shook her fist at him and the others gave him pitying looks, but he didn't notice any of them. There was no policeman in sight.

In a minute he began to move mechanically, making no effort to catch up with his grandfather but merely following at about twenty paces. They walked on for five blocks in this way. Mr. Head's shoulders were sagging and his neck hung forward at such an angle that it was not visible from behind. He was afraid to turn his head. Finally he cut a short hopeful glance over his shoulder. Twenty feet behind him, he saw two small eyes piercing into his back like pitchfork prongs.

The boy was not of a forgiving nature but this was the first time he had ever had anything to forgive. Mr. Head had never disgraced himself before. After two more blocks, he turned and called over his shoulder in a high desperately gay voice, "Let's us go get us a Co' Cola somewheres!"

Nelson, with a dignity he had never shown before, turned and stood with his back to his grandfather.

Mr. Head began to feel the depth of his denial. His face as they walked on became all hollows and bare ridges. He saw nothing they were passing but he perceived that they had lost the car tracks. There was no dome to be seen anywhere and the afternoon was advancing. He knew that if dark overtook them in the city, they would be beaten and robbed. The speed of God's justice was only what he expected for himself, but he could not stand to think that his sins would be visited upon Nelson and that even now, he was leading the boy to his doom.

They continued to walk on block after block through an endless section of small brick houses until Mr. Head almost fell over a water spigot sticking up about six inches off the edge of a grass plot. He had not had a drink of water since early morning but he felt he did not deserve it now. Then he thought that Nelson would be thirsty and they would both drink and be brought together. He squatted down and put his mouth to the nozzle and turned a cold stream of water into his throat. Then he called out in the high desperate voice, "Come on and getcher some water!"

This time the child stared through him for nearly sixty seconds. Mr. Head got up and walked on as if he had drunk poison. Nelson, though he had not had water since some he had drunk out of a paper cup on the train, passed by he spigot, disdaining to drink where his grandfather had. When Mr. Head realized this, he lost all hope. His face in the waning afternoon light looked ravaged and abandoned. He could feel the boy's steady hate, traveling at an even pace behind him, and he knew that (if by some miracle they escaped being murdered in the city) it would continue just that way for the rest of his life. He knew that now he was wandering into a black strange place where nothing was like it had ever been before, a long old age without respect and an end that would be welcome because it would be the end.

As for Nelson, his mind had frozen around his grandfather's treachery as if he were trying to preserve it intact to present at the final judgment. He walked without looking to one side or the other, but every now and then his mouth would twitch and this was when he felt, from some remote place inside himself, a black mysterious form reach up as if it would melt his frozen vision in one hot grasp.

The sun dropped down behind a row of houses and hardly noticing, they passed into an elegant suburban section where mansions were set back from the road by lawns with birdbaths on them. Here everything was entirely deserted. For blocks they didn't pass even a dog. The big white houses were like partially submerged icebergs in the distance. There were no sidewalks, only drives, and these wound around and around in endless ridiculous circles. Nelson made no move to come nearer to Mr. Head. The old man felt that if he saw a sewer entrance he would drop down into it and let himself be carried away; and he could imagine the boy standing by, watching with only a slight interest, while he disappeared.

A loud bark jarred him to attention and he looked up to see a fat man approaching with two bulldogs. He waved both arms like someone shipwrecked on a desert island. "I'm lost!" he called. "I'm lost and can't find my way and me and this boy have got to catch this train and I can't find the station. Oh Gawd I'm lost! Oh hep me Gawd I'm lost!"

The man, who was bald-headed and had on golf knickers, asked him what train he was trying to catch and Mr. Head began to get out his tickets, trembling so violently he could hardly hold them. Nelson had come up to within fifteen feet and stood watching.

"Well," the fat man said, giving him back the tickets, "you won't have time to get back to town to make this but you can catch it at the suburb stop. That's three blocks from here," and he began explaining how to get there.

Mr. Head stared as if he were slowly returning from the dead and when the man had finished and gone off with the dogs jumping at his heels, he turned to Nelson and said breathlessly, "We're going to get home!"

The child was standing about ten feet away, his face bloodless under the gray hat. His eyes were triumphantly cold. There was no light in them, no feeling, no interest. He was merely there, a small figure, waiting. Home was nothing to him.

Mr. Head turned slowly. He felt he knew now what time would be like without seasons and what heat would be like without light and what man would be like without salvation. He didn't care if he never made the train and if it had not been for what suddenly caught his attention, like a cry out of the gathering dusk, he might have forgotten there was a station to go to.

He had not walked five hundred yards down the road when he saw, within reach of him, the plaster figure of a Negro sitting bent over on a low yellow brick fence that curved around a wide lawn. The Negro was about Nelson's size and he was pitched forward at an unsteady angle because the putty that held him to the wall had cracked. One of his eyes was entirely white and he held a piece of brown watermelon.

Mr. Head stood looking at him silently until Nelson stopped at a little distance. Then as the two of them stood there, Mr. Head breathed, "An artificial nigger!"

It was not possible to tell if the artificial Negro were meant to be young or old; he looked too miserable to be either. He was meant to look happy because his mouth was stretched up at the corners but the chipped eye and the angle he was cocked at gave him a wild look of misery instead.

"An artificial nigger!" Nelson repeated in Mr. Head's exact tone.

The two of them stood there with their necks forward at almost the same angle and their shoulders curved in almost exactly the same way and their hands trembling identically in their pockets. Mr. Head looked like an ancient child and Nelson like a miniature old man. They stood gazing at the artificial Negro as if they were faced with some great mystery, some monument to another's victory that brought them together in their common defeat. They could both feel it dissolving their differences like an action of mercy. Mr. Head had never known before what mercy felt like because he had been too good to deserve any, but he felt he knew now. He looked at Nelson and understood that he must say something to the child to show that he was still wise and in the look the boy returned he saw a hungry need for that assurance. Nelson's eyes seemed to implore him to explain once and for all the mystery of existence.

Mr. Head opened his lips to make a lofty statement and heard himself say, "They ain't got enough real ones here. They got to have an artificial one."

After a second, the boy nodded with a strange shivering about his mouth, and said, "Let's go home before we get ourselves lost again."

Their train glided into the suburb stop just as they reached the station and they boarded it together, and ten minutes before it was due to arrive at the junction, they went to the door and stood ready to jump off if it did not stop; but it did, just as the moon, restored to its full splendor, sprang from a cloud and flooded the clearing with light. As they stepped off, the sage grass was shivering gently in shades of silver and the clinkers under their feet glittered with a fresh black light. The treetops, fencing the junction like the protecting walls of a garden, were darker than the sky which was hung with gigantic white clouds illuminated like lanterns.

Mr. Head stood very still and felt the action of mercy touch him again but this time he knew that there were no words in the world that could name it. He understood that it grew out of agony, which is not denied to any man and which is given in strange ways to children. He understood it was all a man could carry into death to give his Maker and he suddenly burned with shame that he had so little of it to take with him. He stood appalled, judging himself with the thoroughness of God, while the action of mercy covered his pride like a flame and consumed it. He had never thought himself a great sinner before but he saw now that his true depravity had been hidden from him lest it cause him despair. He realized that he was forgiven for sins from the beginning of time, when he had conceived in his own heart the sin of Adam, until the present, when he had denied poor Nelson. He saw that no sin was too monstrous for him to claim as his own, and since God loved in proportion as He forgave, he felt ready at that instant to enter Paradise.

Nelson, composing his expression under the shadow of his hat brim, watched him with a mixture of fatigue and suspicion, but as the train glided past them and disappeared like a frightened serpent into the woods, even his face lightened and he muttered, "I'm glad I've went once, but I'll never go back again!"

Frank O'Connor

. . . .

A SET OF VARIATIONS ON A BORROWED THEME

Kate Mahoney was sixty when her husband died and, like many another widow, she had to face the loss of her little home.

Her two daughters, Nora and Molly, were married, and even if either of them had been in a position to offer her a home, she would have hesitated over it. As she said in her patient, long-suffering way to her old crony Hanna Dinan, they shouted too much. Hanna raised her head in mock surprise and exclaimed, "You don't say so, ma'am!" Kate looked at her reproachfully for a moment and then murmured with almost sensual bliss, "Oh, you cheeky thing." The truth was, as Hanna implied, that Kate shouted enough for a regimental sergeant-major, and the girls, both gentle and timid, had learned early in life that the only way of making themselves heard was to shout back. Kate didn't mind that; in fact, she rather enjoyed it. Nor did she shout all the time. She had another tone, which was low-pitched and monotonous, and in which she tended to break off a sentence as though she had forgotten what she was saying. But low-pitched or loud, her talk was monumental, like headstones. Her hands and legs were knotted with rheumatics, and she had a battered, inexpressive country woman's face, like a butcher's block, in which the only good feature was the eyes, which looked astonishingly girlish and merry. Maybe it would be only later that you would remember the hands—which were rarely still—fastening or unfastening a button on her blouse.

Her cottage was in a lane outside Cork. There was high rocky ground behind it that could never be built on, and though as a result it got little or no sunlight and another row of cottages between her and the roadway shut off the view, it was quiet and free of traffic. She wanted to die there, in the bed her husband had died in, but with the rheumatics she couldn't go out and do a day's work, as other widows did. It was this that made her think of taking in a foster child. It was a terrible comedown—more particularly for her, a respectable woman who had brought up two honest transactions of her own, but at her age what else could she do? So she took her problem to Miss Hegarty, the nurse.

Miss Hegarty was a fine-looking woman of good family, but so distracted with having to deal with the endless goings on of male and female that there were times she didn't seem right in the head. "Ahadie!" she would cry gaily to a woman in labor. "Fun enough you got out of starting it. Laugh now, why don't you?"

But Kate found her a good friend. She advised Kate against taking foster children from the local authorities, because they paid so badly that it was no better than slavery. The thing to do was to take the child of a girl of good family who could afford to maintain it.

"Ah, where would I meet a girl like that?" Kate asked humbly, and Miss Hegarty gave a loud, bitter laugh and stood up to lean against the mantelpiece with her arms folded.

" 'Tis easy seen you don't know much about it, Mrs. Mahoney," she said. "What chance, indeed, and the whole country crawling with them!"

"Oh, my!" said Kate.

"But I warn you, ma'am, that you can't rely on any of them," said Miss Hegarty. "They're so mad for men they'll go anywhere for them. And for all you know, a girl like that would be off next month to London and you might never hear of her again. The stick, ma'am, the stick is what the whole lot of them want."

Kate, however, decided to take the risk; there was something that appealed to her in the idea of a child of good family, and Miss Hegarty knew the very girl. She was the manageress of a store in Waterford, who had got entangled with a scoundrel whose name nobody even knew, but indeed he couldn't be much good to leave her that way. When Kate told her daughters, Nora, the flighty one, didn't seem to mind, but Molly, who was more sensitive, wept and begged her mother to come and live with them instead. "Oh yes, what a thing I'd do," said Kate, whose mind was made up. From Nora, who now had children of her own, she borrowed back the old family perambulator, and one spring morning it appeared again outside the door in the lane, with a baby boy asleep in it. "My first!" Kate shouted jocosely when any of the neighbors commented on it, and then she went on to explain, in the monotonous voice she used for solemn occasions, that this was no ordinary baby such as you'd get from the workhouse, without knowing who it was or where it came from, but the child of a beautiful educated girl from one of the best families in Waterford. She went on to tell how the poor child had been taken advantage of, and the neighbors tch-tch'd and agreed that it was a sad, sad story and didn't believe a word of it. The young married women didn't even pretend to believe in Kate's rigmarole. They muttered fiercely among themselves that you couldn't let decent children grow up alongside the likes of that, and that the priest or the landlord should put a stop to it. But they didn't say it too loud, for however embarrassed Kate might be by her situation she was a very obstinate old woman, and she had a dirty tongue when she was roused.

So Jimmy Mahoney was allowed to grow up in the lane along with the honest transactions, and turned into a fat, good-looking, moody boy, who seemed to see nothing peculiar in his mother's being a cranky old woman with a scolding tongue. On the contrary, he seemed to depend on her more than the other kids did on their mothers, and sometimes when she left him with Hanna Dinan and went off to see one of her daughters, he sat and sulked on the doorstep till she got home. One day when Hanna's back was turned, he went after Kate, right across the city to Molly's house on the Douglas Road. Kate, talking to Molly, glanced up and saw him glaring at her from the doorway and started, thinking that something must have happened to him and this was his ghost. "Oh, you pest!" she shouted when she saw that it wasn't. Then she gave him a grin. "I suppose it was the way you couldn't get on without me?"

Molly, a beautiful, haggard woman, gave him a smile of Christian charity and said quietly, "Come in, Jimmy." It was a thing she would not have wished for a pound, for it would have to be explained to her neighbors, and she felt it degraded them all. But after that, whatever she or Nora might think, Kate had to bring Jimmy with her by the hand. It didn't look right—their old mother in her black hat and coat hobbling up to the door with a child younger than their own by the hand.

Even then Jimmy wasn't satisfied. He wanted a brother or sister as well—preferably a brother. He had a great weakness for babies and was mad jealous of other boys who had babies to look after. "Every bloomin' fella in the road have a brudder or sister except me," he said to Kate. But she told him roughly that they couldn't afford it.

All the same, he got his wish. One evening Miss Hegarty came to her and asked if she would take in the child of a well-to-do girl in Bantry. The mother was engaged to marry a rich Englishman, but at the last moment she had thrown herself into a wild affair with a married man who had courted her when she was only seventeen. "Oh, my, my, the things that go on," sighed Kate.

"Mrs. Mahoney," Miss Hegarty cried, "don't talk to me about it! If you knew the half of it, it would make you lose your faith in religion."

Then and there Kate accepted. Later she felt she had been hasty. She needed the money, but not as badly as all that. When Nora came to see her and Kate told her what she had done, there was a terrible scene.

"Ah, Mammy, you're making a holy show of us!" Nora cried.

"*I'm* making a show of ye?" Kate pointed at her bosom with the mock-innocent air that had so often maddened her daughters. "I do my business, and I don't cost ye a penny. Is that what ye call making a show of ye?"

"Ah, you'd think we were something out of a circus instead of an old respectable family," Nora said. "That I can hardly face the neighbors when I come up the lane! Ahadie, 'tis well my poor daddy can't see what you're making of his house! He's the one that would deal with you. A woman of sixty-five! I suppose you think you're going to live forever."

"God is good," Kate muttered stiffly. "I might have a couple of years in me yet."

"You might," Nora said ironically. "And I suppose you imagine that if anything happens you, Molly and I will carry on the good work."

"Ye mightn't be asked," said Kate. "Their people have plenty—more than you'll ever be able to say." This was a dirty thrust at Nora, whose poor husband was not bright. "And how sure you are of yourself! My goodness, that we'd never do anything if we were to be always thinking of what might happen us. And what about my rent? Are you going to pay it?"

"Ah, 'tisn't the rent with you at all," Nora said. "Nor it never was. You only do it because you like it."

"I like it? An old woman like me that's crippled with the rheumatics? Oh, my, that 'tis in a home I ought to be if I had my rights. In a home!"

"Ah, I'd like to see the home that would keep you," Nora replied contemptuously. "Don't be making any more excuses. You love it, woman. And you care more about that little bastard than you ever did about Molly or me."

"How dare you?" Kate cried, rising with as much dignity as the rheumatics permitted. "What way is that to speak to your own mother? And to talk about a poor innocent child in my house like that, you dirty, jealous thing! Yes, jealous," she added in a wondering whisper as though the truth had only dawned on her in that moment. "Oh, my! Ye that had everything!"

The scene upset her, but not because of the row with Nora; the Mahoneys always quarrelled like that, at the top of their lungs, as though they all suffered from congenital deafness, and they got the same pleasure out of it that a baby gets out of hammering a tin can. What really mortified her was that she had given herself away in front of Nora, whose intelligence she had no respect for. It was true that she had taken Jimmy in for perfectly good mercenary reasons; and it was very wrong of Nora to impute sentimental considerations to her—a determined, managing woman, who had lived that long with no thanks to anybody. But all the same, Nora wasn't altogether wrong. Motherhood was the only trade Kate knew, and though her rheumatics were bad and her sight wasn't what it used to be and she had to get Jimmy to thread her needles for her, she felt the older she got the better she practiced it. It was even true to say that she enjoyed Jimmy more than she had enjoyed her own children, but this was natural enough, because she hadn't the same anxieties about him. If you had pressed her hard enough, she would have said that if there was a better boy on the road she didn't know him. And was there anything wrong with that? You could say what you liked, but there was something in good blood.

She might have got angry if you had accused her of being an old dreamer who was really attracted by the romance and mystery of Jimmy's birth—something she had missed in her own sober and industrious life—but that was what she and Hanna enjoyed speculating about over a little glass when Jimmy was in bed. And later, when she had covered him for the night and lay awake in the next room saying her rosary, she would often forget her prayers and imagine how she would feel if one stormy night—one of those nights when the whole harbor seemed to move in on the town and try to push it down—there came a knock to the door and she saw Jimmy's father standing outside in the lane, tall and handsome, with a small black mustache and the tears in his eyes. "Mr. Mulvany," she would say to the teacher (she was always making up ideal names and occupations for Jimmy's father), "your son wants nothing from you." Or, if she was in a generous mood, "Senator MacDunphy, come in. Jimmy was beginning to think you'd never come."

Nora was right. Stupid or not, Nora had seen through her. She was an old fool. And when Miss Hegarty had dangled the extra money in front of her, it wasn't the money that appealed to her so much as the girl who had been ready to throw away her chances with the rich Englishman for the sake of one wild fling with an old sweetheart. "An old fool," Kate said to herself. She didn't feel repentant, though.

But dreamers are forever running into degrading practical realities, and there was one thing about her extraordinary family that Kate could do nothing about. Before she even laid eyes on him, the second boy was also christened James, and, so that Jimmy shouldn't be too upset and that she herself should do nothing against the law, she called him James—an unnatural name for any child, as she well knew. James was a baby with a big head, a gaping mouth, and a sickly countenance, and even from the first day he seemed to realize that he was in the world only on sufferance, and resigned himself to it. But Jimmy could see nothing wrong with him. He explored the neighborhood to study all the other babies, and told Kate that James was brighter than the whole lot of them. He adopted a possessive attitude, and wheeled the perambulator up and down the main road so that people could see for themselves the sort James was. When he came back, he reported with great satisfaction that three people, two men and a woman, had stopped him to admire his baby brother.

A couple of times a year, Jimmy's real mother, whom he knew as Aunt Nance, came to stay with the friends in Cork who had arranged with Miss Hegarty for his being boarded out, and then Jimmy visited there and played with the two children, Rory and Mary. They were altogether too polite for Jimmy, but he liked his Aunt Nance a lot. She was tall and plump and good-looking, with a swarthy complexion and dark, dark hair. She talked in a crisp, nervous, almost common way, and was always forgetting herself and saying dirty words, like "Cripes!" and "Damn!," that only men were supposed to know. Kate liked him to go there, and when he got home, she asked him all sorts of questions about his visit, like how many rooms there were in the house, what he ate, what sort of furniture there was and the size of the garden—things that never interested Jimmy in the least.

When James began to grow up, he too asked questions. He wanted to know what school Rory and Mary went to, what they learned there, and whether or not Mary played the piano. These too were questions that did not interest Jimmy, but it dawned on him that James was lonely when he was left behind and wanted to see the Martins' place for himself. This seemed an excellent idea to Jimmy, because James was a steady quiet kid who would get on much better with Rory and Mary than he did, but when he suggested it Kate only said James was too young and Aunt Nance said she'd see.

It ended by his suspecting that there was something fishy about James. There always had been something unusual about him—as though he weren't a member of the family at all. He didn't like rough games and he preferred little girls to little boys. Jimmy didn't know how you did become a member of the family, but from what he could see your mother had either to go to the hospital or lie up in the house, and he couldn't remember that Kate had done either. James had just been there one morning when he woke. The more he thought of it, the surer he became that James was adopted. He didn't know what "adopted" meant, except that kids it happened to lived with people who weren't really related to them, and he found the idea of this very stimulating.

One evening, when Kate was complaining of her rheumatics, he asked her if she hadn't gone to hospital with it.

"Oye, why would I go to hospital?" she asked sourly. "I was never in one in my life and I hope I'll never have to go there."

James was sitting by the window, scribbling, and Jimmy didn't say anything more. But later, when James was in bed, he asked her casually, "You're not James's mother, are you, Mammy?"

He was surprised at the way she turned on him. "What's that you say?"

"Nothing, only that you're not James's mother."

"Who told you that?" she asked angrily.

"Nobody told me," he said, becoming defensive, "but you never went to hospital, like Mrs. Casey. You told me yourself."

"Don't let the child hear you saying things like that, you caffler!" she hissed.

"I never told him anything," he said sullenly. "But it's true, isn't it? That's the reason you get the money."

"Mind your own business!" she retorted.

Still, she was frightened. "Oh, my! The cunning of him!" she said next day to her old crony. "The way he cross-examined me—that poor Jack Mahoney never did the like! And what am I to say to him? Who will I get to advise me?"

Hanna, who had an answer for everything, was all for telling Jimmy the whole truth at once, but what did Hanna know about it and she an old maid? The other neighbors were inclined to think it was a judgment on Kate for her foolishness. And all the while, Jimmy's behavior got worse. At the best of times it wasn't very good. Though sometimes he was in high spirits and entertained herself and James telling funny stories, more often he was low-spirited and lay on his bed sulking over a comic. After that, he would go out with other boys and return with a guilty air she could spot from the end of the lane, and she would know he had been up to mischief and broken a window or stolen from a shop. At times like that, she was never free of anxiety for him, because apart from the fact that she had a holy terror of the law, she knew his naughtiness threatened the sufferance the neighbors extended to him on her account, and that they would be only too ready to say that it was all you could expect of a boy like that.

Finally, she decided to take Hanna Dinan's advice. But when James was asleep and she and Jimmy were sitting together in the darkness over the fire, she lost courage. She had no notion of how he would take it, and if he took it badly, she'd get the blame. She told him, instead, about James and his mother. She told him how some people, like herself, were lucky, because their fancy never strayed from the one person, while others, like James's mother, had the misfortune to love someone they couldn't marry. She was pleased by Jimmy's silent attention. She thought she had impressed him. But his first words startled her. "All the same, Mammy," he said, "James should be with his own mother."

She was astonished at the maturity in his tone. This was no longer any of the Jimmys she had known, but one who spoke with the sort of authority poor Jack had exercised on the rare occasions when he had called his family to order.

"Ah, how could he be with her?"

"Then she ought to tell him who he is and why she can't have him."

"Is it to be upsetting the child?" she asked complainingly.

"If she doesn't upset him, somebody else will," he said with his brooding, old-mannish air.

"They will, they will, God help us!" she sighed. "People are bad enough for anything. But the poor child may as well be happy while he can."

But it wasn't of James that she was thinking. James might get by, a colorless, studious, well-behaved boy who never gave offense to anybody, but one day Jimmy would beat up another boy or steal from a shop, and some woman would spite him by using the word Kate now dreaded—the word she had so often used lightly herself when she had no one to protect from it. Again she was tempted to tell him the whole truth, and again she was too afraid.

Meanwhile, for a short time at least, she had given Jimmy a purpose in life. Jimmy was always like that, either up or down, either full of purpose or shiftless and despondent. Now he took James over personally. He said it was bad for James to be so much alone, and took him along with him when he went down the Glen with the bigger boys. James didn't like being with the bigger boys. He liked to go at his own slow pace, gaping at everything, and he didn't in the least mind being left alone, but he was flattered by Jimmy's attention. When he came home he repeated his adventures to Kate in the manner of a policeman making a report. "Jimmy showed me a blackbird's nest. You can't touch a bird's nest, because the bird would know and leave the little eggs to die. I think it is wrong to rob a bird's nest, don't you, Mammy?" James collected bits of information, right and wrong, apparently thinking that they would all come in handy someday, and to each he managed to attach a useful moral lesson. No wonder he made Jimmy laugh.

But Jimmy still continued to worry about James's future. He waited till Aunt Nance came to Cork, and when he got her to himself he poured it all out to her in his enthusiastic way. He had managed to persuade himself that Kate didn't understand the seriousness of the situation but that Aunt Nance would. Before he had even finished, Aunt Nance gave him a queer look and cut him off. "You're too young to understand these things, Jimmy," she said.

"But don't *you* think he should be with his mother?" he asked indignantly.

"I don't know a thing about it, and if I did I wouldn't be able to do anything."

Jimmy left her in one of his mutinous, incoherent fits of rage. Instead of taking the bus, he walked, and when he reached the river he stood on the bank in the darkness throwing stones. It was late when he got home, but Kate was waiting up for him. He tossed his cap on the chair and went upstairs.

"What kept you?" she asked after him.

"Nothing."

"Don't you want a cup of tea?"

"I don't."

"He knows about it," Kate muttered to herself. "She must have told him. Now what'll I do?"

After a time she went upstairs to bed, but she heard him from the little attic room next door, where he and James slept, tossing and muttering to himself. She lit the candle and went in. He sat up in bed and looked at her with mad eyes.

"Go away!" he said. "You're not my mother."

"Oye!" she whimpered, sleepy and scared. "You and your goings on."

"You're not, you're not, you're not," he muttered. "I'm like James, only you wouldn't tell me. You tell me nothing but lies."

"Whisht, whisht, and don't wake the child!" she whispered impatiently. "You ought to be ashamed, a big boy like you. Come into the other room."

He stumbled out ahead of her, and she sat on the edge of her bed and put her arm round him. He was shivering. She no longer felt capable of handling him. She was old and tired and bothered in her head.

"What made you think of that, child?"

"Aunt Nance," he said with a sob.

"What did she tell you?"

"She wouldn't tell me anything, only I saw she was afraid."

"What was she afraid of?"

"I asked her to get James's mother to bring him home and she got frightened."

"Oh, oh, oh, you poor misfortunate child!" she said with a wail. "And you only did it for the best."

"I want to know who my mother is," he cried despairingly. "Is it Aunt Kitty or Aunt Nance?"

"Look, child, lie down here and you can sleep with Mammy."

"How can I sleep?" he asked frantically. "I only want to know who my mother is, and ye all tell me lies." Then, turning suddenly into a baby again, he put his head in her lap and bawled. She put her hand under his nightshirt and patted his fat bottom.

"Oh, you poor putog, you're perished," she sighed. Then she raised him onto the bed and pulled the covers about his shoulders.

"Will I get you a cup of tea?" she asked in a loud voice, and as he shook his head she muttered, "I will, I will."

She threw an old coat round her and went downstairs to the kitchen, where the oil lamp was turned low. There was still red ash in the grate, and she blew on it and boiled the kettle. Then her troubles seemed to get the better of her, and she spoke to herself in a loud, angry, complaining tone. " 'Twas the price of me for having anything to do with them—me that was never used to anything but decent people." When she heard herself she was ashamed. And then she shrugged, and whined, "I'm too old." As she climbed awkwardly back up the stairs with the two big mugs of tea, she heard him still sobbing, and stopped, turning her eyes to the ceiling. "God direct me!" she said aloud.

She sat on the edge of the bed and shook him. "Drink this!" she said roughly.

"I don't want it," said Jimmy. "I want to know who my mother is."

"Drink it, you dirty little caffler!" she said angrily. "Drink it or I won't tell you at all."

He raised himself in the big bed and she held the mug to his lips, though he could not keep himself from shivering and the tea spilled over his shirt and the bedclothes. "My good sheet," she muttered, and then took up her own cup and looked away into a corner of the room as if to avoid his eyes. "She is your mother, your Aunt Nance," she said in a harsh, expressionless voice, "and a good mother she is, and a good woman as well, and it will be a bad day for you when you talk against her or let anyone else do it. She had the misfortune to meet a man that was beneath her. She was innocent. He took advantage of her. She wasn't the first and she won't be the last."

He said nothing for a while, then he asked in a low voice, "And who was my daddy?"

"How would I know who he was? Whoever he was, he wasn't much."

"When I find out I'm going to kill him."

"Indeed you'll do nothing of the sort," she said sharply. "Whatever he did, he is your father and you wouldn't be here without him. He's there inside you, and the thing you will slight in yourself will be the rock you will perish on."

"And why did Aunt Nance like him if he was what you said?"

"Because she had no sense," said Kate. "What sense have any young girl? 'Tis unknown what they expect. If they had more sense they would be said by their fathers and mothers, that know what life is like, but they won't be said nor led by anyone. And the better they are the more they expect. That was all that was wrong with your mother, child. She was too innocent and too hopeful."

The dawn came in the window, and still she rambled on, half dead with sleep. Later, when she reported it to Hanna, she said that it was nothing but lies from beginning to end, and what other way could it be when she hadn't a notion how a girl like that would feel, but at the time it did not seem to be lies. It seemed rather as though she were reporting a complete truth that was known only to herself and God. And in a queer way it steadied Jimmy and brought out the little man in him.

"Mammy, does this mean that there's something wrong with James and me?" he asked at last, and she knew that this was the question that preoccupied him above all others.

"Indeed, it means nothing of the sort," she cried, and for the first time it seemed to herself that she was answering in her own person. "It is nothing. Only bad, jealous people would say the likes of that. Oh, you'll meet them, never fear," she said, joining her hands, "the scum of the earth with their marriage lines and their baptismal lines, looking down on their betters. But mark what I say, child, don't let any of them try and persuade you that you're not as good as them. And better! A thousand times better."

Strange notions from a respectable old woman who had never even believed in love!

What it all meant was brought home to her when Jimmy was fourteen and James between eight and nine. Jimmy's mother married a commercial traveller from Dublin who accepted Jimmy as a normal event that might happen to any decent girl, and he had persuaded her they should have Jimmy to live with them. It came as a great shock to Kate, though why it should have done so she couldn't say, because for years it was she who had argued with Hanna Dinan that the time had come for Jimmy to get a proper education and mix with what she called his equals. Now she realized that she was as jealous and possessive as if she were his real mother. She had never slighted Jimmy's mother, or allowed anyone else to do so, but she did it now. "She neglected him when it suited her, and now when it suits her she wants him back," she said to Hanna, and when Hanna replied that Kate wasn't being fair, she snapped, "Let them that have it be fair. Them that haven't are entitled to their say."

Besides, Jimmy provoked her. He had no power of concealing his emotions, and she could see that he had thoughts only for the marvellous new world that was opening up before him. He returned in high spirits from an evening with his mother and his new stepfather, and told Kate and James all about his stepfather's car, and his house outside Rathfarnham, at the foot of the Dublin Mountains. He told Kate blithely that he would always come back for the holidays, and comforted James by saying that his turn would come next. When Kate burst out suddenly, "Yourself is all you think about—no thought for me or the child," he got frantic and shouted, "All right, I won't go if you don't want me to!"

"Who said I didn't want you to go?" she shouted. "How could I keep you and me with nothing? Go to the well-heeled ones! Go to the ones that can look after you!"

By the time he left, she had regained control of herself, and she and James went with him to the station. They were stopped several times by old neighbors, who congratulated Jimmy. At the station he broke down, but she suspected that his grief wouldn't last long. And she had the impression that James felt the parting more deeply, though he was a child who didn't show much what he felt. He seemed to have come into the world expecting this sort of thing.

And yet, curiously, next day, when she woke and remembered Jimmy was gone, she had a feeling of relief. She realized that she wasn't the one to look after him. He was too big and noisy and exacting; he needed a man to keep him in his place. And besides, now that she had become old and stiff and half blind, the housekeeping was more of a trial. She would decide to give the boys a treat, and go to town to get the stewing beef, and suddenly realize when she got back to the kitchen that she didn't remember how to make stew. Then she would close her eyes and pray that God would direct her how to make stew as she made it when she was a young married woman—"delicious" poor Jack used to say it was. James was an easier proposition altogether, a boy who would live forever on tea and sweet cakes, so long as he got the penny exercise books for his writings and drawings.

The loss of Jimmy showed her how precarious was her hold on James, and in the evenings, when they were alone, she sat with him before the kitchen fire and let him hold forth to her on what he was going to be when he grew up. It seemed, according to himself, he was going to be a statue, and sometimes Kate suspected that the child wouldn't notice much difference, because he was a bit that way already. Jimmy had been a great boy to raise a laugh, particularly against himself, and James seemed to think it was his duty to do the same, but if she was to be killed for it she couldn't laugh at James's jokes. And yet she knew that James was gentler, steadier, and more considerate. When you asked him to do anything you had to explain to him why, but you never had to explain it twice. "Jimmy have the fire, but James have the character" was how she put it to Hanna.

And yet she fretted over Jimmy as she wouldn't have fretted over James. From

Dublin he had sent her one postcard, that was all, and he hadn't replied to either of the letters James wrote to him. "As true as God, that fellow is in trouble," she said.

"It's not that, Mammy," said James, "it's just that he doesn't like writing."

"Who wants him to write? All I want is to know how he is. If he was dying that vagabond wouldn't tell me!"

It was a queer way for a woman to feel who had been congratulating herself on having got rid of him.

Then, one morning, she heard a hammering at the front door and knew that the thing she had been dreading had happened. Without even asking who it was, she stumbled down the stairs in the darkness. When she opened the door and saw Jimmy, she threw her arms about his neck. "Oh, child, child!" she whimpered. "Sure, I thought you'd never come home! How did you get here?"

"I came on the bike," he said with a swagger.

"You did, you did, you divil you, you did," she muttered, seeing the bicycle against the wall. And then, her voice rising to a squeal of anguish. "Are them your good trousers?"

"Who is it, Mammy?" James shouted from upstairs.

"Come down yourself," she said, and went to lay the fire. James came down the stairs sedately in his nightshirt. Jimmy went up to him with a grin, and it startled her to see how big and solid he looked beside the frail, spectacled boy.

"Hallo, James," Jimmy said, shaking hands. "I suppose you're sorry I'm back?"

"No, Jimmy," James said in a small voice, "I'm glad you're back. The house isn't the same without you."

"Put on your topcoat, you little divil!" cried Kate. "How often have I to be telling you not to go round like that? That fellow," she said to Jimmy, "he have the heart scalded in me. I'd want ten eyes and hands, picking things up after him. . . . Go on, you little gligeen!"

It was a joyous reunion in the little kitchen when the sun was just beginning to pick out the high ground behind the house. Kate marvelled how she had managed to listen to James all that time and the way Jimmy could tell a story. Whatever James told you, the point of it always seemed to be how clever he was. Jimmy's stories always showed him up as a fool, and somehow it never crossed your mind that he was a fool at all. And yet there was something about him this morning that didn't seem right.

"Never mind about that!" Kate cried at last. "Tell us what your mother said."

"How do you mean?" asked Jimmy, turning red.

"What did she say when you told her you were coming back?"

"She didn't say anything," Jimmy replied with a brassy air. "She doesn't mind what I do."

"She doesn't, I hear," Kate retorted mockingly. "I suppose 'twas jealous you were?"

"What would I be jealous of?" Jimmy asked defiantly.

"Your stepfather, who else?" she said, screwing up her eyes in mockery at him. "You wanted all the attention. And now she'll be blaming it all on me. She'll be saying I have you spoiled. And she'll be right. I have you ruined, you little caffler! Ruined!" she repeated meditatively as she went and opened the back door. The whole hill behind was reflecting the morning light in a great rosy glow. "Oh, my!" she said as though to herself. "There's a beautiful morning, glory be to God!"

Just then she heard the unfamiliar sound of a car in the lane, and it stopped outside the front door. She knew then what it was that had seemed wrong in Jimmy's story, and turned on him. "You ran away from home," she said. "Is that the police?"

Jimmy didn't seem to be listening to her. "If that's my stepfather, I'm not going back with him," he said.

Kate went to the front door and saw a good-looking young man with large ears and the pink-and-white complexion she called "delicate." She knew at once it was Jimmy's stepfather.

"Mrs. Mahoney?" he asked.

"Come in, sir, come in," she said obsequiously, and now she was no longer the proud, possessive mother whose boy had come back to her but the old hireling who had been caught with property that wasn't hers.

The young man strode into the kitchen with a confident air and stopped dead when he saw Jimmy.

"Now, what made me think of coming here first?" he shouted good-humoredly. "Mrs. Mahoney, I have the makings of a first-class detective, only I never got a chance."

When Jimmy said nothing, he tossed his head and went on in the same tone. "Want a lift, Jimmy?"

Jimmy glared at him. "I'm not going back with you, Uncle Tim," he said.

"Oh, begod, that's exactly what you *are* going to do, Jimmy," his stepfather said. "If you think I'm going to spend the rest of my days chasing you round Ireland, you're wrong." He dropped into a chair and rubbed his hands, as though to restore the circulation. "Mrs. Mahoney," he asked, "what do we have them for?"

Kate liked his way of including her in the conversation. She knew, too, he was only talking like that to make things easier for Jimmy.

"I don't want to go back, Uncle Tim," Jimmy said furiously. "I want to stop here."

"Listen to that, Mrs. Mahoney," his stepfather said, cocking his head at Kate. "Insulting Dublin to a Dublin man! And in Cork, of all places!"

"I'm not saying anything against Dublin!" Jimmy cried, and again he was a child and defenseless against the dialectic of adults. "I want to stay here."

Kate immediately came to his defense. "Wisha, 'tis only the way he got a bit homesick, sir. He thought he'd like to come back for a couple of days."

"I don't want to come back for a couple of days!" Jimmy shouted. "This is my home. I told Aunt Nance so."

"And wasn't that a very hard thing to say to your mother, Jimmy?" his stepfather asked. He said it gently, and Kate knew he liked the boy.

"It's true," Jimmy said. "I knew I wasn't wanted."

"You really think that, Jimmy?" his stepfather asked reproachfully, and Jimmy burst into wild tears.

"I didn't say *you* didn't want me. I know you did want me, and I wanted you. But my mammy didn't want me."

"Jimmy!"

"She didn't, she didn't."

"What made you think she didn't?"

"She thought I was too like my father."

"She said you were too like your father?" his stepfather asked incredulously.

"She didn't have to say it," sobbed Jimmy. "I knew it, every time she looked at me when I done something wrong. I reminded her of him, and she doesn't want to think of him. She only wants to think of you. And it's not my fault if I'm like my father, but if she didn't want me to be that way she should have took me sooner. She shouldn't have left it so late, Uncle Tim."

His stepfather said nothing for a moment and then rose in a jerky movement and walked to the back door. "You might be right there, son," he said with a shrug. "But you're not going the right way about it, either."

"All right, Uncle Tim," Jimmy cried. "What is the right way? I'll do whatever you tell me."

"Talk it over properly with your mother, and then come back here after the holidays," his stepfather said. "You see, old man, you don't seem to realize what it cost your mother to bring you to live with her at all. Now, you don't want her explaining why you ran away after a couple of weeks, do you?"

"He's right, Jimmy boy, he's right," Kate pleaded. "You could never go back there again, with all the old talk there'd be."

"Oh, all right, all right," Jimmy said despairingly, and went to get his cap.

"Sit down, the pair of ye, till I make a cup of tea!" cried Kate. But Jimmy shook his head.

"I'd sooner go now," he said.

And it was real despair, as she well knew, not sham. Of course, he showed off a bit, the way he always did, and didn't kiss her when he was getting into the car. And when James in his gentle way said, "You'll be back soon," Jimmy only drew a deep breath and looked up at the sky.

But she knew he really meant it, and that day she had great boasting over it among the neighbors. "A boy of fourteen, ma'am, that was never away from home all the days of his life, coming back like that, on an old bicycle, without food or sleep. Oh, my! Where would you find the likes of him?"

The neighbors, too, were impressed. "Well, Jimmy," they said, when he came back at the end of the holidays, to go to school. "You couldn't do without us, I see."

There was only one change in the relationship between Kate, James, and Jimmy. The day after his return, Jimmy said, "I'm not going to call you Mammy any more."

"Oye, and what are you going to call me?" she asked with sour humor.

"I'm going to call you Granny," he said. "The other sounds too silly."

After a few weeks James said "Granny," too. Though she didn't complain, she resented it. Stumbling about the house, talking to herself, she would suddenly say, "Glad enough they were of someone to call Mammy."

. . . . .

After Jimmy had been back for a year or so, Kate's health began to break up. She had to go to hospital, and Nora and Molly offered to take one of the boys each. But neither Jimmy nor James would agree to this. They didn't want to leave the house and they didn't want to be separated, so they stayed on, and each week one of the girls came to clear up after them. They reported to Kate that the mess was frightful. But it wasn't this that really worried her, it was the wild streak in Jimmy. In the evenings, instead of doing his lessons like James, he was tramping the city with wild young fellows. He had no sense of the value of money, and when he wanted it thought nothing of stealing from herself or James.

She came home before she should have, but even then she was too late to prevent mischief. While she was away, Jimmy had left school and got himself a job in a packing store.

"Oh, you blackguard, you!" she said. "I knew well you'd be up to something when my back was turned. But to school you go tomorrow, my fine gentleman, if I have to drag you there myself."

"I can't go back to school," Jimmy said indignantly. "They could have the law on me if I didn't give a month's notice." He knew she was very timid of policemen, lawyers, and officials and even at her age was in great dread of being dragged off to jail for some crime she didn't even know she had committed.

"Who's the manager?" she said. "I'll see him myself."

"You can't," said Jimmy. "He's on holidays."

"Oh, you liar," she muttered. "The truth isn't in you. Who is it?"

"Anyway, I have to have a job," said Jimmy. "If anything happened to you while you were in hospital, who was going to look after James?"

She was taken aback, because that was something that had been all the time on her own mind. She knew her James, and knew that if she died and he was sent to live with some foster mother who didn't understand him, he would break his heart. In every way he was steadier than Jimmy, and yet he was far more defenseless. If you took Jimmy's home away from him, he would fight, steal, or run away, but James would only lie down and die. Still, though she was impressed by Jimmy's manliness, she wasn't taken in by it. She knew that in an emotional fit he was capable of these big gestures, but he could never live up to them, and in no time he would be thinking how he could turn them to his own advantage.

" 'Tisn't James at all with you," she said. " 'Tis more money you want for yourself. Did you tell your mother first?"

"I'm working till after six every night!" he cried, confounded by her injustice. "What time have I to write to my mother?"

"Plenty of time you have to write to her when 'tis something you want," she said. "Sit down and write to her now, you scamp! I'm not going to be taking the blame for your blackguarding."

Jimmy, with a martyred air, sat at the table and agonized over a note to his mother. "How do you spell 'employment'?" he asked James.

"Listen to him!" Kate said, invoking Heaven. "He wants to give up school and he don't know how to spell a simple word."

"All right, spell it you, so," he said.

"In my time, for poor people, the education was not going," she replied with great dignity. "Poor people hadn't the chances they have now, and what chances they had, they respected, not like the ones that are going today. Go on with your letter, you thing!"

Again his Uncle Tim came and argued with him. He explained patiently that without an education Jimmy would get nowhere. Unless he finished his schooling, he couldn't go to the University. Jimmy, who couldn't stand gentleness in an argument, broke down and said he didn't want to go to the University, he only wanted to be independent. Kate didn't understand what Jimmy's stepfather meant, but she felt that it was probably only the old conflict in a new form: Jimmy's stepfather wanted him to be one of his own class, and Jimmy didn't. Leaving school at that age was what a working-class boy would do. Except for the occasional brilliant boy who was kept on at the monks' expense, there was no education beyond sixth book.

His stepfather seemed to realize it, too, for he gave in with a suddenness that surprised her. "Oh, all right," he said. "But you'd better let me try and find you something better than the job you have. And for God's sake go to night school and learn office work."

When he left, Jimmy accompanied him to the car, and they had a conversation that made Kate suspicious.

"What were you talking to your stepfather about?" she asked.

"Nothing," said Jimmy. "Only asking him who my father was."

"And did he tell you?"

"He said he didn't know."

"How inquisitive we're getting!" said Kate.

"He said I was entitled to know," Jimmy said defensively. "He told me to ask Nance the next time I go up to them." She noticed that sometimes he said "Mother" and sometimes "Nance," and both sounded awkward.

When next he came back from a holiday in Dublin he had discovered what he wished to know. As he described the scene with his mother, Kate was again overcome by a feeling of the strangeness of it all. At first his mother had refused point-blank to tell him anything. She had been quite cool and friendly about it, and explained that she had been only a girl when it all happened and when she had been deserted had cut Jimmy's father out of her life. She hadn't spoken his name since and never proposed to speak it. When Jimmy persisted, arguing and pleading with her, she had grown furious. "Christ, boy," she said, "it's my life as well as yours!" Then she had wept and said she never wanted him in the house again. At this moment, her husband had walked into the room, looking like murder, Jimmy said, and snapped, "All right, Jimmy. Beat it!" He had closed the door after Jimmy, and Jimmy heard the pair of them arguing from the kitchen. Finally, his stepfather had come out and shouted, "Your mother wants to see you, Jimmy," and rushed upstairs. When Jimmy went into the living room, she was standing by the fireplace, pale and dry-eyed. "Your father's name is Tom Creedon," she said coolly. "He had a business in Tramore, but he's left it for years. The last I heard of him he was in London. If you want any more information, you'll have to ask one of his friends. A man called Michael Taylor in Dungarvan is your best chance." And then she, too, had gone out and followed her husband upstairs, and Jimmy had sat by the fire and sobbed to himself till it was nearly out and the whole house was silent. He felt he had outraged two people who cared for him for the sake of someone who had never inquired whether he was alive or dead.

When he had finished his story, Kate felt the same. "And what use is it to you, now you know it?" she asked maliciously.

"I had to know it," Jimmy said with easy self-confidence. "Now I can go and see him."

"You can what?" she asked wearily.

"I can go and see him. Why wouldn't I?"

"Why wouldn't you, indeed, and all the attention he paid to you," she said sourly. "You're never right."

There were times when she almost thought he wasn't right in the head. For months on end he never seemed to think at all of his parentage, and then he would begin to daydream till he worked himself up into a fever of emotion. In a fit like that she never knew what he might do. He was capable of anything—of anything, that is, except writing a letter. One weekend he set off on his bicycle for County Waterford and came back with his father's address. After that it was only a question of getting a friend on the cross-Channel boat to fix him a passage for nothing.

All the time he was away Kate fretted, and, being Jimmy, he didn't even send her as much as a picture postcard. She had the vague hope that he wouldn't be able to locate his father. She thought of it all as if it were something she'd read in a newspaper—how in a terrible fit of anger Jimmy struck and killed his father and then turned himself in to the police. She could even see his picture in the paper with handcuffs on his wrists. "Ah," Hanna Dinan said, "God is good!" But this didn't comfort Kate at all.

And then, one autumn morning after James had left for school, Jimmy walked in. He had had no breakfast, and she fumbled blindly about the little kitchen getting it ready for him, and cursing old age that made it seem such a labor. But all the same, her heart was light. She knew now that she had only been deceiving herself, pretending to think that Jimmy and his father might disagree, when all she dreaded was that they would agree too well.

"Well," she said fondly, leaning on the kitchen table and grinning into his face. "Now you seen him, how do you like him?"

"Oh, he's all right," Jimmy said casually—too casually, for her taste. "He's drinking himself to death, that's all." And instantly she was ashamed of her own pettiness, and tears came into her eyes.

"Wisha, child, child, why do you be upsetting yourself about them?" she cried. "They're not worth it. There's no one worth it."

She sat in the kitchen with him while he unburdened himself about it all. It was just as when he had described to her how he had asked his mother for his father's name, as though he were saving up every detail—the walk across England, the people who had given him lifts, the truck driver who had given him a dinner and five bob after Jimmy confided in him, till the moment he knocked at the door of the shabby lodging house near Victoria Station and an unshaven man with sad red eyes looked out and asked timidly, "Yes, boy, what is it?" As though nobody ever called on him now with anything but bad news.

"And what did you say?" Kate asked.

"I said, 'Don't you know me?' and he said, 'You have the advantage of me.' So I said, 'I'm your son.'"

"Oh, my!" exclaimed Kate, profoundly impressed, though she had resolved to hate everything she heard about Jimmy's father. "And what did he say to that?"

"He didn't say anything. He only started to cry."

" 'Twas a bit late in the day for him," said Kate. "And what did he say about your mother?"

"Only that she didn't miss much when she missed him."

"That was one true word he said, anyway," said Kate.

"He paid for it," said Jimmy.

"He deserved it all," said Kate.

"You wouldn't say that if you saw him now," said Jimmy, and he went on to describe the squalid back room where he had stayed for a week with his father, sleeping in the same dirty bed, going out with him to the pub. And yet through Jimmy's disillusionment Kate felt a touch of pride in the way he described the sudden outbursts of extravagant humor that lit up his father's maudlin self-pity. He described everything, down to the last evening, when his father had brought him to Paddington Station, forced him to take the last five shillings he had in the world, tearfully kissed him, and begged him to come again.

She knew from Jimmy's tone that it was unlikely that he would go again. His father was only another ghost that he had laid.

When he was eighteen, Jimmy took up with a girl of his own, and at first Kate paid no attention, but when it went on for more than six months and Jimmy took the girl out every Friday night, she began to grow nervous. Steady courting of one girl was something she had never thought him capable of. When she learned who the girl was, she understood. Tessie Flynn was an orphan who had been brought up by a staid old couple on the road as their own daughter. They had brought her up so well that every other young fellow on the road was in dread to go near her, and when the old couple discovered that she was actually walking out with Jimmy they didn't talk to her for days. She wasn't allowed to bring Jimmy to the house, and Kate, for the sake of her own self-respect, was forced to invite her instead.

Not that this made her like Tessie any the more. She dreaded Friday evenings, when Jimmy would come in from work, and shave, and strip to wash under the tap in the back yard, and then change into his best blue suit and put cream on his hair.

"You won't be late tonight?" she would ask.

"Why wouldn't I be late?" Jimmy would ask cheerfully.

"You know I can't sleep while you do be out."

It was true. Any other night of the week she could sleep comfortably at her proper time, but when she knew he was out with "that vagabond," as she called poor Tessie, she would lie awake worrying and saying her rosary. Even James reproved her. One Friday evening, he closed his book carefully, raised his big glasses on his forehead, and said, "Granny, you worry too much about Jimmy and his girl friend. Jimmy is much steadier than you think."

But James didn't realize, as she did, that even in his choice of a girl Jimmy was only reliving the pattern of his own life. To anyone else he might seem the most ordinary of young fellows, but she could watch the fever mount in him, and always she was taken aback at the form it took. Once, he lit out on his bicycle to a little town eighty miles away, where his father's brother had a grocery shop. Another time, with the help of his sailor friend, he crossed again to Fishguard and cycled through southern England to the little seaside town in Dorset where he had been born. And she knew that whatever she might say he would go on like that to the end of his days, pursued by the dream of a normal life that he might have lived and of a normal family in which he might have grown up.

James observed it, too, but with a deep disapproval. He thought Jimmy cheapened himself.

"Ah, that's only because you can get away from them, boy," Jimmy said with his toughest air. "Boy, if my family was living in England, I wouldn't worry about them, either."

"Well, your father *is* living in England, and you went to see him," said James. "I daresay I'll see my family, too, one day, but I don't want to see them now, thank you."

"If you have any sense you'll have nothing to do with them," said Jimmy. "They'll only look down on you."

"I don't think so," said James. "At the moment they might, but if they meet me when I'm a professor at the University, or a senior civil servant, they'll behave differently. You see, Jimmy," he went on in the tone he would use when he was a professor at the University, "people like that pay far too much attention to public opinion, and they won't neglect anyone who can be useful to them."

Kate felt that there was a sad wisdom in what James said. While Jimmy, who had something of his father's weakness and charm, might prove a liability to those who didn't understand him, James would work and save, and only when he was established and independent would he satisfy his curiosity about those who had abandoned him. And, though she mightn't live to see it, James would make quite certain that nobody patronized him. She would have given a great deal to see how James dealt with his family.

But she knew that she wouldn't see it. She fell ill again, and this time Molly came to the house to nurse her, while Nora, who looked after Molly's children, came in the evenings, and sometimes one of the husbands. Molly made an immediate change in the house. She was swift and efficient; she fed the boys and made conversation with callers, leaning against the doorpost with folded arms as though she had no thought in the world but of them, though occasionally she would slip away into the front room and weep savagely to herself for a few minutes before returning to her tasks.

The priest came, and Molly invited him into the front room and chatted with him about the affairs of the parish. After he had left, Kate asked to see Jimmy and James. They went up the stairs quietly and stood at either side of the bed. Her eyes were closed and her hands outstretched on the bed. Jimmy took one, and after a moment James took the other. James was never a boy for a deathbed. "Don't upset yeerselves too much over me," she said. "I know ye'll miss me, but ye have nothing to regret. Ye were the two best boys a mother ever reared, and I'm proud of ye." She thought hard for a moment and then added something that shocked them all. "And yeer father is proud of ye, I'm sure."

Molly, who was standing with Nora behind James, leaned forward and said urgently, "Mammy, 'tisn't who you think. 'Tis Jimmy and James."

Kate opened her eyes for a moment and looked straight at her, and her eyes were no colder than the words she spoke. "Excuse me, child, I know perfectly well who I have." Her eyes closed again, and she breathed noisily for what seemed a long, long time, as though she were vainly trying to recollect herself. "Don't either of ye do anything yeer father would be ashamed of. He was a good man, and a kind man, and a clean-living man, and he never robbed anyone of a ha'penny. . . . Jimmy," she added in a voice of unexpected strength, "look after your little brother for me."

"I will, Mammy," Jimmy said through his tears.

Something in that sudden reversion to the language of childhood made Molly break down. She left the room and took refuge in the parlor downstairs. Nora, realizing that something had upset her sister, followed and shouted at her as all the Mahoneys had always shouted at one another. "Wisha, Molly, will you have a bit of sense? Sure you know poor Mammy's mind was wandering."

"It was *not* wandering, Nora," Molly said hysterically. "She knew perfectly well what she was saying, and Jimmy knew it, too. They were her real children all the time, and we were only outsiders. Oh, Nora, Nora, how could she do *that* to us?"

That night, when Kate was quiet at last in her brown shroud, with her hands clutching the rosary beads on her breast, and the neighbors were coming from all parts into the little front room to say a prayer for her, people in every little house around were asking the same question that Molly had been asking herself, though they asked it with a touch of envy. How could a woman who was already old take the things the world had thrown away and out of them fashion a new family, dearer to her than the old and finer than any she had known? Hanna Dinan had the last word. Having sat there for an hour, she took a last look at her old crony on the bed, then pulled her coat about her and said casually, "Wisha, wasn't she a great little woman! She had them all against her and she bested them. They had everything, and she had nothing, and she bested them all in the end."

Amos Oz

. . . .

NOMAD AND VIPER

1

The famine brought them.

They fled north from the horrors of famine, together with their dusty flocks. From September to April the desert had not known a moment's relief from drought. The loess was pounded to dust. Famine had spread through the nomads' encampments and wrought havoc among their flocks.

The military authorities gave the situation their urgent attention. Despite certain hesitations, they decided to open the roads leading north to the Bedouins. A whole population—men, women, and children—could not simply be abandoned to the horrors of starvation.

Dark, sinuous, and wiry, the desert tribesmen trickled along the dirt paths, and with them came their emaciated flocks. They meandered along gullies hidden from town dwellers' eyes. A persistent stream pressed northward, circling the scattered settlements, staring wide-eyed at the sights of the settled land. The dark flocks spread into the fields of golden stubble, tearing and chewing with strong, vengeful teeth. The nomads' bearing was stealthy and subdued; they shrank from watchful eyes. They took pains to avoid encounters. Tried to conceal their presence.

If you passed them on a noisy tractor and set billows of dust loose on them, they would courteously gather their scattered flocks and give you a wide passage, wider by far than was necessary. They stared at you from a distance, frozen like statues. The scorching atmosphere blurred their appearance and gave a uniform look to their features: a shepherd with his staff, a woman with her babes, an old man with his eyes sunk deep in their sockets. Some were half-blind, or perhaps feigned half-blindness from some vague alms-gathering motive. Inscrutable to the likes of you.

How unlike our well-tended sheep were their miserable specimens: knots of small, skinny beasts huddling into a dark, seething mass, silent and subdued, humble as their dumb keepers.

The camels alone spurn meekness. From atop tall necks they fix you with tired eyes brimming with scornful sorrow. The wisdom of age seems to lurk in their eyes, and a nameless tremor runs often through their skin.

. . . . .

Sometimes you manage to catch them unawares. Crossing a field on foot, you may suddenly happen on an indolent flock standing motionless, noon-struck, their feet apparently rooted in the parched soil. Among them lies the shepherd, fast asleep, dark as a block of basalt. You approach and cover him with a harsh shadow. You are startled to find his eyes wide open. He bares most of his teeth in a placatory smile. Some of them are gleaming, others decayed. His smell hits you. You grimace. Your grimace hits him like a punch in the face. Daintily he picks himself up, trunk erect, shoulders hunched. You fix him with a cold blue eye. He broadens his smile and utters a guttural syllable. His garb is a compromise: a short, patched European jacket over a white desert robe. He cocks his head to one side. An appeased gleam crosses his face. If you do not upbraid him, he suddenly extends his left hand and asks for a cigarette in rapid Hebrew. His voice has a silken quality, like that of a shy woman. If your mood is generous, you put a cigarette to your lips and toss another into his wrinkled palm. To your surprise, he snatches a gilt lighter from the recesses of his robe and offers a furtive flame. The smile never leaves his lips. His smile lasts too long, is unconvincing. A flash of sunlight darts off the thick gold ring adorning his finger and pierces your squinting eyes.

Eventually you turn your back on the nomad and continue on your way. After a hundred, two hundred paces, you may turn your head and see him standing just as he was, his gaze stabbing your back. You could swear that he is still smiling, that he will go on smiling for a long while to come.

And then, their singing in the night. A long-drawn-out, dolorous wail drifts on the night air from sunset until the early hours. The voices penetrate to the gardens and pathways of the kibbutz and charge our nights with an uneasy heaviness. No sooner have you settled down to sleep than a distant drumbeat sets the rhythm of your slumber like the pounding of an obdurate heart. Hot are the nights, and vapor-laden. Stray clouds caress the moon like a train of gentle camels, camels without any bells.

The nomads' tents are made up of dark drapes. Stray women drift around at night, barefoot and noiseless. Lean, vicious nomad hounds dart out of the camp to challenge the moon all night long. Their barking drives our kibbutz dogs insane. Our finest dog went mad one night, broke into the henhouse, and massacred the young chicks. It was not out of savagery that the watchmen shot him. There was no alternative. Any reasonable man would justify their action.

2

You might imagine that the nomad incursion enriched our heat-prostrated nights with a dimension of poetry. This may have been the case for some of our unattached girls. But we cannot refrain from mentioning a whole string of prosaic, indeed unaesthetic disturbances, such as foot-and-mouth disease, crop damage, and an epidemic of petty thefts.

The foot-and-mouth disease came out of the desert, carried by their livestock, which had never been subjected to any proper medical inspection. Although we took various early precautions, the virus infected our sheep and cattle, severely reducing the milk yield and killing off a number of animals.

As for the damage to the crops, we had to admit that we had never managed to catch one of the nomads in the act. All we ever found were the tracks of men and animals among the rows of vegetables, in the hayfields, and deep inside the carefully fenced orchards. And wrecked irrigation pipes, plot markers, farming implements left out in the fields, and other objects.

We are not the kind to take such things lying down. We are no believers in forbearance or vegetarianism. This is especially true of our younger men. Among the veteran founders there are a few adherents of Tolstoyan ideas and such like. Decency constrains me not to dwell in detail on certain isolated and exceptional acts of reprisal conducted by some of the youngsters whose patience had expired, such as cattle rustling, stoning a nomad boy, or beating one of the shepherds senseless. In defense of the perpetrators of the last-mentioned act of retaliation I must state clearly that the shepherd in question had an infuriatingly sly face. He was blind in one eye, broken-nosed, drooling; and his mouth—on this the men responsible were unanimous—was set with long, curved fangs like a fox's. A man with such an appearance was capable of anything. And the Bedouins would certainly not forget this lesson.

The pilfering was the most worrisome aspect of all. They laid hands on the unripe fruit in our orchards, pocketed the faucets, whittled away piles of empty sacks in the fields, stole into the henhouses, and even made away with the modest valuables from our little houses.

The very darkness was their accomplice. Elusive as the wind, they passed through the settlement, evading both the guards we had posted and the extra guards we had added. Sometimes you would set out on a tractor or a battered jeep toward midnight to turn off the irrigation faucets in an outlying field and your headlights would trap fleeting shadows, a man or a night beast. An irritable guard decided one night to open fire, and in the dark he managed to kill a stray jackal.

Needless to say, the kibbutz secretariat did not remain silent. Several times Etkin, the secretary, called in the police, but their tracking dogs betrayed or failed them. Having led their handlers a few paces outside the kibbutz fence, they raised their black noses, uttered a savage howl, and stared foolishly ahead.

Spot raids on the tattered tents revealed nothing. It was as if the very earth had decided to cover up the plunder and brazenly outstare the victims. Eventually the elder of the tribe was brought to the kibbutz office, flanked by a pair of inscrutable nomads. The short-tempered policemen pushed them forward with repeated cries of "Yallah, yallah."

We, the members of the secretariat, received the elder and his men politely and respectfully. We invited them to sit down on the bench, smiled at them, and offered them steaming coffee prepared by Geula at Etkin's special request. The old man responded with elaborate courtesies, favoring us with a smile which he kept up from the beginning of the interview till its conclusion. He phrased his remarks in careful, formal Hebrew.

It was true that some of the youngsters of his tribe had laid hands on our property. Why should he deny it. Boys would be boys, and the world was getting steadily worse. He had the honor of begging our pardon and restoring the stolen property. Stolen property fastens its teeth in the flesh of the thief, as the proverb says. That was the way of it. What could one do about the hotheadedness of youth? He deeply regretted the trouble and distress we had been caused.

So saying, he put his hand into the folds of his robe and drew out a few screws, some gleaming, some rusty, a pair of pruning hooks, a stray knife-blade, a pocket flashlight, a broken hammer, and three grubby bank notes, as a recompense for our loss and worry.

Etkin spread his hands in embarrassment. For reasons best known to himself, he chose to ignore our guest's Hebrew and to reply in broken Arabic, the residue of his studies during the time of the riots and the siege. He opened his remarks with a frank and clear statement about the brotherhood of nations—the cornerstone of our ideology—and about the quality of neighborliness of which the peoples of the East had long been justly proud, and never more so than in these days of bloodshed and groundless hatred.

To Etkin's credit, let it be said that he did not shrink in the slightest from reciting a full and detailed list of the acts of theft, damage, and sabotage that our guest—as the result of oversight, no doubt—had refrained from mentioning in his apology. If all the stolen property were returned and the vandalism stopped once and for all, we would be wholeheartedly willing to open a new page in the relations of our two neighboring communities. Our children would doubtless enjoy and profit from an educational courtesy visit to the Bedouin encampment, the kind of visit that broadens horizons. And it went without saying that the tribe's children would pay a return visit to our kibbutz home, in the interest of deepening mutual understanding.

The old man neither relaxed nor broadened his smile, but kept it sternly at its former level as he remarked with an abundance of polite phrases that the gentlemen of the kibbutz would be able to prove no further thefts beyond those he had already admitted and for which he had sought our forgiveness.

He concluded with elaborate benedictions, wished us health and long life, posterity and plenty, then took his leave and departed, accompanied by his two barefooted companions wrapped in their dark robes. They were soon swallowed up by the wadi that lay outside the kibbutz fence.

Since the police had proved ineffectual—and had indeed abandoned the investigation—some of our young men suggested making an excursion one night to teach the savages a lesson in a language they would really understand.

Etkin rejected their suggestion with disgust and with reasonable arguments. The young men, in turn, applied to Etkin a number of epithets that decency obliges me to pass over in silence. Strangely enough, Etkin ignored their insults and reluctantly agreed to put their suggestion before the kibbutz secretariat. Perhaps he was afraid that they might take matters into their own hands.

Toward evening, Etkin went around from room to room and invited the committee to an urgent meeting at eight-thirty. When he came to Geula, he told her about the young men's ideas and the undemocratic pressure to which he was being subjected, and asked her to bring along to the meeting a pot of black coffee and a lot of good will. Geula responded with an acid smile. Her eyes were bleary because Etkin had awakened her from a troubled sleep. As she changed her clothes, the night fell, damp and hot and close.

3

Damp and close and hot the night fell on the kibbutz, tangled in the dust-laden cypresses, oppressed the lawns and ornamental shrubs. Sprinklers scattered water onto the thirsty lawn, but it was swallowed up at once: perhaps it evaporated even before it touched the grass. An irritable phone rang vainly in the locked office. The walls of the houses gave out a damp vapor. From the kitchen chimney a stiff column of smoke rose like an arrow into the heart of the sky, because there was no breeze. From the greasy sinks came a shout. A dish had been broken and somebody was bleeding. A fat house-cat had killed a lizard or a snake and dragged its prey onto the baking concrete path to toy with it lazily in the dense evening sunlight. An ancient tractor started to rumble in one of the sheds, choked, belched a stench of oil, roared, spluttered, and finally managed to set out to deliver an evening meal to the second shift, who were toiling in an outlying field. Near the Persian lilac Geula saw a bottle dirty with the remains of a greasy liquid. She kicked at it repeatedly, but instead of shattering, the bottle rolled heavily among the rosebushes. She picked up a big stone. She tried to hit the bottle. She longed to smash it. The stone missed. The girl began to whistle a vague tune.

Geula was a short, energetic girl of twenty-nine or so. Although she had not yet found a husband, none of us would deny her good qualities, such as the dedication she lavished on local social and cultural activities. Her face was pale and thin. No one could rival her in brewing strong coffee—coffee to raise the dead, we called it. A pair of bitter lines were etched at the corners of her mouth.

On summer evenings, when the rest of us would lounge in a group on a rug spread on one of the lawns and launch jokes and bursts of cheerful song heavenward, accompanied by clouds of cigarette smoke, Geula would shut herself up in her room and not join us until she had prepared the pot of scalding, strong coffee. She it was, too, who always took pains to ensure that there was no shortage of biscuits.

What had passed between Geula and me is not relevant here, and I shall make do with a hint or two. Long ago we used to stroll together to the orchards in the evening and talk. It was all a long time ago, and it is a long time since it ended. We would exchange unconventional political ideas or argue about the latest books. Geula was a stern and sometimes merciless critic: I was covered in confusion. She did not like my stories, because of the extreme polarity of situations, scenery, and characters, with no intermediate shades between black and white. I would utter an apology or a denial, but Geula always had ready proofs

and she was a very methodical thinker. Sometimes I would dare to rest a concili-
atory hand on her neck, and wait for her to calm down. But she never relaxed
completely. If once or twice she leaned against me, she always blamed her broken sandal or her aching head. And so we drifted apart. To this day she still cuts
my stories out of the periodicals, and arranges them in a cardboard box kept in a
special drawer devoted to them alone.

I always buy her a new book of poems for her birthday. I creep into her room
when she is out and leave the book on her table, without any inscription or dedication. Sometimes we happen to sit together in the dining hall. I avoid her
glance, so as not to have to face her mocking sadness. On hot days, when faces
are covered in sweat, the acne on her cheeks reddens and she seems to have no
hope. When the cool of autumn comes, I sometimes find her pretty and attractive from a distance. On such days Geula likes to walk to the orchards in the
early evening. She goes alone and comes back alone. Some of the youngsters
come and ask me what she is looking for there, and they have a malicious snicker
on their faces. I tell them that I don't know. And I really don't.

4

Viciously Geula picked up another stone to hurl at the bottle. This time she
did not miss, but she still failed to hear the shattering sound she craved. The
stone grazed the bottle, which tinkled faintly and disappeared under one of the
bushes. A third stone, bigger and heavier than the other two, was launched from
ridiculously close range: the girl trampled on the loose soil of the flower bed and
stood right over the bottle. This time there was a harsh, dry explosion, which
brought no relief. Must get out.

Damp and close and hot the night fell, its heat pricking the skin like broken
glass. Geula retraced her steps, passed the balcony of her room, tossed her sandals inside, and walked down barefoot onto the dirt path.

The clods of earth tickled the soles of her feet. There was a rough friction,
and her nerve endings quivered with flickers of vague excitement. Beyond the
rocky hill the shadows were waiting for her: the orchard in the last of the light.
With determined hands she widened the gap in the fence and slipped through.
At that moment a slight evening breeze began to stir. It was a warmish summer
breeze with no definite direction. An old sun rolled westward, trying to be
sucked up by the dusty horizon. A last tractor climbed back to the depot, panting along the dirt road from the outlying plots. No doubt it was the tractor that
had taken the second-shift workers their supper. It seemed shrouded in smoke or
summer haze.

Geula bent down and picked some pebbles out of the dust. Absently she
began to throw them back again, one by one. There were lines of poetry on her
lips, some by the young poets she was fond of, others her own. By the irrigation
pipe she paused, bent down, and drank as though kissing the faucet. But the
faucet was rusty, the pipe was still hot, and the water was tepid and foul. Nevertheless she bent her head and let the water pour over her face and neck and into
her shirt. A sharp taste of rust and wet dust filled her throat. She closed her eyes

and stood in silence. No relief. Perhaps a cup of coffee. But only after the orchard. Must go now.

5

The orchards were heavily laden and fragrant. The branches intertwined, converging above the rows of trunks to form a shadowy dome. Underfoot the irrigated soil retained a hidden dampness. Shadows upon shadows at the foot of those gnarled trunks. Geula picked a plum, sniffed and crushed it. Sticky juice dripped from it. The sight made her feel dizzy. And the smell. She crushed a second plum. She picked another and rubbed it on her cheek till she was spattered with juice. Then, on her knees, she picked up a dry stick and scratched shapes in the dust. Aimless lines and curves. Sharp angles. Domes. A distant bleating invaded the orchard. Dimly she became aware of a sound of bells. She was far away. The nomad stopped behind Geula's back, as silent as a phantom. He dug at the dust with his big toe, and his shadow fell in front of him. But the girl was blinded by a flood of sounds. She saw and heard nothing. For a long time she continued to kneel on the ground and draw shapes in the dust with her twig. The nomad waited patiently in total silence. From time to time he closed his good eye and stared ahead of him with the other, the blind one. Finally he reached out and bestowed a long caress on the air. His obedient shadow moved in the dust. Geula stared, leapt to her feet, and leaned against the nearest tree, letting out a low sound. The nomad let his shoulders drop and put on a faint smile. Geula raised her arm and stabbed the air with her twig. The nomad continued to smile. His gaze dropped to her bare feet. His voice was hushed, and the Hebrew he spoke exuded a rare gentleness:

"What time is it?"

Geula inhaled to her lungs' full capacity. Her features grew sharp, her glance cold. Clearly and dryly she replied:

"It is half past six. Precisely."

The Arab broadened his smile and bowed slightly, as if to acknowledge a great kindness.

"Thank you very much, miss."

His bare toe had dug deep into the damp soil, and the clods of earth crawled at his feet as if there were a startled mole burrowing underneath them.

Geula fastened the top button of her blouse. There were large perspiration stains on her shirt, drawing attention to her armpits. She could smell the sweat on her body, and her nostrils widened. The nomad closed his blind eye and looked up. His good eye blinked. His skin was very dark; it was alive and warm. Creases were etched in his cheeks. He was unlike any man Geula had ever known, and his smell and color and breathing were also strange. His nose was long and narrow, and a shadow of a mustache showed beneath it. His cheeks seemed to be sunk into his mouth cavity. His lips were thin and fine, much finer than her own. But the chin was strong, almost expressing contempt or rebellion.

The man was repulsively handsome, Geula decided to herself. Unconsciously she responded with a mocking half-smile to the nomad's persistent grin. The

Bedouin drew two crumpled cigarettes from a hidden pocket in his belt, laid them on his dark, outstretched palm, and held them out to her as though proffering crumbs to a sparrow. Geula dropped her smile, nodded twice, and accepted one. She ran the cigarette through her fingers, slowly, dreamily, ironing out the creases, straightening it, and only then did she put it to her lips. Quick as lightning, before she realized the purpose of the man's sudden movement, a tiny flame was dancing in front of her. Geula shielded the lighter with her hand even though there was no breeze in the orchard, sucked in the flame, closed her eyes. The nomad lit his own cigarette and bowed politely.

"Thank you very much," he said in his velvety voice.

"Thanks," Geula replied. "Thank you."

"You from the kibbutz?"

Geula nodded.

"Goo-d." An elongated syllable escaped from between his gleaming teeth. "That's goo-d."

The girl eyed his desert robe.

"Aren't you hot in that thing?"

The man gave an embarrassed, guilty smile, as if he had been caught red-handed. He took a slight step backward.

"Heaven forbid, it's not hot. Really not. Why? There's air, there's water. . . ." And he fell silent.

The treetops were already growing darker. A first jackal sniffed the oncoming night and let out a tired howl. The orchard filled with a scurry of small, busy feet. All of a sudden Geula became aware of the throngs of black goats intruding in search of their master. They swirled silently in and out of the fruit trees. Geula pursed her lips and let out a short whistle of surprise.

"What are you doing here, anyway? Stealing?"

The nomad cowered as though a stone had been thrown at him. His hand beat a hollow tattoo on his chest.

"No, not stealing, heaven forbid, really not." He added a lengthy oath in his own language and resumed his silent smile. His blind eye winked nervously. Meanwhile an emaciated goat darted forward and rubbed against his leg. He kicked it away and continued to swear with passion:

"Not steal, truly, by Allah not steal. Forbidden to steal."

"Forbidden in the Bible," Geula replied with a dry, cruel smile. "Forbidden to steal, forbidden to kill, forbidden to covet, and forbidden to commit adultery. The righteous are above suspicion."

The Arab cowered before the onslaught of words and looked down at the ground. Shamefaced. Guilty. His foot continued to kick restlessly at the loose earth. He was trying to ingratiate himself. His blind eye narrowed. Geula was momentarily alarmed: surely it was a wink. The smile left his lips. He spoke in a soft, drawn-out whisper, as though uttering a prayer.

"Beautiful girl, truly very beautiful girl. Me, I got no girl yet. Me still young. No girl yet. Yaaa," he concluded with a guttural yell directed at an impudent goat that had rested its forelegs against a tree trunk and was munching hungrily at the foliage. The animal cast a pensive, skeptical glance at its master, shook its beard, and solemnly resumed its munching.

Without warning, and with amazing agility, the shepherd leapt through the air and seized the beast by the hindquarters, lifted it above his head, let out a terrifying, savage screech, and flung it ruthlessly to the ground. Then he spat and turned to the girl.

"Beast," he apologized. "Beast. What to do. No brains. No manners."

The girl let go of the tree trunk against which she had been resting and leaned toward the nomad. A sweet shudder ran down her back. Her voice was still firm and cool.

"Another cigarette?" she asked. "Have you got another cigarette?"

The Bedouin replied with a look of anguish, almost of despair. He apologized. He explained at length that he had no more cigarettes, not even one, not even a little one. No more. All gone. What a pity. He would gladly, very gladly, have given her one. None left. All gone.

The beaten goat was getting shakily to its feet. Treading circumspectly, it returned to the tree trunk, disingenuously observing its master out of the corner of its eye. The shepherd watched it without moving. The goat reached up, rested its front hoofs on the tree, and calmly continued munching. The Arab picked up a heavy stone and swung his arm wildly. Geula seized his arm and restrained him.

"Leave it. Why. Let it be. It doesn't understand. It's only a beast. No brains, no manners."

The nomad obeyed. In total submission he let the stone drop. Then Geula let go of his arm. Once again the man drew the lighter out of his belt. With thin, pensive fingers he toyed with it. He accidentally lit a small flame, and hastily blew at it. The flame widened slightly, slanted, and died. Nearby a jackal broke into a loud, piercing wail. The rest of the goats, meanwhile, had followed the example of the first and were absorbed in rapid, almost angry munching.

A vague wail came from the nomad encampment away to the south, the dim drum beating time to its languorous call. The dusky men were sitting around their campfires, sending skyward their single-noted song. The night took up the strain and answered with dismal cricket-chirp. Last glimmers of light were dying away in the far west. The orchard stood in darkness. Sounds gathered all around, the wind's whispering, the goats' sniffing, the rustle of ravished leaves. Geula pursed her lips and whistled an old tune. The nomad listened to her with rapt attention, his head cocked to one side in surprise, his mouth hanging slightly open. She glanced at her watch. The hands winked back at her with a malign, phosphorescent glint, but said nothing. Night.

The Arab turned his back on Geula, dropped to his knees, touched his forehead on the ground, and began mumbling fervently.

"You've got no girl yet," Geula broke into his prayer. "You're still too young." Her voice was loud and strange. Her hands were on her hips, her breathing still even. The man stopped praying, turned his dark face toward her, and muttered a phrase in Arabic. He was still crouched on all fours, but his pose suggested a certain suppressed joy.

"You're still young," Geula repeated, "very young. Perhaps twenty. Perhaps thirty. Young. No girl for you. Too young."

The man replied with a very long and solemn remark in his own language. She laughed nervously, her hands embracing her hips.

"What's the matter with you?" she inquired, laughing still. "Why are you talking to me in Arabic all of a sudden? What do you think I am? What do you want here, anyway?"

Again the nomad replied in his own language. Now a note of terror filled his voice. With soft, silent steps he recoiled and withdrew as though from a dying creature. She was breathing heavily now, panting, trembling. A single wild syllable escaped from the shepherd's mouth: a sign between him and his goats. The goats responded and thronged around him, their feet pattering on the carpet of dead leaves like cloth ripping. The crickets fell silent. The goats huddled in the dark, a terrified, quivering mass, and disappeared into the darkness, the shepherd vanishing in their midst.

Afterward, alone and trembling, she watched an airplane passing in the dark sky above the treetops, rumbling dully, its lights blinking alternately with a rhythm as precise as that of the drums: red, green, red, green, red. The night covered over the traces. There was a smell of bonfires on the air and a smell of dust borne on the breeze. Only a slight breeze among the fruit trees. Then panic struck her and her blood froze. Her mouth opened to scream but she did not scream, she started to run and she ran barefoot with all her strength for home and stumbled and rose and ran as though pursued, but only the sawing of the crickets chased after her.

6

She returned to her room and made coffee for all the members of the secretariat, because she remembered her promise to Etkin. Outside the cool of evening had set in, but inside her room the walls were hot and her body was also on fire. Her clothes stuck to her body bcause she had been running, and her armpits disgusted her. The spots on her face were glowing. She stood and counted the number of times the coffee boiled—seven successive boilings, as she had learned to do it from her brother Ehud before he was killed in a reprisal raid in the desert. With pursed lips she counted as the black liquid rose and subsided, rose and subsided, bubbling fiercely as it reached its climax.

That's enough, now. Take clean clothes for the evening. Go to the showers.

What can that Etkin understand about savages. A great socialist. What does he know about Bedouins. A nomad sniffs out weakness from a distance. Give him a kind word, or a smile, and he pounces on you like a wild beast and tries to rape you. It was just as well I ran away from him.

In the showers the drain was clogged and the bench was greasy. Geula put her clean clothes on the stone ledge. I'm not shivering because the water's cold. I'm shivering with disgust. Those black fingers, and how he went straight for my throat. And his teeth. And the goats. Small and skinny like a child, but so strong. It was only by biting and kicking that I managed to escape. Soap my belly and everything, soap it again and again. Yes, let the boys go right away tonight to their camp and smash their black bones because of what they did to me. Now I must get outside.

7

She left the shower and started back toward her room, to pick up the coffee and take it to the secretariat. But on the way she heard crickets and laughter, and she remembered him bent down on all fours, and she was alarmed and stood still in the dark. Suddenly she vomited among the flowering shrubs. And she began to cry. Then her knees gave way. She sat down to rest on the dark earth. She stopped crying. But her teeth continued to chatter, from the cold or from pity. Suddenly she was not in a hurry any more, even the coffee no longer seemed important, and she thought to herself: There's still time. There's still time.

Those planes sweeping the sky tonight were probably on a night-bombing exercise. Repeatedly they roared among the stars, keeping up a constant flashing, red, green, red, green, red. In counterpoint came the singing of the nomads and their drums, a persistent heartbeat in the distance: One, one, two. One, one, two. And silence.

8

From eight-thirty until nearly nine o'clock we waited for Geula. At five to nine Etkin said that he could not imagine what had happened; he could not recall her ever having missed a meeting or been late before; at all events, we must now begin the meeting and turn to the business on the agenda.

He began with a summary of the facts. He gave details of the damage that had apparently been caused by the Bedouins, although there was no formal proof, and enumerated the steps that had been taken on the committee's initiative. The appeal to good will. Calling in the police. Strengthening the guard around the settlement. Tracking dogs. The meeting with the elder of the tribe. He had to admit, Etkin said, that we had now reached an impasse. Nevertheless, he believed that we had to maintain a sense of balance and not give way to extremism, because hatred always gave rise to further hatred. It was essential to break the vicious circle of hostility. He therefore opposed with all the moral force at his disposal the approach—and particularly the intentions—of certain of the younger members. He wished to remind us, by way of conclusion, that the conflict between herdsmen and tillers of the soil was as old as human civilization, as seemed to be evidenced by the story of Cain, who rose up against Abel, his brother. It was fitting, in view of the social gospel we had adopted, that we should put an end to this ancient feud, too, just as we had put an end to other ugly phenomena. It was up to us, and everything depended on our moral strength.

The room was full of tension, even unpleasantness. Rami twice interrupted Etkin and on one occasion went so far as to use the ugly word "rubbish." Etkin took offense, accused the younger members of planning terrorist activities, and said in conclusion, "We're not going to have that sort of thing here."

Geula had not arrived, and that was why there was no one to cool down the temper of the meeting. And no coffee. A heated exchange broke out between me and Rami. Although in age I belonged with the younger men, I did not agree with their proposals. Like Etkin, I was absolutely opposed to answering the nomads with violence—for two reasons, and when I was given permission to speak I mentioned them both. In the first place, nothing really serious had happened so far. A little stealing perhaps, but even that was not certain: every faucet or pair of pliers that a tractor driver left in a field or lost in the garage or took home with him was immediately blamed on the Bedouins. Secondly, there had been no rape or murder. Hereupon Rami broke in excitedly and asked what I was waiting for. Was I perhaps waiting for some small incident of rape that Geula could write poems about and I could make into a short story? I flushed and cast around in my mind for a telling retort.

But Etkin, upset by our rudeness, immediately deprived us both of the right to speak and began to explain his position all over again. He asked us how it would look if the papers reported that a kibbutz had sent out a lynch mob to settle scores with its Arab neighbors. As Etkin uttered the phrase "lynch mob," Rami made a gesture to his young friends that is commonly used by basketball players. At this signal they rose in a body and walked out in disgust, leaving Etkin to lecture to his heart's content to three elderly women and a long-retired member of Parliament.

After a moment's hesitation I rose and followed them. True, I did not share their views, but I, too, had been deprived of the right to speak in an arbitrary and insulting manner.

9

If only Geula had come to the meeting and brought her famous coffee with her, it is possible that tempers might have been soothed. Perhaps, too, her understanding might have achieved some sort of compromise between the conflicting points of view. But the coffee was standing, cold by now, on the table in her room. And Geula herself was lying among the bushes behind the Memorial Hall, watching the lights of the planes and listening to the sounds of the night. How she longed to make her peace and to forgive. Not to hate him and wish him dead. Perhaps to get up and go to him, to find him among the wadis and forgive him and never come back. Even to sing to him. The sharp slivers piercing her skin and drawing blood were the fragments of the bottle she had smashed here with a big stone at the beginning of the evening. And the living thing slithering among the slivers of glass among the clods of earth was a snake, perhaps a venomous snake, perhaps a viper. It stuck out a forked tongue, and its triangular head was cold and erect. Its eyes were dark glass. It could never close them, because it had no eyelids. A thorn in her flesh, perhaps a sliver of glass. She was very tired. And the pain was vague, almost pleasant. A distant ringing in her ears. To sleep now. Wearily, through the thickening film, she watched the gang of youngsters crossing the lawn on their way to the fields and the wadi to even the score with the nomads. We were carrying short, thick sticks. Excitement was dilating our pupils. And the blood was drumming in our temples.

Far away in the darkened orchards stood somber, dust-laden cypresses, swaying to and fro with a gentle, religious fervor. She felt tired, and that was why she did not come to see us off. But her fingers caressed the dust, and her face was very calm and almost beautiful.

Cynthia Ozick

THE SUITCASE

Mr. Hencke, the father of the artist, was a German, an architect, and a traveler—not particularly in that order of importance. He had flown a Fokker for the Kaiser, but there was little of the pilot left in him: he had a rather commonplace military-like snap to his shoulders, especially when he was about to meet someone new. This was not because he had been in the fierce and rigid Air Force, but because he was clandestinely shy. His long grim face, with the mouth running across its lower hem like a slipped thread in a linen sack, was as pitted as a battlefield. Under a magnifying glass his skin would have shown moon-craters. As a boy he had had the smallpox. He lived in a big yellow-brick house in Virginia, and no longer thought of himself as a German. He did not have German thoughts, except in a certain recurring dream, in which he always rode naked on a saddleless horse, holding on to its black moist mane and crying "*Schneller, schneller.*" With the slowness of anguish they glided over a meadow he remembered from childhood, past the millhouse, into a green endlessness hazy with buttercups. Sometimes the horse, which he knew was a stallion, nevertheless seemed to be his wife, who was dead. He was sorry he had named his son after himself—what a name for a boy to have come through Yale with! If he had it to do over again he would have called him John.

"Where am I to put my bag?" he asked Gottfried, who was paying the truckmen and did not hear. His father saw a gray-green flash of money. The truckmen began setting up rows of folding chairs, and he guessed that Gottfried had tipped them to do it. Gottfried had organized everything himself—hired the loft, turned it into a gallery, and invited the famous critic to come and speak at the opening. There was even a sign swinging from the loft-window over West Fifty-Third Street: Nobody's Gallery, it said—a metaphysical joke. Gottfried was not Nobody—the proof was he had married Somebody. Somebody had an unearned income of fifty thousand a year: she was a Chicago blueblood, a beautiful girl, long-necked, black-haired, sweetly and irreproachably mannered, with a voice like a bird. Mr. Hencke had spent two whole dinners in her company before he understood that she had no vocabulary, comprehended nothing, exclaimed at nothing, was bored by nothing. She was totally stupid. Since she had nothing to do—there was a cook, a maid, and a governess—she could scarcely improve, and exhausted her summers in looking diaphanous. Mr. Hencke was retired, but his son could never retire because he had never worked. Catherine liked him to stay at home, jiggle the baby now and then, play records, dance, and occasionally fire the governess, whom she habitually suspected of bad morals. All the same he went uptown to Lexington Avenue every day, where he rented an apartment next door to a Mrs. Siebzehnhauer, called it his studio, and painted timidly. Through the wall he could catch the bleatings of Mrs. Siebzehnhauer's Black Forest cuckoo clock. Sometimes he felt tired, so he put in a bed. In this bed he received his Jewish mistress.

The famous critic had already arrived, and was examining Gottfried's paintings. He poked his wheezing scrutiny so close to each canvas that the fashionable point of his beard dusted the bottom of the frame. Gottfried's paintings tramped solidly around the walls, and the famous critic followed them. He was not an art critic; he was a literary critic, a "cultural" critic—he was going to say something about the Meaning of the Work in Terms of the Zeitgeist. His lecture-fee was extremely high; Mr. Hencke hoped his opinion would be half so high. He himself did not know what to think of Gottfried's labors. His canvases were full of hidden optical tricks and were so bewildering to one's routine retinal expectations that, once the eye had turned away, a whirring occurred in the pupil's depth, and the paintings began to speak through their afterimage. Everything was disconcerting, everything seemed pasted down flat—strips, corners, angles, slivers. Mr. Hencke had a perilous sense that Gottfried had simply cut up the plans for an old office building with extraordinarily tiny scissors. All the paintings were in black and white, but there were drawings in brown pencil. The drawings were mostly teasing dots, like notes on a score. They hurtled up and down. The famous critic studied them with heated seriousness, making notes on a paper napkin he had taken from the refreshment table.

"Where am I to put my bag?" Mr. Hencke asked Catherine, who was just then passing by with her arm slung through the arm of Gottfried's mistress.

"Oh, put it anywhere," said Genevieve at once.

"Papa, stay with us this time. You can have the big room upstairs," Catherine said, mustering all her confident politeness.

"I have a reservation at such a very nice hotel," said Mr. Hencke.

"Nothing could be nicer than the big room upstairs. I've just had the curtains changed. Papa, they're all yellow now," Catherine said with her yielding inescapable smile, and through her father-in-law's conventionally gossamer soul, in which he believed as thoroughly as any peasant, there slipped the spider-thread flick of one hair of the horse's mane, as if drawn across his burlap cheek: not for nothing was he the father of an artist, he was susceptible to yellow, he still remembered the yellow buttercups on the slope below the millhouse.

"Kitty, you're hopeless," said Genevieve. "How can you think of shutting up a genuine bachelor at the top of your stuffy old house?"

"Not bachelor, widower," said Mr. Hencke. "Not exactly the same thing."

"The same in the end," said Genevieve. "You can't let them stuff you up, you have to be free to come and go and have people in and out if you want to."

"It's a nice house. It's not stuffy, it's very airy. You can even smell the river. It's an elegant house on an elegant street," Catherine protested.

"A very fine house," Mr. Hencke agreed, though he secretly despised New York brownstone. "Only I feel Gottfried is not comfortable when I am in it. So for family peace I prefer the hotel."

"Papa, Gottfried promised not to have a fight this time."

"What in the world do they find to fight about?" Genevieve asked.

"Papa thinks Gottfried should have a job. It isn't *necessary*," Catherine said.

"It isn't necessary for Rockefeller either," Mr. Hencke said. "You don't see any of the Rockefellers idle. Every Rockefeller has a job."

"Oh, you Lutherans," Genevieve said. "You awful Lutherans and your awful Protestant Work Ethic."

"Papa, Gottfried's *never* idle. You don't know. You just don't know. He goes to his studio every day."

"And sleeps on the bed."

"My goodness, papa, you don't think Gottfried would be having this whole huge show if he never did any *work*, do you? He's a real worker, papa, he's an artist, so *what* if he has a bed up there."

"Now, now," Genevieve said, "that isn't fair, all the Rockefellers have beds too, Kitty's right."

"I wish you would tell me where to put my bag," Mr. Hencke said.

"Put it over there," Genevieve suggested. "With my things. See that chair behind the bar—where the barman's standing—no, there, that man putting on a white jacket—I left my pocketbook on it, under my coat. See it, it's the coat with all that black-and-white geometry all over it? Someone's liable to think it's one of Gottfried's things and buy it for nine hundred dollars," Genevieve said, and Catherine laughed like a sparrow. "You can lay your suitcase right on top of my nine-hundred-dollar coat, it won't be in the way. God, what a mob already."

"We sent programs to *every*body," Catherine said.

"Don't think they're coming completely for Gottfried," Mr. Hencke said.

"Papa, what do you mean?"

"He means they're coming to hear Creighton MacDougal. Look, there's that whole bunch—not that way, over there, near the stairs—from *Partisan Review*. I can always tell *Partisan Review* people, they have faces like a mackerel after it's been caught, with the hook still in its mouth."

"They might be dealers," Catherine said hopefully. "Or museum people."

"They're MacDougal people. Him and his notes, get a load of that! I can hardly wait to hear him explain how Gottfried represents the existential revolt against Freud."

"Gottfried put in something about Freud in the program. Did you see the program yet, papa? He did a sort of preface for it. It's not really *writing*, it's just quotations. One of them's Freud, I think."

"Not Freud, dear, Jung," Genevieve said.

"Well, I knew it was some famous Jewish psychiatrist anyway," Catherine said. "Come on, Gen, let's go get papa a program."

"I'll get one, don't trouble yourself," Mr. Hencke said. "First I'll put away my bag."

"Jung isn't a Jew," Genevieve said.

"Isn't? Don't you mean wasn't? Isn't he dead?"

"He isn't a Jew," Genevieve said. "That's why he went on staying alive."

"I thought he was dead."

"Everybody dies," Mr. Hencke said, looking into the crowd. It resembled a zoo crowd: it had taken the form of a thick ragged rope and was wandering slowly past the long even array of Gottfried's paintings, peering into each one as though it were a cage containing some unlikely beast.

"Like a concentration camp," Genevieve said. "Everybody staring through the barbed wire hoping for rescue and knowing it's no use. That's what they look like."

Catherine said, "I certainly hope some of them are dealers."

"You don't want me to put my bag *on* your overcoat, Genevieve," Mr. Hencke said. "I must not crush your things. I'll put the bag just there behind the chair, that will be best."

"You know what Gottfried's stuff reminds me of?" Genevieve said.

Mr. Hencke perceived that she was provoking him. Her earlier reference to why he chose a hotel over his son's house—what she had said about his having people in and out—clearly meant prostitutes. He was stupendously offended. He never frequented prostitutes, though he knew Gottfried sometimes did. But Gottfried was still a young man—in America, curiously, to be past thirty-seven, and even a little bald in the back, like Gottfried, hardly interfered with the intention to go on being young. Gottfried, then, was not only a very young man, but gave every sign of continuing that way for years and years, while poor Catherine, though socially and financially Somebody, was surely—at sex—a Nobody. Her little waist was undoubtedly charming, her stretched-forward neck (perhaps she was nearsighted and didn't realize it?) was fragrant with hygiene. Her whole body was exceptionally mannerly, even the puppet-motion of her immaculate thighs under her white dress: so Gottfried sometimes went to prostitutes and sometimes—on grand occasions, like the opening of Nobody's Gallery—Genevieve came from whatever city it was in the midwest—Cincinnati, or Boise, or Columbus: maybe Detroit.

"Shredded swastikas, that's what," Genevieve announced. "Every single damn thing he does. All that terrible precision. Every last one a pot of shredded swastikas, you see that?"

He knew what she meant him to see: she scorned Germans, she thought him a Nazi sympathizer even now, an anti-Semite, an Eichmann. She was the sort who, twenty years after Hitler's war, would not buy a Volkswagen. She was full of detestable moral gestures, and against what? Who could be blamed for History? It did not take a philosopher (though he himself inclined toward Schopenhauer) to see that History was a Force-in-Itself, like Evolution. There he was, comfortable in America, only a little sugar rationed, and buying War Bonds like every other citizen, while his sister, an innocent woman, an intellectual, a loyal lover of Heine who could recite by heart *Der Apollogott* and *Zwei Ritter* and

König David and ten or twelve others, lost her home and a daughter of eleven in an R.A.F. raid on Köln. Margaretchen had moved from Frankfurt to Köln after her marriage to a well-educated shampoo manufacturer. A horrible tragedy. Even the great Cathedral had not been spared.

"I was *sure* it was Freud Gottfried used for the quotation thing," Catherine demurred.

"Gottfried would never quote Freud, Kitty, it would only embarrass him. You know what Freud said? 'An abstinent artist is scarcely conceivable'—he meant sex, dear, not drink."

"Gottfried practically never drinks."

"That's because he's a mystic and a romantic, isn't he stupid? Kitty, you really ought to do something to de-sober Gottfried, it would do his work so much good. A little less Apollo, a little more Dionysus."

Catherine tittered exactly as if she had seen the point of some invisible joke: but then she noticed that the truckmen had forgotten to set up the speaker's table, so she excused herself very politely, gaping out at her father-in-law her diligently attentive smile with such earnestness and breeding that his intestines publicly croaked. The father of the artist hated his daughter-in-law, and could not bear to share a roof with her even for a single night; her conversation depressed him and gave him evil sweated dreams: sometimes he dreamt he was in his sister's city, and the bomb exploded out of his own belly, and there rolled past him, as on a turntable in the brutalized nave, his little niece laid out dead, covered only by her yellow hair. Across the room Catherine was supervising the placing of the lectern: he heard it scrape through the increasing voices.

Meanwhile Genevieve still pursued. "Mr. Hencke, you know perfectly well that Jung played footsie with the Nazis. It's public knowledge. He let all the Jewish doctors get thrown out of the psychological society after the Nazis took it over, and he stayed president all that while, and he never said a word against any of it. Then they were all murdered."

"*Gnädige Frau*," he said—and dropped his suitcase to the floor in a kind of fright. Since his wife died he had not once spoken a syllable of German, and now to have such a strangeness, such a familiarity, pimple out on his tongue with a design of its own—and with what terrifying uselessness, a phrase out of something sublimely old-fashioned, a stiff staid long-ago play, *Minna von Barnhelm* perhaps, a phrase he had never said in his whole life—"What do you want from me?" he appealed. "I'm a man of sixty-eight. In sixty-eight years what have I done? I have harmed no one. I have built towers. Towers! No more. I have never destroyed."

He raised his suitcase—it was as heavy as some icon—and walked through the chatter to the refreshment table and set it down behind the chair thickened and duplicated by the pattern of Genevieve's coat. The barman handed him a glass. He received it and avoided the walls, no space of which was unmarked by his son's Aztec emissions. He took a seat in a middle row and waited for the speaker to come to the lectern. At his feet lay a discarded leaflet. It was the program. He saw that the topic of the lecture would be "In His Eye's Mind: Hencke and the

New Cubism." Then he skipped a page backwards and under the title "Culled by Hencke" he read a trio of excerpts:

"Schuppanzigh, do you think I write my quartets for you and your puling fiddle?" *—Beethoven, to the violinist who wailed that the A-minor quartet was unplayable.*

"It is better to ruin a work and make it useless for the world than not to go the limit at every point." *—Thos. Mann.*

"For the people gay pictures, for the cognoscenti, the mystery behind." *—Goethe.*

—All three items had the touch of Genevieve. He looked for the quotation from Jung and found there was none. To Catherine, Beethoven and Freud were just the same, burdens indistinguishable and unextinguishable both. Undoubtedly Genevieve had told her that Schuppanzigh was another Jewish psychiatrist persecuted by the Nazis and that Goethe was a notorious Gauleiter. As for that idiot Gottfried, he read the gallery notes in the *Times*, nothing more, and had a subscription to *Art News*—he was two parts Catherine's money to one part Genevieve's brain, and too cowardly altogether to stir the mixture. Catherine, like all foolish heroines, believed that Genevieve (Smith '48, *summa cum laude*, Phi Beta Kappa) was devoted to her (Miss Jewett's Classes '59, graduated 32 in a class of 36) out of sentiment and enthusiasm. "Genevieve loves New York, she can't keep away from it" was one of Catherine's sayings: alas, she uttered it like an epigram. They had met at Myra Jacobson's. Myra Jacobson (also Smith '48) was a dealer, one of the very best—she *made* reputations, it was said; last year (for instance) she made Julius Feldstein the actionist—and Catherine offered her a certain sum to take on Gottfried, but she refused. "You must wait till he's *ripe*," she told Catherine, who cried and cried until Genevieve appeared like Polonius from behind a Jackson Pollock and gave her an orange handkerchief to blow with. "Now, now," Genevieve said, "don't bawl about it, let me go look at him, you can't tell if he's ripe unless you squeeze." Genevieve was escorted to Gottfried's studio next door to Mrs. Siebzehnhauer, beheld the bed, beheld Gottfried, and squeezed. She pressed hard. He was not ripe. He was still a Nobody.

Hence Nobody's Gallery: Genevieve's invention. It was, of course, to mock Gottfried, who knew he was being mocked, and for spite agreed. Gottfried, like most cowards, had a dim cunning. But Catherine was infinitely grateful: a show was a show. Creighton MacDougal came terribly dear, but you would expect that of a man with a beard—he looked, Catherine said in another epigram, like God.

Applause.

God stood at the lectern, drew a glass of water from an aluminum spigot, sucked up the superfluous drops through the top part of his beard (the part that without the beard would have been a mustache), crackled an esophagus lined with phlegm, and began to talk about Melville's White Whale. For ten minutes Mr. Hencke was piously certain that the great critic was giving last week's lecture. Then he heard his son's name. "The art of Fulfillment," said the critic. "Here, at last, is no Yearning. No alabaster tail-fin wiggles beckoningly on the horizon. There is no horizon. Perspective is annihilated. The completion-complex of the schoolroom and/or the madhouse is master at last. Imagine a teacher with his back to the class, erasing the blackboard. He erases and erases. Finally all is clear black once again—except for a scrap of the foot of a single letter, the letter 'J'—'J,' ladies and gentlemen, standing for Justice, or for Jesus—one scrap of the foot, then, of this half-remaining letter 'J,' which the sweep of the eraser has passed by and left unobliterated. At this point it is the art of Gottfried Hencke I am illustrating precisely. The art of Gottfried Hencke rises from its seat, approaches the blackboard, and with a singular motion, a swift, small, and excruciatingly exact motion, wets its pinkie and smears away the foot of the 'J' forever. That, ladies and gentlemen, is the meaning of the art of Gottfried Hencke. It is an art not of hunger, not of frustration, but of satiation. An art, so to speak, for fat men."

Further applause: this time tentative, as by vulgarians who mistake the close of the first movement for the end of the symphony.

The aluminum spigot squeals. God thirsts. The audience observes the capillary action of facial hair.

"Ladies and gentlemen," continued the critic, "I too am a fat man. I cleverly mask not less than two chins, not more than three. Yet I was not always thus. Imagine me at seventeen, lean, bold, arrogant, aristocratic. Imagine snow. I run through the snow. Whiteness. The whiteness, ladies and gentlemen, of Melville's very Whale, with which I began my brief causerie. All men begin at the crest of purity and hope. Now consider me at twenty-four. I have just flunked out of medical school. Ladies and gentlemen, it was my wish to heal. To heal, my beauties. Consider my tears. I weep in my humiliation before the dean. I beg for another chance. 'No, my son,' says the dean—how kind he is! how good! and his wife is a cripple in a wheelchair—'you will have a long hard row to hoe. Give it up.' Now for thirty years I have tried to heal myself. Allegories, ladies, beauties; allegories, you darling gentlemen: trust me to serve you fables, parables, the best of their kind in season. The art of Gottfried Hencke is an intact art. Was there ever a wound in it? It is healed. It has healed itself, we all heal ourselves, thank you, thank you."

God waved fervently through the exalted shimmer of the final applause.

With inscrutable correctness, as though mediating a bargain in a bazaar, Catherine introduced her father-in-law to Creighton MacDougal. Mr. Hencke was moved. He felt stirred to hope for his son, and for his son's son, who had so far struck him as practically an imbecile. He undertook to explain to the critic about the old planes. "No, no," he said, leaning into a pair of jelly-red eyes, "the Fokker was the fighter as everyone knows, but the Hansa-und-Brandenburger did everything—strafed, bombed, a little aerial fighting, now and then a little reconnaissance over the water to look for your ships. Everything. Very versatile, very reliable. At the end we used a lot of them. In the beginning we didn't even have the Fokker. All we had was the Rumpler-Taube, very beautiful. She was called that because she resembled a lovely great dove. Maybe you know her from the old movies. My daughter-in-law claims she saw one once in a movie at the Museum of Modern Art. I have a little fear of my daughter-in-law—spoils the stock, bad mental genes—a grandson two years old, very pretty boy, nothing mental. You won't mention this, yes? I say it in private. I have a liking for your face. You show a little of my father—the old school, as you say, very strict. Boys nowadays don't stand for that. We had also very strict teachers with the planes. All professors. They knew everything about an engine. The best teachers they gave us. I suppose in an emergency I could still fly something like a Piper Cub. We had the double wing in those days. The biplane, no closed cockpits. We had leather helmets. When it rained it was like needles on the eyeballs. We could go only a thousand feet—the height of the Empire State Building, yes? In the core of a cloud you are quite unaware it's a cloud, to you it's simply fog. Those helmets! In the rain they smelled like a slaughterhouse."

An intense young lady who had just written a book review took the critic away from him: he wiped his mouth. A long thread of detached mucus membrane lifted from its right corner. He snuffed up the odor of his own breath. It confessed that his stomach was not well. On the refreshment table there was a bowl of apples. He thought how one of these would clean the stink from his teeth. The bowl stood next to a platter of cheese sandwiches at the end of the table, near the chair with Genevieve's coat on it. But the coat was not on the chair. It was on Genevieve. She was whispering to Gottfried over the apples. He saw that she intended to leave before Gottfried, to fool Catherine. It was an assignation.

"Gottfried!" he called.

His son came.

"You're not going home?"

"Not for hours, papa. There's a little band coming in. Catherine thought we ought to have some dancing."

"I mean afterward. Afterward where are you going?"

"Home. Home, papa, where else at that hour? Catherine says you won't come with us. She says you're insisting on a hotel again."

"You're not going to the studio first?"

"Tonight, you mean?"

"After the band. After the band you're going to the studio with the bed in it?"

"I can't possibly do any work tonight, papa. Not after all this. Listen, what did you think of MacDougal?"

"The man misunderstands you entirely," Mr. Hencke said. "I talked to him privately, you observed that?"

"No," Gottfried said.

"I want you to take me to your studio," Mr. Hencke said.

"That's a change," Gottfried said. "You never want to see my things."

"You have something worth showing?"

"Oh, for God's sake," Gottfried said. "All ye who seek my monument, look around you. Don't you like a single thing on the wall?"

"I want to see what you keep in your studio."

"Well, I've got a new thing going over there," Gottfried said. "If you're interested."

"A new thing?"

"It's only one-quarter finished. The whole right bottom corner. Seems I've finally worked up the courage to try something in color. Cerulean blue compressed into a series of interlocked ovals and rectangles. Like sky enclosed in the nucleus of the atom. Actually I'm pretty hopeful about it."

"Tell me, Gottfried, who said that?" his father asked.

"Who said what?"

"The sky in the atom. Genevieve? Genevieve's words, hah? A brilliant lady. Very metaphorical. I want to see this sky. Explain to Genevieve that I am always glad to look at any evidence of my son's courage."

"All right, papa, don't get rough. I'll call for you in the morning if you want. It's so damn perverse of you not to come to the house."

"No, no, I have no interest in your house. I abominate high stoops—a barbarism. Tonight I want to see your studio."

"Tonight?"

"After the band."

"That's absurd, papa. We'll all be dead tired later on."

"Good, then we will take advantage of the convenience of the bed."

"Papa, don't get rough. I mean that. Don't get rough with me *now*, you hear?"

"When I myself was a very young man of thirty-seven I addressed my father with respect."

"God damn you, you want to break it up. You really want to break it up. Finally you want to. Why? You kept out of it long enough, a whole year, now all of a sudden it bothers you."

"A year and a half," his father said. "And still you like to call it a new thing. A new thing you call it."

"Do you *need* to break it up? You have to? What's it to you?"

"Poor, poor Catherine," his father murmured.

"Poor, poor Catherine," Genevieve said, coming up behind Gottfried. She was devouring a cheese sandwich, and bits of bread mottled her mouth and sprinkled down on the breast of her coat. Mr. Hencke confronted its design: a series of interlocked ovals and rectangles, dark and light. Looked at one way, they presented a deep tubular corridor, infinitely empty, like two mirrors facing one another. A shift of the mind swelled them into a solid, endlessly bulging, endlessly self-creating squarish sausage.

"He's trying to break it up," Gottfried told her.

"Foolish, foolish boy," said Genevieve, sticking out a cheesey tongue at the father of the artist.

"Are you listening?" said Gottfried.

"Yes, dear. I didn't know the dear knew anything."

"You liar. Big innocent wide-eyes. I told you I told him. I had to tell him because he guessed."

"I am Gottfried's confidant," Mr. Hencke said.

"Mine too," said Genevieve, and embraced the father of the artist. The very slight fragrance of the pumpernickel crumbs on the underpart of her chin—a chin just, just beginning to slacken: a frail lip-like turn of skin pouting beneath it—made a flowery gash in his vision. Some inward gate opened. He remembered still another field, this one furry with kümmel, a hairy yellow shoulder of a field shrugging at the wind. A smear of joy worsened his stomach: at home one used to take caraway for a carminative. "Childe Roland to the Dark Tower came," Genevieve recited, "and broke it up. Gottfried, I vouch for your father. He has never destroyed."

Mr. Hencke marveled.

"I am a deceiver," Genevieve cried, "I too need a confidant, I need one more than Gottfried. Gottfried's papa, let me tell you about my extraordinary life in Indianapolis, Indiana. My husband is an intelligent and prospering Certified Public Accountant. His name will not surprise: Lewin. A memorable name. Kagan would also be a memorable name, so too Rabinowitz or Robbins, but *his* name is Lewin. A model to youth. Contributor to many charities. Vice-president of the temple. Now let me tell you about our four daughters, all under twelve years. One is too young for school. One is only in kindergarten. But the two older ones! Nora. Bonnie. At the top of their grades and already reading *Tom Sawyer*, *Little Women*, and the *Encyclopaedia Britannica*. Every month they produce a family newspaper of one page on an old Smith-Corona in the basement of our Dutch Colonial house in Indianapolis, Indiana. They call it *The Mezuzzah Bulletin*—the idea being that they tack it up on the doorpost. They all four have the Jewish brain."

"Everyone's *looking* at you," Gottfried said angrily.

"That's because I'm wrapped in one of your satiated paintings. Mr. Hencke, did you know that some of the most avant-garde expressionism comes from the Seventh Avenue silkscreen people? But I want to confide some more. Gottfried's papa, some more confidences. First let me describe myself. Tall. Never wear low heels. Plump-armed. Soft-thighed. Perfectly splendid young woman. Nose thin and delicate, like a Communion wafer. Impression of being both sleek and amiable. Large, healthy, indestructible teeth. Half a dozen gold inlays, paid for by Lewin, the Certified Public Accountant. Excellent husband. Now your turn, Mr. Hencke. I've undressed myself for you. It's your turn, that's only fair. Your brother-in-law the shampoo manufacturer that Kitty once mentioned—the one who lives in Cologne, whose house was bombed out?"

Mr. Hencke begged, "What do you want from me? Why do you talk about yourself that way?"

"Tell about him. Confide in me the nature of the shampoo. What did he make it out of? Not now. I mean during the war. Not the war you flew in, the war after that. He was making shampoo in Cologne all the while you were an American patriot architect, raising towers, never destroying. Please discuss your brother-in-law's shampoo. What were its secret ingredients? Whose human fat? What Jewish lard?"

"Genevieve, shut up. Shut up, will you please? Leave my father alone."

"Poor, poor Catherine," Genevieve said. "I just fixed everything up with her. I told her I was going to make the midnight plane home and you had this inspiration and had to stay up all night with it at the studio."

"Just shut up, all right?"

"All right, dear. I'll see you when Mrs. Siebzehnhauer's cuckoo caws two."

"Skip it. Not tonight."

"Who says not? Gottfried's papa?"

"I have nothing against you, believe me," Mr. Hencke said. "I admire you very much, Genevieve. I have absolutely no animus."

"What a pity," Said Genevieve, "every man should have a nice little animus."

"My God, Genevieve, leave him alone."

"Goodbye. I'm going back to Nora Lewin, Bonnie Lewin, Andrea Lewin, Celeste Lewin and Edward K. Lewin, all of Indianapolis, Indiana. First I have to say goodbye to poor, poor Catherine. Goodbye, Mr. Hencke. Don't worry about yourself. As for me, I am sleek and amiable. My gold inlays click like castanets manufactured in Franco Spain. My breasts are like twin pomegranates. Like twin white doves coming down from Mount Gilead, O.K.?" She kissed the father of the artist. The hairy kümmel valley was photographed by flash bulb on the flank of his pancreas. "Your cheek is like barbed wire. Your cheek has the ruts left by General Rommel's tanks."

The artist and his father watched her go from them, picking at crumbs.

"A superior woman," Mr. Hencke said. He felt a remarkable control. He felt as though he had received a command and disobeyed it. "A superior race, I've always thought that. Imaginative. They say Corbusier is a secret Jew, descended from Marranos. A beautiful complexion, beautiful eyelashes. These women have compulsions. When they turn up a blonde type you can almost take them for our own."

His son said nothing.

"Do you enjoy her, Gottfried?"

His son said nothing.

"I would guess you enjoy her, yes? Imaginative. I would guess enjoyment. Superconsciousness."

Still his son held on. Mr. Hencke passionately awaited the confessional tears. He conjured them. They did not descend.

He said finally, "Does she boss you much?"

"Never," Gottfried said. "Never, never. I think you broke it up, papa. God damn you to hell, papa."

His arms clutched across his back, the father of the artist observed the diminishing spoor of visitors. In her bride's dress Catherine glimmered at the top of the stairwell, speaking elegant goodbyes learned at Miss Jewett's. Creighton MacDougal winked and saluted and snapped his heels like a Junker officer. A wonderful mimicry spiraled out of his head: the buzz of a biplane. Simultaneously a saxophone opened fire.

"Dance with me, papa!" said Catherine. "—Oh, no, you're just so out-of-date. Nowadays you're not supposed to even *touch*." She taught him how; he had never seen her so clever. "Mr. MacDougal had to leave, but you know what he said? He said you were a fine person. He said"—her laugh broke like a dish—"you were a natural hermit, and if you ever decided to put up a pillar to sit on top of, it would last a thousand years."

Mr. Hencke copied her but did not touch. "Have there been sales?"

"Not yet, but after all it's only the *opening*. And even if there aren't any that's not the point. It's just so Gottfried can feel encouraged. You have to be noticed in this world, you know that, papa? Otherwise you don't feel you really exist.

You just don't understand about Gottfried. —No, papa, nobody *ever* dips at the end any more. It's so out-of-date to do that. I mean Gottfried works every minute he can. You make him feel awful when you talk the way you did before about Rockefeller. My goodness, papa, he's even going to work when we get through here, he's going over to the studio right afterward."

"I think not. I think he will be far too tired," said the father of the artist.

"But he *told* me he wanted to work tonight. He really meant it, papa. It's not as if I'm the only one he said it to, he's been saying it to everyone—" A scream leaped out of the bowl of apples. "Oh, look, what's the matter with Genevieve?" Catherine, inquisitive as a child, ran.

He delayed and envisioned wounds. In his heart she bled, she bled. He stepped away. He kept back. He listened to her voice—such a coarse voice. The voice or the bass fiddle? A Biblical yell, as by the waters of Babylon. Always horrible tragedy for the innocent. She was not innocent. He suspected what wounds. The saxophone machine-gunned him in the small intestine.

Catherine twitched back. "Someone's stolen Genevieve's pocketbook! She had it lying just like that on a chair, only it was all covered up with her coat, and there was this hundred dollars in it, and her driver's license, and the plane ticket, and a million other things like that. With all these *people*, you wouldn't think there'd be a thief—"

He was bewildered. "Hurt? She's hurt?"

"Well no, she didn't even *leave* yet, she was just starting to go. It's not as if somebody mugged her in the street or held her up or anything. I mean they just *took* it. It was just lying there, so they took it. Can you imagine anybody acting like that?" A vividness disrupted but lit her; his daughter-in-law exulted. She assumed the sheen her wealth deserved: he descried in her at the moment of adventure those canny cattle-buccaneers who had sired her temperament. Booty-getting cannot be bred out: she was just then a true heiress, and the father of the artist was for the first time nearly proud his son had chosen her. What Gottfried had seen, he now saw. Crime rejoiced her, crime loosened the puppet-strings of her terrifying civility. Crime made her intelligent. He himself knew what it was to be one whom crisis exalts. He had once landed with half a wing shot off: his hero's wound afterward seemed sweeter to him than any crisis of lovemaking he was ever to endure.

"Gottfried thinks it must have been one of the truckmen," Catherine said. Ah, she hugged herself.

"Absolutely it was the truckmen," Mr. Hencke assented. "There was no one else here like that."

"The barman?"

"The barman perhaps," Mr. Hencke once again agreed.

"But it couldn't be the barman, the barman's still *here*. If it was the barman we could catch him red-handed. A thief always disappears as fast as he can."

"Then the truckmen," Mr. Hencke said. "The truckmen without question."

"All right, but you know what *I* think, papa?"

"No."

Catherine sucked her lip until it gleamed. "Well, the way that weird man *argued* about his fee when we hired him—I guess you don't say hired for a critic,

CYNTHIA OZICK

but I don't know what else we did if we *didn't* hire him—anyhow he didn't think he was getting enough, especially since that little FM station W-K-Some-thing-Something sent over a couple of men to pick up his speech on a tape re-corder, and he said he doesn't even get royalties from it, so what *I* think"—her beautiful shivery laugh broke and broke, if no longer like a plate then like surf—"is Mr. MacDougal decided to raise his own fee, hook or crook!"

"It was the truckmen," Mr. Hencke said with the delicacy of finality.

"I'm just *fooling.* You always agree with Gottfried, papa. I mean on funda-mentals. I don't know why you argue about everything else."

"Genevieve must be given some money to go home with."

"She's terrifically upset, did you see her? You wouldn't think she could get so upset. She says her husband always tells her not to be highstrung and to carry checks—"

"Tell Gottfried to give her some money," Mr. Hencke said.

"Oh, papa, *you* tell him. If it's something important he never pays attention to any of my ideas."

He looked for Gottfried: there he was, quarreling with the barman, who said he had seen no one and knew nothing.

Genevieve stood chewing on a glove.

"Don't fight with him, Gottfried, it's perfectly irretrievable. It's so silly, and really it's my own stupid fault. Ed'll kill me, not for the money but like they say for the principle. *You* know. He thinks I'm a terrible slob that way, he's a great one for believing in foreseeable actions. I lost the Buick last year, and the year before I lost the baby in the parking lot. God, how I hate people of principle. All the persecutors of the world have been people of principle."

"Genevieve invokes History always," Mr. Hencke said.

She unexpectedly ignored this; at once he regretted it. She said hoarsely, "I'm simply resigned. I'll never get it back. O.K., O.K., so it's irretrievable."

"That is true of so much in life," Mr. Hencke said.

Gottfried darkly turned. "Papa, what do you want?"

The barman escaped.

"I want you to give Genevieve money."

"Money?"

"Under the circumstances." The father of the artist tenderly uncovered his teeth.

Gottfried repeated: "Money?"

"For Genevieve. It's the least you can do, Gottfried."

"I don't give Genevieve money, papa."

He saw the damp creases under his son's nose. Even in America youth is not eternal.

"Ah, but you ought to, Gottfried. Nothing comes free in this life." He felt obscurely delighted by Gottfried's pale charged mouth. His son resembled a pretty little spotted horse spitting disappointing hay. "Airplane rides to Indian-apolis, Indiana, don't come free in this life," he finished in a brief mist of his own laughter.

"Well, look at that," Genevieve said. "Gottfried's papa wants to get rid of me. You were perfectly right about that, Gottfried, he wants to get rid of me."

"No, no," Mr. Hencke protested. "Only of the band. What ugly music. Saxophones frighten. Such a loud lonely forest sound. Why don't you dismiss them, Gottfried? There are no guests left, I think."

"Democracy," Genevieve divulged: Catherine was dancing violently with the barman.

"I see how it is done," Mr. Hencke said. "They move but don't touch. Touching is no longer the fashion. Catherine thinks she is dancing with the thief, yes? Gottfried, give Genevieve some money."

"Catherine can do it," Gottfried muttered; he swam toward his wife as through some thick preventing element.

"He is nearly inaudible when he feels he has been insulted," his father noted. "Did he say he would?"

"It was going to be over pretty soon anyway. How I hate a brouhaha," Genevieve said, staring after Gottfried.

"What an amusing word. After so many years I don't know all the words. Ah, a brilliant lady like yourself, you're bored with my plain-hearted son."

"I'm bored with Kitty. I'm bored with New York."

"And with art. With art too?" He paused desperately. "My son would not say whether it has been a success. He would not say whether there has been enjoyment."

"I wish," Genevieve said, "I just hadn't lost that damn pocketbook. The Certified Public Accountant gave me his last warning. It's the guillotine next."

"Please, please," Mr. Hencke said, "thieves and pickpockets occur everywhere."

"I don't *care* about the money," Genevieve said sourly.

"Dear lady, you care about dignity."

"Yes," Genevieve said, "that's it."

"Sit down," Mr. Hencke said, and scratched toward her the guilty chair. On this chair the stolen pocketbook had lain, and over it Genevieve's patterned coat. The chair was empty. Listlessly Genevieve gathered up the hem of her coat and sat down.

"My bag," Mr. Hencke said, picking it up and putting it at her feet.

"Well, I guess you're lucky they didn't take that too."

"Dignity," Mr. Hencke said. "Dignity before everything. I subscribe to that. Persons tend to assume things about other persons. For example, my son believes I came to New York entirely for this occasion—you understand—to see the gallery, to see the work. For the cognoscenti the mystery behind, yes? In reality tomorrow morning I will be early on a ship. I'm going for a beautiful trip, you know."

"To Germany?" But she seemed detached. She watched the stairwell swallow the musicians. Catherine was using Gottfried's back for a desk, writing something. Her pen wobbled like a plunged and nervous dagger.

"Not Germany, Sweden. I admire Scandinavia. Exquisite fogs. The green of the farmland there. Now only Scandinavia is the way I remember Germany from boyhood. Germany isn't the same. All factories, chimneys."

"Don't speak to me about German chimneys," Genevieve said. "I know what kind of smoke came out of those damn German chimneys."

His eyes wept, his throat wept, she was not detached, she was merciless. "I didn't have the heart to tell Gottfried I'm traveling again. Don't tell him, hah? Let him think I came especially. You understand, hah, Genevieve? To see his things, let him think that, not just passing on the way to travel somewhere else. I have the one bag only to mislead. I confess it, purposely to mislead. In my hotel room already there are four other bags."

"I bet you say Sweden to mislead. I bet you're going to Germany, why shouldn't you? I don't say there's anything wrong with it, why shouldn't you go to Germany?"

"Not Germany, Sweden. The Swedes were innocent in the war, they saved so many Jews. I swear it, not Germany. It was the truckmen, I swear it."

"I suppose it *was* one of the truckmen," Genevieve said languidly.

"The most logical ones were the truckmen. I swear it. Look, look, Genevieve, I'll show you," he said, "just look—" He turned the little key and threw open his suitcase with so much wild vigor that it quivered on its hinges. "Now just look, look through everything, nothing here but my own, here are my shirts, not all, I have so many more in my other bags in the hotel, here I have mostly, forgive me, my new underwear. Only socks, see? Socks, socks, shorts, shorts, shorts, all new, I like to travel with everything new and clean, undershirt, undershirt, shaving cream, razor, deodorant, more underwear, toothpaste, you see this, Genevieve? I swear it must have been one of the truckmen, that's only logical. Please, I swear it. Genevieve," Mr. Hencke said, forcing his fingers rigidly through the depth of his new undershorts, "see for yourself—"

Catherine in her white dress (the wife of the artist was seen in a white dress) jerked into view: she hung like a marionette in the margins of his eye's theater. "Really, Genevieve, Gottfried's so funny sometimes, he has plenty of money in his wallet, but he made me write you this check, he absolutely insisted. Good grief, he's got checks of his own. Can you still make the twelve o'clock plane, Gen?—because look, if you can't, you can easily stay overnight with us, why don't you, that nice room's all ready and papa isn't staying—"

"Oh, no," Genevieve said, jumping up, "I'll never stay overnight!"

She seized the check and ran down the long stairs. The interlocked series of ovals and rectangles scorched into gray. In his tenuously barbule soul, for which he had ancestral certitude, the father of the artist burned in the foam of so much kümmel, so many buttercups, so much lustrous yellow, and the horse's mane so confusing in his eyes like a grid, and why does the horse not go faster, faster?

"My goodness," Catherine said, "why've you got your suitcase open and everything rumpled up like that? Papa, did they steal from you too?" she gave out in her politest, most cultivated, most ventriloquist tone. "Tonight what criminals we've harbored unawares!"—it sounded exactly like a phrase of Genevieve's.

Grace Paley

. . . .

THE CONTEST

Up early or late, it never matters, the day gets away from me. Summer or winter, the shade of trees or their hard shadow, I never get into my Rice Krispies till noon.

I am ambitious, but it's a long-range thing with me. I have my confidential sights on a star, but there's half a lifetime to get to it. Meanwhile I keep my eyes open and am well dressed.

I told the examining psychiatrist for the Army: yes, I like girls. And I do. Not my sister—a pimp's dream. But girls, slim and tender or really stacked, dark brown at their centers, smeared by time. Not my mother, who should've stayed in Freud. I *have* got a sense of humor.

My last girl was Jewish, which is often a warm kind of girl, concerned about food intake and employability. They don't like you to work too hard, I understand, until you're hooked and then, you bastard, sweat!

A medium girl, size twelve, a clay pot with handles—she could be grasped. I met her in the rain outside some cultural activity at Cooper Union or Washington Irving High School. She had no umbrella and I did, so I walked her home to my house. There she remained for several hours, a yawning cavity, half asleep. The rain rained on the ailanthus tree outside my window, the wind rattled the shutters of my old-fashioned window, and I took my time making coffee and carving an ounce of pound cake. I don't believe in force and I would have waited, but her loneliness was very great.

We had quite a nice time for a few weeks. She brought rolls and bagels from wherever the stuff can still be requisitioned. On Sundays she'd come out of Brooklyn with a chicken to roast. She thought I was too skinny. I am, but girls like it. If you're fat, they can see immediately that you'll never need their unique talent for warmth.

Spring came. She said: "Where are we going?" In just those words! Now I have met this attitude before. Apparently, for most women good food and fun for all are too much of a good thing.

The sun absorbed July and she said it again. "Freddy, if we're not going anywhere, I'm not going along any more." We were beach-driven those windy Sundays: her mother must have told her what to say. She said it with such imprisoned conviction.

One Friday night in September I came home from an unlucky party. All the faces had been strange. There were no extra girls, and after some muted conversation with the glorious properties of other men, I felt terrible and went home.

In an armchair, looking at an *Art News* full of Dutchmen who had lived eighty years in forty, was Dorothy. And by her side an overnight case. I could hardly see her face when she stood to greet me, but she made tea first and steamed some of my ardor into the damp night.

"Listen, Freddy," she said. "I told my mother I was visiting Leona in Washington for two days and I fixed it with Leona. Everyone'll cover me"—pouring tea and producing seeded tarts from some secret Flatbush Avenue bakery—all this to change the course of a man's appetite and enable conversation to go forward.

"No, listen, Freddy, you don't take yourself seriously, and that's the reason you can't take anything else—a job, or a—a relationship—seriously. . . . Freddy, you don't listen. You'll laugh, but you're very barbaric. You live at your nerve ends. If you're near a radio, you listen to music; if you're near an open icebox, you stuff yourself; if a girl is within ten feet of you, you have her stripped and on the spit."

"Now, Dotty, don't be so graphic," I said. "Every man is his own rotisserie."

What a nice girl! Say something vulgar and she'd suddenly be all over me, blushing bitterly, glad that the East River separated her from her mother. Poor girl, she was avid.

And she was giving. By Sunday night I had ended half a dozen conversations and nipped their moral judgments at the homiletic root. By Sunday night I had said I love you Dotty, twice. By Monday morning I realized the extent of my commitment and I don't mind saying it prevented my going to a job I had swung on Friday.

My impression of women is that they mean well but are driven to an obsessive end by greedy tradition. When Dot found out that I'd decided against that job (what job? a job, that's all) she took action. She returned my copy of *Nineteen Eighty-four* and said in a note that I could keep the six wineglasses her mother had lent me.

Well, I did miss her; you don't meet such wide-open kindness every day. She was no fool either. I'd say peasant wisdom is what she had. Not too much education. Her hair was long and dark. I had always seen it in neat little coiffures or reparably disarrayed, until that weekend.

It was staggering.

I missed her. And then I didn't have too much luck after that. Very little money to spend, and girls are primordial with intuition. There was one nice little married girl whose husband was puttering around in another postal zone, but her heart wasn't in it. I got some windy copy to do through my brother-in-law, a clean-cut croupier who is always crackling bank notes at family parties. Things picked up.

Out of my gasbag profits one weekend I was propelled into the Craggy-moor, a high-pressure resort, a star-studded haven with eleven hundred acres of golf

course. When I returned, exhausted but modest, there she was, right in my par-
lor-floor front. With a few gasping, kind words and a modern gimmick, she
hoped to breathe eternity into a mortal matter, love.

"Ah, Dotty," I said, holding out my accepting arms. "I'm always glad to see
you."

Of course she explained. "I didn't come for that really, Freddy. I came to talk
to you. We have a terrific chance to make some real money, if you'll only be serious a half hour. You're so clever, and you ought to direct yourself to something.
God, you could live in the country. I mean, even if you kept living alone, you
could have a decent place on a decent street instead of this dump."

I kissed the tip of her nose. "If you want to be very serious, Dot, let's get out
and walk. Come on, get your coat on and tell me all about how to make
money."

She did. We walked out to the park and scattered autumn leaves for an hour.
"Now don't laugh, Freddy," she told me. "There's a Yiddish paper called *Morgenlicht*. It's running a contest: JEWS IN THE NEWS. Every day they put in a picture and two descriptions. You have to say who the three people are, add one
more fact about them, and then send it in by midnight that night. It runs three
months at least."

"A hundred Jews in the news?" I said. "What a tolerant country! So Dot,
what do you get for this useful information?"

"First prize, five thousand dollars and a trip to Israel. Also on return two days
each in the three largest European capitals in the Free West."

"Very nice," I said. "What's the idea, though? To uncover the ones that've
been passing?"

"Freddy, why do you look at everything inside out? They're just proud of
themselves, and they want to make Jews everywhere proud of their contribution
to this country. Aren't you proud?"

"Woe to the crown of pride!"

"I don't care what you think. The point is, we know somebody who knows
somebody on the paper—he writes a special article once a week—we don't know
him really, but our family name is familiar to him. So we have a very good
chance if we really do it. Look how smart you are, Freddy. I can't do it myself,
Freddy, you have to help me. It's a thing I made up my mind to do anyway. If
Dotty Wasserman really makes up her mind, it's practically done."

I hadn't noticed this obstinacy in her character before. I had none in my own.
Every weekday night after work she leaned thoughtfully on my desk, wearing for
warmth a Harris-tweed jacket that ruined the nap of my arm. Somewhere out of
doors a strand of copper in constant agitation carried information from her
mother's Brooklyn phone to her ear.

Peering over her shoulder, I would sometimes discover a three-quarter view of
a newsworthy Jew or a full view of a half Jew. The fraction did not interfere with
the rules. They were glad to extract him and be proud.

The longer we worked the prouder Dotty became. Her face flushed, she'd
raise her head from the hieroglyphics and read her own translation: "A gray-
headed gentleman very much respected; an intimate of Cabinet members; a true
friend to a couple of Presidents; often seen in the park, sitting on a bench."

"Bernard Baruch!" I snapped.

And then a hard one: "Has contributed to the easiness of interstate commerce; his creation is worth millions and was completed last year. Still he has time for Deborah, Susan, Judith, and Nancy, his four daughters."

For this I smoked and guzzled a hot eggnog Dot had whipped up to give me strength and girth. I stared at the stove, the ceiling, my irritable shutters—then I said calmly: "Chaim Pazzi—he's a bridge architect." I never forget a name, no matter what type-face it appears in.

"Imagine it, Freddy. I didn't even know there was a Jew who had such accomplishment in that field."

Actually, it sometimes took as much as an hour to attach a real name to a list of exaggerated attributes. When it took that long I couldn't help muttering, "Well, we've uncovered another one. Put him on the list for Van 2."

Dotty'd say sadly, "I have to believe you're joking."

Well, why do you think she liked me? All you little psychoanalyzed people, now say it at once, in a chorus: "Because she is a masochist and you are a sadist."

No. I was very good to her. And to all the love she gave me, I responded. And I kept all our appointments and called her on Fridays to remind her about Saturday, and when I had money I brought her flowers and once earrings and once a black brassière I saw advertised in the paper with some cleverly stitched windows for ventilation. I still have it. She never dared take it home.

But I will not be eaten by any woman.

My poor old mother died with a sizable chunk of me stuck in her gullet. I was in the Army at the time, but I understand her last words were: "Introduce Freddy to Eleanor Farbstein." Consider the nerve of that woman. Including me in a codicil. She left my sister to that ad man and culinary expert with a crew cut. She left my father to the commiseration of aunts, while me, her prize possession and the best piece of meat in the freezer of her heart, she left to Ellen Farbstein.

As a matter of fact, Dotty said it herself. "I never went with a fellow who paid as much attention as you, Freddy. You're always there. I know if I'm lonesome or depressed all I have to do is call you and you'll meet me downtown and drop whatever you're doing. Don't think I don't appreciate it."

The established truth is, I wasn't doing much. My brother-in-law could have kept me in clover, but he pretended I was a specialist in certain ornate copy infrequently called for by his concern. Therefore I was able to give my wit, energy, and attention to JEWS IN THE NEWS—*Morgenlicht*, the Morning Paper That Comes Out the Night Before.

And so we reached the end. Dot really believed we'd win. I was almost persuaded. Drinking hot chocolate and screwdrivers, we fantasied six weeks away.

We won.

I received a 9 A.M. phone call one midweek morning. "Rise and shine, Frederick P. Sims. We did it. You see, whatever you really try to do, you can do."

She quit work at noon and met me for lunch at an outdoor café in the Village, full of smiles and corrupt with pride. We ate very well and I had to hear the following information—part of it I'd suspected.

It was all in her name. Of course her mother had to get some. She had helped with the translation because Dotty had very little Yiddish actually (not to mention her worry about the security of her old age); and it was necessary, they had decided in midnight conference, to send some money to their old Aunt Lise, who had gotten out of Europe only ninety minutes before it was sealed forever and was now in Toronto among strangers, having lost most of her mind.

The trip abroad to Israel and three other European capitals was for two (2). They had to be married. If our papers could not include one that proved our conjunction by law, she would sail alone. Before I could make my accumulating statement, she shrieked oh! her mother was waiting in front of Lord and Taylor's. And she was off.

I smoked my miserable encrusted pipe and considered my position.

Meanwhile in another part of the city, wheels were moving, presses humming, and the next day the facts were composed from right to left across the masthead of *Morgenlicht*:

! SNIW NAMRESSAW YTTOD
SREWSNA EHT LLA SWONK LRIG NYLKOORB

Neatly boxed below, a picture of Dot and me eating lunch recalled a bright flash that had illuminated the rice pudding the day before, as I sat drenched in the fizzle of my modest hopes.

I sent Dotty a post card. It said: "No can do."

The final arrangements were complicated due to the reluctance of the Israeli Government to permit egress to dollar bills which were making the grandest tour of all. Once inside that province of cosmopolitans, the dollar was expected to resign its hedonistic role as an American toy and begin the presbyterian life of a tool.

Within two weeks letters came from abroad bearing this information and containing photographs of Dotty smiling at a kibbutz, leaning sympathetically on a wailing wall, unctuous in an orange grove.

I decided to take a permanent job for a couple of months in an agency, attaching the following copy to photographs of upright men!

THIS IS BILL FEARY. HE IS THE MAN WHO WILL TAKE YOUR ORDER FOR — TONS OF RED LABEL FERTILIZER. HE KNOWS THE MIDWEST. HE KNOWS YOUR NEEDS. CALL HIM BILL AND CALL HIM NOW.

I was neat and brown-eyed, innocent and alert, offended by the chicanery of my fellows, powered by decency, going straight up.

The lean-shanked girls had been brought to New York by tractor and they were going straight up too, through the purgatory of man's avarice to Whore's Heaven, the Palace of Possessions.

While I labored at my dreams, Dotty spent some money to see the leaning tower of Pisa and ride in a gondola. She decided to stay in London at least two weeks because she felt at home there. And so all this profit was at last being left in the hands of foreigners who would invest it to their own advantage.

One misty day the boom of foghorns rolling round Manhattan Island reminded me of a cablegram I had determined to ignore. ARRIVING QUEEN ELIZA-

BETH WEDNESDAY 4 P.M. I ignored it successfully all day and was casual with a couple of cool blondes. And went home and was lonely. I was lonely all evening. I tried writing a letter to an athletic girl I'd met in a ski lodge a few weeks before. . . . I thought of calling some friends, but the pure unmentionable fact is that women isolate you. There was no one to call.

I went out for an evening paper. Read it. Listened to the radio. Went out for a morning paper. Had a beer. Read the paper and waited for the calculation of morning.

I never went to work the next day or the day after. No word came from Dot. She must have been crawling with guilt. Poor girl . . .

I finally wrote her a letter. It was very strong.

My dear Dorothy:

When I consider our relationship and recall its seasons, the summer sun that shone on it and the winter snows it plowed through, I can still find no reason for your unconscionable behavior. I realize that you were motivated by the hideous examples of your mother and all the mothers before her. You were, in a word, a prostitute. The love and friendship I gave were apparently not enough. What did you want? You gave me the swamp waters of your affection to drown in, and because I refused you planned this desperate revenge.

In all earnestness, I helped you, combing my memory for those of our faith who have touched the press-happy nerves of this nation.

What did you want?

Marriage?

Ah, that's it! A happy daddy-and-mommy home. The home-happy day you could put your hair up in curlers, swab cream in the corner of your eyes . . . I'm not sure all this is for Fred.

I am twenty-nine years old and not getting any younger. All around me boy-graduates have attached their bow legs to the Ladder of Success. Dotty Wasserman, Dotty Wasserman, what can I say to you? If you think I have been harsh, face the fact that you haven't dared face me.

We had some wonderful times together. We could have them again. This is a great opportunity to start on a more human basis. You cannot impose your narrow view of life on me. Make up your mind, Dotty Wasserman.

Sincerely with recollected affection,

F.

P.S. This is your *last* chance.

Two weeks later I received a one-hundred-dollar bill.

A week after that at my door I found a carefully packed leather portfolio, hand-sewn in Italy, and a projector with a box of slides showing interesting views of Europe and North Africa.

And after that, nothing at all.

Cesare Pavese

. . . .

SUICIDES

1

There are days when the city where I live wakes in the morning with a strange look. The people in the streets, the traffic, the trees—everything seems familiar but as if seen with new eyes, like those moments when one looks in the mirror and asks oneself: 'Who is that man?' For me, those are the only days in the whole year that I really enjoy.

On such mornings I get away from the office a little early, if I can, and go down into the streets to mix with the crowd, staring unreservedly at everyone who goes by. One or two of them, I imagine, may stare at me in the same way, for in moments like this I really do feel a self-confidence that makes me quite a different man.

I am convinced that never in my whole life shall I have anything more precious than the revelation of how I can derive pleasure from these moments. One way of prolonging them that I have sometimes found successful is to sit in a modern-style café with wide, clear windows, and from that vantage point to savour the bustle on the pavements and in the streets, the whirl of colour, the babble of voices, and the inner calm that controls all this movement.

For some years, now, I have suffered from delusions and the bitterest remorse, yet I can affirm that my dearest wish is only for this peace, this serenity. I am not made for storms and struggles: and if, on certain mornings, I go down full of zest for a walk around the streets, and my past seems a perfidy, I repeat that I ask nothing more of life than being allowed to watch.

Yet even this simple pleasure sometimes leaves me with the bitter after-taste one normally associates with a drug. Long ago I realised how essential astuteness is to living, and before being astute with others one must be astute with oneself. I envy those people who, before doing something wicked or grossly unfair, or even merely satisfying a selfish whim, manage to pre-arrange a chain of circumstances to make their action seem justifiable, even to their own consciences. Women are especially clever at this. I have no great vices, (unless, indeed, my timorous shrinking from life's battle and my quest for serenity in solitude are the worst vices of all), but nevertheless I know how to be astute with myself and keep my self-control when I enjoy what little pleasure life allows me.

Sometimes I actually stop short in the street, look around me and wonder what right I have to enjoy such self-confidence. This frequently happens when I go out more often than usual. Not that I steal the time from my work; I maintain myself decently and support my niece at boarding school. (She is alone in the world and passes for my niece, but the old woman who calls herself my mother will not have her in the house.) What I wonder is whether I am not being ridiculous when I stroll about so blissfully, staring at people; ridiculous and offensive. I sometimes think such pleasure is more than I deserve.

Or else, as happened the other morning, I may be sitting in a café and find myself watching some intriguing scene that first attracts my attention because the people taking part in it are so normal. Such an incident is quite enough to make me relapse into a guilt-stricken sense of loneliness, a prey to so many desolate memories. The more they recede into the past, the more does their unchanging life reveal their subtle, terrifying significance.

I watched five minutes of byplay between the young girl at the cash-desk and a customer in a light-coloured overcoat, who had a friend with him. The young man explained that the cashier owed him change from a hundred *lire* note. He banged on the desk, pretending to search his wallet and pockets. 'That's not the way to treat clients, my girl,' he said, winking at his embarrassed friend. The girl laughed, and the fellow invented a tale of the trips they would have taken together, with that hundred *lire*, up and down in the lift at the public convenience. With muffled bursts of laughter, they decided they would deposit those few *soldi* at the bank—when they got them.

'Goodbye, my girl,' he called as he finally went out. 'Think of me tonight.' The cashier, laughing and excited, said to the waitress: 'What a man!'

I had noticed that cashier on other mornings, and sometimes I smiled without looking at her, in a moment of forgetfulness. But my peace of mind is too fleeting; based on nothing. My customary remorse comes over me.

We are all dirty-minded in that way, but some of us can be genial about it, smiling and making others smile. Others keep it to themselves, letting it create a void inside them. After all, the first way is not so stupid as the second.

It is on mornings like this that I am surprised by the thought—and every time it strikes me afresh—that all I am really guilty of in life is stupidity. Others perhaps can do something wicked deliberately, with complete self-assurance, interesting themselves in their victim and in the game—and I suspect that a life spent in that way may give a great deal of satisfaction; as for me, all I have ever done is to suffer from a vast, inept lack of confidence, and to react against other people, when I come into contact with them, with stupid cruelty. That is why—and there's no remedy for it—it only needs a few moments of remorse and loneliness to overcome me, and my thoughts go back to Carlotta.

It's more than a year since she died, and by now I know all the ways in which the memory of her can take me by surprise. If I want to, I can even recognise the state of mind that initiates her reappearance and with a great effort distract myself. But I do not always want to. Even now, that remorse offers me dark angles to explore, new points that I scrutinize with the same anxiety and terror that I felt a year ago. I have been so true to her in my tortuous fashion that every one

of those far-off days appears to my memory not as something fixed and un-
changeable, but as an elusive impression that is to me as real as today.

Not that Carlotta had any mystery about her. She was, on the contrary, one of
those women who are too simple, poor things, and grow worried if, for a moment, they stop being absolutely sincere and attempt a subterfuge or a touch of
coquetry. But since they are simple, no-one notices them. I have never understood how she could bear to earn her living working at a cash desk. She would
have made an ideal sister.

What I still haven't fathomed, even today, is the way I felt about her, the restraint I had then. What, for instance, can I say about the evening when Carlotta had put on a velvet dress—an old one—to receive me in her little
two-roomed apartment? I said I would have preferred her in a bathing costume.
It was one of the first times I had called on her and I hadn't even kissed her yet.

However, Carlotta gave me a timid smile, went off into the other room and
reappeared—incredibly—in a bathing costume. That was the evening when I
kissed her for the first time and threw her down on the divan, but as soon as our
lovemaking was finished I told her I always preferred to be alone afterwards and
I went away. For three days I did not let her set eyes on me, and when I went
back I addressed her formally in the third person.

So began a ridiculous love-affair, made up of timid confidences on her part
and an occasional word or two on mine. Once, without thinking, I used the intimate '*tu*' as I spoke to her, but Carlotta did not respond. Then I asked if she had
made it up with her husband. Carlotta answered tearfully, 'He never treated me
the way you do.'

It was easy to make her lean her head on my breast while I caressed her and
told her I loved her. Lonely as I was, why shouldn't I make love to that quasi-
widow? And Carlotta gave in, softly confessing that she'd loved me from the
first moment and thought I was an extraordinary man, but I had caused her a lot
of unhappiness in the short time we had known each other; she didn't know
why, but all the men treated her like that.

'When one is hot and one is cold,' I smiled with my lips in her hair, 'love will
last.'

Carlotta was pale; her enormous eyes often looked tired and strained. Her
body was pale, too. That night, in the darkness of her room, she asked me if I
had left her, that other time, because her body did not please me.

But I had no pity on her this time, either, and in the middle of the night I
dressed myself and told her, without offering any excuses, that I had to get moving and go out. Carlotta wanted to go with me. 'No,' I said. 'I like to be alone,'
and I left her with a kiss.

2

When I knew Carlotta, I was just recovering from a bitter blow that almost
cost me my life; and I felt a grim amusement in going back through the deserted
streets, fleeing from the one who loved me. It had so long been my lot to spend
my nights and days humiliated and infuriated by a woman's caprice.

I am convinced, now, that no passion is powerful enough to change a man's true nature. Even the fear of death cannot alter his fundamental characteristics. Once the climax of passion is over one becomes again what one was before— honest man or rogue, father of a family or a mere boy—and lives one's own daily life. Or, rather, in the crisis one sees one's own true nature. It horrifies us, and normality disgusts us. The insult to us is so atrocious that we would rather be dead, but there is no-one to accuse us except ourselves. It is to that woman that I owe my present condition, reduced to a daily job with no scope and no hope of forging a closer link with the world at large, disliked by the next man, disliked by my mother whom I support, and by my 'niece' whom I do not love. I owe it all to her. But would things have turned out differently with any other woman? Another, I mean, who would be capable of humiliating me as my nature demands?

Anyway, that was the thought that came to me whenever I had done something wrong, something that woman I loved could call faithless, and it gave me some comfort. At a certain stage of suffering we inevitably think we are suffering unjustly; it is a natural anaesthetic; it restores our energies, makes life as entertaining as we could possibly wish, fills us with a sense of our own importance in the face of things in general, flatters us. I have experienced it, and I could have wished that the injustice, the ingratitude, had been even more flagrant. In those long days and nights of anguish, I was conscious of a vague, secret awareness, like an atmosphere or a radiation. I remember my stunned amazement that it could have happened; that that woman was only a woman after all; that the delirium, the agony, the sighs, words, actions, even I myself, could all have turned out as they did.

So, having been treated unjustly, I revenged myself, not on the guilty one but on another woman, as happens in this world.

When I left Carlotta's apartment at night, after indulging my passion to the full, my mind was at ease. It pleased me to wander about by myself, feeling free to enjoy walking down that long avenue, vaguely recalling the sensations and the thoughts of my youth. I have always loved the simple pattern of the night. Street lamps alternating with zones of darkness evoke my most cherished flights of fancy, colouring and heightening them by the contrasts they present. Here I could give free play to the dull resentment I felt towards Carlotta because of her meekness and her lust, unhampered by the restraint I imposed on such thoughts, out of pity, while I was actually with her.

But I was no longer young. I tried to cut myself loose from Carlotta by reviewing in detail her body and her caresses, dispassionately. It seemed to me that, separated from her husband as she was, still young and childless, she might well fancy she had the right to turn to me as a refuge. But, poor girl, as a lover she was too naive. Perhaps that was really why her husband was false to her.

I remember one evening when we were strolling arm in arm through the streets in the dusk on our way back from the cinema. Carlotta said: 'I'm so happy. It's nice to go to the cinema with you.'

'Did you ever go with your husband?'

Carlotta smiled: 'Are you jealous?'

I shrugged. 'What difference does it make?'

'I'm tired,' she said, clinging to my arm. 'This useless chain that binds us is ruining my life and his, too, and compels me to bear a name that has done me nothing but harm. It should be possible to get a divorce, at least when there are no children.'

I felt affectionate that evening, from our long, warm contact and my rising desire. 'Have you any scruples about it?' I asked.

'Oh, my dear,' Carlotta sighed. 'Why aren't you always as nice as you are to-night? Think . . . If I could get a divorce. . .'

I said nothing. At one time, when she spoke to me of divorce I was shattered and exclaimed: 'Please yourself. You're the best judge of that. Do what you like, and I'll bet you'll be awarded alimony, too, if it's true that he was unfaithful to you.'

'I have never wanted anything,' Carlotta replied. 'Since that day I've been working,' and she looked at me. 'Now I've got you, I should think that I wasn't being fair to you if I took money from him.'

That evening after the cinema, I closed her mouth with a kiss. Then I took her to the station café and gave her a couple of drinks. In the dim light from the windows we sat in a corner like a pair of lovers. I had several drinks myself and said to her, out loud, 'Carlotta, let's get ourselves a child, tonight, shall we?'

People glanced at us as Carlotta, laughing and blushing, put her hand over my mouth.

I talked and talked. Carlotta spoke about the film, saying all sorts of silly things, passionately comparing us to the characters in the drama. I went on drinking, knowing that was the only way to make me feel loving towards Carlotta.

The cold air outside revived us and we ran to her home. I stayed with her all that night, and when I woke in the morning I felt her beside me, rumpled and drowsy. She stretched out her arms to embrace me and I did not repulse her. When I got up, though, my head was aching. I felt irritated by Carlotta's air of happiness as she prepared coffee for me, humming to herself. We both had to go out, but remembering the concierge she sent me on first, after kissing and hugging me behind the door.

My most vivid recollection of that awakening is of the trees in the street outside, their boughs stiff and dripping in the fog beyond the bedroom curtains. After all that warmth and affection inside, the keen air waiting for me out of doors stimulated my blood; only I would have rather stayed by myself, smoking and thinking, conjuring up a very different awakening and a different companion.

On these occasions Carlotta drew from me a tenderness that I reproached myself for, the moment I was alone again. I spent frenzied moments trying to purge my mind and free myself from even the faintest memory of her. Again I promised myself to be firmer, harsher, a promise I kept only too well. It must be clear that we made love out of boredom, lust, for any reason except the only one she tried to delude herself existed. It irritated me to recall her serene, blissful look after love-making. It made me furious to see it on her face, while the only woman from whom I wanted it had never given it to me.

'If you take me as I am, all right,' I told her once, 'but get it out of your head that you can be part of my life.'

'Don't you love me?' Carlotta faltered.

'The little love I was capable of, I burned up when I was young.'

But sometimes I grew angry at having admitted, out of shame or lust, that I loved her at all.

Carlotta tried to smile: 'We are good friends, at least?'

'Listen,' I told her seriously, 'that sort of nonsense makes me sick: we are a man and a woman who bore each other, but we get on all right in bed . . .'

'Oh, that, yes!' she cried, clutching my arm and hiding her face. 'I like it, I like it!'

'. . . and there's no more to it than that.'

One such conversation, in which it seemed to me I had been weak, was enough to make me avoid her. If she telephoned me at the office from her café, I replied that I was busy. The first time this happened, Carlotta tried to take offence. Then I made her spend an evening of anguish by sitting coldly beside her on the divan. The shaded table lamp threw a white light over her knees, and from where I sat in the shadow I could feel the barely restrained passion of her glances. The tension was almost unbearable, and I myself broke it by remarking: 'You should thank me, Signora: you will remember this session, perhaps more than many others.'

Carlotta did not move, and I went on: 'You'd like to murder me, Signora? Why not? But if you think you can act the lady with me, you're wasting your time. As for whims and fancies, I can produce those for myself.' Carlotta was panting. 'Not even a bathing costume,' I told her, 'will be any use to you tonight.'

Carlotta leapt in front of me and I saw her dark head flash through the white light like a missile. I threw out my hands to ward her off, but she collapsed at my knees, weeping. I patted her on the head two or three times and rose to my feet. 'I ought to cry, too, Carlotta, but I know it's no use. All you are feeling now, I've felt myself. I wanted to kill myself, but I lacked the courage. Here's the joke: one who is weak enough to think of suicide is too weak to do it . . . So get up, Carlotta, you'll be all right.'

'Don't treat me like this,' she sobbed.

'I'm not hurting you. And you know I like to be alone. If you let me go off by myself, I come back. Otherwise we shan't see each other again. Listen! Would you like me to love you?' She looked up, her face transfigured. 'Then stop loving me. There's no other way. "It's the hare that makes the hunter." '

Scenes like that shook Carlotta to her very roots, so much so that she thought of leaving me. (After all, didn't they show that our temperaments were basically similar?) Carlotta was fundamentally simple—too simple. She was incapable of realising this clearly, but certainly she felt it. She tried—poor, hapless creature—to mollify me by treating it lightly. 'Such is life,' she would say sometimes, and 'Poor little me.'

If she had thrown me over then, and stuck to it, I think I should have felt a little hurt. But Carlotta could not reject me. If I missed two evenings in a row, I found her with swollen eyes; and if sometimes, out of pity or tenderness, I stopped at the cafe and asked her to come out, she would jump up eagerly, confused and blushing, even pretty.

My bitterness did not trouble her; what did hurt her was any restraint, any resentment, that our intimacy tended to create in me. Since I did not love her, it seemed to me monstrous that she should have even the slightest claim on me. There were days when it made me shudder to address her as an intimate friend, an equal. I felt degraded. What was this woman to me, that she should take my arm?

To offset that mood, there were days when I felt reborn; times when I could leave work and walk in the fresh sunlight through the shining streets, free of her and of anything else, my body satisfied, my old griefs lulled to rest, eager to see, to savour, to feel as I did when I was young. The fact that Carlotta was suffering for love of me softened and alleviated my own by-gone sorrows, made me feel rather remote from them and from the mocking world. Away from her I found myself again, unharmed and more experienced. She was the sponge that had wiped me clean again. I often thought of her.

3

Some evenings when I talked and talked, absorbed in the game, I forgot my bitterness and became a boy again.

'Carlotta,' I would say, 'How are you off for lovers? It's a long time since I've been one of them, but, after all, that's the best way. If all goes well, one enjoys it; if badly, one hopes for better luck next time. They taught me to live a day at a time. How does that suit you, Carlotta?' She laughed and shook her head. 'And then,' I went on 'they inspire such fine thoughts! The man we love —who couldn't care less—will never be as happy as we are. Unless . . . ,' and I smiled, 'he goes to bed with some other woman and gets his own back that way.' Carlotta frowned. 'Love's a fine thing,' I concluded, 'and nobody can escape it.'

Carlotta served me as an audience. I talked on my own account, on those evenings, the best kind of talk. 'There's love,' I said, 'and there's betrayal. To enjoy love to the full, it must also be a betrayal. That's a thing boys do not understand. You women learn it more quickly. Did you betray your husband?' Carlotta blushed and tried to smile.

'We boys were more stupid. We fell nobly in love with an actress or a girl-friend and devoted all our finest thoughts to her. Only we forgot to tell her about them. As far as I know, every girl of our age was already well aware that love is a problem of astuteness. It seems impossible, but boys go to the licensed brothels and conclude from that that the women outside are different. What did you do when you were sixteen, Carlotta?'

But Carlotta was thinking on different lines. Before she said a word, her eyes told me that I belonged to her. I hated the firm, possessive care for me that radiated from the look she gave me.

'What were you doing at sixteen?' I repeated, looking at the ground.

'Nothing,' she replied gravely. I knew what she was thinking.

Then she asked my pardon, called herself a poor little thing, said she realised she had no right, but the gleam in her eyes was enough for me. 'You're stupid, you know,' I told her. 'As far as I'm concerned, your husband could have you back,' and I went away feeling relieved.

The next day but one, she phoned me timidly at the office and I replied curtly. In the evening we saw each other again.

Carlotta was amused when I told her about my schoolgirl niece, and shook her head incredulously when I said I would rather have sent my mother away to school and lived with the child. She imagined us as two beings living apart, pretending to be uncle and niece, but in reality sharing a whole world of absorbing secrets. She asked me scornfully if the girl wasn't really my daughter.

'Of course. She was born when I was sixteen. And she would be blonde, just to spite me. How can one manage to be born blonde? To me, fair-haired people are just animals, like monkeys or lions, as if they were always in the sun.'

Carlotta remarked: 'I was blonde, as a baby.'

'I was bald,' I replied.

In those last days I grew mildly curious about Carlotta's past, sometimes forgetting what she had already told me. I scanned her as one scans the gossip columns in the daily papers. I amused myself by puzzling her, asking her cruel questions and answering them myself. In reality, I was just listening to my own voice.

But Carlotta had understood me. 'Tell me about yourself,' she would say on some evenings, squeezing my arm. She knew that to make me talk about myself was the only way of keeping me as her friend.

'Have I ever told you, Carlotta,' I said to her one night, 'that a man killed himself because of me?' She looked at me, half smiling, half dismayed.

'It's nothing much to laugh at,' I went on. 'We died together, but he stayed that way. The dreams of youth . . .' (That's strange, I thought. I've never told anyone about it; and now I'm telling Carlotta.) 'He was a friend of mine, a fine, fair-haired chap. He really did look like a lion. You girls never make friendships like that. You're already too jealous, even at that age. We went to school together, and always saw each other in the evenings. We talked filth, as boys do, but we were both in love with a lady. She must be living still. She was our first love, Carlotta. We spent our evening discussing love and death. No lover has ever been more certain of being understood by his friend than we were. Jean—that was his name—had a haughty sadness that put me to shame. All by himself he created the melancholy that pervaded those evenings we spent walking round in the fog. We had never believed one could suffer so much. . . .'

'Were you in love with her, too?'

'Jean was more unhappy than I was, and that troubled me. In the end I had the idea that we could kill ourselves and I told him about it. He thought it was a fine plan—he who was usually just a dreamer. We had only one revolver and we went into the hills to try it out in case it wouldn't work. Jean was the one who fired it. He had always been the leader in any adventure—indeed, I believe that if he hadn't fallen in love with that beautiful girl, I shouldn't have done so, either. We fired the gun—it was winter-time, and we were in a deserted lane half-way up the hillside—and I was still dazed by the violence of the explosion when Jean put the barrel into his mouth and said: "This is how they do it!" The gun went off and killed him.' Carlotta stared at me, shocked and terrified. 'I did not know what to do,' I said, 'and I ran away.'

That evening Carlotta asked me: 'Did you really love that woman?'

'What woman? I loved Jean. I've already told you so.'

'And did you feel like killing yourself, too?'

'Sure, I did. It would have been a silly thing to do, but it was terribly cowardly not to. I wish I had, sometimes.'

Carlotta often recalled that story and talked to me about Jean as if she had known him. She made me describe him and asked me what I was like then. 'Did you keep the revolver? Not to kill yourself, you know. Haven't you ever thought of killing yourself since?' She looked keenly at me as she spoke.

'Every time a man is in love he thinks of it.'

Carlotta did not even smile. 'D'you still think of it?'

'I think about Jean, sometimes.'

4

Carlotta put me to a lot of trouble at lunch-times. Going to and from my office I had to pass the windows of her café, and hide myself to avoid having to go in and cheer her up a bit. I did not go home at mid-day and I was only too glad to spend that little hour alone in some restaurant or other, smoking with my eyes half shut. Now and then I caught a glimpse of Carlotta perched on her stool, mechanically tearing off counterfoils, nodding, smiling or frowning, sometimes sharing a joke with a customer.

She was there from seven in the morning until four in the afternoon. She wore blue. They paid her four hundred and eighty *lire* a month, and Carlotta was quite happy to spend it all at once. For lunch she had a glass of milk, without leaving her desk. The job would have been easy enough, she used to tell me, if it hadn't been for the slamming of the door every time customers came in or went out. There were times when she felt it was battering on her brain.

After that, I shut the door carefully when I went into the café. When she was with me, Carlotta would try to describe to me those little scenes with the customers, but she couldn't manage to talk as I did, just as she failed to shock me with her suggestive hints about offers made to her by some lecherous old man or other.

'Get off with anybody you like,' I told her, 'only make sure I don't see him. Entertain him on the odd days. And watch out for V.D.'

Carlotta gave a wry grimace. For some days she had had something on her mind. 'In love again, Carlotta?' I asked her one evening, and she looked at me like a whipped dog. I began to lose patience with her, as I had before. The way her eyes shone in the darkness of her little room, the way she kept squeezing my hand, made me burn with anger. I was always afraid of getting too involved with her. I hated the very thought of it.

I grew sullen and boorish. But Carlotta no longer accepted my outbursts of bad temper with the submissive distress she used to show. She would stay quietly watching me, and sometimes she would gently withdraw from the caress I tried to give her to show I was sorry.

That pleased me even less. I found it repugnant to have to court her before I could possess her. The change did not come about suddenly, though. Carlotta would say: 'I've got a headache ... That door! Let's be good tonight. Talk to me.'

When I realised that Carlotta was doing it intentionally, feeling humiliated and dredging up pangs of remorse, I stopped having those violent outbursts. I simply played her false. I started seeing again a woman I had known before, on those dreary evenings when, after visiting a brothel, I would sit and rest in some wretched café, feeling neither happy nor sad, just dazed. To me that seemed fair enough: either one accepts love with all its hazards or turns to the only other thing left—prostitution.

I thought Carlotta was pretending to be jealous and I laughed at her. She suffered, but she was too simple to turn her grief to good account. Instead, as happens to anyone who genuinely suffers, she lost her good looks. I was sorry about that, but I felt I should have to leave her.

Carlotta saw the blow coming. One night when we were in bed and I instinctively avoided any conversation, she suddenly pushed me away and curled herself up against the wall.

'What's the matter?' I asked crossly.

'If I were to disappear tomorrow,' she said, suddenly turning round, 'would it matter at all to you?'

'I don't know,' I stammered.

'And if I betrayed you?'

'All life is a betrayal.'

'And if I went back to my husband?' She meant what she said. I shrugged my shoulders. 'I am a poor woman,' she went on, 'and I'm incapable of betraying you. I've seen my husband.'

'How?'

'He came to the café.'

'Didn't he skip off to Algeria, then?'

'I don't know,' Carlotta replied. 'I saw him at the café.'

Perhaps she didn't mean to tell me, but it slipped out that her husband was with a woman in a fur coat. 'Then you didn't get a chance to talk?' I asked.

Carlotta hesitated: 'He came back the next day but one. He talked to me and brought me home.'

I must admit I felt uneasy. 'Here?' I asked softly.

Carlotta clung to me with her whole body. 'But I love you,' she murmured. 'Don't imagine. ...'

'Here?' I said again.

'It was nothing, dear. He talked to me about his business. Only, seeing him again, I realised how much I love you, and I wouldn't go back to him no matter how much he begged me.'

'He did beg you, then?'

'No, but he told me that if he had to marry again, he'd marry me.'

'Have you seen him since?'

'He came back to the café with that woman. ...'

That was the last time I spent the night with Carlotta. Without saying goodbye to her, without regrets, I stopped running after her or meeting her at home. I left it to her to telephone me and wait for me in the café, not every evening, but now and then. Carlotta came every time, devouring me with her eyes. Her voice trembled as we parted.

'I've never seen him since,' she whispered one evening.

'You're doing the wrong thing,' I replied. 'You ought to try and get him back.'

It irritated me that she regretted leaving her husband, as beyond all doubt she did. It also annoyed me that she had hoped to bind me closer to her by talking like that. Such futile love was not worth Carlotta's remorse or my own risk.

One evening I phoned her to say I would drop in and see her. She seemed incredulous and uneasy as she opened the door to me. I looked around apprehensively. She was wearing her velvet dress. I remember she had a cold and kept pulling at her handkerchief, dabbing her red nose.

I saw at once that she understood. She was quiet and docile, responding to all I said with timid glances. She let me go on talking, watching me furtively over her handkerchief. Then she stood up, came over to me and leaned against my face; I had to kiss her.

'Aren't you coming to bed?' she whispered in her usual voice.

I went to bed, and all the time I found her face objectionable, damp and inflamed as it was from her cold. At midnight I jumped out of bed and started dressing. Carlotta switched on the light and looked at me a moment. Then she put it out and said to me: 'All right then, go.' Puzzled and embarrassed, I stumbled out.

For days after that, I feared a telephone call, but nothing disturbed me. Week after week I worked in peace. Then one evening I was seized with desire for Carlotta, but shame helped me to withstand it. Yet I knew that if I had knocked on her door, I should have brought happiness. That certainty I have always had.

I did not yield, but a day or two later I passed in front of her café. There was a blonde at the cash-desk. She must have changed her hours. But I didn't see her in the evening, either. I thought she might be ill, or that her husband had taken her back. That idea displeased me.

But my legs shook under me when the concierge at the street door stared at me with her hard eyes and told me bluntly that a month ago they had found her dead in bed, with the gas turned on.

Translated from the Italian by A. F. March

THE SAINT

When I was seventeen years old I lost my religious faith. It had been unsteady for some time and then, very suddenly, it went as the result of an incident in a punt on the river outside the town where we lived. My uncle, with whom I was obliged to stay for long periods of my life, had started a small furniture-making business in the town. He was always in difficulties about money, but he was convinced that in some way God would help him. And this happened. An investor arrived who belonged to a sect called the Church of the Last Purification, of Toronto, Canada. Could we imagine, this man asked, a good and omnipotent God allowing His children to be short of money? We had to admit we could not imagine this. The man paid some capital into my uncle's business and we were converted. Our family were the first Purifiers—as they were called—in the town. Soon a congregation of fifty or more were meeting every Sunday in a room at the Corn Exchange.

At once we found ourselves isolated and hated people. Everyone made jokes about us. We had to stand together because we were sometimes dragged into the courts. What the unconverted could not forgive in us was first that we believed in successful prayer and, secondly, that our revelation came from Toronto. The success of our prayers had a simple foundation. We regarded it as "Error"—our name for Evil—to believe the evidence of our senses, and if we had influenza or consumption, or had lost our money or were unemployed, we denied the reality of these things, saying that since God could not have made them they therefore did not exist. It was exhilarating to look at our congregation and to know that what the vulgar would call miracles were performed among us, almost as a matter of routine, every day. Not very big miracles, perhaps; but up in London and out in Toronto, we knew that deafness and blindness, cancer and insanity, the great scourges, were constantly vanishing before the prayers of the more advanced Purifiers.

"What!" said my schoolmaster, an Irishman with eyes like broken glass and a sniff of irritability in the bristles of his nose. "What! Do you have the impudence to tell me that if you fell off the top floor of this building and smashed your head in, you would say you hadn't fallen and were not injured?"

I was a small boy and very afraid of everybody, but not when it was a question of my religion. I was used to the kind of conundrum the Irishman had set. It was useless to argue, though our religion had already developed an interesting casuistry.

"I *would* say so," I replied with coldness and some vanity. "And my head would not be smashed."

"You would not say so," answered the Irishman. "You would not say so." His eyes sparkled with pure pleasure. "You'd be dead."

The boys laughed, but they looked at me with admiration.

Then, I do not know how or why, I began to see a difficulty. Without warning and as if I had gone into my bedroom at night and had found a gross ape seated in my bed and thereafter following me about with his grunts and his fleas and a look, relentless and ancient, scored on his brown face, I was faced with the problem that prowls at the centre of all religious faith. I was faced by the difficulty of the origin of evil. Evil was an illusion, we were taught. But even illusions have an origin. The Purifiers denied this.

I consulted my uncle. Trade was bad at the time and this made his faith abrupt. He frowned as I spoke.

"When did you brush your coat last?" he said. "You're getting slovenly about your appearance. If you spent more time studying books"—that is to say, the Purification literature—"and less with your hands in your pockets and playing about with boats on the river, you wouldn't be letting Error in."

All dogmas have their jargon; my uncle as a businessman loved the trade terms of the Purification. "Don't let Error in" was a favourite one. The whole point about the Purification, he said, was that it was scientific and therefore exact; in consequence it was sheer weakness to admit discussion. Indeed, betrayal. He unpinched his pince-nez, stirred his tea, and indicated I must submit or change the subject. Preferably the latter. I saw, to my alarm, that my arguments had defeated my uncle. Faith and doubt pulled like strings round my throat.

"You don't mean to say you don't believe that what our Lord said was true?" my aunt asked nervously, following me out of the room. "Your uncle does, dear."

I could not answer. I went out of the house and down the main street to the river, where the punts were stuck like insects in the summery flash of the reach. Life was a dream, I thought; no, a nightmare, for the ape was beside me.

I was still in this state, half sulking and half exalted, when Mr. Hubert Timberlake came to the town. He was one of the important people from the headquarters of our church and he had come to give an address on the Purification at the Corn Exchange. Posters announcing this were everywhere. Mr. Timberlake was to spend Sunday afternoon with us. It was unbelievable that a man so eminent would actually sit in our dining-room, use our knives and forks, and eat our food. Every imperfection in our home and our characters would jump out at him. The Truth had been revealed to man with scientific accuracy—an accuracy we could all test by experiment—and the future course of human development on earth was laid down, finally. And here in Mr. Timberlake was a man who had not merely performed many miracles—even, it was said with proper reserve, having twice raised the dead—but had actually been to Toronto, our headquarters, where this great and revolutionary revelation had first been given.

"This is my nephew," my uncle said, introducing me. "He lives with us. He thinks he thinks, Mr. Timberlake, but I tell him he only thinks he does. Ha, ha." My uncle was a humorous man when he was with the great. "He's always on the river," my uncle continued. "I tell him he's got water on the brain. I've been telling Mr. Timberlake about you, my boy."

A hand as soft as the best quality chamois leather took mine. I saw a wide upright man in a double-breasted navy-blue suit. He had a pink square head with very small ears and one of those torpid, enamelled smiles which were said by our enemies to be too common in our sect.

"Why, isn't that just fine?" said Mr. Timberlake, who, owing to his contacts with Toronto, spoke with an American accent. "What say we tell your uncle it's funny he thinks he's funny."

The eyes of Mr. Timberlake were direct and colourless. He had the look of a retired merchant captain who had become decontaminated from the sea and had reformed and made money. His defence of me had made me his at once. My doubts vanished. Whatever Mr. Timberlake believed must be true, and as I listened to him at lunch, I thought there could be no finer life than his.

"I expect Mr. Timberlake's tired after his address," said my aunt.

"Tired?" exclaimed my uncle, brilliant with indignation. "How can Mr. Timberlake be tired? Don't let Error in!"

For in our faith the merely inconvenient was just as illusory as a great catastrophe would have been, if you wished to be strict, and Mr. Timberlake's presence made us very strict.

I noticed then that, after their broad smiles, Mr. Timberlake's lips had the habit of setting into a long depressed sarcastic curve.

"I guess," he drawled, "I guess the Al-mighty must have been tired sometimes, for it says He re-laxed on the seventh day. Say, do you know what I'd like to do this afternoon?" he said, turning to me. "While your uncle and aunt are sleeping off this meal let's you and me go on the river and get water on the brain. I'll show you how to punt."

Mr. Timberlake, I saw to my disappointment, was out to show he understood the young. I saw he was planning a "quiet talk" with me about my problems.

"There are too many people on the river on Sundays," said my uncle uneasily.

"Oh, I like a crowd," said Mr. Timberlake, giving my uncle a tough look. "This is the day of rest, you know." He had had my uncle gobbling up every bit of gossip from the sacred city of Toronto all the morning.

My uncle and aunt were incredulous that a man like Mr. Timberlake should go out among the blazers and gramophones of the river on a Sunday afternoon. In any other member of our church they would have thought this sinful.

"Waal, what say?" said Mr. Timberlake. I could only murmur.

"That's fixed," said Mr. Timberlake. And on came the smile as simple, vivid, and unanswerable as the smile on an advertisement. "Isn't that just fine!"

Mr. Timberlake went upstairs to wash his hands. My uncle was deeply offended and shocked, but he could say nothing. He unpinched his glasses.

"A very wonderful man," he said. "So human," he apologized.

"My boy," my uncle said, "this is going to be an experience for you. Hubert Timberlake was making a thousand a year in the insurance business ten years ago. Then he heard of the Purification. He threw everything up, just like that. He gave up his job and took up the work. It was a struggle, he told me so himself this morning. 'Many's the time,' he said to me this morning, 'when I wondered where my next meal was coming from.' But the way was shown. He came down from Worcester to London and in two years he was making fifteen hundred a year out of his practice."

To heal the sick by prayer according to the tenets of the Church of the Last Purification was Mr. Timberlake's profession.

My uncle lowered his eyes. With his glasses off, the lids were small and un-easy. He lowered his voice too.

"I have told him about your little trouble," my uncle said quietly with emotion. I was burned with shame. My uncle looked up and stuck out his chin confidently.

"He just smiled," my uncle said. "That's all."

Then we waited for Mr. Timberlake to come down.

I put on white flannels and soon I was walking down to the river with Mr. Timberlake. I felt that I was going with him under false pretences; for he would begin explaining to me the origin of evil and I would have to pretend politely that he was converting me when already, at the first sight of him, I had believed. A stone bridge, whose two arches were like an owlish pair of eyes gazing up the reach, was close to the landing-stage. I thought what a pity it was the flannelled men and the sunburned girls there did not know I was getting a ticket for *the* Mr. Timberlake who had been speaking in the town that very morning. I looked round for him and when I saw him I was a little startled. He was standing at the edge of the water looking at it with an expression of empty incomprehension. Among the white crowds his air of brisk efficiency had dulled. He looked middle-aged, out of place, and insignificant. But the smile switched on when he saw me.

"Ready?" he called. "Fine!"

I had the feeling that inside him there must be a gramophone record going round and round, stopping at that word.

He stepped into the punt and took charge.

"Now I just want you to paddle us over to the far bank," he said, "and then I'll show you how to punt."

Everything Mr. Timberlake said still seemed unreal to me. The fact that he was sitting in a punt, of all commonplace material things, was incredible. That he should propose to pole us up the river was terrifying. Suppose he fell into the river? At once I checked the thought. A leader of our church under the direct guidance of God could not possibly fall into a river.

The stream is wide and deep in this reach, but on the southern bank there is a manageable depth and a hard bottom. Over the clay banks the willows hang, making their basketwork print of sun and shadow on the water, while under the gliding boats lie cloudy, chloride caverns. The hoop-like branches of the trees bend down until their tips touch the water like fingers making musical sounds. Ahead in midstream, on a day sunny as this one was, there is a path of strong light which is hard to look at unless you half close your eyes, and down this path on the crowded Sundays go the launches with their parasols and their pennants; and also the rowboats with their beetle-leg oars, which seem to dig the sunlight out of the water as they rise. Upstream one goes, on and on between the gardens and then between fields kept for grazing. On the afternoon when Mr. Timberlake and I went out to settle the question of the origin of evil, the meadows were packed densely with buttercups.

"Now," said Mr. Timberlake decisively when I had paddled to the other side. "Now I'll take her."

He got over the seat into the well at the stern.

"I'll just get you clear of the trees," I said.

"Give me the pole," said Mr. Timberlake, standing up on the little platform and making a squeak with his boots as he did so. "Thank you, sir. I haven't done this for eighteen years, but I can tell you, brother, in those days I was considered some poler."

He looked round and let the pole slide down through his hands. Then he gave the first difficult push. The punt rocked pleasantly and we moved forward. I sat facing him, paddle in hand, to check any inward drift of the punt.

"How's that, you guys?" said Mr. Timberlake, looking round at our eddies and drawing in the pole. The delightful water sished down it.

"Fine," I said. Deferentially I had caught the word.

He went on to his second and his third strokes, taking too much water on his sleeve, perhaps, and uncertain in his steering, which I corrected, but he was doing well.

"It comes back to me," he said. "How am I doing?"

"Just keep her out from the trees," I said.

"The trees?" he said.

"The willows," I said.

"I'll do it now," he said. "How's that? Not quite enough? Well, how's this?"

"Another one," I said. "The current runs strong this side."

"What? More trees?" he said. He was getting hot.

"We can shoot out past them," I said. "I'll ease us over with the paddle."

Mr. Timberlake did not like this suggestion.

"No, don't do that. I can manage it," he said. I did not want to offend one of the leaders of our church, so I put the paddle down; but I felt I ought to have taken him farther along away from the irritation of the trees.

"Of course," I said, "we could go under them. It might be nice."

"I think," said Mr. Timberlake, "that would be a very good idea."

He lunged hard on the pole and took us towards the next archway of willow branches.

"We may have to duck a bit, that's all," I said.

"Oh, I can push the branches up," said Mr. Timberlake.

"It is better to duck," I said.

We were gliding now quickly towards the arch; in fact, I was already under it.

"I think I should duck," I said. "Just bend down for this one."

"What makes the trees lean over the water like this?" asked Mr. Timberlake.

"Weeping willows—I'll give you a thought there. How Error likes to make us dwell on sorrow. Why not call them *laughing* willows?" discoursed Mr. Timberlake as the branch passed over my head.

"Duck," I said.

"Where? I don't see them," said Mr. Timberlake, turning round.

"No, your head," I said. "The branch," I called.

"Oh, the branch. This one?" said Mr. Timberlake, finding a branch just against his chest, and he put out a hand to lift it. It is not easy to lift a willow branch and Mr. Timberlake was surprised. He stepped back as it gently and firmly leaned against him. He leaned back and pushed from his feet. And he pushed too far. The boat went on. I saw Mr. Timberlake's boots leave the stern as he took an unthoughtful step backwards. He made a last-minute grasp at a stronger and higher branch, and then there he hung a yard above the water, round as a blue damson that is ripe and ready, waiting only for a touch to make it fall. Too late with the paddle and shot ahead by the force of his thrust, I could not save him.

For a full minute I did not believe what I saw; indeed, our religion taught us never to believe what we saw. Unbelieving, I could not move. I gaped. The impossible had happened. Only a miracle, I found myself saying, could save him.

What was most striking was the silence of Mr. Timberlake as he hung from the tree. I was lost between gazing at him and trying to get the punt out of the small branches of the tree. By the time I had got the punt out, there were several yards of water between us, and the soles of his boots were very near the water as the branch bent under his weight. Boats were passing at the time but no one seemed to notice us. I was glad about this. This was a private agony. A double chin had appeared on the face of Mr. Timberlake and his head was squeezed between his shoulders and his hanging arms. I saw him blink and look up at the sky. His eyelids were pale like a chicken's. He was tidy and dignified as he hung there, the hat was not displaced, and the top button of his coat was done up. He had a blue silk handkerchief in his breast pocket. So unperturbed and genteel he seemed that as the tips of his shoes came nearer and nearer to the water, I became alarmed. He could perform what are called miracles. He would be thinking at this moment that only in an erroneous and illusory sense was he hanging from the branch of the tree over six feet of water. He was probably praying one of the closely reasoned prayers of our faith, which were more like conversations with Euclid than appeals to God. The calm of his face suggested this. Was he, I asked myself, within sight of the main road, the town recreation ground, and the landing-stage crowded with people, was he about to re-enact a well-known miracle? I hoped that he was not. I prayed that he was not. I prayed with all my will that Mr. Timberlake would not walk upon the water. It was my prayer and not his that was answered.

I saw the shoes dip, the water rise above his ankles and up his socks. He tried to move his grip now to a yet higher branch—he did not succeed—and in making this effort his coat and waistcoat rose and parted from his trousers. One seam of shirt with its pant-loops and brace-tabs broke like a crack across the middle of Mr. Timberlake. It was like a fatal flaw in a statue, an earthquake crack that made the monumental mortal. The last Greeks must have felt as I felt then, when they saw a crack across the middle of some statue of Apollo. It was at this moment I realized that the final revelation about man and society on earth had come to nobody and that Mr. Timberlake knew nothing at all about the origin of evil.

All this takes long to describe, but it happened in a few seconds as I paddled towards him. I was too late to get his feet on the boat and the only thing to do was to let him sink until his hands were nearer the level of the punt and then to get him to change hand-holds. Then I would paddle him ashore. I did this. Amputated by the water, first a torso, then a bust, then a mere head and shoulders, Mr. Timberlake, I noticed, looked sad and lonely as he sank. He was a declining dogma. As the water lapped his collar—for he hesitated to let go of the branch to hold the punt—I saw a small triangle of deprecation and pathos between his nose and the corners of his mouth. The head resting on the platter of water had the sneer of calamity on it, such as one sees in the pictures of a beheaded saint.

"Hold on to the punt, Mr. Timberlake," I said urgently. "Hold on to the punt."

He did so.

"Push from behind," he directed in a dry business-like voice. They were his first words. I obeyed him. Carefully I paddled him towards the bank. He turned and, with a splash, climbed ashore. There he stood, raising his arms and looking at the water running down his swollen suit and making a puddle at his feet.

"Say," said Mr. Timberlake coldly, "we let some Error in that time."

How much he must have hated our family.

"I am sorry, Mr. Timberlake," I said. "I am most awfully sorry. I should have paddled. It was my fault. I'll get you home at once. Let me wring out your coat and waistcoat. You'll catch your death—"

I stopped. I had nearly blasphemed. I had nearly suggested that Mr. Timberlake had fallen into the water and that to a man of his age this might be dangerous.

Mr. Timberlake corrected me. His voice was impersonal, addressing the laws of human existence rather than myself.

"If God made water it would be ridiculous to suggest He made it capable of harming His creatures. Wouldn't it?"

"Yes," I murmured hypocritically.

"O.K.," said Mr. Timberlake. "Let's go."

"I'll soon get you across," I said.

"No," he said. "I mean let's go on. We're not going to let a little thing like this spoil a beautiful afternoon. Where were we going? You spoke of a pretty landing-place farther on. Let's go there."

"But I must take you home. You can't sit there soaked to the skin. It will spoil your clothes."

"Now, now," said Mr. Timberlake. "Do as I say. Go on."

There was nothing to be done with him. I held the punt into the bank and he stepped in. He sat like a bursting and sodden bolster in front of me while I paddled. We had lost the pole, of course.

For a long time I could hardly look at Mr. Timberlake. He was taking the line that nothing had happened and this put me at a disadvantage. I knew something considerable had happened. That glaze, which so many of the members of our sect had on their faces and persons, their minds and manners, had been washed off. There was no gleam for me from Mr. Timberlake.

"What's the house over there?" he asked. He was making conversation. I had steered into the middle of the river to get him into the strong sun. I saw steam rise from him.

I took courage and studied him. He was a man, I realized, in poor physical condition, unexercised and sedentary. Now the gleam had left him, one saw the veined empurpled skin of the stoutish man with a poor heart. I remember he had said at lunch:

"A young woman I know said: 'Isn't it wonderful? I can walk thirty miles in a day without being in the least tired.' I said: 'I don't see that bodily indulgence is anything a member of the Church of the Last Purification should boast about.' "

Yes, there was something flaccid, passive, and slack about Mr. Timberlake. Bunched in swollen clothes, he refused to take them off. It occurred to me, as he looked with boredom at the water, the passing boats, and the country, that he had not been in the country before. That it was something he had agreed to do but wanted to get over quickly. He was totally uninterested. By his questions— What is that church? Are there any fish in this river? Is that a wireless or a gramophone?—I understood that Mr. Timberlake was formally acknowledging a world he did not live in. It was too interesting, too eventful a world. His spirit, inert and preoccupied, was elsewhere in an eventless and immaterial habitation. He was a dull man, duller than any man I had ever known; but his dullness was a sort of earthly deposit left by a being whose diluted mind was far away in the effervescence of metaphysical matters. There was a slightly pettish look on his face as (to himself, of course) he declared he was not wet and he would not have a heart attack or catch pneumonia.

Mr. Timberlake spoke little. Sometimes he squeezed water out of his sleeve. He shivered a little. He watched his steam. I had planned, when we set out, to go up as far as the lock, but now the thought of another two miles of this responsibility was too much. I pretended I wanted to go only as far as the bend we were approaching, where one of the richest buttercup meadows was. I mentioned this to him. He turned and looked with boredom at the field. Slowly we came to the bank.

We tied up the punt and we landed.

"Fine," said Mr. Timberlake. He stood at the edge of the meadow just as he had stood at the landing-stage—lost, stupefied, uncomprehending.

"Nice to stretch our legs," I said. I led the way into the deep flowers. So dense were the buttercups there was hardly any green. Presently I sat down. Mr. Timberlake looked at me and sat down also. Then I turned to him with a last try at persuasion. Respectability, I was sure, was his trouble.

"No one will see us," I said. "This is out of sight of the river. Take off your coat and trousers and wring them out."

Mr. Timberlake replied firmly: "I am satisfied to remain as I am."

"What is this flower?" he asked, to change the subject.

"Buttercup," I said.

"Of course," he replied.

I could do nothing with him. I lay down full length in the sun; and, observing this and thinking to please me, Mr. Timberlake did the same. He must have supposed that this was what I had come out in the boat to do. It was only human. He had come out with me, I saw, to show me that he was only human.

But as we lay there I saw the steam still rising. I had had enough.

"A bit hot," I said, getting up.

He got up at once.

"Do you want to sit in the shade?" he asked politely.

"No," I said. "Would you like to?"

"No," he said. "I was thinking of you."

"Let's go back," I said. We both stood up and I let him pass in front of me. When I looked at him again, I stopped dead. Mr. Timberlake was no longer a man in a navy-blue suit. He was blue no longer. He was transfigured. He was yellow. He was covered with buttercup pollen, a fine yellow paste of it made by the damp, from head to foot.

"Your suit," I said.

He looked at it. He raised his thin eyebrows a little, but he did not smile or make any comment.

The man is a saint, I thought. As saintly as any of those gold-leaf figures in the churches of Sicily. Golden he sat in the punt; golden he sat for the next hour as I paddled him down the river. Golden and bored. Golden as we landed at the town and as we walked up the street back to my uncle's house. There he refused to change his clothes or to sit by a fire. He kept an eye on the time for his train back to London. By no word did he acknowledge the disasters or the beauties of the world. If they were printed upon him, they were printed upon a husk.

Sixteen years have passed since I dropped Mr. Timberlake in the river and since the sight of his pant-loops destroyed my faith. I have not seen him since, but today I heard that he was dead. He was fifty-seven. His mother, a very old lady with whom he had lived all his life, went into his bedroom when he was getting ready for church and found him lying on the floor in his shirt-sleeves. A stiff collar with the tie half inserted was in one hand. Five minutes before, she told the doctor, she had been speaking to him.

The doctor, who looked at the heavy body lying on the single bed, saw a middle-aged man, wide rather than stout and with an extraordinarily box-like thick-jawed face. He had got fat, my uncle told me, in later years. The heavy liver-coloured cheeks were like the chaps of a hound. Heart disease, it was plain, was the cause of the death of Mr. Timberlake. In death the face was lax, even coarse and degenerate. It was a miracle, the doctor said, that he had lived as long. Any time during the last twenty years the smallest shock might have killed him.

I thought of our afternoon on the river. I thought of him hanging from the tree. I thought of him indifferent and golden in the meadow. I understood why he had made for himself a protective, sedentary blandness, an automatic smile, a collection of phrases. He kept them on like the coat after his ducking. And I understood why—though I had feared it all the time we were on the river—I understood why he did not talk to me about the origin of evil. He was honest. The ape was with us. The ape that merely followed me was already inside Mr. Timberlake eating out his heart.

. . . .

EVENTIDE

Mahala had waited as long as she thought she could; after all, Plumy had left that morning and now here it was going on four o'clock. It was hardly fair if she was loitering, but she knew that certainly Plumy would never loiter on a day like this when Mahala wanted so to hear. It was in a way the biggest day of her whole life, bigger than any day she had ever lived through as a girl or young woman. It was the day that decided whether her son would come back to live with her or not.

And just think, a whole month had rolled past since he left home. Two months ago if anyone would have said that Teeboy would leave home, she would have stopped dead in her tracks, it would have been such a terrible thing even to say, and now here she was, talking over the telephone about how Teeboy had gone.

"My Teeboy is gone," that is what Mahala said for a long time after the departure. These words announced to her mind what had happened, and just as an announcement they gave some mild comfort, like a pain-killer with a fatal disease.

"My Teeboy," she would say, like the mother of a dead son, like the mother of a son who had died in battle, because it hurt as much to have a son missing in peacetime as to have lost him through war.

The room seemed dark even with the summer sunshine outside, and close, although the window was open. There was a darkness all over the city. The fire department had been coming and going all afternoon. There were so many fires in the neighborhood—that is what she was saying to Cora on the telephone, too many fires: the fire chief had just whizzed past again. No, she said to Cora, she didn't know if it was in the white section of town or theirs, she couldn't tell, but oh it was so hot to have a fire.

Talking about the fires seemed to help Mahala more than anything. She called several other old friends and talked about the fires and she mentioned that Teeboy had not come home. The old friends did not say much about Teeboy's not having returned, because, well, what was there to say about a boy who had been practicing to leave home for so long. Everyone had known it but her blind mother love.

"What do you suppose can be keeping my sister Plumy?" Mahala said to herself as she walked up and down the hall and looked out from behind the screen in the window. "She would have to fail me on the most important errand in the world."

Then she thought about how much Plumy hated to go into white neighborhoods, and how the day had been hot and she thought of the fires and how perhaps Plumy had fallen under a fire truck and been crushed. She thought of all the possible disasters and was not happy, and always in the background there was the fresh emotion of having lost Teeboy.

"People don't know," she said, "that I can't live without Teeboy."

She would go in the clothes closet and look at his dirty clothes just as he had left them; she would kiss them and press them to her face, smelling them; the odors were especially dear to her. She held his rayon trousers to her bosom and walked up and down the small parlor. She had not prayed; she was waiting for Plumy to come home first, then maybe they would have prayer.

"I hope I ain't done anything I'll be sorry for," she said.

It was then, though, when she felt the worst, that she heard the steps on the front porch. Yes, those were Plumy's steps, she was coming with the news. But whatever the news was, she suddenly felt, she could not accept it.

As she came up the steps, Plumy did not look at Mahala with any particular kind of meaning on her face. She walked unsteadily, as if the heat had been too much for her.

"Come on in now, Plumy, and I will get you something cool to drink."

Inside, Plumy watched Mahala as if afraid she was going to ask her to begin at once with the story, but Mahala only waited, not saying anything, sensing the seriousness of Plumy's knowledge and knowing that this knowledge could be revealed only when Plumy was ready.

While Mahala waited patiently there in the kitchen, Plumy arranged herself in the easy chair, and when she was once settled, she took up the straw fan which lay on the floor.

"Well, I seen him!" Plumy brought the words out.

This beginning quieted the old mother a little. She closed her mouth and folded her hands, moving now to the middle of the parlor, with an intentness on her face as if she was listening to something high up in the sky, like a plane which is to drop something, perhaps harmless and silver, to the ground.

"I seen him!" Plumy repeated, as if to herself. "And I seen all the white people!" she finished, anger coming into her voice.

"Oh, Plumy," Mahala whined. Then suddenly she made a gesture for her sister to be quiet because she thought she heard the fire department going again, and then when there was no sound, she waited for her to go on, but Plumy did not say anything. In the slow afternoon there was nothing, only a silence a city sometimes has within itself.

Plumy was too faint from the heat to go on at once; her head suddenly shook violently and she slumped in the chair.

"Plumy Jackson!" Mahala said, going over to her. "You didn't *walk* here from the white district! You didn't walk them forty-seven blocks in all this August heat!"

Plumy did not answer immediately. Her hand caressed the worn upholstery of the chair.

"You know how nervous white folks make me," she said at last.

Mahala made a gesture of disgust. "Lord, to think you walked it in this hot sun. Oh, I don't know why God wants to upset me like this. As if I didn't have enough to make me wild already, without havin' you come home in this condition."

Mahala watched her sister's face for a moment with the same figuring expression of the man who comes to read the water meter. She saw everything she really wanted to know on Plumy's face: all her questions were answered for her there, yet she pretended she didn't know the verdict; she brought the one question out:

"You did see Teeboy, honey?" she said, her voice changed from her tears. She waited a few seconds, and then as Plumy did not answer but only sank deeper into the chair, she continued: "What word did he send?"

"It's the way I told you before," Plumy replied crossly. "Teeboy ain't coming back. I thought you knowed from the way I looked at you that he ain't coming back."

Mahala wept quietly into a small handkerchief.

"Your pain is realer to me sometimes than my own," Plumy said, watching her cry. "That's why I hate to say to you he won't never come back, but it's true as death he won't."

"When you say that to me I got a feeling inside myself like everything had been busted and taken; I got the feeling like I don't have nothing left inside of me."

"Don't I know that feeling!" Plumy said, almost angrily, resting the straw fan on the arm of the chair, and then suddenly fanning herself violently so that the strokes sounded like those of a small angry whip. "Didn't I lose George Watson of sleeping sickness and all 'cause doctor wouldn't come?"

Plumy knew that Mahala had never shown any interest in the death of her own George Watson and that it was an unwelcome subject, especially tonight, when Teeboy's never coming back had become final, yet she could not help mentioning George Watson just the same. In Mahala's eyes there really had never been any son named George Watson; there was only a son named Teeboy and Mahala was the only mother.

"It ain't like there bein' no way out to your troubles: it's the way out that kills you," Mahala said. "If it was good-bye for always like when someone dies, I think I could stand it better. But this kind of parting ain't like the Lord's way!"

Plumy continued fanning herself, just letting Mahala run on.

"So he ain't never coming back!" Mahala began beating her hands together as if she were hearing music for a dance.

Plumy looked away as the sound of the rats downstairs caught her attention; there seemed to be more than usual tonight and she wondered why they were running so much, for it was so hot everywhere.

Her attention strayed back to Mahala standing directly in front of her now, talking about her suffering: "You go through all the suffering and the heartache," she said, "and then they go away. The only time children is nice is when they're babies and you know they can't get away from you. You got them then and your love is all they crave. They don't know who you are exactly, they just know you are the one to give them your love, and they ask you for it until you're worn out giving it."

Mahala's speech set Plumy to thinking of how she had been young and how she had had George Watson, and how he had died of sleeping sickness when he was four.

"My only son died of sleeping sickness," Plumy said aloud, but not really addressing Mahala. "I never had another. My husband said it was funny. He was not a religious man, but he thought it was queer."

"Would you like a cooling drink?" Mahala said absently.

Plumy shook her head and there was a silence of a few minutes in which the full weight of the heat of evening took possession of the small room.

"I can't get used to that idea of him *never* comin' back!" Mahala began again. "I ain't never been able to understand that word *never* anyhow. And now it's like to drive me wild."

There was another long silence, and then, Mahala suddenly rousing herself from drowsiness and the heat of the evening, began eagerly: "How did he look, Plumy? Tell me how he looked, and what he was doing. Just describe."

"He wasn't doin' nothin'!" Plumy said flatly. "He looked kind of older, though, like he had been thinking about new things."

"Don't keep me waiting," Mahala whined. "I been waitin' all day for the news, don't keep me no more, when I tell you I could suicide over it all. I ain't never been through such a hell day. Don't you keep me waitin'."

"Now hush," Plumy said. "Don't go frettin' like this. Your heart won't take a big grief like this if you go fret so."

"It's *so* unkind of you not to tell," she muffled her lips in her handkerchief.

Plumy said: "I told you I talked to him, but I didn't tell you where. It was in a drinking place called the Music Box. He called to me from inside. The minute I looked at him I knew there was something wrong. There was something wrong with his hair."

"With his hair!" Mahala cried.

"Then I noticed he had had it all made straight! That's right," she said looking away from Mahala's eyes. "He had had his hair straightened. 'Why ain't you got in touch with your mother,' I said. 'If you only knowed how she was carryin' on.'

"Then he told me how he had got a tenor sax and how he was playing it in the band at the Music Box and that he had begun a new life, and it was all on account of his having the tenor sax and being a musician. He said the players didn't have time to have homes. He said they were playing all the time, they never went home, and that was why he hadn't been."

Plumy stopped. She saw the tenor sax only in her imagination because he had not shown it to her, she saw it curved and golden and heard it playing far-off melodies. But the real reason she stopped was not on account of the tenor sax but because of the memory of the white woman who had come out just then. The white woman had come out and put her arm around Teeboy. It had made her get creepy all over. It was the first time that Plumy had realized that Teeboy's skin was nearly as light as the white people's.

Both Teeboy and the woman had stood there looking at Plumy, and Plumy had not known how to move away from them. The sun beat down on her in the street but she could not move. She saw the streetcars going by with all the white people pushing one another around and she looked around on the scorched pavements and everyone was white, with Teeboy looking just as white as the rest of them, looking just as white as if he had come out of Mahala's body white, and as if Mahala had been a white woman and not her sister, and as if Mahala's mother and hers had not been black.

Then slowly she had begun walking away from Teeboy and the Music Box, almost without knowing she was going herself, walking right on through the streets without knowing what was happening, through the big August heat, without an umbrella or a hat to keep off the sun; she could see no place to stop, and people could see the circles of sweat that were forming all over her dress. She was afraid to stop and she was afraid to go on walking. She felt she would fall down eventually in the afternoon sun and it would be like the time George Watson had died of sleeping sickness, nobody would help her to an easy place.

Would George Watson know her now? That is what she was thinking as she walked through the heat of that afternoon. Would he know her—because when she had been his mother she had been young and her skin, she was sure, had been lighter; and now she was older looking than she remembered her own mother ever being, and her skin was very black.

It was Mahala's outcries which brought her back to the parlor, now full of the evening twilight.

"Why can't God call me home?" Mahala was asking. "Why can't He call me to His Throne of Grace?"

Then Mahala got up and wandered off into her own part of the house. One could hear her in her room there, faintly kissing Teeboy's soiled clothes and speaking quietly to herself.

"Until you told me about his having his hair straightened, I thought maybe he would be back," Mahala was saying from the room. "But when you told me that, I knew. He won't never be back."

Plumy could hear Mahala kissing the clothes after she had said this.

"He was so dear to her," Plumy said aloud. It was necessary to speak aloud at that moment because of the terrible feeling of evening in the room. Was it the smell of the four o'clocks, which must have just opened to give out their perfume, or was it the evening itself which made her uneasy? She felt not alone, she felt someone else had come, uninvited and from far away.

Plumy had never noticed before what a strong odor the four o'clocks had, and then she saw the light in the room, growing larger, a light she had not recognized before, and then she turned and saw *him*, George Watson Jackson, standing there before her, large as life. Plumy wanted to call out, she wanted to say *No* in a great voice, she wanted to brush the sight before her all away, which was strange because she was always wanting to see her baby and here he was, although seventeen years had passed since she had laid him away.

She looked at him with unbelieving eyes because really he was the same, the same except she did notice that little boys' suits had changed fashion since his day, and how that everything about him was slightly different from the little children of the neighborhood now.

"Baby!" she said, but the word didn't come out from her mouth, it was only a great winged thought that could not be made into sound. "George Watson, honey!" she said still in her silence.

He stood there, his eyes like they had been before. Their beauty stabbed at her heart like a great knife; the hair looked so like she had just pressed the wet comb to it and perhaps put a little pomade on the sides; and the small face was clean and sad. Yet her arms somehow did not ache to hold him like her heart told her they should. Something too far away and too strong was between her and him; she only saw him as she had always seen resurrection pictures, hidden from us as in a wonderful mist that will not let us see our love complete.

There was this mist between her and George Jackson, like the dew that will be on the four o'clocks when you pick one of them off the plant.

It was her baby come home, and at such an hour.

Then as she came slowly to herself, she began to raise herself slightly, stretching her arms and trying to get the words to come out to him:

"George Watson, baby!"

This time the words did come out, with a terrible loudness, and as they did so the light began to go from the place where he was standing: the last thing she saw of him was his bright forehead and hair, then there was nothing at all, not even the smell of flowers.

Plumy let out a great cry and fell back in the chair. Mahala heard her and came out of her room to look at her.

"What you got?" Mahala said.

"I seen *him!* I seen *him!* Big as life!"

"Who?" Mahala said.

"George Watson, just like I laid him away seventeen years ago!"

Mahala did not know what to say. She wiped her eyes dry, for she had quit crying.

"You was exposed too long in the sun," Mahala said vaguely.

As she looked at her sister she felt for the first time the love that Plumy had borne all these years for a small son Mahala had never seen, George Watson. For the first time she dimly recognized Plumy as a mother, and she had suddenly a feeling of intimacy for her that she had never had before.

She walked over to the chair where Plumy was and laid her hand on her. Somehow the idea of George Watson's being dead so long and yet still being a baby a mother could love had a kind of perfect quality that she liked. She thought then, quietly and without shame, how nice it would be if Teeboy could also be perfect in death, so that he would belong to her in the same perfect way as George Watson belonged to Plumy. There was comfort in tending the grave of a dead son, whether he was killed in war or peace, and it was so difficult to tend the memory of a son who just went away and never came back. Yet somehow she knew as she looked at Plumy, somehow she would go on with the memory of Teeboy Jordan even though he still lived in the world.

As she stood there considering the lives of the two sons Teeboy Jordan and George Watson Jackson, the evening which had for some time been moving slowly into the house entered now as if in one great wave, bringing the small parlor into the heavy summer night until you would have believed daylight would never enter there again, the night was so black and secure.

Alain Robbe-Grillet

. . . .

THE REPLACEMENT

The schoolboy stepped slightly backward and looked up toward the lowest branches. Then he took a step forward, to try to reach a branch which seemed within his grasp; he stood on tiptoes and stretched his hand as high as he could, but failed to reach it. After several fruitless efforts, he apparently gave up. He lowered his arm and merely continued to stare at something among the leaves.

Next he returned to the foot of the tree, where he took up the same position as before: his knees bent slightly, the top of his body twisted to the right, and his head bent over toward his shoulder. He still held his book satchel in his left hand. It was impossible to see the other hand, with which he was no doubt supporting himself against the tree, or his face, which was almost glued to the bark of the tree, as if to scrutinize minutely some detail about a yard and a half above the ground.

The boy had again paused in his reading aloud, but this time there must have been a period, perhaps even an indentation, and he gave the impression that he was making an effort to indicate the end of the paragraph. The schoolboy straightened up to inspect the bark of the tree higher up.

Whispers could be heard in the classroom. The schoolmaster turned his head and noticed that most of the pupils were looking up, instead of following the oral reading in their books; even the one reading aloud kept looking toward the teacher's desk with a vaguely questioning, or fearful, expression. The teacher said severely:

"What are you waiting for?"

The faces were all lowered silently and the boy began again, with the same studious voice, expressionless and a bit too slow, that gave each word equal emphasis and spaced it evenly from the next:

"Therefore, that evening, Joseph de Hagen, one of Philippe's lieutenants, went to the Archbishop's palace on the pretext of paying a courtesy call. As previously stated the two brothers . . ."

On the other side of the street, the schoolboy peered again at the leaves on the low branches. The teacher slapped on the desk with the flat of his hand:

"As previously stated, *comma*, the two brothers . . ."

Searching out the passage in his own book, he read aloud, exaggerating the punctuation:

"Start at: 'As previously stated, the two brothers were already there, so that they might, if need be, protect themselves with this alibi . . .' and pay attention to what you are reading."

"As previously stated, the two brothers were already there, so that they might, if need be, protect themselves with this alibi—a suspect alibi in truth, but the best available to them at this juncture—without allowing their mistrustful cousin . . ."

The monotonous voice stopped abruptly, in the middle of the sentence. The other pupils, already raising their eyes toward the paper puppet hanging on the wall, immediately returned to their books. The teacher turned his glance from the window back to the boy who was reading aloud, on the opposite side of the room, in the first row near the door.

"All right, go on! There isn't any period there. You don't seem to understand what you are reading!"

The boy looked at the teacher, and behind him, slightly to the right, the puppet made of white paper.

"Do you understand, or not?"

"Yes," said the boy without much conviction.

"Yes, *sir*," the teacher corrected him.

"Yes, sir," the boy repeated.

The teacher looked at the printed text and asked:

"What does the word 'alibi' mean to you?"

The boy looked at the puppet cut out of paper, then at the blank wall, straight in front of him, then at the book lying on his desk; and then again at the wall, for almost a full minute.

"Well?"

"I don't know, sir," said the boy.

The teacher slowly looked over the other pupils in the class. One boy raised his hand, near the window in back. The teacher pointed at him, and the boy stood up alongside his bench:

"It's to make people think they were there, sir."

"Just what do you mean? Who are *they*?"

"The two brothers, sir."

"Where did they want people to think they were?"

"At the Archbishop's, sir."

"And where were they really?"

The boy thought for a moment before answering.

"But they were really there, sir, only they wanted to go somewhere else and make people think they were still there."

Late at night, hidden under black masks and wrapped in huge capes, the two brothers slid down a long rope ladder into a small, deserted street.

The teacher nodded slightly a couple of times, as if he were giving his half-hearted approval. After several seconds, he said: "Right."

"Now you will summarize for us the whole reading passage, for the benefit of your friends who may not have understood."

The boy looked out the window. Then he glanced down at his book, then up again toward the teacher's desk.

"Where should I start, sir?"

"Start at the beginning of the chapter."

Without sitting down, the boy leafed through the pages of his book and, after a short silence, began to summarize the conspiracy of Philippe de Cobourg. In spite of frequent stops and starts, he did it almost coherently. On the other hand, he stressed unduly a number of secondary matters, while hardly mentioning, or even omitting, certain crucial events. As, moreover, he was disposed to dwell on actions rather than on their political motives, it would have been extremely difficult for an uninformed listener to puzzle out the reasons for the episode or the connections between the various events described, or between the different people involved. The teacher allowed his glance to travel gradually along the windows. The schoolboy had returned to the spot below the lowest tree branch; he had put his satchel at the foot of the tree and was jumping up and down, stretching one arm upward. Seeing that all his attempts were in vain, he again stood motionless, staring at the inaccessible leaves. Philippe de Cobourg had set up camp with his mercenaries on the banks of the Neckar. The pupils, who were no longer required to follow the printed text, had all raised their heads and were silently staring at the paper puppet hanging on the wall. He had no hands or feet, but only four crudely cut-out limbs and a round head, oversized, through which ran the supporting thread. Several inches higher, at the other end of the thread, could be seen the little ball of chewed-up blotting paper that held it on the wall.

But the boy who was reciting was losing his way among wholly insignificant details, so that the teacher finally stopped him:

"That's enough," he said, "we know enough about that. Sit down and we will take up the reading again at the top of the page: 'But Philippe and his followers . . .'"

The whole class, as one, leaned over the desks, and a new reader began, in a voice as devoid of expression as his classmate's, although conscientiously indicating the commas and the periods:

"But Philippe and his followers were not of this opinion. If the majority of the Diet—or even only the barons' party—were to renounce in this manner the prerogatives accorded to them, to him as well as to them, as a result of the invaluable assistance they had given to the Archduke's cause at the time of the uprising, they would be henceforth unable, either they or he, to demand the indictment of any new suspect, or the suspension without trial of his manorial rights. It was absolutely essential that these negotiations, which seemed to him to have begun so inauspiciously for his own cause, be broken off before the fateful date. Therefore, that evening, Joseph de Hagen, one of Philippe's lieutenants, went to the Archbishop's palace on the pretext of paying a courtesy call. As previously stated, the two brothers were already there . . ."

The faces remained dutifully leaning over the desks. The teacher looked at the window. The schoolboy was leaning against the tree, absorbed in his examination of the bark. He crouched down slowly, as if to follow a line running down the trunk—on the side not visible from the school windows. About a yard and a half above the ground, his movement stopped and he tilted his head to one side, in the same position he had formerly occupied. One by one, the faces in the classroom looked up.

The pupils looked at the teacher, then at the windows. But the bottom panes were of frosted glass, and, above, they could see only the treetops and the sky. Not a fly or a butterfly appeared on the windowpanes. Soon all eyes were again fixed on the white paper cutout of a man.

Translated from the French by Bruce Morrisette

Mercè Rodoreda

· · · · · · · · · · · · · · · · · ·

RAIN

She'd just put the finishing touches on the living room. She stepped back and stood at the door to inspect her handiwork. She'd washed the curtains the night before and ironed them that morning. They looked pretty, all starched. They were cream-colored, with green dots, parted and with a ruffle at the bottom. A green ribbon gathered them at each side.

Beneath the windows sat a divan and two grey velvet easy chairs. On the coffee table, a blue vase with roses. The huge Breton cabinet had just been waxed; facing it, her desk with its books neatly arranged, its clean inkwell and spotless pink blotter.

Everything had been painstakingly scrubbed, dusted, made to look just like new.

On the hope chest, to the right of the door, a crystal decanter of cognac and two glasses sparkled. In the tiny, dazzlingly white kitchen, a tantalizing aroma rose from a tray of pastries. There were six more in the refrigerator: three with custard and three with strawberries.

Everything was ready.

Marta entered the bedroom that, along with a small bathroom, rounded out her apartment. What dress should she wear? Or would a robe be better? That blue one with the flared skirt and white flowers embroidered on the bodice and pockets? She felt so pretty, so alluring in it that she thought: "If anything happens, it'll be the robe's fault." There was also a lacy tulle blouse that she hadn't worn yet . . . At last she decided upon a brown shirtdress and a thick suede belt with gold studs. She washed her face and arms, carefully combed her hair, but put on no makeup. She chose her sheerest stockings and some suede shoes.

Perfume. A last glance over her shoulder at her reflection in the mirror and she returned to the living room. She sat down.

It was early. Barely three. Since she was worn out from fighting the dirt all morning, she'd rest until he came at four. It was the first time Albert would visit her at home . . . and she felt nervous. She got up, walked to the desk, and tried to choose a book to leave on the coffee table. Which one? Maybe Shakespeare? "O my fair warrior!" Othello says to Desdemona as he greets her in Cyprus.

What more pathetically pure compliment could a soldier give his lady? Like Antony when, before his death, he calls Cleopatra "Egypt," imbuing that single word with all her queenly grandeur. Perhaps seeing such a serious book, Albert would think: "She's a snob." Basically she didn't care, but she abandoned the notion and, without further thought, picked *Du côté de chez Swann* and left it next to the roses.

She sat down again. Leaning back against the easy chair, she felt lonely. Lonely and empty. As though her excitement at Albert's visit had melted away and nothing could replace it.

She had no financial problems. A small inheritance on her mother's side gave her just enough to live on. Her job as secretary in an export firm where everyone thought well of her allowed her some comfort and even a few luxuries. She had two or three girlfriends who loved her and on whom she could rely: good, disinterested friends. Why did her heart insist so fiercely on something more?

She'd been in love once before. With all the passion of youth. Now she thought it a mistake and told herself: "With each affair, more bitterness accumulates, and besides, you can get pregnant." When she was twenty, a timely operation had saved her life but left her deathly afraid.

She got up. She couldn't just sit there. She rearranged the roses so the prettiest one faced the window.

It was raining outside. It had been cloudy all day. A stubborn drizzle, the kind that just makes everything muddy.

"Am I in love?" she wondered as she walked to the kitchen. She couldn't resist eating one of the pastries. The coffeepot on the stove was still warm. She poured herself a cup and dropped an aspirin into it. She sat down on the table to drink it.

She liked Albert, of course. Young, at once dynamic and easygoing, simple: an excellent companion. They hadn't known each other long but she often felt she couldn't live without him . . . But love, so complex and vast: could it really be embodied in a nice young man like him? True love was behind her: "Darling, you're the only one, my kingdom . . ." A volcano of words and feelings. Afterwards, the taste of ashes. He'd died far away, and she'd gotten his last letter when maybe not even his corpse existed. That letter had been like poison. A cry of longing that cut her to the quick. A single wish: to go back. It was a cursed time. And now Albert. Very restful, certainly . . . There was no one else around, yet how deep did it go? One day he'd ask her to marry him and they'd rent a big apartment. If he was faithful, he'd be demanding, severe, gloomy. He'd grow old slowly. If he wasn't, he'd be indulgent, broad-minded, he'd have heart trouble and lock himself in a world from which she'd be excluded.

She got off the table and paced to and fro, with a cup of coffee in one hand and a second pastry in the other.

"He'll bring me a bouquet and a box of chocolates. We'll talk about the weather, politics. He'll tell me his philosophy of life but we'll both be thinking of something else. Before leaving he'll tell me how much he loves me and ask for a kiss, which I'll gladly grant him.

"Or maybe he'll storm in looking determined, a little dramatic, and he'll say: 'I can't live without you.' He'll squeeze my arms. 'You hear me? It's impossible;

I can't live without you! I want you every day, every night, beside me all night long.' His eyes will glow, he'll kiss me greedily: my cheeks, neck, and lips. He'll try to unbutton my dress, to get me excited too. Yes, my breasts are pretty and a little attention wouldn't hurt . . . Maybe I'd like it too much. But I don't want to. No, it's not that I'm prudish. I've got my own ideas about many things and a certain notion of how to live, but . . ."

She went back to the bedroom. Then the bathroom. She plucked a hair from the sink. She straightened the bottle of cologne. The mirror had fogged up, so she wiped it and looked at herself.

"Why complicate your life? You feel alone? If he leaves you you'll feel even worse. They're making a dress that'll be my favorite. They're fixing an antique ring that used to be my mother's; it'll be sumptuous, maybe too much for someone as young as me. I've got ten pairs of gloves and an exquisite lingerie collection. This year my bank account has grown considerably. No one kisses me. But kisses often turn out to be costly . . ."

A churchbell rang. It was three-thirty.

She felt like running away, escaping a danger she could scarcely identify. She'd been silly to invite him. She hadn't given it much thought, but he'd be full of hopes she couldn't bring herself to share.

Determined, she put on a felt hat and raincoat and shut the door behind her. As soon as she reached the landing, she smelled the rain. She was down the stairs like a shot.

The street was deserted; on one side was row of single-storey houses, on the other, a garden. When the trees along the wall were bare, she could see a tennis court and swimming pool from her window. In spring, the fragrance from the acacias and honeysuckle made her dizzy. When she left work in the evening, she approached the street slowly, savoring that intoxicating perfume, which at night filtered through her balcony.

It was drizzling. Everything glistened: the sidewalk, the cobblestones, the grass poking between the cracks. Water trickled down the walls and drops fell from tiled roofs. The sky looked like lead, and everything was immersed in milky radiance, as if the trees and houses got their light from an airshaft.

As she started walking, she wondered where she'd go. Where did this urge to flee come from, pushing her through the streets? On a windowsill stood a kitten with a string around its neck. Every time a drop fell on its nose, it looked up. Inside she could hear children screaming.

She walked with her hands in her pockets, her hat pulled down. The streets were deserted. The air seemed still. After a while, a woman carrying milk bottles crossed her path; the bottles clanked together. She passed a nursery school; she could hear the little kids singing. As she approached the center of town, there were more people in the street. Passers-by hurrying beneath umbrellas, with their hopes and their cares. The shop windows were full and some had turned their lights on. A grocer had covered his outdoor fruit stand with a big tarpaulin.

She entered a café. The men were playing billiards and cards. Some whispered and argued, as though they were talking business.

"A coffee."

"Our machine's just gone on the blink."

"Some herb tea, then."

And it kept drizzling. Cars passed, shiny in the rain, a rattling streetcar, a wagon, its drowsy driver wearing a wet sack on his head. People entered the movie house across the street. Inside the bar, a dreamy little boy slowly collected cigarette butts. A lottery ticket vendor asked if she'd like to try her luck; she declined with a weary gesture.

What about going to the movies? But she'd already seen the film. Queen Elizabeth's green feather fan. She remembered Her Majesty's shadow as she descended a staircase. That mirror with a queen inside it . . . She forgot the film. The rain reminded her of those lines by Valéry and she wondered why they were famous: whether Valéry had made them famous or the other way around.

She was beginning to feel tired. She paid and left.

It was still raining. It had been raining since early morning. No downpours; just a calm, steady drizzle. She walked beneath some trees. Their leafy branches met, creating a green, aqueous tunnel. She passed a church. The bells were striking four. Only four o'clock? Every peal stabbed her heart . . . It was absurd, what she was doing. Out of character. She ought to hail a taxi and give the driver her address. But she did nothing. Something stronger than herself held her back.

She couldn't help realizing that the man loved her. Eyes don't lie, and neither do tones of voice. But she had a past. Sooner or later, she'd have to tell him she'd done something crazy. Two things: loving and preventing her child's birth. He'd be four years old by now, and she wouldn't be alone.

But no, that wasn't why she'd left. "Then what was it?" she asked herself impatiently. "Why this fear of a new love? Why this self-absorption, as if you were a crotchety old lady?"

She hurried beneath the dense foliage. She could hear her steps, her breathing, the blood throbbing in her temples. She walked rhythmically. O my fair warrior! There was a bench every hundred yards on the promenade. She felt like sitting down, calmly savoring the undersea light and the sound of rain on the leaves. A kind of modesty held her back. A phrase from she didn't know where had been floating through her mind: *And on just such a night, Queen Dido called out from Carthage to fleeing Aeneas . . . and the lion's shadow frightened him* . . . No, that wasn't right: *And on just such a night, Queen Dido with a willow branch* . . . Now it was Dido who fled. She laughed and muttered: "Idiot!" Tomorrow, seated before the typewriter: "Dear Sir: The shipment of canned sardines, scheduled for mid-September, has been delayed due to circumstances beyond our . . ."

He must have climbed the stairs. Now he was probably ringing the bell with a bouquet in his hand, smoothing his jacket with a swift, unconscious gesture, breathing heavily because he'd mounted the steps quickly. Nothing. Emptiness and silence. He rang again. He grew impatient. He rang again. Nervously. More silence. Finally, with a last glimmer of hope, he'd ring again. Till, disappointed, he'd put on his hat and descend the stairs.

And she walked on. She'd never walked down so many streets in one afternoon. Her feet were frozen, but her face was sweaty. She walked for hours. When the bells struck seven, exhausted, she entered her street. The street said nothing: neither that he'd arrived happily nor that he'd gone away sadly. The shadow of a streetlamp cracked into pieces on the wall and a radio sent out waves of waltz music.

Against the light, she saw the slender needles of rain. The sky was opaque: it would rain all night and then some more.

She groped her way up the steps, like a reveler returning from an orgy. The staircase said no more than the street.

She entered her apartment. A wave of perfume hit her. She'd dabbed some on the easy chairs, the ribbons on the curtains, when she'd finished cleaning. It was a perfume he liked, and she'd done it to please him.

She shut the door and, with a weary gesture, threw down her hat. She left her raincoat in the kitchen. Her head ached, her tongue was white as chalk, her legs hurt.

Everything was the same; the *aubepines* in Proust's book were surely prettier than ever. Who could imagine everything that had happened that afternoon? That is, everything that hadn't happened, everything irretrievably submerged just when it was about to become real? She hardly could herself. Not even her. She knew nothing. Neither why she'd left nor why he'd come. "I can't think about what I don't know; for me it doesn't exist. China suddenly exists when I think of it, when I say: 'Flowering cherry tree, Fire dragon . . .' China or Japan . . . The Dalai Lama's dead if I think he is. The man I expected this afternoon existed because I'd met him, and I existed for him because he wanted me. God, what a headache!"

She entered her bedroom. She'd skip supper. All she wanted was to sleep. She started undressing . . . *Oui, c'est pour moi, pour moi/que je fleuris, déserte!* Now she'd have the imprints of kisses on her shoulders, her arms, her lips; she could hold onto them and they'd keep her company at night. She could slip them beneath her pillow and maybe they'd come out while she was sleeping, returning to the same spots on her arms and shoulders.

She put on her prettiest, most diaphanous, most bridal nightgown. The perfume made her head spin. She turned off the light and opened the balcony doors. The light from the streetlamp entered her room. The monotonous rain fell relentlessly. The night smelled wet. It must be cold.

Barefoot, she went to fetch the decanter of cognac. She was shivering. The bottle was cool against her fingers. "I'll get drunk," she thought. O my fair warrior!? . . . And she drank three glasses in quick succession, all full to the brim.

Translated from the Spanish by David H. Rosenthal

Leon Rooke

· ·

IN THE GARDEN

The woman—the one who stands here at her apartment windows in her blue stockings and blue shoes and a blue raincoat that hangs to her heels—the woman up here behind her windows high over the city's wayward slopes (Oh snow, oh hoary winter's drool!) and over the murky green waters (Needs stirring, I'll say) of Fisherman's Bay . . . is thinking: *What next? What to do with myself today that can be half the fun yesterday was?*

"Life *calls*!" she suddenly trumpets, surprised herself by the sound of her voice and by all the joy that, like a grinning lunatic, has leapt inside her. (I'm chappy as a tick, one might conclude I've been drinkin'.)

She carefully puts down her glass.

"Eleven a.m.," she gloats, "all's well."

She steps out on her narrow balcony, shivering (Merciless winter, oh sweet-jesus will spring never come?), bending low and dangerously over the railing to peer inside the recessed sliding doors of the apartment below.

Feet, feet, she thinks, that's all I've ever seen. Shine your shoes, Mister-Man-Down-There.

No feet today, however. The glass needs cleaning and he ought to throw out those two dying ferns.

"I'll call Estelle," she says. "My good friend Estelle."

Do *do* call Estelle, give the little lady a fine thrill.

But Estelle, it turns out (Dear me, I've split my britches), is not home. (Not in? At this hour? What *is* that elfin horror trying to prove?)

So Rebecca—woman by the window—goes back to the window and again looks out over the close-rippling water (Ten years in this place and I've yet to see a fisherman there, only boats and more boats, teensy putt-putts, you'd think civilized people would have better things to do)—looks out over the city slopes to the high, snowy mountains beyond (Oh fold upon fold upon fold, tedious and exhausting, but rather exquisite; yes, I *do* like it, this is such a friendly part of the world).

Oh, she thinks, what *can* I have been thinking of!

Of course.

She goes into her bedroom and takes her time selecting a nice scarf from her dresser drawer, something in a fetching complimentary blue—

"Yes, this one I think," and ties the silk loosely about her throat.

"Now I'm so pretty," she remarks aloud, "I am pretty enough to *sing sing sing!* And why not, while I'm at it, telephone Estelle?"

Estelle's phone—can you believe it?—rings and rings.

But Rebecca—following a crow's black flight across the bay (Oh look at him swerve and dive, if only I could fly like that!)—is not fooled. Oh, she's *home,* she thinks. Certainly she's home. Where else could she be but at home!

In one of her moods, possibly.

Mustn't discount her elfish moods.

One of her I-don't-want-to-see-anyone days. Doubtlessly nursing old grudges by the ton. Got the brush-off from Harold, could be. Oh, the poor little downtrodden bird.

"None of your business," Rebecca tells herself. "Honey, you stay out of this."

She laughs. Estelle is so funny when she's in her moods. No, one can't help laughing.

A fruitcake, that's what Estelle is on her rainy-day days.

"No way out of it," Rebecca says. "I'd better shoot right over."

A swarm of gnats—fruit flies, she supposes (Genus *drosophila,* dipteria, transparent of mind and wing, oh go away, gnats!)—hangs in the air just short of Estelle's door, which swarm Rebecca steers straight through, thinking surely they will scatter. But they come right along with her, a net of floating black dots. They swirl about, an inch up, an inch down, untouched, as she swats. "Shoo, shoo!" she says, "oh, scat!" Finally she wades through, knocks on Estelle's bright red door.

All the curtains drawn, house sealed up tight. Estelle, honey, is it as bad as all that?

"Yoo-hoo! It's me!"

She can hear music playing over the stereo—or radio—something classical. Harpsichordish, may be. Old Worldish anyway.

Estelle being *grand.*

Grim *church* music to aid and abet the foul downspin.

"Let me in *at once,* darling!"

The door opens an inch and no more. The chain remains in place.

"Why have you kept me waiting here for so long?" Rebecca says. "You should do something about this plague of wild gnats."

All she can see of her friend Estelle is one eye in the crack. She appears to have a bandage of some sort half-covering it.

"Go *away,*" whispers Estelle.

"But I've walked miles," replies Rebecca, not worried in the least by such rudeness. Ooo-la-la, that's Estelle. "My feet hurt. It isn't easy in these high heels. I've probably got a blister, if you want to know. Anyway, I've got to talk to you. It's imperative. You *are* my best friend."

The door quietly closes.

Uncanny. Oh Estelle, why are you treating me this way?

She can hear Estelle's footsteps across the floor, something clattering down

(Temper, temper, oh what a temper she has!)—then the music coming on again, bit louder this time, some kind of silly piano piece, like four birds chirping from a high fence.

Rebecca swatted at the gnats. "Shoo!" she said. "Shoo! Oh, rats! . . ." She walked slowly out to the street, her head down. At the curb she turned and regarded Estelle's house most pensively (Drab, Estelle, very drab. Most shoddy). The house was indeed drab, small and low-slung, like a Crackerjacks box down on its side, and ridiculous with its red door.

Rebecca patted one foot against the pavement. She knotted the scarf tighter against her throat.

Poor Estelle, she thought, how *can* I cheer her up?

She wondered if any of the other people in their houses along the street were watching her. I certainly should be, she thought. I would *continue the investigation* until I knew precisely what was going on. Who *is* that woman? I'd ask myself. What can she *possibly* want? Or, if I were another woman watching me, I'd think: where could she have *found* that beautiful blue coat!

I'd smoke, that's what I'd do. I'd light up a lovely blue cigarette, oh I'd have a killing-good taste of the weed.

I will anyway.

No, no, children might be watching.

An old man, four houses down, was out in his driveway washing his car. Rebecca studied him. Wouldn't it be pleasant, and a nice thing to do, to go and talk to him?

". . . I was dropping in on my friend up the street," she said, speaking from a distance of several dozen yards, "but she does not appear to be receiving."

The man, less old than she had presumed, was down on his knees sudsing a hubcap; he did not look up.

"Her name is E. Beverly Sims," Rebecca went on drawing closer. "She lives in that flat house with the scrawny box hedge by the front porch. I'm sure you must know her well. Estelle is the very outgoing type, and she has a splendid figure. In a nice friendly neighborhood such as this one is everyone must know everyone."

The man, she now observed, stepping up beside him, had a pokey face and practically no hair. He was chewing on the nub of a cigar while squinting up at her. She admired his way of sitting on his heels.

"Where I live it is not the least like that. I live in a small but very efficient apartment down by the Bay. A condominium. You wouldn't believe what it cost. I'm way up on the twelfth floor, and can see for miles. Do you know that huge ships pass my window at night? Far out, of course. But I have a large telescope mounted on a nice tripod. I am continuing my investigation of these ships. It's easily the most interesting hobby I ever had."

"I'm washing this car," the man grumbled.

Rebecca realized that the remark was somehow meant to put her in her place. She laughed.

"I can *see* that. It must have been extremely dirty."

This comment clearly interested him. He rose up off his haunches, backed up a few paces, lit his cigar, and stared appreciatively at the automobile.

"It *was* filthy," he said. "My son had let this car go to the dogs." He spat, very close to his feet, and backed up a bit more. "They tell me young boys like nothing better than sharp cars to show off with the girls, but I give this car to my son and he has not yet got behind the wheel once."

"Oh my," said Rebecca. "That is curious behavior indeed."

Soap suds all along the car side were drying in the sun. But the man seemed more interested in the hubcap. He stooped beside it, buffing up the chrome with his sleeve. "Of course, he doesn't have his license yet. I give this car to him for his sixteenth birthday, but he has some months to go." He peered up at Rebecca. "Do you know Harold?"

"Your son? No, I—"

"You wouldn't like him. He is the most stuck-up boy I ever saw. Something of a sissy, too, you want to know the truth. Bet you can't guess why."

"Hormones, I bet," said Rebecca. "I bet his hormones got sent straight up a tree."

"Not hormones," he said. "His mother. His mother has pampered the little rat since the day he was born." He paused, flipping his cigar in the dirt. Then he walked over and ground at it with his heel. "He is out now at Symphony School. Harold. He plays the oboe." He picked up the cigar, examining its mangled leaves between his fingers. "This cigar," he said, "it's real Havana. I got a pal sends them to me from Canada. Real cold up there. I got maybe twenty, twenty-five these rascals left." He spread the tobacco out in his palm and poked at it with a finger. "Real beauties, these cigars. I bet they cost my buddy a mint. But he owes me. He owes me a fortune, tell you the truth. You know why?"

Rebecca batted her eyes. "Why?" she asked. It had struck her that this man was somewhat *odd*.

"Because I stole his wife. I stole her right out from under his nose. One day there he was, married to the prettiest woman you ever saw, and the next day she wasn't there anymore. She liked me best, you see. I had the real goods but Ralph—old Ralph—well, old Ralph didn't have *nothing* and the next thing he knew he was out in the cold. Yep, between the two of us we really put it to him."

Rebecca considered this. She wasn't sure she liked it.

"Happy?" the man said. "You never saw two people so happy as the wife and me. Regular lovebirds." He shot a hasty look at Rebecca. "Then we had Harold. Beginning of the end."

Rebecca laughed. That phrase had always been one of her favorites.

"You probably know what I mean," he said. "Kids! Look at Job. He had a house full of kids, but what good did they ever do him? Only more misery."

Rebecca felt that she had been silent far too long. She thought it only right that she should point out *there was another side*.

"You would not think that," she told him lightly, "if you were in India, or in Greece, or even in Japan. Suppose you were in China and believed as you do? At the minimum, you'd be ostracized, and probably you'd be shot."

"Fine by me," he replied. "If I had to live in those places I'd *want* to be shot."

Rebecca walked over to the concrete steps leading up to the front door and sat down, crossing her legs prettily. She lit up a cigarette with her gold lighter and closed her eyes, holding her head back, blowing out the first draw of smoke in a long, measured stream.

"Nobody told you to sit there," the man reproached her. "This is private property." He seemed suddenly very angry.

". . . But sit there if you want to. What the hell, who ever listens to me?"

"I'm sure you've a very strong character," said Rebecca. "I'm sure you must dominate any circle you enter."

He puzzled over this a moment, then, shrugging, dropped down on his ankles again and began scrubbing the rear hubcap, his back to Rebecca. She noticed for the first time the baseball cap stuffed into his pocket. She found this intriguing, a strongly personal touch. She wondered what kind of hat he would have stuffed there had he been born in India. She found it charming, where men put their hats. He looked so round and full, stooped like that, a complete little world, total to the point even of where he put his hat. She smiled. She liked the way he bobbed up and down on his ankles, how his heels lifted up out of his shoes; his little grunts, too, were very charming. She could see an expanse of pink skin and now his underpants—swatch of black polka dots—rode up over his hips. She wondered if he would be interested in hearing what she had read about Babe Ruth—not so long ago that she had forgotten—in *The New Columbia Encyclopedia.* Sixty homers, imagine that. And born of people so rag-tail poor he had to be sent away to a training school, made to sweep floors for his daily bread. A pitcher, too. Eighty-seven wins in five years, now that was true pitching, that was real horseshoes.

She became aware after a while that the man was watching her out of the corners of his eyes.

She took off one shoe and held it above her head, shaking it as if to dislodge pebbles. But secretly she watched him.

He dropped his sponge into the sudsy bucket, spinning on his heels. His jacket was wet up to the elbows. "Harold's brother now," he announced sullenly, "he's another case. Been begging me for a car for years, but I wouldn't give him the time of day, not even if he got down on bended knee."

Rebecca nodded. "He must have done something extremely reprehensible," she said.

The man gave her a blank look, then shook his head. "Not *my* son," he explained darkly. "No, Norman's the *wife's* son. I keep telling him he ought to go off live with his *real* father, but he just whines 'Aw, Dad.' Can't even wipe his nose." He picked up his bucket and went around to suds up the grille.

"Estelle is like that, too," Rebecca said.

The man hiked up his pants. He looked off at the closed windows of his house and over at a stunted, leafless tree at the edge of his yard. "That friend of yours," he said gruffly, ". . . that Estelle, she's moved out, you know. That place is *empty* now. No, you'll waste your time knocking on *that* door."

Rebecca decided to let this pass, and the man dropped back down to his bucket. "I wouldn't give ten cents," he grumbled, "to know anybody on this block. Including your long-gone friend."

Rebecca ignored all this. "Beverly was her maiden name," she told him. "She married a man named Sims when she was twenty-eight, and although that union lasted only a short time she and Mr. Sims remain good friends to this day." She smiled mischievously. "Nowadays Estelle has other interests, I understand. She's in love."

"Spit," he said.

"Actually, she's feverish about this particular gentleman, but I have reason to believe the relationship is undergoing its difficult moments."

"Pa-tooey," the man said.

"I'm sure you must have seen him. He drives an orange Toyota."

At this the man perked up. He wheeled about, pointing to a spot on the street vaguely in front of Estelle's house. "Orange?" he said. Rebecca took this to mean that he had seen the car in question parked out in front of Estelle's house through nights too numerous to mention.

"They may be good cars," he said gruffly, "but only a traitor would buy one." He smacked a flat, wet hand against the top of his own automobile. "I've seen him," he said. "He wears a hat."

This news tantalized Rebecca. She had never seen Estelle's lover wearing a chapeau of any sort. She stood up now. She had smoked her cigarette and had her visit and was now ready to leave.

"Where you going?" the man asked her.

She smiled, surprised. "Why, I don't know," she said. "I haven't thought about it."

He strode past her to the side of the house, beckoning. "Come inside," he grumbled. "Something to show you. I bought my son a .22 for his birthday. I've got it on a gun rack in the den. I don't suppose you shoot, being a woman—my wife *hates* it—but what I say is if Harold doesn't go out and shoot something with it the very minute he turns sixteen I'm going to throw him out of the house." He shoved his hands deep into his jacket pockets, scowling back at Rebecca who was lingering. "It beats me," he said, "why women don't like hunting. And fishing. There is not anything more fun than that. Character-building, too. My old man had me out on the marsh with a rifle in my arms before I was two years old. Women! I'll tell you about women. Women have got themselves into this trouble out of their own choosing. They deserve everything they get. Bunch of fools, if you ask me. Silliest thing on two feet. Look at you, for instance. All sky-baby-blue in that silly raincoat and those silly shoes. Well, it's *feminine* all right, but that's all I can say for it."

Rebecca laughed, a low breasty chuckle that brightened her face. She loved insults. She wished he'd say something else—perhaps about her hair or her nice scarf or her blue pocketbook. She wished he'd put on his funny little cap.

"Come on," he ordered. "Want to show you that gun."

Rebecca was tempted. Few things pleased her more than seeing how other people lived. She could imagine herself inside browsing through his cupboards, checking out cereal boxes, opening the refrigerator door to read out the brand names on frozen foods. But she'd been looking at Estelle's house; she was certain she'd seen the front curtain move. "No thank you," she said. "Perhaps another time. I'm often in the neighborhood."

"Buzz off then," he said. "Who asked you? I got better things to do."

The gnats had moved on from Estelle's door. They were now up around the telephone wire where it entered the house, a larger body now, black patch silently lifting and falling, swaying, against the clear blue sky.

"It's me again," Rebecca called, knocking.

The house was silent. Four or five rolled newspapers were on the ground beneath the hedge, soiled and wet, further indication to Rebecca that Estelle's love life had reached the cut-throat stage.

"I've brought you your reading matter!" she shouted, bent at the keyhole, thinking she detected shadowy movement inside.

"I'll huff and I'll puff!" she called. "Stand back!"

Estelle didn't respond.

A tomb.

The back of the house was deserted, too. Curtains were drawn over the windows, and a beautiful spider web had been spun over the upper portion of the door. Crumpled newspaper filled a hole down in the corner of one cracked window. Under the roof line stretched a series of old hornets' nests, or dirt-daubers' sturdy quarters. The garbage can was overturned, but empty. A rusty barbecue stand was down on its side in the tall grass. Numerous tin cans and milk cartons lay about; a huge cardboard box had been flattened by the rain.

Rebecca took her time contemplating the debris, seated in a white metal chair out near where a composting fixture once had stood. She smoked, and pitched her head back to catch the sunshine. She would have been happy if only she had a drink to sip on.

Gloves, she thought. Why haven't I bought myself a pair of nice blue gloves?

The silence of the place fascinated her. She realized she was genuinely enjoying this.

A large fluffy cat, golden in color, hopped up on the picnic table in the neighboring yard. It took turns idly scrutinizing her and, just as idly, licking its fur.

"Gin," said Rebecca. "Gin and tonic, I think."

And she stayed on another ten minutes or so, enjoying the invisible drink.

Someone not far away was calling. A woman's fragile, unhurried voice repeating: "Oro! . . . Oro! . . . Come home, Oro."

Very musical, Rebecca thought.

A breeze played gently across her face, further subduing her mood, and she let herself drift along in a sweet, dreamy doze, seeing the world before her as though through a haze in which all things moved in tranquil, harmonic order, pleasant and kind.

The sun dropped down rays thick as a lattice fence, golden and alluring.

What splendor, she thought. I could be in someone's enchanted garden.

.   .   .   .   .

Afterwards, drawing the blue collar up against her neck, feeling somewhat chilled, she stepped again up to Estelle's rear window. She rapped on the glass, looking for a peephole through the curtains.

"Estelle? Estelle, darling, please open the door."

She heard a quick catch of breath within and could feel Estelle's presence on the other side of the wall.

"It's lovely out here, it truly is. You should come out and talk to me. He hasn't hurt you, has he?" She heard a whisper of footsteps, the creak of floorboards, and beat her knuckles sharply against the window. "Oh don't be unhappy!" she pleaded. "Please let me in. He isn't worth this pining, Estelle . . ."

The floor creaked again.

A cat squawked somewhere in the neighborhood, much as if someone were repeatedly pulling its tail.

Rebecca stiffened; she shivered. She whipped her head around, certain that someone had stolen up and was about to hit her on the head.

No . . .

A very old man with an enormous stomach, wearing a checkered shirt and carrying his shoes in his hands, was out on the steps next door, watching her. He leaned against the door frame, putting on one shoe. Then he leaned the opposite way and put on the other.

"I think she's left that place," he said. "I think she moved out four, five days ago."

Rebecca smiled at him.

The man backed up, slowly withdrawing into the house.

Nearby, someone was singing, or perhaps it was a radio.

Rebecca stared a moment at the dusty, faded newspaper stuffed into the window crack. "I've got my troubles too, Estelle," she said. "My phone rings every night. It's that man I told you about. He refuses to let up. Every night I think, 'Well, tonight he's going to threaten me' . . . but he never quite does. He's extremely cunning. What do I do, Estelle?"

When Estelle didn't answer, Rebecca went up on tiptoe and tugged the stiff paper free. Then she went up again on tiptoe, straightening her arm, and poked her hand into the small opening. She worked her hand past the jagged glass and past the curtain edge and thrust her arm deeper into the room. It felt cold, very cold, in there.

Something brushed or cut or struck against her flesh and with a faint cry of pain, of fear, she snatched back her arm. Shards of glass tinkled down, her heel twisted in the uneven dirt, and she stumbled back, holding in her breath; she staggered, banged one knee against dirt, then lost her balance totally and landed gracelessly on one hip.

Dizzily, she got to her feet. Her coat sleeve was torn, scar in the blue fabric scarcely larger than a dime; a straight line of blood was popping up in droplets across the back of her hand. It stung.

"You've cut me, Estelle," she said, her voice calm, amazed.

She had a clear vision of Estelle inside the cold room, pressed against the wall, eyes slitted, knife poised, waiting for her again to poke her arm through.

But she wasn't sure. It could have been the glass.

She licked the line clean, hastily pulled free her scarf, and wrapped it around her hand.

"That was uncalled-for, Estelle. That was very mean."

She drew back, watching the window.

"But I forgive you."

At the corner of the house she turned, calling again.

"I know you're not yourself today. I really wish you'd let me help you."

She went once more to the front of the house and sat down on Estelle's stoop, brooding on this turn of events.

No, the fault wasn't Estelle's. The fault was Arnold's.

She unfolded one of the newspapers. The moisture had soaked through and the sheet had to be peeled apart. Displayed across the front page was a photograph of Nureyev leaping, his legs flung wide, bare buttocks to the camera, arrow pointing to where his tights had ripped. DANCER SHOWS TRUE FORM, the caption read. But Rebecca shivered at the black headlines. Shivered, and let her head swoop down against the page. 58 DIE IN BLOODBATH . . . OIL RIG GOES DOWN OFF NEWFOUNDLAND, NO SURVIVORS . . . WARSAW ERUPTS.

Yes, she thought, and my mother is dead, my husband has left me, I have no children, hardly any life, and no one knows anything at all—or cares!—about poor Rebecca.

But when her head came up she was ruefully smiling.

Yes, all true, she thought, but we shall continue the investigation.

She turned, peering through Estelle's keyhole.

"Peace Promised for One Zillion Years!" she shouted. "Happiness Lays Golden Egg! . . . Man Steps in Pothole, Breaks Leg!"

She removed the scarf from her hand and closely observed the wound. "Nineteen Stitches Required!" she called. "Noted Plastic Surgeon Called In! . . . Lady Recovers from Heartless Attack!"

The tear in the coat bothered her more. She wondered whether a good seamstress could save the day.

A boy was approaching, yet some distance down the street, slouching, his hands deep into his pockets, small black case tucked up under one arm, his face white as plaster in the sunlight.

Harold.

The man who had been washing the car was no longer in the yard, nor was the car. A woman now stood out in front of the house, arms crossed over her chest. She was looking past Rebecca at the dawdling boy. She wore a print dress, too bold for her thick figure; the hem hung unevenly and the grass cut off her legs. She called wanly to the boy:

"Harold! Harold! He hit me, Harold!"

Harold stopped. Now nearly abreast of Estelle's house, he looked not at his mother but at Rebecca coolly watching from the stoop.

"You don't live there," he said to her. "That place is deserted."

Rebecca loved this frontal approach. He was sullen, nasty even, but she wanted to reach out and hug him. He was abusive, yes, but it seemed to her that

those who were most insulting were also those who most willingly offered enthusiastic praise.

"What's that under your arm?" she asked him. "Is that an oboe?"

The boy's face clouded. He kicked a shoe against the pavement, standing with
his body bent like a quarter moon.

"I wish you'd play for me," Rebecca said. "I haven't heard an oboist play
really well in years."

"Who are you?" he growled. "What are you doing in our neighborhood?"

"*Harold! He hit me, Harold,*" called his mother.

The boy put his case on the sidewalk and, crouching, took the instrument
from it, polishing the bulbous end on his sleeve.

"I give the pitch to the whole orchestra," he said, standing, glaring at Rebecca.

He blew a strong, high note, which then seemed to falter—but the note came
back stronger, more penetrating, thin, only a little plaintive, and it intensified
and kept on coming.

"*Harold!*" called the mother. "*He really hit me hard.*"

His mother now stood at the edge of her yard, her hands twisting around the
narrow trunk of a leafless tree.

The boy scowled at Rebecca. "Sure, I could play," he said. "But I won't.
Harold only plays for money."

Rebecca nodded doubtfully, her thoughts drifting, watching the swarm of
gnats at the side of the house, hovering a few feet above the scraggly grass.

"You're a very good-looking boy," Rebecca said. "I'll bet you must be every
inch of six feet tall."

"*He hurt me, Harold!*"

The boy came up and sat down on the stoop beside Rebecca.

"I'm very advanced for my age," he told her. "I'm very unusual. In fact, I'm
eccentric."

"Well, it is a strange neighborhood," she said.

"Not that strange. The woman who lived here—what was her name?"

"Estelle."

"Estelle was strange. I saw her one night out back of this house, practically
naked—in a flowing gown, I mean—down on her knees in front of that chair
she's got back there, bowing and bowing, like an Arab. *That's* strange."

Rebecca smiled. "Not if you know Estelle," she replied softly.

Across the way his mother advanced a few paces, her footsteps weighted, as if
deep holes were opening in front of her. When she saw them looking at her she
backed up, returning hastily to the tree.

The boy moistened the mouthpiece, allowed his head to settle deep between
his shoulders, then played several quick, rather piercing, notes. "Listen to this,"
he said.

He closed his eyes.

He played.

When the last lingering note faded, Rebecca, only now opening her eyes,
clapped enthusiastically. "Oh God," she sighed, genuinely moved. "You're
going to be immortal."

The boy stretched out one hand, palm upwards.

"*I'm bleeding, Harold!*" his mother called.

Rebecca opened her purse. She looked thoughtfully at her bills, then unsnapped her change purse, and dropped two quarters into his hand.

The boy stared glumly at the coins. "What can this buy?" he asked.

"Happiness," Rebecca said. And she smiled in a bewitched way, as if indeed it had.

The boy walked away, pointing with his instrument to the swarm of gnats. "Those gnats are mating," he said.

At his yard he turned and went on past his mother without a word and entered the house and a few seconds later she left the tree and scooted in after him.

Rebecca leaned back against Estelle's door. "The music was lovely, wasn't it?" she said. "I wonder where such genius comes from."

It seemed to her that from inside the house there came a whispery, half-strangled *yes!*

Rebecca stayed on, pursuing stray thoughts as they popped into her head. Harold's music, unquestionably very beautiful, had put the Garden of Eden into her mind. A kind of dreamy, springtime garden. Yet now several hundred men, no larger than bees, were erecting a barbed-wire fence around the place.

She laughed. How silly.

"A blight has hit the garden," she said.

Men with rifles were up sniping from their towers. *Plunk plunk plunk!* Bullets stirred up soft puffs of dust in the arid soil.

Off in the corner, darkened, the Tree of Knowledge hunkered down, like a rat gone fat from too much wine and cheese. The bullets went on plunking.

Plunk plunk plunk!

Rebecca giggled. It's absurd, she thought, but what can be done about it?

"*Aim over their heads,*" a voice said. "*We don't want to harm anyone.*"

Rebecca's heart caught. She recognized that voice.

"*Well, one or two,*" God said, "*as an example.*"

Two or three hundred of the small bee people began to fall. They rolled down into the grass, kicked and lay still, or they screamed and went limp, snagged on the wire.

Plunk plunk plunk!

Rebecca leaped up, throwing her hands over her eyes. "Estelle," she said, "I've just had the most awful vision!" She knocked again on Estelle's door, and kicked at it, and put her eye against the keyhole, and for a moment believed she saw another eye looking back—but then decided this was nonsense, since Estelle lacked any such curiosity. No, Estelle, after such a busy day, would be spread out on her bed, damp cloth across her brow, claiming headaches, claiming troubles, agony too painful to mention.

I too was once like that, Rebecca thought. I believed I didn't have a friend in the world.

Like something shoved over the edge . . . and still falling.

But she had learned better long ago. People valued her. Friends were ever eager to see her. They let her know without any guile or trickery—without any reservations whatsoever—that their doors were always open.

"*Any time, Rebecca. For you we are always home.*"

She brushed off the seat of her raincoat, fluffed her hair, and started towards the street. "I'm going now!" she called. ". . . Take care of yourself! . . . Enjoyed visiting! . . . See you tomorrow!"

Maybe. Maybe she would see her tomorrow.

At any moment she expected to see Estelle yanking open the door, flinging herself down the path, embracing and pulling her back.

"Chin up, darling! . . . Accept no wooden nickels!"

But the red door remained firmly shut.

She wondered what Harold would be doing. Where Arnold would be in his orange Toyota.

What next? Who to see?

She'd go home first, laze around a bit. Have a quiet smoke, perhaps a nice gin and tonic. Watch the big, distant ships hulking ever so silently by on Fisherman's Bay. Watch the fog—watch darkness—descend slowly over the water.

Think this matter through.

Think about it tomorrow.

Juan Rulfo

. . . .

TALPA

Natalia threw herself into her mother's arms, crying on and on with a quiet sobbing. She'd bottled it up for many days, until we got back to Zenzontla today and she saw her mother and began feeling like she needed consolation.

But during those days when we had so many difficult things to do—when we had to bury Tanilo in a grave at Talpa without anyone to help us, when she and I, just the two of us alone, joined forces and began to dig the grave, pulling out the clods of earth with our hands, hurrying to hide Tanilo in the grave so he wouldn't keep on scaring people with his smell so full of death—then she didn't cry.

Not afterward either, on the way back, when we were traveling at night without getting any rest, groping our way as if asleep and trudging along the steps that seemed like blows on Tanilo's grave. At that time Natalia seemed to have hardened and steeled her heart so she wouldn't feel it boiling inside her. Not a single tear did she shed.

She came here, near her mother, to cry, just to upset her, so she'd know she was suffering, upsetting all the rest of us besides. I felt that weeping of hers inside me too as if she was wringing out the cloth of our sins.

Because what happened is that Natalia and I killed Tanilo Santos between the two of us. We got him to go with us to Talpa so he'd die. And he died. We knew he couldn't stand all that traveling; but just the same, we pushed him along between us, thinking we'd finished him off forever. That's what we did.

The idea of going to Talpa came from my brother Tanilo. It was his idea before anyone else's. For years he'd been asking us to take him. For years. From the day when he woke up with some purple blisters scattered about on his arms and legs. And later on the blisters became wounds that didn't bleed—just a yellow gummy thing like thick distilled water came out of them. From that time I remember very well he told us how afraid he was that there was no cure for him any more. That's why he wanted to go see the Virgin of Talpa, so she'd cure him with her look. Although he knew Talpa was far away and we'd have to walk a lot under the sun in the daytime and in the cold March nights, he wanted to go anyway. The blessed Virgin would give him the cure to get rid of that stuff that never dried up. She knew how to do that, by washing them, making everything fresh and new like a recently rained-on field. Once he was there before Her, his troubles would be over; nothing would hurt him then or hurt him ever again. That's what he thought.

And that's what Natalia and I latched on to so we could take him. I had to go with Tanilo because he was my brother. Natalia would have to go too, of course, because she was his wife. She had to help him, taking him by the arm, bearing his weight on her shoulders on the trip there and perhaps on the way back, while he dragged along on his hope.

I already knew what Natalia was feeling inside. I knew something about her. I knew, for example, that her round legs, firm and hot like stones in the noonday sun, had been alone for a long time. I knew that. We'd been together many times, but always Tanilo's shadow separated us; we felt that his scabby hands got between us and took Natalia away so she'd go on taking care of him. And that's the way it'd be as long as he was alive.

I know now that Natalia is sorry for what happened. And I am too; but that won't save us from feeling guilty or give us any peace ever again. It won't make us feel any better to know that Tanilo would've died anyway because his time was coming, and that it hadn't done any good to go to Talpa, so far away, for it's almost sure he would've died just as well here as there, maybe a little afterward, because of all he suffered on the road, and the blood he lost besides, and the anger and everything—all those things together were what killed him off quicker. What's bad about it is that Natalia and I pushed him when he didn't want to go on anymore, when he felt it was useless to go on and he asked us to take him back. We jerked him up from the ground so he'd keep on walking, telling him we couldn't go back now.

"Talpa is closer now than Zenzontla." That's what we told him. But Talpa was still far away then, many days away.

We wanted him to die. It's no exaggeration to say that's what we wanted before we left Zenzontla and each night that we spent on the road to Talpa. It's something we can't understand now, but it was what we wanted. I remember very well.

I remember those nights very well. First we had some light from a wood fire. Afterward we'd let the fire die down, then Natalia and I would search out the shadows to hide from the light of the sky, taking shelter in the loneliness of the countryside, away from Tanilo's eyes, and we disappeared into the night. And that loneliness pushed us toward each other, thrusting Natalia's body into my arms, giving her a release. She felt as if she was resting; she forgot many things and then she'd go to sleep with her body feeling a great relief.

It always happened that the ground on which we slept was hot. And Natalia's flesh, the flesh of my brother Tanilo's wife, immediately became hot with the heat of the earth. Then those two heats burned together and made one wake up from one's dreams. Then my hands groped for her; they ran over her red-hot body, first lightly, but then they tightened on her as if they wanted to squeeze her blood out. This happened again and again, night after night, until dawn came and the cold wind put out the fire of our bodies. That's what Natalia and I did along the roadside to Talpa when we took Tanilo so the Virgin would relieve his suffering.

Now it's all over. Even from the pain of living Tanilo found relief. He won't talk any more about how hard it was for him to keep on living, with his body poisoned like it was, full of rotting water inside that came out in each crack of his legs or arms. Wounds this big, that opened up slow, real slow, and then let out bubbles of stinking air that had us all scared.

But now that he's dead things are different. Now Natalia weeps for him, maybe so he'll see, from where he is, how full of remorse her soul is. She says she's seen Tanilo's face these last days. It was the only part of him that she cared about—Tanilo's face, always wet with the sweat which the effort to bear his pain left him in. She felt it approaching her mouth, hiding in her hair, begging her, in a voice she could scarcely hear, to help him. She says he told her that he was finally cured, that he no longer had any pain. "Now I can be with you, Natalia. Help me to be with you," she says he said to her.

We'd just left Talpa, just left him buried there deep down in that ditch we dug to bury him.

Since then Natalia has forgotten about me. I know how her eyes used to shine like pools lit up by the moon. But suddenly they faded, that look of hers was wiped away as if it'd been stamped into the earth. And she didn't seem to see anything any more. All that existed for her was her Tanilo, whom she'd taken care of while he was alive and had buried when his time came to die.

It took us twenty days to get to the main road to Talpa. Up to then the three of us had been alone. At that point people coming from all over began to join us, people like us who turned onto that wide road, like the current of a river, making us fall behind, pushed from all sides as if we were tied to them by threads of dust. Because from the ground a white dust rose up with the swarm of people like corn fuzz that swirled up high and then came down again; all the feet scuffing against it made it rise again, so that dust was above and below us all the time. And above this land was the empty sky, without any clouds, just the dust, and the dust didn't give any shade.

We had to wait until nighttime to rest from the sun and that white light from the road.

Then the days began to get longer. We'd left Zenzontla about the middle of February, and now that we were in the first part of March it got light very early. We hardly got our eyes closed at night when the sun woke us up again, the same sun that'd gone down just a little while ago.

I'd never felt life so slow and violent as when we were trudging along with so many people, just like we were a swarm of worms all balled together under the sun, wriggling through the cloud of dust that closed us all in on the same path and had us corralled. Our eyes followed the dust cloud and struck the dust as if stumbling against something they could not pass through. And the sky was always gray, like a heavy gray spot crushing us all from above. Only at times, when we crossed a river, did the dust clear up a bit. We'd plunge our feverish and blackened heads into the green water, and for a moment a blue smoke, like the steam that comes out of your mouth when it's cold, would come from all of us.

But a little while afterward we'd disappear again, mixed in with the dust, sheltering each other from the sun, from that heat of the sun we all had to endure.

Eventually night will come. That's what we thought about. Night will come and we'll get some rest. Now we have to get through the day, get through it somehow to escape from the heat and the sun. Then we'll stop—afterward. What we've got to do now is keep plugging right along behind so many others just like us and in front of many others. That's what we have to do. We'll really only rest well when we're dead.

That's what Natalia and I thought about, and maybe Tanilo too, when we were walking along the main road to Talpa among the procession, wanting to be the first to reach the Virgin, before she ran out of miracles.

But Tanilo began to get worse. The time came when he didn't want to go any farther. The flesh on his feet had burst open and begun to bleed. We took care of him until he got better. But, he'd decided not to go any farther.

"I'll sit here for a day or two and then I'll go back to Zenzontla." That's what he said to us.

But Natalia and I didn't want him to. Something inside us wouldn't let us feel any pity for Tanilo. We wanted to get to Talpa with him, for at that point he still had life left in him. That's why Natalia encouraged him while she rubbed his feet with alcohol so the swelling would go down. She told him that only the Virgin of Talpa would cure him. She was the only one who could make him well forever. She and no one else. There were lots of other Virgins, but none like the Virgin of Talpa. That's what Natalia told him.

Then Tanilo began to cry, and his tears made streaks down his sweaty face, and he cursed himself for having been bad. Natalia wiped away the streaky tears with her shawl, and between us we lifted him off the ground so he'd walk on a little further before night fell.

So, dragging him along was how we got to Talpa with him.

The last few days we started getting tired too. Natalia and I felt that our bodies were being bent double. It was as if something was holding us and placing a heavy load on top of us. Tanilo fell down more often and we had to pick him up and sometimes carry him on our backs. Maybe that's why we felt the way we did, with our bodies slack and with no desire to keep on walking. But the people who were going along by us made us walk faster.

At night that frantic world calmed down. Scattered everywhere the bonfires shone, and around the fire the pilgrims said their rosaries, with their arms crossed, gazing toward the sky in the direction of Talpa. And you could hear how the wind picked up and carried that noise, mixing it together until it was all one roaring sound. A little bit afterward everything would get quiet. About midnight you could hear someone singing far away. Then you closed your eyes and waited for the dawn to come without getting any sleep.

We entered Talpa singing the hymn praising Our Lord.

We'd left around the middle of February and we got to Talpa the last days of March, when a lot of people were already on their way back. All because Tanilo took it into his head to do penance. As soon as he saw himself surrounded by men wearing cactus leaves hanging down like scapularies, he decided to do something like that too. He tied his feet together with his shirt sleeves so his steps became more desperate. Then he wanted to wear a crown of thorns. A little later he bandaged his eyes, and still later, during the last part of the way, he knelt on the ground and shuffled along on his knees with his hands crossed behind him; so that thing that was my brother Tanilo Santos reached Talpa, that thing so covered with plasters and dried streaks of blood that it left in the air a sour smell like a dead animal when he passed by.

When we least expected it we saw him there among the dancers. We hardly realized it and there he was with a long rattle in his hand, stomping hard on the ground with his bare bruised feet. He seemed to be in a fury, as if he was shaking out all the anger he'd been carrying inside him for such a long time, or making a last effort to try to live a little longer.

Maybe when he saw the dances he remembered going every year to Tolimán during the novena of Our Lord and dancing all night long until his bones limbered up without getting tired. Maybe that's what he remembered and he wanted to get back the strength he used to have.

Natalia and I saw him like that for a moment. Right afterward we saw him raise his arms and slump to the ground with the rattle still sounding in his bloodspecked hands. We dragged him out so he wouldn't be tromped on by the dancers, away from the fury of those feet that slipped on stones and leaped about stomping the earth without knowing that something had fallen among them.

Holding him up between us as if he was crippled, we went into the church with him. Natalia had him kneel down next to her before that little golden figure of the Virgin of Talpa. And Tanilo started to pray and let a huge tear fall, from way down inside him, snuffing out the candle Natalia had placed in his hands. But he didn't realize this; the light from so many lit candles kept him from realizing what was happening right there. He went on praying with his candle snuffed out. Shouting his prayers so he could hear himself praying.

But it didn't do him any good. He died just the same.

"... from our hearts filled with pain we all send her the same plea. Many laments mixed with hope. Her tenderness is not deaf to laments nor tears, for She suffers with us. She knows how to take away that stain and to leave the heart soft and pure to receive her mercy and charity. Our Virgin, our mother, who wants to know nothing of our sins, who blames herself for our sins, who wanted to bear us in her arms so life wouldn't hurt us, is right here by us, relieving our tiredness and the sicknesses of our souls and our bodies filled with thorns, wounded and supplicant. She knows that each day our faith is greater because it is made up of sacrifices ..."

That's what the priest said from up in the pulpit. And after he quit talking the people started praying all at once with a noise just like a lot of wasps frightened by smoke.

But Tanilo no longer heard what the priest was saying. He'd become still, with his head resting on his knees. And when Natalia moved him so he'd get up he was already dead.

Outside you could hear the noise of the dancing, the drums and the hornpipes, the ringing of bells. That's when I got sad. To see so many living things, to see the Virgin there, right in front of us with a smile on her face, and to see Tanilo on the other hand as if he was in the way. It made me sad.

But we took him there so he'd die, and that's what I can't forget.

Now the two of us are in Zenzontla. We've come back without him. And Natalia's mother hasn't asked me anything, what I did with my brother Tanilo, or anything. Natalia started crying on her shoulder and poured out the whole story to her.

I'm beginning to feel as if we hadn't reached any place; that we're only here in passing, just to rest, and that then we'll keep on traveling. I don't know where to, but we'll have to go on, because here we're very close to our guilt and the memory of Tanilo.

Maybe until we begin to be afraid of each other. Not saying anything to each other since we left Talpa may mean that. Maybe Tanilo's body is too close to us, the way it was stretched out on the rolled petate, filled inside and out with a swarm of blue flies that buzzed like a big snore coming from his mouth, that mouth we couldn't shut in spite of everything we did and that seemed to want to go on breathing without finding any breath. That Tanilo, who didn't feel pain any more but who looked like he was still in pain with his hands and feet twisted and his eyes wide open like he was looking at his own death. And here and there all his wounds dripping a yellow water, full of that smell that spread everywhere and that you could taste in your mouth, like it was a thick and bitter honey melting into your blood with each mouthful of air you took.

I guess that's what we remember here most often—that Tanilo we buried in the Talpa graveyard, that Tanilo Natalia and I threw earth and stones on so the wild animals wouldn't come dig him up.

Translated from the Spanish by George D. Schade

Nathalie Sarraute

XXII

Sometimes, when they were not looking at him, to try and find something that was warm and living around him, he would run his hand very gently along one of the columns of the sideboard . . . they would not see him, or perhaps they would think that he was merely "touching wood" for luck, a very widespread custom and, after all, a harmless one.

When he sensed that they were watching him from behind, like the villain in the movies who, feeling the eyes of the policeman on his back, concludes his gesture nonchalantly, gives it the appearance of being offhanded and naïve, to calm their apprehension he would drum with three fingers of his right hand, three times three, which is the really effectual lucky gesture. For they were watching him more closely since he had been caught in his room, reading the Bible.

Objects, too, were very wary of him and had been for a long time, ever since, as a little child, he had begged their favor, had tried to attach himself to them, to cling to them, to warm himself, they had refused to "play," to become what he had wanted to make of them, "poetic memories of childhood." They had been brought to heel, these objects had, being well trained, they had the unobtrusive, anonymous look of well-schooled servants; they knew their place and they refused to answer him, out of fear, no doubt, of being dismissed.

But with the exception, very rarely, of this timid little gesture, he really took no liberties of any kind. He had succeeded, little by little, in gaining control over all his stupid little manias, in fact, he had fewer of them now than were normally tolerated; he didn't even collect postage stamps—which normal people did, for all to see. He never stopped in the middle of the street to look—the way he had once done, on his walks, when the nursemaid, come along, will you! come along! had had to drag him—he crossed quickly and never held up street traffic; he walked by objects, even the most hospitable, even the most alive of them, without casting a single look of complicity in their direction.

In short, the very ones among his friends and relations who were keen about psychiatry had nothing to reproach him with, unless, perhaps, in view of his lack

of inoffensive, relaxing whims, in view of his too obedient conformity, it were a
slight tendency towards asthenia.

But they tolerated that; all things considered, it was less dangerous, less indec-
orous.

From time to time only, when he felt too weary, on their advice, he took the
liberty of going away alone on a little trip. And there, when he went walking at
nightfall, in the quiet little snowy streets that were filled with a gentle indulgence, he would run his hands lightly over the red and white bricks of the houses
and, clinging to the wall, sidewise, through fear of being indiscreet, he would
look through the clear panes into downstairs rooms in which green plants on
china saucers had been set in the window, and from where, warm, full, heavy
with a mysterious denseness, objects tossed him a small part—to him too, although he was unknown and a stranger—of their radiance; where the corners of
a table, the door of a sideboard, the straw seat of a chair emerged from the half-
light and consented to become for him, mercifully for him, too, since he was
standing there waiting, a little bit of his childhood.

Translated from the French by Maria Jolas

Isaac Bashevis Singer

. . . .

HENNE FIRE

I

Yes, there are people who are demons. God preserve us! Mothers see things when they give birth, but they never tell what they see!

Henne Fire, as she was called, was not a human being but a fire from Gehenna. I know one should not speak evil of the dead and she suffered greatly for her sins. Was it her fault that there was always a blaze within her? One could see it in her eyes: two coals. It was frightening to look at them. She was black as a gypsy, with a narrow face, sunken cheeks, emaciated—skin and bone. Once I saw her bathing in the river. Her ribs protruded like hoops. How could someone like Henne put on fat? Whatever one said to her, no matter how innocently, she immediately took offense. She would begin to scream, shake her fists, and spin around like a crazy person. Her face would turn white with anger. If you tried to defend yourself, she was ready to swallow you alive and she'd start smashing dishes. Every few weeks her husband, Berl Chazkeles, had to buy a new set.

She suspected everybody. The whole town was out to get her. When she flew into a rage, she said things that would not even occur to an insane person. Swear words poured from her mouth like worm-eaten peas. She knew every curse in the holy book by heart. She was not beyond throwing rocks. Once, in the middle of winter, she broke a neighbor's windowpane and the neighbor never learned why.

Henne had children, four girls, but as soon as they grew up they ran away from home. One became a servant in Lublin; one left for America; the most beautiful, Malkeleh, died of scarlet fever; and the fourth married an old man. Anything was better than living with Henne.

Her husband, Berl, must have been a saint. Only a saint could have stood such a shrew for twenty years. He was a sieve-maker. In those days, in the wintertime, work started when it was still dark. The sieve-maker had to supply his own candle. He earned only a pittance. Of course, they were poor, but they were not the only ones. A wagonload of chalk would not suffice to write down the complaints she hurled at him. I lived next door to her and once, when he left for work at dawn, I heard her call after him: "Come back feet first!" I can't imagine what she blamed him for. He gave her his last penny, and he loved her too. How could one love such a fiend? Only God knows. In any case, who can understand what goes on in the heart of a man?

My dear people, even he finally ran away from her. One summer morning, a Friday, he left to go to the ritual bath and disappeared like a stone in the water. When Henne heard he was seen leaving the village, she fell down in an epileptic fit right in the gutter. She knocked her head on the stones, hissed like a snake, and foamed at the mouth. Someone pushed a key into her left hand, but it didn't help. Her kerchief fell off and revealed the fact that she did not shave her head. She was carried home. I've never seen such a face, as green as grass, her eyes rolled up. The moment she came to, she began to curse and I think from then on never stopped. It was said that she even swore in her sleep. At Yom Kippur she stood in the women's section of the synagogue and, as the rabbi's wife recited the prayers for those who could not read, Henne berated the rabbi, the cantor, the elders. On her husband she called forth a black judgment, wished him smallpox and gangrene. She also blasphemed against God.

After Berl forsook her, she went completely wild. As a rule, an abandoned woman made a living by kneading dough in other people's houses or by becoming a servant. But who would let a malicious creature like Henne into the house? She tried to sell fish on Thursdays, but when a woman asked the price, Henne would reply, "You are not going to buy anyhow, so why do you come here just to tease me? You'll poke around and buy elsewhere."

One housewife picked up a fish and lifted its gills to see if it was fresh. Henne tore it from her hands, screaming, "Why do you smell it? Is it beneath your dignity to eat rotten fish?" And she sang out a list of sins allegedly committed by the woman's parents, grandparents, and great-grandparents back to the tenth generation. The other fishmongers sold their wares and Henne remained with a tubful. Every few weeks Henne washed her clothes. Don't ask me how she carried on. She quarreled about everything: the washtubs, the clotheslines, the water pump. If she found a speck of dust on a shirt hanging up to dry, she blamed it on her neighbors. She herself tore down the lines of others. One heard her yelling over half the town. People were afraid of her and gave in, but that was no good either. If you answered her she raised a rumpus, and if you kept silent she would scream, "Is it a disgrace to talk to me?" There was no dealing with her without being insulted.

At first her daughters would come home from the big towns for the holidays. They were good girls, and they all took after their father. One moment mother and daughter would kiss and embrace and before you knew it there would be a cat fight in Butcher Alley, where we lived. Plates crashed, windows were broken. The girl would run out of the house as though poisoned and Henne would be after her with a stick, screaming, "Bitch, slut, whore, you should have dissolved in your mother's belly!" After Berl deserted her, Henne suspected that her daughters knew his whereabouts. Although they swore holy oaths that they didn't, Henne would rave, "Your mouths will grow out the back of your heads for swearing falsely!"

What could the poor girls do? They avoided her like the plague. And Henne went to the village teacher and made him write letters for her saying that she disowned them. She was no longer their mother and they were no longer her daughters.

Still, in a small town one is not allowed to starve. Good people took pity on Henne. They brought her soup, garlic borscht, a loaf of bread, potatoes, or whatever they had to offer, and left it on the threshold. Entering her house was like walking into a lion's den. Henne seldom tasted these gifts. She threw them into the garbage ditch. Such people thrive on fighting.

Since the grownups ignored her, Henne began to quarrel with the children. A boy passed by and Henne snatched his cap because she imagined he had stolen pears from her tree. The pears were as hard as wood and tasted the same; a pig wouldn't eat them. She just needed an excuse. She was always lying and she called everybody else a liar. She went to the chief of police and denounced half the town, accusing this one of being a forger and that one of smuggling contraband from Galicia. She reported that the Hasidim were disrespectful to the czar. In the fall, when the recruits were being drafted, Henne announced in the marketplace that the rich boys were being deferred and the poor ones taken. It was true, too. But if they had all been taken, would it have been better? Somebody had to serve. But Henne, good sort that she was, could not suffer injustice. The Russian officials were afraid that she would cause trouble and had her sent to the insane asylum.

I was there when a soldier and a policeman came to get her. She turned on them with a hatchet. She made such a commotion that the whole town came running. But how strong is a female? As she was bound and loaded into a cart, she cursed in Russian, Polish, and Yiddish. She sounded like a pig being slaughtered. She was taken to Lublin and put in a strait jacket.

I don't know how it happened, but she must have been on her good behavior, because in less than half a year she was back in town. A family had moved into her hut, but she drove the whole lot out in the middle of a cold night. The next day Henne announced that she had been robbed. She went to all the neighbors to look for her belongings and humiliated everybody. She was no longer allowed into the women's synagogue and was even refused when she wanted to buy a seat for the Days of Awe. Things came to such a pass that when she went to the well to get water everyone ran away. It was simply dangerous to come near her.

She did not even respect the dead. A hearse passed by and Henne spat at it, screaming that she hoped the dead man's soul would wander in the wastelands forever. The better type of people turned a deaf ear to her, but when the mourners were of the common kind she got beaten up. She liked to be beaten; that is the truth. She would run around showing off a bump given her by this one, a black eye by that one. She ran to the druggist for leeches and salves. She kept summoning everybody to the rabbi, but the beadle would no longer listen to her and the rabbi had issued an order forbidding her to enter his study. She also tried her luck with the Gentiles, but they only laughed at her. Nothing remained to her but God. And according to Henne she and the Almighty were on the best of terms.

Now listen to what happened. There was a coachman called Kopel Klotz who lived near Henne. Once in the middle of the night he was awakened by screams for help. He looked out the window and saw that the house of the shoemaker across the street was on fire. He grabbed a pail of water and went to help put it out. But the fire was not at the shoemaker's; it was at Henne's. It was only the reflection that he had seen in the shoemaker's window. Kopel ran to her house and found everything burning: the table, the bench, the cupboard. It wasn't a usual fire. Little flames flew around like birds. Henne's nightshirt was burning. Kopel tore it off her and she stood there as naked as the day she was born.

A fire in Butcher Alley is no small thing. The wood of the houses is dry even in winter. From one spark the whole alley could turn into ashes. People came to the rescue, but the flames danced and turned somersaults. Every moment something else became ignited. Henne covered her naked body with a shawl and the fringes began to burn like so many candles. The men fought the fire until dawn. Some of them were overcome by the smoke. These were not flames, but goblins from hell.

In the morning there was another outburst. Henne's bed linen began to burn of itself. That day I visited Henne's hut. Her sheet was full of holes; the quilt and feather bed, too. The dough in the trough had been baked into a flat loaf of bread. A fiery broom had swept the floor, igniting the garbage. Tongues of flame licked everything. God save us, these were tricks of the Evil Host. Henne sent everybody to the devil; and now the devil had turned on her.

Somehow the fire was put out. The people of Butcher Alley warned the rabbi that if Henne could not be induced to leave they would take matters into their own hands. Everyone was afraid for his kin and possessions. No one wanted to pay for the sins of another. Henne went to the rabbi's house and wailed, "Where am I to go? Murderers, robbers, beasts!"

She became as hoarse as a crow. As she ranted, her kerchief took fire. Those who weren't there will never know what the demons can do.

As Henne stood in the rabbi's study, pleading with him to let her stay, her house went up in flames. A flame burst from the roof and it had the shape of a man with long hair. It danced and whistled. The church bells rang an alarm. The firemen tried their best, but in a few minutes nothing was left but a chimney and a heap of burning embers.

Later, Henne spread the rumor that her neighbors had set her house on fire. But it was not so. Who would try a thing like that, especially with the wind blowing? There were scores of witnesses to the contrary. The fiery image had waved its arms and laughed madly. Then it had risen into the air and disappeared among the clouds.

It was then that people began to call her Henne Fire. Up to then she had been known as Black Henne.

II

When Henne found herself without a roof over her head, she tried to move into the poorhouse but the poor and sick would not let her in. Nobody wants to be burned alive. For the first time she became silent. A Gentile woodchopper took her into his house. The moment she crossed the threshold the handle of his ax caught fire and out she went. She would have frozen to death in the cold if the rabbi hadn't taken her in.

The rabbi had a booth not far from his house which was used during the Sukkoth holidays. It had a roof which could be opened and closed by a series of pulleys. The rabbi's son installed a tin stove so that Henne would not freeze. The rabbi's wife supplied a bed with a straw mattress and linen. What else could they do? Jews don't let a person perish. They hoped the demons would respect a Sukkoth booth and that it would not catch fire. True, it had no mezuzah, but the rabbi hung a talisman on the wall instead. Some of the townspeople offered to bring food to Henne, but the rabbi's wife said, "The little she eats I can provide."

The winter cold began immediately after the Sukkoth holidays and it lasted until Purim. Houses were snowed under. In the morning one had to dig oneself out with a shovel. Henne lay in bed all day. She was not the same Henne: she was docile as a sheep. Yet evil looked out of her eyes. The rabbi's son fed her stove every morning. He reported in the study house that Henne lay all day tucked into her feather bed and never uttered a word. The rabbi's wife suggested that she come into the kitchen and perhaps help a little with the housework. Henne refused. "I don't want anything to happen to the rabbi's books," she said. It was whispered in the town that perhaps the Evil One had left her.

Around Purim it suddenly became warm. The ice thawed and the river overflowed. Bridge Street was flooded. The poor are miserable anyway, but when there is a flood at night and the household goods begin to swim around, life becomes unbearable. A raft was used to cross Bridge Street. The bakery had begun preparing matzos for Passover, but water seeped into the sacks and made the flour unusable.

Suddenly a scream was heard from the rabbi's house. The Sukkoth booth had burst into flame like a paper lantern. It happened in the middle of the night. Later Henne related how a fiery hand had reached down from the roof and in a second everything was consumed. She had grabbed a blanket to cover herself and had run into the muddy courtyard without clothes on. Did the rabbi have a choice? He had to take her in. His wife stopped sleeping at night. Henne said to the rabbi, "I shouldn't be allowed to do this to you." Even before the booth had burned down, the rabbi's married daughter, Taube, had packed her trousseau into a sheet so she could save it at a moment's notice in case of fire.

Next day the community elders called a meeting. There was much talk and haggling, but they couldn't come to a decision. Someone proposed that Henne be sent to another town. Henne burst into the rabbi's study, her dress in tatters, a living scarecrow. "Rabbi, I've lived here all my life, and here I want to die. Let them dig me a grave and bury me. The cemetery will not catch fire." She had found her tongue again and everybody was surprised.

Present at the meeting was Reb Zelig, the plumber, a decent man, and he finally made a suggestion. "Rabbi, I will build her a little house of brick. Bricks don't burn."

He asked no pay for his work, just his costs. Then a roofer promised to make the roof. Henne owned the lot in Butcher Alley, and the chimney had remained standing.

To put up a house takes months, but this little building was erected between Purim and Passover, everyone lending a hand. Boys from the study house dumped the ashes. Schoolchildren carried bricks. Yeshiva students mixed mortar. Yudel, the glazier, contributed windowpanes. As the proverb goes: a community is never poor. A rich man, Reb Falik, donated tin for the roof. One day there was a ruin and the next day there was the house. Actually it was a shack without a floor, but how much does a single person need? Henne was provided with an iron bed, a pillow, a straw mattress, a feather bed. She didn't even watch the builders. She sat in the rabbi's kitchen on the lookout for fires.

The house was finished just a day before Passover. From the poor fund, Henne was stocked with matzos, potatoes, eggs, horseradish, all that was necessary. She was even presented with a new set of dishes. There was only one thing everybody refused to do, and that was to have her at the Seder. In the evening they looked in at her window: no holiday, no Seder, no candles. She was sitting on a bench, munching a carrot.

One never knows how things will turn out. In the beginning nothing was heard from Henne's daughter, Mindel, who had gone to America. How does the saying go? Across the sea is another world. They go to America and forget father, mother, Jewishness, God. Years passed and there was not a single word from her. But Mindel proved herself a devoted child after all. She got married and her husband became immensely rich.

Our local post office had a letter carrier who was just a simple peasant. One day a strange letter carrier appeared. He had a long mustache, his jacket had gilded buttons, and he wore insignia on his cap. He brought a letter for which the recipient had to sign. For whom do you think it was? For Henne. She could no more sign her name than I can dance a quadrille. She daubed three marks on the receipt and somebody was a witness. To make it short, it was a letter containing money. Lippe, the teacher, came to read it and half the town listened.

"My dear mother, your worries are over. My husband has become rich. New York is a large city where white bread is eaten in the middle of the week. Everybody speaks English, the Jews too. At night it is as bright as day. Trains travel on tracks high up near the roofs. Make peace with Father and I will send you both passage to America."

The townspeople didn't know whether to laugh or cry. Henne listened but didn't say a word. She neither cursed nor blessed.

A month later another letter arrived, and two months after that, another. An American dollar was worth two rubles. There was an agent in town, and when he heard that Henne was getting money from America, he proposed all kinds of deals to her. Would she like to buy a house, or become a partner in a store? There was a man in our town called Leizer the messenger, although nobody ever sent him anywhere. He came to Henne and offered to go in search of her husband. If he was alive, Leizer was sure he would find him and either bring him home or make him send her a bill of divorcement. Henne's reply was: "If you bring him back, bring him back dead, and you should walk on crutches!"

Henne remained Henne, but the neighbors began to make a fuss over her. That is how people are. When they smell a groschen, they get excited. Now they were quick to greet her, called her Hennely, and waited on her. Henne just glowered at them, muttering curses. She went straight to Zrule's tavern, bought a big bottle of vodka, and took it home. To make a long story short, Henne began to drink. That a woman should drink is rare, even among the Gentiles, but that a Jewish woman should drink was unheard of. Henne lay in bed and gulped down the liquor. She sang, cried, and made crazy faces. She strolled over to the marketplace in her undergarments, followed by cat-calling urchins. It is sacrilegious to behave as Henne did, but what could the townspeople do? Nobody went to prison for drinking. The officials themselves were often dead drunk. The neighbors said that Henne got up in the morning and drank a cup of vodka. This was her breakfast. Then she went to sleep and when she awoke she began to drink in earnest. Once in a while, when the whim seized her, she would open the window and throw out some coins. The little ones almost killed themselves trying to pick them up. As they groped on the ground for the money, she would empty the slops over them. The rabbi sent for her but he might just as well have saved his breath. Everyone was sure that she would drink herself to death. Something entirely different happened.

As a rule, Henne would come out of her house in the morning. Sometimes she would go to the well for a pail of water. There were stray dogs in Butcher Alley and occasionally she would throw them a bone. There were no outhouses and the villagers attended to their needs in the open. A few days passed and nobody saw Henne. The neighbors tried to peer into her window, but the curtains were drawn. They knocked on her door and no one opened it. Finally they broke it open and what they saw should never be seen again. Some time before, Henne had bought an upholstered chair from a widow. It was an old piece of furniture. She used to sit in it drinking and babbling to herself. When they got the door open, sitting in the chair was a skeleton as black as coal.

My dear people, Henne had been burned to a crisp. But how? The chair itself was almost intact, only the material at the back was singed. For a person to be so totally consumed, you'd need a fire bigger than the one in the bathhouse on Fridays. Even to roast a goose, a lot of wood is needed. But the chair was untouched. Nor had the linen on the bed caught fire. She had bought a chest of drawers, a table, a wardrobe, and everything was undamaged. Yet Henne was one piece of coal. There was no body to be laid out, to be cleansed, or dressed in a shroud. The officials hurried to Henne's house and they could not believe their own eyes. Nobody had seen a fire, nobody had smelled smoke. Where could such a hell fire have come from? No ashes were to be found in the stove or under the tripod. Henne seldom cooked. The town's doctor, Chapinski, arrived. His eyes popped out of his head and there he stood like a figure of clay.

"How is it possible?" the chief of police asked.

"It's impossible," the doctor replied. "If someone were to tell me such a thing, I would call him a filthy liar."

"But it has happened," the chief of police interrupted.

Chapinski shrugged his shoulders and murmured, "I just don't understand."

Someone suggested that it might have been lightning. But there had been no lightning and thunder for weeks.

The neighboring squires heard of the event and arrived on the scene. Butcher Alley filled with carriages, britskas, and phaetons. The crowd stood and gaped. Everyone tried to find an explanation. It was beyond reason. The upholstery of the chair was filled with flax, dry as pepper.

A rumor spread that the vodka had ignited in Henne's stomach. But who ever heard of a fire in the guts? The doctor shook his head. "It's a riddle."

There was no point in preparing Henne for burial. They put her bones in a sack, carried it to the cemetery, and buried her. The gravedigger recited the Kaddish. Later her daughters came from Lublin, but what could they learn? Fires ran after Henne and a fire had finished her. In her curses she had often used the word "fire": fire in the head, fire in the belly. She would say, "You should burn like a candle." "You should burn in fever." "You should burn like kindling wood." Words have power. The proverb says: "A blow passes, but a word remains."

My dear people, Henne continued to cause trouble even after her death. Kopel the coachman bought her house from her daughters and turned it into a stable. But the horses sweated in the night and caught cold. When a horse catches cold that way, it's the end. Several times the straw caught fire. A neighbor who had quarreled with Henne about the washing swore that Henne's ghost tore the sheets from the line and threw them into the mud. The ghost also overturned a washtub. I wasn't there, but of a person such as Henne anything can be believed. I see her to this day, black, lean, with a flat chest like a man and the wild eyes of a hunted beast. Something was smouldering within her. She must have suffered. I remember my grandmother saying, "A good life never made anyone knock his head against the wall." However, no matter what misfortunes strike I say, "Burst, but keep a good face on things."

Thank God, not everyone can afford constantly to bewail his lot. A rabbi in our town once said: "If people did not have to work for their bread, everyone would spend his time mourning his own death and life would be one big funeral."

Translated from the Yiddish by the author
and Dorothea Straus

Susan Sontag

. . . .

UNGUIDED TOUR

I took a trip to see the beautiful things. Change of scenery. Change of heart.
And do you know?

What?

They're still there.

Ah, but they won't be there for long.

I know. That's why I went. To say goodbye. Whenever I travel, it's always to
say goodbye.

Tile roofs, timbered balconies, fish in the bay, the copper clock, shawls drying
on the rocks, the delicate odor of olives, sunsets behind the bridge, ochre stone.
"Gardens, parks, forests, woods, canals, private lakes, with huts, villas, gates,
garden seats, gazebos, alcoves, grottoes, hermitages, triumphal arches, chapels,
temples, mosques, banqueting houses, rotundas, observatories, aviaries, greenhouses, icehouses, fountains, bridges, boats, cascades, baths." The Roman amphitheater, the Etruscan sarcophagus. The monument to the 1914–18 war dead
in every village square. You don't see the military base. It's out of town, and not
on the main road.

Omens. The cloister wall has sprung a long diagonal crack. The water level is
rising. The marble saint's nose is no longer aquiline.

This spot. Some piety always brings me back to this spot. I think of all the
people who were here. Their names scratched into the bottom of the fresco.

Vandals!

Yes. Their way of being here.

The proudest of human-made things dragged down to the condition of natural things. Last Judgment.

You can't lock up all the things in museums.

Aren't there any beautiful things in your own country?

No. Yes. Fewer.

Did you have guidebooks, maps, timetables, stout shoes?

I read the guidebooks when I got home. I wanted to stay with my—

Immediate impressions?

You could call them that.

But you did see the famous places. You didn't perversely neglect them.

I did see them. As conscientiously as I could while protecting my ignorance. I don't want to know more than I know, don't want to get more attached to them than I already am.

How did you know where to go?

By playing my memory like a roulette wheel.

Do you remember what you saw?

Not much.

It's too sad. I can't love the past that's trapped within my memory like a souvenir.

Object lessons. Grecian urns. A pepper-mill Eiffel Tower. Bismarck beer mug. Bay-of-Naples-with-Vesuvius scarf. David-by-Michelangelo cork tray.

No souvenirs, thanks. Let's stay with the real thing.

The past. Well, there's always something ineffable about the past, don't you think?

In all its original glory. The indispensable heritage of a woman of culture.

I agree. Like you, I don't consider devotion to the past a form of snobbery. Just one of the more disastrous forms of unrequited love.

I was being wry. I'm a fickle lover. It's not love that the past needs in order to survive, it's an absence of choices.

And armies of the well-off, immobilized by vanity, greed, fear of scandal, and the inefficiency and discomfort of travel. Women carrying parasols and pearl handbags, with mincing steps, long skirts, shy eyes. Mustached men in top hats, lustrous hair parted on the left side, garters holding up their silk socks. Seconded by footmen, cobblers, ragpickers, blacksmiths, buskers, printer's devils, chimney sweeps, lacemakers, midwives, carters, milkmaids, stonemasons, coachmen, turnkeys, and sacristans. As recently as that. All gone. The people. And their pomp and circumstance.

Is that what you think I went to see?

Not the people. But their places, their beautiful things. You said they were still there. The hut, the hermitage, the grotto, the park, the castle. An aviary in the Chinese style. His Lordship's estate. A delightful seclusion in the midst of his impenetrable woods.

I wasn't happy there.

What did you feel?

Regret that the trees were being cut down.

So you have a hazy vision of natural things. From too much indulgence in the nervous, metallic pleasures of cities.

Unequal to my passions, I fled the lakes, I fled the woods, I fled the fields pulsing with glowworms, I fled the aromatic mountains.

Provincial blahs. Something less solitary is what you need.

I used to say: Landscapes interest me only in relation to human beings. Ah, loving someone would give life to all this . . . But the emotions that human beings inspire in us also sadly resemble each other. The more that places, customs, the circumstances of adventures are changed, the more we see that we amidst them are unchanging. I know all the reactions I shall have. Know all the words that I am going to utter again.

You should have taken me along instead.

You mean him. Yes, of course I wasn't alone. But we quarreled most of the time. He plodding, I odious.

They say. They say a trip is a good time for repairing a damaged love.

Or else it's the worst. Feelings like shrapnel half worked out of the wound. Opinions. And competition of opinions. Desperate amatory exercises back at the hotel on golden summer afternoons. Room service.

How did you let it get that dreary? You were so hopeful.

Rubbish! Prisons and hospitals are swollen with hope. But not charter flights and luxury hotels.

But you were moved. Sometimes.

Maybe it was exhaustion. Sure I was. I am. The inside of my feelings is damp with tears.

And the outside?

Very dry. Well—as dry as is necessary. You can't imagine how tiring it is. That double-membraned organ of nostalgia, pumping the tears in. Pumping them out.

Qualities of depth and stamina.

And discrimination. When one can summon them.

I'm bushed. They aren't all beautiful, the beautiful things. I've never seen so many squabby Cupids and clumsy Graces.

Here's a café. *In the café.* The village priest playing the pinball machine. Nineteen-year-old sailors with red pompons watching. Old gent with amber worry beads. Proprietor's granddaughter doing her homework at a deal table. Two hunters buying picture postcards of stags. He says: You can drink the acidic local wine, become a little less odious, unwind.

Monsieur René says it closes at five.

Each picture. "Each picture had beneath it a motto of some good intention. Seeing that I was looking carefully at these noble images, he said: 'Here everything is natural.' The figures were clothed like living men and women, though they were far more beautiful. Much light, much darkness, men and women who are and yet are not."

Worth a detour? Worth a trip! It's a remarkable collection. Still possessed its aura. The things positively importuned.

The baron's zeal in explaining. His courteous manner. He stayed all through the bombardment.

A necessary homogeneity. Or else some stark, specific event.

I want to go back to that antique store.

"The ogival arch of the doorway is Gothic, but the central nave and the flanking wings—"

You're hard to please.

Can't you imagine traveling not to accumulate pleasures but to make them rarer?

Satiety is not my problem. Nor is piety.

There's nothing left but to wait for our meals, like animals.

Are you catching a cold? Drink this.

I'm perfectly all right. I beg you, don't buy the catalogue. Or the postcard-size reproductions. Or the sailor sweater.

Don't be angry, but—did you tip Monsieur René?

Say to yourself fifty times a day: I am not a connoisseur, I am not a romantic wanderer, I am not a pilgrim.

You say it.

"A permanent part of mankind's spiritual goods."

Translate that for me. I forgot my phrase book.

Still, you saw what you came to see.

The old victory of arrangement over accumulation.

But sometimes you were happy. Not just in spite of things.

Barefoot on the mosaic floor of the baptistery. Clambering above the flying buttresses. Irradiated by a Baroque monstrance shimmering indistinctly in the growing dusk of the cathedral. Effulgence of things. Voluminous. Resplendent. Unutterable bliss.

You send postcards on which you write"'Bliss." Remember? You sent one to me.

I remember. Don't stop me. I'm flying. I'm prowling. Epiphany. Hot tears. Delirium. Don't stop me. I stroke my delirium like the balls of the comely waiter.

You want to make me jealous.

Don't stop me. His dainty skin, his saucy laughter, his way of whistling, the succulent dampness of his shirt. We went into a shed behind the restaurant. And I said: Enter, sir, this body. This body is your castle, your cabin, your hunting lodge, your villa, your carriage, your luxury liner, your drawing room, your kitchen, your speedboat, your tool shed . . .

Do you often do that sort of thing when he's around?

Him? He was napping at the hotel. A mild attack of heliophobia.

In the hotel. Back at the hotel, I woke him up. He had an erection. I seated myself on his loins. The nub, the hub, the fulcrum. Gravitational lines of force. In a world of perfect daylight. Indeed, a high-noon world, in which objects cast no shadows.

Only the half wise will despise these sensations.

I'm turning. I'm a huge steering wheel, unguided by any human hand. I'm turning . . .

And the other pleasures? The ones you came for.

"In the entire visible world there is hardly a more powerful mood-impression than that experienced within one of the Gothic cathedrals just as the sun is setting."

Pleasures of the eye. It had to be emphasized.

"The eye can see nothing beyond those glimmering figures that hover overhead to the west in stern, solemn rows as the burning evening sun falls across them."

Messengers of temporal and spiritual infinity.

"The sensation of fire permeates all, and the colors sing out, rejoicing and sobbing."

There, in truth, is a different world.

I found a wonderful old Baedeker, with lots of things that aren't in the Michelin. *Let's.* Let's visit the caves. Unless they're closed.

Let's visit the World War I cemetery.

Let's watch the regatta.

This spot. He committed suicide right here, by the lake. With his fiancée. In 1811.

I seduced a waiter in the restaurant by the port two days ago. *He said.* He said his name was Arrigo.

I love you. And my heart is pounding.

So is mine.

What's important is that we're strolling in this arcade together.

That we're strolling. That we're looking. That it's beautiful.

Object lessons. Give me that suitcase, it's heavy.

One must be careful not to wonder if these pleasures are superior to last year's pleasures. They never are.

That must be the seduction of the past again. But just wait until now becomes then. You'll see how happy we were.

I'm not expecting to be happy. *Complaints.* I've already seen it. I'm sure it'll be full. It's too far. You're driving too fast, I can't see anything. Only two showings of the movie, at seven and at nine. There's a strike, I can't telephone. This damned siesta, nothing's open between one and four. If everything came out of this suitcase, I don't understand why I can't cram it all back in.

You'll soon stop fretting over these mingy impediments. You'll realize you're carefree, without obligations. And then the unease will start.

Like those upper-middle-class Protestant folk who experience revelations, become hysterical, suffer breakdowns under the disorienting impact of Mediterranean light and Mediterranean manners. You're still thinking about the waiter.

I said I love you, I trust you, I didn't mind.

You shouldn't. I don't want that kind of revelation. I don't want to satisfy my desire, I want to exasperate it. I want to resist the temptation of melancholy, my dear. If you only knew how much.

Then you must stop this flirtation with the past invented by poets and curators. We can forget about their old things. We can buy their postcards, eat their food, admire their sexual nonchalance. We can march in their workers' festivals and sing the "Internationale," for even we know the words.

I'm feeling perfectly all right.

I think it's safe to. Pick up hitchhikers, drink unbottled water, try to score some hash in the piazza, eat the mussels, leave the camera in the car, hang out in waterfront bars, trust the hotel concierge to make the reservation, don't you?

Something. Don't you want to do something?

Does every country have a tragic history except ours?

This spot. See? There's a commemorative plaque. Between the windows.

Ruined. Ruined by too many decades of intrepid appreciation. Nature, the whore, cooperates. The crags of the Dolomites made too pink by the sun, the water of the lagoon made too silver by the moon, the blue skies of Greece (or Sicily) made too deep a blue by the arch in a white wall.

Ruins. These are ruins left from the last war.

Antiquarian effrontery: our pretty dwelling.

It was a convent, built according to a plan drawn up by Michelangelo. Turned into a hotel in 1927. Don't expect the natives to take care of the beautiful things.

I don't.

They say. They say they're going to fill in the canal and make it a highway, sell the duchess's rococo chapel to a sheik in Kuwait, build a condominium on that bluff with a stand of pine, open a boutique in the fishing village, put a sound-and-light show in the ghetto. It's going fast. International Committee. Attempting to preserve. Under the patronage of His Excellency and the Honorable. Going fast. You'll have to run.

Will I have to run?

Then let them go. Life is not a race.

Or else it is.

Any more. Isn't it a pity they don't write out the menus in purple ink any more. That you can't put your shoes outside the hotel room at night. *Remember.* Those outsize bills, the kind they had until the devaluation. *Last time.* There weren't as many cars last time, were there?

How could you stand it?

It was easier than it sounds. With an imagination like a pillar of fire. And a heart like a pillar of salt.

And you want to break the tie.

Right.

Lot's wife!

But his lover.

I told you. I told you, you should have taken me along instead.

Lingering. In the basilica. In the garden behind the inn. In the spice market. In bed, in the middle of the golden afternoon.

Because. It's because of the fumes from the petrochemical factories nearby. It's because they don't have enough guards for the museums.

"Two groups of statuary, one depicting virtuous toil, the other unbridled licentiousness."

Do you realize how much prices have gone up? Appalling inflation. I can't conceive how people here manage. With rents almost as high as back home and salaries half.

"On the left of the main road, the Tomb of the Reliefs (the so-called Tomba Bella) is entered. On the walls round the niches and on the pillars, the favorite objects of the dead and domestic articles are reproduced in painted stucco relief: dogs, helmets, swords, leggings, shields, knapsacks and haversacks, bowls, a jug, a couch, pincers, a saw, knives, kitchen vessels and utensils, coils of rope, etc."

I'm sure. I'm sure she was a prostitute. Did you look at her shoes? I'm sure they're giving a concert in the cathedral tonight. *Plus they said.* Three stars, I'm sure they said it had three stars.

This spot. This is where they shot the scene in that movie.

Quite unspoiled. I'm amazed. I was expecting the worst.

They rent mules.

Of course. Every wage earner in the country gets five weeks' paid vacation. The women age so quickly.

Nice. It's the second summer for the Ministry of Tourism's "Be Nice" campaign. This country where ruined marvels litter the ground.

It says. It says it's closed for restoration. It says you can't swim there any more.

Pollution.

They said.

I don't care. Come on in. The water's almost as warm as the Caribbean.

I want you, I feel you. Lick my neck. Slip off your trunks. Let me . . .

Let's. Let's go back to the hotel.

"The treatment of space in Mannerist architecture and painting shows this change from the 'closed' Renaissance world order to the 'open,' 'loose,' and deviating motions in the Mannerist universe."

What are you trying to tell me?

"The harmony, intelligibility, and coherence of the Renaissance world view were inherent in the symmetrical courtyards of Italian palaces."

I don't want to flatter my intelligence with evidence.

If you don't want to look at the painting, look at me.

See the sign? You can't take the boat that way. We're getting near the nuclear-submarine base.

Reports. Five cases of cholera have been reported.

This piazza has been called a stage for heroes.

It gets much cooler at night. You have to wear a sweater.

Thanks to the music festival every summer. You should see this place in the winter. It's dead.

The trial is next week, so now they're having demonstrations. Can't you see the banner? And listen to that song.

Let's not. I'm sure it's a clip joint.

They said. Sharks, I think they said.

Not the hydrofoil. I know it's faster, but they make me sick.

"The sun having mounted and the heat elsewhere too extreme for us, we have retired to the tree-shaded courtyard." It's not that I loved him. But in a certain hour of physical fatigue . . .

At the mercy of your moods.

Contented sometimes. Even blissful.

Doesn't sound like it. Sounds like struggling to savor.

Maybe. Loss of judgment in the necropolis.

Reports. There's a civil war raging in the north. The Liberation Front's leader is still in exile. Rumors that the dictator has had a stroke. But everything seems so—

Calm?

I guess . . . calm.

This spot. On this spot they massacred three hundred students.

I'd better go with you. You'll have to bargain.

I'm starting to like the food. You get used to it after a while. Don't you?

In the oldest paintings there is a complete absence of chiaroscuro.

I feel well here. There's not so much to see.

"Below the molding, small leafy trees, from which hang wreaths, ribbons, and various objects, alternate with figures of men dancing. One man is lying on the ground, playing the double flute."

Cameras. The women don't like to be photographed.

We may need a guide.

It's a book on the treasures they unearthed. Pictures, bronzes, and lamps.

That's the prison where they torture political suspects. Terror incognita.

Covered with flies. That poor child. Did you see?

Omens. The power failure yesterday. New graffiti on the monument this morning. Tanks grinding along the boulevard at noon. *They say.* They say the radar at the airport has been out for the last seventy-two hours.

They say the dictator has recovered from his heart attack.

No, bottled water. Hardier folk. Quite different vegetation.

And the way they treat women here! Beasts of burden. Hauling those sacks up azure hills on which—

They're building a ski station.

They're phasing out the leprosarium.

Look at his face. He's trying to talk to you.

Of course we could live here, privileged as we are. It isn't our country. I don't even mind being robbed.

"The sun having mounted and the heat elsewhere too extreme for us, we have retired to the shade of an oasis."

Sometimes I did love him. Still, in a certain hour of mental fatigue . . .

At the mercy of your moods.

My undaunted caresses. My churlish silences.

You were trying to mend an error.

I was trying to change my plight.

I told you, you should have taken me along instead.

It wouldn't have been different. I went on from there alone. I would have left you, too.

Mornings of departure. With everything prepared. Sun rising over the most majestic of bays (Naples, Rio, or Hong Kong).

But you could decide to stay. Make new arrangements. Would that make you feel free? Or would you feel you'd spurned something irreplaceable?

The whole world.

That's because it's later rather than earlier. "In the beginning, all the world was America."

How far from the beginning are we? When did we first start to feel the wound?

This staunchless wound, the great longing for another place. To make this place another.

In a mosque at Damietta stands a column that, if you lick it until your tongue bleeds, will cure you of restlessness. It must bleed.

A curious word, wanderlust. I'm ready to go.

I've already gone. Regretfully, exultantly. A prouder lyricism. It's not Paradise that's lost.

Advice. Move along, let's get cracking, don't hold me down, he travels fastest who travels alone. Let's get the show on the road. Get up, slugabed. I'm clearing out of here. Get your ass in gear. Sleep faster, we need the pillow.

She's racing, he's stalling.

If I go this fast, I won't see anything. If I slow down—

Everything. —then I won't have seen everything before it disappears.

Everywhere. I've been everywhere. I haven't been everywhere, but it's on my list.

Land's end. But there's water, O my heart. And salt on my tongue.

The end of the world. This is not the end of the world.

Jean Stafford

. . . .

CHILDREN ARE BORED
ON SUNDAY

Through the wide doorway between two of the painting galleries, Emma saw Alfred Eisenburg standing before "The Three Miracles of Zenobius," his lean, equine face ashen and sorrowing, his gaunt frame looking undernourished, and dressed in a way that showed he was poorer this year than he had been last. Emma herself had been hunting for the Botticelli all afternoon, sidetracked first by a Mantegna she had forgotten, and then by a follower of Hieronymus Bosch, and distracted, in an English room as she was passing through, by the hot invective of two ladies who were lodged (so they bitterly reminded one another) in an outrageous and expensive mare's-nest at a hotel on Madison. Emma liked Alfred, and once, at a party in some other year, she had flirted with him slightly for seven or eight minutes. It had been spring, and even into that modern apartment, wherever it had been, while the cunning guests, on their guard and highly civilized, learnedly disputed on aesthetic and political subjects, the feeling of spring had boldly invaded, adding its nameless, sentimental sensations to all the others of the buffeted heart; one did not know and never had, even in the devouring raptures of adolescence, whether this was a feeling of tension or of solution—whether one flew or drowned.

In another year, she would have been pleased to run into Alfred here in the Metropolitan on a cold Sunday, when the galleries were thronged with out-of-towners and with people who dutifully did something self-educating on the day of rest. But this year she was hiding from just such people as Alfred Eisenburg, and she turned quickly to go back the way she had come, past the Constables and Raeburns. As she turned, she came face to face with Salvador Dali, whose sudden countenance, with its unlikely mustache and its histrionic eyes, familiar from the photographs in public places, momentarily stopped her dead, for she did not immediately recognize him and, still surprised by seeing Eisenburg, took him also to be someone she knew. She shuddered and then realized that he was merely famous, and she penetrated the heart of a guided tour and proceeded safely through the rooms until she came to the balcony that overlooks the medieval armor, and there she paused, watching two youths of high-school age examine the joints of an equestrian's shell.

She paused because she could not decide what to look at now that she had been denied the Botticelli. She wondered, rather crossly, why Alfred Eisenburg was looking at it and why, indeed, he was here at all. She feared that her afternoon, begun in such a burst of courage, would not be what it might have been; for this second's glimpse of him—who had no bearing on her life—might very well divert her from the pictures, not only because she was reminded of her ignorance of painting by the presence of someone who was (she assumed) versed in it but because her eyesight was now bound to be impaired by memory and conjecture, by the irrelevant mind-portraits of innumerable people who belonged to Eisenburg's milieu. And almost at once, as she had predicted, the air separating her from the schoolboys below was populated with the images of composers, of painters, of writers who pronounced judgments, in their individual argot, on Hindemith, Ernst, Sartre, on Beethoven, Rubens, Baudelaire, on Stalin and Freud and Kierkegaard, on Toynbee, Frazer, Thoreau, Franco, Salazar, Roosevelt, Maimonides, Racine, Wallace, Picasso, Henry Luce, Monsignor Sheen, the Atomic Energy Commission, and the movie industry. And she saw herself moving, shaky with apprehensions and martinis, and with the belligerence of a child who feels himself laughed at, through the apartments of Alfred Eisenburg's friends, where the shelves were filled with everyone from Aristophanes to Ring Lardner, where the walls were hung with reproductions of Seurat, Titian, Vermeer, and Klee, and where the record cabinets began with Palestrina and ended with Copland.

These cocktail parties were a modus vivendi in themselves for which a new philosophy, a new ethic, and a new etiquette had had to be devised. They were neither work nor play, and yet they were not at all beside the point but were, on the contrary, quite indispensable to the spiritual life of the artists who went to them. It was possible for Emma to see these occasions objectively, after these many months of abstention from them, but it was still not possible to understand them, for they were so special a case, and so unlike any parties she had known at home. The gossip was different, for one thing, because it was stylized, creative (integrating the whole of the garrotted, absent friend), and all its details were precise and all its conceits were Jamesian, and all its practitioners sorrowfully saw themselves in the role of Pontius Pilate, that hero of the untoward circumstance. (It has to be done, though we don't want to do it; 'tis a pity she's a whore, when no one writes more intelligent verse than she.) There was, too, the matter of the drinks, which were much worse than those served by anyone else, and much more plentiful. They dispensed with the fripperies of olives in martinis and cherries in manhattans (God forbid! They had no sweet teeth), and half the time there was no ice, and when there was, it was as likely as not to be suspect shavings got from a bed for shad at the corner fish store. Other species, so one heard, went off to dinner after cocktail parties certainly no later than half past eight, but no one ever left a party given by an Olympian until ten, at the earliest, and then groups went out together, stalling and squabbling at the door, angrily unable to come to a decision about where to eat, although they seldom ate once they got there but, with the greatest formality imaginable, ordered several rounds of cocktails, as if they had not had a drink in a month of Sundays. But the most surprising thing of all about these parties was that every now and again, in the middle of the urgent, general conversation, this cream of the enlightened was horribly curdled, and an argument would end, quite literally, in a bloody nose or a black eye. Emma was always astounded when this happened and continued to think that these outbursts did not arise out of hatred or jealousy but out of some quite unaccountable quirk, almost a reflex, almost something physical. She never quite believed her eyes—that is, was never altogether convinced that they were really beating one another up. It seemed, rather, that this was only a deliberate and perfectly honest demonstration of what might have happened often if they had not so diligently dedicated themselves to their intellects. Although she had seen them do it, she did not and could not believe that city people clipped each other's jaws, for, to Emma, urban equaled urbane, and ichor ran in these Augustans' veins.

As she looked down now from her balcony at the atrocious iron clothes below, it occurred to her that Alfred Eisenburg had been just such a first-generation metropolitan boy as these two who half knelt in lithe and eager attitudes to study the glittering splints of a knight's skirt. It was a kind of childhood she could not imagine and from the thought of which she turned away in secret, shameful pity. She had been really stunned when she first came to New York to find that almost no one she met had gluttonously read Dickens, as she had, beginning at the age of ten, and because she was only twenty when she arrived in the city and unacquainted with the varieties of cultural experience, she had acquired the idea, which she was never able to shake entirely loose, that these New York natives had been deprived of this and many other innocent pleasures because they had lived in apartments and not in two- or three-story houses. (In the early years in New York, she had known someone who had not heard a cat purr until he was twenty-five and went to a houseparty on Fire Island.) They had played hide-and-seek dodging behind ash cans instead of lilac bushes and in and out of the entries of apartment houses instead of up alleys densely lined with hollyhocks. But who was she to patronize and pity them? Her own childhood, rich as it seemed to her on reflection, had not equipped her to read, or to see, or to listen, as theirs had done; she envied them and despised them at the same time, and at the same time she feared and admired them. As their attitude implicitly accused her, before she beat her retreat, she never looked for meanings, she never saw the literary-historical symbolism of the cocktail party but went on, despite all testimony to the contrary, believing it to be an occasion for getting drunk. She never listened, their manner delicately explained, and when she talked she was always lamentably off key; often and often she had been stared at and had been told, "It's not the same thing at all."

Emma shuddered, scrutinizing this nature of hers, which they all had scorned, as if it were some harmless but sickening reptile. Noticing how cold the marble railing was under her hands, she felt that her self-blame was surely justified; she came to the Metropolitan Museum not to attend to the masterpieces but to remember cocktail parties where she had drunk too much and had seen Alfred Eisenburg, and to watch schoolboys, and to make experience out of the accidental contact of the palms of her hands with a cold bit of marble. What was there to do? One thing, anyhow, was clear and that was that today's excursion into the world had been premature; her solitude must continue for a while, and perhaps it would never end. If the sight of someone so peripheral, so uninvolving, as Alfred Eisenburg could scare her so badly, what would a cocktail party do? She almost fainted at the thought of it, she almost fell headlong, and the boys, abandoning the coat of mail, dizzied her by their progress toward an emblazoned tabard.

In so many words, she wasn't fit to be seen. Although she was no longer mutilated, she was still unkempt; her pretensions needed brushing; her ambiguities needed to be cleaned; her evasions would have to be completely overhauled before she could face again the terrifying learning of someone like Alfred Eisenburg, a learning whose components cohered into a central personality that was called "intellectual." She imagined that even the boys down there had opinions on everything political and artistic and metaphysical and scientific, and because she remained, in spite of all her opportunities, as green as grass, she was certain they had got their head start because they had grown up in apartments, where there was nothing else to do but educate themselves. This being an intellectual was not the same thing as dilettantism; it was a calling in itself. For example, Emma did not even know whether Eisenburg was a painter, a writer, a composer, a sculptor, or something entirely different. When, seeing him with the composers, she had thought he was one of them; when, the next time she met him, at a studio party, she decided he must be a painter; and when, on subsequent occasions, everything had pointed toward his being a writer, she had relied altogether on circumstantial evidence and not on anything he had said or done. There was no reason to suppose that he had not looked upon her as the same sort of variable and it made their anonymity to one another complete. Without the testimony of an impartial third person, neither she nor Eisenburg would ever know the other's actual trade. But his specialty did not matter, for his larger designation was that of "the intellectual," just as the man who confines his talents to the nose and throat is still a doctor. It was, in the light of this, all the more extraordinary that they had had that lightning-paced flirtation at a party.

Extraordinary, because Emma could not look upon herself as an intellectual. Her private antonym of this noun was "rube," and to her regret—the regret that had caused her finally to disappear from Alfred's group—she was not even a bona-fide rube. In her store clothes, so to speak, she was often taken for an intellectual, for she had, poor girl, gone to college and had never been quite the same since. She would not dare, for instance, go up to Eisenburg now and say that what she most liked in the Botticelli were the human and compassionate eyes of the centurions' horses, which reminded her of the eyes of her own Great-uncle Graham, whom she had adored as a child. Nor would she admit that she was delighted with a Crivelli Madonna because the peaches in the background looked exactly like marzipan, or that Goya's little red boy inspired in her only the pressing desire to go out immediately in search of a plump cat to stroke. While she knew that feelings like these were not really punishable, she had not perfected the art of tossing them off; she was no flirt. She was a bounty jumper in the war between Great-uncle Graham's farm and New York City, and liable to court-martial on one side and death on the other. Neither staunchly primitive nor confidently *au courant*, she rarely knew where she was at. And this was her

Achilles' heel: her identity was always mistaken, and she was thought to be an intellectual who, however, had not made the grade. It was no use now to cry that she was not, that she was a simon-pure rube; not a soul would believe her. She knew, deeply and with horror, that she was thought merely stupid.

It was possible to be highly successful as a rube among the Olympians, and she had seen it done. Someone calling himself Nahum Mothersill had done it brilliantly, but she often wondered whether his name had not helped him, and, in fact, she had sometimes wondered whether that had been his real name. If she had been called, let us say, Hyacinth Derryberry, she believed she might have been able, as Mothersill had been, to ask who Ezra Pound was. (This struck her suddenly as a very important point; it was endearing, really, not to know who Pound was, but it was only embarrassing to know who he was but not to have read the "Cantos.") How different it would have been if education had not meddled with her rustic nature! Her education had never dissuaded her from her convictions, but certainly it had ruined the looks of her mind—painted the poor thing up until it looked like a mean, hypocritical, promiscuous malcontent, a craven and apologetic fancy woman. Thus she continued secretly to believe (but *never* to confess) that the apple Eve had eaten tasted exactly like those she had eaten when she was a child visiting on her Great-uncle Graham's farm, and that Newton's observation was no news in spite of all the hue and cry. Half the apples she had eaten had fallen out of the tree, whose branches she had shaken for this very purpose, and the Apple Experience included both the descent of the fruit and the consumption of it, and Eve and Newton and Emma understood one another perfectly in this particular of reality.

Emma started. The Metropolitan boys, who, however bright they were, would be boys, now caused some steely article of dress to clank, and she instantly quit the balcony, as if this unseemly noise would attract the crowd's attention and bring everyone, including Eisenburg, to see what had happened. She scuttered like a quarry through the sightseers until she found an empty seat in front of Rembrandt's famous frump, "The Noble Slav"—it was this kind of thing, this fundamental apathy to most of Rembrandt, that made life in New York such hell for Emma—and there, upon the plum velours, she realized with surprise that Alfred Eisenburg's had been the last familiar face she had seen before she had closed the door of her tomb.

In September, it had been her custom to spend several hours of each day walking in a straight line, stopping only for traffic lights and outlaw taxicabs, in the hope that she would be tired enough to sleep at night. At five o'clock—and gradually it became more often four o'clock and then half past three—she would go into a bar, where, while she drank, she seemed to be reading the information offered by the *Sun* on "Where to Dine." Actually she had ceased to dine long since; every few days, with effort, she inserted thin wafers of food into her re-pelled mouth, flushing the frightful stuff down with enormous drafts of magical, purifying, fulfilling applejack diluted with tepid water from the tap. One weighty day, under a sky that grimly withheld the rain, as if to punish the whole city, she had started out from Ninetieth Street and had kept going down Madison and was thinking, as she passed the chancery of St. Patrick's, that it must be nearly time and that she needed only to turn east on Fiftieth Street to the New Weston, where the bar was cool, and dark to an almost absurd degree. And then she was hailed. She turned quickly, looking in all directions until she saw Eisenburg approaching, removing a gray pellet of gum from his mouth as he came. They were both remarkably shy and, at the time, she had thought they were so because this was the first time they had met since their brief and blameless flirtation. (How curious it was that she could scrape off the accretions of the months that had followed and could remember how she had felt on that spring night—as trembling, as expectant, as altogether young as if they had sat together underneath a blooming apple tree.) But now, knowing that her own embarrassment had come from something else, she thought that perhaps his had, too, and she connected his awkwardness on that September day with a report she had had, embedded in a bulletin on everyone, from her sole communicant, since her retreat, with the Olympian world. This informant had run into Alfred at a party and had said that he was having a very bad time of it with a divorce, with poverty, with a tempest that had carried off his job, and, at last, with a psychoanalyst, whose fees he could not possibly afford. Perhaps the nightmare had been well under way when they had met beside the chancery. Without alcohol and without the company of other people, they had had to be shy or their suffering would have shown in all its humiliating dishabille. Would it be true still if they should inescapably meet this afternoon in an Early Flemish room?

Suddenly, on this common level, in this state of social displacement, Emma wished to hunt for Alfred and urgently tell him that she hoped it had not been as bad for him as it had been for her. But naturally she was not so naïve, and she got up and went purposefully to look at two Holbeins. They pleased her, as Holbeins always did. The damage, though, was done, and she did not really see the pictures; Eisenburg's hypothetical suffering and her own real suffering blurred the clean lines and muddied the lucid colors. Between herself and the canvases swam the months of spreading, cancerous distrust, of anger that made her seasick, of grief that shook her like an influenza chill, of the physical afflictions by which the poor victimized spirit sought vainly to wreck the arrogantly healthy flesh.

Even that one glance at his face, seen from a distance through the lowing crowd, told her, now that she had repeated it to her mind's eye, that his cheeks were drawn and his skin was gray (no soap and water can ever clean away the grimy look of the sick at heart) and his stance was tired. She wanted them to go together to some hopelessly disreputable bar and to console one another in the most maudlin fashion over a lengthy succession of powerful drinks of whisky, to compare their illnesses, to marry their invalid souls for these few hours of painful communion, and to babble with rapture that they were at last, for a little while, no longer alone. Only thus, as sick people, could they marry. In any other terms, it would be a *mésalliance*, doomed to divorce from the start, for rubes and intellectuals must stick to their own class. If only it could take place—this honeymoon of the cripples, this nuptial consummation of the abandoned—while drinking the delicious amber whisky in a joint with a jukebox, a stout barkeep, and a handful of tottering derelicts; if it could take place, would it be possible to prevent him from marring it all by talking of secondary matters? That is, of art and neurosis, art and politics, art and science, art and religion? Could he lay off the fashions of the day and leave his learning in his private entrepôt? Could he, that is, see the apple fall and not run madly to break the news to Newton and ask him what on earth it was all about? Could he, for her sake (for the sake of this pathetic rube all but weeping for her own pathos in the Metropolitan Museum), forget the whole dispute and, believing his eyes for a change, admit that the earth was flat?

It was useless for her now to try to see the paintings. She went, full of intentions, to the Van Eyck diptych and looked for a long time at the souls in Hell, kept there by the implacable, indifferent, and genderless angel who stood upon its closing mouth. She looked, in renewed astonishment, at Jo Davidson's pink, wrinkled, embalmed head of Jules Bache, which sat, a trinket on a fluted pedestal, before a Flemish tapestry. But she was really conscious of nothing but her desire to leave the museum in the company of Alfred Eisenburg, her cousin-german in the territory of despair.

So she had to give up, two hours before the closing time, although she had meant to stay until the end, and she made her way to the central stairs, which she descended slowly, in disappointment, enviously observing the people who were going up, carrying collapsible canvas stools on which they would sit, losing themselves in their contemplation of the pictures. Salvador Dali passed her, going quickly down. At the telephone booths, she hesitated, so sharply lonely that she almost looked for her address book, and she did take out a coin, but she put it back and pressed forlornly forward against the incoming tide. Suddenly, at the storm doors, she heard a whistle and she turned sharply, knowing that it would be Eisenburg, as, of course, it was, and he wore an incongruous smile upon his long, El Greco face. He took her hand and gravely asked her where she had been all this year and how she happened to be here, of all places, of all days. Emma replied distractedly, looking at his seedy clothes, his shaggy hair, the green cast of his white skin, his deep black eyes, in which all the feelings were disheveled, tattered, and held together only by the merest faith that change *had* to come. His hand was warm and her own seemed to cling to it and all their mutual necessity seemed centered here in their clasped hands. And there was no doubt about it; he had heard of her collapse and he saw in her face that she had heard of his. Their recognition of each other was instantaneous and absolute, for they cunningly saw that they were children and that, if they wished, they were free for the rest of this winter Sunday to play together, quite naked, quite innocent. "What a day it is! What a place!" said Alfred Eisenburg. "Can I buy you a drink, Emma? Have you time?"

She did not accept at once; she guardedly inquired where they could go from here, for it was an unlikely neighborhood for the sort of place she wanted. But they were *en rapport*, and he, wanting to avoid the grownups as much as she, said they would go across to Lexington. He needed a drink after an afternoon like this—didn't she? Oh, Lord, yes, she did, and she did not question what he meant by "an afternoon like this" but said that she would be delighted to go, even though they would have to walk on eggs all the way from the Museum to the place where the bottle was, the peace pipe on Lexington. Actually, there was nothing to fear; even if they had heard catcalls, or if someone had hooted at them, "Intellectual loves Rube!" they would have been impervious, for the heart carved in the bark of the apple tree would contain the names Emma and Alfred, and there were no perquisites to such a conjugation. To her own heart, which was shaped exactly like a valentine, there came a winglike palpitation, a delicate exigency, and all the fragrance of all the flowery springtime love affairs that ever were seemed waiting for them in the whisky bottle. To mingle their pain, their handshake had promised them, was to produce a separate entity, like a child that could shift for itself, and they scrambled hastily toward this profound and pastoral experience.

Peter Taylor

. . . .

A FRIEND
AND PROTECTOR

Family friends would always say how devoted Jesse Munroe was to my uncle. And Jesse himself would tell me sometimes what he would do to anybody who harmed a hair on "that white gentleman's head." The poor fellow was much too humorless and lived much too much in the past—or in some other kind of removal from the present—to reflect that Uncle Andrew no longer had a hair on his head to be harmed. While he was telling me the things he would do, I'd often burst out laughing at the very thought of my uncle's baldness. Or that was what I told myself I was laughing about. At any rate, my outbursts didn't bother Jesse. He always went right ahead with his description of the violence he would do Uncle Andrew's assailant. And I, watching his obscene gestures and reminding myself of all the scrapes he had been in and of the serious trouble my uncle had got him out of twenty years back, I could almost believe he would do the things he said. More than one time, in fact, his delineations became so real and convincing it took my best fit of laughter to conceal the shudders he sent through me.

He was a naturally fierce-looking little man with purplish black skin and thick wiry hair, which he wore not clipped short like most Negro men's hair but long and bushed up on his head. It was intended to give him height, I used to suppose. But it contributed instead to a general sinister effect, just as his long, narrow sideburns did; and my Uncle Andrew would always insist that it was this effect Jesse strived for. He wasn't, actually, such a little man. He was of medium height. It was because he was so stoop-shouldered and was so often seen beside my Uncle Andrew that we, my aunt and I, thought of him as little. He *was* extremely stoop-shouldered, though, and his neck was so short that the lobes of his overlarge ears seemed to reach almost to the collar of his white linen jacket. Probably it was this peculiarity along with his bushy hair and his perpetually bloodshot eyes that made me say at first he was naturally fierce-looking.

He wasn't *naturally* fierce-looking. My Uncle Andrew was right about that. It was something he had achieved. And according to my uncle, the scrapes he was always getting into didn't really amount to much. My Aunt Margaret, however—my "blood aunt," married to Uncle Andrew—used to shake her head bitterly and say that Negroes could get away with anything with Uncle Andrew and that his ideas of "much" were very different from hers. "Jesse Munroe can disappear into the bowels of Beale Street," she would say in Jesse's presence, "knowing that when he comes out all he did there will be a closed chapter for 'Mr. Andrew.'" Jesse would be clearing the table or laying a fire in the living room, and while such talk went on he would keep his eyes lowered except to steal a glance now and then at my aunt.

I was a boy of fifteen when I used to observe this. I was staying there in Memphis with my uncle and aunt just after Mother died. The things Aunt Margaret said in Jesse's presence made me feel very uncomfortable. And it seemed unlike her. I used to wish Jesse would look at Uncle Andrew instead of at her and spare himself the sight of the expression on her face at those moments.

But it was foolish of me to waste sympathy on Jesse Munroe, and even at the time I knew it was. For one thing, despite all the evenings we spent talking back in the pantry during the two years I lived there, he never seemed to be really aware of me as a person. Each time we talked it was almost as though it was the first time. There was no getting to know him. Two years later when I had finished high school and was not getting along with my uncle and aunt as well as at first, I didn't live at their house anymore. But I would sometimes see Jesse at my uncle's Front Street office where I then had a job and where Jesse soon came to work as my uncle's special flunky. Uncle Andrew was a cotton broker, and it wasn't unusual for such a successful cotton man as he was to keep a factotum like Jesse around the office. I would see Jesse there, and he wouldn't even bother to speak to me. I am certain that if nowadays he is in a condition to remember anyone he doesn't remember me. I appeared on the scene too late. By the time I came along Jesse's escapades and my uncle's and aunt's reactions to them had become a regular pattern. It was too well established, over too many years, for my presence or my sympathy one way or the other to make any difference. It was the central and perhaps the only reality in Jesse's life. It had been so since before I was born and it would continue to be so, for a while at least, after I left the house.

My uncle and aunt had brought Jesse with them to Memphis when Uncle Andrew moved his office there from out at Braxton, which is the country town our family comes from. He was the only local Negro they brought with them, and since this was right after Jesse had received a suspended sentence for an alleged part in the murder of Aunt Margaret's washwoman's husband, it was assumed in Braxton that there had been some sensible understanding arrived at between Andrew Nelson and the presiding judge. Jesse was to have a suspended sentence; Uncle Andrew was to get him out of Braxton and keep him out. . . . Be that as it may, Jesse came away with them to Memphis and during the first year he hardly set foot outside their house and yard.

He was altogether too faithful and too hardworking to be tolerated by any of the trifling servants Aunt Margaret was able to hire in Memphis. For a while she couldn't keep a cook on the place. Then one finally came along who discovered how to get Jesse's goat, and this one stayed the normal time for a Memphis cook—that is, four or five years. She was Jesse's ruin, I suppose. She discovered the secret of how to get his goat, and passed it on to the maid and the furnace boy and the part-time chauffeur that Uncle Andrew kept. And they passed it on to those who came after them. They teased him unmercifully, made life a misery for him. What they said to him was that he was a country boy in the city, scared to go out on the street. Now, there is a story, seemingly known to all Negro citizens of Memphis, of a Mississippi country boy who robs his old grandmother and comes to town prepared to enjoy life. He takes a hotel room and sits in the window looking down at the crowds. But he can't bring himself to go down and "mix with 'em." The story has several versions, but usually it ends with the boy's starving to death in his room because he is scared to go down and take his chances on Beale Street. And this was how they pictured Jesse. They went so far, even, as to ridicule him that way in front of my aunt and uncle.

As a matter of fact, Jesse couldn't have been much more than a boy in those days. And his nature may really have been a timid one. Whatever other reasons there were for his behavior, probably it was due partly to his being a timid country boy. There was always something of the puritan in him, too. I could see this when I was only fifteen. I never once heard him use any profanity, or any rough language at all except when he was indicating what he would do to my uncle's imaginary attacker—and then it was more a matter of gestures than of words. When the cook my aunt had during the time I was there would sometimes make insinuating remarks about the dates I began having and about the hours I kept toward the end of my stay, Jesse would say, "You oughtn't talk that way before this white boy." If I sometimes seemed to enjoy the cook's teasing and even egged her on a little, he would get up and leave the room. Perhaps the most old-fashioned and country thing about him was that he still wore his long underwear the year round. On Mondays, when he generally had a terrible hangover and was tapering off from the weekend, he would work all day in the garden. I would see him out there even on the hottest July day working with his shirt off but still wearing his long-sleeved undershirt. The other servants took his long underwear as another mark of his primness, and whenever they talked about the light he kept burning in his room all night they would say he never put it out except once a week when he took his bath and changed his long johns.

Yet no matter how much fun they made of him to his face, when Jesse wasn't present the other servants admitted they would hate to run into him while he was off on one of his sprees, and they assured me that *they* didn't hang around the kind of places that he did. And laugh at him though they did, they respected him for the amount of work he could turn out and for the quality of it. He was a perfectionist in his work both in the house and in the yard, and especially in my uncle's vegetable garden.

The cook who found out how to get Jesse's goat shouldn't be blamed too much. She couldn't have known the harm she was doing. And surely Jesse couldn't have gone on forever never leaving the house. The time had to come. And once that teasing had started, Jesse had to *show* them. He didn't tell anyone when he first began going out. The other servants didn't live on the place regularly, and my uncle only discovered Jesse's absence by chance late one night when he wanted him for some trifle. He went out in the backyard and called up to his room above the garage. The light was on, but there was no answer. Uncle climbed the rickety outside stairs that went up to the room and banged the door to wake him. Then he came down the stairs again and went in the house and conferred with Aunt Margaret. They were worried about Jesse, thinking something might have happened to him, and so Uncle Andrew went up and forced the lock on the door to Jesse's room.

The light was burning—a little twenty-watt bulb on a cord hanging in the middle of the room—and the room was as neat as a pin. But there was no Jesse. My aunt, who can always remember every detail of a moment like that, said that from the back-door she could hear Uncle Andrew's footstep out there in the room above the garage. For a time that was all she heard. But then finally she heard Uncle Andrew break out into a kind of laughter that was characteristic of him. It expressed all the good nature in his being and at the same time a certain hateful spirit, too. From her description I am sure it was just like his laughter when he caught you napping at Russian bank or checkers or when he saw he had you beaten and began slapping down his cards or pushing his kings around.

Presently he came out on the stoop at the head of the stairs and, still chuckling in his throat, called down to Aunt Margaret, "Our chick has left the nest." Then, closing the door, he took out his pocketknife and managed to screw the lock in place again. When he joined Aunt Margaret at the kitchen door he told her not to say anything about the incident to Jesse, that it was none of their business if he wanted a night out now and again.

Aunt Margaret could never get Jesse to tell her when he was planning an evening out, and later when he began taking an occasional Sunday off he never gave advance warning of that either. Sunday morning would come and he would simply not be on the place. It was still the same when I came there to live. After a Sunday's absence without leave, Jesse would be working my uncle's garden all day Monday. It was a big country vegetable garden right on Belvedere Street in Memphis. I have seen my aunt stand for a long period of time at one of the upstairs windows watching Jesse at work down there on a Monday morning, herself not moving a muscle until he looked up at her. Then she would shake her head sadly—exaggerating the shake so that he couldn't miss it—and turn her back to the window. When my uncle came home in the evening on one of those Mondays he would go straight to the garden and exclaim over the wonderful weeding and chopping the garden had had. Later, in the house, he would say it was worth having Jesse take French leave now and then in order to get that good day's work in the garden from him.

His real escapades and the scrapes he got into were in a different category from his occasional weekends. In the first place, they lasted longer. When he had already been missing for three or four days or even a week there would be a telephone call late at night or early some morning. Usually it would be an anonymous call, sometimes a man's voice, sometimes a woman's. If a name were given it was one that meant nothing to Uncle Andrew, and when Jesse had been rescued he invariably maintained he had never heard the name of the caller before. He would say he just wished he knew who it was, and always protested that he hadn't wanted Uncle Andrew to be bothered. The telephone call usually went about like this: "You Mr. Andrew Nelson at Number 212 Belvedere Street?"

"Yes."

"Yo friend Jesse's in jail and he needs yo help."

Then the informer would hang up or, if questioned in time by Uncle Andrew, would give a name like "Henry White" or "Mary Jones" along with some made-up street number and a street nobody ever heard of. One time the voice said only, "Yo friend Jesse's been pisened. He's in room Number 9 at the New Charleston Hotel." Uncle Andrew had gone down to the New Charleston with a policeman, and they found Jesse seriously ill and out of his head—probably from getting hold of bad whiskey. They took him to the John Gaston Hospital where he had to stay for nearly a week.

Usually, though, it wasn't just a matter of his being on a drunk. According to my aunt, he got into dreadful fights in which he slashed other Negroes with a knife and got cut up himself, though I never saw any of his scars. Probably they were all hidden beneath his long underwear. And besides, by the time I came along they would have been old scars since by then his scrapes had, for a long time, been of a different kind. There had been a number of years when his troubles were all with women. There were women who fought over him, women who fought *him*, women who got him put in jail for bothering them, and women who got him put in jail for not helping support their children. Then, after this phase, he was involved off and on for several years in the numbers racket and the kind of gang warfare that goes along with that. Uncle Andrew would have to get the police and go down and rescue him from some room above a pool hall where the rival gang had him cornered.

My account of all this came of course from my aunt since my uncle never revealed the nature of Jesse's troubles to anyone but Aunt Margaret. She dragged it out of him because she felt she had a right to know. She may have exaggerated it all to me. But I used to think two of the points she made about it were good ones. She pointed out that the nature of his escapades grew successively worse, so that it was harder each time for Uncle Andrew to intervene. And she suspected that that gave Jesse considerable satisfaction. She also said that from the beginning all of Jesse's degrading adventures had had one thing in common: He never was able or willing to get out of any jam on his own. He would let any situation run on until there was no way he could be saved except through Uncle Andrew's intervention. "All he seems to want," she said, "is to have something worse than the time before for his 'Mr. Andrew' to save him from and dismiss as a mere nothing."

I felt at the time that this was very true, and it tended to make me agree with Uncle Andrew that Jesse Munroe's scrapes were not very important in themselves, and, in that sense, didn't "amount to much." In fact, my aunt's observation seemed so obviously true that it was hard to think of Jesse as anything but a spoiled child, which, I suppose, is the way Uncle Andrew did think of him.

The murder that Jesse had gotten mixed up in back in Braxton was as nasty a business as you hear about. Uncle Andrew would not have had a white man living about his garage who had had any connection with such a business. When *I* finally gave up my room at his house and went to live at the "Y," it was more because of *his* disapproval of my friends (and of the hours I kept) than it was because of my aunt's. And though I couldn't have said so to a living soul that I knew when I was a boy, I used to wish my uncle could have been half as tolerant of my own father, who was a weak man and got into various kinds of trouble, as he was of Jesse. My father was killed in an automobile crash when I was only a little fellow, but, for several years before, Uncle Andrew had refused to have anything to do with him personally, though he would always help him get jobs as long as they were away from Braxton and, always, on the condition that my mother and I would continue to live in Braxton with my grandparents. I was taught to believe that Uncle Andrew was right about all of this, and I still believe that he was in a way. Jesse hadn't, after all, had the advantages that my father had, and he may have been a victim of circumstances. But my father was a victim of circumstances, too, I think—as who isn't, for that matter? Even Uncle Andrew and Aunt Margaret were, in a way.

In that murder of Aunt Margaret's washwoman's husband I believe Jesse was accused of being an accessory after the fact. I don't think anyone accused him of having anything to do with the actual killing. The washwoman and a boyfriend of hers named Cleveland Blakemore had done in her husband without help from anyone. They did it in a woods lot behind a roadhouse on the outskirts of town, where the husband found them together. At the trial I think the usual blunt instrument was produced as the murder weapon. Then they had transported the body to the washwoman's house where they dismembered it and attempted to burn the parts in the chimney. But it was a rainy night and the flue wouldn't draw. They ended by pulling out the charred remains and burying them in a cotton patch behind the washwoman's house, not in one grave but in a number of graves scattered about the cotton patch. (You may wonder why I bring in these awful details of the murder, and I wonder myself. I tell them out of some kind of compulsion and because I have known them ever since I was a small child in Braxton. I couldn't have told the story without somehow bringing them in. I find I have only been waiting for the right moment. And it seems to me now that I would never have had the interest I did in Jesse except that he was someone connected with those gory details of a crime I had heard about when I was very young and which had stuck in my mind during all the years when I was growing up in the house with my pretty, gentle mother and my aged grandparents.) At any rate, it was on a rainy winter morning just a few weeks after the murder that a Negro girl, hurrying to work, took a shortcut through that cotton patch. In her haste she stumbled and fell into a hole where the pigs had rooted up what was left of the victim's left forearm and hand.

In the trial it was proved that Jesse had provided the transportation for the corpse from the woods lot to the washwoman's house. His defense contended that he just happened to be at the roadhouse that night, driving a funeral car which he had borrowed, without permission, from the undertaker's parlor where he worked as janitor, and sometimes as driver. (You can hear the voice of the prosecution: "It was the saddest funeral that car ever went to.") He was paid in advance for the trip, and it was represented to him (according to his defense) that the washwoman's husband was only dead drunk.

It was never proved conclusively that Jesse had any part in the dismemberment or in the efforts at burning. Witnesses who testified they had seen *two* men coming and going from the house to the cotton patch (in the heavy rain on that autumn night) were not reliable ones. Yet the testimony that Jesse's borrowed car was parked in front of the house during most of the night was given by Negro men and women of the highest character. Even Jesse's defense never denied his presence in there. But to me it seems quite as likely that, as his defense maintained, he was kept there at knife point, or at least by the fear that if he attempted to go he might meet the same fate that the washwomen's husband had, as that he willingly took part in what went on. My uncle of course felt that there was no question about it, that Jesse was an innocent country boy drawn into the business by the washwomen and her friend, Cleveland Blakemore (who no doubt guessed he had taken the undertaker's car without permission), and that he wasn't to be blamed. Uncle Andrew even served as a character witness for Jesse at the trial, because he had known him before the murder when Jesse was janitor at his office as well as at the undertaker's.

I never heard any talk about the murder from Uncle Andrew and Aunt Margaret themselves. In private Aunt Margaret would tell me about some of the other troubles Jesse had been in and about how narrowly he had escaped long jail sentences. Only Uncle Andrew's ever widening connections among influential people in Memphis had been able to prevent those sentences. She said that my uncle was such a modest man that he naturally minimized Jesse's scrapes so as not to put too much importance on the things he was able to do to get him out of them.

But my uncle knew his wife well enough to know what she would have told me. Without ever giving me his version of any of the incidents he would say to me now and then that Aunt Margaret was much too severe and that she set too high standards for Jesse. And I did find it painful to hear the way she spoke to Jesse and to see the way she looked at him even after one of his milder weekends. In those days, so soon after my mother died, Aunt Margaret was always so kind and so considerate of my feelings and of my every want that it seemed out of character for her to be harsh and severe with anyone. Before that day I packed my things and moved out of her house, however, I came to doubt that it was so entirely out of character. If I had stayed there a day longer, I might have had even greater doubts. I think it is fortunate I left when I did. Our quarrel didn't amount to a lot. It was about my staying out all night one time without ever being willing to explain where I was. As soon as I was a little older and began to settle down to work and behave myself we made it up. Nowadays I'm on the best of terms with her and Uncle Andrew. And whenever I'm over at their place for a meal things seem very much the way they used to. Even the talk about Jesse goes very much the way it did when he was on the scene and in easy earshot.

When they talked about him together in the old days, especially when there was company around, it was all about his loyalty and devotion to Uncle Andrew. I agreed with every word they said on the subject, and if someone had said to me then that it was Aunt Margaret whom Jesse was most dependent upon and whose attention he most needed I would have said that person was crazy. How could anyone have supposed such a thing? And if I should advance such a theory nowadays to my uncle and aunt or to their friends they would imagine that I was expressing some long-buried resentment against Uncle Andrew. Any new analysis made in the light of what happened to Jesse after he went to work in my uncle's Front Street office would not interest them. They wouldn't be able to reverse a view based upon the impressions of all those years when Jesse was with them, a view based upon impressions received before any of them ever knew Jesse, impressions inherited from their own uncles and aunts and parents and grandparents.

I used to watch the expression on his black face when he was waiting on Uncle Andrew at table or was helping him into his overcoat when Uncle Andrew left for his office in the morning. His careful attention to my uncle's readiness for his next sleeve or for the next helping of greens made you feel he considered it a privilege to be doing all these little favors for a man who had done so many large ones for him. His attentions to my uncle impressed everyone who came to the house. If there was a party, he couldn't pass through the room, even with a tray loaded with glasses, without stopping before Uncle Andrew to nod and mutter respectfully, "Mr. Andrew." This itself was a memorable spectacle, and often was enough to stop the party talk of those who witnessed it: Uncle Andrew, so tall and erect, so bald and clean-shaven, so proudly beak-nosed, and yet with such a benign expression in those gray eyes that focused for one quick moment upon Jesse. And Jesse, stooped and purple-black and bushy-headed and red-eyed, clad in his white vestment and all but genuflecting while he held the tray of glasses perfectly steady for my uncle. It lasted only a second, and then Jesse's eyes would dart from one to another of the men standing nearest Uncle Andrew as though looking for some Cassius among them—some Judas. (And perhaps thinking all the time only that my aunt's eyes were upon him, denouncing him not merely as a sycophant and hypocrite but as a man who would have to answer for his manifold sins before the dread seat of judgment on the Last Day.) When he had moved on with his tray, some guest who had not been to the house before was apt to comment on what a wicked-looking fellow he was. My uncle would laugh heartily and say that nothing would please Jesse more than to think this was the impression he gave. "He gets himself up to look awful mean and he likes to think of himself as a devil. But actually he's as harmless as that boy standing there," Uncle Andrew would say, pointing of course to me.

I would laugh self-consciously, not really liking to have my own harmlessness pointed out. And I wonder if Jesse, already on the other side of the room, sometimes heard my laughter then and detected a certain hollowness in it that was also there when he told me the things he would do to my uncle's imaginary assailant. Because often, when I stood looking at the guest made uncomfortable by Jesse's glance, I could not help thinking of those things. In my mind's eye I would see his gestures, see him seizing his throat, rolling his eyes about, making as if to slice off his ears and nose, and indicating an even more debilitating operation. It may seem strange that I never imagined that those threats might be directed toward me personally, since I was my father's son and might easily have been supposed to bear a grudge against my uncle. But I felt that Jesse made it graphically clear that it was some Negro man like himself he had in mind as my uncle's assailant. When he was going through his routine he would usually be in the pantry and he would have placed himself in such relation to the mirror panel beside the swinging door there that, by rolling his eyes, he could be certain to see the black visage of this man he was mutilating.

It was another coincidence, like their moving to Memphis just when Jesse had to be gotten out of Braxton, that my aunt and uncle decided to give up the house and move to an apartment at just the time when it was no longer feasible for them to have Jesse Munroe working at their house. Uncle Andrew was nearly seventy years old at the time. He was spending less time at his office, and he and Aunt Margaret wanted to be free to travel. During the two years I was with them, there were three occasions when Jesse was missing from the house for about a week and had to be rescued by my uncle. I didn't know then exactly what his current outside activities were. Even Aunt Margaret preferred not to discuss it with me. She would say only that in her estimation it was worse than anything before. Later I learned that he had become a kind of confidence man and that—as in the numbers racket—his chief troubles came from his competitors. He specialized, for a time, in preying upon green country boys who had come to Memphis with their little wads of money. After I had left the house he went to something still worse. He was delivering country girls whom he picked up on Beale Street into the hands of the Pontotoc Street madams.

It was the authorities from neighboring counties in West Tennessee and Mississippi who finally began to put pressure on the police. They threatened, so I have been told, to come in and take care of Jesse themselves. Uncle Andrew moved him to a little room on the top floor of the ramshackle old building that his cotton company was in. Jesse lived up there and acted as a kind of butler and bartender in my uncle's private office, which was a paneled, air-conditioned suite far in the rear of and very different-looking from the display rooms where the troughs of cotton samples were. The trouble was that his "Mr. Andrew" was not at the office very much anymore for Jesse to wait on. And so most of the time he stayed up in his little cubbyhole on the top floor, and of course he got to drinking up my uncle's whiskey. He never left the building, never came down below the third floor, which Uncle Andrew's offices were on, and he never talked to the other Negroes who worked there. I would pass him in the hallway sometimes and speak to him, but he wouldn't even look at me. At last, of course, he went crazy up there in my uncle's office. It may have been partly from drinking so much whiskey, but at least this time we knew it wasn't bad whiskey. . . . When the office force came and opened up that morning they found him locked up in Uncle Andrew's air-conditioned, soundproofed suite and they could see through the glass doors the wreck he had made of everything in there. He had slashed the draperies and cut up the upholstery on the chairs. There were big spots and gashes on the walls where he had thrown things—mostly bottles of whiskey and gin, which of course had been broken and left lying all about the floor. He had pushed over the bar, the filing cabinets, the refrigerator, the electric watercooler, and even the air-conditioning unit. For a while nobody could tell where Jesse himself was. It wasn't till just before I got there that they spotted him crouched under Uncle Andrew's mahogany desk. From the beginning, though, they could hear him moaning and praying and calling out now and then for help. And even before I arrived someone had observed that it wasn't for Uncle Andrew but for Aunt Margaret he was calling.

I was parking my car down in the alley when one of the secretaries who had already been up there rushed up to me and told me what had happened. I hurried around to the street side of the building and went up the stairs so fast that I stumbled two or three times before I got to the third floor. They made a place for me at the glass door and told me that if I would stoop down I could see him back in the inner office crouched under the desk. I saw him there, and what I noticed first was that he didn't have on his white jacket or his shirt but was still wearing his long-sleeved winter underwear.

Fortunately, it happened that Uncle Andrew and Aunt Margaret were not on one of their trips at the time. Everyone at the office knew this, and they knew better than to call the police. They would have known better even if Uncle Andrew had not been in town. They waited for me to come in and telephone Uncle Andrew. I went up into the front display room and picked up the telephone. It was only eight-thirty, and I knew that Uncle Andrew would probably still be in bed. He sounded half asleep when he answered. I blurted out, "Uncle Andrew, Jesse's cracked up pretty bad down here at the office and has himself locked in your rooms."

"Yes," said Uncle Andrew, guardedly.

"He's made a mess of the place and is hiding under your desk. He has a knife, I suppose. And he keeps calling for Aunt Margaret. Do you think you'll come down, or—"

"Who is it speaking?" Uncle Andrew said, as though anyone else at the office ever called him "uncle." He did it out of habit. But it gave me an unpleasant feeling. I was tempted to give some name like "Henry White" and hang up, but I said nothing. I just waited. Uncle Andrew was silent for a moment. Then I heard him clear his throat, and he said, "Do you think he'll be all right till I can get down there?"

"I think so," I said. "I don't know."

"I'll get Fred Morley and be down there in fifteen minutes," he said.

I don't know why but I said again, "He keeps calling for Aunt Margaret."

"I heard you," Uncle Andrew said. Then he said, "We'll be down in fifteen minutes."

I didn't know whether his "we" meant himself and Fred Morley, who was the family doctor, or whether it included Aunt Margaret. I don't know yet which he meant. But when he and Dr. Morley arrived, my aunt was with them, and I don't think I was ever so glad to see anyone. I kissed her when she came in.

I came near to kissing Uncle Andrew too. I was touched by how old he had looked as he came up the stairs—he and Aunt Margaret, and Dr. Morley, too—how old and yet how much the same. And I was touched by the fact that it hadn't occurred to any of the three not to come. However right or wrong their feelings toward Jesse were they were the same as they would have been thirty years before. In a way this seemed pretty wonderful to me. It did at the moment. I thought of the phrase my aunt was so fond of using about people: "true blue."

The office force, and two of the partners by now, were still bunched around the glass door peering in at Jesse and trying to hear the things he was saying. I stood at the top of the stairs watching the three old people ascend the two straight flights of steps that I had come stumbling up half an hour earlier—two flights that came up from the ground floor without a turn or a landing between floors. I thought how absurd it was that in these Front Street buildings, where so much Memphis money was made, such a thing as an elevator was unknown. Except for adding the little air-conditioned offices at the rear, nobody was allowed to do anything there that would change the old-fashioned, masculine character of the cotton man's world. This row of buildings, hardly two blocks long, with their plaster facade and unbroken line of windows looking out over the brown Mississippi River were a kind of last sanctuary—generally beyond the reach of the ladies and practically beyond the reach of the law.

When they got to the top of the stairs I kissed my aunt on her powdered cheek. She took my arm and stood a moment catching her breath before we moved out of the hallway. I thought to myself that she had put more powder on her face this morning than was usual for her. No doubt she had dressed in a great hurry, hardly looking in her glass. But I observed that underneath the powder her face was flushed from the climb, and her china blue eyes shone brightly. Instead of seeming older to me now, I felt she looked younger and prettier and more feminine than I had ever before seen her. It must have been just seeing her there in a Front Street office for the first time. . . . But I still remember the delicate pressure of her hand as she leaned on my arm.

Uncle Andrew went straight to the door of his office and shooed everyone else away. I don't know whether I saw him do this or not, but I know that's how it was. Presently I found myself in the middle display room standing beside Aunt Margaret while Dr. Morley made pleasantries to her about how the appearance of cotton offices never changed. He hadn't been inside one in more than a decade, and he wondered how long it had been for her. Uncle Andrew, meanwhile, in order to be sure that Jesse heard him through the glass door and above his moaning had to speak in a voice that resounded all over the third floor of the building. Yet he didn't seem to be shouting, and he managed to put into his voice all the reassurance and forgiveness that must have been there during their private interchanges in years past. It was like hearing a radio soap opera turned on unbearably loud in a drugstore or in some other public place. "Come open the door, Jesse. You know I'm your friend. Haven't I always done right by you? It doesn't matter about the mess you've made in there. I have insurance to cover everything, and I'm not going to let anybody harm you."

It didn't do any good, though. Even in the middle room we could hear Jesse calling out—more persistently now—for Aunt Margaret to help him. Yet Aunt Margaret still seemed to be listening to Dr. Morley. I couldn't understand it. I wanted to interrupt and ask her if she didn't hear Jesse. Why had she come if she wasn't even going in there and look at him through the glass door? Didn't she feel any compassion for the poor fellow? Surely she would suddenly turn her back on us and walk in there. That seemed how she would do it.

Then for a moment my attention was distracted from Aunt Margaret to myself—to how concerned I was about whether or not she would go to him, to how very much I cared about Jesse's suffering and his need to have my aunt come and look at him! I took my eyes off Aunt Margaret and was myself resolutely trying to observe what a Front Street cotton office was really like when I felt her hand on my arm again. Looking at her I saw that underneath the powder her color was still quite high. While Dr. Morley talked on she gazed at me with moist eyes which made her look still prettier than before. And now I perceived that she had been intending all the time to go to Jesse and give the poor brute whatever comfort she could. But I saw too that there were difficulties for her which I had not imagined. Suddenly she did as she *would* do. Without a word she turned her back on us and went back there and showed herself in the glass door.

That was all there was to it really. Or for Jesse it was. It seemed to be all the real help he needed or could accept. He didn't come out and open the door, but he was relatively quiet afterward, even after Aunt Margaret was finally led away by Uncle Andrew and Dr. Morley, and even after Dr. Morley's two men came and broke the glass in the door and went in for him. When Aunt Margaret had been led away it seemed to be my turn again, and so I went back there and stood watching him until the men came. Now and then he would start to crawl out from under the desk but each time would suddenly pull back and try to hide himself again, and then again the animal grunts and groans would begin. Obviously, he was still seeing the things he had thought were after him during the night. But though he made some feeble efforts at resistance, I think he had regained his senses sufficiently to be glad when Dr. Morley's men finally came in and took him.

That was the end of it for Jesse. And this is where I would like to leave off. It is the next part that it is hardest for me to tell. But the whole truth is that my aunt did more than just show herself to Jesse through the glass door. While she remained there her behavior was such that it made me understand for the first time that this was not merely the story of that purplish-black, kinky-headed Jesse's ruined life. It is the story of my aunt's pathetically unruined life, and my uncle's too, and even my own. I mean to say that at this moment I understood that Jesse's outside activities had been not only *his*, but *ours* too. My Uncle Andrew, with his double standard or triple standard—whichever it was—had most certainly forced Jesse's destruction upon him, and Aunt Margaret had made the complete destruction possible and desirable to him with her censorious words and looks. But they did it because they had to, because they were so dissatisfied with the pale *un*ruin of their own lives. They did it because something would not let them ruin their own lives as they wanted and felt a need to do—as I have often felt a need to do, myself. As who does not sometimes feel a need to do? Without knowing it, I think, Aunt Margaret wanted to see Jesse as he was that morning. And it occurs to me now that Dr. Morley understood this at the time.

The moment she left us to go to Jesse, the old doctor became silent. He and I stood on opposite sides of one of the troughs of cotton, each of us fumbling with samples we had picked up there. Dr. Morley carefully turned his back on the scene that was about to take place in the room beyond. I could not keep myself from watching it.

I think I had never seen my aunt hurry before. As soon as she had passed into the back display room she began running on tiptoe. Uncle Andrew heard her soft footfall. As he turned around, their eyes must have met. I saw Uncle's face and saw, or imagined I saw, the expression in his gray eyes—one of utter dismay. Yet I don't think this had anything to do with Aunt Margaret. It was Jesse who was on his mind. He could not believe that he had failed to bring Jesse to his senses. I suspect that when Aunt Margaret looked into his eyes she got the impression that her husband didn't at that moment know who in the world she was. Maybe at that moment *she* couldn't have said who *he* was. I imagine their eyes meeting like the eyes of strangers, perhaps two white people passing each other on some desolate back street in the toughest part of niggertown, each wondering what dire circumstances could have brought so nice-looking a person as the other to this unlikely neighborhood. . . . At last, when Aunt Margaret drew near the glass door, Uncle Andrew stepped aside and moved out of my view.

For a time she stood before the glass panel in silence. She was peering about the two rooms inside, looking for Jesse. At last, without ever seeing where he was, I suppose, she began speaking to him. Her words were not audible to me and almost certainly they weren't so to Jesse, who continued for some time to keep on with his moaning and praying, though seeing that she had come he didn't go on calling out for her. The voice she spoke to him in was utterly sweet and beautiful. I think she was quoting scripture to him part of the time—one of the Psalms, I believe. Instinctively, I began moving toward the doorway that joined the room I was in and the room she was in. It was the voice of that same Aunt Margaret who had spoken to me with so much kindness and sympathy and love in the days just after my mother died. I was barely able to keep from bursting into tears—tears of joy and exaltation.

Jesse didn't, as I have already said, come out and open the door. But at some point, which I didn't mark, he became quieter. Now there were only intermittent sobs and groans. After a while my aunt stopped speaking. She was searching again for his hiding place in there. Presently, Uncle Andrew appeared again. He came over to her and indicated that if she would stoop down she could see Jesse under the desk. He watched her very intently as she squatted there awkwardly before the door.

If it had seemed strange for me to see her running, a few minutes earlier, it seemed almost unbelievable now that I was seeing her squatting there that way on the floor. I watched her and I thought how unlike her it was. I think I know the very moment when she saw her friend Jesse. I could tell her body had suddenly gone perfectly rigid. She looked not like any woman I had ever seen but like some hideously angular piece of modern sculpture. And then, throwing her hands up to her face, she lost her balance. My uncle was quick and caught her before she fell. He brought her to her feet at once and as he did so he called out for assistance—not from me but from Dr. Morley. Dr. Morley brushed past me in the doorway, answering the call.

Even after she was on her feet she couldn't take her hands down from her face for several moments. When finally she did manage to do so, all her high color and all the brightness in her eyes had vanished. As they led her away it was hard to think of her as the same woman who had rested her hand on my sleeve only a little while ago. Had she really wanted to see Jesse as he was this morning? I think she had. But I think the sight of the animal crouched underneath my uncle's desk—and probably peering out at her—had been more than she was actually prepared to look upon. As she was led off by her husband and her doctor, I felt certain that Aunt Margaret had suffered a shock from which she would never recover.

But how mistaken I was about her recovery soon became clear. I waited around until Dr. Morley's men arrived and I watched them go in and take Jesse. Then I wandered through the other display rooms up to the front office, where most of the real paperwork of the firm was done and where my own desk was. The front office was really a part of the front display room, divided from it only by a little railing with a swinging gate. I knew I would find my aunt up there and I supposed I would find her lying down on the old leather couch just inside the railing. I could even imagine how Dr. Morley and my uncle, and probably one of the office girls, would be hovering about and administering to her. Yet it was a different scene I came on. Dr. Morley was seated at my desk taking down information which he said would be necessary for him to have about Jesse. He was writing it on the back of an envelope. Aunt Margaret was seated in a chair drawn up beside him. She seemed completely herself again. Uncle, standing on the other side of the doctor, was trying to supply the required information. But Aunt Margaret kept correcting most of the facts that Uncle Andrew gave. While the doctor listened with perfect patience, the two of them disputed silly points like Jesse's probable age and the correct spelling of his surname, whether it was "Munroe" or "Monroe," and what his mother's maiden name had been. . . . It was hard to believe that either Aunt Margaret or Uncle Andrew had any idea of what was happening to Jesse at that very moment or any feeling about it.

Dr. Morley had Jesse committed to the state asylum out at Bolivar. They locked him up for a while, then they made a trusty of him. Dr. Morley says he seems very happy and that he has made himself so useful that they will almost certainly never let him go. I have never been out there to see him, of course, and neither has Aunt Margaret or Uncle Andrew. But I have dreams about Jesse sometimes—absurd, wild dreams that are not like anything that ever happened. One night recently when I was at a dinner party at my uncle and aunt's apartment and someone was recalling Jesse's devotion to my uncle, I undertook to tell one of those dreams of mine. But I broke it off in the middle and pretended that that was all, because I saw my aunt, at the far end of the table, was looking as pale as if she had seen a ghost or as if I had been telling a dream that *she* had had. As soon as I stopped, the talk resumed its usual theme, and my aunt seemed all right again. But when our eyes met a few minutes later she sent me the same quick, disapproving glance that my mother used to send me at my grandfather's table when I was relating some childish nightmare I had had. "Don't bore people with what you dream," my mother used to say after we had left the table and were alone. "If you have nothing better than that to contribute, leave the talking to someone else." Aunt Margaret's rude glance said precisely that to me. But I must add that when we were leaving the dining room my aunt rested her hand rather firmly and yet tenderly on my arm as if to console and comfort me. She was by nature such a kind and gentle person that she could not bear to think she had hurt someone she loved.

Michel Tournier

· ·

DEATH AND THE
MAIDEN

Hearing muffled laughter coming from the back of the classroom, the teacher suddenly broke off.

"*Now* what is it?"

The crimson, mirthful face of a little girl appeared.

"It's Melanie, mademoiselle. Right now she's eating lemons."

The whole class roared with laughter. The mistress marched over to the back row. Melanie looked up at her, her face the picture of innocence, its thinness and pallor accentuated by the heavy mass of her black hair. She was holding a carefully decorticated lemon, whose peel was curled up on her desk like a snake. The teacher was perplexed.

This Melanie Blanchard had intrigued her right from the start of the school year. Since she was docile, intelligent, and hardworking, it was impossible not to consider and treat her as one of the best pupils in the class. And yet she drew attention to herself—without being provocative, it is true, and with disarming spontaneity—by ridiculous inventions and strange behavior. In the history class, for instance, she displayed a passionate, almost morbid curiosity about all the famous people who had been condemned to death and tortured. Her eyes shining with alarming intensity, she would recite in great detail the last minutes of Joan of Arc, Gilles de Rais, Mary Stuart, Ravaillac, Charles the First, Damiens, omitting no particular of their sufferings, however atrocious.

Was it merely the fascination with horror so frequently to be found in children, reinforced by a touch of sadism? Other characteristics proved that in Melanie's case it was a question of something deeper and more complex. Right from the beginning of the fall term she had distinguished herself by an extraordinary composition she had written for the teacher. As usual, the mistress had asked the children to describe one day in the holidays that were just over. And although Melanie's account had begun quite tritely with the preparations for a picnic lunch in the country, it came to an abrupt halt with the sudden death of the grandmother, which obliged the family to forgo their outing. Then the story resumed, but on a negative, irreal note, and Melanie went on to describe, imperturbably and in a kind of hallucinatory vision, the various stages of the outing

697

that had not taken place, the birdsong that no one had heard, the preparation under a tree of the lunch that no one had had, and the comic incidents of their return during a storm, which had no rhyme or reason, since no one had set out. And she concluded:

> The family was assembled sadly around the bed on which the grand-mother's corpse was lying; nobody ran off laughing to shelter in the barn, none of them did their hair, jostling one another in front of the only mirror in the living room; they didn't light a big fire to dry their soaked clothes, which therefore didn't steam in front of the chimney like the hair of a horse drenched in sweat. The grandmother had gone off on her own, leaving every-one else at home.

And now it was lemons! Did all the little girl's ridiculous inventions have something in common? What was it? The teacher asked herself this question, and suspected that an answer existed—for there was undoubtedly a certain "family likeness" among all these inventions; they bore the stamp of the same personality—but she could find no answer.

"Do you like lemons?"

Melanie shook her head.

"Then why do you eat them? Are you afraid of getting scurvy?"

Melanie had no reply to these two questions. The teacher shrugged her shoulders and took a stand on more familiar ground.

"In any case, it's against the rules to eat in class. You must write out fifty times: *I eat lemons in class.*"

Melanie acquiesced with docility, relieved not to have to give any further explanation. And indeed, how could she have got other people to understand?—seeing that she barely understood it herself—that she was not treating herself with lemons because she was afraid of getting scurvy, but because she was afraid of a much more profound sickness, both physical and mental, a wave of insipidity and grayness that suddenly came sweeping up over the world and threatened to submerge her. Melanie was bored. She suffered boredom in a kind of metaphysical vertigo.

Though, after all, was it really she who was bored? Wasn't it rather the things, and the landscape, around her? Suddenly, a blinding light came flashing down from the heavens. The room, the class, the street—all seemed molded out of some kind of murky mud into which their shapes were slowly dissolving. Melanie, the only living being in this nauseating desolation, was fighting desperately to save herself from being the next to be sucked down into this sludge.

From her earliest childhood she had discovered a harmless yet very impressive equivalent of this abrupt change of light which modified the very essence of things; and she had discovered it in the spiral staircase which led to the attic rooms in her parents' house. The window that lit this staircase was merely a nar-row loophole containing small multicolored panes of glass. Sitting on the stairs, Melanie had often amused herself by looking at the garden through one particu-lar pane, and then through another of a different color. And each time she expe-rienced the same astonishment, the same little miracle. For though the garden was so familiar to her that she could recognize it without the slightest hesitation, when she looked at it through the red pane it was bathed in the light of a forest fire. It was no longer the place in which she played and dreamed. Both recognizable and unrecognizable, it became an infernal cavern licked by cruel flames. Then she changed to the green pane, whereupon the garden turned into the unfathomable bottom waters of the ocean depths. Aquatic monsters must certainly be lurking in those glaucous profundities. The yellow pane, on the other hand, irradiated, in a profusion of warm, sunny glints, a golden, reassuring haze. The blue one enveloped the trees and lawns in a romantic moonlight. The indigo pane made the most trivial objects look solemn and grandiose. And yet it was always the same garden, though each time with an appearance of surprising novelty, and Melanie was amazed at the magic power she thus possessed which enabled her at will to plunge her garden into a dramatic hell, a paean of praise, or a spectacular ceremony.

For there was no gray pane in the little window on the staircase, and the ashen downpour of boredom had a different origin: less innocent, but more real.

Quite early in life she had identified those elements of an alimentary order that tended to precipitate her fits of boredom and those which, on the other hand, had the power of warding them off. Cream, butter, and jam—the childish food that people were always trying to press on her—foreshadowed and provoked the advancing tide of grayness, the engulfment of life in a dense, viscid slime. On the other hand, pepper, vinegar, and unripe apples—everything acid, sour, or highly spiced—exuded a breath of fresh, sparkling, invigorating air into the stagnating atmosphere. It was the difference between lemonade and milk. For Melanie, these two drinks symbolized good and evil. In spite of the protests of her family, she had adopted, as her morning drink, tea made with mineral water and flavored with a slice of lemon. And with it a very hard biscuit or a piece of nearly burned toast. On the other hand, she had been forced to give up the afternoon slice of bread and mustard she coveted because it gave rise to gales of laughter in the school playground. She had realized that with her bread and mustard she was going beyond the bounds of what was tolerated in a provincial primary school.

There was nothing she detested so much in the climates and seasons as a fine summer afternoon, with its lazy languor, with the obscene, satiated luxuriance of its vegetation which seems to communicate itself both to animals and people. The dreadful act initiated by those muggy, voluptuous hours was that of lounging in a chaise longue with one's legs apart and one's arms raised, while yawning very loudly, as if obliged to expose one's genitals, armpits, and mouth to goodness knew what kind of rape. Against this triple yawn, Melanie cultivated the laugh and the sob, two reactions which implied refusal, distance, and the human being's withdrawal into itself. The weather best suited to this rejection syndrome was a luminous frost, which gave rise to a denuded, frozen, hardened, and brilliant character. At such times Melanie went for rapid, exalted walks in the countryside, her eyes watering on account of the glacial air, but her mouth full of ironic laughs.

Like all children, she had encountered the mystery of death. But in her eyes it had immediately taken on two completely opposite aspects. The animal corpses she had seen were usually swollen and decomposed, and exuded sanious secretions. Such beings, reduced to their last extremities, crudely avowed their basically putrid nature. Whereas dead insects became lighter, spiritual, and spontaneously attained the pure, delicate eternity of mummies. And this did not only apply to insects for, ferreting around in the attic, Melanie had found a mouse and a little bird that were equally desiccated, purified, reduced to their own distinctive essence: This was a good death.

Melanie was the only daughter of a lawyer in Mamers. She had always seemed strange to her father, who had had her late in life and whom she seemed to intimidate. Her mother had been delicate and had died prematurely, leaving Melanie alone with the lawyer at the age of twelve. She was deeply distressed by her mother's death. The first physical sign was that her chest hurt; she felt a kind of stabbing pain, as if she had an ulcer or an internal lesion. She thought she was seriously ill. Then she realized that she was perfectly well, and that it was grief.

At the same time, every so often she experienced waves of tenderness that were quite pleasant. She had only to think intently about her mother, about her mother's death, about the slim, stiff corpse lying in a box at the bottom of an icy hole. . . . Her eyes filled with tears and she couldn't restrain a kind of hiccuping sob that resembled a bitter little laugh. Then she would feel uplifted, freed from the constriction of material things, liberated from the weight of existence. For one brief moment everyday reality became an object of derision, deprived of its self-importance, and no longer an obsessive burden weighing on the little girl. Nothing mattered anymore, since her beloved mama was dead. The obvious truth of this irrefutable deduction shone like a spiritual sun. On the wings of funereal intoxication, Melanie discovered the hilarity in the air.

Then her grief wore off. All that was left of it was a scar which contracted when anyone mentioned the dead woman, or when she couldn't get to sleep at night and opened her eyes wide in the darkness.

After that the days passed, all identical, between an old maidservant who was getting more and more hard of hearing and a father who only surfaced from his papers in order to talk about the past. Melanie grew up without apparently going through any difficult phases. Her family circle found her neither difficult, nor secretive, nor melancholy, and everyone would have been surprised to discover that she was swimming with the energy of despair in a dismal gray void, swimming against the insipid anguish she was caused by that affluent house full of memories, that street where nothing new ever happened, and no one appeared.

When it looked as if a nuclear war might break out between America and the U.S.S.R. over Cuba, Melanie was of an age to read the papers, and to follow the news on radio and television. It seemed to her that a breath of fresh air was sweeping through the world, and her lungs swelled with hope. For, to deliver her from her prostration, it would take nothing less than the immense destruction and appalling hecatomb of a modern war. Then the threat was dispelled, the lid of existence, which for a moment had been half lifted, closed on her again, and Melanie realized that there was nothing to be expected from history.

In the spring, the lawyer was in the habit of turning off the central heating and lighting a fire on those evenings when the temperature was really too low. And this was why, one fine April morning, Étienne Jonchet came to deliver a truckload of logs. He worked for a nearby sawmill in the forest of Écouves—his fifth trade in less than a year—and was one of those handsome, downright jovial fellows who considered the need to work to be an unfair, sordid burden. He smelled of resin and tannin, and his turned-up shirt-sleeves displayed soft, golden forearms covered in obscene tattoos. Melanie had gone down to the cellar to pay him. While she was fumbling in her purse, he looked at her with a strange expression which began to frighten her. It was even worse when he slowly raised his hands up to her shoulders, up to her head, and locked them around her neck. Her knees trembling, her mouth dry, all she could see were the tattooed arms, and a little farther away the young man's smiling face.

"He's strangling me," she said to herself. "He wants the purse and he's going to kill me to get it!"

And she felt herself weakening, going down a path toward death in which terror and voluptuousness were confused.

Finally she collapsed, but he picked her up in his arms, toppled her over a pile of anthracite, and possessed her tender, virginal body in this alcove of darkness.

When she passed her father on the stairs later, she was covered in coal dust, and she amazed him by jumping up at his neck and laughing. She had lost her virginity, she was filthy, but she was happy.

They met again. A month later, pretending she was going to spend her vacation with a school friend, she went to live with her handsome woodcutter, taking with her only the clothes she was wearing.

Étienne was not a very subtle psychologist, but even so the unusual behavior of his new girlfriend surprised him. She turned up at the sawmill more often than was necessary. Instead of packing his lunch in his bag every morning, she chose to take it herself, and to share it with him in the midst of his workmates. He was certainly rather proud of the youth, the beauty, and especially the obvious bourgeois origins of the girl. But she ought to have disappeared when they started work again. Instead, she dawdled around the machines, running her finger over the serrated blades, calculating their sharpness, their cutting edge, the width they sawed, the tension of the steel bands, whose sides were rendered infinitely smooth and shiny by the terrible friction they were subjected to. Then she would pick up a handful of sawdust, feel its fluffy, elastic freshness, hold it close to her nose in order to appreciate its forest odor, then let it trickle down through her fingers. That this velvety snow could be made from compact tree trunks was a miracle that enchanted her.

But nothing fascinated her so much as the brief howls of the circular saws as they cut into the heart of a log, and the crazy, heaving movement of the great frame saw as its twelve blades danced up and down in the soft wood.

The equipment was kept in repair by an old man named Sureau. A former cabinetmaker, he had known better days, but after his wife died he had taken to drink and he made a precarious living sharpening the blades in the sawmill. Melanie decided to win him over. She visited him in his hovel, did little favors for him, insinuated herself into his good graces. In actual fact she knew what she wanted, but no one would have understood the grandiose project she was determined to use him for. She finally got him to take up his tools again—he called them his "clarinets"—to sharpen them, and to return to his trade. True, it might well take him years to produce what would no doubt be his all-time masterpiece.

The summer went by in a nimbus of sun and love, with the underlying mystery of the Sureau project. It seemed as if Melanie and Étienne's embraces would never come to an end. They continued through the autumn mists, through the nocturnal clatter of the rain on the shingle roof of their hut, and under the white mantle of the snow, which that year was heavy.

At the beginning of March Étienne was given the sack after a row with his boss. He went off to look for work. He had heard some talk of vacancies at a nearby stud farm. He promised to come back and fetch Melanie as soon as he was settled. But she was never to see him again. Since it never rains but it pours, old Sureau was hospitalized with pleurisy. It is so true that spring is often fatal to old men.

However, Melanie had no intention of returning to her father, with whom she kept up a parsimonious correspondence. For the moment, the marvelous surprise of her love life, the superb folly of the sawmill, and the Sureau project, which rigorously stemmed from both the one and the other, erected a wall between her present life and the gray waters in which the paternal house seemed to have run aground, like a worm-eaten Ark, in the eyes of her memory.

And yet the void was inexorably closing in on her again, in the piercing, humid breezes of a spring which seemed as if it was never going to end. The shack was invaded by the desolation of the forest as it made its black, haggard way out of the thaw. One day, Melanie surprised herself in the fateful act: She yawned, and recognized with dread the sign that at the same time greeted and summoned up the plashing tide of boredom. The time for childish little gimmicks—lemons, mustard—was well and truly past. Since from now on she was free, she should have run away. But where would she run to? For such is the pernicious force of boredom: It surrounds itself with a kind of universal contagion and sends out its malefic waves over the whole world, over the entire universe. Nothing, no place, and no thing, seems to escape it.

Rummaging around in the toolshed where hatchets, axes, wedges, and saws were awaiting the improbable return of Étienne, Melanie found the solution. It was a rope, a beautiful new rope, still as bright and shiny as it had been when it left the rope factory, and it terminated—on purpose, so it seemed—in a loop. If you passed the end of the rope through this loop, you produced a slipknot, which was the very thing to hang yourself with.

Trembling with excitement, she fastened the rope to the main roof beam. The slipknot swung two and a half meters above the ground—the ideal height, for all you had to do was stand on a chair to put your head through it. And indeed, Melanie placed the best chair she possessed underneath the knot. Then she sat on the only other chair in the house, which was wobbly, and admired her handiwork.

It wasn't that those two objects—the rope and the chair—were particularly admirable in themselves. It was more a question of the perfection of the combination of that seat and that sort of hempen wire, and of its fatal significance. She lapsed into a state of blissful, metaphysical contemplation. In preparing her own death, in raising a visible, palpable barrier against the barren prospect of her life, in building a dam to halt the stagnant waters of time, at one stroke she was putting an end to boredom. The imminence of her death, made concrete by the rope and the chair, conferred an incomparable density and warmth on her present life.

She then experienced several weeks of sinister happiness. The charm had already begun to wear off, however, when the mailman, whom she rarely saw, appeared one day. He brought her a letter from her best friend, Jacqueline Autrain, a schoolteacher who had been appointed to a nearby village for the coming third term of the school year, and who was going to live alone in the apartment over the school. She would be so happy if Melanie would agree to come and spend a few days with her to help her settle in.

Melanie packed her bag, hid the key to the hut in a hole known to Étienne, and went off to stay with her friend.

Jacqueline's welcome, and the springlike radiance of the village, made her forget her obsessions and their funereal remedy. True, she had left her beautiful rope hanging above the chair in the darkness of the locked hut, as if in anticipation, as a kind of pledge against an obligatory return. While her friend was teaching, Melanie took care of their apartment. Then she began to get interested in the children. She started giving private lessons to the ones who found it difficult to keep up. After the love she had experienced all through the summer and winter, in this way, with the coming of spring, she discovered friendship. Between these two celebrations of life was the vast expanse of a bleak desert peopled with exorbitant, nauseating shadows that only a rope ending in the loop of a slipknot rendered habitable.

Jacqueline was engaged to a young man who was at the time serving his apprenticeship with the riot police. Twice during the spring, when she had had a few days off from her job, she had visited him at his barracks in Argentan. One day he turned up with his helmet, his cap, his truncheon, and his big, bulging holster. The two young women were amused by all this paraphernalia.

His leave lasted three days. The first was nothing but a succession of laughter and caresses between the fiancés. When the spectacle became too demonstrative, Melanie tried to slip away unnoticed. On the second day, the young man insisted on going for an outing with the two women, although it was obvious that Jacqueline would have preferred to stay at home and get the full benefit of such rare hours. On the third day she picked a violent quarrel with Melanie and accused her of trying to divert the too naïve policeman's attentions to herself. Coming in unexpectedly, the young man darted into the fray, and by tactlessly trying to defend Melanie he completed his fiancée's despair. When he departed for Argentan he left behind him an accumulation of emotional debris.

Melanie couldn't possibly go on living with Jacqueline. She settled in Alençon, and taught in a private school for the last two terms of the school year.

Then the holidays emptied the schools, the streets, and the whole town, and Melanie found herself alone once again under a white, merciless, piercing sun. On the dusty branches of the plane trees, between the uneven cobblestones of the squares, on the flaking walls tortured by the light there emerged the livid, bloated face of boredom.

Feeling herself sinking, Melanie clung to her most recent memories. When she thought about Jacqueline's fiancé, strangely enough it was always the image of the bulging holster containing his pistol that first entered her mind. She wrote to him at the Argentan barracks and asked him to meet her. He replied, suggesting a day, an hour, and a café.

If he had imagined that this was going to lead to an affair, he was disappointed. Melanie explained that, on the contrary, what she wanted was to clear up any misunderstanding and try to restore the good relationship between Jacqueline and him that she might perhaps have unintentionally contributed toward damaging. She begged him to get in touch with his fiancée again as soon as possible, and to let her know that their reunion had been a success. This would be a great relief to her.

Then she had an inspiration. Why shouldn't he telephone Jacqueline right now, from the café? Then she would know that every attempt had been made.

He put up a feeble argument, then shrugged his shoulders, stood up, and made his way to the telephone booth. He left his cap, his helmet, his truncheon, and his bulging holster on the table.

Melanie waited for a moment. He must be having difficulty in getting through, because the young man was taking his time coming back. Actually, she couldn't take her eyes off the bulging holster, which was innocently swelling on the table. Suddenly she yielded to temptation. She slipped the object into her handbag and rapidly reached the door.

Back in her little room in Alençon, the satisfaction of duty accomplished gave her a few days' peace. But she couldn't forget that by reconciling the fiancés she had permanently excluded herself from their friendship. The pistol, on the other hand, was a source of great comfort. Every day, at a certain hour—she always trembled with impatience and anticipated joy as she awaited it—she brought out the magnificent, dangerous object. She had no idea how to use it, but she was lacking in neither time nor patience. Placed on the table, naked, the pistol seemed to irradiate an energy that enveloped Melanie in voluptuous warmth. The compact, rigorous brevity of its contours, its matt and almost sacerdotal blackness, the facility with which her hand embraced and grasped its form— everything about this weapon contributed to giving her an irresistible *force of conviction*. How good it would be to die by means of this pistol! Furthermore, it belonged to Jacqueline's fiancé, and Melanie's suicide would unite her friends, just as her life had nearly separated them.

The pistol was not loaded, but the holster contained a magazine and six bullets, and Melanie soon found the orifice in the butt where it should be inserted. A click apprised her that the magazine was in place. Then the day came when she felt she could no longer wait to try it out.

She went off very early in the morning into the forest. When she came to a clearing, a long way from any path, she took the pistol out of her bag and, holding it with both hands, as far away from her as possible, she pulled the trigger with all her might. Nothing happened. There must be a safety catch. For a moment she ran her fingers over the butt, the barrel, and the trigger. Finally a kind of protuberance slid toward the barrel, leaving a red spot exposed. That must be it. She tried again. The trigger yielded under her fingers and the weapon, as if seized by a sudden fit of madness, kicked in her hands.

The explosion had seemed tremendous to Melanie, but the bullet had left no trace in the trees or thickets into which it must have vanished.

Trembling all over, Melanie put the pistol back in her bag and resumed her walk. Her legs felt weak, but she didn't know whether this was the result of fear or of pleasure. She now had a new instrument of liberation at her disposal, and how much more modern and practical this one was than the rope and the chair! She had never been so free. The key to her cage was there, in her bag, next to her makeup remover, her coin purse, and her sunglasses.

She had gone about a hundred meters when she saw, coming striding toward her, an old man dressed as a cross between a fisherman and a mountaineer, and carrying a cylindrical botanist's box slung across one shoulder. He approached her right away.

"What's going on? Didn't you hear an explosion?"

"No," Melanie lied. "I didn't hear anything."

"Odd, odd. All the more so in that it seemed to come from your direction. And I had been afraid I was becoming hard of hearing! Ah well. Let's say I had an illusion, then, yes, how shall I put it, an auditory hallucination."

He had pronounced these last two words with a kind of ironic emphasis, and he ended his phrase in a grating little laugh. Then, noticing Melanie's bag:

"Were you looking for mushrooms, too?"

"Yes, that's right, for mushrooms," Melanie lied again, eagerly.

Then, carried away by a sudden inspiration, she added:

"I'd especially like to know how to recognize the poisonous ones."

"Bah! Poisonous! For a real mycologist they're so rare they're practically nonexistent! Do you know that my friends in our learned society and myself often invite each other to dinners in which a whole course consists of mushrooms reputed to be lethal? You only have to know how to prepare them, and also perhaps how to eat them without fear. Apprehension makes the organism more vulnerable; everyone knows that. A game for specialists, that's what it comes down to."

"Then poisonous mushrooms are as harmless as that?" asked Melanie, with a touch of disappointment in her voice.

"For us—for us mycologists! But for the profane—hold on! It's rather like the big cats in a menagerie, isn't it! Their trainer can go into their cage and tweak their whiskers. But woe betide the visitor who allowed himself any such liberty!"

"You're absolutely fascinating!"

Aristide Greenhorn, who owned an antique shop on the rue des Filles-de-Notre-Dame, not far from the house where Saint Teresa of Lisieux was born, belonged to the race of those erudite men, curious about everything, who flourish discreetly in the shade in small provincial towns. He reserved the best part of himself for the learned society, which he regaled with eclectic communications, ranging from the miracles of botany to books of magic spells written by obscure mystics.

He was too delighted at having found a virgin ear to let Melanie go so soon, and for quite a while they walked side by side, chatting. When she got back to her modest lodging, the pistol in her bag was hidden under a perfumed provender of cepes, chanterelles, and parasol mushrooms that they had picked together. But she had also insisted on bringing back—isolated in a plastic bag, it is true—three livid Entoloma and two death cups, the most fearsome killers of the undergrowth.

That evening, she laid out on her table the pistol, stripped of its holster, and a plate containing the five poisonous mushrooms. A dusky silence enveloped her solitude, but these lethal objects irradiated an invigorating warmth with which she was more than familiar. Once again she experienced the same voluptuous excitement that she had felt in the hut in the presence of the rope and chair. But she was now going much further in her intimate relations with death.

She was worried, at first, by the mysterious affinity that seemed to link these two kinds of objects. They had a concise strength in common, a dormant, languid energy seemingly lurking in forms which could only contain it with difficulty, but which were inspired by it. The massive bulk of the pistol—a hand-held weapon—and the muscular curves of the mushrooms also reminded her of a third object that had been hidden at the back of her mind for a long time but which she finally flushed out, not without blushing: Étienne Jonchet's sex organ, which had given her so much pleasure for so many weeks. And thus she discovered the profound complicity between love and death, and that it was the sordid, threatening emblems tattooed on Étienne's delightful arms that had given their embraces their real meaning. Thus Étienne found his proper place in the forest landscape whose center remained the rope and the chair.

The mushrooms, the pistol, and the rope were three keys that each opened a door to the beyond, three monumental doors, whose aspect and style were certainly very different.

The mushrooms were the soft, tortuous keys to a door which displayed the smooth rotundity of a gigantic belly. It was like a vast anatomical altar of repose erected to the glory of digestion, defecation, and sex. This door would only begin to open slowly, lazily. In eating and assimilating these mushrooms, Melanie would have to edge her way through a narrow slit with the obstinate cunning of a baby determined to be born the wrong way around.

The second door was cast in bronze. Black and tabular, unshakable, it stood in front of a blazing secret whose disquieting glow could be glimpsed through the keyhole. Only a terrible explosion, a detonation resonating against Melanie's ear, would open it at one stroke and expose a landscape of flames, the incandescent cleft in a furnace, thick clouds of sulfur and saltpeter.

The third key—that of the rope and chair—concealed beneath its rusticity the abundant richness of a direct affinity with nature. If she put her head through the hempen necklace, Melanie would discover the secret depths of the forest humus, fertilized by rainstorms and hardened by Christmas frosts. This was a beyond which smelled of resin and log fires, which resounded with the rumbling organ sounds the wind made when hurling itself against a cluster of tall trees. In becoming the human weight that would ballast the rope, itself fastened to the main beam of the woodcutter's hut, Melanie would take her place in that vast architecture of balanced treetops and swaying branches, of vertical trunks and entangled foliage, that was called: the forest.

Greenhorn had invited Melanie to visit him. One evening, she triggered off the silvery music of a cluster of tubes that the opening door set in motion. A whole paradise of polychromatic plaster saints welcomed her, either with open arms or with a right arm upheld in blessing. Little Sister Teresa, in a hundred copies of different sizes, clutched a crucifix to her Carmelite uniform as she raised her eyes up to the moldings on the ceiling.

"She was born just a couple of steps from here, you see," Greenhorn explained with fervor. "At number 42 rue Saint-Blaise. If you like, we'll visit her birthplace together."

Melanie's air of consternation as she thanked him couldn't escape him. He realized that he was on the wrong track, and that in this instance the pious antique dealer had to give place to the philosopher. He needed to keep a wary eye open and show signs of humility if he wanted to pin down the personality of this strange girl, who went for solitary walks in the woods shooting pistols, and who had a predilection for collecting poisonous mushrooms. She was certainly someone out of the ordinary. Unfortunately, it turned out to be difficult to make conversation, because she was more interested in learning simple, precise things from him than in talking about herself.

She left him after a quarter of an hour, but she came back two days later, and they gradually became more at ease with each other. With increasing amazement, Greenhorn pieced together the scraps of information Melanie gave him about her brief fate. For the difference in their ages and the soothing atmosphere of the shop reassured Melanie, and encouraged her to reveal herself. He couldn't help giving an involuntary start the day she told him that she taught small children. For she had hinted at the basic elements of her adventure with the handsome, tattooed Étienne, and at her fascination for the rope and its slipknot. "Poor children!" he thought. "Though, after all, people who are completely normal rarely go in for teaching, and it may well be natural and preferable that children, those semilunatics whom we tolerate in our midst, should be raised by eccentrics."*

Later, she told him about the spiral staircase, the narrow window, and the multicolored panes of glass that made it possible for her to see her garden under profoundly different aspects. "Kant!" he thought. "The a priori forms of sense impressions! At the age of ten, without either wanting to or realizing it, she discovered the basic essentials of transcendental philosophy!" But when he tried to initiate her into Kantianism he soon saw that she wasn't following him, and that she wasn't even listening.

Going back even further in her memories, she alluded to the likes and dislikes she had had as a little girl—liking lemons, disliking cakes—to the boredom that

---

* This definition of children is to be found in Jean Paulhan's preface to *The Story of O*. Here it is obviously a question of a vague recollection, and, after all, it is not so surprising that Greenhorn should have read Pauline Réage's novel.

had sometimes submerged her like a gray, greasy tide, to the sparkling and invigorating relief she had found, at first in a small way in corrosive food and drink, and later, in grandiose fashion, in her mother's death.

At this point he no longer doubted that she had an innate metaphysical vocation, which was accompanied by a spontaneous rejection of anything to do with ontology. He tried to get her to understand that she embodied, in the rough, the ancient antagonism between two forms of thought. Since the most distant dawn of occidental humanity, two currents had crossed and opposed one another, the first dominated by Parmenides of Elea, the other by Heraclitus of Ephesus. For Parmenides, reality and truth combine in the motionless Being, single, solid, and unchanging. This fixed vision horrified the other thinker, Heraclitus, who held that flickering, rumbling fire is the primordial substance of the universe, and that the limpid current of singing water is the symbol of life in perpetual flux. Ontology and metaphysics—Being in repose, and Being surpassed—have always, since the beginning of time, opposed two kinds of wisdom and two kinds of speculation.

While he was speaking thus, carried away by his sublime subject, Melanie was staring at him with her huge, dark, passionate eyes. He might have thought she was listening to him, captivated by the amazing portrait of herself that he was drawing. But he was shrewd and lucid; he knew that he had a long, red, curly hair growing out of a wart on his cheek, and he only had to look at Melanie to realize that she had no eyes for anything other than this minute blemish, and that she hadn't taken in a single word of his discourse.

No, decidedly, he had to face facts; Melanie did not have a philosophical turn of mind, in spite of her prodigious talent for spontaneously involving herself, though crudely and quite unconsciously, in the great problems of eternal speculation. The facts of philosophy, by which she was possessed and which were the supreme guidelines of her destiny, could not be translated into concepts and words that she would understand. A metaphysician of genius, she would remain a primitive and never rise to the level of the Word.

Her visits ceased. Greenhorn was not particularly surprised. Since his arguments had had no effect on the girl's mind, he knew that his relationship with her was at the mercy of fortuitous, obscure, and unforeseeable influences. Nevertheless, he finally went and knocked on the door of the little room where she lived. A neighbor told him that she had moved.

What instinctive warning had decided her to return to the cabin in the forest of Écouves? No doubt, a thought that had imposed itself upon her had a great deal to do with it.

The prospect of death—of a certain kind of death, made concrete by a particular instrument—was the only thing capable of rescuing her from being engulfed in the nausea of existence. But this liberation was only temporary and gradually lost all its potency, like a stale drug, so she had to wait until a different "key" came along and promised her a new death, a younger, fresher, more convincing promise whose credibility was still intact. Now it was obvious that this game couldn't go on much longer. Sooner or later all those unkept promises, all those missed rendezvous, would have to be followed by the day of reckoning. Threatened once again by shipwreck in the quagmires of Being, Melanie had therefore decided on Sunday, October 1, at noon as the date and hour of her suicide.*

The idea of this commitment had at first frightened her. But the more seriously she envisaged it, and as the decision ripened in her mind, the more she felt warmed and sustained by successive and increasingly intense waves of energy and joy. It was this, above all, that had dictated her behavior. Death, even when it was still distant, by its very certainty, by the precision of its date and occurrence was already beginning its work of transfiguration. And once this date was fixed, every day, every hour increased this salutary influence, as each step that brings us nearer to a great bonfire enables us to participate a little more in its light and warmth.

And this was why she had gone back to the forest of Écouves, where, first in Étienne's tattooed arms and then in the contemplation of the rope and the chair, she had experienced a happiness that presaged the great final ecstasy.

On September 29 a divine surprise was to crown her joy. A small truck stopped outside the hut. An old man sitting beside the driver got out and knocked on the door. It was old Sureau, whose illness had been only a fairly severe warning sign. The two men got out of the vehicle and carried into the living room a tall, heavy, fragile object, completely enveloped in black veils, like a great widow, stiff and solemn . . .

"If I wasn't afraid of being paradoxical," said the young doctor, putting down his stethoscope, "I would say that she died of laughter."

And he explained that in its first stage laughter is characterized by a sudden dilation of the orbicular muscle of the lips, and the contraction of the musculus risorius, of the canine, and the buccinator, and, at the same time, by a discontinuous expiration, but that in its second stage the muscular contractions could spread to the whole of the network subordinate to the facial nerve and even reach the muscles of the neck, in particular the platysma. And that in its third stage it undermines the whole organism, causes tears and urine to flow, and the diaphragm to contract in painful spasms, to the detriment of the intestines and the heart.

For those gathered around Melanie Blanchard's corpse, this lecture in comic physiology had very different meanings. Knowing Melanie, they were even more aware than the doctor himself that this apparently extravagant theory of death by laughter was pretty well in keeping with the eccentric character of the deceased. Her father, the shy, absent-minded old lawyer, remembered her on that spring day, with her clothes in disarray, her face and arms covered in coal dust, throwing herself at his neck and laughing like a madwoman. Étienne Jonchet recalled her strange and profound smile when she was stroking the most terrifying blades in the sawmill. The schoolmistress thought of the voluptuous grimace that the little girl could not suppress as she took a big bite out of a lemon. Meanwhile Aristide Greenhorn was trying to apply to this special case the the-

---

* October 1 is the feast day of Saint Teresa of Lisieux. Melanie no doubt considered this a touching tribute to her old friend Greenhorn. But we are entitled to wonder whether he appreciated it at its true worth.

ory developed by Henri Bergson in *Laughter*, according to which the comic is a mechanism overlaying a conscious being. Jacqueline Autrain was the only one who didn't understand a thing. Sobbing on her fiancé's shoulder, she was convinced that Melanie, consumed with love for the young man, had sacrificed herself for their happiness. As for old Sureau, he had no thought for anything other than the masterpiece of his career as a craftsman, and under the peak of his cap he was keeping a close eye on its funereal outlines, which encumbered the far end of the room.

Before she died, Melanie had sent them a kind of anthumous invitation informing them of the day and hour of her suicide, taking care to mail the envelopes too late for anyone to intervene. Thus they met, one after the other, in the living room of the forest hut, after Étienne Jonchet—the only one not to have received an invitation—had discovered the corpse when he came to fetch his tools.

The rope still hung from the ceiling, the beautiful new, waxed rope that ended in an impeccable slipknot. On the bedside table were the pistol—with just one bullet missing from its magazine—and a saucer containing five mushrooms that were beginning to dry out. Melanie was lying intact on her big double bed, carried off by a devastating heart attack which had done nothing to obscure the radiant, even hilarious, expression on her face. And, in fact, this dead girl, who had needed no violent expedient in order to cross the threshold, seemed to be floating in the joy of not living.

"And what is that?" the doctor finally asked, pointing to the "widow."

Old Sureau moved, and with the careful, tender gestures of a young bridegroom undressing his bride with his own hands, he began to strip the object of its enveloping black luster veils. They all recognized, with stupefaction, a guillotine, a drawing room guillotine, made with loving care out of the wood of a fruit tree, delicately dovetailed, waxed, polished, weathered—a real masterpiece of cabinetmaking, to which the brightly shining blade with its relentless profile added a cruel, glacial note.

Greenhorn, as an expert antique dealer, noticed that the two uprights along which the blade slid were decorated in the antique fashion with eurythmic foliage, and that the crosspiece above them was in the form of a Hellenic architrave.

"And what's more," he murmured, lost in admiration, "it's in the style of Louis the Sixteenth!"

Translated from the French by Barbara Wright

William Trevor

· · · · · · · · · · · · · · · · · · · ·

BEYOND THE PALE

We always went to Ireland in June.

Ever since the four of us began to go on holidays together, in 1965 it must have been, we had spent the first fortnight of the month at Glencorn Lodge in Co. Antrim. Perfection, as Dekko put it once, and none of us disagreed. It's a Georgian house by the sea, not far from the village of Ardbeag. It's quite majestic in its rather elegant way, a garden running to the very edge of a cliff, its long rhododendron drive—or avenue, as they say in Ireland. The English couple who bought the house in the early sixties, the Malseed's, have had to build on quite a bit but it's all been discreetly done, the Georgian style preserved throughout. Figs grow in the sheltered gardens, and apricots, and peaches in the greenhouses which old Mr Saxton presides over. He's Mrs Malseed's father actually. They brought him with them from Surrey, and their Dalmatians, Charger and Snooze.

It was Strafe who found Glencorn for us. He'd come across an advertisement in the *Lady* in the days when the Malseeds still felt the need to advertise. 'How about this?' he said one evening at the end of the second rubber, and then read out the details. We had gone away together the summer before, to a hotel that had been recommended on the Costa del Sol, but it hadn't been a success because the food was so appalling. 'We could try this Irish one,' Dekko suggested cautiously, which is what eventually we did.

The four of us have been playing bridge together for ages, Dekko, Strafe, Cynthia and myself. They call me Milly, though strictly speaking my name is Dorothy Milson. Dekko picked up his nickname at school, Dekko Deakin sounding rather good, I dare say. He and Strafe were in fact at school together, which must be why we all call Strafe by his surname: Major R. B. Strafe he is, the initials standing for Robert Buchanan. We're of an age, the four of us, all in the early fifties: the prime of life, so Dekko insists. We live quite close to Leatherhead, where the Malseeds were before they decided to make the change from Surrey to Co. Antrim. Quite a coincidence, we always think.

'How *very* nice,' Mrs Malseed said, smiling her welcome again this year. Some instinct seems to tell her when guests are about to arrive, for she's rarely not waiting in the large low-ceilinged hall that always smells of flowers. She dresses beautifully, differently every day, and changing of course in the evening. Her blouse on this occasion was scarlet and silver, in stripes, her skirt black. This choice gave her a brisk look, which was fitting because being so busy she often has to be a little on the brisk side. She has smooth grey hair which she once told me she entirely looks after herself, and she almost always wears a black velvet band in it. Her face is well made up, and for one who arranges so many vases of flowers and otherwise has to use her hands she manages to keep them marvellously in condition. Her fingernails are varnished a soft pink, and a small gold bangle always adorns her right wrist, a wedding present from her husband.

'Arthur, take the party's luggage,' she commanded the old porter, who doubles as odd-job man. 'Rose, Geranium, Hydrangea, Fuchsia.' She referred to the titles of the rooms reserved for us: in winter, when no one much comes to Glencorn Lodge, pleasant little details like that are seen to. Mrs Malseed herself painted the flower-plaques that are attached to the doors of the hotel instead of numbers; her husband sees to redecoration and repairs.

'Well, well, well,' Mr Malseed said now, entering the hall through the door that leads to the kitchen regions. 'A hundred thousand welcomes,' he greeted us in the Irish manner. He's rather shorter than Mrs Malseed, who's handsomely tall. He wears Donegal tweed suits and is brown as a berry, including his head, which is bald. His dark brown eyes twinkle at you, making you feel rather more than just another hotel guest. They run the place like a country house, really.

'Good trip?' Mr Malseed enquired.

'Super,' Dekko said. 'Not a worry all the way.'

'Splendid.'

'The wretched boat sailed an hour early one day last week,' Mrs Malseed said. 'Quite a little band were left stranded at Stranraer.'

Strafe laughed. Typical of that steamship company, he said. 'Catching the tide, I dare say?'

'They caught a rocket from me,' Mrs Malseed replied good-humouredly. 'A couple of old dears were due with us on Tuesday and had to spend the night in some awful Scottish lodging-house. It nearly finished them.'

Everyone laughed, and I could feel the others thinking that our holiday had truly begun. Nothing had changed at Glencorn Lodge, all was well with its Irish world. Kitty from the dining-room came out to greet us, spotless in her uniform. 'Ach, you're looking younger,' she said, paying the compliment to all four of us, causing everyone in the hall to laugh again. Kitty's a bit of a card.

Arthur led the way to the rooms called Rose, Geranium, Hydrangea and Fuchsia, carrying as much of our luggage as he could manage and returning for the remainder. Arthur has a beaten, fisherman's face and short grey hair. He wears a green baize apron, and a white shirt with an imitation-silk scarf tucked into it at the neck. The scarf, in different swirling greens which blend nicely with the green of his apron, is an idea of Mrs Malseed's and one appreciates the effort, if not at a uniform, at least at tidiness.

'Thank you very much,' I said to Arthur in my room, smiling and finding him a coin.

.   .   .   .   .

We played a couple of rubbers after dinner as usual, but not of course going on for as long as we might have because we were still quite tired after the journey. In the lounge there was a French family, two girls and their parents, and a honeymoon couple—or so we had speculated during dinner—and a man on his own. There had been other people at dinner of course, because in June Glencorn Lodge is always full: from where we sat in the window we could see some of them strolling about the lawns, a few taking the cliff path down to the seashore. In the morning we'd do the same: we'd walk along the sands to Ardbeag and have coffee in the hotel there, back in time for lunch. In the afternoon we'd drive somewhere.

I knew all that because over the years this kind of pattern had developed. We had our walks and our drives, tweed to buy in Cushendall, Strafe's and Dekko's fishing day when Cynthia and I just sat on the beach, our visit to the Giant's Causeway and one to Donegal perhaps, though that meant an early start and taking pot-luck for dinner somewhere. We'd come to adore Co. Antrim, its glens and coastline, Rathlin Island and Tievebulliagh. Since first we got to know it, in 1965, we'd all four fallen hopelessly in love with every variation of this remarkable landscape. People in England thought us mad of course: they see so much of the troubles on television that it's naturally difficult for them to realize that most places are just as they've always been. Yet coming as we did, taking the road along the coast, dawdling through Ballygally, it was impossible to believe that somewhere else the unpleasantness was going on. We'd never seen a thing, nor even heard people talking about incidents that might have taken place. It's true that after a particularly nasty carry-on a few winters ago we did consider finding somewhere else, in Scotland perhaps, or Wales. But as Strafe put it at the time, we felt we owed a certain loyalty to the Malseeds and indeed to everyone we'd come to know round about, people who'd always been glad to welcome us back. It seemed silly to lose our heads, and when we returned the following summer we knew immediately we'd been right. Dekko said that nothing could be further away from all the violence than Glencorn Lodge, and though his remark could hardly be taken literally I think we all knew what he meant.

'Cynthia's tired,' I said because she'd been stifling yawns. 'I think we should call it a day.'

'Oh, not at all,' Cynthia protested. 'No, please.'

But Dekko agreed with me that she was tired, and Strafe said he didn't mind stopping now. He suggested a nightcap, as he always does, and as we always do also, Cynthia and I declined. Dekko said he'd like a Cointreau.

The conversation drifted about. Dekko told us an Irish joke about a drunk who couldn't find his way out of a telephone box, and then Strafe remembered an incident at school concerning his and Dekko's housemaster, A. D. Cowley-Stubbs, and the house wag, Thrive Major. A. D. Cowley-Stubbs had been known as Cows and often featured in our after-bridge reminiscing. So did Thrive Major.

'Perhaps I *am* sleepy,' Cynthia said. 'I don't think I closed my eyes once last night.'

She never does on a sea crossing. Personally I'm out like a light the moment my head touches the pillow; I often think it must be the salt in the air because normally I'm an uneasy sleeper at the best of times.

'You run along, old girl,' Strafe advised.

'Brekky at nine,' Dekko said.

Cynthia said good-night and went, and we didn't remark on her tiredness because as a kind of unwritten rule we never comment on one another. We're four people who play bridge. The companionship it offers, and the holidays we have together, are all part of that. We share everything: the cost of petrol, the cups of coffee or drinks we have; we even each make a contribution towards the use of Strafe's car because it's always his we go on holiday in, a Rover it was on this occasion.

'Funny, being here on your own,' Strafe said, glancing across what the Malseeds call the After-Dinner Lounge at the man who didn't have a companion. He was a red-haired man of about thirty, not wearing a tie, his collar open at the neck and folded back over the jacket of his blue serge suit. He was uncouth-looking, though it's a hard thing to say, not at all the kind of person one usually sees at Glencorn Lodge. He sat in the After-Dinner Lounge as he had in the dining-room, lost in some concentration of his own, as if calculating sums in his mind. There had been a folded newspaper on his table in the dining-room. It now reposed tidily on the arm of his chair, still unopened.

'Commercial gent,' Dekko said. 'Fertilizers.'

'Good heavens, never. You wouldn't get a rep in here.'

I took no part in the argument. The lone man didn't much interest me, but I felt that Strafe was probably right: if there was anything dubious about the man's credentials he might have found it difficult to secure a room. In the hall of Glencorn Lodge there's a notice which reads: *We prefer not to feature in hotel guides, and we would be grateful to our guests if they did not seek to include Glencorn Lodge in the Good Food Guide, the Good Hotel Guide, the Michelin, Egon Ronay or any others. We have not advertised Glencorn since our early days, and prefer our recommendations to be by word of mouth.*

'Ah, thank you,' Strafe said when Kitty brought his whisky and Dekko's Cointreau. 'Sure you won't have something?' he said to me, although he knew I never did.

Strafe is on the stout side, I suppose you could say, with a gingery moustache and gingery hair, hardly touched at all by grey. He left the Army years ago, I suppose because of me in a sense, because he didn't want to be posted abroad again. He's in the Ministry of Defense now.

I'm still quite pretty in my way, though nothing like as striking as Mrs Malseed, for I've never been that kind of woman. I've put on weight, and wouldn't have allowed myself to do so if Strafe hadn't kept saying he can't stand a bag of bones. I'm careful about my hair and, unlike Mrs Malseed, I have it very regularly seen to because if I don't it gets a salt and pepper look, which I hate. My husband, Ralph, who died of food-poisoning when we were still quite young, used to say I wouldn't lose a single look in middle age, and to some extent that's true. We were still putting off having children when he died, which is why I haven't any. Then I met Strafe, which meant I didn't marry again.

Strafe is married himself, to Cynthia. She's small and ineffectual, I suppose you'd say without being untruthful or unkind. Not that Cynthia and I don't get on or anything like that, in fact we get on extremely well. It's Strafe and Cynthia who don't seem quite to hit it off, and I often think how much happier all round it would have been if Cynthia had married someone completely different, someone like Dekko in a way, except that that mightn't quite have worked out either. The Strafes have two sons, both very like their father, both of them in the Army. And the very sad thing is they think nothing of poor Cynthia.

'Who's that chap?' Dekko asked Mr Malseed, who'd come over to wish us good-night.

'Awfully sorry about that, Mr Deakin. My fault entirely, a booking that came over the phone.'

'Good heavens, not at all,' Strafe protested, and Dekko looked horrified in case it should be thought he was objecting to the locals. 'Splendid-looking fellow,' he said, overdoing it.

Mr Malseed murmured that the man had only booked in for a single night, and I smiled the whole thing away, reassuring him with a nod. It's one of the pleasantest of the traditions at Glencorn Lodge that every evening Mr Malseed makes the rounds of his guests just to say good-night. It's because of little touches like that that I, too, wished Dekko hadn't questioned Mr Malseed about the man because it's the kind of thing one doesn't do at Glencorn Lodge. But Dekko is a law unto himself, very tall and gangling, always immaculately suited, a beaky face beneath mousy hair in which flecks of grey add a certain distinction. Dekko has money of his own and though he takes out girls who are half his age he has never managed to get around to marriage. The uncharitable might say he has a rather gormless laugh; certainly it's sometimes on the loud side.

We watched while Mr Malseed bade the lone man good-night. The man didn't respond, but just sat gazing. It was ill-mannered, but this lack of courtesy didn't appear to be intentional: the man was clearly in a mood of some kind, miles away.

'Well, I'll go up,' I said. 'Good-night, you two.'

'Cheery-bye, Milly,' Dekko said. 'Brekky at nine, remember.'

'Good-night, Milly,' Strafe said.

The Strafes always occupy different rooms on holidays, and at home also. This time he was in Geranium and she in Fuchsia. I was in Rose, and in a little while Strafe would come to see me. He stays with her out of kindness, because he fears for her on her own. He's a sentimental, good-hearted man, easily moved to tears: he simply cannot bear the thought of Cynthia with no one to talk to in the evenings, with no one to make her life around. 'And besides,' he often says when he's being jocular, 'it would break up our bridge four.' Naturally we never discuss her shortcomings or in any way analyse the marriage. The unwritten rule that exists among the four of us seems to extend as far as that.

He slipped into my room after he'd had another drink or two, and I was waiting for him as he likes me to wait, in bed but not quite undressed. He has never said so, but I know that that is something Cynthia would not understand in him, or ever attempt to comply with. Ralph, of course, would not have understood either; poor old Ralph would have been shocked. Actually it's all rather sweet, Strafe and his little ways.

'I love you, dear,' I whispered to him in the darkness, but just then he didn't wish to speak of love and referred instead to my body.

If Cynthia hadn't decided to remain in the hotel the next morning instead of accompanying us on our walk to Ardbeag everything might have been different. As it happened, when she said at breakfast she thought she'd just potter about the garden and sit with her book out of the wind somewhere, I can't say I was displeased. For a moment I hoped Dekko might say he'd stay with her, allowing Strafe and myself to go off on our own, but Dekko—who doesn't go in for saying what you want him to say—didn't. 'Poor old sausage,' he said instead, examining Cynthia with a solicitude that suggested she was close to the grave, rather than just a little lowered by the change of life or whatever it was.

'I'll be perfectly all right,' Cynthia assured him. 'Honestly.'

'Cynthia likes to mooch, you know,' Strafe pointed out, which of course is only the truth. She reads too much, I always think. You often see her putting down a book with the most melancholy look in her eyes, which can't be good for her. She's an imaginative woman, I suppose you would say, and of course her habit of reading so much is often useful on our holidays: over the years she has read her way through dozens of Irish guide-books. 'That's where the garrison pushed the natives over the cliffs,' she once remarked on a drive. 'Those rocks are known as the Maidens,' she remarked on another occasion. She has led us to places of interest which we had no idea existed: Garron Tower on Garron Point, the mausoleum at Bonamargy, the Devil's Backbone. As well as which, Cynthia is extremely knowledgeable about all matters relating to Irish history. Again she has read endlessly: biographies and autobiographies, long accounts of the centuries of battling and politics there've been. There's hardly a town or village we ever pass through that hasn't some significance for Cynthia, although I'm afraid her impressive fund of information doesn't always receive the attention it deserves. Not that Cynthia ever minds; it doesn't seem to worry her when no one listens. My own opinion is that she'd have made a much better job of her relationship with Strafe and her sons if she could have somehow developed a bit more character.

We left her in the garden and proceeded down the cliff path to the shingle beneath. I was wearing slacks and a blouse, with the arms of a cardigan looped round my neck in case it turned chilly: the outfit was new, specially bought for the holiday, in shades of tangerine. Strafe never cares how he dresses and of course she doesn't keep him up to the mark: that morning, as far as I remember, he wore rather shapeless corduroy trousers, the kind men sometimes garden in, and a navy-blue fisherman's jersey. Dekko as usual was a fashion plate: a pale green linen suit with pleated jacket pockets, a maroon shirt open at the neck, revealing a medallion on a fine gold chain. We didn't converse as we crossed the rather difficult shingle, but when we reached the sand Dekko began to talk about some girl or other, someone called Juliet who had apparently proposed marriage to him just before we'd left Surrey. He'd told her, so he said, that he'd think about it while on holiday and he wondered now about dispatching a telegram from Ardbeag saying, *Still thinking*. Strafe, who has a simple sense of humour, considered this hugely funny and spent most of the walk persuading Dekko that the telegram must certainly be sent, and other telegrams later on, all with the same message. Dekko kept laughing, throwing his head back in a way that always reminds me of an Australian bird I once saw in a nature film on television. I could see this was going to become one of those jokes that would accompany us all through the holiday, a man's thing really, but of course I didn't mind. The girl called Juliet was nearly thirty years younger than Dekko. I supposed she knew what she was doing.

Since the subject of telegrams had come up, Strafe recalled the occasion when Thrive Major had sent one to A. D. Cowley-Stubbs: *Darling regret three months gone love Rowena.* Carefully timed, it had arrived during one of Cows' Thursday evening coffee sessions. Rowena was a maid, known as the Bicycle, who had been sacked the previous term, and old Cows had something of a reputation as a misogynist. When he read the message he apparently went white and collapsed into an armchair. Warrington P. J. managed to read it too, and after that the fat was in the fire. The consequences went on rather, but I never minded listening when Strafe and Dekko drifted back to their schooldays. I just wish I'd known Strafe then, before either of us had gone and got married.

We had our coffee at Ardbeag, the telegram was sent off, and then Strafe and Dekko wanted to see a man called Henry O'Reilly whom we'd met on previous holidays, who organizes mackerel-fishing trips. I waited on my own, picking out postcards in the village shop that sells almost everything, and then I wandered down towards the shore. I knew that they would be having a drink with the boatman because a year had passed since they'd seen him last. They joined me after about twenty minutes, Dekko apologizing but Strafe not seeming to be aware that I'd had to wait because Strafe is not a man who notices little things. It was almost one o'clock when we reached Glencorn Lodge and were told by Mr Malseed that Cynthia needed looking after.

The hotel, in fact, was in a turmoil. I have never seen anyone as ashen-faced as Mr Malseed; his wife, in a forget-me-not dress, was limp. It wasn't explained to us immediately what had happened, because in the middle of telling us that Cynthia needed looking after Mr Malseed was summoned to the telephone. I could see through the half-open door of their little office a glass of whisky or brandy on the desk and Mrs Malseed's bangled arm reaching out for it. Not for ages did we realize that it all had to do with the lone man whom we'd speculated about the night before.

'He just wanted to talk to me,' Cynthia kept repeating hysterically in the hall. 'He sat with me by the magnolias.'

I made her lie down. Strafe and I stood on either side of her bed as she lay there with her shoes off, her rather unattractively cut plain pink dress crumpled and actually damp from her tears. I wanted to make her take it off and to slip under the bed-clothes in her petticoat but somehow it seemed all wrong, in the circumstances, for Strafe's wife to do anything so intimate in my presence.

'I couldn't stop him,' Cynthia said, the rims of her eyes crimson by now, her nose beginning to run again. 'From half past ten till well after twelve. He had to talk to someone, he said.'

I could sense that Strafe was thinking precisely the same as I was: that the red-haired man had insinuated himself into Cynthia's company by talking about himself and had then put a hand on her knee. Instead of simply standing up and going away Cynthia would have stayed where she was, embarrassed or tongue-tied, at any rate unable to cope. And when the moment came she would have turned hysterical. I could picture her screaming in the garden, running across the lawn to the hotel, and then the pandemonium in the hall. I could sense Strafe picturing that also.

'My God, it's terrible,' Cynthia said.

'I think she should sleep,' I said quietly to Strafe. 'Try to sleep, dear,' I said to her, but she shook her head, tossing her jumble of hair about on the pillow.

'Milly's right,' Strafe urged. 'You'll feel much better after a little rest. We'll bring you a cup of tea later on.'

'My God!' she cried again. 'My God, how could I sleep?'

I went away to borrow a couple of mild sleeping pills from Dekko, who is never without them, relying on the things too much in my opinion. He was ti-dying himself in his room, but found the pills immediately. Strangely enough, Dekko's always sound in a crisis.

I gave them to her with water and she took them without asking what they were. She was in a kind of daze, one moment making a fuss and weeping, the next just peering ahead of her, as if frightened. In a way she was like someone who'd just had a bad nightmare and hadn't yet completely returned to reality. I remarked as much to Strafe while we made our way down to lunch, and he said he quite agreed.

'Poor old Cynth!' Dekko said when we'd all ordered lobster bisque and en-trecôte béarnaise. 'Poor old sausage.'

You could see that the little waitress, a new girl this year, was bubbling over with excitement; but Kitty, serving the other half of the dining-room, was grim, which was most unusual. Everyone was talking in hushed tones and when Dekko said, 'Poor old Cynth!' a couple of heads were turned in our direction because he can never keep his voice down. The little vases of roses with which Mrs Malseed must have decorated each table before the fracas had occurred seemed strangely out of place in the atmosphere which had developed.

The waitress had just taken away our soup-plates when Mr Malseed hurried into the dining-room and came straight to our table. The lobster bisque surpris-ingly hadn't been quite up to scratch, and in passing I couldn't help wondering if the fuss had caused the kitchen to go to pieces also.

'I wonder if I might have a word, Major Strafe,' Mr Malseed said, and Strafe rose at once and accompanied him from the dining-room. A total silence had fallen, everyone in the dining-room pretending to be intent on eating. I had an odd feeling that we had perhaps got it all wrong, that because we'd been out for our walk when it had happened all the other guests knew more of the details than Strafe and Dekko and I did. I began to wonder if poor Cynthia had been raped.

Afterwards Strafe told us what occurred in the Malseeds' office, how Mrs Malseed had been sitting there, slumped, as he put it, and how two policemen had questioned him. 'Look, what on earth's all this about?' he had demanded rather sharply.

'It concerns this incident that's taken place, sir,' one of the policemen explained in an unhurried voice. 'On account of your wife—'

'My wife's lying down. She must not be questioned or in any way disturbed.'

'Ach, we'd never do that, sir.'

Strafe does a good Co. Antrim brogue and in relating all this to us he couldn't resist making full use of it. The two policemen were in uniform and their natural slowness of intellect was rendered more noticeable by the lugubrious air the tragedy had inspired in the hotel. For tragedy was what it was; after talking to Cynthia for nearly two hours the lone man had walked down to the rocks and been drowned.

When Strafe finished speaking I placed my knife and fork together on my plate, unable to eat another mouthful. The facts appeared to be that the man, having left Cynthia by the magnolias, had clambered down the cliff to a place no one ever went to, on the other side of the hotel from the sands we had walked along to Ardbeag. No one had seen him except Cynthia, who from the cliff-top had apparently witnessed his battering by the treacherous waves. The tide had been coming in, but by the time old Arthur and Mr Malseed reached the rocks it had begun to turn, leaving behind it the fully dressed corpse. Mr Malseed's impression was that the man had lost his footing on the seaweed and accidentally stumbled into the depths, for the rocks were so slippery it was difficult to carry the corpse more than a matter of yards. But at least it had been placed out of view, while Mr Malseed hurried back to the hotel to telephone for assistance. He told Strafe that Cynthia had been most confused, insisting that the man had walked out among the rocks and then into the sea, knowing what he was doing.

Listening to it all, I no longer felt sorry for Cynthia. It was typical of her that she should so sillily have involved us in all this. Why on earth had she sat in the garden with a man of that kind instead of standing up and making a fuss the moment he'd begun to paw her? If she'd acted intelligently the whole unfortunate episode could clearly have been avoided. Since it hadn't, there was no point whatsoever in insisting that the man had committed suicide when at that distance no one could possibly be sure.

'It really does astonish me,' I said at the lunch table, unable to prevent myself from breaking our unwritten rule. 'Whatever came over her?'

'It can't be good for the hotel,' Dekko commented, and I was glad to see Strafe giving him a little glance of irritation.

'It's hardly the point,' I said coolly.

'What I meant was, hotels occasionally hush things like this up.'

'Well, they haven't this time.' It seemed an age since I had waited for them in Ardbeag, since we had been so happily laughing over the effect of Dekko's telegram. He'd included his address in it so that the girl could send a message back, and as we'd returned to the hotel along the seashore there'd been much speculation between the two men about the form this would take.

'I suppose what Cynthia's thinking,' Strafe said, 'is that after he'd tried something on with her he became depressed.'

'Oh, but he could just as easily have lost his footing. He'd have been on edge anyway, worried in case she reported him.'

'Dreadful kind of death,' Dekko said. His tone suggested that that was that, that the subject should now be closed, and so it was.

After lunch we went to our rooms, as we always do at Glencorn Lodge, to rest for an hour. I took my slacks and blouse off, hoping that Strafe would knock on my door, but he didn't and of course that was understandable. Oddly enough I found myself thinking of Dekko, picturing his long form stretched out in the room called Hydrangea, his beaky face in profile on his pillow. The precise nature of Dekko's relationship with these girls he picks up has always privately intrigued me: was it really possible that somewhere in London there was a girl called Juliet who was prepared to marry him for his not inconsiderable money?

I slept and briefly dreamed. Thrive Major and Warrington P. J. were running the post office in Ardbeag, sending telegrams to everyone they could think of, including Dekko's friend Juliet. Cynthia had been found dead beside the magnolias and people were waiting for Hercule Poirot to arrive. 'Promise me you didn't do it,' I whispered to Strafe, but when Strafe replied it was to say that Cynthia's body reminded him of a bag of old chicken bones.

Strafe and Dekko and I met for tea in the tea-lounge. Strafe had looked in to see if Cynthia had woken, but apparently she hadn't. The police officers had left the hotel, Dekko said, because he'd noticed their car wasn't parked at the front any more. None of the three of us said, but I think we presumed, that the man's body had been removed from the rocks during the quietness of the afternoon. From where we sat I caught a glimpse of Mrs Malseed passing quite briskly through the hall, seeming almost herself again. Certainly our holiday would be affected, but it might not be totally ruined. All that remained to hope for was Cynthia's recovery, and then everyone could set about forgetting the unpleasantness. The nicest thing would be if a jolly young couple turned up and occupied the man's room, exorcising the incident, as newcomers would.

The family from France—the two little girls and their parents—were chattering away in the tea-lounge, and an elderly trio who'd arrived that morning were speaking in American accents. The honeymoon couple appeared, looking rather shy, and began to whisper and giggle in a corner. People who occupied the table next to ours in the dining-room, a Wing-Commander Orfell and his wife, from Guildford, nodded and smiled as they passed. Everyone was making an effort, and I knew it would help matters further if Cynthia felt up to a rubber or two before dinner. That life should continue as normally as possible was essential for Glencorn Lodge, the example already set by Mrs Malseed.

Because of our interrupted lunch I felt quite hungry, and the Malseeds pride themselves on their teas. The chef, Mr McBride, whom of course we've met, has the lightest touch I know with sponge cakes and little curranty scones. I was, in fact, buttering a scone when Strafe said:

'Here she is.'

And there indeed she was. By the look of her she had simply pushed herself off her bed and come straight down. Her pink dress was even more crumpled than it had been. She hadn't so much as run a comb through her hair, her face was puffy and unpowdered. For a moment I really thought she was walking in her sleep.

Strafe and Dekko stood up. 'Feeling better, dear?' Strafe said, but she didn't answer.

'Sit down, Cynth,' Dekko urged, pushing back a chair to make room for her.

'He told me a story I can never forget. I've dreamed about it all over again.' Cynthia swayed in front of us, not even attempting to sit down. To tell the truth, she sounded inane.

'Story, dear?' Strafe enquired, humouring her.

She said it was the story of two children who had apparently ridden bicycles through the streets of Belfast, out into Co. Antrim. The bicycles were dilapidated, she said; she didn't know if they were stolen or not. She didn't know about the children's homes because the man hadn't spoken of them, but she claimed to know instinctively that they had ridden away from poverty and unhappiness. 'From the clatter and the quarrelling,' Cynthia said. 'Two children who later fell in love.'

'Horrid old dream,' Strafe said. 'Horrid for you, dear.'

She shook her head, and then sat down. I poured another cup of tea. 'I had the oddest dream myself,' I said. 'Thrive Major was running the post office in Ardbeag.'

Strafe smiled and Dekko gave his laugh, but Cynthia didn't in any way acknowledge what I'd said.

'A fragile thing the girl was, with depths of mystery in her wide brown eyes. Red-haired of course he was himself, thin as a rake in those days. Glencorn Lodge was derelict then.'

'You've had a bit of a shock, old thing,' Dekko said.

Strafe agreed, kindly adding, 'Look, dear, if the chap actually interfered with you—'

'Why on earth should he do that?' Her voice was shrill in the tea-lounge, edged with a note of hysteria. I glanced at Strafe, who was frowning into his teacup. Dekko began to say something, but broke off before his meaning emerged. Rather more calmly Cynthia said:

'It was summer when they came here. Honeysuckle he described. And mother of thyme. He didn't know the name of either.'

No one attempted any kind of reply, not that it was necessary, for Cynthia just continued.

'At school there were the facts of geography and arithmetic. And the legends of scholars and of heroes, of Queen Maeve and Finn MacCool. There was the coming of St Patrick to a heathen people. History was full of kings and high-kings, and Silken Thomas and Wolfe Tone, the Flight of the Earls, the Siege of Limerick.'

When Cynthia said that, it was impossible not to believe that the unfortunate events of the morning had touched her with some kind of madness. It seemed astonishing that she had walked into the tea-lounge without having combed her hair, and that she'd stood there swaying before sitting down, that out of the blue she had started on about two children. None of it made an iota of sense, and surely she could see that the nasty experience she'd suffered should not be dwelt upon? I offered her the plate of scones, hoping that if she began to eat she would stop talking, but she took no notice of my gesture.

'Look, dear,' Strafe said, 'there's not one of us who knows what you're talking about.'

'I'm talking about a children's story, I'm talking about a girl and a boy who visited this place we visit also. He hadn't been here for years, but he returned last night, making one final effort to understand. And then he walked out into the sea.'

She had taken a piece of her dress and was agitatedly crumpling it between the finger and thumb of her left hand. It was dreadful really, having her so grubby-looking. For some odd reason I suddenly thought of her cooking, how she wasn't in the least interested in it or in anything about the house. She certainly hadn't succeeded in making a home for Strafe.

'They rode those worn-out bicycles through a hot afternoon. Can you feel all that? A newly surfaced road, the snap of chippings beneath their tyres, the smell of tar? Dust from a passing car, the city they left behind?'

'Cynthia dear,' I said, 'drink your tea, and why not have a scone?'

'They swam and sunbathed on the beach you walked along today. They went to a spring for water. There were no magnolias then. There was no garden, no neat little cliff paths to the beach. Surely you can see it clearly?'

'No,' Strafe said. 'No, we really cannot, dear.'

'This place that is an idyll for us was an idyll for them too: the trees, the ferns, the wild roses near the water spring, the very sea and sun they shared. There was a cottage lost in the middle of the woods: they sometimes looked for that. They played a game, a kind of hide and seek. People in a white farmhouse gave them milk.'

For the second time I offered Cynthia the plate of scones and for the second time she pointedly ignored me. Her cup of tea hadn't been touched. Dekko took a scone and cheerfully said:

'All's well that's over.'

But Cynthia appeared to have drifted back into a daze, and I wondered again if it could really be possible that the experience had unhinged her. Unable to help myself, I saw her being led away from the hotel, helped into the back of a blue van, something like an ambulance. She was talking about the children again, how they had planned to marry and keep a sweetshop.

'Take it easy, dear,' Strafe said, which I followed up by suggesting for the second time that she should make an effort to drink her tea.

'Has it to do with the streets they came from? Or the history they learnt, he from his Christian Brothers, she from her nuns? History is unfinished in this island; long since it has come to a stop in Surrey.'

Dekko said, and I really had to hand it to him:

'Cynth, we have to put it behind us.'

It didn't do any good. Cynthia just went rambling on, speaking again of the girl being taught by nuns, and the boy by Christian Brothers. She began to recite the history they might have learnt, the way she sometimes did when we were driving through an area that had historical connections. 'Can you imagine,' she embarrassingly asked, 'our very favourite places bitter with disaffection, with plotting and revenge? Can you imagine the treacherous murder of Shane O'Neill the Proud?'

Dekko made a little sideways gesture of his head, politely marvelling. Strafe seemed about to say something, but changed his mind. Confusion ran through Irish history, Cynthia said, like convolvulus in a hedgerow. On May 24th, 1487, a boy of ten called Lambert Simnel, brought to Dublin by a priest from Oxford, was declared Edward VI of all England and Ireland, crowned with a golden circlet taken from a statue of the Virgin Mary. On May 24th, 1798, here in Antrim, Presbyterian farmers fought for a common cause with their Catholic labourers. She paused and looked at Strafe. Chaos and contradiction, she informed him, were hidden everywhere beneath nice-sounding names. 'The Battle of the Yellow Ford,' she suddenly chanted in a sing-song way that sounded thoroughly peculiar, 'the Statutes of Kilkenny. The Battle of Glenmama, the Convention of Drumceat. The Act of Settlement, the Renunciation Act. The Act of Union, the Toleration Act. Just so much history it sounds like now, yet people starved or died while other people watched. A language was lost, a faith forbidden. Famine followed revolt, plantation followed that. But it was people who were struck into the soil of other people's land, not forests of new trees; and it was greed and treachery that spread as a disease among them all. No wonder unease clings to these shreds of history and shots ring out in answer to the mockery of drums. No wonder the air is nervy with suspicion.'

There was an extremely awkward silence when she ceased to speak. Dekko nodded, doing his best to be companionable. Strafe nodded also. I simply examined the pattern of roses on our tea-time china, not knowing what else to do. Eventually Dekko said:

'What an awful lot you know, Cynth!'

'Cynthia's always been interested,' Strafe said. 'Always had a first-rate memory.'

'Those children of the streets are part of the battles and the Acts,' she went on, seeming quite unaware that her talk was literally almost crazy. 'They're part of the blood that flowed around those nice-sounding names.' She paused, and for a moment seemed disinclined to continue. Then she said:

'The second time they came here the house was being rebuilt. There were concrete-mixers, and lorries drawn up on the grass, noise and scaffolding everywhere. They watched all through another afternoon and then they went their different ways: their childhood was over, lost with their idyll. He became a dockyard clerk. She went to London, to work in a betting shop.'

'My dear,' Strafe said very gently, 'it's interesting, everything you say, but it really hardly concerns us.'

'No, of course not.' Quite emphatically Cynthia shook her head, appearing wholly to agree. 'They were degenerate, awful creatures. They must have been.'

'No one's saying that, my dear.'

'Their story should have ended there, he in the docklands of Belfast, she recording bets. Their complicated childhood love should just have dissipated, as such love often does. But somehow nothing was as neat as that.'

Dekko, in an effort to lighten the conversation, mentioned a boy called Goll-sol who'd been at school with Strafe and himself, who'd formed a romantic attachment for the daughter of one of the groundsmen and had later actually married her. There was a silence for a moment, then Cynthia, without emotion, said:

'You none of you care. You sit there not caring that two people are dead.'

'Two people, Cynthia?' I said.

'For God's sake, I'm telling you!' she cried. 'That girl was murdered in a room in Maida Vale.'

Although there is something between Strafe and myself, I do try my best to be at peace about it. I go to church and take communion, and I know Strafe occasionally does too, though not as often as perhaps he might. Cynthia has no interest in that side of life, and it rankled with me now to hear her blaspheming so casually, and so casually speaking about death in Maida Vale on top of all this stuff about history and children. Strafe was shaking his head, clearly believing that Cynthia didn't know what she was talking about.

'Cynthia dear,' I began, 'are you sure you're not muddling something up here? You've been upset, you've had a nightmare: don't you think your imagination, or something you've been reading—'

'Bombs don't go off on their own. Death doesn't just happen to occur in Derry and Belfast, in London and Amsterdam and Dublin, in Berlin and Jerusalem. There are people who are murderers: that is what this children's story is about.'

A silence fell, no one knowing what to say. It didn't matter of course because without any prompting Cynthia continued.

'We drink our gin with Angostura bitters, there's lamb or chicken Kiev. Old Kitty's kind to us in the dining-room and old Arthur in the hall. Flowers are everywhere, we have our special table.'

'Please let us take you to your room now,' Strafe begged, and as he spoke I reached out a hand in friendship and placed it on her arm. 'Come on, old thing,' Dekko said.

'The limbless are left on the streets, blood spatters the car-parks. *Brits Out* it says on a rockface, but we know it doesn't mean us.'

I spoke quietly then, measuring my words, measuring the pause between each so that its effect might be registered. I felt the statement had to be made, whether it was my place to make it or not. I said:

'You are very confused, Cynthia.'

The French family left the tea-lounge. The two Dalmatians, Charger and Snooze, ambled in and sniffed and went away again. Kitty came to clear the French family's tea things. I could hear her speaking to the honeymoon couple, saying the weather forecast was good.

'Cynthia,' Strafe said, standing up, 'we've been very patient with you but this is now becoming silly.'

I nodded just a little. 'I really think,' I softly said, but Cynthia didn't permit me to go on.

'Someone told him about her. Someone mentioned her name, and he couldn't believe it. She sat alone in Maida Vale, putting together the mechanisms of her bombs: this girl who had laughed on the seashore, whom he had loved.'

'Cynthia,' Strafe began, but he wasn't permitted to continue either. Hopelessly, he just sat down again.

'Whenever he heard of bombs exploding he thought of her, and couldn't understand. He wept when he said that; her violence haunted him, he said. He couldn't work, he couldn't sleep at night. His mind filled up with images of her, their awkward childhood kisses, her fingers working neatly now. He saw her with a carrier-bag, hurrying it through a crowd, leaving it where it could cause most death. In front of the mouldering old house that had once been Glencorn Lodge they'd made a fire and cooked their food. They'd lain for ages on the grass. They'd cycled home to their city streets.'

It suddenly dawned on me that Cynthia was kntting this whole fantasy out of nothing. It all worked backwards from the moment when she'd had the misfortune to witness the man's death in the sea. A few minutes before he'd been chatting quite normally to her, he'd probably even mentioned a holiday in his childhood and some girl there'd been: all of it would have been natural in the circumstances, possibly even the holiday had taken place at Glencorn. He'd said good-bye and then unfortunately he'd had his accident. As she watched from the cliff edge, something had cracked in poor Cynthia's brain, she having always been a prey to melancholy. I suppose it must be hard having two sons who don't think much of you, and a marriage not offering you a great deal, bridge and holidays probably the best part of it. For some odd reason of her own she'd created her fantasy about a child turning into a terrorist. The violence of the man's death had clearly filled her imagination with Irish violence, so regularly seen on television. If we'd been on holiday in Suffolk I wondered how it would have seemed to the poor creature.

I could feel Strafe and Dekko beginning to put all that together also, beginning to realize that the whole story of the red-haired man and the girl was clearly Cynthia's invention. 'Poor creature,' I wanted to say, but did not do so.

'For months he searched for her, pushing his way among the people of London, the people who were her victims. When he found her she just looked at him, as if the past hadn't even existed. She didn't smile, as if incapable of smiling. He wanted to take her away, back to where they came from, but she didn't reply when he suggested that. Bitterness was like a disease in her, and when he left her he felt the bitterness in himself.'

Again Strafe and Dekko nodded, and I could feel Strafe thinking that there really was no point in protesting further. All we could hope for was that the end of the saga was in sight.

'He remained in London, working on the railways. But in the same way as before he was haunted by the person she'd become, and the haunting was more awful now. He bought a gun from a man he'd been told about and kept it hidden in a shoe-box in his rented room. Now and again he took it out and looked at it, then put it back. He hated the violence that possessed her, yet he was full of it himself: he knew he couldn't betray her with anything but death. Humanity had left both of them when he visited her again in Maida Vale.'

To my enormous relief and, I could feel, to Strafe's and Dekko's too, Mr and Mrs Malseed appeared beside us. Like his wife, Mr Malseed had considerably recovered. He spoke in an even voice, clearly wishing to dispose of the matter. It was just the diversion we needed.

'I must apologize, Mrs Strafe,' he said. 'I cannot say how sorry we are that you were bothered by that man.'

'My wife is still a little dicky,' Strafe explained, 'but after a decent night's rest I think we can say she'll be as right as rain again.'

'I only wish, Mrs Strafe, you had made contact with my wife or myself when he first approached you.' There was a spark of irritation in Mr Malseed's eyes, but his voice was still controlled. 'I mean, the unpleasantness you suffered might just have been averted.'

'Nothing would have been averted, Mr Malseed, and certainly not the horror we are left with. Can you see her as the girl she became, seated at a chipped white table, her wires and fuses spread around her? What were her thoughts in that room, Mr Malseed? What happens in the mind of anyone who wishes to destroy? In a back street he bought his gun for too much money. When did it first occur to him to kill her?'

'We really are a bit at sea,' Mr Malseed replied without the slightest hesitation. He humoured Cynthia by displaying no surprise, by speaking very quietly.

'All I am saying, Mr Malseed, is that we should root our heads out of the sand and wonder about two people who are beyond the pale.'

'My dear,' Strafe said, 'Mr Malseed is a busy man.'

Still quietly, still perfectly in control of every intonation, without a single glance around the tea-lounge to ascertain where his guests' attention was, Mr Malseed said:

'There is unrest here, Mrs Strafe, but we do our best to live with it.'

'All I am saying is that perhaps there can be regret when two children end like this.'

Mr Malseed did not reply. His wife did her best to smile away the awkwardness. Strafe murmured privately to Cynthia, no doubt beseeching her to come to her senses. Again I imagined a blue van drawn up in front of Glencorn Lodge, for it was quite understandable now that an imaginative woman should go mad, affected by the ugliness of death. The garbled speculation about the man and the girl, the jumble in the poor thing's mind—a children's story as she called it—all somehow hung together when you realized they didn't have to make any sense whatsoever.

'Murderers are beyond the pale, Mr Malseed, and England has always had its pales. The one in Ireland began in 1395.'

'Dear,' I said, 'what has happened has nothing whatsoever to do with calling people murderers and placing them beyond some pale or other. You witnessed a most unpleasant accident, dear, and it's only to be expected that you've become just a little lost. The man had a chat with you when you were sitting by the magnolias and then the shock of seeing him slip on the seaweed—'

'He didn't slip on the seaweed,' she suddenly screamed. 'My God, he didn't slip on the seaweed.'

Strafe closed his eyes. The other guests in the tea-lounge had fallen silent ages ago, openly listening. Arthur was standing near the door and was listening also.

Kitty was waiting to clear away our tea things, but didn't like to because of what was happening.

'I must request you to take Mrs Strafe to her room, Major,' Mr Malseed said. 'And I must make it clear that we cannot tolerate further upset in Glencorn Lodge.'

Strafe reached for her arm, but Cynthia took no notice.

'An Irish joke,' she said, and then she stared at Mr and Mrs Malseed, her eyes passing over each feature of their faces. She stared at Dekko and Strafe, and last of all at me. She said eventually:

'An Irish joke, an unbecoming tale: of course it can't be true. Ridiculous, that a man returned here. Ridiculous, that he walked again by the seashore and through the woods, hoping to understand where a woman's cruelty had come from.'

'This talk is most offensive,' Mr Malseed protested, his calmness slipping just a little. The ashen look that had earlier been in his face returned. I could see he was beside himself with rage. 'You are trying to bring something to our doorstep which most certainly does not belong there.'

'On your doorstep they talked about a sweetshop: Cadbury's bars and different-flavoured creams, nut-milk toffee, Aero and Crunchie.'

'For God's sake pull yourself together,' I clearly heard Strafe whispering, and Mrs Malseed attempted to smile. 'Come along now, Mrs Strafe,' she said, making a gesture. 'Just to please us, dear. Kitty wants to clear away the dishes. Kitty!' she called out, endeavouring to bring matters down to earth.

Kitty crossed the lounge with her tray and gathered up the cups and saucers. The Malseeds, naturally still anxious, hovered. No one was surprised when Cynthia began all over again, by crazily asking Kitty what she thought of us.

'I think, dear,' Mrs Malseed began, 'Kitty's quite busy really.'

'Stop this at once,' Strafe quietly ordered.

'For fourteen years, Kitty, you've served us with food and cleared away the tea-cups we've drunk from. For fourteen years we've played our bridge and walked about the garden. We've gone for drives, we've bought our tweed, we've bathed as those children did.'

'Stop it,' Strafe said again, a little louder. Bewildered and getting red in the face, Kitty hastily bundled china on to her tray. I made a sign at Strafe because for some reason I felt that the end was really in sight. I wanted him to retain his patience, but what Cynthia said next was almost unbelievable.

'In Surrey we while away the time, we clip our hedges. On a bridge night there's coffee at nine o'clock, with macaroons or *petits fours.* Last thing of all we watch the late-night News, packing away our cards and scoring-pads, our sharpened pencils. There's been an incident in Armagh, one soldier's had his head shot off, another's run amok. Our lovely Glens of Antrim, we all four think, our coastal drives: we hope that nothing disturbs the peace. We think of Mr Malseed, still busy in Glencorn Lodge, and Mrs Malseed finishing her flower-plaques for the rooms of the completed annexe.'

'Will you for God's sake shut up?' Strafe suddenly shouted. I could see him struggling with himself, but it didn't do any good. He called Cynthia a bloody spectacle, sitting there talking rubbish. I don't believe she even heard him.

'Through honey-tinted glasses we love you and we love your island, Kitty. We love the lilt of your racy history, we love your earls and heroes. Yet we made a sensible pale here once, as civilized people create a garden, pretty as a picture.'

Strafe's outburst had been quite noisy and I could sense him being ashamed of it. He muttered that he was sorry, but Cynthia simply took advantage of his generosity, continuing about a pale.

'Beyond it lie the bleak untouchables, best kept as dots on the horizon, too terrible to contemplate. How can we be blamed if we make neither head nor tail of anything, Kitty, your past and your present, those battles and Acts of Parliament? We people of Surrey: how can we know? Yet I stupidly thought, you see, that the tragedy of two children could at least be understood. He didn't discover where her cruelty had come from because perhaps you never can: evil breeds evil in a mysterious way. That's the story the red-haired stranger passed on to me, the story you huddle away from.'

Poor Strafe was pulling at Cynthia, pleading with her, still saying he was sorry.

'Mrs Strafe,' Mr Malseed tried to say, but got no further. To my horror Cynthia abruptly pointed at me.

'That woman,' she said, 'is my husband's mistress, a fact I am supposed to be unaware of, Kitty.'

'My God!' Strafe said.

'My husband is perverted in his sexual desires. His friend, who shared his schooldays, has never quite recovered from that time. I myself am a pathetic creature who has closed her eyes to a husband's infidelity and his mistress's viciousness. I am dragged into the days of Thrive Major and A. D. Cowley-Stubbs: mechanically I smile. I hardly exist, Kitty.'

There was a most unpleasant silence, and then Strafe said:

'None of that's true. For God's sake, Cynthia,' he suddenly shouted, 'go and rest yourself.'

Cynthia shook her head and continued to address the waitress. She'd had a rest, she told her. 'But it didn't do any good, Kitty, because hell has invaded the paradise of Glencorn, as so often it has invaded your island. And we, who have so often brought it, pretend it isn't there. Who cares about children made into murderers?'

Strafe shouted again. 'You fleshless ugly bitch!' he cried. 'You bloody old fool!' He was on his feet, trying to get her to hers. The blood was thumping in his bronzed face, his eyes had a fury in them I'd never seen before. 'Fleshless!' he shouted at her, not caring that so many people were listening. He closed his eyes in misery and in shame again, and I wanted to reach out and take his hand but of course I could not. You could see the Malseeds didn't blame him, you could see them thinking that everything was ruined for us. I wanted to shout at Cynthia too, to batter the silliness out of her, but of course I could not do that. I could feel the tears behind my eyes, and I couldn't help noticing that Dekko's hands were shaking. He's quite sensitive behind his joky manner, and had quite obviously taken to heart her statement that he had never recovered from his schooldays. Nor had it been pleasant, hearing myself described as vicious.

'No one cares,' Cynthia said in the same unbalanced way, as if she hadn't just been called ugly and a bitch. 'No one cares, and on our journey home we shall all four be silent. Yet is the truth about ourselves at least a beginning? Will we wonder in the end about the hell that frightens us?'

Strafe still looked wretched, his face deliberately turned away from us. Mrs Malseed gave a little sigh and raised the fingers of her left hand to her cheek, as if something tickled it. Her husband breathed heavily. Dekko seemed on the point of tears.

Cynthia stumbled off, leaving a silence behind her. Before it was broken I knew she was right when she said we would just go home, away from this country we had come to love. And I knew as well that neither here nor at home would she be led to a blue van that was not quite an ambulance. Strafe would stay with her because Strafe is made like that, honourable in his own particular way. I felt a pain where perhaps my heart is, and again I wanted to cry. Why couldn't it have been she who had gone down to the rocks and slipped on the seaweed or just walked into the sea, it didn't matter which? Her awful rigmarole hung about us as the last of the tea things were gathered up—the earls who'd fled, the famine and the people planted. The children were there too, grown up into murdering riff-raff.

John Updike

· ·

SEPARATING

The day was fair. Brilliant. All that June the weather had mocked the Maples' internal misery with solid sunlight—golden shafts and cascades of green in which their conversations had wormed unseeing, their sad murmuring selves the only stain in Nature. Usually by this time of the year they had acquired tans; but when they met their elder daughter's plane on her return from a year in England they were almost as pale as she, though Judith was too dazzled by the sunny opulent jumble of her native land to notice. They did not spoil her homecoming by telling her immediately. Wait a few days, let her recover from jet lag, had been one of their formulations, in that string of gray dialogues—over coffee, over cocktails, over Cointreau—that had shaped the strategy of their dissolution, while the earth performed its annual stunt of renewal unnoticed beyond their closed windows. Richard had thought to leave at Easter; Joan had insisted they wait until the four children were at last assembled, with all exams passed and ceremonies attended, and the bauble of summer to console them. So he had drudged away, in love, in dread, repairing screens, getting the mowers sharpened, rolling and patching their new tennis court.

The court, clay, had come through its first winter pitted and windswept bare of redcoat. Years ago the Maples had observed how often, among their friends, divorce followed a dramatic home improvement, as if the marriage were making one last effort to live; their own worst crisis had come amid the plaster dust and exposed plumbing of a kitchen renovation. Yet, a summer ago, as canary-yellow bulldozers gaily churned a grassy, daisy-dotted knoll into a muddy plateau, and a crew of pigtailed young men raked and tamped clay into a plane, this transformation did not strike them as ominous, but festive in its impudence; their marriage could rend the earth for fun. The next spring, waking each day at dawn to a sliding sensation as if the bed were being tipped, Richard found the barren tennis court—its net and tapes still rolled in the barn—an environment congruous with his mood of purposeful desolation, and the crumbling of handfuls of clay into cracks and holes (dogs had frolicked on the court in a thaw; rivulets had eroded trenches) an activity suitably elemental and interminable. In his sealed heart he hoped the day would never come.

Now it was here. A Friday. Judith was re-acclimated; all four children were assembled, before jobs and camps and visits again scattered them. Joan thought they should be told one by one. Richard was for making an announcement at the table. She said, "I think just making an announcement is a cop-out. They'll start quarrelling and playing to each other instead of focusing. They're each individuals, you know, not just some corporate obstacle to your freedom."

"O.K., O.K. I agree." Joan's plan was exact. That evening, they were giving Judith a belated welcome-home dinner, of lobster and champagne. Then, the party over, they, the two of them, who nineteen years before would push her in a baby carriage along Fifth Avenue to Washington Square, were to walk her out of the house, to the bridge across the salt creek, and tell her, swearing her to secrecy. Then Richard Jr., who was going directly from work to a rock concert in Boston, would be told, either late when he returned on the train or early Saturday morning before he went off to his job; he was seventeen and employed as one of a golf-course maintenance crew. Then the two younger children, John and Margaret, could, as the morning wore on, be informed.

"Mopped up, as it were," Richard said.

"Do you have any better plan? That leaves you the rest of Saturday to answer any questions, pack, and make your wonderful departure."

"No," he said, meaning he had no better plan, and agreed to hers, though to him it showed an edge of false order, a hidden plea for control, like Joan's long chore lists and financial accountings and, in the days when he first knew her, her too-copious lecture notes. Her plan turned one hurdle for him into four—four knife-sharp walls, each with a sheer blind drop on the other side.

All spring he had moved through a world of insides and outsides, of barriers and partitions. He and Joan stood as a thin barrier between the children and the truth. Each moment was a partition, with the past on one side and the future on the other, a future containing this unthinkable *now*. Beyond four knifelike walls a new life for him waited vaguely. His skull cupped a secret, a white face, a face both frightened and soothing, both strange and known, that he wanted to shield from tears, which he felt all about him, solid as the sunlight. So haunted, he had become obsessed with battening down the house against his absence, replacing screens and sash cords, hinges and latches—a Houdini making things snug before his escape.

The lock. He had still to replace a lock on one of the doors of the screened porch. The task, like most such, proved more difficult than he had imagined. The old lock, aluminum frozen by corrosion, had been deliberately rendered obsolete by manufacturers. Three hardware stores had nothing that even approximately matched the mortised hole its removal (surprisingly easy) left. Another hole had to be gouged, with bits too small and saws too big, and the old hole fitted with a block of wood—the chisels dull, the saw rusty, his fingers thick with lack of sleep. The sun poured down, beyond the porch, on a world of neglect. The bushes already needed pruning, the windward side of the house was shedding flakes of paint, rain would get in when he was gone, insects, rot, death. His family, all those he would lose, filtered through the edges of his awareness as he struggled with screw holes, splinters, opaque instructions, minutiae of metal.

Judith sat on the porch, a princess returned from exile. She regaled them with stories of fuel shortages, of bomb scares in the Underground, of Pakistani workmen loudly lusting after her as she walked past on her way to dance school. Joan came and went, in and out of the house, calmer than she should have been, praising his struggles with the lock as if this were one more and not the last of their long succession of shared chores. The younger of his sons for a few minutes held the rickety screen door while his father clumsily hammered and chiseled, each blow a kind of sob in Richard's ears. His younger daughter, having been at a slumber party, slept on the porch hammock through all the noise—heavy and pink, trusting and forsaken. Time, like the sunlight, continued relentlessly; the sunlight slowly slanted. Today was one of the longest days. The lock clicked, worked. He was through. He had a drink; he drank it on the porch, listening to his daughter. "It was so sweet," she was saying, "during the worst of it, how all the butchers and bakery shops kept open by candlelight. They're all so plucky and cute. From the papers, things sounded so much worse here—people shooting people in gas lines, and everybody freezing."

Richard asked her, "Do you still want to live in England forever?" *Forever:* the concept, now a reality upon him, pressed and scratched at the back of his throat.

"No," Judith confessed, turning her oval face to him, its eyes still childishly far apart, but the lips set as over something succulent and satisfactory. "I was anxious to come home. I'm an American." She was a woman. They had raised her; he and Joan had endured together to raise her, alone of the four. The others had still some raising left in them. Yet it was the thought of telling Judith—the image of her, their first baby, walking between them arm in arm to the bridge— that broke him. The partition between his face and the tears broke. Richard sat down to the celebratory meal with the back of his throat aching; the champagne, the lobster seemed phases of sunshine; he saw them and tasted them through tears. He blinked, swallowed, croakily joked about hay fever. The tears would not stop leaking through; they came not through a hole that could be plugged but through a permeable spot in a membrane, steadily, purely, endlessly, fruitfully. They became, his tears, a shield for himself against these others—their faces, the fact of their assembly, a last time as innocents, at a table where he sat the last time as head. Tears dropped from his nose as he broke the lobster's back; salt flavored his champagne as he sipped it; the raw clench at the back of his throat was delicious. He could not help himself.

His children tried to ignore his tears. Judith, on his right, lit a cigarette, gazed upward in the direction of her too energetic, too sophisticated exhalation; on her other side, John earnestly bent his face to the extraction of the last morsels— legs, tail segments—from the scarlet corpse. Joan, at the opposite end of the table, glanced at him surprised, her reproach displaced by a quick grimace, of forgiveness, or of salute to his superior gift of strategy. Between them, Margaret, no longer called Bean, thirteen and large for her age, gazed from the other side of his pane of tears as if into a shopwindow at something she coveted—at her father, a crystalline heap of splinters and memories. It was not she, however, but John who, in the kitchen, as they cleared the plates and carapaces away, asked Joan the question: *"Why is Daddy crying?"*

Richard heard the question but not the murmured answer. Then he heard Bean cry, "Oh, no-oh!"—the faintly dramatized exclamation of one who had long expected it.

John returned to the table carrying a bowl of salad. He nodded tersely at his father and his lips shaped the conspiratorial words "She told."

"Told what?" Richard asked aloud, insanely.

The boy sat down as if to rebuke his father's distraction with the example of his own good manners. He said quietly, "The separation."

Joan and Margaret returned; the child, in Richard's twisted vision, seemed diminished in size, and relieved, relieved to have had the bogieman at last proved real. He called out to her—the distances at the table had grown immense—"You knew, you always knew," but the clenching at the back of his throat prevented him from making sense of it. From afar he heard Joan talking, levelly, sensibly, reciting what they had prepared: it was a separation for the summer, an experiment. She and Daddy both agreed it would be good for them; they needed space and time to think; they liked each other but did not make each other happy enough, somehow.

Judith, imitating her mother's factual tone, but in her youth off-key, too cool, said, "I think it's silly. You should either live together or get divorced."

Richard's crying, like a wave that has crested and crashed, had become tumultuous; but it was overtopped by another tumult, for John, who had been so reserved, now grew larger and larger at the table. Perhaps his younger sister's being credited with knowing set him off. "Why didn't you *tell* us?" he asked, in a large round voice quite unlike his own. "You should have *told* us you weren't getting along."

Richard was startled into attempting to force words through his tears. "We *do* get along, that's the trouble, so it doesn't show even to us—" *That we do not love each other* was the rest of the sentence; he couldn't finish it.

Joan finished for him, in her style. "And we've always, *especially*, loved our children."

John was not mollified. "What do you care about *us?*" he boomed. "We're just little things you *had*." His sisters' laughing forced a laugh from him, which he turned hard and parodistic: "Ha ha *ha*." Richard and Joan realized simultaneously that the child was drunk, on Judith's homecoming champagne. Feeling bound to keep the center of the stage, John took a cigarette from Judith's pack, poked it into his mouth, let it hang from his lower lip, and squinted like a gangster.

"You're not little things we had," Richard called to him. "You're the whole point. But you're grown. Or almost."

The boy was lighting matches. Instead of holding them to his cigarette (for they had never seen him smoke; being "good" had been his way of setting himself apart), he held them to his mother's face, closer and closer, for her to blow out. Then he lit the whole folder—a hiss and then a torch, held against his mother's face. Prismed by tears, the flame filled Richard's vision; he didn't know how it was extinguished. He heard Margaret say, "Oh stop showing off," and saw John, in response, break the cigarette in two and put the halves entirely into his mouth and chew, sticking out his tongue to display the shreds to his sister.

Joan talked to him, reasoning—a fountain of reason, unintelligible. "Talked about it for years . . . our children must help us . . . Daddy and I both want . . ." As the boy listened, he carefully wadded a paper napkin into the leaves of his salad, fashioned a ball of paper and lettuce, and popped it into his mouth, looking around the table for the expected laughter. None came. Judith said, "Be mature," and dismissed a plume of smoke.

Richard got up from this stifling table and led the boy outside. Though the house was in twilight, the outdoors still brimmed with light, the lovely waste light of high summer. Both laughing, he supervised John's spitting out the lettuce and paper and tobacco into the pachysandra. He took him by the hand—a square gritty hand, but for its softness a man's. Yet, it held on. They ran together up into the field, past the tennis court. The raw banking left by the bulldozers was dotted with daisies. Past the court and a flat stretch where they used to play family baseball stood a soft green rise glorious in the sun, each weed and species of grass distinct as illumination on parchment. "I'm sorry, so sorry," Richard cried. "You were the only one who ever tried to help me with all the goddam jobs around this place."

Sobbing, safe within his tears and the champagne, John explained, "It's not just the separation, it's the whole crummy year, I *hate* that school, you can't make any friends, the history teacher's a scud."

They sat on the crest of the rise, shaking and warm from their tears but easier in their voices, and Richard tried to focus on the child's sad year—the weekdays long with homework, the weekends spent in his room with model airplanes, while his parents murmured down below, nursing their separation. How selfish, how blind, Richard thought; his eyes felt scoured. He told his son, "We'll think about getting you transferred. Life's too short to be miserable."

They had said what they could, but did not want the moment to heal, and talked on, about the school, about the tennis court, whether it would ever again be as good as it had been that first summer. They walked to inspect it and pressed a few more tapes more firmly down. A little stiltedly, perhaps trying now to make too much of the moment, Richard led the boy to the spot in the field where the view was best, of the metallic blue river, the emerald marsh, the scattered islands velvety with shadow in the low light, the white bits of beach far away. "See," he said. "It goes on being beautiful. It'll be here tomorrow."

"I know," John answered, impatiently. The moment had closed.

Back in the house, the others had opened some white wine, the champagne being drunk, and still sat at the table, the three females, gossiping. Where Joan sat had become the head. She turned, showing him a tearless face, and asked, "All right?"

"We're fine," he said, resenting it, though relieved, that the party went on without him.

In bed she explained, "I couldn't cry I guess because I cried so much all spring. It really wasn't fair. It's your idea, and you made it look as though I was kicking you out."

"I'm sorry," he said. "I couldn't stop. I wanted to but couldn't."

"You *didn't* want to. You loved it. You were having your way, making a general announcement."

"I love having it over," he admitted. "God, those kids were great. So brave and funny." John, returned to the house, had settled to a model airplane in his room, and kept shouting down to them, "I'm O.K. No sweat." "And the way," Richard went on, cozy in his relief, "they never questioned the reasons we gave. No thought of a third person. Not even Judith."

"That *was* touching," Joan said.

He gave her a hug. "You were great too. Very reassuring to everybody. Thank you." Guiltily, he realized he did not feel separated.

"You still have Dickie to do," she told him. These words set before him a black mountain in the darkness; its cold breath, its near weight affected his chest. Of the four children, his elder son was most nearly his conscience. Joan did not need to add, "That's one piece of your dirty work I won't do for you."

"I know. I'll do it. You go to sleep."

Within minutes, her breathing slowed, became oblivious and deep. It was quarter to midnight. Dickie's train from the concert would come in at one-fourteen. Richard set the alarm for one. He had slept atrociously for weeks. But whenever he closed his lids some glimpse of the last hours scorched them—Judith exhaling toward the ceiling in a kind of aversion, Bean's mute staring, the sunstruck growth in the field where he and John had rested. The mountain before him moved closer, moved within him; he was huge, momentous. The ache at the back of his throat felt stale. His wife slept as if slain beside him. When, exasperated by his hot lids, his crowded heart, he rose from bed and dressed, she awoke enough to turn over. He told her then, "Joan, if I could undo it all, I would."

"Where would you begin?" she asked. There was no place. Giving him courage, she was always giving him courage. He put on shoes without socks in the dark. The children were breathing in their rooms, the downstairs was hollow. In their confusion they had left lights burning. He turned off all but one, the kitchen overhead. The car started. He had hoped it wouldn't. He met only moonlight on the road; it seemed a diaphanous companion, flickering in the leaves along the roadside, haunting his rearview mirror like a pursuer, melting under his headlights. The center of town, not quite deserted, was eerie at this hour. A young cop in uniform kept company with a gang of T-shirted kids on the steps of the bank. Across from the railroad station, several bars kept open. Customers, mostly young, passed in and out of the warm night, savoring summer's novelty. Voices shouted from cars as they passed; an immense conversation seemed in progress. Richard parked and in his weariness put his head on the passenger seat, out of the commotion and wheeling lights. It was as when, in the movies, an assassin grimly carries his mission through the jostle of a carnival— except the movies cannot show the precipitous, palpable slope you cling to within. You cannot climb back down; you can only fall. The synthetic fabric of the car seat, warmed by his cheek, confided to him an ancient, distant scent of vanilla.

A train whistle caused him to lift his head. It was on time; he had hoped it would be late. The slender draw-gates descended. The bell of approach tingled happily. The great metal body, horizontally fluted, rocked to a stop, and sleepy teen-agers disembarked, his son among them. Dickie did not show surprise that his father was meeting him at this terrible hour. He sauntered to the car with two friends, both taller than he. He said "Hi" to his father and took the passenger's seat with an exhausted promptness that expressed gratitude. The friends got in the back, and Richard was grateful; a few more minutes' postponement would be won by driving them home.

He asked, "How was the concert?"

"Groovy," one boy said from the back seat.

"It bit," the other said.

"It was O.K.," Dickie said, moderate by nature, so reasonable that in his childhood the unreason of the world had given him headaches, stomach aches, nausea. When the second friend had been dropped off at his dark house, the boy blurted, "Dad, my eyes are killing me with hay fever! I'm out there cutting that mothering grass all day!"

"Do we still have those drops?"

"They didn't do any good last summer."

"They might this." Richard swung a U-turn on the empty street. The drive home took a few minutes. The mountain was here, in his throat. "Richard," he said, and felt the boy, slumped and rubbing his eyes, go tense at his tone, "I didn't come to meet you just to make your life easier. I came because your mother and I have some news for you, and you're a hard man to get ahold of these days. It's sad news."

"That's O.K." The reassurance came out soft, but quick, as if released from the tip of a spring.

Richard had feared that his tears would return and choke him, but the boy's manliness set an example, and his voice issued forth steady and dry. "It's sad news, but it needn't be tragic news, at least for you. It should have no practical effect on your life, though it's bound to have an emotional effect. You'll work at your job, and go back to school in September. Your mother and I are really proud of what you're making of your life; we don't want that to change at all."

"Yeah," the boy said lightly, on the intake of his breath, holding himself up. They turned the corner; the church they went to loomed like a gutted fort. The home of the woman Richard hoped to marry stood across the green. Her bedroom light burned.

"Your mother and I," he said, "have decided to separate. For the summer. Nothing legal, no divorce yet. We want to see how it feels. For some years now, we haven't been doing enough for each other, making each other as happy as we should be. Have you sensed that?"

"No," the boy said. It was an honest, unemotional answer: true or false in a quiz.

Glad for the factual basis, Richard pursued, even garrulously, the details. His apartment across town, his utter accessibility, the split vacation arrangements, the advantages to the children, the added mobility and variety of the summer. Dickie listened, absorbing. "Do the others know?"

"Yes."

"How did they take it?"

"The girls pretty calmly. John flipped out; he shouted and ate a cigarette and made a salad out of his napkin and told us how much he hated school."

His brother chuckled. "He did?"

"Yeah. The school issue was more upsetting for him than Mom and me. He seemed to feel better for having exploded."

"He did?" The repetition was the first sign that he was stunned.

"Yes. Dickie, I want to tell you something. This last hour, waiting for your train to get in, has been about the worst of my life. I hate this. *Hate* it. My father would have died before doing it to me." He felt immensely lighter, saying this. He had dumped the mountain on the boy. They were home. Moving swiftly as a shadow, Dickie was out of the car, through the bright kitchen. Richard called after him, "Want a glass of milk or anything?"

"No thanks."

"Want us to call the course tomorrow and say you're too sick to work?"

"No, that's all right." The answer was faint, delivered at the door to his room; Richard listened for the slam that went with a tantrum. The door closed normally, gently. The sound was sickening.

Joan had sunk into that first deep trough of sleep and was slow to awake. Richard had to repeat, "I told him."

"What did he say?"

"Nothing much. Could you go say goodnight to him? Please."

She left their room, without putting on a bathrobe. He sluggishly changed back into his pajamas and walked down the hall. Dickie was already in bed, Joan was sitting beside him, and the boy's bedside clock radio was murmuring music. When she stood, an inexplicable light—the moon?—outlined her body through the nightie. Richard sat on the warm place she had indented on the child's narrow mattress. He asked him, "Do you want the radio on like that?"

"It always is."

"Doesn't it keep you awake? It would me."

"No."

"Are you sleepy?"

"Yeah."

"Good. Sure you want to get up and go to work? You've had a big night."

"I want to."

Away at school this winter he had learned for the first time that you can go short of sleep and live. As an infant he had slept with an immobile, sweating intensity that had alarmed his babysitters. In adolescence he had often been the first of the four children to go to bed. Even now, he would go slack in the middle of a television show, his sprawled legs hairy and brown. "O.K. Good boy. Dickie, listen. I love you so much, I never knew how much until now. No matter how this works out, I'll always be with you. Really."

Richard bent to kiss an averted face but his son, sinewy, turned and with wet cheeks embraced him and gave him a kiss, on the lips, passionate as a woman's. In his father's ear he moaned one word, the crucial, intelligent word: "*Why?*"

Why. It was a whistle of wind in a crack, a knife thrust, a window thrown open on emptiness. The white face was gone, the darkness was featureless. Richard had forgotten why.

Luisa Valenzuela

. . . .

I'M YOUR HORSE IN
THE NIGHT

The doorbell rang: three short rings and one long one. That was the signal, and I got up, annoyed and a little frightened; it could be them, and then again, maybe not; at these ungodly hours of the night it could be a trap. I opened the door expecting anything except him, face to face, at last.

He came in quickly and locked the door behind him before embracing me. So much in character, so cautious, first and foremost checking his—our—rear guard. Then he took me in his arms without saying a word, not even holding me too tight but letting all the emotions of our new encounter overflow, telling me so much by merely holding me in his arms and kissing me slowly. I think he never had much faith in words, and there he was, as silent as ever, sending me messages in the form of caresses.

We finally stepped back to look at one another from head to foot, not eye to eye, out of focus. And I was able to say Hello showing scarcely any surprise despite all those months when I had no idea where he could have been, and I was able to say

I thought you were fighting up north
I thought you'd been caught
I thought you were in hiding
I thought you'd been tortured and killed
I thought you were theorizing about the revolution in another country

Just one of many ways to tell him I'd been thinking of him, I hadn't stopped thinking of him or felt as if I'd been betrayed. And there he was, always so goddamn cautious, so much the master of his actions.

"Quiet, Chiquita. You're much better off not knowing what I've been up to."

Then he pulled out his treasures, potential clues that at the time eluded me: a bottle of cachaça and a Gal Costa record. What had he been up to in Brazil? What was he planning to do next? What had brought him back, risking his life, knowing they were after him? Then I stopped asking myself questions (quiet, Chiquita, he'd say). Come here, Chiquita, he was saying, and I chose to let myself sink into the joy of having him back again, trying not to worry. What would happen to us tomorrow, and the days that followed?

Cachaça's a good drink. It goes down and up and down all the right tracks, and then stops to warm up the corners that need it most. Gal Costa's voice is hot, she envelops us in its sound and half-dancing, half-floating, we reach the bed. We lie down and keep on staring deep into each other's eyes, continue caressing each other without allowing ourselves to give into the pure senses just yet. We continue recognizing, rediscovering each other.

Beto, I say, looking at him. I know that isn't his real name, but it's the only one I can call him out loud. He replies:

"We'll make it someday, Chiquita. but let's not talk now."

It's better that way. Better if he doesn't start talking about how we'll make it someday and ruin the wonder of what we're about to attain right now, the two of us, all alone.

"A noite eu so teu cavalo," Gal Costa suddenly sings from the record player.

"I'm your horse in the night," I translate slowly. And so as to bind him in a spell and stop him from thinking about other things:

"It's a saint's song, like in the *macumba*. Someone who's in a trance says she's the horse of the spirit who's riding her, she's his mount."

"Chiquita, you're always getting carried away with esoteric meanings and witchcraft. You know perfectly well that she isn't talking about spirits. If you're my horse in the night it's because I ride you, like this, see? . . . Like this . . . That's all."

It was so long, so deep and so insistent, so charged with affection that we ended up exhausted. I fell asleep with him still on top of me.

I'm your horse in the night.

The goddamn phone pulled me out in waves from a deep well. Making an enormous effort to wake up, I walked over to the receiver, thinking it could be Beto, sure, who was no longer by my side, sure, following his inveterate habit of running away while I'm asleep without a word about where he's gone. To protect me, he says.

From the other end of the line, a voice I thought belonged to Andrés—the one we call Andrés—began to tell me:

"They found Beto dead, floating down the river near the other bank. It looks as if they threw him alive out of a chopper. He's all bloated and decomposed after six days in the water, but I'm almost sure it's him."

"No, it can't be Beto," I shouted carelessly. Suddenly the voice no longer sounded like Andrés: it felt foreign, impersonal.

"You think so?"

"Who is this?" Only then did I think to ask. But that very moment they hung up.

Ten, fifteen minutes? How long must I have stayed there staring at the phone like an idiot until the police arrived? I didn't expect them. But, then again, how could I not? Their hands feeling me, their voices insulting and threatening, the house searched, turned inside out. But I already knew. So what did I care if they broke every breakable object and tore apart my dresser?

They wouldn't find a thing. My only real possession was a dream and they can't deprive me of my dreams just like that. My dream the night before, when

Beto was there with me and we loved each other. I'd dreamed it, dreamed every bit of it, I was deeply convinced that I'd dreamed it all in the richest detail, even in full color. And dreams are none of the cops' business.

They want reality, tangible facts, the kind I couldn't even begin to give them.

Where is he, you saw him, he was here with you, where did he go? Speak up, or you'll be sorry. Let's hear you sing, bitch, we know he came to see you, where is he, where is he holed up? He's in the city, come on, spill it, we know he came to get you.

I haven't heard a word from him in months. He abandoned me, I haven't heard from him in months. He ran away, went underground. What do I know, he ran off with someone else, he's in another country. What do I know, he abandoned me, I hate him, I know nothing.

(Go ahead, burn me with your cigarettes, kick me all you wish, threaten, go ahead, stick a mouse in me so it'll eat my insides out, pull my nails out, do as you please. Would I make something up for that? Would I tell you he was here when a thousand years ago he left me forever?)

I'm not about to tell them my dreams. Why should they care? I haven't seen that so-called Beto in more than six months, and I loved him. The man simply vanished. I only run into him in my dreams, and they're bad dreams that often become nightmares.

Beto, you know now, if it's true that they killed you, or wherever you may be, Beto, I'm your horse in the night and you can inhabit me whenever you wish, even if I'm behind bars. Beto, now that I'm in jail I know that I dreamed you that night; it was just a dream. And if by some wild chance there's a Gal Costa record and a half-empty bottle of cachaça in my house, I hope they'll forgive me: I will them out of existence.

Translated from the Spanish by Deborah Bonner

Eudora Welty

. . . .

NO PLACE FOR YOU, MY LOVE

They were strangers to each other, both fairly well strangers to the place, now seated side by side at luncheon—a party combined in a free-and-easy way when the friends he and she were with recognized each other across Galatoire's. The time was a Sunday in summer—those hours of afternoon that seem Time Out in New Orleans.

The moment he saw her little blunt, fair face, he thought that here was a woman who was having an affair. It was one of those odd meetings when such an impact is felt that it has to be translated at once into some sort of speculation.

With a married man, most likely, he supposed, slipping quickly into a groove—he was long married—and feeling more conventional, then, in his curiosity as she sat there, leaning her cheek on her hand, looking no further before her than the flowers on the table, and wearing that hat.

He did not like her hat, any more than he liked tropical flowers. It was the wrong hat for her, thought this Eastern businessman who had no interest whatever in women's clothes and no eye for them; he thought the unaccustomed thing crossly.

It must stick out all over me, she thought, so people think they can love me or hate me just by looking at me. How did it leave us—the old, safe, slow way people used to know of learning how one another feels, and the privilege that went with it of shying away if it seemed best? People in love like me, I suppose, give away the short cuts to everybody's secrets.

Something, though, he decided, had been settled about her predicament—for the time being, anyway; the parties to it were all still alive, no doubt. Nevertheless, her predicament was the only one he felt so sure of here, like the only recognizable shadow in that restaurant, where mirrors and fans were busy agitating the light, as the very local talk drawled across and agitated the peace. The shadow lay between her fingers, between her little square hand and her cheek, like something always best carried about the person. Then suddenly, as she took her hand down, the secret fact was still there—it lighted her. It was a bold and full light, shot up under the brim of that hat, as close to them all as the flowers in the center of the table.

Did he dream of making her disloyal to that hopelessness that he saw very well she'd been cultivating down here? He knew very well that he did not. What they amounted to was two Northerners keeping each other company. She glanced up at the big gold clock on the wall and smiled. He didn't smile back. She had that naïve face that he associated, for no good reason, with the Middle West—because it said "Show me," perhaps. It was a serious, now-watch-out-everybody face, which orphaned her entirely in the company of these Southerners. He guessed her age, as he could not guess theirs: thirty-two. He himself was further along.

Of all human moods, deliberate imperviousness may be the most quickly communicated—it may be the most successful, most fatal signal of all. And two people can indulge in imperviousness as well as in anything else. "You're not very hungry either," he said.

The blades of fan shadows came down over their two heads, as he saw inadvertently in the mirror, with himself smiling at her now like a villain. His remark sounded dominant and rude enough for everybody present to listen back a moment; it even sounded like an answer to a question she might have just asked him. The other women glanced at him. The Southern look—Southern mask—of life-is-a-dream irony, which could turn to pure challenge at the drop of a hat, he could wish well away. He liked naïveté better.

"I find the heat down here depressing," she said, with the heart of Ohio in her voice.

"Well—I'm in somewhat of a temper about it, too," he said.

They looked with grateful dignity at each other.

"I have a car here, just down the street," he said to her as the luncheon party was rising to leave, all the others wanting to get back to their houses and sleep. "If it's all right with— Have you ever driven down south of here?"

Out on Bourbon Street, in the bath of July, she asked at his shoulder, "South of New Orleans? I didn't know there was any south to *here*. Does it just go on and on?" She laughed, and adjusted the exasperating hat to her head in a different way. It was more than frivolous, it was conspicuous, with some sort of glitter or flitter tied in a band around the straw and hanging down.

"That's what I'm going to show you."

"Oh—you've been there?"

"No!"

His voice rang out over the uneven, narrow sidewalk and dropped back from the walls. The flaked-off, colored houses were spotted like the hides of beasts faded and shy, and were hot as a wall of growth that seemed to breathe flowerlike down onto them as they walked to the car parked there.

"It's just that it couldn't be any worse—we'll see."

"All right, then," she said. "We will."

So, their actions reduced to amiability, they settled into the car—a faded-red Ford convertible with a rather threadbare canvas top, which had been standing in the sun for all those lunch hours.

"It's rented," he explained. "I asked to have the top put down, and was told I'd lost my mind."

"It's out of this world. *Degrading* heat," she said and added, "Doesn't matter."

The stranger in New Orleans always sets out to leave it as though following the clue in a maze. They were threading through the narrow and one-way streets, past the pale-violet bloom of tired squares, the brown steeples and statues, the balcony with the live and probably famous black monkey dipping along the railing as over a ballroom floor, past the grillework and the lattice-work to all the iron swans painted flesh color on the front steps of bungalows outlying.

Driving, he spread his new map and put his finger down on it. At the intersection marked Arabi, where their road led out of the tangle and he took it, a small Negro seated beneath a black umbrella astride a box chalked "Shou Shine" lifted his pink-and-black hand and waved them languidly good-by. She didn't miss it, and waved back.

Below New Orleans there was a raging of insects from both sides of the concrete highway, not quite together, like the playing of separated marching bands. The river and the levee were still on her side, waste and jungle and some occasional settlements on his—poor houses. Families bigger than housefuls thronged the yards. His nodding, driving head would veer from side to side, looking and almost lowering. As time passed and the distance from New Orleans grew, girls ever darker and younger were disposing themselves over the porches and the porch steps, with jet-black hair pulled high, and ragged palm-leaf fans rising and falling like rafts of butterflies. The children running forth were nearly always naked ones.

She watched the road. Crayfish constantly crossed in front of the wheels, looking grim and bonneted, in a great hurry.

"How the Old Woman Got Home," she murmured to herself.

He pointed, as it flew by, at a saucepan full of cut zinnias which stood waiting on the open lid of a mailbox at the roadside, with a little note tied onto the handle.

They rode mostly in silence. The sun bore down. They met fishermen and other men bent on some local pursuits, some in sulphur-colored pants, walking and riding; met wagons, trucks, boats in trucks, autos, boats on top of autos—all coming to meet them, as though something of high moment were doing back where the car came from, and he and she were determined to miss it. There was nearly always a man lying with his shoes off in the bed of any truck otherwise empty—with the raw, red look of a man sleeping in the daytime, being jolted about as he slept. Then there was a sort of dead man's land, where nobody came. He loosened his collar and tie. By rushing through the heat at high speed, they brought themselves the effect of fans turned onto their cheeks. Clearing alternated with jungle and canebrake like something tried, tried again. Little shell roads led off on both sides; now and then a road of planks led into the yellow-green.

"Like a dance floor in there." She pointed.

He informed her, "In there's your oil, I think."

There were thousands, millions of mosquitoes and gnats—a universe of them, and on the increase.

A family of eight or nine people on foot strung along the road in the same direction the car was going, beating themselves with the wild palmettos. Heels, shoulders, knees, breasts, back of the heads, elbows, hands, were touched in turn—like some game, each playing it with himself.

He struck himself on the forehead, and increased their speed. (His wife would not be at her most charitable if he came bringing malaria home to the family.)

More and more crayfish and other shell creatures littered their path, scuttling or dragging. These little samples, little jokes of creation, persisted and sometimes perished, the more of them the deeper down the road went. Terrapins and turtles came up steadily over the horizons of the ditches.

Back there in the margins were worse—crawling hides you could not penetrate with bullets or quite believe, grins that had come down from the primeval mud.

"Wake up." Her Northern nudge was very timely on his arm. They had veered toward the side of the road. Still driving fast, he spread his map.

Like a misplaced sunrise, the light of the river flowed up; they were mounting the levee on a little shell road.

"Shall we cross here?" he asked politely.

He might have been keeping track over years and miles of how long they could keep that tiny ferry waiting. Now skidding down the levee's flank, they were the last-minute car, the last possible car that could squeeze on. Under the sparse shade of one willow tree, the small, amateurish-looking boat slapped the water, as, expertly, he wedged on board.

"Tell him we put him on hub cap!" shouted one of the numerous olive-skinned, dark-eyed young boys standing dressed up in bright shirts at the railing, hugging each other with delight that that last straw was on board. Another boy drew his affectionate initials in the dust of the door on her side.

She opened the door and stepped out, and, after only a moment's standing at bay, started up a little iron stairway. She appeared above the car, on the tiny bridge beneath the captain's window and the whistle.

From there, while the boat still delayed in what seemed a trance—as if it were too full to attempt the start—she could see the panlike deck below, separated by its rusty rim from the tilting, polished water.

The passengers walking and jostling about there appeared oddly amateurish, too—amateur travelers. They were having such a good time. They all knew each other. Beer was being passed around in cans, bets were being loudly settled and new bets made, about local and special subjects on which they all doted. One red-haired man in a burst of wildness even tried to give away his truckload of shrimp to a man on the other side of the boat—nearly all the trucks were full of shrimp—causing taunts and then protests of "They good! They good!" from the giver. The young boys leaned on each other thinking of what next, rolling their eyes absently.

A radio pricked the air behind her. Looking like a great tomcat just above her head, the captain was digesting the news of a fine stolen automobile.

At last a tremendous explosion burst—the whistle. Everything shuddered in outline from the sound, everybody said something—everybody else.

They started with no perceptible motion, but her hat blew off. It went spiraling to the deck below, where he, thank heaven, sprang out of the car and picked it up. Everybody looked frankly up at her now, holding her hands to her head.

The little willow tree receded as its shade was taken away. The heat was like something falling on her head. She held the hot rail before her. It was like riding a stove. Her shoulders dropping, her hair flying, her skirt buffeted by the sudden strong wind, she stood there, thinking they all must see that with her entire self all she did was wait. Her set hands, with the bag that hung from her wrist and rocked back and forth—all three seemed objects bleaching there, belonging to no one; she could not feel a thing in the skin of her face; perhaps she was crying, and not knowing it. She could look down and see him just below her, his black shadow, her hat, and his black hair. His hair in the wind looked unreasonably long and rippling. Little did he know that from here it had a red undergleam like an animal's. When she looked up and outward, a vortex of light drove through and over the brown waves like a star in the water.

He did after all bring the retrieved hat up the stairs to her. She took it back—useless—and held it to her skirt. What they were saying below was more polite than their searchlight faces.

"Where you think he come from, that man?"

"I bet he come from Lafitte."

"Lafitte? What you bet, eh?"—all crouched in the shade of trucks, squatting and laughing.

Now his shadow fell partly across her; the boat had jolted into some other strand of current. Her shaded arm and shaded hand felt pulled out from the blaze of light and water, and she hoped humbly for more shade for her head. It had seemed so natural to climb up and stand in the sun.

The boys had a surprise—an alligator on board. One of them pulled it by a chain around the deck, between the cars and trucks, like a toy—a hide that could walk. He thought, Well they had to catch one sometime. It's Sunday afternoon. So they have him on board now, riding him across the Mississippi River. . . . The playfulness of it beset everybody on the ferry. The hoarseness of the boat whistle, commenting briefly, seemed part of the general appreciation.

"Who want to rassle him? Who want to, eh?" two boys cried, looking up. A boy with shrimp-colored arms capered from side to side, pretending to have been bitten.

What was there so hilarious about jaws that could bite? And what danger was there once in this repulsiveness—so that the last worldly evidence of some old heroic horror of the dragon had to be paraded in capture before the eyes of country clowns?

He noticed that she looked at the alligator without flinching at all. Her distance was set—the number of feet and inches between herself and it mattered to her.

Perhaps her measuring coolness was to him what his bodily shade was to her, while they stood pat up there riding the river, which felt like the sea and looked like the earth under them—full of the red-brown earth, charged with it. Ahead of the boat it was like an exposed vein of ore. The river seemed to swell in the vast middle with the curve of the earth. The sun rolled under them. As if in memory of the size of things, uprooted trees were drawn across their path, sawing at the air and tumbling one over the other.

When they reached the other side, they felt that they had been racing around an arena in their chariot, among lions. The whistle took and shook the stairs as they went down. The young boys, looking taller, had taken out colored combs and were combing their wet hair back in solemn pompadour above their radiant foreheads. They had been bathing in the river themselves not long before.

The cars and trucks, then the foot passengers and the alligator, waddling like a child to school, all disembarked and wound up the weed-sprung levee.

Both respectable and merciful, their hides, she thought, forcing herself to dwell on the alligator as she looked back. Deliver us all from the naked in heart. (As she had been told.)

When they regained their paved road, he heard her give a little sigh and saw her turn her straw-colored head to look back once more. Now that she rode with her hat in her lap, her earrings were conspicuous too. A little metal ball set with small pale stones danced beside each square, faintly downy cheek.

Had she felt a wish for someone else to be riding with them? He thought it was more likely that she would wish for her husband if she had one (his wife's voice) than for the lover in whom he believed. Whatever people liked to think, situations (if not scenes) were usually three-way—there was somebody else always. The one who didn't—couldn't—understand the two made the formidable third.

He glanced down at the map flapping on the seat between them, up at his wristwatch, out at the road. Out there was the incredible brightness of four o'clock.

On this side of the river, the road ran beneath the brow of the levee and followed it. Here was a heat that ran deeper and brighter and more intense than all the rest—its nerve. The road grew one with the heat as it was one with the unseen river. Dead snakes stretched across the concrete like markers—inlaid mosaic bands, dry as feathers, which their tires licked at intervals that began to seem clocklike.

No, the heat faced them—it was ahead. They could see it waving at them, shaken in the air above the white of the road, always at a certain distance ahead, shimmering finely as a cloth, with running edges of green and gold, fire and azure.

"It's never anything like this in Syracuse," he said.

"Or in Toledo, either," she replied with dry lips.

They were driving through greater waste down here, through fewer and even more insignificant towns. There was water under everything. Even where a screen of jungle had been left to stand, splashes could be heard from under the trees. In the vast open, sometimes boats moved inch by inch through what appeared endless meadows of rubbery flowers.

Her eyes overcome with brightness and size, she felt a panic rise, as sudden as nausea. Just how far below questions and answers, concealment and revelation, they were running now—that was still a new question, with a power of its own, waiting. How dear—how costly—could this ride be?

"It looks to me like your road can't go much further," she remarked cheerfully. "Just over there, it's all water."

"Time out," he said, and with that he turned the car into a sudden road of white shells that rushed at them narrowly out of the left.

They bolted over a cattle guard, where some rayed and crested purple flowers burst out of the vines in the ditch, and rolled onto a long, narrow, green, mowed clearing: a churchyard. A paved track ran between two short rows of raised tombs, all neatly white-washed and now brilliant as faces against the vast flushed sky.

The track was the width of the car with a few inches to spare. He passed between the tombs slowly but in the manner of a feat. Names took their places on the walls slowly at a level with the eye, names as near as the eyes of a person stopping in conversation, and as far away in origin, and in all their music and dead longing, as Spain. At intervals were set packed bouquets of zinnias, oleanders, and some kind of purple flowers, all quite fresh, in fruit jars, like nice welcomes on bureaus.

They moved on into an open plot beyond, of violent-green grass, spread before the green-and-white frame church with worked flower beds around it, flowerless poinsettias growing up to the windowsills. Beyond was a house, and left on the doorstep of the house a fresh-caught catfish the size of a baby—a fish wearing whiskers and bleeding. On a clothesline in the yard, a priest's black gown on a hanger hung airing, swaying at man's height, in a vague, trainlike, ladylike sweep along an evening breath that might otherwise have seemed imaginary from the unseen, felt river.

With the motor cut off, with the raging of the insects about them, they sat looking out at the green and white and black and red and pink as they leaned against the sides of the car.

"What is your wife like?" she asked. His right hand came up and spread—iron, wooden, manicured. She lifted her eyes to his face. He looked at her like that hand.

Then he lit a cigarette, and the portrait, and the right-hand testimonial it made, were blown away. She smiled, herself as unaffected as by some stage performance; and he was annoyed in the cemetery. They did not risk going on to her husband—if she had one.

Under the supporting posts of the priest's house, where a boat was, solid ground ended and palmettos and water hyacinths could not wait to begin; suddenly the rays of the sun, from behind the car, reached that lowness and struck the flowers. The priest came out onto the porch in his underwear, stared at the car a moment as if he wondered what time it was, then collected his robe off the line and his fish off the doorstep and returned inside. Vespers was next, for him.

After backing out between the tombs he drove on still south, in the sunset. They caught up with an old man walking in a sprightly way in their direction, all by himself, wearing a clean bright shirt printed with a pair of palm trees fanning green over his chest. It might better be a big colored woman's shirt, but she didn't have it. He flagged the car with gestures like hoops.

"You're coming to the end of the road," the old man told them. He pointed ahead, tipped his hat to the lady, and pointed again. "End of the road." They didn't understand that he meant, "Take me."

They drove on. "If we do go any further, it'll have to be by water—is that it?" he asked her, hesitating at this odd point.

"You know better than I do," she replied politely.

The road had for some time ceased to be paved; it was made of shells. It was leading into a small, sparse settlement like the others a few miles back, but with even more of the camp about it. On the lip of the clearing, directly before a green willow blaze with the sunset gone behind it, the row of houses and shacks faced out on broad, colored, moving water that stretched to reach the horizon and looked like an arm of the sea. The houses on their shaggy posts, patchily built, some with plank runways instead of steps, were flimsy and alike, and not much bigger than the boats tied up at the landing.

"Venice," she heard him announce, and he dropped the crackling map in her lap.

They coasted down the brief remainder. The end of the road—she could not remember ever seeing a road simply end—was a spoon shape, with a tree stump in the bowl to turn around by.

Around it, he stopped the car, and they stepped out, feeling put down in the midst of a sudden vast pause or subduement that was like a yawn. They made their way on foot toward the water, where at an idle-looking landing men in twos and threes stood with their backs to them.

The nearness of darkness, the still uncut trees, bright water partly under a sheet of flowers, shacks, silence, dark shapes of boats tied up, then the first sounds of people just on the other side of thin walls—all this reached them. Mounds of shells like day-old snow, pink-tinted, lay around a central shack with a beer sign on it. An old man up on the porch there sat holding an open newspaper, with a fat white goose sitting opposite him on the floor. Below, in the now shadowless and sunless open, another old man, with a colored pencil bright under his hat brim, was late mending a sail.

When she looked clear around, thinking they had a fire burning somewhere now, out of the heat had risen the full moon. Just beyond the trees, enormous, tangerine-colored, it was going solidly up. Other lights just striking into view, looking farther distant, showed moss shapes hanging, or slipped and broke matchlike on the water that so encroached upon the rim of ground they were standing on.

There was a touch at her arm—his, accidental.

"We're at the jumping-off place," he said.

She laughed, having thought his hand was a bat, while her eyes rushed downward toward a great pale drift of water hyacinths—still partly open, flushed and yet moonlit, level with her feet—through which paths of water for the boats had been hacked. She drew her hands up to her face under the brim of her hat; her own cheeks felt like the hyacinths to her, all her skin still full of too much light and sky, exposed. The harsh vesper bell was ringing.

"I believe there must be something wrong with me, that I came on this excursion to begin with," she said, as if he had already said this and she were merely in hopeful, willing, maddening agreement with him.

He took hold of her arm, and said, "Oh, come on—I see we can get something to drink here, at least."

But there was a beating, muffled sound from over the darkening water. One more boat was coming in, making its way through the tenacious, tough, dark flower traps, by the shaken light of what first appeared to be torches. He and she waited for the boat, as if on each other's patience. As if borne in on a mist of twilight or a breath, a horde of mosquitoes and gnats came singing and striking at them first. The boat bumped, men laughed. Somebody was offering somebody else some shrimp.

Then he might have cocked his dark city head down at her; she did not look up at him, only turned when he did. Now the shell mounds, like the shacks and trees, were solid purple. Lights had appeared in the not-quite-true window squares. A narrow neon sign, the lone sign, had come out in bright blush on the beer shack's roof: "Baba's Place." A light was on on the porch.

The barnlike interior was brightly lit and unpainted, looking not quite finished, with a partition dividing this room from what lay behind. One of the four cardplayers at a table in the middle of the floor was the newspaper reader; the paper was in his pants pocket. Midway along the partition was a bar, in the form of a pass-through to the other room, with a varnished, second-hand fretwork overhang. They crossed the floor and sat, alone there, on wooden stools. An eruption of humorous signs, newspaper cutouts and cartoons, razor-blade cards, and personal messages of significance to the owner or his friends decorated the overhang, framing where Baba should have been but wasn't.

Through there came a smell of garlic and cloves and red pepper, a blast of hot cloud escaped from a cauldron they could see now on a stove at the back of the other room. A massive back, presumably female, with a twist of gray hair on top, stood with a ladle akimbo. A young man joined her and with his fingers stole something out of the pot and ate it. At Baba's they were boiling shrimp.

When he got ready to wait on them, Baba strolled out to the counter, young, black-headed, and in very good humor.

"Coldest beer you've got. And food— What will you have?"

"Nothing for me, thank you," she said. "I'm not sure I could eat, after all."

"Well, I could," he said, shoving his jaw out. Baba smiled. "I want a good solid ham sandwich."

"I could have asked him for some water," she said, after he had gone.

While they sat waiting, it seemed very quiet. The bubbling of the shrimp, the distant laughing of Baba, and the slap of cards, like the beating of moths on the screens, seemed to come in fits and starts. The steady breathing they heard came from a big rough dog asleep in the corner. But it was bright. Electric lights were strung riotously over the room from a kind of spider web of old wires in the rafters. One of the written messages tacked before them read, "Joe! At the boyy!!" It looked very yellow, older than Baba's Place. Outside, the world was pure dark.

Two little boys, almost alike, almost the same size, and just cleaned up, dived into the room with a double bang of the screen door, and circled around the card game. They ran their hands into the men's pockets.

"Nickel for some pop!"

"Nickel for some pop!"

"Go 'way and let me play, you!"

They circled around and shrieked at the dog, ran under the lid of the counter and raced through the kitchen and back, and hung over the stools at the bar.

One child had a live lizard on his shirt, clinging like a breast pin—like lapis lazuli.

Bringing in a strong odor of geranium talcum, some men had come in now—all in bright shirts. They drew near the counter, or stood and watched the game.

When Baba came out bringing the beer and sandwich, "Could I have some water?" she greeted him.

Baba laughed at everybody. She decided the woman back there must be Baba's mother.

Beside her, he was drinking his beer and eating his sandwich—ham, cheese, tomato, pickle, and mustard. Before he finished, one of the men who had come in beckoned from across the room. It was the old man in the palm-tree shirt.

She lifted her head to watch him leave her, and was looked at, from all over the room. As a minute passed, no cards were laid down. In a far-off way, like accepting the light from Arcturus, she accepted it that she was more beautiful or perhaps more fragile than the women they saw every day of their lives. It was just this thought coming into a woman's face, and at this hour, that seemed familiar to them.

Baba was smiling. He had set an opened, frosted brown bottle before her on the counter, and a thick sandwich, and stood looking at her. Baba made her eat some supper, for what she was.

"What the old fellow wanted," said he when he came back at last, "was to have a friend of his apologize. Seems church is just out. Seems the friend made a remark coming in just now. His pals told him there was a lady present."

"I see you bought him a beer," she said.

"Well, the old man looked like he wanted *something*."

All at once the juke box interrupted from back in the corner, with the same old song as anywhere. The half-dozen slot machines along the wall were suddenly all run to like Maypoles, and thrown into action—taken over by further battalions of little boys.

There were three little boys to each slot machine. The local custom appeared to be that one pulled the lever for the friend he was holding up to put the nickel in, while the third covered the pictures with the flat of his hand as they fell into place, so as to surprise them all if anything happened.

The dog lay sleeping on in front of the raging juke box, his ribs working fast as a concertina's. At the side of the room a man with a cap on his white thatch was trying his best to open a side screen door, but it was stuck fast. It was he who had come in with the remark considered ribald; now he was trying to get out the other way. Moths as thick as ingots were trying to get in. The cardplayers broke into shouts of derision, then joy, then tired derision among themselves; they might have been here all afternoon—they were the only ones not cleaned up and shaved. The original pair of little boys ran in once more, with the hyphenated bang. They got nickels this time, then were brushed away from the table like mosquitoes, and they rushed under the counter and on to the cauldron behind, clinging to Baba's mother there. The evening was at the threshold.

They were quite unnoticed now. He was eating another sandwich, and she, having finished part of hers, was fanning her face with her hat. Baba had lifted the flap of the counter and come out into the room. Behind his head there was a sign lettered in orange crayon: "Shrimp Dance Sun. PM." That was tonight, still to be.

And suddenly she made a move to slide down from her stool, maybe wishing to walk out into that nowhere down the front steps to be cool a moment. But he had hold of her hand. He got down from his stool, and, patiently, reversing her hand in his own—just as she had had the look of being about to give up, faint—began moving her, leading her. They were dancing.

"I get to thinking this is what we get—what you and I deserve," she whispered, looking past his shoulder into the room. "And all the time, it's real. It's a real place—away off down here. . . ."

They danced gratefully, formally, to some song carried on in what must be the local patios, while no one paid any attention as long as they were together, and the children poured the family nickels steadily into the slot machines, walloping the handles down with regular crashes and troubling nobody with winning.

She said rapidly, as they began moving together too well, "One of those clippings was an account of a shooting right here. I guess they're proud of it. And that awful knife Baba was carrying . . . I wonder what he called me," she whispered in his ear.

"Who?"

"The one who apologized to you."

If they had ever been going to overstep themselves, it would be now as he held her closer and turned her, when she became aware that he could not help but see the bruise at her temple. It would not be six inches from his eyes. She felt it come out like an evil star. (Let it pay him back, then, for the hand he had stuck in her face when she'd tried once to be sympathetic, when she'd asked about his wife.) They danced on still as the record changed, after standing wordless and motionless, linked together in the middle of the room, for the moment between.

Then, they were like a matched team—like professional, Spanish dancers wearing masks—while the slow piece was playing.

Surely even those immune from the world, for the time being, need the touch of one another, or all is lost. Their arms encircling each other, their bodies circling the odorous, just-nailed-down floor, they were, at last, imperviousness in motion. They had found it, and had almost missed it: they had had to dance. They were what their separate hearts desired that day, for themselves and each other.

They were so good together that once she looked up and half smiled. "For whose benefit did we have to show off?"

Like people in love, they had a superstition about themselves almost as soon as they came out on the floor, and dared not think the words "happy" or "unhappy," which might strike them, one or the other, like lightning.

In the thickening heat they danced on while Baba himself sang with the mosquito-voiced singer in the chorus of "Moi pas l'aimez ça," enumerating the ça's with a hot shrimp between his fingers. He was counting over the platters the old woman now set out on the counter, each heaped with shrimp in their shells boiled to iridescence, like mounds of honeysuckle flowers.

The goose wandered in from the back room under the lid of the counter and hitched itself around the floor among the table legs and people's legs, never seeing that it was neatly avoided by two dancers—who nevertheless vaguely thought of this goose as learned, having earlier heard an old man read to it. The children called it Mimi, and lured it away. The old thatched man was again drunkenly trying to get out by the stuck side door; now he gave it a kick, but was prevailed on to remain. The sleeping dog shuddered and snored.

It was left up to the dancers to provide nickels for the juke box; Baba kept a drawerful for every use. They had grown fond of all the selections by now. This was the music you heard out of the distance at night—out of the roadside taverns you fled past, around the late corners in cities half asleep, drifting up from the carnival over the hill, with one odd little strain always managing to repeat itself. This seemed a homey place.

Bathed in sweat, and feeling the false coolness that brings, they stood finally on the porch in the lapping night air for a moment before leaving. The first arrivals of the girls were coming up the steps under the porch light—all flowered fronts, their black pompadours giving out breathlike feelers from sheer abundance. Where they'd resprinkled it since church, the talcum shone like mica on their downy arms. Smelling solidly of geranium, they filed across the porch with short steps and fingers joined, just timed to turn their smiles loose inside the room. He held the door open for them.

"Ready to go?" he asked her.

Going back, the ride was wordless, quiet except for the motor and the insects driving themselves against the car. The windshield was soon blinded. The headlights pulled in two other spinning storms, cones of flying things that, it seemed, might ignite at the last minute. He stopped the car and got out to clean the windshield thoroughly with his brisk, angry motions of driving. Dust lay thick and cratered on the roadside scrub. Under the now ash-white moon, the world traveled through very faint stars—very many slow stars, very high, very low.

It was a strange land, amphibious—and whether water-covered or grown with jungle or robbed entirely of water and trees, as now, it had the same loneliness. He regarded the great sweep—like steppes, like moors, like deserts (all of which were imaginary to him); but more than it was like any likeness, it was South. The vast, thin, wide-thrown, pale, unfocused star-sky, with its veils of lightning adrift, hung over this land as it hung over the open sea. Standing out in the night alone, he was struck as powerfully with recognition of the extremity of this place as if all other bearings had vanished—as if snow had suddenly started to fall.

He climbed back inside and drove. When he moved to slap furiously at his shirtsleeves, she shivered in the hot, licking night wind that their speed was making. Once the car lights picked out two people—a Negro couple, sitting on two facing chairs in the yard outside their lonely cabin—half undressed, each battling for self against the hot night, with long white rags in endless, scarflike motions.

In peopleless open places there were lakes of dust, smudge fires burning at their hearts. Cows stood in untended rings around them, motionless in the heat, in the night—their horns standing up sharp against that glow.

At length, he stopped the car again, and this time he put his arm under her shoulder and kissed her—not knowing ever whether gently or harshly. It was the loss of that distinction that told him this was now. Then their faces touched unkissing, unmoving, dark, for a length of time. The heat came inside the car and wrapped them still, and the mosquitoes had begun to coat their arms and even their eyelids.

Later, crossing a large open distance, he saw at the same time two fires. He had the feeling that they had been riding for a long time across a face—great, wide, and upturned. In its eyes and open mouth were those fires they had had glimpses of, where the cattle had drawn together: a face, a head, far down here in the South—south of South, below it. A whole giant body sprawled downward then, on and on, always, constant as a constellation or an angel. Flaming and perhaps falling, he thought.

She appeared to be sound asleep, lying back flat as a child, with her hat in her lap. He drove on with her profile beside his, behind his, for he bent forward to drive faster. The earrings she wore twinkled with their rushing motion in an almost regular beat. They might have spoken like tongues. He looked straight before him and drove on, at a speed that, for the rented, overheated, not at all new Ford car, was demoniac.

It seemed often now that a barnlike shape flashed by, roof and all outlined in lonely neon—a movie house at a crossroads. The long white flat road itself, since they had followed it to the end and turned around to come back, seemed able, this far up, to pull them home.

A thing is incredible, if ever, only after it is told—returned to the world it came out of. For their different reasons, he thought, neither of them would tell this (unless something was dragged out of them): that, strangers, they had ridden down into a strange land together and were getting safely back—by a slight margin, perhaps, but margin enough. Over the levee wall now, like an aurora borealis, the sky of New Orleans, across the river, was flickering gently. This time they crossed by bridge, high above everything, merging into a long light-stream of cars turned cityward.

For a time afterward he was lost in the streets, turning almost at random with the noisy traffic until he found his bearings. When he stopped the car at the next sign and leaned forward frowning to make it out, she sat up straight on her side. It was Arabi. He turned the car right around.

"We're all right now," he muttered, allowing himself a cigarette.

Something that must have been with them all along suddenly, then, was not. In a moment, tall as panic, it rose, cried like a human, and dropped back.

"I never got my water," she said.

She gave him the name of her hotel, he drove her there, and he said good night on the sidewalk. They shook hands.

"Forgive . . ." For, just in time, he saw she expected it of him.

And that was just what she did, forgive him. Indeed, had she waked in time from a deep sleep, she would have told him her story. She disappeared through the revolving door, with a gesture of smoothing her hair, and he thought a figure in the lobby strolled to meet her. He got back in the car and sat there.

He was not leaving for Syracuse until early in the morning. At length, he recalled the reason; his wife had recommended that he stay where he was this extra day so that she could entertain some old, unmarried college friends without him underfoot.

As he started up the car, he recognized in the smell of exhausted, body-warm air in the streets, in which the flow of drink was an inextricable part, the signal that the New Orleans evening was just beginning. In Dickie Grogan's, as he passed, the well-known Josefina at her organ was charging up and down with "*Clair de Lune.*" As he drove the little Ford safely to its garage, he remembered for the first time in years when he was young and brash, a student in New York, and the shriek and horror and unholy smother of the subway had its original meaning for him as the lilt and expectation of love.

Patrick White

· ·

FIVE-TWENTY

Most evenings, weather permitting, the Natwicks sat on the front veranda to watch the traffic. During the day the stream flowed, but towards five it began to thicken, it sometimes jammed solid like: the semi-trailers and refrigeration units, the decent old-style sedans, the mini-cars, the bombs, the Holdens and the Holdens. She didn't know most of the names. Royal did, he was a man, though never ever mechanical himself. She liked him to tell her about the vehicles, or listen to him take part in conversation with anyone who stopped at the fence. He could hold his own, on account of he was more educated, and an invalid has time to think.

They used to sit side by side on the tiled veranda, him in his wheel chair she had got him after the artheritis took over, her in the old cane. The old cane chair wasn't hardly presentable any more; she had torn her winter cardy on a nail and laddered several pair of stockings. You hadn't the heart to get rid of it, though. They brought it with them from Sarsaparilla after they sold the business. And now they could sit in comfort to watch the traffic, the big steel insects of nowadays, which put the wind up her at times.

Royal said, 'I reckon we're a shingle short to'uv ended up on the Parramatta Road.'

'You said we'd still see life,' she reminded, 'even if we lost the use of our legs.'

'But look at the traffic! Worse every year. And air. Rot a man's lungs quicker than the cigarettes. You should'uv headed me off. You who's supposed to be practical!'

'I thought it was what you wanted,' she said, keeping it soft; she had never been one to crow.

'Anyway, I already lost the use of me legs.'

As if she was to blame for that too. She was so shocked the chair sort of jumped. It made her blood run cold to hear the metal feet screak against the little draught-board tiles.

'Well, I 'aven't!' she protested. 'I got me legs, and will be able to get from 'ere to anywhere and bring 'ome the shopping. While I got me strength.'

756

She tried never to upset him by any show of emotion, but now she was so upset herself.

They watched the traffic in the evenings, as the orange light was stacked up in thick slabs, and the neon signs were coming on.

'See that bloke down there in the parti-coloured Holden?'

'Which?' she asked.

'The one level with our own gate.'

'The pink and brown?' She couldn't take all that interest tonight, only you must never stop humouring a sick man.

'Yairs. Pink. Fancy a man in a pink car!'

'Dusty pink is fashionable.' She knew that for sure.

'But a man!'

'Perhaps his wife chose it. Perhaps he's got a domineering wife.'

Royal laughed low. 'Looks the sort of coot who might like to be domineered, and if that's what he wants, it's none of our business, is it?'

She laughed to keep him company. They were such mates, everybody said. And it was true. She didn't know what she would do if Royal passed on first.

That evening the traffic had jammed. Some of the drivers began tooting. Some of them stuck their heads out, and yarned to one another. But the man in the pink-and-brown Holden just sat. He didn't look to either side.

Come to think of it, she had noticed him pass before. Yes. Though he wasn't in no way a noticeable man. Yes. She looked at her watch.

'Five-twenty,' she said. 'I seen that man in the pink-and-brown before. He's pretty regular. Looks like a business executive.'

Royal cleared his throat and spat. It didn't make the edge of the veranda. Better not to notice it, because he'd only create if she did. She'd get out that watering-can after she had pushed him inside.

'Business executives!' she heard. 'They're afraid people are gunner think they're poor class without they *execute*. In our day nobody was ashamed to *do*. Isn't that about right, eh?' She didn't answer because she knew she wasn't meant to. 'Funny sort of head that cove's got. Like it was half squashed. Silly-lookun bloody head!'

'Could have been born with it,' she suggested. 'Can't help what you're born with. Like your religion.'

There was the evening the Chev got crushed, only a young fellow too. Ahhh, it had stuck in her throat, thinking of the wife and kiddies. She ran in, and out again as quick as she could, with a couple of blankets, and the rug that was a present from Hazel. She had grabbed a pillow off their own bed.

She only faintly heard Royal shouting from the wheel-chair.

She arranged the blankets and the pillow on the pavement, under the orange sky. The young fellow was looking pretty sick, kept on turning his head as though he recognized and wanted to tell her something. Then the photographer from the *Mirror* took his picture, said she ought to be in it to add a touch of human interest, but she wouldn't. A priest came, the *Mirror* took his picture, administering what Mrs Dolan said they call Extreme Unkshun. Well, you couldn't poke fun at a person's religion any more than the shape of their head, and Mrs Dolan was a decent neighbour, the whole family, and clean.

When she got back to the veranda, Royal, a big man, had slipped down in his wheel-chair.

He said, or gasped, 'Wotcher wanter do that for, Ella? How are we gunner get the blood off?'

She hadn't thought about the blood, when of course she was all smeared with it, and the blankets, and Hazel's good Onkaparinka. Anyway, it was her who would get the blood off.

'You soak it in milk or something,' she said. 'I'll ask. Don't you worry.'

Then she did something. She bent down and kissed Royal on the forehead in front of the whole Parramatta Road. She regretted it at once, because he looked that powerless in his invalid chair, and his forehead felt cold and sweaty.

But you can't undo things that are done.

It was a blessing they could sit on the front veranda. Royal suffered a lot by now. He had his long-standing hernia, which they couldn't have operated on, on account of he was afraid of his heart. And then the artheritis.

'Arthritis.'

'All right,' she accepted the correction. 'Arth-er-itis.'

It was all very well for men, they could manage more of the hard words.

'What have we got for tea?' he asked.

'Well,' she said, fanning out her hands on the points of her elbows, and smiling, 'it's a surprise.'

She looked at her watch. It was five-twenty.

'It's a coupler nice little bits of fillet Mr Ballard let me have.'

'Wotcher mean let you have? Didn't you pay for them?'

She had to laugh. 'Anything I have I pay for!'

'Well? Think we're in the fillet-eating class?'

'It's only a treat, Royal,' she said. 'I got a chump chop for myself. I like a nice chop.'

He stopped complaining, and she was relieved.

'There's that gentleman,' she said, 'in the Holden.'

They watched him pass, as sober as their own habits.

Royal—he had been his mother's little king. Most of his mates called him 'Roy'. Perhaps only her and Mrs Natwick had stuck to the christened name, they felt it suited.

She often wondered how Royal had ever fancied her: such a big man, with glossy hair, black, and a nose like on someone historical. She would never have said it, but she was proud of Royal's nose. She was proud of the photo he had of the old family home in Kent, the thatch so lovely, and Grannie Natwick sitting in her apron on a rush-bottom chair in front, looking certainly not all that different from Mum, with the aunts gathered round in leggermutton sleeves, all big nosey women like Royal.

She had heard Mum telling Royal's mother, 'Ella's a plain little thing, but what's better than cheerful and willing?' She had always been on the mousey side, she supposed, which didn't mean she couldn't chatter with the right person. She heard Mum telling Mrs Natwick, 'My Ella can wash and bake against any comers. Clever with her needle too.' She had never entered any of the competitions, like they told her she ought to, it would have made her nervous.

It was all the stranger that Royal had ever fancied her.

Once as they sat on the veranda watching the evening traffic, she said, 'Remember how you used to ride out in the old days from "Bugilbar" to Cootramundra?'

'Cootamundra.'

'Yes,' she said. 'Cootramundra.' (That's why they'd called the house 'Coota' when they moved to the Parramatta Road.)

She had been so dazzled on one occasion by his parti-coloured forehead and his black hair, after he had got down from the saddle, after he had taken off his hat, she had run and fetched a duster, and dusted Royal Natwick's boots. The pair of new elastic-sides was white with dust from the long ride. It only occurred to her as she polished she might be doing something shameful, but when she looked up, it seemed as though Royal Natwick saw nothing peculiar in Ella McWhirter dusting his boots. He might even have expected it. She was so glad she could have cried.

Old Mr Natwick had come out from Kent when a youth, and after working at several uncongenial jobs, and studying at night, had been taken on as bookkeeper at 'Bugilbar'. He was much valued in the end by the owners, and always made use of. The father would have liked his son to follow in his footsteps, and taught him how to keep the books, but Royal wasn't going to hang around any family of purse-proud squatters, telling them the things they wanted to hear. He had ideas of his own for becoming rich and important.

So when he married Ella McWhirter, which nobody could ever understand, not even Ella herself, perhaps only Royal, who never bothered to explain (why should he?) they moved to Juggerawa, and took over the general store. It was in a bad way, and soon was in a worse, because Royal's ideas were above those of his customers.

Fulbrook was the next stage. He found employment as book-keeper on a grazing property outside. She felt so humiliated on account of his humiliation. It didn't matter about herself because she always expected less. She took a job in Fulbrook from the start, at the 'Dixie Cafe' in High Street. She worked there several years as waitress, helping out with the scrubbing for the sake of the extra money. She had never hated anything, but got to hate the flies trampling in the sugar and on the necks of the tomato sauce bottles.

At weekends her husband usually came in, and when she wasn't needed in the shop, they lay on the bed in her upstairs room, listening to the corrugated iron and the warping white-washed weatherboard. She would have loved to do something for him, but in his distress he complained about 'wet kisses'. It surprised her. She had always been afraid he might find her a bit too dry in her show of affection.

Those years at the 'Dixie Cafe' certainly dried her up. She got those freckly patches and seams in her skin in spite of the lotions used as directed. Not that it matters so much in anyone born plain. Perhaps her plainness helped her save. There was never a day when she didn't study her savings-book, it became her favourite recreation.

Royal, on the other hand, wasn't the type that dries up, being fleshier, and dark. He even put on weight out at the grazing property, where they soon thought the world of him. When the young ladies were short of a man for tennis the book-keeper was often invited, and to a ball once at the homestead. He was earning good money, and he too saved a bit, though his instincts weren't as mean as hers. For instance, he fancied a choice cigar. In his youth Royal was a natty dresser.

Sometimes the young ladies, if they decided to inspect the latest at Ryan's Emporium, or Mr Philup, if he felt like grogging up with the locals, would drive him in, and as he got out they would look funny at the book-keeper's wife they had heard about, they must have, serving out the plates of frizzled steak and limp chips. Royal always waited to see his employers drive off before coming in.

In spite of the savings, this might have gone on much longer than it did if old Mr Natwick hadn't died. It appeared he had been a very prudent man. He left them a nice little legacy. The evening of the news, Royal was driven in by Mr Philup and they had a few at the Imperial. Afterwards the book-keeper was dropped off, because he proposed to spend the night with his wife and catch the early train to attend his father's funeral.

They lay in the hot little room and discussed the future. She had never felt so hectic. Royal got the idea he would like to develop a grocery business in one of the posh outer suburbs of Sydney. 'Interest the monied residents in some of the luxury lines. Appeal to the imagination as well as the stomach.'

She was impressed, of course, but not as much as she should have been. She wasn't sure, but perhaps she was short on imagination. Certainly their prospects had made her downright feverish, but for no distinct, sufficient reason.

'And have a baby.' She heard her own unnatural voice.

'Eh?'

'We could start a baby.' Her voice grew word by word drier.

'There's no reason why we couldn't have a baby. Or two.' He laughed. 'But starting a new life isn't the time to start a baby.' He dug her in the ribs. 'And you the practical one!'

She agreed it would be foolish, and presently Royal fell asleep.

What could she do for him? As he lay there breathing she would have loved to stroke his nose she could see faintly in the light from the window. Again unpractical, she would have liked to kiss it. Or bite it suddenly off.

She was so disgusted with herself she got creaking off the bed and walked flat across the boards to the washstand and swallowed a couple of Aspros to put her solidly to sleep.

All their life together she had to try in some way to make amends to Royal, not only for her foolishness, but for some of the thoughts that got into her head. Because she hadn't the imagination, the thoughts couldn't have been her own. They must have been put into her.

It was easier of course in later life, after he had cracked up, what with his hernia, and heart, and the artheritis taking over. Fortunately she was given the strength to help him into the wheel-chair, and later still, to lift, or drag him up on the pillows and over, to rub the bed-sores, and stick the pan under him. But even during the years at Sarsaparilla she could make amends in many little ways, though with him still in his prime, naturally he mustn't know of them. So all her acts were mostly for her own self-gratification.

The store at Sarsaparilla, if it didn't exactly flourish, gave them a decent living. She had her problems, though. Some of the locals just couldn't accept that Royal was a superior man. Perhaps she had been partly to blame, she hardly dared admit it, for showing one or two 'friends' the photo of the family home in Kent. She couldn't resist telling the story of one of the aunts, Miss Ethel Natwick, who followed her brother to New South Wales. Ethel was persuaded to accept a situation at Government House, but didn't like it and went back, in spite of the Governor's lady insisting she valued Ethel as a close personal friend. When people began to laugh at Royal on account of his auntie and the family home, as you couldn't help finding out in a place like Sarsaparilla, it was her, she knew, it was her to blame. It hurt her deeply.

Of course Royal could be difficult. Said stockbrokers had no palate and less imagination. Royal said no Australian grocer could make a go of it if it wasn't for flour, granulated sugar, and tomato sauce. Some of the customers turned nasty in retaliation. This was where she could help, and did, because Royal was out on delivery more often than not. It embarrassed her only when some of them took it for granted she was on their side. As if he wasn't her husband. Once or twice she had gone out crying afterwards, amongst the wormy wattles and hens' droppings. Anyone across the gully could have heard her blowing her nose behind the store, but she didn't care. Poor Royal.

There was that Mr Ogburn said, 'A selfish swollen-headed slob who'll chew you up and swallow you down.' She wouldn't let herself hear any more of what he had to say. Mr Ogburn had a hare-lip, badly sewn, opening and closing. There was nothing frightened her so much as even a well-disguised hare-lip. She got the palpitations after the scene with Mr Ogburn.

Not that there was anything wrong with her.

She only hadn't had the baby. It was her secret grief on black evenings as she walked slowly looking for the eggs a flighty hen might have hid in the bracken.

Dr Bamforth said, looking at the nib of his fountain pen, 'You know, don't you, it's sometimes the man?'

She didn't even want to hear, let alone think about it. In any case she wouldn't tell Royal, because a man's pride could be so easily hurt.

After they had sold out at Sarsaparilla and come to live at what they called 'Coota' on the Parramatta Road, it was both easier and more difficult, because if they were not exactly elderly they were getting on. Royal used to potter about in the beginning, while taking care, on account of the hernia and his heart. There was the business of the lawn-mowing, not that you could call it lawn, but it was what she had. She loved her garden. In front certainly there was only the two square of rather sooty grass which she would keep in order with the push-mower. The lawn seemed to get on Royal's nerves until the artheritis took hold of him.

He had never liked mowing. He would lean against the veranda post, and shout, 'Don't know why we don't do what they've done down the street. Root the stuff out. Put down a green concrete lawn.'

'That would be copying,' she answered back.

She hoped it didn't sound stubborn. As she pushed the mower she bent her head, and smiled, waiting for him to cool off. The scent of grass and a few clippings flew up through the traffic fumes reminding you of summer.

While Royal shuffled along the veranda and leaned against another post. 'Or pebbles. You can buy clean, river pebbles. A few plastic shrubs, and there's the answer.'

He only gave up when his trouble forced him into the chair. You couldn't drive yourself up and down a veranda shouting at someone from a wheel-chair without the passers-by thinking you was a nut. So he quietened.

He watched her, though. From under the peak of his cap. Because she felt he might still resent her mowing the lawn, she would try to reassure him as she pushed. 'What's wrong, *eh*? While I still have me health, me *strength*—I was always what they call *wiry*—why shouldn't I cut the *grass*?'

She would come and sit beside him, to keep him company in watching the traffic, and invent games to amuse her invalid husband.

'Isn't that the feller we expect?' she might ask. 'The one that passes at five-twenty,' looking at her watch, 'in the old pink-and-brown Holden?'

They enjoyed their snort of amusement all the better because no one else knew the reason for it.

Once when the traffic was particularly dense, and that sort of chemical smell from one of the factories was thickening in the evening air, Royal drew her attention. 'Looks like he's got something on his mind.'

Could have too. Or it might have been the traffic block. The way he held his hands curved listlessly around the inactive wheel reminded her of possums and monkeys she had seen in cages. She shifted a bit. Her squeaky old chair. She felt uneasy for ever having found the man, not a joke, but half of one.

Royal's chair moved so smoothly on its rubber-tyred wheels it was easy to push him, specially after her practice with the mower. There were ramps where necessary now, to cover steps, and she would sometimes wheel him out to the back, where she grew hollyhock and sunflower against the palings, and a vegetable or two on raised beds.

Royal would sit not looking at the garden from under the peak of his cap.

She never attempted to take him down the shady side, between them and Dolans, because the path was narrow from plants spilling over, and the shade might have lowered his spirits.

She loved her garden.

The shady side was where she kept her staghorn ferns, and fishbones, and the pots of maidenhair. The water lay sparkling on the maidenhair even in the middle of the day. In the blaze of summer the light at either end of the tunnel was like you were looking through a sheet of yellow cellophane, but as the days shortened, the light deepened to a cold, tingling green, which might have made a person nervous who didn't know the tunnel by heart.

Take Mrs Dolan the evening she came in to ask for the loan of a cupful of sugar. 'You gave me a shock, Mrs Natwick. What ever are you up to?'

'Looking at the plants,' Mrs Natwick answered, whether Mrs Dolan would think it peculiar or not.

It was the season of cinerarias, which she always planted on that side, it was sheltered and cold-green. The wind couldn't bash the big spires and umbrellas of blue and purple. Visiting cats were the only danger, messing and pouncing. She disliked cats for the smell they left, but didn't have the heart to disturb their elastic forms curled at the cineraria roots, exposing their colourless pads, and sometimes pink, swollen teats. Blushing only slightly for it, she would stand and examine the details of the sleeping cats.

If Royal called she could hear his voice through the window. 'Where'uv you got to, Ella?'

After he was forced to take to his bed, his voice began to sort of dry up like his body. There were times when it sounded less like a voice than a breath of drowsiness or pain.

'Ella?' he was calling. 'I dropped the paper. Where are yer all this time? You know I can't pick up the paper.'

She knew. Guilt sent her scuttling to him, deliberately composing her eyes and mouth so as to arrive looking cheerful.

'I was in the garden,' she confessed, 'looking at the cinerarias.'

'The what?' It was a name Royal could never learn.

The room was smelling of sickness and the bottles standing on odd plates. 'It fell,' he complained.

She picked up the paper as quick as she could.

'Want to go la-la first?' she asked, because by now he depended on her to raise him and stick the pan under.

But she couldn't distract him from her shortcomings; he was shaking the paper at her. 'Haven't you lived with me long enough to know how to treat a newspaper?'

He hit it with his set hand, and certainly the paper looked a mess, like an old white battered brolly.

'Mucked up! You gotter keep the pages *aligned*. A paper's not readable otherwise. Of course you wouldn't understand because you don't read it, without it's to see who's died.' He began to cough.

'Like me to bring you some Bovril?' she asked him as tenderly as she knew.

'Bovril's the morning,' he coughed.

She knew that, but wanted to do something for him.

After she had rearranged the paper she walked out so carefully it made her go lopsided, out to the front veranda. Nothing would halt the traffic, not sickness, not death even.

She sat with her arms folded, realizing at last how they were aching.

'He hasn't been,' she had to call after looking at her watch.

'Who?' she heard the voice rustling back.

'The gentleman in the pink Holden.'

She listened to the silence, wondering whether she had done right.

When Royal called back, 'Could'uv had a blow-out.' Then he laughed.

'Could'uv stopped to get grogged up.' She heard the frail rustling of the paper. 'Or taken an axe to somebody like they do nowadays.'

She closed her eyes, whether for Royal, or what she remembered of the man sitting in the Holden.

Although it was cold she continued watching after dark. Might have caught a chill, when she couldn't afford to. She only went inside to make the bread-and-milk Royal fancied of an evening.

She watched most attentively, always at the time, but he didn't pass, and didn't pass.

'Who?'

'The gentleman in the Holden.'

'Gone on holiday.' Royal sighed, and she knew it was the point where a normal person would have turned over, so she went to turn him.

One morning she said on going in, 'Fancy, I had a dream, it was about that man! He was standing on the side path alongside the cinerarias. I know it was him because of his funny-shaped head.'

'What happened in the dream?' Royal hadn't opened his eyes yet; she hadn't helped him in with his teeth.

'I dunno,' she said, 'it was just a dream.'

That wasn't strictly truthful, because the Holden gentleman had looked at her, she had seen his eyes. Nothing was spoken, though.

'It was a sort of red and purple dream. That was the cinerarias,' she said.

'I don't dream. You don't when you don't sleep. Pills aren't sleep.'

She was horrified at her reverberating dream. 'Would you like a nice soft-boiled egg?'

'Eggs all have a taste.'

'But you gotter eat *something*!'

On another morning she told him—she could have bitten off her tongue—she *was* stupid, *stupid*, 'I had a dream.'

'What sort of dream?'

'Oh,' she said, 'a silly one. Not worth telling. I dreamed I dropped an egg on the side path, and it turned into two. Not two. A double-yolker.'

She never realized Royal was so much like Mrs Natwick. It was as she raised him on his pillows. Or he had got like that in his sickness. Old men and old women were not unlike.

'Wasn't that a silly one?' she coaxed.

Every evening she sat on the front veranda and watched the traffic as though Royal had been beside her. Looked at her watch. And turned her face away from the steady-flowing stream. The way she bunched her small chest she could have had a sour breath mounting in her throat. Sometimes she had, it was nervousness.

When she went inside she announced, 'He didn't pass.'

Royal said—he had taken to speaking from behind his eyelids— 'Something muster happened to 'im. He didn't go on holiday. He went and died.'

'Oh, no! He wasn't of an age!'

At once she saw how stupid she was, and went out to get the bread-and-milk.

She would sit at the bedside, almost crouching against the edge of the mattress, because she wanted Royal to feel she was close, and he seemed to realize, though he mostly kept his eyelids down.

Then one evening she came running, she felt silly, her calves felt silly, her voice, 'He's come! At five-twenty! In a new cream Holden!'

Royal said without opening his eyes, 'See? I said 'e'd gone on holiday.'

More than ever she saw the look of Mrs Natwick.

Now every evening Royal asked, 'Has he been, Ella?'

Trying not to make it sound irritable or superior, she would answer, 'Not yet. It's only five.'

Every evening she sat watching, and sometimes would turn proud, arching her back, as she looked down from the veranda. The man was so small and ordinary.

She went in on one occasion, into the more than electric light, lowering her eyelids against the dazzle. 'You know, Royal, you could feel prouder of men when they rode horses. As they looked down at yer from under the brim of their hats. Remember that hat you used to wear? Riding in to Cootramundra?'

Royal died quietly that same year before the cinerarias had folded, while the cold westerlies were still blowing; the back page of the *Herald* was full of those who had been carried off. She was left with his hand, already set, in her own. They hadn't spoken, except about whether she had put out the garbage.

Everybody was very kind. She wouldn't have liked to admit it was enjoyable being a widow. She sat around for longer than she had ever sat, and let the dust gather. In the beginning acquaintances and neighbours brought her little presents of food: a billy-can of giblet soup, moulded veal with hard-boiled egg making a pattern in the jelly, cakes so dainty you couldn't taste them. But when she was no longer a novelty they left off coming. She didn't care any more than she cared about the dust. Sometimes she would catch sight of her face in the glass, and was surprised to see herself looking so calm and white.

Of course she was calm. The feeling part of her had been removed. What remained was a slack, discarded eiderdown. Must have been the pills Doctor gave.

Well-meaning people would call to her over the front fence, 'Don't you feel lonely, Mrs Natwick?' They spoke with a restrained horror, as though she had been suffering from an incurable disease.

But she called back proud and slow, 'I'm under sedation.'

'Arrr!' They nodded thoughtfully. 'What's 'e given yer?'

She shook her head. 'Pills,' she called back. 'They say they're the ones the actress died of.'

The people walked on, impressed.

As the evenings grew longer and heavier she sat later on the front veranda watching the traffic of the Parramatta Road, its flow becoming syrupy and almost benign: big bulbous sedate buses, chrysalis cars still without a life of their own, clinging in line to the back of their host-articulator, trucks loaded for distances, empty loose-sounding jolly lorries. Sometimes women, looking out from the cabins of trucks from beside their men, shared her lack of curiosity. The light was so fluid nobody lasted long enough. You would never have thought boys could kick a person to death, seeing their long soft hair floating behind their sports models.

Every evening she watched the cream Holden pass. And looked at her watch. It was like Royal was sitting beside her. Once she heard herself. 'Thought he was gunner look round tonight, in our direction.' How could a person feel lonely?

She was, though. She came face to face with it walking through the wreckage of her garden in the long slow steamy late summer. The Holden didn't pass of course of a Saturday or Sunday. Something, something had tricked her, not the pills, before the pills. She couldn't blame anybody, probably only herself. Everything depended on yourself. Take the garden. It was a shambles. She would have liked to protest, but began to cough from running her head against some powdery mildew. She could only blunder at first, like a cow, or runty starved heifer, on breaking into a garden. She had lost her old wiriness. She shambled, snapping dead stems, uprooting. Along the bleached palings there was a fretwork of hollyhock, the brown fur of rotting sunflower. She rushed at a praying mantis, a big pale one, and deliberately broke its back, and was sorry afterwards for what was done so easy and thoughtless.

As she stood panting in her black, finally yawning, she saw all she had to repair. The thought of the seasons piling up ahead made her feel tired but necessary, and she went in to bathe her face. Royal's denture in a tumbler on top of the medicine cabinet, she ought to move, or give to the Sallies. In the meantime she changed the water. She never forgot it. The teeth looked amazingly alive.

All that autumn, winter, she was continually amazed, at the dust she had let gather in the house, at old photographs, books, clothes. There was a feather she couldn't remember wearing, a scarlet feather, she *can't* have worn, and gloves with little fussy ruffles at the wrists, silver piping, like a snail had laid its trail round the edges. There was, she knew, funny things she had bought at times, and never worn, but she couldn't remember the gloves or the feather. And books. She had collected a few, though never a reader herself. Old people liked to give old books, and you took them so as not to hurt anybody's feelings. *Hubert's Crusade*, for instance. Lovely golden curls. Could have been Royal's father's book. Everybody was a child once. And almost everybody had one. At least if she had had a child she would have known it wasn't a white turnip, more of a praying mantis, which snaps too easy.

In the same box she had put away a coloured picture, *Cities of the Plain*, she couldn't remember seeing it before. The people escaping from the burning cities had committed some sin or other nobody ever thought, let alone talked, about. As they hurried between rocks, through what must have been the 'desert places', their faces looked long and wooden. All they had recently experienced could have shocked the expression out of them. She was fascinated by what made her shiver. And the couples with their arms still around one another. Well, if you were damned, better hang on to your sin. She didn't blame them.

She put the box away. Its inlay as well as its contents made it something secret and precious.

The autumn was still and golden, the winter vicious only in fits. It was what you could call a good winter. The cold floods of air and more concentrated streams of dark-green light poured along the shady side of the house where her cinerarias had massed. She had never seen such cinerarias: some of the spired ones reached almost as high as her chin, the solid heads of others waited in the tunnel of dark light to club you with their colours, of purple and drenching blue, and what they called 'wine'. She couldn't believe wine would have made her drunker.

Just as she would sit every evening watching the traffic, evening was the time she liked best to visit the cinerarias, when the icy cold seemed to make the flowers burn their deepest, purest. So it was again evening when her two objects converged: for some blissfully confident reason she hadn't bothered to ask herself whether she had seen the car pass, till here was this figure coming towards her along the tunnel. She knew at once who it was, although she had never seen him on his feet; she had never seen him full-face, but knew from the funny shape of his head as Royal had been the first to notice. He was not at all an impressive man, not much taller than herself, but broad. His footsteps on the brickwork sounded purposeful.

'Will you let me use your phone, please, madam?' he asked in a prepared voice. 'I'm having trouble with the Holden.'

This was the situation she had always been expecting: somebody asking to use the phone as a way to afterwards murdering you. Now that it might be about to happen she couldn't care.

She said yes. She thought her voice sounded muzzy. Perhaps he would think she was drunk.

She went on looking at him, at his eyes. His nose, like the shape of his head, wasn't up to much, but his eyes, his eyes, she dared to think, were filled with kindness.

'Cold, eh? but clean cold!' He laughed friendly, shuffling on the brick paving because she was keeping him waiting.

Only then she noticed his mouth. He had a hare-lip, there was no mistaking, although it was well sewn. She felt so calm in the circumstances. She would have even liked to touch it.

But said, 'Why, yes—the telephone,' she said, 'it's this way,' she said, 'it's just off the kitchen—because that's where you spend most of your life. Or in bed,' she ended.

She wished she hadn't added that. For the first time since they had been together she felt upset, thinking he might suspect her of wrong intentions.

But he laughed and said, 'That's correct! You got something there!' It sounded manly rather than educated.

She realized he was still waiting, and took him to the telephone.

While he was phoning she didn't listen. She never listened when other people were talking on the phone. The sight of her own kitchen surprised her. While his familiar voice went on. It was the voice she had held conversations with.

But he was ugly, real ugly, *deformed.* If it wasn't for the voice, the eyes. She couldn't remember the eyes, but seemed to know about them.

Then she heard him laying the coins beside the phone, extra loud, to show.

He came back into the kitchen smiling and looking. She could smell him now, and he had the smell of a clean man.

She became embarrassed at herself, and took him quickly out.

'Fair bit of garden you got.' He stood with his calves curved through his trousers. A cockly little chap, but nice.

'Oh,' she said, 'this', she said, angrily almost, 'is nothing. You oughter see it. There's sunflower and hollyhock all along the palings. I'm famous for me hollyhocks!' She had never boasted in her life. 'But not now—it isn't the season. And I let it go. Mr Natwick passed on. You should'uv seen the cassia this autumn. Now it's only sticks, of course. And hibiscus. There's cream, gold, cerise, scarlet—double and single.'

She was dressing in them for him, revolving on high heels and changing frilly skirts.

He said, 'Gardening's not in my line,' turning his head to hide something, perhaps he was ashamed of his hare-lip.

'No,' she agreed. 'Not everybody's a gardener.'

'But like a garden.'

'My husband didn't even like it. He didn't have to tell me,' she added.

As they moved across the wintry grass, past the empty clothes-line, the man looked at his watch, and said, 'I was reckoning on visiting somebody in hospital tonight. Looks like I shan't make it if the N.R.M.A. takes as long as usual.'

'Do they?' she said, clearing her throat. 'It isn't somebody close, I hope? The sick person?'

Yes he said they was close.

'Nothing serious?' she almost bellowed.

He said it was serious.

Oh she nearly burst out laughing at the bandaged figure they were sitting beside particularly at the bandaged face. She would have laughed at a brain tumour.

'I'm sorry,' she said. 'I understand. Mr Natwick was for many years an invalid.'

Those teeth in the tumbler on top of the medicine cabinet. Looking at her. Teeth can look, worse than eyes. But she couldn't help it, she meant everything she said, and thought.

At this moment they were pressing inside the dark-green tunnel, her sleeve rubbing his, as the crimson-to-purple light was dying.

'These are the cinerarias,' she said.

'The what?' He didn't know, any more than Royal.

As she was about to explain she got switched to another language. Her throat became a long palpitating funnel through which the words she expected to use were poured out in a stream of almost formless agonized sound.

'What is it?' he asked, touching her.

If it had happened to herself she would have felt frightened, it occurred to her, but he didn't seem to be.

'What is it?' he kept repeating in his familiar voice, touching, even holding her.

And for answer, in the new language, she was holding him. They were holding each other, his hard body against her eiderdowny one. As the silence closed round them again, inside the tunnel of light, his face, to which she was very close, seemed to be unlocking, the wound of his mouth, which should have been more horrible, struggling to open. She could see he had recognized her.

She kissed above his mouth. She kissed as though she might never succeed in healing all the wounds they had ever suffered.

How long they stood together she wasn't interested in knowing. Outside them the river of traffic continued to flow between its brick and concrete banks. Even if it overflowed it couldn't have drowned them.

When the man said in his gentlest voice, 'Better go out in front. The N.R.M.A. might have come.'

'Yes,' she agreed. 'The N.R.M.A.'

So they shuffled, still holding each other, along the narrow path. She imagined how long and wooden their faces must look. She wouldn't look at him now, though, just as she wouldn't look back at the still faintly smouldering joys they had experienced together in the past.

When they came out, apart, and into the night, there was the N.R.M.A., his pointed ruby of a light burning on top of the cabin.

'When will you come?' she asked.

'Tomorrow.'

'Tomorrow. You'll stay to tea.'

He couldn't stay.

'I'll make you a *pot* of tea?'

But he didn't drink it.

'Coffee, then?'

He said, 'I like a nice cup of coffee.'

Going down the path he didn't look back, or opening the gate. She would not let herself think of reasons or possibilities, she would not think, but stood planted in the path, swayed slightly by the motion of the night.

Mrs Dolan said, 'You bring the saucepan to the boil. You got that?'

'Yeeehs.' Mrs Natwick had never been a dab at coffee.

'Then you throw in some cold water. That's what sends the gravel to the bottom.' This morning Mrs Dolan had to laugh at her own jokes.

'That's the part that frightens me,' Mrs Natwick admitted.

'Well, you just do it, and see,' said Mrs Dolan; she was too busy.

After she had bought the coffee Mrs Natwick stayed in the city to muck around. If she had stayed at home her nerves might have wound themselves tighter, waiting for evening to come. Though mucking around only irritated in the end. She had never been an idle woman. So she stopped at the cosmetics as though she didn't have to decide, this was her purpose, and said to the young lady lounging behind one of the counters, 'I'm thinking of investing in a lipstick, dear. Can you please advise me?'

As a concession to the girl she tried to make it a laughing matter, but the young person was bored, she didn't bat a silver eyelid. 'Elderly ladies,' she said, 'go for the brighter stuff.'

Mrs Natwick ('my little Ella') had never felt so meek. Mum must be turning in her grave.

'This is a favourite.' With a flick of her long fingers the girl exposed the weapon. It looked too slippery-pointed, crimson-purple, out of its golden sheath.

Mrs Natwick's knees were shaking. 'Isn't it a bit noticeable?' she asked, again trying to make it a joke.

But the white-haired girl gave a serious laugh. 'What's wrong with noticeable?'

As Mrs Natwick tried it out on the back of her hand the way she had seen others do, the girl was jogging from foot to foot behind the counter. She was humming between her teeth, behind her white-smeared lips, probably thinking about a lover. Mrs Natwick blushed. What if she couldn't learn to get the tip of her lipstick back inside its sheath?

She might have gone quickly away without another word if the young lady hadn't been so professional and bored. Still humming, she brought out a little pack of rouge.

'Never saw myself with mauve cheeks!' It was at least dry, and easy to handle.

'It's what they wear.'

Mrs Natwick didn't dare refuse. She watched the long fingers with their silver nails doing up the parcel. The fingers looked as though they might resent touching anything but cosmetics; a lover was probably beneath contempt.

The girl gave her the change, and she went away without counting it.

She wasn't quiet, though, not a bit, booming and clanging in front of the toilet mirror. She tried to make a thin line, but her mouth exploded into a purple flower. She dabbed the dry-feeling pad on either cheek, and thick, mauve-scented shadows fell. She could hear and feel her heart behaving like a squeezed, rubber ball as she stood looking. Then she got at the lipstick again, still unsheathed. Her mouth was becoming enormous, so thick with grease she could hardly close her own lips underneath. A visible dew was gathering round the purple shadows on her cheeks.

She began to retch like, but dry, and rub, over the basin, scrubbing with the nailbrush. More than likely some would stay behind in the pores and be seen. Though you didn't have to see, to see.

There were Royal's teeth in the tumbler on top of the medicine cabinet. Ought to hide the teeth. What if somebody wanted to use the toilet? She must move the teeth. But didn't. In the present circumstances she couldn't have raised her arms that high.

Around five she made the coffee, throwing in the cold water at the end with a gesture copied from Mrs Dolan. If the gravel hadn't sunk to the bottom he wouldn't notice the first time, provided the coffee was hot. She could warm up the made coffee in a jiffy.

As she sat on the veranda waiting, the cane chair shifted and squealed under her. If it hadn't been for her weight it might have run away across the tiles, like one of those old planchette boards, writing the answers to questions.

There was an accident this evening down at the intersection. A head-on collision. Bodies were carried out of the crumpled cars, and she remembered a past occasion when she had run with blankets, and Hazel's Onkaparinka, and a pillow from their own bed. She had been so grateful to the victim. She could not give him enough, or receive enough of the warm blood. She had come back, she remembered, sprinkled.

This evening she had to save herself up. Kept on looking at her watch. The old cane chair squealing, ready to write the answers if she let it. Was he hurt? Was he killed, then? Was he—what?

Mrs Dolan it was, sticking her head over the palings. 'Don't like the accidents, Mrs Natwick. It's the blood. The blood turns me up.'

Mrs Natwick averted her face. Though unmoved by present blood. If only the squealing chair would stop trying to buck her off.

'Did your friend enjoy the coffee?' Mrs Dolan shouted; nothing nasty in her: Mrs Dolan was sincere.

'Hasn't been yet,' Mrs Natwick mumbled from glancing at her watch. 'Got held up.'

'It's the traffic. The traffic at this time of evenun.'

'Always on the dot before.'

'Working back. Or made a mistake over the day.'

Could you make a mistake? Mrs Natwick contemplated. Tomorrow had always meant tomorrow.

'Or he could'uv,' Mrs Dolan shouted, but didn't say it. 'I better go inside,' she said instead. 'They'll be wonderun where I am.'

Down at the intersection the bodies were lying wrapped in someone else's blankets, looking like the grey parcels of mice cats sometimes vomit up.

It was long past five-twenty, not all that long really, but drawing in. The sky was heaped with cold fire. Her city was burning.

She got up finally, and the chair escaped with a last squeal, writing its answer on the tiles.

No, it wasn't lust, not if the Royal God Almighty with bared teeth should strike her down. Or yes, though, it was. She was lusting after the expression of eyes she could hardly remember for seeing so briefly.

In the effort to see, she drove her memory wildly, while her body stumbled around and around the paths of the burning city there was now no point in escaping. You would shrivel up in time along with the polyanthers and out-of-season hibiscus. All the randy mouths would be stopped sooner or later with black.

The cinerarias seemed to have grown so luxuriant she had to force her way past them, down the narrow brick path. When she heard the latch click, and saw him coming towards her.

'Why,' she screamed laughing though it sounded angry, she *was*, 'I'd given you up, you know! It's long after five-twenty!'

As she pushed fiercely towards him, past the cinerarias, snapping one or two of those which were most heavily loaded, she realized he couldn't have known that she set her watch, her life, by his constant behaviour. He wouldn't have dawdled so.

'What is it?' she called at last, in exasperation at the distance which continued separating them.

He was far too slow, treading the slippery moss of her too shaded path. While she floundered on. She couldn't reach the expression of his eyes.

He said, and she could hardly recognize the faded voice, 'There's something—I been feeling off colour most of the day.' His mis-shapen head was certainly lolling as he advanced.

'Tell me!' She heard her voice commanding, like that of a man, or a mother, when she had practised to be a lover; she could still smell the smell of rouge. 'Won't you tell me—*dearest?*' It was thin and unconvincing now. (As a girl she had once got a letter from her cousin Kath Salter, who she hardly knew: *Dearest Ella* . . .)

Oh dear. She had reached him. And was given all strength—that of the lover she had aimed at being.

Straddling the path, unequally matched—he couldn't compete against her strength—she spoke with an acquired, a deafening softness, as the inclining cinerarias snapped.

'You will tell me what is wrong—dear, dear.' She breathed with trumpets.

He hung his head. 'It's all right. It's the pain—here—in my arm—no, the shoulder.'

'Ohhhhh!' She ground her face into his shoulder forgetting it wasn't *her* pain.

Then she remembered, and looked into his eyes and said, 'We'll save you. You'll see.'

It was she who needed saving. She knew she was trying to enter by his eyes. To drown in them rather than be left.

Because, in spite of her will to hold him, he was slipping from her, down amongst the cinerarias, which were snapping off one by one around them.

A cat shot out. At one time she had been so poor in spirit she had wished she was a cat.

'It's all right,' either voice was saying.

Lying amongst the smashed plants, he was smiling at her dreadfully, not his mouth, she no longer bothered about that lip, but with his eyes.

'More air!' she cried. 'What you need is air!' hacking at one or two cinerarias which remained erect.

Their sap was stifling, their bristling columns callous.

'Oh! Oh!' she panted. 'Oh God! Dear love!' comforting with hands and hair and words.

Words.

While all he could say was, 'It's all right.'

Or not that at last. He folded his lips into a white seam. His eyes were swimming out of reach.

'Eh? Dear—dearest—darl—darling—darling love—*love*—LOVE?' All the new words still stiff in her mouth, that she had heard so far only from the mouths of actors.

The words were too strong she could see. She was losing him. The traffic was hanging together only by charred silences.

She flung herself and covered his body, trying to force kisses—no, breath, into his mouth, she had heard about it.

She had seen turkeys, feathers sawing against each other's feathers, rising afterwards like new noisy silk.

She knelt up, and the wing-tips of her hair still dabbled limply in his cheeks. 'Eh? Ohh luff!' She could hardly breathe it.

She hadn't had time to ask his name, before she must have killed him by loving too deep, and too adulterously.

Tobias Wolff

. . . .

HUNTERS IN THE SNOW

Tub had been waiting for an hour in the falling snow. He paced the sidewalk to keep warm and stuck his head out over the curb whenever he saw lights approaching. One driver stopped for him but before Tub could wave the man on he saw the rifle on Tub's back and hit the gas. The tires spun on the ice.

The fall of snow thickened. Tub stood below the overhang of a building. Across the road the clouds whitened just above the rooftops, and the street lights went out. He shifted the rifle strap to his other shoulder. The whiteness seeped up the sky.

A truck slid around the corner, horn blaring, rear end sashaying. Tub moved to the sidewalk and held up his hand. The truck jumped the curb and kept coming, half on the street and half on the sidewalk. It wasn't slowing down at all. Tub stood for a moment, still holding up his hand, then jumped back. His rifle slipped off his shoulder and clattered on the ice, a sandwich fell out of his pocket. He ran for the steps of the building. Another sandwich and a package of cookies tumbled onto the new snow. He made the steps and looked back.

The truck had stopped several feet beyond where Tub had been standing. He picked up his sandwiches and his cookies and slung the rifle and went up to the driver's window. The driver was bent against the steering wheel, slapping his knees and drumming his feet on the floorboards. He looked like a cartoon of a person laughing, except that his eyes watched the man on the seat beside him. "You ought to see yourself," the driver said. "He looks just like a beach ball with a hat on, doesn't he? Doesn't he, Frank?"

The man beside him smiled and looked off.

"You almost ran me down," Tub said. "You could've killed me."

"Come on, Tub," said the man beside the driver. "Be mellow. Kenny was just messing around." He opened the door and slid over to the middle of the seat.

Tub took the bolt out of his rifle and climbed in beside him. "I waited an hour," he said. "If you meant ten o'clock why didn't you say ten o'clock?"

"Tub, you haven't done anything but complain since we got here," said the man in the middle. "If you want to piss and moan all day you might as well go home and bitch at your kids. Take your pick." When Tub didn't say anything he turned to the driver. "Okay, Kenny, let's hit the road."

Some juvenile delinquents had heaved a brick through the windshield on the driver's side, so the cold and snow tunneled right into the cab. The heater didn't work. They covered themselves with a couple of blankets Kenny had brought along and pulled down the muffs on their caps. Tub tried to keep his hands warm by rubbing them under the blanket but Frank made him stop.

They left Spokane and drove deep into the country, running along black lines of fences. The snow let up, but still there was no edge to the land where it met the sky. Nothing moved in the chalky fields. The cold bleached their faces and made the stubble stand out on their cheeks and along their upper lips. They stopped twice for coffee before they got to the woods where Kenny wanted to hunt.

Tub was for trying someplace different; two years in a row they'd been up and down this land and hadn't seen a thing. Frank didn't care one way or the other, he just wanted to get out of the goddamned truck. "Feel that," Frank said, slamming the door. He spread his feet and closed his eyes and leaned his head way back and breathed deeply. "Tune in on that energy."

"Another thing," Kenny said. "This is open land. Most of the land around here is posted."

"I'm cold," Tub said.

Frank breathed out. "Stop bitching, Tub. Get centered."

"I wasn't bitching."

"Centered," Kenny said. "Next thing you'll be wearing a nightgown, Frank. Selling flowers out at the airport."

"Kenny," Frank said, "you talk too much."

"Okay," Kenny said. "I won't say a word. Like I won't say anything about a certain babysitter."

"What babysitter?" Tub asked.

"That's between us," Frank said, looking at Kenny. "That's confidential. You keep your mouth shut."

Kenny laughed.

"You're asking for it," Frank said.

"Asking for what?"

"You'll see."

"Hey," Tub said, "are we hunting or what?"

They started off across the field. Tub had trouble getting through the fences. Frank and Kenny could have helped him; they could have lifted up on the top wire and stepped on the bottom wire, but they didn't. They stood and watched him. There were a lot of fences and Tub was puffing when they reached the woods.

They hunted for over two hours and saw no deer, no tracks, no sign. Finally they stopped by the creek to eat. Kenny had several slices of pizza and a couple of candy bars; Frank had a sandwich, an apple, two carrots, and a square of chocolate; Tub ate one hard-boiled egg and a stick of celery.

"You ask me how I want to die today," Kenny said, "I'll tell you burn me at the stake." He turned to Tub. "You still on that diet?" He winked at Frank.

"What do you think? You think I like hard-boiled eggs?"

"All I can say is, it's the first diet I ever heard of where you gained weight from it."

"Who said I gained weight?"

"Oh, pardon me. I take it back. You're just wasting away before my very eyes. Isn't he, Frank?"

Frank had his fingers fanned out, tips against the bark of the stump where he'd laid his food. His knuckles were hairy. He wore a heavy wedding band and on his right pinky another gold ring with a flat face and an "F" in what looked like diamonds. He turned the ring this way and that. "Tub," he said, "you haven't seen your own balls in ten years."

Kenny doubled over laughing. He took off his hat and slapped his leg with it.

"What am I supposed to do?" Tub said. "It's my glands."

They left the woods and hunted along the creek. Frank and Kenny worked one bank and Tub worked the other, moving upstream. The snow was light but the drifts were deep and hard to move through. Wherever Tub looked the surface was smooth, undisturbed, and after a time he lost interest. He stopped looking for tracks and just tried to keep up with Frank and Kenny on the other side. A moment came when he realized he hadn't seen them in a long time. The breeze was moving from him to them; when it stilled he could sometimes hear Kenny laughing but that was all. He quickened his pace, breasting hard into the drifts, fighting away the snow with his knees and elbows. He heard his heart and felt the flush on his face but he never once stopped.

Tub caught up with Frank and Kenny at a bend of the creek. They were standing on a log that stretched from their bank to his. Ice had backed up behind the log. Frozen reeds stuck out, barely nodding when the air moved.

"See anything?" Frank asked.

Tub shook his head.

There wasn't much daylight left and they decided to head back toward the road. Frank and Kenny crossed the log and they started downstream, using the trail Tub had broken. Before they had gone very far Kenny stopped. "Look at that," he said, and pointed to some tracks going from the creek back into the woods. Tub's footprints crossed right over them. There on the bank, plain as day, were several mounds of deer sign. "What do you think that is, Tub?" Kenny kicked at it. "Walnuts on vanilla icing?"

"I guess I didn't notice."

Kenny looked at Frank.

"I was lost."

"You were lost. Big deal."

They followed the tracks into the woods. The deer had gone over a fence half buried in drifting snow. A no hunting sign was nailed to the top of one of the posts. Frank laughed and said the son of a bitch could read. Kenny wanted to go after him but Frank said no way, the people out here didn't mess around. He thought maybe the farmer who owned the land would let them use it if they asked. Kenny wasn't so sure. Anyway, he figured that by the time they walked to the truck and drove up the road and doubled back it would be almost dark.

"Relax," Frank said. "You can't hurry nature. If we're meant to get that deer, we'll get it. If we're not, we won't."

They started back toward the truck. This part of the woods was mainly pine. The snow was shaded and had a glaze on it. It held up Kenny and Frank but Tub kept falling through. As he kicked forward, the edge of the crust bruised his shins. Kenny and Frank pulled ahead of him, to where he couldn't even hear their voices any more. He sat down on a stump and wiped his face. He ate both the sandwiches and half the cookies, taking his own sweet time. It was dead quiet.

When Tub crossed the last fence into the road the truck started moving. Tub had to run for it and just managed to grab hold of the tailgate and hoist himself into the bed. He lay there, panting. Kenny looked out the rear window and grinned. Tub crawled into the lee of the cab to get out of the freezing wind. He pulled his earflaps low and pushed his chin into the collar of his coat. Someone rapped on the window but Tub would not turn around.

He and Frank waited outside while Kenny went into the farmhouse to ask permission. The house was old and paint was curling off the sides. The smoke streamed westward off the top of the chimney, fanning away into a thin gray plume. Above the ridge of the hills another ridge of blue clouds was rising.

"You've got a short memory," Tub said.

"What?" Frank said. He had been staring off.

"I used to stick up for you."

"Okay, so you used to stick up for me. What's eating you?"

"You shouldn't have just left me back there like that."

"You're a grown-up, Tub. You can take care of yourself. Anyway, if you think you're the only person with problems I can tell you that you're not."

"Is something bothering you, Frank?"

Frank kicked at a branch poking out of the snow. "Never mind," he said.

"What did Kenny mean about the babysitter?"

"Kenny talks too much," Frank said. "You just mind your own business."

Kenny came out of the farmhouse and gave the thumbs-up and they began walking back toward the woods. As they passed the barn a large black hound with a grizzled snout ran out and barked at them. Every time he barked he slid backwards a bit, like a cannon recoiling. Kenny got down on all fours and snarled and barked back at him, and the dog slunk away into the barn, looking over his shoulder and peeing a little as he went.

"That's an old-timer," Frank said. "A real graybeard. Fifteen years if he's a day."

"Too old," Kenny said.

Past the barn they cut off through the fields. The land was unfenced and the crust was freezing up thick and they made good time. They kept to the edge of the field until they picked up the tracks again and followed them into the woods, farther and farther back toward the hills. The trees started to blur with the shadows and the wind rose and needled their faces with the crystals it swept off the glaze. Finally they lost the tracks.

Kenny swore and threw down his hat. "This is the worst day of hunting I ever

had, bar none." He picked up his hat and brushed off the snow. "This will be
the first season since I was fifteen I haven't got my deer."

"It isn't the deer," Frank said. "It's the hunting. There are all these forces out
here and you just have to go with them."

"You go with them," Kenny said. "I came out here to get me a deer, not listen to a bunch of hippie bullshit. And if it hadn't been for dimples here I would
have, too."

"That's enough," Frank said.

"And you—you're so busy thinking about that little jailbait of yours you
wouldn't know a deer if you saw one."

"Drop dead," Frank said, and turned away.

Kenny and Tub followed him back across the fields. When they were coming
up to the barn Kenny stopped and pointed. "I hate that post," he said. He raised
his rifle and fired. It sounded like a dry branch cracking. The post splintered
along its right side, up towards the top. "There," Kenny said. "It's dead."

"Knock it off," Frank said, walking ahead.

Kenny looked at Tub. He smiled. "I hate that tree," he said, and fired again.
Tub hurried to catch up with Frank. He started to speak but just then the dog
ran out of the barn and barked at them. "Easy, boy," Frank said.

"I hate that dog." Kenny was behind them.

"That's enough," Frank said. "You put that gun down."

Kenny fired. The bullet went in between the dog's eyes. He sank right down
into the snow, his legs splayed out on each side, his yellow eyes open and staring.
Except for the blood he looked like a small bearskin rug. The blood ran down
the dog's muzzle into the snow.

They all looked at the dog lying there.

"What did he ever do to you?" Tub asked. "He was just barking."

Kenny turned to Tub. "I hate you."

Tub shot from the waist. Kenny jerked backward against the fence and buckled to his knees. He folded his hands across his stomach. "Look," he said. His
hands were covered with blood. In the dusk his blood was more blue than red. It
seemed to belong to the shadows. It didn't seem out of place. Kenny eased himself onto his back. He sighed several times, deeply. "You shot me," he said.

"I had to," Tub said. He knelt beside Kenny. "Oh God," he said. "Frank.
Frank."

Frank hadn't moved since Kenny killed the dog.

"Frank!" Tub shouted.

"I was just kidding around," Kenny said. "It was a joke. Oh!" he said, and
arched his back suddenly. "Oh!" he said again, and dug his heels into the snow
and pushed himself along on his head for several feet. Then he stopped and lay
there, rocking back and forth on his heels and head like a wrestler doing warm-
up exercises.

Frank roused himself. "Kenny," he said. He bent down and put his gloved
hand on Kenny's brow. "You shot him," he said to Tub.

"He made me," Tub said.

"No no no," Kenny said.

Tub was weeping from the eyes and nostrils. His whole face was wet. Frank closed his eyes, then looked down at Kenny again. "Where does it hurt?"

"Everywhere," Kenny said, "just everywhere."

"Oh God," Tub said.

"I mean where did it go in?" Frank said.

"Here." Kenny pointed at the wound in his stomach. It was welling slowly with blood.

"You're lucky," Frank said. "It's on the left side. It missed your appendix. If it had hit your appendix you'd really be in the soup." He turned and threw up onto the snow, holding his sides as if to keep warm.

"Are you all right?" Tub said.

"There's some aspirin in the truck," Kenny said.

"I'm all right," Frank said.

"We'd better call an ambulance," Tub said.

"Jesus," Frank said. "What are we going to say?"

"Exactly what happened," Tub said. "He was going to shoot me but I shot him first."

"No sir!" Kenny said. "I wasn't either!"

Frank patted Kenny on the arm. "Easy does it, partner." He stood. "Let's go."

Tub picked up Kenny's rifle as they walked down toward the farmhouse. "No sense leaving this around," he said. "Kenny might get ideas."

"I can tell you one thing," Frank said. "You've really done it this time. This definitely takes the cake."

They had to knock on the door twice before it was opened by a thin man with lank hair. The room behind him was filled with smoke. He squinted at them. "You get anything?" he asked.

"No," Frank said.

"I knew you wouldn't. That's what I told the other fellow."

"We've had an accident."

The man looked past Frank and Tub into the gloom. "Shoot your friend, did you?"

Frank nodded.

"I did," Tub said.

"I suppose you want to use the phone."

"If it's okay."

The man in the door looked behind him, then stepped back. Frank and Tub followed him into the house. There was a woman sitting by the stove in the middle of the room. The stove was smoking badly. She looked up and then down again at the child asleep in her lap. Her face was white and damp; strands of hair were pasted across her forehead. Tub warmed his hands over the stove while Frank went into the kitchen to call. The man who had let them in stood at the window, his hands in his pockets.

"My friend shot your dog," Tub said.

The man nodded without turning around. "I should have done it myself. I just couldn't."

"He loved that dog so much," the woman said. The child squirmed and she rocked it.

"You asked him to?" Tub said. "You asked him to shoot your dog?"

"He was old and sick. Couldn't chew his food any more. I would have done it myself but I don't have a gun."

"You couldn't have anyway," the woman said. "Never in a million years."

The man shrugged.

Frank came out of the kitchen. "We'll have to take him ourselves. The nearest hospital is fifty miles from here and all their ambulances are out anyway."

The woman knew a shortcut but the directions were complicated and Tub had to write them down. The man told them where they could find some boards to carry Kenny on. He didn't have a flashlight but he said he would leave the porch light on.

It was dark outside. The clouds were low and heavy-looking and the wind blew in shrill gusts. There was a screen loose on the house and it banged slowly and then quickly as the wind rose again. They could hear it all the way to the barn. Frank went for the boards while Tub looked for Kenny, who was not where they had left him. Tub found him farther up the drive, lying on his stomach. "You okay?" Tub said.

"It hurts."

"Frank says it missed your appendix."

"I already had my appendix out."

"All right," Frank said, coming up to them. "We'll have you in a nice warm bed before you can say Jack Robinson." He put the two boards on Kenny's right side.

"Just as long as I don't have one of those male nurses," Kenny said.

"Ha ha," Frank said. "That's the spirit. Get ready, set, *over you go*," and he rolled Kenny onto the boards. Kenny screamed and kicked his legs in the air. When he quieted down Frank and Tub lifted the boards and carried him down the drive. Tub had the back end, and with the snow blowing in his face he had trouble with his footing. Also he was tired and the man inside had forgotten to turn the porch light on. Just past the house Tub slipped and threw out his hands to catch himself. The boards fell and Kenny tumbled out and rolled to the bottom of the drive, yelling all the way. He came to rest against the right front wheel of the truck.

"You fat moron," Frank said. "You aren't good for diddly."

Tub grabbed Frank by the collar and backed him hard up against the fence. Frank tried to pull his hands away but Tub shook him and snapped his head back and forth and finally Frank gave up.

"What do you know about fat," Tub said. "What do you know about glands." As he spoke he kept shaking Frank. "What do you know about me."

"All right," Frank said.

"No more," Tub said.

"All right."

"No more talking to me like that. No more watching. No more laughing."

"Okay, Tub. I promise."

Tub let go of Frank and leaned his forehead against the fence. His arms hung straight at his sides.

"I'm sorry, Tub." Frank touched him on the shoulder. "I'll be down at the truck."

Tub stood by the fence for a while and then got the rifles off the porch. Frank had rolled Kenny back onto the boards and they lifted him into the bed of the truck. Frank spread the seat blankets over him. "Warm enough?" he asked.

Kenny nodded.

"Okay. Now how does reverse work on this thing?"

"All the way to the left and up." Kenny sat up as Frank started forward to the cab. "Frank!"

"What?"

"If it sticks don't force it."

The truck started right away. "One thing," Frank said, "you've got to hand it to the Japanese. A very ancient, very spiritual culture and they can still make a hell of a truck." He glanced over at Tub. "Look, I'm sorry. I didn't know you felt that way, honest to God I didn't. You should have said something."

"I did."

"When? Name one time."

"A couple of hours ago."

"I guess I wasn't paying attention."

"That's true, Frank," Tub said. "You don't pay attention very much."

"Tub," Frank said, "what happened back there, I should have been more sympathetic. I realize that. You were going through a lot. I just want you to know it wasn't your fault. He was asking for it."

"You think so?"

"Absolutely. It was him or you. I would have done the same thing in your shoes, no question."

The wind was blowing into their faces. The snow was a moving white wall in front of their lights; it swirled into the cab through the hole in the windshield and settled on them. Tub clapped his hands and shifted around to stay warm, but it didn't work.

"I'm going to have to stop," Frank said. "I can't feel my fingers."

Up ahead they saw some lights off the road. It was a tavern. Outside in the parking lot there were several jeeps and trucks. A couple of them had deer strapped across their hoods. Frank parked and they went back to Kenny. "How you doing, partner," Frank said.

"I'm cold."

"Well, don't feel like the Lone Ranger. It's worse inside, take my word for it. You should get that windshield fixed."

"Look," Tub said, "he threw the blankets off." They were lying in a heap against the tailgate.

"Now look, Kenny," Frank said, "it's no use whining about being cold if you're not going to try and keep warm. You've got to do your share." He spread the blankets over Kenny and tucked them in at the corners.

"They blew off."

"Hold on to them then."

"Why are we stopping, Frank?"

"Because if me and Tub don't get warmed up we're going to freeze solid and then where will you be?" He punched Kenny lightly in the arm. "So just hold your horses."

The bar was full of men in colored jackets, mostly orange. The waitress brought coffee. "Just what the doctor ordered," Frank said, cradling the steaming cup in his hand. His skin was bone white. "Tub, I've been thinking. What you said about me not paying attention, that's true."

"It's okay."

"No. I really had that coming. I guess I've just been a little too interested in old number one. I've had a lot on my mind. Not that that's any excuse."

"Forget it, Frank. I sort of lost my temper back there. I guess we're all a little on edge."

Frank shook his head. "It isn't just that."

"You want to talk about it?"

"Just between us, Tub?"

"Sure, Frank. Just between us."

"Tub, I think I'm going to be leaving Nancy."

"Oh, Frank. Oh, Frank." Tub sat back and shook his head.

Frank reached out and laid his hand on Tub's arm. "Tub, have you ever been really in love?"

"Well—"

"I mean *really* in love." He squeezed Tub's wrist. "With your whole being."

"I don't know. When you put it like that, I don't know."

"You haven't then. Nothing against you, but you'd know it if you had." Frank let go of Tub's arm. "This isn't just some bit of fluff I'm talking about."

"Who is she, Frank?"

Frank paused. He looked into his empty cup. "Roxanne Brewer."

"Cliff Brewer's kid? The babysitter?"

"You can't just put people into categories like that, Tub. That's why the whole system is wrong. And that's why this country is going to hell in a rowboat."

"But she can't be more than—" Tub shook his head.

"Fifteen. She'll be sixteen in May." Frank smiled. "May fourth, three twenty-seven p.m. Hell, Tub, a hundred years ago she'd have been an old maid by that age. Juliet was only thirteen."

"Juliet? Juliet Miller? Jesus, Frank, she doesn't even have breasts. She doesn't even wear a top to her bathing suit. She's still collecting frogs."

"Not Juliet Miller. The real Juliet. Tub, don't you see how you're dividing people up into categories? He's an executive, she's a secretary, he's a truck driver, she's fifteen years old. Tub, this so-called babysitter, this so-called fifteen-year-old has more in her little finger than most of us have in our entire bodies. I can tell you this little lady is something special."

Tub nodded. "I know the kids like her."

"She's opened up whole worlds to me that I never knew were there."

"What does Nancy think about all of this?"

"She doesn't know."

"You haven't told her?"

"Not yet. It's not so easy. She's been damned good to me all these years. Then there's the kids to consider." The brightness in Frank's eyes trembled and he wiped quickly at them with the back of his hand. "I guess you think I'm a complete bastard."

"No, Frank. I don't think that."

"Well, you *ought* to."

"Frank, when you've got a friend it means you've always got someone on your side, no matter what. That's the way I feel about it, anyway."

"You mean that, Tub?"

"Sure I do."

Frank smiled. "You don't know how good it feels to hear you say that."

Kenny had tried to get out of the truck but he hadn't made it. He was jack-knifed over the tailgate, his head hanging above the bumper. They lifted him back into the bed and covered him again. He was sweating and his teeth chattered. "It hurts, Frank."

"It wouldn't hurt so much if you just stayed put. Now we're going to the hospital. Got that? Say it—I'm going to the hospital."

"I'm going to the hospital."

"Again."

"I'm going to the hospital."

"Now just keep saying that to yourself and before you know it we'll be there."

After they had gone a few miles Tub turned to Frank. "I just pulled a real boner," he said.

"What's that?"

"I left the directions on the table back there."

"That's okay. I remember them pretty well."

The snowfall lightened and the clouds began to roll back off the fields, but it was no warmer and after a time both Frank and Tub were bitten through and shaking. Frank almost didn't make it around a curve, and they decided to stop at the next roadhouse.

There was an automatic hand-dryer in the bathroom and they took turns standing in front of it, opening their jackets and shirts and letting the jet of hot air breathe across their faces and chests.

"You know," Tub said, "what you told me back there, I appreciate it. Trusting me."

Frank opened and closed his fingers in front of the nozzle. "The way I look at it, Tub, no man is an island. You've got to trust someone."

"Frank—"

Frank waited.

"When I said that about my glands, that wasn't true. The truth is I just shovel it in."

"Well, Tub—"

"Day and night, Frank. In the shower. On the freeway." He turned and let the air play over his back. "I've even got stuff in the paper towel machine at work."

"There's nothing wrong with your glands at all?" Frank had taken his boots and socks off. He held first his right, then his left foot up to the nozzle.

"No. There never was."

"Does Alice know?" The machine went off and Frank started lacing up his boots.

"Nobody knows. That's the worst of it, Frank. Not the being fat, I never got any big kick out of being thin, but the lying. Having to lead a double life like a spy or a hit man. This sounds strange but I feel sorry for those guys, I really do. I know what they go through. Always having to think about what you say and do. Always feeling like people are watching you, trying to catch you at something. Never able to just be yourself. Like when I make a big deal about only having an orange for breakfast and then scarf all the way to work. Oreos, Mars Bars, Twinkies. Sugar Babies. Snickers." Tub glanced at Frank and looked quickly away. "Pretty disgusting, isn't it?"

"Tub. Tub." Frank shook his head. "Come on." He took Tub's arm and led him into the restaurant half of the bar. "My friend is hungry," he told the waitress. "Bring four orders of pancakes, plenty of butter and syrup."

"Frank—"

"Sit down."

When the dishes came Frank carved out slabs of butter and just laid them on the pancakes. Then he emptied the bottle of syrup, moving it back and forth over the plates. He leaned forward on his elbows and rested his chin in one hand. "Go on, Tub."

Tub ate several mouthfuls, then started to wipe his lips. Frank took the napkin away from him. "No wiping," he said. Tub kept at it. The syrup covered his chin; it dripped to a point like a goatee. "Weigh in, Tub," Frank said, pushing another fork across the table. "Get down to business." Tub took the fork in his left hand and lowered his head and started really chowing down. "Clean your plate," Frank said when the pancakes were gone, and Tub lifted each of the four plates and licked it clean. He sat back, trying to catch his breath.

"Beautiful," Frank said. "Are you full?"

"I'm full," Tub said. "I've never been so full."

Kenny's blankets were bunched up against the tailgate again.

"They must have blown off," Tub said.

"They're not doing him any good," Frank said. "We might as well get some use out of them."

Kenny mumbled. Tub bent over him. "What? Speak up."

"I'm going to the hospital," Kenny said.

"Attaboy," Frank said.

The blankets helped. The wind still got their faces and Frank's hands but it was much better. The fresh snow on the road and the trees sparkled under the beam of the headlight. Squares of light from farmhouse windows fell onto the blue snow in the fields.

"Frank," Tub said after a time, "you know that farmer? He told Kenny to kill the dog."

"You're kidding!" Frank leaned forward, considering. "That Kenny. What a card." He laughed and so did Tub. Tub smiled out the back window. Kenny lay with his arms folded over his stomach, moving his lips at the stars. Right overhead was the Big Dipper, and behind, hanging between Kenny's toes in the direction of the hospital, was the North Star, Pole Star, Help to Sailors. As the truck twisted through the gentle hills the star went back and forth between Kenny's boots, staying always in his sight. "I'm going to the hospital," Kenny said. But he was wrong. They had taken a different turn a long way back.

Richard Wright

. . . .

BIG BLACK GOOD MAN

Through the open window Olaf Jenson could smell the sea and hear the occasional foghorn of a freighter; outside, rain pelted down through an August night, drumming softly upon the pavements of Copenhagen, inducing drowsiness, bringing dreamy memory, relaxing the tired muscles of his work-wracked body. He sat slumped in a swivel chair with his legs outstretched and his feet propped atop an edge of his desk. An inch of white ash tipped the end of his brown cigar and now and then he inserted the end of the stogie into his mouth and drew gently upon it, letting wisps of blue smoke eddy from the corners of his wide, thin lips. The watery gray irises behind the thick lenses of his eyeglasses gave him a look of abstraction, of absentmindedness, of an almost genial idiocy. He sighed, reached for his half-empty bottle of beer, and drained it into his glass and downed it with a long slow gulp, then licked his lips. Replacing the cigar, he slapped his right palm against his thigh and said half aloud:

"Well, I'll be sixty tomorrow. I'm not rich, but I'm not poor either . . . Really, I can't complain. Got good health. Traveled all over the world and had my share of the girls when I was young . . . And my Karen's a good wife. I own my home. Got no debts. And I love digging in my garden in the spring . . . Grew the biggest carrots of anybody last year. Ain't saved much money, but what the hell . . . Money ain't everything. Got a good job. Night portering ain't too bad." He shook his head and yawned. "Karen and I could of had some children, though. Would of been good company . . . 'Specially for Karen. And I could of taught 'em languages . . . English, French, German, Danish, Dutch, Swedish, Norwegian, and Spanish . . ." He took the cigar out of his mouth and eyed the white ash critically. "Hell of a lot of good language learning did me . . . Never got anything out of it. But those ten years in New York were fun . . . Maybe I could of got rich if I'd stayed in America . . . Maybe. But I'm satisfied. You can't have everything."

Behind him the office door opened and a young man, a medical student occupying room number nine, entered.

"Good evening," the student said.

"Good evening," Olaf said, turning.

786

The student went to the keyboard and took hold of the round, brown knob that anchored his key.

"Rain, rain, rain," the student said.

"That's Denmark for you," Olaf smiled at him.

"This dampness keeps me clogged up like a drainpipe," the student complained.

"That's Denmark for you," Olaf repeated with a smile.

"Good night," the student said.

"Good night, son," Olaf sighed, watching the door close.

Well, my tenants are my children, Olaf told himself. Almost all of his children were in their rooms now . . . Only seventy-two and forty-four were missing . . . Seventy-two might've gone to Sweden . . . And forty-four was maybe staying at his girl's place tonight, like he sometimes did . . . He studied the pear-shaped blobs of hard rubber, reddish brown like ripe fruit, that hung from the keyboard, then glanced at his watch. Only room thirty, eighty-one, and one hundred and one were empty . . . And it was almost midnight. In a few moments he could take a nap. Nobody hardly ever came looking for accommodations after midnight, unless a stray freighter came in, bringing thirsty, women-hungry sailors. Olaf chuckled softly. Why in hell was I ever a sailor? The whole time I was at sea I was thinking and dreaming about women. Then why didn't I stay on land where women could be had? Hunh? Sailors are crazy . . .

. . . But he liked sailors. They reminded him of his youth, and there was something so direct, simple, and childlike about them. They always said straight out what they wanted, and what they wanted was almost always women and whisky . . . "Well, there's no harm in that . . . Nothing could be more natural," Olaf sighed, looking thirstily at his empty beer bottle. No; he'd not drink any more tonight; he'd had enough; he'd go to sleep . . .

He was bending forward and loosening his shoelaces when he heard the office door crack open. He lifted his eyes, then sucked in his breath. He did not straighten; he just stared up and around at the huge black thing that filled the doorway. His reflexes refused to function; it was not fear; it was just simple astonishment. He was staring at the biggest, strangest, and blackest man he'd ever seen in all his life.

"Good evening," the black giant said in a voice that filled the small office. "Say, you got a room?"

Olaf sat up slowly, not to answer but to look at this brooding black vision; it towered darkly some six and a half feet into the air, almost touching the ceiling, and its skin was so black that it had a bluish tint. And the sheer bulk of the man! . . . His chest bulged like a barrel; his rocklike and humped shoulders hinted of mountain ridges; the stomach ballooned like a threatening stone; and the legs were like telephone poles . . . The big black cloud of a man now lumbered into the office, bending to get its buffalolike head under the door frame, then advanced slowly upon Olaf, like a stormy sky descending.

"You got a room?" the big black man asked again in a resounding voice.

Olaf now noticed that the ebony giant was well dressed, carried a wonderful new suitcase, and wore black shoes that gleamed despite the raindrops that peppered their toes.

"You're American?" Olaf asked him.

"Yeah, man; sure," the black giant answered.

"Sailor?"

"Yeah. American Continental Lines."

Olaf had not answered the black man's question. It was not that the hotel did not admit men of color; Olaf took in all comers—blacks, yellows, whites, and browns . . . To Olaf, men were men, and, in his day, he'd worked and eaten and slept and fought with all kinds of men. But this particular black man . . . Well, he didn't seem human. Too big, too black, too loud, too direct, and probably too violent to boot . . . Olaf's five feet seven inches scarcely reached the black giant's shoulder and his frail body weighed less, perhaps, than one of the man's gigantic legs . . . There was something about the man's intense blackness and ungamely bigness that frightened and insulted Olaf; he felt as though this man had come here expressly to remind him how puny, how tiny, and how weak and how white he was. Olaf knew, while registering his reactions, that he was being irrational and foolish; yet, for the first time in his life, he was emotionally determined to refuse a man a room solely on the basis of the man's size and color . . . Olaf's lips parted as he groped for the right words in which to couch his refusal, but the black giant bent forward and boomed:

"I asked you if you got a room. I got to put up somewhere tonight, man."

"Yes, we got a room," Olaf murmured.

And at once he was ashamed and confused. Sheer fear had made him yield. And he seethed against himself for his involuntary weakness. Well, he'd look over his book and pretend that he'd made a mistake; he'd tell this hunk of blackness that there was really no free room in the hotel, and that he was so sorry . . . Then, just as he took out the hotel register to make believe that he was poring over it, a thick roll of American bank notes, crisp and green, was thrust under his nose.

"Keep this for me, will you?" the black giant commanded. "Cause I'm gonna get drunk tonight and I don't wanna lose it."

Olaf stared at the roll; it was huge, in denominations of fifties and hundreds. Olaf's eyes widened.

"How much is there?" he asked.

"Two thousand six hundred," the giant said. "Just put it into an envelope and write 'Jim' on it and lock it in your safe, hunh?"

The black mass of man had spoken in a manner that indicated that it was taking it for granted that Olaf would obey. Olaf was licked. Resentment clogged the pores of his wrinkled white skin. His hands trembled as he picked up the money. No; he couldn't refuse this man . . . The impulse to deny him was strong, but each time he was about to act upon it something thwarted him, made him shy off. He clutched about desperately for an idea. Oh yes, he could say that if he planned to stay for only one night, then he could not have the room, for it was against the policy of the hotel to rent rooms for only one night . . .

"How long are you staying? Just tonight?" Olaf asked.

"Naw. I'll be here for five or six days, I reckon," the giant answered offhandedly.

"You take room number thirty," Olaf heard himself saying. "It's forty kronor a day."

"That's all right with me," the giant said.

With slow, stiff movements, Olaf put the money in the safe and then turned and stared helplessly up into the living, breathing blackness looming above him. Suddenly he became conscious of the outstretched palm of the black giant; he was silently demanding the key to the room. His eyes downcast, Olaf surrendered the key, marveling at the black man's tremendous hands . . . He could kill me with one blow, Olaf told himself in fear.

Feeling himself beaten, Olaf reached for the suitcase, but the black hand of the giant whisked it out of his grasp.

"That's too heavy for you, big boy; I'll take it," the giant said.

Olaf let him. He thinks I'm nothing . . . He led the way down the corridor, sensing the giant's lumbering presence behind him. Olaf opened the door of number thirty and stood politely to one side, allowing the black giant to enter. At once the room seemed like a doll's house, so dwarfed and filled and tiny it was with a great living blackness . . . Flinging his suitcase upon a chair, the giant turned. The two men looked directly at each other now. Olaf saw that the giant's eyes were tiny and red, buried, it seemed, in muscle and fat. Black cheeks spread, flat and broad, topping the wide and flaring nostrils. The mouth was the biggest that Olaf had ever seen on a human face; the lips were thick, pursed, parted, showing snow-white teeth. The black neck was like a bull's . . . The giant advanced upon Olaf and stood over him.

"I want a bottle of whisky and a woman," he said. "Can you fix me up?"

"Yes," Olaf whispered, wild with anger and insult.

But what was he angry about? He'd had requests like this every night from all sorts of men and he was used to fulfilling them; he was a night porter in a cheap, water-front Copenhagen hotel that catered to sailors and students. Yes, men needed women, but this man, Olaf felt, ought to have a special sort of woman. He felt a deep and strange reluctance to phone any of the women whom he habitually sent to men. Yet he had promised. Could he lie and say that none was available? No. That sounded too fishy. The black giant sat upon the bed, staring straight before him. Olaf moved about quickly, pulling down the window shades, taking the pink coverlet off the bed, nudging the giant with his elbow to make him move as he did so . . . That's the way to treat 'im . . . Show 'im I ain't scared of 'im . . . But he was still seeking for an excuse to refuse. And he could think of nothing. He felt hypnotized, mentally immobilized. He stood hesitantly at the door.

"You send the whisky and the woman quick, pal?" the black giant asked, rousing himself from a brooding stare.

"Yes," Olaf grunted, shutting the door.

Goddamn, Olaf sighed. He sat in his office at his desk before the phone. Why did *he* have to come here? . . . I'm not prejudiced . . . No, not at all . . . But . . . He couldn't think any more. God oughtn't make men as big and black as that . . . But what the hell was he worrying about? He'd sent women of all races to men of all colors . . . So why not a woman to the black giant? Oh, only if the man were small, brown, and intelligent-looking . . . Olaf felt trapped.

With a reflex movement of his hand, he picked up the phone and dialed Lena. She was big and strong and always cut him in for fifteen per cent instead of the usual ten per cent. Lena had four small children to feed and clothe. Lena was willing; she was, she said, coming over right now. She didn't give a good goddamn about how big and black the man was . . .

"Why you ask me that?" Lena wanted to know over the phone. "You never asked that before . . ."

"But this one is *big,*" Olaf found himself saying.

"He's just a man," Lena told him, her voice singing stridently, laughingly over the wire. "You just leave that to me. You don't have to do anything. *I'll* handle 'im."

Lena had a key to the hotel door downstairs, but tonight Olaf stayed awake. He wanted to see her. Why? He didn't know. He stretched out on the sofa in his office, but sleep was far from him. When Lena arrived, he told her again how big and black the man was.

"You told me that over the phone," Lena reminded him.

Olaf said nothing. Lena flounced off on her errand of mercy. Olaf shut the office door, then opened it and left it ajar. But why? He didn't know. He lay upon the sofa and stared at the ceiling. He glanced at his watch; it was almost two o'clock . . . She's staying in there a long time . . . Ah, God, but he could do with a drink . . . Why was he so damned worked up and nervous about a nigger and a white whore? . . . He'd never been so upset in all his life. Before he knew it, he had drifted off to sleep. Then he heard the office door swinging creakingly open on its rusty hinges. Lena stood in it, grim and businesslike, her face scrubbed free of powder and rouge. Olaf scrambled to his feet, adjusting his eyeglasses, blinking.

"How was it?" he asked her in a confidential whisper.

Lena's eyes blazed.

"What the hell's that to you?" she snapped. "There's your cut," she said, flinging him his money, tossing it upon the covers of the sofa. "You're sure nosy tonight. You wanna take over my work?"

Olaf's pasty cheeks burned red.

"You go to hell," he said, slamming the door.

"I'll meet you there!" Lena's shouting voice reached him dimly.

He was being a fool; there was no doubt about it. But, try as he might, he could not shake off a primitive hate for that black mountain of energy, of muscle, of bone; he envied the easy manner in which it moved with such a creeping and powerful motion; he winced at the booming and commanding voice that came to him when the tiny little eyes were not even looking at him; he shivered at the sight of those vast and clawlike hands that seemed always to hint of death . . .

Olaf kept his counsel. He never spoke to Karen about the sordid doings at the hotel. Such things were not for women like Karen. He knew instinctively that Karen would have been amazed had he told her that he was worried sick about a nigger and a blonde whore . . . No; he couldn't talk to anybody about it, not even the hard-bitten old bitch who owned the hotel. She was concerned only about money; she didn't give a damn about how big and how black a client was as long as he paid his room rent.

Next evening, when Olaf arrived for duty, there was no sight or sound of the black giant. A little later after one o'clock in the morning he appeared, left his key, and went out wordlessly. A few moments past two the giant returned, took his key from the board, and paused.

"I want that Lena again tonight. And another bottle of whisky," he said boomingly.

"I'll call her and see if she's in," Olaf said.

"Do that," the black giant said and was gone.

He thinks he's God, Olaf fumed. He picked up the phone and ordered Lena and a bottle of whisky, and there was a taste of ashes in his mouth. On the third night came the same request: Lena and whisky. When the black giant appeared on the fifth night, Olaf was about to make a sarcastic remark to the effect that maybe he ought to marry Lena, but he checked it in time . . . After all, he could kill me with one hand, he told himself.

Olaf was nervous and angry with himself for being nervous. Other black sailors came and asked for girls and Olaf sent them, but with none of the fear and loathing that he sent Lena and a bottle of whisky to the giant . . . All right, the black giant's stay was almost up. He'd said that he was staying for five or six nights; tomorrow night was the sixth night and that ought to be the end of this nameless terror.

On the sixth night Olaf sat in his swivel chair with his bottle of beer and waited, his teeth on edge, his fingers drumming the desk. But what the hell am I fretting for? . . . The hell with 'im . . . Olaf sat and dozed. Occasionally he'd awaken and listen to the foghorns of freighters sounding as ships came and went in the misty Copenhagen harbor. He was half asleep when he felt a rough hand on his shoulder. He blinked his eyes open. The giant, black and vast and powerful, all but blotted out his vision.

"What I owe you, man?" the giant demanded. "And I want my money."

"Sure," Olaf said, relieved, but filled as always with fear of this living wall of black flesh.

With fumbling hands, he made out the bill and received payment, then gave the giant his roll of money, laying it on the desk so as not to let his hands touch the flesh of the black mountain. Well, his ordeal was over. It was past two o'clock in the morning. Olaf even managed a wry smile and muttered a guttural "Thanks" for the generous tip that the giant tossed him.

Then a strange tension entered the office. The office door was shut and Olaf was alone with the black mass of power, yearning for it to leave. But the black mass of power stood still, immobile, looking down at Olaf. And Olaf could not, for the life of him, guess at what was transpiring in that mysterious black mind. The two of them simply stared at each other for a full two minutes, the giant's tiny little beady eyes blinking slowly as they seemed to measure and search Olaf's face. Olaf's vision dimmed for a second as terror seized him and he could feel a flush of heat overspread his body. Then Olaf sucked in his breath as the devil of blackness commanded:

"Stand up!"

Olaf was paralyzed. Sweat broke on his face. His worst premonitions about this black beast were coming true. This evil blackness was about to attack him, maybe kill him ... Slowly Olaf shook his head, his terror permitting him to breathe:

"What're you talking about?"

"Stand up, I say!" the black giant bellowed.

As though hypnotized, Olaf tried to rise; then he felt the black paw of the beast helping him roughly to his feet.

They stood an inch apart. Olaf's pasty-white features were glued to the giant's swollen black face. The ebony ensemble of eyes and nose and mouth and cheeks looked down at Olaf, silently; then, with a slow and deliberate movement of his gorillalike arms, he lifted his mammoth hands to Olaf's throat. Olaf had long known and felt that this dreadful moment was coming; he felt trapped in a nightmare. He could not move. He wanted to scream, but could find no words. His lips refused to open; his tongue felt icy and inert. Then he knew that his end had come when the giant's black fingers slowly, softly encircled his throat while a horrible grin of delight broke out on the sooty face ... Olaf lost control of the reflexes of his body and he felt a hot stickiness flooding his underwear ... He stared without breathing, gazing into the grinning blackness of the face that was bent over him, feeling the black fingers caressing his throat and waiting to feel the sharp, stinging ache and pain of the bones in his neck being snapped, crushed ... He knew all along that I hated 'im ... Yes, and now he's going to kill me for it, Olaf told himself with despair.

The black fingers still circled Olaf's neck, not closing, but gently massaging it, as it were, moving to and fro, while the obscene face grinned into his. Olaf could feel the giant's warm breath blowing on his eyelashes and he felt like a chicken about to have its neck wrung and its body tossed to flip and flap dyingly in the dust of the barnyard ... Then suddenly the black giant withdrew his fingers from Olaf's neck and stepped back a pace, still grinning. Olaf sighed, trembling, his body seeming to shrink; he waited. Shame sheeted him for the hot wetness that was in his trousers. Oh, God, he's teasing me ... He's showing me how easily he can kill me ... He swallowed, waiting, his eyes stones of gray.

The giant's barrel-like chest gave forth a low, rumbling chuckle of delight.

"You laugh?" Olaf asked whimperingly.

"Sure I laugh," the giant shouted.

"Please don't hurt me," Olaf managed to say.

"I wouldn't hurt you, boy," the giant said in a tone of mockery. "So long."

And he was gone. Olaf fell limply into the swivel chair and fought off losing consciousness. Then he wept. He was showing me how easily he could kill me ... He made me shake with terror and then laughed and left ... Slowly, Olaf recovered, stood, then gave vent to a string of curses:

"Goddamn 'im! My gun's right there in the desk drawer; I should of shot 'im. Jesus, I hope the ship he's on sinks ... I hope he drowns and the sharks eat 'im ..."

Later, he thought of going to the police, but sheer shame kept him back; and, anyway, the giant was probably on board his ship by now. And he had to get home and clean himself. Oh, Lord, what could he tell Karen? Yes, he would say that his stomach had been upset . . . He'd change clothes and return to work. He phoned the hotel owner that he was ill and wanted an hour off; the old bitch said that she was coming right over and that poor Olaf could have the evening off.

Olaf went home and lied to Karen. Then he lay awake the rest of the night dreaming of revenge. He saw that freighter on which the giant was sailing; he saw it springing a dangerous leak and saw a torrent of sea water flooding, gushing into all the compartments of the ship until it found the bunk in which the black giant slept. Ah, yes, the foamy, surging waters would surprise that sleeping black bastard of a giant and he would drown, gasping and choking like a trapped rat, his tiny eyes bulging until they glittered red, the bitter water of the sea pounding his lungs until they ached and finally burst . . . The ship would sink slowly to the bottom of the cold, black, silent depths of the sea and a shark, a *white* one, would glide aimlessly about the shut portholes until it found an open one and it would slither inside and nose about until it found that swollen, rotting, stinking carcass of the black beast and it would then begin to nibble at the decomposing mass of tarlike flesh, eating the bones clean . . . Olaf always pictured the giant's bones as being jet black and shining.

Once or twice, during these fantasies of cannibalistic revenge, Olaf felt a little guilty about all the many innocent people, women and children, all white and blonde, who would have to go down into watery graves in order that that white shark could devour the evil giant's black flesh . . . But, despite feelings of remorse, the fantasy lived persistently on, and when Olaf found himself alone, it would crowd and cloud his mind to the exclusion of all else, affording him the only revenge he knew. To make me suffer just for the pleasure of it, he fumed. Just to show me how strong he was . . . Olaf learned how to hate, and got pleasure out of it.

Summer fled on wings of rain. Autumn flooded Denmark with color. Winter made rain and snow fall on Copenhagen. Finally spring came, bringing violets and roses. Olaf kept to his job. For many months he feared the return of the black giant. But when a year had passed and the giant had not put in an appearance, Olaf allowed his revenge fantasy to peter out, indulging in it only when recalling the shame that the black monster had made him feel.

Then one rainy August night, a year later, Olaf sat drowsing at his desk, his bottle of beer before him, tilting back in his swivel chair, his feet resting atop a corner of his desk, his mind mulling over the more pleasant aspects of his life. The office door cracked open. Olaf glanced boredly up and around. His heart jumped and skipped a beat. The black nightmare of terror and shame that he had hoped that he had lost forever was again upon him . . . Resplendently dressed, suitcase in hand, the black looming mountain filled the doorway. Olaf's thin lips parted and a silent moan, half a curse, escaped them.

"Hy," the black giant boomed from the doorway.

Olaf could not reply. But a sudden resolve swept him: this time he would even the score. If this black beast came within so much as three feet of him, he would snatch his gun out of the drawer and shoot him dead, so help him God . . .

"No rooms tonight," Olaf heard himself announcing in a determined voice.

The black giant grinned; it was the same infernal grimace of delight and triumph that he had had when his damnable black fingers had been around his throat . . .

"Don't want no room tonight," the giant announced.

"Then what are you doing here?" Olaf asked in a loud but tremulous voice.

The giant swept toward Olaf and stood over him; and Olaf could not move, despite his oath to kill him . . .

"What do you want then?" Olaf demanded once more, ashamed that he could not lift his voice above a whisper.

The giant still grinned, then tossed what seemed the same suitcase upon Olaf's sofa and bent over it; he zippered it open with a sweep of his clawlike hand and rummaged in it, drawing forth a flat, gleaming white object done up in glowing cellophane. Olaf watched with lowered lids, wondering what trick was now being played on him. Then, before he could defend himself, the giant had whirled and again long, black, snakelike fingers were encircling Olaf's throat . . . Olaf stiffened, his right hand clawing blindly for the drawer where the gun was kept. But the giant was quick.

"Wait," he bellowed, pushing Olaf back from the desk.

The giant turned quickly to the sofa and, still holding his fingers in a wide circle that seemed a noose for Olaf's neck, he inserted the rounded fingers into the top of the flat, gleaming object. Olaf had the drawer open and his sweaty fingers were now touching his gun, but something made him freeze. The flat, gleaming object was a shirt and the black giant's circled fingers were fitting themselves into its neck . . .

"A perfect fit!" the giant shouted.

Olaf stared, trying to understand. His fingers loosened about the gun. A mixture of a laugh and a curse struggled in him. He watched the giant plunge his hands into the suitcase and pull out other flat, gleaming shirts.

"One, two, three, four, five, six," the black giant intoned, his voice crisp and businesslike. "Six nylon shirts. And they're all yours. One shirt for each time Lena came . . . See, Daddy-O?"

The black, cupped hands, filled with billowing nylon whiteness, were extended under Olaf's nose. Olaf eased his damp fingers from his gun and pushed the drawer closed, staring at the shirts and then at the black giant's grinning face.

"Don't you like 'em?" the giant asked.

Olaf began to laugh hysterically, then suddenly he was crying, his eyes so flooded with tears that the pile of dazzling nylon looked like snow in the dead of winter. Was this true? Could he believe it? Maybe this too was a trick? But, no. There were six shirts, all nylon, and the black giant had had Lena six nights.

"What's the matter with you, Daddy-O?" the giant asked. "You blowing your top? Laughing and crying . . ."

Olaf swallowed, dabbed his withered fists at his dimmed eyes; then he realized that he had his glasses on. He took them off and dried his eyes and sat up. He sighed, the tension and shame and fear and haunting dread of his fantasy went from him, and he leaned limply back in his chair . . .

"Try one on," the giant ordered.

Olaf fumbled with the buttons of his shirt, let down his suspenders, and pulled the shirt off. He donned a gleaming nylon one and the giant began buttoning it for him.

"Perfect, Daddy-O," the giant said.

His spectacled face framed in sparkling nylon, Olaf sat with trembling lips. So he'd not been trying to kill me after all.

"You want Lena, don't you?" he asked the giant in a soft whisper. "But I don't know where she is. She never came back here after you left—"

"I know where Lena is," the giant told him. "We been writing to each other. I'm going to her house. And, Daddy-O, I'm late." The giant zippered the suitcase shut and stood a moment gazing down at Olaf, his tiny little red eyes blinking slowly. Then Olaf realized that there was a compassion in that stare that he had never seen before.

"And I thought you wanted to kill me," Olaf told him. "I was scared of you . . ."

"Me? Kill you?" the giant blinked. "When?"

"That night when you put your fingers about my throat—"

"What?" the giant asked, then roared with laughter. "Daddy-O, you're a funny little man. I wouldn't hurt you. I like you. You a *good* man. You helped me."

Olaf smiled, clutching the pile of nylon shirts in his arms.

"You're a good man too," Olaf murmured. Then loudly: "You're a big black good man."

"Daddy-O, you're crazy," the giant said.

He swept his suitcase from the sofa, spun on his heel, and was at the door in one stride.

"Thanks!" Olaf cried after him.

The black giant paused, turned his vast black head, and flashed a grin.

"Daddy-O, drop dead," he said and was gone.

Richard Yates

. . . .

THE BEST
OF EVERYTHING

Nobody expected Grace to do any work the Friday before her wedding. In fact, nobody would let her, whether she wanted to or not.

A gardenia corsage lay in a cellophane box beside her typewriter—from Mr. Atwood, her boss—and tucked inside the envelope that came with it was a ten-dollar gift certificate from Bloomingdale's. Mr. Atwood had treated her with a special shy courtliness ever since the time she necked with him at the office Christmas party, and now when she went in to thank him he was all hunched over, rattling desk drawers, blushing and grinning and barely meeting her eyes.

"Aw, now, don't mention it, Grace," he said. "Pleasure's all mine. Here, you need a pin to put that gadget on with?"

"There's a pin that came with it," she said, holding up the corsage. "See? A nice white one."

Beaming, he watched her pin the flowers high on the lapel of her suit. Then he cleared his throat importantly and pulled out the writing panel of his desk, ready to give the morning's dictation. But it turned out there were only two short letters, and it wasn't until an hour later, when she caught him handing over a pile of Dictaphone cylinders to Central Typing, that she realized he had done her a favor.

"That's very sweet of you, Mr. Atwood," she said, "but I do think you ought to give me all your work today, just like any oth—"

"Aw, now, Grace," he said. "You only get married once."

The girls all made a fuss over her too, crowding around her desk and giggling, asking again and again to see Ralph's photograph ("Oh, he's *cute!*"), while the office manager looked on nervously, reluctant to be a spoilsport but anxious to point out that it was, after all, a working day.

Then at lunch there was the traditional little party at Schrafft's—nine women and girls, giddy on their unfamiliar cocktails, letting their chicken à la king grow cold while they pummeled her with old times and good wishes. There were more flowers and another gift—a silver candy dish for which all the girls had whisperingly chipped in.

Grace said "Thank you" and "I certainly do appreciate it" and "I don't know what to say" until her head rang with the words and the corners of her mouth ached from smiling, and she thought the afternoon would never end.

Ralph called up about four o'clock, exuberant. "How ya doin', honey?" he asked, and before she could answer he said, "Listen. Guess what I got?"

"I don't know. A present or something? What?" She tried to sound excited, but it wasn't easy.

"A bonus. Fifty dollars." She could almost see the flattening of his lips as he said "fifty dollars" with the particular earnestness he reserved for pronouncing sums of money.

"Why, that's lovely, Ralph," she said, and if there was any tiredness in her voice he didn't notice it.

"Lovely, huh?" he said with a laugh, mocking the girlishness of the word. "Ya *like* that, huh Gracie? No, but I mean I was really surprised, ya know it? The boss siz, 'Here, Ralph,' and he hands me this envelope. He don't even crack a smile or nothin', and I'm wonderin', what's the deal here? I'm getting fired here, or what? He siz, 'G'ahead, Ralph, open it.' So I open it, and then I look at the boss and he's grinning a mile wide." He chuckled and sighed. "Well, so listen, honey. What time ya want me to come over tonight?"

"Oh, I don't know. Soon as you can, I guess."

"Well listen, I gotta go over to Eddie's house and pick up that bag he's gonna loan me, so I might as well do that, go on home and eat, and then come over to your place around eight-thirty, nine o'clock. Okay?"

"All right," she said. "I'll see you then, darling." She had been calling him "darling" for only a short time—since it had become irrevocably clear that she was, after all, going to marry him—and the word still had an alien sound. As she straightened the stacks of stationery in her desk (because there was nothing else to do), a familiar little panic gripped her: she couldn't marry him—she hardly even *knew* him. Sometimes it occurred to her differently, that she couldn't marry him because she knew him too well, and either way it left her badly shaken, vulnerable to all the things that Martha, her roommate, had said from the very beginning.

"Isn't he funny?" Martha had said after their first date. "He says 'terlet.' I didn't know people really said 'terlet.' " And Grace had giggled, ready enough to agree that it *was* funny. That was a time when she had been ready to agree with Martha on practically anything—when it often seemed, in fact, that finding a girl like Martha from an ad in the *Times* was just about the luckiest thing that had ever happened to her.

But Ralph had persisted all through the summer, and by fall she had begun standing up for him. "What don't you *like* about him, Martha? He's perfectly nice."

"Oh, everybody's perfectly nice, Grace," Martha would say in her college voice, making perfectly nice a faintly absurd thing to be, and then she'd look up crossly from the careful painting of her fingernails. "It's just that he's such a lit-tle—a little *white worm*. Can't you see that?"

"Well, I certainly don't see what his *complexion* has to do with—"

"Oh God, *you* know what I mean. Can't you see what I *mean?* Oh, and all those friends of his, his Eddie and his Marty and his George with their mean,

ratty little clerks' lives and their mean, ratty little. . . . It's just that they're all
alike, those people. All they ever say is 'Hey, wha' happen t'ya Giants?' and
'Hey, wha' happen t'ya Yankees?' and they all live way out in Sunnyside or
Woodhaven or some awful place, and their mothers have those damn little
china elephants on the mantelpiece." And Martha would frown over her nail
polish again, making it clear that the subject was closed.

All that fall and winter she was confused. For a while she tried going out only
with Martha's kind of men—the kind that used words like "amusing" all the
time and wore small-shouldered flannel suits like a uniform; and for a while she
tried going out with no men at all. She even tried that crazy business with Mr.
Atwood at the office Christmas party. And all the time Ralph kept calling up,
hanging around, waiting for her to make up her mind. Once she took him home
to meet her parents in Pennsylvania (where she never would have dreamed of
taking Martha), but it wasn't until Easter time that she finally gave in.

They had gone to a dance somewhere in Queens, one of the big American
Legion dances that Ralph's crowd was always going to, and when the band
played "Easter Parade" he held her very close, hardly moving, and sang to her in
a faint, whispering tenor. It was the kind of thing she'd never have expected
Ralph to do—a sweet, gentle thing—and it probably wasn't just then that she
decided to marry him, but it always seemed so afterwards. It always seemed she
had decided that minute, swaying to the music with his husky voice in her hair:

> "I'll be all in clover
> And when they look you over
> I'll be the proudest fella
> In the Easter Parade. . . ."

That night she had told Martha, and she could still see the look on Martha's
face. "Oh, Grace, you're not—surely you're not *serious*. I mean, I thought he
was more or less of a *joke*—you can't really mean you want to—"

"Shut up! You just shut up, Martha!" And she'd cried all night. Even now
she hated Martha for it; even as she stared blindly at a row of filing cabinets
along the office wall, half sick with fear that Martha was right.

The noise of giggles swept over her, and she saw with a start that two of the
girls—Irene and Rose—were grinning over their typewriters and pointing at her.
"*We* saw ya!" Irene sang. "*We* saw ya! Mooning again, huh Grace?" Then Rose
did a burlesque of mooning, heaving her meager breasts and batting her eyes,
and they both collapsed in laughter.

With an effort of will Grace resumed the guileless, open smile of a bride. The
thing to do was concentrate on plans.

Tomorrow morning, "bright and early," as her mother would say, she would
meet Ralph at Penn Station for the trip home. They'd arrive about one, and her
parents would meet the train. "Good t'see ya, Ralph!" her father would say, and
her mother would probably kiss him. A warm, homely love filled her: *they*
wouldn't call him a white worm; *they* didn't have any ideas about Princeton
men and "interesting" men and all the other kinds of men Martha was so stuck-
up about. Then her father would probably take Ralph out for a beer and show

him the paper mill where he worked (and at least Ralph wouldn't be snobby about a person working in a paper mill, either), and then Ralph's family and friends would come down from New York in the evening.

She'd have time for a long talk with her mother that night, and the next morning, "bright and early" (her eyes stung at the thought of her mother's plain, happy face), they would start getting dressed for the wedding. Then the church and the ceremony, and then the reception (Would her father get drunk? Would Muriel Ketchel sulk about not being a bridesmaid?), and finally the train to Atlantic City, and the hotel. But from the hotel on she couldn't plan any more. A door would lock behind her and there would be a wild, fantastic silence, and nobody in all the world but Ralph to lead the way.

"Well, Grace," Mr. Atwood was saying, "I want to wish you every happiness." He was standing at her desk with his hat and coat on, and all around her were the chattering and scraping-back of chairs that meant it was five o'clock.

"Thank you, Mr. Atwood." She got to her feet, suddenly surrounded by all the girls in a bedlam of farewell.

"All the luck in the world, Grace."

"Drop us a card, huh Grace? From Atlantic City?"

"So long, Grace."

"G'night, Grace, and listen: the best of everything."

Finally she was free of them all, out of the elevator, out of the building, hurrying through the crowds to the subway.

When she got home Martha was standing in the door of the kitchenette, looking very svelte in a crisp new dress.

"Hi, Grace. I bet they ate you alive today, didn't they?"

"Oh no," Grace said. "Everybody was—real nice." She sat down, exhausted, and dropped the flowers and the wrapped candy dish on a table. Then she noticed that the whole apartment was swept and dusted, and the dinner was cooking in the kitchenette. "Gee, everything looks wonderful," she said. "What'd you do all this for?"

"Oh, well, I got home early anyway," Martha said. Then she smiled, and it was one of the few times Grace had ever seen her look shy. "I just thought it might be nice to have the place looking decent for a change, when Ralph comes over."

"Well," Grace said, "it certainly was nice of you."

The way Martha looked now was even more surprising: she looked awkward. She was turning a greasy spatula in her fingers, holding it delicately away from her dress and examining it, as if she had something difficult to say. "Look, Grace," she began. "You do understand why I can't come to the wedding, don't you?"

"Oh, sure," Grace said, although in fact she didn't, exactly. It was something about having to go up to Harvard to see her brother before he went into the Army, but it had sounded like a lie from the beginning.

"It's just that I'd hate you to think I—well, anyway, I'm glad if you do understand. And the other thing I wanted to say is more important."

"What?"

"Well, just that I'm sorry for all the awful things I used to say about Ralph. I never had a right to talk to you that way. He's a very sweet boy and I—well, I'm sorry, that's all."

It wasn't easy for Grace to hide a rush of gratitude and relief when she said, "Why, that's all right, Martha, I—"

"The chops are on fire!" Martha bolted for the kitchenette. "It's all right," she called back. "They're edible." And when she came out to serve dinner all her old composure was restored. "I'll have to eat and run," she said as they sat down. "My train leaves in forty minutes."

"I thought it was *tomorrow* you were going."

"Well, it was, actually," Martha said, "but I decided to go tonight. Because you see, Grace, another thing—if you can stand one more apology—another thing I'm sorry for is that I've hardly ever given you and Ralph a chance to be alone here. So tonight I'm going to clear out." She hesitated. "It'll be a sort of wedding gift from me, okay?" And then she smiled, not shyly this time but in a way that was more in character—the eyes subtly averted after a flicker of special meaning. It was a smile that Grace—through stages of suspicion, bewilderment, awe, and practiced imitation—had long ago come to associate with the word "sophisticated."

"Well, that's very sweet of you," Grace said, but she didn't really get the point just then. It wasn't until long after the meal was over and the dishes washed, until Martha had left for her train in a whirl of cosmetics and luggage and quick goodbyes, that she began to understand.

She took a deep, voluptuous bath and spent a long time drying herself, posing in the mirror, filled with a strange, slow excitement. In her bedroom, from the rustling tissues of an expensive white box, she drew the prizes of her trousseau—a sheer nightgown of white nylon and a matching negligee—put them on, and went to the mirror again. She had never worn anything like this before, or felt like this, and the thought of letting Ralph see her like this sent her into the kitchenette for a glass of the special dry sherry Martha kept for cocktail parties. Then she turned out all the lights but one and, carrying her glass, went to the sofa and arranged herself there to wait for him. After a while she got up and brought the sherry bottle over to the coffee table, where she set it on a tray with another glass.

When Ralph left the office he felt vaguely let down. Somehow, he'd expected more of the Friday before his wedding. The bonus check had been all right (though secretly he'd been counting on twice that amount), and the boys had bought him a drink at lunch and kidded around in the appropriate way ("Ah, don't feel too bad, Ralph—worse things could happen"), but still, there ought to have been a real party. Not just the boys in the office, but Eddie and *all* his friends. Instead there would only be meeting Eddie at the White Rose like every other night of the year, and riding home to borrow Eddie's suitcase and to eat, and then having to ride all the way back to Manhattan just to see Gracie for an hour or two. Eddie wasn't in the bar when he arrived, which sharpened the edge of his loneliness. Morosely he drank a beer, waiting.

Eddie was his best friend, and an ideal best man because he'd been in on the courtship of Gracie from the start. It was in this very bar, in fact, that Ralph had told him about their first date last summer: "Ooh, Eddie—what a paira *knockers!*"

And Eddie had grinned. "Yeah? So what's the roommate like?"

"Ah, you don't want the roommate, Eddie. The roommate's a dog. A snob, too, I think. No, but this *other* one, this little *Gracie*—boy, I mean, she is *stacked.*"

Half the fun of every date—even more than half—had been telling Eddie about it afterwards, exaggerating a little here and there, asking Eddie's advice on tactics. But after today, like so many other pleasures, it would all be left behind. Gracie had promised him at least one night off a week to spend with the boys, after they were married, but even so it would never be the same. Girls never understood a thing like friendship.

There was a ball game on the bar's television screen and he watched it idly, his throat swelling in a sentimental pain of loss. Nearly all his life had been devoted to the friendship of boys and men, to trying to be a good guy, and now the best of it was over.

Finally Eddie's stiff finger jabbed the seat of his pants in greeting. "Whaddya say, sport?"

Ralph narrowed his eyes to indolent contempt and slowly turned around. "Wha' happen ta you, wise guy? Get lost?"

"Whaddya—in a hurry a somethin'?" Eddie barely moved his lips when he spoke. "Can't wait two minutes?" He slouched on a stool and slid a quarter at the bartender. "Draw one, there, Jack."

They drank in silence for a while, staring at the television. "Got a little bonus today," Ralph said. "Fifty dollars."

"Yeah?" Eddie said. "Good."

A batter struck out; the inning was over and the commercial came on. "So?" Eddie said, rocking the beer around in his glass. "Still gonna get married?"

"Why not?" Ralph said with a shrug. "Listen, finish that, willya? I wanna get a move on."

"Wait awhile, wait awhile. What's ya hurry?"

"C'mon, willya?" Ralph stepped impatiently away from the bar. "I wanna go pick up ya bag."

"Ah, bag schmagg."

Ralph moved up close again and glowered at him. "Look, wise guy. Nobody's gonna *make* ya loan me the goddamn bag, ya know. I don't wanna break ya *heart* or nothin'—"

"Arright, arright, arright. You'll getcha bag. Don't worry so much." He finished the beer and wiped his mouth. "Let's go."

Having to borrow a bag for his wedding trip was a sore point with Ralph; he'd much rather have bought one of his own. There was a fine one displayed in the window of a luggage shop they passed every night on their way to the subway—a big, tawny Gladstone with a zippered compartment on the side, at thirty-nine ninety-five—and Ralph had had his eye on it ever since Easter time. "Think I'll buy that," he'd told Eddie, in the same offhand way that a day or so before he had announced his engagement ("Think I'll marry the girl"). Eddie's response to both remarks had been the same: "Whaddya—crazy?" Both times Ralph had said, "Why not?" and in defense of the bag he had added, "Gonna get married, I'll *need* somethin' like that." From then on it was as if the bag, almost as much as Gracie herself, had become a symbol of the new and richer life he sought. But after the ring and the new clothes and all the other expenses, he'd found at last that he couldn't afford it; he had settled for the loan of Eddie's, which was similar but cheaper and worn, and without the zippered compartment.

Now as they passed the luggage shop he stopped, caught in the grip of a reckless idea. "Hey wait awhile, Eddie. Know what I think I'll do with that fifty-dollar bonus? I think I'll buy that bag right now." He felt breathless.

"Whaddya—crazy? Forty bucks for a bag you'll use maybe one time a year? Ya crazy, Ralph. C'mon."

"Ah—I dunno. Ya think so?"

"Listen, you better *keep* ya money, boy. You're gonna *need* it."

"Ah—yeah," Ralph said at last. "I guess ya right." And he fell in step with Eddie again, heading for the subway. This was the way things usually turned out in his life; he could never own a bag like that until he made a better salary, and he accepted it—just as he'd accepted without question, after the first thin sigh, the knowledge that he'd never possess his bride until after the wedding.

The subway swallowed them, rattled and banged them along in a rocking, mindless trance for half an hour, and disgorged them at last into the cool early evening of Queens.

Removing their coats and loosening their ties, they let the breeze dry their sweated shirts as they walked. "So what's the deal?" Eddie asked. "What time we supposed to show up in this Pennsylvania burg tomorra?"

"Ah, suit yourself," Ralph said. "Any time in the evening's okay."

"So whadda we do then? What the hell can ya *do* in a hillbilly town like that, anyway?"

"Ah, I dunno," Ralph said defensively. "Sit around and talk, I guess; drink beer with Gracie's old man or somethin'; I dunno."

"Jesus," Eddie said. "Some weekend. Big, big deal."

Ralph stopped on the sidewalk, suddenly enraged, his damp coat wadded in his fist. "Look, you bastid. Nobody's gonna *make* ya come, ya know—you or Marty or George or any a the rest of 'em. Get that straight. You're not doin' *me* no favors, unnastand?"

"Whatsa matta?" Eddie inquired. "Whatsa matta? Can'tcha take a joke?"

"Joke," Ralph said. "You're fulla jokes." And plodding sullenly in Eddie's wake, he felt close to tears.

They turned off into the block where they both lived, a double row of neat, identical houses bordering the street where they'd fought and loafed and played stickball all their lives. Eddie pushed open the front door of his house and ushered Ralph into the vestibule, with its homely smell of cauliflower and overshoes. "G'wan in," he said, jerking a thumb at the closed living-room door, and he hung back to let Ralph go first.

Ralph opened the door and took three steps inside before it hit him like a sock on the jaw. The room, dead silent, was packed deep with grinning, red-faced men—Marty, George, the boys from the block, the boys from the office—

everybody, all his friends, all on their feet and poised motionless in a solid mass. Skinny Maguire was crouched at the upright piano, his spread fingers high over the keys, and when he struck the first rollicking chords they all roared into song, beating time with their fists, their enormous grins distorting the words:

"Fa he's a jally guh fella
Fa he's a jally guh fella
Fa he's a jally guh fell-ah
That nobody can deny!"

Weakly Ralph retreated a step on the carpet and stood there wide-eyed, swallowing, holding his coat. *"That nobody can deny!"* they sang, *"That nobody can deny!"* And as they swung into the second chorus Eddie's father appeared through the dining-room curtains, bald and beaming, in full song, with a great glass pitcher of beer in either hand. At last Skinny hammered out the final line:

"That—no—bod—dee—can—dee—nye!"

And they all surged forward cheering, grabbing Ralph's hand, pounding his arms and his back while he stood trembling, his own voice lost under the noise. "Gee, fellas—thanks. I—don't know what to—thanks, fellas. . . ."

Then the crowd cleaved in half, and Eddie made his way slowly down the middle. His eyes gleamed in a smile of love, and from his bashful hand hung the suitcase—not his own, but a new one: the big, tawny Gladstone with the zippered compartment on the side.

"Speech!" they were yelling. *"Speech! Speech!"*

But Ralph couldn't speak and couldn't smile. He could hardly even see.

At ten o'clock Grace began walking around the apartment and biting her lip. What if he wasn't coming? But of course he was coming. She sat down again and carefully smoothed the billows of nylon around her thighs, forcing herself to be calm. The whole thing would be ruined if she was nervous.

The noise of the doorbell was like an electric shock. She was halfway to the door before she stopped, breathing hard, and composed herself again. Then she pressed the buzzer and opened the door a crack to watch for him on the stairs.

When she saw he was carrying a suitcase, and saw the pale seriousness of his face as he mounted the stairs, she thought at first that he knew; he had come prepared to lock the door and take her in his arms. "Hello, darling," she said softly, and opened the door wider.

"Hi, baby." He brushed past her and walked inside. "Guess I'm late, huh? You in bed?"

"No." She closed the door and leaned against it with both hands holding the doorknob at the small of her back, the way heroines close doors in the movies. "I was just—waiting for you."

He wasn't looking at her. He went to the sofa and sat down, holding the suitcase on his lap and running his fingers over its surface. "Gracie," he said, barely above a whisper. "Look at this."

She looked at it, and then into his tragic eyes.

"Remember," he said, "I told you about that bag I wanted to buy? Forty dollars?" He stopped and looked around. "Hey, where's Martha? She in bed?"

"She's gone, darling," Grace said, moving slowly toward the sofa. "She's gone for the whole weekend." She sat down beside him, leaned close, and gave him Martha's special smile.

"Oh yeah?" he said. "Well anyway, listen. I said I was gonna borrow Eddie's bag instead, remember?"

"Yes."

"Well, so tonight at the White Rose I siz, 'C'mon, Eddie, let's go home pick up ya bag.' He siz, 'Ah, bag schmagg.' I siz, 'Whatsa matta?' but he don't say nothin', see? So we go home to his place and the living-room door's shut, see?"

She squirmed closer and put her head on his chest. Automatically he raised an arm and dropped it around her shoulders, still talking. "He siz, 'G'ahead, Ralph, open the door.' I siz, 'Whatsa deal?' He siz, 'Never mind, Ralph, open the door.' So I open the door, and oh Jesus." His fingers gripped her shoulder with such intensity that she looked up at him in alarm.

"They was all there, Gracie," he said. "All the fellas. Playin' the piana, singin', cheerin'—" His voice wavered and his eyelids fluttered shut, their lashes wet. "A big surprise party," he said, trying to smile. "Fa me. Can ya beat that, Gracie? And then—and then Eddie comes out and—Eddie comes out and hands me this. The very same bag I been lookin' at all this time. He bought it with his own money and he didn't say nothin', just to give me a surprise. 'Here, Ralph,' he siz. 'Just to let ya know you're the greatest guy in the world.' " His fingers tightened again, trembling. "I cried, Gracie," he whispered. "I couldn't help it. I don't think the fellas saw it or anything, but I was cryin'." He turned his face away and worked his lips in a tremendous effort to hold back the tears.

"Would you like a drink, darling?" she asked tenderly.

"Nah, that's all right, Gracie. I'm all right." Gently he set the suitcase on the carpet. "Only, gimme a cigarette, huh?"

She got one from the coffee table, put it in his lips and lit it. "Let me get you a drink," she said.

He frowned through the smoke. "Whaddya got, that sherry wine? Nah, I don't like that stuff. Anyway, I'm fulla beer." He leaned back and closed his eyes. "And then Eddie's mother feeds us this terrific meal," he went on, and his voice was almost normal now. "We had *steaks;* we had French-fried *potatas*"— his head rolled on the sofa-back with each item of the menu—"lettuce-and-to-mata *salad, pickles, bread, butter*—everything. The works."

"Well," she said. "Wasn't that nice."

"And afterwards we had ice cream and coffee," he said, "and all the beer we could drink. I mean, it was a real spread."

Grace ran her hands over her lap, partly to smooth the nylon and partly to dry the moisture on her palms. "Well, that certainly was nice of them," she said. They sat there silent for what seemed a long time.

"I can only stay a minute, Gracie," Ralph said at last. "I promised 'em I'd be back."

Her heart thumped under the nylon. "Ralph, do you—do you like this?"

"What, honey?"

"My negligee. You weren't supposed to see it until—after the wedding, but I thought I'd—"

"Nice," he said, feeling the flimsy material between thumb and index finger, like a merchant. "Very nice. Wudga pay fa this, honey?"

"Oh—I don't know. But do you like it?"

He kissed her and began, at last, to stroke her with his hands. "Nice," he kept saying. "Nice. Hey, I like this." His hand hesitated at the low neckline, slipped inside and held her breast.

"I do love you, Ralph," she whispered. "You know that, don't you?"

His fingers pinched her nipple, once, and slid quickly out again. The policy of restraint, the habit of months was too strong to break. "Sure," he said. "And I love you, baby. Now you be a good girl and get ya beauty sleep, and I'll see ya in the morning. Okay?"

"Oh, Ralph. Don't go. Stay."

"Ah, I promised the fellas, Gracie." He stood up and straightened his clothes. "They're waitin' fa me, out home."

She blazed to her feet, but the cry that was meant for a woman's appeal came out, through her tightening lips, as the whine of a wife: "Can't they wait?"

"Whaddya—*crazy?*" He backed away, eyes round with righteousness. She would *have* to understand. If this was the way she acted before the wedding, how the hell was it going to be afterwards? "Have a *heart*, willya? Keep the fellas waitin' *tonight?* After all they done fa *me?*"

After a second or two, during which her face became less pretty than he had ever seen it before, she was able to smile. "Of course not, darling. You're right."

He came forward again and gently brushed the tip of her chin with his fist, smiling, a husband reassured. " 'At's more like it," he said. "So I'll see ya, Penn Station, nine o'clock tomorra. Right, Gracie? Only, before I go—" he winked and slapped his belly. "I'm fulla beer. Mind if I use ya terlet?"

When he came out of the bathroom she was waiting to say goodnight, standing with her arms folded across her chest, as if for warmth. Lovingly he hefted the new suitcase and joined her at the door. "Okay, then, baby," he said, and kissed her. "Nine o'clock. Don't forget, now."

She smiled tiredly and opened the door for him. "Don't worry, Ralph," she said. "I'll be there."

Biographical Notes*

· · · · · · · · · · · · · · · · · ·

CHINUA ACHEBE (1930) *Nigeria* Born in eastern Nigeria, Mr. Achebe received his B.A. from University College, Ibadan, and an honorary degree from Dartmouth College. In 1961, he was appointed the first Director of External Broadcasting in Nigeria. He is the recipient of numerous honors, including the Scottish Arts Council's Neil Gunn International Fellowship and the *New Statesman* Award. Mr. Achebe has written five novels; his stories are collected in *Girls at War* and *Sacrificial Egg*.

ILSE AICHINGER (1921) *Austria* Born in Vienna, Ms. Aichinger studied medicine after the war and began reading for S. Fischer Verlag Publishing Company. A novelist and co-founder of the Academy for Design, she received the Group 47 Prize, the Bremen Prize for Literature, and the Austrian State Prize. A selection of her stories is included in *Selected Poetry and Prose of Ilse Aichinger*.

VASILY PAVLOVICH AKSENOV (1932) *Russia* Born in Kazan, Mr. Aksenov is acknowledged as one of the leading Soviet writers of his generation. A prodigious novelist, story writer, dramatist, and screenwriter, he was educated as a doctor and graduated from the First Medical Institute of Leningrad in 1956. Forced to emigrate from the Soviet Union in 1980 when his second novel, *The Burn*, was published in Italy, he now lives in Washington, D.C. He has been a fellow at the Kennan Institute for Advanced Russian Studies and has taught at Johns Hopkins University. Mr. Aksenov is the author of the story collection *Steel Bird*.

MARGARET ATWOOD (1939) *Canada* Born in Ottawa, Ms. Atwood studied at Victoria and Radcliffe colleges. She received the Governor-General's Award and contributes regularly to *The New Yorker*, *The Atlantic*, and *The New York Times*. Her work includes numerous volumes of poetry, several novels, and a variety of critical articles and reviews. Her story collections are *Dancing Girls* and *Bluebeard's Egg*.

---

* Only those story collections that have appeared in English are referred to in these notes.

INGEBORG BACHMANN (1926–1973) *Austria* Born in Klagenfurt, Ms. Bachmann studied philosophy at the University of Vienna. She worked for various newspapers and radio stations, lectured at several universities, and lived in Paris, Munich, Zurich, New York, and Rome. She wrote poetry as well as fiction; her stories are collected in *The Thirtieth Year*.

JAMES BALDWIN (1924) *United States* The son of a revivalist minister, Mr. Baldwin grew up in Harlem and for many years lived as an expatriate in Paris. He has been a writer-in-residence at various universities and is the author of novels, plays, and volumes of essays. His stories are collected in *Going to Meet the Man*.

RUSSELL BANKS (1940) *United States* Born in Newton, Massachusetts, Mr. Banks grew up in New Hampshire and graduated from the University of North Carolina, Chapel Hill. He teaches at Columbia University and Princeton University, and his work has been included in the Best American Short Stories, the O. Henry anthologies, and the Pushcart Prize. Mr. Banks' collections of stories are *Searching for Survivors*, *The New World*, *Trailerpark*, and the forthcoming *Success Stories*.

DONALD BARTHELME (1931) *United States* Born in Philadelphia, Mr. Barthelme grew up in Houston, where he worked for several years as a reporter. After having spent many years in New York City, he has returned to Houston. He is a novelist, a short-story writer, and the recipient of the National Book Award. Mr. Barthelme's stories are collected in *Sixty Stories*.

ANN BEATTIE (1947) *United States* Born in Washington, D.C., Ms. Beattie studied at American University and has taught at the University of Virginia, Harvard University, and the University of Michigan. Her stories are collected in *Distortions*, *Secrets and Surprises*, and *The Burning House*.

SAMUEL BECKETT (1906) *Ireland* Born in Dublin, Mr. Beckett moved to Paris in the late 1920s and has written in French since 1945. He is the author of novels, plays, short stories, poems, scripts for radio, television, and film, as well as a critical study of Marcel Proust. In 1969, Mr. Beckett won the Nobel Prize. His collections of stories are *Stories and Texts for Nothing*, *First Love and Other Shorts*, and *More Pricks Than Kicks*.

HEINRICH BÖLL (1917–1985) *Germany* Born in Köln, Mr. Böll was one of the most influential of the post-war German novelists. He won numerous awards, including the Nobel Prize. His story collections are *Eighteen Stories*, *Children Are Civilians Too*, and *What's to Become of the Boy?*

WOLFGANG BORCHERT (1921–1947) *Germany* Born in Hamburg, Mr. Borchert was a bookseller and an actor before the war. In 1942 he was sent to the Russian front, where he was severely wounded. Because of his outspoken criticism of the Nazi regime, he was returned to the front and imprisoned several times. Although he was chronically ill after his release in 1945, he wrote intensively for the next two years until his death. Mr. Borchert's stories and assorted prose pieces are collected in *The Man Outside* and *The Sad Geraniums*.

JORGE LUIS BORGES (1899) *Argentina* Born in Buenos Aires, Mr. Borges was educated in Switzerland and spent two years in Spain. A political exile and leader of the South American literary movement based on surrealism and imagism, he became Director of the Argentine National Library after the overthrow of Perón in 1955. He has received honorary degrees from Oxford University and Columbia University, and has taught in Europe, the United States, and South America. In 1961 Mr. Borges shared the International Publisher's Prize with Samuel Beckett. His story collections include *Ficciones*, *The Aleph*, and *Dr. Brodie's Report*.

TADEUSZ BOROWSKI (1922–1951) *Poland* Born in the Soviet Ukraine to Polish parents, Mr. Borowski studied at underground universities during the German occupation. He published a volume of poems before he was arrested in 1942 and sent to Auschwitz and later to Dachau. Released in 1945, he published another volume of poems and three volumes of stories about concentration camps before taking his own life. Mr. Borowski's stories are collected in *This Way for the Gas, Ladies and Gentlemen*.

ABDESLAM BOULAICH (ca. 1935) *Morocco* Mr. Boulaich is a writer in the oral tradition. His work has been translated by Paul Bowles.

PAUL BOWLES (1910) *United States* Born in New York City, Mr. Bowles studied musical composition with Aaron Copland, was a music critic for the *New York Herald Tribune*, and wrote musical scores for Broadway during the thirties and forties. An inveterate world traveler, he also explored North Africa during this time, and has lived in Tangier since 1945. The recipient of several awards, Mr. Bowles has written novels, essays, and an autobiography. His collections of stories include *The Delicate Prey*, *The Time of Friendship*, and *Collected Stories*.

T. CORAGHESSAN BOYLE (1948) *United States* Born in New York City, Mr. Boyle currently lives in Los Angeles, where he teaches at the University of Southern California. He has published two novels, as well as two collections of stories, *The Descent of Man* and *Greasy Lake*.

HAROLD BRODKEY (1930) *United States* Born in Staunton, Illinois, Mr. Brodkey has taught at Cornell University and the University of Arizona. He has won several O. Henry Awards, a Prix de Rome and the Brandeis Award. Mr. Brodkey's collection of stories is called *First Love and Other Sorrows*.

DINO BUZZATI (1906–1972) *Italy* Born in Belluno, in northern Italy, Mr. Buzzati lived most of his life in Milan and was an editor and correspondent for *Corriere della Sera*. He was a painter and a writer, and his novels, plays, and short stories have been widely translated. Mr. Buzzati's story collections are *Restless Nights*, *The Siren*, and *Catastrophe*.

ITALO CALVINO (1923–1985) *Italy* Born in Cuba, Mr. Calvino is recognized as one of Italy's foremost contemporary fiction writers. He was an honorary member of the American Academy and Institute of Arts and Letters, and was awarded many prizes in Europe. His story collections include *t Zero, Cosmicomics, The Watcher,* and *Difficult Loves.*

ALBERT CAMUS (1913–1960) *France* Born in Mondavi, Algeria, to Breton and Spanish parents, Mr. Camus grew up in North Africa and traveled to France, where he was a journalist for many years. During the German occupation he was active in the resistance and served as the editor of the clandestine paper *Combat.* Internationally recognized for his essays and novels, Mr. Camus received the Nobel Prize in 1957, a few years before he was killed in an automobile accident. His collection of stories is *Exile and the Kingdom.*

TRUMAN CAPOTE (1926–1984) *United States* Born in New Orleans, Mr. Capote wrote numerous novels and was an experimenter in the field of reportage. His stories are published in *A Tree of Night.*

RAYMOND CARVER (1939) *United States* Born in Clatskanie, Oregon, Mr. Carver is both a poet and short story writer. His story collections are *Furious Seasons, Will You Please Be Quiet, Please?* (which was nominated for the National Book Award), *What We Talk About When We Talk About Love,* and *Cathedral.*

JOHN CHEEVER (1912–1981) *United States* Born in Quincy, Massachusetts, Mr. Cheever studied at Thayer Academy and occasionally taught at Barnard College and the University of Iowa. He wrote a number of novels and was a frequent contributor to *The New Yorker.* His collections of stories include *The Enormous Radio, The Housebreaker of Shady Hill,* and *The Stories of John Cheever,* which won the Pulitzer Prize.

ROBERT COOVER (1932) *United States* Born in Charles City, Iowa, Mr. Coover graduated from Indiana University and the University of Chicago. He has taught at Princeton University and currently teaches at Brown University. His awards include the William Faulkner Award for a first novel, the Brandeis Citation for Fiction, and a grant from the Rockefeller Foundation. His stories are collected in *Pricksongs & Descants.*

JULIO CORTÁZAR (1914–1984) *Argentina* An Argentinian born in Brussels, Mr. Cortazar lived in Paris from 1952 until his death. He was a poet, translator, amateur jazz musician, novelist, and short-story writer. His story collections include *All Fires the Fire, A Change of Light,* and *We Love Glenda So Much.*

GUY DAVENPORT (1927) *United States* Born in Anderson, South Carolina, Mr. Davenport studied at Duke, Oxford, and Harvard universities. A poet, fiction writer, critic, and essayist, he has received, among other honors, the Zabel Fiction Prize, a Rhodes Scholarship, and the Flexner Award for Writing. His story collections are *Tatlin!, Da Vinci's Bicycle, Eclogues,* and *Apples and Pears.*

ISAK DINESEN (1885–1962) *Denmark* Isak Dinesen is the pseudonym of Baroness Karen Blixen, who was born in Elsinore. In 1914 she traveled to British

East Africa, where she lived for seventeen years before returning to Denmark. Her books of stories are *Seven Gothic Tales, Winter's Tales,* and *Last Tales.*

E. L. DOCTOROW   (1931)   *United States*   Born in New York City, where he currently resides, Mr. Doctorow attended Kenyon College and Columbia University. He is a member of the American Academy and Institute of Arts and Letters and the author of plays, several novels, and a collection of stories entitled *Lives of the Poets.*

STANLEY ELKIN   (1930)   *United States*   Born in New York City, Mr. Elkin has taught at several universities, including Washington University in St. Louis, where he presently teaches. His literary awards and honors include *The Paris Review* Humor Prize, the National Book Critics Circle Award, and a grant from the Rockefeller Foundation. Mr. Elkin's stories are collected in *Criers and Kibitzers, Kibitzers and Criers.*

RICHARD FORD   (1944)   *United States*   Born in Jackson, Mississippi, Mr. Ford attended Michigan State University. The first of his three novels, *A Piece of My Heart,* was nominated in 1976 for the Ernest Hemingway Award for Best First Novel of the Year. His collection of stories is entitled *Rock Spring.*

CARLOS FUENTES   (1929)   *Mexico*   Born in Mexico City, Mr. Fuentes grew up in North and South America. He was Ambassador to France, and occasionally lives and teaches in the United States. He is the author of several novels, as well as a collection of stories entitled *Burnt Water.*

MAVIS GALLANT   (1922)   *Canada*   Born in Montreal, Ms. Gallant was made an Officer of the Order of Canada and won the Governor-General's Award and the Canada-Australia Literary Prize. Her collections of stories include *The Other Paris, My Heart Is Broken, The Pegnitz Junction, From the Fifteenth District,* and *Home Truths.*

WILLIAM GASS   (1924)   *United States*   Born in Fargo, North Dakota, Mr. Gass received his doctorate in philosophy from Cornell University. He has taught at a number of universities, including Washington University in St. Louis, where he presently teaches philosophy. The recipient of many literary honors, Mr. Gass has written several novels and collections of essays. His volume of stories is *In the Heart of the Heart of the Country.*

NADINE GORDIMER   (1923)   *South Africa*   A novelist and short-story writer born in the Transvaal, Ms. Gordimer has been awarded many literary honors, including the Booker Prize, the W. H. Smith Commonwealth Literature Award, and the Scottish Arts Council Neil M. Gunn Fellowship. She is a Fellow of the Royal Society of Literature and an honorary member of the American Academy and Institute of Arts and Letters. Her story collections include *Livingstone's Companions, Not for Publication, Friday's Footprint, Selected Stories, A Soldier's Embrace,* and *Something Out There.*

NATALIA GINZBURG   (1916)   *Italy*   Born to Jewish parents in Palermo, Ms. Ginzburg grew up in Turin and married Leone Ginzburg, a Russian Jew active as an antifascist. The Germans restricted the family during the war, and in

1944 Mr. Ginzburg died in prison. After the war Ms. Ginzburg joined the editorial staff of Einaudi, the publishing company her husband had co-founded. She is the author of numerous novels, short stories, and essays, and was awarded the Strega Prize. Her collections of stories are *The Road to the City* and *Dead Yesterdays.*

GRAHAM GREENE (*1904*) *England* Educated at Oxford University, Mr. Greene has written numerous novels, travel books, plays, film scripts, and essays. He was an editor for *The London Times,* a film critic and literary editor for the *Spectator,* and a war correspondent in Indochina for the *New Republic* in 1954. A world traveler who has made his home in France, Mr. Greene was made Companion of Honor by Queen Elizabeth, and in 1967 he was decorated with France's Chevalier de la Légion d'Honneur. His stories are gathered together in his *Collected Stories.*

WOLFGANG HILDESHEIMER (*1916*) *Germany* Born in Hamburg, Mr. Hildesheimer is a freelance artist, dramatist, and fiction writer, and was an interpreter and translator at the Nuremberg trials. He has written novels as well as short stories, which will appear in America for the first time under the title *Collected Stories.*

YASUNARI KAWABATA (*1899–1972*) *Japan* Born in Osaka, Mr. Kawabata graduated from the Tokyo Imperial University in 1924. A novelist and short-story writer, Mr. Kawabata was the first Japanese writer to win the Nobel Prize in 1968. His collection of stories is titled *House of the Sleeping Beauties.*

MILAN KUNDERA (*1929*) *Czechoslovakia* Born in Brno, Mr. Kundera was a student when the Communists came to power in 1948. Also a jazz musician, he was Professor of Advanced Cinematographic Studies in Prague until he lost his position after the Russian invasion in 1968. He has lived in France since 1975. He won the Prix Medicis Award for the best foreign novel published in France, and the Premio Mondello for the best foreign novel published in Italy. His stories are collected in *Laughable Loves.*

TOMMASO LANDOLFI (*1908*) *Italy* Born in Pico, Mr. Landolfi has been called "Italy's Kafka," and he is often linked with the Surrealists. He received a degree in Russian literature at the University of Florence and is renowned for his fine translations of Russian literature into Italian. Mr. Landolfi has written numerous short stories, which are collected in *Cancer Queen* and *Gogol's Wife.*

DORIS LESSING (*1919*) *England* Born in Kermansha, Persia, Ms. Lessing lived in Rhodesia until 1949, when she moved to London. She has written many novels, as well as the story collections *A Man and Two Women, African Stories,* and *Stories.*

MARIO VARGAS LLOSA (*1936*) *Peru* Mr. Vargas Llosa studied at the University of San Marcos in Lima and obtained his degree from the University of Madrid. He has lived in Paris, London, and Barcelona, and has received fellowships from and lectured at a number of universities in the United States. He has written several novels and one collection of stories, *The Cubs.*

NAGUIB MAHFOUZ (*1911*) *Egypt* Born in Cairo, Mr. Mahfouz is considered the foremost fiction writer of the Arab world. He studied philosophy at Cairo University and has written over twenty novels and several volumes of short stories. Although his early fiction was largely historical, his work since 1945 depicts contemporary Egyptian life. *Midaq Alley*, an early novel, has been translated into English, along with a collection of stories titled *God's World*.

BERNARD MALAMUD (*1914–1986*) *United States* Born in Brooklyn, New York, Mr. Malamud studied at City College of New York and at Columbia University, and taught at Oregon State University and Bennington College. He received two National Book Awards, a Pulitzer Prize, and a grant from the Rockefeller Foundation. His collections of stories are *The Magic Barrel*, *Idiots First*, *Rembrandt's Hat*, and *The Stories of Bernard Malamud*.

GABRIEL GARCIA MARQUEZ (*1928*) *Colombia* A journalist, short-story writer, political activist, and opponent of rightist regimes, Mr. Marquez won the Nobel Prize in 1982. He studied at the University of Bogota and has written several novels. His short-story collections are *No One Writes to the Colonel*, *Innocent Erendira*, and *Leaf Storm*.

WILLIAM MAXWELL (*1908*) *United States* Born in Lincoln, Illinois, Mr. Maxwell has received several awards, including the American Book Award and the Senior Brandeis Award. He has written a number of novels and contributes regularly to *The New Yorker*. His short-story collections are *Stories* (which also includes works by Jean Stafford, John Cheever, and Daniel Fuchs), *The Old Man at the Crossing*, and *Over by the River*.

IAN MC EWAN (*1938*) *England* Born in Wales, Mr. McEwan lives in London. He has been a writer-in-residence at the University of Iowa and has won the Somerset Maugham Award. Mr. McEwan has written two novels and two collections of stories, *In Between the Sheets* and *First Love, Last Rites*.

LEONARD MICHAELS (*1933*) *United States* Born in New York City, Mr. Michaels now teaches at the University of California at Berkeley. His collections of stories are *Going Places*, which was nominated for the National Book Award, and *I Would Have Saved Them If I Could*.

YUKIO MISHIMA (*1925–1970*) *Japan* Yukio Mishima is the pseudonym of Kimitake Hiraoka, who was born in Tokyo. He studied at the Imperial University and founded the Shield Society, guardians of Modern Japan in the tradition of samurai warriors. His suicide was public and ritualistic. Mr. Mishima wrote many novels as well as short stories, which are collected in *Death in Midsummer*.

ALBERTO MORAVIA (*1970*) *Italy* Born in Rome, Mr. Moravia is one of Italy's foremost novelists and a prolific short-story writer. His story collections include *Command and I Will Obey*, *Roman Tales*, *Bought and Sold*, *More Roman Tales*, and *The Wayward Wife*.

MOHAMMED MRABET (ca. *1940*) *Morocco* Born in Tangier of Riffian parentage, Mr. Mrabet made his first of three trips to the United States in 1960. In 1965 he met Paul Bowles, who taped and translated his legends and tales, which appear in a number of published books, including *M'Hashish* and *The Boy Who Set the Fire.*

VLADIMIR NABOKOV (1899–1977) *Russia* Born in St. Petersburg (now Leningrad), Nabokov fled to Western Europe during the Bolshevik Revolution. Educated at Cambridge University, he received his degree in modern languages. He lived for a time in Paris and Berlin, and wrote in Russian, German, French, and English. When the Nazis occupied France he escaped to America, became an American citizen, and continued to write, but only in English. He wrote plays, poems, translations, novels, and a memoir. His story collections include *Nabokov's Dozen, Nabokov's Quartet, Tyrant's Destroyed,* and *A Russian Beauty.*

R. K. NARAYAN (1906) *India* Born in Madras, South India, Mr. Narayan now lives in Mysore and has written numerous novels. In 1958 he won the National Prize of the Indian Literary Academy, India's highest prize for a writer. Mr. Narayan's collections of stories are *A Horse and Two Goats, An Astrologer's Day, Lawley Road,* and *Malgudi Days.*

JOYCE CAROL OATES (*1938*) *United States* Born in Lockport, New York, Ms. Oates graduated from Syracuse University. Her honors include numerous O. Henry Awards and publications in *The Best American Short Stories.* She is the author of many novels and volumes of poetry. Her collections of stories include *Night-Side, Marriages/Infidelities, The Wheel of Love, Upon the Sweeping Flood, By the North Gate, A Sentimental Education,* and *Last Days.*

EDNA O'BRIEN (*1931*) *Ireland* Born in western Ireland, Ms. O'Brien lives in London, where she is a playwright and a novelist. Her stories are collected in *A Fanatic Heart.*

FLANNERY O'CONNOR (*1925–1964*) *United States* Born in Savannah, Georgia, and raised in Milledgeville, Georgia, Ms. O'Connor wrote two novels and received three O. Henry First Prizes and the National Book Award in 1971 for *The Complete Stories.* Her other collections of stories are *A Good Man Is Hard to Find* and *Everything That Rises Must Converge.*

FRANK O'CONNOR (*1903–1966*) *Ireland* Born in County Cork as Michael O'Donovan, Mr. O'Connor served briefly in the IRA and directed the Abbey Theatre in Dublin before establishing himself as a writer. He wrote novels, plays, travel essays, political and biographical studies, and numerous collections of stories, including *Bones of Contention, Travellers Samples,* and *The Stories of Frank O'Connor.*

AMOS OZ (*1929*) *Israel* Born in Jerusalem, Mr. Oz studied at the Hebrew University and received an M.A. degree from Oxford University. He served with the Israeli tank force on the Golan Heights in 1973. Leader of Peace Now in Israel, he lives on Kibbutz Hulda. A novelist and short-story writer, he writes in Hebrew and has won several of Israel's most prestigious literary awards. His collections are *The Hill of Evil Counsel* and *Where the Jackals Howl.*

CYNTHIA OZICK (1928) *United States* Born in New York City, where she currently resides, Ms. Ozick has received numerous awards, including two O. Henry First Prizes and a Mildred and Harold Strauss Living Award from the American Academy and Institute of Arts and Letters. She is the author of two novels; her story collections are *The Pagan Rabbi, Bloodshed,* and *Levitation.*

GRACE PALEY (1922) *United States* Born in the Bronx, Ms. Paley studied at Hunter College and lives in New York City and Vermont. She currently teaches at Sarah Lawrence College. Her story collections are *The Little Disturbances of Man, Enormous Changes at The Last Minute,* and *Later the Same Day.*

CESARE PAVESE (1908–1950) *Italy* Born on a farm in the Piedmont, Mr. Pavese studied at the University of Turin, where he obtained a literature degree. He co-founded the Einaudi publishing firm, and was its editor, until he committed suicide in 1950. During the thirties and forties, he was best known as an essayist and translator of American and English authors. Although he wrote several volumes of poetry and numerous novels, novellas, and short stories, he did not receive major recognition until his last novel was translated shortly before his death. His collections of stories are *Festival Night, Told in Confidence,* and *Summer Storm.*

V. S. PRITCHETT (1900) *England* Born in Ipswich and now a resident of London, Mr. Pritchett is a short-story writer, critic, novelist, biographer, and travel writer. He is an honorary member of the American Academy and Institute of Arts and Letters. His stories are in *Collected Stories* and *More Collected Stories.*

JAMES PURDY (1923) *United States* Born in Ohio, Mr. Purdy now lives in Brooklyn and teaches at New York University. He is the author of several novels, plays produced on and off Broadway, and the story collections *Color of Darkness, Children Is All,* and *A Day After the Fair.*

ALAIN ROBBE-GRILLET (1922) *France* Born in Brest, Mr. Robbe-Grillet is well-known as a practitioner of *nouveau roman.* He has written six novels, a volume of essays, a film script, and the story collection *Snapshots.*

MERCÈ RODOREDA (1908–1983) *Spain* Born and raised in Catalonia when it was still a separate and autonomous republic, Ms. Rodoreda wrote numerous novels and short stories between 1932 and 1937. Outspoken during the Spanish Civil War, she lived as an exile in Geneva and Paris from 1939 to 1979, when she returned to Barcelona after Franco's death. In exile, Ms. Rodoreda remained silent until 1959, when she published a volume of twenty-two stories. Available in translation are a novel and a story collection titled *My Christina.*

LEON ROOKE (1934) *Canada* Born in Roanoke Rapids, North Carolina, Mr. Rooke lives in Victoria, British Columbia. He received the Governor-General's Award for his novel *Shakespeare's Dog*. His story collections include *Sing Me No Love Songs, I'll Say You No Prayers: Selected Stories*, and *A Bolt of White Cloth*.

JUAN RULFO (1918) *Mexico* Born in Jalisco, Mr. Rulfo is a major figure in the history of post-revolutionary literature in Mexico. The author of several novels and collections of short stories, Mr. Rulfo writes about the harsh realities and actualities of peasant life. Available in translation are his major novel *Pedro Paramo*, and his story collection *The Burning Plain*.

NATHALIE SARRAUTE (1902) *France* Born in Ivanovo, Russia, Ms. Sarraute received her education in England and France. She has written three novels, an autobiography, and a collection of stories titled *Tropisms*.

ISAAC BASHEVIS SINGER (1904) *Poland* Born in Radzymin, Mr. Singer studied at the Tachkemoni Rabbinical Seminary and worked as a journalist in Warsaw before emigrating to the United States in 1935. In 1978 he received the Nobel Prize. Writing in Yiddish, Mr. Singer is the author of several novels; his collections of stories include *Gimpel the Fool, Spinoza of Market Street, A Friend of Kafka*, and *The Collected Stories*.

SUSAN SONTAG (1933) *United States* Born in New York City, Ms. Sontag has received the National Book Critics Circle Award for Criticism. She is the author of two novels, numerous collections of essays and criticism, and a volume of stories titled *I, Etcetera*.

JEAN STAFFORD (1915–1979) *United States* Born in Covina, California, the daughter of a writer, Ms. Stafford attended the University of Colorado and Heidelberg University. Ms. Stafford wrote several novels; her story collections include *Children Are Bored on Sunday, Bad Characters*, and *The Collected Stories*.

PETER TAYLOR (1919) *United States* Born in Trenton, Tennessee, and educated at Vanderbilt University and Kenyon College, Mr. Taylor now lives in Charlottesville, Virginia, where he taught for many years at the University of Virginia. He has won numerous awards, including a Gold Medal for Fiction from the American Academy and Institute of Arts and Letters. His story collections are *A Long Fourth, Miss Leonora When Last Seen, In the Miro District, The Old Forest*, and *The Collected Stories*.

MICHEL TOURNIER (1924) *France* Born in Paris, Mr. Tournier is the recipient of a Grand Prix du Roman of the Academie Française and of France's most prestigious prize, the Prix Goncourt, for his novel *The Ogre*, the only novel to win that award. His collection of stories is titled *The Fetishist*.

WILLIAM TREVOR (1928) *Ireland* Born in Mitchelstown, County Cork, Mr. Trevor is now a resident of Devonshire, England. He has received many awards and is a member of the Irish Academy of Letters. He has written novels and plays for radio, television, and stage; his books of stories include *The Ball-*

room of Romance, Angels at the Ritz, Lovers of Their Time, Beyond the Pale, and *The Stories of William Trevor.*

JOHN UPDIKE (1932) *United States* Born in Shillington, Pennsylvania, Mr. Updike attended Harvard University and the Ruskin School of Drawing and Fine Arts in Oxford, England. He was a staff member for *The New Yorker* from 1955 to 1957. Mr. Updike has written over twenty-five books, including novels, stories, plays, and criticism. His awards include the Pulitzer Prize, the American Book Award, and the National Book Critics Circle Award. His collections of stories are *The Sand Door, Pigeon Feathers, Olinger Stories, The Music School, Museums and Women,* and *Too Far to Go: The Maples Stories.*

LUISA VALENZUELA (1938) *Argentina* Born in Buenos Aires and now living in New York City, where she is a Fellow of the New York Institute for the Humanities, Ms. Valenzuela is the author of several books, including the story collections *Clara, Strange Things Happen Here,* and *Other Weapons.*

EUDORA WELTY (1909) *United States* Born in Jackson, Mississippi, where she continues to live, Ms. Welty was graduated from the University of Wisconsin. She has received the American Book Award, a Gold Medal for Fiction from the American Academy and Institute of Arts and Letters (awarded for her entire body of work), and the Pulitzer Prize. Her collections of short stories are *A Curtain of Green, The Wide Net, The Golden Apples, The Bride of Innisfallen,* and *The Collected Stories.*

PATRICK WHITE (1912) *Australia* Born in England, Mr. White grew up on a sheep station in the outback of Australia. From the age of 13, he attended school in England and studied at Cambridge University, eventually settling in London. He was an R.A.F. intelligence officer in the Mideast and the Crimea during World War II. Winner of the Nobel Prize in 1973, Mr. White has written several novels and two story collections: *The Burnt One* and *The Cockatoos.*

TOBIAS WOLFF (1945) *United States* Born in Alabama, Mr. Wolff grew up in the Pacific Northwest. He was graduated from Oxford and Stanford universities, and currently teaches at Syracuse University. Mr. Wolff has received many awards and honors, including the P.E.N./Faulkner Award. His two collections of stories are *In the Garden of North American Martyrs* and *Back in the World.*

RICHARD WRIGHT (1908–1960) *United States* Born on a plantation near Natchez, Mississippi, Mr. Wright moved north to Memphis, then Chicago and New York. In the 1930s he became involved in radical politics. He was a reporter for *New Masses,* a correspondent for the Harlem bureau of the *Daily Worker,* and an editor of *New Challenge,* all left-wing publications. An expatriate in Paris from the 1940s on, Mr. Wright wrote several novels and an autobiography. His story collections are *Uncle Tom's Children* and *Eight Men.*

RICHARD YATES (1926) Born in Yonkers, New York, and now a resident of Boston, Mr. Yates has received awards for his work many times throughout his career. He is the author of eight books, including two story collections titled *Eleven Kinds of Loneliness* and *Liars In Love.*